I0766456

REDSTAR RISING

Buried Goddess Saga

I-III

RHETT C. **BRUNO** JAIME **CASTLE**

REDSTAR RISING

©2019 RHETT C. BRUNO & JAIME CASTLE

Print and eBook formatting, and cover design by Steve Beaulieu. Artwork provided by Fabian Saravia. Cartography by Bret Duley.

Published by Aethon Books LLC.

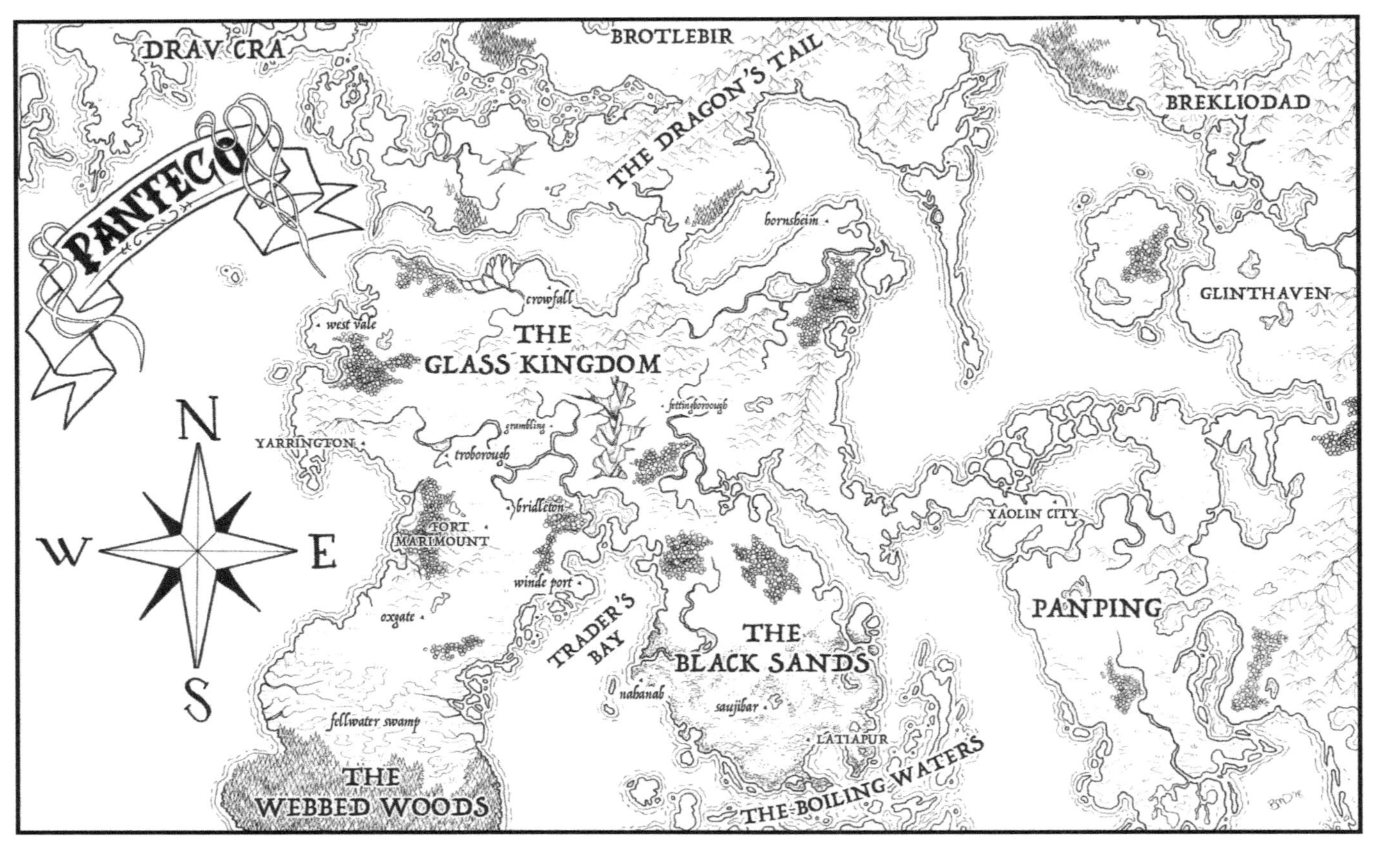
PANTEGO
DRAV CRA
BROTLEBIR
THE DRAGON'S TAIL
BREKLIODAD
hornsheim
GLINTHAVEN
crowfall
west vale
THE GLASS KINGDOM
fettinsborough
grambling
YARRINGTON
troborough
YAOLIN CITY
bridleton
FORT MARIMOUNT
winde port
PANPING
oxgate
TRADER'S BAY
THE BLACK SANDS
nabanah
saujibar
LATIAPUR
fellwater swamp
THE BOILING WATERS
THE WEBBED WOODS
N
W
E
S

BOOK ONE

WEB OF EYES

WEB OF EYES

A Buried Goddess Saga NOVEL — I

RHETT C. BRUNO   JAIME CASTLE

PROLOGUE

An ill King brings circling wolves.

Sir Uriah Davies, Wearer of White, and sworn protector of the Glass Kingdom had been living by those words since the King's health declined. After decades of war, uniting the kingdoms of Pantego under the light of Iam, the one true God, the body of Liam the Conqueror had finally started failing.

King Liam's condition was kept quiet as long as possible, but his absence from assemblies and celebrations brought whispers from all corners. Angry, envious people spoke in darkness about changing winds. For four years, Uriah had been silencing them, praying for the King's restoration. But it never happened.

Foreign lords jockeyed to improve their position with underhanded dealings. Members of the Royal Council bribed the Queen to increase their sway over affairs, all while, she hosted countless grand feasts and masquerades to draw attention away from her dying husband.

Uriah feared the fate of the kingdom hung by a thread when one fitful, early winter night Queen Oleander's brother arrived in the capital city of Yarrington. Redstar, as he was known, was foreign like she had been before the King claimed and married her—a savage from the northern lands of Drav Cra.

King Liam had long rejected Redstar's requests for an audience, but now, with the King barely able to speak, Redstar swept into the city to beseech his sister. He claimed that as chieftain of the Ruuhar Clan, he sought support for his starving people who once were hers.

Uriah knew better than to trust a man like Redstar, a worshipper of false gods and notorious warlock who, along with his Drav Cra brethren, raided and pillaged northern towns within the Glass Kingdom. A man who drew on the foul magics of Elsewhere, as if they were a thing for mortals to wield, using them to sow chaos. Redstar denied such claims, but survivors spoke of a half-red-faced raider wielding fire as viciously as a sword, and Redstar's birthmark—a five-pointed star taking up the whole left side of his face—was impossible to mistake.

Uriah warned Oleander to send him back to the tundra from whence he came, but advising the woman nearly always led her to do just the opposite. Instead, he stood outside the King and Queen's door listening to their hushed argument. It was not his place to eavesdrop, but with the King incapacitated, he found himself doing it more and more. Oleander, more crucial than ever, was young, rash, and harsh as the tundra where she was born. Straining, he heard a clatter.

"This place has made you weak, sister!" Redstar shouted, his voice growing closer. The door nearly smashed Uriah's face, but he repositioned himself just in time.

Redstar glared, lips pursed in anger. He was pale as snow, like his sister, except for the dark red birthmark which had earned him his name. It was said only one of the twin moons smiled on him at his birth, leaving him marked, malformed. Seeing him in person again, Uriah believed it.

"What are you looking at, knight?" Redstar spat.

Uriah held his tongue. He had no love for the man.

Merely a boy when the King took Oleander as his own all those years ago, even then, Redstar was tempted by darkness. Uriah hadn't forgotten the trek home when two of his own men went berserk, killing each other, and Redstar was discovered in his yurt holding a piece of his sister's hair, blood covering his hands.

In spite of his hatred for magic—especially dark, blood magic—King

Liam spared Redstar because of his relation to Oleander. Uriah called it a mistake, though he honored his king's wishes as always.

"This way, my Lord," Uriah said finally, gesturing to Redstar and biting back disdain.

He escorted the Queen's brother back to the guest chamber where he would stay until morning, then retired to his own quarters. But Uriah couldn't sleep.

An ill king brings circling wolves. It echoed in his mind.

So, instead of lying awake, listening through the wall to the moans of his King as Oleander struggled to feed him porridge, he returned to the guest wing. When midnight arrived, his patience rewarded him. Uriah hid, then followed Redstar's glowing torch as he crept through the dark halls of the Glass Castle.

His face screwed in disgust when Redstar turned. It wasn't a torch the man held, his raised hand was wreathed in flame, blood dripping down his forearm.

Blood magic. How dare he taint this sacred castle?

Uriah edged toward a corner, peeking around to see Redstar stopped outside the door of the King and Queen's only son's room. Pi was weak and scrawny, but a sweet boy—a kindhearted and seemingly worthy heir to Liam's great kingdom. Uriah had only just begun to teach him the ways of the sword, but unlike his father, he would rather bury his head in books.

Redstar raised his hand to the lock, sliding it open without even a touch.

"Pi," Uriah whispered, rushing to the door as Redstar slipped through. He listened for a moment but heard nothing. Lowering his shoulder, he burst in to find Redstar looming over the sleeping prince, whispering in his ear.

Then, Redstar looked up. "Shhh, you'll wake him."

"Step away," Uriah demanded.

"You should consider how you address your Queen's brother," Redstar replied, voice as calm as ever, like the world was his playground. His eyes rose to meet Uriah's, mouth curled into a dark grin.

"You should have stayed in your quarters."

"I decided I should leave early. Can't an uncle say a proper goodbye to his nephew?" He drew up the blankets covering the Prince.

Pi groaned, rolled, and pulled the blankets close.

Something was missing. Pi always slept with the crude Drav Cra doll his mother had presented him on his birthing day. The Drav Cra called it an orepul and believed the idols made in their likeness contained a piece of their very souls. Uriah considered it worthless pagan mumbo-jumbo that the King only permitted to placate his wife, but Pi had an attachment to it that Uriah hoped he would grow out of soon.

Presently, Redstar had the orepul clutched in his right hand.

"In the name of Liam and the one true God, return that to your prince at once," Uriah said. "I don't care who you are, *warlock*." The term left his lips with venom but hearing it only seemed to embolden Redstar.

"*Arch* Warlock now," he corrected.

"All the same to me."

"Of course, it is. The Queen forgets her own people." Redstar ran his hand across Pi's cheek, smearing blood from his sliced palm along it. Pi didn't wake, merely twitched as if it were the midst of a nightmare. "Yet still she made him this?"

Uriah drew his sword. "I won't ask again."

"You would threaten a member of the royal family?"

"There is no royalty in you, heathen." Uriah edged closer, making sure to keep a safe distance. The stained glass of the arched window at his back rattled, rain driving sideways with the harsh wind.

"Our Lady and her chosen people are tired of being forgotten," Redstar said. "Your queen is no longer one of us. It is time she stopped pretending."

"Step away, now!"

Uriah extended his sword. The blade nearly touched Redstar's throat, but the heathen ignored it and regarded the orepul, then the Prince. His smirk widened.

"Farewell, my young prince," he said. "We'll be together again soon."

Uriah saw the glint of a dagger as Redstar reached into his robes. He knew harming the Queen's brother wouldn't be overlooked, but he was paid to protect the boy. Uriah thrust his sword at the traitor, but his blade met only air.

Redstar was unexpectedly fast, sliding across the floor and catching Uriah's side. The dagger drew a shallow cut, but it was enough to slow

Uriah. He swung his blade in a wide arc, but Redstar was already by the window.

"Redstar!" Uriah roared as the Arch Warlock smashed the window with his elbow.

Wind and rain like ice sliced in, forcing Uriah to cover his face. Pi's eyes sprung open as if roused from a nightmare, clutching his blanket, frantic in search of the orepul.

Redstar performed an exaggerated stage bow, then fell backward. Uriah reached for his leg, grabbing only silk before the Queen's brother flipped back over the sill and into the night.

Uriah stuck his head out into the driving rain and stared down the castle's tallest spire. There was no falling body, no corpse lying in the courtyard. He was just... gone.

"Sir, what happened! I heard raised voices and... was that Redstar?"

Uriah whipped around to see one of his men, another member of the King's Shield standing in the doorway, claymore drawn.

"Torsten," Uriah said. "Rouse the Queen. The Prince has been robbed."

Torsten's gaze shifted between the frightened prince and Uriah. "What did he take?"

"The boy's soul..."

I

THE KNIGHT

ONE YEAR LATER…

“**F**ilth and braggarts, all of them!” the boy whispered through gritted teeth from beneath his sheets. “Liars, thieves, drunks, and murderers!”

Torsten Unger, the Wearer of White, leader of the King's Shield, had been winding down for the evening when he heard those words in the voice of Prince Pi. Torsten looked around, confused. The boy had refused to leave his room at the highest point atop the West Tower of the Glass Castle since before the last Dawning ceremony when Pantego's two moons passed before the sun and signaled the turning of a new year.

Torsten peeked out of his room, his gaze met by one of the newest members of the King's Shield out on patrol. Sir Rand Langley placed his fist over his heart, as was customary when greeting the Wearer.

“Did you hear that?” Torsten asked.

“Sir?” said Rand.

“The uh… never mind. It's late. Tired is all.”

Rand looked at him, puzzled. “Goodnight, sir.”

Torsten tipped his head and waited for Rand to pass. He'd spent the day overseeing the induction of that very young man into the King's

Shield. The trek down from atop Mount Lister, where Iam was closest and custom dictated the installation take place, had them all exhausted. It was rare that Torsten could shift focus from matters of the kingdom, or filling the needs of Queen Oleander and her sickly husband, so he was happy for the diversion.

Iam had gazed down upon the ceremony with great joy, no doubt. But even with the Vigilant Eye of the one true God watching over them, Torsten knew the Glass Kingdom would soon need all the security it could get. Rand was a promising recruit, young and a bit overeager, which showed as he fumbled through his vows, but Torsten had a hard time faulting anyone for wanting to serve. Especially since, according to the royal physician, King Liam's death was imminent. It didn't matter how much he, or Oleander, or anyone else living in the Glass Castle tried to hide it.

Once Rand turned the corner, Torsten focused back on Pi's voice. It was less of a voice now really, and more like a feeling. He left his quarters, hoping to avoid catching any eyes, but even if he hadn't held the station of the Wearer of White, he was hard to miss. More than once he'd been mistaken for a half-giant. His chest was thick as an iron keg, requiring specially crafted armor from Hovom Nitebrittle, the castle Blacksmith. He stood closer to seven feet than six, and his hands were large enough to pop a man's skull.

As he passed more Shieldsman and castle guards, he saluted each in turn but never spoke a word. How could he say he was following an invisible voice to the Prince's bedroom in the middle of the night?

The arched stone and stained glass door stood a whole head taller than Torsten. He cracked it enough to see a sliver of the Prince's chambers. It felt dirty, wrong—although he had no ill motives. But the Queen had forbidden anyone, even the Wearer of White, from seeing her despondent son. It had been that way since his predecessor, Sir Uriah Davies, caught the Queen's heathen brother whispering madness into Pi's ear and fleeing with his most prized possession.

It took Torsten a moment to figure out where the boy was, then he saw the bulge in the sheets. A moment later, Prince Pi cast off the covers and stood. He was so young, yet his hazel eyes spoke of a lifetime of horrors. His head was cocked to the side while he paced, his messy, dark, hair hanging limply like a wet blanket. One thing was certain, he looked neither sickly nor grief-stricken.

"Yes, they must pay for their sins," Pi said. "The Buried Goddess demands it, and she will do it, not I." His head twitched so hard Torsten worried he'd snap his own neck. Hearing a boy so young speaking of the Buried Goddess startled him.

Torsten instinctively stepped backward as the Prince abruptly crossed the room. There was no doubt he'd heard Torsten's footsteps, but he seemed entirely unconcerned. The pale light of Pantego's moons gushed in through the window. Beyond its arch, Torsten could see Yarrington's twinkling lights—candles, lamps, and campfires. Those paled in comparison to the false light reflected off the castle's spires and the flat, glassy plain of Mount Lister overshadowing them, a monument of the ancient God Feud.

Torsten drew a deep breath before cracking the door a bit more. Countless angular symbols were hastily etched in stone walls, smeared with blood. The Prince may have been young, but it appeared Pi's devotion to the Buried Goddess exceeded even that of her cultists. Torsten had cleared plenty such miscreants from basement shrines throughout Yarrington since having joined the King's Shield, and even more as Wearer of White.

Most believed Nesilia had been dead for thousands of years after Iam brought an end to the God Feud that ravaged Pantego, and Torsten numbered among that lot. Legend was, and so her followers believed, she was not dead, only buried beneath Mount Lister—waiting to exact vengeance upon the One who buried her.

Did the Queen know of Pi's obsession? She'd never mentioned a word of it to Torsten. The Nothhelm family, which had ruled over the Glass Kingdom for centuries, served and revered Iam—the one true God. What would the people of the Glass Kingdom think if they knew the King's only son was a heretic worshipping the false goddess Nesilia?

The voice filled Torsten's mind again, this time louder. He grasped his head, slithering his fingers through his hair, biting back the urge to scream. He rolled his head in sharp circles, gnashing his teeth as the foreign words bombarded his mind. When it was over, he looked up to see the Prince clutching his own head.

"Buried, not dead. Buried, not dead," Pi muttered over and over. "The color crimson and a thousand eyes. I see the color crimson and a thousand eyes!"

Torsten's heart pounded, threatening to burst through his rib cage. He saw large tears flow freely from the young boy's eyes, and his own eyes began to water. The Prince now stood in the middle of his chamber—a room that would dwarf most houses. A circle surrounded him, painted in red on the dark stone floor. Torsten noticed a bloody bandage wrapped around Pi's hand.

He knew blood magic when he saw it.

The Prince raised his voice, beginning a chant. The words drifted in and out like the flight of galler birds in spring, ebbing and flowing, sharp tucks and broad swoops, impossible to know where one word ended and the next began. They would seem nothing more than mindless blabbering to any hearer, and that's what they were to Torsten—nonsense.

Pi's eyes rolled, only the whites showing. He convulsed, head whirling and hands flapping. Torsten flinched and bit back disgust. At that moment, Torsten finally understood the Queen's eternal dourness. It was her brother Redstar's fault, but Oleander blamed herself.

Torsten remembered that day vividly when he found the former Wearer of White in these very chambers after Redstar fled, having attempted some terrible curse on the Prince. The Queen's brother's cold heart matched the bitterness of the northern land from which he hailed. When he visited the castle a year ago, Uriah warned against trusting him. Torsten felt it too, that unsettling feeling just from being in the presence of such a heathen. The Queen still let him in. Blood was blood after all.

As Uriah had expected, he'd betrayed the Queen—*why wouldn't he?* Oleander had been taken from Drav Cra to become King Liam's wife at such a young age. From the tundra to the throne. She had been given a crown while Redstar was left amongst the remnants of their clan after the slaughter, left to pursue his lust for magic until, according to Uriah, he was named the chieftain of his clan as well as Arch Warlock of all the Drav Cra.

Queen Oleander tried to hide her brother's betrayal out of embarrassment, but Torsten was the first to see the boy that next day. He was inconsolable. Redstar had stolen the young prince's orepul and fled to the Webbed Woods, where any who followed soon met their end.

The Queen blamed the loss of the pagan idol for her son's madness, believing it held a part of his soul. She sent Uriah with a small battalion to the woods to retrieve Redstar and the stolen effigy, but they never returned. Torsten was named Wearer in his place, wearing the helm Uriah left behind, with no choice but to follow her orders as she sent more and more to their doom.

Presently, as Pi finished his words, a small spark—an ember—grew in his hand above a spot of blood, but quickly faded. He cursed loudly, words he shouldn't know at his age.

"It won't work without it!" He picked up a wooden chair and heaved it through the open window to the pasture below, no small task for a boy his size.

Pi peered over the edge to find the chair cracked and splintered two stories below. He planted a foot on the sill and pulled himself up, standing there a long while, teetering back and forth. Torsten threw the door open and watched as Pi tilted forward, catching himself at the last instant. Torsten was halfway across the room when without a word, Pi stepped back down, took a few steps, and collapsed on the floor.

Torsten froze. He checked to be sure the boy wasn't conscious. Even the Wearer of White could lose his head for entering the Prince's room unannounced and unwelcome, but he had to figure out what was going on.

Everywhere, strewn across every desk, table, and flat surface were notes upon which were the scribbled writings of a child.

Torsten read them silently. *THE COLOR CRIMSON AND A THOU-SAND EYES.*

Torsten shuffled some more papers and slid open a drawer. Inside, he found a large stack of parchments with the same three words etched on every bit of white space: *BURIED, NOT DEAD.*

Torsten had heard those same words muttered in shadow from the mouths of the realm's cultists, but he couldn't understand where a boy whose life kept him confined to the Glass Castle could have learned them?

If the Queen, a devout—if not a bit lax on her attendance of services—follower of Iam despite her Drav Cra heritage, had known her own son was attempting to commune with the Buried Goddess… Torsten didn't know what she would do. Maybe she'd simply refuse to believe it. Or perhaps she did know, and this was just another of her many secrets? Was that why she refused to have any priest, even Wren the Holy, attend to Pi and try to undo whatever foul influence Redstar's visit had on him?

Torsten regarded the Prince, who now slept innocently like a child should. The sight of the bloody, candle-lined circle surrounding his body sent a shiver up his spine. He sunk back out the way he came, taking care not to be seen as he descended the spiral stairs into the anteroom below.

He reached his chambers without complications and removed his armor while staring out his window on the north side of the castle. Torsten grasped the necklace that had been hanging from his neck for as long as he could remember, a pendant of Iam's Vigilant Eye presented to him by King Liam himself when he'd been knighted. As he looked out over Mount Lister, he let his mind wander to the shocking and blasphemous things he'd seen and heard.

"Iam help us," he said.

II

THE THIEF

"What's the difference between a Westvale whore and a dwarf?" Haam asked from behind the Twilight Manor's worn bar, white shirt stained from a day's work—although he'd likely been wearing it for much longer. "One's short, fat, and has a beard. The other lives in the tunnels of the Dragon's Tail!"

The motley company surrounding him erupted in laughter, slapping the bar and spilling pints all over the faded wood floor. Laughing especially hard was a scruffy, red-haired dwarf, a member of a small mercenary crew hired to guard a trading caravan. Like anyone interesting who found themselves in Troborough, he was simply passing through.

Whitney Fierstown didn't make a sound at the joke, just sat alone at a corner table, nursing his ale. His finger drew circles around the rim of his earthenware mug, mindlessly keeping time with the out-of-tune bard strumming his lute by the hearth.

The Twilight Manor was fuller than usual thanks to the traders, but this wasn't Yarrington or Winde Port. Far from it. The tavern sat in the middle of a cobbled square in the quaint farming village of Troborough.

Whitney stared through the dirty, cloudy window beside his table, completely unsure why in the name of Elsewhere he found himself back in the town he'd grown up. It had been many years since he fled the small life for adventure, so long, nobody recognized him. So long, he learned his parents had both passed a while back at the hands of a plague in the town's water supply. So long their shoddy gravestones were weathered, the names barely legible.

It was tough to say the news made him sad. He'd never been close with them, especially not his ceaselessly grumpy father who cared about nothing except for the next harvest. But a new family now lived in the farmhouse he'd grown up in. A husband and a wife, and two kids who'd never amount to anything in this place. One of the children, a particularly scrawny boy, played swords in the square with his younger sister just as Whitney remembered doing with his only childhood friend, a Panpingese orphan named Sora.

The boy parried and dodged, not just swinging the stick but allowing himself to be stabbed and prodded on occasion as well—the sign of a smart child preparing himself for the harsh realities of life. Any man Whitney had ever met who fancied himself an unconquerable hero found his head on the wrong end of a spike. They were only the stuff of myth and legend, nothing like how he and Sora used to imagine.

The thought of her brought a smile to his lips. He'd only just gotten in that night, and he didn't plan to stay long, but she hadn't shown her face. He'd passed the home where she'd grown up on the edge of town, under the care of the nutty town healer, Wetzel. Nobody was home, and the barely-standing shack seemed abandoned, though it always had.

Whitney only dreamed she'd moved on as he had so long ago, and figured that old Wetzel had probably kicked the bucket by now. He'd been ancient when Whitney was a child. A few times that night, he considered asking Haam about her but didn't feel like getting into a whole thing about who he used to be, or worse, finding out the plague had claimed her too.

He preferred the dream, and not a soul in the tavern remembered him, even Haam. He doubted she would either. It was like he was a ghost visiting his old life.

"Need another, traveler?" Alless, the barmaid asked from a few tables away. Whitney remembered her when he was a boy as well, the stuff of fantasies, or rather, she was. Age had robbed her of much of her beauty.

No fantasies left in this gods-forsaken place.

Whitney waved his hand dismissively, and she returned to the back of the bar and whispered something to Haam. He shooed her away, eager to keep his attentive crowd with more crude jokes, obviously thrilled to have so many visitors. The man had tended the Manor as long as Whitney could remember, and unlike Alless, he'd already been so old back then, he still looked the same save for a rounder belly.

The Twilight Manor served as the center of all things social in Troborough, which was rarely all too much. Throughout the day, it had just been Whitney and few others shuffling in, pontificating, playing gems, and drinking. The farmers would talk about their yield or share rumors of far-off places none of them would ever visit. The same mind-numbing shog everyone went on about when he was a boy.

But the red-haired dwarf and the small band of mercenaries injected a bit of new life into the place when they'd arrived. The little man had spent the better part of the evening boasting to Alless about his prowess with ladies and how many "full-sized" women he'd laid with while serving in the King's army. A gray-skinned Shesaitju gentlemen also serving in the dwarf's mercenary company sat quietly nearby, looking exhausted.

Not to be outdone, Carlo, the town's resident good-for-nothing-but-reminiscing-about-his-days-in-the-Glass-army drunkard spoke of his role in the Third War of Panping, when King Liam himself had led the charge against the heartless Mystic Order. He cursed the dwarves of Brotlebir and how, like cowards, they'd refused to charge that day.

If Whitney didn't know better, the way the man talked, he'd think him a King's Shieldsman. But Whitney did. It was all hog's piss. The same story Carlo had been telling since Whitney was a child. Nobody noteworthy wound up settling down in Troborough, and nobody in Troborough ever did anything noteworthy.

"What's got ye sour, boy? Ye look as dissatisfied as me wife." Whitney hadn't even seen the red-haired dwarf take the chair opposite him, grinning like a madman with his yellow teeth and an eye looking in each direction. Red whiskers, like straw poking out of a barn pile, covered most of his face.

Dwarves… Only thing they're good for is their treasure chests.

"Just tired," Whitney said out loud.

He peered longingly back to his ale, the heady foam finally receding. He was never one to back down from a verbal spat, but the dwarf's question was one he'd been asking himself since he arrived in Troborough. He'd lost track of the years he'd spent roaming Pantego, thieving and swindling his way to being wanted in more cities than he had fingers until, eventually, every score in every land started to feel the same as the last. Some rare treasure no lord or lady even needed.

He missed the challenge. The adventure.

"Tired?" the dwarf scoffed. "What's a pale farmboy like ye got to be tired about?"

Whitney glanced up only with his eyes. If there was one thing he couldn't stomach, it was being lumped into the same meager vocation as his insignificant father. Whitney had seen things nobody in Pantego could imagine, made a name for himself coast to coast.

"Farmboy?" He rose from his seat. "You hear that?" Whitney said loudly to anybody who might be listening. "I think this little half-pint, rock-eating dwarf just called me a 'farmboy.'"

The Twilight Manor went quiet—not dead silent, but enough for Whitney. The bard stopped playing—thankfully. Several regulars turned their attention to him. The members of the trading caravan all slid forward, eager for a show as if used to their mate causing trouble.

"Aye, I did." The dwarf slammed his mug on the table, ale splashing over the side.

"Just making sure you were talking to me," Whitney said. "You dwarves spend so much time down in the dark, sometimes I worry you can't see straight." Whitney hiccuped. He had to use his chair for support.

"At least we can hold our drink, *farmboy*."

"You really don't know who I am, do you? Tell him Haam!"

"Here we go again," Haam grumbled. "Another adventurer who's put down one too many." He threw his towel over his shoulder and climbed down the stairs leading to the storage basement, probably for some peace and quiet.

"Okay… I'll handle it."

After a few tries, Whitney climbed onto the table and stared down his nose at the dwarf. It made the burly little man's features darken in anger. If

Whitney had learned anything a short while back while slumming in the subterranean dwarven kingdom of Brotlebir, it was that dwarves hated when a human drew attention to how short they were. That, and the things they made from gold were gold all the way through.

"My name is Whitney Fierstown! Yes, yes," he said in practiced rhythm, performing an exaggerated bow, "the same Whitney Fierstown of Westvale fame. He who stole the Sword of Grace from right under Lord Theroy's nose while the right bugger slept face-down in a puddle of his own spit. Had myself a throw with his lady daughter that evening as well."

Whitney's laugh was joined by a few others. He hopped down from the table, his voice growing louder after he steadied himself from nearly slipping in a puddle of the dwarf's spilled ale.

"The Mischievous, Master of Mayhem," he continued. "The very same credited for single-handedly delivering the Splintering Staff out of the hands of the Whispering Wizards. You know them, dwarf? Whitney Fierstown, Savior of the Sullen and Surly—that's you. Hope of the Hopeless and Helpless. Thief of all thieves. The Filcher Fantastic himself."

Loud whoops and whistles erupted from the bar. Whitney bowed again, looking up to lock eyes with the fuming dwarf, a humorless smile playing at the edges of his mouth.

"And you call me a *farmboy*?" Whitney asked. "Someone get this sad dwarf another ale. He's either too drunk or not drunk enough."

The dwarf appeared thoroughly unimpressed. Whitney rounded the table, his gaze never leaving the dwarf. He plopped back into his chair, grabbed his ale, and kicked his feet up on the table.

There were a few scattered hand claps before the people of Troborough returned to their business. He wondered how many times they'd heard passers-through boast about similar feats, if he was becoming as bad as the dwarf or even Carlo.

The bard started plucking his lute again, struggling to find the melody. Alless made her rounds, dodging the grabby hands of several toothless men. Haam had returned now, polishing mugs and not paying attention. Even the members of the trading caravan expected more of a show.

The dwarf calmly stroked his beard once, then took his turn climbing the table, even though the thing was nearly the whole height of him.

"And I be Grint Strongiron!" he shouted. The poor bard's notes trailed off from yet another distraction. Grint's companions unenthusiastically tapped their mugs on the bar in support while everyone else ignored him.

"Son of a drunken wife-beater," Grint went on. "Brother of a coward. Me wife's uglier than the south end of a horse-headed north. I got seven fingers, nine toes, and enough spawn to start a small war."

He took two wobbly steps toward Whitney.

"I've broken more bones than I be able to count, many of them me own. I helped dig out the throne room of the Dragon's Tail alongside Brike the Pickaxe when yer great, great, grandfather was still an ache in his own grandfather's britches."

He leaned over, getting as close to Whitney as he could without toppling over.

"Ye say ye've stolen from a lord and some wizards?" he continued. "But ye ain't done nuffin till ye tooken from a king!"

Whitney's head cocked to the side before he laughed deep and hard. He looked around, but not a soul was paying attention any longer. Even Grint's companions had returned to their mugs.

"Ain't thought I said nuffin funny, Thief," the dwarf said. "Even from his bed, the King of Glass still be stealin food from me family's mouth. Ye'd be doin the world a favor, showin the old prick what the feelin be."

"Steal from the King?" Whitney said, incredulous. "What would you have me do, traipse into his throne room and take the Glass Crown right off his head?"

Grint jumped down, missing the landing either for lack of judgment of too much drink. Maybe both. He stumbled into the next table, disturbing two old men in dirt-covered shirts. His Shesaitju friend went to steady him, but Grint shook him off before turning back to Whitney.

"If that's what ye gotta do," he said. "Otherwise, this li'l display of yers is just shog and spit."

"Shog and spit, you say?" Whitney asked.

"Aye. Heard the King of Glass be havin himself another masquerade in a few nights—one of them fancy balls nobles like so much. If yer so good, I be bettin ye could sneak right in, couldn't ye, *farmboy*?"

Whitney let his feet fall from the table and leaned forward, circling the rim of his mug again.

"Steal the Glass Crown," he marveled. Against all odds, he found himself in the town he'd left behind, hoping he might find some inspiration for a new adventure where it all started. And just when he thought life was getting boring…. It happened. Finally, a challenge that might be worth putting his drink down for.

Whitney tapped the top of his head. "All right, dwarf. Next time you see me, I'll be wearing it."

III

THE THIEF

"**S**top, thief!" a Yarrington guard shouted.

Whitney tore around the corner of one of Old Yarrington's winding streets. He accidentally plowed over a nobleman, who fell into his wife and knocked her over as well. Whitney paused just long enough to help her up, peered over his shoulder at the two guards rounding the corner, and dug in again.

"Sorry, milady," he said, bowing his head as he went.

Whitney thrived in chaos. This had been his passion since the day he'd left the farm—the thrill of being chased by guards armed to the eyeballs after snatching some rare treasure. But even as he dodged an especially deep puddle in the cobblestone road, narrowly escaping a third guard new to the chase, he found himself going through the motions.

The massive, armored man splashed face first into the water, arm still stretched out toward Whitney's ankle, The sound that followed told Whitney the other two tripped over the newcomer, but this time, Whitney didn't look back. He veered off toward the stable of one of Old Yarrington's many mansions. The horses inside whinnied, startled by the sound of clanking iron of armor from the recovered guards still in hot pursuit. If that wasn't enough, thunder cracked, sending the equine beasts into a frenzy.

One painted horse burst from its pen. The gate swung open, nearly clipping Whitney's side, forcing him to cut a sharp turn. Wetness plastered his face as he slid in what he hoped was mud. He cursed his luck. He'd already stolen some costly clothing to wear for the masquerade, and now they were ruined.

But that wasn't why the guards were after him. The small gem in his pocket he'd snagged from a noblewoman in broad daylight was enough to get him thrown in the district lockup. Fleeing the guards to the heart of Old Yarrington, however, would land him in the castle dungeon. They'd be too lazy to drag him flailing and screaming anywhere else. It was all part of his greater plan to infiltrate the royal masquerade.

That furry dwarf will eat his words.

The party started in mere hours, and Whitney had to be in the castle when it did. Although intended to celebrate King Liam's birthday, rumors hinted it would be a final send off to the King who'd done more to shape the Glass than any other.

Whitney's mother once told him, "The only thing worse than stealing is stealing from a dying man." Even though the Queen would have a man hanged merely for whispering about the King's alleged condition, Whitney knew there was a bit of truth to every rumor. This year or next, it didn't matter—everyone knew the Glass Kingdom stood on the precipice of a new ruler. The sky seemed to as well. Fog laid like a thick blanket over the streets of Yarrington and rain fell in heavy sheets as if Iam Himself were in mourning.

Good conditions for a thief... usually.

Whitney shook off his stained sleeve and squinted back at his pursuers. While Liam the Conqueror was bedridden, his guards were very much alive, and he couldn't let them catch him yet. Though, from the sound of it, they weren't fairing much better in the wet conditions.

He jumped back to his feet, and as he ran, he scoured the map of Old Yarrington he'd purchased down in South Corner. It was yellowing and brittle—and apparently out of date. Whitney turned another corner and wound up face to face with a wall made of solid stone piled three meters high.

This was supposed to be a garden.

He slid to a stop before the towering wall, kicking up mud. He used to love this part, thinking on his feet, improvising in the face of certain doom. But lately, it had all become so mundane, whether it was a lord's mare or a lady's gem. He found himself disheartened, frozen, wondering if he should just slip away and end this wild boar chase.

Whitney shook the thought away, unwilling to chance facing the dwarf in defeat. He shoved the mud-slick tip of his boot into an almost imperceptible notch in the stone and pushed himself up just enough to wrap his fingertips around the lip of the wall. One hand slipped on the smooth, wet stone. He squinted back after he caught his balance to see the guards closing in, but the heft of their armor slowed them. If he had trouble climbing the wall, those lumbering fools wouldn't stand a chance. Besides, he didn't want to escape, or else he would have by now. But if they caught him now, it would make it seem too easy. He needed them angry to ensure he'd make the castle dungeon.

Once more, he dug in and thrust upward. This time his fingers found purchase, and he yanked himself up. Wiping his face and glancing back at the guards, he decided it hadn't been mud he'd slipped in earlier. He fought back the urge to vomit over the edge of the wall.

This isn't worth it, he thought. Nothing seemed to be worth it anymore. *Piss in the wind and shog in my mouth.*

Again, he forced himself to focus. He could only count two guards through the driving rain now, both struggling to pull themselves up the wall, shouting up at him to stop. He looked in all directions for the third guard before swearing and hopping down the other side. Again, his foot slipped in what definitely wasn't mud, sending him into a split. He used the momentum to roll, thoroughly tarnishing his new clothing. Nonetheless, he was soon on his feet again, running.

Mud spattered below, rain fell from above. Visibility wasn't great, but he could just make out the outer wall of the Glass Castle now, looming in the distance as if taunting him.

He peered back again. Now, none of the city guards could be seen. When he turned back around, the third and missing one stood in the path before him. He was a hulking brute with a scar from what appeared to be a bad burn covering the bulk of his face and neck.

Why is it always the big one?

The guard reached for Whitney with both hands.

Whitney easily dodged the man's thick, sausage-like fingers and threw a punch of his own. The guard smiled down at him mirthlessly as his blow landed harmlessly against his boiled leather armor. Whitney put on a nervous grin, then aimed for the man's bare elbow with his next punch, just below where the arm pads stopped.

His fist cracked hard against bone. Whitney yelped and flexed his hand. He probably broke a knuckle, but the blow forced the guard to stop momentarily and shake out his arm.

A moment was all Whitney needed.

Behind him, he heard the clatter of the other two guards who'd decided to take the long way around the wall. Whitney slipped past the hulking guard and ran. So far, in spite of a couple hitches, the plan was working. Only one thing remained. It needed to look absolutely real.

He reached a locked, iron gate at the end of a street serving some Royal Councilman's absurdly large mansion, still under construction. He shook the gate, a family crest—a ship and a coin—rattled against the metal. The fence was so high he'd never be able to climb over it, but this was a dead end he'd prepared for.

At least that old map was good for something.

He stopped, feigning surprise, frantically looking for a way out. He attempted to scamper up the slick iron bars in futility, then turned back toward the guards.

He dug his hand into his wet, muddy pocket and produced the little gem he'd swiped. "Look, fellas," he shouted over the din of rain as he walked toward them. "I think this is a misunderstanding."

"Lady Holliday's jewels jumped into your pocket then?" the hulking guard asked. The others bellowed in laughter.

"Here, you can have it back. No harm done, right?"

"Wrong." The big guard approached slowly, the other two behind him.

Whitney held his breath. There were plenty of joys to be found in thieving, but the next few minutes would not count amongst them.

When the brute was only paces away, Whitney feigned left, then spun and went right instead. He knew it wouldn't work, but it needed to appear like he wasn't ready to give up just yet. As expected, the hulking guard planted his feet. Whitney braced for what he knew was coming. The man reared back, and a second later, Whitney Fierstown was swept off the streets of Old Yarrington.

I V

THE KNIGHT

Queen Oleander wore a pale blue gown, low cut and high-collared, with white lace and frills along the edges. On her left wrist, she wore a glass bracelet adorned with diamonds, shiny and glinting in the bright room. She wasn't alone, but powdered her face in the vanity as if Torsten wasn't there. The sweet aroma of flowers filled the room—oleanders, her namesake. To call her beautiful would be as understating as calling Brotlebir cold.

While he waited for an answer to a question he'd asked, Torsten eyed the Queen with the same look any man would but forced himself to remember his place, shifted his weight and cleared his throat.

"Oh, yes," she said. "You're still here. You were saying?"

He gathered his thoughts. "Since the King's illness took and he stopped appearing publicly, we've noticed a shortage of tax payment from the Shesaitju. I spoke with Lord Darkings, the Master of Coin—"

"I know who he is," she snapped, although Torsten wasn't sure she did.

"Yes, of course." These sorts of political conversations seemed to repulse her, so it had become a habit for Torsten to ensure that she knew the names of all the Royal Councilman. "As I was saying, he swears all is well with the coffers, but I believe we should send a royal emissary south to the Black Sands."

Oleander's fingers snaked along a necklace—a long, silver chain with prongs grasping a blue crystal.

"Come, Torsten, hold up my hair," she demanded.

"Your Grace?"

"You heard me. Since we excused Tessa for this *titillating* conversation, I require assistance."

Torsten approached, his heart pounding as she wafted her hair up, exposing her slender neck and shoulder blades. Her gown's back plunged into a deep **V**, and the curve of her spine drew his eyes so low it caused a sudden pang of shame.

Torsten now stood as Wearer of White, head of the King's Shield and commander of his royal army, but he hadn't always been on the road to such prestige. He had been born a harbor rat to a pair of Glintish traders, con artists really. He lived off scraps discarded by South Corner fishermen —stuff no right-born man, not even dogs, would have eaten. But for Torsten, it was picking meat off scales and bones or die.

"The King is going to love this celebration, Your Grace," he said as he approached.

"Don't be daft, Torsten. My husband won't know this night from a night spent watching lightning bugs twinkle in the bailey."

Torsten's heart, perhaps more than any, broke for the King. It had been he who'd rescued Torsten from a life of squalor after a fortunate childhood misstep thwarted an assassination attempt on the then-young-and-virile King Liam. Bumping into the Black Sands archer hidden in the adoring Yarrington crowd while Torsten was trying to steal bread had been an accident, but the King refused to see it that way. He called it Iam's hand at work and immediately made Torsten an armiger under Sir Uriah Davies.

Still, none of it ever made him feel comfortable while alone with nobles, least of which, Oleander, the 'Flower of Drav Cra,' as she'd become known. He reached up and gingerly held the Queen's hair in place while her willowy fingers reached back and drew open the clasp of her necklace. He felt guilty as the scent of her perfume greeted him, flowing through his nostrils, touching a portion of his mind that drove him wild with desire.

"Shall we?" Torsten asked, refocusing.

"Shall we, what?" The Queen's mind was clearly elsewhere. She picked up her costume for the masquerade and absent-mindedly stroked the fabric, letting her fingers play over the embroidered flowers.

"Send an emissary to the Shesaitju Caleef."

"Don't be silly, Torsten. The Black Sands have been faithful to the Glass Crown for more than a decade since Liam's war. Caleef Sidar visited the court not too long ago. I am confident all is well."

"I still think it's prudent for us to consider—"

"Where were you last night?" Queen Oleander asked abruptly.

Torsten swallowed so hard he thought she'd heard the spit go down. "I'm sorry?"

"Last night," she repeated. "I sent for you in your quarters, but you could not be found."

"I'm afraid I don't know when you're referring to. I finished knighting a few new Shieldsmen and returned straight away to my bed."

"I had one of my servants come to your chambers, and she reported them empty."

"Oh, of course, I must have been sneaking a bite of food from the kitchens. Hiking Mount Lister works up the hunger."

He hated lying to her, but he couldn't allow her to find out about his trip to Pi's room. The Queen was most known for two things, her beauty, and a temper sharp as broken glass and just as fragile. Many said that, other than Prince Pi, her son, the only thing in all the world she was kind to was her pure white, prize horse from the far east. King Liam once had a knack for calming her, but in his current condition…

"I would prefer if the Wearer could be found when needed," she said.

"Apologies, Your Grace," Torsten said.

"Luckily, your new man… Rory was it?

"Rand, actually," Torsten corrected.

"Ah, yes, Rand. He's a good boy. He helped in your… absence."

Torsten couldn't help the twinge of jealousy passing through him, good a soldier as Rand might've been. Torsten was now the Wearer of White because of his king. It was the last coherent order Liam had given a year ago after Uriah went off after Redstar and never returned. Now his king clung to this life like a beggar to his last autla. Torsten worried what might happen if Oleander no longer found him, Torsten, useful.

Oleander started to pull away, and Torsten allowed her hair, soft, silky and the color of the sun, to flow through his hands. Torsten stepped backward, inching toward the corner of the room. Suddenly, her demeanor changed and her features darkened.

"When was the last time we sent men to find my son's orepul?" she questioned, a harsh edge creeping into her tone.

"It has been long enough," Torsten said. "If they were successful, they'd have returned by now."

"Send more."

"But Your Grace—"

"But what?" she spat, terse.

"It's just… I am sickened by the thought of how many have been sent to their deaths. Our army dwindles, and we need to—"

"What we need," she interrupted again, "is to help my precious boy get back to normal. He will soon take his rightful place on the throne, and he hardly wants to leave his room, all thanks to my thieving brother."

More talk of the orepul, but now Torsten knew the truth. He wanted to shout it at her—to tell her that her son was not overwhelmed by grief, but instead, he was locked up in his room trying to resurrect the Buried Goddess, possessed by the same dark desires as her brother's people, that Redstar's lies had likely sent him on this mad quest when he visited a year ago.

Her son was the heir promised by God after Oleander struggled so long to produce a son. Only, now that Torsten had seen the object of Pi's passions, he questioned which god.

Torsten drove the thought away. *Nesilia is dead. Only Iam remains.*

He kept quiet, told himself he couldn't bear to share information that would bring her pain. Even that, he knew, was a lie. He merely didn't want to chance being on the receiving end of her anger. He'd seen men beheaded for far less, and his future was foggy. If Queen Oleander knew the truth and was trying to keep it secret, who knew what she'd do to keep him silent.

"We've been sending soldiers for a year now, Your Grace," he said. "Since Sir Uriah Davies failed to return from the woods." It pained Torsten to speak the name. Uriah had been a brilliant fighter and mentor, and even he was claimed by the Webbed Woods. Every father in Pantego was guilty of telling tales to their young ones about the place, about the evil, giant spider that devoured anything which dared enter its domain.

"Because they're weak!" the Queen shouted.

"Any more loss will leave *us* weak. Our enemies will take advantage of the first opportunity they have once they discover the true weight of the King's condition—if they haven't already."

"Don't be such a fool, Torsten. We have not been at war for many Dawnings. We have no enemies left, thanks to him."

An ill king brings circling wolves, Torsten thought to himself. Uriah had spoken those words often at the first sign of the King's waning mind.

"A kingdom, as long as it rules over conquered peoples, will always have enemies," Torsten said. "King Liam spent a lifetime spreading the word of Iam, but he can no longer speak. For all we know, the Shesaitju, Panpingese, or any countless others have already begun plotting."

"As if we don't have a strong enough army to thwart any uprising?" Oleander asked. "Has Yaolin City not been secured? Has the entire Panping Region not flown the Vigilant Eye for thirty years?"

"Of course, Your Grace. I am simp—"

"Enough of this," she said, waving her hand. "You know I hate politics."

It was true, she preferred to pry, and taunt, and seduce, and that was precisely what she was doing at the moment. She turned toward Torsten, applied a liberal amount of shimmer to her neck and collarbone, then reached down to lift the mask she would wear to the masquerade that night celebrating King Liam's birthday. It was frosted white glass lightly adorned with a filigree of gold. She placed it against her face, her full lips still visible.

"Do I look okay?" she asked, wearing a crooked smile.

"My Queen," he said. "You look perfect."

"Yes, yes," she droned, pulling the mask away from her face.

She strolled to her window and lifted a glass of wine with a stem so thin it was barely visible from the sill. She swirled the contents before taking a long pull. Again, her features twisted with concern.

"Is it not true that the Prince hasn't left his room since the orepul was stolen?" she said, turning back to Torsten, lips stained a deeper red.

Torsten held his tongue again. This conversation with the Queen seemed endless. The doll didn't hold a piece of the boy's soul. It was ancient, Drav Cra hogwash that she too didn't truly believe in. Pagan folklore that she'd happily forgotten until she needed something to blame beyond only her wretched brother.

No, what Pi needed more than anything was faith in Iam. Torsten had seen that first hand, but he said nothing.

"He grows old," she continued, "and hardly remembers why he is so sad. You speak of lost men, but can you stomach another king who cannot rule? My son is destined for the throne, and yet, he cannot sit upon it thanks to my rotten brother."

Oleander ambled toward Torsten, rising to the same height as him. All Drav Cra were tall and lean, but for a fleeting moment, he felt like she'd grown.

"You will recover what was stolen from your beloved future king, or I will find a new Wearer who can," she said.

Torsten bowed as low as his armor would allow. "Yes, my Queen," he said through his teeth. When she got like this, he knew it was best not to press.

"Good. Now, leave me," she demanded.

Torsten turned toward the door.

"And knight," she said, stopping him. "Do not disappoint me."

He bowed again and exited her chambers.

V

THE THIEF

Yarrington, the capital of the Glass Kingdom, practically sparkled like the waves on the Torrential Sea. Whitney could only guess that's how the kingdom's name was derived. It was a city that had stood the test of time, whose winding, spindly streets appeared in constant motion as people from all over Pantego went about their daily business. It was a city whose architecture proved the melding of these peoples—buildings with tall arches designed to allow giants passage, small homes bore into boulders for dwarves, but mostly those more appealing to humans.

The towering, white walls surrounding it had helped it survive innumerable wars and sieges over the ages—at least until King Liam had established himself and conquered those threatening the peace.

Mount Lister could be seen standing tall and proud from anywhere in the city. Anywhere, except the spot where Whitney found himself. From there, he could only see the gray, damp walls of a cell somewhere in the castle dungeons. He wondered why dungeon cells always had to be so dark. Motes of dust floated about, dancing in a thin ray of fading sunlight pouring in through a small, barred window set so high he could only see a slice of the sky. He wiggled his fingers, creating shadows on the dirty floor.

"Ah, fresh meat," said a voice from the darkness.

Whitney had been listening to the old man snore from the adjacent cell for what seemed like an hour. He'd wondered when he'd wake up.

"Hello, stranger," Whitney said, applying his best impression of nobility.

"A bit overdressed for a place like this, dun't ye say?" The man stepped out of the darkness, his bony limbs creaking, shaking, and wobbling with each step. He wore a filthy, tattered, gray tunic like he'd just been draped with a sack. The few teeth he had left were yellow and thick with grime.

"Prince Breynard of Gilly Gale," Whitney said with a flourish. That was his go-to identity in times like these. Gilly Gale was the name of some forgotten stronghold at the base of the Dragon's Tail, the mountains in the North where the dwarves dug their hollows. Whitney stumbled upon the ruins while running from an angry Breklian lord after he'd spent a night with the man's favorite concubine. It was manned by a group of monks who worshipped a god they called the Lord of Eternal Silence. It was no wonder no one had heard of it, the crazy bastards had all taken a vow of silence.

"Never heard of no Gilly Gale," the man said.

"Oh, it's a beautiful land. Tall mountains, lush valleys. You know the sort."

A good lie was the very essence of thievery, and a lie was most easily told and believed when it was sprinkled with bits of truth. Whitney thought lying to be an art, not a skill, taking great pride in crafting his tall tales.

"He ain't a prince!" a guard shouted, voice distant and removed. A series of laughs followed.

Whitney counted four distinct voices.

He moved closer to the bars separating him from the geezer.

"They're right," he whispered, looking around as if trying to keep a secret.

The old man's cackle turned into a wheeze, followed by a moist hacking. He almost fell over before finally recovering.

"What's your name, old man?" Whitney asked, casually leaning against the prison bars.

In response, the man simply lowered himself to the hard stone floor. Whitney cringed when the man stretched his wiry legs, his aging bones popping. Old people were the worst. They smelled—their bodies half-decayed already. They were difficult to communicate with, always having trouble hearing.

"Since you're likely too old to hear me, allow me to be the first; my real name is Whitney Fierstown, perhaps you know the name?" It didn't matter if a withering old prisoner knew the truth. He needed the man to trust him if he planned on getting out.

The man cackled more. "I been in this cell longer than ye've been alive, boy. Every day passes I wonder why they ain't hanged me yet. No, I never heard of ye."

He probably wasn't exaggerating. He was ancient. Probably knew the Buried Goddess before she got buried.

"How about a different question, then?" Whitney turned his back and took a few steps away before returning his gaze to the man. "What's an old man like you done to deserve the cell?"

The man eyed Whitney, his face beginning to soften if only for a moment. His eyes scrunched and his mouth curled into a snarl.

"That's two questions, ye biff," he said. "I seen a hunnerd of ye come and go from these cells and not one of ye deserved to be here more than me."

"For all you know," Whitney said, "I caused a riot and killed the Queen."

"Ye dun't."

"That's true, I didn't." Whitney smiled. "But I might've. Actually, all I did was steal one little gem."

Whitney pushed himself away from the bars and fell backward into a roll, head over feet until he was seated on the floor with his back against the wall.

The old man stared at him but didn't seem the least bit fazed.

The sun was beginning to set outside, the blue-purple light of night painting the cells the same color. Whitney settled against the wall with one leg propped up, arm on his knee, examining dirty fingernails.

"So, ye dressed like a fruitcake?" the old man asked after a brief silence.

"When in Old Yarrington… they say."

He looked down at the tattered hems of his pants and swore under his breath. It was all part of the plan to get into the King's soiree, but he hadn't counted on the sky unleashing a torrent worthy of the gods and his outfit getting completely ruined. When he escaped, he would have to find someplace to clean up if he was going to fit in at any masquerade—royal or no.

The old man harrumphed and laid down on the bench that would be both seat and cot. Whitney rose and did the same. It was hard stone and completely unacceptable in terms of comfort, but Whitney had suffered more for less. After a while, he felt a familiar feeling in his stomach. He stood and strode toward the cell door.

"Can I get a menu?" he shouted. "There a barmaid available?"

No one answered.

"Stew and mead, then," he decided.

"Ain't time for eatin," the old man said without stirring. "Ye missed the meal, and that's that. Ye'll have to wait till supper time."

Whitney sat again.

"I don't plan to still be here at supper time," he said under his breath.

"Neither did I me first day. Look at me now. Get comfortable, kid." He cackled his way into a coughing fit once more.

Whitney rolled his eyes and peered back through his tiny sliver of a window—his only connection to the outside world. For now.

From his pocket, he pulled out a key he'd snagged off a guard on his way into the dungeons and rolled it between his thumb and index finger. Every cell across the world had two things in common, they left the promise of being free right there to drive men mad, and not one had ever been able to hold Whitney Fierstown for long.

The Glass Crown was soon to be his.

VI

THE KNIGHT

Torsten stood at the opposite end of the Grand Hall, watching as Queen Oleander took her place beside King Liam on the dais. Once upon a time, the Nothhelm's were the picture of royalty. The Glass Throne stood as a monument to Liam's power, a tangible reminder of his accomplishments and deeds. They say that it was half the size when his father died in the First War of Panping and Liam the Conqueror was named king. Everything in the Glass Kingdom was half the size.

The Queen's throne, nearly as impressive, was elaborately decorated with glass flowers of her namesake. But it paled in comparison to the woman herself. She looked even more stunning in contrast to the decrepit King. It was a sad sight to behold. He'd been struck down in the prime of his life by a disease even the best of the realm's physicians couldn't name. Oleander had spared no expense, even bringing healers from as far as Panping to bring with them the wisdom of their lands. Still, nothing could heal the King.

What remained of his hair was stringy and peeked out in thin wisps from below the Glass Crown. His amber eyes appeared to have life, but they stared blearily, his mouth hanging open, drool playing at the corners.

Torsten ached for his once-mighty Lord. The days he'd spent at Liam's side were his best; first wearing the mail of a Glass soldier and then, donning light blue and white of the King's Shield. Now, he was Wearer of White—King Liam's personal sentry and the kingdom's most respected military authority outside of the King himself.

He'd watched the King's steady decline and had been there with Uriah when the King was still cognizant enough to question it all.

"What's happening to me, Uriah?" Liam's voice was still strong in those days—now he didn't possess one at all.

"It will pass," Uriah would lie to him, told him it was probably from stress over desiring a worthy heir or a dalliance in one of the faraway lands they'd conquered.

Then and now, Torsten's most important job was to keep the King safe and alive. It wouldn't be long before both his and Uriah's failures were complete. There was sadness in King Liam's golden eyes, and by order of the Queen, this would not be an evening for tears. She reached out from her throne and adjusted his Glass Crown, which had drooped at some point along with his face. Torsten sighed, turning his attention from Liam before it drowned him in sorrow.

With the King's condition, these types of events were nerve-wracking. So many within an arm's length of mead and striking distance of the Notthelms, and all of them in disguise.

Sir Wardric Jolly, the King's Shieldsman posted closest to the entrance, raised his left arm in a purposeful gesture meant for Torsten. Torsten knew the signals; he'd helped Uriah develop them. Torsten responded by scratching the stubble on his chin. Another noble with violent history with the kingdom had arrived. That made Iam knows how many.

The Grand Hall filled to near capacity, the whole of the Yarrington court there to celebrate the King's fiftieth year—although he looked a hundred. Lords and ladies pranced around, their faces covered by masks. Torsten thought it was a perfect picture of the kingdom's most noble houses. Glass faces for a Glass Kingdom.

They were schemers and sycophants. Half of them came from king-doms forced to bend the knee at the tip of a sword. Others did so preemp-tively before Liam brought the wrath of Iam to their doorsteps. In those days, when he arrived at a kingdom's wall, the Vigilant Eye of Iam painted on his shield, it was either kneel or have your entire history erased.

Torsten wasn't sure what would happen when King Liam died and the crown passed to Pi. He was too young to begin with, and far too troubled to rule effectively—not to mention a blasphemer—meaning Oleander would be the true power in Yarrington. Every morning Torsten woke, he could feel Pantego growing smaller. He could taste the coming battle on his tongue like blood after being on the wrong end of a hard punch. Would those conquered peoples remain loyal to the Glass or would they renounce the grace of Iam as Pi seemed to? Would the Shesaitju, or Panping, or whoever else return to their heathenistic ways?

Arriving musicians tuned their instruments on a makeshift stage in the center of the hall, pulling Torsten from his worry. Above them hung a grand, glass chandelier adorned with hundreds of little flames, their light being cleverly magnified and spread throughout the room using the glass and mirrors.

Watching the servants scurrying around like ants was almost like watching a dance performance in one of the city's finest playhouses. They weaved in and out between the guests, stopping to offer drinks or lavish foods. Torsten had often fantasized about being one of those nameless servants. An anonymous face in the crowd, only noticed if performing poorly. How could one perform such a mundane task poorly? He wanted desperately at times like this to be able to wake in the morning, put on servant's attire like he was destined to before King Liam knighted him, then clean, bake, or sew without a worry for anything but coin.

The thought shamed him. He knew he should be eternally grateful to Liam for raising him up.

He was just tired. Tired of lying awake at night fearing for the fate of the Glass Kingdom, wondering what would happen when it no longer had a king.

Queen Oleander may have ensnared the masses with her appearance, but she made decisions rashly and based upon emotion, not rationale. It was the savage, Drav Cra blood in her. She'd all but ignored the kingdom's Royal Council since Liam lost his ability to communicate, and she hadn't even been crowned Queen Regent yet.

Taxes had gone up to finance extravagant parties like this, designed to pretend all was right with the kingdom. A drought, unlike any Torsten could remember, had food stores lower than ever, and in light of rumors that the Shesaitju had refused full payment on the year's taxes, the army was restless. Oleander didn't seem to notice any of it. All she concerned herself with was her son's worthless, lost doll.

Growing frustration had Torsten's mind racing, making it difficult to concentrate but the soft flow of music starting up soothed him a bit.

Couples circled one another, eyes locked and chests inflated like birds flashing their colors for potential mates. A lute played melodious and fast. Cymbals crashed, a crescendo. He watched one couple in particular as they moved with the music. It always amazed Torsten how much a good dance mimicked battle. She advanced, he retreated, then they switched roles, never breaking eye-contact, always mindful of footing. Torsten was no dancer, but you'd have to sail across the Torrential Sea to find anyone who hadn't heard of his skill with a sword.

His eyes wandered around the Grand Hall to all the other nobles. No one acted as though this was a night for the King, least of all Queen Oleander. She sat quietly, her many ringed fingers tapping in time with the music. Her gaze momentarily drifted to Liam. Torsten saw something in her eyes but couldn't place it. *Pity? Sorrow? Relief?* In public, she played the role of adoring wife to the man who stole her from her homeland and forced her to marry him, but in private they argued often. Especially after she took so long to produce an heir.

Torsten had been at the King's side that day—little more than a young man himself when they traveled to the far north, across Winter's Thumb, to the place where the nomadic Drav Cra roamed. Their boats were legendary—even mythological—sailing Ice Deep and the Torrential Sea, raiding and pillaging to survive. Nomads and pirates, their lands were too hard with frost to offer much in the way of resources, and most civilized men had long since fled those wastes.

Liam sought to conquer all of Pantego in the name of Iam, but even he was ready to turn from those harsh lands until he spotted the young daughter of the powerful Ruuhar Clan dradinengor, long before she'd bled. The moment the young King laid his eyes upon Oleander, he had to have her as his queen despite a kingdom of right-born women from which to choose. Her father protested, fought, but when Liam had something in his sights, no army could stand in his way.

Her acceptance did not come easily, the commoners and nobles alike whispering in the streets and court. Some spoke too loudly and ended up without tongues. Oleander had been festooned with many titles: The Northern Whore, The Wild Queen, and others worst still. Likewise, the King was no fool, giving her a name of his own: "The Flower of Drav Cra." Torsten watched as the young girl grew into a queen and forgot her savage ways. He watched her carry and lose two of Liam's daughters in the womb, had been there when the King nearly shattered his own throne in anger over lack of an heir.

The entire court thought their foreign Queen accursed. Many believed the stress of having a worthy heir to be the catalyst for Liam's descent toward the haggard man now seated upon the Glass Throne, a shell of his former self. And then, one day, by stroke of luck or the hand of Iam, she became pregnant with Prince Pi.

Torsten had never seen Queen Oleander happier than when she'd carried him. Maybe it was because the King had finally left her alone for those nine months, or perhaps she knew the connection she'd have with the child even during gestation. He missed how she was then. So full of hope, not refusing to see her son for what he'd become and blaming stolen trinkets. Now, all he could do was hope those days might return sooner than later.

He decided it was time for him to stop studying the room for danger and to find his place near the Queen's side. If he waited any longer he'd risk falling out of her good graces, and if there was anywhere in the world he needed to be now, it was there.

For the good of the Glass.

Torsten made eye contact with a few more of his men posted around the hall. After receiving a nod from each that the King and Queen were safe, he strode across the room, his heavy armor clanging with every step. The crowd parted. He hardly knew the difference between fear and respect and didn't care which of the two he received. Both served the same purpose: order.

He lifted his foot onto the first step of the royal dais. He could already smell Queen Oleander's perfume, and it was intoxicating.

"My Queen," he said, bowing low.

"Torsten, come," she said. "Stand with me and keep me company."

Torsten covered the paces remaining and found his place between the thrones and one stride behind.

"If only he could still keep me company." She threw a woeful glance at the King. "If only you were upon that throne," she said, flirtatiously grazing Torsten's forearm down to his hand.

Torsten knew better than to react. Uriah had taught him well before he left. The Queen could be cruel in her mocking. He had good reason to believe she knew how he looked at her when he thought she wasn't paying attention—everyone did. He wished he could help it. She found delight in coaxing him on, and a weaker man may have given in. But she was married to his king, and that was a sacred vow made under the Eye of Iam. One which he'd never break.

"Oh, come now," she said. "Don't be such an uptight prude."

"I'm sorry, Your Grace," was his only retort.

She rolled her eyes. "Oh, look, the real entertainment has arrived."

The head of a troupe entered to a chorus of fanfare. He strutted up to the dais and bowed low, his loose, frilly sleeves nearly brushing the floor.

"Your Highnesses," he said, annunciating each word like he was in a coliseum. "On this most auspicious day, the Westvale Troupe are pleased to present to you a recreation of one of the King's most remarkable conquests. The siege of Latiapur!"

He extended an arm back toward the entrance and his group flooded the Grand Hall with the over-the-top kind of flourish only an acting troupe could. A line of actors dressed in the blue and white of the Glass and others, skin painted gray, wearing tan and black of the Shesaitju's Black Sands soldiers followed closely behind. Torsten eyed a few of the gray-skinned Shesaitju nobles present, their mouths showing signs of scowls growing beneath their masks. He trusted their kind the least.

Their disdain only lasted until they thought better of it and joined the rest in applause. Barely a noble present was from a land which hadn't faced Liam's crusade, and they were, all of them, better off under the grace and prosperity of Iam's chosen kingdom.

The Queen let out a soft giggle and slapped Torsten on the arm. "I do believe that one's supposed to be Uriah," she said, pointing to a man wearing a white helmet like the one Torsten now held under his arm. Uriah had been Wearer of White during that war and nearly every other.

Torsten was appalled. The man was excessively fat. He waddled around the dance floor like a buffoon. The whole court stifled laughter until the Queen burst out in applause. Those attending followed her lead.

"He looked nothing like that," Torsten said under his breath.

"It's just a show," the Queen said, shushing him.

That was easy for her to say. She was portrayed by a young lady almost equally breathtaking as she was—almost. The troupe undoubtedly scoured the land in search of someone beautiful enough to not offend Her Royal Highness.

When the actor playing Liam arrived, the crowd's applause grew deafening. The man had a chin like an anvil and feathered black hair, same as Liam used to. He took several bows and was met by whistles and cheers. Torsten peered at the Queen with the corner of his eye, not turning his head. Her brow furrowed, but only for a moment. She cleared her throat, smiled humorlessly, and joined in with the same gentle applause.

The night carried on, the troupe depicting more epochs from the King's grand life. Although he'd accomplished far more than could be covered in a single night, they did a fabulous job honoring him. From bringing the scheming Panping mystics to justice after they poisoned his father, to the first and only Shesaitju War. They ended the evening with the siring of his heir—they, of course, graciously withheld the more private portions of the event.

The Queen's expression soured at the sight of the babe playing Pi. Torsten found himself doing the same.

Even knowing who Pi spoke of in the cover of darkness, Torsten cared for Liam's son and couldn't believe that he wasn't present on the evening the kingdom paid, what might be, their final respects to his father. Had he really been that obsessed? Tormented? Could he not snap out of his madness long enough to eat, drink and be merry?

"Will the Prince not be joining us again?" he asked the Queen, leaning in just enough that his cheek brushed her golden hair. "He should be here for his father."

She whipped around sharply.

"You know better than to ask about my precious boy at a time like this!" She bolted upright, stormed off the dais, and headed outside. Several attendees took notice but returned to their food and drinks when Torsten's scowl found them.

"My Queen," Torsten said. He took a step to follow, then thought better of it and stood his ground beside the King. After all, he was the head of the King's Shield, and his king was not yet dead.

The revelry continued. Tables were carried out by servants for a feast the likes of which Torsten would have killed for growing up poor in South Corner. Now, seeing the Great Hall filled with such finery sickened him. Barely a soul in the entire room even glanced over at Liam while they ate without Oleander present, fed from the gold in coffers he'd fought a dozen wars to fill. Fewer still said grace to Iam for providing this bounty, even as High Priest Wren tried to lead them.

Why would they? Few were of the Glass, and now no one of importance watched. Oleander may have been brash, but the people needed to see a Nothhelm capable of command upon the throne.

Unable to stomach the discourtesy any longer, Torsten finally left his post.

"Sir Nikserof," he addressed the Shieldsman standing guard at the western courtyard door Oleander had exited through. "Keep an eye on things for a moment."

"Is everything all right?" Nikserof asked.

"Fine, but the Queen should be seen up here at his side."

Nikserof saluted, then opened the door for Torsten. Two flowerbeds flanked a dirt pathway in the castle's west courtyard. Deep gouges dappled the dirt where long, thin stilettos had punctured the wet earth. It had been the first night in as long as Torsten could remember where the rain accompanied sunset.

The spire above, a long spindle of twisting glass, reflected and refracted the light of Celeste, the bright moon, and spread a false light over the whole city of Yarrington. Torsten looked beyond it at Mount Lister. Its glassy upper plain also reflecting the light of the moons to create a silvery aura. In his mind, he could almost imagine the God Feud long ago atop that cloven peak—gods and goddesses throwing spears and bolts of lightning and the crackling of Elsewhere's fire. He tried to imagine this land before the Glass Castle was erected, before the first kings left the northern lands to find peace in the south.

He flicked his gaze back to the hazy courtyard before him. At his feet were the Queen's heels and her mask, sticking up from the soil like unnaturally shaped flowers blooming in the night. She must have become tired of pulling them free of the mud and removed them.

Torsten peered up from the pile of the Queen's effects and saw her seated at the large fountain in the middle of the courtyard—a stone-carved dragon, each of its ten-thousand scales chiseled expertly. The smell of fresh jasmine wafted through the crisp night air.

She looked at peace, watching as the water dribbled from the dragon's mouth to join the rain. Torsten cautiously took a few steps, the soft sound of the fiddle playing in the Grand Hall became even softer. He saw her hand snaking through the cascading waters, breaking like the Boiling Waters against the rocky southern coast.

Then, suddenly, her head spun. She rose and hurried toward the West Tower. Her long dress dragged through the puddles and she didn't even bother to lift it, which wasn't like her. Rain trickled again from the sky that was quickly going from dour gray to midnight blue. Torsten expected thunder and lightning, but instead, the rain broke into a downpour. Torsten picked up his gait, the cold droplets drumming against his skin and armor.

A shrill scream erupted in the distance, carried on the wind across the courtyard, rising over the gale of the storm. The cry of the Queen, too far for any guard to hear. Torsten hated how the sound of her anguished voice caused him such pain. She was still queen only because she bore Liam a son, not because her people loved her. And she was neither kind nor loving—she was the opposite of all Torsten had ever wanted on the throne… yet he cared.

His boots crunched against the gravel walkway as he ran in the direction of her cry. All he could think of were the many nobles who'd entered that evening; the many possible assassins with their sights set on ending the Nothhelm reign. Masked faces spun like a carousel through his mind.

His anger grew as he heard her sobs. It was so dark, and the rain fell in such thick sheets, he could have been right on top of her and wouldn't know until it was too late. He slowed for just a moment, trying to find his bearings.

"My Queen!" he shouted. He knew if enemies stalked nearby he'd reveal himself, but he didn't care. If Queen Oleander was in trouble, it was his fault.

He drew his blade—a fine, glaruium claymore with the Eye of Iam adorning the pommel. The blade itself was nothing overly extravagant, just a sword that brought death when swung or stabbed. And Torsten was prepared to bring death.

"Torsten!" Oleander shouted in response. Even that single word broke into several syllables as she struggled to speak through sobs.

Torsten followed her voice and saw the source of her grief.

He sheathed his weapon and dropped to his knees beside Prince Pi, splayed out on the wet grass. He looked up and saw that the window of his chambers swung in the wind. Torsten remembered seeing him swaying on the windowsill on the night he'd felt a drawing to the boy's room, and this time he must have stepped out.

What have I done? I should have told her.

Torsten placed his ear against the boy's chest. "He's still breathing, but barely."

He grabbed the boy, intent on delivering him to the infirmary. A current shot through him like he'd been struck by lightning. His vision blurred, and he felt suddenly as if he was flying. The world whirled past him. He could feel the wind pulling at his face, and then it all came to a halt as if time itself had slowed. When the world came back into focus, Torsten stood at the edge of darkness. Tall trees rose before him bathed in shadow. Tiny, glowing orbs pulsed within the darkness—white spheres hanging, defying the laws of nature itself.

He reached toward one when a sense of vertigo stole over him. His eyes lost focus again, and all he could see was dark red—crimson. He closed them to blot out the color, and when they reopened, he stood again at the base of the West Tower, holding the Prince as the Queen sobbed at his feet.

The very air seemed to be sucked from the Queen as her cries turned to low wails. She shook violently, struggling even to breathe.

Torsten's heart burst with sadness for her, but more than that, for his kingdom. The poor boy was meant to be the next great King of Glass. If the vision Torsten saw was something the boy lived with, it was clear he wasn't simply distressed over a lost doll, or driven mad with an obsession over communing with the Buried Goddess. Something dark and terrible afflicted him. Dark magic, a curse, unlike anything Torsten had ever felt— magic few but a Drav Cra Arch Warlock like Redstar were capable of.

A sudden flash of lightning split the sky. The thunderous crack that followed couldn't mask the sound Torsten hoped he'd never hear. A bell chimed three times from the castle's tallest spire. It meant the King was in danger, and with all the masked strangers around, his heart filled with dread.

VII

THE THIEF

The Yarrington dungeon remained dank as ever. The smell of rotting flesh and excrement never lifted, even after hours of waiting. It was no wonder since there was a steaming pile of shog just sitting in the corner of the old man's cell.

Whitney sighed loudly.

"Would ye rather me hold it in, yer royal highness?" the old man asked, followed by a cackle and a hack.

Whitney ignored him.

Celeste and Loutis, Pantego's twin moons, peeked through the high barred window, offset against the star-speckled sky. There was some legend about them being Iam's first followers. Celeste, the follower who stayed true, was the larger of the two, bright and golden. Her counterpart, Loutis was said to have turned his back on Iam, thus cursed to be pale and gray like a haggard skull. Like anything to do with gods and curses, Whitney thought it was a pile of horse shog.

Their appearances, however, told Whitney the time was near.

He stuck his nose between the bars, ignoring the stench, pointed and said, "It appears that staircase over there is unguarded."

"Goes to the kitchens where they make that yig they call food," the old man replied.

It was true. Whitney's first, and hopefully only meal in this pit, was awful. It was a paste—like something a potter would wipe from his hands at the end of a long day of molding clay.

Whitney smiled, happy the old man was finally speaking again. He'd begun to fear the man had finally bit the dust in his sleep, which would undermine his entire escape plan. A series of creaks and groans echoed as the gaunt old man dragged himself to the spot where the guards left his food. Half of it puddled around the edges of the bowl.

"Disgusting," the man said, which didn't stop him from scooping the floor food up and shoveling the slop into his mouth.

"Are you going to tell me your name?" Whitney asked. "Or should I just continue thinking of you as 'that haggard old man?'"

"Reese Gladsby," he answered between mouthfuls. "The finest house ye ain't heard of."

"Ahhh, Reese," Whitney said as if he'd just discovered the secret to immortality. "How about why you are imprisoned?"

It appeared Reese just needed a bit of food in his belly before he would be willing to speak. Not that Whitney really cared about the answer, but a little familiarity and he could persuade most men to do nearly anything.

"Ye asked me last night why I ain't been transferred yet," Reese said. "That be a better question to answer em all."

Whitney nodded.

"Ye ever met former guard captain, Donova?" Reese asked.

Whitney shook his head.

"Long afore your time, sure'n. I's young in them days. Old rat bastard left a message I wasn't to leave this cell just hours afore he croaked. Idiots thought it meant forever. Alls I did's tell him his mum's ugly. Tryin teach me a lesson, he was."

Whitney stared at the man, incredulous.

"Worst part," Reese continued, bits of gruel spilling from his lip, "Never got to say goodbye to me boy. He was only a half-dozen years them days. Now he himself'll be a man—if he ain't dead yet."

"The new captain wouldn't listen?" Whitney asked.

"Ye ever met one of these bolt-headed lot? All they do's take orders. Don't think, they don't. Donova says I stay in the cell, they keep me in the cell. Simple as pie. Not like'n any of them's even met the fellow."

Whitney couldn't help but laugh under his breath.

"Think it's all a big joke, huh, *Prince*?" Reese questioned.

"No, not at all," Whitney said, sincerely sorry. "It's just that I was waiting to make sure it really was you."

The man stopped mid-chew. "What'chu tryin'a say, boy?"

"That door." Whitney pointed toward the kitchens. "The stables are through there too. Your son is waiting for you with two steeds, prepared to whisk you away from here. Said to look for a man named Reese when he paid me to get myself thrown in here."

Reese's face went pale. "My son?" he asked, breathless. He recovered quickly. "My son dun't even know where'n I be. Ain't never visited me, at least." Reese waved in dismissal. "Bah!"

"Yes, that's because he has been working hard to move up in the world. He's finally become a stableboy for the castle—I suppose he'd be a stableman at this point."

"A man..." Reese's scratchy voice trailed off with the possibilities. Then he crept closer to the bars, a glimmer of hope touching his features for the first time since Whitney met him. "He handsome like his father?"

Reese flashed nasty, rotting teeth.

"Like a prince," Whitney said, burying the urge to cringe.

Reese's grubby paws wrapped the bars, drawing as close as he could, but then he sank back. "Dun't matter none," he groaned. "There ain't no way outta these cells."

"Yig and shog," Whitney said with a sing-song flourish. "You just haven't met me yet."

Whitney strolled over to his cell door and leaned into it, shielding Reese's view of what he was doing. He made believe he was just examining the door, but he fished the key he'd filched from the guard out of his pocket. There was a soft scraping sound, then a click as Whitney pushed the key into the lock and turned it. He shook the bars, careful the door stayed shut.

"I told ye, no way out," Reese said.

Whitney strode across the cell, opened his hand, and showed Reese the key.

"Had you known who I was," Whitney began, "you would know the name Whitney Fierstown is synonymous with 'world's greatest thief.'

Swiped this from the fat one—well, they're all pretty fat—the fat one with the burn mark when they threw me in here."

The old man fumbled over a response, his bloodshot eyes bulging.

"Your son paid a handsome fortune for me to get myself arrested," Whitney said. "Don't squander this opportunity. You've only got a couple of minutes left. Right now, the guards are over there, and the kitchen is empty."

Reese shifted his gaze from the key to the bars of his cell, then back. That was all the consideration he needed. "Gimme, gimme, gimme," he begged, nearly coming out of his skin to reach for the key.

"Ah, ah, ah," Whitney said, pulling the key out of the man's reach. "First, promise me you'll make sure your son doesn't skip town without paying me the rest of what he owes me." He wasn't out of the woods yet. A master thief knows that you never give up the grift until the grift is through.

"Anything!" Reese shouted.

"Keep it down in there!" came the distant voice of one of the guards.

"Anything," the old man said in a desperate whisper.

Whitney handed over the key, and Reese wasted no time rushing to the door of the cage he'd called home for Iam knows how long. The door unlocked with a soft click. Reese looked back at Whitney. Whitney saw a new sense of life on the man's face and almost regretted what he was about to do until the old man cackled.

"Thanks, Mr. Thief, but ain't no way you'll be collecting anything from me in there."

Reese tossed the key out of the window of his cell, then threw open the door and scurried up the stairs toward the kitchen. He was so excited he panted like a dog in heat.

Whitney waited until the old wretch reached the exit. "Guards!" he shouted. "Oh, guards! The prisoner escaped!"

The guards peeked into the cells, expecting it was a lie. When they saw the sprung cell door, they scrambled for their gear.

"He went up those stairs, just there!" Whitney said.

All four guards rushed past him. When the sound of boots on stone faded, Whitney casually walked to his cell door, swung it open, and released a satisfied sigh, relieved he hadn't trusted the man and opened his own cell in advance.

He only had a few minutes before they caught Reese and tossed him back into the dungeon for the rest of his miserable life. It was hard to pity a man so swift to ignore his debts—even if they were lies to begin with. Whitney imagined the old guard captain had a good reason for locking him up in the first place.

Closing his eyes, Whitney conjured up his memory of the castle from the last time he'd escaped. He was in the castle's upper dungeons, but still on the first level—the only level with windows. He'd been dragged in from the left staircase, and the right staircase led to the kitchens.

He went left, away from where the guards chased Reese, pausing for just a moment in their station. Their desk was empty except a bit of parchment and a cup of what smelled like mead. Whitney threw back the remainder of the amber substance and swallowed hard. He coughed.

Not mead...something harder. Much harder.

He shook out his head and took the stairs. They were obviously not the only guards on duty in the royal keep of the largest kingdom this side of the Torrential Sea, so he had to be careful. The floor leveled out to a gracious hallway lined with crystal candelabras which led into the keep's Great Hall.

He skulked down the hall at a brisk trot, careful to avoid any windows or openings. A tall arched door framed the far end of the passage, and beyond it, the exit from the keep and entrance to the West Tower.

He spotted two King's Shieldsmen talking with a dwarf near a doorway. Whitney thought there'd be more of the King's Shield around. It was all a bit too easy. The Shieldsmen spoke harshly to the little man, shoving him out of the way before taking several steps outside to make sure he didn't try anything.

Whitney took off running, then slid for the far doorway just before the Shieldsmen turned again. He let the door quietly close and leaned flat against it, breathing heavily.

Once his heart settled, he regarded his clothing, dry now, but still stained with crusting mud and... other stuff. The neckline of his shirt sagged, and the bottoms of his pants were torn. There was no way he would fit in at a royal masquerade. He needed a new plan.

He trotted down the long loggia adorned with creeping vines. He stayed close to the wall and kept his eyes peeled for guards that never came.

A shouldered arch led into what he remembered should be the western courtyard. As Whitney crossed the threshold, he listened to music playing through a door across the way leading into the Great Hall—a fiddle. Of all the countless instruments he'd heard in his travels across the world, he hated the fiddle most of all. Above the distant music, he heard the gentle cascading of water.

He canvased the area for guards. Again, not a soul was in sight. From his new position, the soft sound of water now sounded more like the steady gurgling of a fountain. He crossed the greenway, and there he saw it —a gorgeous fountain and fresh water. It was carved in the form of a dragon, wings spread wide, eyes of brilliant crystal. In his last foray through the Glass Castle, the impressive statue surely hadn't been there.

From its mouth, water spouted into a shallow pool. Whitney dipped down low and splashed his face, sucking in mouthfuls. After the food he'd endured in the dungeon, it provided a needed boost in energy.

For a brief moment, the music grew louder. He glanced up and saw none other than the Queen of Glass herself, still wearing her mask. She burst from of the Great Hall's side entrance and stormed toward him. He ducked behind the fountain and covered his mouth.

The Queen's heel got stuck in mud, and she cursed it before ripping her foot free and throwing down her mask. She crossed the greenway and sat at the edge of the fountain. Whitney thought he could hear her crying, but the rain had picked up again and made it difficult to hear.

He peaked around the fountain again. The Queen's necklace alone was probably worth enough to buy a castle in the Dragon's Tail. He knew he was in the castle for the King's crown, but he couldn't help himself.

Before he had the chance to further consider the heist, her head snapped around, and he ducked again. She gasped, then stood and ran in the other direction. At the same time, a King's Shieldsman exited the Great Hall and sprinted after her.

With the rain picking up again, Whitney knew this was the perfect cover to get what he came for. He bent down, spread a bit of mud on his face, and tore off through the downpour. Now he invited the mud to further splash up and conceal his outfit's many tears.

He spotted the Queen's pair of glittering heels and a mask outside the Grand Hall. He thanked some good fortune most people would call Iam, and snagged up the mask, smearing mud on it as well to diminish its opulence. Frosted glass with gold trim was an excellent way to make him stand out, and a thief always fared better blending with the crowd.

He opened the door to the Great Hall, and the sound of joyful music amplified. Fiddles and drums, lutes and lyres. The nobles danced and ate, wine flowed freely. No one seemed the slightest bit aware that the Queen was outside in distress. Maybe they wouldn't care. Men who frequented the kind of places Whitney did knew how people spoke about their "Savage, Whore Queen," when they thought they weren't heard.

Whitney had escaped the Glass Castle once or twice before, but one look around the Great Hall, decorated for a party, and Whitney finally understood why the kingdom bore its name. Everything sparkled. Small flames flickered in a dozen glass chandeliers, prisms of light dithering across the walls, ceiling, and floor. Twisting crystal columns reached up and met the glass spire above.

Few men without old names or old money had seen the magnificent spire from this angle, although it could be seen from nearly anywhere in the city, reflecting the light of the sun or moons, casting its glow over Yarrington. So close to the bay and there wasn't even a need for a lighthouse. From this angle, however, its immensity made Whitney speechless —which was a rare occurrence.

Stained glass painted beautiful pictures onto the walls like tapestries telling the stories of great kings and their dedication to Iam. In the center of the room, King Liam sat in a glistening throne made of glass. Its legs sprawled out like translucent hands clutching the dais below. Atop his thinly-haired head was the prize—the Glass Crown.

For the first time in his life, Whitney wondered if he'd gone too far. Had he finally accepted a challenge even he couldn't pull off? The King was an invalid, the rumors were true, but there were King's Shieldsmen everywhere, including directly behind and to the side of the King. Whitney held the mask up to his face just in time to see a Shieldsman approach, so young the man couldn't even grow a proper beard yet. Not that Whitney could either.

"My Lord," the Shieldsman said. "You are quite disheveled."

"Quite observant of you," Whitney feigned a ridiculous eastern accent. "I was resting in the peace of the gardens when a quick and sudden downpour threatened to drown me where I lay. I miss the drought already."

"You smell rather… ripe. We can get you some new clothing if you follow me, my Lord."

Whitney caught a whiff of himself. His face scrunched up. "Thank you, Sir…"

"Sir Rand Langley, my Lord."

Whitney didn't squander the chance to further survey the hall as he followed the Shieldsman into an adjoining chamber. Rand spoke in a hushed voice to a young handmaiden inside. The girl blushed as he stroked her arm. Whitney pretended not to notice.

"Stay here," the guard said, returning his attention to Whitney. "Tessa here will bring you fresh clothes."

"Tell her to make it quick," Whitney replied.

Impatience was a stable of nobility, so he had to play the part. He waited, tapping his foot as if to appear anxious though it was really just in time to the music.

"My Lord, your clothes?" the handmaiden said after a short while. It sounded like a question.

Whitney turned around to see her place a pile of clothing more exquisite than anything Whitney had ever worn on a chair in the corner of the room. She curtseyed before leaving him in privacy.

He peeled the wet, mud-and-shog-crusted clothes off his body. From the castle stables to the dungeon, and now the very castle itself, they'd seen more than most noble's clothing did in a lifetime. The handmaiden had brought him cloth with which to dry himself as well, which he was thankful for. He dried off before slipping on the silk clothes. The young lady had thought of everything, even bringing him a new mask.

He now wore the white and pale blue colors of Iam and the Glass Kingdom. He regarded himself in the large looking glass and found himself simultaneously impressed and disgusted. He looked exactly the part of all those wretched gold-mongers he'd dedicated a lifetime toward robbing.

Just then, screams erupted from the Grand Hall. He threw open the door and found himself in the midst of chaos. Shieldsmen shoved their way through flocks of nobles, knocking over servers and their trays. It took Whitney a moment to realize what was going on but when his gaze fell upon the dais where the King slumped, he knew.

He fought through the frantic crowd. His plan to get close and distract the guards was no longer needed. Everyone was more than distracted.

He pushed forward lightly, but with enough force to make a path. As he neared the stage, he watched the whole of the King's Shield surrounding the King.

Three bells rang out. King Liam's head hung slack to the side, his withering, gray hair twisting over a liver-spotted forehead and with the Glass Crown no longer atop it. Air rattled through his throat, a sound like a wheezing zhulong. One final breath and then Liam went silent.

The King's Shield raised their shields and blocked everyone else in the party from seeing, but Whitney was behind them, now just feet away from the raised platform. Heads bobbed frantically as guests tried to get a good view. That's when he saw it. Glimmering on the dance floor not five paces away—the Glass Crown. It must have fallen off the King's head and rolled. No one was even paying attention to it.

Whitney pushed again, closer and closer. He stopped just in front of the crown and stepped on its edge, turning it upright. He hooked his foot around it and slowly lifted his knee, trying to draw as little attention to himself as possible before reaching down and grabbing hold of it. It was light as a feather, even with all the flawless gems embedded in the thin band. The image of Iam's lidless eye bulged front and center, the pupil a diamond so large Whitney nearly lost his breath.

He took a deep breath to compose himself, shoved it under his shirt, and backed away.

Well, that was easy.

"Hey, you! Stop!" someone shouted from somewhere behind Whitney.

He cringed before glancing back. An older, scarier looking Shieldsman stalked toward him, drawing his sword from his scabbard. Just as Whitney prepared to run, he realized the knight wasn't looking at him. He swept by, nearly bumping the priceless crown under Whitney's shirt, then reached out and grabbed one of the Shesaitju emissaries by the collar and yanked him down from the dais.

"They don't need your help, and you don't need to be up there," the Shieldsman said, escorting the gray-skinned man from the throne.

Whitney didn't wait around any longer. He fell in with the mob being forced from the Grand Hall and kept his head low until he was on the streets.

Whitney Fierstown had just stolen the Glass Crown from King Liam the Conqueror and gotten away with it.

VIII

THE THIEF

After days of travel, for the first time in his life, Whitney was relieved to see the town he'd grown up in. Troborough in all its boring glory loomed on the horizon as he stopped to drink. The water felt chilly as it went down, autumn in full swing. He tried not to think about how he and the rest of the town had used the Shellnak River to bathe and piss in daily.

The water *tasted* pure, and that's all that mattered.

His horse whinnied behind him. It wasn't his horse per se—he'd nipped it from an Old Yarrington stable in the chaos following the King's death—but he'd ridden enough to know their various sounds. The old beast probably just wanted a sip of water, which it deserved after the long trek from Yarrington. After he'd fully sated his thirst, Whitney grabbed the reins, leading the horse to the river. It stepped in, the light brown hair darkening where the water lapped against its legs.

"That's a good girl," Whitney said, then looked the horse over. "I mean boy." He laughed and excused the horse for not joining in.

"Not much farther," he said, still talking to the horse as if it cared to listen. It was the kind of company he got used to in his line of work. Anyone he ever ran too close with either screwed him over on a job or vice versa. No honor amongst thieves.

After giving the horse a drink, he climbed up and gave a soft kick.

"Over there is where Sora lived with old man Wetzel all those years ago," he said, almost absentmindedly. He pointed to a tiny, thatched hovel sitting along the river. She had been a friend—more than a friend, probably. But he was so young it was difficult to have called her anything else. That was all before he'd left home to pursue a life of thrills at the expense of others. Now, it seemed odd to even mention her home with such familiarity.

He slowed the horse to a trot without thinking and watched the home until it was out of sight. It looked completely abandoned, just as it had a few days ago, overgrown with weeds, and the windows blocked by clutter. He thought about her from time to time, though rarely, and he imagined she hadn't given him much thought either over the years. The day he left, he may as well have been dead to the people of Troborough, his own family included.

"Still nobody home."

A pile of books falling away from the window stole the words from Whitney's lips. There was movement within, then the gaunt face of old Wetzel appeared. He looked like a walking corpse, skeletal and pale. And somehow, he seemed grumpier than ever. His pale eyes fixated on Whitney as he went by, giving him goosebumps. The only thing he felt comfort in was that the rest of the shack was empty, and there was little space to hide.

"Sora really must have married and moved on at least," he said, patting the horse. "Good for her. Can't believe that old codger outlived the King though."

He took a deep breath and looked around. He'd never noticed the pleasant beauty of the land surrounding Troborough. When he'd lived there, he hardly ever left the farm—milking cows, plowing fields, and feeding chickens. When he'd returned to spend a few nights drinking himself silly, he'd come in at night and spent most of his time with blurry vision. Hadn't even left the Twilight Manor. They had beds and booze, what more did one need?

Now, in the light of day, he saw the rolling fields and the flowering meadow. The birds soaring above without care. It was so peaceful.

In the distance, a thatched roof rose up from the hills—Farmer Branson's place. And next to that, the Julset twins and the Whelforks. He laughed out loud, remembering old Charles Whelfork and the way he waved his walking cane anytime he caught anyone on his property.

The horse let out a snort.

The town's chapel appeared over the horizon, a two-story structure bearing a single steeple with the Eye of Iam carved in bronze now patinated. He remembered it being much larger, but after seeing the castle, and the mansions, and the cathedrals of Yarrington, the place looked like little more than a pointy hovel.

"Hey, Farmer Branson!" Whitney shouted and waved at a man toiling in his field. He glanced up, wiped his sweaty, furrowed brow, and went right back to work.

Whitney hadn't expected anyone to remember who he was, not really. He scratched at his neck and heard the hairs against his fingernails. When he'd left, he couldn't even grow stubble.

The horse plodded along past Wetzel's little healer's stand in town. Usually covered by potions and herbal concoctions, it stood empty save for some beads hanging from the canvas. It looked nearly abandoned, like the man's shack. He probably was so old he couldn't even leave his home. Whitney could remember many times as a child having to force down whatever remedy the old coot concocted while Sora told him to be a man.

Even though Wetzel still clung to life like a mad hermit, Whitney wondered how many others had passed on from his hometown? He already knew about his parent's fates, and that plague surely couldn't have been merciful. The fact he'd never get a chance to rub his many adventures in his father's face was the saddest part though. He knew that was wrong, but it was true. His father made it clear enough before Whitney left that he was no longer worthy of the good Fierstown name, and his mother always took his father's side no matter what. Now, there was precious little he could do apart from kicking some dirt over their graves.

Shog on him. Shog on them both. This Fierstown carries the Glass Crown instead of manure.

In the middle of the village, between the chapel, the bailiff's house, and the Twilight Manor was a large town square. As always, it was the busiest place in a town that rarely was. Hitched outside was the armored trade caravan run by the no-good, wobbly-eyed dwarf Grint Strongiron who'd challenged Whitney.

Everyone stopped as Whitney arrived on his horse. Hushed voices broke out all around him.

"Is this about King Liam?" asked Carlo, the town drunk.

"By Iam, it's true… he's gone."

News normally traveled to fringe towns slowly, but word had apparently already reached them. Even long expected, the death of King Liam was sure to cause great waves of change throughout the kingdom.

Whitney glanced down at his outfit and realized why Liam was all that came up. It was sewn from silks only a noble or an envoy of the Crown could afford. So, he walked the horse directly in front of the Twilight Manor and stood on the stirrups.

"Grint Strongiron!" he shouted. "Come out of your drinking hole and behold your thorough defeat!"

After a few beats, the door to the tavern thudded open, and the dwarf came waddling out beside his mates. Whitney barely remembered what they looked like, and definitely not their names. There was the reedy, Shesaitju fellow with skin the color of ash, two scarred-up mercenaries who looked like twins, still wearing so much armor it must have been filled with sweat despite the temperature, and a plump old man in silks. The trader they all protected, no doubt.

"What say ye, farmboy?" Grint asked, wobbling from too much drink already. Only thing he'd be able to protect the poor sap from was an angry ant.

Whitney produced the Glass Crown from the folds of his cloak, its gems gleaming in the sunlight.

"Gaze upon my greatest achievement." He placed the crown on his head. It was a perfect fit.

"Bah!" the dwarf said. "Anyone could buy one of them fakes. Ain't no one—including you—done robbed the King."

"The King is dead," Whitney said, then immediately regretted it.

The crowd gasped as all the rumors were confirmed. A woman started crying as if she'd ever even laid eyes upon Liam the Conqueror. The town's priest fell to his knees and traced circles of prayer around the white cloth covering his eyes. Whitney didn't recognize him, but the same plague that killed his parents probably took the priest he remembered. The church usually cared for people in such times of crisis, often getting themselves sick when nothing could be done. It was things like that which led Whitney to believe that if there ever was an Iam, he wasn't looking down on his so-called children anymore.

"Ye killed the King over a bet?" the dwarf asked, incredulous. "I knew I liked ye!"

"No that's not—"

"Blasphemer!" Carlo barked. All his blabbering about serving in the King's army, judging by his expression, maybe it was true. He could barely hold back tears.

"The Grace of Iam is dead because of you?" asked a woman.

"No, no," Whitney said. "I didn't do it."

The town's confusion over Whitney's arrival gave way to anger. Troborough had no militia, only a worthless bailiff stationed there by the Crown, but he forgot that these were small-town folk who likely believed all the grand stories about their king. Worshipped him as much as they did Iam, maybe more. Grint and the caravan watched in bewilderment as the townsfolk, all wearing scowls, closed in around Whitney's horse. All that was missing were pitchforks and torches.

Whitney hadn't even gotten to the part of his triumphant romp where he tossed the crown's many gems to the children so they might seek out more for their lives like he had.

He backed his horse away slowly, then noticed flakes of something wavering in the air above him.

Early in the season for snow.

Then, the smell came. It was like a campfire but far stronger. Ash fluttered on the currents of a southern breeze. He craned his neck to see around the chapel and found billowing smoke filling half the sky.

A pair of screams stole the mob's attention.

Whitney fell back down in the saddle and pushed his horse toward the smoke. The sky grew darker and the pungent, yet sweet smell of burning wood and thatch met his nostrils.

Where the path opened, just beyond the delta, he saw it. Sharp, whipping tongues of fire reaching like demons of Elsewhere, devouring the eastern side of town. He couldn't even see the now-empty farm where he'd grown up, tears welling in his eyes from the heat, a thick cloud of darkness looming over the community.

"The Black Sands are attacking!" a man screamed as he ran down the road. "The Black Sands are—" He hit the dirt and flipped, head over heel, an arrow sticking out of his back.

Whitney wasn't sure if he'd heard correctly, but the arrow was revealing enough. The town square exploded into panic. Whitney tried to turn his horse around, but frantic villagers darted everywhere, causing it to rear back. The crown flew off his head and fell at Grint Strongiron's feet. The dwarf glanced up with his drunken, crossed eyes, grinned, and picked it up.

"Thieving, runt," Whitney swore under his breath. He tried to push his horse forward through the chaos when an arrow tipped with fire shattered the Twilight Manor's window.

The wood caught fast.

"Time for us to leave, boss!" one of the trading caravan mercenaries said. He and his twin grabbed the old trader and hurried him onto their wagon, Grint following close behind. Their Shesaitju companion tried to do the same, but Carlo grabbed him. By the looks of his cherry-red cheeks, he was drunk as they were.

"You bring your ash-skin friends here?" Carlo said. "Eager to lose again?" He reared back and punched the man across the face. The Shesaitju hit the dirt hard, then reached out for the wagon. Grint hauled him up just before they raced away. The trader thrashed on the reins, and they took off in the direction opposite the fire and screams.

Whitney finally convinced his horse to leap over a fallen villager and took off after them. Grint hung onto the side of the wagon with one hand and admired the crown in the other as if the sounds of death filling the air were merely another day at work.

"No good son of the mountain!" Whitney grabbed the other side of the crown and tried to pull it free as he rode. The dwarf was stronger than his size suggested.

"Let go of it, farmboy!" Grint yelled.

Whitney felt his grip slipping, then the elegant crown snapped in two. The recoil sent him sliding off the saddle, and as he tumbled, he saw the damnable dwarf grinning and waving with half the crown on his head. A villager screamed for them to let her on, but one of the armored mercenaries kicked her away.

Whitney slammed into the side of Liora Dodson's pig farm, the roof already alight. The smell of pork greeted his nostrils, confusing his stomach. Flames lapped at him from the windows of the farmhouse as the wood burned and popped. The heat was overwhelming, and sweat soaked him through. He couldn't hear anything over the sounds of fire and screaming townsfolk, so he squinted through the heaviness of the smoke back toward the chapel.

He looked around for his horse, but it was smart enough to flee.

"Traitorous beast," he whispered, stowing his half of the crown.

He spun a slow circle, trying to figure out his next move, then quickly jumped back behind cover and peered back around the corner. An army stampeded his way, numbering in the dozens, carrying the standard of the Kingdom of the Black Sands. The tattered banner—nothing more than solid tan with specks of black—flapped tauntingly above the helpless Troborough villagers. It was the very same flag the Shesaitju had flown before being conquered by Liam and the Glass Kingdom.

Whitney cringed as he heard the screams of men and women, many of which he'd grown up with. Leaning out further, he saw the gray hands of Black Sands warriors groping Troborough women and slaughtering the men.

He drew a breath of air and stifled a cough as the black smoke filled his lungs. A group of Shesaitju shouted as they set fire to the chapel.

What are Black Sandsmen doing in The Glass Kingdom?

The two peoples hadn't been at war since he was a child. When Liam marched on them, they suffered significant losses and eventually, the Kingdom of the Black Sands bent the knee. Fair trade, yearly annuity, and an agreement to send troops to the Glass Kingdom's aid whenever they asked for it were the foundation of an alliance that greatly favored one side. Rebellions among their people who refused the terms were frequent in the early days of Liam's reign, but not since.

An alliance was only an alliance until the interests of one party outweighed the benefits of the union.

Presently, one Black Sandsmen stood apart from the horde of ash-skinned warriors, riding a beast with orange scales, a mane of the same color, and thick legs like a warthog. It had a snout, wet and turned up but it was the size of a horse with the face and tail of a dragon. Whitney knew the creatures well from his travels in the Shesaitju lands. The zhulong rider gave orders which Whitney couldn't hear over the loud snap-crackle of the fires, now threatening to set the surrounding forest ablaze.

He sucked in another breath, ignoring the sting, and leaned back against the wall. It was time to go. The King was dead only a few days and the Shesaitju were already rebelling?

This isn't my fight. Whitney turned to bolt toward the other end of the alley, away from the fight, when he heard a cry from the middle of the road.

"Mama!"

The girl couldn't have been more than five years old. Whitney peaked around the corner and saw a crew of Black Sandsmen pointing her way.

Move girl! Whitney thought. *It's time to move.*

He looked back at the attackers. The zhulong rider sat, head above most roofs, galloping toward her, but she merely stood there and cried.

"Don't be a hero, Whitney," he whispered to himself as he stared at her. "Just run like she ought to." Flames grasped for her from the building, causing her to shriek as it licked her arms. Still, she didn't move.

"Shog in a barrel," Whitney cursed before taking a step, then another, willing each foot to do its part. He begged his limbs to move faster, but he was used to fighting in the shadows, not in open battle. He didn't even have a weapon.

The zhulong and its rider closed in, the latter screaming something in Saitjuese. Whitney grabbed the little girl and ran, but the mount picked up speed behind him. Its thick paws hammered the earth as quickly as Whitney's heart did his rib cage.

He glanced back.

Never look back, you dolt!

Dust kicked up, and the sound of the man's roar was so near, it overpowered the sound of flames. He twirled a razor-sharp scimitar high above his head.

Whitney turned away and drove his feet harder into the ground. It was no use. The shadow of the beast arced in front of him, and as he prepared to dive, a *whiff* passed by his ear followed by a *thunk.* The rider screamed and crashed to the hard dirt path. An arrow stuck out of his neck, still wobbling.

The great beast continued running, knocked Whitney off his feet, and continued aimlessly. Whitney was able to shield the girl just in time to absorb the brunt of the fall. She escaped his grip and fled so fast he wondered why she ever needed him to carry her.

He rolled over, still in a daze, until he felt something sharp dig into his side. He threw open his cloak and saw the half of the Glass Crown. A curse bubbled up from his lungs as he remembered the thieving dwarf.

A loud clash of metal drew Whitney's attention to a legion of Glass Kingdom soldiers on horseback just arriving. They crashed into the Shesaitju raiders, and Whitney found himself caught right in the middle of the fray.

A Black Sandsman spotted Whitney and charged. His blade sliced down toward him, but Whitney rolled, ignoring the sting of the crown poking him. He reached and grabbed the sword of the fallen zhulong rider, then brought it to bear, surprising his attacker. It caught the man across the neck, but dug in at an odd angle and got stuck.

The gurgling corpse dragged Whitney as it collapsed, but Whitney yanked on the hilt until the blade came free. Blood saturated his face and he dropped the sword to paw at his face, desperate to wipe the blood from his eyes and lips, willing the vomit to stay in his stomach.

It wasn't the first time he'd seen a man die in battle, not by a long shot, but it was the first time he'd been holding the weapon. Killing was a thief's last resort, and Whitney was good enough to avoid doing it.

His gaze darted from side to side at the fighting soldiers. He'd never seen such chaos. Dirt swirled in the air, dyed red from blood and the glow of flames. Clashing blades sparked, screams echoed, and it was impossible to tell who was winning. He went to take a step, then an archer lost his head to a Glass soldier.

Whitney spun, searching for a way out. He heard movement beside him and turned. A gray fist plowed into his jaw and sent him sprawling to the ground.

"As brittle as glass without your king, eh, *my Lord*?" said a heavily accented voice, laughing. The Shesaitju brute was a towering stack of corded muscle.

Whitney rolled onto his shoulder and used his momentum to shoot back to his feet. The warrior closed in on him. Whitney took a step back and tripped over a bow. Now that was a weapon he was proficient with. In one fluid motion, he grabbed an arrow from the quiver on a dead man's back and notched it. The warrior brought his sword up just as Whitney let the arrow go. It stabbed through the Shesaitju man's chest, but he didn't slow a bit. Instead, he grinned as he snapped the shaft, stalking forward. Whitney groped for a second arrow but found none. The warrior pressed a heavy boot down on Whitney's chest and drew back his sword.

This is how the greatest thief in Pantego is going to die? On my back, with the broken crown of a dead conqueror in my pocket, in a fight I have no horse in.

A part of him felt it was fitting. The other part closed his eyes and prayed to Iam for a miracle. Whitney wasn't a religious man, but a good thief always hedges bets.

The weight suddenly lifted. He reopened his eyes and found the man's tree trunk of a neck without a head on it. He collapsed on top of Whitney, hard, knocking what little breath he had left in his lungs right out of them.

Hooves *clip-clopped* behind him, then skidded to a halt, dust kicking up.

"I don't think that belongs to you, thief," said that same young King's Shieldsman who'd had the handmaiden fetch new clothes for Whitney. Sir Rand Langley sheathed a fine longsword and hopped down from his steed. Behind him, Whitney heard the cheers of Glassmen as the Black Sands attackers were forced into retreat.

Rand knelt and reached into Whitney's open cloak without bothering to free him from the heavy corpse first. His eyes went wide as he grasped the Glass Crown and only one half came out.

"The Black Sands stole it," Whitney wheezed. "Was just on my way to return it, I swear."

The man ground his teeth in frustration, glanced up at his fleeing foes, then back at Whitney. "Tell it to the Wearer of White," he said, right before bringing his foot down into Whitney's head.

IX

THE KNIGHT

King Liam was dead, and Queen Oleander shed real tears, though not for him.

Torsten had trouble sleeping ever since he'd carried Pi's nearly lifeless body up the West Tower to the Queen's chambers, out of sight. He couldn't get that gruesome vision out of his head. The poor boy, driven to attempted suicide by Redstar's curse, and now he lay in fitful sleep from the fall.

I should have listened to her about him…

For once, Torsten actually wanted to engage Oleander in a discussion regarding Redstar and that night a year ago. He had been plotting for a way to broach the subject without angering her but couldn't find a moment alone. King Liam's funeral overwhelmed the capital while Pi's fate remained secret.

Torsten watched the servants toiling to transform the Grand Hall into a viewing chamber. The casket itself was crafted out of glass and ornately decorated. The King's body was covered by a thin sheet of light blue silk. It was all employed to ensure that Liam would be remembered as he was when Torsten fought at his side and not as he now was—frail and rotting.

Flowers filled the hall, hydrangeas and larkspur, always blue and white. Incense burned; a sweet, almost too-sweet smell. At least the room no longer stank of death.

Once everything was set, Torsten took his place at Oleander's side.

"Your Grace," Wren the Holy, High Priest of Iam, addressed her on her throne which had so long stood beside Liam's. The Glass Throne itself remained empty. "Is the Crown Prince coming?"

The old man had been High Priest since before even Liam was coronated. His long, white beard was likely a foot shorter then, and hadn't needed to walk hunched over with a cane. Scorch marks around his eyes left them white and useless, for as any ordained priest of Iam, he had taken a vow of sightlessness. His was the Eye of Iam and no other. Some priests chose to cover their burned-out eyes with a cloth, but Wren left his bare for all his flock to see.

"My son mourns in private for his beloved father," she answered, not missing a beat.

"But, Your Grace, it is customary for the Crown Prince to be present at the burial of his father. And being that Pi is Liam's only—"

"My son, your future king, wants to be alone."

"I understand, Your Grace. These times of loss are never easy for the young." He bowed, then turned to face the amassed crowd. They were nobles of the Glass Kingdom, from the wealthy families within the walls of Yarrington to the members of the Royal Council.

"Esteemed people of Yarrington and beyond!" he bellowed with timbre and clarity not expected from a man his age. "We gather here under Iam. May he watch over us and guide our steps."

He raised his scepter topped with the Eye of Iam. The crowd echoed his words, then traced their eyes with their fingers and bowed their heads, as was customary.

"Long has Liam lifted our people to fulfill the will of the one true God. A thousand years ago, Iam watched from the Gate of Light as his brethren battled each other over who might rule Pantego. For the Vigilant Eye of Iam saw the trouble in their hateful ways, just as his chosen son Liam saw it here. Our King fought, in His name, to bring peace to fair Pantego. Praise be the Vigilant Eye."

The assembly repeated those words.

Another blind priest shuffled over and presented Wren with King Liam's claymore, known across Pantego as *Salvation.*

Wren lowered his cane, then balanced the sword across his hands. The weight made his arms shake as he made his way to the open casket.

"With this sword, Liam brought this kingdom to new heights," Wren said. "And so shall it join him in the Light, and *we* must never forget the greatness he has left in our hands."

Torsten watched Oleander with a heavy heart as Wren laid the blade over Liam's chest and folded his liver-spotted hands over the golden hilt. Pi's nearness to death had made her inconsolable, and with him to be named the new king, in no condition to rule, it would leave her the most powerful person in Pantego. The Queen Regent.

Wren stretched out his back, retrieved his cane, then turned back to the crowd. "It is with a heavy heart we bid farewell to our kind and pure King, but he is with Iam now, watching over us for all of time, in darkness and in light. And he has not left us alone. For we are fortunate that Liam has left us with a fine, young heir."

"Then why is the Crown Prince not here?" asked Yuri Darkings, Master of Coin. The handsome, if not rotund, gray-haired man from Winde Port stood at the front of the Royal Council, where he'd served since before Torsten was born.

Oleander seemed to be in a fog until those words caused her to sit up, eyes smoldering.

"We haven't seen him in months," Yuri continued. "Should the Crown Prince not attend his own father's funeral?"

Murmurs flared through the crowd, filling the Great Hall like a swarm of angry bees.

"Yes, where is he?" asked another.

"They say he's locked away in his room like a mad hermit," said the Master of Rolls, Frederick Holgrass, earning a glare from Oleander that could stop hearts.

"Pi Nothhelm is the one true heir of Liam Nothhelm," Wren stepped forward and declared before Oleander could react. "He is our rightful king, and when he is done mourning the loss of his great father, the Glass Crown shall be placed upon his head, as is the will of Iam."

Oleander made a weak attempt to smile, though her glower never left the council members who'd spoken out. Torsten's heart plummeted further. The upcoming coronation would be merely symbolic of course. Pi was king the moment Liam's heart stopped beating, and the faces of many of the Glass nobles glowed with the hope of another great leader.

They were all being lied to, and Torsten could do nothing about it, even if he wanted to.

The truth would do more harm than good. If the people found out that Liam's only living heir might be dying already, or had spent the last year in a fog of madness and not rooted in studies as Oleander always claimed, Torsten couldn't imagine where new enemies might spring from. For Iam's sake, even the Glass Crown itself had gone missing, stolen or lost in the confusion of the masquerade. Torsten loathed to think how people might react to such a failure of the King's Shield, or his queen whom he'd decided not to tell until the search ran dry.

Wren returned to Liam's casket and lay a hand upon it. He whispered a prayer first, then turned his attention back to the crowd. "Until Celeste is full once more, we join the future King in mourning the loss of his father. Then, at the crest of Mount Lister, under the full moons and Iam's Vigilant Eye, Pi's coronation will be complete. Praise be the Vigilant—"

Suddenly, Sir Rand Langley barged through the side doors. He was supposed to be off inspecting Fort Marimount but entered the Grand Hall instead, ready to speak until he realized what he'd interrupted. A bit of blood stained his right pauldron.

Torsten lowered his hand from the handle of his sword, then stood quietly, waiting for an explanation.

Oleander's glare hardened.

"Sir… I've been sent to fetch you," Rand stuttered as all eyes fixed on him. "It's important."

"Enough to interrupt the funeral of my late husband, your king?" Oleander questioned.

"I… uh."

The poor kid looked like he was going to piss himself.

"Your Grace," Torsten whispered to her. "Allow me to go with him. I assure you, you're in good hands."

"What is the meaning of this, Your Grace?" Yuri Darkings questioned.

Oleander regarded the longstanding Master of Coin, then nodded. "Go,

Torsten, and show him what happens to those who can't follow orders," she said. "I will be fine. Your men are trained well…. Most of them."

It was the closest thing to a compliment Torsten had ever received from her. He bowed low, his gaze falling upon King Liam's glass casket.

I'm so sorry, Your Grace, he thought, looking to his king's casket. All those years of service to the man who raised him from the dirt, and now he would miss watching his body committed to the Royal Crypt. But duty, as always, came before personal feelings, and a young Shieldsman like Rand wouldn't barge in on so sacred a ceremony unless it was urgent.

Torsten turned to follow the petrified knight, who required a firm nudge to get moving. They quietly but hastily traveled through the servant's tunnels. It was the quickest route to the Shield Hall. The circular war room was carved into the cliffside upon which the castle stood, with a clear view of Mount Lister.

Tapestries telling tales of Liam's conquests hung from the walls surrounding a long, shimmering table. Statues were placed around the edge of the room, not of kings like in the Grand Hall, but of former Wearers of White. Men who'd served the Glass Kingdom before Liam was even a thought. Like the Shieldsmen armor and swords, each of the effigies was carved from glaruium—a potent ore found only in the belly of Mount Lister herself. The circle wasn't yet complete. Although Uriah's likeness had been formed of glaruium, his was the only one not holding a sword, as his body had never been found after he disappeared into the Webbed Woods.

Two other Shieldsmen huddled over the massive sheet of glass, intricately etched, engraved with a map of the kingdom and beyond. Torsten noted the sand-blown glass flames positioned on the map in at least a half-dozen locations southeast of Yarrington.

"What is this?" Torsten asked.

"Go on boy, tell him," Wardric, the gruffest of the Shieldsmen, addressed Rand. The Wearer of White had no official second in command, but if anyone were, it would have been Wardric. He'd served long before Torsten, before Uriah was even Wearer of White, but had been passed over for Wearer of White when Uriah died after Liam personally chose Torsten. The oversight never seemed to sit well with him.

Rand swallowed hard. "Sirs Nikserof, Mulliner, and I were doing a routine inspection on Fort Marimount in the South, as Taskmaster Lars assigned us when we saw smoke rising. We followed it and engaged a raiding party razing Troborough."

"Where are they?" Torsten asked.

"Still dealing with the aftermath in Troborough. They sent me back to tell you."

"We also received galler birds from Lilith's Mill and Flatpost at the start of the ceremony—said they also were hit but not nearly as complete." Wardric pointed to another small farming town south of Yarrington and then another.

"Who?" Torsten asked.

"The Black Sands," Wardric said with the venom of a man who'd fought the Shesaitju on more than one occasion.

"I saw them myself," Rand said. "We tried but..."

He hung his head. Torsten patted him on the shoulder. It was a tough first ask for any new recruit to do better. "It's all right, lad," he said. "Who could have imagined they'd do this with King Liam only freshly in his casket?"

"Those heathens will do anything to keep their gold," Wardric spat.

Torsten drew a deep breath and let the information settle. Burning defenseless towns seemed like a random act of hatred, but the Shesaitju had clearly learned from losing to Liam. Cities, no matter how large, were fed by farms, and they'd just laid waste to countless yards of them; enough to cause unrest in the population. They were feeling out their enemy first instead of charging carelessly as they'd tended to do in the past.

Had Liam incidentally taught all of Pantego how to win a war?

A dead king, a dying heir, an act of rebellion—what else could go wrong?

"Did we capture any raiders?"

Rand shook his head. "None alive."

Torsten cursed under his breath. "How about survivors?" he asked. "Did anyone see anything that might help us figure out where they attacked from? If they managed to raid that many towns, it means there might be an army gathered somewhere. They aren't Drav Cra. They never stray far from their numbers and their warlords."

"Townsfolk and farmers who don't know the Black Sands from Brekliodad mostly," Rand replied. "Nobody of interest except for one. He's in the dungeon. But sir…"

"What?" Torsten snapped without meaning to.

Rand produced a bag and dumped the contents onto the table. Half of the recently lost Glass Crown tumbled out.

"I found this on the man," Rand said. "I recognize him from the masquerade. He came in from the courtyard soaking wet, but nothing seemed out of the ordinary."

Torsten lifted it, eyes wide as he noticed a few gems missing.

"Nothing out of the ordinary?" Wardric reprimanded, causing Rand's features to sink back. "He stole the crown right off our king's still-warm corpse. For Iam's sake boy, he might have even poisoned him!"

Wardric raised a hand to smack the young Shieldsman, but Torsten stopped him. "The royal physician assured us it was natural causes," he said.

"You know the gray men and their poisons. Perhaps it's something new they concocted in their sand pits."

"Why poison a man on his deathbed? They wouldn't risk being caught trying to assassinate him when they could merely wait."

"Did you not become a Shieldsman by thwarting an assassin from those very lands?"

Torsten regarded the old man. His face didn't show it, but the resentment in his tone was clear. Whether it was in regards to Torsten's humble origins, or Wardric's desire for the White Helm, Torsten wasn't sure. He decided to let it go.

"Those were different times," Torsten said. "He could still lift a sword."

Wardric grumbled but didn't disagree. "Then what? They sent a thief to show us how vulnerable we are?"

"Their warlords are brazen, you know that," Torsten said.

"I'm not sure," Rand said. "I had to keep one of the Shesaitju bastards from gutting him on the battlefield."

"So, he isn't with them?" Torsten said.

"Or he betrayed them and got caught," Wardric said.

"We can't rule anything out. Where's the rest of the crown?"

"That's all we recovered," Rand said.

"Well, a man doesn't stroll into the holy King's masquerade and steal the crown for no reason. Whether the theft and raids are connected or not, it's clear our enemies smell blood. We must stand strong now brothers."

"What are your commands, sir?" Wardric asked, fist to his chest. He could be difficult, but Torsten never questioned his loyalty or his talents.

Torsten leaned on the table, closed his eyes and drew a long breath. "Have the Royal Council request a surplus shipment of grain from the Governor of Yaolin City to make up for what was lost," he said. "Do it quick, we must maintain control during this transition. Have Taskmaster Lars quietly inform the King's Shield that we are under attack. We must reinforce the southern forts around Winde Port and have a unit sent to every farming village in the southern reach."

"And what of our response to the Shesaitju aggression?" Wardric asked.

"First, have the Master of Coin detail a full report on the Shesaitju's delinquent taxes, so I gain a full understanding of the situation. Then, dispatch gallers to the Caleef in Latiapur. Demand explanation for these unprovoked attacks."

"A letter?" Wardric said, incredulous.

"They killed all those people," Rand protested. "We have to do something about it. Don't we?"

"I agree with the boy, Torsten," Wardric said. "They kneel to the Glass no matter who died. We should remind them of that, lest our new king appear weak."

"And we will," Torsten said. "But before we declare open war, we must decide if this was an action sanctioned by the Caleef who declared his fealty and mortality before Liam, or an overeager warlord acting of his own accord. For now, we must quietly secure our own borders and appear unshakeable."

"If King Liam was alive—"

"He isn't," Torsten interrupted. And for the first time, the dire circumstances of his kingdom felt real. More than just nightmares. "The Queen Mother does not need the stress of open rebellion at the moment. Not with our new king…" He nearly let the truth of Pi's condition slip. "In mourning."

"He should be eager to live up to his father's name."

"Just move the troops," Torsten ordered. "The Shesaitju merely prod because they fear us. A display of force in the South should keep them at bay until we can assess the state of the kingdom."

"Whatever we can do to keep the fragile mind of the *Flower of the Drav Cra* comfortable you mean?" Wardric said.

Torsten stood proudly. "I'll pretend I didn't hear that, Shieldsman. Liam may be dead, but I'm still the Wearer of White. Follow your orders, or I'll find someone else who can." Torsten almost stopped himself before that last sentence. He sounded just like Oleander.

Wardric ground his teeth and saluted. "Right away, sir."

"Good." Torsten turned to Rand. "Now, take me to the thief who stole the crown."

"With respect, sir, towns are burning," Rand replied. "Can't he wait?"

Torsten exhaled. This is what happened during times of unrest after Liam's slow descent started. Everyone wearing Shieldsman armor forgot that they didn't wear the white helm. They started doubting and asking questions. Uriah never stood for it. He commanded, and the King's Shield obeyed. Torsten had only been Wearer for a year, but he'd had two great mentors show him how to lead.

"With or without respect does not change the fact that you are questioning my command, boy," Torsten said.

"Yes, sir. Sorry, sir," Rand stammered. "I'm only trying to understand."

"I intend to find out what kind of thief would be so bold as to steal the royal crown only to get caught a few days later in a Shesaitju ambush."

"Not a very good one," Wardric remarked.

Torsten let his eyes carry over the glass-blown flames donning the war table. "Or one who intended to be caught."

X

THE THIEF

"I'd wondered if I'd ever see you again, scag."

Whitney had hoped he never would. He stared at the same scarred, ugly mug of the brutish guard who'd flattened him for stealing jewelry on the day of his last incarceration in Yarrington.

"Looks like it's your lucky day, then," Whitney said. The comment was met with a swift punch to his gut.

The guard then shoved Whitney into the small cell before he got a chance to swipe the key from his belt again.

"Not my lucky day… stuck down here with the likes of you, thief," the guard said, taking his time with his terrible retort. "But, it looks like yours is far worse." "Really?" Whitney said, finding the wind in his lungs again. "I like it way down here. I was hoping for a darker cell."

"Well, get used to it. Our great King is dead, which means nobody will have time to worry about filth like you." The guard laughed, deep. "Thieves rot down here, forgotten with the dirt and shog."

"Last guard who said something like that had a nice view of my hind-quarters on my way out. I forget, was that you?"

"Try to escape again. I beg you. I've been waiting for an excuse to put you down for good." He dangled a key in front of the cell, then quickly snatched it back.

"Oh, you found your key. I knew I'd misplaced that."

The guard lips pursed in frustration. "You got lucky. Never again." The guard banged on the bars in a futile attempt to give Whitney a fright, then lumbered away grumbling.

Whitney groaned. Guards never realized what kind of challenge they were issuing when doing such things. But as the guard left, Whitney sat down, resigning himself to the cell. His mind wandered back to Troborough, his once-home.

Never before had he seen battle up close like that. He blinked as he remembered the feeling of blood-soaked dirt in his eyes, shuddered at the sight of the nearly black stuff under his fingernails. He closed his eyes to drive out the images and banged the back of his head against the stone.

This cell was different from the last, which had been dark, wet, and gray—this one was as well, but it was somehow darker, wetter, and grayer. Here, there were no windows or even an adjoining cell. This was the lower dungeon, where only the worst of Pantego were thrown; heretics and assassins, witches and conspirators—the worst. And then, of course, one quick-fingered thief who'd managed to break a priceless crown that'd been in the Nothhelm family for centuries.

A rat squeaked by him, brushing his leg and causing him to flinch. It stopped and circled back toward him. Whitney had a fondness for rodents. They shared the streets with him all these years—free spirits. He figured they must have known he was like them, too, as they rarely feared him like they did other humans.

Whitney stuck his arm out, palm up like a bridge from the ground. The little creature crept up on him, slowly at first, then, without reservation, crawled up to his shoulder. Its little whiskers bobbed as it sniffed the skin of his neck. It tickled, and Whitney shivered a bit. They really did have a lot in common. Even growing up on his parents' farm, he'd often found grander company in the field-mice than other people—especially with any child his age not named Sora. The rodents seemed smarter. When they needed food, they found it. When it rained, they sought shelter, even if that meant braving old Wetzel's broomstick.

Determined little creatures.

Whitney lifted a finger to scratch the rat on its brown head. The rodent lashed out with sharp teeth and bit him, drawing blood. Whitney reeled his hand back and sucked on his finger. The rat scampered away.

"Even friends bite," he whispered to himself in the dark.

Figured after all that'd happened, he'd learn a lesson from a rodent. In the end, people, like animals, were only interested in one thing: their own interests.

What had it all amounted to? Every heist, grift, and pocket picked? Living it up in Winde Port or Yaolin City until his last autla was spent. Even his time in Latiapur, on the black sands was disappointing—except for the brothels. The brothels never disappointed. Not one bit.

Seeing the world and experiencing all its decadent pleasures, some of it was just as amazing as Whitney had hoped. But now he was alone in a cage all the same, without a soul in the world wondering where he'd gone, and this time he hadn't planned on being there.

Piss in the wind.

He let his head fall back again, lightly bumping the wall this time. He breathed deeply, lungs still burning from the smoke caught in there. On the bright side, he wasn't chained to the wall. Plenty of holding cells around Pantego did that. In Latiapur, the Shesaitju capital, the cells opened right up to the Boiling Waters, inviting criminals to take the chance and drown. Nobody had ever made it out that way... well... nobody but Whitney.

Snap out of it, Whitney.

If nothing else, it was fun, the life he led—it was exciting. It wasn't putting one's shoulder to the plow and barely scraping by for no good reason.

He stood and stretched, then strode toward the bars, a new vigor overtaking him.

"Guard!" he shouted. When none came, he shouted even louder.

The hulking guard peeked around the far corner, knowing better than to get too close. "Aye?" the guard said. "Gotta piss? Hole's in the corner. Don't fall in."

The man shamelessly laughed at his own joke.

"No sir," Whitney answered, buttering him up. "Hoping you could tell me what happened to all those at Troborough?"

The guard's face scrunched up into a vengeful sneer. "You'll find out soon enough, Thief."

"I'm also wondering why you jailer types are always such shogs?"

"I told you, you ain't stealing the keys from me this time." The guard chortled and went back to what he had been doing. Probably practicing his next awful comeback.

Whitney couldn't imagine what would've been done with the refugees of Troborough, assuming there were any. With King Liam dead and the kingdom under attack, Whitney could be left rotting in that cell forever. Forgotten.

He sighed, closed his eyes, and slumped back down against the walls of his newest temporary lodging. He was about to nod off when he heard the clatter of heavy armor. "Who's there?" The guard jarred awake, apparently attempting to nap as well. "M...my Lord," the massive man stammered, an even more massive knight of the King's Shield standing before him. "What're ye—shouldn't ye be at the funeral?"

"I was," the Shieldsman said. "Now I'm here waking up guards."

"I wasn'—"

"Enough. Where is the crown thief?"

"Crown... Oh, aye. Right piece of work, him."

The guard led the Shieldsman by torchlight to Whitney's cell. A few other prisoners pled for freedom and grasped at him through their rusty bars.

"This is him," the guard said. "Ey, thief! Wake the yig up." He rattled on the bars until Torsten grabbed him by the forearm. The guard reached for his cudgel with his other hand, but the Shieldsman stuck out his arm.

"That's enough," the knight said. "Unlock it and leave us."

The guard eyed him, confused, but when the Shieldsman's face didn't waver, the guard did as asked. Taking the torch and sticking it through the bars, the Shieldsman squinted to get a better look inside. He was enormous, a mountain of armored muscle with a strong jaw. His head, which appeared to be bald, was covered by a shiny white helm that had to be made from glaruium metal. He was of obvious Glintish decent, which seemed rare for a Shieldsman, with skin brown as mahogany and eyes even darker.

There was no questioning that he was impressive, but Whitney had met plenty of men who looked the part. He pretended to yawn himself awake and fully stretched out like a stray cat in Latiapur. He glanced up, smacking his lips as if he'd been waiting for dried meat instead of rotting in a dungeon.

"Another *guard* come to take his shots?" he asked. "Right then, let's get it done."

"Stand up," the Shieldsman demanded.

"I think I'm good right here."

"I am Torsten Unger, the Glass Kingdom's one and only Wearer of White. You will obey my commands."

"Wish I could, but my legs are a little tired from battling all those Sandsmen. You people are basically useless against them."

"Really? I heard my men found you being crushed under one of their gray heels."

"People tell tall tales."

"Why did you take it?" Torsten asked.

"You're going to have to be more specific."

Torsten slammed on the bars. "You know exactly what I am talking about!"

"I've taken lots of things from lots of rich people in lots of cities. Visit one. You'll see this beautiful face on posters in half the barracks in Pantego. Some of them even captured my nose in all its perfection."

Torsten bit his tongue, reached into the satchel dangling from his belt and produced the half of the Glass Crown Whitney had in his possession when the last Shieldsman he met took him in.

Whitney grinned. "Oh, that."

"Oh, that?" Torsten said. "Do you realize what this is?"

He shrugged. "I was just enjoying a party when it rolled right into my foot. I couldn't help myself."

"This is the King's crown!"

"*Was.*"

Torsten swung the cell door open and rushed in. His thick fingers wrapped around Whitney's throat, and he lifted him and pinned him against the wall, feet dangling. "You are guilty of stealing from the Crown. You'll be in a noose by morning, so I suggest you start talking."

Whitney pawed at his neck like he wanted to say something. Torsten let up.

"I can't talk when you do that," he rasped.

Torsten flung him to the floor and paced the cell. "What's your name?"

Whitney coughed, but drew himself to his feet and performed an exaggerated bow. "Name's Whitney Fierstown. I'm sure you've heard of me."

"Can't say I have."

Whitney sighed, then drew in a deep breath. "He who stole the Sword of Grace and the Splintering Staff from the Whispering Wizards? The very same who lifted the Ring of Pandula from the Latiapur Vaults and now, of course, my finest accomplishment, the Glass Crown."

"Finest failure. In case you forgot, only half of the crown is sitting here in my pocket, and the other is nowhere to be found."

"The way I see it, I successfully stole that crown. My mistake was stopping to gloat about it long enough for thieving dwarves and murderous sandsman to get the jump on me. I guess we both have new enemies."

"Did you really think you would get away with this?"

"I never think."

Torsten punched the wall right over Whitney's shoulder. The stone cracked around his gauntlet. "Why did you take it, thief?"

"I told you, it came to me. It was like… fate. Iam's will and all that."

"If it were fate, you wouldn't be locked up like a hog in a pen."

"Unless this is exactly where I want to be." He put on a grin like he was in on some joke, which only served to vex the Shieldsman more. In truth, Whitney wasn't sure where he'd hoped to be after showing Grint his quarry, but it certainly wasn't back below the Glass Castle.

"Who put you up to this?" Torsten asked. "Does Valin Tehr think he can turn more of the city into his own personal playground again with King Liam gone? I already know you aren't with the Sands, so who else? The Panpingese want revenge for their Mystics?"

"I saw something shiny and wanted it," Whitney stated. "Simple as that."

"Who's your fence? Thieves don't work alone."

"This one does."

Torsten's fingers balled into fists. "You really expect me to believe you did this by yourself?"

"I don't care what you believe."

"I could say you poisoned King Liam to get the crown if I wanted. One look at you and not a soul would doubt it."

"Go ahead. As you've said, I've got a date with a noose either way."

"There are worse fates than death, thief."

"If you say so. Can I get back to my nap now?" Whitney groaned, making himself comfortable on a loose stone like it was a pillow.

"It'll be your last," Torsten said. He let himself out of the cell and called for the guard to come and lock it.

"Let him rot and starve until he's ready to be honest," Torsten said.

"My pleasure," the guard snickered, almost salivating on getting vengeance for his failure. Torsten took a few steps down the long, dark hall when Whitney stopped him.

"There was nobody left to steal from," Whitney said.

"What?" Torsten turned and found Whitney with his eyes closed.

"That's why I took it. There was nothing left."

XI

THE KNIGHT

Word on the condition of the young King Pi found its way across Yarrington. Torsten wasn't sure who let the news out, but with so many wolves circling it was impossible to know. Any of the whispering sycophants on the Royal Council could have been behind it, and Oleander had already threatened to have any of them executed if it was found that they did.

The story spun to the public by Wren the Holy through sermons in the market and the cathedral square was that Prince Pi, distraught over the loss of his father, accidentally slipped and tumbled down the stairs of the West Tower, but would survive.

The news seemed to sate the masses, but it didn't stop the rumors from stirring—a hornet's nest of stings and accusations about the foreign Queen Mother at the top of the mill. Many said she'd poisoned her husband and tried to kill her son in an attempt to usurp the throne. Torsten, on her command, had been so busy arresting anyone caught speaking such blasphemies he hadn't even had a minute to address Redstar's role in Pi's condition with her or consider the Black Sands situation.

Presently, he approached Oleander's chambers upon her request—always the Shield. She'd been appointed Queen Regent after Pi's condition was made public, so it was even more difficult to deny her now.

He was just about to enter when the royal physician, Deturo, stormed out, his long, gray beard swishing.

"That woman is going to be the death of—" He caught himself upon noticing Torsten. "Ah, Sir Unger."

"Is everything all right?" Torsten asked.

"Just examining our young King. I was hoping to take him to my study where I could try forcing him to ingest a rare herb concoction from eastern Panping. I've heard of great results. The Queen Regent, however, won't allow me to risk giving him anything but water."

"Does he seem in pain?"

"He doesn't seem anything. Still, he wheezes but does not wake. If we do not try something more drastic, I fear we might lose him."

"Pray, Deturo," Torsten said, laying a hand on the agitated man's shoulder. "Beg for Iam's light as I have every night since Liam passed. There is no better salve for the wounded."

"I am a man of..." He stopped and drew a deep breath. "Just try to get through to her, Sir Unger. She nearly had me hanged assuming I spread news of Pi's condition. I fear she won't heed my advice that rest alone is not improving anything."

"I'll try."

"Good. I'd rather not prepare the body of another king for eternal rest."

He walked away, grumbling under his breath, and Torsten continued on his way to Oleander's chambers.

"You called for me, Your Grace?" he asked before entering.

"Did I?" she replied.

"I... Yes. You sent Rand for me."

"Well, come in then, my Wearer. Sit."

Torsten entered, but remained standing by the door.

Oleander sat, her hair freshly washed and being combed by her favorite handmaiden Tessa, barely aware of Torsten's presence. Torsten watched, but his gaze listed continuously toward the Queen's bed where Pi lay, his small head poking through the covers, eyelids sealed and face tranquil for the first time in longer than Torsten could remember.

"Tessa," Oleander said, addressing her handmaiden. "What do you believe about my husband's untimely death?"

Torsten could see the discomfort on the poor girl's face as she took a moment to collect her thoughts.

"Your Grace," she answered in a thick accent from the northern regions—maybe Crowfall or Fessix. Each word was a bit slow and drawn out. "Twas a shame, right forward. I dunno how it could be seen any other way."

Oleander smiled. "And of my son?"

"I, myself, cried at the news," she said. "He was a sweet boy."

"Is." Oleander snapped. "He *is* sweet."

"Y…yes, of course. Tis what I meant."

She settled down, cleared her throat. "A result of your simple mind, I'm sure." It was as if Oleander had wholly forgotten her roots in the savage North.

Tessa's hand shook now as she continued combing, glancing periodically over at Pi.

Smart girl, calling the boy sweet. No one who knew Pi in the last year would have called him sweet, and Torsten hadn't known him much before since he was too busy serving the kingdom elsewhere. Uriah said there'd been a time he was kind, quiet, and studious, but since the day Redstar betrayed them, Pi was disturbed and often violent, especially toward the help. Even the simple act of knocking on his door could cause him to throw anything he could get his hands on.

Torsten always figured Uriah was exaggerating about the boy's former nature for Oleander's sake, but he was starting to feel foolish for doubting. The more he thought about it, he almost blamed himself for not barring Pi's windows after the night he'd witnessed him teetering on its edge.

Incapacitation is better than worshipping a fallen goddess.

Torsten quickly admonished himself for having such a cruel thought. It wasn't the way of Iam.

"Tessa, I'd like some honeyed wine," Oleander said, breaking the awful silence.

The servant placed the brush down immediately and curtsied. "Yes, Your Grace."

Torsten watched with pity as Oleander picked up the brush and continued where the girl left off. He could see her reflection in the mirror before her. Her puffy eyes started watering again. She slammed the brush down on the vanity, startling Torsten.

She moved to sit beside Pi, brushing his moppy hair like she would her own. Torsten followed but kept his distance.

"I can feel him fighting still, Torsten," she said.

"He comes from good stock, Your Grace," Torsten said. "Liam's blood runs through his veins."

"That didn't stop him getting sick."

Torsten's lip twisted. "No, but he lived a glorious life before. I'm sure Pi will wake soon and we will again have a king worthy of the Glass."

"He won't."

Torsten fumbled over a response. "Your Grace?"

"He won't wake until we find my depraved brother and retrieve his orepul. Something you continually fail to do."

Again, with the doll.

Torsten had to stifle a groan lest he further anger her. "We've tried time and time again. Some of my best Shieldsmen—"

"Try harder! This is the only way, I know it in my heart. Send more men. He is your King!"

"Your Grace, this has nothing to do with a doll. Pi threw himself from a window because Redstar used dark, warlock magic to plague him with visions. A worthless doll can't wake a boy from such awful ailment, only Iam can help him now." He wished he'd spoken more calmly. He'd been trying for years to break Oleander of her fixation, but nothing ever got through to her and with all the stress he was now under, it came bubbling to the surface.

She turned to him, eyes like a pair of smoking, blue coals. She stood to her full height, her Drav Cra frame towering as if she were something more than human.

"Worthless?" she said. "It is an *orepul*—not a *doll.* I sewed it for Pi when he was born, my beautiful, baby boy, and my brother stole it! Stole a piece of him. That is what is wrong."

Torsten did his best to stand his ground. The Drav Cra were a superstitious people but, Torsten had also seen their ways fail enough to know they were folly. All the sacrifices they made to their Buried Goddess in the hopes of fending off Liam did nothing for them. He left those lands to their infighting and barbarity because there was nothing of worth there. Nothing left to save.

"My Queen, I heard him whispering in the night. Words of some concern," Torsten said. It was time to confront her about everything. Torsten was nothing if not loyal, but it was growing difficult to coddle the Queen Regent and reposition the Glass army without her knowing.

She spun. "Speak plainly."

"I no longer blame your son, but he spoke of the Buried Goddess, my Queen. Communing with her. We've wasted a year seeking out your heathen brother rather than considering that he cursed Pi and left for good. That the answer to the young King's salvation was here all along. Now that he is bedridden from injury caused by Redstar's curse, we should place our faith in Iam, not in the black magic of a broken people. Let Deturo attempt to coax him from slumber more aggressively. Invite Wren the Holy and the Yarrington priests up here to—"

"Redstar!" The back of her hand crashed into Torsten's cheek, unexpectedly powerful for how slight she was. Torsten swallowed his pride and the copper taste of blood drawn by one of her rings. "He wounded Pi's soul because he thinks I've turned my back on my people. On tundra and suffering. I should wipe the rest of them off the map!"

"Your Grace, we have more dangerous enemies to worry about," Torsten said.

"Liam is dead, and Pi cannot speak," Oleander said. "Am I not your Queen?"

"You are."

"And are you not the commander of the Glass army?"

Torsten bowed his head. "I am, Your Grace."

"Then I command you to stop sending worthless cowards. Lead our entire army into the Webbed Woods, burn it to the ground if you must. Bring my brother to justice, return what was stolen from my son, and restore him."

"I can't." Torsten knew what her reaction would be before he said it, but it came out anyway. Her eyes went wide, flabbergasted that the Wearer of White would deny anything she asked. Ever since Uriah disappeared,

Torsten had served her every need, no matter how ill-advised, but he couldn't anymore. The Glass was in danger, and he alone seemed interested in saving it.

"What did you say?"

"The army must remain nearby Yarrington, my Queen," he stated firmly. "We need all of them to secure our borders against rebellion."

Oleander laughed. It was an unsettling sound. "Rebellion?"

Torsten shifted his weight, his head staring at his feet. "Two day's past, the Black Sands razed a handful of our villages."

Her glare hardened. The sight made Torsten's spine quiver.

"Why was I not aware of this?" she asked.

"You've been at Pi's side where you belong," he replied. "I hoped to spare you the news until he recovered from his unfortunate… accident."

"Spare me news of treason? That bastard Sidar had dinner in my royal court not half a year ago!"

"And he will answer for it. I have already sent a demand for an explanation. We have to proceed carefully now to avoid a war we're ill-prepared for."

"We? You have conspired to mobilize the Crown's forces without informing me?"

"To defend us."

"I defend us! I told you, Torsten, if you cannot perform the duties of the Wearer then I will find someone who can. You've failed your new king. Kept secrets from me, his mother!"

Oleander ripped the white helmet from Torsten's head and flung it at the door. Tessa entered with a crystal vial of wine at the same time and it clattered to the polished floor, spilling everywhere.

"My mind is not so fragile it cannot handle the truth of war!" Oleander bellowed. "I am the Queen!"

"Your Grace..."

"You are a relic of my husband, Torsten. Nothing more. Another failed servant like Uriah."

"You must listen to me, Your Grace. The kingdom needs stability now more than ever. We can't march our entire army south and leave ourselves even more vulnerable. Uriah said he went to the Woods, but that was a year ago. Redstar's playing games, and those games have cost us dozens of Shieldsmen. The order is thin now, filled with new recruits whose names I barely know.

She raised her hand before he could say another word. "I am done listening to you. I should have you hanged for treason."

"And I wouldn't blame you. But—"

"Out!"

"Your Grace, we heard shouting," said Rand as he rushed through the door. He nearly tripped over Tessa who was busy soaking up wine with her dress and trying not to cry. He paused to help the young woman, apologizing profusely, before Oleander stole back his attention.

"You," Oleander said. "Take Torsten outside the walls and strip him of his armor. He is not to set foot within the walls of Yarrington again."

Rand nearly choked in confusion. "Your Grace. He is the Wearer."

"Not anymore." Oleander rushed across the room and lifted the white helmet off the floor. Then she presented it to Rand. "Take it."

"My Queen. I… I'm not—"

"He's been wearing the Shield for a barely a week," Torsten said. "Surely Wardric or Nikserof would be better suited."

"No. If you have proven anything it's that a rat could do this job better than you," Oleander said. "Take the helmet, boy, or you'll join Torsten outside these walls."

Torsten met Rand's gaze and tried to calm him. "Do as she asks," he whispered, nodding slowly, assuredly.

"But sir?"

"Your kingdom needs you," Torsten said.

"I'm surrounded by infants," Oleander groaned. She placed the helmet over Rand's head, scraping his nose in the effort. "There. Now take this traitor out of my sight and leave me with my son!"

"Yes, Your Grace." Rand took Torsten's arm, though he grasped without conviction.

Torsten stopped in the doorway, regarding Oleander. She stood, fuming, wine pooling around her gem-encrusted heels. If ever there looked a queen it was her, but Rand hadn't seen war, let alone led one. And now she provoked the Black Sands to full-scale rebellion with him in charge of the army.

Torsten couldn't believe it but knew the only person with the authority to save his kingdom was in that room, lying unconscious. A boy he barely knew, who'd spent a year scrawling heathen symbols on his walls in blood, cursed.

"I will always serve the Glass, Your Grace," Torsten said, bowing.

"If I see you again, you will join the Black Sands for treason," she said. "Take him."

Rand didn't wait to hear any more orders. He pulled Torsten out of the room, and after a few steps through the citadel, Torsten realized he'd become the one towing Rand. The sound of Oleander scolding Tessa now echoed down the halls, making the young Shieldsman wince.

"Sir, what was I supposed to do?" he asked, voice trembling.

"You did fine, lad," Torsten said. "Don't worry about me."

They reached the main hall where Wardric stood guard. He eyed Torsten and Rand, brow furrowing when he realized who wore the distinguished White Helm. Rand quickly removed it and tried to hand it back to Torsten.

"Sir, I don't want this," Rand whispered.

"Neither did I," Torsten said, pushing the helm back. "Listen to the others. Nikserof, Reginald, and especially Wardric, the grouch that he is. They can help you keep the kingdom in one piece."

"What about you? By Iam, we need you."

"As long as our new king sleeps, the kingdom isn't safe. I'm going to do what his mother thinks I must to save him. Even if it is folly."

"I don't understand."

Torsten seized the boy by his shoulder and drew him close. "Rand, focus," he said. "I need you to do me one last favor as your Wearer."

"Anything."

"Before the Queen Regent's edict becomes known, take me to the lowest dungeon and leave me the key."

"What? Why?"

Oleander believed that Pi's orepul was the key to his health and sanity. For the year after Uriah failed, Torsten had sent some of the finest soldiers after him into the cursed Webbed Woods. None ever returned. But Torsten knew now that if he wanted to make Oleander see reason, earn her trust, and reclaim his helm—if he wanted to protect the Glass, as he swore to

Liam he would so many moons ago—then he'd have to be the first. Even if Pi were truly beyond help, he'd have to bring Redstar to justice and steal back that doll or die trying.

"I need a thief," he said.

XII

THE THIEF

Whitney couldn't remember when last he sat in a cell without plotting a way to break out, whether it was studying the possible routes or digging his way under the guard's skin to drive them to open the door and attempt to provide a beating. Pissing people off was probably his greatest skill, if he had to choose one.

This time, he quietly accepted the slop they called food with barely a jab at the hulking guard's stupidity. Barely. He couldn't help himself there. But then he settled against the mold-laden wall and let his mind turn off as he shoveled the shog down.

Whitney caught glimpse of his rat friend watching him from across the cell. His finger still stinging from the bite he'd received earlier, he considering shooing it, but flicked a bit of glop onto the floor instead. Sharing had never been his issue, it just rarely occurred to him. All the things he'd stolen were hidden in buried caches across Pantego or left beyond in new places for some lucky soul to stumble upon. It'd never been about the things themselves, he just wanted to be able to say he took them.

He'd returned to Troborough because he'd run out of places to go, and as he sat in the darkness, he figured it was time to move on. He'd stolen the crown of Liam the Conqueror. It didn't matter for how long, he'd done it. A visit from the current Wearer of White himself made that pretty damn clear.

The rat finished its meal and inched a little closer.

"Now you want to be friends?" Whitney asked.

He threw down another morsel, and then it dawned on him: all those hidden treasures were likely worth more in gold than whatever was in the Yarrington vaults. If he broke free… when he broke free… he could go to every small town in the world and distribute wealth in ways no proper king ever had. He could give young fools like he had once been the chance to be more.

Just imagining the bard's songs about the 'Noble Thief of Troborough' made him smirk. He wondered how they'd embellish his exploits. It'd be tough to make them better than the truth, but they'd find a way. Maybe they'd add a great dragon or some other mythological beast.

"Thief," a gruff voice called, clearly addressing him. Whitney thought he recognized it, but the stark, stone walls of the deepest dungeon made everything echo in strange ways.

"I prefer hero," Whitney replied.

"Then find a new occupation."

A torch lit the bars of Whitney's cell, and he saw the Wearer of White once more. Only, Torsten no longer wore the helm of his station, and the dark bags beneath his eyes spoke of days of restless slumber. The lock clicked, the rusty door squeaked open, and the rat scurried between a crack in the wall.

"You look worse than I do," Whitney said.

"On your feet," Torsten commanded.

"I told you last time, I'm quite comfortable here."

"I said, on your feet. We have no time to waste."

"To hang me? Is the Crown short on rope?"

"Listen, you worm. You can either rot in here, or you can come with me and be useful to the kingdom for once in your worthless life."

"Well, that's just rude," Whitney said. "Here I am thinking about how to give back to the people, and you call me worthless."

"Come with me, now. That is an order."

"Where's your helm?"

Torsten zipped across the room in one healthy stride, grabbed Whitney by the collar, and heaved him to his feet.

"Are you the greatest thief in Pantego like you claim?" he asked. "Or are you a talker like all the others?"

"Depends on my mood," Whitney replied.

"Do you know what happens to the criminals who get thrown down here? They get lost. Forgotten. Until the porters are sent down to sweep up the bones. The Crown needs a thief, and the best I can find on short notice is you."

"I'm on a bit of a vacation." Whitney flourished his arms wide to draw attention to the cell.

"I…" Torsten drew a long, exasperated breath. "I knew it. Just like all the rest."

Torsten threw him down and stormed out of the cell. He didn't even lock the door behind him.

Whitney dusted off his pants and stretched his shoulder. Then he caught the rat staring at him from the corner of the room.

"What?" Whitney asked it.

Torsten's heavy boots echoed down the hall, drawing Whitney's attention back toward the exit. The rat took the opportunity to sprint out, grab his bowl and shove it toward his little hollow in the wall.

"Son of a—" Whitney took a hard step toward it, then stopped and grinned. The rodent tilted the bowl to get enough of it through the crack that the rest of the food spilled out of reach. In comparison, the crafty bugger robbed a human exponentially larger than any of the giants Whitney had stolen from.

"It can't hurt to ask, right?" He shrugged. "What's one more?"

He tipped his head to the rodent, as if he were wearing a hat, then hurried after Torsten. The Shieldsman moved slowly, clearly expecting him.

"What's the catch?" Whitney asked.

"I thought you were on vacation?" Torsten muttered.

"I am. Let's just say I'm curious."

"Hey!" the lumbering guard watching the dungeon hollered from his post. "He's not supposed to—"

"The Queen Regent needs him," Torsten said.

"Regent?" Whitney said. "Didn't the King have some sort of crazy son? Didn't leave his room since the last Dawning?"

"You speak of your new king!" Torsten snapped.

"Hey, I'm just saying what I've heard."

"Your new king has fallen ill, and his mother rules in his stead until he is healthy. That is all you need to know."

"What could the Queen possibly need with filth like this street rat?" the guard asked.

"I could think of one thing," Whitney said as he adjusted his pants.

Torsten sent a glower so fierce it nearly caused Whitney to bite his tongue. The Wearer of White was a bore, but the claymore on his back wasn't deckled with scratches and dents without reason. Whitney knew when he was outmatched in a fight.

"It concerns only the Crown," Torsten said to the guard before he continued on his way.

"I meant no offense, sir," the guard said. "But…wait. The royal keep is that way."

Torsten didn't answer. Whitney tapped the guard on the shoulder, causing him to spin. Whitney swiped the keys from his belt as he did, then jingled them right in front of his face.

"Farewell, my friend," Whitney said. "The Queen Regent needs me." Whitney tossed the keys at the guard's feet, then scurried on after Torsten, ignoring the flurry of curses at his back.

"Can you focus for two seconds?" Torsten said, exasperated.

"I'm just trying to figure out what the Crown could possibly want from me."

"Some time ago, the Queen Regent's estranged brother, an Arch Warlock named Redstar, stole a priceless heirloom from King Pi."

"What kind of heirloom?" Whitney said, eyes glinting.

"It's called an orepul. It's a doll sewn by the Queen herself in Pi's likeness. Those of Drav Cra descent believe is enchanted with a piece of the owner's soul, and that stealing it curses the owner."

"Of course they do…" Whitney rolled his eyes.

"I know how it sounds, and it doesn't matter. Redstar did something to taint the boy, and I have my orders. Her brother fled into the Webbed Woods with the orepul. The Queen Regent needs us to return it and bring the traitor to justice. She believes this will help King Pi recover. All I know, is that we need to find Redstar."

Whitney stopped in his tracks, causing Torsten to do the same. "The Webbed Woods?"

A Drav Cra warlock was bad enough news, but everyone knew about that awful forest where the trees formed a canopy so thick it was like eternal nightfall. Where the horror of the beasts roaming its swampy floor was only surpassed by a giant, cursed spider ever stalking, ever feeding. The bards said it devoured men instead of insects, but only after it drove them mad first.

Whitney had been almost everywhere in Pantego, but never there. There were no men to rob there after all. Nothing but death, if the stories were to be believed. They rarely were.

"Are you afraid, master thief?" Torsten asked, a hint of playfulness entering his tone for the first time.

"No," Whitney protested.

"Then what happened to your face?"

"This is my thinking face."

"We've sent dozens of soldiers and Shieldsmen after Redstar. None returned. Help me find the wretch who robbed our new king, and you will be pardoned of all your crimes. You can go back to what got you locked in here for all I care if we return alive."

"It's the alive part I'm concerned about."

"This is your chance to do something with your life. A long time ago, King Liam gave me a similar chance, and I never looked back."

Whitney didn't care about that. The idea of him becoming a servant of the Crown or worse, a King's Shieldsman, was laughable. His legs were desperate to carry him back to his cell, but he didn't budge.

Arch Warlocks, cursed spiders, and certain death? Whitney was already wanted in every corner of Pantego. He'd already stolen the Glass Crown, among countless other achievements, but as he stared at the knight who somehow hadn't heard of him, an idea for his next mark popped into his head. His plan to spread wealth to Pantego's unfortunate children would have to wait.

"I'm in," Whitney said, fighting his reluctant tongue to get the words out. "But only on one condition."

Torsten glared at him. "What now?"

"If we get back, the Crown has to anoint me with a new name."

"A new name?"

"Yeah. Fierstown is great and all, but something with a better ring to it. Something noble that rolls off the tongue."

And something that belongs to me, he didn't add. That would be his greatest theft ever. Stealing a new name to replace the one left to him by his good-for-nothing father.

XIII

THE KNIGHT

"You think the Crown would consider ennobling a man like you?" Torsten asked the vagabond standing in front of him. He could see the wheels of inspiration turning in Whitney's head.

"What's wrong with a man like me?" Whitney said.

Torsten didn't even bother answering.

"I think that if the Crown wants my help, it better consider what a man of my enormous talent is worth," Whitney went on.

Whitney's clothes were crusted with dirt and blood, torn at every joint. The handsome devil had eyes, weightless, warm and inviting like he belonged in a brothel, but Torsten knew his kind. Get drawn too close by his silver tongue and he'd find a knife in his back and the autlas swiped from his pocket.

Torsten couldn't believe it'd come to this: recruiting scum to help him save his kingdom. Giving in to demands. But what choice had he? After Oleander's ruling on Torsten was made public, not a soul of worth would follow him, and Rand was too inexperienced to disagree with her. If Wardric didn't throw a coup first to claim the White Helm he always wanted, Rand would let her keep sending soldiers to the Webbed Woods, or at the Black Sands, or wherever her heart desired until there was nothing left. Only Torsten knew the truth of her grief, and only he could fix things.

Torsten and the scag standing in front of him. This Whitney was a braggart and a fool, but he didn't seem insane. He was simply the kind of vermin that got loose when chaos took hold.

"Fine," Torsten conceded. "If we make it back in one piece with Redstar and the orepul in hand, I'll make sure that you are…" He paused to swallow back the bad taste filling his mouth. "Granted a name of noble air." He couldn't technically promise anything now that he too was a man without station, but he couldn't waste any more time either.

The corners of Whitney's mouth lifted into a mischievous grin. "I've never met something I couldn't steal."

"King Liam never lost a battle either, and now he's gone."

"Aren't you a follower of Iam?" Whitney asked.

"Of course, I am. What true Glassman isn't?"

"Then why is it you believe death to be a loss?"

Torsten bit his lip. "This won't be as easy as you think, thief."

"By Iam," Whitney sighed. "It's like you want us to fail."

"I don't. But if the greatest thief in Pantego got caught napping through a Black Sands attack, Pantego must be filled with worthless thieves. Now let's go."

Torsten gave Whitney's arm a tug and continued through the dank tunnels. The thief staggered in tow for a moment, then caught his balance.

"I still say that doesn't count," Whitney said.

"For our sake, I hope you're right," Torsten replied.

"Where are we going anyway? Isn't the way out supposed to smell better?"

"Just be quiet and follow me."

He didn't listen. At every turn throughout the warren of tunnels beneath the castle, he whispered some comment under his breath. Again, Torsten couldn't believe it'd come to this. He feared he'd have to cut Whitney's tongue out before they ever reached the Woods.

"I have one question," Whitney said as they rounded into the catacombs.

"What?" Torsten grumbled.

"Redstar?" He guffawed. "What kind of name is that."

"You'll see when we find him."

They stopped at an entry sealed by a heavy stone. The old entrance to the Royal Crypt buried beneath Mount Lister was ancient and it both looked and felt it. It took all his might to slide the large stone aside.

Whitney didn't offer a hand. Though, he did feign a gagging noise as they entered.

"Show some respect!" Torsten snapped. His voice echoed, reflecting off a domed ceiling that was coated in a thick layer of formed glass that swirled to create the Eye of Iam. A thin beam of light shot through an oculus set inside the pupil, then splayed out to wash the room in a dim veil of light.

"Me?" Whitney said, incredulous. "I'm not the one who neglected this place so long that it now smells like death's doorstep. Where are we?"

"The Royal Crypts. Resting place of the Nothhelms."

"So, death's doorstep."

Torsten ignored him. He stopped before the light, fell to his knees, and traced a circle around his eyes. Through rounded fingers, he gazed around the circular space. Bodies lying vertically behind glass lids wrapped the space as if frozen in their caskets, all perfectly preserved, staring ahead blankly, their hands wrapped around the gilded hilts of swords.

"These are all past kings, queens, princes, and princesses," Torsten said. "The men and women who forged the Glass Kingdom. Yet only one name will be remembered for all of time."

"Pretty sure Autla's gonna be remembered," Whitney said. "Currency named after him and all."

Torsten ignored him, stood and approached the newest casket. Liam Nothhelm lay within, clutching the claymore known as *Salvation* which he'd wielded in so many battles. He was dressed in the light blue armor he wore to every celebration of a victory, not a spot of blood or vein of rust. His long, graying hair was combed for the first time in years, and, but for the absent look in his amber eyes, Torsten might have mistaken him for being amongst the living.

"How do they do that?" Whitney asked.

"What?" Torsten said.

"Make them look so alive. The King looked far worse at the masquerade." Whitney poked one of the lids, and a rusty piece of metal fell from an adjacent sconce.

"Don't touch anything!"

"Smart. I think that one looked at me." Whitney shuddered. "Not going to lie, I've seen plenty of weird places in my life, but this might beat them all."

"Would you just be quiet?"

Torsten returned his attention to King Liam. He reached into the satchel hanging from his side and removed the half of the Glass Crown. Kneeling, he held it near the foot of the casket in front of a placard bearing Liam's name and title.

"Maybe this is a sign," Torsten said, staring at it. He placed what was left of the crown down gently. Laying his palm over Liam's name, he took a deep breath. "You gave me more a life than I ever deserved, Your Grace," he said softly. "I would have followed you without question into any battle, until the bitter end. It has been an honor wearing the white in your name. Though I've never understood why you chose your queen, I will uphold your legacy no matter what the cost. You may be gone from this world, but we will never forget."

He leaned forward to kiss the foot of the casket.

"I think I might cry." Whitney fake-sniveled and pretended to wipe his eyes.

Torsten stopped and turned to send another glower his way. He was about to say something when Sir Wardric stepped through the crypt's main entrance. His hand rested on the pommel of his longsword.

"I had a feeling I'd find you down here," he said.

"I couldn't leave without saying goodbye," Torsten said, rising.

Wardric stepped in cautiously, skirting the edge of the room. "You always were his favorite. Maybe even more than Uriah."

"I never asked to be."

"That's probably why."

"Is anyone going to tell me what's going on here?" Whitney asked.

"Who is this?" Wardric said.

"He's coming with me," said Torsten.

"The Queen Regent's orders are known throughout the Shield. You shouldn't be here."

"We were just leaving." Torsten nodded to Whitney, and they took a step toward the exit.

Wardric positioned himself in front of it, his hand slowly wrapping the handle of his weapon. "Why do you still wear that armor?"

"I'll need it where we're going," Torsten said.

"You're really going to walk away from this? War is coming."

"I have no choice. Now please, move aside and let us pass. The kingdom depends on what I must do."

"You couldn't just keep your mouth shut and leave her in her own little bubble? Always the loyal dog, begging for food, even from the plate of the foreign Queen."

Torsten reached for his back-scabbard and gripped his claymore. Whitney took a step back, but with his other hand, Torsten grabbed the thief by the arm and squeezed tight enough to keep him from doing anything foolish.

"Please, Wardric," Torsten said. "I know we've had our differences, but the kingdom needs you. It needs both of us right now."

The old, bitter knight leveled his glare and didn't budge. Wardric's chest heaved as he drew long steady breaths. His stance widened into a defensive posture. Then, suddenly, he released his weapon and stepped aside. Torsten released a mouthful of air.

"She's in charge of us with the Boy-King unable to wake," Wardric said. "Whatever you think you need to do to change that, do it quick and return. Take two horses and food from the stables. Nobody will stop you. The Glass needs the King's Shield more than ever now. All of them."

"I'll do my best," Torsten said. "Watch over Rand. He's a good lad, but he won't be able to handle her like this."

"Liam barely could," Wardric snickered. "I'll keep him in line."

"Good. You have to try and convince her to let the young King receive whatever treatment Deturo prescribes. He was cursed, Wardric, all that time. Now his body merely needs healing."

"I will try. I may have been passed over as Wearer twice over, but I serve the Glass, always." He straightened his back and banged his chest-plate in salute. "We are the right hand of Iam. The sword of His justice, and the Shield that guards the light of this world."

Torsten circled his eyes in reverence for the words of their holy order, then bowed his head. "Farewell, Sir Jolly."

"Farewell."

Torsten rushed out of the Royal Crypt, pulling Whitney along behind him. Whitney eventually squirmed free and rubbed his arm.

"I've met a lot of knights, but you might be the worst," he griped.

"If you don't hurry up I'll make sure that's true," Torsten replied.

"You know, you should be kinder to someone who's helping you out of the goodness of his heart. What was all that back there anyway?"

"Politics."

"*Blech*, My worst subject. For Iam's sake, let's go steal a doll then and save the kingdom. I'm growing tired of this adventure already."

Whitney sped up, so he was leading the way even though he had no idea where he was going. Torsten rubbed his temples with his large thumb and index finger.

"You and me both," he muttered. "Iam, save us all."

XIV

THE THIEF

Whitney looked south and the day seemed colder, but it was just the breeze once the walls of Yarrington no longer confined them. The foothills rolled and rose into Mount Lister, lording over the city. The grain fields to the east stretched for a kilometer, marked every so often by lone trees swaying in the wind like worshipers in the Cathedral.

On a quiet day, Whitney wondered if he could hear the Torrential Sea to the west where the bluffs plunged. Within the high walls of the city, he'd rarely paid much attention to the docks or their many bars and taverns. He'd preferred the cobbled streets and the more upscale inns and their elegant rooms.

He also preferred his hands to be free. He and Torsten both rode horses, but the Shieldsman's stayed out front, and he held its reins with one hand and the rope binding Whitney's wrists with the other.

"Is this really necessary?" he asked Torsten. "Rope? Really? I said I'd help you get the Iam-forsaken doll."

"You said it yourself," Torsten replied. "You're wanted in every city in the realm. What makes you think I'd trust you to keep your word?"

"A man's word is his bond!" Whitney cried out in mock protest.

"I prefer a physical bond."

"The ladies must love you."

A dirt path snaked through the eastern fields, slithering toward farmlands and small towns like Troborough, where Whitney grew up. It was a far cry from the big city, but Whitney couldn't deny the charm the country carried with it for simple folk. Too bad Troborough and so many other towns like it had been burned to the ground just days before.

He looked out into the distance and saw a column of smoke still rising from the south.

"So, are you telling the people who did it?" he asked.

"Did what?" Torsten asked.

"Burned all those towns to the ground."

"The people will believe whatever they choose to. Black Sands, Panping, it doesn't matter who attacked, only that we *were* attacked. The people are scared with King Liam gone."

"Only the people?" Whitney couldn't help but grin at his comment. Torsten gave his restraints a hardy tug.

"I've dedicated my life to their safety."

"By hiding the truth? You may as well just tell everyone it was dragons if you want to lie to them. At least that's exciting."

"What would you know about protecting anything? Let me guess, you were born a Yarrington street rat, so you turned to thieving. Not only food to survive, no, but the very things people cherish. Their treasures. Just to get back at them because you were born in the shog and thought the world owed you. That about sum it up?"

Whitney's gaze drifted back to the thin line of smoke on the horizon. Maybe it belonged to Troborough—what was left of it, at least. That cluster of tiny hovels where he was raised in obscurity. The place didn't even have a street for him to be a rat on.

"Exactly right," he said.

Torsten scoffed. "I thought so. Let me and Iam worry about the people."

"Hey, the only thing I'm worried about is myself. But I wonder, when's the last time you stepped down from your pretty halls and had a drink at a tavern."

Torsten opened his mouth to respond, but nothing came out.

"That's what *I* thought," Whitney said. "King's Shield. Born to some noble family, I bet. Got to live thinking gold was as common as stone. So, protect people all you want, but you aren't one of them."

"Better than being a fool."

Torsten gave him another tug, and Whitney smiled. He'd gotten under the big man's skin. He may have been tied up, but he'd make sure the knight remembered one thing above all else: this was Whitney's chance for infamy. The Crown beckoned a thief for help, not the other way around.

He scratched his chin, lifting both hands as far as his bindings allowed. He still wasn't used to feeling stubble there. It was in that moment he realized just how big a toll the last few days had taken on his body. He hadn't had a decent night's sleep or a substantial meal since winding up in a bloody battle. As if to remind him, his stomach rumbled.

"Don't think we should have a quick bite before we start off, eh?" he asked.

In response, Torsten kicked his heels into his horse's side, clicking his tongue. The horse started off, and Whitney felt a tug before his horse followed.

"Okay, fine," Whitney said. "I wasn't very hungry anyway. Just thought you might be. Have I told you how good the dungeon cuisine is? When we get back, I have to meet the chef."

What he wouldn't give for a piping hot bowl of stew or a sweet, creamy, apple pie with bourbon and cheese. Drool pooled in the corners of his mouth. He shook away the thought, especially once he realized he was chewing on his lip. Whitney hated the taste of blood.

Great, I'm thirsty now too.

"Did we even bring bread?" Whitney asked.

Torsten turned slightly in his saddle, his face silhouetting against the brightness of the sun.

"Are you going to complain like a child at every turn?" he asked. "Should I bind your mouth as well?"

"I assure you, Shieldsman," Whitney said. "Many have tried."

Torsten snorted and prodded his horse forward, so hard Whitney had to focus on not falling face-first off his mount. That and excruciating hunger kept him quiet.

They rode on the Royal Road in silence until it began to narrow. They were leaving the Glass Prairie and entering into the surrounding farmlands. No patrols, no city guards, just crops for kilometers and the occasional scattered village, less of them now.

Whitney's gut wrenched at the thought that they might end up passing through one of the ravaged villages. He hadn't experienced a time in his life where he'd felt more hopeless than when Troborough was under siege. He wished he could say he played the part of one of the old legends, whipping out a sword, felling each Black Sandsmen one by one, but even he couldn't spin a lie that good. Worse even, if it hadn't been for Torsten's men, he'd had fallen to one of the Shesaitju curved blades. Not that he could ever admit that to the hulking Shieldsman towing him along.

They entered a copse of trees, large trunks towered far above on each side of the pathway—spruce and redwoods, cypress and sequoia. Whitney loved the smell of pine and dirt. It reminded him of every successful theft he'd ever undertaken when he escaped the walls of society and found a quiet place to admire or hide his haul.

"Oh, slave master!" Whitney called out. "There's some nice shade. How about a bite to eat now?"

Torsten pulled back on the reins. Without a word, he tossed his leg over the horse's side and hopped down. When he started rummaging through the saddle sacks, Whitney joined him. The slap of a hard gauntlet met his bound hands.

"Ouch!" Whitney whined, shaking his hand.

"Hands to yourself, thief," Torsten said, terse. "You get what I give you, now sit down."

Whitney backed up but didn't back off. "This partnership isn't going to work if you don't trust me."

"This is no partnership, street rat. You are with me only because the Crown demands it. You should be honored."

"Me? Do you know how many would kill for the services of Whitney Fierstown? They'd tie me up just to keep me close… sound familiar?"

Torsten spun, grabbed hold of Whitney's tunic, said, "Listen, boy… I've stood by the side of both king and queen while the most famous jesters in Pantego performed their mindless nonsense. They didn't amuse me, nor will you."

He shoved a handful of dried meat into Whitney's chest and stormed away. Whitney collected himself and took a bite of the salty snack. It was chewy, like leather, but it was the best thing he'd eaten in days.

"Back on the horse," Torsten said. "It's not time for resting. Eat and ride."

"Are you always so cheery?" Whitney asked. "Warn me now, because I have a tough time with happy people."

If Torsten heard him, he didn't show it.

"I'll take that as a 'yes,'" Whitney said, and tore another bite out of the tough meat.

"Let's go. Certain death awaits us."

"Who's making jokes now?" Whitney asked.

"Wasn't a joke," Torsten said, climbing onto his horse. "No one's ever escaped the Webbed Woods with their sanity, and I doubt we'll be the first."

"So, you're a goblet half-empty kind of guy then?"

"Best get on your horse before you find yourself running." To accentuate his point, Torsten gave his horse a little kick, and the rope tugged, causing Whitney to stumble.

"You know, this is no way to treat an innocent man." Whitney dug his feet into the Earth and yanked on the rope. Torsten, atop his horse, didn't budge even an inch.

What is he made of stone?

"You're far from innocent," Torsten said.

Whitney gave up pulling and Torsten willed his horse backward to give Whitney enough slack to mount his steed. He was already coaxing the horse to a steady trot by the time Whitney situated himself on the saddle.

"I forgot; I've got to take a pi—" Torsten cut Whitney off by kicking his horse and leading them onward.

"Piss in your saddle."

He didn't, though, it took a fair amount of concentration not to. Especially after his meal was finished. The dried fruit was military rations, overly salty and dreadful tasting. He couldn't imagine how anyone could march across Pantego and fight with their bellies full of such garbage.

How would he possibly handle the Webbed Woods on such a diet?

Whitney found his mind wandering to dark places as the time passed, towering trees and eight-legged monsters...

"They call the beast 'Bliss,'" Torsten said as if reading Whitney's mind. "The 'Spider Queen.' Hog's piss and horse shog if you ask me. Just another monster needing to be sent to Iam."

"How did you—" Whitney began.

"If you have any sense, you must be thinking about the Webbed Woods and every story you'd ever heard about it. I haven't stopped thinking about it since we left, and I'm prepared to not return. You should be the same."

"All this for a doll?"

The knight tugged the reins and brought both steeds to a halt. "All this for the Glass," he said sternly. Then he snapped them, and the horses took off again.

"Nobles," Whitney muttered under his breath. "How they love their trinkets."

XV

THE KNIGHT

Torsten peered through the canopy of leaves and branches, sunlight glinting through the breaks like a thousand specks of gold. Dusk had arrived in the Haskwood Thicket, which meant night was coming. Torsten knew better than most to stay off the roads in the dark. Even at the height of King Liam's power, bandits and worse made their home on the roads between cities.

"It's getting late," he said. He gave a tug on Whitney's rope to make sure he was paying attention. He thought he heard the thief snort awake as if he'd fallen asleep.

"Observant," Whitney said.

"We'll make camp here for the night." Torsten was quickly growing accustomed to ignoring Whitney's witless comments. "We'll head out in the morning."

"Good, I can feel my fingers freezing off, and we'll need them."

"Well, get rubbing them together. No fires tonight." With the Shesaitju on the prowl, Torsten knew they couldn't afford to take chances.

"You can't be serious."

"I am always serious. Vile folk troll these lands at night. We can't draw attention to ourselves."

"We aren't even that far from the city!" Whitney protested. "What's the point of adventuring with a King's Shieldsman if we have to hide like everyone else."

For the first time since they left Yarrington, Torsten remembered that he was no longer a member of the King's Shield—not in the eyes of the Crown at least, and those were the only eyes that presently concerned him.

"I never met a thief who didn't prefer the dark," Torsten remarked.

"It's not the dark I'm worried about." Whitney exaggerated a shiver. "It's the things *in* the dark. Plus, it's freezing."

"You think this is cold?" Torsten said. "You wouldn't have lasted an hour marching on the Drav Cra."

"Is that why you're so dour?"

Torsten hopped off his horse. He secured Whitney to a tree, tying the rope around a thick branch before sitting down on a nearby rock.

"This is ridiculous," Whitney said. "Where do you think I'm going to run off to?"

Torsten rummaged through his supplies once more, ignoring the question, pulled out some cheese and more dried meat.

"What are you going to do when we get there?" Whitney asked. "Won't be much good against Queen Bliss with my hands bound together."

"Bliss."

"What?"

"It's just Bliss. There's only one Queen."

There was silence for a while. Out in the country, it was a different kind of quiet. Torsten hadn't been this far from Yarrington and the Crown since King Liam's last war against the Panping. Yet here he was, in the wilderness again. He had to make Oleander see reason again—if for nothing else, for the sake of the kingdom and Liam's legacy. Even if his son was beyond saving.

"Hey, knight." Whitney snapped his fingers. "See any nefarious folk out there?"

Torsten shook away the thoughts. He tossed the food at Whitney with intentional zip. The thief couldn't catch with his hands bound, but he batted it down into the grass.

"No," Torsten said. "But try to keep your mouth shut."

"Tough to do that and eat at the same time."

"You'll find a way."

The buzz of night bugs began as they ate in silence. It was almost peaceful. Torsten had grown so used to the din of Yarrington—carriages on stone roads, drunkards stumbling and rambling, shopkeepers howling —he'd forgotten what the country sounded like, forgotten what it was like to live where most of the people did.

He cursed Whitney inwardly for being right. He'd spent too much time like a hand-servant attending to the Oleander's every need. He hadn't even realized how much he'd missed the openness of the field, the smell of the camps the night before battle. Somehow, with Liam leading, he was never afraid of waking up and falling into the charge. But this mission did not feel like those had. Liam was not at the lead. Sadly, he never would be again.

Torsten snapped back to the present when he heard a snore come from Whitney's direction. The young thief finished his meal and had passed out almost immediately, lying on his side in the middle of the grass like an infant.

Torsten scoffed, then heard another snore. Only this one stirred the horses. They stomped in place, neighing as they backed up toward the tree, a haze of dirt rising.

"Calm down." He swatted at them with one hand and wiped dust from his eye with the other. "It's only the kid."

Torsten heard what he thought was another snore, but this time it sent the horses into even more of a frenzy.

"Hey now," he said, drawing himself to his feet. He was consoling the horse he'd been riding when he realized the sounds weren't snores at all.

Yellow eyes glinted in the moonlight all around them, piercing eyes that seemed to shred the darkness. Wolves.

"Whitney," Torsten whispered as calmly as possible. At the same time, he reached back and slowly wrapped his hand around the grip of his claymore.

A sliver of light caught the face of one of the approaching beasts. Its back was as high as Torsten's waist, with paws the size of his head. The shaggy, brown hair along its spine stood tall as it bore fangs as long and sharp as daggers. These were no ordinary wolves.

Dire wolves. Further south than he'd ever seen them.

Torsten took one long step toward his sleeping companion. The pack leader snarled, saliva dripping from its black lips.

"Whitney," Torsten whispered. The thief rolled over and nestled against his hand as if enjoying a pleasant dream. "Would you wake up." He kicked him in the thigh.

"I'm leaving, dad!" Whitney shouted himself awake. He sprung up, panting and searching from side to side as if he were lost. When his gaze found Torsten, he scowled. "I thought noblemen were supposed to be raised with manners, you—"

Torsten raised a finger to his lips. "Move slowly. We're not alone."

The pack leader growled, a sound like the rumble of thunder. Whitney's eyes went so wide they seemed ready to pop out of his head.

"Iam's shog!" he yelped.

"Watch your tongue."

"Forget that. You have to untie me. Those are wolves."

"Dire wolves." The correction made Whitney's cheeks pale. "Just move slow. They don't usually roam this far south. They're tentative." The dire wolves were closing in. It was dark and, without a fire, Torsten had to rely mostly on his sense of hearing.

"Says the man with armor."

Whitney crawled backward slowly.

The alpha released a sound so unnatural, Torsten's arms were coated in gooseflesh.

"Tentative my ass. I love food way too much to be dinner!" Whitney scurried to his feet and bolted to the tree where the horses were tied. Torsten went to yank on his restraints, but there was too much slack.

One of the horses got spooked and thrashed its head so hard the rope fastening it snapped. It bolted off through the forest, drawing half the wolves in pursuit. The pack leader and two others remained focused on human prey.

"By Iam, you're useless," Torsten said. He backed toward the tree and drew his claymore.

"Throw me a sword, and I'll join you!" Whitney hollered.

Torsten glanced back and saw that Whitney had somehow scaled the tree with his wrists tied and sat atop a thick bough. Torsten had half-a-mind to tug the end of the rope and give the wolves a proper feast, but he was focused on his footwork. The remaining horse reared back and roared, but this one couldn't break free.

"This sword has slain giants, beast," Torsten threatened the pack leader as it bore down on him. "You think it fears fangs?"

"I've heard talking tough to monsters really works," Whitney called down.

Torsten ignored him and tightened the grip on his sword. The beast was so hulking, each one of its footsteps made the ground quake. Torsten had encountered dire wolves in the northern lands of the Drav Cra and wondered if Redstar had anything to do with their presence.

"Back!" Torsten bellowed, swinging his sword at the wolf. It wasn't even fazed. The thing looked ravenous like it hadn't eaten in days, and considering how far from home it was, that was probably true.

Torsten heard a shuffle to his right and glimpsed a smaller—by comparison—gray wolf circling him. The crafty leader used the distraction and leaped. Torsten got his arm up just in time as its teeth clamped down on his armor. Any other suit, the teeth would've sunk through into his flesh, but King's Shield armor was crafted by the finest smiths in Pantego and hewn from glaruium.

It didn't, however, stop the momentum of the beast from bowling him over. They tumbled through the grass until Torsten was on his back, the wolf gnashing at his arm and spitting all over his face. The other wolves went for the horse, slowly circling it as its cry filled the night.

Torsten pawed through the blades of grass for the hilt of his sword. It'd been too long since he saw battle, or even sparred for that matter. He could feel his muscles wilting under the weight of the great beast.

He found his sword and let his arm dip. The dire wolf's fangs slid down his bracer, and one found the weak spot behind the forearm. As it bit down, Torsten jabbed it in the side of the head with his sword's pommel, the Eye of Iam with a spike at the end. It howled, and Torsten was able to spin free and slash wide, drawing a thin line of blood across its chest.

Any regular wolf would have backed down from the blow, but this one's skin was thick. Torsten regrouped and dropped into a battle-ready crouch. Blood trickled down his wrist and stained the rope bound to his cowardly companion hiding in a tree.

"Leave!" Torsten roared. "The Glass will not fall at the hands of wolves!"

He raised his sword high and brought it crashing down toward the wolf's head, but it lurched out of the way. The claymore twirled with it, coming around for another strike that caught it in its hind-quarters. Blood sprayed the grass, but still, the wolf didn't back down. It pounced, and just before it crashed into Torsten's side, he felt the rope wrapping his hand pull taut. Then he was yanked out of the way. His feet struggled to find a hold but kept him from being thrown to the ground. Whitney sat atop Torsten's horse, his wrists still bound, but the horse cut free.

"What are you waiting for, wolfslayer?" he shouted.

Torsten looked back at his foe, now flanked by the two smaller, gray dire wolves that could still tear him to pieces with claw or maw. He ran for the horse while Whitney held her steady, then hopped up behind him.

Whitney whipped on the reins with both his bound hands to spur the horse along at full speed. The wolves gave chase.

"Look who decided to stop hiding," Torsten said.

"All part of the greater plan," Whitney replied.

"Right."

"Only way to mount a panicked horse is to drop down from above. Better than your bright idea to have a sword fight with one of those things!" Whitney's voice went shrill on the last word as the pack leader caught up and snapped at their feet.

"This would be a lot easier if I could use my hands," he said.

"Not happening," Torsten replied. He twisted his body and got a good grip on his claymore. One of the smaller wolves raced around and leaped at them from atop a fallen trunk. He smacked it away, the weight nearly breaking his wrists as he struggled to hold onto the giant blade.

The beast squealed, writhed across the ground, but the others continued on. The alpha's gaze was fixed as if prepared to devour their very souls.

"Hold on tight," Torsten said.

"Oh no, what this time?" Whitney asked.

Torsten squeezed his armored calves against the sides of the horse and propped himself up as high as he could. He lifted his sword and scanned the trees. When he spotted a thick enough bough hanging in their path, he brought the blade crashing through it. Wood splintered as the branch split into two. Torsten hung onto Whitney's back to keep the momentum from flinging him off the horse, and luckily the thief finally listened to his orders and held them steady.

They glanced back at the same time. The obstruction slowed the wolves down long enough for the horse to put some distance between them, and they made sure to keep building it.

After what felt like an hour, when they were finally sure they'd lost their pursuers, Torsten and Whitney exhaled at the same time.

"So, now when do we get to sleep?" Whitney asked.

Torsten gritted his teeth and rubbed the cut on his arm, but didn't answer. Barely a day into their trek and they'd already nearly been devoured. He would have preferred running into bandits or a coven of witches, but one thing was sure—Dire wolves south of Crowfall… the kingdom he'd known was no longer the same.

XVI

THE THIEF

The shimmer of small flying insects weaving in and out of the tall grass was Whitney's only company as morning came, white specks like dust being swept up by servants. The silhouettes of birds passed overhead. They'd likely been there all along, one flock after another, but the darkness made them impossible to see.

He struggled to keep his eyes open, and occasionally Torsten broke into a snore. But they were exhausted and stopping again in the forest seemed like a bad idea with dire wolves about.

Of all his wild adventures, this was starting off as the strangest yet—running from giant wolves with a giant Shieldsman bouncing behind him. The tremendous man didn't leave much room for him on the saddle either, and the constant clattering of his armor made it a challenge to catch a few winks while their horse trudged along down the dirt trail.

Whitney watched a squirrel scurry by and felt his stomach rumble. In the right hands, it could make a wonderful stew, but Whitney had never been a great cook. He closed his eyes and pictured himself back in Yarrington, wearing a flamboyant looking disguise, enjoying a feast fit for nobles. Then, Torsten's loudest snore yet sent crows fleeing from the boughs above. The large man's weight drifted back, nearly dragging Whitney with him.

"Ey," Whitney groaned. He gave Torsten's pauldron a smack. The Shieldsman nearly broke Whitney's neck as he woke in a violent panic.

"Iam's shog!" Whitney yelped. "It's just me."

"You should know better than to wake a knight," Torsten said.

"Yeah, well if I don't get real sleep, neither do you," Whitney replied. "I'm all about equality."

"We can switch if you'd like."

"Oh, so I get to play fair maiden?"

"In case you forgot," Torsten said, "there was only one of us who fought anything back there."

"And I rode to your rescue like the great King Liam himself."

Torsten's lip twisted. "Well, you look like you can use the sleep, fragile as you are. Come on. We've got a lot of ground to cover, and not all of it will be as easy as the Haskwood Thicket."

"Easy?" Whitney scoffed. "Was it only me that almost got eaten by wolves last night?"

"As I told you before, those were dire wolves," Torsten corrected.

"Well, they've all got teeth. Double the size, double the appetite." Whitney shuddered at the thought of winding up a meal. "How about this: I let you back up front, so your manhood isn't threatened, and you untie me."

"So, you can knock me out in the night and flee? Not a chance."

"In case you forgot, you invited me on this mad quest because you needed the best thief around. Why would I run from the chance to prove it?"

"Because that's what thieves do. You think I was born some satin-pantsed noble? I grew up on the same streets you did, boy. Scrumming for food in the garbage."

"Your high and mighty father trying to teach you a life lesson?"

"My father was a cur. Came over on a wagon from Glinthaven and never left. Spent his days hungover and his nights at the taverns trying to swindle men out of gold until one bashed his head in. My mother was a brothel wench who could care no less I existed. It was King Liam who gave me my name, raised me from the rabble. So next time you think to utter his name, don't."

Whitney swallowed back a response. He never found it easy to still his tongue—he could talk plaster off a wall—but a Shieldsman born so common? No, not just a Shieldsman, the Wearer of White himself. He'd asked to be given a new name back in that cell to escape his father's, but that didn't mean he believed a man could rise above his caste, from street urchin to commander of armies.

"Who'd you kill to move up?" Whitney finally decided on, feeling there was no other plausible reasoning.

"That's exactly what's wrong with people like you. I didn't move anybody aside. I prayed to Iam every waking moment until finally, he saw fit to bless me. He came in the form of our great King Liam who saw worth in me I never had."

"Yeah well, sadly, that king's dead now."

"A new one will wake upon our return, and he will remember what stock he comes from, or Iam save us all."

"All I'm saying is that I sat in that cell talking to a rat and I didn't pray a lick, and look at me now." Whitney gave a tug on the horse's reins, forcing it to stop walking. He spun and presented his bound wrists. "On my way to becoming a free man. Look at that expression. I can tell how much it pains you to stare at the back of my gorgeous head."

"Better than your face."

"Pretty please?" He raised his hands further.

Torsten's features darkened. He groaned and lifted Whitey down from the horse as if he were light as a child. Then, he grabbed his wrists, leaned down, and used the claymore hitched to his back to cut the ropes.

"Sweet liberty!" Whitney exclaimed.

He stretched his arms, not even realizing how much his wrists burned from trying to squirm free. He usually escaped from bindings much more quickly, but the Shieldsman tied one yig of a knot.

His jubilation was cut short when a cold, armored hand fell upon his shoulder. "You try to flee, the King's Shield will hunt you to the ends of Pantego."

"What's one more group after me?" Whitney smirked. Torsten remained staid as a stone wall. "Relax my giant, brooding friend. If I wanted out, I would've left you for the wolves."

Whitney ducked around Torsten, and on his way, snagged a bit of dry meat out of his satchel. He swung up onto the back of the horse and took the largest bite he could possibly fit in his mouth.

"Are we going?" Whitney asked, crumbs spilling from his lips.

"Try that again, and you'll lose a hand," Torsten said.

"You hired me to steal a magical doll. I won't be much good without two of them."

"It isn't magical."

"Some might think so."

Torsten pulled himself up onto the front of the saddle and spurred the horse ahead with a light kick. "Let's cover some ground before night falls again," Torsten said, digging his heels into his horse.

"You're not telling me that counted as sleep?" Whitney protested, mouth still crammed.

Torsten didn't answer, and they continued along in silence until arriving at a small stream. The cool water lapped at their feet as the horse trudged through. When they reached the other side, they stopped a moment to give the horse a drink.

"You know, it's not winter yet," Whitney said. "We could try our hand at fishing. They must teach you that sort of stuff. Have ourselves a real meal…"

Whitney's words trailed off when Torsten reached for his head. At first, Whitney thought he was so annoyed he'd finally lost it, then the Shieldsman released some manner of shrill groan and then collapsed from the horse into the mud.

Whitney stared. He hadn't seen such a reaction since finding his way into a cultist blood mage's dungeon and watching the man dig through people's minds like they were old, battered tomes. It took him a few moments to realize he should do something.

"Torsten!" Whitney called out. He ran over and slapped him across the face. Nothing. He just continued to mutter under his breath like a madman, eyes closed like he'd seen some terrible monster.

"Buried…" it sounded like, and then something else indiscernible over and over again.

Whitney took a deep breath, reared back his arm, shouted, "Wake up!" and punched Torsten across the jaw.

"Not dead!" Torsten roared. His eyes sprung open, and he threw

Whitney back so hard he splashed through the stream. Torsten panted like a wild animal.

"What in Elsewhere was that?" Whitney asked, brushing off his pants.

"The color crimson and a thousand eyes," Torsten whispered, squeezing his eyes.

"Hey!" Whitney got to his feet, stormed over and shoved Torsten's chest. The brick of a man barely budged, but some form of clarity washed over his gaze. He regarded Whitney "What does that mean?"

"What are you—what happened?" Torsten squeezed his eyelids. "Is this your excuse for an escape plan?"

"Are you daft? You fell and started rambling like a lunatic. Threw me so hard I nearly broke my back!"

"I don't…"

"Are you dying on me, knight? Because your little story was getting me excited about a new name."

Torsten managed to roll onto his side, coughing. He looked down and seemed to notice a bit of blood on his hand from where his armor pinched flesh. He quickly wiped his palm against the grass, still moist with morning dew.

"Just help me up, boy," he grated. "I fell off my horse, who knows what I'm saying?"

Whitney reached down, grabbed Torsten by the elbow with both hands, and used all his energy to heave him to his feet.

"Seriously, are you going to tell me what happened?" Whitney asked. "You suffer from night fits? I promise I won't tell any of the other Shieldsmen."

"Probably dozed off and had a nightmare."

"You have those?" Whitney asked.

"When you've seen the things I have, boy, every dream turns into one."

"Well, then I think it's time we actually rest. You look worse than shog."

"Fine," Torsten conceded, terse. He climbed back onto the horse. "Oxgate should be just over that hill. I hoped to speed through, but we should be able to find lodging for a few hours."

"Lodging." Whitney rolled his eyes.

"What?"

"You noble folk and your fancy terms." Whitney drew himself back onto the horse and stuck his arm out. "Onward to lodging! And keep those eyes open."

They continued riding until a basso wailing sound broke the silence. Torsten glanced back confused, then sent the horse into a gallop. When they reached the crest of the hill, they saw its source.

The charred remains of Oxgate spanned before them, still smoldering in some areas. Embers flitting in the wind. There wasn't a house or shop standing. No fields of corn or wheat remained. There wasn't even a sign of horse or cattle. The only thing left standing was a lone tree in the middle of the village.

"By Iam," Torsten said. "They took Oxgate too."

"How did one tree survive a fire that destroyed a whole village?" Whitney asked.

"That's no tree."

XVII

THE KNIGHT

A man nailed to a crucifix in the center of the razed town screamed a blood-curdling scream. Even from such a great distance, Torsten could see the anguish contorting his face.

"We've got to get him down from there," Whitney said.

Torsten lifted a hand. "Wait. We don't know who did this."

"What are you talking about? It was the Black Sands!"

"The town, maybe, but that isn't how they kill. Whoever did this might still be around."

Whitney leaned forward, regarding Torsten with eyes like a begging hound. "We *are* going to get him down, right?"

"It might be best to keep our distance and leave him for the gallers. We have our mission."

Torsten had seen war. He'd known battle from every angle, and this one wasn't worth the fight. The man was soaked in blood, his lungs likely already collapsing. Torsten was no physician, and whoever had played healer for the people of Oxgate now lay scattered amongst the ashes.

"I'm getting him down from there," Whitney said, "with or without you."

With that, Whitney leaped from the back of the horse and bounded down the hill. Torsten called after him in a raised whisper but to no avail.

He considered, for more than a moment, letting the young thief play hero and find his own fate in the middle of Oxgate by the cross of a helpless man, but that wasn't the way of the King's Shield. His order was a part of him even if the Queen Regent had stripped him of his title. He snapped the reins and took off after his reckless companion.

By the time Torsten's horse matched Whitney's stride, the latter slowed, eyes wide as he looked upon the poor, tortured soul. The man's cries sent a chill up even Torsten's hardened spine. It was always his least favorite part of combat, hearing the groans that followed. After every major battle, hundreds loosed their death cries as if a mob of spirits escaped Elsewhere, but one was enough. Torsten had always been fine with taking a man's life in the name of the Glass, but when it came to watching men suffer, he hadn't the stomach for it.

"Horrible," Whitney said under his breath.

"Damned street rat!" Torsten spat. "I told you, we need to move." His eyes scanning the smoke and embers for movement. If this were an ambush they'd run headlong into, whoever planted it was taking their time springing the trap.

"Just help me get him down." Whitney grabbed hold of the side of the crucifix to get a better look.

The man howled in pain, impossible to understand.

"We should just stick a sword through his gut and end it," Torsten said.

"Will you do the same to me if that warlock gets his hands on me?" Whitney questioned.

"If mercy begs it of me." Torsten shoved Whitney aside, then drew his claymore. He raised it high above his head, but just before it fell, the crucifix went up in flames. Tongues of fire swept over the man and the wood as if they'd been doused in oil.

The horse flailed, throwing Torsten off and knocking into Whitney as it galloped away. Torsten's shoulder hit the ground hard, but there was no time to worry about pain. He clawed through the dirt, looking for his sword, the crackling fire so hot he could feel his skin blistering under his gauntlets. He found the blade and flipped over to search for what caused the fire. Whitney was on the ground holding his leg and squeezing his eyelids like he was in terrible pain.

Torsten was about to help him when, from all directions, a dozen figures, maybe more, in unmarked, hooded robes poured out of the smoke. Their heads were lowered, so their faces were completely shrouded in darkness.

Torsten's hands tightened around the grip of his claymore. "Walk away, and nobody has to die," he addressed them. "We have no autlas or anything worth your lives."

The hooded strangers didn't answer. They circled the duo and drew nearer, weaponless hands clasped together in front of their chests.

"Are you planning on helping me up?" Whitney groaned.

"I'll handle this," Torsten answered.

"At least give me your dagger!"

Torsten backed up until he was so close to the flaming crucifix he felt his hairs singe. Seared wood crumbled, the charred man collapsing to the dirt with it.

Torsten spun to better appraise the situation. Thirteen of them were closing in. Torsten had faced worse odds against better-armed enemies. Things weren't dire enough to hand a blade to a back-stabbing thief who could easily be behind this ambush. His glaruium armor and claymore were more valuable than a gold mine.

"You guys looking to get rich?" Whitney asked the assailants. "I've got a ring buried a few leagues east of here. It's precious. Leave us alone, and it's yours."

"They clearly aren't interested in your—"

Torsten lost his train of thought when the hooded figures suddenly stopped. He and Whitney exhaled in relief at the same time.

Maybe he is good for something, Torsten thought.

Then the assailants stopped and raised their heads. Each of their faces was covered by a white ceramic mask—a smooth, expressionless human face with a red teardrop under the right eye. The sight gave him goosebumps. He'd seen masks like them in hidden, cult-shrines discovered from time to time in Yarrington basements.

They were Glassman who turned their backs on Iam's light and instead worshipped Nesilia, the Buried Goddess. Torsten's heart skipped a beat. He'd been wondering what had caused him to relive the flurry of visions which had struck him the night Pi fell—remnants of Redstar's curse. Now he knew. The same believers in occult magic being nearby must have been the cause.

"Oh, you've got to be kidding me," Whitney said. Torsten glanced back at him to find his eyes bright with horror. The thief struggled to stand on his wounded leg.

"Step back in the name of Iam and the Glass Throne, heathens!" Torsten bellowed. He brandished his claymore and glowered at his enemies. They were heretics. Thieves and braggarts like Whitney were troublesome pests, but there were few as wicked as those who'd willingly chosen to worship fallen gods in the shadows.

"Good idea," Whitney remarked. "Stare at them until they cower in fear."

The closest masked assailant reached into the folds of his robe and removed a dagger, its blade curved twice in a wave until it reached the razor-sharp point. He raised it over his hand, then slid the blade along his palm. Blood poured out along his wrist and pooled in the dirt around his feet.

Torsten dug his boots into the earth, now mixed with soot and charred wood. A sudden burning sensation began in his favored hand. Starting from the inside, unimaginable heat radiated along his fingers until he could no longer bear the weight of his claymore. It slipped from his grip, and he fell backward, howling in agony. He threw off his gauntlet to observe the damage.

"What in Elsewhere is wrong with you!" Whitney protested. "I have to handle everything."

He pushed a leg off the ground to launch himself toward the claymore. The renowned thief apparently couldn't handle a sword worth a yig. He swung at the robed figure, who parried and disarmed him in one smooth motion.

"Let me go!" Whitney shouted as a pack of them grabbed hold of him.

A few more came for Torsten. The burning pain in his hand was beginning to dissolve, but it had him seeing stars. Sliced, cut and stabbed in countless battles, he'd never felt such a tremendous discomfort. He could barely describe it, yet on his now-bare hand, there wasn't even a mark.

A mess of hands grasped his arms, trying without success to restrain the mountain of a man. He threw his weight forward and tore free, grabbing one by the neck and flinging him through what little was left of the crucifix.

He spun again, grabbed another by the folds of his robe, and unleashed a heavy fist straight to the face. With his gauntlet off, it hurt, but he knew it felt better than the attacker's face must have. The ceramic mask split down the middle before its wearer stumbled backward, landing with a forceful thud.

Torsten took a hard step toward another, but as soon as his foot landed, searing heat coursed through it. His leg gave out and sent him slipping through the blood-puddled mud. When he was able to, he looked up to see the same armed assailant with blood dripping from a long cut across the top of one of his bare feet.

Torsten tried to fight the burning sensation, but his armor was designed for armed combat—as heavy as it was durable, exhausting to wear in a hand-to-hand brawl.

The men reached down for a second time, trying to haul Torsten off the ground. It went just as poorly as their first attempt. Finally, they got one of his arms wrenched behind his back and smashed him in the back of the skull with something solid.

White spots flashed across Torsten's vision, and he collapsed face-first into the mud. Blood and ashes filled his nostrils. Fresh embers stung his flushed cheeks. More hands drew him upright before binding his wrists and towing him along like a dog on a leash. He offered as much resistance as he could, but his muscles were too strained and his head too foggy. He cursed Whitney for cutting into the few precious minutes of sleep he was able to get over the past day.

Whitney, he remembered. Now he understood how he had felt when his hands were bound. The young thief spat a long strain of curses, and in his peripheral, Torsten saw his arms flailing wildly as they hauled him along.

"Cut it out, kid," Torsten muttered.

Whitney ignored him. "You have the wrong guy!" he said. "I love wearing masks too."

Torsten could hear the whispers of the robed figures holding Whitney. They spoke plainly, but he didn't understand them. As former Wearer of

White, he knew of every language in Pantego, but this one caused his lungs to deflate.

Drav Crava.

The harshness of the language of Redstar's people could not be mistaken. The worst southern cultists to the Buried Goddess often learned it as they longed for the savagery of the Drav Cra, but some of their captors spoke it without a hitch like they were born in the far north.

"Seriously, if you all were smart, you'd take me up on that ring," Whitney said, then pointed to Torsten. "Do you know who that is?"

"Be quiet!" Torsten snapped.

"You're lucky a lightning bolt hasn't struck you yet. That's Iam's own Wearer of White you're hauling. "

The one leading the processional, the one who'd cut himself twice, raised his hand. His followers stopped. The others parted to allow him passage. He stopped in front of Whitney. Torsten swore inwardly. He could see the man's eyes, as dark as wet earth, through the slots in his impassive mask. The steam of his breath leaked from the bottom on the crisp, fall air.

He closed in on Whitney, hand curled around the handle of his curved dagger. Whitney steeled himself and strained his neck, lifting his chin. Torsten thought he saw the boy quiver just a bit.

"That's not what I hear," the cultist whispered to Whitney.

Then, before Whitney could respond, one of the figures hit him hard on the side of the head, and he fell limp.

"The Queen Regent will have your heads!" Torsten shouted and drew on all the energy left in his body, yanking until the ropes dug into his wrists.

He didn't get far before two sets of hands squeezed his arms together so hard the pain of the clashing bones became unbearable. Someone grunted something in Drav Crava. A foul-smelling cloth sack descended over Torsten's head. Torsten labored for breath. They were relentless as they walked, tugging so hard Torsten struggled to maintain his footing.

Silhouettes of light and shadow became his world. All he could make out was the twisting canopy of branches above, waving in the wind as if taunting him. They moved down a sharp, steep slope winding back and forth as even the shadows of trees disappeared.

"Where are you taking us?" he asked, his voice muffled.

The sound of rushing water echoed. He heard a cranking sound followed by a *bang* that made him flinch. A gust of air caught his legs before he was shoved onto the first plank of a rickety suspension bridge. He hesitated for a moment but was pulled so hard he stumbled over a gap.

The bridge swung spasmodically beneath his weight, and it took him a few steps to realize that the planks were made of metal rather than wood. He tried to stop, but his captors allowed him no rest, moving along until his feet hit solid ground and further still, until the sound of water was but a distant memory.

They were entering a cave… no a fortress. The stone beneath his feet was much too smooth to be natural. Even through the cloth, he could see torchlight painting sharp corners and stilted archways. He only knew of two places that designed arches like that: cathedrals of Iam, and the underground dwarven cities of the Dragon Tail.

They stopped.

Torsten opened his mouth to speak but was promptly shoved to the ground. He gasped and coughed, desperate to catch his breath. One of the hooded men tilted him upright, tore the sack off his head and forced him into a cage along the wall. The space was so cramped he had to crouch not to hit his head. Whitney was dumped in another cage beside him.

"Where have you taken us," Torsten said, still winded. The roomy hollow beyond the brass bars of the cage was unexpectedly ornate. Columns hewn from the rock filled the space, spottily clad in gold and bronze that looked like it had tarnished centuries early. They wrapped a circular basin situated below a domed ceiling as smooth as Glass.

It all reminded Torsten of the Royal Crypt, and that was because the people that constructed this place had constructed that one as well. A dwarven fortress, manned by their kind eons ago when their kingdoms ruled Pantego before man descended from the Drav Cra and drove them underground. The place may have lost all its luster, but the dwarven ruins scattered throughout Pantego remained sturdier than half the castles in the kingdom.

The assumed leader of the cultists stepped toward the basin, flicked his hand, a slow stream of blood still pouring from the wound. A blazing fire erupted from the pit at its center, nearly licking the ceiling with its tendrils.

The bloody, hooded man barked something at the others in Drav Cra. One by one, they filed out until only Torsten, and an unconscious Whitney were left with him.

He turned from the flame, lowered his hood, and slowly removed his mask, revealing the face of a man—pale as parchment and nearly as thin. His nose was long and crooked, like a carrion bird. Torsten tried to get a sense of the man's age, but it was impossible. Flaking, black paint was smeared across the top half of his face with a thin line of red just around his eyes. A thick necklace of sharp teeth and bones rattled around his skinny neck.

He was a true warlock—the mortal servants of Nesilia, their heathen Buried Goddess—like Redstar was. There was only one reason such a wicked man of the Drav Cra would be so far south masquerading as a cultist.

"Where is he?" Torsten asked through clenched teeth. He wrapped his hands around the bars of his prison and pressed his nose through the narrow opening.

The warlock spoke to the flames in the language Torsten didn't understand. Torsten's head suddenly began to ache, like the inside of his skull was put to the torch. The warlock's words morphed, shifting into the common tongue in the midst of a phrase.

"—a blot, a stain upon this land," he said. "She must be eradicated, and he will do it. A knight, a master of shadows, and a—"

"Where is your master?" Torsten growled, interrupting him. "Where is Redstar!" He banged on the cage with what little strength he could muster.

The warlock turned to him. The sight of his painted face made Torsten uneasy.

Whitney was just beginning to stir and jolted upward, hitting his head against the low ceiling of his dwarven cage. Torsten couldn't imagine any other reaction to waking to see such an unpleasant façade.

"He won't get away with this," Torsten said.

The warlock stopped and leaned down in front of the cage, his dark eyes boring directly to his core. Out of nowhere, he grasped Torsten's hand, pulled it through the cage, and sliced the tip of his finger. The cage shook as Torsten tore free and slammed against the back wall.

The warlock brought a bit of Torsten's blood to his lips, his tongue lashed out, staining it red. It reminded Torsten of a lizard or a toad catching its prey.

"Interesting," he said, voice like a serpent. "I sense that you have already been in contact with our lady below. The master will want to see you." He stood, turned, and left without another word.

"Get back here, heretic!" Torsten rattled the cage, but he was answered only by his own echo.

XVIII

THE THIEF

"This is hog's piss," Whitney said, scratching at a line in the stone wall at the back end of his cage.

Torsten grunted an indecipherable reply.

"You realize this is the third time in almost as many days I've found myself locked up in a cage?" Whitney asked. He banged on the low ceiling. "And a Dwarven one to boot? I'm starting to hate them."

"You're a bloody thief," Torsten said. "What do you expect?"

"Oh, and you're so noble, are you, Shieldsman?" Whitney crawled across the cage to look through the brass bars that separated them. "I'm no idiot. I know a Nesilia cult when I see one. What did you do to anger the Buried Goddess and get us all thrown in here?"

"There is only one god's opinion which matters."

Whitney scoffed. "I've been to every corner of Pantego, friend. Seen men worship everything from silence to flowers. It was all as real as Iam to them, but say it out loud, and you'll find yourself in a dungeon just like this one."

"And now you see why. There is only one God who loves mankind. The others spread and corrupt like a virus. All they seek is power."

"I know of a guy who conquered just about everyone in Pantego for a god you say, 'loves mankind,'" Whitney said. "Doesn't sound too loving to me."

"He loves enough to pursue," Torsten said, resolute.

Whitney made a raspberry sound with his lips. "If Iam gave a lick about us we wouldn't be in here. Now it's up to me to find us a way out."

Torsten leaned his head against the back wall, then closed his eyes as if nothing was wrong. Whitney wanted to punch him, but couldn't reach. More importantly, he wanted to bash that damned dwarf from the tavern in his wobbly-eyed face. "Rob the King," he'd said. "It'll be fun. Hog's piss."

Whitney crawled the length of the cell, which didn't take long. If he laid down and stretched his hands, every limb would be sticking through the bars.

What am I doing?

Chasing after a baby's toy toward the most dangerous place in Pantego. He'd have been better off falling down a dwarven mineshaft… one they still inhabited at least. They might have had the decency to offer him an ale at the bottom.

He glanced back at his companion who'd constantly cursed his being and spat on him the way knights tended to do to thieves. The man who'd done the total opposite of offering a drink—tied his hands and dragged him along like a badly behaved pet. It hadn't been much longer than a day, and they'd been attacked by dire wolves, found a man crucified in a burning town, and now been nabbed by some psychotic Buried Goddess cult practicing blood magic. Torsten had never said that's what it was, but Whitney had seen plenty of magic before.

All that, yet the thing his mind kept drawing back to, was how quickly the brave Shieldsman pretending to nap in the neighboring cage was able to condemn the crucified villager to death—like it was just another day at work.

Whitney preferred to do *his* work alone. Even if his partner wasn't a justice-hungry, obey-the-authorities-at-all-costs, goody-goody like Torsten, being involved meant another life to worry about.

Whitney preferred only worrying about himself.

Stealing may have been the only thing he was good for—and he was damn good at it. Why did he need to prove himself by stealing a silly little toy from an insane Drav Cra warlock and his made-up spider queen? Whitney had stolen the crown off the King's very head.

I'm not going to sit around, waiting for Torsten to feed me to the spider just to save his own hide.

He searched the cage walls, ceiling, and floor, for anything that would help him break out, but found nothing.

He swore and kicked the rock wall at the back. A piece of stone broke off. It pinged off one of the bars of his cage and struck him in the thigh.

A smile crossed his face. He rushed over to the fragment of rock and picked it up. He took a step toward the wall between him and the Shieldsman.

"Torsten," Whitney whispered. The man didn't stir. Exhausted enough to fall from his horse, his fake nap had turned real very fast. *"Torsten,"* Whitney said lilting his voice like a child playing street games.

Finally, asleep.

Whitney squeezed his hand through the bars into Torsten's cage. He prodded the Shieldsman's only remaining gauntlet and checked to make sure it didn't wake him. All that hard work keeping him awake on their horseback ride was paying off. Taking a deep breath, he ripped the gauntlet free, wincing as he pulled it into his own cage. Torsten continued snoring, snorted, and turned his head away.

"Some knight," Whitney mumbled under his breath.

Giving the room a quick scan, he stretched the gauntlet out along the floor. The rock made a dull *clunk* as it banged on the jointed metal of the pinky finger. He continued, cringing with each hit, worried he might rouse Torsten or draw the attention of one of those freaks. Finally, the end piece of plating broke free.

"Would you keep it down?" Torsten grumbled. "I'm trying to think."

"Sorry," Whitney answered. "Cages give me jitters."

Whitney waited a few minutes until he heard the steady rasp of snores again. Then he continued banging. He paused, then did it again, and again, flattening the metal into as thin a sliver as possible.

It wasn't the finest lock-pick he'd ever crafted, but not the worst either. Considering the hooded cultists had seen fit only to have a guard pass through to observe the cages on rotation, they were either not used to holding prisoners, overconfident, or both.

Not a good combo while trying to confine Pantego's greatest thief!

Whitney twisted his hand between bars and lifted the lock with the other. The angle killed his wrist, but he clenched his jaw and got to work. The tip of the gauntlet's finger-piece just barely fit. He lowered his ear and listened for the familiar clicking of tumblers in the lock.

He had it the first try but was interrupted by footsteps. A cultist entered the room holding a candle, probably drawn by the sound of him slamming the gauntlet. Whitney snapped backward and lounged, the gauntlet stuffed beneath his back and digging into him.

"Any chance on getting a meal down here?" he asked.

The man turned, stared his way from behind his expressionless mask. Whitney always thought the depictions of demons were the stuff of nightmares, with their horns, eyes of fire and disfigured faces. He was wrong. This was.

The cultist then continued on his way without responding.

"What is with people and not wanting to eat?" Whitney groaned to himself, loud enough for the cultist to hear him. He leaned forward as the man went by, and the second he was around the corner got back to work.

It took longer than he cared to admit the second time, taking breaks only to rest his hand or bang on the piece of metal again to reshape it. Occasionally, he glanced up to see if Torsten had awoken and to make sure no more of the cultists were approaching.

Whitney's fingers were shaking by the time he heard the lock click and fall open.

"Got you!" he exclaimed, then realized how loud he'd been.

With the lock disarmed, he took a moment to admire his handiwork. The makeshift pick was barely in one piece, but it had worked.

Making a lock-pick out of a piece of glaruium to escape a cult of fanatics and the Wearer of White was one for the records. He'd barely have to add any flair when he told it at taverns across Pantego.

Sidling through the cage door, he stopped. Footsteps were approaching again, and Whitney hurried across the circular space toward the single, poorly lit passage leading out. It felt good to be able to stretch his neck. That was the thing about dwarves, only their prisons suited their size. They built everything else in a way that dwarfed giants.

He peeked around the corner. The cultist and his candle were heading his way, no way around them. Whitney ducked back down and scanned the room for loose stone. His heart started to race.

Damn those dwarves and their craftsmanship!

Old as the place was, he didn't find a piece of stone big enough until right before the cultist entered. It'd been a while since he had to make a move so drastic, but if he could battle Shesaitju, he could handle this. He waited until he saw the shadow of the man go by, wavering in the candle-light. The cultist froze in the doorway, facing Whitney's now empty cage. The beginnings of a word were on his lips when Whitney bashed him in the head just like they had done to him earlier.

The cultist didn't go down easy. He turned, and Whitney struck him again in the face, cracking his mask in two. Whitney caught both him and the candle before it hit the floor. He glanced over at Torsten, who was so exhausted he still hadn't woken. Only then did Whitney finally exhale. He placed the candle down, then dragged the man off to the side and lowered him.

"How do you like being hit?" he whispered in the unconscious man's ear. He considered stealing the robe, but the man's mask was unusable and getting the cumbersome robe off a limp body would take too long. Instead, he stole the man's wavy dagger and used it to tear off a piece of the sleeve to stuff in the man's mouth.

"You should have made better life choices," he said as he hauled the man over his shoulder and carried him to his cage. He slowly lowered the man in, checking Torsten every so often. The massive knight snored so loudly he gagged, then turned over in the other direction.

Whitney locked the cultist in and checked on Torsten one last time. He noticed the homemade lockpicking tool on the ground where he left it.

"Good luck, oh noble one," he whispered as he slid it into the Shields-man's cage. "You'll need it."

Even if Torsten woke up at that moment, Whitney would have a head start—and that's all he ever needed. It was the least he could do for the man who'd sprung him from the Glass Castle dungeons.

Whitney stood, dusted off his pants, then he returned to the hallway and continued his escape. There wasn't much activity in the next large chamber he passed, but what he saw made him even more curious.

Etched into a slightly curved wall on the far side of the room, wrapping behind a crumbling throne, was a mural pieced together from stone shards. It depicted a woman with a spear in the center, one foot planted firmly on the chest of some enemy. He didn't have time to see who it was before he heard movement and drew himself back into the hallway.

He held his breath and squeezed the dagger's grip as one of the robed cultists passed, not more than a meter from where he stood hidden. He couldn't afford to get caught for admiring artwork. He pressed on through the room after the man's footsteps faded. Whitney moved cautiously, finding cover where he could.

He arrived at another hall, only this one wasn't long and empty. It looked like a corridor at an inn, only the open doorways spaced along it had curtains instead of doors. Living quarters.

How does anybody live in a place like this? Might as well get locked in a dungeon.

He cursed his luck. A good thief always avoids sleeping quarters unless there's good reason.

What better reason than survival?

Whitney pushed forward, stopping before each room to check for watching eyes before passing. The first few went by without incident, no one home. He had almost decided they would all likely be empty when he came across one that wasn't. An old man stood naked inside, face aimed up at the ceiling with his eyes closed. His back and arms were covered in faded scars.

Whitney didn't have time to linger—nor did he want to. He took two leaping steps across the curtain, then made a break for it. Carefully monitoring the sounds of his footsteps, making sure they landed heel-to-ball so he'd go unheard, he reached the end of the hallway and peered around the corner. No time to catch his breath. Ahead of him was an open gate. A bridge beyond it spanned a narrow ravine. Water gushed somewhere amongst the shadows at the bottom, and he could hear the bronze wheels of a mill turning in the current, still operational.

He'd hoped to escape the ancient dwarven fortress without incident, but with each step, it seemed less likely. Now he knew why they hadn't bothered leaving a guard by the cages. There was only one way out, through their entire hideout. But they hadn't encountered Whitney Fierstown before.

His heart beat steadily, rhythmically. It took him a second to realize it wasn't his heart, but actually a distant drum beat. Whitney skulked toward the bridge, staying low. It crossed to a clearing at the bottom of a narrow valley. The fortress was apparently built into the cliffside, hidden. A perfect place to bury a cult of the Buried Goddess.

Pesky dwarves and their hiding places.

He stuck his foot out to test the brass planks. Satisfied they seemed sturdy enough and grateful for the sound of the rushing water below to muffle any noise he made, he swung his legs over the edge. He couldn't uprightly cross it in front of everyone, so he placed the dagger in his mouth, grabbed onto the side of the bridge and hung down. Making sure not to look down as his feet dangled, he sidled along, hand over hand.

One of the planks at the halfway point was loose, and he lost grip with one hand. His body swung, and the dagger fell from his mouth, causing him to look down at the rapids far below. He quickly grabbed back onto the next plank and continued along. He expected his recent luck to run out and someone to have heard. They didn't.

Once he was safely across, he climbed up, ducked into the shadows, and began to plot out his next move.

A dozen of the robed figures were in the clearing illuminated by the light of the moons. They were distracted by what he imagined was an unholy ritual taking place around a fire pit. A narrow path behind them skirted up the bluff, dotted by torches. It was the only way unless he wanted to take a swim in the rapids and see where they dumped him out.

Always go up.

It would've helped if he could've understood a word the cultists spoke, but he had no such luck. While they chanted and drummed, he tiptoed around the clearing, back pressed against the rock, keeping to the shadows. He wrapped back until he could see the front of the dwarven fortress carved into the opposite side of the ravine.

Two massive relief sculptures of dwarven warriors stood proudly on either side of the open gate, their axes crossed above it. They were so large, their eyes were literally windows. He could tell by the flicker of flame through them.

He reached the path and didn't bother looking back. He picked up his pace, sticking to the wrinkles to avoid torchlight. A chilly breeze hit his cheeks when he got high enough to see the heads of the dwarven statues. When he turned back to the path, he noticed a torch bobbing towards him.

Someone was approaching.

He backed up into a shallow nook that barely concealed him and listened for footsteps. It was impossible to hear anything that subtle over the echoes of drums pounding below. Ducking low and counting on the minimal throw of torchlight to keep him hidden, he waited until the time was right to strike. Now without a weapon, he was at a clear disadvantage, but these cultists only seemed to wield daggers, and he'd slipped by guards with halberds plenty of times.

The figure rounded the corner and Whitney sprung into action. He threw a punch into the groin of whoever it was. A cheap shot, sure, but only fools like his father valued honor over survival. The only problem was, the person he punched didn't go down like he should have.

That complicated things. Whitney wasn't one to hit women, but this one took full advantage of his confusion by lashing out with a perfectly targeted chop of her hand. It connected with Whitney's upper arm, and it felt like a bone had snapped.

"Ow!" Whitney yelped as he leaped back. "Okay, we're really fighting then."

"Stop talking, fool," the woman snapped. Her voice had a softness, despite her tone.

Whitney swung at her with his fresh arm, and she dodged him with ease. Then again. He tried one last punch, and she absorbed the blow, grabbed his forearm and flipped him. He landed hard on his back. His hood fell off, and his head dangled off the edge of the bluff so he could hear just how far a fall awaited him. She drove her knee down into his chest, twisting his arm to the side.

Whitney gazed up at his defeater, expecting to see one of the ceramic masks of his captors, but instead found a familiar face. Shrouded in the shadows of a hood or not, it was a face he could never forget.

"Sora?" he said.

XIX

THE THIEF

"Sora!" Whitney sprang to his feet and wrapped his arms around her without thinking. His joy at seeing his old friend dwindled when he realized she wasn't squeezing him back. He held her at arm's length and saw that she didn't look happy either.

"Wait, why in the world did you hit me?" he asked, releasing her.

"You hit me first," she said. "In the balls."

"But it didn't hurt you!" he said, brushing the dust off his pants and rubbing his lower back where he'd landed. "What are you doing here? Oh, shog. You're one of them?"

She gave Whitney a light shove. "Do you want to stand here and talk, or get out of here before they find us?"

"So, you're not one of them?"

"Move!"

She shoved Whitney harder this time, sending him stumbling down the path.

"All right," he groaned. "Still as impatient as ever, I see."

She led him to the top of the winding path where they came across the bodies of two cultists, spilled tankards of ale between them. One wore robes, the other, nothing. At first, Whitney feared they were dead, but their chests rose and fell.

"You did this?" Whitney asked.

"I needed a robe, and they were standing guard," she replied matter-of-factly. "Slipped some of Wetzel's sleeping tonic into their drink."

"I… wha…"

"They weren't planning only to punch a woman in the balls if they caught me sneaking about."

Woman. Hearing her say that gave Whitney momentary pause. The last time he saw her back in Troborough, she was far from a woman.

Whitney collected himself. "Smart," he said, then squatted down and grabbed the small, curved dagger from the still-clothed body. The other cultist's weapon was deposited next to his stripped body. He raised it for Sora to take.

"I have my own," she said.

"More for me." Whitney tucked both daggers into his belt, then leaned in further to check the robed man's pockets.

"Seriously?" Sora said.

"Once a thief, right?" Whitney winked but doubted Sora could see him in the dim light.

She shrugged, lifting a small pouch of autlas out of her robes with one finger and rattling it. "Well, you're too late. Let's go."

After giving him a shove, they delved back onto the path up through the cliffside, moving faster this time. When they rounded the last bend at the top, Whitney saw Pantego's moons hanging high above the tree line. Ice-cold water from a light drizzle splattered on his cheeks.

He stopped and drew a lungful of fresh air. He always forgot how dank and foul the air could get deep underground until he smelled the surface again. Fresh grass and a cold autumn breeze which, for once, he welcomed. He let out a hearty laugh.

Sora threw her hand over his mouth and shushed him. "We aren't free yet, you dolt. C'mon."

They avoided the roads and kept to the trees in case they were followed by cultists—or Torsten in the off-chance he'd managed to escape the ruins. Once they built a safe distance, Whitney turned to Sora, and the sight of her back in his life gave him momentary pause.

He'd nearly forgotten what she looked like. The years had been kind to her. The young Panpingese woman was somewhere between cute and beautiful, with a turned-up nose and almond-shaped eyes bearing just the right amount of wrinkles at the corners. She wore her jet-black hair long and straight, the pointed ears indicative of her heritage poking through on the sides. She could have been deadly gorgeous, but she barely tried, and Whitney had a thing for the effortless.

"Okay, now can you tell me what in the name of Iam's, shog-yigging sake you're doing here?" he asked, finally.

"Saving you, apparently," she replied.

"I was well on my way to escaping before you attacked me, in case you forgot."

She glared at him with her piercing, amber, almost yellow, almond-shaped eyes. Whitney felt like their color was even more vibrant now than he remembered them being. Those eyes always spoke of her uniqueness. Most other Panpingese he'd ever met had brown eyes, but hers were the color of the rising sun.

"You're lucky it was me you ran into," she said. "The way you fight, it could have been one of them with their knee at your throat and a dagger through your eye."

"I had you right where I wanted you." He chuckled. "I meant, how in Elsewhere did you know where I was or that I needed saving?"

"I saw you in Troborough the other day and followed."

Whitney stopped. "You were there when—"

"Yes," she said solemnly, looking to the ground. "I'd just returned after a few weeks visiting Yarrington when the Shesaitju attacked. I only wish I'd spent one less day there and maybe… maybe I could have helped stop those traitorous animals."

"Imagine that. After all this time, we were minutes from running into each other on the road."

"Imagine." She seemed far less enthused.

"So, you saw me fighting off those Black Sands savages then?" Whitney asked, puffing out his chest.

"I saw something, but it didn't look like fighting."

Whitney dismissed her comment with a playful wave of his hand. "Yet you decided not to help? Doesn't sound like the Sora I know."

"Knew," she corrected, and Whitney noted her harsh tone. "Someone had to get the children to safety. Besides, I wasn't completely sure it was really you until you went for my nethers back there. Thought I was seeing things from breathing too much smoke in the attack. You're much taller now."

A moment passed.

"Still can't grow a beard, though," she remarked.

"What, you don't see it?" Whitney smirked, scratching at stubble. A brief bit of laughter passed between them until suddenly his smile faded and he realized what her being in Troborough might mean.

"So, you still live in Troborough then?" he asked as if it were the worst possible thing he could imagine.

"Lived," she said, terse. "Not all of us are deserters willing to abandon everyone who loves us."

Whitney could have kicked himself for embracing her back on the cliffside as if no time had passed. Of course, Sora would feel abandoned. All these years later and Whitney rarely had a chance to think about her, but there was a time they were the closest of friends; perhaps, the only friend he'd ever really had.

"Sora, I'm—"

"It doesn't matter now," she interrupted. "I got to hear your mother weep for weeks and your father curse the name of their only child. Did you ever even say goodbye to them?"

"In my own way," Whitney lied. His teenage self said goodbye the moment he hit the road, slipping out in the dead of night. Same way he'd said bye to Sora. Without a word.

"Lucky them," she muttered. "You know they died, right?" She didn't let him answer. He could tell she had something she needed to get off her chest before they got anywhere. "A plague. Even Wetzel's cures couldn't save them, their illness got so bad. I thought you'd come riding in proud on a great steed after some unexpected adventure took you away. I watched the road the entire night, but you never showed."

"I only heard about them when I came through Troborough a few weeks ago," he replied, throat going dry.

"So that *was* you," Sora said, as if it were the answer to a riddle.

"Wait, you knew I was there, and you didn't come say 'hi?'" Whitney asked, desperate to veer the conversation in a new direction.

"I could say the same for you."

"I passed by Wetzel's place, and it looked abandoned! I figured nobody was home." It wasn't the whole truth, but Whitney had perfected the art of half-truths.

"Well, I stay away from that awful tavern. Hamm doesn't even have decent bards anymore. You know how many drunks and vagabonds stop by to bloat their legends? I didn't imagine the bragging thief passing through who everyone wished would pack up and leave was you."

Whitney scratched his chin. "Weird, I'm never one to leave out my name." Nearly everything about that night with Grint was a blur. All he really remembered was the dwarf challenging him, and then him setting off for Yarrington. Grint was so drunk he probably remembered less, and now he had half the Glass Crown and Whitney nothing.

"Nobody seemed to care about it if you said it," Sora said, shrugging. "Even Haam couldn't remember."

"Now you're just being hurtful."

"Good. A part of me still thought it was you, but by the time I got away from helping Wetzel with his work the thief was gone."

"I was sent on an important quest by a trader, which I completed by the way."

"I'm sure. It must have been something earth-shattering for Whitney Fierstown to return home twice after ten-and-a-half years."

"It's been that long?" Her glare made the end of his sentence trail off. He honestly hadn't realized it'd been that long. For him, the moment he saw her it was like no time at all had passed.

The rain started to pick up. Sora brought up the hood of her stolen robe, making Whitney wish he'd taken the time to take one for his own.

"What about me?" Whitney asked, breaking the uncomfortable silence and desperate to change the topic.

"I'm sure you learned how to weather a storm or two out there frolicking in the *real world*," she replied.

All he'd accomplished was making things more awkward. Her pace became brisker in response to the weather, forcing him to keep up.

"So, you spot someone you thought could be me in Troborough and followed him all the way here?" Whitney asked, finally. "I'm flattered."

"I had to do something. I tracked the Glintish Shieldsman back to

Yarrington after they took you prisoner. Next thing I knew, you were back on the road with that…"

"Torsten," Whitney said.

"What?"

"His name is Torsten. He's the Wearer of White."

Her eyes went wide. "The what? And *you're* with him?"

"I'm moving up in the world," he said, putting on an air of sophistication. He held his breath, hoping she'd kept her distance enough not to notice that Torsten had him tied up for half the journey.

"I've got to hear this. You go from stealing bread from Big Ben Barenstein to leaving all of us behind to become some sort of… noble?"

"Noble?" Whitney scoffed. "Gods no! I'm still the same me you remember. The Queen pretty much had to beg me for help. She needed someone with my… particular talents, and after I stole King Liam's crown right off his head for that trader in Troborough, even they couldn't deny I'm the greatest thief in all of Pantego."

Sora laughed. "You're the greatest thief in Pantego? I haven't heard of you since the day you *left* Troborough."

Whitney's lip twisted, but he kept his cool. "I wouldn't be a very good thief if you had, would I?" He reached into his pocket and displayed the same bag of coins Sora had stolen off a cultist.

She patted her pants, then shot a glare his way. "Why in Elsewhere would the Queen need a silver-tongued devil like you?"

"Must be for my quick fingers." Whitney winked.

"You're gross."

"Or maybe she just couldn't resist my charm. Either way, Torsten and I were heading south to the Webbed Woods when that oaf of a Shieldsman got us captured by cultists."

"The Webbed Woods?" Sora asked. It sounded like her breath got caught in her lungs. Whitney didn't recall her being afraid of anything, but only a fool wouldn't fear those cursed woods.

"The Queen wanted us to retrieve the Prince's… or King's… whatever he is now. She wanted me to steal his special doll back from a Drav Cra Arch Warlock who happens to be the Queen's brother or something like that. Somehow, it'll help him recover from sickness. Highborn and their trinkets."

Sora just stared at him, dumbfounded. Whitney couldn't help but smirk.

"I think that's enough, you? They won't be catching up. Let's rest."

"Thought'd you'd never ask," Whitney said.

They found a relatively dry spot under a thick canopy of trees to block the rain. Whitney took a seat on a fallen tree trunk, and Sora sat beside him, scooting in close. She smelled like a farm, which wouldn't have been awful if not for the fact that it was now a smell so foreign to him. He was used to city folk and city smells—shog and piss and everything worse.

"So, what now?" Sora asked.

"I'm not sure," Whitney said, "but I'm sure as Elsewhere not going to die for some Shieldsman."

"You're going to abandon him?"

"Better me do him before he does me."

"Good to see some things never do change."

"That's not fair," Whitney argued. "He hired me to steal, not to fight. He was supposed to be the muscle, and he goes and gets us captured by a mob of crazies who probably wanted to cut our throats to please a goddess that's not even listening? How do you think he'll fair against Arch Warlocks or giant, bloodthirsty spiders? He'd throw me at them to save his hide." Whitney shivered at the thought.

"What's the pay?"

Whitney had plans to continue his rant, but her response caught him off guard. "Excuse me?"

"The pay," she repeated. "In exchange for helping."

Whitney grinned, turned his cheek and said, "I swore I wouldn't say."

"Oh, c'mon, Whit." She nudged his side playfully. "Clearly you're getting paid. What is it? How much?"

"Why? It doesn't matter anymore. Torsten's locked in a cage, and without him, I barely know who or what I'm looking for."

"So, you give up?" It wasn't a really a question.

"No, I move on to greener pastures. I'm out of dungeons and ancient dwarven ruins, in the clean air. I'm thinking a vacation is in order. I *did* just steal the Glass Crown you know."

"You still haven't answered. What was the price?"

"My freedom, which I now already have, and some riches."

"You're lying." She shifted her body and leaned forward so she could stare straight into his eyes. He tried to look past hers, but the brilliant, golden flecks in her irises kept drawing him back.

"I swear."

"A swear from a man who fears no gods is no swear at all." Her breath on his skin brought a feeling familiar and strange all at once. "And furthermore, I don't believe you. You were a sad liar when we were kids, and you still are." She lay her hand on his thigh and nudged in closer. "Just tell me. What does the greatest thief alive get offered for his services?"

Her hand slid further and further up his leg until finally, Whitney blurted, "A name."

She pulled away immediately.

"A name?" she asked.

"Yes. A name. Happy?"

"What does that mean?"

"If we made it back alive, Torsten was going to have me ennobled the head of a new house, and I wouldn't have to share a name with that sorry bumpkin I called Dad."

Sora seemed disappointed. She sunk back, all the glimmer stricken from her eyes.

"But it's not worth dying over," Whitney went on. "A name doesn't matter much in a profession where you're not meant to be seen or heard. It was a stupid idea, really."

"You haven't changed one bit." Sora sprung to her feet and took a few healthy strides away before Whitney reacted.

"What is it now?" he whined.

"Was it really so awful back home with all us *bumpkins*?"

"That's not what I meant."

Sora folded her arms and continued facing away from him.

"Look," Whitney sighed. "There are enough men after me to fill a barracks right now and trust me, I've had my fill of dungeon food. I have a friend in Winde Port. He's one of the only decent dwarves I've ever met. We can head there for now."

"What makes you think I want to go anywhere with you?"

"For one, you followed me all the way to Oxgate. Two, there's no Troborough to go back to…"

He hadn't sooner said the words than regretted saying them. There was no more Troborough. Her home had been burned to the ground for no good reason.

She turned to him, tears pooling in the corner of her eyes. "You're a real bit of shog, you know that?" She walked off. Whitney chased her.

"Sora," he called. She didn't stop. "Sora!" He tugged on her shoulder. She whipped around, grabbed his wrist, and wrenched it so hard the pain forced him up onto his toes.

"I should have left you to rot in that cage!" she bristled, then released him.

"Probably, but now we're here. Whitney and Sora, together again." Whitney figured it was best not to mention he'd already expertly escaped the cage when she found him. Instead, he placed a hand on each of her shoulders, smiled, and said, "Don't you remember when we got Pavlo's dad to believe his pigs ran away?"

Sora continued glaring for a few seconds, but her lips betrayed the slightest hint of a smile. That was enough for Whitney.

"He searched frantically, screaming out to them each by name," he said, holding back a snicker.

"Until he heard the snorting in his cellar," she said.

"Must have smelled like shog in his house for a week." They shared a laugh, and Whitney used the moment to rub at his sore wrist. For such a small woman, she had a grip like a vice.

"And then you left," she said, her smile vanishing.

He sighed. Ever since that day he'd worked alone. It was how he liked it. But as he regarded her, now so many years older, he couldn't help but imagine what it might have been like if he'd invited her along, had a partner in crime. Would he still have found himself jaded enough to go back home for inspiration and drink himself silly all alone?

"I'm back now," he said. "We've all done things we aren't proud of, no? Why don't we put the past behind us for now and go somewhere far away from here? See what kind of trouble we can get into?"

Sora moseyed back to the fallen log and lay down, staring at the canopy above. From that angle, Whitney could really tell how much she'd grown up. He pretended to cough, hoping she hadn't noticed him staring.

"You know what I want?" she said.

"What's that?" he said.

"I want to see what you learned all those years away from home. I want you to find the new King's doll and get that name of yours. And since I have no more home to go back to, I'm going to help you."

Whitney stifled a groan. He leaned against a tree, facing away from her, trying to find words that wouldn't trigger her again. "Look, Sora. I don't know if the stories about the Webbed Woods are true, but this is a job for professionals. Drugging some cultists is one thing, but this—"

He lost his train of thought when he felt a burning sensation in his side. He looked down and realized that the bottom of his shirt was burning. He tore at it, slapped at it, but it kept burning. He grabbed it by the collar and ripped downward, removing it entirely. Then, he cast it to the ground and stamped on it until the fire suffocated.

The sound of Sora laughing drew his eyes up. She stood grinning, her expression more sinister than playful. She gripped a small knife in one hand and had the other raised toward him. A thin, fresh line of blood dripped down Sora's palm, with a tiny ball of flame hovering in front of it.

"Don't you worry about me," she said. "You're not the only one who's been training."

Whitney's eyes very nearly popped from his head. He knew what he was witnessing, but found the words difficult to muster.

"B...b...blood magic?" Whitney stammered. "You are a blood mage?"

The smile still hadn't left Sora's face as Whitney's shirt lay smoldering on the ground.

"Are you crazy?" he said.

"What?" she said. "You can galavant off into the world stealing staves from wizards, but I can't learn a bit of magic?"

"So, you *have* heard of me?"

It was dark, but Whitney was pretty sure Sora rolled her eyes. "Maybe once or twice. Traders whisper and bards sing, especially those who've been robbed. And apparently, you're never smart enough to leave out your name. No wonder you want a new one."

"There are songs about me?"

"Not very good ones."

"Very funny. We're getting off topic. How in Iam's name did you learn…" He lowered his voice even though they were alone. "Blood magic."

"It's not really an interesting story. Not like one of your grand, exaggerated epics of stealing crowns and serving the Queen."

"I'll have you know that every one of my feats is one-hundred-percent, perfectly true. It's not my fault I was gifted with the ability to enrapture minds."

Sora's eyes rolled so far this time Whitney couldn't miss it.

"Just tell me," He pointed to a spot on the ground beneath the boughs of an aged oak tree. "We can stop here for the night. The ground's damp, so it looks like we're going to have to snuggle up close to keep warm. Where better to talk?"

"You do remember what I just did to your shirt?"

Whitney glanced down at his bare chest. Seeing it also made him notice how cold the air was. "Right. I'll get you some wood."

"You think I'm going to cut myself again just so you don't catch a chill?"

Whitney started to respond, but Sora's giggle made him realize she was chiding him. He laughed nervously along with her and began gathering wood.

"What are you doing?" she asked.

"Helping you start a fire," he said.

"You really don't understand how this works, do you?"

She stood and searched the ground until she found a spot in between two thick, fallen branches. She squeezed her hand into a fist, and a droplet of blood dripped to the earth from her last cut. She closed her eyes and spent a long moment deep in focus, then fire sprung from the wet dirt.

She plopped down and waved her hand through the spikes of flame. It reached out for her palm as if she were controlling it, keeping it from spreading to the boughs of the tree above.

Whitney took a step back, aghast. He'd seen magic before. Most humans weren't adept at it, and dwarves never were, but he'd seen more insane miracles than making a fire. He imagined his amazement was more over the fact that it was Sora. He'd always hoped he could learn a trick or two, but not everyone was born with an affinity with Elsewhere, both the source of magic and the underworld realm filled with demons, spirits, and far worse which Iam created for them after the God Feud.

"Okay." Whitney joined her by the fire. "You're seriously going to have to tell me where you learned that."

"Troborough," she answered as if that should be expected.

"Not a chance," Whitney said. "I grew up in that goat-shog town. C'mon, really, where?"

"Like I said, Troborough."

"And you thought my stories sounded crazy?"

Sora swiped her hand through the fire, causing it to lick Whitney's boots. He yelped and shimmied further away.

"Wetzel," she said.

"What? He was an old nutter who played with medicines, not blood magic!"

"He wasn't just some 'old nutter,' he was a healer. And if I remember correctly, he sewed up more than a fair share of your cuts."

"I can pull a thread, Sora. I don't bleed fire."

"That's not how it—" She exhaled. "Wetzel taught me everything he knew."

"This isn't adding up," Whitney protested. "How could you have practiced *blood magic* in the middle of our little town without anyone knowing?"

"Oh, now it's *our* town?" Sora scoffed with a smile. "Wetzel knew— plus, he'd been doing it for gods know how long under his shack, and no one has found out. It's not legal you know, using the magic of Elsewhere. What better place to learn than in a town barely anybody has heard of?"

"Were you… even when I was still there?"

She shook her head. "I was too busy getting into trouble with you. But he saw my potential after you left."

"I always knew there was something off about him."

Her features darkened. "Was…" she whispered softly. She raised her knife and stared longingly upon the wooden handle, the end carved into the shape of a dragon's head. Whitney recognized the weapon as the one Wetzel used to use for surgery.

He swallowed back the lump forming in his throat. It was clear Wetzel meant more to Sora than being just some old coot who took her in as an orphan and let her live in his tool shed so long as she helped him with his work.

"He died in the attack, didn't he?" Whitney asked.

Sora didn't answer, but she didn't need to.

Whitney stood to walk over and comfort her but stopped, thinking better of it. She might be talking freely, but it was too soon. She obviously hadn't forgiven him for leaving without so much as a goodbye all those years ago, when he disappeared like so many of the treasures he'd stolen from their owners.

"None of that matters anymore," she said. "My old life is over." She turned her head and tried to subtly wipe her cheek as if it were an itch that drew her hand and not a tear. She didn't fool Whitney, but the way her hair framed her face in the darkness made it look like she was still wearing a hood, and flicked a spark in Whitney's mind.

After giving her a moment, he said, "Sora, I have to ask you something."

"I already told you, we aren't cuddling," she replied.

"No… it's just…. Those cultists back there were blood mages too. And… and you just happened to follow me there?"

Sora stood to meet Whitney's gaze, the arms of the fire rising with her.

"Are you *accusing* me of helping capture you after I just rescued your worthless hide?" she said.

"No, not at all. I'm just saying, it is pretty coincidental."

"Yes…yes, it is quite coincidental that Whitney Fierstown would find himself thrown in prison for *stealing the King's crown* on the same night the King died. It is also *coincidental* that he was somehow released from jail to adventure across the land accompanied by the Wearer of White. Or maybe that after ten years you returned to Troborough right when the Shesaitju decide to rebel. There are a lot of coincidences going on around here, Whitney, but unlike the others, this one is exactly that."

He had to admit, his story seemed unlikely. Maybe even more than hers. As he thought back over the past ten-day, it all seemed awfully strange. He'd been wanted in every major city and most small towns, but breaking free of his third imprisonment in as many days had to be a new record. He was rarely caught unless he planned to be.

"Must be the hand of Iam, eh?" Whitney said, grinning.

"A blood mage and a thief," she said. "I'd wager Iam isn't too fond of us."

"If there's one thing I've learned in every part of Pantego, it's that the gods don't give a yig about us. Doesn't matter what name they go by. We're still alive, that's all that matters."

"You sound like Wetzel."

"Must have been a brilliant man."

Sora answered with a soft grunt. She returned to her seat by the fire and lay her head back against a thick root. "We should get some sleep. We'll need it for the Webbed Woods."

"Hey, I don't remember agreeing to that," Whitney protested. "I can think of a million better places to go."

"Goodnight, Whitney Fierstown. Maybe when I wake up, you won't have run off again."

She turned onto her side, facing away from him, and tried to make herself comfortable. Sleeping in the dirt wasn't hard for Whitney—not that he preferred it over a nice, soft bed—but after sleeping in a dungeon, anything is possible. She had the look of someone who'd never slept without a thatched roof over her head and a cushion under it.

Whitney lay back himself, listening to her struggle to find a good position. "I'm sorry," he whispered after a brief period of silence, not sure if she was still awake. For one of the few times in his life, he really meant it. Not for leaving her behind—the places and things he'd done were nothing a young girl should've experienced—but for not at least saying goodbye. He'd been so intent on getting out of Troborough, leaving behind his worthless life and every part of it, he'd never even considered his only childhood friend might actually care.

"For which part?" Sora answered after several heartbeats.

"All of it, I suppose," he lied. Sometimes it was the best way.

No answer.

He turned his head and lowered his gaze toward the fire.

How can she complain when she got to stay home and learn how to make that without even a stick?

He couldn't believe he found himself jealous of someone who stayed to live in Troborough while he watched the embers wafting across the night sky, disappearing as they passed by Celeste, the bright moon. He tried to clear his mind when a clump of cloth landed on his face.

"Hey!" he protested, pulling down the ball of clothing. He held it up and realized it was the cultist's robe she'd stolen. She'd had a plain tunic and leather pants on underneath, clothing fit for a peasant of Troborough and not adventure.

"In case you get cold," she said. "Next time, bring a spare shirt, thief."

XX

THE KNIGHT

Torsten's head was foggy from the beating he took, but he was still sharp enough to deduce what had happened when he woke up to find the adjoining cell empty. His one remaining gauntlet lay in Whitney's cell, as battered as Torsten's own body. Beside his foot lay a thin shard of glaruium and a small stone.

"That thieving son of a—"

Torsten heard movement. He grasped the stone and tucked it beneath his leg. There was some shouting in Drav Crava, and a moment later, several cultists returned with the warlock in their lead, no longer bothering to hide what he was.

"Please, I did what I was told!" one of them sniveled before being forced to his knees. He too wore no mask, only blood dripped down his face. This man looked to be a Glassman, and far too young to be involved with cults. The tears streaming down his cheeks furthered that assumption.

"Where is he?" the Drav Cra warlock questioned, pointing to Whitney's empty cell.

"I do not know," Torsten said. "He was gone when I woke up." If Torsten had to guess, Whitney was headed as far northeast from Yarrington as possible—Hornsheim or even Brekliodad, away from the

Webbed Woods, away from a chance at doing good by the kingdom. The coward's path.

"Liar!"

"I do not lie. Though I can't imagine there would be a reason I should tell you heathens anything."

"Then you will continue to rot in that cell."

"Am I to believe that you'd have let me go had I told you where the boy went?"

The warlock stared blankly.

"Thought so," Torsten said. "Now, why don't you get on with it and crucify me like that poor man in Oxgate?"

"He was no innocent," the warlock said. "And you were interfering with our judgment."

"And what was his crime?"

"He was an infidel and a liar," he said. "That is what we do to liars and failures." His gaze flicked toward the man on his knees, who didn't dare speak. Sweat now poured from his forehead to mix with the blood.

"It appears you'll have to crucify all of the Glass Kingdom then," Torsten said. "If Iam doesn't strike you down first."

"Iam's eye is blind."

"I pity those who can't feel his light."

He could tell the warlock wanted to reply, but he bit his lip instead. "The Grand Maester will handle you," he growled. He spun, snapped his fingers, and he and the others departed, leaving Torsten alone again. The bleeding one screamed his innocence as they carried him away, fighting to break free. The moment they were around the corner, he went silent. Torsten didn't have to think hard to imagine why.

He wasted no time before picking up the shard of glaruium broken off his gauntlets. After so many years in the Shield, he knew a lockpick when he saw one. His arms, however, were too thick to fit through the bars to reach the lock even with his gauntlets off.

Maybe the kid has a few skills after all.

He tried to maneuver himself for a better angle. Still unable, he leaned back and placed his booted foot firmly against one of the bars. He thought maybe he couldn't finesse his way out like that pestering thief, but this cage was intended to hold a dwarf, not a man anywhere near Torsten's size. Now that his muscles weren't completely exhausted from lack of sleep, falling from his horse, and fighting, nothing was going to keep him from getting out.

He pulled his leg back and kicked. He repeated this until the bar began to bend out at the center, the space between them now just wide enough to fit his arm.

He jiggered the lock as steady drum beats began reverberating throughout the cavern again. Torsten didn't know what it meant, but it couldn't be good. He wondered if Whitney had been caught trying to escape.

It would serve him right; leaving a brother at arms behind.

The drums intensified. Torsten continued to prod with the thin piece of metal, but he had no idea what he was doing. By the time he could feel the vibrations of the drums in his bones he still hadn't gained any headway. His frustration mounting, he stood, lowered his shoulder and rammed into the gate as hard as he could. He backed up and went again harder this time.

He could feel the metal starting to give when a procession of the masked cultists entered the hollow area and parted around the central node. A man emerged from the heart of them wearing an unmarked robe like the others but without a mask or hood. At first, Torsten thought it was the warlock again, but a braided, white beard fell below this man's collar.

This new stranger raised a fist, and the drumbeat stopped. He took a step toward Torsten. Torsten expected to be regarded with disgust, but instead, the old man appeared confused.

"Torsten?" he said.

A response got caught in Torsten's throat as the man stepped into torchlight and his face was illuminated. Of all the people to show up in such a foul place, Uriah Davies was the last he'd expected to see. No one had heard from him in over a year, but Torsten was sure it was him. Especially once he saw the one-of-a-kind sword sheathed at his side. The blade, crafted from glaruium hewn from Mount Lister, bore a mighty lion's head carved on the pommel.

Hard lines creased his forehead and the corners of his eyes. Dark, heavy bags hung from his eyes like ripe fruits straining their branches. A web of scars spread from a barren patch in his beard up to his right eye and across the cheek. But that's how he'd always looked. As a matter of fact, he didn't look a day older than when Torsten had last seen him.

"Uriah?" Torsten had done everything but bury his predecessor's body, yet here he was, holed up in with blasphemers and heretics.

"Yes, my friend. Though now they call me Grand Maester Ur." His staid, wrinkled face settled into an emotionless stare.

The memory played in Torsten's mind: a broken-hearted Uriah Davies, haunted by what Redstar had done, intent on finding him no matter what the cost.

"Open the door," Uriah commanded. A cultist stepped forward, unlocking the cage Torsten had expended so much effort trying to bash through. The mangled bars labored to pass each other.

Torsten backed away.

"Old friend," Uriah said. A soft smile spread across his face, but Torsten was unconvinced. "You have no reason to fear. I am sorry for how you have thus been treated."

Torsten inched toward his former compatriot until one of the masked cultists beckoned Torsten to step through. The moment he was free, Uriah wrapped him in a tight hug. Then he held him at arm's length, smiled, and asked, "How long has it been?"

"Too long," Torsten said. "Have you been…" He looked around, "…here all this time?"

"Are you hungry?" Uriah asked, ignoring the question.

After a moment Torsten nodded. "Starved."

"Grand Maester," the warlock interrupted, now masked. "His companion escaped. Shall we send anyone after him?"

"Don't waste our time with him," Uriah said. "He's worthless." He turned back to Torsten. "Let us feast old friend."

Before he could ask any more questions, Torsten was led upstairs to a celebratory hall. Torsten had gone from being beaten and stuffed in a cage meant for dogs, to being treated like royalty. He couldn't help but be skeptical, old friend or not.

A long, bulky table made of bronze awaited them, covered in biscuits soaked in sausage grease, pickled herring and cod, boiled apricots and honeyed hams. The dessert table was just as grand with rich foods Torsten would have been impressed by, had he not lived in the Glass Castle and had the walls not been adorned with banners and idols to the Buried Goddess. Her unholy sigil was everywhere, a droplet of blood buried within a triangular shape similar to either a mountain or an arrowhead. On the far end of the room, two massive, eye-shaped apertures looked out over a ravine, as if they were within the empty head of a giant.

"All this food..." Torsten said, averting his eyes from the devilry. Every attempt to ask Uriah what had happened was ignored, so he decided starting with small talk was the best course. "Where does it come from?"

"Oh, this place and that," Uriah said, licking his fingers after trying a sugared dough ball. "The servants of the goddess deserve only the best."

Torsten cocked his head. "The goddess?"

"You don't need to play coy with me. I'm sure you know exactly where you are. Any Shieldsman would."

"And, I also know that we took an oath to destroy places like this. To save those who would stray from Iam's blessed light."

"You have so much to learn, old friend." He pulled out a chair for Torsten and sat in one beside it. "Sit. Eat. There is much to discuss."

Torsten eyed the finely crafted dwarven chair and then cast his gaze upon all the masked heretics patiently awaiting his next move, wondering which of them was a warlock serving Iam's sworn enemy. He'd witnessed their profane magic, and now they wanted him to take his guard down. He sat with one leg on the chair, and his feet planted and ready to shoot him upright. Uriah had served Liam and the Glass Kingdom longer than Torsten had been alive, so he deserved an opportunity to explain himself.

"Uriah, what are you doing here?" he asked, this time making eye contact so he wouldn't be ignored.

"I could ask you the same. A Wearer of White beyond the Yarrington walls is a rare sight indeed."

"Same reason you left. The Queen sent me to track her brother into the Webbed Woods and retrieve what he stole from Pi."

Uriah smirked, torchlight catching the shine of the scars on his cheek. "So, the Flower of Drav Cra finally ran out of grunts and once again sent her best to his doom."

"I'm sorry, Uriah," Torsten said. "I never should have allowed you to go. I told her it wasn't wise after—"

"Allowed?" Uriah spat, his features darkening, wrinkles between his eyes appearing. "I was your Wearer. It was my choice to go in the name of your queen."

Torsten didn't miss the fact that Uriah had referred to Oleander as Torsten's queen and not his own.

"If anything," Uriah continued, "I am grateful. Had she never sent me, I'd be blind as the rest of you."

"Blind? How could one who once served under the vigilant eye of Iam now stand in halls wet with the blood of blasphemy and call anyone blind? You do know that one of those heathens no mere cultist, but a Drav Cra warlock, don't you?"

"I'll explain everything Torsten, but please, eat. It would be a shame to have all this good food go to waste."

Torsten pushed the food away. "I will not defile my body with food sacrificed to her."

"Always cautious," Uriah laughed, mouth full of bread. "The goddess does not require the blood of beasts. None of the food before you has been *tainted* as you might believe. Please, friend: eat."

Torsten hesitated still, but his growling stomach finally got the best of him. He tore into the buffet as if he'd not eaten in a fortnight. The meats were tender, the bread moist. How these people managed to cook such a decadent feast, Torsten couldn't understand, but Uriah was a noble since birth and knew how food should taste. He was humble, brave, and selfless —Torsten had never known a better knight.

"I never found Redstar after I left, but I saw evil in the Webbed Woods that no man should witness," Uriah said. "My men were lost. I watched as their eyes were torn from their sockets and their bodies wrapped to be devoured by Bliss and her unholy spawn."

Uriah took a bite from a chicken leg while Torsten's stomach lurched at the thought.

"Their eyes…"

"Gouged out," he said, nonchalant. "She says its eternal damnation."

"She…Bliss?"

"Aye. From that day forward, I knew such evil couldn't be allowed to exist; feeding, growing, preparing to wipe us all away. I knew that the moment your queen stopped sending her food in the form of knights, that the woods would no longer contain them."

"No great spider has ever left those woods," Torsten said, testing a bit of pudding with the tip of his tongue, "in legend or otherwise."

"So we all thought, and then I looked into the beast's eyes and saw true evil. Ancient evil, Torsten; the likes of which Iam and his followers believe no longer exists. It must be destroyed."

"And why didn't you return and tell us?"

"Would you have returned had you failed to find Redstar? I knew Oleander wouldn't listen to me and she was the only one who could. Too obsessed with the curse her brother put on Pi, she is."

Torsten leaned forward. "So, he was cursed?"

Uriah stopped chewing for a moment. "That's what I assume. She believed it was the orepul he stole, but I knew Redstar as a boy. There was no evil he wouldn't turn to."

"We could make her see together if you'd come back. You left us alone. The King, Pi... me. For this? Hiding like a mad hermit amongst cultists and Drav Cra."

"None of you would have understood. I couldn't risk being locked up for speaking what I saw. For I have learned that Redstar himself asked for her help in destroying Bliss. That is what started all this. The color crimson and a thousand eyes, my friend. I saw it, everywhere, in all our futures."

"What did you just say?"

"Ah, so you've heard those words spoken before? I can see the fear in your eyes."

"Yes. King Pi said something like it before he fell ill." He didn't mention the vision he'd seen on the road or in the Glass Castle courtyard thanks to coming in contact with the cursed boy.

"A warning, sent from our Lady Goddess, Nesilia. Though she is buried, she is not dead. But Bliss grows in power, Torsten. Emboldened by this new wave of attention. Waiting to feed on the flesh of all mortals if we do not strike her down as Redstar intended."

Torsten almost choked on his next bite. "So, you're working with Redstar?"

"Redstar hasn't been seen since I left chasing him," he said, terse. "He doesn't matter any longer. Bliss is the true enemy, and she must be stopped lest all Pantego fall to her swarm."

"Redstar cursed Pi, you said it yourself! How could you turn from your own people to chase a mindless beast?"

"Ah, you still don't believe. Let me show you." Uriah stood. Torsten didn't know why, but even after everything, he still trusted the man.

They rose, and he guided Torsten back down into the depths of the fortress.

"Do you all live here?" Torsten asked.

"Not all, but most."

"Do *you* live here?"

Uriah's gaze sunk to the floor. "I have no home anymore."

The passage opened into a large hall. On the far end sat what little was left of a stone-hewn throne once meant for a dwarven king. A smooth, painted wall was behind it, rising high up through a rift in the ceiling. Sunlight poured down through the slit, its soft glow cast along the top of the space like a crown.

Uriah pointed to the smooth wall. Upon closer inspection, Torsten realized it was composed of numerous stone pieces all fitting together like a puzzle to form a mural depicting a mountain and other figures. An inscription wrapped the borders written in a language Torsten didn't recognize. A few characters seemed similar to Drav Crava hieroglyphics Torsten had seen, only vastly more ancient.

"What is this?" Torsten asked.

"A painting from the first men, long before our time," Uriah said.

"I never took you for a collector of artifacts."

"Alas, it was not me. It must have taken years for Redstar to find all of the pieces." He lay his hand upon the wall with reverence. "His followers led me here after he abandoned them and disappeared into the Webbed Woods. They were desperate for a new leader, you see. He forgot his purpose as both the Ruuhar dradinengor and the Arch Warlock of all Drav Cra, and unleashed something terrible."

"Arch Warlock. Listen to you, Uriah, you sound like one of them. They're all the same."

"All the same? The Arch Warlock is chosen to speak for all of them, Torsten. He survived beneath the dirt for three days in their Earthmoot. They trusted him to destroy Nesilia's enemy and preserve this world, and instead, he allowed vengeance to cloud his mind after his very sister denied him. He decided that if Oleander wouldn't help him, he'd bring the orepul containing a piece of a royal soul and offer it as a gift to Bliss so that she may help him show his sister how wrong she was to deny him."

"Once a traitor. Always a traitor."

Torsten reached out to trace one of the lines of the mountain in the center of the mural with his finger. He knew which one it was meant to depict, although Mount Lister's tip was presently a flat plain. Flames etched all around it were filled with soldiers and instruments of war. Nesilia, the Buried Goddess, lay in the center of it all. She was locked in a losing battle with a deity legend referred to as the One Who Remained.

Torsten had seen similar imagery before, only here the beauty of Nesilia was inscribed in detail, strikingly gorgeous. The churches of Iam usually painted her as the grotesque witch she was. Here, her wild, luscious black hair cascaded to the ground and even amidst the fierceness of her losing fight there was a softness to her features.

The One Who Remained was equally striking, depicted here as a female when Torsten had mostly seen her as male. Her armor was spiked along her spine and limbs almost like an insect's carapace. She gripped the spear piercing Nesilia's chest on its way to cracking the top of Mount Lister.

A fracture coruscated down from the tip of the spear into the heart of the mountain where the Eye of Iam was etched in black. One of Nesilia's arms was being pulled down through the fissure.

Torsten stepped back and examined the mural in its entirety. In typical portrayals of the God Feud, Iam brought an end to the battle from above, not below. The god's battled over who held the right to reign over the realm of Pantego, ravaging the land in their selfishness. Nesilia and the one who buried her beneath the great mountain were the last remaining, while Iam, in his wisdom, stayed out of the pointless feud. Instead, he protected the mortals over which the gods watched, and when the fighting stopped, he banished the weakened victor from the world. The One Who Remained, remained no more, and Iam's light could finally shine upon Pantego unhindered.

"The language around the border is ancient," Uriah said. "Predating the Glass Kingdom, even the dwarves. Redstar had translated the fable it tells before he vanished. Would you like to hear it?"

"Spare me," Torsten said.

Uriah sighed. "Essentially, it tells that Nesilia will return when the blood of the enemy, the One Who Remained, is spilt. Redstar and the Drav Cra have lost hundreds to the cause before he chose vengeance instead, your queen too in sending our people there to find him. All I know for sure is Nesilia is the key to destroying this great evil."

"You believe that this… spider—"

"Queen Bliss," Uriah interrupted.

"Fine… you believe she is the One Who Remained?" Torsten asked.

"I know it. And she is not just a queen—she too is a goddess. Yes, deformed, a remnant of her former self, but a goddess nonetheless. It was a punishment by Iam. He mutated and mutilated her for piercing the heart of the one he loved."

Torsten wished he wasn't so concerned or he would have laughed. "You have truly lost it, Uriah. It was Nesilia who began the feud by her selfishness. The one who slew her was banished from this realm by Iam, and both of them deserve what they got. Iam does not punish out of lust or love. He protects us, guides us."

"My friend, you must listen to me. Nesilia is not who you've been made to believe. She is not the enemy." Uriah laid his hand upon Torsten's shoulder, but it was promptly shaken off.

"I pity you, Uriah. You have turned your back on Iam, your people, and it's clear there is no changing that. These are carvings etched by warlocks and heretics, like Redstar, who want nothing more than to see us burn. They lie, they sin, they sacrifice their own—I will not be party to it."

"The Second God Feud is coming, Torsten, and the warlocks have predicted a far different outcome. Nesilia was taken from Pantego, sealed below Mount Lister at the hands of her enemy, but only she and Iam together can help us."

"Iam," Torsten clarified. "And she is the enemy."

Uriah shook his head. "Bliss is. There is much we have been taught which we must unlearn."

"Blasphemy!"

"I have seen—"

"Enough!" Torsten bellowed. "I am going to the Webbed Woods on command of *our* queen. I will accomplish what you could not and put an end to Redstar's influence over the royal family for good."

"You think him still in the woods?" Uriah laughed. "He is dead, Torsten."

"How do you know this?"

"No man could survive there for a year, and no offering would drive Bliss to help the children of the gods who smote her. All he has done is stirred her hunger. No, he has to be dead. Even his own followers gave up on him and came here."

"I thought you were dead, yet here we are."

Uriah exhaled. "Will you not listen to reason? Redstar is irrelevant. Pi is irrelevant. There is a greater evil working in that forest. One that needs banishment. Together we might be able to uncover the key to vanquishing her. Perhaps we can also learn Redstar's fate and reclaim what he stole from Pi while we're there."

"Redstar brought ruin upon this realm with his malfeasance—not some spider. I will go into those woods and find that which the Queen desires."

"You will die there unless you let us help you."

"Then I will die in service to my kingdom."

Uriah hung his head. He walked over to a nook and returned holding Torsten's claymore and other effects. "Then I will not stand in your way. Take your things and go, Torsten, but as Bliss hangs you from her web, I hope that you remember it didn't need to be so."

Torsten tore his weapon from Uriah's hand and hung it on his back. "It is only because of who you are that I won't tell the crown about this place. I'm only glad King Liam isn't alive to see what you've become."

The news appeared to catch Uriah off guard, but before he could say anything, Torsten grabbed him by the collar. He leaned in so close he could smell the stench on the man's breath. "Get caught sacrificing another man to fallen gods again, and my mercy will run out."

Torsten pushed him aside and stomped toward the exit. He was nearly out when Uriah spoke again.

"If King Liam is dead, then the last great Nothhelm is gone," he said. "Redstar already corrupted Pi's mind. There is no helping him now. But we can stop Bliss from covering the world in darkness."

Torsten stopped for a moment, his hands balling into fists. "Just stay out of my way, Uriah," he growled, then continued on his way.

XXI

THE THIEF

"Y ou sure this is a good idea?" Sora asked.

"It's my idea, how couldn't it be good?" Whitney laughed as he studied the town from the hillside. It wasn't Yarrington, but it wasn't Troborough either. Three sprawling roads made up the bulk of Bridleton, and in its center, Iam's temple—a tall, thin structure made of old, grey wood and iron—cast a long shadow over the community.

"If we are going to travel together, I'm certainly not wearing this." Whitney gestured toward the unmarked cultist's robe draped over his body, a dab of blood on the sleeve. "And if you recall, it's your fault we are in this position, Ms. Plays-With-Fire."

"Okay, fine," Sora said. "We go in, get you some clothes. Then it's straight to the Webbed Woods. Quick and painless."

"You're really not going to drop that idea, are you?"

She stroked his chest and put on sultry inflection. "Oh Whitney, I'm just dying to see your famed thieving skills for myself."

Whitney couldn't hide his grin. Maybe it wasn't a vocation one should be proud of, but that had never stopped him. "I appreciate the flattery, Sora, but it won't get you what you want."

"We'll see."

She sidled up next to him, her hip rubbing against his. The moment he turned to face her she hopped back, the cultist's coin purse again strung around her finger.

"Now, let's go buy you a shirt," she said.

"Buy clothes?" Whitney scoffed. "Do you remember who I am?"

"You plan to steal clothes from some poor merchant when we have the coin to purchase it? Is that what you've been up to all these years?"

"If I only stole that which I didn't have the coin to purchase, I'd never have the coin to purchase anything."

Whitney sensed Sora formulating a response but started off down the hill before she had a chance.

"I'll buy them for you," she shouted. "As a gift!"

"We both know we aren't on gift-giving terms," Whitney shouted back over his shoulder.

She hurried to catch up with him. "Clothing wasn't really on my mind when I said, 'renowned thief.'"

"C'mon, it'll be like old times."

"No, it's just cruel."

Whitney stopped and looked her over. There was no room for softness in his game. No room for morality. From the smallest to the most ludicrous heist, any hesitation could get him killed, or worse, slammed behind more bars.

Her brow furrowed as he continued to stare. She had a slender build, long fingers, and the ability to craft fiery distractions on a bloody whim. Whitney had never willingly worked with a partner—the mess with Torsten excluded—and now that he was free of the Shieldsman and done wallowing in boredom, he knew for sure, taking on an apprentice was precisely what he needed to keep things fresh. Just the prospect of stealing a shirt alongside Sora had him more exuberant for a job than even the crown heist.

"Would you stop staring at me!" Sora bristled.

"I'm sizing you up," Whitney said. "You say cruel, yet you want to take on giant spiders and warlocks. I say I won't consider going into those woods with you unless I know you can handle snagging something as simple as a shirt. Doesn't matter if you can snap your fingers and make fire."

Sora glanced at her fingernails, then nodded. "Fine, but I choose the mark."

Whitney allowed a smile to play at the corner of his mouth. "That's the spirit! But, first things first. You'll draw about as much attention here as a giant in Brotlebir." Whitney drew one of the dagger's he'd taken from the unconscious cultist, and sliced the top of his robe and held the hood out to her. "Here."

"What's this for?" she asked, not taking the cloth.

"Tuck the frayed ends of the hood into your collar and pull it up to cover your ears. Keep your head down, so nobody notices your eyes unless they're really looking."

She took a step back, aghast. "Excuse me?"

"Look, I don't know how well-received you're going to be here. Not everyone in Pantego is like the people of Troborough."

"What, simple?"

Whitney squeezed the bridge of his nose with his thumb and forefinger. "No, accepting. You were displaced young—really young. And with your parents… gone, Wetzel and much of the town took you in like one of their own."

"You were barely older than me," she said. "Don't act like you remember."

"I remember how even my dad used to talk about you."

Her expression soured, and he knew he probably went too far even though it was true. His dad hated her people after losing his brother in one of the Panping Wars, and while he held his tongue whenever he permitted Sora around, the insults flowed once she wasn't.

"All I'm saying is that not everyone in the Glass Kingdom has forgotten the Panping Wars," Whitney said. "They were bloody, and they touched this area of the Glass heartland. I'd bet a lot of blood was spilled near here."

"You're overreacting. Panping is part of the Glass now."

"Barely more than Drav Cra is."

"This is ridiculous. I'm not a child. I can take care of myself."

"Sora, how many times have you left Troborough?"

She grimaced. "A few."

"Well, I've been to every corner of Pantego. I've seen hate in every form, and it's the quickest way to get too many eyes on you."

"You're being ridiculous."

"Would you just trust me?" He shoved the hood into her gut, so she had no choice but to grab it. She squeezed it so hard her knuckles went white, then she dropped it.

"I'm sick of hiding everything," she said.

Sora set off down the hillside at a brisk pace without looking back. Whitney tried to keep up, but she had long legs and sprinting into a town for no reason was the best way to seem like you were up to no good. It reminded him of his childhood, chasing her down to the ravine where they'd play together until his mother called for supper. She wound up eating with his family as often as his father and desperate-to-appease-him mother allowed since Wetzel kept a bed for her in his shack but little else... well, except for apparently a bevy of tomes on blood magic.

"Would you slow down!" Whitney said in a raised whisper. He couldn't help but see the irony in being on this end of the discussion.

She kept going, right toward Bridleton like she was on a mission. There were no gates—but two soldiers sat on stools, drinking ale and guarding the road through the town. They wore the blue and white of the Glass, Iam's eye painted on leather armor. But judging by their grungy appearance, they were locals turned sentries for the crown, paid to watch out for another potential Black Sands attack while the real soldiers waited in forts. And judging by the ale dripping from their beards, they were doing a terrible job of it.

The guards perked up the moment Sora got near. It wasn't an abnormal reaction to seeing a beautiful, unfamiliar woman. But Whitney could see their eyes narrow in disgust after they gave her a thorough look over. The fatter and grungier of the two nudged the other. They both stood and clomped over in front of Sora.

"Aye there! Knife-ear!" the fatter guard barked. Sora stopped as suddenly as if she'd been petrified. People didn't talk like that out loud in tiny farming villages so near the capital. The war never reached that far.

Whitney cursed under his breath.

"What business have ye in Bridleton?" the fat guard asked.

Sora's fists clenched as she said, "Just passing through."

"Ye could just as easily *pass around*."

Sora took a step forward. They moved to block her, one of them giving her a healthy shove with his arm that was definitely not accidental.

"Yeah, we don't see yer kind much round here," said the other.

"Especially ones so pretty."

"Please, I'm just looking for somewhere to spend the night," Sora said. She might as well have been mute because they didn't hear a word.

"I'm sure we can work that out." The fat guard squeezed her arm.

She leaped backward, her hand falling toward the knife sheathed in her belt.

"Knife-ear goin for her knife," one of them chortled.

"I'm beggin ye," the fat one said. "Give us a reason to show you how accommodating Bridleton can be."

Whitney quickly turned and tore a strip of cloth from his crummy robe, then tied it over his eyes like a proper priest of Iam. The threading was so poor he could see shapes and a bit of detail through it if he squinted. Enough, at least, to not trip over his own feet or get surprised.

"Gentlemen, she is a child of Iam just as you are," Whitney said before Sora could do anything stupid. He added a raspy effect to his voice, the kind Iam's priests use in sermons to make each word appear to be bursting with wisdom.

The men gave her an appraising once-over.

"Ain't nothin bout her like us," one said.

Whitney lay a steadying hand on Sora's shoulder. With the other, he lightly guided her hand away from her weapon.

"What more do you want, my sons?" he asked. "Her people renounced their lands and their false gods and now serve the One True. Should we not rejoice together in his light?"

Whitney was impressed with himself for coming up with that on the spot, but that was nothing new. His only hope was that nobody questioned his knowledge of the Panping much further because he honestly couldn't remember the name of any of the gods Sora's people prayed to. She wouldn't either. Sora was so young when war left her a displaced orphan in Troborough, she was raised by Iam's followers.

"Little young for a father, ain't ye?" the fat guard asked.

"Those robes ain't look like nothin we seen Father Anyon wearin," said the other.

"Ah, please forgive my appearance," Whitney said without missing a beat. His hand moved to where his daggers were hidden, hoping to not have to use them. He made a mental note to hide them better if he made it through this encounter. Priests didn't carry weapons. Though they couldn't see either and if these men decided to tear off his blindfold he'd be made in an instant.

"We fell upon hard times over our long journey," Whitney continued. "Wolves tore off my hood on a quest for my throat. This young lady happened to hear my cries and saved me."

"This puny girl took on wolves?"

"I'm quite handy with a knife," Sora said sharply.

Whitney gave her a nudge in the side on his way in front of her. "She merely searches for a bit of respite amongst your good people," he said. " Tell me, did… Father Anyon was it? …teach you well enough to help a stranger in need? After all, you never know when Iam's eye is upon you."

"Ain't no way Iam gives one bit of horse shog about her kind."

"Iam cares for all who tread the path of light," Whitney said. He bowed and traced the area around his eyes with his fingers like a good, loyal servant of Iam would do. "Where can I find Father Anyon?"

"Father Anyon died last week."

Whitney counted to five, not wanting to give away his excitement.

"Ah, yes. Of course, how could I be so stupid? I am his replacement, Father Gorenheimer."

"Yer here to replace him and ye didn't know he died?"

"I knew he was *dying*. I was sent by the clergy as soon as I heard the news. I am sad to hear he finally passed."

"He was run over by a goods wagon."

"Yes, quite the tragedy," Whitney said, lowering his head. "Agonizing way to go."

The man appeared momentarily suspicious from what Whitney could tell in his blurred view of the world but eventually stepped aside. "All right, move along, but we'll all be keeping an eye on her. Wouldn't be the first time some Panping wench came along, tryin to impose her heresies on us. Them Panpingese mystics are worse than snakes."

"Priest's lodgins are by the church," the other guard said.

"Thank you, kind children of Iam. Praise be the Vigilant Eye in all His mercy." Whitney again performed the standard appraisal gesture to Iam. He was so close to the men they had no choice but to return the gesture.

"Come, my daughter," he addressed Sora. "For your help, you deserve a night in proper lodging."

He strode by the men and held out his hand so that Sora would take it and guide him since he was blind. Anything to get her hand off her knife. The guards whispered something in her ear on her way by that had her teeth grinding in anger, but this time she kept quiet until she reached Whitney.

"If you say, 'I told you so,' I'm going to burn off your nethers," she whispered.

"I wouldn't dare," Whitney replied. "But I do recall a similar conversation."

She groaned. "Where in Elsewhere did you drum up that name?"

"Lesson one, long names make stupid people feel even more stupid. Gets them to shut up faster."

"Noted. But what happens when the people realize you're a fraud with eyes?"

Whitney chuckled. "You think this is the first time I've posed as a priest?"

The next day began with a pounding on the door. Whitney grunted something incoherent and saw light pouring in through the thin veil of his eyelids. He threw his feet over the edge of the bed as another series of knocks came. Although the old chapel house adjoined to Bridleton's church creaked and groaned the way old houses tended to do, Whitney hadn't slept so well in weeks.

"I'm coming!" he growled in his affected voice.

The room was small, barely space for a bed and kitchen. There were two doors. One led outside and was currently under attack and the second led to the church. Whitney's bare feet dragged across the cold wood floor.

He was about to open the door before he remembered to cover his eyes first.

"Father, I apologize for disturbing…" the lady in the entry said. She looked over Whitney's shoulder and saw Sora lying in the bed. "Oh, I… I'm so sorry. I—"

Whitney had forgotten about *that* part of taking Iam's cloth. Though, he may as well have been honest; somehow he and Sora had managed to sleep back to back all night without ever turning over. It was a part of the story he'd leave out of his own recounting of the time he'd posed as a priest in Bridleton.

"It's not how it appears, my daughter," Whitney said as piously as he could manage. "After saving my life, I've decided to take her on as my altar server. She took the bed and I the hard floor. I could do naught but accept Iam's will. It's as if He wanted us to meet."

"Of course, how noble of you, Father…" She hesitated, brow furrowing as she tried to recollect the ridiculous name Whitney had come up with. It took a few seconds for his own groggy head to dredge it up.

"Gorenheimer," he said.

"Yes. We are so pleased to have you here."

"Thank you, my dear. Now, how may I help you?"

Whitney couldn't tell if she was attractive or not through the fibers of his thin blindfold, only that she was young. Her golden hair was tied up in two buns, one on each side of her head, and she dressed like a proper noble, something Whitney didn't expect to see in Bridleton.

"My name is Nauriyal. When it is convenient for you, my father, Constable Darkings, desires to meet you."

"Where can I find the good constable?"

"Good is not a term generally associated with my father," Nauriyal said, offering a bemused smile. She motioned for Whitney to follow her a few steps outside of the threshold and pointed to a large house atop a shallow hill just beyond the perimeter of town.

"We live there," she said. "You're new here, and it's nice to have such a *young* Father, so please don't keep him waiting. He isn't a patient man."

"The will of Iam is never rushed. We enact it precisely as He means us to."

"Even still, it will make things far simpler."

"Very well. I'll be there within the hour."

"Thank you, father." Nauriyal bowed, then departed. Whitney promptly shut the door and removed his blindfold.

"Altar server?" Sora asked. "Isn't that for children?"

Whitney turned around to find Sora peeking over with one eye open. "What? You look young."

Sora popped upright so fast Whitney flinched. He laughed nervously. "It's a compliment.

"Sure." She relaxed her shoulder and rubbed her bleary eyes. "What do you think that was about?"

"Who knows, but that's our potential mark, if you agree. Constable Darkings… Even his name invites theft."

"'Please don't keep him waiting,' to a priest of Iam?" Sora put on a wry grin. "I have a good feeling about this one."

Whitney couldn't tell if it was forced or not, but he was glad to see her getting in the spirit of things. Every so often, when he caught himself looking at her, he could see the forlorn look in her eyes of a person who'd lost their home. Whitney had met plenty of people in his travels who had, both to war or disasters. He worried that she was throwing herself into all of this simply to distract herself from the pain of loss, but even if that were so, he'd do his part to keep up the distraction. He owed her that much.

"So do I," Whitney said, smiling in return.

A short while later, he and Sora stood before the tall iron gates of Constable Darkings impressive home. The emblem of a ship sitting atop a coin marked the entrance. If Whitney knew one thing, it was that men who erected walls around their houses in towns the size of Bridleton were always of a bad sort.

Whitney tilted his head back to peer through the bars under his blindfold. It brought back memories of his last few days, first in the Glass Castle dungeon, and then in the Glass Castle dungeon again, and finally, the cultist's hideout.

Shog, am I losing my touch?

He wondered briefly what had come of Torsten. They hadn't grown into best mates, but Whitney had to admit, he was kind of taking a liking to the rigid, humorless Shieldsman. Enough, at least, to hope he'd made it out alive.

They'll probably sell him for ransom, he thought. *Serves the giant oaf right for getting us captured.*

Whitney shirked the thought, then shoved his face against the bars of Constable Darkings' gate. "Constable Darkings!" he shouted.

After a moment, a man dressed in chainmail armor descended the steps of the mansion. This one wasn't a conscript of the Glass army. Whitney had seen finer armor, sure—Torsten's came to mind—but never anything like it in such an insignificant place.

"Quite a house for such a humble town," Whitney whispered to Sora.

"Make's Wetzel's place seem like a barrel," she replied.

"Just about anything makes Wetzel's place look like a barrel."

She shot him a glower.

"No offense," he said.

The armored guard stopped at the base of the stairs. He had a nose so flat it looked like he'd taken a hammer straight to the face, and a scar that whitened one of his eyes. Here Whitney was pretending to be blind, meeting a man who was halfway there. The guard would be extra upset if he discovered the truth.

"Who goes there?" he questioned.

"I'm the new town clergy," Whitney replied. "Whi—uh, Gendrel Gorenheimer."

"Who's the knife-ear?"

"Definitely our mark," Sora whispered as she pinched Whitney's arm.

"Keep calm this time," Whitney said under his breath and pushed his way in front of her. "This is Penny, my new altar server."

"Hah!" the one-eyed man cackled. "A Panpingese, *and* a woman at that?"

"The times are changing, my son. We are here by invitation of Constable Darkings. He is expecting us."

"You wasted no time getting here did you, Father Gorenheimer? Anyon passed only days ago. We weren't expecting Yarrington to dispatch a replacement for some time with all that's going on in the kingdom."

"Bridleton was in luck, Praise Iam." Whitney performed Iam's appraisal. Sometimes he swore he could make it in a traveling troupe. They could even perform some of his own adventures.

"I was in Oxgate," he went on, "helping with the aftermath of the

Black Sands attack—heretics, they are." He left out the part that unlike Troborough, not a soul in Oxgate had survived. He purposefully made sure he and Sora hadn't passed by there to stir up any memories in her, and had to hope a larger town like Bridleton hadn't suffered the same fate.

"Lucky for us, they sent a whole regiment to Fort Marimount up the road. They won't dare touch us now," the guard said as he strolled forward and opened the gate. "Follow me."

He led them up the staircase, Sora taking Whitney's arm to guide him as if he were really blind. Whitney noted through the bottom of his blind-fold that the stairs were made of marble. The thick columns supporting a second-floor balcony were as well, with ornately carved capital at the top that belonged in Old Yarrington.

"Must be good to be the constable around here," Whitney said.

"It's not good to be anything around here," the man responded.

"I didn't catch your name."

"I didn't say it."

The large doors swung open.

"Your apprentice should stay out here," he said. "Because of the… you know?" He pinched his fingers at the tips of his ears.

Whitney bit back a response, knowing that the man didn't think he could see the gesture. He squeezed Sora's arm to keep her quiet.

"Where I go, Penny goes," Whitney said. "She saved my life."

"The constable lost a lot at their hands," the guard replied. "We all did."

"The war was long ago, and I assure you, Penny was not involved. Now we are all the children of Iam. Praise be his Vigilant Eye and thanks be to Him for mercy."

The guard groaned. "If you insist."

They entered a vast greeting hall. It wasn't overly cluttered with trinkets but for a few pieces of well-made furniture hewn from stained mahogany.

A curved staircase lined by a wooden railing carved like fruited vines led to the second floor. Whitney knew the constable's sleeping quarters would be up there—as well as his closet. Public affairs at the ground level, private above, servant's quarters buried below. That was the way Yarrington nobles designed their homes, and it was no different here.

Whitney didn't even have to spot the portrait of the constable hanging above the stairs with his obscured vision to know it was there.

He took it all in through his blindfold that barely worked, memorizing everything, the location of every guard, the places where the constable might have locked up his more prized possessions.

"You're the new priest?" Constable Darkings said, appearing as if from thin air. Whitney would have mistaken the voice for an old woman's had he not seen him. The middle-aged man wore a satin tunic, crimson, although it could have been brown, it was tough to tell through the linen holes. The bit of gold flair on the collar, however, was unmistakable and it drew attention away from his rotund belly and jowls. An exquisite piece fit for the royal court, and with the pants and belt to match.

"Gendrel Gorenheimer," Whitney said, bowing his head while purposefully facing the wrong way.

"Constable Darkings," he said, licking his lips. "The church allows servants now?"

Whitney heard a hard exhalation but didn't bother to look back at Sora.

"This is Penny, my altar server," Whitney said, emphasizing the end of the word.

"A woman?" He laughed. "And a knife-ear too? Iam's lost his yigging mind, has he?"

"Are we not all created equal beneath his all-seeing eye?"

"Not in my experience."

"The High Priest Wren has begun to see things differently."

Darkings barely let him finish before he scoffed. "I couldn't care less about those pansies in the capital. I invited you here to make sure you understand how things work out here." He stopped at the base of the stairs, smiled, and smoothed his pants. "Care for a drink?"

He snapped his fingers in the direction of a nearby doorway, and a servant hurried out carrying a cask on a silver platter. Again, Whitney heard Sora make a dissatisfied noise. The servant was a Panpingese boy, barely more than ten.

Darkings filled and offered it, but Whitney raised his hand in polite refusal.

"The love and mercy of Iam are not for sale, Constable," Whitney said.

"Cut the yig-and-shog. We both know you're here for the same thing I am. I collect taxes, and you collect tithe. I have a house, free of charge; as do you. As long as you and the church don't stick your fingers into my coffers, I'll leave yours be as well, and I won't inform the clergy about your unusually fulsome altar *child*." He gave Sora a once over, and Whitney quickly realized what he was implying.

"I think you misunderstand my motives, Constable Darkings. I'm here for the good of the people of this fair town."

Darkings' chortle echoed throughout the room. "It's your lie, priest. Tell it how you want to." He stepped in front of Whitney and appraised his robes with two fingers.

"Shoddy things, these," he said. "There's a tailor on the western side, tell him I said to have new ones made for you on my coin. He'll make them white as snow like a proper Yarrington Father."

"I think I'll kindly pass on your offer. I prefer to wear the mud of the world over my shoulders."

Darkings moved forward until Whitney could smell the alcohol on his breath. "You're new here," he whispered. "You'd do well to play nice. It would be a shame for Bridleton to lose a second father so soon."

"Indeed," Whitney said.

"All I ask is that you keep church business within the walls of your chapel and stay out of my way. These are simple folk who have never left these fields. They wouldn't know Yarrington from Westvale. This place…" he raised both hands and gestured to his grand hall, "…might as well be the Glass Castle itself, and I like it that way. You play your cards right, you can have a place just like it."

Whitney circled his eyes and bowed. "Under the watchful eye of Iam, I have no intention of interfering with your matters of business, Mr. Darkings. Though I needn't a shelter of this… grandeur."

"Good enough for me."

Behind the cover of his ineffective blindfold, Whitney shifted his focus upstairs. With the right play, he could pilfer an outfit, and they could be on their way before sundown. If Darkings would wear his current outfit to meet with a mere man of the cloth, Whitney could only imagine what finery he dressed in for formal events. He cleared his throat and asked, "May I use your facilities?"

"You can use your own facilities, priest," Darkings replied. "Our time here is concluded." He turned to his daughter, who Whitney hadn't even realized was standing beside them. "Nauriyal, escort the father and his *friend* back to their hovel."

"Of course, daddy," she said, curtsying.

It's never easy, Whitney thought to himself as they were led outside. *Why can't it ever be easy?*

When they'd cleared the front doors, Nauriyal placed her hand on Whitney's arm. "I'm sorry about him. He can be a bit extreme at times. I do hope you won't hold it against me, Father?" She smiled bashfully.

"I condemn no child for the sins of their parents. You are always welcome in the house of Iam."

"Thank you, Father."

Whitney stopped and took her hand. Now, up close and in the sunlight, if he squinted through the blindfold, he could make out her face in more detail. 'Pretty' was barely adequate to describe her. "You never have to thank me," he said softly.

Whitney felt Sora's elbow jab against his ribs and quickly released the young woman's hand.

"Yes, yes, thank you, Nauriyal," he said, clearing his throat. "I will remember your kindness."

A pair of the constable's guards opened the iron gate. It slammed shut the moment Whitney and Sora were outside. Nauriyal remained behind the bars, staring.

They walked a short distance before Sora whispered, "Priests don't get flirty. Don't screw this up."

"I wasn't *flirting,* I was being polite," Whitney said.

"I know what your flirting looks like. It's painful."

"Trust me, if I ever flirted with you, you'd be swooning."

"Oh really? 'Can I use your bathroom?' Some master thief you are."

"Worth a shot," Whitney said. "Lesson two: always start a job by testing the route of least resistance, then plan accordingly. Consider this on the job training."

"Oh, making me endure the insults and prying eyes of those bigots was training?"

"Now that I've got the lay of the land, it won't be hard to return tonight."

"You did see how many guards there were, right?"

"Four inside and at least two outside," Whitney answered. "Your point?"

"That's too many to risk for a shirt."

"I've snuck past twenty wizards, broken out of castle dungeons, and robbed a dragon of his gold. You think a handful of small-town thugs is going to stop me?"

"Dragons? Now I know you're mad. They've been extinct longer than we've been alive."

"You will see how mad I am when I return this evening wearing the finest silks in the region."

Whitney rounded the Bridleton streets toward the ramshackle cottage beside the church. He tugged on his blindfold to reach an itch on his cheek. "I can't wait to get this thing o—"

A high scream echoed across the town square. "Father! Father! Please come quick!"

Whitney turned to see the outline of a young boy charging toward them. His face was streaked with red.

"My f-f-fath-f-f-fath—"

"Slow down," Sora said, kneeling to meet the child eye-to-eye.

The boy froze momentarily as he regarded Sora's ears, then he drew a deep breath. "My father was b-b-bit by a wolf," he said. "P-please come help."

"Wolf?" Sora asked. "This close to town?"

Sora followed the boy toward a ranch at the edge of town, giving Whitney no choice but to follow. He ducked under the rickety wooden fence. Whitney nearly tumbled over the top in his heavy robes, but Sora caught him.

A herd of cattle clustered by the farmhouse, but the closer they got Whitney could make out the low groans of the man stolen amidst the tall grass over.

"I've found help, pa," the boy said as he kneeled beside him. "Don't worry."

The rancher held a wound on his side to keep the blood from gushing, but his hand wasn't nearly large enough. Four deep cuts wrapped his torso, rent by the claws of no normal sized wolf. Had the beast extended its claws even a fraction more and the man's intestines would be forcing their way out.

Whitney placed his hand over the wounds, still pretending to be blind even in crisis. *Never surrender the grift until the grift is through.* "This wasn't done by a normal wolf," he said, remembering his and Torsten's encounter in the woods.

"I s-saw it. It was huge!" the boy said.

"Redstar," Whitney whispered and shook his head.

"What?"

"Nothing. Careful with him," Whitney said to the boy. "Don't agitate the wound."

"What do we do, Father?"

"That doesn't look like it came from a wolf at all," Sora whispered in Whitney's ear. "And it's too late in the season for bears."

"It was neither," Whitney said.

"So, the boy was seeing things?"

"Dire wolf," Whitney said.

"There's no way. They don't come this far south... ever."

"Tell that to the ones that attacked me and the knight just a couple of days past. You were following, didn't you see."

Her eyes went wide. "I saw you too break camp and rush away one night for no reason. I didn't see why."

The rancher released a hair-raising cry and kicked his legs, drawing their focus back from their bickering. The boy sprung at Whitney and shook him. "Please, Father Gorenheimer, you have to help him!"

Whitney finally felt a tinge bad for pretending he was a priest. Earning the cloth of Iam meant some training in the healing arts, but Whitney knew about as much about that as his bumpkin father. The rancher's eyes were closed, his breathing was shallow, and sweat beaded on his forehead even though it was mid-autumn. Even looking at the bubbling, bloody gashes across the man's ribs made Whitney's stomach turn.

"Fever has already set in," Sora said.

"What am I supposed to do?" Whitney whispered, turning himself toward her and away from the boy. "I'm no priest, much less a healer."

"Please, Father. Would you pray for Iam to heal him?" The boy hugged his father, tears freely flowing again.

"Take the boy over there," Sora said. "Pray the most believable prayer you've ever prayed. I'll take care of the rest."

"This is not why we are he—" Whitney began before she cut him off.

"So, you want to let this little boy's father die when we might be able to help? Wetzel taught me a few things."

Whitney surveyed the boy. A part of him felt he'd be better off without a father forcing him to stay at the farm like his own always wanted. Of course, Whitney got the chance to choose to be orphaned and not be made one.

"Where's your mother?" Whitney asked.

"He's all I got." He wiped snot from his nose. "Please, you gotta help him."

"Oh, shogging exile." Whitney kicked the dirt. The boy looked stunned at his language. "Okay, come over here with me and let my friend here examine him. She's an expert on the healing arts."

He wrapped his arm around the boy's shoulder and led him away, so his back was turned to Sora. He instructed the boy to close his eyes tight and believe really hard. As Whitney muttered what he knew must have sounded like incoherent religious jargon, he glanced back and peeled up his blindfold a bit to watch Sora pull Wetzel's knife from its sheath. The dying man didn't move, barely breathed. Sora grabbed hold of the blade and winced, this time drawing far more blood than she'd done when she made fire.

With her other hand, she scooped up a handful of the rancher's blood, then clasped her bleeding hand over it.

Whitney struggled to continue praying with the boy as he saw wispy, blue smoke rising from Sora's hand and the bloody mixture. Her face contorted in agony as she clenched her fist and placed it against the man's heart. There was a pulse of light. The man lurched, then shook. Sora started to convulse with him, but before Whitney could run to her, the rancher bolted upright.

Sora collapsed next to him.

"What happened?" the man asked, breathing heavily.

Whitney raced to Sora's side while the boy embraced his father.

"Pa! You're okay?"

"Son, what happened? The wolf…"

"The new father prayed, and you were healed!"

The man looked up, but Whitney barely noticed. "Thank you, Father. I… I don't know what to say."

He said something else, but Whitney didn't care to hear a word of it. Sora wasn't moving, and her breathing had slowed to a crawl.

"Sora?" Whitney shook her. "Sora, are you okay?"

XXII

THE KNIGHT

Several lonely days passed trekking south from the dwarven ruins, and Torsten hadn't run into as much as a titrat or squirrel. His feet were sore and blistering, but at least one thing was going for him: silence. The self-proclaimed 'greatest thief alive' had been nothing but a ceaselessly-chattering bother. Torsten was happy to hear birds again. Insects, the blowing wind, anything but Whitney's mindless blabbering.

Being alone wasn't an unfamiliar feeling. It was the way he'd felt since Liam grew too ill to give sensible orders and the way he was damned to continue onward. Everyone he'd ever trusted seemed to be losing their minds; from Liam to Oleander, and now good Sir Uriah Davies—one of the finest King's Shieldsman he'd ever had the pleasure of knowing. The man who'd taught him the art of swordsmanship might as well be dead. He let Torsten leave with enough food to reach the Webbed Woods, but every time he bit into the stale bread he felt a deep chasm growing in his belly.

He couldn't remember how many times he'd knelt beside Uriah under the gilded Eye of Iam in Yarrington Cathedral, how many battles he'd marched to at his side in the name of the Glass Kingdom. Now, he worshipped fairy tales in the cult-dens of fallen gods.

"Iam," Torsten whispered toward the moon one night, "if this is a test, I do not understand."

He sat at the edge of a small bear cave, arms wrapped around his torso to stay warm. He didn't want to risk a fire again and had forgotten to ask for a blanket when he'd left the cultist's compound. The night air bit at his cheeks, growing colder every hour. Soon the bears would be returning to their hollows for hibernation, but until then, he had cover from the wind.

He reached beneath his undershirt and grabbed his necklace—an Eye of Iam made of blown glass. He could still remember the day Liam had given it to him. It rained the day Torsten was sworn into the King's Shield. Liam told him Iam was weeping with joy.

Torsten closed his eyes and squeezed. "Since the day I felt your light upon me, never have you led me astray. You saw fit to take Liam from this plane, and I did not question your wisdom. But these last few days… what have I missed, my Lord? What sins have I committed to earn this heartbreak? Send me a sign, oh, Vigilant Eye, that I still number among your champions."

Torsten released the amulet and opened his eyes. Silence reigned but for the rattling of bare branches silhouetted against the night sky. Almost the last of the leaves had fallen, and Torsten noted Pantego's moons. Celeste was full and orange like an orb of flame, but Loutis, the gray, lifeless, rock was crested on its side as if, together, they were the eyes of a winking giant.

Their proximity to Iam's Star—always pointing north, the brightest in the sky—meant it was winter's first day. A rough time to be stuck in the wilderness. That helped explain the quiet. Tinkers and traders who might generally travel the roads were hunkered down until spring. Farming villages, like Oxgate had been, were stagnant, their peoples cuddled for warmth, hoping theirs wouldn't be the next target of Black Sands, or worse.

Torsten couldn't help but feel like the sight was fitting for his straining kingdom. The branches, like the hands of a bony army, wagged their fingers, taunting him.

He shook the thought away.

"Give me a sign," he whispered. A gust of wind tore through the cavern and sent a shiver. He tucked his arms tighter around his torso. "Let me feel your light."

Just then he heard an outlandish snort—wet, almost like a sneeze. He raised his hand to the handle of his claymore, then crawled forward to poke his head out of the cavern. If it were a bear returning home, his night's rest would come to a swift end. He hadn't the stomach to fight any more hulking beasts.

He brushed aside a bit of shrubbery, and that was when he saw the unnatural, soft, green light glowing like a beacon and drawing nearer. He'd fought in enough skirmishes against the Black Sands to know what it was.

A long pole rose up. On its end, a lantern made of glass and bone housed sloshing water and a luminescent creature. The nigh'jels dotted the surface of the Boiling Waters, the sea south of Latiapur, the Shesaitju capital city. They were like any other jellyfish by day, but at night their tentacles glowed as green as emerald, oscillating along their wiry tentacles.

Torsten drew his head back into the shadows of the cave just as a set of giant paws pounded by. A wet spray of mucus arched from the gargantuan snout of a zhulong, narrowly avoiding contact with him.

The zhulong wasn't alone. Upon its back sat a man with ash-gray skin, clothed in boiled leather armor and wrapped in layers of ratty cloth for warmth. Neither the zhulong nor the Shesaitju warrior had spotted him. The green light from the nigh'jel lantern cast a sickly shadow that Torsten thought fitting.

Black Sands, here?

By now, he was on the western fork of Southern Pantego—a wild place with little but sparsely occupied villages, and further south, the Webbed Woods. Across the bay, the Shesaitju made their home on Pantego's eastern fork. There was nothing over here for them. Attacking Oxgate and Troborough and other towns nearer to Yarrington made strategic sense, but the capital wouldn't even likely hear of a raid in the mostly inhospitable region in the shadow of the Webbed Woods.

He crept out further, staying low.

The zhulong stopped at the crest of a nearby hill, and Torsten froze. He loosened his claymore from the scabbard strapped to his back. Then, a second mounted beast arrived from the other side of the hill. The glow of two nigh'jels coalesced and danced against the darkness as the men exchanged words in old Saitjuese.

Between the wind and other night sounds, he could only hear every few words, and understood even less. With every conquest, Liam made sure to impose the language of Iam. "Understanding your potential enemies," he would say, "is the key to any victory."

What would he think of me now?

Torsten didn't have time to dwell on the thought. The two men clasped arms, then took off in opposite directions, one toward him and one away. Torsten stayed quiet until both nigh'jels were at a safe distance, then hurried up the hill.

The grass was wet with slobber. Claw tracks ran down the slope, vanishing into darkness and muck. One rider's nigh'jel faded like the stars at dawn just at the edge of the vast, wetness of the Fellwater Swamp which bordered the Webbed Woods. It was a foul place, so Torsten had heard. He'd never been there himself, never had any reason to go so far south, so far from real civilization. But so many of his men—good men— would have had to pass through the muck as they followed his orders to find Redstar in the Webbed Woods.

The rank stench of stagnant water assailed Torsten's nostrils. In the daytime, insects would be nipping at his neck, refusing to surrender to winter's chill. There was nothing else in this fetid place, no reason at all for the Shesaitju to be there.

Torsten was exhausted, but rest could wait. His bag of food secured, he set off after the zhulong heading south and its Shesaitju master. At the base of the hill, the tracks disappeared in mud and mire. He didn't need them. The still-visible, gentle, green glow of the nigh'jel lantern was enough.

He started to jog. Eventually, the zhulong would outpace him, but swamps slowed beasts and men without favor. He kept his steps choppy so his boots wouldn't sink in too deep, and made sure to breathe through his mouth.

With all that had befallen the kingdom, Torsten knew he had to find out what the Black Sand's scouts were doing so far from home. The Shesaitju were once a militant people. They worshipped battle, ascending through victory, and respecting those who claimed it. Their battles with King Liam had been fiercer than any other, but when he brought them to their knees, they respected him for it.

Respected *him*, not his queen.

Liam's body wasn't even cold before the Shesaitju Caleef, Sidar Rakun, had apparently set his forces out to raze more than half a dozen defenseless villages to the ground. Villages filled with men, women, and children. Torsten was exiled before he had a chance to learn how many had died, or how many others were displaced, forced to find refuge in places already too populated and underfed.

The glory of the Glass was at stake.

A cold fog swept through as the moons reached their peak, moistening his skin, even beneath his armor. The nigh'jel he'd been following was lost now, so all he could do was hope he remained headed in the proper direction.

Eventually, he grew accustomed to the stench, same as his younger self had with the smell of waste buckets when he lived among the shanties in South Corner, Yarrington. The cold air made his throat sore, and his ears feel like they could be snapped in two like a fresh carrot.

In an attempt to distract himself from the miserable trek, he found himself wondering where Whitney had run off to. He hated himself for it but wondered nonetheless. He imagined the thief was sitting by a warm hearth, enjoying a nice meal, bragging about all the impossible feats he'd likely never accomplished. *That's what cowards do when the world crumbles around them.* He probably wasn't even a real thief. Just talked his way out of his cell while Torsten was desperate.

Torsten was busy cursing himself for being so foolish when one of his feet sunk knee-deep into mud.

"You've got to be kidding me," he said, the thick sludge working its way into the crevasse in his armor where the greaves met the kneecap. He looked up, but the fog was so thick now, even the moons hid behind it.

He grabbed hold of his leg and tugged. Nothing. He repositioned himself, bent at the waist, and pulled with all his strength. The ground gave out under his limb. A mound of mud collapsed and sent him sliding into a pool of stagnant water as thick as molasses.

"*What was that*?" someone said in Saitjuese—words Torsten was barely able to translate.

He slowly lifted his head from the mud. Two nigh'jel lanterns hovered nearby, the only things visible in the smog. Their wielders sloshed toward him.

Torsten remained still, feeling wet mud rippling around him as they neared, so covered in muck he may as well have been a log. He waited until he could see the shadow of a leg. He grabbed it and swept the man off his feet. A quick elbow to the head knocked the man unconscious. Torsten let out a roar as he rolled over the body and tackled the other one.

A long fauchard thrust at him from the second Shesaitju warrior. He sidestepped, catching it between his arm and hip before twisting to yank it free. Torsten grabbed the man by the throat as he fumbled for balance, forcing him to his knees. He snagged the lantern and held it between them.

"What are you doing here?" Torsten asked through gritted teeth.

The ash-skinned warrior gargled for air. Torsten loosened his grip as the man grated something in Saitjuese.

"Speak common, knave," Torsten said. "You're far from home. Scouting out more villages to slaughter?"

The Shesaitju warrior regarded him, eyes as gray as his flesh. His thin, painted lips creased into a grin. "*Afhem* Muskigo has surprise for you, Glassman."

"That wasn't an answer," Torsten barked, tightening his grip again. "Tell me why you are here, or I will squash you like an ant."

"The time of Glass is over. Like tides from Boiling Waters, this will not stop."

The man drew a blade from his boot and sliced at Torsten. The knife drew a thin line of blood on the side of his neck, but he pulled back just in time, so it didn't cut deep enough to be fatal.

Torsten got his two massive hands around the man's head. The Black Sandsman thrashed and flailed, slopping mud everywhere. Then Torsten wrenched his hands to the side, and a sickening *snap* brought silence as the body crumpled into a heap at his feet.

He'd hoped it wouldn't come to killing, but he knew better than most how stubborn the Shesaitju were. Warriors until the bitter end. They bowed to Liam in their defeat out of respect, but many of their afhems didn't support the decision. They abandoned their lands with their loyalist followers to become swords for hire.

Are these mercenaries working for Redstar?

He couldn't imagine a more likely reason they'd be so far south but for gold.

Or did the Queen... he didn't finish the thought. He wouldn't put it past her, seeing an opportunity for more men to feed her obsession with the Webbed Woods. Hiring the very people who'd just caused so much unrest.

Torsten knelt beside the other warrior, still unconscious. It might be morning by the time he woke. Torsten seized their weapons, tossing them across the swamp, then picked up a lantern again.

He trudged forward, staying as low as possible. The one benefit of being in the muddy waters was there were no fallen leaves for his boots to crunch. Although the fog was thinning with every step, it was still difficult to make out his surroundings. He was moving downhill, and the sound of water lapping at the coast greeted his ears.

It wasn't long before another set of sounds came. Voices and splashing, the sounds of a forge—hammers on anvils. He slowed his pace and ditched the lantern. Then, finally, his altitude lowered enough for the fog to break completely. He'd expected to see a small encampment fit for a mercenary crew, but what he found stole the breath from his lungs.

Boiling Waters met the coast, and in the soggy delta was an army in waiting. Nigh'jels illuminated their camp as if it were morning but in that sickly, shimmering green. Black Sands ships were moored throughout the delta, sails sweeping over their bows like the tail feathers of the great gallers. Zhulong filled a series of stables, snorting and rolling gleefully in the muck. Tents numbered in the hundreds, and lanterns hung from warrior's hips weaved between them—fireflies at dusk. Thousands of them.

"By Iam," Torsten whispered.

Another sight drew his attention: men and women of the Glass Kingdom draped in rags, weary and transporting supplies from the ships. They carried lumber and iron to forge siege weapons, spears, and bows. Black Sandsman snapped whips at their backs while they worked. It appeared not all those caught in the Shesaitju raids were sent to rest at Iam's bosom.

Suddenly, it made sense how the Shesaitju could have attacked so quickly after Liam's passing without anybody spotting them on the move. They'd come from this dank, awful place where no sane soul would ever search.

Torsten had been in charge of the kingdom's army and security, and he'd failed. He'd been so distracted by Liam's last days, and the Queen's obsession with Redstar, her troubled son, and the doll, he'd allowed this force to amass in the shadow and fog. This was no army meant to pillage, raid, and burn like biting insects stirring unrest, it was the largest Torsten had seen in a decade.

An army meant for rebellion. To bring the Glass Kingdom and everything he held dear to its knees.

XXIII

THE THIEF

"What do I do? What do I do?" Whitney said to an unconscious Sora once he got her back into the priest's cottage.

He thought back to every experience he'd had with sickness or disease, but nothing helped. Throughout his life, those things usually led to the death of those affected. Healings were rare and, even with Wetzel's medicine, people rarely made miraculous recoveries.

There was no Wetzel to count on here. And even if there were, no one could find out what she'd done. As far as everyone in Bridleton was concerned, the new father performed his first miracle. The only thing worse than a knife-ear around these parts was a knife-ear practitioner of cursed and forbidden arts.

He paced the room, occasionally glancing out the window. All the sick and injured in Bridleton were gathering for a visit with their new 'miracle father.' The newly-whole rancher and his son stood out front making sure no one got too close.

"Step aside!" one man shouted at him. "You got your healing; my daughter needs hers!"

"Don't be so selfish!" cried another.

Finally, Whitney had enough. He put his blindfold on and threw open the door, narrowly avoiding hitting the rancher's son with it.

"Enough!" Whitney bellowed. "The work of Iam is taxing, and I need to rest. Go home!"

Murmurs erupted throughout the crowd.

"Please, Father," said an old lady as she stepped forward. She hunched over, using a cane to steady herself. Her skin seemed like it was made of century-old parchment found in the trash. "We need a blessing from Iam."

"The drought was long, and the coming winter will be harsh," said another.

Whitney slammed the door and sunk back against it all the way to the floor.

"You heard the father," the rancher said through the door. "Time to go home."

The murmurs turned sour, and Whitney feared the rancher would be in further need of Sora's healing if things escalated. A glance at Sora lying on the bed told him he'd be out of luck. She was breathing, but still unconscious.

Whitney sighed in frustration. They didn't have much time before Bridleton's *real* new father would arrive. Whitney hoped Sora would be recovered by then, but it was impossible to know.

So much for working with a partner. It'll be the end of me.

Two townsfolk exchanged heated words outside, a fistfight inevitable. Bridleton seemed happy, but like any small, meaningless place toiling under the boot of a despot like Constable Darkings, they were a powder-keg waiting to blow.

Whitney picked himself up off the floor, then moved to Sora's side. The bed's dressings were soaked with sweat. She'd stopped convulsing, and it looked like a bit of color was returning to her cheeks.

"Come on Sora," he whispered. "Hurry up."

He fixed her pillow, then returned to the front door with his priest garb back on. Sunlight beat against his face and the crowd hushed as the door opened again. The rancher and another man had their hands on each other's collars and were ready to exchange blows, but stopped at the sight of him.

Whitney knew he needed to stall them while Sora was recovering. If the town burned itself to the ground, she'd be caught in it.

"Your name again?" Whitney asked the rancher.

"Pherry," he replied.

"Bring them next door to the chapel, Pherry, and I'll convene with them momentarily."

The door shut again. Whitney ensured Sora was adequately tucked in and comfortable, then made sure he looked pious enough before exiting the cottage through the back door, which led directly into the chapel's altar.

By Glass Kingdom standards, the church was quaint. But compared to any other building in the town, save for the constable's mansion, it was a palace. The vaulted ceiling was framed with thick, wood cross beams, and painted with scenes from scripture. Iam's gift of sunlight to humanity, which thrust them out of darkness, his molding of the first human, and, of course, the God Feud—that terrible war of legend where Iam had to watch as his brethren slaughtered each other out of selfishness, and was left alone with Pantego after banishing the One Who Remained.

The Eye of Iam hung against the back wall, surrounded by stained glass, just above a raised dais upon which a golden podium—one worth more than most of these humble folks would have made in a lifetime —stood.

The doors opened, and people flooded the room, filling the long, hard pews. Whitney quickly lowered his blindfold before anyone saw him. Aside from the occasional groan or the wailing of a baby, they remained quiet as they sat in hopeful anticipation.

Whitney surveyed their many faces. Even with his vision obscured he could see how coated they were with grime. Elderly, children, the maimed and the broken; they all stared at him as if he'd brought rain to the desert lands in the far east. It was then he realized he'd never paid attention to a sermon in his life. He'd stolen gold-clad Eyes of Iam from plenty of churches across Pantego but never listened.

Poor saps... Came here for guidance and instead found me.

"Children of..." He had to pause to clear his throat and properly affect his voice. "Children of Iam. Long has the world stood and longer still it shall remain. The remaining of this world will be long, and it will stand."

Good one, Whitney.

He hoped the over-zealous inflections he used to punctuate every sentence would distract the people from his improvised drivel.

"We work and toil, the land itself bringing pain upon its back," he said. "Pantego is no easy place, far less, Bridleton!"

Many of the townsfolk nodded and whispered their agreement, which started to give him confidence. He knew that was probably a bad thing, but he always acted at his finest when he had a captive audience.

He took a few steps closer to the people until a man in the front pew coughed so hard he could hear the phlegm gurgling. He cringed, making no effort to hide it. The man appeared about ready to keel over.

"I—uh—Iam sees you!" Whitney exclaimed. "His Vigilant Eye is upon you, yet you seek His hand? What good then, is a hand without an eye? And what eye has no face? Seek not His hand, but His face! He looks down upon these sick and hurting with compassion, but not all can be set free of their afflictions!"

More whispers, less of them agreeing this time.

"Why him?" a man shouted, pointing to the rancher.

"Is it for any one of us to question the ways of Iam?" Whitney said. "Are His thoughts not deeper than what we can contrive? Allow His peace to wash over you, children. Whether healed on this plane or the next, we shall all bask in His eternal peace."

Someone threw a hunk of bread at the dais. The crumbs peppered Whitney's robe. He wondered what kind of impoverished dullard would waste good food because they thought they were deserving of a miracle, then recalled all the awful people he'd met throughout his years traveling the realm.

"Wait! Wait!" Whitney shouted. "You misunderstand! You shall all receive your healing!"

The glares of his onlookers softened, though many brows remained furrowed. He needed to keep them happy just a short while longer until he and Sora could hit their mark and disappear. Then they'd be some other charlatan's problem.

Sure, his visage would don another wanted poster in a place which he'd never return, but he was featured in about as much artwork throughout Pantego as there was in Yarrington Cathedral. What would be the harm in one more?

"Once a day, come one at a time after midday," Whitney said. "Until all are healed. My friend, here," he pointed to the rancher, "will schedule your visits based upon need."

The rancher nodded.

"I will do all I can to bring Iam's benevolent mercy upon Bridleton, where it has been lacking so long!" Whitney pronounced. "Have patience, and you will all be rewarded. Now please, go, I need my rest." He performed the circling of his eye and turned to walk away, and that was when the front doors of the chapel swung open.

In the entrance stood a proper priest of Iam, thinning hair as white as the robes he wore, his face weathered by time and study. Like Wren the Holy, he didn't bother covering his seared, useless eyes, his vow of sight-lessness was laid bare for all the world to see. A cane topped with the Eye of Iam helped him move about.

The two worthless Glass soldiers who had been watching the town's entry flanked him, swords resting atop open palms. All three looked like they'd just stepped in steaming shog.

"Father, uh..." Whitney paused. "You're just in time."

He bolted for the back door and burst into his cottage to find Nauriyal hovering over a waking Sora.

"What the yig are you doing in here?" Whitney snapped as he turned to lock the door.

"Please," she said. "I'm here to help." She lifted Sora's arm so she could get her sleeve on. Sora stared at Whitney as she accepted the aid, her lips trembling, silent.

"How did you know I was here?" Nauriyal asked.

"Never mind that," Whitney said. "How did you get in here?"

She didn't press him any further as she waved a key over her shoulder with one hand as the other continued its work. "Daddy has a key to every building in the town." Her features darkened. "You both seem so nice. You have to leave this place before it's too late, Father."

"Trust me, I know. The real fath—" Whitney caught himself. If she'd called him that, it meant she didn't know the truth yet. He was glad he didn't take a moment to remove his blindfold. The real father must have been led straight to the chapel by those two goons in front of Bridleton. That meant Whitney was short on time and severely lacking allies.

"A bad feeling struck me when I met your dad," he said. "As if Iam Himself were issuing a warning."

A sudden pounding came from the chapel-side door behind him, and he knew it would be only moments before they were at the front door as well. He rushed over to help Nauriyal.

"Open up in the name of the Glass, *father,*" the fat soldier from the town entry said. His sarcasm was obvious, but luckily Nauriyal didn't pick up on it.

"Why help us?" Whitney asked.

"Like I said, you seem like nice people," Nauriyal replied. "My father has terrorized this place long enough. Do you know how many priests have mysteriously died since he became constable?"

Whitney didn't respond, only packed his and Sora's bags—careful to grab the daggers he'd hidden when they'd first arrived. He placed Sora's arm around his neck to lift her. She winced and tried to whisper something.

"Six," Nauriyal answered for him. "Six priests over the past two years."

"It's about to be seven if we don't get out of here," Whitney said. "Those men outside, they think I did something wrong."

"I know. Word about your miracle healing reached my father's ears. Miracles like that don't fly around here. No one is allowed to be more respected than him."

A grin touched Whitney's lips. He thought better of it and cursed under his breath. If Darkings felt threatened by a miracle of Iam, that meant his ruse had worked flawlessly. It wasn't his fault the man was a self-conscious prick, or that the real priest decided to arrive ahead of schedule. It was a perfect storm of plans going sideways, but that didn't mean they weren't planned to perfection.

"There's a horse out back for you," Nauriyal said. "I'm tired of watching him ruin good people."

"I won't ask again!" the fat soldier shouted, slamming on the chapel-side door a few more times.

Then another knock came at the front door, causing Whitney to nearly drop Sora as he spun.

"Open up, Gorenheimer," said an angry voice belonging to the one-eyed, bigot guard he and Sora had met guarding the constable's house. "Mr. Darkings would like to speak with you about what happened at that ranch. Now!"

Yep, a perfect storm.

Enemies battering at the gates from all angles, each blaming Whitney for something else. He'd been caught in pincers like this before, but usually by two women.

"What's going on," Sora said blearily. "Whitney?"

He was too frantic to be excited to hear her voice again. "It's fine Sora." He studied the room for another way out. There was a window, but it was high, and there was no way she'd be able to make it out in her state. The front door was the best option. Ram it open hard, knock the guard back, and make a run for the horse.

More clatter came from both doors of the cottage. Whitney looked to Nauriyal. "You have been very kind," he said. "Iam will not forget, and neither will I."

The girl smiled meekly, then bowed and traced her eyes. Whitney almost forgot to return the gesture but offered a halfhearted version that would never have passed in Yarrington. Again, she took no notice. Whitney checked his hold on Sora and moved for the front door. Nauriyal stopped him in his tracks.

"When Father finds out, he's going to kill me," she said.

Whitney stopped and turned.

Sora groaned. "Leave it alone," she whispered.

Whitney ignored her. He took a few steps and kicked the table beside the bed. The old wood hit the floor and snapped in two. Nauriyal jumped back.

"What are you doing?" she yelped.

"Get on the floor and make it look like you've been punched," he said.

Her brow furrowed. "You're a priest. You wouldn't—"

"Trust me, your father will believe it."

"I've never been punched... I... I don't know."

"Just lay down and groan. Look, I'd do it for you, but I wouldn't want to damage such a pretty face."

Nauriyal's cheeks momentarily went pink, until a realization struck the color away. "Wait, how do you know what my face looks li—"

Sora suddenly lashed out with her fist, catching Nauriyal on the chin. The young woman slammed into the wall before toppling over onto the bed.

Whitney stood, stunned.

"You're welcome," Sora said in Nauriyal's direction. "If I had to hear any more of you two I was going to puke."

Whitney threw off his blindfold and gawked at her. "How in Elsewhere did you learn to hit like that?" he asked. The poor, young woman was completely limp, the side of her face red and already swelling.

"I learned a lot after you left. Now let's do the same."

Whitney regarded the motionless heap that was Nauriyal, then circled his eyes one last time. Sora elbowed him in the ribs, spurring him to help her toward the front door. It appeared much of her former strength had returned, as if Father Gorenheimer had performed his second miracle.

They paused in front of the door and drew some deep breaths.

"Ready?" Whitney asked.

Sora grunted her agreement.

Whitney quietly unhinged the door's bolt lock and counted. At three, they threw all their weight against it. The door swung open as they burst through, sending the guard sprawling through the mud. Another of the constable's cronies froze between trying to decide whether to help his comrade or give chase until the former barked the orders to seize them, mouth filled with dirt.

They were too late. Nauriyal's horse was hitched right around the corner, just as promised. Whitney gave Sora a boost onto the saddle then followed her up. One of the constable's goons grabbed his leg and earned a boot to the face, then Whitney snapped the reins, and they took off.

A *thunk* followed a *zip* and Whitney turned to see an arrow quavering, the whole head buried in the wood of the wall where they'd just been. The one-eyed guard stood, bow in hand.

"Shooting at a priest?" Whitney said. "Shame on you!" He led the horse around a few wooden hovels to avoid the man's aim.

"You're still going with that?" Sora answered.

"Lesson three," he shouted. "Never surrender the grift until the grift is done!"

Sora snorted and said, "There are at least a dozen more coming down the hill!"

Whitney glanced right to see the silhouette of the constable's mansion painted against the failing sun. On his left, the real priest and the other thugs rounded the far side of the church. Enemies closing in from every angle. Even without horses, the guards gained on them. The winding roads of Bridleton didn't allow his horse to build up much speed. He'd have to lose them in the woods outside of town.

"Think he pays well?" Whitney asked. An arrow bore into the wall of a house as they skirted by, just missing. "I bet he pays well."

"Shut up and get us out of here!" Sora yelled.

"You didn't want to stay for tea?" He kicked the horse's sides to spur it faster, then bent into the horse's mane and held on tight.

Sora dug her nails into his ribs.

"They should be calling you knife-fingers!" he yelped. "Yig!"

They narrowly avoided several more arrows. Whitney steered the horse down a hill and for a moment the constable's men disappeared.

"The woods are just up there," Whitney said. "If we can get there, I think I can lose them."

The men crested the hill. The voice of the one-eyed bigot from the constable's mansion's carried. "I want that liar and his knife-ear pet on a stake!"

"That wasn't very nice!" Whitney shouted back to them.

The naked trees drew nearer as they galloped on. Just another minute or two and they'd be safe within cover. Whitney had ridden plenty of horses in his day, but he wished he were more of an expert. The woods were dense, and in there, at full gallop, steering would be down to the horse.

He closed his eyes as they whipped into the forest. Low branches snapped all around them, their sharp tendrils slapping against his face and neck.

When he could no longer take the pain, he pulled the reins. Once they were at a manageable speed, he glanced back at Sora, whose face, which had been hidden behind his back, remained clean of cuts.

"How are you feeling?" he asked.

"Is this really the time to worry about my health?" she replied.

"Just answer the question! Are you in pain?"

"No."

"Good." Whitney turned and angled his arm awkwardly around Sora. "Ready?"

"Wait! What?"

He pushed off the horse. Together, they slammed against the forest floor and rolled, the landing softened by a layer of fallen leaves.

"Why did you do that!" Sora flipped over and punched his arm. "We had a horse!"

"Just be quiet and stay low," he said. "Hurry before they see us."

Whitney took her hand, led her to a fallen tree, and they laid behind it. She started to scold him again, but he placed his hand over her mouth. The ragtag mob of the constable's men entered the forest, their boots crunching atop fallen leaves. When they reached the spot where Whitney had abandoned their horse, he thought he saw a faint hesitation by their leader, but they continued following the horse, cursing under their breath.

"I can't believe that worked," Sora said once the men were at a safe distance.

"You doubted me?" Whitney said.

"You haven't given me a lot of reason not to."

"Well, maybe now you'll trust me. C'mon, this way."

"That's the wrong way," she said. "That'll take us right back to town."

"I know. I've still got clothes to steal."

"You're joking."

"I don't joke," Whitney said.

"Whit, you're going to get us killed over a shirt."

Whitney stopped and leveled his gaze. "You really don't believe me, do you? I stole the Glass Crown from Liam the Conqueror's own head. In the middle of a crowded party. At the Glass Castle. And you think we're going to get killed stealing a shirt from some wish-he-were-king, backwoods constable?"

"You really don't need to prove anything to me."

"To you? This was your test, remember? To see how we work together."

"It wasn't my idea to play priest."

"No, but things went sideways. That's how this works, Sora. Remember lesson two? You make a plan, abandon it, improvise."

"That's the dumbest thing I've ever heard."

"Yet it's the only way. Now, let's go before they realize that horse is riderless. Unless you'd rather fail?"

"I never fail."

"Good." Whitney helped her up, and they started back toward Bridleton. Some birds flapped through the brush, but that was the only sound save for the distancing cries of the constable's brainless men.

They emerged from the forest onto a relatively flat plain. "This is about the place the kid brought us to his dad, right?" Whitney asked.

Sora stopped and surveyed the area. Mostly grass with a few lonely looking trees looming, branches rattling like dancing skeletons. "Over there," she said.

The rancher's blood still stained the ground and the bark of the tree.

"What exactly happened here?" Whitney asked.

"What do you mean?"

"You," he said. "You ended up in bed for the better half of the day, and now you're fine. Nothing wrong in the least."

"It's just how it works," she said. "Blood requires blood, and only through that sacrifice can I draw on the power of Elsewhere."

"Every time?" Whitney stuck out his tongue in disgust.

"Yes, every time. Wetzel said I had an affinity with fire and had me focus on that, but I taught myself a few other tricks with his books. I've only ever tried to heal rodents or cuts before, so that's probably why it drained me so much. I was able to save them… most of the time."

"You mean to tell me that while we were undercover, you decided to put a man's guts back in without knowing what might happen?" he asked. "What if you didn't wake up!"

"I had to try something. He was dying."

"Well, next time you're going to magic yourself unconscious, we should at least discuss it first."

"You don't get to ask me to do that."

"I just mean." Whitney sighed. "If we stop to heal all the wounded folk in Pantego we'll never get anywhere. I can't carry you everywhere and pretend your wicked magic is the work of Iam."

"Look, I know my limits."

"Do you?"

She swallowed, then pursed her lips. "I don't think we have time to go into the fundamentals of blood magic. Had you stayed in Troborough maybe you could have learned from Wetzel too. But now he's gone."

Her stare grew unfocused, longing. Whitney did his best to try and hold his tongue and move on.

"It doesn't matter anymore," she said after a long silence. She pointed across the field. "The constable's place is just beyond the farm. Do you have a plan?"

"Of course," Whitney said. "Haven't you been listening? Steal some clothes."

XXIV

THE THIEF

Whitney knelt in the cover of the garden bushes just inside the constable's wall, pulling thorns from the hem of his robes.

"There's gotta be a thousand of them!" he groused. "Why can't priests wear pants like the rest of us?"

Sora poked a sharp elbow into his ribs to hush him. "Would you be quiet? You don't know all the guards are gone."

"Well, of course not *all* the guards are gone. There's bound to be a few dolts still patrolling the grounds. Maybe even one or two inside."

"Okay, so honestly, what is your plan?"

Whitney poked his head up and pointed. "See that window?"

"That's your grand plan? Climb through an open window?"

"And out of that one upstairs," he pointed to another window with a trellis running next to it. "Master thievery doesn't have to be complicated. I already led all his men on a wild horse chase through perilous woods."

"By accident!"

"Was it?" He grinned. "Look, just wait here. Let me know if you see anyone coming."

"How am I supposed to do that?"

Whitney was already sneaking toward the mansion. "I'm sure you'll come up with something."

"Whit, wait!"

He heard her but didn't respond.

Staying low, he trod lightly through the garden and pressed his back up against the wall nearest the window. He leaned forward enough to get a look inside. The room was empty, as he'd hoped. He hiked up his robe —he couldn't wait to wear clothes that didn't feel like a dress—then carefully threw his leg over the window sill, and pulled himself into the house.

The room was dimly lit, and the moons were already rising outside, so very little light poured in through the open window. Whitney took note of his surroundings and began drawing a map in his mind. The last time he'd entered the mansion was through the front doors. It was clear he was now on the side of the house close to the backyard. To his left, a door was propped open, revealing a kitchen. To his right appeared to be a staircase descending into the servant's quarters.

Commotion from the stairwell startled Whitney, and he realized dinner time was fast approaching. The house cook would be making his way up soon. Whitney swore and hurried toward the kitchen. He'd only taken one step into the veritable maze of counters and cabinets when an adjoining door to the backyard opened. He ducked behind an island bar.

Plan, abandon, improvise.

He took a deep, steadying breath.

"Your grounds are impressive for so humble a town," Bridleton's new priest said as he stepped in, tapping the floor with his cane to guide himself.

"I'm glad you like it," Darkings replied, right behind him. "And thank you for coming to meet with me so promptly. I do apologize for the confusion, Father."

"It is no matter. Any man who would falsely claim the cloth of Iam does not deserve his grace."

Whitney stayed low and peeked around the corner. They stood just outside the kitchen, too close for Whitney to make a move.

"I couldn't agree more," Darkings said. "These are hard times, with the kingdom in such turmoil. You never know what sort of miscreant rabble will wander into town."

"I am so sorry to hear about your daughter, Constable. I do hope those dregs will be brought to justice. In all my years, I've never heard of such disrespect."

"She will recover. And I assure you, justice shall be served in the name of Iam."

"Praise the Vigilant Eye." He circled his useless eyes. "I hear of much suffering here in Bridleton, Constable. Together, I hope we can offer ease to some of those who have too many times seen their lands ravaged by war."

Whitney heard footsteps on the stairs from the servant's quarters at his back. At the same time, the heeled boots Darkings wore to make himself appear taller clacked onto the kitchen tile.

Shog in a barrel!

Whitney held his breath and listened as closely as he could to figure out which way around they were going through the kitchen. Slowly, he sidled around the cabinets on the opposite side.

"I believe we can do good things here, Father," Darkings said. "Hopefully this little mess will be sorted out before morning. I wouldn't—Ah, chef Tagred, there you are."

The chef emerged from the stairs and now stood on the other side of the kitchen. Whitney was about to be caught between them.

"My Lord," the chef said. "I was about to seek you out regarding your preference for supper."

"Father, would you do me the honor of staying for dinner?" Darkings asked. "You must be starving after your journey. We can discuss our plans for the future of Bridleton."

"It would be an honor, Lord Darkings."

By then, Whitney had nearly flipped sides of the kitchen with them as he edged along, but now they all stopped to talk.

"Don't let Chef Tagred's humble appearance fool you, Father," Darkings said. "He makes the most delicious rabbit's foot stew in all Pantego."

Whitney hoped they would get on with it, but the chef went on to describe all the ingredients in his dish. Whitney's mouth would have been watering if he weren't so offended.

I didn't get offered dinner…

He ignored his starving belly and tried to figure a way out quick. He scanned the room until he homed in on a hatch. He'd seen similar ones in castles and the homes of those who lived in the upper crust of society. The dumbwaiter, a system designed to make it so easy for a noble to receive his meal that he didn't even have to get out of bed, was open and buried in the corner of the room. Whitney could climb the rope inside straight up to Darkings' chambers, he hoped. All he needed to do was distract the men from their mind-numbing conversation for the second it would take to reach it.

He reached up over his head and behind, pawing the counter above until he found a small enough object to throw. A wine cork. He dabbed the wet end on his tongue just to get a sense of the vintage—he'd never met a villain without impeccable taste in wine. Poking his head up, he flung it at a plate propped up on a high shelf on the other side of the kitchen.

The soft cork plunked almost soundlessly off it. The plate wobbled a few times as if taunting Whitney before it finally fell and shattered. The sound drew their attention, and Whitney took off for the dumbwaiter without looking back.

Within it, he found a board and a rope as expected. It was an incredibly tight fit, but Whitney hopped in. As he shut the hatch behind him, he checked to make sure nobody had seen him. Darkings, the priest, and the chef all stood around the broken plate.

"You'd think my servants are trying to kill me the way they arrange things!" Darkings barked.

"It's no problem, my Lord," the Father said.

"They don't seem to understand that things cost autlas. Tagred, I want you to find the last person who so precariously tidied my kitchen."

Whitney didn't wait to hear the rest. Judging from what he'd seen from the constable, he'd just gotten whoever that was in a world of trouble.

That's what happens when you stay in a place where you'll never be anything.

He grabbed hold of the rope inside the dumbwaiter and began climbing. The tiniest sliver of light pierced the shaft just a few meters above. Whitney's hands burned, and his robe kept getting caught beneath his feet. He slipped more than a couple times before finally reaching the second-floor hatch.

He pried it open just enough to see through. His view was limited, but he didn't see anyone. He heard nothing either. The hatch slid open with a screech. Whitney cringed and waited to see if anyone came running. When they didn't, he opened it fully and pulled himself through.

He was in the constable's quarters, which were as opulent as he'd hoped. A large bed—which was nearly as big as the whole priest's cottage—sat in the middle of the room. Iron bars formed a canopy above it, and plush, luxurious silk sheets and pillows adorned its top. A finely crafted armoire made from mahogany stood erect against one wall, with a vanity cut from the same wood across from it.

There was enough wealth in this one room to feed Bridleton for a year, but Whitney knew he didn't have time to take anything other than what he'd come for. There was no telling how quickly the constable's men would give up the hunt.

A closet joined the bedroom. Whitney approached it with caution and a smile spread across his face when he saw what was inside. It was brimming with clothing. He could have his pick of the lot.

He didn't bother being careful, yanking clothing down from the racks and out of drawers. Finally, he settled upon an exquisite silk doublet with gold trim, leggings just the same, and a broad, brown leather belt. It made even his masquerade outfit back in Yarrington seem like rags.

Another voice stirred him. He pulled the closet door shut just in time to see two Panpingese servants enter the room. He left the door open a sliver to peek through.

"Another priest to impress already," one said. "I can hardly remember their names."

"'Make sure everything's spotless.' Even though there'll be a new one next week."

The servants laughed, spreading out, dusting and sweeping. One reordered the papers on top of the vanity, the other set the bed pillows straight. Before moving on, they snuck a sip from a bottle of wine on the constable's nightstand. Lowering the bottle to the table, a servant headed straight for Whitney and the closet he'd just ransacked.

He'd hoped to be able to get out of this without any more fighting, not that these skinny servants were much a threat. Judging by the way they talked about Darkings, they probably hated him more than anyone. Yig, they'd probably invite him to steal more.

He sunk back into the racks of clothing and checked his footing.

"Ey, who left this open?" the servant called over from the dumbwaiter. The one in front of Whitney stopped mere seconds from opening the closet, then went over to his mate.

"Weren't me," he said.

"Mr. Darkings and his late-night snacks," the other sniggered.

"You think he's eating them priests?"

They shared another laugh, then slammed the hatch shut and continued out of the constable's quarters, luckily forgetting about the closet.

Whitney released a mouthful of air. Once sure they were gone, he exited the closet and peered around the corner. An odd light entered through the window, drawing his attention. He cautiously approached the window to find a tall flame rising from the garden and Sora jumping up and down waving her hands. Even from this distance, he could see blood glinting on her palm.

It was her warning. Someone was coming, and whether she'd intended to use it to tell him about the servants or someone new, he wasn't sure.

He spun a one-eighty, his head snapping side to side, surveying the room one last time. Something shimmering on the vanity caught his eye. A golden amulet was strung up in a small glass display. It was molded into the shape of an arrowhead, the surface etched with lettering in some unfamiliar language and the point dusted with diamond bits. A flawless gem cut to the same form was encrusted in its center, amber in color and practically glowing with beauty.

Without question, even considering the priceless art adorning the walls, this was the most valuable object in the whole room. Whitney had a knack for knowing such things. He tried to open the case, but it was locked. He examined it further, but there was no time to waste picking locks. Sora's terrible form of warning was sure to earn the suspicion of the entire town.

He grabbed a pewter goblet from beside the half-full wine bottle, raised it high, and brought it down swift upon the glass. A hairline crack appeared. He did it again. The crack grew.

"What's that racket?"

Whitney recognized the one-eyed guard's voice, back from the chase. He brought the goblet down a third time and the display shattered. He threw the goblet aside and snatched the amulet, allowing himself a moment to marvel at the craftsmanship, then shoved it into his pocket and ran for the window.

"Aye! Stop, ye!"

Whitney threw open the window before realizing how large Sora's flame had grown. Wind blew hot embers inside. He ducked as they caught the curtains and began to burn bright and hot.

"Thief! Stop where yer at!"

Whitney retreated from the window and away from the guard. The flames overtook the room, drawing a clear line between him and his pursuer.

"Sorry, friend," Whitney said. "It's getting hot in here, and I could do with some fresh air."

The guard pressed against the flames but didn't try to go through. Whitney found a door on the other side of the room leading to another short corridor. There were no windows and only one door on the opposite end, but it was locked. He shouldered it, but nothing happened.

Whitney swore and devised a plan.

He grabbed the belt he'd stolen and folded it back until the metal clasp broke free and only the pin remained. Throwing the leather aside, he leaned in and began work on the lock. It was much simpler than the one on the amulet display, just a simple pin-tumbler. He shimmied the makeshift lockpick, allowing it to slide up and down and after a series of clicks, the door popped open.

Whitney heard the guard behind him shouting to the others, and the crackling of flames escalated to a roar. He ran for a staircase at the end of the hall and took the steps three at a time. The door at the bottom opened easily, but the moment he burst through he realized where he was.

The passage was a hidden servant passage so that, Iam-forbid, Darkings didn't have to see his help unless he wanted to. Whitney had emerged in the dining room. The table was only half-set. On the other side of the absurdly long table sat Darkings and the priest, with two guards flanking them in response to the bedlam.

"You!" Darkings muttered, incredulous. His features contorted like he'd just fallen into a Yarrington sewer.

Whitney flashed him a smile, then bolted the other way toward the grand hall. At least he knew where he was now. Guards flooded down from the second floor, smoke hot on their trails. The one-eyed bigot he'd encountered upstairs waited at the front door, two hands on his sword, sneering.

Whitney ran straight at him. If he'd learned anything from avoiding battles over the years, a fighter approached from the sides knew what to do instinctively, but straight on forced them to think. The man swung, and Whitney hit the floor. Another thing about the rich: they always have their wooden floors polished and sanded, so he was able to slide right under the attack.

As he twisted back, the guard was able to stick out a hand and get two fingers on Whitney's leg. He stumbled into the front door, which burst open, then tripped down the marble stairs outside.

"Get back here!" the one-eyed guard yelled.

He leaped as Whitney hit the ground, but just before he could bring his sword down, a pair of hooves sent him flying into the wall of the mansion.

"I guess they caught the horse!" Sora yelled.

She stuck her leg down from the top of the mount and helped Whitney up onto the saddle. He felt a blast of warm air from the blazing fire that now enveloped an entire side of the mansion.

"I said to warn me, not play Black Sandsman!" Whitney said.

"Improvise!" she replied.

He smirked. "Not bad for a knife-ear."

A few more guards hurried down the stairs, but she swung the horse around fast. Its hindquarters sent them all bowling over one another. Constable Darkings appeared in the doorway. When he saw them on a horse, his eyes went wide.

"I'll find you and kill you!" he shouted.

"Consider yourself honored, Constable!" Whitney shouted. "You've been robbed by Whitney Fierstown, the greatest thief alive." He was in the midst of performing an exaggerated bow of his head when Sora urged the horse to take off. The whole yard was in flames now, building a barrier around the property.

"What now?" Whitney asked.

"Hold on!" Sora shouted.

The horse jerked into a gallop, barreling toward the inferno.

"Sora, you're not thinking—"

"Just hold on!"

She reached down and sliced her thumb on the base of her dagger, then raised it toward the flames. Whitney closed his eyes and let out a primal scream as she muttered under her breath. The heat was so intense he couldn't breathe, but he didn't burn. He snuck a peek and saw flames bending all around them, a tunnel of safety within a sea of fiery death.

The horse hurdled the constable's wall and the heat dissipated. Whitney looked back, eyes tearing from the smoke. The constable's mansion was now a glowing, orange beacon soaring over Bridleton. All Whitney wanted were clothes, but it was tough for him to feel bad. Whatever Darkings had done to get so rich in so small a town, not a bit of it was good.

He whooped in excitement, then turned back to find Sora regarding the burning mansion with a thousand-meter-stare.

"You didn't mean for the fire to get that big, did you?" he asked.

He could see in her eyes that she considered denying it before settling on shaking her head.

"Don't worry, he got what was coming," Whitney said. "Daughters don't betray kind fathers."

Sora nodded, inhaled the crisp autumn air and then a few quiet seconds later released a laugh unlike any Whitney had ever heard from her as their mount tore across the plains. Half terrified, half thrilled, all the signs of a successful heist.

"We make a half-decent team, don't we?" she said.

"Sloppy, but decent," he said, smirking.

"You said you liked improvisation."

"Sure," he said, "but let's keep the fire to a low roar next time."

"It's hard to keep focus with you getting caught all the time!"

"I assure you, every time I get spotted it's completely intentional."

Sora sighed. "I can't wait to see you looking all prim and proper in Darkings' clothing."

"Anything will be better than wearing this dress. He really does have great taste, but I'd have to eat this whole yigging horse for them to fit properly. Oh, well, it'll all go to ruin in the Webbed Woods anyhow."

Sora eyes glinted like gold beneath the light of the moons. "So, you've decided to go?" she asked.

"I don't think I have much of a choice after that performance."

"The great Whitney Fierstown, letting a *woman* boss him around?"

"Hey! I'm not like those guys. I love women—I mean… I don't have a problem with—I uh."

Sora gave him a playful nudge with her elbow. "Whatever, tough guy. That was some scream back there."

"War cry," Whitney corrected, leaning forward. He pointed to the smaller of Pantego's two moons. "And, if you're intent on sitting up front, you might want to head that way. The Webbed Woods are south."

For a woman who'd barely left Troborough, heading in the right direction was likely something she'd never had to worry about.

She grumbled something under her breath, then gave the horse a hard kick in the side. It turned so sharply Whitney was almost thrown off. His arm brushed against the amulet folded in with the stolen clothes as he clutched the saddle.

For a moment, while Sora giggled, he found himself wondering how it would look on her, then shook the thought away.

Only a fool would head to the Webbed Woods on purpose, but with Sora at his side, two fools would be more than enough. The glow of the burning mansion slowly faded, and he realized that not once during the heist had he found himself bored or just going through the motions. Even though it was only clothing and jewelry he'd stolen, doing it with Sora was more exciting than robbing the Glass Crown. Of course, he'd never tell her that.

He'd get that doll, march it right up to the Queen herself, and demand his new name from her. Anyone had to be more reasonable than Torsten. Then he'd see where his new partnership with Sora led, and for the first time in a long time, he couldn't wait to find out.

XXV

THE KNIGHT

All of Torsten's fears for his kingdom had come to pass, sooner than he could have imagined. So many nations had been conquered under Liam's rule; they feared and respected him so immensely that even as his mind decayed, nobody dared make a move against the Glass Crown. Torsten hoped those loyalties would linger longer after his death, but it wasn't to be.

The Glass sat on the precipice of war as thousands prepared to march on the heart of the kingdom, and Torsten was as guilty of it as any. Who knew which allies the Black Sands had already scrounged up—how many scorned and broken kingdoms. They'd been shown the light of Iam through Torsten's beloved King Liam, but if Torsten had learned anything in his years, it was how easily people reject blessing. How easily they sin.

I must warn Oleander, he thought, then realized how foolish that was. He'd been exiled. Cast out of the kingdom, stripped of his rank despite the armor he clung to. He'd sent so many men through the Fellwater on a perilous mission into the Webbed Woods. He couldn't say if any of them had stumbled upon this army hiding in the fog or when it started gathering, but if any did, fear of upsetting their queen likely urged them onward instead of back with the news. Like them, Torsten couldn't abandon his quest. It was the only way to make the grief-stricken Queen Regent see reason enough to put an end to this.

He glanced up at the murky sky. Judging by the faint glow of the moons lost behind the veil of fog, he had a few hours until morning. A few hours of smothering darkness. He couldn't do much to sow unrest in the camp without fire—he remembered the annoyance of the Shesaitju reliance on nigh'jels from their wars—but he could send a message.

He scanned the camp for the slaves and found dozens, mostly dedicated to lugging supplies. Surrounded by so many soldiers, they'd be difficult to target. Others dumped buckets of Shesaitju piss and shog into the swampy waters, but Torsten had his attention on those dealing with a different kind of shog.

The zhulong may have looked part wingless dragon, but they acted more like their hog half. They ate constantly and rolled in mud that, if not properly kept, wound up being mostly their own excrement. It took more than a few hands to keep one of their pens in order. Torsten grew up in a wretched place, but he didn't truly know what an assault on the nostrils felt like until he raided his first Shesaitju zhulong stable under Liam.

He hurried down the slope toward the camp. Staying low wasn't easy for a man his size. However, with his dark skin and his bright white armor now covered in mud, he had the night as an ally. He hugged the edge of the delta in case any part of his armor wasn't covered, hoping it might seem like a ripple in the fetid waters.

The Shesaitju were used to the warm, humid nights of the southern, black, sandy beaches bordering the Boiling Waters. The cold of early winter nipped, and the nigh'jels provided only a nominal bit of warmth, not like fire… not that one would even stay lit in such a damp place. The nearest pen wasn't far, but it was on the other side of a large, covered area; the rec-tent judging by the hubbub coming from it. Even the war-hungry Shesaitju needed a place to blow off steam.

Off-duty soldiers drank and caroused throughout, playing games of chance—evidently trying to distract from the harsh cold. The tent, open on all sides, was edged by countless barrels of food and drink, and in its center: a Shesaitju tradition—a roped off arena where soldiers could show off their prowess in Black Fist, a hand-to-hand martial style unique to the Black Sands and without rival in Pantego.

Presently, a large, raucous crowd cheered on two warriors in the arena. They traded blows and grapples, the dance of battle. Torsten preferred the feel of cold steel in his hands when it came to combat. It was said no man could best a Black Fist Master in one-on-one combat, but Torsten had proven that untrue many times over at the end of his claymore.

He ducked behind a stack of barrels and slowly shuffled around them in the direction of the pen. He could no longer see the makeshift arena, but bodies hitting the dirt and myriad expressions of both pain and excitement told him nothing had changed. When the fight ended, there was such revelry it was as if they'd just sacked Yarrington.

Celebration before victory. Typical.

In Liam's camps, all that was celebrated before battle was Iam. They'd beg his forgiveness for the bloodshed to come in His holy name, and because of it, they never lost. Ale and games were reserved for the victorious.

Torsten reached the end of the supply stacks where there was an open gap between him and the pen's fence. At least a ten-meter strip of swampland without anything for cover and fully illuminated by the nigh'jel lanterns hanging along the rim of the tent.

The soldiers were distracted, but not that distracted. Torsten found himself wishing he still had a thief with him, someone soft on his feet and used to skulking through shadows. To make things worse, his armor had already begun squeaking a bit from drying mud. He quickly shook his head.

Only Iam is with me now.

He waited for an opening. So long in fact, that his boots began to sink into the muck. Every time new combatants sparred in the arena there was a ton of movement, only the tables never emptied. More soldiers cycled in and out, from an army that he now realized was even bigger than he'd first thought. More than ten thousand men, easy.

Torsten considered making a break for it when suddenly, everyone beneath the tent went silent. He peeked over the top of a barrel to see a man arriving, flanked by masked warriors in gilded armor. He himself was wrapped head to toe in flowing silk, gold chains dangling from his neck and elaborate white tattoos covering his ashen, gray, bald head.

He was young and, Torsten had to admit, handsome, with a sharp jawline that ended in a braided beard adorned with gold jewelry. His eyes were black as pitch. His cheekbones rose high and, along with his forehead, were covered with gold flakes that shimmered against his ashen skin. Shesaitju royalty, and judging by the jewel-encrusted hilt of the scimitar hanging from his belt, an afhem warlord.

The tent's occupants bowed low in reverence as if the man were a god. To the heathen Shesaitju, he may as well have been. Liam's conquest converted a great many of their people, but there were those who still worshipped the afhems and the Caleef himself standing as the chief of their living pantheon—the God of Sand and Sea. Their temples bore fewer images of gods like Iam or Nesilia than fallen warlords.

The afhem walked as if on air, like the whole world beneath him.

A soldier greeted him in Saitjuese, then said in common, "Afhem Muskigo, we are graced by your presence."

"Farhan Uki'a, commander," Muskigo replied. His voice was soft and calculating. He pronounced every syllable in both languages as if he'd be cursed if he messed up. "I have come to see if my afhemate is prepared."

"We are prepared. In the name of my ancestors I swear, we will stain the Glass red."

Torsten prepared to move while everyone was focused on the afhem, but Muskigo's gaze froze him. He looked both at his commander and around him all at once, face aimed toward the path Torsten needed to take. Muskigo reached out and grasped his commander's chin, turning his head as if grading livestock.

"Show me," he said.

He raised his arms, and his guards removed his silk wrappings first, then his shirt. His body was laced with muscle like he was carved from stone. More white tattoos covered every inch of him, many of them bearing the same gold flecks as the ones on his head. His breath billowed in the cold, but it didn't seem to affect him.

He stepped into the arena, parting men like a curtain at one of the Queen's plays, but this was no acting troupe.

"My Lord, I c-can't—" Farhan stammered.

"Am I not your afhem?" Muskigo said. "You will do as I command."

He stretched his arms high and fell into a Black Fist grappling stance, left arm fully extended, hand as flat as a dagger's blade. He looked like a bird of prey and Torsten knew, just as deadly.

Farhan, the commander, eyed his men in turn, then finally stepped in. Cheers rained down on them as he met the Afhem's stance and they circled each other, every pair of eyes in the tent fixed on them.

Curious as he was, Torsten used the opening to creep along the outside of the tent to the next batch of supplies piled up beside the zhulong pen. When he made it, he glanced back over, and again found himself captivated. He had a perfect view of the fight now.

Muskigo waited until the commander made the first move and slid gracefully out of the way. As his right leg swept behind him, dust clouded up at his feet and fell just as quickly. Farhan swiped and grappled, but Muskigo was a blur. His hands both thrust forward so gracefully, Torsten wondered how they could have done any real damage, but the cry of pain that escaped the Farhan's lips left nothing to question.

Muskigo slid back, nearly floating again. His muscles weren't even tensed. Farhan rose and brought his leg around in a spinning kick.

"The moment we underestimate our enemies…" Muskigo said, ducking and sweeping the commander's grounded foot "…is the moment we fall again."

Farhan sprang up and charged. Fluid as a master painter, Muskigo slapped away every blow. Then he grasped the Farhan's forearm and wrenched his arm behind his back.

"Our fathers thought themselves invincible, and that was their folly," he said.

He shoved Farhan forward into the line of warriors. They spun him and sent him right back into the fight. Farhan was tired now, panting. He leaped forward with what little energy remained, swung at Muskigo's head, and caught only air. Muskigo fist pistoned into Farhan's solar plexus and sent him reeling back.

The afhem pressed, and the crowd parted. Muskigo hit the man again, and again until they were both outside the arena. Farhan's feet found mud, and he slipped, spinning in time to get his hands out beneath him. He rose to all fours like a dog and sloshed through the slurry into the feet of his men, and stayed there, hoping for protection.

Muskigo shook the grime off his hands, then gestured to his guards to clothe him. He wasn't even breathing heavy.

"The Glass is fading," he said, "but we must fight every battle as if it is our last. If we do not, we will join our fathers beneath the sand. So, you will all sleep here, in the freezing cold, until your bones are near shattering. Because, until one of you can best me in combat, we will attack nothing. We will starve if we must because mediocrity will not do."

The crowd stared in silence and Torsten couldn't help but join them. The Black Sandsmen he'd battled were arrogant and eager to charge full-tilt into Liam's wall of shields. They believed that in death they'd join their fallen ancestors in the depths of the Boiling Waters, and they acted like it. This man was different. As he strolled out of the tent, Torsten felt a very human chill run up his spine.

At least that means there's time, he decided.

This young, impressive afhem was an enemy for a different day. He turned and peered into the crate behind him. The smell wafting out was rank. Raw meat for the beasts. That would come in handy later. He climbed over the fence and into the pen where the smell was even worse. Even on four legs, the zhulong's backs were as high as Torsten's chest. The mane along their reptilian necks ran down into a body sheathed in rust-colored scales. Hoglike-snouts, complete with tusks that could gore a man straight through, snorted and dripped. But despite their appearance, they were mild creatures, happy to lounge and roll in the mud—so long as the temptation of fresh meat was far from them.

Torsten snaked his way through the bulky beasts, not daring look down, for even in the darkness he knew what he was slogging through. He pushed forward until he spotted a human slave kneeling amongst a cluster of zhulong, scooping shog into a bucket. She was young, too young for such work, her dress tattered, stained and wet. She lifted the bucket and went to walk toward the water when Torsten lay his massive hand on her shoulder. She shrieked as she whipped around, dropping the bucket onto one of the zhulong's massive paws, causing a few others to respond as if threatened.

Torsten could only imagine what he looked like to her: a giant, mud-covered monster. He held a finger to his lips as she stared at him, wide-eyed. "I'm here to help you, girl," he whispered.

"By Iam, You're a…a…a…" she stammered.

"A Hand of our Lord, brought here to save you from this place. Were you from Oxgate?" She nodded. "They'll pay for that. But for now, I need you to do something for me."

"You're not going to free us?"

"I am, but King Pi needs you."

"Surely you mean King Liam?"

She doesn't know. Is it possible none of them do?

"That is a discussion for another day," he said. "For now, when I leave, you must gather the others in here. When the time is right, run north and don't look back."

"How will I kn—"

"You'll know. I need you to move, fast as you can. Go to Yarrington and ask to speak with Ran—with Wardric of the King's Shield."

Rand was a good kid, but he was young and an impressionable. Torsten knew better than most what even less than a week trying to appease Queen Oleander could do to a man. But Wardric had served under Liam. He may have been dour, but only because he'd seen so many of the horrors in Pantego under the flag of a true leader.

"Show this at the gates, and they'll let you in." Torsten removed his necklace. He took one long look at the glass pendant, his Eye of Iam given to him by Liam himself, before handing it over. "What is your name?" he asked.

"Abigail," she squeaked out.

"I'm trusting you with this. The Queen Regent is trusting you. Tell the King's Shield what you saw here. Spare no detail. Do this, and you will never want for anything again in your life, I swear it by the light of Iam."

The girl marveled at the necklace as it rested in her shaking palms. She was common born judging by the gauntness of her cheeks. Probably had never seen a piece of jewelry so fine in her life.

"What about you?" she asked.

"I must continue on. But do not fear, Abigail. Iam is with us, even here. He will guide you home. Now, gather the others and prepare to run. Stick to the shadows and let nothing stop you from warning the kingdom."

She looked terrified. But Torsten knew fear was a better choice than slavery. He held her gaze until finally she nodded and turned.

He grabbed her arm. "The fate of the very kingdom is in your hands, Abigail."

She nodded slowly and headed off. Torsten watched her go until she vanished behind the haunches of a zhulong. Putting his faith in others hadn't been easy lately, but, yet again, he had no choice. He had to trust she wouldn't abscond from duty as Whitney had.

There is still decency in this world, he told himself. *Iam hasn't abandoned us yet.*

He hurried back to the portion of fence running along the rec-tent. He crouched by the wood and removed his claymore from its back-scabbard. Then he slid the sword through a gap, careful to not make a sound. Although the warriors were still very much affected by their leader's speech, that didn't mean they were deaf.

He poked the blade right under the lid of a crate filled with raw meat for the zhulong, then pushed. He took his time, remaining quiet until the crate tipped and the meat spilled out. All at once, a dozen snouts snorted. Torsten could feel the heat of the zhulong's breath on the back of his neck. He chose to ignore the spray of mucus that accompanied it.

A small company of the Shesaitju heard the crash and stood to find its source. They'd be too late. Torsten raised his sword and brought it crashing down on the makeshift fence, cleaving the entire panel in two. A swift kick sent it folding over.

Zhulong stampeded through the opening. Torsten dove out of their path moments before being trampled. The smell of the meat sent them into a frenzy, smashing into each other in a mad scramble. One smashed into the tent's corner support and yanked the canvas down. Hanging nigh'jel lanterns fell and cracked, allowing the jellies to squirm out.

The gentle zhulong were gentle no more. Tusks clashed, gargantuan bodies slammed, and Torsten had the distraction he needed. He turned and saw Abigail with a group of slaves sprinting across the far edge of the pen. He caught her eye and gestured toward the hill from which he'd come.

He traced his eyes in the name of Iam, and before the group picked up their pace, Abigail returned the holy gesture. The sight lifted Torsten's spirits.

Not all bad after all.

Now he just needed to keep the Black Sands distracted long enough for the slaves to put a reasonable distance between them and their captors. If they were caught escaping, their fate would be far worse than shilling shog.

He backed up behind the mess of zhulong, searching for the most bashful. He spotted one—young by the looks of it, its tusks still coming in —waiting at the back instead of joining the fray.

Torsten had never ridden a zhulong, but he'd spent a lifetime on horse-back. He approached it from the side so he didn't make eye contact, grabbed its tusk, and gently tilted its head down until it could see him with one eye. The young beast remained docile and permitted Torsten to climb onto its back. As immature as it was, it still proved difficult for Torsten's armored legs to wrap around its thick sides. He now understood why the Shesaitju wore leather and cloth instead of metal greaves.

Torsten grasped a handful of its mane with one hand, then gave it a kick. It was like striking steel. The beast tore forward through the mud so fast he nearly toppled off. Sinking down, he used the mane to guide it through the opening in the fence. With his other hand, he brandished his claymore, a sword so large it would require two hands from any ordinary-sized man.

"*Abbat mos!*" A Shesaitju shouted over the din of feeding beasts. "Abbat mos!"

"Iam, forgive for what I must do in your name," Torsten whispered to himself. Then he slashed down from the back of the zhulong at the man. No sooner did the soldier hit the mud than horns rang out all across the camp. A murder of crows, frightened, rose up from naked trees, a cloud of black blending into the dark sky.

Torsten turned right, and his mount bowled through a table covered in freshly tanned and stretched leathers. Soldiers scattered. Others ran for spears and bows. They all shouted, "Abbat mos!" but Torsten swept his massive claymore from side to side like a scythe in harvest season. There was no formal declaration of war against the Shesaitju, but he felt no remorse as his blade rent flesh and split bone. Men from this camp had slaughtered innocent villagers for little but to send a message to the Glass Castle.

He rounded a corner and a host of spears stabbed up at him. He parried two with a single swipe, and the rest snapped against the tough hide of his zhulong. The wealthiest Black Sandsmen made armor out of the creatures' scaly hide, and now he knew why. Its tusk split a man's stomach and lifted him through the air, his body sliding off like meat from a kebab.

When he was out of the way, Torsten saw Muskigo and his Serpent Guard standing ahead, waiting. Unlike the rest, these men wore gilded plate armor with zhulong hide hauberks beneath. They formed a circle around Muskigo with their round shields raised, spears sticking out. It was certain death if Torsten charged them, even atop a zhulong, but a chance at an afhem was tough to pass up.

Torsten stared straight into the man's eyes as he neared and they stared back, black as night. Neither cowered or showed interest in doing so. Muskigo straightened his shoulders, rolled his neck, and stood tall. Torsten waited until the last minute, then guided his mount to veer right, avoiding the spears. Even as he passed, he and Afhem Muskigo never broke eye contact. Then, just as he went to turn away, Muskigo's black lips creased into a smile.

He would have to wait. Torsten's quest was more important than claiming the life of one vengeful afhem.

Someone ahead bellowed something in Saitjuese. Torsten turned just in time to see a mounted zhulong bounding toward him. A spear plunged toward his head, but he dipped left, swinging his sword in a full arc that caught the attacker across the forehead.

The zhulong slammed into each other and sent Torsten's mount into a wild spin. He squeezed its mane and hung on tight until the beast found its footing. A slew of arrows promptly zipped past his head, one nearly nicking his ear another glancing off his pauldron. A few stabbed into the zhulong's haunches just above its long serpentine tail.

They didn't pierce the beast's hide, but it was startled and took off at full speed, squealing. Torsten was along for the ride now. Fortunately, they were headed south out of camp just like he wanted. He glanced back and saw three more mounted warriors hot on their tail. Their older zhulong closed the distance quickly.

One launched an arrow that found a soft spot in Torsten's armor and burrowed into the meat of his right shoulder. Another closed in from his left and stabbed at his zhulong with a spear. The Shesaitju knew their beasts well. It howled as the blade sunk through the fleshy underside of its hind leg. Torsten fought the pain in his shoulder and swung down, chopping the spear in two. He leaned out and grabbed the sharp side of the broken weapon, another arrow missing his throat by centimeters.

He released the zhulong's mane to transfer his sword to his off-hand. With the other, he flung the spear. It pierced the bow-wielding warrior through the chest and sent him tumbling into the swamp.

Torsten quickly tossed his sword back to his right hand. Sharp lines of pain shot down the arm as he moved it into position to parry the attack of the third warrior.

"Run, beast!" he roared and kicked his zhulong in the sides as hard as he could.

The fog and the darkness were stifling, but ahead he saw a patch of blackness deeper than everywhere around, growing taller and wider. The form was jagged, ever-changing, like waves around a ship long at sea.

The Webbed Woods. He was so close. The two riders caught up, forcing him to fight them off at the same time. He clenched his jaw as he worked his blade, deflecting every blow.

He could see the form of the trees now. An endless warren of towering trunks taller than he'd ever seen and hanging vines as thick as his legs. The place looked like the foulest realm of Elsewhere, yet nowhere had ever seemed so inviting.

His mount didn't feel the same way.

It stopped short at the first root protruding from the woods. Torsten flew over the zhulong's head and rolled between two trees as tall as the Glass Castle. The shaft of the arrow sticking from his shoulder snapped in two as he rolled and popped to his feet, whipping around with his sword in both hands.

His zhulong turned and ran perpendicular to the row of trees, never daring to get within an arm's length of the place. The pursuing warriors had stopped dead in their tracks as well. Their mounts squealed in fear, and their eyes spoke of dread.

They watched Torsten as he slowly backed into the forest. After a few steps, the Shesaitju warriors were gone. After a few more, he could barely see the sword in his hands, or the broken end of the arrow protruding from his armor, only a layer of copious darkness enveloped him. Darkness only found in the Webbed Woods.

XXVI

THE THIEF

It wasn't the darkness of the Webbed Woods that had Whitney's flesh rising into little bumps. It wasn't even the overwhelming silence but for the gentle rattling of a canopy far above and the occasional scuttle of unseen creatures. It was the fetid smell of dried blood and old flesh. Death. Like he'd just stepped into the largest graveyard known to man.

He shuddered. "I've got a bad feeling about this."

He'd had one since the moment they arrived. It was a straight shot south to the Webbed Woods from Bridleton. No more interruptions from dire wolves, ghosts of the past or crazed cultists. Their horse sloshed through the Fellwater Swamp, cutting through a layer of fog so copious Whitney could barely see its mane in front of him. The tremendous trees of the infamous woods loomed like strong towers.

Whitney and Sora didn't run into a soul even though the echo of screams rang through the air like ghosts were about. Their stolen horse, likely smarter than either of them, hurled them off instead of entering. It was on foot from there, into darkness that was somehow worse than the blanketing fog. Searching for someone and something for which Whitney had no idea where to start looking or even what exactly to look for.

Whose bright idea was this? He couldn't even remember any longer.

"Quit being a baby," Sora said. "I thought you've robbed a *dragon*?"

"I never said it was alive." Whitney couldn't see Sora's face well, but he'd come to know her eye roll by memory and was sure it accompanied her groan. "Besides, this is different. You can *see* a dragon. We've been walking in near-darkness for half a day after the horse ran away and we haven't seen anything. Have you noticed there hasn't even been a bird chirping, or a night bug, or anything? It's just quiet. Eerie quiet."

"If you were a bird, would you live in here?"

"If I were a bird I'd be an even better thief—Eek! Was that you?"

"What?"

Whitney didn't get a word out before he felt something slither around his gut. It tightened suddenly and yanked him against a tree.

"Sora!" he yelped.

He reached for his dagger, but whatever the thing was wrapped one of his wrists and blocked the weapons around his waist. It moved like a tentacle or a snake, but it wasn't slimy. It felt almost like…

"The vines!" Whitney said.

He tried to pull himself free, but a vine wrapped his ankle and squeezed it against the trunk. Another found his throat.

Sora's raised her bandaged hand in front of his face. A fresh streak of blood stained it, and from her fingers roiled an orb of flame so perfectly round it was as if she held a glowing crystal ball. The vine immediately retreated.

"Took you long enough," Whitney said, panting.

"Are you okay?" she asked. Whitney saw a momentary flicker of concern on her face, which vanished as soon as he nodded. "You should have heard yourself squealing. And I thought I was the girl."

"You're just jealous of my incredible singing voice," he said, rubbing at his neck.

"You're insane."

"Maybe, but remember what I said about sneaking around in here without fire to avoid attention? Ignore me."

She turned, her hand casting flickering orange light on the trunks of towering cypress trees. A slew of vines draped all around them shriveled away in hiding. Whitney stared up but could see nothing but darkness beyond the glow of her magic once they were gone. There was no sky. There wasn't even the tree-top canopy. Just night eternal.

Whitney gripped the amulet he'd stolen from Constable Darkings as they walked, rolling it absentmindedly between thumb and forefinger.

"I still can't believe you nearly got us killed for that ugly thing," Sora said.

"What?" Whitney said.

"That stupid thing," she said pointing to the amulet. "You don't even know what it is."

"I know what it is!" Whitney whispered as loudly as he dared.

"Yeah? What?"

"It's a…" he flipped it over a few times. Even in the dim light of the flames, the amber stone glimmered. "It's a… an arrow-shaped amulet with a gem worth more than Troborough. And look, little flecks of something else, probably diamond, on the tip."

"It's useless, and we could have died."

"What about you? You were supposed to set a signal fire not burn the entire house down."

"Oh, *now* you care?"

"I think we should talk about it before anything happens here and you bring a tree down on top of us."

"I just… I lost control. It won't happen again."

"Your fire may be magic beyond my *unmystical* comprehension," he said, exaggerating the word, "but I'm going to need more than that. What if next time you take the entire town with you, just like Trobor—" Whitney froze before the word came all the way out.

Sora stopped mid-step. "What?" she said, seething. "Say it."

"All I'm saying is that part of being a thief is being inconspicuous. If we start leaving a trail like that?"

"You seemed pretty happy when you got out of there with your stupid necklace, shouting your real name like a boastful…a boastful…" She threw her hands up and groaned in frustration.

Whitney knew he'd struck a nerve, but he could tell by her lack of punching him in the arm that her frustration wasn't solely directed at him. He remembered her expression as she watched the fire consuming the

Darkings' house from afar. He thought then that it was pity, but now he realized there was fear there too.

Fear over what she was capable of. Fear over what she couldn't control.

"Just forget it," he said. "If you say it won't happen again then I believe you."

"No, you don't," she said.

"I swear, I d—shhh, did you hear that?"

"You're not going to trick me out of this conversa..." Her words trailed off because Whitney's hand was suddenly covering her lips.

"I'm being serious," he whispered. "Put out the fire."

When the crackle of the fire stopped, the sound of a branch snapping echoed.

"Was that—"

"Footsteps," Whitney finished for her.

"Who would be here?" Sora said.

"The knight said Redstar was here, but he didn't know where. Might be him or one of his followers. Go hide over there. We'll get the drop on whoever it is."

"*You* go hide," she bristled.

Whitney gave her a light shove and said, "This isn't the time for chivalry."

A few moments later, a hulking shadow fell over Whitney. He drew his daggers and turned to face the giant.

"Come on then," he said, voice quavering just a bit. "Let's do this."

The figure stepped forward. It was a meter away, and Whitney felt sweat beading on his forehead and the small of his back even though the air was brisk.

"I knew you were a bloody fool," said the giant, "but I had no idea you were this stupid."

He lunged forward and snatched Whitney by the collar. Whitney brought his blades down, but they clanked against steel.

"Quit that, thief!"

"Torsten?" Whitney asked, but it was too late.

Sora leaped down from a low-lying tree branch onto Torsten's back.

Torsten grabbed her arm and plucked her off before she could stab him with her knife.

"Enough!" he roared.

"Okay, okay," Whitney squawked—which wasn't easy under the crushing force of the meat hook Torsten called a hand.

"I ought to crush you where you stand, coward."

"This is the knight?" Sora grated, her throat being squeezed by his other hand.

"There was only time to get one of us out, I swear," Whitney gargled.

"Say what you will, but Iam sees through your lies," Torsten said.

"It's true! I'm here, aren't I? Finishing what we started."

Torsten drew him so close Whitney could actually see his face in the dark. And smell him. He was coated in mud, blood, and gods know what else. It made the stench of the swamp seem like an oleander blossom in retrospect.

Torsten growled, then finally dropped them.

"Gods, your hands are freezing!" Whitney groaned a moment after he landed hard on the moss-covered forest floor.

"Maybe they wouldn't be had you not destroyed my gauntlets," Torsten said.

Whitney's lip twisted. "Sorry about that."

Torsten rubbed his shoulder, wincing as he did. Whitney thought he noticed something sticking out of the metal through the oppressive darkness, but didn't have time to ask.

"What in Iam's name are you wearing?" Torsten asked.

Whitney stood, brushed off his silks, and said, "I think I look rather dapper, what's your excuse?"

Sora moaned.

"You look like a jester," Torsten said. "Who's she? Trick some knife-ear harlot into helping you? Plan to leave her for dead too?"

Fire erupted in Sora's hand again. She held it to Torsten's face, and Whitney could see the fear rippling through his features as he backed away slowly. Whitney wasn't sure if it was the fire or the realization that he was standing before a blood mage.

"Put that out, now," Torsten said through clenched teeth.

"Call me a knife-ear again," she said.

"Really?" Whitney said. "Of those two insults that's the one you care about?"

She shot a glower his way.

"All right," he said. "Your call."

"If I saw that flame, how many other things in these woods do you think are now keenly aware of your presence, witch?" Torsten asked.

"Better than being strangled by… by living vines," she spat.

"Legends speak of evils here that swords cannot cut. If you fear vines, you've come to the wrong place."

Whitney swore. "He's right."

Sora growled and extinguished the fire. "Well, I still don't like that name."

"Didn't you just learn about it the other day?"

She punched Whitney in the arm. "I'm not a harlot either," she added.

"What you both are, is stupid," Torsten muttered. "Holding a beacon of cursed fire in your hand like an invitation to a masquerade! Black magic is like a candle to demonic creatures."

"What about you?" Whitney asked. "Your footsteps are about as soft as a zhulong's."

"Why did you say that?" Torsten asked with unexpected urgency. "Did you encounter them as well?"

Something shrieked from the bushes, so shrill it raised the hairs on Whitney's neck. The three went silent and backed up against each other. Torsten drew his claymore and held it at the ready, Whitney his daggers.

"You two just couldn't keep your mouths shut!" Sora snapped. Fire wreathed her bleeding hand again.

"Did I mention I hate forests?" Whitney said.

Suddenly, a slew of demonic cackles issued from every direction, echoing up through the dense canopy. Whitney's hairs already stood on end, but now his heart was clamoring within his chest. Years of adventuring across Pantego, and he'd never heard a sound so purely wicked.

"Show your faces, cowards!" Torsten barked, claymore gripped tight.

"It's too dark, they can't," Whitney whispered.

The hidden creatures moved in concentric circles around them, slowly closing in. Whitney couldn't see them, but he heard every movement. At times they sounded like frolicking children, at others something far more sinister.

"I told you that fire was going to draw attention," Torsten said.

"Oh, and you think it had nothing to do with the volume at which you berated us?" Sora spat. "Get off your high horse, Shieldsman."

"I remember when we had a horse," Whitney said.

"Not now!"

"Everyone, be quiet!" Torsten shouted.

Just then, one of the creatures passed close enough to be illuminated by Sora's magic.

Its piercing, red eyes glowed, reflecting the searing brightness of the firelight. Two horns, short and stubby, jutted out of the top of its skull. Hair framed its face, peppered its upper body, and smothered its lower half which ended in a pair of hooves.

Whitney knew what it was immediately, though he couldn't believe his eyes. Satyrs were mischievous, vile creatures who were said to be able to smell fear. He had never come into contact with one before, only heard of their evil in songs by the bards throughout Pantego—and gods know their tales could never be trusted.

"What is that?" Sora gasped.

"Satyr," Whitney and Torsten responded simultaneously. They shared a look. Torsten's expression betrayed a modicum of approval, but he quickly returned his attention to the beast... which Whitney promptly realized wasn't an apt description. It stood only three feet tall.

"It's so small," Sora said. "Is it a baby?"

"If that's a baby, I'd hate to see its parents," Whitney replied.

"Well, I'm afraid you're about to," Torsten said, leveling his sword.

Two more of the creatures appeared from within the brush. These stood nearly the height of Torsten. Their horns curled around like a goat's and ended in a nasty looking hook. The child was unpleasant, but these creatures were hideous beyond compare. Their sharp, narrow features gave their faces the look of vultures, everything tapering toward the point of their aquiline noses. A neat row of jagged teeth glinted in the fire. And their eyes were red as hot embers.

They spoke, words a gallimaufry of grunts and neighs.

"What are they saying?" Whitney asked, but no one answered.

Movement behind him and to each side told him they were surrounded. Satyrs were as legendary for their agility as they were for their tricks. If they wanted, they could have all three of them sliced and skewered before they even managed to take out the child. The creatures were said to live in dens, and Whitney would bet all his hidden treasures around the world they'd accidentally stumbled upon one.

"Uh, Torsten?" Whitney said. "Any knightly plans for this?"

"They smell fear," Torsten said.

"Then I must stink."

"How many more?" Torsten asked, not daring take his eye off the three in front of him.

"At least nine," Sora said.

"Of all the ways I thought I would die…" Whitney said.

"We mean you no harm," Torsten stepped forward and said. "If we are trespassing on your grounds, we will leave."

The larger of the three hopped forward twice, then crouched.

"Get ready," Torsten said.

"For what?" Whitney asked, voice cracking.

As if in response, the rest hopped forward, forcing Whitney, Sora, and Torsten back to back. Sora's flame grew larger. Whitney's hands were so sweaty he could barely hold onto his weapons. Fighting Shesaitju warriors suddenly seemed preferable.

Torsten swung his sword in a horizontal arc, not intending to make contact. A warning. Satyrs were the spawn of fallen gods and Elsewhere, but they were intelligent enough, Whitney hoped, not to want any of their family to die senselessly at the hands of a mighty Shieldsman.

The leader whistled sharply. Whitney heard scattering from all directions. The baby in front of them turned tail—literally—and fled.

"The little ones are leaving," Sora said.

"That's a good sign, right Torsten?" Whitney whispered. "Right?"

The leader shuffled again.

"Put the weapon away, knight, it will do you no good in any case," said the largest of them. His voice was high and felt like gravel against Whitney's ears.

"Your manipulation won't work on me, demon," Torsten said.

"A pity," the beast said, "I thought this would be quick."

"We do not desire a fight, although I will not hesitate to send you sprawling back from whence you came. Return to the dark planes of Elsewhere, or find yourself in the fires of exile."

The cackling came again. "If a fight is not what you desire, a shred of respect would carry you a long way. These are our woods." As if to solidify his claim, he raised his hands, and several vines snapped upward, cracking against the air like whips. "What could possibly bring such feeble humans into our domain?"

"Another human," Whitney said. "You seen him?"

"Ah, so your friends can speak?" the beast said.

"We can do far more than that," Sora said. Flames erupted in Sora's hands, painting the forest bright orange for barely a moment before her fire was squelched. Sora gasped.

"Do not deceive yourself, young blood mage," the satyr said, his own preternatural light emanating from his body. It was a soft glow but provided enough light to see their surroundings clearly. "Your powers are useless against us. Did you think drawing on the magic of Elsewhere would do you good against those who have tread on its planes?"

"I've heard enough of your poisonous words, demon," Torsten said. "Leave now and be spared the wrath of Iam!" He lunged and thrust his claymore. He caught only air. The satyr lashed out and scratched Torsten's cheek with razor sharp claws, sending him staggering backward.

It grunted twice and bared its teeth, yellow and barbed. Faster than Whitney could register the movement, it fell to its hands and kicked out with both hooves catching Torsten in the midsection. His armor had likely saved his life. Two dents, roughly the size and shape of the hooves, remained. Still, even with the armor, it seemed to steal the air from his lungs.

He clambered back, grunting in pain and clutching his shoulder. From the satyr's light, Whitney now realized blood dripped from the area. The creature moved so fast he didn't even see it strike him there.

"Okay, okay, I'm sure we can talk this out," Whitney said. Words were difficult to get out. None of the other satyrs attacked. He and Sora remained back to back while the beasts looked on from a safe distance, shifting their weight between hooves as if ready to charge.

"What are they doing?" Sora asked.

"Taunting us," Whitney said. His hand brushed Sora's, and for a second he considered dropping a dagger and grasping her hand before he remembered how bloody it was.

"What do you want?" Torsten questioned the leader, breathless.

"I already posed my question, why are you in our woods?" the satyr leader said. "You answered with an attack. Is this fight not what you wanted?"

"We are here to find an Arch Warlock of the Drav Cra." Whitney blurted. Nothing else was working, so he went to his last resort in negotiating. The truth.

"A warlock you say?" The satyr glanced across the circle at one of its brethren. "Have you seen a warlock in these woods?"

They laughed again together. Whitney tilted his head and clamped down, grinding his teeth against the sound.

"I assure you, anything that stepped foot into these woods did so only by our knowing." the satyr said. "If an Arch Warlock had been here, we would know. These are our woods, after all."

"I'm confused," Whitney said. "I thought some giant spider named Bliss owned these woods. You have a ledger you can show us?"

The satyr spread its arms wide, lowered its head, and released a spine-tingling hiss. "Do not speak that name!" When it dropped its hands, a vine swung around from a nearby tree and wrapped tight over Whitney's mouth. Two more restrained his arms.

"Let him go!" Sora demanded, raising her knife to her arm. Before she could draw blood, a vine wrapped her wrist. It squeezed so hard she dropped the weapon and fell to her knees.

"Both of you keep quiet!" Torsten said, biting back pain and anger.

"You are a knight of Iam, are you not?" The satyr stood erect again. The others followed his example.

Torsten nodded and circled an eye with one finger as if a demon would care whether or not he could prove it.

"Yet you travel with a blood mage?" it asked.

"We only just met," he said. "I don't even know her name."

The satyr closed its eyes, then whispered, "Sora." Its voice seemed to resonate all the way up through the canopy.

Sora yelped. Whitney might have too if he could open his mouth.

"What business is it of yours who I travel with, demon?" Torsten asked. If the demon knowing her name had shocked him as well, he didn't let it show.

"Her link with Elsewhere is strong," it said. "Stronger than I have felt in some time." Another vine shot out and grabbed Sora by the ankle, heaving her into the air. She hung upside down, face to face with the satyr.

Whitney frantically screamed into his gag and swung his arms.

Torsten raised a hand to quiet him.

"If you only just met her," the Satyr said. "Then you would not mind if we kept her. With her bond, she would likely produce formidable offspring."

Whitney's stomach turned over. The satyrs were mysterious creatures, but he remembered from the songs about them that all satyrs were male—using *lesser* races to bear their young. He'd thought it ridiculous at the time.

"Sora!" Whitney cried. He pulled free, got his daggers up, and sliced the vine off his face. Three satyrs hopped in front of him as he tried to run to her. One of them threw a hard fist across his jaw and knocked him off his feet. The beast hit harder than any guard he'd ever encountered.

"I cannot, with a clear heart, allow you to take her," Torsten said. "No matter what she is."

"Then it is a fight you want, Torsten of Yarrington?" the satyr leader said.

Now it was Torsten's turn to show how unsettling it was for a demon to know his name without him ever having spoken it. Whitney could tell he was struggling, trying to keep calm.

"We wish only to pass deeper into the… *your* woods," he said.

Good one, Shieldsman. If Whitney knew two things about demons. Never trust them, and that flattery was the best way to bargain with them. He only wished he hadn't been so overcome by fear and thought of it sooner.

"Have you anything else so magnificent to offer?" The satyr extended a hand and ran one of its sharp claws across Sora's cheek. She squirmed, but the blood rushing to her head from being upside down, and the fear visibly gripping her kept her quiet.

The satyr leaned forward and sniffed her. "Fear," it whispered, dragging out the word.

"I have this!" Whitney said from the ground, stealing the beast's attention. He raised the amulet he'd stolen from Darkings over his head and tossed it to the satyr. The creature studied it, the thick line of hair across its forehead furrowing.

"It's a precious amulet. It belonged to the great mystic… uh… I forget her name."

Do not waste my time with ugly, mortal trinkets," the satyr said, then flicked the necklace back at Whitney's feet.

"Seriously?" Whitney said, lifting it back over his head and glanced between the shiny amulet and Sora. "It's not ugly."

Torsten shifted his stance and tried to bring his sword to bear. One of his arms shook as he did. The satyr had already made him look foolish when he tried to strike it last, but a fight seemed inevitable, and their best chance at fighting was too injured to get his sword higher than his hip.

Whitney remained on his hands and knees and slowly edged toward Sora, hoping none of the demon eyes would notice. She stared down at him, terrified, more than he could ever remember her being. He could rip her free and make a run for it, let Torsten fend for himself. It wasn't the best plan, trying to outrun demons, but he'd only just started to enjoy his line of work again with Sora involved. He didn't want to lose that already.

Right before he made his move, Torsten lowered his weapon to the ground. "The thief is right. Somewhere, in these woods, there is an Arch Warlock more powerful than she will ever be," he said pointing to Sora. "So powerful, he has masked his presence from you. Help us locate him, and you will be rewarded."

The satyr laughed. "And what, mortal, could you possibly reward us with. Your silly gold autlas? Garish jewels? You mortals have no idea how worthless your riches truly are."

Torsten didn't answer. What could he offer? A demon wouldn't have any need to ask for a name, or a title, or a castle. Whitney wasn't sure what they really wanted.

."You can have the warlock," Whitney said. Torsten's gaze snapped toward him.

"No, he belongs to the Crown," Torsten said. "He must answer for his crimes."

"Sorry, Torsten, I know they're all the same to you, but if it's between some traitor named Redstar and Sora, it's an easy decision." He flashed her a nervous grin. He couldn't tell if she sent one back, as being upside down so long had her looking faint.

"That was not our arrangement."

"Then keep your name." Whitney faced the satyr. "Maybe you can't mate with the warlock…or whatever you do… but I'm sure you'll find a way to use him."

The satyr's brow furrowed again as if intrigued. The fact that he hadn't dismissed the offer immediately had Whitney feeling optimistic.

A guttural sound from the woods suddenly drew the satyr's focus. The vine wrapping Sora's ankle shriveled to its natural form, and she fell. Whitney dropped his daggers, sprawled out and caught her before her head hit the ground.

The satyr backed up. "What is this? What trick are you playing?"

Whitney didn't know what was happening either. He helped Sora sit upright while she clutched her head.

"Was that you?" Torsten asked her.

She shook her head.

The satyr glanced over his shoulder in both directions, panic twisting his goat-like features.

"What's happening?" Whitney questioned

Another deep growl resonated from the depths of the darkness. Whitney had one arm around Sora and the other squeezing her bloody hand without noticing, then the gnashing snout of a dire wolf broke through the black. It crashed into a pair of satyrs, catching them off guard and throwing them to the ground. Their screams could have even curdled the blood of King Liam himself.

It pounced onto the lead satyr, but the demon batted it away but received a long gash across its chest for the effort.

A whistle sounded from the woods. The shaggy, brown, dire wolf responded by pressing a massive paw firmly against the satyr's chest, claws drawing thin lines of black blood. The other satyrs scrambled and retreated.

"What the… what?" Whitney said under his breath. At the same time, he noticed that he was holding Sora's hand and quickly released it. He hoped she was too lightheaded to realize.

"Torsten, my friend!" Uriah Davies stepped out of the woods, monk's robe swishing at his heels, a torch in his hands.

"Uriah?" Torsten said.

He whistled again, and the dire wolf stepped off the satyr. Then he walked up to it, drew his sword, and positioned the blade against the demon's throat.

"They are under my protection," he said. "Is that understood?"

The satyr's hooves kicked, and he bleated. The dire wolf growled and snapped, a stream of saliva spattering from its lips. It was then Torsten realized the wolf was the very same pack leader he'd fought off days ago. His sword had left a thick, hairless scar across its massive chest.

"Yes," the satyr said. The word came more like the hiss of a serpent. It stumbled to its hooves and hopped away, limping.

XXVII

THE KNIGHT

While Whitney attended to the Panpingese witch, Torsten stared at the hulking wolf standing behind his old friend and former Wearer of White, Uriah Davies. He had no idea what to say, or even think.

Uriah extended his torch in front of Torsten's face. "What's the matter, old friend?" he asked. "You look like you've seen a ghost."

"Only a friend I no longer recognize."

"I hope to change that," Uriah said. "I've been tracking you long enough to see the licking you gave those gray-skinned curs. I decided I couldn't let you march down here and get yourself killed alone like a fool."

Torsten swallowed the lump forming in his throat. "How, Uriah?" he asked.

Uriah glanced from side to side as if surprised by the question, then realized where Torsten was looking. "The wolf? The goddess' tongue fares well with them. Far more efficient than a sword."

Before Torsten could answer, he heard Sora snap, "I'm fine!" at Whitney. Then she stomped over. "Is that a dire wolf in South Pantego?" she questioned.

"I told you before, the warlock named Red—hold on." Whitney

plucked his daggers off the ground, then turned to face Uriah with both pointed at him. "What are you doing with this beast? You involved with Redstar?"

The growl of the wolf shut him up quickly.

"Ah, you must be Whitney," Uriah said. "We narrowly avoided each other in my encampment outside Oxgate, but I hear you are not shy about professing your name and your cunning."

"Sounds like me." He chuckled nervously and backed away as the wolf circled in front of Uriah, never averting its piercing gaze.

"Whitney, let me handle this," Torsten said.

"This is a friend of yours?" Whitney asked. "Cult leaders, thieves, and blood mages… you really should work on the company you keep."

Torsten clenched his jaw.

"I'm so sorry for how you were treated," Uriah said, still looking at Whitney. "I am former Wearer of White, Uriah Davies. The knight and I are old friends."

"If cages and blades are how you treat friends, I'd hate to be your enemy," Whitney said.

"Wait," Sora said. "This man leads the cult that captured you?"

"What do you want, Uriah?" Torsten interceded. "I already told you, I will not be party to… whatever darkness it is you have turned to."

"It is the light, brother. The truth that I have found. This mad search for the Queen's lost brother is a waste of time and effort. He lost his way. We should be focusing our efforts on killing Bliss."

"I appreciate your help, Uriah…" Torsten said, beginning to walk away, "…but our lives no longer travel the same path. This is where we part ways."

"Please, Torsten. Trust me as you once did. There is evil in this place that doesn't care what god we whisper to in the darkness."

"I do not worship in secret as you do, *friend.*"

"You must listen to reason," Uriah said. "The spid—"

Torsten stuck out his massive arm and clutched Uriah by the throat. The wolf snarled, but the old former knight waved it down. "Enough!" Torsten bellowed. He was so irritated he tried to heave Uriah off his feet, but pain flowered in his shoulder again. He clutched the arrow wound he'd carried since escaping the Black Sands and fell to a knee. He had to use his sword to stay upright.

"By Nesilia, your wound," Uriah said. He helped him take a seat against a tree. He lifted the plating of Torsten's pauldron to reveal the wound. Half of an arrow's shaft stuck out of the back of his shoulder, surrounded by puss and blood.

Whitney released a gagging sound. "That blood was from an arrow? How in Elsewhere did you get that?"

"Did you learn nothing under my tutelage?" Uriah said, ignoring the thief. "You let a wound like this fester with no dressing?"

"I was a little preoccupied trying to save the kingdom," Torsten said, pain making his voice hoarse. He couldn't even lift his arm any longer. "Something you wouldn't know anything about."

"Mine is the work of all mortals. Now stop being so stubborn. If we don't clean that wound, your kingdom, along with the rest of us, will perish."

Uriah positioned himself with firm footing and wrapped a hand around the broken stump of the arrow. Torsten winced and stared at his old friend. A messy gray beard hugged his chin, masking wrinkles deep as the caverns of the Dragon's Tail. He looked exactly the same as the day he'd left to chase Redstar into these very woods… except in his eyes. Something was different there, darker maybe, now that he'd turned to the Buried Goddess.

"It's a Shesaitju thorn arrow," Uriah said. Torsten nodded in understanding. Shesaitju arrows were four-pronged, with backward facing spikes. They didn't fly as far or as accurately, but once they went in, they couldn't be yanked out without causing a heap more damage. They were especially effective in naval combat, clinging onto enemy ships.

"Shesaitju?" Sora asked, eyes going wide.

"Yeah, I second that question," Whitney said. "There are Black Sands. Here? I mean, as the King's Shield knows, fighting them is my specialty, but…"

"They're camped in the swamp, to the far east along Trader's Bay you fool," Torsten growled, the pain making Whitney even more insufferable. "An army, prepared to attack the Glass Kingdom with nobody left to defend it. So, the faster we get on with this, the faster we might have a chance to stop them."

"We didn't see a camp," Whitney said, looking to the ground as if he were insulted. Like he even could be.

"Of course, you didn't. You couldn't find a—"

Uriah suddenly pushed. Torsten didn't even have time to scream as the arrow plunged all the way through his shoulder. He just sat, shaking, as the shaft fell to the ground.

"There you go, old friend." Uriah patted his other shoulder. "Now's the fun part. Thief, use my torch to heat your blade."

Hearing Uriah issue orders brought Torsten back to simpler times following Liam into battle, though it may have been the pain.

"I'm sorry, since when do you give me orders?" Whitney said.

"Just listen to him," Torsten moaned.

"If we do not seal the wound, infection is likely," Uriah said. "That will kill him quicker than any satyr or spider—Bliss or not."

Whitney took the torch, eyed it quizzically. "You want me to…"

"Men," Sora sighed. "Don't do it, Whitney, unless you want his screams to attract whatever out there is worse than satyrs. I can heal him. I won't let the Shesaitju kill anybody else."

"Sora, last time you almost—"

"Last time, the wound was fatal. This is just one hateful knight being a baby."

"I don't want to have to carry you."

"You won't." Sora blew by Whitney toward Torsten. At some point, she'd retrieved her knife and now held it over her bandaged palm.

"What is this?" Torsten asked.

"You're sure you are capable?" Uriah asked.

Sora nodded.

"Capable of what?" Torsten said.

"I could sense how special you were the moment I saw you, blood mage," Uriah said. "Nesilia would welcome you with open arms."

"Good for her," Sora said.

Uriah placed a hand on Torsten's good shoulder to keep him steady. Torsten watched in horror as the Panpingese witch knelt in front of him, then slowly slid her blade across her hand. She cut deep, flinching as the blood oozed out.

"What is this madness?" Torsten said. He fidgeted as Sora reached toward him, but Uriah held him steady. "In the name of Iam, don't you lay your accursed hand on me!"

"I am sorry if you're not a fan of blood magic. But yours is not the only life at risk here. Now hold still."

"Watch out, he's bigger than that rancher," Whitney said. "And infinitely more bullheaded."

Torsten continued to resist. "I will not be party to this heresy!"

Sora lay her bloodied hand over the wound even as Torsten protested. The moment the bond was made, Torsten was rendered still. Cool blue smoke rose from the bloody hole and Sora grimaced as if in incredible pain. Immediately, it stopped hurting, but he felt a deep chill spreading up his arm and across his chest—cold like he'd been half-buried in Winter's Thumb.

"Iam protect me," he whispered over and over... though he realized he was saying no words. His throat was closed, and he couldn't speak. He pawed for his necklace of Iam's Eye before remembering he'd given it to Abigail.

Then, as suddenly as it had appeared, the feeling was gone. Sora fell back into Whitney's waiting arms, panting uncontrollably.

Torsten sprang to his feet. He gasped, then glanced down. Where there had just been a hole, only a streak of red and dried mud remained around a barely visible scar on either side of his shoulder. He stretched his arm, rotating it in wide circles. No blood. No puss. No gaping wound. He felt completely fine.

"Where did you learn to do that?" a wide-eyed Uriah asked.

"My teacher says it comes naturally to me... said..." Sora muttered, barely able to speak above a whisper. The magic left Torsten feeling like he could face any foe but left her unable to stand without Whitney's help.

"I would like to meet—"

"What is this devilry?" Torsten barked, his shock finally waning enough for him to speak.

"I healed you, you ungrateful triss," Sora said.

"With the powers of the fallen gods themselves!"

"You could show a little gratitude, Torsten," Whitney said. "That takes a lot out of her."

"To her?" Torsten said, aghast. "I don't even know who *she* is, but she has no place here."

"She's an old friend from the homestead that wanted to help," Whitney said.

"Why am I not surprised that you are friends with a witch?"

"Better than a knight turned cult leader, no offense." Whitney nodded in Uriah's direction.

Sora pulled herself free of Whitney. Beads of sweat rolled down her forehead as she huffed. She looked like she was ready to pass out. "You are the most insufferable, hateful, ignorant—"

Exhaustion sent her back into Whitney's arms. Before she fell, Torsten could have sworn he saw small flames bursting in her hazel eyes, more gold than brown. He saw something in them—something familiar.

"Everyone stop." Uriah's voice was soft but authoritative. It was almost as if the very words were a spell. Torsten couldn't help but comply with his old mentor.

"This is helping no one, Torsten," he said. "If you only heed my advice once more, heed this, thank the lady, and let us destroy Bliss together— like old times."

Torsten shifted the aim of his ire. "There is nothing about this that resembles 'old times.' My mission is to find Redstar, and forgive me, but I will not take the word of a deserter. I don't care who you are."

"I don't know, I think we let him tag along," Whitney said.

"He locked us both in cages! Lies spew from his mouth now as if it is his very nature."

"He saved our skins this time. Plus… a dire wolf? There's a good chance we are going to need him."

"Then go with him. Go with both these heretics. My soul is with Iam and the Glass alone." Torsten snatched up his sword, placed it in his back-scabbard and started trudging away.

"You promised me a name!" Whitney shouted. Torsten didn't even slow down.

"Stop," Uriah said. "Let me lead you to where I know Redstar was last seen."

"Why would you know that?" Whitney asked.

Torsten stopped and spun back. Uriah stood, calmly stroking the neck of his wolf. "Yes," Torsten said. "Why would you know that?"

"Don't misunderstand," Uriah replied. "I never did find the man after Oleander sent me after him, but I've heard of his exploits. His followers left him to die here after they learned their Arch Warlock planned to make an offering to Bliss and betray their mission for vengeance. Now, as you know, we continue the great cause he abandoned."

Torsten stormed back, hand on the grip of his sword. The giant wolf at Uriah's side crouched and let out a low growl, the hair on his back rising. "You said he abandoned them to come here, not that they were with him."

"I'm sorry, Torsten," Uriah said. He rested a hand on the wolf's head. The beast calmed immediately. "I wanted to tell you everything, but you wouldn't listen to reason. I didn't want you to go chasing ghosts."

"That doesn't surprise me," Sora muttered, still using Whitney as a crutch.

"You betrayed me and the Glass," Torsten said. "You betrayed Iam. Your King!"

"Do you serve Queen Oleander?" Uriah said.

"I serve all the royal family."

"Even her?"

Torsten nodded.

"Why?" Uriah asked. "What has she ever done for you?"

"She is the wife of Liam and the mother of *our* present king—if Liam trusted her, so shall I."

"She's not bad to look at either," Whitney added. Torsten and Sora shot daggers his way. "What? I met her."

"You did not," Sora said.

"Well, I saw her. Running. From a great distance."

"I tried to tell you the truth in the ruins," Uriah continued. "The truth on many things, but you would not see. Nesilia is not who you believe her to be, Torsten. Imagine Iam to be like King Liam."

"More than any man who ever lived," Torsten said, back straight and head tall.

"Now imagine Nesilia as the Queen."

"Blasphemy!" Torsten shouted.

"The answers were all there on that ancient mural. You didn't want to hear the legend then, but now you must. When I heard it from Redstar's lost disciples, I finally saw. I knew what I had to do."

Uriah cleared his throat and began to sing softly. His voice was raspy, coarse, but Torsten and the others couldn't help but listen.

> *When last the dew drops come to dry*
> *Clouds and heavens unleash a cry*
> *Dragons bellow, thunder cracks*
> *When truth's forsaken, the sky grows black*
>
> *The fire levels meadow plains*
> *And smoke devours; ne'er wains*
> *Beneath the earth her death she feigns*
> *The God and Goddess cease their reigns*

"This is absurd," Torsten interrupted.

Whitney hushed him. "Let him continue, I liked the tune."

Uriah smiled and went on.

> *Nary a whisper; nary a word*
> *Nary a flight of galler bird*
> *It ended terse with his anger unleashed*
> *The One Who Remains turned into a beast*
>
> *Eye always wary and never known fear*
> *Abruptly disrupted by a single shed tear*
> *Beneath soil and stone, the Lady awaits*
> *The heart of her lover shall ne'er abate*
>
> *Biding her time, her pain like a flood*
> *Alone in the darkness, she longs for the blood*
> *In the name of the Lady, in the name of the Lord*
> *Shall settle the score with power and sword*
>
> *Then she may arise, in glorious day*

Through will and through fire, her enemies slain
Forgotten, abandoned, but no longer bound
From Elsewhere and exile, she'll receive her crown

When he was done, the silence was palpable. Not even Whitney spoke.

"That could be about anything," Torsten finally rebuked. "Bard's songs and poet's musings."

"Sounds pretty clear to me," Whitney said. Sora slapped his arm.

"They were lovers, Torsten," Uriah said. "It is the lie we've all been taught. That Iam stood alone in defense of man during the God Feud as his brethren destroyed each other in their arrogance. But he was not alone. She was there, and she sacrificed herself so he may end the feud. You see, to follow Iam is to follow Nesilia. They are bound eternally like you to your king and country. Why shouldn't even Iam find love?"

Torsten stared, incredulous.

"I'm not asking you to believe fully at this moment," Uriah continued. "But please, trust the man you once knew?" He extended his hand. "It is the One Who Remained who is the root of all evil in this world. Redstar's followers showed me that after I survived her wrath. She is spider, she is satyr, she is every foul demon loosed upon our world from Elsewhere. But most of all, she is Bliss, and we must snuff out that evil in the name of the light."

"I'm confused," Whitney said after a brief silence. Torsten's head whipped toward him like a powder keg had gone off. "Aren't we here to steal a doll?"

"A powerful Drav Cra orepul cursed by a rejected brother," Uriah clarified. "Redstar sought to bring it as offering to Bliss. If he truly did so, it would be where his followers claim they abandoned him, at the lair of The One who remained. The lair of Spider Queen Bliss."

"Blasphemy," Torsten said again, but no one was listening anymore.

"Then we have to go there," Sora declared. Her strength seemed to have returned, leaving Whitney's side and standing on her own, dark eyes glimmering.

She appeared to care more about the quest than the thief even without any promised reward. But Torsten had encountered enough blood mages in cults and covens throughout the kingdom—followers of Nesilia and other fallen gods, or worst of all, followers of nothing at all, those who simply desired power for power's sake. Only demons were more dangerous.

"I will take you there," Uriah said. "But only on one condition."

"And what might that be?" Torsten said through his teeth.

"That if you find what you're looking for there, you will consider helping us destroy Bliss. I will not judge should you walk away, but when you see what wickedness she is capable of, I believe you will see as I do, holy knight. Forget Nesilia or Iam. If you are truly tasked with shielding the Glass Kingdom, you will know that such evil cannot endure, as I do."

"I know what I'll choose," Whitney said.

"A fight?" Sora said.

He scoffed. "Of course, it seems fair to me."

The teachings of Iam warned against any mortal who would turn to Elsewhere for power, but as Torsten scanned the ranks of the three unexpected people he'd found company with in the Webbed Woods, he realized the truth. If he had to risk the wrath of Iam to save the Glass, then so be it. If the grief-stricken Queen allowed that heathen army of Black Sands to invade, the kingdom of Iam would fall regardless. They were the true power to fear, not an imagined goddess spider.

Torsten clasped Uriah's hand and pulled him in close. "Do not betray us."

"We serve the same side." Uriah snapped his fingers, and five cultists emerged from behind trees. They wore those same terrifying, expressionless masks as they had in Oxgate, except the one in the middle. The pale, gaunt, Drav Cra warlock no longer bothered to hide what he really was.

Whitney spun, one hand on the hilt of a dagger and the other holding Sora. "Oh, not these guys again."

Torsten's hand instinctively went to his weapon as well.

"Relax," Uriah said. "They work with me now. We will lead you."

Uriah, the dire wolf, and his followers set off through the forest. Torsten eyed Whitney and Sora who, like him, hesitated to follow a fallen knight and a bunch of the Buried Goddess' followers further into the blackness of the Webbed Woods. Sora's uncertain expression made Torsten feel better that, at least, maybe she wasn't a murderous cultist like them, and was merely a young, displaced Panpingese woman who'd been tempted by the dark arts and gone astray.

Torsten took a deep breath, lowered his hand from his sword, and waved them along. Finding anything in the Webbed Woods except for killer vines and demonic satyrs seemed impossible without guides.

What choice was there?

XXVIII

THE THIEF

"There's another!" Whitney said, pointing at one of the red blisters on a tree trunk. None of his companions knew what they were, but they seemed harmless enough, and it was passing the time.

"No one else is playing this stupid game," Sora said.

"We've been walking through the canvas of the world's most boring painter. Just dark greens and black and then suddenly… look, darker green! Over and over again. I have to do something to stay sane."

"It's only been a couple of hours, Whit."

"Longest of my life," Whitney complained.

"Won't be much farther," Uriah said. His pet—the scariest pet alive—a dire wolf, still stalked beside him, occasionally sniffing at shrubs shrouded in darkness. His cultist followers kept a wide perimeter, nothing but shadows moving with them.

Uriah stopped suddenly. He said something in Drav Crava and his followers gathered, then sprinted off in another direction.

"What did you say?" Whitney asked.

"I told them to scout ahead," Uriah replied. "We're not far."

"You're sure where we're going is where Redstar was last seen?" Torsten said.

"I'm sure you'll find his rotting remains, yes."

"Lovely thought," Whitney said.

"I didn't say it would be lovely or easy," Uriah said. "I've made it clear from the start: this quest is not smart. Bliss is the true enemy."

Torsten grunted but kept plowing forward. His sword was out now, and he used it to carve a path through vines and branches. The deeper they delved into the woods, the more congested they grew. Maybe it was the smothering darkness making Whitney imagine it, but he could barely stretch out his arm in any direction without hitting a tree, as if they were closing in all around them. The smell of death and decay surged stronger the deeper into the woods they traveled.

"When you say, 'we're not far,' what does that mean to you?" Whitney asked after Iam knows how much longer walking. His legs were beginning to grow sore.

"Do you ever stop talking?" Torsten spat. "Keep quiet, or we're going to end up attracting more enemies."

"Are you forgetting about the giant wolf flanking us?"

"You can call him Gryff," Uriah said.

"It's got a name?" Whitney said.

Uriah raised one hand to stop everyone. One of his cultists suddenly appeared from around a tree and nearly gave Whitney a heart attack.

Whitney squeezed Sora's arm. Her glare frightened him further. She wasn't lightheaded and docile from being hung upside down anymore.

The cultist said something in Drav Crava. Uriah replied, then thanked him. He pointed over Torsten's shoulder. "See that ridge? Her lair is just beyond, but we don't believe her to be there."

"Why is that?" Torsten asked. "I'm not fluent in Drav Crava."

"Who cares? Count your blessings, holy man," Whitney said.

"A Wearer should be fluent in all language of the realm, Torsten," Uriah said.

"You're in no place to lecture me on how to serve the Glass," Torsten growled, though he knew Uriah was probably right.

"We've been studying Bliss since Redstar woke her to make his offering. She has several nests throughout the woods and tends to move when her babies are in danger."

"Her babies—geesh," Whitney scoffed.

"My men had orders to go to another nest and draw her attention."

"You're just telling us this now?" Torsten questioned. "Is that true?"

The masked cultists nodded, wordless.

"They appear to have done their jobs. If Bliss were here, her children would already be upon us. Now, let us move hastily and search her lair for Redstar before the distraction wears off. Then you'll see what I've been trying to tell you."

"I doubt it," Torsten said.

They continued on, but something ate at Whitney. After a short walk, he gave Uriah's shoulder a tug.

"I just have one question," Whitney said, keeping his voice low.

"Yes, thief?" Uriah answered.

"What if we decided not to let you tag along? I mean, I don't plan on sticking around to fight any Spider Queens for a guy who locked me in a cage, but you seem pretty confident *he* will." He gestured to Torsten who was up ahead slashing a path through more vines.

"I've known your leader for many years. I was certain he would press onward no matter what. All roads lead to this place. If chasing Redstar's ghost is what's needed to open his eyes, so be it. Your quest, mine, it is as if we were all—"

"Fated to meet," Sora finished for him.

He turned back and smiled like the old cotter in every village. That one you can't help but love and listen to as he rambles on. Like old man Wetzel who'd somehow turned Sora into a blood mage. Whitney wasn't sure if he liked that smile.

"He's not our leader," Whitney remarked.

"Do not fool yourself, boy," Uriah said. "Sir Torsten Unger is every-one's leader in the Glass."

"Ah, hog's piss," Whitney spat. "Only reason I'm in this shog is me."

Torsten stopped at a clearing and looked back. "Iam's hand is in every-thing that happens on Pantego," he said. "It's not our place to question it."

Whitney's eyes nearly rolled through the back of his head. He didn't think Torsten had been listening, but it didn't matter. He wasn't about to take anything back.

They reached Torsten's side and saw why he'd stopped. In the small clearing of trees was a protrusion of rock with little more than a narrow hole in the side. There was no way it could be Bliss' place. Whitney had expected something more, something grander—like a dragon's lair. Truth be told, he'd never seen a dragon's lair, not even that of a sleeping one. The one he'd once snuck by was a tiny wyvern stuck in a birdcage. A curiosity belonging to some Panping mystic in a monastery that smelled like incense and loneliness.

"Welcome to Bliss' lair," Uriah said. "This is where Redstar led his followers before they discovered his true intentions and left him for dead. If Pi's orepul is anywhere in these woods, it will be here."

"Then let us find it!" Torsten all but shouted as he began trekking forward again.

"Wait," Uriah said.

"What now?" Torsten growled.

"Even if Bliss is not present, it's not wise for us to traipse in there like we own the place and draw her attention back. Her senses are nothing like ours. They are divine."

"What do you suggest then?" Torsten said, seething.

"You brought a thief for a reason, didn't you?" Uriah placed a hand on Whitney's shoulder. "You see? Fate is again with us."

Whitney was barely paying attention. "Wait, what?"

"I believe you should go in alone, search the lair for Redstar—or what remains of him—and find what you came here for."

"No way. I am a thief, not a monster slayer."

"This should be nothing after Darkings' place," Sora added with a snicker.

"You go in then! I can't summon fire."

"As I've said, Bliss has been drawn away by the others," Uriah said. "Her children follow her like chicks to a hen. There shouldn't be any monsters to slay."

"Shouldn't? *Shouldn't* be any?" Whitney took a step back.

"I hate to say it, but he's right," Torsten said. "By Iam's Light, this is clearly the reason I broke you out of prison, *greatest thief in Pantego*. If you still want that name, this is how you earn it."

Whitney folded his arms. "It's 'world's greatest thief.'"

"Pretend it's only a dragon." Sora gave him a playful slap on the back.

He released a nervous chuckle. They were right. All that boasting that he could steal from a mythical spider, and now he'd be forced to prove it.

You and your big mouth, Whitney.

Running seemed like the smarter option, if not for the warm breath of Gryff the dire wolf against his back.

They all began walking again, slower this time, and he scurried to keep up.

"What am I supposed to do if I get in there and a massive spider attacks me?" he asked.

"Were you taught to pray as a child?" Torsten asked.

"Was that a joke, Sir Knight? I'm so proud of you."

"What a blessing," Torsten grunted.

Whitney sighed. "Fine. I'll pop in for a—hey look! The stars are finally peeking through." Lights glittered around the stray branches and vines bridging the break in the canopy over the cavern's narrow entry.

"Are those stars… swaying?" Sora asked. They visibly swung back and forth, like the crystal balls in the Glass Castle during the masquerade.

"Those aren't stars," Uriah said. "Those are eyes."

Now that the Celeste's light illuminated the woods, Whitney could see thousands of eyeballs hanging by threads of webbing everywhere he looked. He retched. Sora cursed as some of his stomach contents splashed onto her boot.

Knowing what they were made the smell of death became nearly over-whelming, even if he imagined it. Whitney pulled the front of his silly, silk shirt up over his nose but if it helped at all, it was minimal. He regretted not choosing something more practical from Darkings' house.

"This is it?" he said, stalling outside the entry. "I expected something more like when I raided the ancient tombs at the Brotlebir borders. You've never seen their equal."

"In you go," Torsten said. "This is why you were hired."

"I might have to renegotiate my price," Whitney said.

"You left me for dead," Torsten bristled. "You're lucky if you get anything at all."

"I didn't—you know, if something happens to me in there, you're going to miss me."

Torsten replied with a chortle, then grabbed the back of Whitney's shirt and gave him a shove. Whitney hesitated in the maw, then felt a hand on his elbow. He turned to see Sora standing there.

"Just be careful?" She didn't look him in the eye, just cleared her throat and said, "Go on, oh great one."

"Right," Whitney said, turning. He cracked his knuckles. "So, I just…" He motioned with his hands to indicate crawling inside. "Feet first? Head first? How does one crawl into the den of a murderous, giant spider?" When nobody offered a good idea, he decided to go with the latter and managed to squeeze halfway in. "Tight… fit…"

"Just hurry up," Torsten said, his voice muffled and barely audible from inside the hole.

The tunnel was narrow and grew narrower. His hand brushed up against something soft and squishy. The red blister burst, a shower of clear liquid spraying out and covering his arm and chest. Tiny, transparent-looking spiders poured out, scurrying in every direction. He fought back the urge to throw up again.

"Just keep crawling," he whispered to himself. "They're babies. What's more harmless than a baby?"

Where there weren't egg sacs, the walls perspired with murky water. His mind raced back to just how many blisters he'd seen on their way into the heart of the woods. They must have numbered in the hundreds or even thousands. If each of them was this full of spiders….

A shiver stole any warmth he had left in him.

His mind raced back to the day at the Twilight Manor when he'd met that little ale-keg of a dwarf, Grint. It seemed a lifetime ago. How would things have turned out had he not boasted quite so proudly? *Steal the crown from a king? Yig and shog, what a stupid idea.* From dead and dying kings, to probably dying in the lair of a spider queen.

Whitney arrived at a fork. Without a coin to flip to decide which way to go, he simply closed his eyes and chose. He had one arm in when he realized the ground beneath his hand was supple, like a web.

Exactly like a web.

His elbow tore through, and he plummeted, bumping and scraping flailing appendages, too shocked to scream. He braced for impact. It was impossible to tell how far down he'd gone when he finally crashed into a pile of sticks. They clamored against the wall, banging and tapping in an almost melodic, musical tune.

"'You're lucky if you get anything at all,'" Whitney said like a child, imitating Torsten's voice. Then, "I'll give you luck."

Something dug into his lower back. He reached around and wrapped his hand around what felt like a smooth, thick branch. He tugged, and it came loose.

A dim light came from somewhere. He couldn't find its source, but it was bright enough for him to make out what appeared to be a femur bone —a human femur bone. Grossed out again, he wriggled free, the ground beneath him shifting with each motion. More rattling; a symphony of death. Not sticks, but skulls, bones, ribcages, and even rusted remnants of armor from Glass soldiers rolled around below as Whitney scrambled to find his footing. It was almost as if he was swimming.

He finally found stable ground a few meters away and hopped between both feet to shake the smaller bones off his body.

"Perfect," he said to no one. "Just perfect."

Whitney looked up and saw the passage he'd fallen through, shuddered. Somehow the cave was even colder now. He could see his own breath. He tried not to think about how many adventurers had fallen to their deaths. Enough to create a pile of bones so high that he didn't join them.

He searched the room. Every square centimeter of the walls and ceiling were covered in egg sacs. From above, more eyeballs hung like ornamental orbs. Each one stared at Whitney. As he turned, he found the tiny shaft where the light was coming from. Whitney thought twice, then decided anything was better than being stuck with corpses.

He checked the ground to make sure it wasn't another hole, then shimmied inside and thanked any gods who might be listening that it was just a short tunnel which opened into a big, dark, auricle-shaped room.

Moonlight sifted in through several man-sized holes above. They looked like pinpricks from this distance. He crouched just in case, although there wasn't any sign that anything other than him was alive in the whole space. Even the sacs of unhatched baby spiders were missing. He shivered again at the thought.

As he delved further into the room, he saw thick stone columns at the center connected by thinner, stone protrusions. While there were no egg-sacs in this room, the stone was covered in puffy, white blotches.

He climbed three shallow steps into the middle of the chamber. His heart thumped against his ribcage as he looked upward. From his new vantage, he realized that the columns and protrusions weren't that at all. They formed the shape of a massive web spanning out to all corners of the room.

Then one of the puffy white spots stuck to it moved. Whitney drew his curved daggers and spun, ready to fight before he realized that half the spots were moving. They were food, beasts and men strung up to the grand web like how normal-sized spiders string up flies.

"'It'll be empty,'" Whitney whispered to himself, now mocking Uriah. "'Bliss won't be around anywhere.'"

Last time Whitney checked, no one leaves their food for too long, and it was clear that Bliss' dinner resided in those puffy white sacks. His throat was dry, and he felt sick. He searched the room for any route of escape.

He didn't become the world's greatest thief by running away from a challenge. He did, however, run away from giant scary monsters. If he didn't, he'd have had an awfully short career.

Taking a deep breath, he switched his targeting from a place of escape to making sure he was alone but for Bliss' squirming, unfortunate prey. As far as he could tell, there wasn't even a sign of smaller spiders or rodents.

If the rats are afraid of this place...

He drove the thought out of his mind and reminded himself of the mission; find some stupid, little kid's stupid, little doll. Get back to Yarrington, and be crowned the hero of the day. Earn a new name to muck up in future adventures with his promising new partner in crime.

"Where does a giant spider keep a doll?" he asked. There was no chest filled with loot, which was the image he'd conjured up throughout the journey. Though, he wasn't sure what a spider might need with gold and jewels.

What am I looking for? Dead bodies?

There were plenty of those.

Rusted old chestplates?

Definitely those too.

One thing was for certain, he needed to get out from beneath the web and explore the massive room.

How big it really was didn't become clear until he realized the specks against the far wall were piles of human remains. His feeling of nausea returned in full force. He'd become somewhat used to the smell of the death that enveloped him—but every time he saw new sources, it returned with a fresh fire.

A full set of pearly Shieldsman armor similar to the one Torsten wore, sat against a pile of more Shieldsman armor. Whitney knew plenty of Glass Kingdom men had been sent on this mad quest before, so it was as good as any place to start.

He took one step, then heard a sound like a tarp unfolding. He looked up but saw nothing. As he went to glance behind him, something fuzzy stroked his jaw.

"So, you're the newest in a long line of failures to enter my lair? How handsome."

The voice came from behind him. It was smooth, sultry even. Whitney's whole body froze, and he clamped his eyes tight. Whatever it was tilted his head from side to side as if studying him before releasing him.

"You can open your eyes, Mr. Fierstown," she said. "I won't bite… yet." Her laugh was infectious, like one of the ladies of Old Yarrington.

Whitney complied, and a creature that could be none other than Bliss circled around in front of him.

"My, my, aren't you handsome?" she said.

Whitney just stared at her, mouth agape. The one thing no one prepared him for was how gorgeous Bliss would be. Gorgeous and… naked. Sure, her lower half was a gruesome, horrid, massive, bulbous, spider body, but her top half was all woman.

"Go on, say something," she said, licking her lips.

"You—you weren't supposed to be here," he mustered the courage to say.

She laughed again, this time it wasn't quite as charming. "You steal your way into my home and then complain that I'm here? And here I thought you were supposed to be some great thief."

"How… how do you know who I am?"

"Did your traveling companion tell you nothing?" She reared up on her back four legs, the front four waving in the air. "I am a Goddess!"

She came down hard, and the ground shook. Dust and loose webs poured from above, coalescing into the light from the holes above. A loud thump drew Whitney's attention, and he glanced over to see one of the bodies who'd been rolled up in webbing fall from above, landing just a few meters away.

Whitney took a step backward. His foot slipped off a short step, twisting his ankle. He tumbled, and one of his daggers fell loose, sliding across the floor.

"Try to keep your feet, mortal," Bliss said. "It's no fun without a struggle."

She strode forward and used one of her legs to flip him upright. The movement was so fluid and otherworldly it made Whitney's heart pause. He'd never seen anything to compare. It was less like she'd walked and more like she glided toward him. She leaned in close, and he could smell her rotting breath.

"You're going to be delicious," she said. "Impure meat is so much... juicier."

Whitney took off, gritting his teeth through the pain of his ankle. Her laugh continued, and by the sound of it, she wasn't pursuing.

"Oh, I do love a chase!" she said.

Before Whitney could register the movement, she stood on the wall in front of him, peering down like an owl from a perch or, he supposed, like a spider from its web. She lowered her abdomen, and a spray of webbing shot out and landed at Whitney's feet.

He dodged and strafed sideways, then searched frantically and spotted the nearest tunnel. There were many of them all around the lair, a dozen ways Bliss could've snuck up on him. When he looked back, she was gone.

He pushed his legs as fast as they could go. The tunnel wasn't far, but it might as well have been Winde Port. He was closing in when he heard her cackle echoing all around him, sounding almost as if it originated within his head.

He kept running.

One of her spiny feet pressed against his chest when he was only a few strides away. He collapsed onto his back, gasping for air. He wished he hadn't. The smell gagged him and made it even harder to catch his breath.

"Good show, boy," she said, "but I tire of games."

"Are you sure?" he said. "I can think of a few more."

"Quiet now. If you struggle, it will only be worse."

Her legs wrenched their way beneath him and forced him onto his stomach.

Whitney momentarily broke free of her grasp, gripped his remaining dagger and slashed upward. He caught only air, but she stumbled backward. He hopped up and thrust at her.

"Now, you listen," he said. "Let's come to some sort of deal, and I promise I won't cut you into pieces." He thrust again, and as he did, she whipped her body around. A thick spray of webby paste glued his mouth shut, and as she came back around, one of her legs smacked the blade out of his hand.

"You talk far too much for such a useless creature," she said.

She brought her full body over him, towering. Whitney tripped again as he cowered, landing on his rear.

He pawed at his mouth.

She yanked at his legs.

He began rolling at a nauseating rate, seeing the floor and then the ceiling, over and over. He felt it on his calves first, the thick webbing drawing them closed so he could no longer kick. He tried to fight, slapping at her legs at any chance he could find. It was no use. His arms were bound, his left tight against his side, the right pinned uncomfortably against his chest. She reached his neck before stopping.

"Now, I will take your eyes just like all the rest," she said. "You will forever watch as the world passes you by, damned to never leave this plane."

Whitney wasn't sure what he screamed into his sealed lips. Curses or prayers, anything he could think of. But she couldn't hear him. No one could. He was all alone and was going to die at the hands of a spider goddess.

She lowered her face until it was mere centimeters from his. Up close, her beauty was even more undeniable. Her eyes were dark and deep purple, mesmerizing, and her face as fair as any maiden he'd seen across

Pantego. Only instead of hair and ears, a silver carapace wrapped her head and stuck out on either side like the points of a crown.

"Be still," she said. "Your friends will be with you soon. All you pathetic mortals will be."

She pressed her lips against his, the paste covering his mouth melting away at her touch. He felt her tongue against his teeth, tasted blood.

When she pulled away, he found himself growing sleepy and numb, like he'd imbibed an entire bar's worth of ale.

"We haven't even… haven't even gone on our first date yet," he slurred.

The next thing he tried to say was a garbled mess. Bliss smiled down at him as her web stretched over his face and everything went dark.

XXIX

THE KNIGHT

"It's been too long," Sora said. "I'm going in."

She stood, but Torsten grabbed her arm. "Relax, nothing can kill that man," he said. He almost felt bad when he added, "He's like a cockroach."

Her face betrayed her guilt.

"He's going to be fine," Torsten assured.

"We sent him in there alone," she said. "What if Uriah is wrong? What if Bliss is in there waiting for him?"

"There are many things Uriah Davies is, but I have fought at his side many times. There is no finer commander."

Sora glanced over at him, and Torsten did the same. He paced back and forth in front of the cave, murmuring to his dire wolf under his breath. Torsten had to admit, he was far from the Wearer he'd once admired and served beneath. Far from a man worthy of being King Liam's right hand.

"I just don't trust him," she said.

"If I remember, you supported inviting him along," Torsten said.

"Still..." She ran a hand through her hair. "It's been too long, and those guys give me the creeps." She nodded toward Redstar's unmasked follower, the warlock with his painted face. He sat alone a few strides behind them, legs folded and hands resting on them. Silent.

"As far as I can see, you both serve the same fallen gods."

"I don't *serve* anybody," she retorted.

"Well, we can safely say that none of us trusts one another."

"That's for sure," Sora muttered.

"Two weeks ago, I stood beside the throne. King Liam was sick but alive. Now, I'm out here with a thief, a blood mage and a cult-leading ghost who's seemingly lost half his mind. I don't have to like it, but this is all we have. Iam wouldn—"

"Why do you say it like that?" she interrupted.

"What?"

"Blood mage. Like just saying it makes you want to throw up."

"Because I have fought those who call on the wicked magic of Elsewhere, girl. In all forms. Iam created Elsewhere as a realm between here and the Gates of Light. A place to banish those of his brethren who sought power over peace, to send the abominations and demons they crafted to fight in the god feud."

"I know what Elsewhere is," Sora said, a harsh edge to her tone.

"Then you know why I can never abide by anyone who would wield the power of that place to alter our world. Conjuring fire or demons, or even healing wounds meant to heal naturally; it is all a perversion of the gifts Iam gave us."

"Easy to say from up there in glass spires. All Yarrington ever was for me was a blur on the horizon." She raised her bandaged hand. "This is all I have. All the man who raised me left for me."

"And did he teach you what happens when a demon possesses you through your connection to Elsewhere? Or when you decide summoning flames isn't enough?"

"We aren't all bad, you know."

"Power is a dangerous thing," he said. "I've seen the Panping mystics mutilate men for their experiments. 'Learning how to heal the body through the sacrifice of others,' they claimed."

Sora tried to speak, but he didn't let her.

"And I've seen how whatever magics Redstar used corrupted the mind of a little boy until he chose to jump from a window rather than hear the whispers. I've felt the curse's remnants myself. It is the unholy power you draw on that is the very reason we are here. So no, blood mage, I don't trust you, and I never will."

Her lip twisted. "Well, you can at least thank me for saving your arm."

Torsten folded his arms. A part of him wanted to say it. She was still young and didn't seem to be overtaken by the lust for power blood mages often fell for yet, but the words didn't come.

"You two should try to keep it down," Uriah said as he strode over.

"That's fine. We're done talking." Sora stood, arms crossed, and walked a few steps away.

"You should open your mind a little, old friend," Uriah said, laying a hand on Torsten's shoulder.

"So, I can be like you?" he said. "Hiding in caves with depraved cultists? Crucifying people in the name of fallen gods?"

"Nothing seems more wicked than that which we do not understand."

Gryff started barking at the sky. Uriah clapped his hands and hissed to silence him. "That girl has a part to play in all of this. I know not what it will be, but there is both light and darkness in all the affairs of gods and men."

Again, Gryff started barking. Uriah was about to reprimand the beast when Sora shrieked.

"Ick, what was that!"

Torsten turned to see Sora shaking her leg. A small spider flew off. Well, small in a relative sense. He was hoping to avoid a giant, but this one was the size of his hand, which still made them the largest spider he'd ever seen. He leaped into action and crushed it beneath his heel.

"I thought they weren't home?" Sora said.

"They are now," Uriah said.

Torsten turned back to him and saw Uriah was staring up. Before he could do the same, another hand-sized spider landed on his shoulder. He flung it off, then followed Uriah's eyes. Beyond the display of human eyeballs, hundreds—maybe thousands—of the creatures crawled down strings of webbing hanging from the canopy. It was as if the trees themselves had come alive.

"Bliss returns to protect her nest," Torsten said. He dug in, clenching his sword.

"Whitney is still in there!" Sora shouted above the din of thousands of scurrying legs.

"Then we must keep them out!"

The creeping spiders on the webs were small, but Torsten saw a new wave appearing through the darkness. Bulbous, black eyes filled the trees surrounding them, countless in number, and belonging to spiders the size of hounds.

"He was bait, wasn't he?" Sora said to Uriah. "Just a means for you to get us to help you!"

"Why would I want to face a goddess when we aren't at our fullest strength? Please, Torsten, talk some sense into your companion."

"The longer we argue, the more danger he'll be in," Torsten said.

"Like you care," Sora said.

"I may not like the kid, but he's an ally, and a soldier never leaves his allies behind."

The giant spiders poured through the trees as if they were a tidal wave. Thousands of them, the color of midnight. More continued dropping from above, blotching out what little moonlight there was to be seen. They fell on the warlock, crawling under his clothes and grasping at his painted face. He screamed and slit his hand. A spark of fire ignited, but never grew as one of the larger spiders sunk its fangs into the back of his neck.

"Brother!" Uriah shouted.

"We're surrounded!" Sora sliced her palm and raised her arm. A stream of flames burst forth, searing dozens of the descending arachnids, but not before they'd already dragged the cultist away into oppressive blackness.

"Ignore the babies!" Torsten grabbed Sora's arm and aimed it forward. The larger spiders on the ground backed away from the heat.

"You're okay with magic now?" she said, terse.

"Form up!" Torsten said, ignoring her.

He fell back beside Uriah at the mouth of the cave, both their swords raised. Gryff was beside them, hair raised along his back as he growled. Sora ended her spell and joined them. She panted, sweat pouring down her forehead and blood dripping from her hand. The spreading flames kept the creatures at bay, but a few trickled through. One seized the leg out from under Sora, but Torsten and Uriah were there to meet them with cold steel before she was pulled away. Torsten ducked as one leaped at him, slicing it open thorax to abdomen from below. He caught another by the leg and flung it into the fire.

They were large, but he was larger. He spun, coming face-to-face with a pair of glistening fangs. He didn't want to imagine what their venom might be capable of. Gryff slammed into its side before it struck.

Sora turned another into a charred husk, keeping it from attacking Torsten from behind. He glanced back and saw her hands on her knees. The cost of blood was draining her fast. A spider rushed, flanking her. Torsten leaped over a fresh corpse and swung down, cleaving the spider in two.

He grabbed her arm. "We have to go through the lair! There's no other way. If we beat Bliss to Whitney, we can all find a way out." He slashed left, slicing off a bundle of legs. "They can't swarm us in tunnels."

"I'm afraid you're already too late," said a woman's voice, low and matronly. It was both comforting and chilling, and as soon as she spoke all the spiders froze where they were and watched, twitching.

Torsten, Sora, and Uriah turned to see Bliss mounting the rocky walls outside her lair. Half-spider, half-human, she was an abomination Torsten could barely fathom. And the fact that her woman half was as stunningly beautiful as Oleander somehow made it worse.

"Another knight, come to die," Bliss said. Her voice carried across the woods, making the very leaves tremble. "I hope you'll prove more formidable than your friend."

"Whitney!" Sora screamed. "I swear if you hurt him." She drew a deep cut over her forearm and fire wrapped her whole arm.

"It seems our battle with the beast will come sooner than expected," Uriah said.

"Beast? You of all people should be careful throwing around names." She shimmied down to the ground.

He stroked the back of his snarling wolf, sword at the ready, a mad grin plastered across his face. "Take her! Take her now!"

Gryff sprung at her, fast as lightning. His fangs sunk into her shoulder and his claws tore at her. Sora launched a ball of flame at her chest that exploded into sparks as bright as Celeste. It blinded Torsten before he could aim a blow. Uriah rushed forward and slashed at Bliss' chest.

Torsten's vision finally settled, and he went to join them, but one of Bliss' arms caught his leg and threw him backward. With two others she flicked Uriah and Sora away like rag dolls.

Her children grasped at Torsten as he tried to recover. His armor held their fangs at bay, and left him grateful they hadn't bitten his hands or face. He roared and whipped his claymore in a full circle, driving them back, all the while watching as Bliss clutched Gryff with all four of her front legs and lifted him off her. The dire wolf had to weigh at least a ton, and she wasn't even struggling.

The wolf bit and snarled, but she leaned close in front of him and blew a puff of something acrid and yellow into his mouth.

"Release him!" Uriah yelled. A spider crashed into his back and sent him staggering. He ripped off one of its legs, but he was too slow.

Gryff's veins grew thick and black under his shaggy coat. His eyes went the color of pitch, down to the whites, and she dropped him. He landed in a heap of tangled legs at Uriah's feet, body shriveled like a grape left out in the sun.

Bliss released a laugh that commanded silence, carrying across the woods and making the very leaves tremble. Torsten felt it resonating in his chest, like a vice squeezing away all hope—like Iam himself abandoned this foul and horrid place.

"You puny, mortal children of Iam really think you can defeat me?" Bliss said, still amused. "I'm glad I saved my appetite."

XXX

THE THIEF

Whitney didn't remember having a drink, but when he woke up, it felt as if he'd cleared the Twilight Manor of their whole stock. He groaned and struggled to open bleary eyes. They wouldn't even budge. He tried to throw his legs over the side of his bed, but they wouldn't move either.

Shog, he thought, his memory beginning to return.

Eyes still closed, he wriggled the fingers on his right hand because that was all it seemed he could move. They brushed a silky, sticky substance. A cold, feverish feeling stole over him. He struggled, his face growing hot until he could separate one of his eyelids a hair. A semi-transparent film blocked his vision, but he could make out the shapes of columns and slivers of waning light from the top of Bliss' lair.

He thrashed left and right like a grounded fish desperate for water. His neck craned, simultaneously trying to find Bliss and hoping not to. His daggers were gone, his arms secured by the webbing.

Panic overwhelmed him. Breath wouldn't come. He felt as if he could die of suffocation. Letting out air and slowly drawing it back in, he calmed himself and let his head fall back. The stone floor hurt, but he didn't care. He was going to die soon anyway. What a fitting end to his legend. Why shouldn't the world's greatest thief die in some daring attempt to steal from a goddess?

At least, that was what he told himself to keep from hyperventilating.

He flopped his body over onto his side and heard something jingle. He stretched for the sound with the fingers of the hand pinned to his chest, and his index tapped the amulet he'd stolen from Darkings hanging from his neck. It wasn't a dagger, but if he could manage to break the gem free of its casing, it might just be solid and sharp enough to cut through the webbing.

Good thing those demons thought it was worthless.

He continued rolling until he was face down. Then he stretched his fingers as far as he could. His elbow stung from being bent the wrong way, but he used the ground to push it until he was able to get two fingers around the amulet.

He took a moment to catch his breath, then stuck his fingernail between the gem and the frame. He used the momentum from rolling his body to tweak the amulet. His fingers bled, sharp metal digging beneath his nails, but he ignored the pain. Again, he rolled, and this time the framing bent slightly. One more time and the gem broke free of the set.

He squirmed along the ground, pawing with his two longest fingers until he found the arrow-shaped gem safely nestled within the web. He fidgeted until he got the right leverage, then sawed into the webbing with the point.

It caught at first, and he dropped it several times before finally starting to progress. The process was slow, but he eventually opened a gap that allowed him to move his right arm.

Immediately, he freed his face, thankful to no longer feel like he'd been smothered by a very thin blanket. The webbing constricted the rest of his body like a woman's skirt pulled too tight. He couldn't lean forward any further without first releasing his hips and waist. He focused his attention on his belt line and made quick work of it. After that, it wasn't long before he released his upper body and was completely free.

Whitney gasped for air as he crawled out of his silky tomb, even though his face had been free for some time. It somehow still felt like he was drowning. He sprawled across the floor, staring up at the web-adorned ceiling. He knew he should get up and run, but he couldn't stop himself from laughing.

"'I still can't believe you nearly got us killed for that ugly thing,'" he said, imitating Sora's voice. He raised the gem to his face and gave it a kiss. "Oh, I love you, I love you, I love you."

"Whitney!" a distant scream echoed through the cavern, full of panic.

He rolled over. "Sora?"

He jumped to his feet, but his legs were wobbly. He rested his palm against a column, steadying himself. Now that he was free, he could better remember what brought him to the position he was in. He remembered running. He remembered Bliss spinning him round and round. He remembered... the kiss. He wasn't sure how long it had knocked him out, but it still had his body feeling funky.

He staggered forward to another column and looked around. Dozens of other creatures were stuck in the webs surrounded him. Some strung up from the ceilings, others wrapped against the cavern walls. Somehow his web-sack had been left on the ground as if someone interrupted her lunch.

He'd considered trying to cut some of them loose, but other than a couple of unmoving ones, none were within reach.

Suddenly, his mind cleared for a moment. "Sora!"

If they'd all come looking for him when he didn't return, that would mean Bliss... "Oh, shog."

It was impossible to know which of the many tunnels would lead him to his friends, which ones would bring him to certain death, or which would do both. One thing he knew, the route he'd entered through would send him to an impossible climb.

He heard some more distant shouts and closed his eyes to try block out everything else and pick a direction. When he had his best guess, he bolted... or rather, tried to. His legs felt like reeds of cattails sticking up out of the river he'd grown up playing in with Sora. It took a moment for the blood to return to them after being wrapped up so tightly, but after a few clumsy steps, he was surefooted as ever.

Clearing the tremendous lair took some time. He stopped for a breather when he nearly stepped on one of the daggers he lost battling Bliss. As he bent over to reclaim it, he realized he was standing near the poor saps in shiny armor who'd lost their skin and flesh to the giant spider.

The corpse out front clutched a raggedy old doll against its chest with a sterling, glaruium gauntlet that looked like Torsten's before Whitney ruined them, but had the image of a lion carved on the top. He wasn't sure what Pi's magical orepul was supposed to look like, but this doll was a strange enough thing to be in a spider goddess' lair in the possession of a fallen Shieldsman.

"Sorry buddy," Whitney said as he bent over and pried the doll lose. What little was left of the corpse's brittle bones crumbled. Its head toppled forward and rolled from its shoulders. The gauntlet grasping the doll clanged onto the floor. Whitney winced, hoping the clatter wouldn't cause Bliss to return. When it didn't, he took a moment to study the doll. It looked like something a beggar might make his son because he has nothing else—vaguely human in shape, but barely identifiable, with bits of yarn for hair.

"All of this for a piece of trash?" He wasn't sure what he'd expected, but surely something more, like one of those exquisite mannequin dolls rich girls loved. At least something that didn't look like a shrunken scarecrow.

He sighed. It wouldn't be easy to embellish the prize he stole from a goddess' lair, but the story of how he got it was grand enough. He stuffed the doll into his waistband, took measure of the armor, and decided to slide the gauntlets over his forearms. He figured he owed Torsten that much after ruining his pair back in the ruins.

He continued toward the tunnel through which he could best hear the hollering of his companions. If he believed in gods and curses—the thought stopped as soon as he realized he'd just met an apparent goddess who knew his name. In that case, Whitney cursed himself for what he was about to do.

Why must I always be such a hero?

The tunnel led him into a snaking corridor. He slashed at sticky cobwebs with his dagger as he pressed forward blindly. As the corridor narrowed, he felt the egg sacs brushing against his arms. It wasn't long before he heard the clear sounds of battle, the explicit sound of Sora's voice, and grunts that could only belong to Torsten.

"I'm coming!" Whitney shouted, earning a mouthful of webs.

Just then, the corridor split and something slammed into Whitney from the side. He felt one of the red blisters pop as his shoulder collided with the hard wall. Hundreds of tiny, little legs drooled all over him.

He swatted them as he whipped back around. A faint, orange glow illuminated the labyrinth of tunnels, revealing eight glittering eyes and venom-coated fangs prepared to drive their needles into him. Whitney brought his dagger up, and the steel drove hard against the biting chelicerae. A spider, the size of a mule, was repositioning itself for another strike, but Whitney got a leg up and kicked. He'd expected the creature's body to be soft because of all the hair, but his foot felt as if it was planted firmly against hard stone. He pushed against the bulb of its abdomen and slipped. It was slick like oil.

The creature knocked him back, poking and prodding with eight sharp claws. He managed to pull one arm free and drove the point of his dagger into the spot where a leg met the cephalothorax. The spider let out a humanlike cry, and then Whitney realized the sound was coming from his own mouth. One of the spindly legs managed to find a home in his supple flesh, digging into his bicep. He chanced pulling his dagger around and slicing at the leg. It found its mark, chopping it off at one of its forty-eight kneecaps.

Off-balanced, the spider toppled slightly, allowing Whitney to wriggle free enough to swing with his other arm. He used the corpse's gauntlets like a crude, blunt weapon and whacked the side of the spider's head. The creature shrieked, its legs shriveling.

Whitney leaped and drove his daggers down in the center of his many eyes.

He stumbled away from the dead monster, arms covered in black goo. "It's official, I can't stand spiders." He shook his hand off, then headed toward the flickering orange glow that could be none other than Sora's fire.

XXXI

THE KNIGHT

Torsten twisted his frame just in time to dodge Bliss' strike. Her many legs—each of them covered in tiny spikes—fell upon him in a flurry.

He parried one leg thrust with the flat of his blade and tried to stab, but she batted his claymore aside like he was a child with a stick. He'd fought a giant in the Third Panping War, and even its strength paled in comparison. Slaying a dire wolf was no simple task and Bliss had done it without throwing a punch.

"Uriah, forget him and help me!" Torsten shouted.

Uriah and Sora were busy fending off countless spiders of all sizes intent on devouring Gryff's desiccated corpse. They'd found a break in Sora's slowly spreading blaze and funneled through.

"My children will keep them occupied at least until you are dead, Torsten Unger," Bliss said. "Iam has forsaken all of you. And I, the One Who Remained, shall feast on all men."

Torsten's eyes went wild, his shoulders squared, and his nostrils flared. He was smart enough to know she was trying to taunt him into making a mistake, but he didn't care. He might not have cared about Uriah's mad quest to destroy her before, but now that he had looked upon her, he knew he was where he belonged. Even if they all died. This abomination. This evil. He couldn't just stand idly by and let her prevail now that Redstar had stirred her and given her a taste for men.

He understood Uriah, even if he could never forgive him.

He planted his right foot and pushed off, driving the sword toward her. She laughed and easily avoided the blade by circling up onto the rocks. She was toying with him, and there was nothing he could do. Bliss snapped her leg toward him. It cracked against his chestplate and sent him reeling, short on breath.

"Come now, knight," she said. "Where is your god now?"

Behind him, Sora shrieked. He took a second to glance back. She and Uriah were surrounded. She no longer wielded flame, so they stood back to back, slashing with their blades while the thorny legs of spiders tore at their clothes.

In that split second, Bliss pounced, knocking Torsten's claymore free. He punched, but her carapace was like plate mail. With his other hand, he grabbed one of her legs and held it back.

The only way he was going to make any headway was to attack her human-like upper body, but she had been doing a flawless job of protecting herself. She drew back onto her hind legs and brought her weight down. Torsten rolled, barely escaping her dagger-like appendages and grabbed his sword along the way.

"I do not fight for myself, monster," he roared as he spun back around to face her. "In the name of the Glass and Holy Iam, today your reign of terror in these woods shall end." He charged straight through her razor-sharp appendages and shouldered her in the thorax, his brazenness catching her unprepared. It was the first time he'd seen her tripped up.

"Torsten!" The voice came from somewhere near the tunnels, and Torsten had never been happier to hear it. Whitney had been a pain in his backside, but they were outnumbered and outmatched. Another set of hands could be the difference between victory and death.

But Whitney, as Torsten should have expected, lost what could possibly have been his only opportunity to surprise Bliss. She had retreated up on top of the cave's entry, and somehow, he didn't see her. Instead, Whitney's gaze fell upon Uriah.

"You son of a shog-eating shrew!" Whitney yelled, charging at Uriah. "She was in there waiting for me!"

Bliss swept her legs down and knocked the dagger from Whitney's hand. It skidded across the ground toward Torsten.

"How dare you think you could escape!" Bliss roared, anger emanating from her like white hot heat. She stretched down from her vantage and met him face to face.

"Yig!" he yelped as he tripped backward. He scrambled away until he bumped into Torsten's leg.

"Are you blind!" Torsten lifted Whitney to his feet and shoved his dagger into his gut. Then he pushed him right back down into a crouch as two of Bliss' arms zipped over their heads.

It was a kill shot.

Whatever Whitney had done to anger her, she wasn't toying anymore. He had a knack for enraging others, and while missing his opportunity to catch Bliss unawares was the stupidest thing he could do, riling her was a close runner-up.

"Torsten," Uriah bellowed, "we aren't going to be able to hold these things back much longer!"

Torsten peered over his shoulder and saw Uriah and Sora still fending off the spiders. They looked exhausted, clothes bloody and tattered.

"Hang in there, Sora!" Whitney called.

"Whit?" she replied. "You're alive!"

"Yeah, I'm here to save the day."

Torsten didn't hear her response if there'd been one. Bliss extended her back end and spouted out a stream of sticky webbing. He scarcely avoided getting hit by it.

"Keep her busy," Torsten told Whitney.

"Keep her wha—" He dove out of the way of another of Bliss' legs.

While the goddess was occupied trying to impale Whitney, Torsten decided to change his strategy. He carved a bloody swathe toward Uriah and Sora. He swatted an arachnid the size of a wagon-wheel, then slashed one off Sora's back.

He grabbed her shoulder and pulled her to the path he'd opened through the beasts. Her breathing was labored from using so much blood magic.

"We need to take her together," he said. "Find whatever strength is left in you. Uriah, it's time to finish what you started."

Now together, Torsten and Uriah fought their way back to Whitney. They let Sora stay in front, as she was so weak she could barely lift her knife. Ahead, Whitney dropped to the dirt under Bliss' leg and rolled out of the way of another. As he came to a stop, a third leg crashed toward his head.

Torsten reached him just in time and deflected the blow. He dragged Whitney back as another slashed the dirt between his legs, then lifted him again.

"It's like fighting someone with eight swords," Whitney complained.

The four of them now stood side by side, Sora leaning on Whitney like a crutch. Bliss stretched out before them, purple eyes fuming with rage. The patter of her largest children closing in behind them grew louder and louder.

"Can we run yet?" Whitney asked.

"No. We hit her in the heart or the head," Torsten said.

The spider queen rushed once more. Torsten and Whitney both thrust their blades, barely nicking her armored underbelly but both taking hits from her spiny legs. They landed on their backs, hard, but recovered fast to charge back at her. Sora was on her knees, struggling to raise her knife and make another cut so she could help. Out of the corner of his eye, Torsten saw Uriah take her hand and place it aside.

"No. This must end now." Uriah used her knife to slice both of his palms. Then he dropped to the ground, crossed his legs, closed his eyes, and clasped his bloody hands together.

"What are you doing!" Torsten questioned.

"I didn't know we could take breaks," Whitney said, panting hard before he was forced to duck under another massive leg. A second one caught him from the other direction and sent him flying into the wall of the cave.

"Whitney!" Sora rasped and stumbled.

Uriah began muttering under his breath in Drav Crava. A swirling cloud of black smoke rose around him, and a bright red light glowed as if he himself were a beacon.

"What is this, Uriah?" Torsten questioned.

Uriah didn't answer, but he began to levitate.

"Uriah!" Torsten shouted.

Bliss' expression revealed concern for the very first time.

"This will not work," Bliss spat, venom lacing her words.

"Torsten, ready your blade." Uriah's voice was… different. It carried on the air, surrounding them like Bliss' had.

Torsten lifted his claymore. Bliss was so distracted by Uriah that there would be no better chance. She lashed out at Uriah's floating body, but the black smoke swirled around her limbs, holding them in place and exposing her human half.

"Strike her, now!" Uriah shouted.

Torsten bounded forward and slashed, drawing a deep gash along her belly. Half a dozen spiders promptly tore their way through the bloody hole and leaped at him. One bit down on his bare hand.

Whitney came too and rushed to Torsten, hacking at the spiders with his dagger. There were too many. A small fireball raced by, pathetic compared to Sora's usual magic, but enough to hit several of them at once. They shrieked in pain as they shriveled. "My babies!" Bliss writhed, her spider legs struggling to hold her belly together.

"Again!" Uriah called. "I cannot hold this much longer!"

Torsten lunged, this time plunging the sword all the way through. Her legs battered him, but he stood firm, drove deeper, and twisted his blade. Black blood poured out, coating his arms and flooding down his torso.

She stopped fighting and pulled him in closer until her gorgeous face was his whole world. Torsten remembered what happened to the dire wolf when she blew on him. He closed his eyes, preparing for her to drag him into death with her when Uriah's blade joined his in her chest. The former Wearer of White had descended and now stood at his side, flaying her wide. That same black mist swirled around his hands and exuded from his mouth.

Bliss' scream shook the earth beneath their feet as she lurched. She pushed them away, and the blades slid out. Blood gushed from her like a castle fount as her legs fumbled for traction.

"Fools!" she bellowed. "I will slaughter every last one of you. I will devour your children. Even Iam could not destroy—"

Torsten roared and swung his sword with all his might, spinning as he did, and cleaved her neck mid-sentence. Her legs crumpled, and her head teetered before tumbling down along with them. The forest hushed when it came to a stop. Then an ear-piercing cry echoed all around them. The children, mourning the loss of their mother. It was sharp and sudden and gone just as quickly. Then they all scattered into the trees.

"That's right, you better run!" Whitney hollered.

Torsten looked around. Sora was spent, barely able to stand. Whitney's filthy clothes were drenched in blood and he, like Torsten, was covered in bruises.

The only sounds in the darkness were sharp, labored breaths, the crackling of the dying flames at their backs, and the sizzle of black magic surrounding Uriah.

XXXII

THE THIEF

"Congratulations, old friend," Uriah said. "You have slain even what your God could not. The One Who Remains is no more."

Whitney stared at Uriah as the black cloud surrounding him dissipated. He stretched his arms and drew a calming breath as if everything was fine. It was then that Whitney remembered what had happened and his blood started to boil.

"You used me as bait!" Whitney shouted. He jumped at the old man and pointed his dagger at his throat.

"Put the blade down, Whitney," Torsten said.

"Why? He used me so we'd have no choice but to fight his monster. Your men didn't draw her away, did they? This was all to get us to distract her so that you could do... that. Whatever the shog that was."

The old man merely smiled, wrinkles splaying at the corners of his lips.

"Is that true, Uriah?" Torsten said.

"Of course, it is!" Whitney growled. "Bliss was waiting to drain me." The thought made him shiver. "Do you know what it's like down there?"

"I knew something was off," Sora said softly, still on one knee struggling to catch her breath, exhausted from using magic.

"I ought to make you go down there and lay with the corpses!"

"Whitney, stop!" Torsten bellowed. "Uriah, is it true?"

The old man sighed. "I did what was needed to rid this world of great evil. The potential sacrifice of one man does not compare to what we have accomplished here together."

"I'll give you sacrifice." Whitney went to hit him, but Uriah was too smooth. In a flash, he had Whitney disarmed and his arm wrenched behind his back.

"Please," Uriah said. "I do tire of all this arguing." He shoved Whitney into Torsten.

"I trusted you," Torsten said, holding Whitney back.

"And your trust was not misplaced. Look." He gestured to all the carnage around them. Bliss' corpse plugged the entrance to her lair, legs tossed haphazardly like a marionette on the strings of a puppeteer. The bodies of her children covered so much of the surrounding area that the forest floor could no longer be seen. "We have victory. Who cares what it took to achieve it. Didn't Liam teach you that in all his bloody conquests?"

"We?" Torsten said. "That spell, whatever you did. You didn't need us."

"Oh, but I did."

"I've never seen magic like it," Sora added. "Not even from Wetzel."

"What happened to you?" Torsten asked.

"I called upon the gifts of my goddess," Uriah said. "You too could be teeming in her power, if only you'd see the truth about the beings we worship."

"You were a servant of Iam! You believed in him even more strongly than I."

"Whatever he did, it did save our lives, oh holy one," Whitney remarked. Torsten glared at him. "What! The guy sent me to die. If anyone should be mad, it's me."

"Stop being so stubborn and listen," Uriah said. "Nesilia, Iam, together, after all these countless years, we faithful have brought their enemy to her bitter end."

"Together we have done nothing," Torsten snapped.

"Do you not remember the song, old friend?"

"Again with songs of fancy and fantasy?" Whitney said.

Biding her time, her pain like a flood
Alone in the darkness, she longs for the blood
In the name of the Lady, in the name of the Lord
Shall settle it all with power and sword

Then she will arise, in glorious day
Through will and through fire, her enemies slain
Forgotten, abandoned, but no longer bound
From Elsewhere and exile, she'll receive her crown

"Riddles and nonsense," Torsten said.

"How do you not feel it?" Uriah said, looking to the sky and closing his eyes. "Their union, deep in your soul like a… like a mounting storm."

"You guys both sound insane," Whitney said. Of course, nobody paid him any attention. He was getting used to it.

"Do not make me a party to your heathen worship of the Buried Goddess," Torsten said. "It was Iam who guided my blade. You may have tricked us into helping you, but we are done now. We will find King Pi's orepul, and then you will return to Yarrington and answer for your sins."

"You cannot deny what happened here!" Uriah roared, his calm façade slipping.

It was then that Whitney realized how foolish he was for charging the former Wearer of White.

He just called on shadows to kill a goddess, you idiot.

"Why don't we just let him leave," Whitney said. "I have the damn doll anyway. We can all go on our merry way." He removed the orepul he'd found in Bliss' lair from his belt and held it up.

Torsten and Uriah grabbed it at the same time, their hands covered in Bliss' black blood, so much that it soaked the poor doll's crude face through.

"Hey!" Whitney ripped it back and patted the head before he stored it back underneath his belt. "Didn't either of you ever learn to share?"

"Where did you find that?" Torsten asked.

"In the big chamber he sent me into with the… you know, spider webs and dead bodies."

"So Redstar really is dead," Torsten said. It was not a question.

Whitney shrugged. "I suppose. There was a body holding it. Well, it used to be a body. It was really just a pile of white armor and crumbling bones. Like yours, see." He raised his forearm to show off the gauntlets he'd taken.

Torsten's eyes went wide. "Those are glaruium gauntlets," he said. He clutched Whitney's arm and pulled it close. "Where did you find these?"

"They're yours if you want them. I figured it was the least I could do after I… uh… damaged yours back in the ruins."

There was silence.

"Really, that was his fault," Whitney went on, pointing to Uriah.

"You found these in the same place as the doll?" Torsten asked.

"Yeah, cradled right in these things like it was a baby."

Torsten's eyebrows rose slowly and his gaze leveled on Uriah. Whitney did the same.

"The lion's head?" Torsten said.

A smirk played at the corners of the old man's lips. He clicked with his tongue and shook his head. "This could have been a smooth transaction. In and out. Both our needs fulfilled. You got the orepul and I… I get what she asked of me."

"What is going on?" Whitney asked.

"Watch out!" Sora suddenly sprawled in front of them with her hand raised as if to block something. When nothing happened, she glanced up with her weary eyes and said, "I felt…"

Uriah snapped his fingers. Whitney winced, then, when he looked again, Uriah was gone. Where he had just been standing, a pale, gangly man now stood. The scarred, left side of his face was covered by a deep red, almost crimson birthmark with a few points stretching over his forehead and nose.

Whitney was dumbfounded. Sora froze in her place.

"It's you," Torsten said softly. "You son of a—" He lunged at him, but the man sliced his palm on his sword and raised the hand. Torsten went stiff.

The man waved his arm aside and sent Torsten slamming hard into the cavern's outer wall, his head cracking against the stone.

Whitney lifted his hands in surrender. He was no fool. Torsten hadn't told him a thing about what Redstar looked like, but a birthmark like the one this man had made it pretty obvious. And anyone who could use magic to change their appearance like that was a warlock not worth messing with.

"Hey, man. Listen, we're friends, right?" Whitney said. "You sent me to my doom, no sweat. This really has nothing to do with me." He nodded to the doll. "You want this? Fine, no skin off my bones."

"You really think this was all about the orepul?" Redstar said. Even his voice changed. It was stronger, more dignified.

"Don't, Whitney," Torsten groaned as he struggled to recover. "He is behind everything. He'll never let you leave alive."

"Unfortunately, he's right about that."

Redstar raised his bloody hand, but so did Sora. She stood tall in front of Whitney and fire erupted from her own newly bleeding hand. Redstar didn't even bother moving. As the ball of fire leaped from her palm, he snapped his fingers. The flame turned to ice mid-flight, then fell to the ground and shattered. He then extended a hand toward both Whitney and Sora and threw them into the same wall as Torsten.

They all lay in a heap, staring at Redstar. Whitney felt a new level of fear that even Bliss didn't instill in him. She needed a leg to throw him across the room, but Redstar didn't even need to touch him.

Torsten drew himself up. "Redstar, I am here under the command of your sister, the Queen Regent. Stop this madness."

"She's not my ruler!" he shouted. "I came to her a year ago. Begged her to see the truth of what lived in these Woods and to help us destroy it. She treated me as a stranger—worse than a stranger. The sister who I witnessed being ripped from our home and forced to the Glass Kingdom died that day in Drav Cra. Your King defiled her."

"So, you cursed a child?" Torsten spat. "We can talk with her. Reason with her."

"I will not waste any more time with her. My faith belongs to another Lady; one who holds real power. My goddess will soon return with a vengeance, and it's all thanks to you."

"Me?" Torsten stomped forward, but Redstar flexed his hand again and shoved him back down.

"Didn't you pay attention to anything I've been telling you?" Redstar asked. "'One of the Lady and one of the Lord.'"

"We all heard your dumb song," Whitney said.

"Only true believers of Iam and Nesilia, together, could truly vanquish Bliss and undo what she has done. And your faith was proven so predictably at the ruins. Now, Torsten, she will rise again. No longer forgotten!"

"Not on my watch," Torsten declared. "Not in the Glass."

"If only that were up to you. I no longer need you or these filthy little creatures you find company with."

Behind him, three of his masked cultists appeared, only they weren't wearing masks any longer. Their faces were pale, black painted across the top halves with thin lines of red around their eyes. They had all the features of men from the Drav Cra tundra, not Glassmen. They were, all of them, real warlocks pretending to be cultists.

"Drad Redstar, Arch Warlock of Nesilia, condemns you each to death," they said in perfect unison. "May the dirt take you."

One waved his hand and Whitney went flying. Another did the same to Torsten. Redstar raised his hand in Sora's direction, and with it, she floated, pushed hard against the rock wall. She groaned in agony as her back was crushed.

"And you… little blood mage." Redstar took a few steps forward. "I hate to see such raw talent wasted, but I cannot take any risks."

"You're pure evil," she said through her teeth.

"Young lady… there is no evil—only power." He squeezed his fist into a ball, and she writhed.

"Stop!" Whitney shouted from wherever he'd landed. One of the cultists slowly walked toward him with a dagger in hand, robe sloshing through Bliss' pooling blood.

"Redstar, let them go!" Torsten pleaded. "They are not your enemy."

"You don't understand, do you, knight? You wouldn't." Redstar squeezed harder. "I enjoy this."

Sora's eyes opened wide, and she looked as if she were about to burst. Torsten closed his eyes and prayed, asking for Iam's light to deliver them from evil and give his kingdom a second chance. Whitney found his footing and charged at Redstar, ignoring the cultist. Redstar raised a bloody hand his way and paralyzed him mid-stride. Then he focused back on Sora. Her moans of pain grew louder and louder until it was all he could hear. He wished he could look away, but Redstar held every part of him still. A soft glow began to form in her irises and then it grew brighter.

Then Sora screamed.

Blinding light and fire surged from every pore of her battered body. Whitney, Torsten, and the cultists bore down. The light was so bright and the heat so sweltering, Whitney had to close his eyes. When he opened them again, Redstar lay ten meters away, his clothes smoldering. His three warlocks were charred to a crisp. Whitney rolled over and tried to stand, but his head was ringing, and he fell back over. Torsten stumbled a few feet then did the same.

"Sora!" Whitney grated. The heat on the air made it hard to breathe. She lay on her back against the cavern wall, arms draped off to the side, eyelids twitching. Whitney crawled the rest of the way to her.

"Sora," he repeated. "Are you okay?" She wasn't moving. He grabbed her by the jaw and rolled her eyelid open, but only saw the whites of her eyes. "Sora wake up." He dragged her down from the wall, laid her down flat and started slapping her cheek. "Sora!"

"I..." she coughed and rolled her head. "I'm okay."

Whitney released a mouthful of air and pulled her close. She was too weak to speak, but that was better than dead. "That was incredible, Sora. Where did you learn to do that?"

"I didn't..."

"He's still breathing," Torsten said. He crouched at Redstar's side with his hand on the man's throat. "Barely."

"So, drive that sword into him and be done," Whitney said.

"I can't do that. The Queen will want him. If I bring him back, she might restore..." his voice trailed off.

"Restore?" Whitney said.

"Hope in the kingdom. No, he still must be returned alive to answer for these crimes. To show Yarrington that Iam remains with us."

"So, what happens when our friend wakes up and goes all drunk with power again?" Whitney asked.

"He won't," Sora said softly.

"How do you know?"

"His hands," she strained at first, but her words gained strength as she spoke. "See those little cuts? He's just like me… a lot stronger, but just like me."

"By the look of things, there aren't many stronger than you," Whitney said.

She blushed. "I got lucky."

"There's a word for it. You were like a powder keg."

"I think... maybe I somehow drew on Bliss' blood."

"Is that possible?" Whitney asked.

She was able to shrug one shoulder. "Wetzel didn't know everything."

"No," Torsten declared. "It was His light—Iam's light—that came through her. I know it. That is why we were spared."

"Now her powers are all fine and dandy?" Whitney said.

"We cannot say why or how he will choose to act through his vessels, but of this fact, I have no doubt. I prayed to him as death closed in around us, and I felt him in my heart when the light arrived. Perhaps your friend has turned toward the Light, but he has not turned from her."

Sora rolled her head over to face Torsten. Whitney couldn't quite discern what her expression meant, but he was sure it wasn't anger. Maybe it was hope. It didn't last long before her exhaustion returned in full force.

"Whatever you say." Whitney lifted Sora's head to keep her from fainting. "So how do we keep him in check?"

"Bind his hands and legs," she said. "Gag his mouth, too. He shouldn't be able to perform any spells like that."

"I don't know if this is something we want to chance."

Torsten was already tearing Redstar's robes to use as makeshift bindings. "It's a chance we'll have to take."

Whitney laid Sora down, retrieved Wetzel's dragon engraved knife to tuck into her belt, then went to the knight's side to help. A long rasp sounded as he tore more fabric. Torsten went to grab hold of Redstar's hands, but his arms froze. He started to rise into the air again.

Redstar groaned, "You will not—"

Whitney threw a sharp right hook into the side of the Arch Warlock's head. His eyes closed for good.

"Good punch," Torsten said.

"Thanks," Whitney said, shaking his hand.

They finished tying up Redstar, then stood.

"You're carrying him," Whitney said.

"There are two of us, Thief," Torsten replied. "And we have a long road back to Yarrington."

"Well, someone has to help her!" He pointed at Sora, who had passed out at some point while they were binding Redstar. Torsten's gaze moved from her, then froze on the gauntlet covering Whitney's outstretched hand.

"Ah, right." Whitney went to remove them, but Torsten stopped him.

"I dare not wear them. I doubted Uriah's faith and I have to live with that forever."

"Redstar was a good actor." Whitney rolled his shoulders, then handed the gauntlets over anyway. They barely fit, and even though the armor of a former Wearer was quite the treasure, he had no desire to be reminded of nearly being devoured by a giant spider every time he looked down at them. For all his preaching, Torsten seemed plenty satisfied as he strapped them on.

"So, that was the real Uriah I found down there?" Whitney said.

"Yes." Torsten bent over and picked up Redstar's sword—Uriah's sword—the pommel sculpted into a lion. "The monster stole his sword and everything, all to deceive me."

"About that. I still don't really understand what in Elsewhere he wanted."

"What does any heathen want? Chaos. To blot out the light in this world because there is no light in theirs."

Whitney looked up and considered making a remark about how little light the woods had, even with the glittering eyeballs hanging all around them and reflecting Celeste's light, but he decided against it. "Well, if it's all right with you, I'm ready to get out of this place."

"Yes. For too long the Webbed Woods have haunted our kingdom thanks to this madman. It's time to leave for good."

"Finally." Whitney patted the Drav Cra doll in his belt. "I'll hold onto this until we're back, just in case you decide to go rotten."

"I gave you my word under Iam's Vigilant Eye."

Again, the swinging eyeballs caught Whitney's gaze, and he stifled a gag. "Please don't mention eyes… ever again."

Torsten sighed. "I will stand by my promise."

Whitney flashed him a grin. "But it's so much more fun not to."

XXXIII

THE KNIGHT

Yarrington.

Torsten swore he'd never been so happy to see the glory of the capital in all his life. From the dark, towering trees of the Webbed Woods, to the white-stone spires and crystal spindle swirling atop the distant castle—he'd been to war in plenty of places but never had the difference been so stark. Mount Lister's snow-dusted, flat top glistened under the bright winter sun as a backdrop to it all.

He sat atop his steed staring down upon the city from a nearby hill. It seemed more peaceful than ever. Redstar was slung over the back of his saddle, bound, gagged, and so far he hadn't tried any tricks. Uriah's sword was strung along the side of it, finally able to be returned to its proper place.

Whitney and Sora sat on the horse behind him, the thief finally quiet for once in his Iam-forsaken life, and Sora finally at full strength after Torsten had felt Iam appear through her to save them all. He was sure of it. And because of that, he was about to allow a known blood mage to enter the capital.

The world really has changed...

They'd traded for two horses at the first stable they found outside the Webbed Woods. There were few southern villages left that hadn't already been razed by the growing Black Sands army, so stocky, southern short-hairs were the only option. Whitney hesitated to give up his stolen arrow-shaped amulet in exchange for such inferior beasts, but he eventually gave in when he realized walking was the only alternative.

Torsten couldn't help but feel like the young man was finally starting to see the weight of their actions. How a quest, so foolish in its description, could help save the Glass Kingdom.

"Are you planning on sitting up here all day?" Whitney asked. "Sora can really use a bath."

"Excuse me!" She smacked him in the back of the head.

"What? We all can. Nice, warm, castle water. A fresh rack of lamb. Rosemary potatoes."

Torsten glanced back at him, incredulous. Then his stomach rumbled. He'd eaten nothing but the stale bread Uriah—Redstar—had given him for days.

"We're heroes, Shieldsman," Whitney said, clearly protesting the look Torsten sent his way. "It's the least we deserve. We rescued a hand-sewn damsel—dame?—in distress, thwarted an Arch Warlock, and slew an evil, goddess, spider... thing."

"Is a name of worth not enough?" Torsten questioned.

"You have met him, haven't you?" Sora said. "Nothing is ever enough."

"You're learning," Whitney said.

"Stop." Torsten held out a hand and nodded toward the doll tucked into Whitney's belt.

"I said you'd get it when we reached Yarrington."

"This is close enough. We will be better received if it is in my hands."

Whitney looked to Sora, who seemed too preoccupied marveling at the great city to care. He sighed and handed it over.

"It's a creepy little thing anyway," Whitney said. "Not to mention all the gross, spider-woman blood you got all over it."

Torsten raised Pi's Drav Cra orepul in front of him—the boy's supposed soul. The thing was a wreck. A year or so in Queen Bliss' lair hadn't been kind to it. An eye was missing, and the dark stains of blood—both old and new—and dirt would never wash out.

That the entire kingdom could rely on something so small and worthless...

Torsten tucked it away. "Let's go home."

"Your home maybe," Whitney muttered.

Torsten spurred his horse on down the paved road into Yarrington. The farms outside were quiet, touched by winter's frost. A few lonely, old farmers tilled the soil to keep it fresh, but naught for that, only stubborn crows disturbed the stillness. Smoke climbed from the mills and homesteads, firelight glowing through hazy windows.

Torsten always enjoyed winter. Quiet. Fewer foreign traders to monitor, and the people were usually too cold to cause much of a stir. It made his job easier, and coming back from Liam's war campaigns had always exhausted the King's Shield.

It was different now, like so much else. The city may have looked peaceful on the outside, but as soon as they reached the gate, Torsten knew Yarrington wasn't the same place he'd left. The main eastern gate into the city hadn't been sealed in ages, yet now the tremendous, oak doors were closed and the steel portcullis lowered.

He brought his horse to a snorting halt.

"Who goes there?" A voice shouted down from the stony ramparts.

"Where are the trumpets?" Whitney whispered.

"Torsten Unger!" he shouted up. "King's Shieldsman. The Wearer of White." It was only as the words left his lips that Torsten remembered he was lying. He'd never actually said out loud what he no longer was.

"Sir Rand Langley's the Wearer now!" the guard replied. "I don't believe you're supposed to be here."

"Did I just hear him right?" Whitney said.

"Quiet," Torsten snapped. He looked back up. "Fetch Sir Wardric Jolly! He'll be expecting me. I bring a gift that may very well save our young, ailing king."

The guard hesitated, but soon disappeared, leaving them to wait in the cold. A northern breeze bit at Torsten's nose and cheeks, though it was welcome compared to the fetid stench of swamps and cursed woods. He took a moment to inhale the chilly air through his nostrils when Whitney tapped his shoulder.

"I'm sorry, Rand?" Whitney said. "He's the way-too-young knight who took my crown. What is that guy talking about?"

"It wasn't *your* crown, and it's complicated."

"No, *alchemy* is complicated. This is simple. Are you the Wearer or did you lie to me when I agreed to this insane adventure?"

"The Queen Regent is impulsive. When we return, she will see reason, and you'll get everything we agreed upon. You have my word."

"Your word? Are you even a knight?"

"Well..."

Whitney's jaw dropped.

It hadn't occurred to Torsten until they defeated Bliss that he may not be able to offer what he promised should they succeed. He didn't care about disappointing Whitney— the thief had done more than enough to deserve disappointment—but a vow made under the light of Iam was a sacred thing.

"I knew I didn't like him, Whitney," Sora said. "We should leave right now, before he turns on us, too."

"Look," Torsten said. "The Queen Regent sent me off in anger. When she sees what we return with, all will be forgiven. I will ensure you get what was promised, thief."

Whitney took a long hard look at the road from whence they came and scratched his chin. "Fine. But I swear: if you go back on it, I'll burn that doll. Or maybe I'll sneak back into your Royal Crypt and turn your beloved King's old crown back into sand."

"My word is my bond. If I'm unable to anoint you, I have friends in the castle who will honor my final request."

"What about her?" he asked, nodding to Sora.

"I agreed upon nothing with her."

"We'd be dead without her, and you know it."

"Perhaps there is redemption for you, thief. Whether you fled and left me to die in those ruins or not, you returned and stood by to the end. But no Shieldsman, I, nor any other, can, in good conscience, bestow a name upon a known practitioner of the dark arts."

"But you said it yourself, you're not a Shieldsman anymore."

Torsten bit back his anger. "All I can offer is that she may walk free. I will say nothing of her malfeasance and see to it she is rewarded appropriately in autlas, as any aid to the Crown would be. Perhaps enough that she may pursue a decent art." He eyed her disapprovingly with the last words. "Her fate rests in Iam's hands now, and after what I witnessed in that forest, I have faith she'll find the right path."

"She saved us all! You said it yourself, 'Iam worked through her', or some mumbo-jumbo."

"It's okay, Whit," Sora interrupted Whitney. "I don't need a name or gold. The Crown's never offered a poor, outsider like me anything anyway."

"Well, then what do you want?"

Chimes from Yarrington Cathedral rang out before she could answer. Then the gate creaked as old gears inside the wall slowly turned, grinding against one another. The doors opened to reveal Sir Wardric atop a strong, regal-looking stallion. It had only been a few weeks, and the already-elder statesmen of the King's Shield looked as if he'd aged a decade. His graying hair and beard were haggard, his face creased like a stone quarry.

"Wardric, you have no idea how good it is to see a familiar face," Torsten exclaimed cheerily. He chose not to dwell on how the two of them left things, almost killing each other. As Torsten stretched out his arms in greeting, Wardric's expression was as solemn as it had been then.

"I figured you weren't coming back," he said.

"I have captured the Queen Regent's traitorous brother and returned what was stolen. Please, I must speak to her."

Wardric bit his lip. "You should come with me, Torsten."

"What happened?"

"I dare not speak it here. Come."

Torsten urged his horse forward, looking down upon it with shame in the light of Wardric's tall steed. Whitney and Sora followed.

"Who are they?" Wardric asked.

"They helped me bring Redstar to justice and are to be rewarded justly." Torsten glanced back at them. Whitney wore that same wry grin he'd been found wearing in the Yarrington dungeon on the day they'd met. Sora's scowl, on the other hand, made him reach for his holy pendant he no longer wore. "They can be trusted."

"So be it."

Wardric spun his horse, and Torsten caught up. It was only once he passed the guard's tower he realized the state of Yarrington. He'd seen many cities, and—outside of the docks—the capital had always been the cleanest. No longer. It was as if the citizens had stopped working. Horse shog stained the streets. Beggars and paupers donned the porches of every shopfront, crowding the usually bustling entry plaza. Commotion broke out down one of the avenues, armed soldiers holding back a mob of rag-clad citizens hollering that they were starving.

"The Black Sands hit many granaries when they raided those towns," Wardric explained as they rode as if reading Torsten's mind. "As if the poor harvest this season from the drought wasn't enough. Stores are low, and we had to send as much as we could to fortify our fortresses throughout the kingdom against possible uprising."

"We should fortify the South first," Torsten said. "I sent riders with news about the afhem gathering an army in the Fellwater. Did they reach you?"

"Yes." Wardric reached into a satchel and removed Torsten's necklace. It was covered in grime, barely recognizable as the holy eye. He handed it over.

Torsten exhaled as he took it and threw it back over his neck. He hadn't realized how exposed he felt without it until it was back.

"I worried they wouldn't make it," he said.

"They're safely locked up for spreading lies and fear-mongering."

"Lies? Fear-mongering? I saw the force with my own eyes, Wardric. It's the largest army we've faced in a decade, I swear to you."

"It's not me you must convince."

"Oleander," Torsten muttered to himself, hanging his head. "Surely Rand—"

"Is a spineless whelp," he said, finishing Torsten's sentence. "He stands guard outside her locked door while she sits with her son. Half the men whisper of a coup, the others lose faith in Iam and the White."

"How is the boy?"

Wardric brought his horse close and leaned over to whisper. "He still has not woken. The physicians say nothing more can be done, and now the Queen Regent won't allow anybody in. He could already be dead for all we know."

"Don't speak like that!" Torsten snapped, less because he was angry, and more because if Pi was dead than his entire quest was in vain.

"Hey, what're you two whispering about?" Whitney hollered from behind.

Torsten's hands squeezed his reins so tight his knuckles went white as Brotlebir snow.

"Well, you know her better than anyone left," Wardric said. "If that really is her brother, sate her with revenge, and then, maybe, she'll open her damned eyes. Otherwise, we're doomed to wind up like the others."

"Others?" No sooner had the word left Torsten's mouth than they reached the walls of the Glass Castle itself. Bodies hung by their necks from the parapets facing the street, some in robes, some stripped bare. At first, he hoped they were all cultists or traitors but then recognized one.

"Deturo? What in the name of Iam?" Torsten traced his eyes.

"He couldn't heal Pi after she waited so long," Wardric said. "Nor could the others."

Torsten didn't know the royal physician well, but the old man had always been kind and as knowledgeable as his white beard was long. His left eye was missing. A raven sat upon his shoulder, blood on the tip of its beak.

Others were more doctors, healers, or clerics of Iam. There were also soldiers. Not King's Shieldsmen, but many of them wore the armor of castle-guards. All dead. He rode slowly, down the line, absentmindedly staring into all their bulging, blank eyes. Then, another stuck out; The Master of Rolls, Frederick Holgrass, the noose fresh around his neck. A member of Royal Council, hanged for all of Yarrington to see. Yet, it was not him which made Torsten's throat go dry.

Swinging beside him, directly beside the castle gates, was the body of Oleander's favored handmaiden, Tessa. Her dress was torn, and her cheek bore a red mark with the distinctive shape of one of Oleander's rings.

"I must speak with her," Torsten said, voice shaking.

"You're the only one who can," Wardric replied.

Wardric knocked on the iron gate, and it groaned. Torsten turned back to Whitney and Sora, who stared at the swinging bodies.

"You two might want to stay out here," Torsten said.

"We should wait here," Whitney said at the same time. "Smart. I'm beginning to think we should have stayed in the Woods."

"I'll call for you when this business is concluded." Torsten whipped back around and gave his horse a kick. He zoomed beneath Tessa's limp legs through the malodorous stink of death.

"I'll be right out here!" Whitney called after him. "Waiting for what was promised!"

XXXIV

THE THIEF

"How long are you planning to wait?" Sora asked.

It had been only a few minutes but felt eons longer. The wind picked up after Torsten went inside, causing the many strung up bodies to batter the citadel walls like the drummers of a traveling troupe. If that wasn't bad enough, there was the stench, and then still, the pair of King's Shieldsmen who'd arrived to guard the gate.

For what could have been any number of reasons—from his fanciful yet tattered outfit to her ears—their gazes never left Whitney and Sora. Or it could have been because they were the only two people foolish enough to be loitering on the street. Everyone else rushed by, going out of their way to pretend the public display of punishment wasn't there.

"Just a few minutes more," Whitney said, rubbing his hands together. The cold of winter was settling in, and his thin, silk outfit didn't help.

"You really think he'll give you what you wanted?" she said. "A noble like him will never give a shog about two criminals."

"You help steal one outfit, and you're a criminal now?"

"After meeting him, I'm starting to understand why Wetzel taught me underground."

"You're learning. Thieves, mystics, and bastards—there's nothing in the Glass Kingdom hated more."

"What about knife-ears?" She smirked.

"I have a feeling the Shesaitju are in the lead these days."

They laughed, then Sora shivered. "C'mon, Whit. He used you. Both of us. You're really going to stand out here waiting for a name because of some decade-old feud with your dead father?"

"Torsten will come through. Have you met the guy? He's about the only person in Pantego pious enough to believe a promise is sacred."

"True, but that doesn't mean we have to wait outside." She nodded toward a tavern across the street called The Lofty Mare.

Whitney had never been inside. On this side of town, it was where rich men went to get away at night. Stuffy folk.

"Buy a girl a drink?" she said.

"With what?" he said.

She raised the small pouch filled with coins they'd lifted from Redstar's unconscious follower in the ruins near Oxgate. It rattled around in her bandaged palm.

"I thought I lost that back in Bridleton!" Whitney exclaimed.

"You did lose it," she winked and shook the bag again.

"Wait, you made me waste that amulet getting us horses while you had that?"

"That thing was worthless."

"It saved my life. It was lucky!"

She drew herself in close, rubbing his arm with one hand while she placed the pouch in his palm and slowly closed his fingers over it. "Maybe I'm the good luck charm."

Whitney leaned forward until their faces were centimeters apart, then whispered, "No, you're a pest." He tossed the gold over her head and caught it on his way toward The Lofty Mare. A horse-drawn cart raced by and almost made him drop it, but he kept his balance and strode on as if nothing happened.

"You coming?" he hollered back. "I'm thirsty."

Her groan was louder than the thumping of the swinging bodies against the castle walls. She caught up just in time to step into the tavern with him. The inside was as barren as the street. A few ragged drunks here and there, but mostly, the tavern was spotless. Never a good sign for a place of imbibing.

Whitney strolled right up to the counter and slammed two autlas down in front of the bartender, a chubby fellow dressed far too extravagantly for the homely décor.

"Two of your finest ales, my good sir!" he declared.

The bartender didn't acknowledge. He was too busy staring dumbfounded at Sora. Again, Whitney wasn't sure if it was her ears, or how filthy they were.

"We don't serve their kind here," he said.

"What, women?" Whitney replied. He went on before the tender could answer. "Don't worry, she can handle an ale good as any man. Besides, business seems slow what with the corpses staring at your door."

Whitney plopped onto a stool and pulled one out for Sora. She glared right back at the man, even as she sat and leaned over the bar.

Whitney said, "Did I mention she also single-handedly defeated the most powerful Drav Cra warlock alive?"

Finally, the bartender gave in and filled a mug for each of them. "It'll be two autlas for hers."

"How about one for both?" Whitney took one of the coins away. "Thanks, friend. Money's tight after all. Just got back from a special assignment from the Wearer of White himself."

"You expect me to believe that?"

"Look at my outfit. Storm on the way in mussed things up, but you're speaking with Constable…" Whitney realized he did know the man's first name and hoped it hadn't spread this far north "… Phineas Darkings of Bridleton. Now I suggest you put those down before I lose my cheery disposition."

The bartender grimaced, then placed them down harder than necessary and went to go clean the other end of the bar.

"City folk," Whitney shook his head.

"Phineas?" Sora whispered.

He shrugged, grabbed his mug and guzzled half in a single gulp. He missed the froth and the bitter taste. Ever since he'd left the farm, he had a tradition to enjoy a drink—or six—after a successful job.

Sora wasted no time either. She grabbed her mug and winced. With the dozens of little cuts littering her palms, Whitney wasn't surprised. She bit past the pain and drank, though she glowered at the bartender over the rim of her mug the entire time.

A large man with a broom bumped Whitney's stool.

"Excuse me, my Lord," he said, then the chubby man's eyes went wide. "Sora?"

"Hamm, what in the world are you doing here?" Sora asked.

"Everything okay over there?" the bartender asked.

Hamm gave the man a thumbs up and turned back to them.

"Just trying to earn a bit of coin to rebuild the Manor. It's little more than ash now, but the people are working hard to restore the whole town."

Whitney struggled not to ask why they'd waste the time. They'd all be far better off in Yarrington. But he knew it'd earn him a punch and a glower.

"That's great to hear, Hamm," he said instead.

"Do I know you?"

"Wait." Sora snickered. "You really don't remember him?"

"Should I? Oh right, you're that adventurer? Yeah, that's it. The one who got into a pissing match with Grint Strongiron."

"His name you remember?" Whitney snorted.

"Well, I'm glad to see you made it out of that raid alive too and are keeping our fair Sora company."

"She's my apprentice now."

"Oh?" Hamm asked.

"I was Wetzel's apprentice, *my lord.* But there's always work to find for those practiced in the healing arts.*"*

"Whatever you say," Whitney grumbled.

"I was sorry to hear Wetzel didn't survive the attack." Hamm laid a hand on Sora's shoulder. Even dressed like a noble and posing as a constable, he moved right on from Whitney like he wasn't there.

"He was an odd one," Hamm went on, "but he patched up more than his fair share of drunkards. And it was a good thing he did, taking in a girl without a home."

"It was," Sora said softly.

"Well, he had a good long life. I only wish he'd come in a few more times and told more about it. A man doesn't live that long without a tale or two to tell."

"Oh, I'm sure he could have taught you some magical things." Whitney was expecting the nudge he earned from Sora, and he didn't mind it. The sight of Hamm had first made her look like she was seeing ghosts, but his words about Wetzel seemed to calm her.

"I'm sure. Well," Hamm tapped his bloom on the floor, "if your new friend isn't keeping you too busy, we could always use a healer in Troborough. Though, right now, I fear the people need someone who could mend their souls, not their bruises."

"I'll see what we can do," Sora said, cutting Whitney off right as he opened his mouth. "It's good to see you, Hamm."

"And you." Haam turned to continue sweeping, but Whitney called for him.

"Haam, do you remember a boy named Whitney Fierstown by any chance?" Whitney asked.

He stopped and scratched his chin. "Old Rocco's boy right, Iam bless his soul? Ran off, I'd say, well I can't remember. A long time ago."

"What are you doing?" Sora whispered.

Whitney ignored her. "I see. Sora here keeps talking about him, so I wanted to know if I should be worried."

"Whitney and Sora…" He laughed to himself. "I remember you those trying to break into my stores when you were young."

Whitney feigned shock. "Sora? Of all people?"

"They were quite the troublemakers back in the day. Sora here turned into a fine lass though. Wherever young Whitney is, I hope he found whatever it is he was looking for." He stared at Whitney for a few seconds, as if he was about to realize who he was, then turned and nodded toward Sora. "I hope Iam's light brings us together again."

Sora stifled a laugh as he walked away. "How does it feel to be completely forgotten?"

"Forgotten? Didn't you hear him? He remembers some of my early work." Whitney wiped his mouth.

"Then maybe you need a more memorable face, not name."

"Very funny. But enough playing around. It's time to evaluate your first job. See if you'll be a worthy apprentice."

"Me?" Sora said, the ale seemingly taking off her usual edge. "I'm not so certain you're a worthy teacher after all I've seen."

"Then you had your eyes closed. C'mon. Whitney Fierstown worked alone, but Whitney Blisslayer doesn't have to. I'll be the greatest thief ever born twice over!"

The bartender glanced over. Whitney smiled and raised his mug to him.

"Blisslayer?" Sora asked.

"Has a nice ring, doesn't it?"

Sora rolled her eyes. "Is that really what this is all about?"

"Of course. How many people get to compete with themselves. I was getting tired of the same old thing, but then I had this brilliant idea. Now, will you come along for the ride or not?" He wrapped his arm around her and stared into the distance, waving his glass in an arch over an imagined horizon. Some ale spilled over on his sleeve.

"We can be legends," he said. "Thieves that even the Crown calls upon for help when all hope is lost."

"Only if you tell me one thing first," she said.

"Anything."

"Why did you really leave Troborough? No yig and shog this time."

Whitney reeled his arm back and lowered his mug. He'd hoped Sora had moved on from that, that over the course of their adventure she'd forgotten how mad she was at him for abandoning their childhood friendship.

Whitney closed his eyes. "'I don't want you hanging around with that knife-ear runt,'" he said, adding a rasp to his voice.

"What?"

"My father said that to me once after I was late to supper. My mother silently agreed."

"You never told me they didn't like me."

"They didn't like anybody," he muttered. "You were just an easy target."

"That's why you left?"

"Don't flatter yourself." He grinned. "That was just one of a million little things. It's like I said, my father spent a lifetime grousing about everyone from better places and never once left his farm. Every trader that came through was a crook. Every knight, a noble born into his armor, when I know now that's not true. He always did just enough, barely enough to live, until they died of what, water poisoning in their own shog-hole home? I'll be damned if I'm gonna live the same way."

"So, why didn't you invite me in the first place? After all our talks about seeing the world together, getting out of Wetzel's smelly shack and off the farm."

Whitney peered up at her over the rim of his mug. She didn't look angry like when they'd first reunited, just confused. Her brow furrowed in that particular way that made the tip of her nose wrinkle along with it. Her pointed ears twitched, and he wondered if she knew they did that.

"Honestly… I don't know," he admitted. "I think I just had to give life a go on my own. Prove to my dad that the world doesn't owe us a yigging thing; we have to go and take it. Didn't seem right to ask you to come on such a foolhardy quest with me, because I knew you would've followed without thinking."

"I guess… that's fair."

Whitney released an exaggerated mouthful of air. "Thank Iam."

"You're not completely off the hook. You still should have told me."

"You're right. I tend not to think about things until after I do them, but I swear, Sora, I never wanted to hurt you. I just wanted to be gone without ever looking back. I—"

"It's okay, Whit," she said, laying her hand over his. "We found each other again."

"Even the gods themselves couldn't keep the team of Whitney and Sora apart!" Whitney proclaimed, earning a laugh from Sora. Whitney went to raise his mug, then paused. "While we're in the honest spirit I have a question too."

"Here we go..."

"You've never been to Yarrington, have you?"

"What?"

"I could see it written all over your face when you came in,. the wonder of a place where you can't see hills through all the buildings. You said you were on your way back when the Shesaitju attacked, but it's not true is it?"

Sora's features went pale. She stared longingly over Whitney's shoulder as if she were expecting something to be there. "The truth?"

"Unless the lie is better." Whitney smiled. She laughed nervously.

"It was the truth... sort of," she looked sideways at Hamm who was sweeping nearby. The man nodded. "I really did hear there was a legendary thief for hire in town who wouldn't shut up about every amazing thing he'd ever done. Sounded like you, but aren't all thieves arrogant bastards?"

They shared a laugh.

"I decided to see for myself like I'd said, but when I got there, you'd already left. I don't know what happened. Something snapped in me after so long in the same place maybe, but I took off after you without even knowing if it was you. I just wanted to believe you'd come back."

"Seriously... nobody remembered my name from that night?" Whitney interrupted. She went on as if he hadn't spoken.

"I went further than I'd ever been from Troborough," she said. "Made it far enough to see the Glass Castle and Mount Lister on the horizon. Then I just... froze. It was the furthest from home I'd ever been. At first, I was glad for the break from Wetzel, I got so tired of him bossing me around, you know? Telling me I couldn't leave until I had full control of my abilities or I'd risk being caught by the King's Shield. Telling me anywhere outside Troborough was dangerous for *something* like me."

She cleared her throat and took a sip of ale, trying to fight back tears.

"Ah, so he wouldn't have approved of barging past Glassmen in Bridleton," Whitney said, giving her a break.

"Let me finish."

Whitney didn't dare push her further.

"I wasn't like you I guess, able to put the past behind me so easily. I saw the city and thought I'd want to run down and experience all the things I never had. But all I could think about was Wetzel. He was the closest thing to a father I ever had, and he was getting sickly in his old age. Could barely remember how to brew his potions. His hands shook. Sometimes, I wondered if he even knew who I was. He needed me, and before I knew it, I found myself heading back home. To Troborough and Wetzel. I told myself that if I wasn't important enough for you to come see on your visit, you probably didn't want to see me anyway."

"Sora—"

"No, it's okay, I get it now. I don't believe that anymore."

She took a moment to gather her breath. Tears welled in the corner of her eyes. Whitney thought better of letting the quip bouncing around in his head come through his lips.

"I returned at the same time the Black Sands were driven away, when the King's Shield carried your limp body back to Yarrington. There was smoke everywhere from the fighting. Wetzel's shack was up in flames, and when I found him, he'd already suffocated on smoke. I... I... I ran away, and I wasn't there to help him because I thought I wanted to leave. I didn't even have a chance to say goodbye. I should have been there."

Whitney reached out to take her hand, thought better of it, then decided to do it anyway. Her gaze snapped toward him like he'd stabbed her, but he held on. "The only good being there would have done is gotten you killed or worse, caught by Glassmen for using dark arts."

"I could have saved him."

"I know you could have. But do you think he would have wanted you to miss out on our glorious reunion?" He got her to crack a smile.

"See?" he said. "I didn't know the old coot well, but if he cared about you at all, he would've wanted more than for you to be stuck in that town all your life. You took down an Arch Warlock for Iam's sake, whether Torsten admits it was you or not. Wetzel may not have known if you were ready to be out on your own, but I do."

Her gaze turned to her mug as she blushed, her smile widening. The sight of it invigorated Whitney so much he wrapped his arm around her back and pulled her tight like he used to when they were children.

"It wasn't your fault," Whitney said.

"Yeah, yeah."

"It wasn't. It was the Black Sands who destroyed your home, but not just them, the Glass too. All these shog-eating lords and ladies and their ancient rivalries, thinking we commoners give a yig."

"Soon to be not-commoners. At least, one of us."

Whitney released her and raised his mug. "Right. To forgetting the past, and to new beginnings."

"To new beginnings."

They clanged their mugs together and were about to each take a sip when the sound of a bell reverberated through the tavern. It chimed three times. The bartender's face immediately knotted with concern. Whitney had heard the castle bell ring in that pattern only once before—the night he'd disappeared with the late King's crown.

It only happened like that when a ruler of the Glass Kingdom passed.

Whitney and Sora exchanged a nervous glance.

Did Torsten kill the Queen?

Whitney thought what they dare not say aloud. If Torsten was willing to lie about his position, he could have been lying about everything else. It seemed unlikely, but Whitney knew a thing or two about pretending.

XXXV

THE KNIGHT

Torsten skidded to a stop at the entry of the Glass Castle, kicking dust at the guards stationed outside. They lowered their halberds as Torsten hopped down. He only realized then that while he was still wearing his white armor, it was so caked by mud and blood it was impossible to recognize. The people of Yarrington hadn't seen men return from war in nearly a decade, and he looked like he'd seen war.

"You will lower your weapons in his presence," Wardric ordered. "Now!" The guards retreated so quickly they almost dropped their polearms. "This armor still holds some respect."

"Take Redstar," Torsten said. "It's time to fix all of this."

"Is he dead?"

"Unconscious." Torsten spoke the word with venom.

Sora had found a combination of herbs along the road she'd ground to dust and force fed to the Arch Warlock, keeping him in a barely-alive state. Never had Torsten known a man who deserved death more. Cursing a child, impersonating and tainting the memory of Uriah, a good and loyal servant of Iam—it wasn't easy to spare him, but he knew the Queen Regent would want to deal with her brother in her own way.

Wardric slung Redstar over his shoulder, then they entered the castle side by side. Torsten clutched Pi's effigy in his hand.

The Grand Hall was as barren as the rest of the city. No visiting dignitaries or nobles seeking the ear of their king. A thin film of dust covered glass sculptures of old kings, and the throne was in a similar state of disrepair. Two King's Shieldsmen stood on either side of it, but its seat was unoccupied.

"The people are being ignored, Torsten," Wardric said. "She hasn't held audience with a soul since you left. Not our emissary from Panping, not the head of the mining guild, not even a farmer. Plans for Pi's hopeful, public coronation have been delayed, and when Lord Holgrass tried to broach the subject of drafting legal succession papers just in case Pi didn't wake, well... It didn't go well."

"There is no grief like the fear of loss," Torsten said. "I felt it every day as I watched Liam suffer."

"This is more than grief. It's as if Iam has turned his Eye from us."

"No. Never that. He twisted the darkness into light in the Webbed Woods and saved us all, I felt it. This is the work of his enemies: Redstar, Nesilia. It's over now." Torsten lay a hand upon Wardric's shoulder. They weren't close, never had been, but they were brothers in arms. "He is still with us."

They continued to the castle's main tower and climbed. Light refracted through the crystal at the top, painting the stairs with a rainbow as it so often did when the sun peaked. Torsten had no time to admire how much he missed the color. He took three steps at a time, and nobody arrived to stop them. The castle seemed abandoned, as if everyone were hiding.

A large, generous hallway lined with glass candelabras awaited him at the top. Broken glass and cracked tableware covered the floor. At the end of the lush, blue carpet, stood Rand and two other members of the King's Shield outside Pi's chambers.

Whereas Wardric looked like he'd aged terribly since Torsten left, Rand didn't look a day older. And he still looked scared, like a boy off to battle who'd freeze in camp at the first sign of winter. The white helm he wore lolled off to the side, barely fitting.

"Halt!" he shouted, voice cracking. "Nobody is permitted on this floor."

They didn't listen, striding right up to him until his eyes went wide with concern upon realization of who Torsten was.

"You're back?" he said.

"Step aside, boy," Wardric said. "He's here to see the Queen Regent."

Rand drew his longsword. One of the other guards did the same, but the second hesitated with his hand on the hilt.

"You're not supposed to be back," Rand said.

"We won't ask again. It's time to end this." Wardric went to draw his weapon, but Torsten stopped him.

He stepped forward until Rand's sword brushed against his chestplate. The boy quaked. Torsten reached onto his back. The other guards took hard steps forward, but Torsten didn't grab his weapon. Instead, he unlatched his back-scabbard and let his claymore clang against the floor.

He was sick of fighting. All he saw as he stared into Rand's wet eyes was a kid in over his head. A kid forced to have innocent men hanged by the demands of the Queen Regent. He saw himself, lifted out of shog of the docks by King Liam and made into a man.

"I'm so sorry, Rand," he said softly. "This is not where you belong."

"Her Grace asked to not be disturbed," he said, lips trembling.

"I return with a chance to show the Queen Regent the error of her ways. To help her see the light again. All you need to do is step aside." Torsten raised the orepul.

Rand eyed it like it was as worthless as it really was, and he didn't budge.

"You were exiled," he said. "Please leave, Torsten. Don't make me force you."

"Don't be a fool, kid," Wardric said. "Just move."

"The Queen Regent was not in the right mind," Torsten said.

"Her word is law now," Rand said. "No matter what state her mind is in."

"Do you have a family, Rand?"

"What?"

"A family; do you have one?"

"Well... yes. A sister down in Dockside. What does that have to do with anything?"

"Since I was younger than you, I've dedicated my life to the Glass.

Liam, Oleander, Pi, they are all that I have. I would do—have done—anything to protect this throne. So, you see, the Crown is my only family."

"I still can't let you in. She… she… demanded it."

"And she demanded someone find this orepul and bring her brother to justice." He gestured back at Redstar, whom Wardric had deposited on the floor in case it came to fighting. He noticed that the Arch Warlock's eyes were open again, flitting side to side to figure out where he was.

"I have finally done both after far too long. I can reason with her." Torsten stepped forward, but Rand angled his sword up at his throat.

"Stand down, Sir Ung… Torsten!" he ordered.

"If I have learned one thing in my many years, it is that the Crown is fallible. All of Iam's children make mistakes, even Liam. I have known Queen Oleander since the day he claimed her as his own. Since she was half your age. She has grown into a woman unlike any other, but she *has* made mistakes in her grief. All those men out there, hanged, they aren't on you."

"I am the Wearer of White," he sniveled. "I passed the sentence."

"No, I did. The moment I left on a fool's errand instead of standing my ground. The moment I lost faith in the Queen Regent because she wasn't her husband, and I didn't believe she could see reason without a miracle. Let me bear the weight of her mistakes, as I should have before."

He extended an open hand toward Rand's white helm. Rand's sword pressed against Torsten's neck until it drew a pin-prick of blood.

"Go. Be with your family, Rand," Torsten said. "Let me handle mine."

He stared straight into Rand's eyes. He'd seen the same look on the faces of young soldiers after battle a thousand times before. Soldiers who weren't yet numbed to the horrors of war—and there was a war on its way from the South.

He held Rand's gaze, even as a stream of red ran down his neck. Then, suddenly, Rand lowered his sword. He reached up, lifted the helmet off his head and dropped it at Torsten's feet. He didn't say a word. He just left it there and walked down the hall. He didn't cry, at least not while he was within sight.

The other two guards sheathed their weapons and stepped aside. Torsten regarded the helmet, his helmet. He considered putting it on, but without the blessing of the Crown, he'd be wearing a lie.

"Now what?" Wardric said.

Torsten drew a deep breath, then opened the door a crack.

"I said not to bother me, you insolent child!" Oleander shouted, and something shattered against the wall inside.

Torsten didn't miss getting scolded by her. He swallowed hard, then pushed the door until he was fully inside. She sat at Pi's bedside, stroking his head. Even with her hair and clothes in disarray, she was as stunning as ever. Beautiful as her namesake.

"I said leave!" she whipped around. Her hard glare softened the moment she saw who it was. "Torsten?" she whispered.

He fell to a knee and bowed his head. "My Queen."

"Torsten where have you been? I've been calling and calling for you, but instead I've had to deal with that useless boy, Ralph."

Torsten didn't bother correcting her. "You sent me away, Your Grace."

"Did I?"

"You did."

"Well, I didn't think you'd be so soft. It is your job as Wearer of White to know when I need you."

Torsten took a moment to gather himself upon learning he never even had to leave. That she had no idea she'd stripped him of his station. *She needed this closure anyway,* he told himself.

"I have captured your brother, My Queen. And I have reclaimed what was stolen from your son."

"You did what?"

He presented the doll. She eyed it a long moment before a smile stretched across her face.

"His orepul!" she exclaimed. "I knew I could count on you, Torsten! My loyal Wearer of White. Bring it here!"

Torsten stood, and it only took two strides toward her before he noticed that the room smelled like the outside of the castle. Like death. She snatched the doll out of his hands, and he didn't fight it. He was too busy staring at Pi. The boy's flesh was a sickly shade of light purple, and he didn't look to be breathing.

"Your soul is complete again, my sweet," Oleander whispered. She stroked Pi's hair and placed the doll in his hands. There was no strength in them. She had to pry open his fingers just to place the doll in, but it kept slipping away, so she had to help him hold it.

"Now my awful brother's curse may be lifted."

Torsten slowly circled to the other side of the bed so that he could lean over for a better look. The boy's chest didn't rise, and the stench was so foul Torsten had to force himself to stifle a gag.

"How long has he been like this?" Torsten whispered, barely able to get words out.

Oleander continued to smile as she pulled him close and rocked with him. "None of the castle doctors could do a thing for him, but I knew we could trust you. Loyal Torsten."

Torsten felt like he'd been punched in the gut. Oleander had been so convincing in her obsession with Pi's orepul that a part of Torsten hoped it could bring him out of his sleep. In truth, he was a child that fell from a window after the curse of the Drav Cra's Arch Warlock drove him mad. A child whose mind and body were broken.

"Iam, let not his sinful dalliance be remembered," Torsten said, tracing his eyes with his fingers. "Shower him in your light, oh Vigilant Eye."

"Come now, my sweet," Oleander said. "Wake up. It's time for your eyes to open."

Torsten returned to her side.

"There's no reason to be afraid," she said.

Torsten reached out to lay his hand upon her shoulder, and only then realized he was shaking as much as Rand had been. She didn't even seem to notice his touch. She just kept stroking Pi's hair.

"He's dead, Your Grace," he said. "Liam's only son is dead."

She turned toward him. He expected to face her wrath as he had so often but instead saw something he never expected. A tear ran down from her crystal blue eyes and anguish gripped her features. Oleander looked… shattered.

Perhaps it was hearing him say it that ended her denial. Honesty with her was always one of his gifts. As honest as one could be with their monarch that is.

"I'm so sorry, Your Grace," he said. "I was too late."

"My baby boy…" she stuttered. "Have all the gods forsaken us." Despite the filth of his armor, she threw her arms around Torsten's waist and wept. He didn't even know she was capable of it. She hadn't even cried when her husband passed. Not even a tear.

He drew her tight against his armor and squeezed. "I should have been here. I should have been stronger." He wanted with all his heart to join her in grief, but for her sake, he held back.

His head whipped around at the sound of a cackle. Redstar lay against the door, arms drenched in blood, a dagger in his hand. His gag was removed, and the bindings around his wrists were surrounded by embers as if they'd been burned away. The bodies of the two guards were outside, blood pooling around their throats.

"You traitorous cur!" Torsten roared. "He's your nephew!" He released Oleander and charged Redstar. The Arch Warlock merely grinned as Torsten lifted him by the throat and squeezed.

"He got the jump on me," Wardric groaned from the hall. He leaned against the wall, rubbing his head.

"I should crush the life out of you," Torsten grated.

"My work is already complete," Redstar gargled.

Torsten felt the man's trachea beginning to collapse, and right before it did, he dropped him.

"No," he muttered. "All of the kingdom will watch you burn for poisoning the mind of your nephew. They will see what evil is wrought from those who follow false gods and idols." He glanced back at Oleander, expecting her to be watching intently but she only continued cradling Pi like her hated brother had never shown up.

"In the name of the Queen Regent, and as Wearer of White, I Torsten Unger, sentence you to death." Before Redstar could get another word out, Torsten's boot crashed into his face and knocked him out.

Torsten reached over him, grasped the white helm of the Wearer, and placed it over his head. Then he turned to Wardric. "Throw him in the dungeon and chain every part of his body to the stone. Then tell Wren the Holy to ring the bell. King Pi Nothhelm is dead. Long live the Queen."

XXXVI

THE KNIGHT

King Liam's public ceremony was attended en masse by dignitaries from around Pantego. Former enemies, allies, foreign and domestic. At Pi's, Torsten could hear the coughs in the small crowd dappling the castle hall as Wren the Holy gave his eulogy. A eulogy for a boy nobody knew, driven mad by the whispers of his uncle's curse. Even Torsten only knew him in his brokenness, but now he believed the stories Uriah used to tell about how smart and kind Pi was before Redstar's curse.

Presently, Torsten and Wardric followed while Wren and the priests of Iam carried Pi's crystal casket down the dark catacombs to the Royal Crypt buried beneath Mount Lister. The Queen strode just ahead, long, azure dress swishing across the stone. She neither wept nor spoke, merely stared blankly ahead as she clutched her son's Drav Cra orepul—his soul —against her chest.

"Rand never came back," Wardric said as they walked.

"He should have never been asked to wear this helm," Torsten said.

"Is it wrong to say I'm glad it never came to me?"

"If only it were up to us. Perhaps it was not Iam testing Rand's fortitude, but instead, His hand that brought me back to free him after evil was invited into our home."

"You still believe Iam is with us?"

"If we falter in our faith, what else do we have?"

"It's just... ever since Liam fell ill, it's as if the darkness has slowly been surrounding us. I've had this strange feeling for a long time."

"What kind of feeling?"

"That maybe Liam struck a deal with the fallen gods of Elsewhere to reach his fame. That all this is punishment."

Torsten stopped and clutched Wardric by the shoulders. "Bury that thought deep," he whispered sharply. "King Liam spread light where there was only night. This is the work of the faithless. Wretches and heretics like Redstar who sow discontent wherever they go. Now is the time to stand strong, brother."

"For who? Her? Liam's bloodline died with the boy."

"Union under Iam is as sacred as blood," Torsten said. "The Queen is still young. There will be no shortage of worthy suitors."

"What about you? You're already worthier than any to be king."

Air caught in Torsten's throat, and he coughed. Oleander turned and glared back at them. The look sent his heart sinking into his stomach. A common-born man like him shouldn't even have been permitted to look upon royalty, let alone joke of such things.

Torsten had no chance to respond before they reached the domed hollow of the Royal Crypt. From crystal caskets, all the kings watched through perfectly preserved eyes as another was brought to join them. With the royal physician hanged and no replacement set, Pi hadn't been given the embalming treatment and his little body, pale and limp, was hard to look upon. His casket was placed in the very center beneath the shaft of light coming through an oculus.

"His eyes, are your eyes, for all Iam's children watch over us." Wren recited. Even he, the mortal vessel of Iam on Pantego, spoke without his usual vim. He drew circles around Oleander's eyes.

Torsten could barely watch. And, if not for Oleander, he wouldn't have. She stood silently beside her son, looking just as Liam did in his final days. Not her appearance—the servants had her looking as lovely as ever—but in her face. Cold, dejected, broken. Tears flowed freely as she placed the orepul, cleaned of as much spider blood as possible, over Pi's still chest. Then, she leaned over and kissed his cheek, smearing her tears onto his face.

All Torsten could do as he struggled to watch was imagine the Shesaitju army growing in the South, fueled by decades of resentment. He pictured all the conquered peoples and all their allies throughout the kingdom smelling blood in the water. Would the hidden Panping mystics recapture the minds of their people? Would the dwarves of Brotlebir refuse to open their vaults?

Things were simple when he was hunting down Redstar, but now the full weight of being the Wearer again was almost more than he could bear. Wardric was right, he may as well have worn a crown. Queen Oleander was inconsolable, though that was preferable to her hanging doctors, hand-maidens, and members of the Royal Council.

"Oh, Vigilant Eye, we pray that you see this loyal servant to your side," Wren said as he signaled for the boy's body to be sealed in and prepared for his slot in the eternal wall.

It was then, out of the corner of his eye, that Torsten noticed a shadowy figure standing in an adjoining tunnel, watching. It was the same one he and Whitney had escaped the dungeon through.

That no good, rotten scoundrel!

Torsten skirted his way around the gathering of the highest Lords in Yarrington who hadn't died or fled, King's Shieldsmen and priests. Of the Royal Council, only the Master of Husbandry showed, the Queen had apparently scared off too many others while Torsten was absent. Even Master of Coin, Yuri Darkings, the most longstanding member, had appar-ently fled the capital to avoid her ire.

"How did you get down here?" he snapped as he rounded the corner. The thief was already facing the other way but stopped at the sound.

"You guys really should work on your security." Whitney turned and lowered his hood. His grin made Torsten's skin crawl.

"This is a holy ceremony. It is no place for the likes of you."

"It's been more than a day, and you still haven't called for me. I was worried."

"On my list of things to do as Wearer of White, rewarding you is far at the bottom."

"Congratulations on getting your title back, by the way."

"Save it." Torsten raised his hand to the grip of his claymore. "Now leave, before I throw you back in a cell."

"You'll need to make a new one. They're all full."

"What are you talking about?"

"You haven't been down there? Your beloved queen was awful busy while we were gone."

Torsten glanced back over his shoulder. Pi was placed in the wall, and Wren was positioning gold autlas over the boy's eyes, the embedded Eye of Iam facing outward. There was nothing to be gained by staying while all those in attendance paid final respects, as was custom.

"It seems like ages since we met down here," Whitney said.

"Quiet," Torsten said, pushing by Whitney.

The closer to the lower dungeons he got usually meant an onslaught of silence, broken by the occasional screams for freedom or ravings of madmen. But now, it sounded like entering the barracks mess hall. Bowls clattered, conversations echoed.

A guard lay by an open gate into the dungeons, hand in a bowl of chow, snoring.

Torsten glowered at Whitney. "How did you?"

"He'll be fine. Just helped him take a long nap."

"I don't even have words."

"What? I was worried about you." Whitney lowered his head in feign submission.

"It truly amazes me that you're still alive."

"Iam loves me."

Torsten grunted in response. Then he rounded the corner and saw what the thief was talking about. The lower dungeon was overflowing. There were two to three people to every cell, and not all of them looked like vagabonds.

There were more doctors, likely being prepared to join the others hung over the wall. There were soldiers and handmaidens, priests and cultists. People from all walks of life who might inhabit all the corners of Yarrington and the castle.

"Guess I picked the wrong week to get locked up," Whitney remarked. "It's like a party."

Torsten ignored him.

"Hey!" he shouted to the two more guards sitting at a table inside, half-asleep. The larger of the two nearly fell as they roused, and the other had half a complaint out of his mouth before noticing Torsten's helmet.

"Another new Wearer?" one guard questioned.

"That's the old one, numb-skull." The big one nudged him.

"Why are there so many prisoners?" Torsten asked.

"Failed the King, the last one said."

"Or spoke out against his mother," said the other.

"It's no wonder the streets are dead. Can't share a proper pint anywhere these days," said the first.

"This is—"

"Hey, don't I know you?" A guard asked, pointing a stubby finger at Whitney.

"You're that yigging crown thief!"

"Finally, someone remembers me," Whitney remarked.

"As much as I would love to see him behind bars," Torsten said, returning the conversation to himself, "he's no longer your concern. I want detailed reports. Why and how everyone wound up down here."

"That will take forever," one guard bristled.

"Then you'd better get started."

Torsten ran his fingers along the bars, looking into each cell. It had always been easy to tell who belonged behind bars. But not this time. It didn't seem to matter who they were or where they were from, they were all lumped in together because they couldn't save Pi. Torsten may as well have been right in there with them.

"Torsten?" a small voice muttered.

He whipped toward it. Inside the cell, a young girl and a few other mud-coated men and women shivered. She was the slave he'd freed from the Black Sands, whom he'd been too busy to remember until then. Abigail. She and the others were locked up because... well, there was no good reason. They delivered a message to deaf ears because he asked them too.

"By Iam," Torsten whispered. "Guard, open this cell right now!"

"What! They get freed without even having to go to the Webbed Woods?" Whitney said.

"Guard!"

The big guard fumbled with his keys on his way over. It took him a few tries to unlock the cell door. The moment he did, Torsten barreled past and held the girl at arm's length. She was emaciated. A long journey back plus dungeon food wasn't a recipe for health.

"I'm so sorry," Torsten said. "You will all have a room in this castle for as long as you need. Your service to the Crown will not be forgotten, however little good it did."

"T… t… thank you, my lord." Abigail leaned up on the balls of her feet and kissed Torsten's cheek. Then she and the others slowly filed out of the cell.

"You leave me in the street with corpses, and they get a room?" Whitney said.

Torsten's head snapped around. He could have wrung the thief's neck, but then a familiar cackle stole both of their attention. Torsten swept out of the cell, and down the hall. Chained in the very same cell where he'd found Whitney on that fateful day, was Redstar.

His wrists and ankles were cuffed to the ceiling and floor, stretching his limbs to make him appear like his namesake. A steel muzzle covered his mouth and nose so he couldn't bite, a few tiny holes allowing him to breathe.

"Remind me again how that guy is related to the gorgeous Queen?" Whitney asked. "He gives me the creeps."

"I think it's time you leave," Torsten said.

"Me?"

"Come to the Throne Room tomorrow, and you will have your reward."

"Torsten, I—"

"I said leave!" Torsten slammed on the bars.

It startled Whitney, making his foot slip on the slick floor, but he caught his balance. He dusted off his pants and acted like it was on purpose. "Tomorrow, Throne Room. I'll be there. See ya, Red Moon." He offered a lazy salute into the cell.

Torsten watched him saunter away, not a care in the world. On the way by, he spooked the hulking guard who was busy checking on a prisoner, then vanished into the dark before he earned a cudgel to the head.

Torsten turned back to Redstar. He couldn't see his mouth but could tell by the way his forehead wrinkled the crimson birthmark covering half his face that he was grinning.

"You'll never be able to hurt that boy again now," Torsten said. It took all his willpower not to burst through the door and snap the traitor's neck right there and then. "Do you hear me? All your twisted games are finished."

Redstar laughed. "My work is already complete," he said. The mask gave his voice an unnatural, muffled basso.

"No, you failed. The Glass Kingdom still stands, Nesilia remains buried even with your Bliss destroyed, and your sister will watch you burn at the stake."

"My sister loves games more than I. Or do you think it coincidence that as she grew old enough to flower, the great King Liam grew weaker? Slowly decaying from the inside."

Torsten knew he was just trying to get in his head. Plant seeds of doubt about the Queen. "The only traitor in your family is you."

"You simple, foolish knight. Glass, Drav Cra, Black Sands, they all mean nothing. A reckoning is coming. Are you sure you're on the right side?"

"Whatever side destroys monsters like you is the right one. May Iam's light never find you."

Redstar released a cackle so hideous it raised the hairs on the back of Torsten's neck. "You really don't understand anything, do you?" He looked to the floor. "I know, my Lady… they'll see soon enough."

Torsten maintained eye contact with the madman until it became too uncomfortable.

"Guard, I want two men posted right outside his cell at all times," he said. "Ignore every word out of his mouth, and if you can't, cut out the bastard's tongue."

He then turned and headed back toward the Royal Crypt, Redstar's laugh echoing all throughout the hall, and inside his head.

XXXVII

THE THIEF

"Let's get this over with," Torsten said. If it was possible for him to appear more grim than usual, the death of King Pi had done it. Whitney wasn't stupid. It meant that their entire quest was pointless. But, at least, the surly knight wore his white helm again.

"Oh, c'mon my friend, this is a big moment!" Whitney put his hands up on Torsten's shoulders, and the look he received made him instantly regret it. "Look, I know things aren't looking too bright. Your kings are dead, rebel armies amass… but it's times like these you have to celebrate the little things."

"Or break them in two."

Whitney swallowed and removed his hands. "So, yeah. Rewards."

He dropped to one knee and stared at Torsten's boots—as clean as they should be now—then he glanced from side to side. The throne was empty as the Queen grieved, and there were only a few Shieldsmen with Torsten. Whitney realized he'd never been in a room like it without being in some ridiculous guise.

All the statues and banners honoring the kingdom's great past remained in their places. Countless heroes had kneeled on the same floor to receive the honor Whitney was about to. Even Torsten, a common-born man himself, had. Whitney couldn't think of a more fitting, ironic end for the legend of Whitney Fierstown.

"Stand up, you fool," Torsten said. "You aren't being knighted."

"Right," Whitney replied, cheeks getting a little hot.

"In the name of Iam and the Kings—and Queen—of the Glass, both past and present, I Torsten Unger, Wearer of White, stand before you. For your heroic deeds in service to the Crown, you are henceforth ennobled, Whitney…" He hesitated, then cleared his throat. "Blisslayer of Troborough. First of his name."

He heard Sora stifling a chuckle behind him.

"Since the Master of Rolls is no longer with us, I have had his young apprentice draft this letter patent as proof of your estate," Torsten continued.

He reached back, and one of his men handed him a piece of rolled parchment. He slapped it into Whitney's hand. Whitney went to take it, but he didn't let go at first.

"Try not to lose it," he said. "There is nobody here to craft records now." He released it.

Any witty response died on Whitney's tongue as the page unfurled. Below all the sloppily scrawled legal jargon was the seal of the Nothhelm family itself. Iam's Eye set in the center of a crested helmet surrounded by an intricate floral pattern that was almost impossible to counterfeit… almost.

Whitney knew the Shieldsman before him would never do something like that.

He felt as if he were floating on air. For so many years he pushed to outdo himself. But now, he'd stolen the one thing that couldn't be grasped or seen. Respect. Because all throughout Pantego, no matter where he lived, all anyone ever really cared about was who your parents were. But every great house came from somewhere, and now he was the first.

"Now, leave the throne room, thief, and don't come back," Torsten said.

"Is that any way to treat the head of a noble house?" Whitney retorted. He rolled the writ back up and tucked it into his belt.

"Do not try my patience, Whitney."

"Let's go, Whit," Sora said. "Maybe if we look hard enough we can find a place where people are more grateful."

Whitney held out a hand. "One second. I believe the lady was promised fair compensation, for her loyal service to the Crown?"

Torsten turned back.

"Wardric?" he addressed one of the other Shieldsmen. The gray-haired knight handed him a pouch stuffed with golden coins engraved with the seal of the Glass Kingdom. Torsten dropped it in Whitney's hand. The weight dragged his arm down.

"Is this enough, Sora?" Whitney asked.

"This is not a market," Torsten snapped. "This is more than fair compensation for a woman like her."

"What's that supposed to mean?"

"It means I have other things to do, and I don't have any more time to waste with games."

Whitney was thinking of some witty retort when he saw the briefest break in the knight's stern façade. He sighed. "I really am sorry we couldn't do anything for your king."

"I'm sure you are," Torsten said. "Is that all?"

Whitney held his tongue, then performed an exaggerated bow as he backed away. "It has been an honor and a pleasure, Sir Torsten. I don't look forward to it again."

"And I hope Iam sees it in his heart to show you two mercy. There is no soul beyond hope if you but open your hearts to the light."

"Mine's plenty open and hers; you said it yourself, Iam worked through her."

Torsten grimaced.

Whitney slapped the coin purse into Sora's bandaged hand. "Here you are, milady."

"Can we please get out of here now?" she asked.

"Not a moment too soon. Until the Crown calls on us great heroes again!" Whitney raised his arms as he shouted, voice echoing along the towering, stone walls and vaulted, stained glass ceiling. "I've always wanted to try that in one of these places," he whispered in Sora's ear as he turned.

She held Torsten's gaze for a few seconds longer, rage percolating behind her eyes, then finally turned. Torsten and his Shieldsmen did the same. Whitney glanced back at the giant man's back before he vanished behind the empty throne.

I'll miss him, was his first thought. He wasn't exactly sure why, and he knew nothing good would ever come of seeing him again, but a part of him enjoyed traveling with someone who seldom agreed with a single thing out of his mouth. It was one of the greatest challenges he'd ever faced. Even more so, was getting the stubborn knight to give in to his charms. Torsten would never admit it, but Whitney knew it'd be a long time before he forgot him.

Guards led them out the front gates and across the castle grounds. A few others stood on ramparts, removing the corpses from the castle walls. Carts carried away piles of bodies that had already been taken down.

They reached the street and Whitney looked from side to side. "So, where to next?" he asked, breathing in deep and immediately regretting it. Just because the bodies were leaving didn't mean the stench had yet.

"What's the furthest city away from this awful place?" Sora said. "Away from the Shesaitju, and hateful knights, and murderous queens."

"That depends. Above or below ground?"

"Above." Sora nodded her head repeatedly as if she'd initially doubted herself. She smiled. "Yeah, definitely above."

"Shog… I did love the Dragon's Tail. Dwarves love to gamble."

"What about Panping?" she asked.

"Bringing me to meet the parents already?" Her glare gave him goosebumps. "Sorry…"

"How about it?" she asked. "I figure, the way Torsten looks at me, it must be the most fun place in the world. Any place he dislikes must be amazing."

"He does despise a good time, doesn't he?" Whitney scratched his head. "It's a fine city. A bit too many soothsayers for my taste though. They have a way of looking through you."

"Well, now you have me. C'mon. Don't I deserve to see why they call us knife-ears?"

"Look in the mirror."

"I'm serious," she said.

"You just want to figure out how in Elsewhere you performed that spell in the Woods, don't you?"

She blushed.

"Well, I'm not sure that sort of answer is something we can steal," Whitney said, "but I've never been one to turn away from an impossible job."

"Like stealing that doll was really that hard?"

"Please, that was a cinch compared to my last foray in Yaolin City. But first things first."

"What is it this time?"

"Let's get out of these rags. I'm tired of smelling spider blood."

Sora picked a few coins out of her new purse. "This should do it, and take us the whole way there."

"Where's the fun in that?" In one motion, he pulled his dagger and slit the bottom of the bag, the gold tumbling out into his hand. A few pieces clanged against the cobblestone street. Sora lunged at him, but he side-stepped and skipped backward.

"Lesson number three, my young apprentice," he said. "Never accept gold from the Crown."

"That's lesson four," she said.

"So, you *are* paying attention! Alright, off we go."

He took a few coins and tossed them at a ragged man sleeping under an overhang, covered in mud from wagon wheels.

"There is no better place to start then from the beginning."

XXXVIII

THE KNIGHT

Torsten stood before Uriah Davies' likeness in the Shield Hall, overlooking the smooth, snow-covered slope of Mount Lister. Celeste, the bright moon, was nowhere in sight. A strange sight, Loutis, haggard and plain being the only faint light that could be seen that night.

The Shield Hall wasn't anywhere as glorious as the Royal Crypt, but it was where men like Torsten were buried under the watchful gaze of Iam. Men who'd dedicated their lives to the Crown.

URIAH DAVIES, WEARER OF WHITE.

Unlike the tombs of the other Wearers, there was no body buried within his. The statue was made, but he'd never returned. Now, at least, Torsten knew he was at rest through the Gate of Light.

Torsten drew the longsword that had belonged to Uriah before Redstar stole his visage. He lay it across the statue's palms, admiring the black-smithing. The blade was elegant, cleft down the center, but sharp as a wolf's fang.

"I'm sorry I doubted you, old friend," he said, placing the sword vertically between the hands of the statue. He noticed the gauntlets which had once belonged to Uriah on his hands. He'd decided he would wear them in

Uriah's honor, though they needed the attention of Hovom Nitebrittle, the Castle Blacksmith to be properly fitted.

"There is no greater honor than to die in service to God and Crown," Torsten said. "I pray you are at peace up there beside our great King in the Light. One day, by the grace of Iam, I might join you. But for now, guide me, as you once did Liam. Please…"

A deep tremor suddenly shook the ground. Torsten heard glass shattering in the castle as he was rocked from side to side. He had to grab onto the statue just to keep from being tossed. It didn't last long, and the moment it ended, cries for help echoed all around.

He jumped to his feet, searching the area. His gaze fell on Mount Lister, where a sliver of moonlight revealed a new gash running down the length of its side. It was like nothing he'd ever seen. He wasn't sure why, but he felt compelled toward it, beckoned.

He left the screams and the chaos of the castle at his back, descended the stairs leading outside and headed toward it. The closer he got to the base of the mountain, the louder the whispers in his head, the unflinching desire to head for the heart of the quake, grew.

He climbed over a pile of fallen rocks and found himself standing before an opening in the earth. Where Mount Lister met the plain, the ground had caved, revealing the heart of the Royal Crypt within. The oculus cutting through the side of the mountain had been smashed to shards.

Torsten crept to the edge and stared down. Too many caskets to count had been cracked open, Liam's among them. His sword, Salvation, had been cracked into three pieces, the hilt pinned between rocks. The remaining half of his Glass Crown lay in the center of the room, glimmering under the moons glow until a shadow covered it.

Torsten's eyes went wide.

Bending to pick up the broken crown, was Pi. Breathing, moving, he stared at the half-circlet as if it were the first thing his young eyes had ever seen. In the other hand, he clutched the bloody, ragged orepul Torsten had gone through so much to recover.

Pi Nothhelm, first and only son of Liam the Conqueror and the Flower of the Drav Cra, had been buried, but he wasn't dead.

BOOK TWO

Winds of War

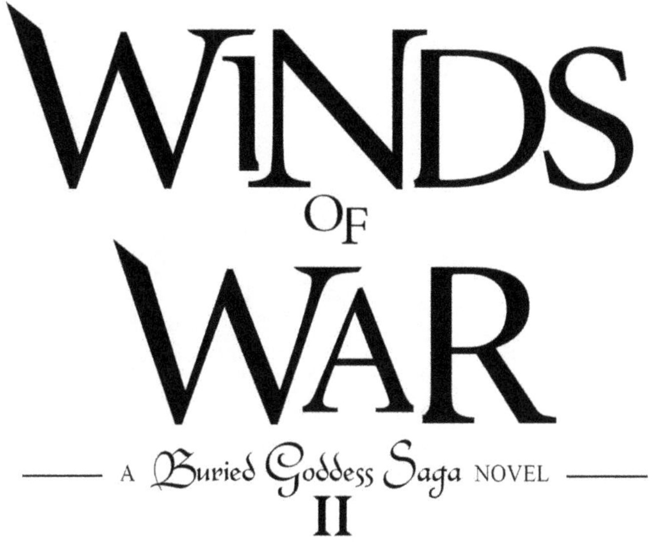

RHETT C.
BRUNO

JAIME
CASTLE

PROLOGUE

Wooden planks coated in a thick layer of moss creaked under Bartholomew Darkings' heavy boots. He closed the paint cracked and weather-worn doors behind him. The Church of Iam was enveloped by darkness but for a faint light filtered in through a circular stained-glass window, so covered in dirt the imagery was impossible to distinguish. A long aisle separating the pews was abandoned. The pews themselves were askew, and the gilded Eye of Iam had fallen from its perch over the altar. Shards of its glass core lay scattered across the floor, coated in dust.

"Hello?" Darkings called out, crossing the threshold. Only his echo answered.

He brushed a string of cobwebs from his hair, yelping like a man on fire, flailing to break free. He struggled to dignify himself, catching his breath and straightening his silk tunic. He removed a note from his pocket. On one side was a red hand and on the other, an unsigned invitation to the church with a time and day scrawled beneath.

"Another one of your made-up stories, isn't it father?" Darkings said to nobody. "The Dom Nohzi… I should have known better."

He crumpled up the note and tossed it aside, then turned toward the door. Just as his fingers wrapped the handle, he heard rustling behind him.

He whipped around to find a man shrouded in a dark cloak holding the note. The man drew back the hood, revealing hair as white as the snow sprinkling the streets just beyond the doors. His pale skin didn't show even the slightest wrinkle, not even at the corners of his eyes which were so dark it was as if they had no whites at all.

"What resolve you show, Bartholomew Darkings of Winde Port," the man said. "Waiting all of three minutes?"

Darkings had met men from Brekliodad before, but none with accents so harsh.

"Th… there was no one here," Darkings said. He wasn't sure what to expect when he used his father's contact to reach out to the Dom Nohzi, but just the sight of the man made him feel like his heart had stopped. "Where did you come from?"

"You called for us. You do not get to ask the questions here, Southerner."

"Yes, I…" Darkings drew a deep breath so he'd stop coming off like a blathering fool. His was one of the wealthiest families in Pantego, he could deal with a glorified hitman. "I have heard when it comes to eliminating enemies, your order is the best there is."

"What do you seek? And I warn you, waste my time, and you will leave here without a tongue."

Darkings swallowed the lump in his throat. "I need you to kill a man."

"Every poor soul stuck on this plane wants a man dead. The Sanguine Lords are neither man nor god, and we are their silent hand. If he is worthy of their judgment, then it will be so. If he is not, then yours will be the life forfeited. Do you accept?"

"You'll kill me? That wasn't part of my fath—"

"A man who marks the death of an innocent deserves not to live."

Now Darkings' throat went dry. He knew he should have further studied his father's notes about this ancient order of killers, but he was in such a rush. After what happened in Bridleton, losing everything he'd worked so hard to build, he'd been desperate. He pictured the flames devouring his home, all thanks to that damnable thief. He was through waiting.

"The man posed as a priest of Iam to rob me of my mother's last remaining memory. Then, he used a Panpingese witch to burn everything I loved to the ground. He is the foulest, most inso—"

The cloaked man raised a finger to silence him again. "A mystic?" he said.

"I suppose. You can kill them both if you want, but all I ask for is her companion, Whitney Fierstown. I want him delivered to me. Alive, so that I may see the life flee from his eyes."

The man inhaled through his nose and closed his eyes as if someone had just laid before him the most delectable meal imaginable. He looked at the ceiling and smiled. "The Sanguine Lords accept this offering."

Before Darkings could get out another word, the man was less than an arm span away, closing the long distance in a second. He pulled a knife from his cloak and slashed Darkings across the arm.

Darkings howled in pain. "You said they accept!"

The man raised Darkings' arm. He held a vial between two fingers and allowed the blood to trickle into it until it was full.

"Blood given, for blood required," he said. "This is our pact. If you fail to fulfill your end of the arrangement, my order will hunt you to the ends of the world. They will find you anywhere with this." He plugged the vial, then shook it in front of Darkings' face before stowing it.

"Clearly, you have never heard of my family. Whatever you ask for will be paid in full and then some for every minute you add to that bastard thief's suffering. Gold, gems, anything."

"I have no need for riches."

"Then what do you want?"

The man leaned forward, allowing Darkings to see beneath the folds of his cloak. A row of knives was strapped to his chest, sharp as galler talons. He raised Darkings' chin with a single finger, so their eyes met, then answered.

"Power."

I

THE KNIGHT

Torsten knelt atop Mount Lister, flattened centuries ago in the God Feud. Ice and snow gathered within the Eye of Iam carved into the plain, shimmering like glass when the clouds broke. White flakes danced down from a blanket of gray that hadn't waned in weeks. King Liam Nothhelm the Conqueror had ruled over the Glass Kingdom for all those years, yet now Pi stood in the center of the plateau, his mother Oleander beside him in a blue, velvet dress. Lush, white furs draped over her shoulders to fight the cold wind. She'd been unable to take her eyes off her beloved child since the moment he awoke from death. Unable to stop smiling, even though he hadn't muttered a single word since.

The boy was twelve years old, but he didn't look it. Even weeks later, the color hadn't returned to his gaunt cheeks. But it was his hazel eyes, so much like his father's, that made him seem so much older. They bore the struggle of a whole lifetime. Dark bags hung from them like sacks of wheat, and crow's feet jutted from the sides as pronounced as a man five times his age.

Wren the Holy, the blind High Priest of Iam, held a newly crafted Glass Crown above the boy's head. It was even grander than Liam's had been. An Eye of Iam in the center was set with a large diamond gleaming as a pupil. By Oleander's demand, there was a thin line of glaruium laced around it, ensuring that her son's crown not suffer a similar fate as her late husband's.

Wren spoke, but Torsten couldn't focus enough to hear the words. He could only think of how much had been lost since Liam's illness and subsequent death. Uriah Davies, Torsten's true predecessor as Wearer of White and Commander of the Glass Army, had been lost at the hand of the Queen's traitorous brother. Without Liam on the throne, an insurgency the likes of which Torsten hadn't imagined possible had arisen. A rebel Shesaitju force had even sprung up in the south, waiting to strike, ready to take back what they felt was theirs.

And the Queen... that stunning, proud woman standing beside her miracle son, she had left a swathe of death amongst her own people under the guise of trying to save Pi. Even if Torsten understood how the love of her son could drive her to such awful things, he knew the kingdom would never be the same.

He could feel it in his bones as he watched the coronation. He expected more enthusiasm—a fraction of joy, even. This was the day a new king was formally recognized; the king of the most vast and wealthy kingdom Pantego had ever known. But as Wren lowered the Glass Crown over the Miracle Prince's head, properly declaring him king beneath Iam, people cheered in presentation only. Torsten could see it in their faces; they were doing so out of fear and not love. And for all the realms Liam had brought under the rule of the Glass, no foreign dignitaries showed.

The Queen embraced her son when the ceremony was through, and then Torsten. She whispered something in his ear that he missed. The new king offered nothing, just received the crown and left wordlessly, leaving Torsten and Oleander behind to catch up.

The boy was now king, both legally and in the eyes of the Holy Lord. A boy Torsten knew little about beyond his having spent the last year cursed by Redstar to see nothing but the horrors of the Buried Goddess, Nesilia.

It all felt like a bad dream.

Once they made it back to Yarrington and returned the boy safely to the castle, Torsten left his white armor behind and found himself wandering the streets as he'd so often done as of late. He listened to the people as he walked, how they talked about the Crown now compared to when Liam was king, or more unsettling, avoided talking about it. They were scared. All of them.

His stroll took him to a tavern he'd been frequenting down in Dockside, not far from the spot in South Corner where he'd grown up. The Maiden's Mugs was like any other tavern in the area—dark, dank, and filled with the kind of riffraff with which the King's Shield was above dealing. Tired old men drinking until their vision went blurry, grasping at barmaidens, cursing their rotten luck.

It was the kind of place Torsten's father loved. A godless place smelling of sweat and sorrow. And every time he visited, he couldn't help but imagine how his life might have turned out had Liam not raised him from the muck.

He was just happy to get out of the snow. Winter had fallen upon the Glass Kingdom in a way not seen in a decade. It was as if Pantego still wept frozen tears for the greatest king Pantego had ever known instead of celebrating the newly crowned Miracle King.

Torsten supposed that's how Pi would be named: King Pi the Miraculous. It brought a shiver not caused by the cold.

The Maiden's Mugs was raucous as usual, but as the weeks went on, more and more were driven in at night to escape the weather. Torsten wasn't concerned. Even without his armor, he outmatched any dozen men in the bar twice over.

The hearth was warm, and beside it sat a cross-eyed bard strumming a lute, keeping the myriad conversations private. A sign hung on the wall and read, Order any drink ye like, so long as it's ale. But Torsten wasn't here for that. He'd seen so many soldiers turn to drink to drive out their demons, but Torsten could thank his wretch of a father at least for teaching him the evils of alcohol.

He sat in a corner booth and watched the staircase leading to the apartments upstairs, waiting for Sigrid Langley to come down. When she finally did, he sank further into shadow. Skulking wasn't like him. In fact, it reminded him too much of that rotten scoundrel, Whitney.

A drunkard grasped at Sigrid's behind and earned her elbow to his gut. She flashed him a forced grin on her way by, then slid behind the bar to start her shift serving the dregs of Yarrington. Torsten shimmied out from his seat and tried to blend in. Not an easy task for a man his size.

He was mere paces away from the stairs when he heard her voice. "My Lord, Wearer, I can't imagine what ye could be doing here."

Torsten stopped. His gaze drooped slightly, but he recovered before he spun to greet her with his best smile. She held a tray of sloshing mugs for eager customers. She was well-kept, fiery-red hair in a bun, face clean. Her beer-stained dress, however, was cut so low Torsten felt he was sinning just by looking. His father had his mother do work like this to earn autlas before she passed from fever. Dressing like that was the best way to get tips in a place like Dockside.

"My lady," Torsten bowed his head, "the pleasure is—"

"He don't wanna see ye," she interrupted. "How many times ye gonna come around?"

"Until you allow me to pass."

"Ye expecting me to be believing I'm stopping ye?"

"Your brother took an oath. I'm already ignoring the law by not dragging him before the throne, so if you'd please just—"

"Dragging him before the throne to see who? The true king is dead, Wearer, and there ain't no one fit to rule in that castle. Rand told me all that went on in that Iam-forsaken—"

Torsten placed his palm over her mouth. He must have moved too hastily, or maybe it was just his size, because she flinched in terror, tray nearly toppling.

He was always shocked at how openly Dockside folks would speak ill of the Crown—as if they didn't realize they were committing treason. Maybe they just didn't care. Dungeons had food after all, and they were warmer than wooden shacks rattled daily by the bitter, oceanside breeze.

"Ye know what?" she continued. "Be my guest. Go on. See what ye sorry old lot did to my dear brother. Don't come back down here looking to wash yer regret in a pint though."

Torsten held his tongue and turned to climb the rickety old flight, the wood groaning. He rounded a corner to a corridor of tightly clustered doors. The housing above the tavern was cheap, and rightly so. Cobwebs lined the planked ceiling and the floor sagged in the corners. To Torsten, it wasn't worth a single autla to live in such a place. Maybe he had forgotten his roots.

The door to Rand Langley's apartment was a few planks of wood poorly fit together. If the purpose of a door was to maintain privacy, his failed on every account. Through the large cracks, Torsten could see Rand sitting at the table, staring into a withering flame, hand wrapped around a mug of ale, but Torsten knocked anyway.

When no answer came, he drew a deep breath and pushed the door open. His hand clutched the Eye of Iam pendant hanging from his neck.

It was the sight, not the smell that made his stomach turn.

Torsten's quarters in the castle were far from opulent, but Rand's home could fit in one corner of it. A candle flickered on a table cramped against a mattress stuffed with hay. The whole of it was nearly a thick pool of wax, cooling quickly as a cold draft poured in from a frost-coated, cracked, glass window.

"Rand," Torsten said softly from the entrance. "It's good to see you again."

"Torsten?" The young man broke from his daze. "Torsten!" He jumped up from his chair, then toppled backward, knocking it over. He burped as bent to pick it up. "Forgive me," he said, speech slurred. "I wasn't expecting such a noble guest."

"I'm far from noble."

"Nonsense! You're the Wearer of White again." He extended his arms wide and banged his knee on the table, then stumbled a few more paces and placed his hand on Torsten's shoulder for balance. His breath reeked of ale. The stuff in Dockside was so strong it masked the ocean stench. Torsten remembered stealing a sip when he was a child and nearly vomiting. Even before he took the Shield vow, he never touched it again.

"Come, let's sit," Torsten said. "I have an important matter to discuss with you." Torsten wrapped him and guided him back to his seat. It was only in the candlelight he noticed a few stale shreds of bread, thick with mold, in the basket near the window.

Rand plopped down. His eyes lit up at the sight of his ale as if only just realizing it was there. He pawed at it a few times before gaining purchase and raising it to his lips. He took a long sip, then stopped, peering at Torsten over the rim.

"Will you have a drink with me, sir?" he asked. "I think I have another mug around here some…" His words trailed off as he reached out and rifled through an open cabinet.

"That's okay, I'm here on behalf of the Crown." It wasn't strictly forbidden by the King's Shield for a man to drink, assuming it didn't grow into a vice. So long as they remained true to Iam and the Glass, and put duty above all things, even themselves, their oath was upheld.

"Oh." Rand burped. He clanged his mug down hard on the table, spilling some all over his hand. He slurped it up and reached for his basket of bread with his dry hand.

"Bread?" he asked, tearing a piece off the stale loaf with his teeth. A small puff of mold rose, but Rand didn't seem to notice.

Torsten shook his head. He considered sitting across from him, but the rickety wooden chair looked like it'd crumble beneath the weight of him.

"I'd like you to consider returning to your post," Torsten said. "The King's Shield needs its best men for the days ahead."

Rand laughed. "Then it doesn't need me."

"No, you're exactly who we need. It was Liam who decided our order needn't have armigers of noble knights and gentlemen, but the best men the Glass Kingdom had to offer. The most loyal. This is no place for a man of your quality to live."

"Why not? I like it." He laughed again and took another swig. "The best part of living above a tavern." He raised the mug.

Maybe Rand was permitted to drink, but Torsten knew a dangerous vice when he saw one. He only hoped he wasn't too late. "I haven't been Wearer long," he said, "but you were the finest of the few recruits I trained myself."

"And my sister is the finest barmaiden this side of the gorge." He snickered and went to take another drink. Torsten ripped the mug out of his hands and flung it against the door.

"Would you listen to me, Rand!" he shouted. "You took an oath. To shield Iam's chosen king and Country from whatever evils would seek to undo them. Until your dying breath, it cannot be broken."

"Then hang me!" Rand snapped. His grin faded and his face contorted with anger that instantly rendered Torsten silent. Beyond his training, Torsten didn't know the young man personally, but he'd always been restrained, disciplined. Always followed orders.

"Do you know what I did when I was Wearer?" Rand whispered, lips trembling. A tear rolled down his flushed cheek. "I hanged them all. Everyone who disagreed with *her*. Everyone who couldn't save her precious boy. Because that's what we're supposed to do, isn't it? Serve the Crown? I wasn't the Wearer; I was a gods-damned executioner!"

"Rand, I…"

"You're what? You're what!" He slammed the table. That was when Torsten realized his hand was quaking as well. "You're sorry you weren't there?"

"You weren't ready."

"And you are? Ready to hang men simply for doing their jobs? Then you might as well do the same to me because I'm not coming back."

"The Queen was grieving," Torsten argued.

"The Queen deserved to be strung up over that wall with the rest of them."

"By Iam, keep your voice down! That's treason."

"Iam turned his back on us, Torsten. Don't you see that?"

"No, he is still with us. I saw it with my own eyes, Rand. He sent the prince back to us. Offered us all a second chance."

Rand scoffed. He leaned back in his chair, eying the bit of spilled ale pooling across the floor. "Did you visit their graves?"

"Pi's? I was there, Rand! I saw the miracle of his rebirth with my very eyes."

"Not him," Rand whispered. "All the people she hanged—I hanged. Deturo, and Holgrass, and Tessa…If Iam is with us, why didn't he bring them back, too? Why only bring back a mad prince who mutters evil in the dark."

Torsten's heart leaped into his throat.

"You thought you were the only one who ever heard him?" Rand asked, clearly noticing the change in Torsten's expression.

"It was the curse of Redstar that made him do such things," Torsten offered.

"No, that boy is cursed. Everyone who goes near him... they... they end up dead. I'm never going back to that place. I don't care what you do to me." He swung his hand as if shoeing Torsten but fell off his chair.

Torsten's fist clenched, but he bit back his response. Instead, he watched as Rand pawed at the cabinets again, searching for something else to drink on his hands and knees like an animal.

Torsten wasn't sure why he kept returning to this tavern. Perhaps it was because he too had risen from the shog of Yarrington's poor to the height of King's Shieldsman, But the boy he helped train was clearly gone —deader even than King Pi ever was. In some ways, deader than King Liam. Only a sniveling coward remained.

Without royal edict stating that one was no longer fit, either by age, injury, or worse, serving the King's Shield was a lifelong vocation. Deserting the post, as Rand had, was punishable by death. Had he cursed the Crown so profusely in public, Torsten would've had no other choice but to drag him to the dungeons. But they were alone, with only the soft whistling of wind through the cracked window and the sizzle of a candle nearing wick's end for company.

Torsten couldn't help but pity him. He knew Rand never should have been left alone to deal with Oleander's unhinged fury, and if Torsten hadn't chased Redstar to the Webbed Woods, perhaps he could have kept her from killing so many. It was only that guilt which prevented him from turning Rand in.

"The light of Iam is with you, brother, whether you feel it or not," Torsten said as he backed away. "Should you ever find the strength to hold it again, there will always be a shield waiting for you in the Glass Castle."

Rand grunted an unintelligible response without looking back. His tear-filled eyes went wide as he found another jug of ale.

The young man looked much like Pi had when Torsten found him pacing his room, muttering madness, thanks to Redstar's curse. As Torsten backed out of the tiny apartment in the shog-end of Yarrington, he couldn't help but trace a circle around his eyes and ask Iam to forgive the boy.

The worst curses come from within.

He could imagine no worse fate than having his faith shattered. He'd rather deal with twisted Arch Warlocks like Redstar any day. Because, try as they might to break him and the faithful masses, he knew they would always fail as Redstar had. The man who tried to unravel the Glass Kingdom now sat chained beneath the castle awaiting execution. And now that the coronation had passed, the time had come to rid the world of him and turn the pages on a new chapter.

II

THE MYSTIC

"This is a stupid idea," Sora said.

"Just trust me for once?" Whitney groaned. "'World's Greatest Thief' twice over, remember?"

"That's great, except I feel like I am doing all the real work."

"You're right, looking pretty must be really difficult for you."

Sora punched Whitney in the arm. "No, but acting helpless is. Why are we targeting these men again?"

"Because," Whitney said, feigning exasperation, "they have a horse and a wagon, and I'd rather not walk the rest of the way to Winde Port. I'm tired from slaying monster-gods."

She punched him again, harder this time. "And what, we just leave them stranded in a gorge? I told you, we're only going after people who deserve to lose what they've got. Like Darkings."

"But where's the fun in that?" Whitney smirked.

Every time Sora saw that look on his face, she wanted to slap it right off, but the next thing she knew she was knee-deep into one of his asinine plans.

"I don't like it," she said.

"Trust me, Sora. I've dealt with a million caravans like that." Sora raised an eyebrow. "They stop in small towns like Troborough and swindle everyone with worthless 'trinkets.' They can keep their wagon and trash if it makes you happy. All we need is one horse, they have two. Would you rather steal one from some poor stableman?"

"If you didn't toss all our gold onto the streets of Yarrington we could have just bought one."

"Sora!" he playfully shook his head. "I never thought you'd be so against my autlas-giving nature."

"I... You are the most maddening person I've ever met. A single gold autla, that's all we'd have needed."

Whitney crossed his arms. "There's no lesson in that! I promised to help you become the second best thief in Pantego, and that's what I plan to do."

"I don't remember that promise."

"It was something like that."

Sora sighed. "Fine, but this better be worth tearing my tunic. I liked this one."

"There she is!" Whitney clapped his hands, then wrapped his arm around her. "Now, do you remember the plan?"

"Of course. 'Use my assets,' as you so eloquently put it."

It was lesson number who knows how many since she found Whitney in that dwarven ruin, kidnapped by Redstar's Drav Cra followers posing as cultists. When she decided to go with him to steal the Prince's lost doll, she didn't think he'd treat it like a real apprenticeship. But his 'lessons' were endless—and endlessly obnoxious—as if thieving were some great art.

Back in Grambling, the last town they passed through, he'd swindled a drunken tailor out of boots. Played him in a game of gems, even though he'd swiped all the good cards before and hid them up his sleeve. Sora asked what the lesson was in that and he might as well have shrugged when he said, "Always check your stack before you deal."

It wasn't that he'd changed terribly since their time together as children in Troborough, but now, he had a one-track mind. In her experience, all young men had one track minds, but Whitney's was different. All he seemed to care about was stealing and making a name for himself. And none of what he took even mattered, he was happy just to throw it away. It was an obsession.

What's worse, in the thrill of their few jobs together she'd forgotten herself, but afterward, she always questioned if Wetzel had spent the final years of his life training her so she could become a thief. She'd grit her teeth and look up to the sky, then sigh and follow along behind Whitney. Because she cared about exactly one person in the world, and as incredibly irritating as he could be, he now stood right beside her wearing that goofy smile he always did when he thought he had a bright idea.

She had nowhere else to go. Nobody else to be with. No home.

"Sora." Whitney snapped his fingers in front of her face to get her attention.

"What?" she asked.

"I'm going to be just over there." He pointed to a large boulder dotting the side of the dirt trail where the path fell off down a sharp slope into the Jarein Gorge. The rift in the land was massive and deep, a canvas of red and russet rock where snow didn't cover it. At the far bottom, a river connected Winde Port with the Walled Lake which was half frozen by winter's touch, and eventually through tributaries to Yarrington or east into the Panping Region.

"If they try anything—"

"I won't be far," Whitney interrupted.

"I was going to say I'm going to roast you alive." She smiled. She couldn't help it around him, even when he was being a pest.

"I'd expect nothing less from the great and mighty Sora. We need to get you a name."

"Can we steal that next?" she joked before realizing he might take her seriously. She had no interest in being ennobled. She had no parents that she knew of, no family connections, and she'd been fine living that way her whole life.

"It's on my list. And don't worry, this is a merchant caravan with a guard or two. No way they're going to try anything too nefarious."

"Easy for you to think while hiding behind a rock."

"You'll be fine," Whitney assured her. "When the time is right, you know the plan."

Sora took a deep breath and let it out. She could take care of herself. She drew a thin line of blood along her leg with her knife which once belonged to her late teacher Wetzel.

Then she slapped it into Whitney's waiting hand, harder than she needed to. Not only would the cut help with the illusion of being a damsel in distress, along with her purposefully ripped clothes, but it provided ready access to a font of sacrifice which would allow her to tap into the magic of Elsewhere.

Blood drawn is never wasted, she told herself. *Power from sacrifice.* That was the main lesson Wetzel imparted in his teachings. The image of him crushed and charred under the roof of his shack after the Shesaitju raided Troborough flashed through her mind. She did her best to force it away.

She stepped out onto the Glass Road which connected Yarrington, the capital of The Glass Kingdom, and Yaolin City in the eastern region. The further from the capital they got, the less impressive the road grew until it was just a narrow line of dirt skirting the cliffs and a peppering of gravel for footing. She scraped away the thin layer of snow with her hands, always gloved when in public to cover her blood mage scars, then lay across the road as if she'd been beaten and left for dead. She tore the shoulder of her tunic a bit more after she got comfortable, just in case, then closed her eyes.

A few minutes later she was shivering. As she lay there, alone and vulnerable, she realized how much a gamble this was so far out in the middle of nowhere. The Jarein Gorge wasn't safe territory for anyone, let alone a young lady. It was the quickest route to Winde Port by land and Sora remembered talk back in Grambling about bandits who nestled up in caverns along the bluff.

She thought about building a tiny fire in her palm for both warmth and protection when she heard the creaking of wagon wheels and the thumping hooves of the leading horses.

A harsh voice cried out. "Whoa!"

The wagon rumbled to a stop. The horses snorted in protest, metal clanked, and footsteps approached.

"She dead?" one voice asked.

"She's a pretty little thing," said another, then added, "for a knife-ear."

"Knife-ears shag as well as the next, I say," said a third.

She could imagine the disgusting man's grin as he spoke, but she held her tongue. Although she'd only been outside of Troborough a few times, she wasn't naive. Her small village had its fair share of traveling bands and troupes passing through the Twilight Manor over the years, the kind of people who thought they were better because they'd seen things, who thought every woman in town was theirs, ripe for the plucking.

Sora much preferred stealing herself away into the hollow below Wetzel's shack, reading the dusty old tomes on magic he'd gathered throughout his long, friendless life.

"She dead?" repeated the first one.

"Dun't think so. She's breathing."

Sora moaned, putting as much desperation into it as she could muster.

"Well, don't just stand there, help her into the wagon!" Hands fell upon her, sliding and groping around unnecessarily. Her muscles tensed involuntarily but she relaxed them and stuck to the plan.

She cried out in mock pain. The men backed off. "Don't move me, p-please. I-I think I've broken s-som-something."

She made believe the noon sun was blinding her like it'd been ages since she'd opened her eyes.

"What happened, my dear?" asked a portly fellow in orange silks. He had the look of a trader—combed gray hair under a feathered cap and a calming smile. His accent reeked of Old Yarrington arrogance as he annunciated each syllable of every word.

Two hunks of muscle and armor stood off to the side, whispering and grinning with one another. They were nearly identical. One made crude gestures toward Sora, the other snickered. Another man with ash-colored skin and a scaled leather cuirass knelt beside her. A Shesaitju... a Black Sandsmen like the ones who had ravaged her hometown.

The sight of him made her lose her train of thought. She could feel the cut on her leg burning as if Elsewhere were begging her to draw on it and turn the man into crispy flesh like his kind had done to Troborough.

Stick to the plan, she told herself. She'd felt terrible about robbing a group she knew nothing of, but a part of her now considered how nice it would be to ride south on two horses instead of one.

"My wagon's h-horse got sp-spooked," she said. "Drove off the ledge. I-I barely... I barely j-jumped in time." She eyed each one, in turn, looking for signs of suspicion but found none.

"Over there?" asked the old man in silks, pointing toward the ledge which emptied into the gorge.

Sora let out a soft moan and nodded.

The twin brutes stopped joking long enough to walk with their leader toward the ledge. Their plate armor was impressive, but unmarked, meaning they were swords for hire keeping the wagon and its owner safe. Which also meant there might be something worth taking inside.

Sora cursed herself for thinking like Whitney.

The Shesaitju stayed by her side. He inspected her, eyes pale and gray like the sky after a rain shower. He said nothing, but Sora nearly shuddered under his gaze.

"I see nothing at the bottom!" one of the mercenaries called back. "Nothing at all."

"H-how could you?" she asked. "'Tis only shadow down there."

"Oi, you know what it looks like down there? What'd you first crawl to the ledge to see the remains of your cart before you flopped over, girl?"

The big men laughed.

"And pray tell, what was a knife-ear wench like you doing out here all alone so far from your home?"

"Looking for a real man, I say," said one of the guards with a grunt.

"Pick her up," the trader ordered. "We can't leave her here in this state."

Sora began to sweat more than she already was. The Shesaitju continued to stare, silent.

The armored men grabbed her and yanked her to her feet about as gently as if they were hefting a dead warthog. She maintained her composure and groaned, even though her blood was beginning to boil.

She could hear Whitney's voice in the back of her mind, "Lesson three: never give up the grift until the grift is done!"

She swore silently, wondering what he was waiting for.

"Another member of our merry band?" one of the mercenaries said to the trader.

A large hand slid over her breast and squeezed hard. She whimpered, experiencing real pain this time. Her eyes fell toward the cut on her leg. She imagined what it would be like to light the man on fire starting from his boots.

"Something funny, girl?"

She hadn't realized she'd been grinning at the thought.

"P-please," she begged, "I'm just trying to get to Winde Port. M-my cart went over—"

The mercenary squeezed her jaw and tilted her head up to get a better look at her like she was a prized steed. "You already said that."

"Enough," the trader said.

"Why? You think a pretty little thing like this wound up out here alone? What's your game knife-ear?" He turned her head again, this time more forcefully. Instinct kicked in, and Sora bit down on the soft bit of flesh between his thumb and forefinger. He howled, and she broke free.

"You wench!"

The other twin grabbed her and threw her down near the wagon. Her head bounced off dirt and gravel and had her seeing stars.

"Stop this, now," the trader said.

"You hired us to protect you. The way I see it, knife-ears on the road are nothing but trouble."

One of the twins placed a knee against the small of her back to hold her down. She heard the other's belt clasp come undone. The trader protested but neither listened. A familiar tingle ran through her spirit as she felt a hand against her thigh. The area around the cut went simultaneously cold and hot. The rest of her was disembodied. Numb. She felt fire crackling on the tips of her fingertips when the cart shook and down stepped a stocky, little, red-haired dwarf. He held a mug in one hand, ale dripping down his scraggly beard.

"What in Meungor's Axe is goin on out here?" He looked at Sora, his eyes each looking in different directions, then at the mercenaries. "Pull yer pants up, animal."

He shoved the mercenary in the chest, and even though the man towered over the dwarf, he backed down. As Sora rolled over, she noticed a strange sort of a hat topping the dwarf's shaggy hair. When he got closer, she realized it wasn't a hat, but a half-broken circlet made of blown glass.

"I was not going to allow it, Grint." The voice came from beside Sora. She hadn't even noticed the soft-spoken Shesaitju standing beside her with his scimitar drawn in defense of her. She instantly felt sorry for wanting to torch him.

"By the look of it, ye were outnumbered."

The twin mercenaries had their hands hovering over the grips of their weapons. Grint and the Shesaitju stepped in front of her.

"Fellows, I do believe it's time we moved along," the trader said.

"Just leave her be an' get yer horny hinds back aboard," Grint growled. "Ain't helpin her, nor hurtin her. Just move along."

"We're tired of listening to you, dwarf," one of the mercenaries said, his belt still undone.

"Too bad. I made better men shut their traps than ye, *Dorblo*." He spat the name like it was an insult. "And I be in charge of keeping this here caravan safe."

Grint grabbed Sora by her ripped tunic and shoved her aside without even an attempt to be careful. So much for her savior.

"Get inside!" he barked.

"You're not paying me," Dorblo said. "He is."

The old trader stammered over a response.

"Plenty more gold to go round if we lose the two of ye." Grint stroked the battle axe hanging from his belt.

"I dare you," Dorblo said.

"What ye be, is needin to get in the wagon." They stood face to face, the dwarf up on the balls of his feet. To his credit, he made himself nearly as tall as the man, but Sora hadn't seen a battle of testosterone like this in her entire life.

"You ain't worth my time," Dorblo huffed, finally backing down. He nudged his twin, and they stormed off together toward the ledge and away from the dwarf. The old trader dripped with sweat, eyes darting back and forth between them. By the looks of his carefully manicured fingers, he'd never been in a scrap in his life.

Sora went from wanting to burn them all, to feeling like she was watching a play performed by the school children in Troborough.

Whitney where the yig are you?

"She needs help, Grint," the Shesaitju said, his sword still drawn.

"We ain't a charity," Grint said.

"We aren't monsters either."

"We got no room for another. 'Specially not her kind."

"You know it's not safe here after dark. That's why we were hired."

"I said, there ain't room. Ye be wantin to walk all the way to Winde Port?" The dwarf gave the gray man a shove.

"Do not strike me," the Shesaitju man said.

"Don't make me, then."

The dwarf shoved him again, and the Shesaitju retaliated.

Sora crawled back slowly and was about to run when she heard someone whisper her name.

The horses snorted, and the wagon creaked as it lurched forward, causing Sora, and all five men to stop bickering to look over. Whitney Blisslayer sat at the reins of the wagon. The armored twins and the trader were far enough to be of no concern, but the dwarf, nose now bloody and probably broken, and the Shesaitju, in far worse shape, were both close enough to be trouble.

Sora scrambled to her feet. Whitney grabbed hold of her hand and yanked her up beside him.

"Took you long enough," Sora bristled.

"Take the reins!"

"What?"

"Just take the reins!" Whitney said as he gave them a vigorous snap and the horses shot forward. He let go, and Sora fumbled to grab them. Heavy flakes of snow stung at her cheeks and arms as the carriage was pulled along.

Whitney rose and leaned over the side of the carriage. The dwarf took a swing at him with his battle axe but, dizzy from his fight, missed. Whitney reached out, plucked the half-crown from the dwarf's head and pulled himself back up.

"All right, on the horse and we'll cut the carriage free," Whitney said. Sora glanced back at the men chasing after them and remembered how they'd treated her—a lost soul on the road in need of help. Even if her state was a ruse, she couldn't believe strangers would treat a person in such a way.

She said nothing, only snapped the reins and propelled the entire carriage around a sharp turn on the cliff-side trail. It tilted onto one wheel and drifted on the icy, slick path. Sora closed her eyes, fearing they would suffer the fate of her own lie, sliding off the edge and into the canyon below, but the horse whipped around the corner and yanked the carriage down so hard Whitney almost lost his Glass Crown.

"Thanks for the carriage!" Whitney shouted. "And Grint, Whitney Blisslayer thanks you for the crown!"

Sora tightened her grip on the reins as if somehow she knew he'd take his attention off the road to offer his usual bow and flourish. One hard bump or sharp turn would have sent him flying off the cliffside. And after leaving her with those rotten men, a part of her wanted to pull back on the reins.

"I thought you just wanted to take a horse?" Whitney said as he climbed back to sit beside her. She squeezed the reins so hard her knuckles went white as a corpse. "What? I'm not complaining."

"You're a bloody pile of shog, you know that?" Sora snapped. "How long were you going to wait? Those men were about to..." She couldn't even get the word out.

Whitney, on the other hand, grinned ear to ear. He had the broken circlet in his hands and marveled at it. Now that the dwarf's messy hair didn't cover it, she realized it was much more than a circlet. It was a crown—half of one—with flawlessly cut gems set into every point. The glass was so pure it caught the high sun and painted an area of his leg with a prism.

"Are you even listening?" Sora said.

"Of course, I am," Whitney replied. "I knew you had nothing to worry about."

"No, *you* had nothing to worry about, watching me get tossed around from five hundred paces away." Now that enough distance had been put between them, Sora allowed herself to take her heated glare off the bumpy road and back on Whitney.

"I watched you single-handedly stop one of the most powerful warlocks in the known world. You know what that makes you?"

She didn't answer.

"The most powerful blood mage in the whole world. Huh, how about that? 'The World's Greatest Thief' and the 'World's Most Powerful Blood Mage' riding together into the sunset."

"It's noon, you fool."

"It's a figure of speech." Whitney placed the half-crown over his head and leaned in front of her. He bobbed back and forth, trying to get her to say something.

"You should be grateful you know," he said.

"Are you serious?" she asked, incredulous. "For what exactly? You using me as bait? Forcing me to play along with the stupid games of a child looking to prove himself greater than a father long past? What? Tell me."

"Wow, that hurt," Whitney said, but his smile told a different story. "Look, we just scored something big. Really big. And what's best about it is who we stole it from."

"They were just a couple of… of… there's not a harsh enough word for them."

"Except the Black Sandsman, he looked like he had a little crush on you. First, they destroy your town, now you're falling in love with one." Whitney shook his head in mock disappointment.

Sora's cheeks went hot. She wished Whitney wouldn't have noticed even though she could tell he did. It wasn't that she found the ash-skinned man attractive. She just felt terrible for grouping him in with others who looked like him, like all the sorry men who'd cursed her simply for being a knife-ear since she left home.

"At least *he* was willing to stand up for me," she said.

"Like he stood up for Troborough?"

"What?"

"That sorry lot. They were there in Troborough the day it was burned down."

Her brow furrowed and for an instant, curiosity replaced her anger, then a sharp turn in the road drew her attention back to the horses. The way grew so narrow that there wasn't half a meter alongside the carriage separating them from certain doom. And on the other side was a sheer cliff, the rock as red as blood. She was grateful the horses seemed to know the way.

"That's how the dwarf had what's left of the King's crown I stole." Whitney pointed to his head. "They *all* fled the place when the Shesaitju attacked, including your would-be-savior. I think I remember seeing him kick a helpless woman begging for a ride so they could speed away."

"And you knew about this?"

"Came up with the plan the moment I spotted their wagon across the gorge. I never forget a group that deserves to be robbed."

She took her hands off the reins to slap him on the arm with the back of her bandaged hand. "This partnership isn't going to work if you don't trust me."

A thousand different answers flickered across his face, all of them probably warranting another slap. Sora was glad he took his time. "You're right," he said, finally. "I'm sorry. I thought it would be better if you thought it was just another mark. I didn't want you to go all, you know, explody because these men might have been responsible for…"

His words trailed off. She knew what he was about to say. He'd been good about not bringing up Troborough too much. The wound was still too fresh for her. A mercenary group like that one might have been able to save dozens of townsfolk if they hadn't run. *They might have been able to keep Wetzel from being...*

"I wouldn't have killed them all," she mumbled. She wasn't sure if she believed those words, which frightened her. She could feel that tingle of energy on her arm and hand again, pulsing in her blood. Even the Shesaitju who came to her defense. She wasn't sure what she would have done.

"I'll believe that when you tell me how you beat Redstar," Whitney said.

She had no response. Torsten thought what happened when she released enough energy to stop the Arch Warlock was the work of Iam. She thought maybe she'd drawn on Bliss' godly blood. But the spider's corpse had been meters away from her, and neither she nor Wetzel had ever been able to draw on any blood but their own before.

"Exactly," Whitney said.

"Did you know?"

"Know what?"

"That they were the kind of men who'd do... that... to me."

Whitney swallowed the lump in his throat. "All I knew was that they were thieves and cowards," he said.

A smirk played at the corners of her lips. "You're a thief, and if I remember the woods correctly, you yelp like a coward."

"But I do it with style! That bastard dwarf challenged me to steal the crown, then swiped it during the attack and fled. I am many things Sora, but you should have seen me fighting off Black Sandsmen until the Glass soldiers arrived to save the day."

"Didn't they arrest you?"

"Which time?"

They shared a laugh, and Sora felt the itch of tension fading. It was the same every time he did something wrong. She'd scold him, and then a few wisecracks later and he'd have her smiling and forgetting why exactly she'd been so angry. Not this time.

She leveled her gaze at him until he had no choice but to make eye contact. "If you ever lay me out like fresh meat again, Whitney Fierstown—"

"Blisslayer," he corrected. Her scowl stole the color from his cheeks.

"If you ever do that again, I'll burn your hands so deep you'd never steal another thing. Do you hear me?"

"I hear you."

"I'm serious."

Whitney circled his eye with one finger. "I swear to Iam and all the fallen gods. Never again." She kept her lips straight and continued staring until finally, he frowned. "I didn't think it would go that far. I promise."

Sora exhaled through her teeth. "It's okay. We'll consider using my assets one of your more forgettable lessons."

"You just have to keep working at it."

"Forget it."

He smirked, then leaned back and made himself comfortable. "Oh, Sora, we'll make a thief out of you yet."

"Yeah…"

She stared off into the distance where a watchtower rose over an outcrop of rock, and the road twisted back around toward a colossal stone bridge crossing the gorge. The columns and arches supporting it sank into the shadow of the rift. Others sprung out from anchors in the snow-covered rock. It made the old wooden bridge crossing Troborough's portion of the Shellnak River seem like a plaything. She didn't even know man could build such a wonder, yet here she was, growing further and further from the home she knew with every second.

"So, that's the bridge to Panping?"

"Yeah. Older than the Glass Kingdom itself. Dwarves built it... I think."

"And why aren't we crossing it?"

"It's a long way to Yaolin City and the roads are filled with things worse than Grint Strongiron. Like I've said, it'll be a quick ride down to Winde Port. We'll sell the silks and whatever else is back there, buy passage on the first ship to Yaolin City, and be there in half the time."

"What about the crown? I bet we could purchase our own ship with that."

He looked at her, appalled. The last time she'd seen him appear so concerned about anything was right before he delved into Bliss' lair, which meant this wasn't just one of his games.

"So, that really did belong to the late king?" she said.

"Plucked it off his holy head."

"Then you might want to consider hiding it." She gestured to the watchtower standing proudly on their side of the bridge where the road bent south. Another waited on the other side, blue and white banners of the Glass Kingdom draped from the tops. Archers waited on the walls, and more soldiers stood at the base. They searched another wagon waiting to pass.

Whitney sprung upright. He yanked the crown from his head, looked at her, then back at it.

"You're right," he said. "If they recognize this we're dead."

"Recognize what? I've never seen it before in my life."

"Very funny. Slow down." Whitney crawled into the wagon and dug through a pile of fine silk blankets, wrapping the half-crown in one.

"You better hurry up!"

Sora snapped on the reins, and the jolt sent him tumbling into the back of the carriage.

"Sora!" he yelped. He lost the crown in the pile of sheets and scrambled to find it. She couldn't help but chuckle as she noticed the great Whitney Blisslayer beginning to sweat. It was the least he deserved for almost getting her killed just to get the relic back, after all. And if she was stuck with him on this journey to see the world and the home of her ancestors for the very first time, she was done doing everything on his terms.

III

THE KNIGHT

I t was no easy task, repairing the Royal Crypt after an earthquake
split the ceiling, leaving a zigzagging gash down the base of Mount
Lister. Canvas and wooden scaffolding covered it, but snow flurries
still found their way in where pilgrims and worshippers tried to peak in at
the site of Iam's latest miracle.

The entire wall, which once housed the caskets of Liam Nothhelm and
his son, Pi, had ruptured. And so, Liam's corpse was placed off to the side,
coin-covered eyes staring up through the lid of his glass sarcophagus. The
casket beside his was empty, fractured by the quake before Pi stumbled
out that fateful night.

"Lord Wearer?" the dwarven foreman said.

Dwarven artisans were summoned to perform the repairs, for they
alone possessed the skills to undertake such a task quickly. The tunnels
were older than the castle, older even than the Glass itself having been dug
thousands of Dawnings before humans migrated south from the Drav Cra
tundra.

Torsten's focus was so lost between the remains of his great king and
the site of Pi's rebirth, he barely registered the dwarf's words. As a Hand
of Iam, he was not one to question the one true God, but he couldn't stifle
the questions echoing around in his head over the last weeks.

Why not Liam? Why not both of them? *Why him? Only him?*

He knew how horrid it was to think. No father should be forced to live in a world where his son had already passed, but the Glass Kingdom needed a leader—a true leader—now more than ever. The wolves were waiting to pounce, and once the wonder of Pi's triumphant return to the realm of the living and subsequent coronation wore off, Torsten knew they would.

The dwarf shook Torsten's arm. "Me Lord."

"What?" Torsten snapped, too late to adjust his tone. He breathed deeply. "Apologies."

"Ain't no matter, me Lord." The dwarf pointed toward the heaviest bit of construction. The burly little dwarf's beard drooped down to his belt, and his biceps were as wide as Torsten's, even though he was a third his height. "Just lettin ye know we're gonna need a bit of extra support in that sector. Struts be makin things uneven—"

"Do what you must," Torsten interrupted. "I just want this place closed in so nobody can disturb them."

"Aye. Bad luck disturbing the buried and the dead."

Torsten nodded.

The dwarf didn't leave, only shifted his weight to the other foot and scratched his head.

"Was there something else?" Torsten asked.

"It's uh…. All this work's gonna take longer than expected."

"How much longer?"

"A fortnight? Maybe three."

"If you need more men, there are plenty of folk in South Corner who can use the coin. Trust me."

"Won't help. With the mountain so damaged, we gotta work slow or risk cavin the whole yigging thing—excuse me words, Lord."

Torsten motioned for him to continue.

"Then there's matchin the architecture, and I tell ye, even we dwarves don't build em like this no more. The stonework's impeccable."

Torsten ground his teeth. "The Crown hired your crew because you're one of the best in the Dragon's Tail."

The dwarf clicked his tongue. "The best willin to travel so far south to work on a crypt. Ye humans do love yer dead. We burn ours and give em to the air. Fires keep us warm and the demons away. Just bein round em gives me the willies."

Torsten bent to meet him face to face, knowing how much the dwarves hated being reminded of their stature. He grabbed him by the collar. "I don't want to hear your excuses," he bristled. "You're being paid handsomely. Get it done or we'll find someone else who can."

The dwarf didn't back down. "Ain't no one better than dwarves, Glassman. And ain't none of em other than me who'd be wantin to risk bein slung over a wall by the throat by the Queen Mother."

Torsten squeezed tighter, then decided better of it. He shoved him away. "Just get it done."

The dwarf bowed excessively low. "O'course, yer Highness. We won't stop til the job's done or yer coffers be dry."

"Dwarves," Torsten grumbled. As he turned to leave, he thought he heard the foreman mutter something about 'flower-pickers' under his breath.

The new Master of Masons, Leuvero Messier was instructed to find the best and Icarus deToit, the new Master of Coin, to pay whatever it took, but the new Royal Council lacked experience, among other necessary virtues. Of all those who'd served directly under Liam, only Torsten remained. The others had been dismissed, executed, or fled the Queen's rage while he was off to the Webbed Woods.

Even Uriah had to start somewhere, Torsten told himself.

Being the Wearer wasn't an easy job, and it wasn't his place to question his station. Still, he longed for the days when Uriah wore the white helm, and the only worry was if news of the late king's condition would leak beyond the castle walls. Things were simpler then.

Instead, he now had business in the dungeons, facing one of those Royal Council members who'd fled and now returned. The warren of dwarven-built tunnels deepened and grew less ornately carved until it was no more than plain, efficiently stacked blocks of stone. Somehow, even the room full of corpses found a way to smell more pleasing.

Torsten turned into the lower dungeons. Sir Nikserof stood with a torch before one of the cells. He noticed Torsten and struck his chestplate in salute.

"Wearer, he's in here," he said. "They say he strolled right into the prefect's estate in Winde Port, begging for his old station back." Torsten returned the salute. He wasn't sure of the soldier's name as he had traveled all the way from Winde Port.

In the cell sat an older gentleman wearing fat mustache. He dressed like a noble because he was one.

"Sir Unger!" the prisoner exclaimed. He jumped at the bars and poked his head into the opening. "There's been some sort of mistake."

"No, Lord Darkings, there hasn't been," Torsten said. Yuri Darkings was the former royal Master of Coin, handler of finances. He had the tanned skin of a man from the great port city to the southeast, and no man knew more about the Yarrington coffers than he. "You abandoned your kingdom in its time of need."

"Oh please, Shieldsman," he countered, his sense of nobility returning. "It was a matter of survival. Oh wait, you wouldn't know. You were sent away before she'd really lost it."

"I did what I had to for the Glass."

"So did I. You think it would have helped anybody had I stayed and wound up hanged like Deturo and the others? Now we have some pimple-faced Royal Physician no good to anyone. Now let me out, and we can put all this behind us."

"Your role has already been filled."

"What, by some pup from the market district? One of my assistants? I was hand-picked by King Liam before his body failed. I never imagined how much I'd miss him being around."

Torsten didn't want to voice his agreement, but his expression betrayed his thoughts. Yuri seemed to gain confidence in seeing he was getting through.

"He kept me too busy to breathe with all his conquests," Yuri said, "but at least those made sense."

"King Pi has returned," Torsten said, mustering his most authoritative tone. "Everything is as it should be, yet I'm told you were in no rush to return. You would have been in Winde Port for a week or two before Prefect Calhoun says you walked through his doors."

"Would you have been scrambling to return here?"

"Am I not here now?"

Yuri sighed and backed away. "You've made your point, locking me away down here. But be smart, Sir Unger. I know what it takes to fund a war. I hear the rumors. I know what's coming."

"I am merely a member of the Royal Council," Torsten said. "I don't decide who sits on it."

"Ah, but you have her ear."

"There is a new king now."

"Please, I may have just returned, but I have ears all over the city. I know the 'Miracle King' hasn't spoken a word since he was returned to life, if that's even what happened."

"It was. I was there."

"Relax. I'm not questioning anything these days. All I know is that everyone who disappointed Oleander wound up dead or down here, but all she did was kick you from the castle and onto some insane quest. Don't be a fool, Unger. I can help, just as I have for decades."

"I'm sure you could. But how could we ever trust a man who'd abandoned his post?"

"I hear the Caleef is visiting soon. I know exactly how much they owe us in delinquent taxes, how much they've been skimping since the late king's condition became public. Down to the autla. And I know how much it costs to arm a Glass Soldier for war. Who is in charge now, deToit, my apprentice?" He laughed when Torsten's face betrayed the answer. "He can barely grow a beard. You need me."

Torsten wanted to curse the man, but he knew he was right. As much as he loathed merchant-types with all their scheming and counting coins, men like Yuri were all that kept the Crown from drowning in debt. War was expensive, if it came to that, and another loan from the Iron Bank in Brotlebir was out of the question. Liam funded more than half his campaigns through them, paying the dwarves back when another foreign city was sacked and absorbed by the kingdom.

Investing in Liam had been a smart decision, and his ability to settle debts had forged strong alliances with the dwarven kings, especially King Cragrock of Brike's Hollow. Investing in the unpredictable Queen and a child, however; that was far riskier. The fact ever more proved by the quality of artisans willing to travel to Yarrington. In the days of Liam, dwarves would have fought one another for the chance to build something for him. Now they sent their leftovers.

"Your reinstatement is not for me to decide," Torsten said. "But I'll speak with her."

"I suggest you do it fast. It's never a good idea to be in a castle surrounded by strangers. You know me at least, and you know I know what I'm doing. Can you say the same for anyone else in the new Council?"

"I said I'd talk to her." He turned to Sir Nikserof. "See to it he is fed well and made comfortable during his time here."

"Sir." Nikserof saluted.

"We're all that's left, Torsten," Yuri said as Torsten turned to leave. "We can't let her mar Liam's legacy any further before the boy is even old enough to lead."

Torsten grunted a response, then continued along. He knew Yuri only as well as he needed to, being that they served on the same Council for the last year, but he also knew the old dwarven saying that the demon you know is better than the demon you don't. And Yuri was right. There was nobody in Yarrington better with money.

Torsten reached the other end of the dungeons when he heard a cackle. The sound of it made his blood boil and his heart race.

"My, my. My dear sister really has made a mess of things," Redstar said through the metal mask covering his face to keep him from drawing blood with his teeth. All that was visible beyond it were his dark eyes. It was the playfulness in them Torsten found most unnerving. Locked in the deepest dungeon, to be executed any day now, yet everything seemed like a game to him.

"Quiet!" one of the two guards posted outside his cell snapped.

Torsten stopped and bit his lip. He told himself not to turn and face the manipulating heathen. It never led to anything good.

"Why don't you let me out and I'll talk with her? I can join the fair prince. Miraculous, what happened to him, wouldn't you say? It is like he has some strong tie to the Lady. Two souls beneath this mountain were once buried but not dead, not really. How… poetic."

Torsten couldn't hold it in. He turned to engage when Sir Wardric Jolly arrived and slammed on the bars in front of him. The gray-haired Shield-sman was the unofficial second in the King's Shield, having served since before Torsten was born.

"You'll hang soon enough, knave," Wardric said. He turned to Torsten and saluted. "Sir, I need to talk with you."

Torsten held Redstar's gaze for a moment longer.

"Buried, not dead. Buried, not dead," Redstar sang, snickering.

"Torsten," Wardric said, finally earning Torsten's focus. He guided him around the corner. "When are you going to get rid of him already?"

"The Queen did not wish to besmirch the miracle of Pi's rebirth by spilling the blood of her brother before the coronation," Torsten replied.

"Well, that's done with now, and nothing boosts the people's spirits like a good execution."

Torsten smiled and patted him on the back. "His time will come. Now, you seemed in a hurry. Is everything all right?" He'd become used to things going awry. When someone of any stature approached him, he assumed the worst. However, the old, weathered Shieldsman appeared calm.

Wardric led the way through the labyrinthine tunnels beneath the Glass Castle. "Queen Oleander is requesting your presence in the Throne Room," he said. "He's arrived. A day late and with no notice."

"Naturally. The Black Sands want to see Yarrington as it is, not as we would present it to be for the coronation. Afhem Muskigo tested us with fire, and now Caleef Sidar Rakun will test us with his eyes."

"*If* they're working together," Wardric offered.

"If Muskigo truly did attack without blessing, Caleef Sidar will have no choice but to align with us."

Wardric sighed. "I tire of these games."

"Brace yourself, my friend. I fear the games have only just begun."

"Iam save us all."

"So, you have faith He's with us again?" Torsten asked.

"The only legitimate heir of Liam Nothhelm rose from the dead. Wren the Holy believes it a miracle, why shouldn't I?"

"A miracle, indeed," Torsten said.

But whose?

He couldn't keep the thought from popping into his mind. Every time he pictured Pi standing in the Royal Crypt, crown and bloody Drav Cra orepul in hand, Torsten thought of those last words he'd heard the boy whispering in darkness—Redstar's words.

Buried, not dead… buried, not dead.

"You went to see him again?" Wardric asked as they rounded a corner into the castle's east wing. Tall, pointed-arched windows lined the hall, stained glass shining like precious gems beneath the winter sun.

"See who?" Torsten asked, happy to be stirred from impure thoughts.

"The boy, Rand."

"He's a boy no longer."

"You're wasting your time, Torsten."

"I refuse to let another worthy soul abandon his post."

"Then consider the reason he left," Wardric pleaded. "Consider the reason the Royal Council is sparse, and those who remain are grossly under-qualified whelps."

Torsten shot a glower his way. Wardric took him by the shoulders and stopped him outside the door to the Throne Room. "How long will the miracle steal everyone's attention? Eventually, we have to address what happened while you were gone. How can the people trust leaders who hang physicians and servants for merely speaking truth? Our dungeons still overflow, and we don't even know who really belongs there."

Torsten lightly shrugged Wardric off. They'd grown closer in the weeks since he'd returned from the Webbed Woods. Of all the Shields-men, Wardric had given Torsten the hardest time after he'd taken over for Uriah Davies, his long-time predecessor. It took horrid times, but Torsten now knew that if he could trust anyone throughout the kingdom, it was the gray-haired Shieldsman standing before him.

"Let us deal with one problem at a time," he said. "We were all lost after Liam passed. A new king doesn't change that. None of what happened was right, but we can only look forward now. Agreed?"

Wardric drew a deep breath, then backed away. "Agreed. Now, go make sure the Caleef answers for what was done."

"He will, my friend. You have my word."

Torsten turned, but Wardric grabbed his arm. "Don't let her cause a war we cannot win. We've lost enough already."

Torsten nodded, then stepped into the Throne Room. Pantego's ulti-mate seat of power, a Glass Throne possessed by a juvenile king, towered over the room. By the new king's side stood Queen Oleander, and behind her the Council of nobodies her unbridled rage had left them with. Torsten was the only among them who'd seen war while serving under Liam. For Iam's sake, he was the only one who'd ever even held a sword.

Glass Soldiers lined the hall along with a handful of Shieldsmen. The former remained at attention, stoic, disciplined. The latter saluted Torsten, fists against their chests as he passed. Torsten recognized only a few of the Shieldsman beyond Nikserof who remained downstairs. Sir Mulliner, Reginald, a few more faces he couldn't put to names.

His own fingerprints upon the Shield, compared to Uriah's, were nearly imperceptible after he spent so much time catering to the Queen's will and sending others to their deaths at the hands of Bliss. And now there were fewer within the walls of Yarrington than ever before. Following the death of Liam, dozens had been dispatched to strongholds throughout the kingdom by Wardric when Oleander wasn't looking. All across the southern reach, they trained the Glass armies and fortified, preparing for another attack by the Black Sands. Then there were those like Rand and Lord Yuri Darkings who had fled Oleander's wrath and deserted their post.

"You're late," Oleander said from beside the throne. She was easily one hundred paces away, but her voice carried down the vaulted ceiling like a galler in flight.

Torsten bowed low. "I had some affairs of the state to address, Your Grace."

She slowly shook her head. "You know I don't like waiting when I call."

"Apologies, Your Grace. It won't happen again."

"You always say that." She held her stern glare for a few seconds before it gave way to a smile.

Just the sight of it gave Torsten pause. Her late husband had named her the Flower of Drav Cra, and never had an epithet been apter. A month had passed since Pi was reborn, and since that day she was as confident as ever, never leaving her quarters without a veritable army of handmaidens preening her.

Presently, she wore a blue gown—always blue—more extravagant than any Torsten remembered having seen her in. It was cut low—always low cut—revealing the lines of her collarbone, then sweeping up around her slender shoulders like peacock feathers. The bottom cascaded down the throne's dais. With Tessa dead at the hands of her wrath, Oleander's new favored handmaiden—he wasn't sure of her name—was busy unfurling the ends, so it appeared like a waterfall cascading down glass steps.

Torsten couldn't help but remember when he found Oleander at Pi's bedside, shattered by grief after the boy died. It was as if she too had experienced a rebirth through his resurrection, the whole castle even. The court went from cowering from her grief-stricken wrath, to impossibly busy with the coronation and other affairs. And now, the royal entourage of the Shesaitju Caleef was arriving in the heart of Pantego. On the surface, everything seemed back to normal, but one look around, and it was painfully clear how much it wasn't.

As Torsten took his position to the left of the throne, he realized he'd never attended an audience with any but Liam seated upon it—even when the King was sick and his body rendered useless, it was him.

As usual, Pi slumped to one side of the glass seat three sizes too big for him. The chair's arm was so high it could have served as a headrest. He dressed in an elegant satin tunic, his long, dark hair combed as his mother spent so much time doing every night. Torsten found himself growing angry at the sight of the boy's beautiful crown, so much more extravagant than Liam's but fought it off.

"The Shesaitju are a proud people," Torsten whispered to Pi while they watched the main doors of the castle. "Choose your words carefully, but do not give an inch."

King Pi half-turned his head to regard Torsten with a single eye. Torsten averted his gaze. The boy's expression didn't change. Not a word. Not even a nod. His mother would tell him to take his time finding his voice again as she stroked his hair every night. But Torsten remembered his voice—the voice which whispered to the Buried Goddess in the night; thanks to Redstar.

"The Shesaitju will learn humility," Oleander said, standing on the opposite side of the throne. "Don't worry, my precious child, they are here to grovel and apologize to their new king, nothing more."

"We must distill more information about the attacks," Torsten implored. "Find out if that afhem was acting alone so we can pit them against one another."

"Nothing more." Oleander shot Torsten a cold glare he knew was meant to silence him. As beautiful as she was, even Liam the Conqueror couldn't wield a glower with such vinegar.

Torsten swallowed the lump forming in his throat, but didn't back down. He couldn't. The Miracle King didn't talk, and so the Queen Mother had been his mouthpiece. When Rand Langley failed to contest during his short run as Wearer, all who spoke ill in her presence found themselves on the wrong end of a noose.

"He will declare his fealty," Torsten said, "but first, please consider a tactful approach. The caleefs once fancied themselves living gods. Appeal to their dignity and we can use the truth to our advantage."

"Weren't you there when Sidar Rakun bent the knee to Liam and renounced his deification?"

"I was," Torsten said proudly.

"The *greatest* warlords in the world, and we crushed them. The Caleef knows his place, unlike some of us."

"My Queen… I—"

Before Torsten could finish, the double doors opened. Light poured in, shimmering off the gold clothing and beads of the Caleef's entourage. Wardric arrived to greet them and disarm the guards. When he was finished, he nodded at Torsten, who waved them to approach.

Torsten glanced at King Pi who didn't even budge at the sight of them. Oleander, however, grinned wide, her lips a dark shade of violet. Torsten turned back to the hall to watch the entourage of dignitaries and shirtless servants approaching. A handful of them carried the Caleef on a golden platform, plumed at the back with broad palm leaves, the veins painted gold.

Unlike the rest of his people, Sidar Rakun wore all-black, head to toe. Even his dark gray skin had two bars of paint, black as the beaches his people came from, running down from his eyes to his chin. And though Liam's longtime, defeated rival was as old as he had been, his dark hair didn't show a touch of gray.

They stopped in the middle of the hall. An afhem barked something in Saitjuese. From behind the Caleef's chair, his Serpent Guard—the elite defenders of the Caleef and his afhems, masters of the Black Fist combat technique—silently fanned out to form a line on either side of him.

Their name was well-earned. According to legend, they were just as slippery and impossible to strike as snakes—though Liam had little trouble. Golden leather armor covered them head to toe. Gilded masks, bearing the shape of a snake's head, hid their faces from their hairlines to the tips of their noses. Rumor had it they filed their teeth into fangs, though their mouths remained closed.

Servants lowered the Caleef's platform. Two took his hands and helped him down. Torsten struggled not to roll his eyes. Last time he saw Sidar Rakun, more than a decade ago, he groveled on the floor and declared his mortality. Liam never needed a servant to hold his hand when he could still walk. Even after his legs failed him, he never needed to be carried or fanned. The man had dignity unto death.

"So, it's true," Sidar said as he approached, staring at King Pi. His voice was deep and full of timbre, but Torsten knew it was all bravado. He'd heard his true voice when he'd surrendered the first time.

Sidar stopped before the dais and stood tall. Oleander's face twisted with rage.

"You stand before Pi Nothhelm," Torsten said. "Son of Liam Nothhelm, first of his name, the Miracle of Iam, and High King and Lord of the Glass Kingdom."

"'The Miracle King,'" Sidar said as if imitating someone. He remained standing straight.

Torsten coughed and looked toward the Caleef's legs.

"Ah, yes, my apologies." The Caleef bent his knee, though never allowed it to touch the floor before standing proud again. "I am so very pleased to see you well again, King Pi."

"Turns out no one believes in punctuality," Oleander said, eyeing Torsten.

"Your Grace?" Sidar said.

"We expected you here yesterday on the day of my son's coronation under Iam."

"We set out from Latiapur the moment we received Sir Unger's galler bird. We ran into a few delays at Marimount, however. I wish I could have been here, but your son wears the crown of his father proudly."

"The crown is his own," Oleander corrected.

"Yes, it is, isn't it? It is a great pleasure to see you again as well, Your

Grace," he addressed Oleander. "I believe the last time I saw King Pi, he was this tall." He held his hand just under his kneecap.

Oleander stepped forward, her hand falling upon the arm of the throne. "Yes, I believe it was the day you wore the white of surrender to these very halls and cowered before my husband."

Torsten coughed from shock.

"Your Grace, today is a day of celebration," Sidar said.

"No, yesterday was a day of celebration," Oleander interrupted.

"Ah, yes," Sidar said, tipping his head slightly. "But Liam's great son has returned to us. Iam smiles upon you again. Must we dwell on a bitter past?"

"Iam smiles upon us all," Oleander said. For once, Torsten agreed with her. Showing the godless Shesaitju the way of Iam after they were conquered wasn't easy. Many of them still clung to their old ways of worshipping their ancestors and warlords.

"Yes, of course. I will admit, I have struggled to feel his light since my heart was opened to him, but seeing your son alive and well, sitting right in front of me after hearing of his unfortunate fate…. It truly is a blessing."

"Enough pandering, Sidar. You are going to make me sick. Do not pretend you were only invited here to share a feast in the name of our new king. The Wearer of White sent for you because your people raided villages under the protection of the Crown."

"When I heard what happened, I prayed for the well-being of your people. Whoever raided your lands did so without my knowing."

"Ah, of course. Then who should I blame for killing my people?"

One of Sidar's afhems whispered something into the ear of another. They smirked.

"I do not see the humor in this," Oleander snapped at them. "What did they say?"

"I didn't hear, Your Grace," Sidar said. "But my people would be wise to remain silent whilst I converse with their queen." He glared back at his entourage, and they immediately fell silent.

Torsten's understanding of Saitjuese was rough, but it was enough for him to put together the comment. *I hear she kills her own,"* they said. Torsten decided it was better not to translate.

"Your Grace, have I done something to offend the young king?" Sidar asked, clearly in an effort to change the subject. "He has avoided looking at me since I entered."

Oleander wrapped her way around the throne and sat on the armrest. She ran her fingers through Pi's hair, then stroked the crown. Pi continued staring blankly at the wall.

"My son, your King, does not wish to look upon you until you swear fealty to him," she said.

"I do not understand your meaning, Your Grace."

"'Your Grace.' 'Your Grace,'" she mocked. "Are you so kind to all your friends before you stab them in the back?"

"Your Gr—Queen Oleander. The Kingdom of the Black Sands remains loyal to Yarrington. Our lands have prospered under the rule of your late husband."

"Torsten?" the Queen said. He preferred Sir Unger in such a public setting, but she never was one for the ceremonial.

"Yes, my Queen?" Torsten replied.

"In your vast experience, do loyalists delay tax payment and then burn a handful of innocent farming villages to the ground, destroying crops that would help this city... oh, how did he put it... 'prosper' through the winter."

Torsten feared where her bluntness would lead, but there was only one clear answer: "No."

"Then you see why I hesitate to believe a word out of your mouth, Sidar." She turned back to him, and Torsten saw him shudder slightly. "Perhaps you came here to discuss the weather, but you were summoned here to answer for your transgressions."

"Your Grace, you must understand," Sidar said. "Storms in the Boiling Waters ravaged us this year and cost us greatly."

"How convenient."

"If the Master of Coin lists all discrepancies we will fulfill our obligations as we are able."

"You think I care about a few loose coins? You walk up to this throne, up to your holy King, as if nothing is wrong. You wear black when white is more appropriate. The smelting of your little platform would pay for all your *discrepancies.* But would payment and apologies put those villages back together?"

"As I said, the perpetrator of those attacks is unknown to me."

"So, it is a mystery to you that one of your afhems is secretly raising a vast army west of the bay? What did you hear them call him, Torsten? Mosquito was it?"

"Muskigo, Your Grace," Torsten said.

"Indeed."

A flicker of emotion passed over Sidar's face. Whether it was confusion, guilt, or surprise the Queen knew, Torsten wasn't sure. There was a reason Muskigo raised his army in the fog of the Fellwater Swamp. He didn't want to be known.

"My Queen," Sidar whispered, "perhaps we should continue this conversation in private."

"Anything you want to say, you can say here in front of my son, your King, and his Royal Council. Do you admit the afhem called Muskigo was acting on his own authority when he attacked my lands?"

"I was not aware of his intentions. I was led to believe he raised a fleet to answer the call of the Breklians who have been under the heavy hand of pirates."

Torsten studied his face as he talked. Either Sidar was the best liar he'd ever met, or Torsten had his answer. Muskigo was acting entirely of his own accord, and Sidar Rakun was as shocked as Torsten had been when he stumbled upon the army.

"Strange, we've heard nothing of the plight of the Breklians," the Queen sneered. "Unless my loyal Wearer and scouts are lying, he is camped in the Fellwater, preparing to ravage my kingdom even further."

"I swear to you in the name of Iam, this news comes as a surprise to me."

"Then, do you renounce him as one of your own? Will you raise your forces with us and remove the stain of his being from Pantego?"

Sidar exhaled. "It is more complicated than you might think, Your Grace. His is a respected family that has walked the black sands for centuries."

"Then you endorse his slaughtering of innocents while my people mourned the loss of my husband?"

"No, never, my Queen, but if I raise arms against an afhem I—"

"Enough," Pi said softly.

Torsten thought himself hallucinating, but the Queen spun a full circle toward her son. Even the nearest guards broke their discipline and turned their heads.

Sidar too was stunned speechless. Even had he not known of the boy's lingering silence, for a ruler of Sidar's age and stature to be addressed so boldly by a child was a rare thing.

"Excuse me, Highness?" Sidar asked.

Pi placed his feet beneath him and rose to a standing position on the throne. Torsten felt a chill so cold it was as if the doors had been opened and Winter's Thumb had migrated south. The King's eyes had been little more than a blank stare for months, but now they glinted with the same passion and vigor his father's once did.

"I said, that's enough. Your queen asked a simple question. Will you declare the traitor an enemy and stand with us, or are you our enemy as well?" Even his voice had changed. It was smooth and confident, carrying across the hall like a practiced orator. He sounded like his father.

Sidar stuttered over a response.

"My Queen, perhaps the Caleef was right and we should proceed privately," Torsten tried to whisper to her behind the throne, but she was too preoccupied staring at the hard features of her baby boy to hear him.

"It isn't difficult," Pi said.

"I can strip Muskigo of his title and demand he surrender," Sidar said. "But I cannot order my people to stand against one of their own. You must understand."

"I understand that Afhem Muskigo is an enemy of the Crown, and unless you lie, a traitor to you as well."

"And he will be given the chance to remedy his mistakes. Please, Your Grace, I beg you not to act rashly. Be reasonable. Let us address this misunderstanding diplomatically before resorting to war."

"An act of war has already been committed," Pi declared. "My foolish mother was merely too distracted to notice."

For the first time since he spoke, Oleander stopped marveling and winced, shaken by the harshness of his words.

"My precious boy, certainly you don't—"

Pi held out a hand to silence her. Her lips sealed immediately, something Torsten thought was impossible.

"Sir Unger," Pi said. He turned to face Torsten.

"My King?" Torsten could barely get the words out. A year as Wearer of White and he'd never actually had a conversation with the boy.

"Until the Caleef reconsiders, he and his followers are to be confined to this castle. As of this moment, I declare the Kingdom of the Black Sands enemies of the Crown."

Sidar staggered back a few steps, then looked to the Queen. "Your Grace, I was invited here to celebrate your son's coronation. This revelation complicates things, but I am prepared to discuss the situation peaceably. However, we will not stay here as prisoners."

Pi stepped to the edge of the seat where he stood a good head taller than Sidar and stared down his nose at him. "You will proceed to your quarters, or you will be forced there."

Torsten was busy thinking of how to de-escalate the situation when he felt suddenly compelled to reach for his sword. It was like he wasn't even in control of his own body, years of service instinctually willing his muscles to serve his king.

He removed it a few inches from his back scabbard, and every Glass soldier and Shieldsman present followed his lead. The sharp rasp of metal hummed through the hall.

A Serpent Guard sprang into action, hurried to the Caleef, pulling him down from the dais to be surrounded by his men. They were unarmed, but as the Serpent Guards dropped into fighting stances, Torsten knew they needed no weapons to be a threat.

Torsten fully drew his claymore. His men did the same, surrounding the Shesaitju entourage with halberds and longswords. One young, overeager soldier stomped hard toward them. A Serpent Guard disarmed and turned his own weapon on him in a single motion.

"Stop this!" Torsten barked. He moved before Pi and the Queen and lowered his voice. "Your Graces, I do not think this wise. He tells the truth about Muskigo, I am sure of it. Perhaps he can talk the rogue afhem down, but if we do this, war is certain."

The Queen remained too consumed with her son to answer. Pi, on the other hand, reached out and laid both his hands on Torsten's shoulders. He may have appeared frail, but Torsten felt unexpected pressure from them, felt small beneath them.

"Sir Unger," Pi said. "Your name was featured in many great tales my father told me before his days of illness. I would hate to see one of our finest commanders exiled again for defying orders."

Torsten's heart sank. The boy had been in a deep sleep when Torsten had been sent away by the Queen on a fool's errand, yet somehow he knew. And to retrieve his worthless doll nonetheless. Now, as Torsten stared upon Pi's face, despite the boy's size, he saw a child no longer. The boy didn't just sound like Liam, it was there in his eyes, too.

Torsten turned to face the Shesaitju Caleef, unable to deny his new king. He could barely control his own breathing he was so overwhelmed, so confused.

"Caleef Rakun, your king has spoken," he said. "Order them to stand down, and there will be no bloodshed."

Sidar glanced back and forth. His men formed a wall around him, but halberds closed in from every side. Wardric had taken up position with a contingent of Shieldsmen at the Throne Room's entry. His sword was drawn, but he looked as tentative as Torsten knew he should be.

Taking the Shesaitju leader captive—a man many of them still believed to be a living god—was an unsound decision only a fledgling king would make, one he knew he should counsel more vehemently against.

"Stand down and come with me," Torsten demanded.

"It's not too late to stop this, Oleander," Sidar said. "He's just a child; you are a queen."

Torsten felt a sudden surge of rage and energy. He stormed forward. One of the Serpent Guards went to impede him, but he grabbed the man's arm before it struck his throat, snapped it at the elbow, and flung him into the others. Then he hefted his heavy claymore with one hand, extending it toward the Caleef's neck.

"He is your King," he bellowed. "And you will stand down."

Sidar raised his hands in surrender and nodded for his followers to do the same. His men obeyed without question. Glass soldiers promptly aimed their halberds at the gray men's chests and directed them toward the exit.

"Are you all insane?" Sidar shouted. "My people will not forgive this!"

Unable to control himself, Torsten grabbed the Caleef by the arm and yanked him along more roughly then he'd intended to. It wasn't until they were nearly out of the room that his anger subsided enough for him to breathe again.

Sidar continued protesting, cursing in common and Saitjuese. Pi remained standing on the throne. His mother stood to his left, stunned into silence, staring as blankly as her son had been only minutes earlier. But Pi looked to his right, smiling as if someone were standing in the empty space beside him telling a hilarious joke.

IV

THE THIEF

"This is Winde Port?" Sora asked, clearly unimpressed.

"Oh, I've missed this place," Whitney drew a deep breath. He could smell the salt of Trader's Bay even from the other side of the city. They were on the main road heading in, Merchants Row. It was dotted with mobile trading posts and merchant caravans, not unlike the one they'd stolen.

The city itself was built on a small peninsula jutting out into the mouth of the bay where it narrowed to Winder's River. Northerly, it cut up to the Jarein Gorge, through the Great Ravine. A web of manmade canals ran through a hodgepodge of buildings. Unlike Yarrington, where all the stone matched, or in the Dragon's Tail where everything was undeniably dwarven, Winde Port was just stone, clay, and wood—some from the North on Winter's Thumb, Crowfall, Fessix and the like, and some black, like the trees of the Shesaitju lands. Thatched roofs and Panping tile. In fact, the only thing that gave the place even the slightest resemblance to a city of the Glass Kingdom was the tremendous cathedral standing proudly in the skyline, its Eye of Iam glistening under the morning sun.

Whitney leaned over the side of the wagon and snagged a large chunk of meat skewered on a stick from a vending cart whose owner's back was turned. He held it out, offering Sora a bite. She recoiled in disgust.

"Don't know what you're missing," he said with a full mouth.

"This place is disgusting," she bristled.

"This place is freedom."

Whitney meant what he said, but saw her point. It wasn't Old Yarrington—it was hardly South Corner—but it was the one place in the Kingdom where race and heritage didn't matter. Everyone was welcome so long as they had a few autlas and a dream.

"You should love this place," Whitney said. "No difference between me and you here."

"So what? Here nobody will call me *knife-ear*?"

"Well, I wouldn't say that, but they won't say it with such... I don't know... scorn."

Sora rolled her pretty, amber-colored eyes and reached out for the stick.

"I knew you'd come around," he said.

She took a bite and juice dribbled down her chin. "Oh, by Iam, that is delicious," she garbled.

Whitney just smiled and turned back to the road. She reached for it again, but he pulled it away. "Get your own."

He waited a few seconds for good measure, then offered the stick again only to find that she was no longer next to him.

"Sora?"

He spun until he saw her walking toward the meat vendor. He clicked the horses to a stop, and hopped down, hastily looped the reins around a post.

"Wait up!" he shouted, running to catch up. "I was kidding. Have a bite."

"No, you're right. I want my own."

She reached into a small bag they'd found in the carriage and pulled out a silver autla. "One, please."

The vendor, talking and chiding with another customer, turned only a little faster than it had seemingly taken Whitney and Sora to get to Winde Port in the first place. His face scrunched up at the silver, and then, Sora.

"Ain't from round here?" the vendor asked.

"Just rolled into town," Whitney pointed at their caravan.

"Oh, you picked a bad time to visit Winde Port. Glass transferred a bunch of soldiers just last week. Been rounding up all the *rainclouds*."

"Rainclouds?" Sora asked.

"Ya know, the Shesaitju, gray skin and all." He laughed, then said, "Been a mess, so, price is twice that until the threat dies down. Just not enough people buying any more."

Whitney and Sora exchanged a sidelong glare.

"What threat might that be?" Whitney asked.

The man laughed again. "Where you been, in the woods?"

"Actually—" Whitney started, but Sora slapped him in the arm. "That spot is getting sore!" he snapped under his breath, rubbing it.

"Please, continue," Sora said.

"You ain't heard about the Black Sands rebel army mounting?" the trader asked as he lifted a butcher knife and sliced a chunk of carcass—looked like deer. "There's been attacks. Towns burned to the ground."

Whitney couldn't believe they'd somehow forgotten what Torsten said about a giant army of Shesaitju gathering in the swamp. Of course, Winde Port would be feeling the consequences of the Black Sands attacks. It was the largest trading hub in Southern Pantego, along Trader's Bay, with tributary access into Eastern, Western, and even Central Pantego through Winder's River and the Walled Lake.

"Rumor was some noble from Bridleton came to the city since his estate was turned to ash," the trader went on before turning to grab another piece of meat.

Whitney swallowed hard, then mouthed the name, "Darkings," to Sora.

She nodded.

"Anyway, do yourselves a favor and leave town. Especially you." He pointed to Sora with his cleaver. "When people get scared of one foreign face—they get scared of all of 'em."

Sora's features darkened. Whitney imagined after the bigots she'd endured in Bridleton and beyond, she was a bit more wary of warnings such as that. She feigned a smile, and turning to Whitney said, "You're right. I *should* love this place."

Whitney thought he saw her eyes begin to water as she pulled up her hood and walked a few steps back to their carriage. He brushed flecks of swiftly accumulating snow off the carriage bench as he climbed. He'd spent many a winter month in Winde Port and couldn't remember another so cold. At least there was one thing to be thankful for—in the snow, Sora's drawn cloak would look less conspicuous.

After a few moments of silence, Whitney leaned in and said, "Look, let's just get to the harbor and charter a boat. We'll be out on the open sea and away from all this in no time at all."

"Fine," Sora said, offering no argument.

Their wagon rolled down Merchants Row toward the city proper. Winde Port might have been part of the Glass Kingdom, but it had always been far from the grasp of the law. It was never uncommon to find a table where dwarf, Shesaitju, Panpingese, and regular old Glass folk like him could sit down and enjoy a game of gems.

It appeared all that had changed.

A palisade wall now wrapped the city all the way to the coast on either side. The northern end was still under construction. It covered one of the canals that ran out alongside Merchants Row to make transport easy, and he only then realized the water on their side was dried out by a makeshift dam.

The wooden walls boasted blue and white standards, and soldiers from Yarrington were everywhere. It made Whitney queasy. He wondered if Torsten might be fumbling around in his bright white armor, ruining yet another thing Whitney loved.

Ahead, several Glass Soldiers gathered at a gateway. *A gateway in Winde Port.* Whitney scooted closer and put his arm around Sora, slowing their pace so as not to draw attention.

"Aye!" one of the soldiers shouted. He was more decorated than the others, with a feathered helm and shiny, King's Shield armor. And Whitney knew, when Shieldsmen were watching the gates, that was when things in the kingdom were about to run afoul. "Stop the cart."

Whitney exhaled. "Another one of these," he mumbled, remembering how impossible Torsten could be. "What can I do for you today, Sir Knight?" he asked, bowing his head with a flourish.

"Commander Citravan of the Winde Port legion," the man corrected. "You heading in?"

"No, we're g..." Whitney cut off his sarcasm before getting them into trouble. "Yes, sir," he said instead. "Silk traders on our way to Yaolin City."

"Don't care where you're going." The commander signaled to one of his men, and a soldier hopped up onto their wagon without even asking. He peeled open the canvas and rifled through some of the goods inside. Sora seemed nervous, but Whitney wasn't sure why. He'd already stashed his half of the Glass Crown somewhere nobody would ever think to look.

The guard stepped out and nodded to the commander.

"All right, move along," Commander Citravan said.

"Thank you, Sir," Whitney replied. "Keeping the Realm safe. There's no higher calling under Iam's Eye."

"Move along."

Whitney bit down hard, forcing himself to not test the man. He looked to Sora as their wagon rolled forward, expecting her to be joining him in frustration. Instead, she stared off to the left.

Another shorter, spiked barricade bowed away from the main wall on the opposite side of the city. Pikemen stood guard at every entrance into a vast camp filled with gray-skinned Shesaitju. Men, women, and children all huddled together in wooden shacks and tents, despite the cold. No warm hearths, just fire pits out in the open to keep warm.

"So much for freedom," Whitney said.

Sora didn't answer. She simply stared, expressionless.

"Serves them right for what they did," Whitney said, thinking of the day they'd burned Troborough and taken from Sora everyone she'd ever known and loved—though he wasn't sure he meant it.

He locked eyes with one of them, a little gray-skinned girl of about five years, eating scraps of rotten meat by a dwindling fire. That little girl had done less to Troborough than he had.

"Yeah..." Sora said softly.

"By all the fallen gods, what did you do with my Sora? You're supposed to be telling me we should abandon all our plans and try to help them."

Sora was silent, again.

Shesaitju were led in a long single-file line through the gate and toward the detainment camp. Rusty, silver chains strung them together at the wrists and feet. The sound was horrifying, like they were all being led to execution. Behind the line, a soldier of the Glass poked and prodded them.

"In you go, rainclouds," he chortled. One of the Shesaitju cursed at him in his native tongue and earned a club to the stomach. The guard reached down and wrenched the man's hair back as he heaved for breath, and spoke directly into his ear loud enough for Whitney to hear. "My sister died in Oxgate, you swine. You'll rot in here."

"Aye!" Commander Citravan shouted. "I said, move along."

"Sorry, sir," Whitney said. "It's just... my wife is from around here and she's never seen the city... well... like this."

"All Shesaitju west of the Great Ravine are to be detained until the rebel Afhem Muskigo surrenders," he explained. "It's for their own good. They'd get torn to pieces otherwise. Now, I said move along. I won't ask again."

Whitney got the wagon rolling, but Sora didn't stop staring at the sad state of the Shesaitju until they were beyond the palisade.

"Just forget about it, Sora," Whitney said once they were in.

She glared at him. "Typical Whitney Fierstown—"

"Blisslayer."

"Would you shut up with that already! Just because you got some letter sealed by the Crown doesn't mean you can just throw away who you've always been."

"Technically, it does, but that's beside the point. I—we—worked hard for that name. You can't just go forgetting it."

"Well, it's not right, locking them out there. It's cold."

Whitney sighed. "There she is. A second ago you wanted to burn their whole camp to the ground."

"It wasn't their fault."

"No, it wasn't. But out in the world, it starts to get hard telling, doesn't it, knife-ear?"

He winced impulsively, but she didn't strike him. Instead, she shot a glower his way that made him feel like shriveling into a cocoon.

"I'm just making a point," he said. "Out in the world, if you stay somewhere too long you'll wind up wrapped up in the affairs of lords and ladies. It's the same thing I told you back in Yarrington."

"What, and there are no lords in Panping? What'll we do when we get there and my people are locked up thanks to some rebel warlord thinking about no one but himself?"

"We move on to the next place." He placed his arm around her, knowing full well the risk he was taking considering her mood. "You think I fancy myself a Glassman because I was born outside Yarrington? I'm as much one as you are Panpingese."

"Not according to that piece of paper in your pocket." Sora either cleared her throat or chuckled, Whitney wasn't sure which.

"All I'm saying is that in our line of work, we're all on our own. Yeah, make that lesson number… whatever number we're on: it's us against the world."

"And what exactly would you call our line of work?" Sora asked. He could tell by her tone she was starting to cheer up. Which was good, because a month-long voyage across the Boiling Waters to the land of her ancestors would be worse than Elsewhere if she was in a sour mood. And if seeing a group of Shesaitju forced to live in a camp, thanks to a possible rebellion, was the worst she'd ever seen... she had no idea what she was in for if pirates attacked.

"Thieving?" she went on. "That's too simple. We did burn down Darkings' mansion. What about scoundreling. Is that a word?"

"We're beyond description."

"Scoundreling it is, then," she said.

He slowed the wagon down beside an amassed crowd watching a street performer—a Panpingese kid juggling torches. He let the fire come as close to his face as possible, egging on a crowd of wealthy Glassmen in the merchant district. After he finished and earned a chorus of applause, he pointed to Sora.

"You!" he called. He had the voice of a proper showman, booming, yet inviting all at the same time. Impressive for his age. Whitney had run with a few performing troupes in his time. The acting was fun, but distracting a whole crowd of men and women with full pockets was even better.

Sora glanced between Whitney and the kid, then laughing, stopped the wagon.

"Go on," Whitney said. "You're part of the act now."

The crowd parted to let Sora pass. Whitney heard a few lewd

comments about her looks. Lucky for them, he couldn't see who'd said them. He hopped down and watched from the back.

"I uh... wow…. she's gorgeous enough to be Empress of Panping, isn't she?" the kid asked, earning a mixture of laughter and cheers. Sora's cheeks went as red as the walls of the Jarein Gorge. Whitney gave a nod of approval, even though he knew the kid wasn't watching him. He was probably half her age, he was so young, but he was good.

"Now, stand right here." The kid took her by both hands and led her to a tiny stand.

"Here?" she asked, so embarrassed she could barely get the words out.

He gave her one last adjustment. "Right here." He bent down, and from beneath the stand, drew two curved daggers. They looked Shesaitju in design.

Only in Winde Port, Whitney thought, smirking.

Sora's face drained of color. Two Glintish women dressed in feathery gowns yelped.

"Now, whatever you do," the kid said, "just don't move."

Sora looked to Whitney, but there was nothing he could do. The performer began juggling the blades all around her. She closed her eyes as one twirled up over her head, the kid catching it on the other side. *Ooos* and *ahhhs* filled the air as he danced with blades, each one closer to cutting her than the next. Until one sliced her arm. Just barely, but enough to make her howl. Half the crowd lunged forward to help her, but Whitney didn't budge. He waited patiently until he felt the faintest pressure against his side. Reaching back with cat-like speed, he caught the hand of a pickpocket.

He shook his head in disapproval as he looked down at the performer's younger running mate. The boy looked like he was going to fill his trousers with shog. It was probably his first time getting caught. Whitney remembered his younger days of honing his quick fingers on the streets of Winde Port. Traders and wealthy shoppers were the easiest targets around —easily distracted and usually with too many things on them to notice if something went missing.

Whitney however, was neither. "C'mon kid, oldest trick in the book. Never go for the man at the very back of the crowd because he clearly has trust issues." He released the boy's arm and gave him a light shove. "Now scram."

Whitney continued watching for a moment, then bulled his way through the crowd toward Sora. She was hunched over, holding her arm while the performer tried to assess the damage. He looked nervous too, and Whitney could see why. A stream of blood ran from the cut down her arm, trickling over the hem of her glove. He'd nicked her far deeper than was planned.

Whitney wanted to smack the kid upside the head, but his attention was drawn elsewhere. Smoke poured out of Sora's clenched fists. It was faint, but there was no question it came from her.

Within her?

He still barely understood how magic worked, blood-based or not, only that it drew on Elsewhere, the realm of banished gods and demons created by Iam after the God Feud.

The fabric over her fingertips began to sear. Whitney quickly hooked his arm around her and rushed her back through the crowd. The performer grabbed at Whitney's arm, asking if she was okay.

"You juggle knives like my grandmother," Whitney said, then added. "And your little brother has fingers as light as a zhulong. I sent him running that way if you're looking."

The performer looked both ways, then snagged his tin of autlas donated by the gathered crowd and bolted. Whitney leaned Sora against the carriage.

"You okay?" Whitney asked. "You need me to chase down the knife-ear?"

She managed to break her grimace for a second and smirk. Then shook out her arm. There was a long cut across her forearm over a row of ghosted scars he'd never noticed before.

"Seriously though," Whitney said. "You're not going to explode again, are you?"

"I'm fine. That area is just tender from… growing up."

She flexed her arm and a bit more blood oozed out. Whitney had to turn away to avoid gagging. He made it look like he was just getting one of the silk blankets from their wagon. He wrapped it tight around her arm.

"There you go…" He coughed, again to cover for the sick feeling in his stomach. "Most expensive bandage ever." Blood soaked through the fabric quickly. "Those scars—"

"Are where Wetzel used to cut me to help me tap into my abilities. It brings up bad memories."

"Of him dying?"

She nodded. "And living. Unlocking a link to Elsewhere isn't easy. I hated him every day until it worked and then even still, for a while."

"Well, let's make sure and leave these fine folk intact. Using blood magic in public in the Glass Kingdom is a one-way ticket to the gallows, even here."

She groaned. "I'm starting to hate this place, too."

"Oh c'mon." Whitney pulled her in tighter and pointed over her shoulder at Winder's Wharf where the tops of masts soared high over the city skyline like tree trunks stripped of their boughs.

"We're in paradise," he said as he took a great big whiff of the salty air. To him, it was the smell of freedom and relaxation. There was nothing in the world further from the worthless town he grew up in than sailing upon open seas.

V

THE KNIGHT

"Well, that was certainly unexpected," Wardric said. They stood in the Shield Hall. Snowflakes swirled in through an open, arched aperture overlooking Mount Lister and the Torrential Sea, carried by an icy breeze.

"I'm still trying to understand," Torsten said.

"What's there to understand?" Wardric walked toward the opening. "Apparently, our timid prince wasn't so shy after all."

Torsten gripped the railing. His eyes fell on Mount Lister. The top of the mountain was a mere silhouette through the low clouds but the area at its base where the earth crumbled into the Royal Crypt below, remained visible. The tarpaulin covering it flapped, and he could imagine the tiny dots of dwarven artisans flitting about inside.

"I know," Torsten said. "It was like Liam was alive all over again. I swear to you Wardric, I could literally feel him next to me. Before I knew it, my sword was drawn…"

"You won't see me complaining about the new king growing up fast. I haven't seen anyone put her in her place like that since Liam. Apparently, Pi was paying attention all those many years ago."

"He declared war. There's no question of the state of the kingdom now."

"Like the boy said, they acted first. The last time we stood in this chamber I told you we had to teach the Shesaitju a lesson in force. You were wise to delay that while the Queen Mother was unstable, but we can't be cautious forever."

"It won't just be Muskigo. He'll rouse more afhems seeking to 'free' their Caleef."

"Good, let all the traitors show their colors so that we may put them in their places."

"You did not see Muskigo fight. Nor did you see his innumerable army."

"Are you losing your faith, Sir Unger?"

Torsten sighed and turned away from the overlook toward a large, slate table. Eyes of Iam, spiked flames, and other sculptures covered the slate table like the parts of some elaborate game. Each blown-glass figure represented an army, thousands of young men whose lives were now in jeopardy thanks to the impulsiveness of a twelve-year-old.

Torsten reminded himself that Liam too had been stubborn in his youth. He wouldn't have conquered the world, wouldn't have brought glory to the name of Iam if he hadn't been. Like Pi, Liam's father had died when he was still young, leaving Liam as king at only sixteen. Though four years might as well be a lifetime that early on.

"How long do you suppose we have until word gets out?" Wardric asked.

"Days," Torsten said. "Maybe less. I trust the Shield, but our numbers are thin, and I don't recognize half the people in the castle anymore."

"Another thing for which to thank our lovely Queen Mother."

"And what thanks is that, Sir…" Oleander appeared in the entry. Pi stood in front of her, barely reaching her waist with the top of his moppy hair. The fire in his eyes was gone, and he looked every bit as tired and disinterested as he once had.

"Sir Wardric Jolly, Your Grace." He bowed low, but Torsten could sense the bitterness in his tone. He'd been a pillar of the King's Shield for longer than she'd been queen and she still didn't know his name.

"Your Grace." Torsten bowed. "We were discussing the potential… consequences of the King's decision."

"He was brilliant, wasn't he?" She smiled and patted his head. He didn't react in the slightest. "Why should we have to play coy with those who should be kissing our feet?" She led Pi to the stone seat at the head of the table and helped him onto it. He slumped back, barely able to see the map.

"We must consider the implications carefully." Torsten turned to the map. "From my scouts, we know that Afhem Muskigo remains in the Fellwater with his army. They have completed numerous siege engines—"

"Breaching towers, catapults," Wardric explained.

"I know what that means," Oleander snapped. She took a step toward Wardric, her tall, Drav Cra frame looming over him. All the confidence Pi had stripped from her when he scolded her seemed to have returned in full. "Torsten, who is this man who addresses me as if I need his explanations?"

"He has served the King's Shield for decades, Your Grace," Torsten said. "Longer even than I. He fought faithfully by your husband-King. He's the most loyal sword in the Glass."

"Well, tell him to keep his tongue sheathed in my presence."

Torsten grabbed the back of Wardric's armor and guided him away. If fury could manifest in flames, the room would be ablaze.

"Muskigo's army seems prepared to march at his command," Torsten said, refocusing the conversation. "News of their Caleef's detainment will most certainly expedite things. We can only guess at his exact numbers since they are hidden by the swamp's fog, but it's enough to know Muskigo has been preparing this coup since the moment Liam fell ill."

"Oh, Torsten. Sweet, loyal… *gullible* Torsten," Oleander said. "You really believe the lies spun by Sidar Rakun?"

She positioned herself before him. They were the same height, but they rarely saw eye to eye. He couldn't help but be rapt by her lips, glistening a deep indigo that matched her dress, by her long blonde hair, so fair it shone silver under a certain light.

Torsten took a moment to gather his breath. "It doesn't matter what I think, Your Grace. The King's decision will inspire others to the rogue afhem's call." He gestured to the area on the map where Pantego forked off into the rocky and black sand-ridden beaches of the Shesaitju. "These cities southeast of the Walled Lake have large, concentrated Shesaitju populations. When word—"

"The Master of Rolls has already sent word across the kingdom that all gray-folk are to be placed under armed watch," Oleander interrupted.

"I'm not sure…" His voice trailed off. He shook his head, frustrated. "How? The audience only just concluded."

"Don't look at me," she said. "Your king gave the order the moment we stepped out."

"Taking such a harsh stance will only encourage revolts, Your Grace." Torsten regarded the boy, but Pi remained emotionless. "We must focus on the true enemy south of us."

"Better to root out all insurgents now than wait until the army is nearer," Wardric said. "Why don't we sail a fleet down from Winde Port, catch them napping in Fellwater?" He smiled proudly like he expected Oleander's approval. Instead, she ignored him.

"The Shesaitju have been fighting within their islands for centuries," Torsten argued. "They are renowned for their naval combat. In that shallow water and fog, so far from home, we would be at a great disadvantage, especially if their scouts see us coming."

"And how could anyone miss a mass of ships sailing down Trader's Bay?" Oleander remarked.

Wardric bit his lip. Torsten could tell he was growing frustrated and tried to urge him with his expression to relax. Nobody knew better than Torsten how hard it was to get and stay on Oleander's good side.

"Does it benefit you, keeping fools around, Torsten?" Oleander asked.

Wardric was squeezing the table now. But before he said anything stupid, King Pi said, "Excuse me, Mother, but why exactly are you here?"

Torsten glanced up and saw that the boy now stood and stared down at the map. That fierce look in his eyes had returned.

"What was that, my dear?" Oleander asked.

"I said, I'm curious why you are here? You are not king and have no experience with war, yet you insult this soldier who served beneath Father in numerous campaigns."

Her whole body tensed but she maintained a calm expression.

"As Queen Mother, it is my duty to help look after your kingdom. I learned a lot watching your father, Iam rest his soul."

Torsten traced his eyes in prayer to Iam. Wardric did the same, though there was no missing the mirth tugging on the corners of his mouth. Pi did not—Torsten noted.

"If you paid attention to Father," Pi said, "you would know the best course of action is to rely on the expertise of the Royal Council when its outside your own specialties. Of course, because of your actions, Sir Unger is the only man of proper resource who remains on *my* council."

"Pi..." Oleander's lips started to tremble. The muscles on her long, slender throat contracted as she fought back tears.

"Now, please," he lifted a hand, palm out, "allow them to continue without interruption."

Oleander stared at her son a few seconds longer, her eyes welling. His façade didn't falter, stern, cold, the way Liam was with irritators. Torsten wasn't Wearer when the man could still walk, so he didn't have as much insight into how he was with Oleander, but Uriah had always said how rigid he could be when she spoke out of turn.

Oleander stood and curtsied. She didn't weep aloud, but Torsten noticed her shoulders bobbing on her way out of the room. He couldn't help but feel sorry for her despite everything she'd done, despite turning Yarrington into Elsewhere while he was gone. She'd done it all for Pi.

"So, attacking them first is out of the question," Wardric said. He lifted a statue of a zhulong—the pig-dragon beasts the Shesaitju were so fond of —which represented Muskigo's army then placed it back down.

Torsten forced himself to return his focus to what was important. "Agreed. Only zhulong would be able to handle mud that deep, and he has many."

"You told me that the afhem seemed brash, proud," Wardric stated.

"He is bent on revenge for the wars their fathers lost."

"Then he won't sit idly after he learns of the Caleef's imprisonment."

"No," Torsten said. "He'll seek to destroy the seat of Liam." He looked to Pi, who remained attentive. "I understand the choice you made in light of their attacks, my King, but you have to understand how so many of them view their Caleef. You are the Word of Iam. For many of them, he remains a living god."

"Then they must be shown the error of their ways," Pi said. "There is only one true God."

Torsten nodded, smiled. It wasn't long ago that the boy had been cursed by his uncle with thoughts of the Buried Goddess, yet now he sounded like a true king of the Glass.

"We will do everything in our power to prepare," Torsten continued. "Muskigo will have two choices." He stretched across the table and tapped two Eyes of Iam. "He can head straight north and take Fort Marimount."

"It is a mighty fortress, Your Grace," Wardric explained. "Half-built by the ancient dwarves themselves."

"And it's all that stands between him and a full-scale invasion of Yarrington. If he takes it, they can dig in and reinforce themselves. With your edict against the Shesaitju enacted, they won't be difficult to find."

"You did not approve of my decision, did you?" Pi stopped him.

"Your Grace?"

"You can be completely honest with me without fear of hanging, Sir Unger."

Torsten drew a deep breath. He'd never known what it was like to serve someone he didn't have to walk on eggshells around. "I would have appeased and distracted the Caleef with finery while we first handled Muskigo. Then reprimanded Sidar Rakun for such loose control of his people."

"Feigned complacency before striking like a snake in the weeds? Careful, tricks are the craft of the fallen gods."

Torsten's brow raised. Pi was smirking now, and Torsten realized it was the first time he'd ever seen the boy do it. He didn't sound like he was only twelve, and just like in the Throne Room, he barely looked it.

"That is true, Your Grace," Torsten said. "But Liam taught us to learn from our enemies in defense of the faithful. First, we win, and then, beg Iam for forgiveness."

"Then I do apologize for my reaction, Sir Unger."

"You need never apologize to me, Your Grace. The Black Sands had to be dealt with, one way or another." Torsten's gaze jumped between the young King and the map a few times before he was able to gather his thoughts.

"Marimount would be option one," Torsten continued, "or turn his army along the bay and sail for Winde Port."

Wardric nodded in agreement, running his finger along the river running north from the trade port. "It's not as defensible as the Fort, but the winters aren't so harsh there, and it would allow him easier access to Eastern and Western Pantego."

"It's exactly halfway between here and Latiapur, and it would provide him with a port to the West."

"A strategic location, sure, but they'd sacrifice a lot of men taking a city so far from Yarrington when they could close the distance better at Marimount. You said it yourself, the afhem was brash and confident."

"Brash, confident, and willing to have his men train in the wet and the cold until they could be called ready."

Wardric scratched his chin. "We don't possess the men to properly reinforce both potential targets."

"We don't have the men to meet Muskigo's army in open battle at all. Our legions in the East must remain to ensure a similar situation doesn't evolve in the Panping Region—Governor Nantby has already begun building defenses against such an attack, however unlikely. In the North, they defend against Drav Cra marauders who don't believe in allegiance. In the Northeast, we continue to honor contracts with the dwarven King, Cragrock, assisting with the grimuar scourge and to secure the borders with the Breklians."

"You just named our only forces with any experience in battle. We've been sitting on our fat asses ever since Liam got sick." Wardric laughed a mirthless laugh.

"It's time to consider a conscription. Bolster our numbers."

Torsten could see Pi listening, but the boy remained quiet.

"More untested men to join an army that hadn't been tested in a decade?"

"Muskigo's men are angry, loyal, and worthy, but only a small percentage of them probably ever served as mercenaries, and none of them are used to our winters. If he cuts a straight line for Yarrington, we should be able to defend Fort Marimount against whatever he throws at us."

"And if he heads northeast to Winde port?"

"Then I pray to Iam we can overwhelm him with numbers. The King's miracle has the people in good spirits after all the foulness that preceded. If we issue a call now and focus on a chance for vengeance for the villages Muskigo slaughtered, we should have success."

"It's winter, and grain stores throughout the region are low. People might eagerly take up the sword knowing they'll get their bellies filled in the legion."

"Then it is decided?" Torsten asked. "I'll have scouts watch for the first sign of movement from Muskigo's forces so we can reinforce his target. Galleys will be sent out into Trader's Bay in case he does move by water. Perhaps they can slow down his much larger fleet to buy us time. Frederick Holgrass will issue a conscription edict from here to Westvale, and then again to Hornsheim."

"Holgrass the new Master of Rolls?" Wardric asked.

Torsten sighed, they were all new. "Yes. All men of proper age and health will be beckoned to the call of their king. Are you in agreement, Your Grace?"

Torsten and Wardric both turned their attention back to Pi, but found that he no longer stood at the table. He was sunken back into his chair, half-asleep. He nodded his head listlessly but said nothing.

"It's settled then," Torsten said. "I'll bring word to the Royal Council and have the proclamation prepared immediately."

Wardric nodded in agreement. Torsten, however, couldn't stop staring at the young king who looked so dejected.

Now he sees how many more lives might be lost in war because he was too eager.

Oleander never learned from or admitted her mistakes, but Liam never forgot his. He used that knowledge to crush his enemies. It was then that Torsten realized he may have underestimated Pi, that there may have been even more of Liam the Conqueror in him than he'd ever imagined.

VI

THE THIEF

hitney pulled the wagon over at the edge of Winder's Wharf and took in the sight. Like the rest of Winde Port, nothing in the place matched. It stretched the whole of the peninsula, from a stone platform carved into the low bluffs to the north down to creaking wooden planks atop the sandy, southern beachfront. Canals branched off at random intervals like fingers stretching out into the city. They alternated with paved roadways, making it simple to ferry supplies. The locals even traversed them with gondolas during warmer months when they weren't frozen over.

Ships of all sizes, from every corner of Pantego, moored in the harbor. He even spotted a Breklian corsair vessel, its fanning sails like a stack of daggers from his angle. Brekliodad was one of the few places the Glass Kingdom's influence didn't reach, yet here they were in Winde Port.

Everything looked as it had the last time he'd visited, except one new addition: three Glass Kingdom warships floating out in the bay, keeping watch.

"So, which one should we steal?" Whitney asked.

Sora snorted. "Don't be ridiculous."

"What? We just stole the caravan and that was easy enough. A ship can't be much harder. My eye's on that one." He gestured to the small, agile ship from Brekliodad.

"You can't sail a ship with two people."

"Says the woman who can summon fire."

"How about for once we just pay for something? It's not like we can't get the autlas." She looked back into the wagon at all their stolen goods. "If we sell it all we could probably buy a small ship. If you let us sell that yigging crown, we could probably get a galley and a crew."

"Don't even look at it." Whitney lunged forward and reached under one of their horses. He had the crown pinned under its stomach using the strap from the saddle. He removed it, wrapped it in a silk blanket, and stuffed it into a fold in his clothing. The points poked into his ribs but he didn't care.

"What do you even plan on doing with that thing?" Sora asked.

"I'm not sure yet, but I'll know it when the time comes."

"Well, I still say we sell off all of this stuff and get out of here before those monsters we stole it from come back."

"You know, you're no fun at all. This wouldn't be the first time I've stolen a ship."

"Oh boy, here we go. Please, Whitney, oh glorious and grandmaster thief, tell me the story I know you'll tell me no matter what." Sora folded her arms across her chest.

"Many moons ago I found myself first mate to Grisham 'Gold Grin' Gale, king of the pirates and master of the seas. But he knew as well as I did that he wouldn't even have a ship had it not been for me."

"And where is this ship now?"

He rolled his shoulders. "Who can say? Likely at the bottom of the Torrential Sea."

"You know you're not old enough to have done everything you say you've done, right?"

"Age is but a number." He sighed and looked at the ground. "Fine, let's see if we can't go charter a ship." Whitney grabbed one of the horses by the lead and started off toward the docks.

"Charter is a strange way to say steal."

"Nope, this time you're right. I may be many things, but I'm not the one to try sailing a ship through the Boiling Waters. It would be tough to teach you any more all-important lessons if we're stranded on a rock."

"No more lessons." Sora closed her eyes, smiled, and let out an exaggerated breath. "Almost sounds like paradise."

Whitney ignored her and led the wagon to a tailor at the end of the docks. There wasn't a type of trade hard to find in Winde Port. They rifled through Grint's gang's belongings. Mostly it was silks, but there were a few other trinkets as well. Nothing so opulent as the Glass Crown, but Sora seemed eager to add it all in as a bonus. They threw in the horses as well. The portly merchant looked like his eyes were going to bulge out of his head as he took in his haul. Whitney knew they were getting an awful deal, but it would be more than enough to catch a ride like royalty aboard the finest ship sailing east. They'd leave nothing but an empty, horseless carriage for Grint and the others to find.

When they reached the harbor, the wind and cold had hulls groaning, and that was as close to the sound of waves as there was in Trader's Bay. The water was like a sheet of glass, with portions of the coast so still, they might have been frozen. Whitney couldn't remember the last time it got cold enough to turn the bay half-solid. It was such a harsh juxtaposition to the murky waters of the Torrential Sea bordering Yarrington where massive waves pommeled into Mount Lister and towering sea walls.

Down by the beach, along the splintering deck, stood Whitney's favorite watering hole in all Pantego, Winder's Dwarf. He stopped outside and looked to Sora.

"All right, if there's anyone I trust to get us to the Panping Region in one piece, they're in this room," he said. "I know these people. Just stand there and look pretty and the deal will keep getting sweeter."

Sora groaned and rubbed her temples between her index finger and thumb. "You have a strange way of complimenting a lady."

"Oh, you're a lady now?" Whitney then flung the door open and shouted, "Tum Tum!"

Everyone in the tavern repeated the words and slammed their tankards twice on the bar or tables. Raucous laughter followed.

"I thought we were here to charter a ship?" Sora whispered after she took a good look around the place.

Like most of Winde Port, the bar's interior was unimpressive. But like any good tavern, it was crammed with sloppy drunks. But unlike most, Winder's Dwarf had no need for a bard. Those slovenly, unassuming men were from every corner of Pantego, even beyond the Glass—well, except the Shesaitju, Whitney noticed. Which was fine with him, he'd always found their culture to be incredibly formal and drab.

But there were Dwarves and Panpingese, men from Brekliodad and the far north. There was even a half-giant hunched over in the back of the room with women draped all over him, though it wasn't clear how he even got through the front door.

"No better place to strike a deal than within these walls," Whitney said. "Plus, Tum Tum is a stand-up dwarf. Nothing like Grint. You'll love him."

"Tum Tum is a name?" she asked, incredulous.

Whitney parked himself on a stool furthest from the door and Tum Tum waddled over. He was so short and his belly so round that he looked like a pufferfish. His coal-black beard grew in patchy, with whiskers sticking out from his nose and ears that he never cared to trim. Grint Strongiron made all dwarves seem like thieving, backstabbing cowards, but Whitney had known Dwotratum "Tum Tum" Goodbrew for years and he was the finest dwarf there was.

"Whitney Fierstown!" Tum Tum said. "Thought ye were dead."

"Not dead. Reborn!" Whitney exclaimed. "Whitney Blisslayer now. First of my name."

"Yer yanking me beard."

"Nope." Whitney reached into his pocket and slapped down the writ given to him by Torsten himself. Tum Tum leaned up over the bar and scoured the paper. "Got the seal of the Crown and everything."

"By Meungor's axe it does! How in Elsewhere did ye manage a thing like that?"

"If I started that story we'd be here all night."

"That's for sure," Sora mumbled.

"Let's just say a member of the Royal Council owed me big time."

"Well, I'll be." Tum Tum folded the writ up and handed it back to Whitney, then stepped onto a low stool that helped him see over the bar.

"Aye! Everyone!" he shouted. "We got ourselves a noble in the house!" More laughter rose and tankards slammed. "I suppose that means ye can pay double now?"

"You should be paying me to drink in this shoghole you call a tavern," Whitney said."

"Watch yer mouth. There's a lady present."

"Finally, someone notices," Sora said, deciding to take a seat.

Tum Tum reached out and took her hand between his chubby fingers. "And what may I have the pleasure of callin ye, my lady?"

"Sora."

"Blisslayer?" Tum Tum finished for her. The look on her face made him question what he said before he even finished. "You two aren't?"

"Married? Gods no!" Whitney burst out laughing and earned a well-deserved elbow into his ribs.

"He should be so lucky," Sora said through clenched teeth. "We're friends from childhood, catching up on old times. Sora, with no other name and proud of it."

"Well, any friend of Whitney the Filcher Fantastic is a friend of mine. First round's on me." Tum Tum opened a tap and ale poured freely into a couple of earthenware mugs.

"Afraid there'll only be time for one round, my friend," Whitney said. "We're hoping to catch passage to Panping—Yaolin City, in fact—before things around here heat up any more."

Tum Tum threw his head back and released a hearty laugh from deep in his belly. "Ye ain't goin nowhere without a temporary trader's license issued by the prefect. All ships be grounded, as ye can right see. Only ones leavin be those tradin essential goods and able to prove it."

"Well then, a second round it is!" Whitney said, slapping the bar.

"That's it?" Sora asked. "You give up?"

"If you call a night in the best pub in Pantego 'giving up,' then we really need to reconsider my lessons."

Sora slid her ale away and said, "Tum Tum, why are all ships grounded? Any word on when things might let up?"

"Just got into town I be guessin? Saw the Black Sandsmen in lock up on the way through? Rumor is there be a war brewin and the Boilin Waters ain't safe, that there be some group of rebels waitin out there, wantin vengeance for the new king lockin up Caleef Rakun."

"So, we're stuck here?" Sora asked.

"As a pickaxe in mud."

Whitney threw his mug back. Half the ale wound up dribbling down his chin. "Very simple really," Whitney said between swigs. "Just gotta find someone with papers heading that way who wouldn't mind a couple of fine-looking stowaways."

"Are you confused about what simple means?" Sora asked.

"Ye might be in a bit of luck," Tum Tum said.

"Why's that?"

"That there's Tayvada Bokeo. Not likely many be crazy enough to risk both the Boilin Waters and gettin shredded by a Shesaitju fleet, but he be a member of the Winde Traders Guild. And nobles always be welcome at the guild. Tayvada!" the dwarf called to him even before Whitney could respond.

A thin, Panpingese man sauntered over, smiling and shaking hands with all those he passed. His hair was the color of a Dawning midnight, and he wore it pulled back so that his pointed ears were unmistakable.

"Tum Tum, the place is lively as ever," he said. "Good fortune to you."

"Aye. Here's someone I'd be wantin you to meet." He put an ale down in front of Tayvada and continued. "Whitney Blisslayer, first of his name."

"Ah, Mr. Blisslayer, a pleasure. Tayvada Bokeo at your service." He bowed, then turned to Sora, took her hand, and kissed it. She seemed so stunned by what he was, she barely reacted. "And your wife? Stunning! So good to see a Lord of the Glass and a Lady of the East in matrimony together."

"Oh, she ain't—"

"It's an honor to meet you as well, Lord Bokeo," Whitney interrupted Tum Tum. He bowed low in return, sneaking a glance over at Sora. Her glower looked like it could slice through glaruium.

"What brings you both to town?" Tayvada asked.

"I've—*we've* heard great things about your guild and hoped to enter the fold," Whitney lied.

"So good to know our reputation has carried all the way to… Yarrington raised I'd say?"

"So right you are!" Whitney forced a nauseating laugh. Sora tittered and smiled with the grace of a proper lady. He had to give her credit. If he didn't know any better, he'd have thought she hadn't grown up in a crummy shack on a dried-up river.

"And you, my dear, when did you leave our beloved Panping?"

"Actually—" Sora started, but Whitney cut in.

"Actually, we were planning to catch a ship there before hearing of the horrible things happening in your fine city and the slowdown in the harbor. We have business in Yaolin City. A potential import deal with her family. We grow barley on a plantation north of the city, you see."

"An exceptional crop," the man remarked.

"But it appears we are without the temporary license needed to charter passage. And to travel by land, at this point, would delay things beyond what we can afford."

"I see. Prefect Calhoun issued the edict shortly after the new king declared war against the Black Sands."

"So we heard. I attempted to meet with the prefect and get all this sorted out, but all this has him too busy for unexpected audiences and we're not from around here."

Tayvada shook his head. "Of course. In general, that man is notoriously hard to meet with and these are rough times here in Winde Port. Haven't seen everyone up in arms like this since the Panping Wars. What was that... has to be more than twenty years ago?"

"And some change now," Whitney said as if the man didn't know. Liam's War, which brought down their Council of Mystics and absorbed all the Panping Region under the Glass, had been two-and-a-half decades ago. He knew because that was when Sora arrived in Troborough on a caravan finding homes for children orphaned by the fighting.

"Such a shame. Normally it wouldn't have mattered at all. Would have merely cost you a few more autlas to charter east as passengers."

"Which is what I told my wife on the ride here. Much safer sailing to Yaolin City from here then all the way around by way of the Torrential Sea. Alas, it seems that was the better option."

Tayvada scratched his chin and took a look around the room. Then, he leaned in closer and lowered his voice. "I'll tell you what, I like a couple that proves our peoples can live harmoniously after so much bloodshed. These days, that's more important than ever."

"There's no one in the world I'd rather be with." Whitney took Sora's arm and gave it a loving squeeze. Her false smile deepened while she returned the gesture, but she dug her nails into his back at the same time.

"Well, why don't you come by the Guild Hall later this evening. Find me and I'll see what can be done to get you to Yaolin City in fair time—short of hitching a wagon—yes?"

"That would be superb, Lord Bokeo."

"Please, call me Tayvada."

A soft purring sound emanated from the man. Whitney nearly let a laugh sneak out at the thought of a man as proper as Tayvada gassing up the place. Then a pair of reptilian wings flapped behind him. Whitney didn't even try to hide his surprise.

"Whoa!" he shouted, taking a step back and bumping into the bar. A few glasses rattled as he looked to Sora, whose jaw dropped.

"I am so sorry," Tayvada said. "I sometimes forget she is there." A dark brown creature about the size of a large sack landed on his padded shoulder. Scales covered every bit of its body, with frills around its head plate. A pair of small wings stretched out acting also as front legs, claws serving both as joints and feet.

"Is that… a dragon?" Sora stammered. The creature blinked at her inquisitively. Its piercing, snake-like, yellow eyes had two sets of eyelids. A thin, translucent layer which closed sideways beneath a normal, vertical pair.

The man laughed. "Dragons are long gone, my dear. This here is Aquira. She's a wyvern—a distant relative of the dragon found in the Pikeback Mountains. She is nearly full-grown and mighty friendly… unless she considers you dangerous. You're not dangerous, are you Lord Blisslayer?"

"Not toward a beauty like her," Whitney said. "That's for sure." He grinned and again glanced toward Sora. Her face was like stone, unmoving from awe. He'd seen a few wyverns before in Panping whereas, she'd clearly never seen anything like it. They were extremely rare and valuable. They didn't, however, burn down villages and eat men as they couldn't sustain flight for long with their small wings.

After a long moment, she finally whispered, "May I touch her?"

"It is doubtful she'll let you. She may be friendly, however, wyverns are notoriously proud. But by all means, try. She won't bite."

Sora reached out. Aquira backed away and stuck out her serpentine tongue. Whitney was about to tease Sora when the wyvern suddenly leaned back in and nuzzled her head against Sora's outstretched hand.

"Bravo!" Tayvada said, giddy.

"Her scales are so dry!" she exclaimed.

"Let me see. A friend of mine had one and he loved me." Whitney went to pet Aquira, but the wyvern hissed at him before flying back and hovering behind Tayvada. Her breath was hot, like the hazy air just above a roaring fire.

"Don't fret, my friend." Tayvada lay his hand on Whitney's shoulder. "She has a soft spot for women."

"She just has good taste," Sora said.

Whitney crossed his arms, then plopped back down on his stool. "So, the Guild Hall, tonight?" he asked.

"Yes, tonight," Tayvada said. "I shall see you there. And do wear something… fitting?"

Whitney looked down at his tattered cloak. "My apologies. It has been a long journey."

"I understand. Until tonight, my Lord and Lady." He bowed, then nodded Tum Tum's way. "Come Aquira!"

Whitney turned to Sora as the man walked away, Aquira flapping to keep up with him. Sora was finally able to turn off her smile, but Whitney's remained ear to ear. He raised a fresh tankard of ale to both her and Tum Tum.

"See?" he said. "Simple."

VII

THE KNIGHT

Torsten could almost taste the energy in the air the night of Pi's declaration. A flurry of genuine activity passed through Yarrington the likes of which not seen since the passing of King Liam. People active not because they felt they had to be, such as had been for his coronation, but out of true desire.

He could hear the great King Liam's voice imparting wisdom before yet another war, "Common people don't revel in the fear of the royals behind walls," he said. "They crave an enemy they can reach. Villains that breathe their air, walk their dirt… spill their blood."

It was a simple concept, but as Torsten looked out upon Yarrington, he understood better than ever. For months, the city had been obsessed with things they couldn't control; a dying king, a queen driven to the brink of madness, unprovoked raids, hunger, a miracle—but now the taverns bustled. Together, young men and fathers drank and cursed the Shesaitju. They flooded the barracks across the kingdom, volunteers on top of conscripts.

All that time, trying to avoid war and Torsten forgot what the Glass Kingdom was founded on. Half a century ago, they were just another kingdom in the corner of Pantego. Then a young king was called on by

Iam to take up the sword, to bear His name, to bring greater Pantego under a single crown.

Liam had been older than Pi, yet Torsten couldn't help but wonder if history would repeat itself, would give a second chance, granted by Iam, to stay true, to keep spreading his light.

"Shouldn't you be planning?"

Torsten whipped around to see Oleander in the doorway of his chambers. It was neither modest like Rand's apartment nor luxurious like the King and Queen's, but it suited him. Instead of paintings and sculptures, the flawlessly cut stone walls were covered in weaponry. The shield of Sir Roderich of Cornhovel—a city no longer on the map thanks to so many battles, the Spear of Sir Von the Valiant—relics of great Shieldsmen he could aspire to.

It was, however, no place fit for the Queen Mother.

"Your Grace." Torsten bowed. "I wasn't expecting you."

"At least someone still bows to their queen."

She entered the room, her long legs carrying her to Torsten's bedside in only a few strides. She sat on the edge and her handmaiden made sure her dress didn't bunch—not a dress, Torsten realized. She wore a negligee as extravagant as any gown in Pantego. The frills were woven with gold, and the blue fabric was stitched in a tight floral pattern. The light of the moons poured through Torsten's window and caught it, allowing him to clearly see the silhouette of the lithe figure beneath.

Torsten averted his eyes, wondering if she knew. Then, he realized that he too was out of uniform, wearing only the sweat-laden, baggy tunic worn beneath his armor. He could only imagine the stench. The audience with the Caleef had every ounce of perspiration rolling down his back and from his shaven head.

"Forgive me," Torsten said. "If I knew you were coming I would be dressed appropriately."

"Can you stop being such an insufferably honorable man for once?" she groaned.

"And you…" She spun on her handmaiden. "If I wanted you to follow me in here I would have asked."

The young woman froze and stuttered, "Your Grace, I—"

"Get out!"

The young handmaiden scurried out of the room like a rat caught foraging at a banquet. Torsten watched the young lady's retreat and caught a glimpse of the Queen making herself more comfortable. His heart raced. There had never been a woman on his bed, let alone her.

"Your Grace, is there anything you need…" His words trailed off when he heard her snivel. His eyes lifted and found her face buried in her palms, crying.

Torsten rushed to her side. "What happened?"

"He's so… cruel," she whimpered.

"Who?"

"He wasn't like this when he was younger. Before everything. He was a sweet, kind boy. Uriah always said so, too. Now, I… I don't even know him."

Torsten sat beside her. He was a hair's breadth from laying his hand over hers but thought better of it. He slid away a bit, where the overpowering scent of her flower-blossom perfume wasn't so intoxicating.

"Oh, him," he said. "He's been through a lot, Your Grace. He's just figuring things out."

"I should've never let Redstar anywhere near him."

"None of us should have, but he can't poison Pi's mind any longer. He's locked up and won't be seeing day's light anytime soon."

"Don't you see, Torsten? I've been caring for a stranger ever since that day." She turned to him, tears causing her makeup to run. The last time he saw her so affected was when he found her cradling Pi's corpse. Now the boy was alive, yet she cried all the same.

"I only knew him from afar before then, so I cannot say."

"He loved to read. I'm not sure where he got it from. His father was a man of action, and I… I didn't learn to read until Liam brought me here. There's no reason for a woman to study in the far North."

"Then I'm glad you're here, Your Grace."

"Do not spin lies. Do you think I've not heard the whispers all these years? About the 'foreign whore Queen.' Do you think I don't know how they talk about me now? The murderous witch who lost her mind. I was only trying to save him."

"And Iam heard your prayers and returned him to us," Torsten said before thinking. He didn't believe that. The people prayed, maybe, but

Iam didn't reward senseless killing. In the corner of his mind, ever since that day, Torsten always wondered if he'd been the one who'd caused the miracle. If it had been his unwavering faith that broke whatever curse Redstar had laid upon Pi and inspired Iam to return him to the realm of the living.

He never presumed to know the machinations of Iam. All he knew for sure was Oleander's rampage wasn't the cause of it. It couldn't have been.

"I thought everything would be back to normal when you found him in the crypt," Oleander said. "But now, when he starts talking, all I see in him is his father."

"Liam was a great man."

"He was. From the moment I saw him in the tundra, I knew he had no equal. Redstar couldn't understand why I left without a fuss. He still doesn't."

"I remember."

"You were there?"

Torsten nodded. "I was Uriah's squire."

How could he forget that day? Liam sought to conquer the Drav Cra before he realized he never could. The land beyond Winter's Thumb was wild and always would be. But then Liam saw the stunning daughter of a chieftain, barely of proper age. She stuck out like a flower growing through the ice.

Oleander ran her fingers along her tear-covered cheeks. "Oh, how time has ravaged me since then."

"You are more radiant than ever, Your Grace." That, he meant. How Liam fell for someone so young, he would never understand, but the man had an eye for seeing beyond what others could. Somehow, he knew the marvel Oleander would blossom into. A fierce queen and the greatest beauty in Pantego... now sitting on Torsten's bed.

"How in Iam's name are you not betrothed, Torsten?" She smiled, though her swollen eyes made it pitiable, and sidled closer.

"The Crown is a Shieldsman's only love, Your Grace."

"Right, of course. You're not still chaste though, are you?"

"My Queen?"

"A virgin, Torsten."

"I know what it means, Your Grace. I just—"

"You are, aren't you!" Oleander said, seemingly forgetting about her tears.

"Of course not!" Torsten exclaimed, cheeks red as cherry plums.

"No, how could you be? Conquering all those foreign lands with my husband. I'm sure you were treated like a king by all the whores he brought in."

Torsten choked on his next breath.

"What? You think I don't know?" She laughed. "He had enough mistresses to fill the Great Hall."

"I… the King kept to his tent…."

"My sweet Torsten, you don't have to lie to me. I know who my husband was. Within these walls, I was the love of his life, but out there? Every time he returned from some great battle, it wasn't blood I smelled on him."

"He loved you, my Queen," Torsten said softly. He could think of nothing else, and even those words barely managed past his lips.

"I know he did. And I loved him when I could. But the others were all beautiful, faultless and fleeting loves. Only *I* suffered under the weight of his honesty. As I now suffer under the weight of my own son's—his son."

"For a boy his age to have been through so much… I can't even imagine. I truly believe he's simply still figuring things out, Your Grace."

"Torsten, please do away with the formalities. We are alone in this room."

"Of course, Your Gr—Oleander." He didn't need the reminder of their solitude, it was all he could think of.

She rested her head against Torsten's shoulder. He quaked with conflicting emotions. He had never—could never—deny how stunning she was, how powerful, but he'd been on the receiving end of her wrath far too many times.

"I did it all for him," she said quietly after some time had passed.

"I know."

"No, you don't!" She removed her head from his shoulder, but her anger quickly subsided and she returned it again. "How could you?" she continued, calmly this time. "You have no child of your own. You're like all the rest. You think I'm some crazy, murderous shrew."

This time, Torsten was the one to break the connection. He stood, hands balled into tight fists. "I think you were broken by grief and made mistakes. And I may not have a child, but my quest to bring young Pi back to this realm showed me terrors no man should see. Included are your brother's torments, masquerading as a man I respected, and a beast so grotesque her visage assaults me in my dreams."

He stared off into the shadow of his room and imagined her there. The Spider Queen Bliss, her eyes like amethysts staring back at him, wanting to devour him.

"Torsten." The Queen took his hand, pulled him toward her. When he drew his gaze away from the shadows and back toward her, he found her solemn again. Bliss was said to be a goddess, and at that moment Oleander seemed her equal.

Before he knew it, they were sitting so near one another, their legs touched. Her long, painted nails ran up his arm and along the bare flesh of his neck. All the tiny hairs on his body rose with it.

"My greatest mistake was losing faith in you. Sending you away," she said softly, leaning in. Her perfume wafted around his nostrils, making it impossible to retreat.

"I'm here now," he said, voice quavering.

"Of course you are, my loyal, handsome, knight. I never properly thanked you for stopping my brother." Her other hand gripped the back of his neck. Her fingers were cold, but her breath was warm.

"You can start by finally executing the bastard." His voice shook and his breath came in spirts. "The coronation is over now. I cannot bear another day knowing his shadow looms over us. Especially with war to come."

"Tonight, then? I'll let you hold the sword." She drew herself closer, throwing one leg over his, her knee resting between his thighs. Her negligee stretched, falling off one of her slender shoulders as her body contorted. "I've heard Pantego has no finer swordsman. Surely, you could *handle* it."

Torsten knew he should back away, but he'd never seen her so intimately. Her milky skin was supple, without blemish. Her eyes bore so many different shades of blue it made the summer sky seem dreary. There wasn't a man in all the Glass and beyond who hadn't dreamed of this. He wasn't sure what Oleander was up to—she was always up to something—

but he couldn't stop. His heart beat so fast he felt like it would drive him to an early grave. Her lips fell upon his. They tasted as wonderful as her perfume smelled.

He didn't lean into it. He couldn't even move. But she did all the work. One of her long legs wound its way around him and squeezed until their chests pressed together.

He could deny her no longer.

He kissed her hard in return. His hand found its way to the small of her back, and as he prepared to lay her down and give into the silent, sinful cravings that had been building in him for so long, out of the corner of his eye, he saw someone familiar pass by his chamber. Realizing the door was still open made his eyes go wide, but the man he thought he saw caused him to release the Queen.

"My Queen, stop," he panted. He tried to remove her leg, but she only stretched the other around him, laid back on the bed, and tried to reel him in again. "Oleander, stop."

Hearing her name gave her pause enough for Torsten to break free without having to lay his hands on her.

"What?" she said. "Liam can have all the fun in the world but his sweet, widowed queen can't?"

"No… I… it's him."

Torsten sprinted to one of many racks filled with various arms. He grabbed his most trusted claymore, then swept out into the corridor.

"Redstar!" he bellowed.

He wasn't sure he was right until halfway down the passage, the man stopped and turned. It was Redstar no doubt, free of chains. A luxurious robe now fell around his feet, the same color crimson as the birthmark covering his face. A mischievous grin split Redstar's face. If he feared being caught, it didn't show. By the looks of him, he'd even found time to have a bath.

"Torsten, my old friend!" he exclaimed. "I was hoping to stumble upon you first."

"Show me your hands, now."

Redstar raised them without protest, not even a spot of blood on his scarred palms.

Torsten rushed him, pressing his sword to his throat. "On your knees."

He advanced the blade, pulling it back before drawing blood, only just realizing how dangerous that could be. "If you try anything, I swear to Iam I will—"

"Torsten what is the meaning of this?" Oleander called from his room.

He glanced back just long enough to see her features darken as she realized the situation. Her negligee was still askew, her hair as wild as the land from whence she came.

"Redstar?" she whispered.

Redstar's brow furrowed. "Oh, now this is interesting."

"Quiet!" Torsten growled. He extended the sword further, until the tip put an indent in Redstar's skin. "How did you escape?"

"Escape?" he cackled. "I was set free."

"On whose word?"

"Mine."

Torsten whipped around. Further down the hall, past the entrance to his room, stood Pi. Oleander straightened her clothing before turning to see him as well. His frame was cloaked in darkness. What was easy to see, however, was how serious he was—as stern as Liam Nothhelm on the eve of battle.

VIII

THE MYSTIC

Sora couldn't remember her long trek from the Panping Region to Troborough. She was far too young all those years ago. However, she'd been told she was a part a large group of refugees, orphans, mostly, whose parents were slaughtered in the Third Panping War. Somehow, she'd never been angry with the Glass, not really. Maybe it was Wetzel's influence and teaching, but she understood war. She realized the Glass wasn't really the enemy any more than her own people. Besides, had it not been for Wetzel, a Glassman, she'd likely have died, starved and exposed to the elements.

Her childhood was pleasant, but in light of recent events, she started to see how she'd been treated differently from the rest of the children. She'd thought it was just because of weird, old Wetzel. But now she knew it was more. An inherent distrust of her kind by nearly everybody in the western Glass Kingdom, whether they realized it or not.

The only times she'd really felt normal was when she was with Whitney. He didn't look at her like she was a great, big mistake. Whether they were splashing in the Shellnak, or nabbing little cakes from the baker— that was Whitney's favorite. Sora's favorite was sneaking into the Twilight Manor to listen to the traveling bards spin melodic yarns about far-away places, but that was hers alone. Whitney never believed her when she said she'd done it and she'd never showed him how, even though he practically begged her. To Whitney, she was just Sora, the girl from downstream with funny ears.

Music always had a way of making Sora feel comfortable when she was among all the older folk of Troborough. Some people had long walks in the fields, or riding horses, or thieving, but for Sora, it was the sweet tones of a lute expertly plucked. She didn't play an instrument, but always wished she had.

Standing there in the entrance to the Winde Traders Guild Hall, Sora realized that all the best bards who came through Troborough—Fabian "Feel Good" Saravia, Dudley "Dreamboat" Blanco—they'd all been nothing compared to what Winde Port had to offer. As she listened to the notes, she felt like she really stood before the golden arches of Glinthaven, birthplace of the bardsong.

"Sora!" Whitney's voice snapped her back to reality. "Let's go see what fortune holds for us!"

Whitney tapped his foot, waiting for her, clutching his letters patent, the document the Glass Master of Rolls had drafted for him. They somehow proved him nobility, even though she knew his parents were simple farmers. The stupidity of the entire situation constantly astounded her.

She knew from Wetzel's dusty, but limited library that in the land of her ancestors, there weren't any papers to prove a person was of worth. *They* proved it. From great mystics to great minds, any man or woman could rise... at least until the King of Glass took hold.

She sighed.

At least these papers might help get them to Panping faster. She tried not to show it around Whitney, but she'd never been so anxious to get anywhere in her life. Something had awakened in her when she defeated Redstar. Torsten thought it was Iam, she'd said it was the blood of Bliss, but somehow, she knew there was more to it. And she knew the answers had to be somewhere in Yaolin City, a land where mystics once freely drew on the powers of Elsewhere without blood sacrifice or condemnation.

For now, she needed to play the role of Mrs. Whitney Blisslayer. She certainly looked the part of nobility. They'd received quite a handsome sum from the goods in Grint's wagon. Enough to buy her a sparkling gown with lace trim fit for the Queen of Glass herself. Long, fingerless silk gloves covered her up to her elbows, assuring no one would discover her dark secrets by spying the many scars crisscrossing her hands and forearms.

Had she been wearing the Glass Crown, she could have passed for royalty. She hated to admit to herself that Whitney could as well. High, leather boots met his green, silk tights at the knee. He wore an exquisite doublet marked with intricately embroidered filigree. The whole ensemble was inexplicably both dashing and ridiculous all at once, much like the man who wore it.

But that was nothing compared to the others eating and drinking within the guild. Ladies wore unnaturally-colored hair high in plumule fashion, layer upon layer. Their faces were masked by makeup worthy of a masquerade. And the men looked no better, wearing puffy white wigs and collars so thick and ruffled they looked like they were being strangled by fluffy kittens.

Whitney had told her on the way over that the longstanding merchant families of Winde Port put the nobles of Yarrington to shame with their pomp and circumstance. The real thing made her feel more out of place than ever before, regardless of what she wore.

Whitney, on the other hand, sniggered as they passed by a table of four men all wearing puffy, patterned shirts.

"Hush, Whit," Sora warned. "You'll embarrass us."

"Yeah, because we're the ones who should be embarrassed."

"For once in your irreverent life, would you just try and behave yourself?"

Whitney stopped at a table in the corner, bent at the waist, and beckoned her forth. "Why, of course. Right this way, milady."

"Better than knife-ear," she grumbled.

They sat down and ordered drinks. It was such a normal-seeming thing, yet Sora realized she'd never been waited on before. In all the taverns she'd ever visited—a total of two—she had to carry herself up to the bar.

Presently, the server returned carrying oddly-shaped glasses filled with violet liquid.

"This is no ale I've ever seen," Sora said.

"It's a Winde Port delicacy called a cocktail," Whitney said. "Ridiculous name, I know, but it's fruity. You'll love it."

Sora lifted it and studied the liquid. It looked like poison out of some fairy tales she'd found on Wetzel's bookshelf. But all around the room, nobles were throwing them back. She gave it a whiff. It smelled like the first lavender blossoms of spring.

"Would you just try it already?" Whitney griped.

Sora brought it to her lips and took the tiniest sip imaginable. Her eyes went wide. She tilted the glass and downed half in a single gulp.

"It tastes like the plums Farmer Branson grew in the fields across from my house!" she exclaimed. "I can't wait to have another..." Her voice trailed off. Sadness came like a deluge at the thought of that field, now black and burnt at the hands of the Shesaitju.

"Enough of that look in your eyes, Sora. This is about trying something fresh and new. Drink up. The bottom of that glass is the start of a new one."

Sora forced a smile. "Are you trying to get me drunk, *husband*?"

"Never." Whitney laughed. "So, do you see Tayvada anywhere?"

"No," Sora answered. "But I hope his drag... wyvern is here. I've never seen anything like it."

"I have," Whitney said, finishing his drink in one mouthful. He raised a finger for the waiter to bring more.

"Is this another of your tall tales?" Sora asked.

"I don't tell tall tales. I speak history."

Sora rolled her eyes before she too finished the rest of her drink. Whitney went to request another, but she waved him down. She'd never drank much more than a single ale or a sip of honeyed wine from Wetzel's cupboard. The old badger didn't like her losing control when she was still getting a handle on her abilities. And after what happened in the Webbed Woods, she wasn't too keen on it either. One "cocktail" and her head was already feeling light.

"I wonder where Tayvada is," she said while Whitney tried another beverage, this one, a sickeningly bright shade of orange. "We need to get going."

"What's the rush?" Whitney asked. "Look at this place, it's beautiful. I used to have to sneak into places like this, come up with a whole elaborate backstory and name. If only Torsten could see me now." He kicked his feet up on the bench across from him.

"He'd probably want to burn those as much as me," she said, referring to his boots she'd just shoved off the bench. "Now c'mon, we should find him."

"You need to learn to relax. Oh, shog…"

"What?"

"Don't turn around," Whitney said. "I said *don't* turn around!"

It was too late. She was already craning her neck to see behind her. She cursed herself for not listening to him, but it was his fault for making it so impossible.

"Darkings…" She whipped her head back around. The sight of him stole the breath from her lungs. "Did he see you? I think he saw you. He did. He's coming this way."

"What do we do?" Sora whispered.

The man sauntered over, eyes poring over Whitney and then, Sora. He carried himself like one who'd never done an honest day's work, and he likely hadn't. His face and hands were smooth as a man half his age. There was so little grit in his voice, Sora could imagine the demon ears of Elsewhere perking up when he spoke. Her hand instinctually fell toward the handle of the knife in her belt.

"Father Gorenheimer, wasn't it?" he said. "Oh wait, Whitney Fierstown, that's right. Though, now I hear it's Lord Blisslayer. How many names can one man have?"

In the weeks since they'd last seen him, he'd grown bushy mustache which looked like a fuzzy caterpillar resting on his upper lip. Chest hairs poked out from beneath an expensive looking tunic, and when he smiled, Sora recoiled. Yellowing teeth poked out over his bottom lip.

"Constable Darkings!" Whitney exclaimed. "How's your daughter?"

Sora felt all the color drain from her cheeks. She couldn't believe that after they robbed and burned down the Constable of Bridleton's home, that was the first thing Whitney would say. Then Sora remembered how she hit the poor girl to keep their flirting from getting everyone killed.

It wasn't her finest moment.

"I've shipped Nauriyal to a convent in Hornsheim," Darkings said.

"Turns out she played not-so-small a role in the destruction of my home—but you already knew that, didn't you? Maybe a little hard work in the bitter cold will teach her to respect her elders."

Whitney's beaming smile didn't fade in the least, but his eye twitched.

"No matter," Darkings continued. "I promised you last time I saw you that I'd have my revenge."

"And here you are! Should I expect you'll gut us, here and now?" Whitney asked.

"This is a room for gentlemen. I would never tarnish the good name of Darkings. Not here in the very guild my grandparents helped build so many Dawnings ago. You see, Darkings is not a name you should have meddled with. Do you even realize the enemies you've made?"

"What do you want, Constable?" Sora asked, exasperated.

He slid into the booth next to them and his face turned deadly serious. "Do not speak to me in such a flippant manner, *knife-ear!*" he hissed. Now her fingers wrapped firmly around the wooden grip of her knife.

Darkings faced Whitney. "You burned everything I built to the ground," he said. "My father served as Master of Coin to the Crown for twenty years, and he will be reinstated under the new king in short time. If I even breathed word of this to him, the King's Shield would have your heads on pikes."

Sora looked to Whitney. She didn't have to ask out loud if he knew that Darkings was the son of a member of the Royal Council. She did it with her eyes, and his said, "no."

The worldliest thief in Pantego and he doesn't know a thing!

She wanted to explode at him but somehow kept quiet.

"If I were you, I wouldn't bother daddy," Whitney said calmly. "Turns out, people thought it was another act of the Black Sands. Sounds more plausible to me than a couple of nobles rolling into Bridleton for a bit of respite, no? Plus, the Wearer of White already *is* reinstated, and he's a good friend of m—"

"You are no more noble than the shog on my boot!" Darkings spat.

"I have papers saying otherwise. Bearing the royal seal itself."

"A piece of paper won't keep you…" He cleared his throat and stroked his mustache. "Are you a gems playing man, Mr. Fierstown?"

"*Lord* Blisslayer. And, yes I fancy myself rather good at all games of chance. Up for a game or two?"

Darkings scoffed and leaned in. "You have shown your hand, boy, and it is not a winner. I, on the other hand, keep mine close to my chest. When you are least expecting it, you and your Panping witch will find yourselves drowning in your own blood and piss."

Whitney brought his drink to his lips and before taking a sip, said, "I've always enjoyed a swim. I'll be looking forward to it."

"Don't you worry. You'll be seeing me again soon enough."

Whitney opened his mouth to speak but a server approached the table.

"I'm sorry, I didn't know it would be a party of three," he said. "Can I get you something, Lord Darkings?"

"No, thank you. I was just leaving. Please, get this special couple a round of your finest Breklian brandy, on me. It might be their last," he paused, "in Winde Port."

Darkings stood, grinned, and walked away.

"Was that a threat?" Sora asked, finally feeling like she could breathe. She didn't release her weapon until he was completely out of sight.

"An ominous warning, I'd say," Whitney said, taking another sip of his drink.

"This isn't funny, Whit. We are on lockdown in an unfamiliar city with an apparently powerful family after us."

"This city isn't unfamiliar to me. We're going to be absolutely fine."

"How in Elsewhere did you not know who his father was!"

"I'm supposed to keep track of every twit on the Royal Council? They're in and out like flies, and with the mad Queen, I barely know who's king anymore."

"Why am I not surprised?"

Whitney didn't answer. He leaned over the table, tilted one of his empty glasses and watched it sway back upright. "You hungry?" Whitney asked.

"You're thinking about food at a time like this?"

"You're not? We haven't had a decent meal since Grambling, back at the Walled Lake."

"Aren't we here just to get some papers from Tayvada?" she asked.

"Do you see Tayvada?"

"No." Sora's face scrunched. "Should we ask someone?"

Whitney sighed, then rose. "I'll be right back."

Sora sidled a little further into the booth, wary of leaving her back exposed. Darkings was an obtuse fool but he wasn't accepting like the rest of the people here. And he didn't seem to care about all the fineries. She glanced over each shoulder and saw plenty of others like her—*knife-ears*. She tried to just relax and enjoy the music. After a few tunes went by without him returning, she started to worry that Darkings had exacted his revenge on Whitney already and she'd be next.

A sudden movement made her yelp. Whitney slid back into the booth from the other direction, carrying what looked like a leg of lamb. He stretched it toward her but she declined.

"You had me worried sick and you were getting food?" she asked.

"Sora, you've gotta learn to relax a little. Take it all in. We are exploring the wide world together. No agenda. No worries!"

"Except the little bit about a man wanting us dead. Oh, and the mounting army. Oh, and—"

Whitney groaned. "Do you want to know what I found out about Tayvada or not?"

"Fine."

"Turns out one of his servants came about an hour ago to leave message that he fell ill and wouldn't be..." Whitney puffed out his chest and put on a distinguished effect, "'...attending any of his appointments this evening.'"

Sora threw her hands up in frustration. "Great. Now we have to wait for him?"

Whitney took a bite of lamb, then with his mouth still full said, "Nope. I got his home address."

IX

THE KNIGHT

"Your Grace, please help me understand," Torsten said to Pi, keeping his voice low. "Why would you free him?"

They were in Pi's old chambers now, high up in the Glass Castle's West Tower. He hadn't yet found reason to move to his father's quarters—besides, Oleander still occupied them. There were bars on the window, an unpleasant reminder of Pi's fall.

"You could just ask me," Redstar said. He sat at Pi's desk, the same smug grin plastered on his face that he'd worn when revealing his true self in the Webbed Woods.

"Silence!" Torsten snapped. He stood behind him, claymore in both hands, the tip grinding into the stone floor.

"Pi, my precious boy, don't you remember what he did to you?" Oleander sat beside him on a bed two sizes too large for him, stroking his hair.

He remained indifferent.

"I forget, sister, which of us has more of your people's blood on our hands?" Redstar remarked.

"Sir Davies was worth a thousand of any of us!" Torsten said. "He died because of you."

"Just kill him, Torsten," Oleander spat. "I will not have him poison these halls any further."

"You will do no such thing, Wearer," Pi said, calm and collected. He turned to face them, head and neck only. "No harm will befall my uncle."

"He tried to kill you! To destroy everything inside of you."

"What, with this?" Pi reached across his bed and lifted the tiny, Drav Cra effigy sewn for him by Oleander at his birth. By the ancient customs of her former people, an orepul was said to bear a piece of its owner's soul.

The young King lifted it, then without a second of hesitation, ripped the head from its stitches. The Queen gasped as it fell to the floor in two pieces. Torsten's heart sank with it. Not that he believed it wielded any power—such would be heresy—but he'd been through exile and back to retrieve it for the Queen.

"Not with that, Your Grace," Torsten said after a brief silence. His fingers squeezed so tight around the handle of his sword it hurt. "He put a spell on you with blood magic. A spell that had you seeing awful visions of darkness and terror and the Buried Goddess. I know because I felt them too shortly after you fell from this very window."

"Excuse me for trying to open his eyes by showing him the truth," Redstar said. "How was I to know that children grow up so soft here in the capital that he wouldn't be able to handle it?" He walked across the room as he spoke and lifted the two pieces of the orepul to study them more closely. Torsten imagined seeing an effigy supposedly holding a piece of Pi's soul would unnerve him, but he didn't seem so in the slightest.

"Because of your dark magic, my son, your king, leaped from that window!" Oleander shouted. She tried to stand, but Pi extended one of his short arms in front of her.

"My uncle acted vindictively because *you* refused him," Pi said. "Because you forgot that the ice of the Drav Cra runs through your veins, as it does mine. I may not approve of what he did to me, but I do understand."

"What have you done, Brother?" Oleander asked. "How have you twisted his mind this time?"

"Oleander, I'm hurt." Redstar stuffed the orepul into a pouch, then placed his hand over his heart in mock-surprise. "I've been locked away safe and sound. Pi came to me."

"You don't deserve to breathe the same air as him!" Oleander grabbed a small letter opener off the bedside table, sprung to her feet, and charged him. Torsten caught her just in time, the blade only inches away from Redstar's eye. A heartbeat later, he wondered what in Elsewhere he was thinking by stopping her.

Redstar didn't even flinch. "Now we both owe each other, Sir Unger," he said. His grin deepened as he stood and patted Torsten's back.

"Torsten, don't let him do this," Oleander said. "He can't be trusted. He tried to kill my son." She tried to squirm free, but Torsten's brawny arms didn't give. "He tried to kill my son!"

"I know, Your Grace," Torsten whispered. "But not like this."

"Guards!" Pi called. Not a second later, the door flew open and two members of the King's Shield entered, weapons drawn. "Please remove my mother to her chambers until I see fit. She is feeling ill again and I worry what she might do."

The guards glanced between the King and Torsten.

"You will not lay a hand on me," Oleander hissed. "I am your Queen."

"They will do as their king asks, *Mother*, and so will you," Pi said, a man's timbre in his tone. "When I met with Redstar, he called on the names of Iam and his goddess in heartfelt apology. He has repented for what was done out of spite and anger." He lowered his voice and said, "When will you?"

Torsten felt all the fight leave Oleander. Her arms went slack. The words were harsh, yet partially true. An apology from a deceiver like Redstar meant as little as one made in the name of the Buried Goddess, but Oleander too had acted from a dangerous place.

"Pi…" Oleander's voice cracked. "He's a monster. You have to trust me."

"Our weakness after Father grew ill has emboldened our enemies," Pi said. "Perhaps monsters are exactly what we need now."

Torsten regarded Redstar. He'd manipulated the entire kingdom to help him destroy Bliss, the apparent enemy of his people's own fallen deity, but doing that didn't even seem to compare to how self-satisfied he now appeared.

"Just go, Your Grace," Torsten whispered in Oleander's ear. "I'll make sure he never sees daylight again."

She turned and took Torsten's hands. Hers were quaking.

"Oh, Torsten," she sniveled. "Loyal, Torsten. Show him the light of Iam that breathed life into him again." Her fingers slid apart from his, then she slowly backed away between the two guards.

Torsten nodded the Shieldsmen along but didn't break eye contact with Oleander until she was through the door. She'd been a terrible queen when she was in charge, one who had senselessly murdered so many of her loyal servants. But at least Torsten knew why. Perhaps she was a monster too, but if that were true, there was no term foul enough to describe her brother.

Redstar sighed. "Perhaps now we can discuss how to handle the Shesaitju situation in peace and quiet, Nephew."

Torsten lashed out and grabbed him by the collar. He pulled him close. The Drav Cra were inherently tall, but Redstar was the runt of his family. Torsten towered over him.

"You will address him as your King," Torsten growled, then shoved him back into the chair.

"Relax, Sir Unger." Pi stood and paced in front of his window. His head barely reached over the sill, but Torsten wasn't foolish enough to believe he was a child anymore, even if he looked it. Whatever had happened between his death and rebirth, he was as much a man as they were.

"I understand your hesitance to trust my uncle," Pi said.

"Beyond being a murderer, he is a heretic and practitioner of blood magic," Torsten said. "He is the enemy of the faithful and the scorn of Iam's vigilant Eye."

"And he is not only one of the most respected leaders in Drav Cra as dradinengor of the Ruuhar Clan, but also named High Warlock by the rest of his order."

"Arch Warlock," Redstar corrected.

Torsten scowled his way. "That is not a title we of the Glass should abide."

"Maybe so, but it is a title which allowed him to gather thousands of capable warriors to our cause in only a month. My father turned from their lands because he knew they were a hard, unconquerable people. Yet the tomes of history teach us that all men descended from the tundra. Drav Cra is in all our blood, and it is half of mine."

"Liam knew they couldn't be trusted. He knew how far Iam was from their hearts."

"Yet he brought one home. Made her queen. Because my father knew that worth could be found in the strangest of places. He knew that the wild tribes of the North would have bowed to my mother if only she remembered them. That was how he planned to conquer them. Through blood, not by blood."

"How do you know that's what he planned?" he asked, even though it sounded exactly like something Liam would do. He hadn't only been a fearless commander who charged into battle and inspired his own men, but a tactician without equal.

"Sir Davies said as much when I was very young," Pi said. "But then Father grew too ill and our borders stopped expanding. My mother could have been useful to him then. Instead, she remained a cruel, foreign treasure locked up in this castle scaring everyone away."

"Your Grace, she gave birth to you. She sat at your side every night while you were ill."

"And she let the kingdom crumble. You said it yourself, our armies are weaker than ever. We don't trust any of our allies in Panping or Brotlebir to come to our aid. Instead, we're calling on conscripts who've done nothing but plow fields for a decade."

"And drink," Redstar added. "For centuries, my people have been battling cold that makes this seem like summer. Scraping and clawing for leftovers of the few beasts that still roam the tundra."

"After two decades as queen, my mother's failure will be rectified," Pi declared. "The mighty warriors of the Drav Cra will march at our side."

"The heathens should never be allowed into this city," Torsten bristled.

"I sent for them weeks ago." Pi stopped at the window and had to lean up on the balls of his feet to look down over the sill.

Torsten rushed to his side and threw open the window. Cold air and flurries blasted his cheeks but he craned his neck over the edge so he could see the castle's entry bailey. Snow and clouds dulled the light of the twin moons but there was no mistaking the gathering. Hundreds of tall, pale Drav Cra men wearing heavy furs and axes stood waiting. Enough of them to slaughter everyone inside, King and Queen Mother as well.

Among them were others dressed in ragged robes of layered animal furs, wearing necklaces festooned with strange totems and bones—true Drav Cra warlocks, not just in the capital, but within the walls of the castle. They didn't even bother to pretend they were cultists to the Buried Goddess or cover their faces with hoods and white masks like the ones who followed Redstar in the Webbed Woods. They let their faces show, black paint covering their eyes with a line of red over the lids. Cracking, white paint covered the rest of their faces and ran down their necks as if they needed to make their pale skin paler.

"By Iam, what have you done?" Torsten's voice shook.

"I'm finally using every advantage at our disposal," Pi said.

"Had I known how wise the young King was, I would have come straight to him a year ago and skipped all the nonsense," Redstar said.

"You call that nonsense?" Torsten growled as he whipped back around. "Your Grace, I am your Wearer of White, commander of your armies. Why wasn't I told about this?"

"You are loyal and you are respected, Sir Unger," Pi said. "But I knew your piety would hinder your ability to see the benefit of this alliance."

"And the only pay they require is food," Redstar said, grinning so wide Torsten wanted to slap it off his face with his spiked, glaruium gauntlet.

"You expect my men—you expect *me* to march beside these heathens? Those are warlocks of the Buried Goddess down there." Torsten took Pi by the arm and the glare he received sent him reeling back. "If my men cannot trust their brothers in arms, I cannot lead them effectively."

"And you will not have to," Pi said. "As part of this arrangement, I have named my uncle Emissary of Drav Cra. You will command the armies, but he will lead his people under you. You will work together to bring this Shesaitju rebellion to an end. Then, my father's blessed work will be continued."

Torsten fell to his knees. "My King, I beg you, don't trust this man. The things he's done. The things he can do. He is a snake in the flesh of a man."

"'Iam is mercy. Iam is compassion. Light.' All my life I've heard this, yet all those who love gods of other names are ridiculed and condemned. I spent a great deal of time reading as a child. The holy texts beg for peace in Pantego. And here, those of Nesilia stand ready to fight by our side. Wren the Holy speaks of her evil. Redstar however, says that she was as close to Iam as skin to bone."

"Lies from the mouth of a deceiver."

"Possibly. Yet the God Feud teaches us that fighting amongst each other helps no one. And so, Torsten Unger, you will find a way to work with my uncle for the good of the kingdom, or you will find yourself exiled again."

Torsten glanced back at Redstar, at a man so wicked Iam sought to mark him eternally with the red of blood. A man who wore the guise of Sir Uriah Davies after luring him to his death. A man who'd been willing to risk everything to vanquish the Spider Queen Bliss, and for what?

Now he had the ear of the young, impressionable king after he drove the boy mad with dark magic. Torsten's fists clenched. He knew he could take Redstar down right then, ending whatever game he played. But as he looked back to Pi, he also knew that wasn't the way of Iam.

Perhaps Pi wasn't as ready for rule as Torsten had thought earlier that day, but he was right about what Iam stood for. And Torsten would be there when Redstar's true nature was revealed to him again. As he always would be.

He bowed his head. "I will serve in whatever way you see fit, Your Grace. But I will never trust him after what he did to you and neither should you."

"That is why I have a Shieldsman who served my father for so long at my side." Pi laid a hand on Torsten's shoulder.

For a moment, Torsten felt silly being so proud of receiving the praises of a small boy. Then Pi's arm fell away and he longed for it to return. The young king lay back onto his bed, all energy seeming to fade in an instant as the color drained from his face. It might have been the light, but Torsten thought the dark rings around his eyes seemed more pronounced than ever.

"Now leave me," Pi said weakly. "Both of you."

"Of course, Your Grace," Torsten said, rising. "You must be exhausted."

"Yes, seeing reason can be so tiring." Redstar bowed exceedingly low.

It reminded Torsten of the way the thief, Whitney, used to praise him in jest. Just the sight of it had him nearly swinging his sword in a wide arc across Redstar's neck. He controlled himself for Pi's sake.

They started off out of the room, side by side until Redstar stopped. "Ah, Your Grace, before I forget," he said. "I spoke with Yuri Darkings in the dungeon—the former Master of Coin who fled your mother's scorn. He is eager to return to his post, and in this time of war and uncertainty, it seems wise to have an experienced hand in charge of finances."

"You eavesdropped on my—" Torsten was cut off by the gentle voice of the King. He remained staring up at the ceiling with his limbs stretched out, now totally drained.

"Excellent idea, Uncle," he groaned. "Have him reinstated immediately."

"At once." Redstar bowed again and hurried out of the room.

Torsten seized him the moment they got outside and slammed him against the wall. His nostrils flared. His blood felt like it was on fire. It took all his willpower not to crush the traitor's neck.

"'Excellent idea,'" Redstar gurgled, repeating Pi's words. "Thank you for shedding light on the Council's needs. I needed to build a little faith."

"I don't know what you're up to, but I swore to you I wouldn't let you hurt him again," Torsten snarled, squeezing tighter.

"Can't..." he gurgled again, "...can't a loving uncle do what's best for his nephew?"

"Every word out of your mouth is poison." Torsten released him. Redstar fell to the floor, coughing and rubbing his neck. Once able to breathe again, he looked up, wearing that same annoying smirk.

"As I told you in the dungeon the day you brought me back, my work is already complete. Nesilia smiles upon me, and now she wants me here, serving my new king. Who are we to question her?"

"The name of the Buried Goddess will never be uttered here with impunity."

"I believe I just heard Pi *utter* it in the same sentence as your loving, wonderful Iam."

Torsten shoved a boot against his chest and pinned him back against the wall. "Don't you dare use His name."

"Or what?"

"Or I will do what I should've done in the Webbed Woods."

Redstar grinned through the pain of Torsten's full weight. "You can try," he said.

Suddenly, Torsten felt heat on his shin and looked down at a smear of blood on Redstar's hand. A glimmer of fire swirled around it. Blood magic, being used in the very halls of the Glass Castle.

Torsten's grip on his sword tightened. He couldn't stop it. A moment of weakness washed over him, or perhaps it was Iam guiding his hand. The King might banish him, or worse, but at least they'd be free.

Redstar grabbed Torsten's leg with his fire-wreathed hand. His pants burned away and his skin blistered. He didn't care.

"Iam forgive me for what I must do," he whispered under his breath. Then, he raised his blade.

At the same time, Redstar bit his other hand, drawing fresh blood. He raised his palm and Torsten felt all his muscles tense. He remembered the woods, how Redstar flung him and his companions around like rag dolls.

The Arch Warlock was clearly weakened from his time in a cell since Torsten still felt a twinge of control. It stung as much as the fire on his leg to try and move his muscles against the magic but he gritted his teeth and fought to try and break free.

"Sir Unger!" someone hollered from down the hall.

Torsten couldn't turn his head but he peered over with his eyes. Wardric stood in the corridor, fully armed. Beside him was a female Drav Cra warlock, her wild hair threaded with jagged beads made of bone. She sliced her hand and raised it. Her power, combined with that of Redstar, flung Torsten back, slamming him hard against the wall. His claymore clattered to the floor.

"Release him!" Wardric drew his sword and raised it to the warlock's neck.

"He assaulted Drad Redstar," the woman hissed.

Torsten's entire body seized. His back was crushed against the stone so hard he felt his ribs beginning to snap inward. A scream bubbled in his throat, one that would certainly rouse Pi if he hadn't been already.

Redstar stood, then dusted off his clothes. "Ah, my dear Freydis," he addressed her. "I was wondering when you and the others would arrive."

"Shall we send him to the goddess, Drad Redstar?" she asked.

"No, my over-eager friend. Release him. They're our allies now." Redstar lowered his own hand.

Torsten crumpled to the floor. Somehow, he'd forgotten what it felt like to be manipulated by blood magic—like an infant in the arms of its mother. It was a feeling he'd hoped never to experience again.

"My apologies, fair Shieldsman," Redstar said. "It was only a misunderstanding."

Freydis lowered her bloody hand as well, but Wardric still wielded his blade.

"It didn't look like it," Wardric said. "Why does that monster walk free?"

Torsten tried to stand but his muscles were as sore as they'd been on his first day of King's Shield training. He stared ahead at Pi's chambers. In a moment of weakness and fear, he had nearly broken the oath he made to the boy beyond its finely carved door.

"It's fine," Torsten said, panting. "Stand down, Wardric."

The Shieldsman didn't listen, only extended the blade further underneath the flaking white paint on Freydis' slender neck.

"What is the meaning of this, Torsten?" he asked. "I rode to bring you urgent news from the Southern Reach and find a barbarian horde camping at our doorsteps. This woman claimed to have been invited."

"By the King himself," Redstar pronounced with a flourish.

"Don't speak, knave!"

It took all the energy Torsten had to gesture to Wardric to lower his weapon. "It's true," he began through labored breaths. "Our young king has decided to free Redstar and make an alliance through him with the Drav Cra."

"That's madness," Wardric said.

"But true."

"You see? Just a squabble amongst new friends," Redstar said. He sauntered over, abounding confidence in every stride, then hoisted Torsten up by the shoulders. He brushed his own shoulder, and gave Torsten a playful slap on the cheek. "Good as new."

Torsten's stomach churned at his touch but he was too exhausted to push him away.

"Now, Sir… Jolly, I believe?" Redstar said. "What news do you bring from the South?"

Wardric slowly lowered his blade, but didn't drop his guard. Freydis on the other hand remained still and silent, her pale, gray eyes seeming to glow from the black paint smeared across the top half of her face.

"I bring news for the Wearer, and him alone," Wardric said.

"It's fine," Torsten grumbled, rubbing his temples. Now that the dominating magic had worn off, his head was starting to ache. "What is it?"

Wardric's gaze darted nervously between Freydis and Redstar until eventually, he took a step forward. Disgust contorted his features but he continued anyway.

"Muskigo's army is on the move," he said. "They've left their ships to drift into the swamp's fog and march north under the light of nigh'jels, straight toward Fort Marimount."

"And then Yarrington," Torsten finished.

Muskigo had made the first move, and if he took the ancient dwarven fortress, he'd have a stronghold within direct reach of Yarrington. The villages he'd already raided would be nothing compared to the slaughter he could unleash around the capital.

Torsten wasn't sure what to say next. He'd fought in many wars, but never at the helm. His mind was racing when Redstar clapped loudly.

"Looks like we won't have to wait to test the King's brilliant plan," he said. He turned to Torsten. "I so look forward to getting to know you better."

The crimson half of his face creased like parchment as his smile formed, deeper and more gleefully than ever before. And it was then that Torsten knew he'd missed his best chance. Because now, he truly did need the traitorous leech.

"Come Freydis. We have much to catch up on since I left for the Woods." Redstar went to Freydis' side, and she sneered at Wardric before they continued on down the hall together. Two warlocks, free in the Glass Castle, yet somehow that wasn't Torsten's biggest problem.

In only days, Muskigo had apparently learned of his Caleef's detainment and was on the march. There was no time for conscriptions to be filled out or properly trained, unlike the throng of hunters and heathens at the castle gates who were already prepared for battle. Now there was no way out of it. Torsten would have to march beside the man whose curse had once killed Pi only for him to breathe again; the man whose actions led to Uriah Davies' death, Oleander's breakdown, and Torsten to experience fear at the hands of Bliss like he'd never imagined before.

X

THE THIEF

I t was dark by the time they'd left the Guild Hall. The moons, Celeste and Loutis, hung high above the city. Celeste shone orange and bright through a thick fog, but Loutis could barely be seen peeking through. Whitney still couldn't believe how chilly it was so far south. He saw Sora shiver out of the corner of his eye and absent-mindedly shed his cloak to wrap around her.

She smiled, then asked, "You know where we're going?"

"Yeah, I've never been to the Panping District, but it's not far from the bay."

"The Panping District?"

"I'm sure there's another name for it, but that's what I've always called it. C'mon this way."

They passed shops and houses all locked up for the evening. Some still had wares up for display and Whitney had to keep his hands in his pockets to control himself. Furs from Hornsheim, globes from Yaolin City, and a suit of armor forged from dwarven bronze that might have made even Torsten jealous. Nigh'jel lanterns from Latiapur hung from posts along the way, the tentacles of the amorphous creatures within pulsing a soft green light. The Shesaitju may have been locked up, but apparently, the people of Winde Port were happy to keep using those.

Whitney followed the lights to a rickety bridge crossing over a canal. Beyond, the light grew scant with only a candle here or there glowing in windows rotting off their hinges. Women dressed in clothing far too slight for the weather beckoned Whitney and Sora toward dark alleys. A portly Northern merchant chatted with one down on a gondola docked in the freezing water.

"His place should be just around the corner," Whitney said.

"Good, I don't like this side of town."

Wharf Street and Delanie Road crossed at a lightless church. It seemed all but abandoned. Snow covered the carved, wooden gates. Nobody even bothering to have swept it away. The stone was chipped, and the stained glass along the façade and up the spire was so dusty, the design was indecipherable. It was always unusual to see a Church of Iam be so forgotten in the Glass Kingdom. But Whitney had seen it before, and he knew that although they'd pledged themselves to Liam and the Vigilant Eye, the Panpingese people it was constructed for simply never showed up.

"Come on," Sora said. "I'm cold."

"Light a fire." Whitney began walking again but stopped when he saw Sora standing at the end of the street, staring.

"What is this?" she asked.

Ramshackle, wooden row houses were crammed along a narrow street that, beyond the church, cheapened to dirt. Ropes covered in drying clothes were hung from one window to the next, some hanging lower than Whitney's head, barely able to dry in the cold. A few Panpingese men and women lay huddled in a structure that didn't look like it'd had a roof for a century.

The air reeked of smoke from the chimneys so tightly clumped together they created a thick cloud. Beneath the scent of burning wood was something else less pleasing.

"It smells like shog and piss," Whitney said.

"Looks like it too." She scanned from one side of the street to the other, incredulous. "This is the Panping District?"

Whitney knew what to expect. There were certain… amenities… that could only be found in a place like this, and he'd spent plenty of drunken nights in Winde Port. He didn't have the heart to tell her that the real name of the place was the Panping Ghetto.

"According to the city map," he said.

"I don't understand," Sora said. "Tayvada was dressed nicely. He is a trader in the guild. Surely he has enough money…" Her voice trailed off before she said, "He *has* to live here, doesn't he? They make all of my people live in this… this filth."

"I'm sure he's just a man of the people." Whitney took a few steps and Sora followed. A man bundled beneath a stack of furs groaned and rolled over onto the path. As they went around him, another woman in a candlelit window stared at Whitney, her almond-shaped eyes unflinching.

"Supposedly, he lives just over there." Whitney pointed to a larger row house at the end of the street. It was in much better shape than the buildings flanking it, with patterned wood panels at the second story, but it was still far from luxurious.

"Sora?" Whitney asked.

He looked back and noticed that she'd fallen behind. She kneeled in front of a pair of skinny children. The older of them coughed while the other leaned against him, wrapped in a ratty blanket. Whitney couldn't tell if they were faking. Begging was a full-time occupation in some parts of the world, and nobody earned better than children.

"Sora," Whitney said. "Leave them be."

She ignored him, and instead, opened one of the full coin purses they'd earned for selling Grint's stuff. She placed a gold autla in each of their hands and smiled, watching as their eyes went wide. They'd probably seen bronzers or even silver before, but never gold.

They said something to Sora in Panpingese, the words rattling off their tongues so choppy and fast that Whitney didn't pick up any of it. He knew a bit of the language from his travels, but Sora, on the other hand, knew none.

Whitney took her arm and gently guided her away. "C'mon, Sora. Tayvada's house is right up here."

She shook him off. "Are you heartless? No one should have to live like this."

"We can't help them all."

"Oh?" She lifted the purse, removed a coin, and flung it up through an open window. "Are the people of Yarrington more deserving of our riches?" She took another and flicked it onto the ground.

"No, but we didn't need money then."

"We don't *need* all of this." She went to dump out more coins, but Whitney grabbed her arm. He could see the rage in her amber eyes, that same rage she used to release an explosion of light and energy that defeated Redstar. He was just glad she wasn't bleeding.

"We don't know that. It won't be cheap if we need to purchase passage at a time like this. And if we need to buy a ship ourselves, it'll be even more."

"We can go by land," she said softly.

"War's coming. There's a merry band of mercenaries on the road back that likely want us dead, plus an incredibly wealthy ex-constable who definitely wants us dead. We need to leave here as fast as possible, and nobody can touch us on a boat. We'll go see your homeland and maybe after, you can come back here and we'll load up as many children as you want, bring them to Panping so they can starve there instead."

Sora was stunned by his words. He wasn't sure if it was because of the harshness, or because she'd become accustomed to him joking, but he was an expert on the ugly truth of the world. It was never an easy thing to realize.

"You give one coin to each of them, and they'll eat for a week," he said. "Then we'll be long gone, and it'll be back to normal for them. Some people are just plain unlucky, Sora. But we're living, breathing proof that it doesn't have to be that way. It's all up to them to fight for more."

"Oh, yes," she said. "Growing up with a loving family on a farm was so difficult for you."

"There's more opportunity in a city, that's for sure. Now, let's just do what we came here to do."

He risked putting his hand on her back. She didn't fight it as he guided her toward Tayvada's house.

"Now, when we get in, let me do the haggling," Whitney said. "I know these types. They're vultures in gentlemen's clothing, traders. The moment you think you're their friend is the moment they bend you ov..." The words trailed off as Whitney remembered what had happened on the road with that lecherous dwarf. He winced ahead of time, expecting to feel Sora's scorn, but she didn't hear him.

"Seriously?" Sora asked after taking one disgusted look at Tayvada's house. "This is the city you talk so highly of. The place so accepting of all peoples and cultures?"

"A lot of people got displaced by war," Whitney said. "They needed homes quick, and they lost so…"

"I get why we need to leave, but you're really defending this?"

"No, I'm just saying that not everything is so black and white. Look at me." He grinned. "I don't even have a home."

"Would you stop comparing yourself to these people?"

"I compare myself to everyone. You know that." He gave her a friendly nudge, but she wasn't having it. Her whole face had been stuck scowling since the moment they crossed the canal.

"I don't want to talk about this anymore," she said. "Let's just speak with Tayvada and get out of here."

"Fine by me," Whitney replied, relieved.

He approached the man's door and slammed on the knocker while shouting his name. A thin line of flickering light came from beneath the door, but nobody came. He tried again. Still nothing. A stray cat hissed and leaped out from the browning bushes, giving them both a scare. The thing set Tayvada's front gate squeaking on its rusty hinges. Whitney couldn't help but notice his was the only home on the whole street with a perimeter fence and gate.

"He's probably asleep," Sora said.

"Let's go find out," Whitney decided.

"We're just going to go in uninvited?"

"Uh… thief, remember?"

"You're supposed to be acting like a noble, if that's possible for you."

Whitney tried the door and found that it was unlocked. He shot a smile at Sora and pushed it open. "I am. We found the door ajar, and like any good citizens, wanted to check if everything was all right. The richest man in a place like this?"

"Somehow, you're going to make an enemy out of the only man who can help."

"C'mon." Whitney peered through the opening. A single candle burned on the mantle, nearly down to the wick. He waved for Sora to follow.

"Tayvada!" Whitney called. "You home?"

There was a thud upstairs, then Aquira came screeching down a flight of a dozen or so stairs. Whitney was up on the dining table, daggers drawn before he knew what happened.

Sora jumped in front of the door before the wyvern could escape.

"What's wrong, girl?" she asked, kneeling down. Aquira hid behind her leg and hissed at the staircase. Whitney thought he saw a speckling of embers spew from her mouth like spit, a failed remnant of the majestic, extinct dragons it devolved from.

"The sound came from upstairs," Whitney said, pointing with a wavy blade.

"Well, are you going to get down from there and check it out?" Sora asked.

"I'm pretty sure he's not home."

Sora released an exasperated sigh, then removed her fancy glove, pulled out her knife, and drew a line of blood across her palm. She crept toward the stairs and started climbing. Aquira, however, didn't go further than the first step.

"Smart girl," Whitney said to the wyvern before reluctantly following Sora.

As they climbed, the dim light from the candle burning downstairs became even dimmer and was replaced by the orange glow of Celeste's light gushing in through open windows.

They split up at the top, Whitney going to the left, toward where the sound might have originated. Sora went right.

Whitney found nothing but rooms, empty of life but packed with valuables. He could almost see gold autlas dancing before his eyes, but his visions were abruptly ended by the sound of Sora's scream. He turned and took off down the hall. If anyone was in the house, they were now fully aware of his and Sora's presence.

Clearing the threshold of what was clearly Tayvada's bedroom, Whitney saw what had frightened Sora. Hanging from the ceiling like a butterfly's cocoon, was what remained of a Panpingese man. Blood stained the body all the way down from a slash on his neck, still dripping from his jet-black hair, pooling across the floor, and seeping through the planks in the wood.

"Shog in a barrel," Whitney whispered.

"Is that…" Sora could barely get the words out.

"Yeah, it's him."

Whitney sheathed his daggers and moved in for a closer look, covering his mouth and nose with the collar of his shirt to ward against any potential smell. People about to die tended to make a mess of themselves. Those who did die always did.

Tayvada's skin was whiter than snow, the veins on his neck like blue spider webs. He hung upside down from a rope looped around a crossbeam. His body had been drained of blood like butcher's meat.

"Watch the door. Whoever did this might still be around." Whitney closed his eyes before shoving a hand into Tayvada's doublet.

"What are you doing?" Sora asked, terse.

"We came here to find passage. His papers can get us that."

"Do you ever steal from anyone who's still alive? You're going to get us cursed!"

Whitney rooted around and found a small envelope in the man's front pocket. It was exactly what they needed—a temporary trader's export license issued by Prefect Calhoun of Winde Port.

"Mumbo jumbo," he said. "Trust me, if I'm not cursed yet, I never will be."

"How did you know that was in there?"

"At Tum Tum's, he said it was always on him, remember? Lesson four hundred twelve—always pay attention. Now let's get out of here."

"You're just going to leave him like that? This is barbaric."

"Welcome to Winde Port, home of deals gone sour," Whitney whispered.

"Whitney," Sora said, stern, "we can't leave him."

"Sometimes it's best to stay out of bad business. Besides, nobody knows we're here. Nobody saw us."

"Oh, but I did," spoke a voice from within the darkness of the room.

Whitney spun toward the sound and watched as a man emerged from the shadows. He wore boiled leathers with an absurd number of buckles and clasps over his torso, each of them holding sharp looking knives. Long, white hair fell far below his shoulders, but the man didn't look anywhere near old enough to be so gray.

"It is funny how the fish can sense the hook but cannot deny the bait," he said as he strolled forward. His thick, bold accent informed Whitney that the color of his hair wasn't due to age but was indicative of the people from the northeastern land of Brekliodad. "Its allure surpasses the wisdom of even the brightest of creatures."

"Look fellow, I don't know who you are or what you're talking about, but you'd better turn around," Whitney said. He drew his daggers and took a step back to get his footing before realizing his back was against the rickety wall. Sora was beside him, and the mysterious intruder stood between them and the room's only window and door.

"How can you not see how outmatched you are, pathetic little man?" The white-haired devil stopped beside Tayvada's hanging body, ran a single finger through the man's bloody neck and marveled at the shiny red liquid, smearing it between his forefinger and thumb.

"You murdered him!" Sora shouted.

The mysterious man shrugged. "Bait is bait."

"Bait for wha—" Whitney didn't have time to finish before he heard the familiar wincing sound of Sora cutting her already bleeding hand even deeper, fueled by rage. Ever since they arrived in Winde Port, he could see her affinity with her race growing, and seeing one hanging out to dry had put a look in her eye unlike any he'd seen there before.

She thrust her hand forward, fire erupting from the tips of her fingers. It struck the white-haired man in the chest and exploded with a blinding flash. It temporarily blinded Whitney, but when he could see again, the man was enveloped by smoke and flurrying embers. The expulsion of such energy left Sora doubled over, panting.

Whitney saw motion in the cloud and expected to see a body topple over. Instead, when the smoke cleared, the man rose from a crouch and rolled his shoulders like it was nothing. The only visible damage was a small scorch in his armor. The blades of his many daggers glowed red hot, and his dark, thin lips curled into a nightmarish grin.

"I knew I was right about you," he said to Sora, who was as shocked as Whitney. "So much untapped potential. So much raw… power."

"Sora, run!" Whitney charged at the man, swinging one of his daggers. The man moved so swiftly it was like swiping at air. Whitney staggered, then came whipping around with his second dagger. For a moment it looked like he'd catch the man's stomach. But again, it was almost as if the man disappeared into nothingness. Whitney tripped over a loose floorboard and scrambled for the door.

Sora and Whitney reached the door at the same time, but two knives stabbed into it right in front of their faces, the force of the throw causing it to slam shut. They looked back and saw the white-haired man holding more knives, fanned out like cards in a game of gems.

"Now, now, don't run," he said. "Things are just starting to get fun."

"Stay away from us!" Sora screamed. She raised her hands and released fire again, only she was so drained from last time, it came out as little more than a sputter. The man spun out of the way, flames catching the end of his cloak, then dropping to the floor. The dry wooden planks beneath him caught fast, but the man removed his cloak and snapped it, extinguished the fire in one smooth motion. He shook it out and calmly placed it back over his shoulders.

"Our friend here is no good to anyone cooked," he said, slapping Tayvada's corpse on the arm. "

"Whitney..." Sora whispered as if he had any answers.

He was lucky he could even hold his weapons his hands were so sweaty and shaky. His heart raced so fast he could no longer feel it beating, just a steady rock in his throat. "If you wanted us dead we would be, so j...just tell us what you want," he managed to say.

"You small, insignificant fool. You could not comprehend what I want in one hundred lifetimes."

"Try me," Whitney replied, finding his last bit of courage. He found himself thinking the oddest thought, wishing Torsten were there. But the man chuckled and stole Whitney's focus back to the moment.

The Breklian darted at them. It all happened so fast, Whitney wasn't sure whether he actually tried to defend himself or simply closed his eyes. When they opened again, the man was gone. A breeze wafted in through the now-open window, curtains flapping in the wind. All that was left in the room was the lingering sound of the man's haunting laugh.

"Who the yig was that?" Whitney asked after a moment. He turned to Sora, only to find that she too was gone.

Three hard raps on the front door startled him.

"Whitney Blisslayer, we know you're in there!" someone called up from the street. "Surrender in the name of the King!"

"No, no, no," he said. He peeked out of the window and saw at least a dozen Glass soldiers spread out in front of the home. A crowd of ghetto locals gathered to watch as if they'd never seen soldiers in their district before.

The townhouse was so narrow, there was no way out through any upstairs window except the one they'd clearly see him leaving. Whitney sheathed his weapons and swept out into the hall and downstairs, searching for a side door, back door, anything—even a basement. Nothing. The Panping Ghetto was contained, its row homes facing straight onto the streets, backs of the homes butting up to the back of others on the adjacent street. His back was literally against the wall.

He patted his clothes and found Tayvada's trading papers before also realizing he still had his half of the Glass Crown hidden beneath his cloak. Swearing, he removed both, wrapped the papers around the circlet, and ran to the hearth. The soldiers knocked again as he shoved his hand up the flue. He found a bit of loose stone and hung the Crown from the ledge along with the papers.

The front door flew open.

Whitney leaped upright and raised his hands in surrender as the soldiers poured in, spears and swords drawn and aimed at his throat. Out of the corner of his eye, he saw Aquira zipping out the front door behind them.

Lucky little... he cursed inward. Then he grinned. "Hey fellows," he said. "I think I saw who you're looking for upstairs."

XI

THE KNIGHT

"I am, hear me," Torsten whispered. He clutched his holy pendant—the same one given to him by King Liam, nearly lost only weeks ago—against his chest while looking upward. The great Vigilant Eye towered in the apse of the Yarrington Cathedral. The holy symbol was cast in gold with a pupil of glass that, when looked at from the east, framed Mount Lister in all her glory.

Light poured in through stained-glass windows above and behind it. They depicted the story of the God Feud and Autla Nothhelm, the First King of Glass, the one for whom their currency was named. In the depiction, he was being anointed on the flattened summit of Mount Lister by Iam himself thousands of years ago after the Feud ended, given the task to spread His light to all creatures.

Torsten imagined that King Liam, young and healthy, once kneeled in this very spot gazing upon the legends of old before deciding to bring an end to the incestuous squabbling that had, for so long, confined the Glass Kingdom to its own little corner of Pantego. Now, their sphere of influence extended from Latiapur in the South to far east Panping, well beyond Yaolin City, and up to Winter's Thumb at the foot of Drav Cra. Pi had only been king for a month, yet already he was following in his father's footsteps by bringing Redstar's people into the fold.

It just felt so… different this time.

"A trickster and heathen has been invited within these very walls," Torsten said to Iam. "Only ruin follows in his wake. Never has Your light led me astray, but please, help me understand why he should be counted amongst Your holy kingdom. Show me, oh, Vigilant Eye, what am I missing?"

"Something troubling you, Wearer?"

Torsten turned to see Wren the Holy shuffling toward him. His cane clacked across the marble floor, echoing down the cathedral's soaring nave as he navigated the room. He looked more weary than usual, even considering his age. Dark rings wrapped his eye-sockets, scorched from taking the vow of sightlessness. Heavy white robes and the clunky necklace of interlocking Eyes of Iam around his neck seemed to weigh him down.

Pi's resurrection had left the cathedral inundated with worshippers, come to see the place where he had been reborn and where, long ago, Iam ended the God Feud and took man under His sheltering wing. They came to hear the words of Wren, the mouthpiece of Iam in Pantego. The High Priest's voice usually carried with vim and vigor, but today, it was raspy from his many sermons.

Torsten had come at sunrise to try and give the old man time to rest before the doors opened to the public, but Wren was ever vigilant.

"It's nothing, Your Holiness," he said. Torsten went to stand, but Wren lay a hand on his shoulder. His aim was true despite having no use of his eyes.

"Please. I have been around long enough to know when a man is feeling exceedingly… mortal." His thin lips creased into a smile. In a kingdom where war had left so many children orphans, perhaps his greatest gift of all was a fatherly smile. Of course, Torsten's father was a lecherous cur who'd never served, but there was still something about Wren that made him feel at home.

Torsten sighed and lifted himself onto the front pew before the altar. Wren sat beside him, his old knees popping.

"We leave to quell the Shesaitju rebellion today," Torsten said.

"So I have heard."

"Then you also know who the young king has invited to march at our side?"

Wren nodded.

"Then please, Your Holiness, tell me how I can march beside a heathen like that?"

"My son, when Liam sought to bring all of Pantego under a single banner, he knew he could not force the people beyond this realm to see the light of Iam. He could only show them the way; they had to do the rest. Now the world is a brighter place for his many efforts."

"I don't question anything Liam did."

"But you fought alongside him for a long, long time. Beside allies old and new, men and dwarves from different corners of our world. Not all of whom believed Iam to be the source of light in their soul. Yet you fought with them nonetheless."

"Redstar is different. I know it may be a sin to think, but I don't believe his soul is redeemable."

"Every soul is redeemable."

"What about all the fallen gods who have been banished from this realm. What about Nesilia and Bliss?" Wren's brow furrowed at the name of the latter. "The One Who Remained," Torsten corrected. That was the name people were familiar with when speaking of her. Torsten realized then that Redstar was the one who claimed Bliss and the One Who remained were one and the same, that Bliss had defeated Nesilia, the Buried Goddess before the feud ended. And that Iam had then punished her by transforming her into a beast and condemning her to that foul place, a vindictive act against the very nature of the God whom Torsten loved.

Redstar also claimed that Nesilia and Iam had been lovers, not mortal enemies and that everything he knew about the God Feud was a lie.

More of his lies and games.

Bliss was likely a demonic creature of Elsewhere, similar to any other. All Redstar's talk of serving the Buried Goddess by slaying her; in the end, he was clearly just trying to keep Torsten away from Yarrington while Oleander suffered from the wicked curse placed upon Pi. All a part of Redstar's plot to get Torsten killed so that, in her grief, Oleander would lead the Glass Kingdom, which left him behind and forgot him, into ruin.

As Torsten's darkening thoughts twisted his features, Wren's smile deepened.

"All *mortal* souls are redeemable," he said. "We are all the children of

Iam, and His word is mercy. His word is peace. I cannot say why He has brought Redstar to us, just how I cannot say why He saw fit to afflict Liam with so wretched an ailment though his hair had only just begun to gray. But to say it wasn't his time is folly."

"Can His enemies not upset His designs? Redstar poisoned King Pi's mind and led him to suicide."

"Yet, he lives again by the Hand of Iam." Wren groaned as he used his cane to rise from the pew. "They can certainly try, Sir Unger, but so long as we faithful remain, they cannot shake us."

Torsten turned from the High Priest of Iam to regard the massive eye set before him. He ran his fingers around his own eye sockets in prayer, then stood.

"Thank you, Your Holiness, for helping show me the way."

Wren shook his head. "I am only an oracle of Iam. The path of light is always within you." He tapped Torsten's chest with his cane.

"I hope I don't lose it. You'll look after King Pi while we're gone? I worry about him, up in that castle. He barely left his quarters as a boy. Even those few on the Council who remain from serving his father are strangers to him."

"Always. In these times of peril, it will help the young king to turn to his holy studies."

"Thank you, Great Father." Torsten bowed and traced his eyes again.

"Thank Him," Wren said, gesturing to the gargantuan Eye of Iam. He needed no sight to find it. "I am but a vessel."

Torsten turned to leave the cathedral, suddenly feeling lighter. It still didn't feel right, what he had to do, but Wren and the lofty cathedral had a way of calming him, of making him realize he was but a small part of Iam's plan.

He pushed open the massive front doors, two hunks of iron with patterned rifts cut out and filled with frosted glass. Crisp, cold air greeted him, even though the sun shone brightly that morning, making him long for summer.

A small cohort of King's Shieldsmen awaited him, though he had come to the cathedral alone. He was about to ask why they weren't at their posts or with the rest of the army outside the city walls when Oleander hopped down from her beloved white horse and ran to him, wearing tall, spiked heels despite the cobblestone streets of the Royal Avenue.

"Torsten." She threw her arms around him before he could say a word.

He got caught halfway between embracing her in return and pushing her away. He wasn't sure when their relationship had become so informal, and he could see the prying eyes of his men over her shoulder, struggling to stay at attention as they likely thought the same thing.

"Is everything all right, Your Grace?" Torsten asked. He peeled her off him, and Torsten started walking, so they didn't linger. The Queen Mother out on the streets was a rare thing indeed. He saw no need to inform the whole city of her presence. She hadn't made many friends, and he wasn't sure who might seek retribution.

"Is everything all right?" Her expression soured. "I had to beg my newly brazen son to let me out of my room. It's as if he has forgotten who was really in charge after Liam forgot how to speak."

"He spent that time in a cloud of horrid visions, Your Grace."

"Yes, yes. Put there by that bastard I call 'Brother.'"

"I don't like the way you're treated any more than you, but Pi is King now. Would you prefer him unconscious and clinging to life again?"

"Of course not!" Her raised voice brought the attention of a few passersby.

Any other month, the end of the Royal Avenue, the grand plaza in Old Yarrington within which the Cathedral of Yarrington stood, would be full of flowering trees, but now it was barren. Instead, pilgrims from afar filled it with tents, waiting for their chance to hear a sermon from Wren the Holy.

A young man, the father of several, pointed back at the Cathedral, his wife and children smiling. Torsten stopped and followed his finger to the snow-covered summit of Mount Lister, visible through Iam's Eye, standing proudly at the peak of the roof. The pupil was made from glass similar to the one at the altar, but this one was segmented, like a cut diamond. As the sun rose over the mountain, the prism cast a rainbow across the plaza. The pilgrims flocked to the vibrant strips of light, praising Iam, kissing the very street upon which His light touched.

"It's been a difficult year, hasn't it?" Torsten said.

Yet there was Iam's light, still shining bright—an arm of warmth against the bitter onslaught of cold.

"Torsten," Oleander said, clearly irritated. She shook his arm.

"Yes, Your Grace?" Torsten replied.

"Did you hear a word I said?"

"I'm so sorry, Your Grace. I must have missed it. My mind is on the forthcoming battle."

Oleander groaned. "Is there a man in this world that isn't just like my husband?"

"There is no man like him."

"Hey, careful with her or I'll have your hands!" she snapped at the stablehand who had taken the reins of her horse to walk her behind them. She slapped the young man's hands, then ran her fingers through the horse's mane. Torsten couldn't remember the last time she let her favorite horse out of the royal stables where she kept her locked up and safe like a piece of jewelry.

"I… I'm so sorry, Your Grace," the young man stuttered.

"A light touch, and grace. If I hear a whinny from you pulling her…"

"You won't. My apologies."

Oleander rolled her eyes and returned to Torsten's side. "The age of great men is clearly over."

Torsten forced a chuckle but didn't respond. He'd been on the receiving end of her seemingly senseless scorn enough times to know how it felt. He snuck the stable hand a nod of approval before they continued down the Royal Avenue, flanked by Shieldsmen. Mansions belonging to Yarrington's noblest families stood, nearly all of them for generations, the stone of their foundations hewn from Mount Lister itself. The newest belonged to the reinstated Master of Coin, Yuri Darkings. It was at the end of the row, still partially under construction but even more magnificent than the others.

Yuri came from a family of no-names who rose up the ranks of the Winde Traders Guild until he was running the accounts. That was the greatness of Liam, he looked beyond established houses to raise men like Yuri and Torsten beyond their station. Now, Yuri had a crew of human laborers constructing the newest wing of his Old Yarrington home, including a giant for a foreman who was busy hefting a wood column as thick as the trunks in the Webbed Woods.

A giant, yet the Crown could barely entice an experienced group of dwarves to repair the Royal Crypt. He blamed Oleander's wrath for their lack of respect, but the truth was, it would've happened anyway. The people didn't know all the real reasons behind why she had so many loyal servants hanged and most would fear their rulers regardless. Kings and Queens across Pantego had done far worse and been feared far more.

Pi had been revived by a miracle of Iam and was greatly revered in the weeks leading up to a coronation barely anyone of worth showed up for. Nothing really changed. In the end, the people were thankful to Iam, not a child-king they barely knew. Oleander could have been the most beloved queen in history, and still, nothing would have changed. Because neither of them was Liam.

"Forgive me if it is not my place to ask, but do you ever miss him?" Torsten said.

"Who?" Oleander replied.

"Liam. I know he didn't always make your life easy, but…"

"Of course, I do. Is there a reason you are so interested in my relationship with my late husband?"

"It's only that… I was there… at his funeral. The kingdom wept, yet you didn't even shed a tear."

"Do you know how long I spent feeding him? Changing him once he fell ill—probably thanks to one of his dirty, foreign whores? How many times I watched Tessa clean him after he…" She drew a deep, solemn breath, and Torsten wasn't sure if it was because she was finally stricken by what she'd done to her former handmaiden, or over the memory of Liam. He hoped both.

"I was waiting for him to die and was relieved when he did," she went on. "I bid farewell to that man long before his kingdom did."

Torsten's head hung a little lower.

"I never cared that he took me from my home and my people when I was but a girl because I had never seen a man so mighty," she said. "It was as if Iam Himself had come to the Drav Cra in the form of a man."

"I remember thinking the same thing when I saw him down on the docks as a boy," Torsten replied. "With his white armor shimmering, wondering how we could both possibly be counted among men. He was like a god."

"I hated seeing him so weak. I would miss the way he scolded me for not presenting myself appropriately for an audience or when I failed to produce a worthy heir for so long. By the end, I couldn't bear to look at him. All I cared about was Pi and him getting healthy again, helping him become even a fraction of the man Liam was."

"He seems to be finding his footing."

Oleander frowned. "Yes…."

"My Queen, I know you're concerned for him; I am too. First, leaving no option but war without even consulting his Council, then allying with Redstar and warlocks. Whatever happened after his body died, it's as if he feels he is all alone."

"It's the Drav Cra in him," Oleander said. "In the far North, a boy his age is sent out into the wilderness to survive on his own. To battle the wolves and bitter cold."

"He's half Liam too. I didn't know our great King at that age—I wasn't even born—though I'm sure it took him some time to find his way, too. Pi can't do it alone. You need to try to get through to him while I'm gone."

"His father would have broken his neck if he'd talked to him the way he does me."

Her horse neighed, and she shot a look back at the stablehand so fierce it could've frozen the air between them.

"May I speak frankly, My Queen?"

Oleander eyed him from head to toe, then nodded.

"Don't push him away," Torsten said. "Endure his insults. Show him how much you love him. I've seen it firsthand the lengths you're willing to go for the slightest chance at helping him."

They were in front of the castle fortifications now. Torsten made sure not to let his gaze stray toward the ramparts, where less than a Dawning ago, the Queen had strung so many up to die.

Hers, on the other hand, flitted there, and just for the briefest moment, Torsten thought he saw a wave of regret pass like a shadow across her face. A sight he thought impossible.

"Get him to open up, My Queen," Torsten said, "so that we may begin to understand what he went through and what's now going on inside him. If there is one strength within you to which even Liam paled in comparison, it is your undying love for your son. Show him that."

Oleander's features grew hard as she folded her arms. "Do you have no fear, Wearer? Speaking so openly to the Queen Mother?"

"I have many fears, but there is not one of them I wouldn't face for this kingdom."

Oleander stalked forward, her smoldering blue eyes enough to make a man feel small. Not to mention that with her heels on she was taller even than Torsten.

"Even me?" she asked. She lay both her hands on his shoulders, her nails clacking against his armor.

"Anything," he said, voice shaky. His mind took him back to the night in his chambers when she threw herself at him. To even think of Oleander in that manner made him feel ill, dirty.

"Then do something for me, my honest Wearer." She leaned in, her warm breath tickling his ear. "Slaughter those rebels in the name of your king and remind Pantego who his father was. And when you're finished with him, see to it that Redstar never returns here. I care not how."

Torsten backed away, incredulous. "Your Grace?"

"You know what must be done, so do it. And when you return victorious and free of this blight, I'll see to it that ours is the only advice my precious boy will care to hear." She grabbed him by the back and pulled him close. Then, she kissed him on the cheek. "Good luck, my knight."

She whipped around, her long, cerulean dress kicking up the powdered snow. "Come boy!" She clapped her hands, and the stablehand allowed her horse to trot to her side. She stroked the magnificent creature's mane as she sauntered back behind the walls of the Glass Castle. Her guard went with her, not daring look at him or mutter under their breath about how close the Queen Mother was with the Wearer of White.

It confused Torsten as well. When last he left Yarrington, he had been exiled by Oleander in her unchecked fury. When he returned, she was shattered mind and spirit until Pi came back to her. Now, he left in her good graces, somehow knowing that of anyone in the castle with Pi's ear, she was perhaps the one he could trust the most, the one with the most honest of intentions—protecting him.

Yet there was no denying what she'd just asked of him. Stabbing Redstar in the back was less than the man deserved but to do so was to betray the will of his king.

Torsten looked at the statue of Liam in the castle's entry bailey and remembered how simple things were with him alive. His eyes moved down the line of statues: Remy the Revealer, Tarvin the Fair-Handed, and even King Autlas the First. He wondered if any one of them acted as rashly as King Pi had.

Then the castle gates closed.

"Your horse, Sir Unger?" the stablehand offered, returning from the bailey.

Torsten nodded and waited for the young man to return with his horse, then he rode down through the heart of Yarrington. Wardric met him in the markets, which were simultaneously more crowded and quiet than usual.

"Did you find what you were looking for in the cathedral?" Wardric asked.

"Always… and never," Torsten replied.

"Sounds about right." Wardric laughed, then grew stern. "I went to the kid's home to see if he'd march with us, just like you asked. Sister didn't even let me through the door."

"She's tough, that woman."

"Aren't they all? At least Rand's got a better chance of surviving here."

Torsten surveyed the market. The people were roused, but none haggled, hawked wares, or exchanged autlas. Instead, they watched as soldiers flocked through open city gates. Mothers embraced their conscripted sons, father's their wives and young children. They begged Iam for protection and for victory.

Torsten, like Wardric, knew how many of them would never return. How many would die in the name of Iam and His chosen kingdom?

"I never thought I'd live to see another war," Wardric said.

"Let's hope this one ends quickly so we can rid our castle of unwanted guests," Torsten said.

"I wonder, do you mean the Caleef or them?" He nodded toward the gate. Redstar leaned against the stone in the opening, biting a chunk off a loaf of bread. Beyond him, a group of Drav Cra warriors knelt around the warlock Freydis, her breasts exposed. Her body was covered in white paint, chipped and cracked from the cold. Her head was black except for two streaks of blood under her eyes which dripped down her cheeks and neck. A circle of blood, bright against the snow, was painted over the frozen farmland and in its center stood a goat. Freydis held a knife to its throat; a sacrifice to their Buried Goddess in the name of victory.

Redstar glanced back, noticed Torsten and Wardric, and smiled while he waved with his bread. Not a care in the world.

XII

THE MYSTIC

Sora gasped awake, her heart racing as she scanned her dark surroundings. The air stank of mildew. Light from the moons filtered in through a circular panel of stained glass, a film of dust covering most of the imagery. She could just barely make out the Iam's Eye sprawling across it in gold.

A church?

She'd only been in Troborough's chapel, but she recognized the stone walls and glass windows when she saw them. Cobwebs glistened in the faint light, draping from every corner. The memory of the giant spiders in the Webbed Woods gave her a shudder.

She tried to get a better look around but felt something tight against her wrists. Her arms were stretched taut above her head and spread apart, her feet dangling. She hung from two chains running down from a structure beneath the hipped roof clearly meant to hold a bell. When she stretched her neck to look behind her, she noticed it, a cracked bell on the floor, infested by spiders.

She whimpered softly.

She was in a church steeple, abandoned by the look of it. She felt so exposed under the blurred Eye of Iam, still wearing her glittering evening gown, arms and legs bare. She still had the coin purses they'd earned from selling that trader's silks, which meant whoever did this to her had no interest in money.

"Help!" she screamed. "Help!"

"Nobody will ever hear you way up here." It was the voice of the white-haired man from Tayvada's house. The harsh accent could only be Breklian, far in the northern portion of the continent, beyond even the Dragon's Tail and Brotlebir. Traders from the area had passed through Troborough very rarely, but their kind were hard to forget.

Sora's head whipped toward him, her skin crawling with fear. He wasn't there.

"I've waited so very long for you to wake," he said.

She felt a hand stroke her back, a cold finger tracing the line of her spine. She shuddered but didn't give him the benefit of hearing her scream. But she wanted to. More than ever before, she wanted to.

His voice was bad enough, very harsh consonants hanging in the air like the hiss of a serpent. But his touch... it was like what she felt every time she called upon the powers of Elsewhere, like there was some great evil trying to take her over.

"Get away from me," she spat.

He chuckled. "You will learn to appreciate me." His tongue ran up the side of her jaw. She wanted to crawl out of her skin.

"You're a monster."

"That very well may be true." The man backed away and sat across from her on a moldy barrel. He removed two knives from his bandolier, one being Sora's. Sora flinched, but he merely set them against each other as if preparing to carve roast duck.

Sora closed her eyes and focused on Elsewhere, on that haunting feeling she knew so well. The man was right about power coursing through her, just as her old master Wetzel had been, and with all her willpower she begged for it to come to the surface.

But the wound she'd earlier traced across her hand was sealed and freshly bandaged. Whoever the man was, he knew how to block her.

"What do you want from me?" she asked.

"Everything." Sparks flew out from Sora's blade as he used the other to start sharpening it. Sora wished more than anything she could summon sparks of her own and burn the floor out from under him.

"Is this about Whitney?"

"There you are, mystic. Smart and powerful. When that grotesque little man hired me to kill the thief, he severely underestimated you."

"Darkings," she realized, all her fears coming true. She was right to be afraid of that vengeful wretch. Whitney had calmed her back at the Traders Guild, but she was right. "Is Whitney…" She couldn't even bring herself to say it.

"Not until sunrise, unfortunately for me. Darkings wants to make a public show of it, fool that he is, and until the kill is made I cannot touch my quarry. I may ignore many of my order's doctrines, but the blood pact is sacred. I may neither eat, drink, nor… play, until his life on this plane is over."

"Well, you're wrong. I'm no mystic."

"I think I'll keep this." He raised Sora's knife, spun it, then grinned as he stowed it. In the faint light filtering through the stained glass, Sora could see now how young he was despite his white hair, how handsome. Yet beneath all his striking features was menace unlike any she'd seen before. Not even Bliss, with her eight eyes and eight legs, could compare.

"You are so much more than you know," he said. "Your blood radiates energy only so few of your people are born with. I could smell it across the city, not like any blood mage or Drav Cra warlock who can't so much as make a spark without gashing themselves. Tainting themselves."

"That's exactly what I am."

"No, you are raw, unfocused power—with a master who either did not see so or was, himself, too weak to properly instruct you."

"How do you know about him?" she questioned. The idea of him digging through her mind had her wriggling, desperate to shake free. But her struggle only seemed to entertain him.

"Relax, my dear. I'm capable of many things but reading minds is not one of them. However, I have walked this plane for a long, long time. I know what it is to see wasted potential."

She shook again. "When Whitney breaks free he's going to kill you!"

"Kill me? I am beyond life and death, but your friend? He will die. There is no escaping it. Because I must have you."

"Please, no. You can take every autla on me and leave, I won't tell a soul. It's…it's enough to buy a ship."

"I already have one." In an instant he was before her, dark eyes piercing her soul. His hands grasped her waist, and he slowly leaned in toward her neck. She turned her head away, but there was nowhere to go.

"His death is the only way," he said. Then, hovering there beside her neck, he exhaled into her flesh, his breath cold as freshly fallen snow.

He backed away, closed his eyes and shivered. His eyelids flickered as if just the scent of her was enough to give him a rush. He licked his lips, and as he did, she noticed fangs as sharp as any dire wolf.

"What are you?"

He drew a deep breath to calm himself. "I am Kazimir."

"What…"

"My kind have been called many things throughout the ages. You may know us as fangs, vampires, even some call us undead. I prefer upyr, the name Brekliodad gives us. Call me sentimental."

Sora swallowed the lump forming in her throat. Wetzel's text mentioned the upyr from time to time. Men and women trapped between Pantego and Elsewhere, unable to die, yet not truly alive, thirsting for the blood of man lest they lose their tether to the mortal realm and go insane.

Most books thought them a myth—or extinct. The terrible feeling in her gut told her he spoke truthfully.

"You look horrified," Kazimir said, a trace of disappointment passing across his face. "You have no reason to be afraid. Your blood is too precious for me to waste. For centuries upyr took the mystics as wives, using their blood so they may cross the light at will."

"You want me to marry you?" She spat at his feet. "I'd rather die!"

Rage twisted his features. The dark of his eyes grew darker still and his fangs extended. He glared up at her, and at that moment, she knew she was alive only because he needed her for more than a rush. She didn't understand exactly why, but it was clear he could devour her at any time.

His icy breath upon her ear, he whispered, "As I said, you will learn to appreciate me. Together we can do great things."

Kazimir took one last euphoric whiff of her, then backed away. His monstrous face softened once again to the preternaturally handsome Breklian he'd been just moments ago. He turned and peered through the stained glass, where the amber light of the sun filtered through and a purplish glow of dawn washed over the room.

"But for now," he said, looking back at her. "I have an execution to attend."

The thought of Whitney's neck snapping filled her thoughts even more than her captor's horrifyingly pale face. "Please," Sora said, her voice now brittle from unrelenting fear. "Please spare him."

"It doesn't work that way."

"It can. Please, Kazimir, I'm begging you. I'll… I'll try to be whatever you want."

"You will. After his life is given."

"No, please, no!"

"We will see each other soon, my lady." He grinned and bowed, then vanished through a door into the stairwell leading down from the steeple.

Sora shook again, as hard as she could.

"Help!" She screamed at the top of her voice, but by now, she'd realized she was in the abandoned church at the edge of the Panping Ghetto—where her cries for help would be lost amongst the beggars, even if anyone could hear her through stone and glass.

"No, no, no…" If she couldn't break free, they were both doomed. Whitney would be hanged, and she would be forced to marry an upyr for whatever dreadful reasons Kazimir desired.

She searched the room for anything within reach of her feet that might help her. Nothing. Then she noticed the scars on her hands.

Blood for power…

Her captor may not have meant to, but he'd given her an idea. She twisted her neck to try and reach her arm so that she could bite into it. She wasn't sure if she'd be able to clamp down hard enough to draw blood, but she had to try.

She stretched and wrenched her body, but it was no use. The chains cuffing her wrists had her arms spread too far apart to get the right angle.

Her heart sank, and her gut roiled. She bit her lower lip and fought back tears, and then had another idea. The very thought had her wanting to vomit, but she bit down harder on her lip until the taste of copper filled her mouth. Then, she looked inward, reaching out with invisible arms for the vast well of power contained in Elsewhere.

She reached into that dark place which both scared and astounded her. Warmth tickled the tips of her fingers… but nothing more. The sacrifice wasn't enough. She stuck her tongue between her teeth instead. Biting off the tip might be enough, but she couldn't bring herself to do it.

A tear ran down her cheek. She freed her tongue and gasped for air. The upyr was wrong about one thing—she was no better than the warlocks of the Drav Cra drawing on blood. No more powerful.

"Help!" she screamed again. It was all she could do.

XIII

THE THIEF

Whitney was beginning to get used to the feeling of having his wrists squeezed by rope. Ever since his triumphant return to Troborough, he'd found himself bound more often than he changed undergarments.

"I'm sure we can work out this little misunderstanding," he said to one of the Glass soldiers. "This isn't what it appears to be." They held him outside Tayvada's house while they ransacked the place. He crossed his fingers in hopes that they wouldn't shove their heads up the chimney.

"It appears like you were standing just downstairs from the drained corpse of a respected member of the Winde Traders Guild."

"I found him that way."

"Aye," said another soldier walking behind him, "and my wife's half-gray son really *is* mine!"

Whitney would've usually been able to think of some snappy remark, but the face of his and Sora's white-haired assailant flashed through his mind. Those dark, soulless eyes, that nightmarish grin.

"All right, move it."

Whitney felt a shove on his back and stumbled forward. "I swear it though, I didn't do it," he pled. Another push came, this time harder.

"Shut your thieving, murdering mouth, or I'll shut it for you."

Whitney believed the man. He'd been wanted for many things and been placed in far more precarious situations, such as battling a goddess with Torsten in the Webbed Woods but never before was he accused of murder.

The guards finished up inside, then dragged him down the dark streets of the Panping Ghetto. He wondered where they were taking him, but he dared not ask. He simply walked, trying hard not to think about what might have happened to Sora.

Whitney didn't know who that man she'd disappeared with was. He only knew where he was from. And if he had to guess at his occupation, hired blade was a good start considering he was covered in them. But what was he after? Whitney had seen all kinds of men in his life, but never one with eyes like his. They were… soulless.

Poor Sora, he thought. And then, *Poor me.*

He looked around the streets he thought he knew so well as they emerged from the Panping Ghetto. The Shesaitju rebellion had the whole city on their toes. Unlike more normal times, the blue and white of the Glass Kingdom actually seemed to mean something, which meant he'd be under stricter watch and escaping would be even more difficult.

"Shog in a barrel," Whitney said out loud. He received a hard shove for it.

As they approached the barracks, Whitney noted how it paled in comparison to Yarrington—or even Westvale. He'd seen more of their insides than he cared to admit.

"I hope you're ready for the gallows, murderer," one guard said.

"I'm all for new experiences," Whitney replied.

"The guy was just a *knife-ear*, why does anyone care?" the other guard said, low to keep Whitney from hearing. But he heard. He also heard the response, which made his intestines clench.

"Lord Darkings cares, and I heard his father is Master of Coin for the whole kingdom again. He'll probably be prefect of Winde Port as soon as old Calhoun kicks the bucket, so you'd best be caring too."

Darkings Cares?

Whitney recalled how the bastard spoke to Sora—like she was a stain on Pantego. That meant one thing. *This was a setup…*

The realization that he'd been played bounced around like daggers in

Whitney's skull. Fantasies of killing Darkings were washed away only by the fantasy that Sora's fire would have devoured him back in Bridleton. That quickly had Whitney wondering why that white-haired Breklian devil took Sora and not him.

"Hey, where are we going?" Whitney asked as they led him right by the barracks. "Aren't you going to throw me in a cell for the night? I'll break out, and you'll spend the next week wondering how I did it."

"Not today, scag."

"That's okay," Whitney said. "I've seen nicer barracks in Fessix."

"Move."

"So where are we going?" Whitney was shoved hard into a barrel. He toppled over, hitting his head on the rim, then rolled off onto the stone. He didn't even have time to breathe before being hoisted back up and moved along.

"You know, I'm not resisting," Whitney groaned.

"Try it. Make my night."

"Your mother said something similar last evening."

Whitney winced, expecting a cudgel to the gut, but none came. Instead, they silently walked him toward the northern sector. He'd already worn into them so much they were growing numb.

Step one.

There was always a calm before the storm. Now he just had to figure out how to push their buttons enough for one of them to snap, try to release all that pent-up rage, and make a mistake.

They steered away from the wharf, instead, climbing up the hill toward the wealthiest district in the city, positioned at the height of its northern bluff, overlooking all of Trader's Bay. Whitney spent his younger days pilfering the area, but after a few occasions in Winde Port, he found the challenge wasn't there. There were too many distractions in the city and unlike presently, spotting a Glass Soldier or guard used to be a rarity.

They dragged him up a gravel path which turned to brick at the top. The haphazard nature of the city gave way to a neighborhood reminding him of Old Yarrington. Stone and wood mansions, heavy on ornament, only here many of them had balconies sticking out over the bluff, challenging nature to do its worst.

He was led to the biggest home of all, the door bearing the Darkings family crest. The constable's place in Bridleton belonged in the Panping Ghetto by comparison. Whitney cursed himself for not looking deeper into the man's history. He remembered wondering how Darkings came to such power in that little town and now he knew.

His family was in power everywhere.

Half a dozen of Darkings' private guards stood out front, one of which Whitney recognized.

"Oi! Scar-Face!" Whitney called, unable to help himself.

The one-eyed guard he and Sora had escaped in Bridleton growled like a bear. His knuckles turned white around the shaft of a spear.

"Count yourself lucky the constable… former constable… wants you alive," he said.

"I always count myself lu—"

The butt of the spear whipped across Whitney's chin with bone-crunching speed. He spit out a mouthful of blood, glad no teeth came with it.

"He said nothing about your quality of life." The one-eyed guard cackled. "Can't wait to watch you squirm." He raised his free hand to his throat, stuck his tongue out and forced his eye wide, then laughed some more.

He went to take Whitney, but the Glass soldier holding him positioned himself between them. "I believe your boss owed us something for bringing him straight here."

"Aren't you men of the Glath thupposed thu be honorable?" Whitney said, mouth still filling with blood.

"Not for free."

The one-eyed guard grunted under his breath. He reached back and was handed a plump coin-purse. The Glassmen took a peek inside, then handed Whitney over, saying, "Give Darkings my regards."

"You thure you don't wanth thu join uth?"

He was flung through the entry of the house. Somehow, this mansion was more elaborate yet just as sparsely decorated as Darkings' former home in Bridleton. Probably because it was double the size. What hadn't changed was the giant portrait of Darkings hanging front and center. Only, it wasn't *this* Darkings in the painting.

"My father, Yuri," former Constable Darkings said, once again showing up as if from thin air from a side entry. "He is quite a handsome man. I'm told I got his good looks."

Good looks was a stretch, but it was true, they could have passed for twins. If not twins, it was obvious they were father and son. Both had bellies that hung well over their belts. Darkings the younger's new mustache was an obvious homage to Yuri, his father, as well.

"Father was so kind as to lend me his winter home since mine was *burned to the ground.*" His tone bore such venom Whitney expected to be hit. "Somebody get him a towel," Darkings ordered instead. "He's bleeding all over the marble."

A moment later, a young Panpingese boy returned with a hot towel. Begging for coins on the corner of the Panping Ghetto seemed preferable to having to heed the beck and call of such a wretch. The one-eyed guard took the towel and forcefully wiped Whitney's face. Whitney spat on the floor when he was finished.

Darkings clicked his tongue and shook his head. "Always the rebel."

"You knew I wath gonna go afther Thavatha," Whitney lisped. "You killed him and thet me up, didn'th you?"

"Please stop. You sound like a fool." Darkings snapped again, and another servant arrived with two cups of wine. He offered one to Whitney.

"Don't be proud," he said. "This will clean out your mouth."

"Like you care," Whitney said. He took it with both his cuffed hands and lifted it to his lips anyway. It burned his cut gums on the way in, then quickly began to numb the pain.

Darkings pulled down on his collar to get a look at his chest.

"Whoa," Whitney protested. "I'm sure you like seeing me cuffed and all, but at least gimme a meal first."

The wine was helping, but now his mouth was beginning to swell.

"Where is the necklace you stole from me?" Darkings asked.

"Sold it for a horse back in… I forgot what town."

"You sold that priceless artifact for a horse?"

"Two horses, actually. But they were shorthairs so, really—"

"Shut up!" Darkings shouted.

Whitney rolled his shoulders. "My legs were tired," he whispered under his breath.

Darkings raised the back of his hand, stopping himself right before smacking Whitney across the face. His whole arm quaked. "Tell me, did you think you'd get away with it?" he asked.

"I wouldn't have done it if I thought otherwise."

"I have been watching you since you entered my city," Darkings said. "You and your little pet. Where is she now?"

"You tell me. She disappeared along with that white-haired killer who I assume you hired to come after me."

"Ah yes, Kazimir. I must say, when I employed him, I didn't imagine how excessively thorough he would be."

Whitney pictured the man again, that awful, nightmarish grin. "What are you doing with her?"

"What he does with your *knife-ear* is none of my concern. I offered more wealth than you could imagine for him to track you down, yet the moment he knew of her, she was the only prize he wanted."

"Prize?" Whitney scoffed. "He's in for a rough night."

"Heavens no! You think he's that sort of hired blade?" Darkings chortled. He strutted over to a seat by the stairs, right below his father's portrait. It may as well have been a throne.

"Well, you hired him. I just have to figure he's scum."

Darkings took a long sip of wine, grinning impishly as he licked his lips. "Have you ever heard of the Dom Nohzi?"

Just hearing the name had Whitney swallowing the lump in his throat.

He nodded.

Anyone who'd been to the big cities of the world had, though most thought them a myth. But Whitney had been to Brekliodad, and he'd seen their work first-hand. The Dom Nohzi were an order of assassins whose work was legalized amongst their people by blood pact. If one went to them and provided a case of why a man should die, and some deities they called the Sanguine Lords accepted, that was the end. It was all heaped in layers of mystery but what was known was that upon being employed, their order was ruthless, calculating, and apparently, now operating this far south.

"I'm sure you would have, being the worldly thief you are," Darkings went on. "It was only when I got here and looked through father's ledgers that I found a contact there. The business of coin can be so cutthroat after all."

"And people insult *my* profession," Whitney scoffed.

"Swindling people is a fool's profession. And fools die."

"Yet here I am," Whitney said, "alive and breathing."

That was the thing about the Dom Nohzi, if you were unlucky enough to be chosen as one of their targets, it was said you never saw them coming. One night you were carousing at a tavern, and then the tip of a knife found its way into the back of your skull.

Burning down a man's house after robbing him was certainly enough to get their gods to approve the blood pact, yet, somehow, Whitney lived. And it was then that he realized; he hadn't burned down the house. That was Sora.

"All right, all right, Darkings, you got me." He clapped his hands, chain jingling as he did. "So why don't you let Sora go. The whole her-burning-the-house-down thing? It was an accident." He released a nervous chuckle. "Seriously, you should have seen her face after."

"You think I don't know that you were the ringleader of that little escapade? As I said, what Kazimir does with your knife-ear girlfriend is not up to me. Though I can only imagine what use his order might have for a blood mage with no family to care about her."

Before Whitney could think better of it, his eyes shot open with horror. Darkings had challenged him to that game of gems, and Whitney's bluff was already shot. After looking into Kazimir's horrible face, he couldn't imagine. He didn't want to.

"Darkings, look—"

"It is Lord Bartholomew Darkings to you!" he roared, springing up from his seat. He slammed his drink down on a table and approached Whitney. "I want you to hear me, boy," he said. "I own you. I *own* you."

He squeezed Whitney's puffy jaw tight between his fingers. Whitney winced, feeling like a barrel of pins had burst in his mouth. "You're still here because that is how I want it."

"Just… let… Sora… go," Whitney forced out.

"I wouldn't even if I could. She is a perversion, a taint of Elsewhere that we loyal followers of Iam cannot abide."

"Now… you're so… pious?"

"You'll never see her again. The blood pact on your head is complete.

She is payment and now, your death is going to earn me the trust of the entire Panping citizenship."

He released Whitney's jaw and sauntered back to his seat, grabbing his wine on the way. The one-eyed guard promptly grabbed Whitney and shoved him to his knees.

"To think," Darkings said as he sat back down. "I simply wanted to destroy you. I wanted to sully the name of Whitney Fierstown, or whatever you call yourself. Now, I get to drag two of your names through the mud, watch you hang, and further my foothold in this city." He took another sip of wine, savoring every last drop. "You are the most useful pile of shog I've ever come across."

"And you're the ugliest."

The comment earned Whitney a right hook across his already injured jaw from the one-eyed lackey. He would have gone down, but the other guards forced him upright.

"We hang him at dawn for the murder of Tayvada Bokeo," Darkings ordered. "Such a sad city these days. They will revel in the entertainment. Throw him in a cell and tie all his limbs. We don't want any miraculous escapes."

Whitney spat out another gob of blood. "Then you captured the wrong man. Miraculous escapes are my specialt—" A cudgel to the back of the head had him on his knees and seeing bright lights. By the time he could see clearly again, Darkings was crouched in front of him.

"You're nothing, boy." He reached into Whitney's jacket and removed the letters patent presented to him by Torsten and sealed by the Crown itself. On it, was proof of his noble name and house: Blisslayer. To his horror, Whitney remembered that in the chaos created by Queen Mother Oleander, there was no time for the newly named Master of Rolls to add a copy to the archives.

It was just a name and a worthless piece of paper, yet as Darkings raised it to one of the candles mounted on the wall, Whitney felt his heart sink. Fire caught the corner and spread, the ink melting away as it flaked into ember and ash.

"You will die as nothing," Darkings said as he dropped the papers to the floor to finish burning. Then a second blow to the head sent Whitney face first into cold marble, and his whole world went black.

XIV

THE KNIGHT

It was two days marching before the stone of Fort Marimount shone under the light of the moons against a sea of darkness. It was said that the natural portion had been excavated by dwarves and used as a foothold for hunting the ancient dragons that stalked the region. The fortress itself was built across a shallow valley, half-sunken into the rock with a stone stronghold rising from its edges. The Glass Road, running north and south, led right through it like an armored bridge with a gate on either side. The farmland they passed on the west side helped feed the capital, and on the east was the Haskwood Thicket where Muskigo's men were said to be waiting.

The valley didn't cut across all the Southern Reach like the Jarein Gorge did up north, but Torsten knew Muskigo wasn't foolish enough to go around it. He'd looked into the afhem's eyes after all.

Marimount guarded the Southern Reach, the last bastion of defense before Yarrington. Muskigo had already ambushed many of the surrounding villages when the Glass was distracted by Liam's death. Taking the Fort would make it easy for him to invade the heart of the realm without risk of being surrounded, to impede trade routes from the south and east, then put Yarrington under siege and to starve them out.

Redstar zipped up a nearby hill on his black horse, two gray dire wolves flanking him along with a Drav Cra dradinengor and the warlock, Freydis. Torsten felt like he was stuck in a nightmare every time he saw the man, still dressed in robes like a heathen instead of being armored properly like a Glassman off to war ought to be. Flame wrapped his hand for light. A torch would have been easier, would've required no drawn blood, but Redstar seemed intent on unsettling Torsten's men with his dark magic… or perhaps he thought he was impressing them.

"Torsten," Redstar said. "I bring news from the valley."

"Nobody asked you to," Wardric grumbled.

The dradinengor led his horse in a circle around Wardric. He didn't speak, only stared. The man had a beard so thick it was hard to tell where it ended and the furs draped over his shoulders began. Torsten recognized him. He was Drad Mak the Mountainous, leader of the southernmost Fyortentek clan. Torsten didn't know many of their kind by name, but this one was larger even than Torsten and had led so many successful raids against the towns surrounding Crowfall over the years that, as Wearer, Torsten had been forced to help bolster defenses.

Now they marched together.

"I prefer to rely on scouts that know the land, Shieldsman," Redstar said. "Not fools with eyes."

"Just spit it out," Torsten said.

Redstar said something to Mak in Drav Crava.

"Yes, Drad Redstar," the dradinengor grunted in response, then sneered at Wardric before riding to their people. Redstar then fell in beside Torsten.

"I had my followers in that ruin—you remember it, don't you Torsten?" Redstar said.

"I remember the face you wore."

Redstar referred to the dwarven ruins southwest of their current position where, not too long ago, Torsten had been deceived into believing Redstar was his long-lost mentor, Uriah Davies.

"Ah yes. You know, I always did dream of being some great knight after King Liam stole my sister. I always imagined what it would have been like if he took me too."

"Perhaps you should have thought of that before trying to stop him with blood magic," Wardric bristled.

"Stop him?" Redstar snickered. "Liam invaded in the name of his *peaceful* god and stole a young daughter from the hands of her father… yet, somehow you paint me the villain? I swear, the hypocritical nature of you people never ceases to astound me."

"You're welcome to leave at any time," Torsten said. "Now what did you want to tell me?"

"You won't like it."

"Spit it out, I said!"

"My followers called on the Buried Goddess to listen. To hear the rumblings through the earth. They tell me that Marimount is not the Shesaitju's only target."

"And where else might they attack?" Torsten asked.

"Nesilia does not reveal all, only glimpses from so deep below. She speaks of grating mud, of river water sloshing beneath the feet of great beasts."

"I thought you said your work in bringing your goddess back was complete?"

"I am her vessel, I only do as she asks."

"What would you do then?" Torsten asked.

"The only logical targets for the afhem and his afhemate are here and Winde Port. I suggest you send a portion of your army east to the port city just in case. My men can go if you'd like?"

"And miss the battle?" Wardric said. "You truly are a worm, Redstar. Are you that frightened at the thought of fighting?"

"The armies of mortals are nothing compared to the goddess we slew in the woods. I am merely trying to help my nephew."

"How quick your loyalties turn," Torsten said. "Now, are you finished?"

He nodded.

"*My* scouts inform me that Muskigo's army gathers before the fortress and he, himself is in the lead. Siege towers and catapults are preparing to breach the walls, and Prefect Calhoun of Winde Port sent word by galler, just this morning, that the only ships in Trader's Bay are anchored merchants and our fleet."

"And what does Iam tell you?" Redstar asked.

"He tells me that the sick feeling in my stomach is from being next to you, not doubt in our strategy. As we speak, Commander Citravan of the Winde Port guard rides this way. We will surround Muskigo here at Marimount, and we will end this rebellion before all the Black Sands decide to fall in with him in the name of their Caleef."

"You shifted forces from the east?" Redstar asked, incredulous. "Why was I not informed about this?"

"Because you're not the leader of this army, heathen," Wardric said. "You're here to do what Sir Unger tells you, then go home to your ice."

Redstar slowly drew his dagger and held it over his lap. "Torsten, I would advise your man not to speak to me in such a manner, lest he experience pain no mortal should know."

"You dare threaten a member of the King's Shield?" Wardric reached for his sword.

Torsten raised his hand. "Enough. None of this is up for debate. The King placed me in command. Redstar, you will take the Drav Cra west around the fortress and through the valley. When the flaming arrow hits the sky tonight, our cohort from Winde Port will charge from the east and you from the west. With the enemy surrounded, we will flood out of Marimount, surround them, and end this."

"You have a fortress, yet you want to initiate the attack?" Redstar asked.

"This victory must be swift if our new king is to appear strong. Muskigo will expect us to dig in, but he will not be expecting Drav Cra allies. We'll catch them preparing for a siege."

"And this is what Iam tells you to do?"

"It is what Liam would have done."

Redstar chuckled. "Of course. Bold and unexpected Liam. Well, you may be a fool, Torsten, but at least you're not a coward. We'll follow your plan for now, but I hope, for your sake, it works. You may hold the ear of the Queen Mother, but her son's remains open." He lowered his voice to a whisper. "And you can't sleep with him."

Torsten's arm shot out and wrapped Redstar's throat. Choking him was becoming like second nature. It took every ounce of his being not to fulfill Oleander's desires.

"Just do what you're asked to," he said, seething. "Fire a flaming arrow into the sky when you're in position."

"I think I'll just use my hand." He purposefully sliced his thumb on the way to stowing his dagger, and a flurry of embers formed in his palm. "My Wearer."

He bowed his head low, then muttered something in Drav Crava to Freydis. A horde of warriors and more warlocks branched away from the Glassmen, their heathen tokens rattling, furs billowing in the wind. As they vanished into the darkness of the valley, it was impossible to tell them apart from the dire wolves they ran with.

"Circling wolves," Torsten muttered.

"What was that, sir?" Wardric asked.

"Nothing. Just something Uriah used to say."

"Would that he were here. It would make him sick knowing we are fighting beside these savages."

"You have no idea."

"Well, I don't trust any of them," Wardric grumbled. "If Redstar's trying to curry favor with King Pi, who knows what he might try."

"Save your eyes for the Shesaitju. I'll keep the corner of mine on Redstar."

"I know, you're right," Wardric said, lowering his head. "It took me long enough, but I do trust the man Uriah trained to take his place."

"Trust in Iam, my friend. We're just here to do his work."

Torsten kicked the sides of his horse and spurred it on ahead. The northern gate of Marimount clanked open to greet him. Soldiers ran out to help the traveling army with supplies. Lord Eveliss, Duke of Marimount, rode out to greet them. Gentry Eveliss came from a distinguished house of Yarrington who presided over the southern reach. His father and his father's father had served the Kings of Glass for generations.

Eveliss himself, on the other hand, was about as green as they come. Barely able to grow a beard, he reminded Torsten of Rand.

"Sir Unger," Eveliss saluted. "Everything is prepared to your specifications."

"What of Black Sands?" Torsten asked.

"They remain out of range behind the tree line, preparing their siege engines. The man you described as Afhem Muskigo is in their lead."

"Excellent," Torsten said. "Wardric, ready the first legion at the southern gate. At my command, we charge their camp and end this."

Wardric saluted and continued on ahead with Eveliss to prepare. Torsten dismounted and headed up onto the ramparts. Archers used pulleys to haul wood buckets of arrows up from the courtyard. Others carried food and water stores up from Marimount Keep. Torsten had no intention of withstanding a long siege but learned long ago it was always better to be prepared.

He climbed the watchtower, the highest point in the southern reach. From there beside the gate, he looked upon what was to be his canvas for battle. On a clear day, he might be able to see all the way to the mists of the Fellwater and along the coast of Trader's Bay, but presently, the sight was even more ominous.

The greenish glow of nigh'jel lanterns stole away the darkness. Thousands of them—creatures born in the vastness of the Boiling Waters now confined to small, glass and bone lanterns—stretching across a vast swathe of forest. There seemed like even more than when Torsten had stumbled upon the Shesaitju camp in the swamp.

In their light, he could see the charcoal-colored wooden planks of siege towers—that unmistakable wood from the palm trees littering the black, sandy, Shesaitju coast. Massive stones were being loaded into catapults.

"Lord Eveliss could have lent more urgency to his words," Torsten said to the archers posted around him as if any of them were listening. The siege wasn't just being prepared. From what Torsten could see, Muskigo appeared to be planning to unleash the fury of his forces that very night.

There was no time to waste.

Torsten leaned out over the ramparts. "Muskigo!" he bellowed. It carried across the cold night air, and at the sound of his voice, all his men stopped what they were doing. It grew so quiet he felt he could even hear snow flurries bouncing about on the light breeze.

Torsten saw motion behind the cover of the thicket. He kept his peripherals on the alert, waiting for the other units to get in position.

A thunderous rumble was the first indication that Muskigo had answered the call. He rode out alone into the clearing. His zhulong mount let out a roar that, combined with its heavy footsteps, shook earth and sky. Gold plating wrapped its tusks, but it wore no armor. Its thick, rust-colored scales and rock-hard hide were all the protection it needed.

Muskigo himself wielded a long glaive, staff made of blackened wood and a flawless emerald set in the curved blade. It caught the light of the nigh'jel hanging from the post on the back of his mount, which made it glow as if there were some great power sealed within the gem.

Even from so far, Torsten recognized the afhem. He could never forget that intense glare. The Shesaitju were from a place where winter never brought snow, yet Muskigo barely wore a hint of armor, tattoo-covered body bare against the cold.

But Torsten had seen the man fight in the Fellwater Swamp, and there was no better way to measure a man. He was a true showman who would freeze to death if it meant intimidating his enemies.

"Muskigo!" Torsten roared again. "Surrender now, and you alone will be tried for your crimes. Spare your men!"

Muskigo didn't answer. He moved closer still, until he was so near a single arrow could easily end it all. Now Torsten's men atop Marimount's walls could see, in detail, the great zhulong and the man's corded muscles. Torsten heard some of the archers already beginning to mutter about how he didn't need armor.

"Stop this!" Torsten shouted. "No one need die here today. We can all find peace in the light of Iam."

Finally, Muskigo stopped and looked up at Torsten, his eyes boring through him.

"The time of the Glass is over," he said. His voice was calm, like the rising of a wave carrying with it the threat of devastation.

"Caleef Rakun swore fealty to the Nothhelm's in perpetuity. Stand down, and he will not be harmed. We will continue in the prosperity of King Liam that has helped both our lands flourish."

"It is too late for that. Your child-king thinks he can insult the mighty Sidar Rakun? His flesh, borne from the Black Sands—our beaches themselves. His blood, fused from the waters of the Boiling Waters. You've sealed your fate; all afhems will stand with me now. We will carve through you, straight to the capital, and free our great Caleef ourselves."

"In the name of Iam and *your* king, you will lower your arms and surrender. This is your final warning."

"The boy is no king of mine! I will string him up in the Boiling Keep and bleed him over the waters as his father did to mine so long ago. Pray to your god, Glassman. You will see him soon."

Muskigo snapped on the reins of his zhulong and raced back toward the forest, leaving Torsten with a hundred different responses on the tip of his tongue. He hadn't expected diplomacy to be an option—not with the size of Muskigo's army—but he didn't expect such coarseness either.

He looked to the sky, his blood boiling. A flaming arrow arced across the inky darkness to the west.

Commander Citravan.

The green lanterns in the forest suddenly drew back his attention. All at once they began to stir, their bearers falling into formation. As they spread apart, the numbers seemed to swell, ranks stretching across the breadth of Fort Marimount, extending deep into the thicket.

There was some shouting in Saitjuese, then a crank and a loud *snap*.

"Hold ranks!" Torsten yelled. He grabbed onto the parapet as Celeste illuminated two chunks of rock soaring through the air. They slammed into the walls, chewing out stone, and causing the entire keep to buckle.

"It doesn't appear catching them napping is still an option!" Wardric called up from the bailey.

"Hold!" Torsten answered.

He looked back to the eastern sky and braced himself for another round of catapult fire. One of the boulders smashed into the base of the tower on which he stood. He reeled with the impact, feeling the vibrations in his glaruium armor and his bones. In the forest, the siege towers begin to budge, and through the two in the center, a pair of zhulong charged, a massive battering ram being hauled between them.

Time was running out. If the Shesaitju advanced, they'd trap his forces within the keep. Their only route of escape would be funneling through the South Gate straight into Muskigo's hands while he held off the smaller forces to the east and west.

"Redstar!" Torsten screamed, and just as he finished the word, a ball of fire traced across the sky like a shooting star. He never thought he'd be so relieved to see magic.

His head rang from the crashing of stone, but he gathered himself and raced downstairs to the South Gate where Wardric waited with his horse.

The rest of the King's Shieldsmen sat atop their own horses at the front of the mass of Glass soldiers—their mighty cavalry.

"Open the gate!" Wardric shouted. "Archers, loose!"

Torsten caught Lord Eveliss' attention. "My Lord, barricade yourself and your most loyal guards in the keep. If we fail, hold them off as long as you can."

He glanced between Torsten and the slowly rising gate. Another bang of rock on stone sent Eveliss into to a crouch. Torsten hoisted him back up by his fanciful collar and shoved him toward the keep, then turned to take his position at the head of the army, claymore drawn.

Green tinted dust swirled about in front of the gate as it rattled, colored that way by the distant nigh'jels. All he could hear was the chattering of armor and rapid breathing as some of the less experienced soldiers behind him shivered in fear.

Torsten, however, was calm, his hand steady. It had been a long time since he saw battle but there was nowhere else where he truly felt at home. The simplicity soothed him. Kill or be killed, in the name of God and Crown.

"Men of the Glass!" he yelled. "The Vigilant Eye falls upon us today, forgiving of what we must do. Our enemies pillage and raze. They would slaughter our women and children, destroy our very way of life. But their master is only mortal, as our great King Liam proved so many moons ago.

"I beg you now, find the strength of light in your heart, for we are the sword of peace. Let us show now that the Glass will neither bow nor break. Our lives for Iam!"

"Our lives for Iam!" Wardric repeated along with the entire army. Nervous as so many of them might have been, together the boom of their voices shook the walls. Torsten didn't wait for the echo to quiet. He snapped on his reins and charged forward, the thundering sound of pounding hooves and footsteps just behind him.

A volley of Glassmen arrows momentarily blotted out the light of the moons before they went stabbing into the forest to a chorus of screams. Then came the *snap-hiss* of another round being loosed from atop the keep. Torsten closed the distance on the tree line and could now see the silhouette of men within the green glow.

His gaze was fixed on only one: Muskigo atop his beast. The afhem barked orders in Saitjuese, sounding panicked, clearly having expected a long siege and not to fully unleash his army so soon.

Suddenly, a cluster of trees straight ahead went up in flames. Their naked boughs were too powdered with snow for it to spread but it was enough to burn the bark fast and hot and coat the forest in a thick fog of smoke.

Whale oil, Torsten realized.

"They're trying to split us!" he shouted. "Forward. Charge through with all your might Glassmen, and let Iam's light shield you!"

The red radiance of flames coalescing with that of the nigh'jels made it seem as though he were charging into Elsewhere itself. But he didn't slow. His horse leaped over a tendril of flame and into the Shesaitju ranks.

His claymore arced down, gashing one of the battering-ram-pulling zhulong across its thick hide. He swept it to the other side, expecting to find a soldier, but it was only a silhouette in the smoke. His men rushed through the blaze at his rear. Torsten whipped his horse around, trampled another Shesaitju soldier, but again, wasn't able to quickly find a second target.

He spun, searching the smoke, expecting to hear the clash of metal and the unforgettable shrieks of death as two great forces collided but the cries were scattered, drowned out by the sound of feet on earth as the unit from Winde Port and the Drav Cra converged from the east and west.

Something was strange. The last Shesaitju he slew had a post sticking up from his back, but that wasn't it. That was normal. They hung their lanterns from tall poles attached to their rear armor at night so that their hands would be free—but this one was positioned horizontally in a way that would make it difficult to traverse the dense woods and impossible to fight effectively. A half-dozen lanterns hung from it alone, each filled with a nigh'jel hanging at different heights, tentacles pulsing green.

"Torsten!"

Wardric dove from his horse and tackled a Shesaitju drawing back a bowstring. The man's arrow sped over Torsten's shoulder, and the thought of having to remove another of their barbed projectiles stopped his heart. He watched it stab into a burning tree, then noticed more of the lanterns strung up between boughs.

His men raced by, plowing through only a handful of enemy soldiers who had abandoned their posts at catapults to take down as many Glassmen as they could before dying.

"Torsten, where are they?" Wardric asked. He unsheathed his sword from a gray chest and stood.

A Drav Cra horn sounded, followed promptly by fur-clad warriors swarming the forest. From horseback, Torsten could see, but down in the fog of smoke, everyone was a shadow.

"Stand down!" Torsten ordered! "Fall back. It's a trap! Fall back!"

Wardric echoed his command and Torsten spurred his horse out of the woods. He coughed as he emerged on the plains, smoke filling his lungs.

"Drad Redstar, where are the enemies?" Freydis said, her hair wild as the fires.

"What is the meaning of this?" Redstar questioned as he approached.

All Torsten could manage was to shake his head.

"Must I do everything?" Redstar moaned. He hopped down from his horse and advanced toward the burning trees. Glassmen and Drav Cra poured past him in full retreat. He stopped, removed his dagger, and drew a deep cut across his hand. Blood dribbled onto the snow-covered grass.

He whispered something, then swiped his wounded hand to the side. In an instant, all the fire was snuffed out, and the smoke swirled out to either side. Then, a soft light bloomed in his palm as if holding a star. Murmurs of confusion broke out across both armies until Redstar laughed.

Torsten jumped down and ran to his side. With the smoke and fire cleared, Redstar's illumination spell revealed the entirety of Muskigo's camp amongst the trees.

A single boulder sat by two operational catapults, and all the rest were simple planks of wood balanced to appear like weapons. The siege towers were hollow, with wheels that barely worked. The battering ram didn't even have a ram under its cover. Thousands of nigh'jel lanterns were strung up everywhere as well as littering the ground by corpses.

There were no supplies alongside their tents. No food or water, none of the essentials needed to man a successful siege. And amidst it all, were the bodies of no more than one hundred Shesaitju warriors and a handful of Glassmen.

That was all.

"What sorcery is this?" Torsten snapped at Redstar. "What have you done!"

"What have *you* done, Shieldsman?" he replied. "It appears to me that Muskigo's army is not here."

"You think I can't see that!" He whipped around. "Wardric, send scouts out in every direction. Find where they went. We won't be caught out here in the open. Everyone, return to Marimount!" He went to take a step, but Redstar stopped him.

"What of the men you summoned from Winde Port?" he asked. "I see no new faces among these men."

"He signaled his approach. They're likely still in the for…" The words got lost in his throat when one of his men shouted and pointed east. Sitting on his zhulong, atop the hill, moons at his back, was Muskigo. He fired a flaming arrow straight up into the sky, then disappeared over the peak.

"That treasonous scag," Torsten swore. He rushed back to his horse and took off toward the afhem.

"Sir, it could be a trap!" Wardric called.

"Don't follow," he called back. "Get them all back to the keep!" He snapped his reins as hard as he could.

A horse appeared next to him carrying Redstar. Two dire wolves dashed at his sides.

"I said don't follow!"

"You're not the king," he answered.

They crossed the hilltop and Torsten could hear the echoing snorts of the zhulong long before he saw them. A full regiment of mounted Shesaitju raced across the plains, so far now they were only shadows. Muskigo was chasing after them, all headed east toward Winde Port.

Between Torsten and Redstar and the Black Sands riders, was the unit of a thousand men he'd summoned from Winde Port to surround Muskigo. They looked like they'd been hit by an avalanche, trampled and broken, groaning and in need of physicians.

Massacred.

Commander Citravan was at the front, his helmet caved into his skull.

Torsten wasn't sure how they didn't hear it happen until he remembered the chaos in the smoking forest, his men screaming in the heat of battle as they fought to kill barely a hundred men—Shesaitju warriors who had sacrificed their lives to be a distraction.

Marimount was never the target at all.

Torsten glanced at Redstar, speechless. The Arch Warlock looked back. He didn't smile like usual, but he wasn't mournful either. In fact, he didn't look surprised at all.

"The eye far above is blinder than the one beneath our feet," he said, calmly. "May She save us all."

XV

THE THIEF

"Oh, One-Eye?" Whitney called out.

Darkings' scarred lackey ignored him like he had during Whitney's previous twenty attempts at gaining his attention.

"Buried a bit north of here and to the east, there is a ring so precious you've likely never seen its equal," Whitney went on. "Let me out, and it's yours. You'll never work in a shoghole like this again."

He considered bringing up the broken crown stuffed into a chimney in the middle of the Panping Ghetto but hated the idea of giving up his greatest prize. Even in half, it once sat upon the head of Liam the Conqueror.

"Shut your mouth!" the guard finally grunted from his seat down the hall. "Ah, yigging shog, look at what you made me do." He threw down a deck of cards and the guard across from him plucked a few autlas off the table.

Whitney poked his head as far through the bars as he could, pulling the chains on his wrists and ankles tight.

"Don't blame me. You threw an anvil down against the archer? You need that ring if you're expecting not to lose all your money in gems."

"Enough, thief. Pray to whoever you think'll care and eat your last meal. Dawn is coming, and it'll be the last one you see."

Whitney stared longingly back into his cell. "That slop is my last meal? I thought I'd at least get chicken. Looks more like what the chicken ate for supper."

He turned and climbed up a bench to peer through the tiny window slot at the back. It was dark as pitch outside, which would only mean one thing; dawn was about to break. Never before had Whitney been so sure he was going to die. He'd always had a plan, but right now, he had nothing and no allies to speak of. He could usually get guards to come around and take a bribe, but these guys weren't biting. Probably because they worked for Darkings and not the Crown, and that meant they were well paid.

C'mon Whitney, think! But nothing came. All he could imagine was that Sora… poor Sora… was in the hands of a ruthless assassin while he was left to hang.

He found himself subconsciously grabbing at his throat, swallowing hard.

"The ring and the Splintering Staff," he said. "I have them both hidden nearby. I can take you there right now. They're yours. Worth more than you'll make in a lifetime. Just let me out." He emphasized those last words, shaking the cell door.

The guard rose and silently began unlocking the cell.

"Oh, thank you," Whitney said. "Thank you. You won't regret this. I will—"

"Shut it, thief!" the guard said. He reached through the bars, grabbed Whitney by the scruff of his neck, and pulled him hard into the bars. Whitney's head cracked against the metal before he staggered backward.

"You ain't going nowhere but to your death," the guard growled.

His gems partner arrived as well, along with another of Darkings' goons. They unlocked Whitney's chained limbs and dragged him along. He tried to fight, but he could barely stand, his head was ringing so loud. Plus, each act of resistance only furthered their resolve to injure him more. By the time they'd hauled him out of Darkings' basement, down the street, and to the upper wharf where the gallows had been set up, he had been kicked, punched, and otherwise beaten more than a dozen times.

A gathering had amassed. Word about hangings always traveled quickly within big cities. Nothing roused the common-folk more than watching one of their own flail at the end of a rope. Usually, it was cultists, leaders of rebellions, bandit crews, or—apparently murderous folk. Or in Whitney's case, men set up to look like one.

Through swollen eyes, Whitney saw people of all shapes and sizes, most of them poor, and most Panpingese. Light, bronzish skin, pointed ears, and expressions of profound sadness.

"All right, last chance," Whitney said to Darkings' lackey. "I'll get you the ring, the staff, and... I can't believe I'm saying this... the Glass Crown of Liam Nothhelm."

"I'm going to enjoy watching your neck snap, scag."

Whitney was handed off to the city guard, proudly donning the blue and white of the Glass Kingdom. He was promptly shoved through the growing crowd. The looks of sorrow among the Panpingese quickly transitioned to rage as vegetables and hard chunks of bread slammed into his body from every direction. What appeared to be a turnip clipped his ear and even drew blood. The soldiers made as little effort to shield him as was physically possible.

Everyone with pointed ears wanted to take a shot at the bastard who killed Tayvada, even if it meant spoiling much-needed food. It appeared Tayvada was loved dearly. He was probably the pride of their community, using the wealth of the Traders Guild to provide food and other necessities. For the first time since finding his drained corpse, Whitney felt a hint of remorse over the man himself. None of them realized they blamed the wrong guy. From their viewpoint, he agreed.

The soldiers walked him up a small flight of stairs and tossed him down on the wooden planks. Raising his head, he watched as many of the onlookers spit toward him. Whitney never cared whether he was liked before, but now he knew he hated being so reviled. Thieves who meet their end usually did so rotting in a cell or falling from a rooftop. Public execution was never what Whitney expected, or deserved.

He watched Bartholomew Darkings ascend the steps from the opposite side of the platform, donning his best formal silks. He licked his lips beneath thick mustache and edged toward Whitney and his detainers. A hush fell upon the gathering mass as the former constable of Bridleton and son of the Master of Coin positioned himself at the front of the platform.

"Nice shirt," Whitney remarked. Darkings didn't even pay him a passing glance. "Did your mother sew that—" He lost his train of thought when, out of the corner of his vision, he saw someone familiar watching from the shadows. Standing under the pitched roof of a bell tower was the white-haired assassin who'd taken Sora. He leaned against a column, grinning.

"Good people of Winde Port," Darkings announced. "Especially the fine folks of the Panping Ghe..." He cleared his throat. "District"

"Welcome!" he shouted.

Thunderous applause rained down on him.

"Yes, yes," he continued, motioning for the crowd to quiet. "My name is Bartholomew Darkings, beloved son of our great Master of Coin. My family helped build Winde Port centuries ago, and so I stand here today, a man of the merchant city just like each of you."

Yeah, minus the fact that you live in a mansion on a hill the whole ghetto could fit into. Whitney scoffed internally.

"I hope for today to be more than the execution of one worthless whelp," Darkings continued. "I hope it to be a day of eternal memory. One we can look back upon as the beginning of a new era. For too long, you've been forced into obscurity. This fact accented by the death of one of the greatest men in all of Winde Port being brutally murdered in a place where, with even the slightest presence of city guards, it could have been prevented."

Murmurs of agreement carried across the crowd. Whitney would've rolled his eyes if they weren't so fixated on the assassin. Never in his life had just seeing a man made his throat clench. All the hope that his good luck would get him out of this drained away.

"Had it not been for my personal guards receiving a tip about this... scoundrel being in our fine city, Tayvada Bokeo's death may have gone days without notice."

"I didn't even do it!" Whitney finally drew enough focus to shout. The last word came out as a grunt, one of the guard's boots finding his ribcage.

"But no more!" Darkings shouted, inviting an uproar from the crowd. "The Darkings have returned to Winde Port. Returned home. And we will fight to make our city safer for everyone!"

Darkings turned to face Whitney, eclipsing the menace watching from a distance, and winked.

"It all starts now," he said. He raised his hand, and the soldiers roughly pulled Whitney to his feet. They gave him a shove toward the center of the gallows where a noose hung.

"This man is a fraud!" Whitney shouted, but no one could hear him over the cheers. Without the dark eyes of Kazimir upon him, he felt like himself again.

Darkings came close and said, "No one cares about you, thief. Your name means nothing. You will go down in history only as the man who sealed my hold on Winde Port. And nobody but I will ever know."

Darkings turned back to his captive audience and waved his arms for them to quiet. "Ladies and gentlemen, I give you the man who stole Tayvada Bokeo's life in cold blood. Whitney Blisslayer!"

The crowd cursed his name. The executioner wrapped a coarse rope around his neck, then stepped back to a lever, ready to plunge Whitney into Elsewhere. Things got so crazy it sounded like a riot until a lone, gruff voice cried out.

"Stop!" Whitney couldn't find its owner in the crowd. "Ye ain't got the right to hang a noble at these gallows."

The people parted, revealing Tum Tum. The rotund dwarf stood tall, however short he was.

"He deserves to stand before the prefect for his actions and defend himself, aye?" Tum Tum said, looking around for support.

To Whitney's shock, a few of the wealthier onlookers in their posh outfits agreed.

"And who might you be to question a Darkings?" Bartholomew said.

"I be the true voice of the people, standing up to those who think themselves above the law because their daddy's a big shot in Yarrington."

Bartholomew laughed humorlessly, then his face contorted into a scowl.

"I assure you, my bearded friend, that the prefect is busy securing the region against possible rebellion and has vested in me the power to take this unfortunate matter into my own hands. Tayvada was…" He closed his eyes and feigned sincerity, "…a dear friend."

"Tayvada fed my children when we had nothing!" a Panpingese man hollered from the back.

"Hang the bastard!" A cacophony of onlookers voiced their agreement.

"And someone will pay for his death!" Tum Tum said. "But, I've known Whitney for years, and the man be gentle as they come."

"Hey, I'm not that..." Whitney said, before realizing how stupid it would be to argue that. "Yeah, he's right! I can't even hurt a spider."

"This man was found in Tayvada's very home," Bartholomew shouted, "blood on his hands."

"Yeah, so I hear. So ye say he slit the poor bloke's throat—let the blood drain from him. The Whitney I know retches at the sight of a cut." Tum Tum hopped—or, rather, rolled—up onto the stand. A kind onlooker even rushed to help him to his feet after watching his struggle. "My Panpingese brothers and sisters, I know ye are angry, and why shouldn't ye be? But is this really Winde Port justice?"

"Maybe the dwarf has a point," that same highborn in front said. Whitney thought he recognized him from the Guild Hall. "Should we not hear the accused's defense before he is sent from this world?"

"Yeah, what he said!" Whitney cried out. "I'm weak and harmless. But maybe there's someone else who gets something out of painting a new villain. Maybe he's right here among us."

A mixture of approval and distaste spewed forth from the non-Panpingese members of the crowd. Bartholomew leaned in close to his one-eyed guard. "Kill the dwarf as soon as we're gone," he whispered so only Whitney could hear.

He turned back to address Tum Tum.

"Your complaints are duly noted, Dwarf," he said. "But this decree has already been made and signed by Prefect Mortimer Calhoun." He unfurled a piece of paper from the folds of his jacket. Whitney couldn't see it, but he could see Tum Tum's features darken and knew his fate was sealed. And even worse, he could once again see the grin on the assassin's face now that Bartholomew had moved, teeth and hair white against the shadow.

"Today," Bartholomew pronounced with renewed vigor. "The murderer, Whitney Blisslayer die—"

A sudden scream rang out. "In the bay!"

Whitney turned toward the water. A flaming rock crashed into one of the Glass Kingdom warships floating in the bay. Then, suddenly, an arrow exploded through the chest of the noble that had taken Whitney's side. For a moment, Whitney thought someone was coming to spring him, but then he realized… only a Shesaitju barbed arrow could tear through a man with such force.

A frenzy broke out as more arrows trickled down, men and women tripping over one another. Even the Glass soldiers overseeing the execution dispersed.

Whitney saw his opening. The executioner no longer stood on the platform, and Bartholomew's guards were otherwise occupied. Just as Whitney began to duck out of the noose, one of the lumbering brutes bumped into him. In turn, he bumped another guard, who bumped into Bartholomew, and finally, the man's fat ass struck the lever. In an instant, the floor fell out beneath him and Whitney was hanging.

He gurgled and strained. As he struggled, he wondered why his neck hadn't snapped, though he wasn't complaining.

His vision grew blurry, blood rushing to his eyeballs. He could feel drool against his cheek before he went lightheaded. His ears rang, but he heard a loud *crack-boom,* and suddenly, he was falling again.

It took a moment for him to figure out what happened. A shower of wood fragments rained down on him as, somehow, he lay safely on the ground. He stood beneath the gallows, sides broken but for a few supporting struts. Beyond the structure where the crowd had just been, was an open marketplace. Everyone was busy running for their lives.

The Shesaitju are attacking again?

Whitney didn't wait around for an answer. He went to run, but Bartholomew grabbed his ankle and sent him sprawling.

"You won't escape me again!" Bartholomew hissed.

"You're right, I won't." Whitney kicked him across the jaw. Then he rolled over and jumped on the man. He used the rope that still bound his hands and pulled it taut against Darkings' neck. "Where is she!"

"Unhand him!" The loyal, one-eyed guard grabbed Whitney and flung him off.

Before either could make a move, another volley of arrows rained down. The guard raised a chunk of broken wood and kept an arrow from shredding Bartholomew's head. Another landed in the dirt, right between Whitney's legs.

He stared at it, frozen by fear. He knew firsthand what the barbed arrows could do. All the while, Bartholomew's men lugged their master away while he vowed revenge again and again.

With them gone, the sight of Kazimir standing through an open doorway across the plaza finally stirred Whitney. While everyone fled for their lives, the Breklian assassin stayed in the darkness, calmly juggling one of his many knives.

Whitney rolled and hopped to his feet, then ran, arms bound and severed noose flapping behind him. He saw the source of his salvation in a massive ball of stone that had apparently been catapulted into the city. There was no time to celebrate his renowned luck. He needed to get out of the target zone, lest another boulder or arrow come crashing down.

Kazimir was now nowhere to be seen, and none of the city guards paid any attention to the escaping prisoner. Whitney sprinted as fast as he could and only stopped once he knew he was free of the threat of discovery. Ducking into an alley, he slid the noose from his neck and worked the rope until his hands were untied.

He rubbed his neck. Knowing there'd be a mark, he pulled his collar up tight against his ears. Only then did he finally allow himself to catch his breath. Once he had his fill of the precious, life-giving air, he peered around the corner toward the bay. From the morning fog along the shore, emerged hundreds of dark rowboats cracking through the ice toward Winder's Wharf. Each of them carried gray-skinned rowers by the dozens, so many that some were even hanging off into the freezing cold water.

On the back of each, stood an archer, loosing arrow after arrow into the city. Glass soldiers fired back and formed along the wharf, but boulders from catapults soared out of the fog. They came from the direction of the coast as if somehow an entire army had snuck right onto Winde Port's doorstep overnight.

The Shesaitju mounted the wharf, descending upon the shields of the Glassmen like a tsunami.

Bells tolled from all around him. Whitney felt the breath catch in his lungs. This was no mere raiding party with a lust for bloodshed. It was an army. The biggest Whitney had ever seen. And once again he was in the wrong place while they were attacking.

He backed away and as he did, noticed Kazimir on a sunken balcony on a neighboring building, staring out at the bay. The assassin was enraptured by the sight of the invaders, same as he was. Whitney used the man's distraction and sunk all the way back into the alley. He found a sewer cover nested at the base of a building and weaseled his way in.

Darkings, Panping—they could all wait. He had to find Sora before the whole city burned down around them… or Kazimir killed them both.

XVI

THE MYSTIC

By the time sunlight filtered in through the stained glass, Sora's throat felt like tree bark.

"Help!" she grated. She thrashed her body and clenched the muscles in her stomach until they finally gave out and she hung slack.

Multi-colored light painted the cobwebs like splintered diamonds hanging from rotting beams in the otherwise empty room that would be her grave. A spider flitted across one. It was tiny, but it still brought her back to the Webbed Woods and the last time she thought she was going to die.

She tried to force herself to think about the same things she had when Redstar was killing her—when she lost control and the energy of Elsewhere coursed through her like a hot spring. About all the places in the world she'd missed out on seeing while hiding beneath a shack. She considered every scar. How Wetzel used to cut her mercilessly, bidding the darkness within her to rise up.

She begged her body to bring that power back to bear.

But it never came.

"At least I'll die in a church," she groaned, sardonic.

She'd never been religious. Wetzel didn't care for anything but his studies and his potions. But as a child, she'd gone with Whitney and his family to the Troborough church house. Her first few visits, everyone stared at her. Whitney's mother told her it was because she was "just so cute." But his father's eyes shot daggers sharper than her ears.

But she'd watch the other families leave service, their eyes circled by luminous white paint once a year during the Dawning, when the moons blotched out the sun, and the people of the Glass were forced to look inward for Iam's light. Tears speckled her eyes as she recalled how they smiled and caroused, mothers hugging their daughters, fathers tussling their sons' hair.

She'd always longed for that. One year, Whitney's parents even took him to Yarrington for the ceremony led by Wren the Holy at Yarrington Cathedral. She remembered being the loneliest she'd ever been in her life, sitting by the stream staring at the empty Troborough chapel while Wetzel called for her to help with his potions.

No matter how many times Whitney told her what a load of shog it all was, she always wanted to belong. Wetzel cared for her the best he knew how, but he wasn't her real father.

She hung her head and closed her eyes. Wetzel didn't believe in any Gate of Light, didn't believe that the dead would be delivered into the waiting arms of Iam. Like her ancestors, he believed that after death, the spirit went to Elsewhere. To linger without purpose, watching until the essence of one's soul would one day be returned to the world of the living. She wondered if she might find her true parents on that eldritch plane.

In truth, she only hoped death would bring relief from painful memories. That when her eyes shut for the last time, she would no longer have to remember the pain of abandonment, the shame of her heritage, or the brutality she'd experienced at the hands of men like Kazimir.

She swore. There were no men like Kazimir.

The steeple door creaked open.

"I won't go with you," she said. She opened her eyes and expected to see Kazimir, only the entry was empty. She searched from side to side, trying to keep her heart from beating through her rib cage. She'd seen him move like this, like a shadow. "You might as well kill me because I won't come with you."

A faint clicking noise drew her gaze to the floor, and there, sniffing her dangling feet was a wyvern.

"Aquira?" she said, incredulous. "What are you…"

The creature blinked. She stood up on her hind legs and stuck her forked tongue at Sora's feet.

"You need to leave right now before he returns. You need to go home…" The words trailed off as she realized that, like her, Aquira had no home to return to. Her master had been murdered for merely being in the wrong place at the wrong time. Just like Sora's own parents.

"I'm so sorry girl," Sora said. "You didn't deserve any of this. Neither of us did."

Sora stretched her foot to pat the wyvern on the head. Aquira's frills rippled as she closed her eyes, purring softly in a series of rhythmic clicks. Sora could feel the heat radiating off the creature, even through her heels.

The corners of her mouth rose.

"Aquira," she said. "Do you want to help me out of here?"

The wyvern merely stared up at her and blinked again.

"The chains. Can you melt them?" Sora shook her arms, and in doing so, her entire body. Aquira scurried away, and Sora cursed under her breath.

"Why don't I speak wyvern?" she groaned. Aquira stopped a few paces away and turned to look back at her. Sora inhaled slowly and remembered one of Wetzel's lessons about ancient Panping mystics who learned how to dominate the minds of lesser beings. Sora couldn't do that but the birds her old master always tested his concoctions on always favored her.

"Aquira," she whispered. "I know you can't understand me, but if you don't break me free, I'll lose everything."

A chorus of distant screams echoed, then a loud crash outside kicked dust off the ceiling and made Aquira dart for the door.

"Aquira!" Sora shouted. "Please, stop!"

The creature stopped in the entry near the stairs and turned.

Another crash, louder than the first, made the entire steeple rumble. Aquira tilted her head and before Sora could say another word, rushed back to her.

She flew up onto Sora's leg, claws poking into her.

"Good girl," Sora said, gritting her teeth. "You can do this." Aquira's needle-like claws wound their way up her body until she was sitting on Sora's shoulder.

Sora shook her right arm, so the chain holding her bound to the ceiling rattled.

"Right here," she said.

Aquira's strange, yellow eyes blinked in Sora's face, then she growled and turned to the cuff.

"Yes!" Sora exclaimed. "That's right."

Aquira's scaly tail wrapped the back of Sora's neck for balance. It was like wearing a campfire for a coat the wyvern was so warm. Then, she flapped her wings to hover just overhead. The weight made Sora's already sore shoulder feel like it was going to tear from the joint.

Sora squeezed her eyelids shut to stifle the groan festering in her throat, not wanting to scare her reptilian savior again. A sweltering brush of air wrapped her forearm. Fire spewed from Aquira's mouth, bright and hot. It was aimed at the chains, but Sora's hand blistered anyway.

The metal wilted like the wax of a candle. Even Sora's magic couldn't compare. When half her body swung free, Aquira used the momentum to leap up onto the other chain. In an instant, the second was reduced to molten slag as well.

Sora crashed to the floor, one of her heels driving a hole in the old wood plank. She gasped for air. She hadn't quite been crucified, but with both arms stretched she hadn't realized just how labored her breathing had become until she had a lungful. She clutched her chest. Against her cheek, she felt a dry, coarse tongue.

She threw her arms around Aquira. The wyvern didn't fight it, just nuzzled against Sora's neck, frills tickling her chin. More screams and banging noises sounded from outside, but Sora couldn't bring herself to let go. She squeezed harder and Aquira's purring intensified.

Before she knew it, she was sobbing. Her tears trickled down onto Aquira's scales and turned to mist. Her whole body, inside and out, grew warm from holding the wyvern but she didn't care. Her life had been so chaotic since the Black Sands took everything away from her that she hadn't even really had time to stop and let it all out.

Wetzel. Troborough. Seeing Whitney again and dealing with his 'jobs'—tears over all of it poured from her eyes like a dam had been broken. It took all her effort to pull away and momentarily focus her blurry vision on the lizard-like face of her unexpected rescuer.

"I promise, you'll never be without a home again," she sniveled.

Aquira went to lick her again when the bang of the church doors slamming shut downstairs made her heart sink. She waited for the loud thumping of boots against the stairs, same as she'd heard when Kazimir left her earlier.

"C'mon," she said, scrambling to her feet. Her legs were numb from hanging, but she didn't let that stop her. She ran to the stained glass window, she wrapped her fist with the hem of her dress, then bashed on it as hard as she could. The glass vibrated but didn't break. If there was one thing for which the Glass Kingdom was proficient, it was hardened, stained-glass panels.

Sora struck it again and again until Aquira released a snarl that raised the hairs on her arms. She turned around, and in the entryway, saw the white hair and dark, callous eyes of her captor. Her hand fell toward a knife she didn't have—a knife Kazimir had stolen from her.

He strolled forward calmly, clicking his tongue in disapproval. He purposefully avoided the beam of sunlight flooding in through the high window, but as he turned, she noticed that, unlike before, he was now covered in grime. His hair was unkempt, and a few of his knives were missing from his bandolier.

"Where are you going, my dear?" he asked. "We were just starting to get along." The sound of his voice made her spine tingle, but she also noticed something new in it. For once, he seemed flustered.

"I'm not going anywhere with you," she said.

"You are going to help me find your friend and honor my pact."

He's alive?

Hoping Kazimir wouldn't see the relief on her face, she looked down as she unwrapped her hand from her dress and balled it into a tight fist. Aquira snarled at Kazimir. Only a spark came out of her mouth, clearly drained from melting the chains.

"And who is this adorable, new friend?" Kazimir asked. "I swear, today is just full of surprises."

"Stay away from us!" Sora screamed. She drew back her bare hand

and punched through the glass. It was only a small hole, but when her hand recoiled, it was sliced all over.

Bleeding.

Now she felt it, that dark, unexplainable power inside. All at once, she was unstoppable and vulnerable, as if she, herself, were walking the planes of Elsewhere. Fire erupted from her injured hand and blew the entire window open just before Kazimir was able to grab her.

Wind howled, and light flooded the steeple. Kazimir leaped backward into the shadows, wincing as if in pain. It was then that Sora remembered another of the lessons in one of Wetzel's old books. The upyr were fearsome, but immortality came with drawbacks... the insatiable need for blood, and a horrible allergy to sunlight which turned their skin to ash.

Sora grabbed Aquira and backed away slowly. The lust in Kazimir's eyes was replaced by terrible rage. She lifted her leg over the sill and stepped out onto the slanted roof, her eye never leaving her captor.

The racket in the city was deafening. Metal clashing, screams of agony and war—death all around her. Out of her peripheries, she saw the low palisade wall on the landlocked side of the city. Gray-skinned Shesaitju from the detainment camp swarmed over it like ants from a nest.

The image of Troborough burning at the hands of the Black Sands flashed through her mind. She tripped on a loose tile and rolled to the roof-ledge. Aquira flew from her arms, but Sora caught her by the tail.

As Sora struggled to pull the squirming, squealing wyvern back up, she stared through the steeple's broken window. Kazimir stood in the light, his skin flaking away, smoking like parchment under the heat of flame. He clenched his jaw but never made a sound. Instead, he knelt, scraped his knife along the ground to coat it with Sora's blood, and lifted it to his lips.

Sora felt a nibble on her finger and looked to see Aquira fluttering below. She let go, and the wyvern drifted downward.

She quickly returned her attention to her assailant. His eyelids flickered as he licked off every last drop. His skin seemed to shift a to a lighter shade. The sun's blisters slowly faded as he stood and rolled his neck with a series of pops.

"Your blood is like a storm," he said with renewed vigor. "Come, my dear. We have so much to accomplish together."

Sora panicked. She looked down, then back up at the monster bearing down on her. The sunlight dried and cracked his skin, but the marks healed faster than they could form.

Sora didn't think. She pushed off the wall of the church with her feet and let go. Air rushed up around her as her heart sank into her stomach. The fall ended abruptly as she crashed onto the flat roof of a Panping Ghetto home. Her ankle banged off something, a sharp line of pain streaking up her leg. Her back felt like it had broken in two. She thanked the gods she'd crashed through a galler bird cage and into in a pile of feed. It wasn't soft, but it was better than the unforgiving ground. Groaning, she flipped over and noticed Aquira had already taken to stalking one of the freed birds.

She wanted to lay there forever, exhaustion tempting her to close her eyes and pass out, but one look back at the broken-down church and she saw Kazimir preparing to make the leap.

"C'mon!" She grabbed Aquira and swung her up onto her shoulder just as the wyvern went to snap at her unsuspecting prey.

Behind them, Kazimir made the jump like it was as easy as walking. He stretched his arms out wide, like a bird in flight, and then at the last moment, flipped head over heels, landing with the grace of a prince.

Sora's ankle burned, but she pushed her legs as fast as they could go. Blood coated her hand from the glass shards digging in, and she flung a ball of flame back over her shoulder. Kazimir spun out of the way and kept moving. She'd never seen anyone move like him.

She jumped between two flats. Where only the day before she found herself cursing how the Glass Kingdom had crammed together the houses of her ancestors, now she was grateful for it. From roof to roof she went, not daring to look back. Kazimir's footsteps—if they even made a sound —were drowned out by the unseen chaos overtaking the streets of the city.

"Running is futile," Kazimir said, not even panting as he chased her. "With me, you'll be so much more than some thief's plaything."

Sora glanced back, and her foot crashed through a tarp covering a devastated structure at the edge of the ghetto. She crashed through wooden beams, then through a flimsy floor. Aquira slipped from her shoulder, but not before one of her claws ripped off a small chunk of skin.

By the time Sora stopped falling she was at street level, covered in dust and bits of wood. Her dress was torn at the seams, half her scratched torso exposed, one sleeve missing.

"Aquira?" she moaned. Her vision was spotty at best, but she didn't see her new friend anywhere.

"Alva shueth!" someone barked in Saitjuese. Before she could see where it came from, a gray hand pulled her from the rubble. Her gaze met those of a Shesaitju soldier wearing scaled leather armor and a waist-coil of black wooden plates.

Sora was in so much pain she couldn't think straight. She knew she had to keep moving, but the sight of a Shesaitju again transported her weary mind back to that fateful day Troborough burned.

"Get off me!" she snapped, tearing free of the soldier and igniting a fire around her hand. There was so much blood it enveloped nearly her whole arm, burning hot and bright. A second soldier aimed a spear at her neck and cursed her in Saitjuese.

Before any of them could make a move, a knife sliced across each of their necks. Blood squirted as they fell to their knees, pawing at their throats.

"Nobody but I will ever touch you again," Kazimir said.

Sora spun and fell backward, her magic abandoning her. The white-haired devil emerged from the ruined structure, mindlessly flipping a throwing knife by the blade.

"G… get away from me," Sora stammered. She reached inward for that well of power she so often relied on but was too petrified.

"I—" Kazimir was cut off when Aquira appeared on his shoulder and dug her teeth into his neck. He howled and fell to one knee, smoke sizzling out of the wound as if the wyvern's teeth themselves were made of fire.

Kazimir ripped her off him and held the flailing creature by its neck. Rage contorted his features. His fangs extending like swords. He drew another knife and raised it to Aquira's throat.

"Enough!" he roared. "I tire of chasing you, mystic. Perhaps killing your friend here will show you that I will not be denied."

"Please don't!" Sora begged. "Don't hurt her. I'll… I'll do anyth…" She didn't finish because she noticed that while the marks from Aquira's bite were healing, Kazimir's flesh was beginning to flake away again from the sunlight. His hand crackled, allowing Aquira to squirm free and hide between Sora's legs.

"Just leave us alone!" The chance to fight back energized her. Sora raised both bloody hands, and a pillar of flame exploded from them. It struck Kazimir on the hip and sent him flying back into the rubble.

Smoke and embers danced, but he didn't stay down. He flung a plank off his body and hopped back to his feet. Now, from the shadows, he watched her.

Before she could catch herself, Sora's eyes lowered toward a stain on the floor. His followed, and what he saw made him grin.

He knelt down to the tiny pool of Sora's blood gathering around his boots. Sora looked deep into herself. Her whole body was numb from pain, but she drew on all her worst memories. She knew summoning another flame so soon might make her pass out. Elsewhere sapped her body like it'd spent a week harvesting barley every time she did it.

But she had no choice. Fire swirled around her hands once more as Kazimir raised her blood to his lips.

She heard another voice behind her, sharp and sudden. She glanced back, just for a moment, and saw a cluster of Shesaitju warriors staring at her, clad in golden armor and faces were covered by masks in the visage of snakes. At their center stood a breathtaking warrior unlike any she'd ever seen. Despite the chill in the air, he was shirtless, his gray skin covered head to toe in white tattoos.

When she turned back, Kazimir was gone.

Sora scanned the shattered remains of what appeared to be a home in the middle of the Panping Ghetto. Fear had her crippled, both physically and magically. She turned back toward the impressive Shesaitju man.

"Who are you?" she asked.

"I could ask the same of you?" His gaze wandered momentarily toward her exposed midriff before he caught himself.

"I… I…" Between sheer exhaustion, relief that Kazimir was gone, and the overwhelming presence of the man standing before her, she could hardly speak.

The man looked down at the two dead Shesaitju warriors, then to the smoldering wake left behind by her magic where Kazimir had stood only moments before. Some cloth smoked amongst the embers as if she'd completely vaporized another attacker.

"You did this?" he asked.

Sora hesitated. If she said no, she'd need to tell them about Kazimir. Who would believe there was an upyr chasing her through the streets of Winde Port? If she said yes, they might lash out and kill her on the spot. Again, she was rendered silent.

"Very impressive," he said. "My people were ordered not to touch a single dwarf or Panpingese. They clearly deserved their fate. Am I right men?" The soldiers flanking him said nothing. They stood silent beneath terrifying, golden, serpentine masks.

"Our people have no qualms with you or yours, mystic," the man continued. He went to touch her shoulder, but, instinctively, she recoiled. However impressive he seemed, she couldn't ignore the rage growing inside of her. His was the gray skin of the people who had senselessly slaughtered Troborough.

"You deny me, mystic?" he questioned, his features hardening.

She was about to correct him—to tell him she was no mystic and he was responsible for burning down the town she called home. She was also about to summon fire to the tips of her fingers and burn him to a crisp. Then she remembered Whitney and the man after them.

"No, my head is just fuzzy from the fight," she lied. If she tried anything rash, she'd die with him. Which meant Whitney, wherever he was hiding, would be left alone against Darkings, Kazimir, and an army of Shesaitju who wanted all Glassmen dead.

"Well, I assure you, I will have word spread that any of my men caught harming one of your people will be punished in kind." He lay his hand upon the dilapidated wall and closed his eyes in deep thought. "This place… it is a graveyard for your people. A cesspool of filth and no place for one of such stunning beauty to dwell."

Just then, Aquira skittered out from behind a pile of rubble. The snake-faced warriors moved to attack.

"No, stop!" Sora shouted. "She's mine."

"Yours?" the man said, raising his hand for his men to obey. "No one can own a dragon."

"She is my companion," Sora corrected. "But she is also no dragon.

She's a wyvern. I know as well as anyone, dragons are no longer with us on this plane."

"In that, I'd argue you are wrong, mystic. My people believe there are plenty of dragons who remain, but like so many in Pantego, they've retreated into solitude in response to the heavy hand of the evil, vile, King Liam and his ilk."

"Is that what this is?" she asked. "A battle for freedom?"

"That is how it began." He took a step toward her. "But then the Child-King Pi dared imprison our great Caleef. His unprovoked attack—"

"Unprovoked?" Sora interrupted. "Your people burned towns to the ground. Homes and businesses—destroyed people's lives."

"How dare you speak to Afhem Muskigo with that insolent tone!" One of the snake-faced men moved toward her, readying the back of his hand to strike her.

"Stop," Muskigo demanded. The soldier froze immediately. Never had Sora seen a man command such respect. His baritone voice even raised the hairs on her arms. "She is right."

Sora wasn't sure who was more surprised at the response, her or his men.

"War makes villains of us all" Muskigo said. "I'm not proud of that which must be done."

"What must be done?" She recognized the name Muskigo from so many rumors on the road to Winde Port. He was the rebel who caused it all. Again, the rage built in her, the storm now crashing upon the shores, tearing trees at the roots and foundations from the earth. She could feel Elsewhere reaching through her very pores, the energy desperate to explode out of her and claim vengeance for Wetzel and so many others.

And then Muskigo spoke again. "You saw those villages?"

Sora thought carefully about how she would answer, and as she did, she noticed the unmistakable pangs of sorrow in his eyes. She didn't know many people throughout her secluded life, but she'd seen that same look every time after Wetzel used to scold her.

"No, but we hear horrible things here at the center of the world," she said, trying to fight back the surge of energy in her fingertips. If she told Muskigo she was in one of those villages, he might know that she was as unimportant as the folks living in the Panping Ghetto. But she still wore her fine dress from the guild, tattered as it was. And he'd seen her with a wyvern, using magic like a true mystic of old—he didn't have to know it took leaking blood for her wounded body to summon it.

Use my assets, she thought.

Suddenly Whitney's lessons didn't seem quite so asinine. She remembered the way Muskigo had eyed her figure when he first saw her. The same way the boorish mercenaries in the caravan by the gorge did. If Whitney—the most cynical and sacrilegious man she'd ever known—could pretend he was a priest of Iam, she could pretend she was more than a girl from Troborough. Until the time was right.

"But I suppose you're right…" Sora said, edging closer and standing up straight, no longer cowering. "They've held us down for far too long. There are likely many of my people in this city who are grateful for your… interference. I would count myself among the lucky for my powers to be put to use against the petulant King and his crazed Queen Mother."

Muskigo exhaled. "It is good to see someone with reason. May I ask, are you from this city? I don't mean to presume, but… a wyvern… practicing magic, you don't—"

"I am not," Sora interrupted. She knelt and extended her arm toward Aquira. The wyvern quickly slithering into the crest of her arm, terrified. "I'm from Yaolin City, but I moved here with my husband, Tayvada Bokeo when we joined the Winde Traders Guild." She hated using poor Tayvada's name like this, but at least it may help her stay alive long enough to get vengeance on the man who murdered him.

"The Traders Guild?" Muskigo said. "I hadn't realized they took on people of your descent. You and your husband must have great influence in your homeland with the Order of Mystics dissolved."

"Late husband," Sora blurted, almost forgetting to hang her head in sadness.

Stupid, Sora. Remember what Whitney would do—keep the subject of your lie wanting.

Despite her mistake, the word "late" put a sparkle in Muskigo's eye which he couldn't mask even if he'd tried.

"I'm so sorry to hear that," he said. "I hope it wasn't due to this unfortunate fighting?"

"No, he was murdered. Some time back. But he lives on in Elsewhere, always waiting until the day I may return to him." A bit of truth never hurt the illusion. She wasn't sure if Whitney had told her that, but was sure she'd learned it from watching him. Tayvada was indeed murdered, and from her studies, she knew that her ancestors didn't fear Elsewhere—the spirit realm—the way the children of Iam and other gods did. To them, it was merely the next step in the soul's journey reflective of a life lived on Pantego.

"I hope that day is long from now," Muskigo said. The sincerity in his voice was unmistakable. "We came here to strike the heart of the Glass Kingdom. Yet seeing how your people are forced to live beneath them, the glory of your ancestors thrown aside, forced into churches of a God in which you don't believe, forced to ignore the flicker of power so many of you are blessed with—I see now that perhaps we have come here for more people than my own."

Sora stuck her chest out and stated, "Or have you merely come here for more allies?" She felt ridiculous, the way she fully annunciated each syllable like the men and women she'd seen in the guild that night. Like she'd grown up in some fancy mansion on the right side of town and not in a basement below a dilapidated shack.

Muskigo's cheeks went a darker shade of gray. "You see right through me…"

"Sora," she said, bowing slightly.

Muskigo returned the bow. "Beautiful name. Though it doesn't sound Panpingese? And your speech; even I can hear you have not the slightest hint of your home in your voice."

Sora's heart raced as she somehow maintained a stoic façade. She knew her chances of survival were slim if she didn't play her cards right. Maybe the Shesaitju were sparing her kind, but not those who try to trick their ahfem. Especially not those who wanted him to pay for his crimes.

"My parents were worldly, or rather… they had to be after the Glass Kingdom disbanded the Order."

Muskigo's dark eyes lit with wonder. "They were Council Mystics?"

Sora nodded and cursed herself inwardly. *Stop spiraling further!* All Whitney's dumb lessons were garbled around in her head, but she knew that the more layers she added to her lie the easier it'd be to slip up. *Simple is better.*

"What surprising things we find here at the edge of despair." Muskigo went to wrap his arm around her waist, earned a growl from Aquira, then lightly took her arm instead. Even the way he stepped was not so brazen anymore, which meant Sora had him intrigued... she hoped. The noblest man she'd ever met was Torsten Unger, and he was impossible to read.

Muskigo regarded her arm, sliced and bleeding in more than one location. "My men did this to you?"

She lowered her head. "They were not so kind as their leader."

"Again, I cannot express how sorry I am. What can a simple afhem do for a true daughter of the mystics to make amends?"

"I... I could use a good meal and some rest."

"Of course, where are my manners? If you waited any longer, you might mistake me for a Glassman. The men of the Black Sands treat our women as we treat the palms..."

His words trailed off there as if he expected her to finish. She tilted her head, then regarded Aquira, who was now starting to get more relaxed.

A crooked smile formed on Muskigo's face.

Is he nervous?

"...We never shake them."

"Now," he continued, "join us within the prefect's estate, and you'll have all the food and rest you need. And I'll ensure one of our physicians examines and cleans your injuries immediately. In fact, all Panpingese men and women are invited to share in the festivities while we will finish the work we've begun; bringing Yarrington to its knees."

Without so much as another thought, Sora took a step forward, and Muskigo's men parted, inviting her into the inner circle. They led her through the city, past the carnage of their wake. She'd missed it from the rooftops of the ghetto because Muskigo wasn't lying, his people didn't seem interested in that place. And her people probably barred their doors shut and closed the shutters like they did every time there was a ruckus in the better parts of town.

Glass soldiers littered the ground like trash. But not just them, civilians too. Merchants, chimney sweeps, anyone born west of the Great Ravine who got caught in a wave of Shesaitju warriors. A few of their ashen bodies stained the ground, but more of them stood. Hundreds, everywhere, being forced to stack the bodies of the dead on carts to wheel them off to

Iam knows where. Sora couldn't help but scan every single one for Whitney's ridiculous Traders Guild outfit.

"So many dead," she muttered. The air felt trapped in her lungs. She squeezed Aquira for comfort without meaning to, but the warm creature didn't seem to mind. Suddenly, Troborough felt so small and far away, and all Muskigo's talk of heroics, which actually had her questioning her dark desires, melted away.

"A forgettable foundation of blood for a brighter future," Muskigo replied.

"Are the lives of these people so frivolous?"

"That is an unfair word. Their deaths will be with me forever. It is the weight I bear, so others don't have to. But it is not only the lives of my enemies who mar these streets and will stain them further tomorrow."

Muskigo stopped and knelt beside a Shesaitju warrior, writhing on the ground, a spear through his gut. He extended his palm and one of his men handed him their sword. He leaned in, cupped the dying warrior's neck, and whispered something into his ear.

Sora knew what was coming. She fought her best intentions to stay quiet. With enough of a blood sacrifice, she knew she could heal him. It would drain her so much she'd probably pass out, but she could. However, it would show Muskigo that she was little more than a blood mage. Plus, why him and not another?

While indecision wracked her mind, Muskigo plunged the blade into the man's heart. Sora had to look away as the life fled his eyes.

"You see?" Muskigo said as he wiped the blade on his skirt and returned it to his guard. "You may look away, for only I need wield the blade that brings their end."

He rose, and they began walking again.

"You could have not brought them here in the first place," Sora said.

"They've pledged their lives to this cause and were all too eager to fall for the glory of our Caleef."

"It must be nice to be so devoted to one man."

Muskigo stopped and in doing so, brought their whole company to a halt.

"Caleef Sidar Rakun is no mere man," he said. "He, like all those who came before him, was birthed from the depths of the Boiling Waters and the churning sand. He is the embodiment of god."

"Which god might that be?" she asked. She knew she might be pushing her luck but couldn't help herself. As much as she hated him for what he'd done, as much as she wanted to give in to the power begging to leap from her body... so too did she hope to understand why her home had to be destroyed, and everyone she knew had to die. "I've heard of many so-called gods, but none of them have lived up to the hype."

Muskigo's dark eyes fell upon her. For a moment, she thought the man would lash out at her, bringing a swift end to her the way Kazimir had to her attackers. Instead, he laughed. "That does not surprise me, Sora of Yaolin City. You have not seen the likes of the God of Sand and Sea."

"I thought your Caleef is your god?"

"He is, and he is so much more. He does not hide behind a name or scripture like Iam, but instead, walks amongst us.

They started moving again over Winde Port's grand, central canal. She ignored the Glass Soldier lying face down on the frozen water but then, she saw worse. All down Merchants Row, the palisade wall surrounding the city was visible. The heads of soldiers dotted the stakes, overlooking where she and Whitney ate on their first day in the city. Her stomach did a spin.

"Speak your mind, Sora of Yaolin City," Muskigo said. Apparently, she hadn't been as proficient at concealing her disgust as she'd hoped.

"It's just..."

"Yes?"

"These people... what did they do to deserve this? The towns you burned. Those were lives, families, people like you and me."

They stopped again, and Muskigo placed his hands upon Sora's shoulders. She winced.

"This is war, mystic. You should know as well as any the consequences of battle. Are you too young to remember the Third Panping War?"

She wondered the same of him. His beard was dark and thick, and his skin was smooth—signs of youth—but his eyes held great depths within. Having lived in Troborough most of her life, she didn't have tremendous experience with Shesaitju. Did they age slower? She wasn't sure if Afhem Muskigo was twice her age or less… or more.

"My parents fled after the war, but I was so young I remember very little of it," she said, allowing herself to look up at the heads.

Crumbs of truth.

She didn't remember a thing of her true parents, but she had a single memory of her ancestral lands. Chaos and screaming… It was why she never cared to go back until her memories of Troborough were forced to be the same.

Muskigo finally decided to wrap his arm all the way around her. Aquira grumbled in disapproval, glare fixed upon the afhem's hand as if daring him to try hurting her. Sora again flinched at his touch, but she didn't fight it as he guided her away and continued their walk toward the palace.

"My father died at the hands of that wretched killer, Liam. To his people, Liam was the great conqueror—uniting Pantego under the banner of his God. In *peace.*" The word left Muskigo's mouth as if it were poison. "But what about us? Did we ask to worship Iam?"

"I suppose not," Sora admitted.

"And now they've imprisoned our Caleef. Would the Glass not have done worse to get their own king back? What would their crazed queen do?"

Sora remembered the bodies hanging from the Yarrington walls in the Queen's mad quest to save her son. It was her first, and she hoped only impression of the Glass Castle.

Before she had a chance to respond, they stopped in front of a beautiful two-story estate. Marble columns supported a balcony that jutted from the upper story. Vast, green, gardens were visible in the courtyard through the lower floors arcade—lush despite the bitter cold.

"Welcome," he said, spreading his arms. "My new home belongs to you. It belongs to all who have long suffered under a Glass boot."

The inside of the palace was as grand and luxurious as the exterior. In the center of the lofty greeting hall was a great hearth set in stone. Shesaitju soldiers sat around the blaze, drinking and laughing as if it were any other day. As if there weren't dead bodies littering the streets of a foreign city just outside the door.

Muskigo snapped and a handmaiden, dressed in clothing more appropriate for a desert than the land north of the beaches, approached them. He whispered something in her ear, and she bowed. Her face was covered by a shawl, but the skin around her eyes was creased with age.

"Now, I have business to attend to preparing our defenses," Muskigo said. "Shavi will take care of anything you need. We shall speak soon, Sora of Yaolin City."

He fell in with a group of gold-armored guards and left the estate. Sora was too overwhelmed by the majesty of the place to muster more than a faint curtsy to bid him farewell.

"Come, dear," the old handmaiden named Shavi said, leading Sora deeper into the place.

Sora followed along. She wasn't excited about the prospect of temporarily sharing the home of an enemy, but she knew it was her best chance at finding Whitney—her best chance because it was the only option that seemed to promise her life. With all the soldiers around, and the daylight filtering in through the great arches of the courtyard, Kazimir wouldn't be able to touch her.

She glanced down at Aquira, who looked up at her. Sora was no expert on wyverns or their facial twitches. Her frills undulated, and her mouth was crooked, with one sharp fang hanging out over her lip. She didn't appear overly nervous, and Sora couldn't blame her.

"Can't be worse than being drained by an upyr," she whispered to the wyvern. Then they entered.

XVII

THE KNIGHT

"By Iam," Torsten said. It was all he could manage as Winde Port appeared on the horizon. It didn't take long leading his army along Muskigo's tracks for him to realize he'd underestimated his enemy. A mass of refugees swarmed the hill. Traders and civilians, guards and dockworkers—anyone who could escape the port city before the wrath of the Black Sands fell upon it. Some were bloodied, many crying, others being carried with Shesaitju arrows protruding from their backs or limbs.

Torsten reached down from his perch atop his horse and grabbed a fleeing city guard by the shoulder. The man looked petrified, hands shaking and sweat pouring from his brow. "Soldier, what happened?"

"The Black Sands… th-they… they…" the man stuttered.

"Spit it out," Wardric grunted.

"They came from the f-fog… thousands of them." He finally seemed to remember the world around him and grabbed Torsten's leg. "My brother. He's still in there. You have to save them."

"We will," Torsten said.

"Only Nesilia can save them now," Redstar remarked.

Torsten glared back at the scourge of his life, then spurred his horse ahead of his army to get a better view. Every thud of his mount's hooves made the refugees shudder. He hadn't seen such frightened people since the Third Panping War, after their great mystics were vanquished and the people were left to clean up their dead.

He rode his horse up a promontory and stared down at the city. Words failed him at the sight. The late King Liam had once called Winde Port 'the key to Pantego,' the fulcrum upon which the East and West swung. It wasn't heavily fortified, even with the defensive measures taken after Torsten returned to Yarrington with news of Muskigo's betrayal more than a month ago. Wooden palisade walls now wrapped the city where it met land, though they remained unfinished at the city's north.

It wasn't anything insurmountable, and that was half the reason Torsten never expected Muskigo to center his invasion of the Glass heartland on it. But he had forgotten the Shesaitju of his youth—the ruthless, godless warlords whom it took every ounce of Liam's brilliance to defeat.

Glass Soldiers were hung by their necks over the palisade walls in the very same manner Oleander had used, some still squirming and alive. The heads of more soldiers crowned many of the pointed stakes comprising the wall itself, and piled in front of it were the decapitated bodies, fortifying defenses with a layer of flesh. Muskigo's savagery made Oleander's killing spurt seem like child's play. Blood rushed to Torsten's head. It was almost as if the afhem mocked her.

And yet, of all of it, that wasn't the worst. From his vantage, Torsten could see a fenced area protruding from the wall, surrounded by spiked barriers. Thousands of Glass civilians were packed inside a camp that appeared as though it had been ransacked. Innocent people tied together by chain and rope like cattle on their way to the slaughterhouse. Grayskinned Shesaitju warriors stood guard like shepherds over sheep.

Or worse, like butchers.

Not warriors, Torsten realized. They wore little more than tattered rags, and every one of them wielded weapons stolen from the Glass Soldiers. The young King had issued an edict to detain any Shesaitju civilian west of the Walled Lake, and in an instant, Torsten knew that these were those people, spurred to revolt by Muskigo's invasion and making it even easier for them to gain ground.

The King's edict, meant for protection, had collected all those potential enemies in one place. With that, and Torsten falling for the deception of

Marimount as the primary target, they'd handed over Winde Port on a silver platter.

"I tried to tell you not everything was as it seemed," Redstar said from behind him. Just the sound of his voice had Torsten clenching his jaw. "Nesilia is many things, but a liar she is not."

"I'm getting tired of hearing about her," Torsten growled, not bothering to look back.

"And I suppose your men will quickly grow tired of a commander who lost a battle without even being present. Where was the all-seeing Eye of Iam when Winde Port needed him?"

"Distracted by snakes in our ranks."

Redstar laughed. "Blame me all you want, but it was your scouts who missed this." He rode up beside Torsten and pointed to the coast of Trader's Bay, south of the city. A light mist loomed over it as it always had in this region. And within that veil of white, tremendous shadows loomed. "That is their fleet, dragged up the coast in the cover of night and fog by their beasts."

He was right. One by one they were being turned by zhulong and heaved into the water, completely blocking off the bay. That was how nobody noticed their fleet sailing in from the south because they hadn't sailed at all. They'd exhausted their beasts hauling their ships, siege weapons and supplies up the oft-rocky, and always foggy coast.

"Whispers. Rebellion. Spiders," Redstar said. Torsten turned back and saw him, calm as could be despite the horrors arrayed before them. "It is what lurks in the darkness that we fear more than anything, isn't it?"

"This is what you hoped for all along; to watch us fail, all because King Liam took your sister and gave her a life worth living in a place worth living in. Do you know why he and Uriah left you behind?"

"Because I committed the awful sin of seeking power that is freely available for those willing to grasp it."

"Because you were a wretched boy, more interested in playing blood magic than caring for your sister. It was your fault. She needed you in a strange new world, and you couldn't shut your mouth, keep your weapon down, and help her."

"Playing?" Redstar sniggered. "Tell me, Torsten Unger… King Liam died of a long, terrible sickness. I wore the skin of Uriah Davies, his

Wearer of White after the Goddess Bliss drained the blood from his body. Does that sound like a game to you?"

"Are you admitting to regicide?"

"Heavens no. But *my* goddess is just." He patted his horse's neck like their conversation was nothing more than talk amongst friends. "You were there that fateful day when your 'great' king stole a girl from her home and made her a wicked woman, hanging her own from the parapets. I wonder what will happen to you next?"

Redstar sidled his horse close and laid his hand on Torsten's shoulder. His other hand pointed with the flat edge of a dagger toward the bodies piled and staked before the walls of Winde Port. "How poetic would it be for you to join them?"

Torsten hoisted his claymore off his back scabbard and held it at Redstar's neck. "I could kill you right now for your words."

"I'd be careful if I were you, Sir Unger," Redstar said calmly. "My people are fiercely loyal."

"Are you two ever going to stop bickering?"

Torsten and Redstar whipped around to see Wardric. Behind him, the front ranks of the army stared intently. The Drav Cra warriors squeezed the handles of spiked clubs and spears. The eyes of the Glassmen darted nervously from side to side.

Redstar lowered his blade first. "Not bickering," he said. "Merely discussing strategy."

"Well, tell your savages to back off," Wardric demanded.

"Of course." He bowed his head. "The true enemy is behind those walls, after all." He shot Torsten a smirk, then led his horse back toward his forces.

Torsten could feel the tension in the air like a thick paste, and he realized the mistake he'd made. Driving a wedge further between their combined forces after allowing himself to be fooled was the last thing he needed. He wasn't ignorant to the whispers as they marched through the bodies of Citravan's slaughtered legion from Winde Port. Redstar's people, saying how Nesilia predicted this, his own, fearing that Iam had abandoned them.

"Wardric," he said.

"Yes, sir?"

"Set up camp on this hillside," Torsten said. "I will ride into the city."

"For what?" Wardric asked, clearly perturbed by the idea.

"I plan to speak with the rebel."

"You've already heard all he had to say at Marimount. Look at the wall. This man has no honor. If he gets the chance, he will string you up with the rest of them."

"Then the Shield will be left in your capable hands."

"Sir, it is the King's decision who serves as his Wearer of White." He shot a sidelong glare Redstar's way. "If you are lost, there is no saying who would replace you."

Torsten brought his horse right before Wardric's and leaned in close. "Barely a man outside the King's Shield has fought in a war. Even fewer of them against the Shesaitju, and already, we have lost a battle."

"That was barely a battle, it was a sacrifice."

"We lost to one hundred ghosts in the fog. What do you think is running through their minds, seeing that city overrun? It's exactly what Muskigo wants."

"How do you know?" Wardric asked.

"Because it's what Liam would have done—sewn fear until our army sees them as more than men. It started when they burned down villages during the sacred cycle of mourning. Lights in the trees. Fire. We only lost a handful of soldiers yet half of those remaining shiver in fear."

"Losing you won't help."

"No," Torsten agreed, "but it will show them that one of us Glassmen isn't afraid. Now, follow your orders." He sped off toward Winde Port before he could be dissuaded. Unclasping his cape as he rode, he raised it in the air as he headed straight for the gate.

A westerly breeze blew out from the bay, making the hanging bodies swing and bang against the wall like bamboo wind chimes. It also carried with it the fresh stench of chaos and death. Screams still echoed from the city as the Shesaitju's conquering of Winde Port was made complete.

Torsten instinctually reached for his necklace and squeezed the Eye of Iam hanging from it, the gift from his former king which he'd only once removed—never again.

And he prayed.

He prayed for all the poor souls hanging because he shifted all his cards toward Marimount. He prayed for his kingdom, King, and Queen Mother. And mostly, he prayed for himself. He brought his horse to a halt at the gate and swung his legs down, then removed his helmet, leaving his sword sheathed in its back scabbard. Approaching the gate with his hands raised in front of him, he heard bow strings creak and tighten in the hands of the Shesaitju glaring down at him from atop the wall. Chains of their new captives rattled from the detainment camp, the sound of whips ringing across the foul air any time one of them tried to speak.

"Muskigo!" he bellowed. "This is over." How recently had the situation been reversed? It had only been a matter of hours when Muskigo arrived at the base of Marimount threatening to bring the Glass Kingdom to its knees. Now, Torsten stood, the one looking up at walls—only these were far from a dwarven fortress. Winde Port's construction was slapdash, barely reinforced but for the corpses stacked before them.

The heavy iron grated open and the doors swung wide. It was only then Torsten saw that the Winde Port cathedral was defaced. The golden Eye of Iam atop its roof was shattered and all its intricate stained-glass windows just a latticework of shards.

Heathen monsters.

A dozen Serpent Guards, all clad in gold filed out, scimitars in hand, faces covered as if they were scaled demons from Elsewhere. From between them, rode Muskigo atop his prodigious zhulong.

His bare, tattooed torso was covered in gooseflesh from the cold winds and the blood of his enemies. And now that Torsten could see the man's dark eyes, he remembered how intense they were, like a storm brewing over the Torrential Sea.

"Do you like what I've done with the place?" Muskigo asked. "I took some inspiration from your queen, but the rest was me. Just one last finishing touch." His hands came out from behind his back, revealing the two severed heads he gripped.

Torsten recognized them.

One belonged to Winde Port's Prefect, Mortimer Calhoun, a distant cousin of the Nothhelms who'd presided over the city for many decades. The other was the city's priest. Torsten regretted not knowing the man's name, but the cloth covering his brow made his position unmistakable.

He raised them both by their gray hair. "I couldn't decide which would look better hanging from the gates."

Torsten stared at the gaping mouth of the priest and couldn't help but trace his own eyes in prayer for the poor soul. Muskigo shrugged and rolled them both across the mud and snow.

"So, I took both."

"You will pay for this," Torsten said.

"And here I thought you came to debate the finer points of decor. My lights in the forest were a nice touch, I thought."

"You won't last in there, Muskigo. This is our land. You'll starve and freeze until your own people would rather hand you over than keep fighting this futile rebellion."

"I don't think so, Wearer. See, news of your weakness spreads like wildfire across the Black Sands. Soon, all will throw off their shackles and join us. So long as we own the bay, we will eat like caleefs. And I may only just be getting acquainted with this city, but I've found the old prefect's estate quite hospitable."

Torsten bit his lip in frustration. "This doesn't end with you surviving, you must know that."

"Our ancestors believed that death in the glory of combat was the only way to reach the shores of paradise. If that is my fate, I will not blink an eye. Will you? Will your Iam forgive you all this bloodshed?"

"If it means stopping a monster?"

"Monster?" He raised his arms to gesture to all the swaying and decapitated bodies. "A monster stands beside your throne, and Iam rewards her by breathing life back into her son. I hear he whispers to himself in the night as if he's lost his mind."

"Enough, Muskigo," Torsten snapped. "It's time we end this. Let all those innocent people go. Face me, on that field, the right hands of our respective kings."

"You dare mention my Caleef whom you hold captive within your walls?" Muskigo swung his legs off his zhulong and approached. He too wielded no weapon. In stature, he was a head shorter than Torsten, but his entire frame was laced with muscle. And now that Torsten saw him even closer, he noticed more scars than he could count speckled amongst the white tattoos.

The arms of the Shesaitju archers, still holding arrows at the ready, shook as their leader stepped into their aim. He didn't stop until Torsten could feel the warmth of his breath.

"Long ago, Liam Nothhelm issued my father the same challenge," Muskigo said. "I was just a child then, you probably no more than a squire. And do you know what happened?"

Torsten's hands balled into tight fists within his glaruium gauntlets. He could reach out and break the man's neck if arrows didn't shred him first. Instead, he stood, unspeaking. Defiant.

"My father was foolish enough to accept," Muskigo continued. "He died that day, his afhemate fell, and the Glass Kingdom crept ever nearer to the Caleef's sacred seat in Latiapur, which, of course, was conquered as well."

"At least he had the honor to spare your people," Torsten said.

"The heads of the afhems were hung from the palms like so many coconuts. Our wives were cast into exile—likely raped by your savages. My mother took her own life in shame. All my father did was help grow the legend of Liam the *Coward*." He spit.

Torsten ignored the insult.

"Then defeat me," he said. "Prove you're better."

"There is not a doubt in my mind I would slice your throat open before you could even cry in protest. But you are not Liam Nothhelm. You are not even Uriah Davies, who, as Wearer, earned so many victories in the name of king and God. You are a disgrace to that helm. Nobody. Less than nobody—the hand of a murderous shrew."

Torsten reached for his claymore. The Serpent Guards unsheathed theirs in unison. The archers, whose grip had slackened, drew their strings back farther.

"Do it," Muskigo whispered, smiling. "Do. It."

More than anything, Torsten wanted to oblige him. His hand shook with rage. Sweat poured down his neck only to be kissed by the bitter wind. The entire city went quiet watching, waiting until finally, he lowered his hand.

Muskigo shook his head. "How far the Glass has fallen. Return to your people, Torsten Unger. Tell them they can bring Drav Cra, Panpingese, even the damnable dwarves… you will all die together." He turned to walk back to his zhulong.

"Do not turn your back on me, heathen!" Torsten ordered.

"Go back to your people and pray to your God," Muskigo said, hand upon the saddle of his terrifying beast. Raising one arm toward his throng of chained captives, he shouted, "Because the moment you try and retake this city, every single one of them will help me finish decorating this wall."

He led his zhulong through the gates, never turning to face Torsten. He did, however, snap his fingers and arrows zipped into the ground at Torsten's feet, purposely missing but forcing him back to his horse before it fled. As he pulled himself onto the saddle, thousands of captives were whipped and forced to move, bound together in bunches, and one by one sent to spread across the length of Winde Port's palisade walls—to sit upon the piled corpses of soldiers.

A human barrier.

Torsten could charge, his army could surmount the clumsy walls, but doing so would mean sacrificing his own people. And it was then, as his horse backed away, he understood just how long a game Muskigo was playing.

If Torsten brought his army east over the Jarein Gorge to maintain control over the Shesaitju lands, the Glass heartland would be exposed. If he stayed, Muskigo would dig in and sew unrest throughout the Shesaitju cities until the Crown's control over his conquered people eroded.

They were at an impasse. Muskigo denied his challenge because he knew that as well as Torsten did. There was only one clear choice for Torsten, impossible as it may have been. He had to do whatever it took to cut the head off the serpent. To kill Muskigo.

XVIII

THE MYSTIC

Sora stared down into the warm water of a bath in one of the prefect's estate's many luxurious chambers. Afhem Muskigo's handmaidens drew it for her, giving her no choice but to try it. Before she knew what was happening, she was spinning out of her tattered dress and covering her privates with her hands and forearms, simultaneously hiding the countless scars on them.

She did her best not to protest. A woman of wealth and circumstance like she'd claimed to be would have experience with warm baths. In reality, she'd never cleaned off with anything but running river water.

Aquira had no problem getting comfortable. She was as calm as Sora had seen her since the moment they met. She lay, her long, scaled body sprawled out along the rim of the opposite side of the bath. Her eyes were closed, tail and one wing hanging down, swishing through the water. Thin lines of smoke escaped her thin nostrils every time she snored.

"Go on, dear," Shavi said.

Sora sighed, then stepped in one leg at a time. The water stung the many wounds striping her body as she lowered herself. She gritted her teeth, the pain didn't last long and after it dissipated, was well worth it. The warm water was like a healing salve now that her adrenaline wasn't pumping and she realized how beaten and bruised her body was from fleeing Kazimir. She could draw on her own power and sacrifice to heal others, but she'd never been able to do the same for herself.

Kazimir...

Her eyes flitted toward the window behind Aquira. Sora had ordered them not to be covered by the cascading, velvet drapes. He was somewhere out there, hunting. The only thing that allowed her to try and stay calm was the fact that she was now in probably the safest place in all of the city. Wherever Muskigo was, those gold-clad protectors were with him.

She sunk back further until her entire head was submerged and the window was just a pale light beneath the rippling water. All the sounds of the world were drowned out. It was like she was weightless. She tried to close her eyes, but every time she did, all she could see was Kazimir's devilish grin.

So, from beneath the water, she screamed. She screamed at the top of her lungs until face was surrounded by bubbles. When she returned to the surface, it was like a weight being lifted off her shoulders. She could finally relax and enjoy a luxury she never imagined she'd know.

Shavi knelt behind her, grabbed a clump of her now wet hair, and ran a comb through it.

"Your hair is knotted like I've never seen, my dear," she said, ignoring the scream. Her voice rattled with age.

"I travel too much," Sora replied softly.

"A woman like you shouldn't have to."

Sora turned to face her so Shavi would stop brushing, startling the old women. "Does the afhem treat all of his guests like this?"

"I could lie and say yes."

"I just... it seems so wrong being in here bathing while people are suffering out there."

"People are suffering everywhere, at all times, my dear—"

"Sora."

Shavi's shawl lifted revealing a soft smile. "Sora," she said as if in wonder of the name. "Take every rare chance at reprieve you can. Trust me, I've been around a few years."

"As a servant," Sora remarked, then immediately regretted it.

"I am no servant. I could walk through that door anytime I wish, and not a soul would touch me. I've willingly served the family of Muskigo Ayerabi since I was as young and pretty as you are."

"I... thank you. I meant no offense."

"I take none." Shavi took Sora's hair and again began brushing it. "We women of the Black Sands may not be warriors, but the depths of the sea are not unreachable. Our men die in battle to please the God of Sand and Sea, but we bring those men into this plane through womb and water. We feed them. Ensure their houses do not fall. And a life lived in service to our people is as worthy as one lived in war."

"I'm sorry, I don't know much about your people," Sora said. In fact, the only thing she really did know is that their warlords like Muskigo were renowned and that his men slaughtered Troborough and all those other innocent villages, seemingly without a second thought.

"There is more to us than war, my de—Sora."

"It seems like that's all there is to anybody these days."

"It comes in tides like the rising of the sea. Men are born, they fight, they die, and we are left to make the ruin in their wake shine. And people say us women are powerless." She leaned forward and winked. "We're all that really matters."

"Talking another girl's ear off, Shavi?" Muskigo asked from the doorway. Now that they were out of public sight, he had furs over his bare shoulders. His scimitar hung from his hip, harmless.

Shavi wasn't alarmed in the slightest by the sight of him, but Sora threw her arms over her body as if she could even be seen over the gold-trimmed rim of the tub. Aquira sprung awake, flipping over and nearly slipping into the water. Her frills went back, and she showed her teeth at the uninvited guest.

"You should know better than to interrupt a woman's bath, Muskigo," Shavi scolded. No titles, no proper names or bowing. She talked to the afhem as if she was his mother.

"My apologies." Muskigo raised a bowl. "I came to offer our esteemed guest a proper meal before it runs out."

Shavi stood, walked over to him to take the bowl, and returned to Sora. She didn't even bow or offer thanks.

"Here you go, dear," she said to Sora.

Sora glanced back at the afhem before taking it. He didn't smile, but he watched with an anxious look on his face. His features only seemed to relax when she grabbed it as quick as possible so her arm wouldn't be visible above the water long.

"What is it?" she asked.

"A Latiapur delicacy. It was my mother's recipe."

"You cooked this?"

Shavi laughed. "That boy hasn't made a meal in his entire life."

"Enough, Shavi," Muskigo said. "Let her eat."

Sora took another look at the afhem. He still stood in the doorway, but she couldn't believe how eager he seemed. He, the rebel who had ordered the destruction of her home, who had sacked Winde Port and staked the heads of his enemies at the gates, was waiting on her… to see if she liked his food.

Sora cursed herself inwardly for feeling such pride over that fact. Her chin was held high as she raised the bowl to her lips and took a sip of the chunky stew. An involuntary moan of pleasure escaped her lips as the broth hit her tongue.

"Good, no?" Muskigo asked.

"Deli—" she cleared her throat. "It's not bad," she said, a bit of the stuff spilling over her bottom lip and down her chin. Out of the corner of her eyes, she noticed that he'd crept further into the room.

"You're a terrible liar, Sora of Yaolin City." He chuckled.

She looked back. He took another step forward but Aquira objected, soaring over the tub and up onto Sora's shoulder. Sora had to quickly lift the bowl to keep it from spilling. The wyvern's sharp claws dug into her skin, drawing pinpoints of red. Her body was so used to being cut she barely felt it.

"And your friend needn't be so protective," Muskigo added.

"She's been through a lot," Sora said. "We both have."

"I only sought to help clean your mouth with a meal that *wasn't bad.*"

He pointed to his chin. Sora did the same and realize a chunk of stew was stuck there. Her face grew hot—first, because she was blushing, then from anger because she realized she was blushing.

Keep it together. You're not a little girl playing princess. This man is a murderer.

But who was she to talk? Did she not recently trick a caravan full of men into aiding her and then rob them of everything they had? She considered the men in the caravan. It was the Shesaitju among those brutes who treated her with respect, just as Muskigo was now. But she also remembered what Whitney told her—how they were at the attack on Troborough ordered by Muskigo and did nothing to help.

They deserved it, she thought.

"Leave her be, Muskigo," Shavi said, continuing to brush Sora's hair. "Women are permitted to eat however they please."

"Of course, Shavi," Muskigo said. "I would never think otherwise. I simply want to be sure the lady enjoys some of the finer things our people have to offer."

"Well, *be sure* over there." Shavi pointed to the door. "How did I help raise such a man who would pry on a stranger in a bath?"

Now it was Muskigo's turn to blush.

Aquira crept down from Sora's shoulder as he backed away, but she didn't go far, and she kept her piercing yellow eyes on him. Sora took another sip of her meal. The stew wasn't quite like anything she'd ever tasted, and Wetzel had been no stranger to whipping together random concoctions for her to try. His famous rabbit foot soup could make a pig vomit, and his herb mixes, which he said would help her "unlock her powers," were even worse.

"What is this anyway?" Sora asked.

"Zhulong stew," Shavi answered.

"It's so tender though," she exclaimed. "I would expect zhulong to be tough." They were dirty, smelly, scary beasts. Not the kind of animal she was used to eating.

"You will find it is not only the zhulong whose outward appearance is a poor reflection of what lies inward," Muskigo said with a smile, lips crooked, all the confidence oozing off him as his commanding façade faded.

Sora nearly choked on her next mouthful. She wasn't sure if Muskigo was just being kind to her because he thought she had worthwhile connections in Panping, but now she knew it was much more than that. The way he regarded her wasn't lecherous like drunks in a tavern either. It was the same way someone else looked at her in those rare moments of vulnerability… Whitney.

"Anyway, I'm glad to see you are satisfied," Muskigo said, breaking her train of thought. "When you're finished, Shavi will find proper clothing and somewhere you'll be able to sleep."

Sora glanced up from the bowl.

"Nothing nefarious, you have my word. There's not a man within these walls who would trifle with you now that we are friends."

This time she actually did choke. She had to hit her chest to get the piece of zhulong to tumble down her throat.

Friends.

Playing this role was all fine and good for survival's sake, but hearing him call her that had rage mounting within her again. She could feel the water around her begin to boil.

"Sora?" Muskigo said.

She hadn't realized he'd been speaking, so caught up in her thoughts as she was. "Oh, sorry…" she muttered.

"I have more planning to attend to with my commanders, but I'm glad to see you cleaned up. Tomorrow, if you are ready, I hope we may discuss plans for inviting your people to this fight for freedom. I have been in need of a liaison with the ability to reach out to Panping, and I believe I may have found that in you. Sleep well."

"Of course," Sora said softly. "I'm looking forward to it."

He smiled again, that same reticent look that spoke of many more intentions than wanting an ally. Then he turned to walk away, a host of faceless warriors in the hall falling in around him.

"He's more bark than bite," Shavi said once he was gone.

"The headless bodies outside might not think so," Sora snapped before she could stop herself. "Sorry, it's just… seeing all of that… I remember what happened to my people."

"No need to apologize, dear. Sometimes when I look at him, I still see the young boy I cared for while his father was out fighting King Liam. He's not that anymore, is he?" She laughed, and Sora couldn't help but smirk.

"Not at all."

"No, but he is a better man than the horror you see outside. Now, lay back. I'll get your hair so cleaned out you won't have to worry about it for years."

Sora did as she asked. While Shavi went to work, her gaze listed back toward the window where the occasional scream of pain rang out thanks to the war outside. Perhaps Muskigo wasn't the horrible monster deserving death who she'd been imagining since the day she left Troborough behind, but just because he wasn't Kazimir didn't mean Whitney's views on people like him were wrong.

Lords and ladies always appear impressive, but they don't care a lick for the people they step on to get what they want—no matter how much they claimed to. Whether in the name of gods or freedom, the ends were always the same... and only the people suffered for them.

Even if Sora could never bring herself to be the one to drive a knife into his heart, she'd never help him. And she'd certainly never sit at his royal side and become a person like him. No matter how much of his wealth, wiles, or charms he threw at her.

XIX

THE KNIGHT

Torsten tested the ropes on a newly-erected tent. They were loose, the fabric flapping in the wind. What better could he expect from an army that had never set camp before? Untried. Untested.

He lay his hand on the arm of a soldier. "Stake those in deeper," he said. "Or you'll be sleeping in the cold."

"Yes, sir," the young man saluted.

"And you," Torsten pointed to another, "get a fire started. Staying warm is the difference between life and death."

"Wouldn't want the puny Glassmen getting cold," murmured Drad Mak as he strolled by, a cracked battle axe propped against his shoulder.

"Ignore them," Torsten said. "Out here, the Black Sands aren't our enemy. The elements are. The Shesaitju aren't used to being so far north. With Iam on our side, we'll outlast them."

"A weak god, for a weak people. You should hear their villagers squeal and run when my warriors arrive to take their crops. Not a man among them." Mak laughed again.

Torsten paid him no mind. He couldn't, even as arguing broke out between them and some nearby Glassmen. If he stopped every time one of Redstar's men insulted one of his own he'd be busy for days.

The men remained shaken by what happened at Marimount. The bodies dangling from the walls of Winde Port didn't help either. Nor did the biting cold.

Torsten sighed and pulled his cloak a bit tighter. He remembered something King Liam used to say to former Wearer Uriah, "War has no schedule, no fixed times of meeting. The better prepared army always wins, and it is a leader's job to have his men ready for anything, at any time."

Like most of Liam's lessons, it was quite simple, at least until panic settled in. And fear of loss and life. Uriah, however, was never rattled. He'd walk the camp before battle, and just the sight of him in his pearl-white armor was enough for Torsten to know they couldn't fail.

As Torsten strolled by, offering nods of encouragement to different groups of soldiers, he wondered if he instilled that same courage.

How could I after Marimount?

Riding fearlessly to meet with Muskigo at the gates might have helped, but until they defeated him in battle, Torsten knew he was no Uriah. Not even close.

"Hang the traitor!" a voice cracked through the nervous din of preparations. Torsten turned and saw a bit of commotion. He expected to see another brawl between Drav Cra and Glassmen but realized that a few of them stood side by side, yelling at something together. He hurried over.

"What is the meaning of this?" he asked, pushing some men aside.

"Look what we found, sir," a Glass soldier said. He had a Shesaitju on his knees and kicked him in the back so hard the man hit the dirt. "A rain-cloud sneaking about."

"One of Muskigo's spies, no doubt," said another.

"I do not know what you are talking about!" the Shesaitju man protested, earning another boot to his spine. He had the look of a fighter—strong jaw, hard body, only he wore furs and boiled leather armor that looked western in origin. His black lips trembled with real fear.

"And who are they?" Torsten asked. Also kneeling in the mud behind the Shesaitju were two identical-looking men in unmarked armor who were unquestionably mercenaries, a stocky, red-bearded dwarf, and an old man dressed in silks that appeared to have at one point been of excellent craftsmanship. Now his clothing was tattered and his features just as ragged, with all the others not faring much better.

"We be silk traders ye no-good, flower pickin—" The dwarf's rant was interrupted as Mak the Mountainous arrived to spit on him.

"Go crawl back underground, dirtmonger." Mak said as he walked by and went to punch him but Torsten caught his arm. He knew there was no love lost between the two peoples. Their lands shared a border in the north, and even though the dwarves lived beneath the mountains, that didn't mean their riches were any less sought after.

"Enough," Torsten said. Drad Mak turned, daggers in his eyes. Torsten didn't flinch.

The men halted their barrage on the odd group of travelers but kept them on the ground—especially, the dwarf, who thrashed and cursed in ways Torsten didn't think were possible.

Torsten approached the old man and knelt. "Who are you?"

"I…I'm a simple merchant," he stammered.

"He's helping the spy!" someone shouted from the quickly growing crowd. Torsten glared back at him, then turned his attention back to the merchant.

"I swear in the name of Iam! These men are my protection, Grint Strongiron's company."

"Who is that?" Torsten asked.

"Me ye dolt!" the wobbly-eyed dwarf barked. "Finest company west of the lake."

"A merchant?" Torsten asked. The man nodded emphatically. "Where are your goods?"

"We were on our way to Winde Port to meet with the Traders Guild when we were set upon by bandits. They stole our caravan, my wares, everything. We hoped to find them in the city, but then this…"

"Finest company, yet you were taken by a couple of bandits?"

"Wouldn't have happened if anybody listened to me," the dwarf grumbled. "Never stop on the road to help a pretty woman, I tell ye. Especially not a knife-ear witch."

Torsten's brow furrowed. "Did you say Panpingese witch?"

"I said *knife-ear*. Her pretty boy mate stole the caravan while we tried to help her. By Meungor's axe, that's what we get for trying to be good citizens."

"Keep telling yourself that Grint," the Shesaitju said.

"She wasn't no witch," another one said.

"Might as well've been, the way she conned ye," the dwarf said.

"Conned you, too."

"Not another word out of you, spy!" the soldier restraining him snapped and shoved him back into the dirt.

Torsten looked into the terror-stricken eyes of the old trader, then couldn't help but smirk. It wasn't that he endorsed thieving, but he had a feeling he knew exactly who was behind what happened. It was Whitney, the newly minted noble, and Sora, the Panpingese blood mage who Iam saw fit to use as his vessel back in the Webbed Woods, saving them from Redstar's wrath.

"All right, everyone off them," Torsten ordered. "They're telling the truth."

His own men looked at him, perplexed. Mak the Mountainous scoffed.

"The gray man stays," he grizzled. "By edict of *your* king."

"Don't you see what happened to Winde Port because of that?" Torsten said. "We're safer with him far away from here."

"I promise, we will go far... very far..." the Shesaitju mercenary stammered.

"Safer still with him dead!" Mak shouted to a chorus of agreement from all those present. "Why should we listen to you anyway? It wasn't the King's choice to go to Marimount, I hear."

Torsten kept his head high. "No, but that doesn't mean locking every Shesaitju behind a wall is right."

Mak laughed and turned to a crowd of his people. A warlock stood, emotionless, amongst fur-clad warriors. Torsten wasn't sure he'd fully realized how much of his army wasn't his own until then. How many weren't even faithful to Iam.

"So now the Wearer doubts his own king, the beloved nephew of Arch Warlock Redstar!" Mak announced. "Yet we're supposed to follow him into battle, bells on our ears?"

"He'll let the gray men slaughter us!" shouted another. "I say kill the spy!"

Mak brandished his axe while others held the trading crew down. Grint's company writhed and shouted in protest. The axe went up, but before it fell, Torsten swung his giant claymore to stop it.

"Enough!" Torsten's thunderous roar combined with the clang of metal brought an abrupt end to the fighting. "We are together in this fight, whether any of you likes it or not. King Pi shares the blood of both our peoples. Can we not work together to bring glory to his name?"

Everyone watched in silence. Drad Mak didn't let off his axe or soften his glare. The Shesaitju warrior scurried away through the dirt toward his crew.

"We'll play nice when you get on your knees, kiss the ground, and thank the goddess for your existence," Mak said, seething.

"How dare you speak to our Wearer that way!" the Glass soldier holding the dwarf yelled.

"He is nothing to me."

Both sides erupted. Punches were thrown. Someone tackled someone, and Torsten couldn't see much more in the cloud of dust and snow that formed as a scrum broke out. All he was sure to do was shove the dwarf, trader, and the mercenary crew out of the way.

"Winde Port is under occupation," he told them. "I suggest you head back the way you came." He regarded the Shesaitju man who was clearly shaken. Torsten was smart enough to know the man had nothing to do with this rebellion. Lost on the road without a wagon thanks to Whitney, they probably didn't have any idea there even *was* a rebellion. "And I'd suggest keeping him out of any taverns."

"Flower picking humans," the dwarf groaned. "This is why I prefer the Dragon's Tail. Let's go, boys. Leave the knights to their foolish quarrels." He gave the old trader a nudge, shocking the man who was busy staring at the brawl.

Torsten watched them leave, then squeezed the grip of his sword. The sounds of fighting and cursing were deafening. He went to turn, to demand order when a familiar voice stayed his hand.

"Better off letting them vent, sir," Wardric said, approaching on horseback from the side.

"They'll kill each other before we get anywhere," Torsten replied.

"They won't," Wardric assured him. "I've been thinking—yeah, I do that from time to time—if we lose, Redstar loses. The Black Sands will wipe him out as well and whatever influence he plans on gaining over the Crown will die with him."

"Is it wrong that a part of me thinks that might be preferable?" Torsten looked across the field to Redstar who was barely fazed by the chaos. He sat in a circle beside Freydis and a group of Drav Cra warlocks all covered head to toe in furs and small, heathen tokens and bones. A dire wolf lay at his back, sleeping. They had candles arrayed in a circle between them, lines of blood crossing between them.

"I fear that man's devotion to his goddess above any army in this land," Torsten said.

"I'm with you sir, but if we face all our enemies at the same time—"

"They'll pick us off like wolves, I know. Which is why I hope not to fight a battle here."

"But starving Muskigo out won't work."

Torsten looked up the hill they were camped on. A group of horses clomped in from the northwest along with a gold-trimmed carriage. They flew the blue of the Glass Kingdom, but flying proudly above the carriage was another standard—a family crest, a ship with a coin.

"Right on schedule," Torsten said. "Come with me, I have a plan."

They returned to the center of the camp where several tents stood in a defensive position. The King's Shield tents were more lavish than the rest, but Torsten was beginning to appreciate why. Most of the men of his order had spent years training. They needed to stay warm and well-fed if there was any chance of defeating Muskigo's rebellion.

A map of the Winde Port region was unfurled atop a small, round table. There was no need for figurines to show where Muskigo was. He owned the entire city, from Merchants Row to Trader's Bay.

"You invited me?" Redstar said as he approached, a gray dire wolf at his side. The giant creature weaved in and out of a line of King's Shields-men, making each of them quiver.

"The time to decide our next move has come," Torsten said.

"For someone so loyal to Iam, you spend an awful lot of time believing you have any control over our next move."

"A man who walks no path cannot be steered to a new one."

"A convenient sentiment." Redstar clapped his hands, then plopped down on the seat at the end of the table. A seat reserved for Torsten during war meetings. "Now, I can't wait to hear this plan."

Wardric scowled at him. Torsten raised a calming hand. A seat was no more than a seat so long as they all worked in concert.

"Muskigo is everything," Torsten said. "His ruse has inspired his followers to believe they can win even though they lost more than we at Marimount. He thinks he can dig in here and hold us while more Shesaitju rebellions spring up across the southern peninsula. And he's right."

"Sir?" Wardric asked, incredulous.

A flicker of interest showed on Redstar's birthmarked face. He leaned forward and started twirling the tip of his dagger on the table.

"To attack head on is to sacrifice the lives of his captives and a vast portion of our combined army," Torsten said. "I won't allow the King's people to die in chains."

"How very unlike your benefactors," Redstar remarked. "Liam would've trampled them himself if it meant victory. And my sister... well... we've all seen firsthand how she feels about her subjects."

"That's enough out of you!" Wardric growled. "If you have nothing to add, you might as well leave."

"Shall I take my people with me?"

Wardric bit his lip. "Just show some damn respect to your Wearer."

"My apologies." Redstar pointed his dagger with a limp wrist. "Proceed, my Lord."

Torsten caught himself staring at Redstar. Normally, one with such a grotesque birthmark covering half his face, making the eyebrow scraggily and gray, wouldn't have been so confident. Torsten had been waiting since the moment they departed Yarrington for him to drop his smirk, yet it seemed permanently affixed.

"Yes," Torsten sighed, tearing his gaze away. He pointed to a spot on the map: the heart of the city. "The prefect of... late prefect of Winde Port... lived on this estate. Our scouts on the ridge tell me that Muskigo's Serpent Guards stand outside as he makes himself comfortable within."

"A conqueror with taste," Redstar remarked, back to spinning his dagger. "I like him already."

"We have a chance to end this before it escalates, to kill Muskigo and persuade the Caleef to sign a new treaty aimed to spare his people the same fate."

"Sir, that estate is old as the Glass itself," Wardric said, "in the most well-defended portion of the entire city along Merchant Canal."

"And that's why we will come from beneath," a new voice said.

Yuri Darkings entered the tent and lowered his hood. His finely embroidered leather jacket could be confused for armor, but Torsten knew it was all for show. Just one of the puffy sleeves could feed South Corner for half a year.

The longtime Master of Coin was back where he belonged. No longer hiding from the wrath of the Queen, he was every bit the picture of the wealth the Glass Kingdom brought with it to the lands it touched. His gray hair was perfectly combed, mustache trimmed above his lip. But more importantly, he had the tanned skinned of a man from Winde Port where the sun shone but for a few months of winter and when the morning fog rolled through.

"Lord Darkings, I'm glad you could finally join us." Torsten bowed.

"Apologies for the wait, Wearer," he replied. "I didn't stop even for a bite to eat after receiving your message." He turned to Redstar. "Ah, and the royal uncle. I hear you are the one I should thank for talking sense into our young king and getting me my old post back."

"I have an eye for men of value," Redstar said. He nodded, but for a moment Torsten thought he could see a flicker of surprise in the man's features—as if Yuri's arrival wasn't something he'd calculated into his plans.

"Yes, well, Lord Darkings is from Winde Port," Torsten said. "In fact, before Liam named him Master of Coin for the whole kingdom, he served as such for Prefect Calhoun."

"How is the old badger?"

Torsten hung his head. "He is with Iam now." He decided it best not to elaborate on how Muskigo had rolled the man's head across the ground like no more than a worthless piece of trash.

Yuri traced his eyes in prayer. "I'm sorry I couldn't be here sooner."

"There is nothing anyone could have done. The man now enjoying the comfort of his halls is a monster bent on vengeance."

"And now, so am I." Yuri bent over the map and scanned it intently. He ran his finger back and forth, then stopped at a bluff a short way north of the city on the western side of the Winder's River. "Here," he said.

"What is it?" Wardric said.

"There is an old tunnel that leads out here, branching off the sewer lines. Merchants once used it to smuggle contraband before the Winde Traders Guild took control."

Redstar chuckled, purposefully loud.

"What?" Torsten questioned.

"Nothing. I'm simply amused by his use of the word contraband. You Glass folk are so terrified to admit what you truly are, it's maddening."

"And what is that?" Wardric said.

Redstar grinned. "The same as everybody else."

"Are you finished?" Yuri said before anybody could respond, a harsh edge to his tone. "I don't care what you are to the King, or what recommendations you stole from Sir Unger and claim as your own. In regards to me, you have no title, and you will not interrupt a member of the Royal Council again."

Torsten coughed in shock. Redstar's dagger spun too far and fell off the table.

"Now, if I may continue." Yuri cleared his throat. "These tunnels lead beneath Winder's Wharf and tie into the sewers leading directly beneath the prefect's estate. The Shesaitju haven't the luxury of building atop dwarven ruins. The sands do not permit sewers, leaving their… filth to be funneled through an aboveground system. They will not be mindful of the tunnels beneath them."

The man had a gravitas which even Redstar seemed to respect. Torsten had never seen him speak out much while Liam was alive, but that was no longer the case. Now, he was the oldest on the Royal Council by decades, old enough to remember when the Glass Kingdom only comprised a small corner of Pantego. When even Winde Port was a lawless, free-trading city without a Crown.

"Precisely," Torsten said. "Yuri has a contact in the city who will lead me and a small cohort of our finest men beneath the estate. We will end Muskigo's reign of terror before they know what hits them."

"And if you fail?" Redstar said.

"We won't."

Redstar stood and circled the table, his glare fixed on Yuri. "The city teems with gray skins. If any spots your torches before you make it, they'll be on top of you in seconds. Are you really going to hand me lead over this great army so easily?"

"No, because you and your wolves and your finest men are going to come with us. They will help Yuri's men navigate the dark without need of torches, and I've seen what you are capable of. If we're unable to take Muskigo down by blade, you'll bring the entire estate down around us."

"My, my, Sir Unger, now you're so willing to abuse my unholy gifts?"

"Countless lives are at stake. I have to believe Iam brought you to our side for a reason. But with our finest warriors working together, I have no doubt we will succeed."

"So, let me get this straight. You want me to sacrifice my best people for this impulsive plan, and if things go wrong, which knowing you they no doubt will, give my life for the Glass?" Redstar chuckled.

"If it's meant to be."

"My apologies, Sir Unger. But I must reject this plan."

"You don't get to."

Redstar chuckled again. "You see, Wearer, that is where you are wrong. I've beseeched my goddess for guidance, and hers are the only orders I will heed. She warned me you would send us on a suicide mission. She tells me that if we wait and pray, we will know the time to strike when the cold is driven away by wind and flame."

"You would cower back here until spring?" Wardric said.

"If the goddess wills it. Or do you forget the last time we ignored her warning and allowed Torsten here to lead us astray."

Torsten's anger was cooled only by noticing a few of the King's Shieldsmen surrounding the tent, watching. "The cryptic messages you concoct aren't a warning, Redstar. They are an excuse for cowardice. We were all deceived, and now is our chance to make it right. We need our best men to carry this out, yours and mine. That is an order."

"Unfortunately, I still must decline."

"That is treason," Yuri said. "You're worse than your sister."

"Careful, my Lord. Saying that, I might accuse you of the same."

Torsten looked down and realized he'd been squeezing his fists so tight his palms were sore. He stepped in front of Redstar but didn't draw his dagger. Instead, he stared into the man's eyes—the man who'd tried to murder him in the Webbed Woods, and had hurt so many countless others.

"Redstar, I know we don't trust each other, but this is our chance," he said. "Do it for your sister or your nephew. By Iam, do it for yourself. Even if we die killing him, you'll be remembered as more than the uncle who cursed a child. You'll be a legend, remembered forever for saving the lives of thousands."

"Just as Nesilia was remembered for giving her life so Iam may end the God Feud?" he said. "Excuse me if I have a hard time believing you."

"Forget gods," Torsten said, unable to believe his own words. He took Redstar by the shoulders. "Do this, and I will forgive you for everything you have done. I might even begin to trust you."

Redstar closed his eyes. His lips twitched at the corners as if he were picturing what it might be like to experience a triumphant return to Yarrington. Torsten thought he finally got to him until he opened his mouth again.

"Whilst I'm touched by your sentiment," he mused. "I cannot so easily throw aside the will of my goddess."

"Damnit Redstar!" Torsten released him and slapped aside a group of tankards sitting on the table. "What must I do to get you to fight beside us? Every minute, one of your people starts a brawl and you do nothing. You're a member of the royal family, and if you would just demonstrate the worth of this alliance, we could return peace to the kingdom."

Redstar backed away and strolled around the table. He stopped behind Yuri and massaged the man's shoulders before being promptly shrugged away. "It has been made plainly apparent that neither I nor my goddess are your equal," he said. "But my army is to yours, and they will follow me no matter what. We will not risk fighting again. I must obey my goddess."

"Then you are a coward!" Wardric slammed on the table.

"The King will hear of this upon my return," Yuri said. "You have my word."

"I'm sure he will," Redstar said. "Right after you tell him of my future victory. Now, you must excuse me, my Lords. We must continue praying to the one below so we do not fail again." He bowed absurdly low while leveling his gaze upon Torsten. It reminded him of the sarcastic way the thief Whitney used to acknowledge him, only this wasn't playful. There was something curious in the gesture—as if it were meant to be the last bow he ever gave. Then, he walked away.

"How dare you turn your back on your Lords!" Yuri hollered.

"Forget him," Torsten said. "If he wants to hide, then we're better off without him. I was wrong to stake our chance at victory on the foul powers he calls upon by blood and sacrifice."

"Agreed," Wardric grumbled.

Torsten turned to Yuri. "Can your man quickly lead us through the dark alone?"

"Nobody knows these tunnels better," Yuri said. He was stuck staring at Redstar until he became just another fur amongst the ranks of his people.

"Then take us to the passage. I will lead a cohort of Shieldsmen beneath the city and end this."

"No," Wardric said. "I will lead them."

"Wardric, I refuse to argue with someone else about this," Torsten said.

"Then don't. Redstar is a bastard, but he's right about one thing. This may well be a suicide mission. It's not like riding to the walls under the banner of peace. You are our Wearer, and I cannot in good conscience allow you to take on this burden."

"That is why it must be me."

Wardric pulled Torsten aside and lowered his voice. "This is exactly what he wants, don't you see? He's gambling that you will die on this mission and he can step into command. By Elsewhere, he might burn the entire city to the ground while you're in there just to do it."

"I know what he wants."

"Then don't risk it! I have served the King's Shield for decades—far longer than you. Now, I may not be the same warrior, but I knew Uriah and King Liam just as well. I never wanted to be Wearer, I only wanted to serve my kingdom. But now I'm asking you… use me for this. Stay behind with the army."

Torsten swallowed the lump forming in his throat. To think, he once worried old Wardric would be a thorn in his side when he took on the mantle. Now, he wished he had an army of the man.

"It has to be me, Wardric," Torsten said. "If you fail, Redstar will use it to contest my leadership either way. He wants the King's favor more than anything. He thinks me dying will make him Wearer but he's wrong. If I fail, it will be you who takes over… I know it."

"You know that's not true. Like we said, it is the King's dec—"

"What do you think I spent my time doing while you two were gone?" Yuri interceded. "The young King will heed my counsel. If Torsten fails, I will tell him who deserves to wear the white."

"And if I don't, even his own people will learn to respect us," Torsten said. "You've been to Drav Cra. They respect only strength, nothing else. They'll see Redstar for the coward he is when his beloved goddess is wrong."

Wardric looked to the ground. Tears welled in the corner of his eyes but he slowly began to nod. "Don't fail, sir," he said softly. "Don't fail."

"I don't plan to. Iam hasn't forsaken us. Not yet." Torsten pounded his chestplate in salute. Wardric returned the gesture.

And then, they embraced.

"I don't care what anyone says," Wardric said after they released, "you're as brave as Uriah was."

"And twice as stupid." Torsten grinned. "Look after the men while I'm gone?"

"Oh, I plan to. And if my sword accidentally finds it's way into Redstar's back, I'll say it was an accident."

"And I'll support you in that as well," Yuri added.

"Try to keep him alive," Torsten said. "I can't wait to see his ugly face when I return with Muskigo's head."

"I'll try," Wardric chuckled.

"Now, you know the men even better than I. Send me one hundred of the most experienced Shieldsmen we have, but leave some for yourself. No wolves. No dark magic." He shook the pommel of his sword, sculpted into the form of Iam's Eye. "Iam will guide us beneath the rebel, and we will bring him swift justice."

XX

THE THIEF

Whitney gagged as his feet splashed up shog and piss. The Winde Port sewers reminded him of the Fellwater Swamp… and he hated the Fellwater Swamp. A thin beam of light slashed in from the small hole above and the sounds of battle echoed through the tunnel. He couldn't help but laugh.

Did I really almost finally get hanged?

Of all the adventures he'd had since leaving the homestead, his last couple of months were the craziest. He'd been purposely imprisoned after accepting the world's stupidest challenge to steal the Glass Crown off the head of a dying king. A challenge in which he'd succeeded.

He'd been at the wrong place at the wrong time when the same enemy that now attacked Winde Port laid waste to his hometown of Troborough. He narrowly escaped but only thanks to yet another capture at the hands of Glass soldiers.

He'd been commissioned by the Wearer of White to journey into certain death where he was captured—again—by cultists before finding himself face to face with a Spider Queen goddess. He was spun up in her web, fought giant man-eating spiders… and somehow survived.

Now, he thought all that was behind him until the one part of the adventure that felt just like every other caught up to him—a spoiled, entitled, good-for-nothing, has-been constable named Bartholomew Darkings and his hired assassin from some mysterious land in the North.

Whitney peered upward at the slime-coated, moldy, dripping ceiling.

"Gods and yigging monsters! What have I done to deserve this?" he shouted. His voice boomed, his words echoing, returning to him again and again. He kicked the wall.

"Shog in a barrel." Now his foot hurt on top of everything else.

As he trudged through what resembled dwarven-dug channels, Whitney found himself wishing he really was far up north in the Dragon's Tail, gulping down tankards of ale. Those dwarves knew how to drink.

He glanced down at the ropes still binding his wrists together. They were tight, and it wasn't until that moment he realized pins and needles were running up and down his arms. He heard the squeaking of a rat, and straining his eyes, spotted the little critter gnawing on what appeared to be leather.

Whitney was proud, but not too proud to admit when he saw a good idea. Raising his wrists to his mouth, he began to bite at the ropes. By the time they unraveled, his teeth were in agony, but otherwise, he was no worse for the wear, and his arms were free of pain and restraint. He silently thanked the rat and sludged on.

There was so much going on in the city above that Whitney couldn't prioritize his own thoughts. Sora was missing. A hired assassin was loose with his knives trained on him, and the Shesaitju were overrunning the place.

Way to defend your cities, Torsten.

He'd missed being able to blame the once-and-present Wearer of White for his bad luck. Against all odds, it actually helped him feel like things were normal. And normal helped him realize that he was standing in the one place in the whole city that could likely get him out alive. The sewers had to run somewhere—probably straight into the bay. And since no good city planner would allow the muck he presently stood in to filter out too close to the city, he might actually find himself on his pathway to true freedom.

He closed his eyes and felt his chin sink into his chest. There was no way he could abandon Sora—even if there was a good chance she was already dead.

"Being heroic is a pain," Whitney sighed to another rat hunched over in a corner. He had made a decision to take on a partner when she found him in the western forest. Her training on thievery and the ways of the world wasn't done yet, he realized, ignoring the second thought that popped into his head about how perfect "On Thievery and the Ways of the World," would be for the name of a book on his life.

He resolved to not leave Winde Port without Sora. And to someday write a book.

He had no idea where to find her, but if she was in the city, he had two ideas. She was still in the Panping Ghetto, either captured by Kazimir, or she was able to escape in the chaos and knew that would be the best place to disappear. In a district where others looked like her, and where the fighting would be minimal she'd find rest. There were no soldiers or guards for the Black Sands to fight there.

His other thought was that Darkings had her somewhere in his mansion, waiting to sell her off to Kazimir as some sick gift after Whitney kicked the bucket... only he was still alive, which meant the blood pact was open and Sora remained Bartholomew's offering.

With newfound gumption and faith that she remained alive, he set off down the tunnels. At a fork, he turned against the slow current of the muck, toward where the smell was fouler and not diminished by the salt of the bay. He had to hold his nose. This was far from his first foray into city sewers, but the people of Winde Port who could afford it were known for revelry. Which made for smellier garbage.

He kept going until he reached a wider tunnel with a trough down the middle connected to one of Winde Port's many canals. He couldn't see which one, only that it wasn't grand enough to be the Merchant Canal running through the heart of the city. Shouting echoed from beyond it in too many languages for him to discern a word.

Whitney hopped across the trough and made his way to the canal. An arched opening led out to the frozen surface, and since from so low all he could see were stone walls, he decided it was time to figure out where in the city he was. He'd already been circling the sewers for Iam knows how long.

He lay back and pulled himself through the opening along the ice. Cold stung his back through his sodden shirt, but the fresh air was a welcome reprieve. He kept his legs spread wide to form a sturdy base on the ice, then leaped up and grabbed a loose stone on the canal wall. A drain pipe leaked icicles, and jutted out. From there, he was able to grab onto the lip of the canal and slowly pull himself up to peer over the edge.

He was at the opposite side of the square where he'd faced execution.

He stole a glance toward the coast. Even on the small portion of the wharf visible from so far, there were dozens of rowboats bearing the tan and black standard of the Shesaitju army. Hundreds of gray men lined up, marching down the streets, fauchards and spears erect. Dead and dying Winde Port citizens and soldiers were scattered throughout the plaza. The battle for Winde Port was already finished, and the Black Sands were in complete control.

A loud *thwack* drew his attention to a barbed arrow still trembling in a wooden docking post to his right. His eyes went wide as he spotted a cluster of Shesaitju warriors on their own, bearing down on him. Probably performing clean up duty while they secured their new city.

Whitney ducked just before another arrow zipped overhead. He leaped along the wall to another pole, then looked down. A fall from up so high might send him plunging through the ice to a watery doom. And if it didn't, he'd been leading the blood-thirsty soldiers right into the sewers after him. So, he did the unexpected, didn't overthink it because a second guess about rolling up into the open and he wouldn't have done it. An arrow slashed through his sleeve, drawing a thin line of red once he was up. He sprinted straight at the soldiers who emerged from the nearest alley.

A spear whipped over his head as he slid.

Just like running from angry Yarrington guards, he told himself. Only these ones had the intent to kill.

He planted his foot against the wall and shoved off. A scimitar clanged right behind him. Reaching the wall opposite he did the same, and again, back and forth until he'd scaled up to the tile roof.

The warriors chattered in Saitjuese, several pointing upward.

"Sorry to disappoint," Whitney shouted, "but I've a meeting to attend. Good luck with the whole invasion thing!"

As he cleared the lip of the rooftop, a spear careened through the air right in front of his nose. He rolled onto the flat of his back, taking a moment to catch his breath and keep his heart from bursting. Then, he peered off to his right and realized his mistake. Beyond the square, the army amassed, and it would only be seconds before he was spotted by one of the thousands. Or even worse… Kazimir. In all the insanity, he'd forgotten about the wretch hunting him.

He stood, backed up enough to gather some speed and then leaped across the chasm to the adjacent rooftop. Below, he heard armor clattering. He peered back over the ledge. The Shesaitju group had done precisely as expected, rounding the corner of the building Whitney had climbed to wait for him on the other side. He quickly slid down a balcony, dropped to the plaza, and darted back for the canal behind their backs.

He slid down the first docking pole he saw, earning a couple of splinters on the way. His feet tapped lightly against the ice. Enough to cause some shallow cracks. Whitney didn't bother to be careful the rest of the way. He clambered through the porthole back into the sewers, his feet digging out chunks of ice in his wake.

Darkness returned, and the awful smell returned with force. "Better than being skewered by Black Sands arrows," he panted, sitting in the stale water and happy to be there. Now that he knew how thoroughly Winde Port had been conquered, he knew there was no more surfacing to figure out where he was.

He'd have to endure the warren of tunnels and troughs crisscrossing beneath the city. He'd figure out landmarks—a misplaced stone here, a chunk of moss there, and rely on looking straight up through grates to find his bearings. His foray into the plaza had him all spun around, so he decided he'd head for the Darkings' mansion first. It was closer than the Ghetto, straight to the north, somewhere where it looked down upon the wharf with the rest of the city's high nobility.

Whitney set off. The deeper he delved, the colder it got. The ends of his sleeves were literally starting to freeze. He had to hold his hands tight against his chest to keep from shivering.

The smell grew worse too, like death and decay now. The corpses dotting the surface surely didn't help, nor the blood tricking through grates here and there. His eyes were fully adjusted now, able to distinguish between grime and blood. His sense of hearing was heightened as well as he listened for which direction the wind was coming from, which direction the bay was.

He'd always prided himself on his senses and their ability to get him out of a jam. When he was just a boy, he and his family had traveled to Yarrington to witness the Dawning at Yarrington Cathedral with a view of the sun over Mount Lister. It was one of the few times they'd left Troborough. At the turning of every new year, Pantego's two moons drifted side by side in front of the sun, blotting out its light like two eyelid's closing over the world.

His father made them get there early to attend the ceremony led by Wren the Holy himself. At the end, the High Priest made them focus their senses inward. That was what the Dawning was all about, a test at each passing year when, for a short while, Iam's light was blocked, and humanity was left to look inward to find it.

With their eyesight all but stolen from them, Whitney found he could hear snails inching along the wet ground, or the grass grow. Wren explained it all with his mumbo jumbo about faith, but to Whitney, it always felt like a magical power.

Then, he met real mystics and blood mages and realized it was nothing like magic.

The thought of Sora picked up his pace. He ignored the swishing of human excrement beneath his boots and tickling the hem of his pants. He'd been walking for what could have been minutes or hours.

As he shivered, he caught himself daydreaming of a warm bed and a blazing hearth. Without even being aware of it, he'd been imagining the Twilight Manor, the tavern and inn located in the middle of Troborough. Or at least, it had been there before the gods-damned Shesaitju came in and razed it to the ground.

Whitney's desire to drive a dagger into the skull of every gray-skinned bastard in Winde Port and avenge Sora grew. Torsten would be proud. "For Iam!" he would yell before hefting his absurdly large claymore high above his equally oversized head.

Something weird was happening, something Whitney wasn't used to. He found himself caring about people in a way he never had. Sora was a given—they'd grown up together. But with the occupation of the city above, he couldn't help wonder if the Wearer of White would arrive in time to save the day.

He laughed and shrugged the thought away.

Then, a sound not unlike an earthquake rumbled through the sewer and focused his wandering mind. Several screams replaced it when it stopped. Against his better judgment, Whitney bolted in the direction from which it had issued.

You're not a hero, you fool! Stop acting like one.

"I helped kill a goddess," Whitney said to no one but himself, then ran faster.

The amber light flickered up ahead, reminding Whitney of Sora's fire. As he rounded the corner, he saw the back of a Panpingese woman with long black hair, with the exact same stature as Sora. His eyes bulged until she turned around. He couldn't deny his disappointment. She was a bit older than Sora, and the man beside her was older still.

"Please," she begged. "Help my son. Help us!"

She shifted her weight, and the movement revealed a little boy, barely ten years old. He looked strangely familiar, but he could have been any number of beggar children Whitney had seen since entering the city.

The man Whitney presumed was the father was working hard to extract the boy from a large pile of crumbled stone. Whitney glanced up. The source of the noise was revealed in the gaping hole in the ceiling and the mound of stones beneath.

"What happened?" Whitney asked as he rushed to the man's side and began removing large hunks of rock.

"Cave-in," he said. "Must have been the catapults. By Iam, I hoped I'd never see another war."

"Then you don't know much about kings and queens."

Whitney kneeled before the mound of debris to better appraise the situation. "We're going to get you out of there, kid."

By the looks of the situation, he couldn't help feeling like he was lying.

The boy moaned—deep and agonizing.

"What are you doing down here?" Whitney asked his parents.

"Those tunnels lead out of the city," the woman said, pointing toward a crude opening in some loosely stacked stones. Beyond it, was a tunnel that no longer looked to be a part of the circular sewer-ways, but instead, rough and carved through rock.

"Our master is a cruel man. We thought we could escape," the woman continued. She bent over to do as much as she could to help remove the stones, but they were too heavy.

"You're slaves?"

She shook her head. "No slaves this far in the heartland, but we may as well be the way he pays us. That very passage was created to smuggle our peoples in and out of Winde Port after the Third War of Glass."

Whitney recalled that was how the Panping people referred to the Panping Wars. It made sense. In their eyes, Liam and the Glass were just foreign invaders come to take yet another land that didn't belong to them. They'd always made the excuse they were fulfilling the will of Iam—free them from their unholy mystic rulers—hog shog.

How many lives across Pantego had been taken in the name of some unseen god or goddess? Whitney had almost been one of them, fighting to find some cursed doll for a mad prince. Well, this wasn't going to be just another casualty added to a long list.

"You're coming out of there," Whitney said, even though he knew he should've just tucked tailed and run. "You hear?"

Whitney fought every ounce of his survival instincts, bent his knees, and grabbed a particularly large boulder. As he pulled, more dirt settled and the pile shifted, threatening to come down on all of them.

"Fate is determined to kill you, Whitney Fierstown," said a pitchy voice from behind him. "And you? My best servants. So sad it had to come to this... your boy always was my favorite. Never spilled a drop of brandy."

Whitney glanced over his shoulder to see Bartholomew Darkings, then back at the boy.

That's how I know him! He'd brought them wine after Whitney was forcefully escorted to the mansion somewhere above them.

"It's not the time for this," Whitney growled, continuing working to help free the boy. During his quick glance, he'd seen Bartholomew's one-eyed lackey. Whitney huffed a curse but didn't let it stop him.

"Fenton," Darkings addressed his man. "Mr. Fierstown needs to finally learn his place."

"*Fenton?*" Whitney laughed. "How proper. I think I'll stick with One-Eye."

Whitney heard shuffling behind him and fully expected to feel the clammy hands of One-Eyed-Fenton on him at any moment, but it never came. Instead, he heard a scream as the guard seized hold of the boy's mother and dragged her toward Bartholomew. He removed a hunting knife from his boot and held it to her throat.

"Turn to face me, or we make this father and son watch as Fenton does to her what he likely already does to her every night," Bartholomew said, eliciting a chuckle from Fenton.

Whitney didn't know if he'd ever hated anyone more than he did Bartholomew Darkings. The woman's husband wiped tears from his eyes and spun on Darkings.

"Don't worry about me!" the mother cried. "Save Ton'kai!"

Her husband didn't listen. He stomped toward Bartholomew, but before he'd come within a meter of them, Fenton's fist hit his stomach with such force he crumpled to the ground like his legs had disappeared.

"That's enough *Barty*!" Whitney shouted. "This kid is going to die if we don't get him out of there."

Bartholomew stuck a fat finger out toward Whitney. "I *own* that boy! If I want him to die, that is my choice."

The boy's mother was sobbing now and the boy, Ton'kai, had stopped making noise altogether. His pale Panpingese skin was even paler, and Whitney feared they'd already lost him until he saw a finger twitch.

"Fenton," Bartholomew said, "bring the thief to me. He'll die in these tunnels like so many of his whore-girl's ancestors."

Whitney clenched his teeth as he hauled off a couple more rocks, finally seeing the boy's legs, crushed and bloody. He bided his time, waiting until the perfect moment. Listening to Fenton's footsteps, he counted under his breath…

Three…

Two…

One…

He spun around, gripping a heavy stone with both hands. It connected with the side of Fenton's face with a bone-crunching crash. His knife flew from his hands, and Whitney snagged it out of the air as Fenton hit the stone floor. He wasn't dead, but he was definitely no longer an immediate threat. Bartholomew stood staring, incredulous.

"Whitney," he stammered. "Just calm down. We can work this out. Let's help the boy out, together."

"Lord Blisslayer, to you," he said, pointing the knife his way. "You're lucky I don't carve up your pudgy little face." He looked to the boy and then to his blubbering parents. "But we need all the hands we can get."

"You can't expect me to—"

"Help him!" Whitney brought the knife toward Darkings' face, stopping only inches away.

The worthless wretch looked like he'd pissed himself.

"I won't ask again," Whitney said, seething. He grabbed him by the collar with the other hand and shoved him toward the pile.

All four went to work. There were a couple of close calls, clouds of dust spilling down from the loose ceiling, but they managed to avoid catastrophe. When the final hindrance was removed, Whitney pulled Ton'kai out. His father grabbed him immediately and cradled him tightly. His mother sobbed louder when she saw the state of his legs. One was crushed and bruised. The other was bent backward at the knee, clinging on by a thread of skin with a bone sticking out.

Whitney turned his head to hide his retching. Out of the corner of his eyes, he noticed Bartholomew doing the same. The big tough man who treats his servants like proper slaves didn't even have the stomach to watch them suffer.

Whitney shoved him. "Lead the way," he demanded.

Bartholomew glanced at him, then at the suffering family. His lips curled into a wicked grin. "Your heart is going to get you killed."

A small stone whacked Whitney in the side of the head before he could react. It wasn't enough to knock him out—not with Bartholomew's flabby arms—but it sent him sprawling as the former constable took off into the smuggling tunnels.

"You said that about my tongue," Whitney groaned, rubbing his head. "Follow him!" he called to the family. "Save the kid."

The father passed Whitney, chasing Bartholomew, Ton'kai draped across his arms. His mother tried to keep up but fell behind, losing so much of her strength to tears. Whitney gathered his wits and gave chase, knife in hand.

Bartholomew maintained a healthy lead. Whitney was amazed that the man could keep up the pace for so long with all his excessive weight. He seemed as determined as any to escape the city before the Shesaitju killed them all.

After a multitude of turns, they followed him around a corner, the amber light of Celeste reflecting off the river outside. Bartholomew was the first one through but stopped the moment he emerged. Whitney soon found out why. Before him, stood a host of King's Shieldsmen. At their helm was one familiar face Whitney wasn't sure he wanted to see. Torsten Unger, the Wearer of White.

The first thing Whitney thought to do was grab Bartholomew and raised the knife to his throat. "Of all the smuggling tunnels in all the world," he said. "Here you are."

XXI

THE KNIGHT

"Get them to the camp and wrap his wound!" Torsten picked out two Glass soldiers escorting his company of King's Shieldsmen. They got to quick work, grabbing the injured Panpingese boy who'd emerged from the tunnels and rushing him up the hill. His parents followed close, faces streaked with tears.

"Now, Whitney, drop the dagger," Torsten demanded. Of everyone he'd have been glad to see emerge from their secret path into Winde Port, there wasn't anyone lower on the list. The thief held a dagger to the throat of a middle-aged man. He looked familiar to Torsten, but he couldn't place him. He wore the clothing of a noble… had the gut for it, too.

Whitney's eyes darted nervously at all of the armed King's Shieldsmen surrounding them.

"I don't think so," Whitney said, sliding the blade closer along his captive's throat. It was so quiet Torsten could hear the metal scraping across the man's stubble. "By the way, it's nice to see you, too."

"Bartholomew Shelley Darkings, what have you gotten yourself into?" Yuri asked before Torsten could respond.

Both Torsten and Whitney snapped toward him. Whitney stifled a laugh. Torsten's head cocked, his mind racing over how strange a reunion this was. Almost as if there were another, greater hand at play.

"You've been in the capital too long, Father," Bartholomew said. "This is the filth infesting our city now."

"So, this is your big, famous Pa?" Whitney said. "Kind sir, I mean this with all due respect, but where in Iam's name did you go wrong raising him?"

"How dare you speak to him like—"

"Quiet boy!" Yuri bristled. "You were supposed to meet us here to let us know whether or not the tunnels are clear. Why am I not surprised you somehow managed to find trouble doing even that?"

"Your son is the contact?" Torsten asked. He didn't know much about Yuri's family beside how fabulously wealthy they'd grown under Liam's rule. In fact, he didn't know much about many of the Royal Council, old and new. His focus, since the day he took the white helm, had been Oleander, her dying husband, and her cursed son. He made mental note to study those closest to Pi, should he survive the coming battle.

"Unfortunately, it wasn't enough that you allowed my favorite house in Bridleton to burn, was it?" Yuri said.

"I thought that was *your* house?" Whitney asked Bartholomew, barely able to contain himself.

"I swear, thief. When this is over, I'm going to revel in watching you suffer," Bartholomew said. "I'll boil your tongue."

"Pretty foolish thing to say to the man with a knife at your throat," Yuri reprimanded.

"Whitney, I know you're barely sane, but are you really going to murder a Darkings?" Torsten said. "In front of the Wearer of White, no less?"

"This one I might," Whitney replied.

Torsten sighed. He'd forgotten what it was like to deal with the intolerable thief Whitney Fierstown, now Blisslayer. "After all we went through, you haven't changed a bit, have you?"

"Why mess with perfection?"

"Whitney, for Iam's sake, just put down the knife."

"What, so he can stab me the moment I do?"

"He won't."

"Trust me, Shieldsman," Bartholomew said. "I would."

"You two are standing in the way of a royal operation." Torsten lifted his hand to graze the pommel of his claymore. "You will stand down, or you will both find yourselves occupying dungeons in the Glass Castle!"

"Relax, Sir Unger," Yuri said, extending his arm. He calmly paced before Whitney and his son, hands clasped behind his back. "What sort of mess did you get yourself into Bartholomew?"

Bartholomew went to speak, but Whitney angled the blade just under his chin.

"C'mon, Barty," Whitney said. "Tell him."

"If you insist. This whelp masqueraded as a blind priest of Iam before burning down the Bridleton estate."

Torsten's jaw dropped when he heard that. He knew Whitney was no favored son of Iam, but posing as a priest?

"Then, he stole my mother's—your wife's—favorite necklace, and who knows what else," Bartholomew continued. "Is that not enough?"

"Okay, I admit that sounds bad," Whitney said, "but burning down the house was an accident."

"An accident carried out by a Panpingese witch illegally practicing blood magic!"

"A priest?" Torsten mouthed, barely able to get the word out.

"That's the part you…" Whitney caught himself. "Look, none of it was my finest moment, but we were desperate."

"To steal from my dead mother!" Bartholomew bellowed. He turned his head to get a glimpse of Whitney, ignoring the knife as it drew a thin line of red across his neck.

"I can promise you that pendant saved everyone's life in the Webbed Woods when we…" Whitney turned to Torsten. "Am I allowed to say, or…"

"These are high crimes, Whitney Fiersto—" Torsten's glare shut him up halfway through correcting the name. "And that's besides me wanting no explanation of why you were deceiving the people of Bridleton when we were on a sworn quest to find the Queen's brother! You should be hanged, not thrown in a cell."

"Trust me, I tried," Bartholomew sneered.

"Quiet you," Whitney said, wrenching the man's head back into place.

Yuri held up both hands to silence everyone before the yelling continued. Torsten had plenty more he wanted to say, considering

Whitney had abandoned him in their quest to play thief in Bridleton for a time.

"Are you referring to the pendant I gave your mother on her half-century? The piece of heartstone hewn from Brike's Passage in the Dragon Tail?"

Bartholomew nodded.

"Then you should have guarded it better!"

"Father I—" Bartholomew stammered, smug smile disappearing.

"Don't speak," Yuri cut his son off. "Do not speak. We are Darkings men. We don't stoop to the level of thieves and brigands, yet here he is with a knife at your throat rather than running from your justice. So I'm going to ask once because I have no idea… what have you been up to in my city? And do not lie."

Whitney actually felt a lump bobbing in Bartholomew's throat. "I've been trying to track this man down so I may return mother's necklace."

"Really?" Whitney asked. "Because for all your dungeon-throwing, gallows-hanging, and speech-giving, this is the first I've heard of it."

"Because who knows what a monster like you would have done with it if you knew it meant something."

"I don't care about a necklace!" Yuri roared.

Torsten felt the hair on the back of his neck stand. He had no idea a man with hair so gray could have a voice that carried so thunderously. Even the eyes of the other King's Shieldsmen watching went wide.

"Tell me, thief, what slight did my hopeless son offer you?" Yuri asked. "We must all move on and focus on this war."

"Lord Darkings, I know this man," Torsten whispered in Yuri's ear. "I'm sure your son has good reason."

Yuri's only response was to hold up a finger before turning back to Whitney and Bartholomew. Torsten wasn't used to being dismissed like that by anyone but the Queen, however, he allowed Yuri this one. He had no son, so he didn't know what it was like to be disappointed in one.

But he did know Whitney. The thief was a man capable of instilling an endless well of disappointment.

"Well, for starters, he treats his servants like common kitchen trash," Whitney said. "Oh, and he hired a Dom Nohzi to kill me in exchange for Sora. So there's that."

Yuri took a hard step forward and raised his hand with the intention of collaring his son. Whitney reeled them back and further angled his blade.

"You went to the Dom Nohzi?" Yuri asked, face flush with unbridled rage.

"The assassins from Brekliodad?" Torsten asked. He'd never dealt with the order of legal killers, as their lands were beyond the realm of Glass, but he knew of them. It was said they were richer than any kingdom or guild after centuries of killing. That they had toppled kings of old without a soul knowing.

"I told you about this runt," Bartholomew said. "You were too busy to listen, so I took things into my own hands. This man assaulted our family."

"The Dom Nohzi are animals!" Yuri shouted. "We deal in gold, not blood, favors and whatever else they ask for. Do you know what it means to hand them your blood? If you do not hold up your end of the pact, even if it isn't your fault, they can find you anywhere in Pantego and make things even. You will have tied my hands!"

"And you promised him Sora?" Whitney said. He chuckled. "If I know her, she's probably already slipped him, and now he'll be coming for you."

Torsten saw a flicker of doubt on Whitney's face even as he tried to act brashly. It'd always been evident that he cared for the blood mage—as much as a thief could care for anything—which meant there was no question of how much danger she was in.

"Whitney," Torsten said. Three sets of eyes darted to face him as if he'd set off an explosion. "Maybe we can all find a way out of this."

"I can't imagine where this is going." He rolled his eyes.

"Sora is still in the city?"

Whitney nodded. "Wherever that killer is keeping her."

"Where is that, Bartholomew?" Yuri demanded.

"You think I know?" Bartholomew answered. "The Dom Nohzi find you or invite you, they don't get dropped in on, and they're always on the move."

"He can't have her until I'm dead, or something," Whitney said. "So he can't run even if he wants to. That's how their deals work, right?"

Bartholomew kept his mouth shut.

"Answer him!" Yuri hissed.

"Yes, that's how it works," Bartholomew hissed. "This one is loose with the rules though. He probably already had his way with her and tossed her in the bay."

"How many stories did I tell you about the Dom Nohzi growing up boy?" Yuri hissed.

"Too many," Bartholomew said. "How do you think I found him?"

"Then you know, until he kills the promised target, he would not dare."

"You're sure she's alive?" Whitney asked, eyes glinting.

"I'm sure that my son is an idiot. But they are as strict as they are exacting. The man will hunt you to the ends of the known world to fulfill the blood pact."

"Can it be rescinded?" Torsten asked.

"Once the pact is made? I don't know. You are among a very lucky few. The Dom Nohzi typically act swifter than a man can reconsider and are usually not interrupted by war."

"Bartholomew?"

"I don't know," he grumbled.

"You will draft a writ immediately, informing them that the deal is annulled," Torsten said. "You will offer to compensate them for time lost, and Whitney and his friend are to live."

"After everything he's done? I'd rather die."

"This is not a debate!" Torsten thundered. "The Dom Nohzi are killers, but from what I've read, they are honorable. The blood pact is over by command of King Pi's Royal Council, and they will obey it."

"I knew I liked this guy," Whitney remarked.

"I'm not finished. Burning the home of a noble and robbing him of his mother's heirloom? Posing as a priest? When I had the Master of Rolls ennoble you, I was unaware of these unspeakable atrocities."

"About that," Whitney said with a sly grin. "Any chance the Master of Rolls can draft up a new one? *Someone* burned what was apparently the only copy."

"I can't say you didn't deserve it," Torsten said. "But no son of Iam deserves to die without fair trial. And so, as punishment, you will help us in our quest to end this war. You will lead us back through these tunnels and create a distraction like I know only you are capable of. Cover our ambush."

Torsten looked to Yuri. "This is our best chance at Muskigo, and the more men drawn from his side, the more exposed he'll be."

"You expect me to go back in there?" Whitney asked.

"I do. Sora is still in there, and if you do this, I will ensure that when we retake the city, we search for her, and present the assassin with Bartholomew Darkings' resignation."

"And if I say no?"

"Then you will be arrested for high crimes, nobleman or not. I'm growing tired of seeing you in a cell, but I will make sure the next is one you won't escape from."

"You can't be serious," Bartholomew groaned. "This man can't be trusted! Father, it was my duty to lead them through these tunnels. I've played in them since I was a child, nobody knows them better than I."

"Played?" Whitney said. "Did you push children in front of collapsing walls back then, too?"

"Enough Whitney," Torsten said.

"I'm just saying. I've seen how this guy likes to pla—"

"I said, enough! If Lord Darkings agrees, that is how this is going to go. You've insulted the wrong family, Whitney, but here is a chance, once again, to show that you're out for more than yourself."

"I agree," Yuri said. "Clearly I can't let my son out of my sight for even a minute. If you think the thief can lead you back through and under the prefect's estate, then I won't stand in the way."

Torsten stared into Whitney's eyes. They were full of terror no matter how hard he tried to mask it. Torsten wasn't sure why he trusted Whitney wouldn't lead them astray, yet he did. Reuniting with him like this, with everything in the balance… it really did feel like something—someone—greater was at work.

"Sure, I can," Whitney said. "But are you really sure you want to go back in there? I've seen it Torsten. It's a war zone."

"I have no choice," Torsten said. "But you do. If you won't help to serve your kingdom, then at least do it for her. I've seen the way you look at her, Iam knows why. If we don't retake Winde Port, there isn't a soul in there that'll be safe."

"You have to be kidding me," Bartholomew said. "Father, you're really going to leave this in the hands of this scoundrel?"

Yuri didn't even bother to respond.

Whitney started to let up on his grip of the man, his dagger sliding down to around his shoulder. "You promise you'll help me look for Sora?"

"To any extent I can, *after* we handle Muskigo," Torsten said.

"No, you have to swear on him. Swear to Iam, and I'll give you the best yigging distraction anyone's ever seen."

"My word is my bond," Torsten said.

"You bond needs to be stronger if I'm going back into that shoghole."

"You're not in a place to bargain, thief."

Whitney slowly brought the dagger back to Bartholomew's throat.

Torsten growled. "Forgive me, Iam." He fell to a knee and traced his eyes with his fingers. "I swear to Iam, beneath the Vigilant Eye. Help me, and you have my word."

Whitney's gaze arced across the faces of all the King's Shieldsmen, then to Yuri, and back to Torsten. His hand momentarily tensed, then he chuckled and pushed Bartholomew away.

"You son of a—" Bartholomew whipped around but was promptly seized by his father. Yuri took him by the ear like he was a petulant child and drove him to his knees.

"My son will draft the annulment at once," Yuri said, twisting further.

Whitney watched gleefully as Bartholomew moaned in pain, slapping the ground.

"With my seal upon it," he continued, "the Dom Nohzi are more likely to acquiesce. You've placed me in a precarious situation, boy. We can only hope they don't ask anything of me in exchange, or for your worthless life."

"Thank you, Lord Darkings," Torsten said. "For everything."

"I live to serve the Crown, my Wearer. Thank you for suffering through this family matter."

Torsten strode forward and took Whitney by the arm. It almost felt a dream that the thief was back in his life until he touched him. The Webbed Woods, Bliss… it had only been a month, but it all seemed like eons ago considering how much had changed since then. Again, Torsten was placing the kingdom's future in the hands of a thief, but he was never one to ignore the silent hand of Iam at work.

"Are you ready for another quest in the name of the Glass, Blisslayer?" Torsten asked. As the words left his lips, he couldn't even believe how accepting he was of the notion.

Whitney shrugged. He was still busy marveling as Bartholomew received the punishment he so deserved. "Just let me enjoy this for a few more minutes," he said, "then we can go be heroes again."

XXII

THE THIEF

"So, this is what it feels like to lead an army," Whitney said, glancing back at the line of King's Shieldsmen. It was impossibly dark, but a few pricks of light filtering in through cracks above allowed him to see their gleaming armor. Torsten wore his white helm, face guard open, which meant things were serious.

"Feels good," Whitney continued. "Maybe if you die up there…"

"You're lucky to not be living out the rest of your days in a cell, thief," Torsten replied. The word came out with extra venom as he stepped over a lumpy pile of something in the narrow passage. All that he could be sure of was it didn't smell good.

"Oh, c'mon, we've got to be on a first name basis by now."

Torsten gave him a grunt, nothing more. Whitney knew the big lug was glad to see him though. There was no reason the King's Shield needed Whitney to lead them through these secret passages when a Darkings could do it, which meant Torsten must have trusted him more.

The thought had him grinning.

"Think you could get me on royal retainer?" he said. "You know, for whenever you need my special skills?"

Torsten scowled but didn't answer.

Whitney led them further through the warren of smuggling tunnels, trying to remember the path he'd taken following Bartholomew. He was nearly at the point of praying he'd led them the right way through the stifling darkness when they reached a break.

Rock turned to carved stone, buried tunnels intended for sneaking horrible things became sewers intended for shipping shog. A false wall of stone blocks lay dislodged and around the corner. Whitney raised a hand. The troop stopped behind him. He craned his neck to hear better. Something was wheezing just on the other side.

"What is it?" Torsten asked.

"Wait here."

He hurried through the opening. What sounded like wind weeping through cracks was really Fenton on his hands and knees trying to gather his bearings. A few thin lines of light seeped in through a ruptured portion of the ceiling above. He saw the wet spot of blood where Ton'kai nearly died. Whitney couldn't help but hope Kazimir would decide to end that fat slob Bartholomew when he caught wind of the proposed annulment.

He patted his pocket to make sure the papers hadn't fallen out into the muck below.

Fenton looked up at him, eye lulling, blood coating the side of his head. "You… it's—"

Whitney kicked him hard in the head. His body flopped over onto the collapsed rock, unconscious again.

"The first one was for them," Whitney said, shaking out his foot, "but that was for me."

"Who was that?" Torsten questioned. He appeared behind Whitney, sword in hand.

"Nobody now."

"Whitney."

"Just one of Darkings' boys who deserved way worse."

Torsten grabbed Whitney by the arm and forced him back to the front of the line. "No more games, Whitney. I want you in front at all times. Is that clear?"

"Fine, fine. I got it out of my system anyway." He pointed to the right, into the sewer tunnels, toward where the air smelled fouler. "This way is the city sewer system. I don't think any gray skins saw me go down here but we should be on the lookout."

"I wouldn't worry about that," Torsten said. "The invasion is complete. As far as they or anyone else knows, the sewers are confined to the city limits and empty into the bay, which they control. They'll be covering exits, but no longer the tunnels themselves."

"How do you know that?"

"Their focus is defense. They're digging in to wait out the winter."

"Just be on the lookout."

Torsten regarded the King's Shieldsmen at his back. "These are the finest warriors the Glass has to offer. *If* we see anyone, they won't live long enough to bring word to a soul."

"It's your funeral. We run into trouble, I'll be swimming across the bay."

They continued, now wading through slosh. Whitney was more accustomed to the smell this time, but behind him, he heard a few of the King's Shieldsmen gag. Torsten, however, was barely affected.

Maybe he really did grow up in South Corner.

"I just don't understand, Whitney," Torsten said after a while.

"What's that?"

"You proved yourself worthy of a new name. You helped save so many people from Redstar and that beast. How could you so quickly return to your shystering ways?"

"'Once a thief, always a thief.' You know the saying."

"Enough of your foolish jokes. I am your Wearer, and I'm being serious."

"As am I, Shieldsman. You may have been born in the shog, but you've been living pretty for most of your life. I'm not ashamed of who I am. Made a name for myself and it's my name to do what I want with."

"Do not presume to know a thing about how I've lived," Torsten said.

"All I'm saying is I'm going to do what's right for me."

"All sin can be traced back to selfishness," Torsten said.

Whitney spread his arms and looked toward the ceiling. "Then Iam strike me down."

Torsten slapped his hands down. "He might. You posed as a priest. What greater sin could you commit?"

"I could think of a few." He sighed. "I do what I must to survive. You weren't too concerned about my practices when it benefited you and the

Crown back there in the Webbed Woods. And you don't seem too concerned now, sneaking through hidden tunnels toward the prefect's estate, not even concerned about how I know my way there."

"I do what I must for my kingdom," Torsten countered. "If that means placing my trust in you, then I can only walk the path Iam puts before me."

"I'll tell you this, if there is an Iam, and I'm not saying I believe in any of that mumbo-jumbo, he's got a great sense of humor because he keeps bringing us together."

"Indeed."

"I mean, here I thought I'd never get to see your dour face ever again, and there you are, right in front of me when I'm about to exact my vengeance on old Bart Darkings."

"There is no road back from murder, Whitney. If I stopped you from crossing that line, then I too am glad we had to be reunited."

"Aww, touching sentiment," Whitney reached back and rubbed Torsten's pauldron. He earned a glare that sent his stomach sinking into his ass. "Wouldn't be my first time killing. I took a few of these gray men down back in Troborough. I'm not sure if your men told you the stories before they captured me."

"They left out the details." What followed was a sound Whitney couldn't quite place.

"Is that a chuckle I hear?"

"No," he said, stern. "Besides, that's not the same. That was battle. Kill or be killed. But to slit the throat of an unarmed man... it's something you can't undo."

Whitney looked back, met by Torsten's thousand-meter stare.

"You say that like you have experience," Whitney said.

"There are many things I've had to do in the name of king and Crown. Not all of them bring joy to think of. Not all of them make me proud. All I can hope is that when Iam receives me at the Gate of Light, he sees my intentions were pure."

"If you don't wind up in Elsewhere," Whitney offered.

"If I do, I'll spend the rest of eternity haunting you. And maybe one day, I'll make you into a decent man."

"I don't think eternity is long enough for that."

This time, Whitney was confident he heard a chuckle. He wasn't sure why he felt so proud at that. Maybe because it'd never once happened during their quest to the Webbed Woods. Or perhaps it was that he knew, as well as Torsten, that beneath all their bickering, there was a bond. The kind only a team who had battled a giant spider goddess together could forge.

"Giant spider goddess," Whitney said under his breath with a laugh.

"What's that?" Torsten asked.

"Nothing."

Whitney stopped when they reached the widest tunnel yet. A flowing trough ran down its center, flanked by branching tunnels. If the Shesaitju were anywhere in the sewers, this was where they'd be. But there was nothing except scurrying rats hiding from the cold.

Short bridges led over the stream of water and shog which emptied out through a porthole into Winde Port's largest canal along Merchants Row. Whitney stared through the barred opening. He could see the many gray legs of an army marching by on the walkway above. It was only then he realized if a single soldier spotted them, they'd be slaughtered.

"We're in the heart of the city now," Whitney said. He pointed to the porthole. "That's the Merchants Canal. If you follow that, the prefect's estate should be up a ways, somewhere on the north side."

"You're sure?" Torsten asked.

"Chasing Darkings down here wasn't my first run through the Winde Port sewers. I've been getting into trouble here since before you were Wearer."

"That's only been a year."

"Then way before. See how experienced I am?"

Torsten exhaled through his teeth. "How far up do we go?"

"Without being able to pop my head through that grate? Beats me."

Torsten gave him an encouraging look and nodded his head toward the opening.

"No way, not again," Whitney said, shaking his head. "I got you here without a hitch. You can check all the offshoots until you're under the courtyard. You've probably been there, so you'll recognize it. Lowly thieves aren't usually invited to meet prefects."

"Fine."

"Then this is where we split up. The wharf is down that way, and I have a plan that'll get every eye in Winde Port on them."

"Just don't destroy the city."

"When Whitney Blisslayer gets hired to make a distraction, he goes all out. You don't get to hold me back now." Whitney turned to walk away and felt a heavy gauntlet on his shoulder.

"Iam willing, we will meet up after the fighting is through." Torsten's tone was solemn, heartfelt. Whitney was sure it was the first time he'd ever spoken to him that way. "Do not die, thief."

"Let me worry about dying. I have a great plan for when that day arrives, and it isn't today. Just wait for my signal."

"How will I know?"

Whitney sighed. "Haven't you ever done this before? The answer is always, 'you'll just know.' I take distractions seriously."

"I'm sure you do." Torsten went to turn, and this time Whitney grabbed him.

"But remember, I'm not doing this for free. Sora is up there somewhere, and you gave your word that you'll help me find her after you end Muskigo."

"And I stand by it. I know you're not doing this for the Crown, but maybe you're not so selfish after all."

Whitney pulled away. "Don't go getting soft on me."

"Just do me a favor? When we find her again, stop being a fool for once."

The lumbering Shieldsman turned to his men and raised his voice just above a heavy whisper. "All right, the prefect's estate is down this trough. I want a man on every grate. We know what we're looking for."

Whitney watched the Wearer of White get to work.

Did he just tell me to make a move on a Panpingese blood mage?

He thought he might have been dreaming considering the way he'd treated her on their last adventure.

"Yep, he's definitely gone soft."

Whitney sighed. It couldn't be a dream because only the real world could smell so awful. He regarded the stubborn Shieldsman one more time, then turned to continue down the shog-covered sewers toward the wharf.

He couldn't tell Torsten what to look for because he honestly had no idea how he was supposed to distract an entire army. Genius usually struck for him in the heat of the moment, so he decided to turn off his brain and allow instinct to take over.

Before long he was standing at a large, barred opening at the bay. The smell of salty air greeted him along with a freezing gust of wind. It smelled like freedom, but he knew it couldn't be. Even if he'd decided to bail on Torsten and take his chances with Kazimir, Sora was still somewhere within the city, and he refused to leave without his apprentice.

He took inventory of the area. From the opening, he could see the wharf, lined with trader's ships. They swayed to and fro as a heady wind blew, battering the docks with small waves of water cold enough to stop a man's heart. Lonely chunks of ice floated, broken by the churning bay.

The Shesaitju rowboats littered the sandy coast south of the wharf. And further down, massive galleons made of black wood, with bowing, triangular sails floated menacingly. Some still had catapults on their decks, stuck in launch position. A herd of zhulong traipsed around in the mud where they were moored under the watch of stablemen.

Whitney squeezed through the bars and pulled his body up so he could see atop the wharf. He moved slowly, quietly, unable to escape the sinking feeling that the moment his head popped up he'd be target practice again. Only now, at least, he had the cover of night.

Several Shesaitju warriors stood guard along the coast, but since none of the hiding Winde Port citizens would dare attempt an escape, they weren't paying much attention. Many of them were engaged in some kind of game under the green light of a cluster of nigh'jel lanterns. It involved a large sheet of zhulong skin and throwing spears.

Merchant ships and personal vessels lined the wharf, packed in tight like a deck of cards due to the grounding of ships. He watched them rock back and forth, the ropes holding them going loose and taut in rhythm with nature's song. An idea popped into his head as he watched them. It was insane, but thinking twice was a thief's worst enemy.

He pulled himself up onto the wharf and slinked down the edge. The heavy winds coming from the west made such a racket of water and creaking wood that nobody would ever hear him. However, if any one of the hundred Shesaitju soldiers posted decided to look in his direction, they'd no doubt see a scruffy thief climbing aboard one of the ships under the light of the moons.

He chose the largest vessel, a western galley big enough to transport a herd of cattle and with sails the size of the Darkings mansion. Tall deck walls kept Whitney mostly hidden as he crouched and ran toward the bow. His plan was as simple as it was crazy, but he hoped it would be effective.

"Pssst."

Whitney whipped around, saw no one. He heard it again and spun in the direction it had come. A stout but muscular dwarf with a dark, patchy beard popped up from a corner behind a spool of rope.

"Tum Tum!" Whitney nearly exclaimed before he caught himself. "What are you doing?"

"Got stuck between a rock and a hard place, I did," he replied. "Yiggin gray men have been keepin watch all afternoon. And after what they did to me bar, I ain't for takin no chances."

"You mean the Winder's Dwarf is..."

"Infested." Tum Tum pointed across the way to his bar. The front windows were bashed in, and Shesaitju were everywhere. They had full run of the place, but not one of them drank. The Black Sandsmen did so hate enjoying life.

*All that wasted ale...*Whitney frowned. "These Black Sandsmen are intent on ruining everything, aren't they?"

"Aye. They barged in askin if the dwarf who owned the place would support the fall of the Glass. O'course, I told em to stop botherin me customers and blades started takin away all the Glassmen. What good be a tavern without downtrodden men to drink at em?"

"Oh, Tum Tum, silly dwarf. You always say 'yes.' War makes even the best men drinkers and peacetime... well, that's even worse."

"I know, I know. But I was drunk when they asked," he chortled.

"Of course, you were," Whitney said. "Well, since you're here, wanna help me win the war and get your place back?"

"Me fightin days are long gone, me Lord," Tum Tum replied. "Ain't for sayin I can't be tossin some fists round, but I'd be doubtin we could handle hunerds of them gray men."

"I've got a plan, and we shouldn't even have to ball our fists." He leaned in to whisper. "I'm working with the King's Shield again."

"By the sharp axe of Meungor!"

"Keep your voice down," Whitney scolded. "Now, gather up all that rope and tie it around the mast."

"What's the plan?"

"You'll see."

Whitney looked out over the rails at the city he used to love. Suppertime along the wharf was usually the most fun place one could be in all of Pantego. It wasn't just Winder's Wharf, but bar after bar, packed with people ready to spend. There were some of the finest restaurants, including the Winde Traders Guild at the end of the row. Now, anywhere that wasn't swarming with Shesaitju invaders was empty. Not a drink being poured.

Unable to bear the sight anymore, Whitney turned to look down the wharf. The ships were tightly packed between pilings and floating walkways ramping down from the wharf. From the vessel they were on, there were ten more docked down to the sandy shores where the zhulong and Shesaitju rowboats occupied. Enough to make a racket even the gods might hear.

"Done yet?" Whitney asked after some time had passed.

"Me legs ain't as long as yers be," Tum Tum groaned in response. "Hold yer saddle…" Then, a few minutes later, "There, done."

"Okay. You sit tight and stay low."

"Ain't no other way I can be." Tum Tum laughed, and his belly rolled.

Whitney placed a finger against his lips to shush him.

"When I give the signal, raise the sails, then get your ass to the sewers, or inside. Anywhere but the docks."

"Aye, aye, Cap'n."

Whitney sighed in relief. Tum Tum was no thief, but he'd helped Whitney try and woo a fair share of pretty women in the Winder's Dwarf over the years. Enough time to know that when Whitney offered a signal, it was best to wait and see what that might be.

Torsten could learn a thing or two.

The spool Tum Tum had used for a hiding place was nearly all they would need for this ship. Whitney took the free end, tied it to a bucket, and threw it to the ship docked in the next slip. He winced, expecting to hear clanging metal that might alert the guards, but the wind was causing such a ruckus, even he couldn't hear it.

"Wish me luck," Whitney said to the dwarf.

"With what?"

Whitney ignored him and leaped from deck to deck. He found the bucket, removed the rope, and tied the end around the ship's mast. Then, he found another spare rope and affixed it to the mast as well before using the same bucket to fling it to the next ship. He continued on down the line of ten ships to the one nearest the southern coastline where the zhulong grazed.

Just as Celeste and Loutis reached their climax in the night sky, he tied his last knot. Sweat poured down his forehead despite the cold. All that jumping and crouching... thieving was a younger man's game. Not even three decades, he was already on the decline.

He peered over the railing and saw a couple of gray-skins doing rounds down the length of the wharf. He waited for them to pass, then slung the end of the rope not affixed to the mast over the side of the ship. He slid down it onto a floating walkway and shimmied toward the wharf. Miraculously, the Shesaitju were still unaware of his presence, and he hoped to keep it that way. When his feet hit the wharf, they were already running.

He hopped down to the muddy shores and toward the zhulong herd. In the darkness, the Shesaitju were easy to spot with their green, glowing nigh'jels. There were a few care-keepers scattered about, but Whitney made sure to steer clear of them.

"All right," he said out loud to no one. "They're just big pigs. Nothing to worry about—just big pigs with spiked tails and massive tusks."

As he got closer, he realized they were far bigger than he remembered. He was actually quaking now, his knees weak. Sweat still poured off him, threatening to freeze on his face.

"Shogging exile, Whitney," he cursed. "Get a yigging grip."

He sidled up to an exceptionally large male—he could tell by the length of its tusks—and patted its side. Its head turned, eyeballs the size of Whitney's fist, maybe bigger. It leaned down to sniff Whitney's pants, shog-stained from the sewers.

"Hey, boy, think you could help me with something?" Whitney stammered. "Yeah, attaboy."

Whitney grabbed the reins hanging from a bit in its mouth and gave them a soft tug. The beast thrashed its head in protest, causing Whitney to back away, arms in the air. The zhulong followed him, stuck out its short, coarse tongue, and licked his calf.

"More pig than dragon, eh?" Whitney said.

He strode a few meters, then turned and noticed the zhulong following him, its massive snout huffing.

The patrolling warriors were on the opposite side of the wharf, so the time was right to get to work.

"Stay," he said to the zhulong. It didn't listen. As he went to climb back up, it hooked him with a tusk to get at his pants.

"How come only ugly beasts want to get in my pants?" he groaned. It made a deep rumbling noise. "Okay! You're not ugly. I'm sorry." He weaseled out of its clutches, then reached down and tore off a strip off his sodden pants. He tried to imagine they were only wet with water as he raised the cloth.

The beast grabbed it from him and started chewing.

"Good boy." Whitney shrugged and made his way back beside the nearest ship. He found the loose end of the rope he'd slid down and carried it to the zhulong. It was still busy chomping on his pants when he knotted it to its saddle.

Just then, he heard shouting. A Shesaitju warrior fell off the side of the ship Tum Tum was supposed to be hiding on, splashing into the ice-cold water. A contingent of warriors sprung into action and headed for the ship. Before Whitney could even make a move, he saw the towering sails go up, accompanied by a cacophony of Saitjuese cursing.

"Tum Tum!" Whitney shouted.

He had to think fast. He ripped the stained piece of fabric from the zhulong's mouth and tossed it down the beach. The zhulong's giant nostrils flared with rage, and Whitney had to summon all the courage he had to give it a slap on the hindquarters like he was playing. He closed his eyes, half-expecting to be gored, but the mighty beast turned and ran toward the cloth.

Mission accomplished.

It tugged on the rope, which was bound to the mast of the nearest ship, which was connected to the one adjacent, and so on until the compromised galley.

The sails Tum Tum had raised caught the strong westerly winds, and with the zhulong also pulling with its substantial strength, the row of ships tipped, slamming into one another. There was a series of cracks, loud as thunder, and the zhulong herd went frantic. The rope on Whitney's friend snapped free, whipping across and taking out Whitney's legs.

They stampeded toward the city, throwing sharp, hooked tusks as they charged. Whitney had to roll back and forth to avoid being trampled. Giant, clawed paws smashed into the mud all around him, and when he finally was able to look up, he saw a mass of Shesaitju along the docks, half staring, aghast, at the toppled ships and others trying to calm the zhulong.

Whitney kept waiting to hear shouting about a dwarf but heard nothing. He dug himself deeper into the mud to hide. All he could do was hope Tum Tum had abandoned ship and hid before it was too late. Used to the deep cold of the northern mountains, dwarves were resilient, maybe enough to survive that water for a few minutes.

What was certain, however, was that Whitney's distraction had worked. His service to the Crown was complete, with exceptional success if he had to say so. Now it was up to Torsten to handle his end so they can get started trying to find Sora and the monster who held her.

XXIII

THE MYSTIC

havi didn't have to give Sora any clothes after she dried off. Her chamber in the prefect's estate was already full of them. The old handmaiden quietly finished cleaning and straightening her hair, told her to rest while she could, and left the room—but not without first asking countless times if Sora needed anything. She was warm and welcoming like a mother should be... not that Sora knew much about mothers. Wetzel was called many things back in Troborough, matronly not numbered with them.

Sora watched her leave, then dug through a wardrobe for something appropriate to wear. As she did, she couldn't help but wonder who the countless clothes belonged to and what had happened to her.

It wasn't hard to discern the answer. Winde Port's prefect was gone, probably a head on the city walls. There wasn't a soul with pink skin or round eyes from the heart of the Glass Kingdom to be found. No servants, or wives, or children.

Sora ruffled through more exquisite clothing than she'd ever seen in one place until she found the plainest dress available. It was tree bark brown and barely hugged her figure. There was no finery along the seams of tan, threaded trim. It wasn't servant attire or anything, but she was tired of playing the role of a fancy royal. She strapped the fat coin purse she and

Whitney got from selling the silk trader's goods to her thigh underneath the folds, then, she found a pair of long, satin gloves to pull up all the way over her forearms to hide her scars.

She turned and saw the luxurious bed waiting for her opposite the bath, begging her to get lost in the impossibly soft sheets. Aquira was already curled up in a ball on one of the pillows. Sora didn't dare join her. Not even for a moment, knowing that if she hit the cushion, she'd be passed out for hours. And she couldn't do that.

The sun was falling, its protection against Kazimir with it. Whitney was still somewhere out there, and as soon as the light was gone, he'd be in more trouble.

Maybe he fled, Sora thought. *Maybe he left me behind just like when he ran from home.*

It was a thought that would have usually pained her, but now, all she did was hope he was as bad a man as he sometimes seemed—worse even. She hoped he'd stolen a ship in the chaos and was already sailing the Boiling Waters on another mad adventure.

Then she remembered Kazimir's terrible grin and what he'd said about the sacred nature of a blood pact. He'd hunt Whitney to the ends of Pantego if it meant getting her. Yet still, she had no idea why. There had to be countless other Panpingese magic-users hiding around the world. Her people were supposed to share the closest affinity with Elsewhere, whether through blood or otherwise.

No more hiding. I need to find him.

"Aquira, let's go," she said. The wyvern raised her head and blinked wearily in her direction. "C'mon girl. He may be a pain, but he's all I've got." Aquira stood and stretched, arching her spine and looping her tail around to brush her neck frills. A puff of smoke poured from her mouth as she coughed, then she hopped down and followed behind Sora.

It was a short walk down the hall to a huge anteroom, arched windows along the side looking out upon the bay. Dusk was made even darker by a thick layer of clouds and snow flurries.

Sora stopped in the entry when she realized Muskigo wasn't lying. The hall was filled with homeless Panpingese men, women, and children wrapped in blankets. A few Shesaitju guards stood silently at the entries but kept to their own.

It was an odd sight; the room, so luxurious and lavish, and a people so much the opposite. Velvet covered chairs were parked before intricately marked tables upon which were myriad varieties of food and drink. Maybe the people didn't have a warm bath or hearth to stay warm, but even a roof overhead was a far cry from how so many of them were living in the ghetto.

She stepped in and immediately recognized two children sleeping on their mother as the ones she'd tossed coins to back in the Panping District. Her hand instinctually fell to the purse beneath her dress, filled with more gold then anybody in this room had seen in a lifetime combined.

"You need something?" the mother asked.

Sora shook her head, not even realizing she had been staring. "No sorry, I recognized your sons," she said.

"Ah, you must be 'beautiful angel' that gived that gold autla."

"I...uh... yeah. They looked like they could use it."

"Could have used more." The woman wore a glare for a few seconds, then her features softened and she said, "Thank you."

Her skin creased like leather as she smiled, even though she didn't seem very old. Within her dark, almond-shaped eyes, Sora saw peace. It was strange for anyone to seem peaceful during these times, but as she looked around the room, at the other Panpingese refugees, it was a common attribute.

"That is Tayvada's wyvern," the women stated.

Sora glanced down and saw the wyvern calmly sitting at her heels. Her heart sunk, but she nodded. "You knew him?"

"Every Panpingese in Winde Port knowed him. He didn't go around tossing out gold, but did what he could to feed us."

Sora eyed the Shesaitju guards to make sure they weren't listening to her. She was supposed to be Tayvada's widow after all. "I wish I had a chance to know him better, but Aquira found me in the chaos and won't leave my side."

"You must be a decent one then. She was his pride and joy, and she has eye for troublemaker. Always growled at these two for causing ruckus." She shook her children a bit and laughed.

"Ouch, momma," one of them groaned. He rolled over and rubbed a cut on his arm. It wasn't deep, but Sora knew cuts better than anybody. It was the kind that stung but wasn't bad enough for anyone to heal. Sora recalled many times when Wetzel scolded her for being a weakling. This mother did the same.

"Oh, quiet," she said. "It just a scratch. You're lucky that's all we got in the fighting."

Sora knelt in front of them then sliced her thumb on her shoe buckle and ran the blood gently over his wound. A bit of blue smoke rose, and the boy's cut began to seal until all that was left was a line of irritated skin. Sora released a mouthful of air and panted a few times. Healing took more out of her than anything, but the wound was so minor she recovered quickly.

The boy was too tired to notice what had happened, having fallen asleep almost immediately after changing positions. The mother, on the other hand, gawked at her like she was from another world.

"Are you a—"

"Mystic," Sora finished for her, keeping her voice low so as not to wake the children or earn more attention. "No, I just learned a few tricks with blood magic in the west."

"Tricks, eh? Think you can get my leg to stop aching? Knee pops every time I stand." She grabbed her knee cap and wiggled it around more than was natural.

Gross as it was, Sora couldn't help but chuckle. "I don't think so."

The woman waved her hand in dismissal. "Bah, what good are you?"

"Still figuring that out." Sora smiled and sat, legs folded in front of her. Now that the woman had warmed up to her, she figured she might be able to get some real information. "So, you have lived here in Winde Port your whole life?" she asked.

"Born and raised in ghetto. Never been anywhere."

It explained her accent and broken way of speech. Sora imagined most of the district dwellers stayed among their own.

"Why do you call it that?" Sora asked, her eyes narrowing. "It's such an awful word."

"What more is there to call it?" an old man leaning against the wall beside them spoke up, suddenly paying attention. "We count ourselves lucky to even have a place of our own. So many of us died after the Third War of Glass… better here in Winde Port than in Elsewhere."

He spoke with elegance. More like Tayvada than the others.

"Or some backwater village," added another. "Here we get to see world, even if only through eyes of travelers."

"Or invaders," Sora muttered.

Everyone looked to the gray men lining the entries. They all wore weapons, but none were drawn. Several just laughed with one another, shoulders against the walls.

"They've treated us better than others has," the mother said, shrugging, almost apathetic as if the slaughtering of so many outside meant nothing.

"Aye," said the old man. "These warriors have spared us, given us food and shelter in a place bigger than the whole Ghetto. They are no enemies of mine. If the mystics would stop hiding, maybe we could join them."

The mother slapped the man's arm. "That is enough, Nijo. Council is gone, and every time they're bringed up I have to explain it to my children."

"Good. They should learn exactly why we're here kissing boots." The old man stood, huffing. His bony legs shook for a moment before he decided to sit back down and continue enjoying his free meal.

"Sorry about him," the mother said. "Talk of war stirs up rotten memories."

"I don't remember it, really…" Sora said. "Well, I have one memory actually."

"That is enough for lifetime."

"It's of my mother." Sora wasn't sure why she started explaining. She'd never told anybody about the memory; not Wetzel, or Whitney. Nobody. But she'd never been amongst so many people that didn't look at her like she was misplaced, or delicate.

"I can't recall my father, but her," Sora continued. "I can almost picture her face. I think I look like her except my eyes; those must have been my dad's. Maybe it's just a dream, but she cradles me and tells me she loves me. She's crying. I think I am too. She kisses me on the forehead. Then she's gone."

Sora could feel her eyes starting to well up. The woman, however, barely seemed moved. "Sometimes, it is better to barely remember," she said.

"It's always better," Nijo scoffed. "My wife was burned for using magic. My daughter, chained up and sold. Last I saw she was being dragged away by her hair and I was too broken to help them."

"It's not competition, Nijo." The woman took Sora's hand. "It is beautiful memory, dear. But that's all it is. We here now, eating, thanks to these people. What more is there to ask?"

"These people destroyed my home," Sora said, softly.

"Welcome to the club," Nijo groaned

Sora bit her lip upon realizing how foolish she sounded. She couldn't expect any of these people to feel bad for her. She was delivered to a home after the war. It wasn't perfect, but Wetzel looked after her, fed her, gave her shelter. And she had a friend who helped her through so many hard and lonely times. He may have abandoned her for a while, but he was back now. Whitney was counting on her, and she'd wasted enough time on her own curiosity over her people's living situation.

"You say you knew Tayvada?" Sora said. The woman nodded. "The man they said murdered him, Whitney Fierstown. Did you see what happened to him?"

"I was not there," she said.

"I was," Nijo said. "Bastard escaped when the gray men attacked. Slipped right into the sewers."

Of course! Sewers.

They were a thief's best friend according to one of his lessons if she remembered correctly. The one place in the world where Whitney could hide and never be found. Probably not even by Kazimir. But the upyr couldn't summon a fire that never dwindled in a place that wet. And he didn't have a Wyvern who'd met Whitney and could no doubt sniff him out.

"Thank you," Sora said. She stood and bowed. "Thank both of you."

"Don't think I've ever been bowed to befo—"

Nijo was interrupted when the grand, central doors to the anteroom swung open. Muskigo appeared, flanked by his gold-clad guards. Gone was the look of calm Sora had seen on his face since they first met.

"All civilians must vacate the estate at once," he commanded. All the Panpingese folk glanced up at him, then returned to their meals. "Now!

His men flowed in, ripping the people from their meals and shoving them toward the exits. All around the room, soldiers did the same. Nijo's chair was kicked out from under him. The mother's children awoke, startled.

Sora stormed toward the afhem. Aquira caught her leg on the way and used it to get a boost up to her shoulder. "What is the meaning of this?" she questioned. "These people aren't hurting anybody."

"Sora, I don't have time," Muskigo responded. He wouldn't even look at her, too busy watching his men bully the homeless.

"You promised these people shelter."

"I don't have time!" he thundered. Now he stared straight at her and in his pale gray eyes, she saw storm clouds. He drew a deep breath. "It is no longer safe here. The Glassmen are coming."

"It's safer here, protected, then out there if battle is coming."

"I don't have time to explain. Take them back to their district and stay inside."

"I don't lead them."

"Someone needs to. Now go, Sora of Yaolin City. Our conversation will have to wait." He turned to leave without even a second glance, but it was what he clutched in his hands that drew her attention. It was a letter bearing the unmistakable seal of the Darkings Family—a ship and a coin. She recognized it from the ring Darkings wore, and from the door of his house in Bridleton.

"Was this all just to impress me?" she shouted as more of her people were shoved by.

Muskigo stopped but didn't look back. "No, this is war."

Sora watched as he hurried to the railing around the courtyard and looked down. She watched as armed guards pushed her people around no matter how young or frail they were. Only a moment before they felt safe for once in their lives, and now, children were crying.

A hand fell upon Sora's shoulder. She looked left and saw Shavi.

"You must listen to him, Sora," she said. "If he believes danger is coming, it is. Fighting. It's all he's ever trained for."

"Apparently," Sora replied. "Go, I'll be right there."

"Trust him." She went to leave, stopped to help an elderly man up, and they continued out of the room.

"I don't," Sora muttered. She turned and spotted the mother and her children hurrying to gather their blankets. Sora ran to them, reached under her dress, and shoved the coin purse into the woman's chest.

She stared down, eyes wide with confusion.

"I don't need it anymore," Sora said. It was true. There were no merchant ships left to charter. And even if Whitney was right that she couldn't make a difference in these people's lives by handing out gold, she was done not trying.

"Take it. Be the new Tayvada, or give it out. There's enough there to fill a dozen flats with new beds and more."

"I… I don't…" The woman fumbled over a response until there was a booming crash. It was like thunder, only the sound repeated a few times and was immediately followed by shouting in Saitjuese.

Sora grabbed the woman and guided her toward the exit. "Just go!"

Her eyes darted between her children, Sora, and the money. Then she ran. She ran with enough gold to buy a ship.

Whitney won't mind, Sora told herself. And she also told herself that he wouldn't mind one more detour before she went after him. She glanced back up at Muskigo, still staring down into the courtyard. The sight had the rage she'd been holding down bubbling back to the surface.

Whatever that bang was, it signaled war. More killing. Muskigo forcing the Glass Kingdom to attack. Her people may have survived their surprise invasion, but nobody would survive an all-out war in the city.

All his talk of fighting for freedom, yet he was clearly working with Darkings, a man wicked enough to turn to the upyr and blood pacts. Sora suddenly realized how foolish she was to believe there was more to Muskigo. They were royals, helping each other, and the people be damned.

The series of crashes had drawn all the soldiers' attention to the courtyard. All the refugees and handmaidens were cleared out.

Sora was alone.

She picked up a shard of a broken clay plate which must have fallen in the chaos. Aquira dug into her shoulder and growled as if she could read Sora's mind. Then, they headed straight for Muskigo.

Sora knew now that she could help her people. She could end the looming war and keep what happened to Troborough from happening again. Maybe not forever, as there would always be greedy lords and ladies wanting more, but at least enough to make fewer orphans and refugees.

She could end the fighting.

XXIV

THE KNIGHT

Torsten raised a hand, stopping the legion—one hundred of his finest King's Shieldsmen at his back. They had been trained during Uriah Davies' reign as Wearer, by Wardric as the eldest in the order, and by Torsten himself, after he took on the mantle. Not since King Liam turned the entire army of Glass into a hammer of faith had the Shield led an operation like this.

Yet, perhaps the most astounding thing about where they now stood was that Whitney, the damnable thief without a filter hadn't failed in leading them.

Torsten looked up through the grille of a gold-clad grate and into the courtyard of the prefect's estate. He placed a finger over his mouth as a pair of gray legs passed, then regarded his men. He knew a few of their names—Mulliner, Reginald, Nikserof—but he wished he knew them all. He wished he'd been forced to spend less time at Oleander's side or watching to make sure Liam wasn't taken advantage of after he'd grown too ill to speak. In fact, he longed for the days when he had been one of them—an anonymous face in the great order, following a worthy Wearer whose accomplishments were so vast he'd never be contested by a murderous, Drav Cra Arch Warlock.

This will change everything, he told himself.

"Muskigo is somewhere above us," he said aloud, voice low, but carrying down the narrow passage. The dwarves, although small in stature, developed spacious tunnels to accommodate men and even some giants. Torsten was thankful for that as he traveled through the main lines, but now that they were within the estate's infrastructure, things were tight. They were forced into a long line, no more than two men crammed across, and the ceiling so low he had to crouch. A pain in his neck now but it would help them swarm into the courtyard when the time was right.

"We are with you until the end, Wearer," the man nearest him said. "Or let Iam strike me down."

He was young but hardened. Three lines of scars ran across a chin like an anvil. His eyes glinted with a healthy blend of fear and resolve, proving he was not a man driven by bloodlust but a true warrior. Torsten recognized him but wasn't sure of his name.

No more heeling like a dog at the feet of royals. This is your order. These are your men.

"What's your name, Soldier?" Torsten asked.

"Xander Corsocova, Sir," he saluted.

"Where are you from?"

"I… Westvale, Sir. Born and bred. Trained by Sir Wardric Jolly under the command of Sir Uriah Davies a few Dawnings back."

"It's an honor to be here beside you, son. Can you do something for me?"

"Anything, sir."

"Ask the name of the man on either side of you, who trained them, where they're from. Then, tell them to do the same." He knew some of them might already know each other, but these were the finest, selected by Wardric. That meant they were posted all across the western half of the kingdom.

"Sir, the—"

"There's time. We await a signal from Winder's Wharf to move. It's an order. Here we stand, ready to die in Iam's name, I would like to better know the brave men at my side."

Xander nodded and turned to Nikserof, the Shieldsman beside him, to ask the same questions. Then on and on down the line. Torsten listened to the answers of those nearest and watched the rest. Some were calm like

Xander, others more visibly taken by fear. But, as a few men joked in their answers and earned low laughs, the terror began to dissipate.

Liam's armies were a unit. Thousands of men unified in resolve and their trust in him. Uriah's King's Shield was an extension of that. No single member mattered, only the unit as a whole. Alone, they were only drops of rain, but together, a great hurricane.

But the time of great and famous men was over. Torsten had led for a single battle and been deceived. He had to argue with a heathen imposter for every move, under the orders of a king whose voice had yet to lower, in the shadow of a Queen Mother now best known for killing her own people.

"What about you, sir?" Xander asked while the rest continued.

"Excuse me?"

"Sorry, sir. If I overstep…"

Torsten looked up into the courtyard, flakes of snow danced by, melting just beyond the grate. Then, he turned his gaze down upon the sewer and the layer of muddy water running past his feet. He remembered why the stench and darkness of such a place barely affected him.

"South Corner, Yarrington," Torsten said finally, eyes closed. "Born to a no-name father and a streetwalking mother. Iam saw fit to lead me into the arms of Liam Nothhelm and never once have I looked back."

He regarded Xander, who stared at him in disbelief.

"We are all Iam's children," Torsten said. "No matter where we come from." He reached out, took the man by his pauldron and shook. "Now we are ready."

A crash echoed in the distance, followed by a bell, and shouting in Saitjuese. Dust trickled off the ceiling as footsteps pounded across the ground above.

Torsten grinned. "Maybe there is still hope for the boy," he whispered to himself and above. Not only had Whitney led them successfully but his distraction appeared to be working as well.

Torsten positioned himself below the grille. His fingers twirled the Eye of Iam hanging from his neck. "Forgive me Iam, for what we must do. Watch over us, but do not judge, for in the name of peace we take up arms against those who trespass against Your light."

As he prayed under his breath, so too did his men, each in their own way. Some mouths moved silently while others took a knee, speaking to the inside of their eyelids. He let them all finish in their own time, and when he saw the whites of all their eyes, he traced his own.

"We are the armor of Your holy kingdom," he said, raising his voice enough for his men to hear. They quietly echoed every word—the words of the King's Shield, which Torsten couldn't remember the last time he'd had the opportunity to recite.

"Our lives," he continued, "are given freely under the sight of your Vigilant Eye so Your children may thrive in this world You have blessed us with."

Torsten raised his hand to the sewer grille, then raised his voice even louder. His men did so as well. "We are the right hand of Iam. The sword of His justice, and the Shield that guards the light of this world."

He shoved the grille with all his might and jarred it from its setting. Xander gave him a boost and his feet fell upon the snow-filled courtyard, the first of all his men—as it should be. If Liam had taught him anything of war, it was that no leader inspires his men like one willing to head the charge.

The rest flowed in after him, men with long swords and heater shields at the front, spears and pikes at the back—the wedge and hammer.

Torsten spun to study the yard wrapped on four sides, at two levels by an arcade utterly devoid of Shesaitju. Bells rang louder in the distance, accompanied by a series of crashes. Whatever Whitney had done, it cleared the entire place.

Torsten signaled to Xander. "Secure the front door," he ordered. "Muskigo is somewhere in here. We take him now, or we die trying."

Xander saluted, then led a smaller unit toward the palace doors. Torsten surveyed the courtyard again, trying to decide the next move. And that was when he heard a scream of agony too near to be Whitney's doing. He drew his claymore and swung back to face the direction it'd come from.

A bar of spikes had swung across the Arcade's central passage from one side. Xander screamed and flailed, trying to free himself from the bar which had him pinned against the wall. The sound of Saitjuese orders cracked the air, the voice familiar. Standing on the walkway right above where Xander met his fate was Afhem Muskigo, arms crossed, eyes fixed on Torsten.

The moment he saw him, Torsten knew Redstar's betrayal was complete. He had warned Muskigo, sending any and all competition for command of the Glass Army to their doom.

Muskigo barked something and archers flooded in from surrounding rooms. They lined the second-floor balconies overlooking the courtyard as well as the roof.

"Ambush!" Torsten shouted. "Form up. Form up!"

King's Shield armor was durable, laced with the glaruium of Mt Lister herself, but it was not impregnable. At the right angle, the Shesaitju's barbed arrows could pierce it, as Torsten knew too well. And now his men would learn too.

Arrows zipped around the courtyard from every direction like angry hornets in a stirred nest. They stabbed at angles, stung shields. The Shieldsman right in front of Torsten took one to the weak, flexible mail around his throat as they all closed rank. Another arrow glanced off Torsten's white helm, sending him staggering and knocking the helmet off his head.

"Wearer!" one of his men shouted. Whoever it was grabbed him and raised a shield, but was stung from behind by another projectile. Torsten went to pull him back and received a mouthful of innards as another arrow erupted through the man's stomach.

He wiped blood and bits of flesh from his eyes. Metal clanked all around him as the King's Shield formed a circle of shields.

"Shields…" Torsten coughed, the tang of copper heavy on his tongue. A wave of frantic bodies crushed him in the center of the circle, pressing against his chest, stampeding his feet. He could hardly breathe.

Of all the battles he fought under Liam, he'd never felt so… hopeless.

Every arrow clashing against their shield wall stole a bit more breath from his lungs. And those were the ones that didn't sneak through the cracks, shredding flesh and sinew of one of the men he'd foolishly led to their dooms.

He pawed at his chest for the pendant of Iam—something to squeeze as he prayed for a miracle. But his arm was pinned between two of his men jockeying for position under the umbrella of shields being slowly picked apart. He was able to loop a finger around the necklace when someone banged into his side and caused the chain to snap off his neck. The pendant cracked as it hit the ground, then shattered beneath a boot.

Torsten fell to a knee, finally able to gasp for air. He pawed at the shards, and in the reflection of the largest piece, he caught a glimpse up into the balcony. All the breath he'd only just regained fled his lungs at the sight of Muskigo standing there.

The gray man watched like a galler bird, eyes set upon floundering prey, so focused that he didn't see what was coming up behind him.

The blood mage—from a village razed at his very command—walked up behind him, something sharp in hand. A strange, scaled creature, which looked like it could be a newborn zhulong sat perched on her shoulder.

Iam is still with us!

Anger contorted her features just as it had in the Webbed Woods when Redstar pushed her to the brink of death. Torsten watched her weapon sink into Muskigo's shoulder blade, and then his mass of soldiers shifted and obscured Torsten's view. Swimming through the mess of legs and armor, Torsten clambered for a better view. Arrows battered the metal on the other side, but he lifted his head regardless.

Now he saw Muskigo hulking over Sora, sword to her throat as she crawled back across the floor.

"Muskigo!" Torsten roared. "Come down here and face me like a man!" The barb of an arrow slashed his cheek on its way by. His men pawed at his shoulders in an attempt to drag him back to safety.

He stood strong.

Muskigo momentarily turned his attention from Sora to meet Torsten's glare. The girl grabbed the sword by either side of the blade with her bare hands. Blood leaked from her palms as she squeezed and fire swirled around her. The scaly creature on her shoulder leaped at Muskigo and dug sharp fangs into his shoulder. The afhem released a roar, sword slipping from his grasp.

The attempt to kill their afhem had some of his men distracted, but others rallied. Arrows flew at Sora, flaking to ash before they reached her flame-covered body. Another charged her from behind and swung a curved sword, but a flick of her finger sent fire hurtling into the man's face.

Muskigo ripped the creature from his flesh and threw it back at Sora. It screamed loud enough to be heard over the din of battle as it skidded to a stop. Muskigo backed away slowly, lowering into a Black Fist fighting stance.

"This is for my master," Sora said. "This is for my home!"

Fire exploded from her hands. At the same time, it shot forth from the scaly creature's mouth. Both streams merged together.

Muskigo spun out of the way, but a part of the blast caught his side and sent him flying backward so hard he broke through a wooden post. The rest hit the structure of the roof and courtyard, igniting the wood rafters and melting the stone columns of the arcade as if they were iron under the smelter.

The entire half of the building sagged, then began to crumble away. The devastation rippled across the entire building, wood catching everywhere. Torsten and Sora's eyes met for but a moment before the ceiling caved in around her. She grabbed her scaly friend and vanished.

"We're not alone!" Torsten hollered. He could feel the energy flooding his muscles, his despair fading beneath the blinding glow of fire. "Fight toward the exit. Push!"

Half of Muskigo's men surged across the crumbling upper walkway to dig him out of the rubble. The others continued the assault, but Torsten's men seemed reinvigorated by the spreading inferno.

The mass of shields and armor shuffled out of the courtyard and into the entry hall. Walls collapsed around them, and the ceiling fell away. Torsten never felt such incredible heat, but he took comfort knowing the Shesaitju hadn't either. They preferred their nigh'jels to fire, and this fire was unnatural. Its arms licked and spread as if fueled by the rage of the very girl who ignited it.

Shesaitju soldiers fell upon them as they reached cover. "Shift!" Torsten ordered. The men at the edges of the formation turned their shields and those behind thrust spears through the openings.

"Wall!" Torsten said, the shield closing once more with a thunderous clap.

"Push!" They pressed forward toward the front entry as if one unit. Less than half the men he'd come with remained, but in the King's Shield, that counted for hundreds.

A large portion of the ceiling crashed down, breaking their formation.

Torsten didn't wait for Shesaitju to flood the gap. He leaped over the bodies, his claymore carving a bloody arc across the chests of his enemies. He parried a spear, then ducked under another. A Shieldsman—Sir Nikserof Pasic—jumped forward, blocked an attack from his flank and pulled him back to cover.

Another chunk of the ceiling gave way ahead of them, crushing a mass of Shesaitju warriors. Torsten, seeing an opening, waved his men onward, over the smoldering rubble. He lowered his shoulder, and cold air filled his lungs as he broke through the estate doors, finally feeling like he was able to breathe. Icy snow and burning embers met in a macabre dance, sweeping across the entry. Dark clouds swirled in the darkening sky, bringing with them a robust and west-blowing gale that felt like daggers upon his bleeding cheek. The prefect's estate was wholly consumed, but it wasn't alone.

The strong wind rapidly carried flames across the city. At the same time, a strange voice echoed through the air. The words were long and trailed off, but it sounded like Drav Crava, as if he could hear Redstar chanting across the battlefield.

The wind allowed the inferno to bridge Winde Port's canals like forest wildfire. Building after building caught, even though it was snowing—an unstoppable force of nature's wrath.

Torsten turned his attention to the streets. They were out of the cauldron, but Muskigo's army still filled the city. A cluster of unmanned zhulong stampeded through the streets, throwing massive tusks in every direction.

"We are the right hand of Iam!" Torsten shouted as his men formed rank again. "The sword of His justice and the shield that guards the light of this world!" The zhulong crashed into them, throwing Nikserof aside like a rag doll. Another couldn't dodge the pack, taking a long tusk through his abdomen.

"Fight toward the gate!" Torsten ordered after the beasts passed. "We shall make it out of here alive, men. Iam is with us!"

Torsten emerged from the shield wall and brought his claymore down upon a Shesaitju warrior's skull. He heaved Nikserof to his feet by the forearm, and they fell back into cover. In and out of the formation he and others went, taking five with them for every Shieldsman that died.

But they were dying.

Torsten knew they wouldn't last long surrounded by enemies and fire, but now he wasn't afraid.

Just like in the estate, their formation slowly ebbed west through the overwhelming force. The finest men the Glass had to offer would only die if they took hundreds more with them. The further west they edged, the louder Torsten could hear Redstar's voice, as if the warlock was directly beside him.

The wind grew stronger as well, and Torsten saw the fire hopping across the rooftops. The distraction helped give them breadth through the army, and now it was beginning to catch the palisade wall surrounding the city.

Torsten's giant hands snapped the neck of a Shesaitju, cracking like a branch underfoot, then he spun, pulling his sword free and bringing it down through the shoulder of another. A blade slashed his thigh, but his armor dulled the blow. He grabbed the man by the neck, and as he raised him, a ram's horn filled the air. One long blow.

'We will know the time to strike when the cold is driven away by wind and flame.' The words Redstar had spoken before he left suddenly filled Torsten's mind. That horn belonged to the Drav Cra, and suddenly, all around them, Torsten's men were no longer the Shesaitju army's target.

Shouting echoed all over in common and Saitjuese. Torsten could make out the meaning of some, like 'wall' and 'charging"—enough to know that Redstar was about to do whatever it took to be the hero while Torsten and his men failed, damned be to the innocent citizens being used to shield the city.

Redstar would claim it was Nesilia who sparked the fire that took the walls even though Torsten knew it was Sora. He knew Iam was working through the girl though he knew not why. As a blood mage and descendant of mystics, she was everything Iam's scripture preached against, but he knew it to be so.

He crushed the throat of the man in his grip. His men cheered as the horns of reinforcement sounded and Shesaitju warriors flowed by to meet the army at the burning wall. Torsten's heart, on the other hand, sank again. He looked back toward the estate and searched.

Muskigo was being helped out of the crumbling building and led toward a zhulong. He shook one of his Serpent Guards off and hopped up. Half his chest was seared, his usually-gray skin bubbling, exposing the pink of muscle and sinew.

"To the wall!" Torsten shouted. He helped Sir Nikserof take down a Shesaitju soldier, then pushed him in the direction of the walls. "Go!"

He and the rest of his men rushed by. Torsten stayed put. He leveled his sword, its tip pointing down the street at Muskigo.

"Muskigo!" he bellowed. The afhem's dark eyes spotted him through the smoke and embers. "Will you cower from me again?"

One of his Serpent Guards threaded a bow, but Muskigo raised a hand to stop him. He slid his scimitar out of his sheath and pointed it back at Torsten. "Defend the city," he ordered. "The Wearer is mine!"

XXV

THE THIEF

From his perch atop the tilted mast of the black galleon, the reality of Winde Port's fate was all too clear. The hundreds of buildings and businesses lining Merchants Row were being destroyed. Fire raged along the road as the wind blew, hopping the city canals and burning both sides. The strong western wind fanned it along so it couldn't spread to the wharf, but it rapidly pushed toward the city walls. It was as if the gods themselves were blowing upon it and Whitney thought he could hear eldritch chanting in the air.

The Shesaitju army stormed toward the palisades to defend their captured city, vanishing in the smoke. War cries and battle drums were all Whitney needed to hear to know what was happening. The Glass Army was charging.

"Torsten," he said under his breath. The inferno spread fast, but Whitney was sure it began at the prefect's estate where Torsten was making his ambush.

He ran down from the boat and onto the quay. The Shesaitju remaining were so distracted trying to saddle the dozens of zhulong roaming the streets, they didn't even see Whitney as he bolted passed them.

As he reached the place where Winder's Dwarf used to stand, he thought about Tum Tum. The look on the dwarf's face as they watched his livelihood be overrun would stay with Whitney forever. Tum Tum had always been a good friend. If Whitney believed in life after all this chaos, he'd hope to be wherever Tum Tum ended up—even if it meant the Great Hall of Meungor.

"For you, good buddy."

He stopped at the turn onto Merchants Row. Fire licked at the streets from all sides, but the wind kept Whitney's face free of smoke. That was when he realized he had no idea what to do next. He could barrel into the burning prefect's estate and find Torsten, his best chance at standing up to Kazimir. Or he could continue searching for Sora in the most logical places he could think of—the Panping Ghetto and the Darkings Mansion.

Both were on the north side of the city, beyond where the fire was spreading. But the Darkings Mansion was atop a hill and mostly stone. The Ghetto was down at the base, and if a single ember reached those shoddy, wooden flats, the place would go up like a bonfire.

Torsten can handle himself, he decided. If starting this fire was part of his plan to ambush Muskigo, he'd have a lot to answer for to Iam.

Whitney went to cross the canal when, from the direction of the prefect's estate, a mob of Panpingese men and women raced toward him through the smoke.

Whitney turned and pushed through into the heat and smoke. "Sora?" he questioned. In all the smog, half the women looked just like her. He coughed and called for her again. His eyes were burning now, tears streaming down his face.

"Sora!" He stopped, placed his hands on his knees, and tried to take a breath as the crowd fully passed him by. Instead, he just made himself cough even more. He watched them, unsure what to make of the exodus. He wasn't even sure why he imagined Sora might be with them. He'd spent the whole trip trying to prove to her that it didn't matter what she looked like, that the only *people* she had were the ones she chose to stand with.

Wetzel and himself, namely. Half the reason Whitney was so okay with taking her to her ancestral homeland was so she could see that it had nothing to do with her. It was just a place with a name and similar looking people. It also had a great deal of strange and magical treasure to steal, especially if they stumbled upon any underground mystic covens. But that was beside the point.

He sighed, pulled his shirt up over his mouth, and backed up out of the smoke.

Focus Whitney. You'll find her.

He went to turn and continue back on his path across the canal when he heard a low growl.

"Aquira?" he said. The little wyvern stood on the ash-and-snow-covered street blinking its big, yellow eyes at him. Whitney fell to his knees in front of her.

"Aquira!" He went to pick her up but she growled even louder, and he wisely redrew his hand. "Aquira? Where is Sora? So-ra." He pronounced both syllables. "You remember her, right?"

He patted himself down, searching for anything he had that might contain her scent. There was nothing. A month together and he realized he had nothing of hers. If she died in the city or was already dead, he'd have nothing to…

A woman burst through the gathering smoke and fell to the ground. She hacked and coughed, sounds that would have made Whitney vomit if not for realizing the mouth they came out of.

"Sora?" he said softly. His eyes went wide. He scrambled over and pulled her further out of the smoke so she could catch her breath.

"Whit," she rasped. She threw her arms around him and he her. They held each other there in the middle of the street as the city came undone around them. Whitney went to pull away so they could get moving, but she squeezed tighter.

"We need to move," he said.

A group of Shesaitju warriors rumbled by, half of which were mounted on zhulong. They must not have seen Whitney or Sora as enough of a threat to stop.

"C'mon, Sora." Whitney forced them apart, took her hand and led her over the canal to the side where the fire was less rampant. Aquira flew up and dashed along the railing in pursuit.

Whitney leaned Sora against the side of one of the few buildings still standing in that district. He coughed and breathed, and then, again.

"Are you okay?" he asked. Now that she was in front of him, he realized tears were streaming down her face. And not just from the heat of the fire. Her shoulders bobbed like she was trying not to weep.

"Me?" She wiped her eyes. "Are *you* okay?"

"I'm fine, just breathed in too much smoke. Wasn't my first time. There was that time with the dragon—wait a second."

"What now?"

"Why were you coming from the prefect's estate?"

One corner of her lips pulled slightly into a smirk. It was a half-hearted attempt, one that couldn't mask a deeper layer of sorrow, but it was there. Whitney looked up at the flame devouring all the buildings up Merchants Row ahead of them.

You fool, Whitney!

He wasn't sure how he missed it. There was no mistaking her distinct brand. It wasn't like an ordinary flame that billowed and grew gradually. Hers was like a tsunami, chewing through wood and stone like parchment.

"This was you, wasn't it?"

She glanced at Aquira. "I had some help. We found the man who destroyed Troborough. Who killed Wetzel."

"Iam's light, Sora. Did you forget that this isn't his home to get revenge on?"

"I… I lost control." She hung her head.

Whitney took her by the shoulders and smiled. "Merchants Row needed remodeling anyway. Oldest part of Winde Port and it shows."

Sora looked up with only her eyes.

"So, is he dead?" Whitney asked.

"I'm not sure."

"Well, Torsten will finish the job. He was headed there too."

"I know." A genuine grin finally broke out on her face. "I saved his life," she said, and then a second later, "again."

"Oh, he won't like that at all."

"No, I wouldn't think so," she said.

"If Muskigo is still around—"

"Don't forget the assassin after us."

"Ah, yes, how could I?" He laughed. "Shogging exile, I think it's time we get the yig out of here."

"Remember when you said I'd love it here?"

Whitney rolled his eyes. "Well, the gates are burning, thanks to you. So now both armies are killing each other. I'd rather avoid that, so, same plan as ever?"

"Which is?"

"Steal a ship," Whitney said, matter of factly. "There are a few smaller ones docked on the northern wharf that I didn't knock over. Just gotta get our papers and we can be on our way."

"Papers? Seriously? You think anyone is going to be concerned with papers at a time like this?"

"The law is the law, Sora." He winked.

"Everyone's a bit preoccupied right now. I doubt anyone is going to be stopping us to see our papers."

"It's not for here. We'll be crossing Shesaitju waters, and if you haven't noticed, they're in the middle of a rebellion. The Winde Traders Guild isn't going anywhere, however much their home city is hurting. They have pull."

"I don't know," she said. "We are in this mess over those stupid papers."

"Did I mention pirates? Only the worst ones will hit a member of the Guild. Which reminds me, do you still have our gold?"

"I… uh." Her gaze flitted toward the burning cinder that was the prefect's mansion lost in a cloud of smoke across the canal. "Lost it while uh… running from Kazimir."

"Shog in a barrel," he said. Then, he clapped his hands together, smiled and said, "Then we really need those papers. Give a pirate enough gold, and they'll leave you alone. Give them nothing, they'll take your ship and leave you for sharks."

"They can do that even if we have papers."

"But they're less likely to. Trust me, they are in a safe place. We'll be in and out."

"Where?"

"Tayvada's house."

Whitney saw a wave of fear wash over her face.

"What's wrong?" he asked.

"It's nothing…"

"Sure, doesn't look like nothing," he said. "What's going on? Oh, him."

He was ashamed he'd so quickly forgotten their last experience at the guild member's home. He could only imagine what horrors she'd suffered at Kazimir's hand.

"It's fine," Sora said. "Let's go get some yigging papers."

"There's my girl!" Whitney took her hand again, and they took off.

The further from Merchants Row they got, the less forgiving the chill in the air became. Lucky for the city, the fire seemed contained to that avenue, the strong wind keeping it focused. Merchant fronts and governmental buildings, the places the owners could afford to rebuild.

The more residential districts were left mostly untouched, baring the arrows and spears stuck in their walls—and the haphazardly discarded corpses littering the ground from the fighting. Smoke, fog, and snow mixed to create a thick haze at street level. It was like a ghost town.

"How did you escape Kazimir?" Whitney asked as they ran.

"He went to watch you be executed," she answered.

"As if that were possible."

"Then, Aquira showed up and freed me." The wyvern screeched from her perch on Sora's shoulder. "Kazimir chased me until I found Muskigo."

"And you decided to go after revenge instead of finding me?"

"I...I..."

Whitney laughed, then stopped walking and looked her in the eyes. They stood on the opposite side of the canal leading into the Panping Ghetto now.

"I'm kidding. You were trying to survive, and you did, which means my lessons really are working."

"Don't flatter yourself."

"I am glad you didn't kill Muskigo though. I had the chance to take down Darkings too, but embarrassing him was way better. Torsten told me there's no coming back from murder, and for once, I think he might be right."

"That self-righteous oaf?"

"I know, right?"

"He'll take care of Muskigo," she said. "They'll all hang for what they did. The ones who deserve it."

"Your mouth to Iam's ears." Whitney bowed with a flourish and beckoned Sora over the canal toward the run-down church on the edge of the ghetto. "My lady."

Sora didn't move. She stared in the direction of the church and the dilapidated homes of her people, and Whitney thought he noticed her legs start to tremble.

"You want to wait here?" he asked.

"Shogging exile, no."

"Don't worry about Muskigo." He patted his pocket, feeling the writ issued to Kazimir and the Dom Nohzi requesting they rescind the blood pact in the name of Yuri Darkings. "Darkings' father called them off, so I think old Barty is in more danger from Kazimir than us."

"Bartholomew?"

"Right? That's his name. I know, ridiculous. Anyway, I've got the papers right here. If Kazimir shows up, we flash them, and we'll be fine."

"More papers?"

He stuck out his chest. "It's the way of greater men."

"Well, let's be quick anyway."

The Ghetto was nearly untouched by battle but for a couple of homes near the front, across from the church. Their roofs were caved in, probably just due to shoddy craftsmanship. For once, the streets were empty of the homeless. There wasn't a lighted candle or even a sound.

The door to Tayvada's remained ajar, so they pushed their way in. Whitney's own memories flooded back so he could only imagine what Sora would be thinking. Tayvada swinging, dripping blood. Kazimir's nightmarish grin as he emerged from the shadows and made their lives living exile.

"I hid it over there," he said, pointing to the chimney.

He reached up and pulled down the makeshift package—the crown wrapped in the trading papers. Opening it, his eyes gleamed like he'd won the pot in a game of gems. In a way, he sort of had.

He felt a hard fist against his shoulder.

"Are you *kidding* me?" Sora shouted. "That's what this is really about!"

He heard a hiss and nearly toppled over when Aquira popped up over Sora's shoulder, a flicker of fire in her open mouth.

"Call off your dragon!" He smiled.

"This isn't a joke, Whitney Fierstown. You dragged us back here to this… place… just so you could get your beloved crown?"

"No, it's not like that. I swear. Happy accident. We just needed the papers and I happened to leave them with the crown."

Sora folded her arms and huffed. Whitney went to place his hand on her shoulder, but Aquira hissed again.

"I promise, Sora," Whitney said. He extended his hand with the crown. "You can trash the crown if that'll prove it to you."

"Okay," she reached for the crown, but he swiftly reeled it back.

"Come on, is that necessary?"

"You just said—"

"Fine, it was a little about the crown, but it was more than that. We have no autlas now, and we're sailing war-ravaged waters. We need a bargaining chip in case of—"

"Shesaitju ships, I know."

"Or pirates." He sighed. "And I wanted you to come back here. Look." He took her by the hand and led her outside. To his surprise, she let him. He pointed to all the dilapidated buildings. "I think you should burn it to the ground. The whole place. Make sure no one ever has to live under these conditions ever again."

Sora just stared.

"You said it yourself," he continued "'No one should have to live like this.'"

He could see wheels turning in Sora's mind.

"No," she said, finally. "Let's just go get a ship."

"Wait, what do you mean? Yesterday you were ready to do whatever it took to make sure these people didn't live this way. I thought…"

"I don't want to talk about it," she said and started walking.

"Sora."

She spun around. "Fine, if you need to know. I followed every one of your dumb lessons. I used my 'assets' to get into Muskigo's inner circle. I pretended to be Tayvada's wife, and he bought it."

It was now Whitney's turn to stare.

"While I was with him," she continued, "I saw so many of my people being treated with far more respect by them than I ever have by the Glass.

But even so…it was just a ploy by Muskigo to get more allies so more can die in this war."

"War is what forced my kind here," she said. "This isn't their realm. This is foreign territory. Same as when I came to Troborough. I lived in a basement below a shack, Whit. But you know what? That was leagues better than not having any home at all. What if I burned this place down and the Glass didn't care? Actually, they won't care. This isn't Merchants Row."

"But Sora—"

"But nothing. Muskigo burned down my little shack, and now I have no home. What would make this any different?"

Whitney tilted his head, looked back into Tayvada's empty home and said, "Fine, it's the gesture that counts, then. Let's go."

"One second." Sora returned to Tayvada's door and knelt before it. Whitney couldn't help but listen in. She set Aquira down in front of the house. "You deserve a chance to say goodbye, girl."

The wyvern trotted up to the door and gave it a whiff—enough, Whitney assumed, to remember the scent of her former master forever. She let out a squeal and looked back at Sora with her big, yellow eyes.

"I know, girl," Sora said. "This place will miss him, too. But things will get better, I know it. Now, c'mon." She extended her arm, and Aquira darted back onto her shoulder. Sora closed the door, then drew a deep breath.

"All right, what are you waiting for?" she said, turning to Whitney. "We've got a ship to steal."

"You have no idea how proud I am to hear those words," Whitney said. "And Muskigo's inner circle? By Iam, I demand to know every detail of that story and how you used your *assets*."

"Is that jealousy?" she asked.

"Professional curiosity."

"Shut up." She chuckled and punched him in the arm again. He had no idea he could miss a sore spot so much.

XXVI

THE KNIGHT

Torsten shifted his stance. Despite the heat beating down on his body from all around, the street was slick with melting ice. His fingers tightened around the grip of his claymore until it felt like an extension of his arm. He drew slow, steady breaths, the air thick with smoke. He wasn't afraid. So much of his world had become a mystery but this, he understood. Battle. And as he watched Muskigo's zhulong charging him, gold-clad tusks thrashing, he was both there and at the beginning. His mind recalled when he was but an armiger, and those first few bouts training under Uriah Davies. He remembered the sting of the wooden sword upon his back. Being slammed to the dirt over and over. And of course, he remembered the first time he landed a strike on the then-Wearer.

Kings, queens, and ancient feuds were one thing, but this he understood. This was kill or be killed.

He waited until the last possible moment, then shifted to the right and swung his sword wide, low to high. The side of a tusk smashed him in the ribs just as the tip of his claymore cut through the zhulong rear haunch. Any ordinary sword wouldn't have pierced its thick, scaly hide, but the glaruium of Mount Lister was strong and its sharpness never dulled.

Torsten caught himself before hitting the ground and turned, half-crouched. His chestplate had a dent the size of a fist, the pain of the blow pulling at his entire left side. The zhulong, on the other hand, went down hard. Muskigo flew from its back, rolled across the street and found his footing in one smooth motion.

"I'll give it to you, Shieldsman," he said as he flicked snow off his scimitar. "You are brave as you are foolish." His left half was horribly burned, and blood oozed out of the wound in the back of his other shoulder where Sora stabbed him. If the pain affected him, he didn't show it.

"I am a vessel," Torsten said, having to growl just to cover for the fact that every breath he drew made his ribcage feel like it was going to pop through his skin. "Now, you will see the power of faith."

Another plangent moan of a Drav Cra horn sounded, and with it, the din of battle escalated. Every clash of metal like thunder creeping ever-closer. Footsteps like raindrops pounding on stone. The coming of a storm.

"Do you hear that?" Muskigo said. "It's the sound of your army failing. And when they do, I will bring everything I have crashing upon Yarrington."

"Not if you are dead."

"Spoken like a true follower of Iam. Peace?" he scoffed. "Your god is a bringer of death. So come, vessel, and do what he does best!"

Muskigo brandished his sword, and Torsten charged. Torsten was larger, as was his weapon, but even with his many injuries, Muskigo was impossibly fast. He ducked right, then spun out of the way of a furious swipe. Torsten immediately recognized the Black Fist style. Muskigo never let the full brunt of Torsten's claymore land upon his sword, but deflected blow after blow downward. He used his scimitar more like a shield than a weapon, and his lack of encumbering armor always had him one step ahead.

That was the essence of the style—to be as unshakable as a balled fist. To wait, absorb, exhaust your enemy until the time was right to land one perfect, deadly punch.

Muskigo caught a thrust between his blade and hip, then slid forward, slicing Torsten across a weak spot of armor behind one knee. Torsten roared and whipped around, his scimitar cracking the street as it barely missed Muskigo.

"You want to know what I learned from my father?" Muskigo asked, pacing out of range, barely breathing heavily. "Patience."

Torsten turned with him, struggling to hide his windedness. Between the bruised rib, exhaustion from the ambush, and the weight of his glaruium armor, his muscles were being pushed to their limits. He vowed, should he make it from Winde Port alive, to train more often and focus less on politics.

"The zhulong is a stubborn beast, you see," Muskigo continued. "When it feels threatened it charges—no matter what. But the sand serpents that inhabit the beaches outside Latiapur, you would barely know they were there, even if you were staring right at them."

"Are you going to keep talking? I've been looking forward to this since the moment I saw you in the Fellwater."

Torsten took a hard step and swung low at Muskigo's shins. The afhem's agile body allowed him to hurdle the sword. He landed, and before Torsten could bring his sword back around, the man had darted forward and sliced his elbow.

It was as if Muskigo's blade were precisely drawn to Torsten's armor joints. He pulled a sharp breath through his teeth.

"The serpent buries itself and waits," Muskigo continued, keeping his distance and circling Torsten like a hunting wolf. "Sometimes for days, sometimes until it starves. It waits for prey to stroll by, unassuming, and then... it strikes like a bolt of lightning." Muskigo feigned attack.

"Fight me!" Torsten bellowed.

"There is honor in charging like the zhulong as my father did but they are clumsy, mindless creatures happy to be ridden. The serpent, on the other hand, won't move a muscle. And by the time you realize it's still alive, its venom is coursing through your veins."

"No!" Torsten said. "Your rebellion ends here, today."

Torsten went at him again, throwing every bit of his remaining energy into every attack. Muskigo didn't even use his sword this time. He dipped and evaded, and as Torsten went high with his claymore, Muskigo's gray fist shot forward and struck in the center of his chest.

Torsten's armor caved, and he careened backward, the sword slipping from his grasp. He looked down when he landed. He had taken hits from battle hammers and not suffered such damage. His time for amazement ended swiftly as Muskigo's scimitar raced toward his head. Torsten did the only thing he could. Used his strength.

He caught it with both hands, the blade driving through the joints of his gauntlets and slicing his hands. He held it there, the edge only inches from cleaving his skull. Now it was Muskigo's turn to look surprised.

Torsten shifted one hand, allowing the scimitar to continue into the ground at the side of his head. With the other he punched Muskigo hard across the face, the spiked knuckles of his gauntlet splitting his lip. A second shot tore chunks of flesh from his cheek.

Muskigo staggered back. Torsten fought the sharp pain racking his limbs as he scrambled to his feet and drove his armored shoulder into the afhem. They tumbled across the slick street, their tangled bodies spinning. They punched and kicked all the way until their bodies slipped over the edge of Merchants Canal.

They landed on their backs. The thick ice covering the water splintered but didn't break. Torsten's ears rang from countless blows to the head. The sounds of battle at his back were louder than ever, as if the armies were now warring within the city itself.

Muskigo didn't seem to be faring much better. And as they both got to their feet, ready to engage again, the ice cracked more.

Half the man's gray face was carved up and drenched in blood like his torso, but Muskigo's confidence never waned. "I wonder which one of us will go through first?" He spread his sandaled feet wide to disperse his weight.

Torsten looked down. Cracks snaked away from his armored feet like the webs of a spider. It didn't matter how he shifted his weight. He reached for the pendant hanging from his neck, only to be reminded it was no longer there.

But he never needed it, not really. Iam was in his heart, always—right there along with the King who helped forge him into the man he was.

"You forget, afhem," he said. "Only one of our deaths matters!"

Torsten darted forward. He could feel the slick surface giving way under his heavy feet, but he kept pushing. Muskigo got his sword around a fraction of a second too late. Torsten's massive body barreled into him, and when they hit the ice, this time it gave way.

Icy water and darkness enveloped Torsten as he clung to Muskigo's waist to try and drag him under. The afhem clawed at the unbroken ice, desperate to stay above the surface. His lack of heavy armor made him fast, but even seconds below the surface might stop his heart.

Torsten could feel it; bitter death seeping through the cracks in his armor. Pushing against his lips to reach his lungs. Yet even with his weight and armor, they didn't sink. Instead, they began to rise through the ice.

His head emerged from the water. Two of Muskigo's Serpent Guards had thrown a rope wrapped to a gondola post to the afhem and were hauling him up.

"Yo—u d—die… here," Torsten said, shivering.

Another warrior, standing at the lip of the canal, threaded his bow. It took every bit of his strength for Torsten to move his head out of the way of an arrow. Muskigo then thrashed and caught Torsten in the face with a foot. His numb arms gave out, and the leader of the rebellion wriggled free.

As he plunged into the water, Torsten watched Muskigo be heaved to the surface and wrapped in leathers. Torsten could hear nothing but the slowing rhythm of his own heart, but he saw the afhem's now-purple lips rasp orders.

Muskigo stared down into the depths of the canal for a moment. He didn't seem proud or satisfied, just bowed his head in respect as he was escorted away.

It was Torsten's last clear sight before the cold started to blur his vision. His entire body went numb, toes to skull. Even his heart was silent. And as the water closed in around him, he couldn't help but feel this was his path to Elsewhere. He had dedicated his life to the light of Iam, and here he would die, weightless in the dark. A failure.

A spear stabbed through the surface. Torsten couldn't feel his fingers, but he was able to get a few around the staff. Then the tip of another spear hooked around the back of his armor. Before he knew it, the reddish glow of fire filled his vision. A dozen hands grabbed at him, rolling him up onto the surface.

He couldn't speak, couldn't even move. He could do nothing but shiver as the world came into view again. Shesaitju forces were in a full retreat, pursued by the combined army of Glassmen and Drav Cra. The fire, which had carved a path of destruction all the way to the walls was dwindling as snow fell harder.

A familiar face leaned down over him, pale and half-covered by a spiky, red birthmark. Redstar spoke, but Torsten couldn't hear a thing. He could only watch as Redstar extended his hand for the warlock Freydis to slice. He placed his bloody palm against Torsten's chest and began to mutter under his breath until the hand glowed red. His eyes were shut, lids flickering.

Warmth built within Torsten's heart. He could feel it spread through his veins like a tree laying roots. First, his fingers and toes thawed, then the limbs themselves, and then he gasped for air. Water spewed out, literally steaming thanks to Redstar's blood magic.

Redstar withdrew his hand. "There you are," he said. "Breathe. Nesilia tells me it is not yet your time."

Torsten brushed him aside and rolled over. He still couldn't find the ability to speak, but he leaned back on perched elbows and stared down toward the docks. The Shesaitju were fleeing to their ships and rowboats, abandoning Winde Port. And now the streets were filled with Torsten's own people... and the Drav Cra.

They beat their chests and cheered, and on the lips of both peoples, Torsten heard a name that had a part of him wishing he'd drowned.

"Redstar, Redstar, Redstar..."

XXVII

THE THIEF

As Whitney, Sora, and Aquira crested the hill of mansions overlooking Winder's Wharf and the rest of the city, Whitney was sure of one thing—Winde Port would never be the same. That free-loving, gold-flipping place he'd loved had seen the wrath of war. Not just the fire that burned its finest shops and most stately buildings, but a terror would hover over the place that would change it.

Whitney felt it in Panping any time he was there—this weight, as if the spirits of the dead were constantly whispering to the survivors of Liam's war that they were left behind.

War would ruin another place he loved, but as he looked down upon the battle-filled streets at the walls and heart of the city, he couldn't help but feel a bit of pride that he'd helped the winning side. It was difficult to see through the lingering smoke in the night, but the Shesaitju were clearly starting to retreat, eyes set on their rowboats and ships moored on the southern beaches. The Glass Army charged through the city walls like a nail through a ship's hull.

"He did it," Whitney said, not even trying to hide his joy. "He really yigging did it!" The war was stupid, a pointless squabble between rich lords over land and forgotten slights. But Torsten, his friend, led this battle. And after everything that had happened to the kingdom he loved for whatever Iam-forsaken reason, Whitney knew the Shieldsman deserved a win.

"Praise be," Sora said, her voice dripping with sarcasm. "I suppose he'll give all credit to Iam for saving his hide once again?"

"Oh, you know he will. Never to you… unless… are you Iam and you didn't tell me?"

"If I were, I'd have created you without a mouth. Now let's move before the docks are overrun again." Her fingernails dug into Whitney's forearm as she pulled him down the hill. Aquira looked back and screeched at him as if warning him not to test her.

"Are you sure you don't want to take a moment and knock another mansion off Darkings' board?" Whitney pointed left, at the highest point in the city upon which the homes of Bartholomew and Winde Port's richest families stood. With the glow of dwindling flames so far off, they were drenched in darkness. A corner here or there glowed under whatever slivers of moonlight slipped through the clouds, but not a candle was lit. Snow piled up in front of their heavy doors.

Most of their inhabitants probably got out safely through their own tunnels like the Darkings. Or they threw their slaves at the Shesaitju and ran. Now, the homes stood as great, big gravestones for the city.

"I think we should stop making enemies," Sora said, pulling him harder.

"That's a great lesson," Whitney answered. "Write that down: friends are better."

The road flattened out, and he pulled Sora back against a building on the edge of the wharf. A cohort of Shesaitju ran by, screaming and cursing. Whitney noticed, out of the corner of his eye, they were leaning against the Winde Traders Guild Hall. Through a shattered window, he could see all the velvet-cushioned chairs were overturned and plates of delectables strewn across the floor.

Sora peeked around the corner. "Most of the ships are tipped!" she exclaimed.

"About that…" Whitney said. He stole a look as well. The ships used in his distraction were in rough shape. With the snow picking up, a few of the smaller ones were weighted much too heavily to one side, others were half-sunken in the shallow water from ruptured hulls.

He cursed himself as he looked down toward the beachfront.

The Shesaitju vessels remained in fine condition, awaiting the return of their respective crews out on the bay. It looked like a choreographed dance upon the waters, rowboat oars plunging and pulling in perfect harmony as gray men made their way to freedom. Zhulong and their riders plunged into the ice-cold water, where the hulking beasts proved to be unexpectedly agile swimmers.

A volley of arrows cascaded overhead, then rained down upon the waters, many finding their places buried within the boats and their pilots. The Glassmen were advancing, while brave Shesaitju warriors still on the wharf gave their lives to allow for a thorough retreat.

"What about that one?" Sora pointed toward the small, black corsair vessel at the north end of the dock. It was right next to the one Whitney and Tum Tum had started the chain reaction of devastation upon. Its low stature kept it safe even as the adjacent ship's hull angled up and over it.

"Good enough." The small, nimble ship would be easy to maneuver through the crowded bay, even, hopefully, by a crew of only two. "All right, on my count, we run for it."

Sora regarded the wyvern on her shoulder. "Ready?" Aquira clicked her tongue in response.

"Three…two… one…"

They hurried out onto the quay. Sora's foot slid out on the icy surface, but Whitney was there to catch her. The heaviest fighting was south of them, by Merchants Row and the beach. They made it to the ship without a hitch and climbed up the lowered ramp. It was only when they were onboard that they noticed the four gray men already on the deck.

"This will be our ship we are having!" one of them said in broken speech. They raised their curved blades.

"I've got these," Whitney said, holding out his arm.

"What a gentleman," Sora replied.

Whitney was just about to say something smart when he saw one of their knees snap inward. Tum Tum stood behind him, a giant hammer in hand.

"Not without me ye ain't," Tum Tum shouted.

Whitney charged while they were distracted. He lowered his shoulder, and it connected with one of their stomachs. Luckily, Tum Tum noticed him and dropped to hands and knees at the last moment. The Shesaitju propelled backward, tripped over Tum Tum, and flipped over the railing into the icy waters of the bay.

The remaining two went back to back. One kept their sword trained on Tum Tum and the other on Whitney.

"If ye'd told me your plan it'd saved me a heap of trouble," Tum Tum said.

"But you love trouble," Whitney replied.

The warrior swung at Whitney, who rolled aside and came up wielding the dagger he stole from Fenton. Tum Tum slammed his hammer down on the deck with all his might. The wood planks nearby came unsettled, and Whitney's opponent lost balance when he went to take another swipe.

"Watch the ship! We need it!"

Whitney ducked to the side, then darted forward and delivered a deep slice through his opponent's hamstring. At the same time, Tum Tum raised the handle of his hammer into his target's groin, then flipped him, legs first. His head slammed into the floor, knocking him out cold.

"Uh, Whitney, when you boys are done!" Sora said.

Whitney looked back. Several more Shesaitju were bounding down the wharf toward the ship, desperate for any suitable vessel.

"Tum Tum, hoist the mainsail!" Whitney ordered.

"I won't be able to reach, ye dolt," he said. "This ship was made for taller men."

"Must I do it all?" Whitney groaned. "Fine, just help Sora."

Whitney tossed her his dagger before hurrying to help Tum Tum prep for launch.

Sora drew a cut along her palm, then raised her bloody hand toward the attackers and screamed. No ball or pillar of flame exploded from her hand as Whitney was used to. Only a smattering of pathetic embers spewed out.

Whitney stopped by the mast. "Where's your magic?" he hollered.

"I… I don't know," she said, suddenly sounding faint. "I can't manage even a spark."

Whitney was about to run back to help when Aquira soared off her shoulder. She swept in front of the Shesaitju, blowing a line of fire between the ship and the wharf. She didn't pack much of a punch, but the heat was palpable.

Tum Tum waddled over to the ramp to hold them off. The ramp was securely attached, but the dwarf brought his hammer down on it as one Shesaitju braved the flame. Just then, Whitney unfurled the sails, and they snapped up, catching the heady winds.

The ship pulled away from the dock. The weakened ramp snapped in half, the Shesaitju upon it plummeting into the icy depths. A second later, the vessel jarred to a stop.

"Sora," Whitney shouted. "Forget them, get that rope!" He pointed to the single rope still attached to a cleat on the wharf. The Shesaitju must have untied the rest before they overtook them. Sora nodded her understanding. She panted as she slashed at it twice, sending two frayed ends into the wind. A Shesaitju dove toward the ship and grabbed onto the stern before his fingers met Sora's knife.

"Jolly fine departure everyone!" Whitney exclaimed.

"Whit!" Sora screamed.

Whitney turned quickly to face her as a sword swiped only inches from his head. He heard a hum, felt a sting, then blood sprayed in front of his face. He dropped to his knees and saw a Shesaitju behind him. His knee was a mangled mess, but he stood upright on his good leg. He didn't get his sword back around before the dwarf finished the job, crushing his skull against the deck.

"Whitney," Sora said, running toward him "Are you okay?"

"What?" He placed a hand on the side of his head. It was bleeding profusely, and his head rang.

Tum Tum came around in front of him, holding the top half of Whitney's ear. He lifted it to his mouth and shouted, "Can ye hear me?"

Whitney ripped it out of his hands. He held it to the portion of ear still attached, and only when they touched did he realize how much it really stung.

"My yigging ear!" he shouted.

Sora knelt in front of him. She couldn't mask her concern, but Aquira looked like she wanted to lick up the blood.

"Is it bad?" Whitney said.

"I've seen worse…" she lied.

"Can you fix it?" he asked Sora, holding the ear up.

"Not right now I don't think." She looked down at her bloody hand. "I think I'm completely drained."

"Well, you did just light half the city on fire..." His words trailed off. He looked back at Tum Tum, who not only had no idea she could do such magic, but it was his city that burned. If he took offense, he didn't show it. The Black Sands had overtaken the place, regardless.

"So ye be a mystic?" Tum Tum asked.

Sora shrugged. "I'm something. We're going to Yaolin City if we make it out of this bay alive."

"Hello!" Whitney interrupted. "My ear!"

"Oh, quit whinin ye flower picker," Tum Tum said. "It's only a piece." He slapped him in the side of the head. Whitney yelped.

"Here." Sora took the chunk of flesh from Whitney's hands. Then she buried it in a bit of snow piled around the mast. "We'll keep it fresh, and I'll see if I can help after we have some rest."

"Sure, I'll just sail around, earless," Whitney said. He stood and drew a long breath of the chilly air.

"You two dump these bodies off the ship. Tum, I'm guessing you're okay with going to Yaolin? Otherwise, I can drop you off in the Boiling Waters."

The dwarf stood at the rail and stared longingly back at the wharf and his city, glowing red. "Aye. All I gots be gone anyway," he said, sadness heavy in his voice.

"Then I hope you're ready for a fun ride." Whitney grabbed hold of the wheel and spun it. The ship lurched and changed course.

"How do you—" Sora began.

"What part of 'I sailed with Grisham "Gold Grin" Gale' did I not make clear?"

He knew she didn't believe him about half the things he said he'd done —which was probably smart on her part—but this one was the cold, hard truth. He knew how to run a ship, though he was glad to have Tum Tum and Sora onboard to help with things. Who knows, maybe by the time they reached Yaolin City, Sora would be a right good sailor.

First, they had to weave their way through a number of Shesaitju warships and rowboats. He hoped they were too preoccupied with their escape to worry about a small corsair vessel. Still, he kept their course southeast, so it seemed like they were Shesaitju soldiers part of the retreat. At his first opportunity, he could cut the sails to steer them behind the Breakwaters—a tight clumping of dagger-like stones sticking up from Trader's Bay.

For a large ship, the boulders would be catastrophic, but this corsair would slip right into the strait with no difficulty. Then, it would be off toward the Boiling Waters on the fastest route to Panping.

"We don't want to be spotted, so everyone stay low," Whitney said. "Or, well, Tum Tum, you can just stand."

"Very funny, one ear."

Whitney grinned and steadied the wheel, feeling the weight of the ship and waters fighting back. "I think we finally found my pirate name."

"Too bad you can't grow a beard!" Sora hollered over from the other side of the deck.

Whitney glared back at her, then smiled. He'd never been so happy to see someone sliding a body off the deck of a ship before. He'd never been so happy to see anyone.

XXVIII

THE MYSTIC

"I must say, Sora," Whitney began, "ever since you found me, these have been adventures for the record books. Of all that happened in that gods-forsaken city, being pivotal pieces in a battle for Pantego's soul will be tough to top."

Whitney stared over the starboard side of the deck back to Winde Port. He barely paid attention to the wheel now that they were passed the retreating Shesaitju army and heading for the strait out of the bay. Tum Tum was busy angling the ship's single, triangular sail to catch what little breeze there was. After that focused gust that fed Sora's fire and felt so much like magic, the air was still. The water may as well have been frozen it was so flat, tiny ripples wiggling like glowing snakes under the light of the moons.

"Clearly, I attract trouble," Sora said.

"And rebel afhems," Whitney muttered.

"I knew you were jealous!"

"Just that I missed such an incredible display. I was worried you were too uptight to act." Whitney flinched, clearly expecting her to punch him. When she didn't, he turned and found Aquira leaning over the boom of the sail, glaring down at him. "We're never going to be alone again, are we?"

Sora reached up and stroked her new friend's tail. "Nope. She's part of this scoundreling crew."

"Going with scoundreling, then? Perfect."

For a short while, they quietly watched the retreat. The Shesaitju vessels were already unloading at the docks of a small village on the opposite side of the bay. Back in Winde Port, the Glass army celebrated victory. Or at least, that's what the tiny, shiny dots flitting around the wharf looked like they were doing.

"Do you think Torsten made it out?" Sora asked.

"Of course, he's too stubborn to die. Look." Whitney pointed to the wharf. "That's probably him right there. Of course, it is; no one else has such blinding armor at night. Happy to be of service again, Torsten!" He waved.

"Why were you helping him, anyway?"

"He was supposed to help me find you after Muskigo was eliminated. Clearly, since I found you well enough by myself, he still owes me one."

"That makes two of us. Did I mention I saved him and his men from an ambush in the estate when I started that fire?"

"Yeah?"

"They walked right into it."

Whitney sighed. "What is that man going to do without us?"

"Probably lose a war."

"You're right. We should go back." He pretended to start spinning the wheel.

"Whitney, stop!" Sora laughed.

"What? You're right, we can't leave him behind. He needs us."

"Whit." Her hand fell upon his, and they turned toward each other. She stared at him while he wore that same, goofy grin that hadn't changed since he was a boy. He still couldn't grow a beard, but for a runt from Troborough, he was handsome as a prince. The standards weren't high. The only difference was one of his ears now had a chunk taken off.

"I'm sorry," they said at the same time.

"For what?" they said at the same time again.

They chuckled.

"You first," Whitney said.

"No, you go ahead," Sora replied. "I want to hear this."

Whitney stole a page out of Sora's book and rolled his eyes.

"Fine," he began. "I'm sorry I let you get taken back at Tayvada's place. I'm sorry for dragging you into this life. It's not safe. It's no place for a… lady."

"Hah! A lady? Don't let my tattered clothes fool you. Plus, you didn't *let* me be taken. You couldn't have stopped that heinous creature even if you wanted to. He's a yigging upyr, Whit. You know what tha—"

Whitney held out an arm. He held his stomach like he was going to vomit. "Vampire," Whitney said with a shudder.

"Let me guess, you worked with them a few years back. Cue some ridiculous story."

"No, my dear, Sora. This one will be a first, and one I'm glad to be rid of. No wonder he avoided sunlight."

Sora nodded.

"Yigging gods. If I knew that was what Barty sent after us maybe I would have killed the slob. He didn't want to…"

"Drink my blood?" Sora asked. "He did, but Aquira wouldn't let him."

"Thank the fallen gods for her."

At the mention of her name, Aquira craned her neck down from the sail toward Sora.

"You were scared, weren't you?" Sora scratched the wyvern under her chin. Aquira's wings expanded, and she stuck her head out, the thin flap of skin underneath stretching taut.

"I'm sure it was only her," Whitney remarked.

Sora regarded him and her heart sunk. "I wanted to find you," she said, not looking him in the eye. "But so much happened so fast. I was worried you died, then running from Kazimir, Muskigo, seeing my people. It all—"

He placed a finger over her mouth. "Sora, you don't have to explain a thing to me." He craned his neck and gestured to the red mark ringing his neck. "The gods seem to want me alive no matter what. I think I might be invincible."

"By Iam, Whitney." She pulled him closer and examined the dark red ring around his neck. "I didn't notice that. It looks awful. Kazimir said you survived execution, but he didn't say you were already strung up to die when you did. How did you get out of it?"

"You've got magic, and I've got my own secrets." He puffed out his chest and went to playfully run his hand through his hair. His finger grazed the sliced part of his ear, and he winced.

"Smooth," Sora chuckled. "We're going to have to do something about that soon. It's going to get infected." She reached up toward it. Her thumb hit a piece of his hair, and a thick, wet paste rubbed off. "Ick! Is that, shog?"

"Long story," Whitney said.

"Oh, c'mon, I finally want to hear a story and you're holding out?" When she looked down, she realized how close to him she'd gotten to examine his wounds. She could feel the warmth of his breath. They locked eyes, and on his face, he wore an expression unlike any she'd ever seen him wearing. Her heart started to race, and she didn't know why.

He smiled, but he didn't back away—not even as Aquira growled from up above. Instead, she could feel him slowly growing closer. "Well, we do have plenty of time," he said softly.

"I wouldn't be so sure of that," said a voice from behind them, accent thick as blood.

Sora and Whitney fell apart from each other and whipped around. Kazimir emerged from the shadows of the open captain's quarters. He clicked his tongue in disapproval.

"Did you think I would so easily allow you to leave?" he asked. "After all we've been through together?"

"Who the yig be that!" Tum Tum shouted from the bow.

Aquira flew down to Sora's shoulder and growled. Sora raised her hand. It was still bleeding, but she couldn't feel an ounce of that dark power roiling within her. No matter how she willed on Elsewhere, she felt... empty within.

Whitney's arm extended in front of her as he stepped forward. "No need to burn down the ship." He reached into his pocket and removed a roll.

"Kazimir," he began in diplomatic fashion, "I have a writ signed by Yuri Darkings himself. You are released from your blood pact with Bartholomew Darkings, so we can just all move on."

In the span of a second, Whitney was on his back, and Kazimir straddled him like a mare. Whitney turned away from the man and clenched his eyes tightly. But still, he held up the paper. "You wouldn't want to upset your bosses," he said. "The Master of Coin could be a powerful ally."

"Not a soul will know what happens here."

"Your Sanguine Gods will," Whitney grated.

"*Lords*. And they know that a pact cannot be rescinded. Not even by a king, let alone some Council member. This paper is as worthless as you are." Kazimir ripped it from his hands. His nightmarish grin widened as he released it to the wind.

"Damn that family," Whitney swore under his breath.

"I don't understand, Whit," Sora said. "You said the pact was ended." Her voice shook. Even having Aquira on her shoulder, ready to fiercely protect her, didn't make her feel brave. All she could do was stare at those terrible, soulless eyes, frozen.

"Clearly, father Darkings lied so I wouldn't kill his son. I knew I should have gone with my gut."

Sora's stomach went tight. She knew precisely why Whitney didn't go with his gut. Why he delved back in the city, helped Torsten... everything. For her.

"This is no longer about you, thief," Kazimir snapped. "In time, Bartholomew Darkings will pay for his attempted retraction with his own blood. But I'm here for her."

He regarded Sora, breathed in deep, and released a moan. The way his lower lip trembled made Sora's skin crawl.

"Yes," he said, a twinge of ecstasy lacing the word. "Cut, dash, slice, rend. The smell alone gives me a strength I haven't felt in years."

He leaned down and spoke softly in Whitney's ear—something Sora couldn't hear. Whitney's face lost its color, and he stopped fighting like he was petrified into stone by the gorgons of legend.

"I suggest ye get off him and off our ship," Tum Tum demanded. He stood beside Sora now, hammer in hand.

Kazimir rose but kept a boot on Whitney's chest.

"My ship actually," he said. "An entire night wasted hunting the two of you, and you come right to me." He laughed, then looked back at Sora. "It's almost as if our union were destiny."

"Even still, yer outnumbered. Leave, or I'll make ye."

"Remain where you are, Dwarf! We have no quarrel, and that fact need not change. Besides, do you think your lumbering body is any match for me?"

Again, before Sora could blink, Kazimir changed locations. Aquira hissed and went to bite him, but he slapped the poor wyvern aside and sent her into the wall of the ship.

"Aquira!" Sora gasped.

The wyvern groaned but was still breathing. Sora tried to run to her, but Kazimir wrapped her midriff in a soft caress with one hand and placed the other against her neck.

"Take your hands off me!" she screamed, squirming, but it was no use. He was too strong.

Kazimir's hand slid down from her neck, fingertips tickling her shoulder, then her forearm before finally coming to rest around her wrist. She let out a squeak. She couldn't help it, his strength was unimaginable.

He extended his arm and with it, hers. Then, he licked a line of half-dried blood off her forearm. "We will be so happy together."

Whitney sat up but remained silent. Whatever Kazimir said had to be horrific to still his tongue for so long. Tum Tum stood like a statue, watching in horror as the upyr called Kazimir had his way. A simple tavern owner from Winde Port had likely never seen magic, let alone a man move so impossibly fast.

"I will die before marrying you," Sora said.

That seemed enough to shake Whitney. "Marry?" he asked. "Shogging exile, what are you talking about? This *creature* wants to marry you?"

"Watch your tongue, thief, or I will devour it," Kazimir said.

"Whit, what do I do?" Tum Tum asked quietly.

"Just stay still." The ship was beginning to lilt with nobody at the helm. Whitney slowly stood and wrapped his fingers around the steering wheel. Kazimir squeezed Sora tighter.

"I don't think you understand, Kazzy," Whitney said. "Can I call you that?"

That was when Sora saw that mad glint in his eye when Whitney was about to do something monumentally stupid. *Please don't,* she willed him. *Please.*

"Just weeks ago, we killed an actual goddess," Whitney continued. "She wasn't some two-bit joke wearing leather and silver clasps, flitting around the night like a bat. She was a real yigging goddess, and we gutted her like a fish."

Kazimir chuckled. "If the spirits are correct, it was the dark-skinned Wearer of the Glass and the marked orphan of the Drav Cra who brought doom to Bliss. You were merely a distraction and she… oh, the power within you." Kazimir again took a break from the conversation to take a whiff of Sora's neck. She could feel his fingers fluttering from the joy of it.

Hate welled inside of her. It felt like Elsewhere, yet it wasn't readily at her fingertips. No spark or preternatural heat. She cursed herself, cursed Wetzel for not training her better. In the distance was Winde Port, ravaged by the work of her hand. The fire seemingly fed on her anger and connection to Elsewhere even after it left her fingers. She had nearly won the battle for the Glass Kingdom all on her own, but now, faced with mortal danger, she couldn't even help herself or her closest friend.

"Let them go, and I'll come with you," she said. Her natural instincts screamed at her, but she said it anyway. "Be with you. Whatever you want."

"Sadly, dear, the time for courtesy has passed. You don't need to want to be mine for me to take you."

His breath was hot on her neck now. She could feel him against her back, an animalistic aura pulsating from him. His sharp fangs brushed her neck.

"Stop!" Whitney said. "Take me instead."

"What?" everyone asked at the same time.

"Take me, right? I'm a Lord now, technically... I'm not one for bureaucracies. But that's gotta count for something. The Wearer of White owes me, too. I can give you power, wealth."

"Whitney what are you doing?" Sora asked. "It's my blood he needs."

Kazimir seemed amused. "I rejected a Darkings. What could street filth possibly offer?"

"How about this?" Whitney slowly reached into the folds of his clothing, leaving his other hand raised. Kazimir grew tense until Whitney pulled out the broken half of the Glass Crown. All the precious gems set in its point glimmered even under the dull moonlight. "This here is the Glass Crown worn by Liam Nothhelm himself. Well, half of it."

"Meungor's axe!" Tum Tum exclaimed, stirred from his trance.

Kazimir approached it, dragging Sora along with him. Even his dark, soulless eyes seemed to brighten with wonder. Whitney shot her a subtle wink.

"I stole it right off his head," Whitney said, edging closer. "It broke while I escaped, but still has to be worth a damn fortune." Kazimir went to grab it, but Whitney pulled it back. "Not so fast. You drop this pact and leave us alone, it's yours. You can wear it for all I care."

"Why should I not just take it?"

"Honor?" Whitney audibly swallowed the lump forming in his throat. "Honestly, I was just trying to buy a second or two." Whitney jerked the wheel to the side. "Ah hah!"

The ship lurched a bit, and everyone took a small step to the left, but little else happened.

"Shog in a barrel. I really thought that would have done more."

Sora growled and used the minor distraction to kick Kazimir in the shin and escape his grasp. Whitney tossed her his dagger, and she caught it mid spin and whipped it around to plunge it into Kazimir's chest. Her strike met only air.

"Hands off him, demon," barked Tum Tum, brandishing his hammer.

Sora turned back around to see Kazimir somehow already holding Whitney.

"You children don't seem to understand how this all works!" the upyr snarled, a knife to Whitney's throat. Sora's knife. "Every single one of you is going to die. The only question now is how fast."

Kazimir pushed down on Whitney's shoulder and with his free hand put pressure on his forehead, stretching the skin of his neck.

"You kill me, and your bosses will be quite mad," Whitney taunted. "There's no blood pact on me anymore. You should be going after Bartholomew."

Kazimir laughed. "The Sanguine Lords didn't request the life of Tayvada Bokeo either, yet he is dead."

Whitney swallowed hard.

"How dare you speak his name after what you did," Sora snapped.

"Do you think anyone controls whom I send to Elsewhere? The Dom

Nohzi's days are numbered. Only I can lead them away from the fires of exile. We no longer need to hide in the shadows."

"It's okay, Sora," Whitney said, smiling, trying to stay brave. "Just blow us both away. I know the power is in you. Sail off to your people and see where you came from."

Sora knew what she wanted to say; that he was the only people she ever really had. But she couldn't bring herself to.

"Just leave him alone," she managed. "You've got what you want!"

Kazimir leaned down and licked Whitney's wounded ear. Whitney writhed in pain. The sight made Sora sick. All he'd done for her, and this was how he was going to die. He could have sent her on her way back in the forest all those weeks ago when she found him, but instead, he brought her into his way of life. He promised to show her things she'd never dreamed of. Accepted her. Gave her a purpose, even if she didn't love what it was.

Kazimir tore the crown from Whitney's fingers and shoved it onto the front of his head so hard it drew lines of blood on his temples.

"I've always wanted to taste the blood of a king," Kazimir whispered. Then, he sunk his fangs into Whitney's shoulder.

"No!" Sora yelled as Whitney cried out.

She felt a sudden rage bubbling again deep within. There was a familiar taste on her tongue—a mingling of iron and ash. She'd tasted it before, felt it before, but something was different this time. It was pure —unbridled.

"Leave him alone!" she bellowed.

She wasn't bleeding any longer, but she raised her hands anyway. She could feel the energy crackling around her fingertips. A blinding light bloomed around her hands—not just her hands, her entire body.

The light intensified and with it, all the strength fled her muscles like Elsewhere was sapping her. It was similar to conjuring a ball of flame or when she healed another's wound, only exponentially more intense. Even when she summoned the blast that stopped Redstar in the Webbed Woods, it paled in comparison.

She almost couldn't continue standing, yet she couldn't fall. Somewhere in the distance, she heard screams. Familiar screams, but altogether preternatural. Her name. Someone was screaming her name, but she could barely hear it over the sound of a rushing wind. Her face hurt like she stood in the middle of a hurricane. But at that moment, she realized she was the hurricane.

A deep rumble shook the deck beneath her. Then, a *crack, boom!*

Her eyes opened, and Tum Tum stood beside her shielding his face with his arm, beard and hair in tangles. The compass beside the ship's wheel spun wildly. Wind flapped the sails even though the bay remained flat as glass.

She fell to her knees, barely able to see, straining her eyes to focus on Whitney, but he was gone. Kazimir was gone. Where they had just been, there was now nothing more than scorched wood, two piles of clothes with her knife laying atop them, and the King's Glass Crown teetering on its edge. Aquira limped over to the spot, sniffing the air as if something were missing.

"Whitney?" Sora whispered. And then she collapsed, accepting sleep like an old friend.

XXIX

THE KNIGHT

Torsten stood on Winder's Wharf, staring out upon the moonlit bay. He wore a wolf pelt over his shoulders for warmth, given to him by Redstar after he was pulled from the canal. Everyone was cheery now that the battle was won even though they were surrounded by death and destruction, Glassmen and Northmen patting each other on the back.

What have we won?

Afhem Muskigo was alive thanks to Torsten's failure. He'd called the retreat early, and now most of his army crossed Trader's Bay to the eastern banks, and there were few ships intact to follow them before they regrouped. Torsten wasn't surprised Whitney's distraction wound up doing almost as much harm than good. All the vessels moored directly in the harbor were tipped onto one another, hulls and masts shredded by a chain of ropes.

A sole Breklian corsair ship headed south apart from Muskigo's army. It was far, but Torsten could see a man waving from the wheel and knew exactly who he had to be. What he didn't expect, however, was how much he hoped Sora, a blood mage, had made it on safely as well. He could only trust Whitney had changed enough to genuinely care about someone other than himself. He owed her that much after saving his life for the second time.

"Smile, Wearer," Redstar said, stepping up beside him. "Muskigo may live, but it is a victory nonetheless."

"Winde Port will never be the same," Torsten said.

"So it is with war. You should know better than any. How many cities did Liam ravage as he reached further across Pantego?"

"That was different. He fought to brighten the world."

"It wasn't different for those he… *brightened*."

"What do you want Redstar?"

"Must I want something to speak with my Wearer?"

"You're here to gloat," Torsten said. "I led my men to their doom while you stole the glory."

"I did nothing. The Buried Goddess showed me the moment to strike, I merely obeyed and called upon her strength."

"You warned Muskigo I'd be coming, didn't you?" Torsten snapped, his hand clutching Redstar by the collar before he could stop himself. Over the man's shoulder, he noticed a handful of men watching, concerned for the Arch Warlock and uncle of the King. More than a few of them were of the Glass.

Redstar lowered his voice. "If I wanted you dead, I wouldn't have fished you out of that canal after *you* failed to kill the only Sandsman whose death mattered."

"I don't know what you want, but saving me was the biggest mistake you'll ever make." Torsten shoved him and stormed away. His men parted for him to pass, though they were too fixated on Redstar to salute.

"Where is Sir Wardric?" he asked.

Nobody had an answer. He'd been searching for the man who'd been left in charge of his army since the fighting stopped. He imagined that he and both Darkings, father and son, were back at the camp. Noblemen like Yuri didn't have a taste for battle.

So, Torsten walked back through the city, now cautious to take a true measure of things. He still felt cold and pulled his pelt tight, but the anomalous warmth in his chest didn't wane. It even dulled the pain of his many wounds.

The prefect's estate was a pile of glowing rubble like coals in a fire that had burned too hot and too long. A line of homes west of it were charred husks of buildings. It would take half the gold in the royal vaults to undo the damage. Bodies filled the streets—Shesaitju, his own army, civilians unfortunate to have been caught in the invasion in the first place.

On his way by, Torsten noticed something white glinting in the wreckage. He trudged through the ash and debris and lifted his own white helm, nearly in perfect shape but for a dent on the side. Pure glaruium was a difficult thing to break. His armor was similar to the other members of the King's Shield, though slightly more ornate, but that helm had been worn by Wearers for decades before even his mentor Uriah. Torsten lifted it, dumped the ash out, then continued on his way with it tucked under his arm.

The densest stacking of corpses was by the palisade walls, or rather, what remained of them. The wind had spread Sora's fire before the snow had time to extinguish it. The dry, wooden walls caught in an instant. Barely a segment still stood, the rest ashes.

"Sir, you're alive!" someone shouted.

Torsten turned and saw Sir Nikserof Pasic, one of the old guard, a member of the King's Shield who'd been in the ambush, sitting on a chunk of burned wood. His steel armor was coated in blood, most of it probably belonging to his own people. A barbed arrow protruded from one arm.

Torsten approached, and the man went to salute, but he stopped him. "You don't need to stand for me."

"Thank you, sir." He winced.

"You should see the physicians."

"I'm in good shape compared to the rest. Can you believe what happened here? They say the King's uncle summoned wind and fire to take the walls. A moment slower, we would have died in that courtyard."

"He didn't summon any fire." That much was true, but Torsten recalled hearing Redstar's incantation echoing in the air after they escaped their ambush, as if he was willing the fire along.

Nikserof's gray brow furrowed. A few more nearby soldiers and Shieldsmen started to eavesdrop. "Then who did?"

Torsten bit his lip. He couldn't say that it was the work of a Panpingese blood mage he knew, even if he believed Iam was working through her—then they would not only think him a failed general, but a madman.

"Iam reached down to save us," Torsten said. "Redstar may have charged at the right time, but at what cost? We were supposed to save those prisoners."

"You haven't heard, sir?" Nikserof asked.

"What?"

"Their bonds were tied to the walls. When they burnt, the people of Winde Port were able to break free, and the gray men couldn't give chase because our army charged. They're all back at camp, mostly. Many of them will need new homes but still… it's a miracle."

Torsten looked closer at the remnants of the wall and all the bodies covered in ash. They were almost entirely soldiers from either side, stacked in twos and even threes where the fighting was fiercest.

"The Buried Goddess is with Drad Redstar," Mak said from nearby. It seemed he was always around to stir up trouble. "Lucky for you, Wearer."

"There is no such thing as luck," Torsten snapped.

"The way I hear it, they had to scoop you out of the canal after you let Muskigo survive. Without Redstar, you'd be an icicle. Sounds lucky."

"Watch your tongue," Nikserof said. "That is your Wearer."

Mak smiled and bowed. "My apologies. What a fine job he's been doing." He laughed and continued on his way. After a few paces, he looked up to the sky. "Where's your light now!" he shouted, laughing some more.

"Ignore him," Nikserof said. "If we didn't distract Muskigo, they wouldn't have accomplished a thing."

The truth was, Torsten knew that wasn't true. Perhaps with Muskigo able to lead his army in the defense, they would have lasted longer, but they still would have lost because there was no accounting for a fire like what Sora caused. More of them might have even perished instead of calling an early retreat to fight another day.

No, Torsten's distraction helped with nothing. Sora still would have tried to kill the man she blamed for destroying her home. She still would have failed in the face of a mighty warrior like Muskigo and been forced to use magic. And the fire still would have spread on Redstar's other-worldly, west-faring wind.

Torsten merely answered with a grunt and a nod.

"Have you seen Wardric?" he asked.

Nikserof shook his head. "Can't bring myself to climb the hill. I've lost a lot of blood, as have many. I think Sir Austun Mulliner headed up there though."

Torsten left him, wading through the piled bodies, careful to show the proper respect. Then, turning his head to the sky, he whispered, "Where *is* your light now?"

He caught a whiff of something foul and glanced back down. A pile of dead Drav Cra warriors was being burned across the field while the warlock Freydis stood before them chanting. Her words were as foreign as the rattling of her tokens.

Priests of Iam would arrive soon to help lay the fallen Glassmen to rest as well, as they did after every battle so the dead may be committed to the Gate of Light. But all the soldiers and refugees standing atop the hill over-looking a victorious battlefield would first see the warlocks of the Buried Goddess staining it. Torsten could barely look without thinking impure thoughts; however, as he went by, he noticed a silvery sheen amongst the corpses.

A King's Shieldsman?

"Stop this!" he barked as he ran over. He shoved Freydis out of the way. A few warriors pulled their weapons on him before they realized he was kneeling by one of his own.

"How did this man wind up in here?" he questioned.

The shaggy-haired warlock seemed as confused as he was. The black paint on her brow cracked as it furrowed "An accident, I suspect," Freydis said. "There are so many bodies."

"This was no accident." Torsten reached through the fire and grabbed the body by the arm. He tried to pull, but it wouldn't budge. A fur-clad hand fell upon his shoulder.

"It is too late," a warrior said. "His ashes will join the others in the dirt as his soul is passed to Skorravik, where he may spend eternity in glorious battle."

"He is a soldier of Iam." Torsten went to pull him out again, but this time, the warrior wasn't so gentle, grabbing Torsten and pushing him away. Torsten reached for his sword before he realized it was at the bottom of a Winde Port canal. A gathering of Northerners glared at him, knuckles whitening on the grips of their axes.

Torsten backed away slowly, then returned on his path to the camp. His blood was boiling with rage. A few more warlocks were burning their dead. Ashes into the dirt. Torsten tried only to look at the ground. If he saw one more of his people caught up in their heathenistic ways, he wasn't sure what he would do.

Iam's followers were buried in death so their mortal vessels would be hidden from the sight of the Vigilant Eye while their souls rose to Iam's waiting arms. The process was longer, and with all these bodies, it would take a new graveyard to do, but his people deserved eternal rest for sacrificing their lives. Redstar, his followers—all they wanted was to take the easy way.

Civilians filled the camp, both refugees and the thousands who had escaped thanks to Sora's fire. Only one name was on their tongues being praised: Redstar. Torsten could even hear it over the screams echoing from the hospital tent where the wounded were being treated and amputated. He never thought he'd prefer that terrible sound over anything.

He made his way up to the Shieldsmen's camp. A few soldiers recognized him along the way and offered a salute. Most were too busy commending heathens to notice.

"Wardric!" Torsten called. "Wardric!"

He found the main tent where they'd planned their attack. A few younger Shieldsmen sat inside, sharing a drink and laughing like they were common soldiers and not the best the Glass Kingdom had to offer.

"Where are Sir Wardric and Yuri Darkings?" Torsten asked the only one he somewhat recognized, a blonde with a crooked nose. He wasn't sure of his name with his head so fuzzy, but he was a young Shieldsman too green to be dragged along on Torsten's ill-fated ambush. Torsten was sure he had overseen a few sessions of the man's training before he took the vows.

"Sir?" the blonde Shieldsman scrambled to come to attention, spilling his drink in the process. "You made it."

"A surprise to everyone it seems."

"I—with the fire—we—"

"It's not important," Torsten said. "Where are they?"

"I haven't seen them since they got back from leading you to the tunnels, sir."

"Any of you?"

The other two Shieldsmen shook their heads.

"He was temporary commander of the King's Shield," Torsten said. "You charged without orders from him?"

"It all happened so fast," the blonde Shieldsman said. "One moment, Redstar and all those crazy warlocks were lined up in the field, kneeling and chanting and cutting themselves. The next, the walls took to flames, and the King's uncle called the charge. If we didn't listen, all of the civilians fleeing the gray men would have died."

"You don't have to explain yourself to me. You men made the right decision for those people. But the battle is done. I need to find Sir Wardric so we can discuss the next move. Muskigo remains at large, and now he is east of the ravine, near the ancestral lands of his people and ready to spread his uprising."

"I swear, sir, none of us have seen him."

Torsten's gaze turned to their drinks, then back to the blonde Shieldsman's eyes. "Keep an eye out, all of you. If you find him, send for me."

"Yes, sir," said all.

Torsten thought he heard a snicker as he walked away but ignored it. Members of the King's Shield, drinking and carousing as if one battle ended a war? Torsten wondered if he was still in the freezing depths of the canal, dreaming before his body gave out. Or perhaps death had taken him to another plane entirely.

Is this Elsewhere? Is this my eternal exile?

He left the white helm in his tent, then swept through the other tents of his order, searching for Wardric but only finding more of his men celebrating victory. It was as if his army had raided the abandoned taverns of Winde Port for all their ale.

He stopped and spun a tight circle, unable to stop hearing the whispers of praise for Redstar. His breathing picked up. The warmth in his chest was dissipating now, so he felt the chill of the air once more. He was near ready to drop to a knee and give up when he noticed the luxurious carriage Yuri Darkings had arrived in. The reins for its two horses were sliced, the animals nowhere to be seen. But Torsten's eyes were drawn somewhere else, to a small smattering of red on the entry's frame.

One of his men said something to him from behind, but Torsten ignored it and approached the carriage. His legs were still incredibly sore, one of them gashed deep. He fought the pain and pushed forward. The door wasn't locked, which he found odd considering the wealth and importance of the man who owned it. He swiped his hand over the red spots. *Dry.*

He slowly pushed the door in and what he saw made his stomach turn over. This time he fell to his knees and had to fight with all his willpower not to retch. Wardric lay on the lush, silk bed—or rather, his body did. His throat was slit end to end, blood so dark it looked like pitch stained the sheets and pooled across the wooden floor.

Torsten's fingers slid through the liquid on his way to investigate the body. He wasn't sure why he needed to check if Wardric was alive. Maybe instinct. Maybe he was hoping for a miracle. But it was clear from the moment he entered, his friend was dead.

Torsten crawled backward. He was breathing so fast it felt like his lungs were going to pop.

"Iam guide me," he rasped. "Iam guide me..." He repeated that over and over as he clutched at his chest. His armor was there, stained red and still tight against his frame. He had to unstrap his chestplate just to feel like he could draw air. A few of his men saw him floundering in the snow and ran over. Their faces were blurs, their words, muted.

All he could focus on was the man blithely strolling across the battle-field. His crimson robes flapped in the wind. His pale skin blended with the snow, the mark on his face like a bloodspot.

Torsten went blind to everything else in the world. He rose, threw off his chest plate and stormed at the man.

"Sir Unger," Redstar said as he approached. "You should see one of my healers. They'll sew you up in no time."

"You killed him!" Torsten thundered. He seized Redstar and slammed him to the ground. The Arch Warlock went for his dagger, but Torsten ripped it away from him and held it at his throat.

"What are you talking about?" Redstar grated.

"Wardric. I found him, Redstar. I found him slaughtered like swine so that you could lead the charge."

Redstar closed his eyes and let his head fall back into the snow. He looked exhausted but not afraid, which only propelled Torsten to press the edge of the blade tighter against his skin.

"Deny it!" Torsten shouted.

Redstar tilted his head and looked toward the ground. "He doesn't know."

"Don't talk to her," Torsten snapped, yanking Redstar's head back straight. "This is between me and you."

"This is between you and you, Sir Unger. Look around. I have just taken Winde Port back, and all you want to do is drive us away because we don't follow your god."

"What do you want, Redstar? The King forced you at my side. Is that not enough?"

"Torsten, I suggest you get off me." His eyes signaled for Torsten to look around. A crowd had gathered around them. Drav Cra and Glassmen, King's Shieldsmen and warlocks of Nesilia. Drad Mak stood amongst a group of fur-clad warriors, each one more tremendous than the next, but none more than him. He gripped his axe in two hands. Freydis and two other warlocks held their daggers to their palms, black face paint making their eyes bright with rage

"You think I'm afraid of them?" Torsten looked up but never let the knife shift. "This man killed Sir Wardric Jolly! He left his body to rot in that carriage!"

Nobody answered.

"Reach into my pocket," Redstar said.

"What?"

"Wardric was nothing but a lap dog. Why would I kill him? Now, reach into my pocket and find the answers you already know."

Torsten pressed against Redstar's throat with his elbow and did as instructed. He removed a stack of letters.

"What is this?" Torsten said. "What are these."

"Correspondence between Yuri Darkings and the rebel afhem. A lot of yammering about the Glass Kingdom's fortunes fading and the unworthy heirs of Liam the Conqueror. Riveting stuff really, but I'll let you decide."

Torsten leafed through them with one hand. Some were written in ink on parchment, the seal of the Darkings house at the top. Others were etched into dark gray sheets of paper made from the black palms of the Shesaitju beaches, signed by Afhem Muskigo. Page after page. He spotted instructions that Torsten was planning to head to Marimount, ways to avoid Glass scouts as his armies were moved into position.

"Sir Wardric caught Yuri and his son sending a galler bird into Winde Port. He wasn't able to stop them warning Muskigo of your ambush, but he detained them and sent for me. When I got there, I found his body and them fleeing."

"And you just let them run?"

"I sent my wolves after them, but they haven't yet returned. I had to make a choice. The traitors, or take advantage of our summoned wind and flame and charge on Winde Port."

"A blessing called upon from Nesilia herself by the hero of Winde Port," a Drav Cra warrior said.

"What did you say?" Torsten said. He yanked Redstar upright and stood, knife still at his neck. "This man is no hero!" He looked to his own men, whose faces were twisted by concern—even the King's Shieldsmen watching. "He turns to dark arts and fallen gods. His every breath is an insult to Iam."

"Torsten, put down the weapon," Redstar said.

"Don't you all see? Every word out of his mouth is a lie! These letters, forgeries meant to spoil a house that has loyally served the Glass for decades so he may deceive us all; just as he wore the face of Uriah Davies to fool me." He flung the letters onto the ground.

"Wore a face?" Redstar laughed. "I am one with the magic of Elsewhere, but even I cannot *wear* a face."

"Lies! Shieldsmen, I want you to arrest this traitor for the murder of Sir Wardric Jolly."

The men of his order looked to each other, but not a soul moved. Torsten searched the faces for a familiar one. Sir Nikserof Pasic or any of the most celebrated Shieldsmen he'd led into the ambush, but there were none present. They were all dead or injured. And all that remained were men he hadn't yet fought beside and whom he'd barely been a part of training.

"That is an order from your Wearer!" Torsten said.

"Control yourself, Torsten," Redstar whispered. "Look to your God."

"Look to my God? *Look to my God?* I'm going to do something I should have done back in the Webbed Woods. It's time this kingdom is free of—"

Redstar slid his head forward, catching the side of his neck on the dagger. Blood leaked out, but the slice didn't catch anything vital. As Redstar collapsed, Torsten knew what was coming, but he was too slow. The Arch Warlock whipped around, extended a hand, and all Torsten's muscles became paralyzed. Redstar tore the blade out of his hand with a thought and Torsten couldn't do a thing.

Northerners ran to Redstar to stop the bleeding. He pushed them away. The more blood, the stronger his hold on Torsten would be.

"I took Winde Port!" Redstar shouted, the rage in his voice making the very air vibrate. "With this power and faith you eschew, I took it. Perhaps, Sir Unger, you too have been swayed by Muskigo to betrayal. Perhaps that is why the rebel Afhem still lives."

"I..." Torsten opened his mouth to speak, but Redstar closed his fingers, and with it, Torsten's lips went rigid as stone.

"Do not speak." Redstar turned to the crowd. "This is the man who you would follow as Wearer? A man who would kill your King's unarmed uncle just because he's too frightened to accept help from a goddess who loves all of you just as she loved Iam? How many lives among you did she just save!"

Redstar swiped his arm down and forced Torsten to his knees. He begged his muscles to move, but even trying made his entire body burn.

"Shieldsmen," Redstar went on. "You charged with me. Clearly, your Wearer is broken. If I release him, he will kill me. So, I ask you, as the royal uncle and the only man who can lead this army effectively, arrest him. We will drag him before the King, and there, he shall be weighed justly for his actions. Perhaps even he can be saved of whatever it is that haunts him."

His men seemed petrified as they looked to each other, none willing to make the first move. Then, finally, the blonde Shieldsman Torsten had scolded for drinking back at camp stepped forward. He was emboldened by alcohol, and Torsten dug through his mind to find a name with which to beg. He couldn't.

So instead, he just struggled to squeeze a single word through his magically sealed lips, "P… please."

The Shieldsman took Torsten by the arms. Redstar released those limbs of his magic so they could be wrenched behind Torsten's back.

"I'm sorry, Sir," the Shieldsman said, "but he's right. He saved this city while you were gone. You aren't thinking clearly."

Redstar smirked. "Thank you, Sir Mulliner," he addressed the Shieldsman.

The sense of pride in Redstar's voice as he spoke the name Torsten couldn't find made Torsten feel ill. Never in his life had he wanted to kill someone so badly. Even Muskigo he respected for his prowess, but Redstar was a trickster demon in human form. Whether or not anything he said about Wardric was true, he could have told Torsten on the docks about what happened with the Darkings. He could have revealed the truth then, but instead, allowed Torsten to make this spectacle.

"I'm sorry it had to come to this, Torsten," Redstar said. "But you are in need of help. He leaned down, his breath hot on Torsten's ear. "Pi may breathe now thanks to the Buried Goddess, but it seems Iam favors me now, too," he whispered. He turned to walk away, releasing his mystical hold of Torsten's body.

Torsten had been waiting for that exact moment. "I'll kill you!" he roared. Sir Mulliner tried to restrain him, but Torsten used his massive body to tear free. Another of the Shieldsmen who'd been drinking with Sir Mulliner grabbed him, but Torsten tossed him aside like a doll. The man's face smashed against a rock.

Sir Mulliner ran to his friend, and Torsten tore the sheathed longsword off the Mulliner's belt while he was distracted and sprung at Redstar. He didn't get far. The pommel of a sword bashed against the back of his head and knocked him face first into the snow and dirt. The last thing he realized before he spun into oblivion was who had taken him down like the raving lunatic Redstar made him seem.

One of his own men. A King's Shieldsman, but not Sir Mulliner or another relative stranger. It was Nikserof, a man of the old guard with whom Torsten had endured a crucible of blood, barely able to stand from his wounds. Nikserof watched in horror, and as Torsten's vision began to go fuzzy, he knew that he'd given him no choice.

XXX

THE THIEF

G ray mist swirled around Whitney as he was jarred back to consciousness. There was no telling how long he'd been out, but nothing looked as it had just moments ago. Where there were night skies, there was now a vibrant red expanse, as if fire filled the heavens. Strangely, the sound of waves was still there, though he no longer felt wood beneath him. Instead, dry chalk billowed with each movement as he coaxed himself to rise.

Before him, the shore of an endless ocean stretched out to the horizon. The fog rolled along it like the wheels of a chariot. But something about the water was… off. It was black—the color of old blood.

"Where the…" Whitney exhaled.

"How did we?"

Whitney spun toward the accented voice behind him.

"You!" he shouted, then lunged at Kazimir with abandon. "This is your fault!"

Somehow, he tackled the impossibly fast upyr and brought him down. Whitney mounted him and was able to drive one fist into his nose. Kazimir caught his next punch, and while he waited for his hand to be crushed, Whitney noticed the blood pouring from Kazimir's nose. Whitney was so stunned to see it, he allowed Kazimir to push him off.

The upyr wiped his nose with the back of his hand. The look on his face would have given Whitney enough joy to sustain him for a lifetime, had he known where the yig he was.

"No, this isn't possible," Kazimir said. "Not again."

"All things are possible here," said another voice.

Whitney whipped around again toward the voice. It was frail and withering.

"Oh great," Whitney said. "Who the yigging exile are you, now?"

The man was nearly doubled in half he was so hunched over. A robe hung down, whipping back and forth in the black waters along the shore. He stood beside a tiny rowboat that somehow didn't float away despite not being moored. A hood covered his head, casting a deep shadow over his face. If he even had a face.

"You may call me the Ferryman," the stranger said.

"Right, and I'm the world's greatest thief," Whitney replied.

"I know exactly who you are, Mr. Fierstown."

Whitney took a step back, eyes wide. "Then you'll know that's not my name anymore."

"A man cannot escape who he is. I've been waiting for you... both of you."

The mysterious new presence nearly made Whitney forget the upyr behind him.

"Yeah? Then who is he?" Whitney said, pointing to Kazimir.

"Who is he... that is a question with a far longer answer," the Ferryman said.

Whitney shot a glance at Kazimir. The upyr's gaze drifted downward.

"He has gone by many names," the Ferryman continued. "Haven't you?"

"What do you want, old man?" Kazimir asked.

Whitney stepped forward and threw open his arms. "Can everyone take a deep breath and explain what the yig-and-shog is going on? Where is Sora? Where is Tum Tum? Where is—"

"Whatever your mystic friend did has sent us to Elsewhere, you fool," Kazimir said. "The world between worlds."

"We're..." Whitney paused to take a deep breath. "Dead?"

"Some would say so. Some would say not. Much like him." The

Ferryman stepped up onto the tiny boat and lifted a long oar just like the ones gondolas used to navigate the canals of Winde Port.

"Now join me," the Ferryman said. "The Sea of Lost Souls is no place to linger."

Kazimir approached without a fuss. "You didn't keep me here last time, spirit," he grumbled as he climbed up. "You won't this time, either."

"Give me one good reason for getting in that boat with him," Whitney said.

The Ferryman raised his hand. Spectral arms reached up through the shallow water, dozens of them, pawing at Whitney's ankles. They passed through his flesh and bone, yet he could feel a chill with every one.

Whitney was on the boat so fast he wasn't even sure how he got there.

"Well put," Whitney said.

"Let's make this quick," Kazimir said.

"No need to rush," the Ferryman said as he pushed his oar through the water. "We have eternity."

The sea lapped against the sides of the boat as they moved forward. Specters teemed beneath the surface, their moans like broken lutes playing on a loop.

"Shog in a barrel," Whitney said as fog enveloped them like a shroud of death.

BOOK THREE

WILL OF FIRE

RHETT C. BRUNO

JAIME CASTLE

PROLOGUE

TWO YEARS AGO

Devlin Boremater stood before the altar in Fessix, just east of Crowfall. Beside him, blind Father Morningweg leaned wearily upon his cane, blessing the townsfolk as they entered. It was a small village settled along the water in the Northern Glass Kingdom. Like every day before and every day that would come, the sun rose, and a sliver of its light shot through a pinhole in the back wall, beaming directly through the Eye of Iam hanging above him. The light refracted through the glass, painting vibrant colors down the central aisle.

Devlin, the altar server, acted as the Father's eyes, watched as the flock filed in one by one to hear the morning sermon. It was the same as always in the sleepy town as the cold of winter set in upon an already frigid landscape. Devlin whispered each name to the father as men and women approached. Father Morningweg smiled at each of them and listened to the town gossip.

He never could help himself, even though Iam would disapprove.

Fishermen spoke of how the fish stopped biting as ice covered the Strait of Bautim. Most others complained about the deepening chill in the air. More than a few discussed the latest town scandal that Mistress Falhua had been unfaithful to her husband, the bailiff. A man, dressed in Yarrington fashion, said he'd heard whispers during the last feast at the

Glass Castle. Apparently, King Liam had toppled from his chair and was rushed away. His wife, Queen Oleander, then had a public meltdown, slamming tableware against the wall until every noble in the Great Hall left.

Devlin wasn't sure he believed them. Although he wasn't yet a man and was an orphan without parents to take him to see the great city of Yarrington, he'd heard enough stories about the Queen from passersthrough. The way they talked of her beauty, he couldn't imagine her suffering from fits of rage. Besides, rumors about Liam's declining health had been rampant for years, and High Priest Wren discredited them as stirs of dissension from enemies of the Crown.

"Welcome all," Father Morningweg said as the pews squeaked. Devlin took his own seat on the platform. "The light of Iam shines upon you this morning. Winter may be on its way, but that does not mean we let darkness set into our souls. Iam the all-knowing gave us this harsh season so we may learn to find the strength within to endure. So we might never grow soft in this, His world, and forget to count all the blessings he bestows. We are fortun—"

A shrill scream reverberated from somewhere outside, loud enough that all those who'd just sat down leaped up and studied the door. A woman burst through, face drained of all color, terrified.

"The Drav Cra—they—their ships emerged through the fog and cloud," she stuttered.

"You are sure?" the village bailiff questioned. The woman managed a nod, and the bailiff hastened to her. "Everyone stay here."

"Stay here?" a man protested. "Last time they slaughtered my cows."

"Better than your children, aye?" The bailiff stuck his head outside. A bell from the docks chimed. "Everyone in!" he bellowed. "The house of Iam is our protection. Come now!"

Stragglers—all those late to morning service—sprinted through the doors before they were slammed shut and locked. It was impossible to know if the entire village made it in.

"Is everyone here?" Father Morningweg asked.

"I… I think so," Devlin said, scanning the faces of the huddled crowd. His heart raced. He'd never been through a raid before, though he'd heard the horrifying tales parents told their children at night to frighten them.

"Are you sure, boy?"

"As best I can be," he said, putting on his bravest face.

"It is all right, my children," Morningweg said to the entire congregation. "What do we do when the devils come?"

"Shield ourselves with Iam's light," many of them replied in unison, Devlin amongst them.

"Good. Here, within these walls, we are shielded by the light of Holy Iam. The heathens come only for our food and supplies because they live in shadow without fortune. Let them have it. For His love protects us and they are like infants thrashing in the darkness."

The sound of ships cracking against the docks was loud enough to hear through the stone walls. Everyone winced, even Father Morningweg. Devlin felt the man's hand on his shoulder and immediately all fear dissipated. Although the father's touch might have calmed Devlin, the screams and whimpers of fear still coursed through the church.

The bailiff worked to restore peace, but there was really no saying if, with all the panic, someone had been left outside. Mothers and fathers searched through their crowd for their children, and when finding them, pulling them close. Others called out for family members or friends who may have arrived separately.

Outside, heavy footsteps rumbled like thunder. There was shouting in what Devlin imagined was Drav Crava. Father Morningweg hushed his flock and pointed them toward the Eye of Iam. With his fingers, he circled his eye sockets, empty after his vow of sightlessness, and whispered a silent prayer. Devlin did the same, then rose to stand next to the priest, grasping the man's forearm with both hands. The room grew eerily quiet save for the sniffles of small children.

Despite being locked, the thick, worn, wooden doors swung open. Dust and snow swirled, and through the fog stepped the savages. There were two in front. One had her face painted, half white at the bottom, half black on top with red around her eyes, so their fury shone. Bones and trinkets rattled from within a nest of raven-black hair. She was a warlock. If the tales Devlin had heard could be believed, they painted themselves to evoke fear. It worked. Devlin tightened his grip on the father's arm, and his heart thumped even faster. Beside her was a more refined man, garbed in a robe of crimson. His face didn't need paint, for a red birthmark stretched across his face into five points.

"It is okay, my son," Father Morningweg said. "Stand, therefore, and see the salvation of Iam."

"You do not belong here, heathens," the bailiff called, standing at the doors and in front of the people of Fessix. "Begone or the wrath of King Liam will befall you as it once did."

Before he could get out another word, the female warlock slashed his throat with a crude knife. Devlin flinched. The villagers gasped as the bailiff fell to his knees and the warlock climbed over him up onto one of the pews. She hopped from one to the next, glaring down at the innocent people.

"What happened?" the father whispered.

Devlin couldn't find any words.

"Silence." The birthmarked man calmly spoke as crying broke out once more. "It will all be over soon."

A group of hulking, fur-clad warriors strode into the room, axes and spears in hand. They shoved the people aside and made way for their apparent leader to stroll down the aisle. Devlin watched in horror, then looked up at Father Morningweg. The man's face remained stoic. All the talk of Drav Cra Raiders and how they were like walking demons on Pantego were true, but seeing the real thing was even worse.

When Devlin came into the service of the priest, he'd been told of the many raids the father had endured since the church sent him to serve the people of Fessix. He'd assured Devlin that the raiders always kept out of the church. As if though they worshiped the Buried Goddess, they feared what might happen should they anger Iam.

Not this time.

The villagers all watched in silent horror as the heathens passed. Parents held their children, covering their mouths to stifle the cries.

Devlin Boremater winced as the female warlock leaped down in front of him, then circled him. The sight of her eyes, bright against her black face paint, sent a shiver coursing down his spine.

"Drad Redstar," she said, addressing the birthmarked man before rattling off words in Drav Crava.

"My dearest Freydis," the man replied, gently stroking her cheek. "Their time will come soon enough."

He moved to shove by Father Morningweg toward the nave and the Eye of Iam, but the priest blocked him and spread his arms wide. "Please, there is nothing for you here."

Devlin hadn't noticed, but he'd been cowering behind the father, shaking.

"Out of my way, priest," the man named Redstar said, "or you will join your bailiff."

Father Morningweg kept his nerve for a few seconds longer, then shrunk out of the way, dragging Devlin with him. Redstar strolled by, ignoring Devlin. Instead, he turned and headed down the stairs of the crypt.

In the back of the church, a man panicked and ran for the door. He made it outside where a brown wolf, big as a horse, pounced on him. His screams could've curdled blood as the great beast dragged him out of view. More cries sounded.

"Nobody else move!" Father Morningweg shouted. He turned to Freydis. If the man had eyes, Devlin imagined he'd see fear there, too. "Please, take whatever you want. No others must die."

"But Father," she said, voice heavily accented. "Wouldn't we be doing a favor sending them to the Gate of Light?" A few of the Drav Cra raiders laughed.

"If it is our time, but I beg you." He fell to his knees. Devlin took the opportunity to shrink back behind the altar. "They have families, children who still need guidance."

"Relax, priest," Redstar said. He returned from the crypt carrying a broken shard of stone with unfinished, ancient artwork painted on it. From his studies, Devlin knew it was one of the few relics left over from the age of the God Feud. It had been stored in Fessix, kept in a sealed reliquary, in hopes of remaining hidden in an unremarkable town, but Redstar's hand was now bloody as if he'd somehow bashed through the thick glass.

"The tablet," Devlin squeaked before he could help himself.

Father Morningweg's head turned toward the sound, and Freydis' did too. Devlin crouched down further.

"How dare you touch that!" Father Morningweg snapped, drawing the warlock's attention. "That is a holy relic."

"Not to me." Redstar stopped in front of the father. "It is the final piece of a story. Ancient priests, men like you, broke this story to pieces and hid them around their land until they too forgot the truth." He tenderly ran his fingers across the engraving, wiping away a layer of dust. "It has taken a lifetime to gather, but this is the last."

Devlin watched with admiration as Father Morningweg found his nerve again, standing to block the Drav Cra's path once again. "I... I won't let you leave this church with it. You—you'll—have to kill me."

"Now what fun would that be?" He swiped his bloody hand through the air, and heathen magic sent Father Morningweg sailing into the wall.

"Father!" Devlin cried out, running toward him. Freydis smiled, then spat on them both.

Redstar grabbed Devlin and drew him in close, placing a knife against his neck.

"Leave him be, heathen!" Father Morningweg cried. "Kill me, but leave him be."

"How will any of you see the truth of the Dawning if I kill you now?" Redstar said. "I suppose you won't see much of anything though would you, priest?" He dragged the tip of his blade up Devlin's cheek. Devlin's body went stiff, petrified from fear.

Redstar lowered the blade and handed the piece of sacred stone to one of the raiders. In response, the man asked a question in Drav Crava.

"Freydis, burn the church and let them pray to the ashes," Redstar said. "Then, return to the north and prepare the clans. It's time I pay a visit to my sister. I shall summon you when the time comes."

"We await the death of the enemy," Freydis replied.

Redstar strolled out of the room, and his men followed behind. Freydis then kneeled before Devlin and Father Morningweg, and a sinister grin spread across her face. "Where is your god now?" she asked as she drew her crude knife, slid it across her palm and squeezed blood over their heads.

"You will help the priest see the truth that will come, boy," she said, standing.

Devlin shivered. He was crying now. He wasn't sure when it started, but he couldn't help it.

"But you will only need one eye for that." She placed her hand over one side of Devlin's face. Her skin was as hot as a roaring fire. Her fingers covered his eye and burned it, branding his skin. Devlin cried out, falling to the ground, clutching his eye.

"Now you are halfway to priesthood. You're welcome."

Father Morningweg wrapped his arms around Devlin and held him tight as she left. After a few moments, the townsfolk stirred and shrieked, and the acrid smell of smoke filled Devlin's nostrils.

I

THE KNIGHT

Torsten heard the rumble and watched the familiar streets of Yarrington bounce by through the bars of a prison carriage. His ankles and wrists were cuffed, chained to the floor as if he were any other prisoner of war. Others, most of them afhems or commanders of the Shesaitju, judging by the number of their elaborate tattoos, shared the carriage.

One of Afhem Muskigo's Serpent Guard sat across from him, mask removed to reveal a face too soft to belong to a grown man. Torsten wasn't sure why they kept him alive. Serpent Guards had no tongues and wouldn't be giving up any secrets.

Down at the end sat a wiry boy from the Glass heartland. He had the extreme misfortune to have been an assistant to Yuri Darkings before the traitor murdered Wardric Jolly and fled. Torsten could tell he knew nothing.

"Where are they taking us?" the boy asked as the carriage banked. His face was pressed against the bars, his body trembling.

"The Glass Castle, Shield barracks," Torsten answered. "Doesn't matter. There'll be bars either way."

"I swear… I didn't know what my master was plotting."

"I believe you. A week ago, that might have been enough."

The boy glanced at the white helm sitting between Torsten's legs, left there by Redstar as if part of some cruel joke. "But you're the Wearer of White," he said.

The gazes of all the captive Shesaitju snapped toward Torsten, bright with anger. As if he didn't have enough problems. Somehow, they'd made it the entire journey without his identity coming up. Without wearing his full suit of armor, the gray men had no way of knowing what the helmet signified. The Serpent Guard's hate-filled eyes opened and now fixed on Torsten's throat.

Torsten ignored them and raised his chained hands. "A week ago, that might have been enough, too."

"It's a mistake though, right?" the boy said. "Everyone always talks about how honorable you are. What they claim you did, it can't be—"

"It is," Torsten snapped. The boy shuddered, his whole body slammed back against the carriage wall. If any of the Shesaitju wanted to go for him, he wouldn't stop them. Countless times in his mind he'd replayed those moments after the battle, and every time the truth was evident.

He'd killed one of his own men.

After finding Wardric's body and accusing Redstar, Torsten publicly attacked the King's supposedly-reformed uncle, having to be restrained to keep from killing him. But that wasn't why he found himself chained up in a carriage. In his rage, Torsten threw a King's Shieldsman aside like a rag doll. The boy was just trying to keep Torsten in check, and for his efforts, his head hit a rock. Dead on impact.

Torsten deserved to be where he was. He was meant to lead an order whose sole purpose was to shield the followers of Iam from evil and darkness, and he'd failed them. Torsten didn't even know the fallen Shieldsman's name. He'd played so spectacularly into Redstar's hands that they were now the same thing. *Murderers*.

"I… I don't want to die…" the boy whimpered.

"If you are truthful," Torsten replied, "Iam will not let you."

"His light… it—is it gone?"

"Never."

The boy hung his head against the bars and began to weep. Torsten knew he was telling the truth. *Nobody is that good an actor—except perhaps Whitney Fie—Blisslayer.*

Torsten cursed himself for thinking of Whitney at a time like this, yet simultaneously wished the thief were there. He'd have known how to pick the locks holding Torsten in place, how to smooth-talk his way out of a mess of his own making.

Torsten recalled watching him flee Winde Port by ship after helping with the failed ambushing of Muskigo. The thief had no reason not to. He'd only helped in exchange for Torsten aiding in the search for Sora, and judging by how his blood mage friend burned down all of Merchants Row, she was in perfectly good health and in no need of aid. Whether she truly was touched by Iam, Torsten didn't know, but there was something special about her. He'd seen it in her eyes.

She'd stopped Redstar in the Webbed Woods, survived being captive to the Dom Nohzi, single-handedly ended Muskigo's brief occupation of Winde Port, and in doing it all, saved Torsten's life twice when he was supposed to be saving hers. The memory helped Torsten cling to the faith that Iam remained with him despite his failings. For whatever reason, He was working through her; using that same wicked magic Redstar used for evil to do good. To make light from darkness.

It has to be a sign.

And Torsten needed one.

Through the bars, he could see the faces of Yarrington citizens celebrating their victorious return. Afhem Muskigo and his rebel army had been battered and forced to retreat. The price, in gold and lives, was grave, and his influence would continue to spread amongst the people of his conquered homeland. Much of the Glass army and their Drav Cra allies remained in Winde Port to prepare for an extended campaign into the Shesaitju lands to end the rebellion, but it was a victory nonetheless.

Only, the cheering citizens didn't praise the Glass soldiers or King's Shieldsmen who had died in the fighting. They celebrated Redstar. The man who'd 'summoned wind and flame to drive the gray men away.' And Redstar, in turn, heaped all credit upon Nesilia's shoulders, never mentioning once that the fire had sprung from Sora's hands. Torsten even wondered if the unnatural wind Redstar's magic appeared to be behind had actually been Sora's doing—Iam protecting Winde Port from invaders through her hand.

There was nobody to tell them it was all a lie. Even the King's Shieldsmen marching back with them remained silent as Redstar's name dripped from the crowd's lips. Thanks to Torsten, they had no leader to guide them, to show them that they were being deceived.

Torsten hadn't seen the masses in such jubilation since Liam's last war nearly a decade ago. Even the snow couldn't keep them indoors. Sure, mothers wept for those lost, but the victory had been swift and overwhelming. More fathers were left to embrace returning sons than expected. Priests of Iam thanked their God for success and prayed for the souls sacrificed in defense of the Kingdom of Glass. However, they weren't alone.

Men and women dressed in crimson, hooded robes, wearing white, expressionless masks with a single line of red running down from one eyehole dotted the crowd. It was the garb worn by cultists to the Buried Goddess. Torsten had broken up plenty of rings in his day as a Shieldsman, rooting them out of basements in the city or caves beyond. Never had he seen them openly on the streets unless guards were chasing them.

Presently, nobody else even seemed to notice them. They blended in, and why wouldn't they? For riding at the front of this victorious army were the true followers of Nesilia, the Buried Goddess. They needn't hide behind masks. The warlocks and dradinengor chieftains of the Drav Cra, and their Arch Warlock, Redstar, uncle to a king he'd once cursed and tried to kill.

Torsten couldn't believe he hadn't seen Redstar's plot.

The carriage turned onto the Royal Avenue and drove along the walls of the castle. Only months ago, the Queen Mother, Oleander, thrown into a frenzy by the condition of her son, had lined that wall with the hanging dead for no reason good enough to excuse. Now, Glass soldiers and city guards stood along it, cheering and carousing.

Torsten knew that with Liam gone, the people, more than anything, were starved for a hero. A name to revere as they had him before he fell sick, before all these dark times of rebellions and broken faith. Redstar had given that to them. While Torsten failed to subdue Muskigo, Redstar had turned air and a spark of fire into a miracle victory.

Even if it wasn't true, Torsten didn't blame the people for believing it. He blamed himself. He was the one who refused to end Redstar's life in the Webbed Woods so that he could return him to Oleander as a gift and reclaim his title as Wearer. He was the one who thought respecting the commands of King Pi to be more important than striking down evil.

Selfish, foolish, murderer.

The carriage stopped. Yuri's assistant's crying grew louder as he realized what would come next. The Shesaitju stirred and tried to get a better look through the narrow openings. All but the Serpent Guard, still quietly staring.

The doors opened and the King's Shieldsman, Sir Nikserof, appeared along with a few others. Lines of regret wracked his face.

"This is where you get off, Sir," he said as he stepped in, hand on his sword and ready for any of the Shesaitju to make a move.

"You don't have to call me that," Torsten said.

"You're still Wearer until the King says otherwise, Sir." He knelt in front of him and unlocked the chains on Torsten's ankles, then his wrists. "We won't have you appear before him chained up like a dog."

Torsten stretched out his limbs. He lay a hand on Nikserof's armored shoulder. "Thank you."

"Don't. I must believe it was an accident, Sir. Stress from the ambush, from nearly drowning and freezing to death. You should have been with a healer, not finding more bodies and trying to lead an army."

Torsten opened his mouth to respond, but nothing came out. He stared longingly upon the face of a good, loyal Shieldsman, a man who'd followed him into battle without question and barely made it out alive. Accident…. He couldn't say. In that moment, he saw red, and whoever got in his way would have met the same fate as that Shieldsman. Nikserof was just lucky he was behind him.

"All right, up you are." Nikserof lifted him. "And don't forget this." He shoved the white helm into Torsten's chest and then helped him toward the exit.

"W… what about us?" the boy at the back of the carriage asked.

"Quiet," Nikserof said. Torsten was surprised at his tone. It was kind but authoritative. He liked Nikserof and wished he'd known him better, like so many of the other Shieldsmen. The saddest part was that of all the Shieldsmen left alive, he knew Nikserof the best.

"I've got him," another Shieldsman bristled. Sir Austun Mulliner yanked Torsten down as hard as he could. He'd been friends with the

Shieldsman Torsten killed, so Torsten didn't blame the man for rough treatment.

He couldn't even bear to look Mulliner in the face. Instead, he watched Yuri's assistant's terrified eyes through the bars as the rolling prison rumbled away. There was no saying what would happen to him during an interrogation, but this much was clear: both were accused of being complicit in the death of a King's Shieldsman, and only the man responsible stood unchained before the castle.

"Ah, Sir Unger. I hope the ride wasn't overly dreadful." Redstar approached from behind him, flanked by Freydis. She was as menacing as ever, and still hadn't even bothered to wash the blood from her knotted hair after the battle. Redstar snapped at a few of his warriors, and they led a collared dire wolf toward the outer stables. He and his people, making themselves at home.

Torsten's insides began to boil just from the sound of him. "Let's just get this over with."

"You must understand, Torsten. This is not what I wanted."

"Oh, I think it's exactly what you wanted. The ear of the King. You're not different from Bliss, spinning your lies about your fallen goddess."

Redstar leaned in. "I spin nothing, old friend. This heart knows only truth."

Torsten's fists clenched, and his brow furrowed. He stared at the high doors of the castle, unwilling to look Redstar in the eyes. "Did you tell Uriah that before he died?"

"We didn't have a chance to speak. I did not kill your friend, and I didn't ask him to chase me. Regardless, in killing Bliss, we have already avenged his death. You should be thanking me."

Torsten finally whipped around to face him, and it took every bit of his willpower not to strangle the man. Freydis stepped between them, her hand on the hilt of her dagger. The fingernails of Torsten's free hand dug so hard into his palms they drew tiny arcs of blood. Somehow, he held back. He had no desire to make Redstar's case for him further, that he was an unhinged murderer incapable of donning the white helm.

"One day, your blood will stain my sword," Torsten said. "For now, our king awaits us."

Redstar laughed, clapped his hands. "I look forward to it." He walked on ahead, Freydis returning to his side. The doors swung open and in they went, foreigners and heathens. King's Shieldsmen who'd remained behind stood on either side, features twisted by confusion.

"Sir, what is—"

"Just watch the doors," Torsten told them. "Everything is fine."

"Let's go," Austun Mulliner said from behind, giving Torsten a light shove.

"Enough, Sir Mulliner," Nikserof snapped as he caught up. "He's still your wearer."

Austun looked between Torsten and Nikserof, bit his lip, then marched off toward the Throne Room on his own.

Torsten drew a deep breath and continued through the soaring greeting hall. Vibrant colors painted the carved stone walls, and light filtered in through the grand, stained windows illustrating the history of the kingdom. The statue of Liam Nothhelm the Conqueror seemed like it was staring at him as he went by, stoic. He couldn't imagine how the great King would have looked upon him now. He'd trusted Torsten to be Wearer after Uriah passed, and look where he'd led them.

Redstar's grin stretched from ear to ear as they headed straight into the Throne Room. King Pi sat slumped on the Glass Throne, the Glass Crown sitting crooked upon his head, tangled in long hair. The Royal Council watched from behind. Among them was not one familiar face except Wren the Holy who'd gone pale at the sound of Freydis openly wearing her heathen trinkets in the Throne Room. He looked like he was going to faint.

Queen Oleander stood directly at Pi's side, gorgeous as ever. A long dress the color of a clear sky hugged her figure, stopping just above her ankles. Her silvery hair was pulled back into a braid that fell to her hips, accentuating her perfect jawline. Her cheeks were no longer red and puffy from crying as they'd been the last time Torsten saw her, tormented over dealing with her unpredictable son. Again, that trademark confidence Torsten knew so long oozed off her.

"Welcome, brother," Oleander announced. "And Sir Unger." Her glower fell upon Torsten and his heart sunk to his stomach. He'd instructed her before leaving for war to regain her son's trust, and judging by where she now stood and the demeanor she wore, her time in Yarrington had been fruitful. She, in turn, had tasked Torsten with eliminating Redstar, yet her traitorous brother strode down the hall alive and well, a bounce to his step.

"My lovely sister." Redstar strode up to the dais and swept his arms low into a bow. "I trust you've heard news of our glorious victory."

"Your victory over the Shesaitju was expected. Other developments, were not." She spoke to Redstar, but her heated glare never left Torsten.

Torsten reached Redstar's side and fell to a knee. "Your Graces," he whispered.

"Rise, Wearer," Pi groaned, still slumped and staring off to the side. "We need not waste time with formalities. There is much to address in the wake of what happened at Winde Port."

"Your Grace, if I may—"

"You may not." Pi's head finally turned to face Oleander. "Mother, inform them of what has transpired."

"Uh, Your Highness," Wren interrupted. He used a cane topped with the Eye of Iam and shuffled forward to reach Pi's ears. "Should this be discussed with them here?" He pointed to the warlock standing in the shadow of Redstar, then to the Drav Cra warriors standing at the entry to the room.

"His Holiness is right," Oleander said. "Please send your dog outside, brother."

"But of course." He murmured something in Drav Crava, and Freydis turned to leave, sneering at Torsten on her way out.

"How forgetful of me," Redstar said. "I wouldn't want to stain these hallowed halls."

"Thank you, Your Grace," Wren whispered to Pi.

"Step back and do not interrupt my son again," Oleander snapped. The lump bobbed in Wren's wrinkled throat as he slid backward. He traced where his eyes should have been with his fingers, then kissed the top of his cane.

"Go on, mother," Pi said.

"Of course, my precious boy." She took a step forward, swaying her hips as if to draw all the guards present into a trance. "It appears the betrayal of Yuri Darkings was more thorough than we'd ever expected. The chambers of Caleef Rakun were left unlocked before he departed for

Winde Port. Many King's Shieldsmen were lost battling off his Serpent Guards, and Caleef Rakun was able to escape into the wilderness, alone."

Redstar cackled.

"You find that humorous, brother?" Oleander questioned.

"Not at all. It's just what I've come to expect when the King's Shield is placed in charge of something. You've really let the order go to waste, haven't you Sir Unger?"

"How dare you!" Torsten growled before being immediately silenced.

"Quiet," Pi ordered, low but authoritative. "I dispatched you to work together in ending this rebellion and clearly that has not happened."

"Not for lack of trying, nephew," Redstar said.

Torsten stepped forward and again fell to a knee. "Your Grace, this man tried to undercut me at every turn. I know you asked me to work with him in leading this army, but how could I trust him after everything he's done, with him questioning my every move?"

"Choose better moves," Redstar whispered.

Torsten rose and pointed to the Arch Warlock. "Do you see? This insufferable heathen stood in my way at every turn!"

"The army speaks of his heroics in retaking Winde Port whilst you fell into a trap laid by the traitor Darkings," Pi said. He leaned forward in the oversized throne. "Do you deny that?"

"I deny nothing. He would place all the credit at the feet of the Buried Goddess, but it was Iam who shed His light behind us. I felt it there, as we were surrounded by death, as I once felt it fighting beside your father."

"You would blame Iam for reducing half of Winde Port to ash?" Redstar asked.

"I would credit him for seeing this kingdom restored to its rightful glory!" Torsten approached Oleander and took her hands. She didn't fight it.

"My Queen, you know him," Torsten said, referring to Redstar. "You know what he is capable of. I know I failed you, but do not fall for this deception."

Her ruby lips parted, but no words came out. Torsten could see the flicker of doubt in her features, finally. That vulnerability she'd revealed before he set off for Winde Port when her son eschewed her.

"You do not appeal to her, knight," Pi said. "You appeal to me, and me alone."

"Watch out, Your Grace," Redstar said to the King. "He might try to bed you, too."

"How dare you!" Oleander snapped. Finally, her mask of composure slipped to the floor. She lunged at her brother, but Torsten was there to intercept her. He refused to let another fall prey to the trickster.

"Is this not a hall for speaking truth?" Redstar demanded. "Do you not see the way he lusts for your mother, King Pi? I wouldn't be surprised if that were how he weaseled himself into the post of the Wearer after your father fell ill and Sir Davies died when it is widely spoken that the late Sir Jolly was far more qualified."

"He never wanted to wear the white helm," Torsten said.

"Or perhaps he wasn't as adept at fulfilling my sister's… baser needs when Liam couldn't."

"And how would you know?" Torsten said. "You were too busy fleeing to the Webbed Woods chasing monsters and cursing the Prince. Your current king!"

"Opening eyes is never easy."

"Quiet!" Pi thundered. His voice filled the hall, louder and with more timbre than any boy his age should be capable of. He stood upon the throne now, piercing golden eyes, so like his father's, fixed on Torsten.

"Sir Unger," he said, calculating. "I am blind to nothing that happens in these halls. Your attempted dalliance with my mother would be enough to have you hanged if I decide so, or if I was foolish enough to believe that it was not she who took the first step."

Oleander looked aghast, leaving Torsten unsure at how much headway she'd actually made in earning back the boy's trust.

"And Redstar," Pi continued, "if I am not mistaken it was you who advised I restore Yuri Darkings' position upon the council."

Redstar didn't miss a beat. "Alas, I am ashamed to admit that I over-heard Torsten and Lord Darkings discussing that very arrangement while I was in the dungeon. I hoped to win your favor in improving your Royal Council."

"Is this true, Sir Unger?"

"I will not lie to you, Your Grace," Torsten said. "It was my intent. But nobody could've predicted Yuri's motives, even Redstar's Goddess. It was all our failures in allowing him back into power. So, use me. Send me to hunt down the Caleef and fix this."

"As you hunted Muskigo?" Redstar said.

Torsten sunk away from the dais.

"Your Grace," Redstar said, taking a few steps closer. "I believe we have wasted enough time pretending that our situation has not changed. The rebel army remains at large, and soon Muskigo will inspire more afhems to his cause whether we find the Caleef or not. The bulk of our armies remain in Winde Port preparing to march on the Shesaitju lands, but they are leaderless now. I sent a report of what the Wearer has done, and I believe it is time he is stripped of his command. Would you trust a man capable of coming so unhinged to bring justice to Muskigo, and restore order to your great kingdom?"

"Your Grace, I will make no excuses for what I have done, but this man is attempting to deceive you," Torsten said. "Do not forget that it was he who poisoned your mind and led you to leap from that window! It is only by the grace of Iam that you returned to us when Redstar would have seen the Nothhelm line ended."

"You speak of magic as if you understand it," Redstar said. "I did not curse the boy; I merely allowed him to see what the rest refuse to. The true power which watches over us. You claim I destroyed our king's mind, yet there he sits, alive and well. Stronger than ever. All thanks to me. For it was not Iam who brought him back, but the hand of my Lady."

"That is blasphemy!" Wren shouted. "Your Highness, I agree with the Wearer of White. Redstar may be your uncle, but from the moment he arrived in the capital a year ago, we have seen naught but suffering."

"Queen Mother," Torsten addressed Oleander. "Do you not remember what he reduced your son to? How he had him rambling on about nonsense in the darkness?"

"Of course, I remember," Oleander replied, still diffident after her son's verbal attack.

"Then how could you, how could any of us listen to a word he says?"

"My uncle explained his intentions to me before I released him, Wearer," Pi said. "He helped me see in the only way he knew how and has already been pardoned. We are not here to discuss his place in my kingdom; we are here to discuss yours."

"Your Gra—"

"If I must ask one more time not to be interrupted, you will hang."

Silence filled the hall, thicker than any sound could.

"The truth, Sir Unger, is that you allowed Winde Port to be taken in the first place by ignoring Redstar's warning," Pi said. "You invited Yuri Darkings to Winde Port of your own accord. And you failed to eliminate Muskigo while Redstar was forced to take action and reclaim the city. And perhaps worst of all, you killed one of your own Shieldsmen in a blind rage directed at my uncle despite his heroics leading an army that was meant to be under your command. These are the reports I have received. Do you deny any of it?"

Torsten swallowed hard. He glanced back over his shoulder and saw his Shieldsmen. Not one of them spoke up in his defense, and only Nikserof's expression revealed the slightest grief. Sir Mulliner didn't smile, but his satisfaction at Torsten's facing of justice was evident.

"I do not," Torsten said, "but—"

"Stop." King Pi held up his hand. "You were sent to subdue Muskigo while he was removed from his people. Now he is back among them to stir the hornet's nest, and our coffers lack the gold to both go after him and repair Winde Port. You speak against my uncle, yet without him, we would be in a far worse situation. Winde Port would remain occupied, and Yuri Darkings likely still in his post ready to bury us."

"As I said, it is clear Sir Unger was unfit to inherit the helm from his predecessor," Redstar said. "We are lucky I was there to pick up the pieces."

Torsten lost what little restraint he possessed. He swung the white helm of his post into the side of Redstar's face. His birthmark split open at the cheek as he hit the ground. Torsten pounced onto him, punching him again and again. This time Redstar didn't use magic to fend him off. He merely cackled as Torsten struck him.

Sir Mulliner and other members of the King's Shield arrived to pull him off. It was the battlefield of Winde Port all over again, only now he was in front of the King, Queen Mother, and High Priest of Iam. All those important to him, present to see him acting like a wild beast.

Redstar crawled backward against the throne's dais. "Behold," he rasped, still cackling. He spat blood onto the marble. "Your Wearer, my King."

"He's using you!" Torsten shouted as he tried to break free. Sir Mulliner shoved him hard onto his chest and held him there. "He's using all of you, can't you see!"

Nobody could bear to watch. Wren prayed under his breath. The other worthless members of the Royal Council cowered. Even Oleander turned to the side and closed her eyes.

All but Pi. His unwavering stare remained on Torsten, the small boy who looked a giant upon his throne. "I see a man broken by his failings," he said. "In the name of Iam and the Glass Throne, I strip you of your position as both Wearer and Shieldsman. Your vows are nullified. And for the murder of Sir Havel Tralen, you will be imprisoned until I can think of what to do with you."

Sir Havel... Now he knew the name of the Shieldsman he'd murdered. He stopped fighting Sir Mulliner and stared toward the throne, eyes wet with tears. He didn't look to Pi or Wren, but to Oleander. The Queen Mother who'd hurt so many in the name of her son; the only person who might understand him.

"Please, Oleander," he said, imploring her by her own name. "You know me. I would never purposely bring harm to this kingdom. I am, as always, your loyal servant. But him?" He hadn't even the energy to point to Redstar. "He'll destroy us all."

Finally, Oleander half turned. He noticed the glint of a tear on her cheek, but she never moved enough to look Torsten in the eye.

She drew a deep breath. "The demands of my son, your King, are final," she said weakly. "You served this kingdom well during my husband's illness, and for that, you have my gratitude. I can offer no more."

Torsten felt like he'd been punched in the gut. "And what esteemed Shieldsman is to replace me?" he asked. He could hardly move, but he angled his restrained arm to point at Sir Nikserof who stood near the entry. "It may mean nothing, but Sir Nikserof's bravery in Winde Port was commendable."

Pi hopped down from the throne and began to pace. Now on the floor, it was clear how small and fragile he was, but he didn't walk like it. He moved with the swagger of a conqueror, shoulders high and proud like his father's always were.

"It is clear to me that the old ways are no longer working," Pi said. "I have been left with an unfit council, unable to complete a task as simple as having a crypt repaired on time. My father had no family to trust and had to see the worth in others, but I do. As of this moment, my uncle will be named my prime minister, closely overseeing the roles of all the Royal Council."

Murmurs broke out amongst the members behind the throne.

"And," Pi continued, louder as to quell the din, "he will assume the role of royal commander of my armies for the time being. We will install a new Wearer and generals who will honor and respect our alliance with the Drav Cra, and together, we will end all talk of rebellions."

The murmuring grew louder. Even Sir Mulliner and the other Shieldsman holding Torsten seemed confused. But Redstar remained lying on the marble wearing a bloody grin.

"Your Grace, the position of High Priest responds only to the will of Iam," Wren said. "I am his mouth and hand in Pantego. Your uncle is a servant to Nesilia, the Buried Goddess. I will not allow him to oversee our holy church."

"You will do as instructed!" Pi snapped. "It was my father's willingness to force our faith on others which leads now to an uprising. Redstar will have no control over the Church of Iam, worry not, but so long as he and his people are here, they are members of the Glass Kingdom. They will not be persecuted for speaking the name of a goddess whose magic helped save so many in Winde Port."

"You would allow these warlocks and blood mages to poison the ears of our people?"

"If Iam is the one true God," Pi answered, "then our people will not be shaken."

"This is an outrage." Wren stormed down from behind the throne and out of the room. Torsten had never seen the blind priest move so fast; he barely used his cane.

"Too long have we relied on old customs," Pi announced. "Under my father, the Glass Kingdom was a shining beacon in a dark world. Together, we can make it that again."

"Please, Your Grace!" Torsten shouted. "Think about what you're doing. He is her servant, not yours. He belongs to Nesilia, and she will bring ruin to us all."

"Yet Redstar tells me that Nesilia and Iam were of one flesh. That it was together, the God Feud was ended, not apart."

"He would say anything to gain more power. Don't do this."

"Ask yourself this, what if he's right? What if together, we can bring Pantego to greater heights than ever?"

"And we shall, Your Grace." Redstar stood, slowly climbed the glass stairs, and lay his hands upon the King's shoulders. "There is so much work to be done. Now, why don't you meet me in the Shield Hall and we can discuss our options."

"Yes, come Pi," Oleander said. "I can't bear to watch this any longer." She guided her son off the dais and toward the tower up to the private wing. She didn't even look back. Torsten had failed her, more than anyone else. He'd promised to bring Redstar down and instead allowed him to ascend to the side of the King.

Redstar stayed behind. He bent to pick up the bloodied helm of the Wearer of White. Then he raised it over his head and lowered it. It looked ridiculous without the rest of the armor, but he didn't seem to care. It was just a game to him, like everything else.

He regarded Torsten, still grinning. "You don't approve?" he asked. "Did it look better on Uriah?" He swiped his hand in front of his face, and for a moment his appearance changed to that of Torsten's mentor. The same face Redstar wore to trick him into helping him in the Webbed Woods. In a moment, his ugly, blemished façade returned but just seeing him mar the memory of Uriah again fueled Torsten.

"You won't get away with this!" He roared and thrashed, but Austun pushed down again.

"All right. Lock him up, Sir Mulliner." Redstar tapped on the helm. "That's an order."

Austun tried to get Torsten under control, but his massive body was too strong. A few more Shieldsmen jumped in to help.

"I have to handle everything," Redstar groaned. He brushed some blood off his face, then raised his palm. The Shieldsmen were yanked off Torsten by unseen magic; then the warlock flicked his wrist and Torsten slid all the way across the hall, striking the wall just beside Nikserof. Freydis stood beside him, a wicked grin smeared across her white-painted lips.

The Royal Council members, guards, and Shieldsmen remaining watched, utterly flabbergasted by the open use of blood magic in the Throne Room of the Glass Castle, a place blessed and occupied by the faithful to Iam for centuries. But Redstar didn't have to hide what he was anymore, and it was all thanks to Torsten.

II

THE MYSTIC

Sora hadn't left the captain's quarters of the Breklian corsair she and Whitney had stolen from Winde Port for a fortnight. She laid in a bed made of the softest material she'd ever felt, but she still couldn't sleep. Every time her eyes closed, visions of Whitney and that monster, Kazimir, danced through her mind. It was mental torture worse than any physical pain she could imagine enduring.

Her dwarven companion, Tum Tum, had long since given up on trying to stir her. The fact they hadn't sunk yet told her the dwarf knew the intricacies of sailing. It's not like she knew how, anyway.

As the ship rocked then dipped, her stomach rose into her throat, and she wondered if they'd already reached the Boiling Waters south of the Black Sands. The thought of stepping out into sunlight brought an overwhelming sense of panic. For a reason she couldn't put her finger on, she felt like anything more than darkness would be like screaming to the gods that she'd forgotten about Whitney.

She hadn't. She never would. And she couldn't forget how she'd...

What had she done? Was he dead, banished, evaporated like water on a hot day? All she knew was that one moment he and Kazimir were there, the next they'd vanished. She'd felt the energy of Elsewhere crackling in the area where they'd been. It made the blood coursing through her body tingle. Eventually, it dissipated, but not on Whitney's stolen half of the Glass Crown. She'd had to cover it with a blanket because every time she looked at it, she felt that same overwhelming sensation of Elsewhere seeking to work through her. If she touched it, her entire body, from her fingers to her neck, tensed.

Not for the first time, she rolled over and screamed into a pillow, beating it unmercifully with her fists. It always managed to make her feel a little bit better. But she knew what came next. Tears. Exhaustion. And finally, after her eyes were spent of the stuff, she'd drift off into nightmares.

Aquira heard her and squirmed up right beside her. The wyvern's body was like a furnace, and even though her scales were dry and coarse, Sora appreciated the company.

She couldn't say how long it'd been before the cabin door swung open and sunlight poured in. Aquira bolted upright, growling until she realized who it was. A stout dwarf appeared in the entry, with a nose like a pear and a beard that seemed not to have seen a blade in years.

"All right, lass," Tum Tum's gruff voice said. "The time for sleepin and depressin be over."

"Please, leave me alone," Sora said, and rolled over.

"Not happenin. I know ye ain't a bit happy bout our situation and neither be I, but we be lost and nearly out of food."

Sora sat up. "We're lost?"

"As a giant in Hornsheim," he said with a chuckle. "What did ye expect? All I know about sailin I learned watchin the wharf from me bar and ye've been pissin the days away in here. Not that I be complainin, if ye'd been of the right mind we'd be out of food long ago."

Sora swore.

"Just give me a few minutes to get properly dressed," she said.

"As I said, not happenin. I know if I leave here, yer just gonna flop back down on that soft, comfy bed and drift off again."

She knew he was probably right. She grunted and got out of bed. She wasn't naked, but she wasn't dressed either. It was dark, and the dwarf turned around to give her privacy, especially after Aquira screeched at him.

After wiggling into a pair of pants and pulling on a sack-like tunic—

both she'd found in the quarters—she said, "Okay," and they went out onto the deck. Aquira flapped up and landed on her shoulder.

The sunlight hit her full in the face, causing her to squint. Water sprayed her cheeks, reminding her she was still alive. Climbing the five stairs from the cabin doorway, she breathed in the salty air. She had to admit; it felt good to get out of that room.

"Where are we?" she asked.

"In the middle of the ocean," Tum Tum said.

He wasn't lying. There was blue everywhere—blue ocean, blue sky—except to what she thought was east where the skies were beginning to darken. Sora had to grab a railing to keep grounded and avoid feeling dizzy. All around them, there was no land or steady horizon. It vacillated with the crests of waves, up and down, side to side, an interminable wall of water.

She swallowed hard. "That doesn't look good," she said.

"That's why I be waking ye," Tum Tum said, "Easy to sail alone when ye let the boat do the drivin, but now there be a storm comin and I ain't barely good on a bright day."

Sora's head hung a little, and her shoulders followed.

"What's left for food?" she asked.

"Still got some fish I caught, but since the previous owner didn't eat nothin dead, there wasn't much in the way of stores."

"Please don't remind me about him." Any thought of Kazimir, the upyr who'd hunted her and Whitney through Winde Port, would make her remember how he'd wanted to feed on her blood until she was dried out. Which would remind her of her unbridled rage as he threatened Whitney's life, and then what had happened to both of them.

"Apparently, he had a love of apples cus there was a bunch of em," Tum Tum said. "Most be dried up and rotten by now though. If ye be wantin some sweet fish stew of me own invention, there's some on that pot over there."

He pointed toward the galley, which was really just a covered, flattened portion of the ship with three walls and a cauldron.

The thought of food had her stomach rumbling. She'd only eaten every few days and only when she couldn't manage any longer. She imagined if she had a looking glass, she'd barely recognize the woman in the reflection.

"I must be gaunt," she said to no one in particular.

"Fair as the day I met ye," Tum Tum responded.

What he hadn't said was that they'd only met about two weeks ago, and even then, just a day or so before they'd ended up on this ship together.

She quietly made her way toward the food, all the while eyeing the steadily approaching storm.

Tum Tum trailed a bit behind her.

"I'm sorry, Tum Tum," she said softly.

"Sorries be for the past," he said. "Let's just get off this damned boat."

Sora laughed and nodded as she ladled some of the food onto a tin plate. She raised another spoonful for Aquira, who devoured it in a single gulp, nearly breaking the spoon too.

"Looks great," Sora said. "Aquira seems to like it."

"Trust me; it's not." Tum Tum laughed this time. "I serve drinks. Leave the food for me cooks. Or well… left."

Sora pursed her lips and raised her bowl to him in solidarity. If there was one thing she understood, it was losing one's home. Then they took a sip of the stew together, and she stifled a gag. Tum Tum wasn't lying. The fish was dry and filled with bones, and the broth was tart.

"Where do you think Whitney is?" Sora asked after a long silence and forcing herself to get half the bowl down.

"Not here," he answered. "Not here, lass, and that's all we be knowing. Best not dwell on what we can't change."

Tum Tum returned to the helm while she ate, eyes closed, ready to nod off. She'd have cried if she still had tears left, but instead, she stood and walked back out onto the deck. By now, a dense fog had rolled in. The storm still loomed a bit off in the distance, but it was approaching at an uncomfortable rate, and the wind was picking up. The ships sail flapped loudly.

Sora regarded Tum Tum, seated at the helm. It was he who slept now, and she hated him for it, imagined he was dreaming of snow-covered mountains and far-away lands, pretty dwarven women and gold-filled mines. She knew it was unfair. Tum Tum knew Whitney too. He might have even known him better than she had. It was easy to forget that between him leaving Troborough without saying goodbye, and her finding him escaping Redstar's prison, was nearly a decade of adventures. She'd give anything to hear him exaggerate about another.

Piss in the wind, as Whitney would have said.

What mattered now was how to get to where they wanted to go so she might be able to figure out where they were. It was her magic that disappeared them. She knew it wasn't Kazimir's because he had no interest in Whitney. No. Whatever had happened sprung from her fingertips, and the strange power growing within her. Her abilities had always come with the cost of blood. It allowed her to keep them in check, but occasionally, like in the Webbed Woods, or when she lit Winde Port on fire, she lost control. She'd promised Whitney she wouldn't let that happen again, and she'd lied.

"You're out there somewhere," she whispered into the wind. "I know it."

She couldn't, however, answer the question of where without first finding land before she and Tum Tum starved. That was step one. Don't starve. Then she could figure out a way to get to Yaolin City, where she and Whitney were headed before everything went south. Based on everything she'd learned from Wetzel, only her Panpingese ancestors, and their great mystics, fully attuned to drawing on the powers of Elsewhere, could help—if any who still knew anything even remained now that the Glass Kingdom ruled their lands.

As she stared quietly upon the continually shifting horizon, white crests rising and falling, a mass of what seemed like land peeked through the rolling fog.

Maybe we're in Panping already?

She'd never sailed before so had no idea how fast it should go. This was by far the furthest from home she'd ever been, and thanks to Afhem Muskigo and the Shesaitju rebellion she had no home to go back to for the second time.

"Tum Tum!" she called.

"Aye?" he said, sleepily.

She thought about the stories she'd heard over the years when sailors would occasionally pass through Troborough and hunker down in the

Twilight Manor on their way to Yarrington. Sora would usually sit and listen to the bards play their songs and overhear some of the tales. What was it they would shout when they spotted land?

"Land, whore!" she cried.

Tum Tum muttered a curse as his head sprung up from resting on a spoke of the wheel. Then he laughed. "It's land ho, lass." He waddled over to Sora by the bow. He squinted and said, "I dun't see nothin."

"Right there," she pointed. "Just beyond the veil of…"

Her voice trailed off at the same time she'd realized her mistake.

"It's not land, it's another ship!" she yelled. "That might be even better than land."

"Unless they be pirates," Tum Tum remarked.

"Those are just tall tales told by sailors looking for attention," she said. "The Glass Kingdom drove them all out… right?"

They both stood and watched the approaching ship which was more than twice the size of theirs and had three times the sails. As its silhouette grew, it pierced the veil of fog and Sora's heart sank into her stomach. The sails were dark as night, and the flag flapping in the now buffeting winds bore the image of a chipped skull with blood leaking from its eye-sockets and mouth.

"Are those…" Sora couldn't finish.

"Not just tales, lass," Tum Tum said quietly.

They both swore.

"Mayhaps they won't be seein us," he added.

"I think it's too late for that," Sora replied.

The ship lurched, the boom and sail swinging over their heads. The sound as the wind caught the fabric was loud as thunder, and Sora and Tum Tum realized they were both crouched in fear. Aquira's claws dug into Sora's shoulder, only one leg still on as she flapped with all her might to combat the gust.

"We've got to get you inside." She grabbed Aquira and tucked her under her elbow before running to the captain's quarters.

Cold, wet rain slashed against Sora's skin like needles as she ran. They were far enough south to escape the bitter cold of winter, but the rain still came down like ice. She locked Aquira inside before it got even worse, the wyvern screeching in protest.

In a matter of minutes, it went from a light sprinkle to a deluge. Their ship rocked uncontrollably in the growing waves, even as Tum Tum took the helm to try and keep them steady. The dark, pirate vessel maintained a straight on approach.

"Best be preparin for what's to come," he said.

"Which is?" Sora said.

"The end."

The seconds ticked by like hours, and the sky turned a sickly shade of green. The ocean lost its blue, as if somehow it could become even less inviting. Now it was gray like death and decay, the waves rising high all around them, blotting out even the clouds.

"We can't just sit here and wait for them to board us," Sora said. She turned and raced back to her cabin. She returned a moment later with Wetzel's knife in hand.

"Are ye plannin on us hackin down twenty pirates all by ourselves?" Tum Tum asked. "Face it, lass, whatever they be wantin, they'll be gettin. We may as well play coy and ask to join the crew."

"Don't underestimate me, dwarf."

"Long as you don't underestimate them," he retorted, pointing a stubby thumb toward the ship that was now only fifty meters away.

Sora walked out to the center of the deck and drew a thin line of blood across her hand. Sacrifice, to draw on the powers of Elsewhere. She raised her hand toward the boarding vessel. Flame sizzled at her fingertips as she pulled on that haunting, indescribable power within; but it never formed further.

Driving rain stung at her wound and washed the blood away, and after whatever she'd done to Whitney, her body was still weak. She could usually feel the energy of Elsewhere percolating in her gut, but now it was distant, fleeting.

"C'mon," Sora willed her body. "Don't do this again!" She cut her bicep, deeper this time. Her hand and forearm were numb to the abuse, but as the soft skin split apart, it came with a forgotten pain. She fell to a knee, wincing, but she didn't give up. A pathetic stream of fire swirled around her hand, then arced off into the pirate ship.

The rain quickly extinguished even the magical flame, and all that was left was a singe on the ship's hull.

Several dirty men peered over the side of the rail. The frigate or galleon—Sora knew nothing about the names of ships—drifted close and it occurred to her that their vessel could literally fit inside of it.

"Prepare to be boarded!" a gruff voice shouted, barely audible over the whipping winds. Grappling hooks soared over the watery expanse and found purchase in the wood of the corsair. Several pirates swung across, landing and rolling to a standing stop before drawing short, curved swords.

Rough hands seized her from all directions. Sora swung at them with her knife, but it was pointless. The men were stronger, and no matter how she tried, she couldn't get the fire to come. She told herself it was the driving rain keeping her spark at bay before it formed, but she knew that was a lie. Every time she looked inward for the call of Elsewhere, Whitney's face flashed through her mind.

Tum Tum protested even louder as they ripped him from the helm, lashing out with curses she didn't even know existed. A plank lowered with a loud *thunk* when the two ships were close enough to one another.

The pirates jeered at her, and she found herself wondering why evil men were always so gross. Rotting teeth, messy beards, scars going every which way. Last time she'd been faced with a situation like this, Whitney had shown up just in the nick of time, stealing a caravan from a bunch of vile mercenaries, and together, they rode off into the proverbial sunset. Not this time. She would have to handle this on her own.

"There's nothing worth taking here," she said, throwing one of them off her arm. The end of the sleeve tore.

"I beg to differ, little lady," one said, looking her up and down like a piece of steak. He went to wrap her arms around her waist.

"Get your hands off me!" She squirmed, but it was no use against so many of them. And even as her fresh blood mixed with the rain, she couldn't will Elsewhere to respond beyond the tips of her fingers.

That would have to be enough.

She grabbed her assailant's arm and he squealed like a stuck pig in response to the heat of her palm. "Iam's light, what was that!"

Sora slipped under the grasp of another and ran toward the captain's quarters. Tum Tum was by the helm, still fighting to break free. She could hear Aquira inside making a racket over the storm. The wyvern might be enough to change the tide.

Sora looked back at the ruffians in pursuit, and when she turned to the door, her path was blocked. The man before her cut an imposing figure. He stood more than a head above Sora and three above Tum Tum. A long, thick beard fell from his chin, black with strips of white running vertically at nearly perfect intervals. His heavy, silver clasped boots landed on the deck of the small ship with a horrifying thud.

"All hail Grisham 'Gold Grin' Gale!" one fat lump cried from behind. "Scourge of the Seas, Ward of the Waters, and King of the Pirates!"

"All hail!" the rest echoed.

Sora didn't know how to react.

Of all the pirates in the world...

Whitney boasted about his time spent with Gold Grin a few times. She didn't usually believe him about these kinds of things, but she had to admit, a bit of hope coursed through her body.

"Aye, let go of me ye shog bucket!" Tum Tum screamed as they tried hauling him toward her.

"Just relax," Sora said, but it was too late. One of the pirates clubbed Tum Tum hard over the head, and the dwarf collapsed to the ground, unconscious.

"Tum Tum!" Sora lunged for him, and a mess of grimy hands pulled her back.

The hulking man who could be none other than Gold Grin looked down at her. He grinned, and Sora learned how apt his name was. Lots of men had yellow teeth, but his were gold as autlas and sparkled just the same.

"Where's yer cap'n?" Gold Grin asked, scanning the ship over Sora's head.

"We don't have a captain," she answered.

The men laughed. All but Gold Grin.

"Where's the rest of the crew?" he asked.

"We don't have anyone else."

A few men laughed again, but most took the cue from their leader who remained stone-faced.

"Ye thinking this a joke?" he asked.

"No joke, my Lord," Sora said. "It's just the two of us. We were three—someone I believe you may know."

If the pirate were listening, he didn't show any sign of it. He strolled off toward the captain's quarters and threw the door wide open.

"Fortist, Hestor," Gold Grin shouted to two of his men. "Tear it apart!" He leaned into Sora and grinned even wider. His breath smelled of ale and fish. "And I ain't no lord, pretty lass."

Two of the pirates began giving orders to the rest, and in seconds they had fanned out like ants from a mound. Gold Grin joined them and headed down the stairs into holding.

"Please!" Sora yelled. "Just listen!" She went to step, but the deck was slick and rocking side to side with the tremendous waves. She slipped, and was immediately hoisted back up by a couple of men. As could be expected, their hands wandered wherever they desired.

"You don't understand!" she started.

"Naw, ye don't understand, wench," one of her captors said. "This be our ship now, and ye might stay alive to keep us company."

Everyone within earshot laughed, but Sora finally had enough. The familiar surge of Elsewhere returned, and this time she forced herself to think of Kazimir, Muskigo, and Redstar; all those who'd ever tried to hurt her. Anyone but Whitney. The gash on her arm itched, begging her to draw on blood offered. Flames erupted from her and scorched the men on either side. They cried out, and even those holding Tum Tum backed away.

The pirates shouted about witches and demons, but one voice broke through the din of insanity.

"Aren't ye a special one?" Gold Grin clomped back toward Sora and stood, eyes fixated on her. In his hand he twirled half of King Liam's crown, fingering the glass. "This be a mighty good fake."

"That's no fake," Sora said, panting. Gold Grin approached her as if her hands weren't currently wreathed in embers. "That belonged to King Liam himself."

"Only one king around here," one of the pirates said, voice shaking.

Sora looked at Gold Grin and smiled. "You're the king of the pirates, huh?"

"The ones that matter," he chortled.

"Aye! Boss, look what I found!"

Sora turned toward the captain's quarters where a skinny little runt of a man came running out holding Aquira by the neck. She flapped and squirmed but couldn't get free. He had a singed sleeve for what it was worth, and the one next to him was full of bite marks.

"Leave her be!" Sora shouted, her fire growing brighter and stronger.

"A Panping mystic with a wyvern?" Gold Grin said. "Now there be a story I'd like to hear."

"Put her down," Sora demanded. "I won't ask again."

Gold Grin motioned for the pirate to release Aquira. The wyvern turned and snapped at the man. He drew his hand back, fearful. Two long flaps brought Aquira to Sora, and she tucked under her arm where the wind wouldn't send her flailing. She coughed, sparks dribbling down her chin to join Sora's flame.

Last time their powers combined, half of Winde Port went alight. She knew what would happen if she released energy like that on a ship, but a part of her didn't care. A part of her wanted to send all these grimy souls who thought they could do whatever they wanted to anyone with no consequences to the bottom of the ocean, even if she went with them. But then she'd never find out where Whitney was.

"What's a pretty, powerful woman like ye doing out at sea with naught but a dwarf for company?" Gold Grin asked, moving closer. She raised her flaming hand, but it didn't stop him. The man showed no fear as if her magic was just the beginning of the wonders he'd seen.

Despite her having the perceived upper hand, Sora was fearful of any man who didn't flinch in the presence of magic.

"Whitney Fierstown," she blurted as Gold Grin drew close enough for her to smell the fish on his breath.

He leaned back. She could tell from the change in his features that the name meant something to him, just what was yet to be determined.

True to his name, a wide grin began to stretch across his sun-beaten face. It looked like leather stretched across Mr. Gregor's tanning frames.

"What did you say?" he asked, slowly examining the faces of his men.

Sora still couldn't judge which direction her choice to invoke the name of Whitney Fierstown would take her.

"You know him?" she asked.

Every last one of the men nearly doubled over with laughter. Gold Grin merely stood there, same grin plastered across his face.

"Do we know him, boys?" Gold Grin shouted.

None stopped laughing long enough to provide an answer.

"Aye," he said, leaning in again, "I know him weller than any man be wanting to know any lying, thieving, picaroon. Had a date with Stump-maker Jack, he did." The man motioned to his neck and drew his finger across his throat. "Escaped with more than his life that day."

They all laughed again, and Sora swore to herself.

"Left this crew as the only man to ever steal from Grisham 'Gold Grin' Gale, he did!"

Gold Grin took one last step forward. Aquira growled, but Sora's flame began to weaken from drawing too long on the power. She knew she'd made a mistake. *I should have known better than to think Whitney left a good impression on anybody.*

"Left here with the respect of each and every one of us too!" Gold Grin exclaimed after a brief silence. "Where be that carousing rapscallion?" He grabbed her by the shoulders and shook her.

"What?" she asked, stunned.

"He be on this crew? This ship? He be a bucko of yers?"

"I—he—I," she couldn't manage more than a stammer until Gold Grin stumbled backward, chuckling.

"He was. I—I don't know where he went. He just… disappeared."

Still laughing, the pirate king said, "Sounds like Whitney Fierstown, the scalawag! Bet he stole this crown as well, didn't he?"

"Yes." She hoped her face didn't betray her sadness. "At least, that's what he claimed."

"Then we've all been flimflammed by the same rotten scoundrel. What be yer name, love?"

"Sora," she said, then added, "and this is Aquira."

The wyvern growled.

"And that," she pointed to the still-unconscious dwarf, "is Tum Tum."

"Aye, he'll be fine," Gold Grin said. "Throw a bucket on him, Nevin!"

A hunched over, well-fed pirate Sora assumed was Nevin grabbed one of the buckets Tum Tum had been using to swab the deck and tossed it on the dwarf.

Tum Tum awoke in a startle, scrambling to his feet, and readying his fists.

"Where they be? I'll kill em all," he muttered as he stumbled around the deck.

"It's okay, Tum Tum," Sora said over the laughter of the pirate crew. "They know Whitney."

Tum Tum grumbled something, but Sora couldn't make it out. He plopped down on the deck, clearly exhausted.

"What are ye doing on here all on yer own?" Gold Grin asked. "Gods. Whitney didn't drive ye to kill him and toss him overboard did he?"

"It'd be about time!" one of his men hollered.

"We were sailing for Yaolin City before getting lost," Sora said. "I'm… I'm a trader."

"I'm all for liars girl, but usually traders be… well… having something to trade!"

More laughter came.

Sora didn't overthink. Whitney taught her not to when spinning a lie. She reached into the folds of her clothing and removed the sealed writ she and Whitney had taken from Tayvada Bokeo in Winde Port after he died. The one that indicated him a member of the Winde Trader's Guild. Sora had used it on Afhem Muskigo to trick him into helping her, and now the poor, murdered man would ensure her life again.

Gold Grin took the sopping wet papers and shook them off. "Winde Trader's Guild, eh?"

"Yes, with my… uh. My husband. He died in the Shesaitju attack on Winde Port. Gave his life so that I could escape alive. I need to reach Panping as soon as I can to settle his affairs." A tear rolled from her eyes even though she wasn't trying to cry. *Pieces of truth.* That was how Whitney had taught her to lie, and now she realized that she'd partly been talking about him.

"You hear that, Gold Grin?" the grungy, wiry pirate beside him said, missing an eye and more than a few teeth. "She's available."

Gold Grin's slapped him in the back of the head.

"Ye can see all the wonders in the world, but you can't teach a scoundrel manners," Gold Grin said, "My condolences, me lady."

Sora sauntered toward him. She knew she couldn't hide the grief and fear wracking her face, but she let her figure do the talking. Out to sea for Iam knows how long, with only disgusting men for company, Gold Grin was easy prey. She lay her hand gently upon his forearm.

"Please," she said meekly. "All me and my friend want is to sail to Yaolin City unharmed, and bring some closure to Tayvada's family." As the words left her lips, she vowed that if she made it, she'd do just that. Let them know he died a hero to his people, and that he'd saved her life twice now.

"You plan on heading through them waters?" Gold Grin asked, pointing to the east. "Not likely this little ship will take ye through unscathed with only two of ye. Plus, there be pirates about!"

The man he'd just hit chuckled.

"I'll tell ye what," he said. "Give me this here crown, and we'll take ye where ye be going, right boys?"

"Aye!" they all shouted.

Sora bit her lip. She knew Whitney would freak out if he knew she'd bartered the crown, but what choice did she have? Neither she nor Tum Tum had a clue what they were doing out on the open seas. And as much as she didn't want to admit it, Whitney was gone, maybe not dead, but somewhere else. The only people who might know where were through the torrent.

A tear welled at the corner of Sora's eye. The crown was all she had left to remember him by. But it wouldn't do her any good at the bottom of the ocean. She lowered her head, closing her eyes against the thought. *He wouldn't want me to die out here all alone, or give up on finding him.*

She stuck out her hand. "Deal."

Gold Grin grabbed hers and shook. She tried to avoid staring at his stained fingernails. "I don't suppose them papers can get me and me boys into Yaolin without the guards taken shots at us. Haven't been to a proper city since I sunk my first Glass galleon."

"I… I'm not sure."

He leaned in and flashed his golden teeth once more. "Well, it won't hurt to try… us at least." He laughed, then snapped his fingers to his men. "Prepare a bed for our new guests and strip this vessel for all she's worth."

"Aye!" his men echoed.

He placed his hand on Sora's back and led her to the plank so she could look upon his galleon. "Welcome to the *Reba*!" he said, spreading his arms wide. "There be one rule and one rule only; None of that fire magic on me ship and we'll get along just fine. Wood and flame don't exactly make the best of friends."

Sora swallowed the lump forming in her throat. Riding with pirates wasn't the way she expected to reach Yaolin City, but it was too late to turn back now. She couldn't help but think that Whitney would approve.

"No fire?" she said. "I think I can manage that."

III

THE THIEF

"Thee's a very simple explanation for all of this," Whitney said. "It's a dream. It's a yigging dream. Tomorrow, I'll wake up, and I'll be in some inn on the shog side of Yarrington. Or better yet, a brothel in Latiapur."

Whitney looked over at the pale, terrifying man beside him. They were in the boat that beached ashore when they arrived in what he'd been told was Elsewhere, courtesy of one of Sora's unpredictable spells.

Well, he looked over at the apparition of a pale man because he still believed he had to be asleep.

Kazimir, the white-haired upyr, hadn't said more than two words together since they boarded the rickety boat. Whitney kept an eye on him the entire time, waiting for when the man would try to throw him overboard and finally succeed in killing him.

"No, really," Whitney continued to himself, "you don't understand how much sense this makes. I think I must be in some sort of extensive sleep. Maybe I've been poisoned—I've never been poisoned. Huh, I'd always thought it would hurt more."

The boat creaked as the dark, robed figure who stood upon the bow paddled through the endless sea with a long, knotted oar. He answered only to the name the Ferryman, but he too hadn't spoken since they set off. The silence drove Whitney mad.

"There's no way I was rescued from a jail cell by the Wearer of White after stealing the King's crown, just coincidentally ran into my childhood friend Sora, slew a yigging goddess in a gods-forsaken forest, and then ended up in Elsewhere next to a gods-damned upyr," Whitney decided. "I'm asleep. It's the only reasonable answer."

A foot connected hard against Whitney's arm. He yelped.

"Can't feel pain when you're asleep," Kazimir said.

"I doubt that's true," Whitney said.

"Just be silent," Kazimir growled. "Your tongue is the only thing that could make Elsewhere worse."

"You're not too great a companion either, Kazimir," Whitney grumbled under his breath as he laid back. "*Kazi*mir. What kind of name is that anyway?"

The upyr ignored him, as he had for the last how many hours. So, Whitney stared up at the night sky. It wasn't any sky he'd ever seen. No stars twinkled. If Celeste and Loutis were present, they were hiding well.

"It's kind of a reddish-purple," Whitney said. He looked at Kazimir again, who was pointedly looking away, off toward the horizon. "The sky," Whitney continued. "Makes sense. The water is dark and bloody, why wouldn't the sky be the same?"

Whitney laughed nervously to himself as waves gently lapped against the side of the boat. He'd long since learned to ignore the cold, spectral hands reaching over the side of the boat. They grasped but could never grab hold of anything. The deep wailing echoing off the surface of the Sea of Souls was nearly a lullaby now that they'd proven to be harmless.

"I remember someone telling me the ocean wasn't really blue," Whitney said after a brief silence. "The real ocean that is. Can you believe that? They said it's just a reflection of the sky."

Whitney didn't care if anyone listened. He loved to hear his own voice.

"But this, I can't believe its real. Do you know how long I've been ignoring priests' words about the punishments of Elsewhere? My whole life—yet, here it is. The Sea of Souls. That is, of course, assuming I'm not asleep."

"Where are we going, old man?" Kazimir finally questioned the wizened old Ferryman.

When he didn't respond, Kazimir launched himself to his feet and stepped over Whitney. The little boat rocked furiously, and Whitney had to grab the sides to steady himself.

"Hey, watch it!" Whitney complained.

"Will you answer me, Ferryman?" Kazimir barked. "I've already been through this gauntlet. I refuse to play these games again. Do you hear me!"

He reached out to grab the Ferryman by his robe. As if he were one of the lost souls beneath the surface, Kazimir's hand went right through him. He let out a cry of frustration that barely sounded human. It occurred to Whitney it was likely because the man wasn't human.

"Just settle down," Whitney said. "It'll all be over soon when I wake up."

"You think this a game, thief?" Kazimir spat. "You have no idea what kind of torment awaits you on the other side of this sea."

"And you do?" Whitney asked with a smile.

"Explicitly."

A sudden movement beneath the waters stole Whitney's breath and sent the boat into a spin. Kazimir stumbled, nearly flailing over the edge and into the deep, his otherworldly grace and agility gone. Whitney scrambled again to grab hold of the vessel. The Ferryman didn't respond in the least.

"What was that?" Whitney asked.

"You're about to get a taste of Elsewhere, boy," Kazimir replied.

Water, red as wine, rose up on both sides of the boat and showered over them. If the blue Torrential Sea was a mere reflection of the sky, this was nothing like it. The thick liquid stuck to Whitney like blood, making him hope it wasn't. Something whipped across the waters and slapped down, causing another spray and a swelling wave that threatened to overturn their vessel.

Whitney swore.

Again, the thing rose up and slapped the surface of the deep. One end of the boat sailed into the air and slammed back down. When the onslaught of sea spray ended, Whitney shuddered and stumbled backward.

The creature had pulled up alongside them and leveled the gaze of one giant, black eye upon Kazimir. Whitney couldn't see any more of it through the thick water, but that was enough to know how enormous it was.

A shadow cast over them and Whitney looked up to see another tentacle the size of a church steeple rising. Right before it crushed them, a bright light burned from the top of the ferryman's oar. Whitney shielded his eyes—then, just as quickly as it all started, it stopped. The creature was gone.

Heart pounding, Whitney said, "Shogging exile, what was that?"

He turned to Kazimir, who looked paler than before, now a sickly white, like the haggard moon Loutis. Whitney imagined he looked similar, but if a ruthless upyr was frightened, then he couldn't even imagine what else would come. Whitney turned to the Ferryman.

He was gone, only his oar left where he once stood. Whitney swore again as he crawled toward the edge of the boat to peer down into the dark water.

"Hello!" he shouted. The only reply was his echo and a pair of spectral hands reaching up toward him which sent him stumbling back into the boat.

"Gone," Whitney whispered. "He's yigging gone. Just like that? He yigging left me alone with you?"

"Yes," Kazimir sighed, still refusing to look at Whitney. "He tends to do that and, in this case, we're lucky."

"All right, that's it." Whitney stomped his foot. The boat swayed, and he thought better of doing it again. "Who in Elsewhere are you really and how do you know about… Elsewhere?"

"Just row the boat," Kazimir said.

"What, so you can shove me off and fulfill your blood pact?"

Whitney promptly found his throat closed off by a powerful hand. Kazimir was close enough for him to have smelled his breath if the overwhelming stench of the Sea of Souls wasn't vying for the award for worst smell ever.

"If I wanted you dead, you never would have stepped foot on this boat," Kazimir said. "Best not to be alone in Elsewhere."

Whitney spent the whole trip so far trying to get under Kazimir's skin

—hours, maybe an entire day, it was impossible to tell—now, he'd welcome the neglect. The upyr's dark eyes bore into him as if piercing his very soul. Only when he turned his head away did Kazimir release him.

Whitney crumpled in a heap. Kazimir kicked the oar into his gut.

"Why do I have to row?" Whitney murmured, more to himself than his dreadful companion.

"Because someone has to." He returned to his seat and went back to staring at the vast nothingness.

Whitney absentmindedly started rowing. Nagging the upyr was all fun, but seeing that rage again reminded him how near he'd come to having his body drained of blood while he was still alive. Or Sora's. He shuddered.

Wherever they were, dream or not, at least here, in the middle of nowhere, he couldn't hurt her. But if all of this was a figment of his imagination, he had to think that their reunion was as well. Which would mean that the only woman in the world he cared about still harbored years-old hatred toward him for leaving Troborough without so much as a goodbye.

He focused on rowing to take his mind off all of it, but it just brought new concerns. The feeling of the oar against the water was unsettling. He could sense the wood smacking against the bodies of all the lost spirits teeming beneath the surface, which was odd since they couldn't touch him.

"Are we even going the right way?" Whitney asked. "You know we got all turned around when that thing hit us?"

"The right way for what?" Kazimir asked. "Who knows where that wretch was bringing us this time. Any direction is as good as another."

"Okay, Mr. Deadman with all of the answers, what was that thing that attacked us then?"

Kazimir exhaled sharply and said, "It is a wianu. We call him Dakel un Ghastrin."

"And that is?"

"Roughly translated. 'Guardian of the Dead.'"

"A friend of yours?" Whitney asked.

"Hardly," Kazimir said. "He's hunted, trying to kill me for a thousand years."

"Why didn't it?"

"Apparently, the Ferryman wants you to see the other side."

"Iam's light you are cryptic." Whitney sighed. "So, is the old man dead?"

"Has been for longer than Pantego has existed."

Whitney gave up expecting answers from the upyr, rolled his eyes and turned back to the sea.

He wasn't sure when he'd resolved himself to the idea of talking to an upyr in the middle of Elsewhere, but here he was. Somehow, in the grand scheme of things—Kazimir trying to murder him, kidnapping Sora, working for Darkings—things on Pantego seemed unimportant.

It wasn't that Whitney wanted to make friends—the man was a monster unlike any he'd known before—it was just that, surrounded by the bloody ocean, any company seemed preferable to being alone.

"What about food?" Whitney said. "What if we get stranded at sea?"

"Hunger is an illusion here for mortals like you. You will ache and crave because that is what you were used to, but here, you will never eat your fill, and you will never starve."

"Dreaming," Whitney muttered to himself as he paddled. "I'm dreaming."

"You're not dreaming, thief. I promise you this, we are here, and we aren't leaving anytime soon."

"If you can't feel anything in Elsewhere, then we aren't in Elsewhere," Whitney said after a long spell of silence."Kazimir let his head fall back as he exhaled. "I didn't say you feel nothing. Trust me; you will long for the days where you felt less."

"Well, that makes sense because I feel terrified. I'm pretty sure I just urinated in my pa—where the yig are my pants?" Whitney glanced down and realized he wasn't wearing any clothing. "There's no way. We've been naked this whole time?"

How in shogging exile did I not realize?

He shifted his frame, suddenly acutely aware of his shame. His cheeks went red. He covered his nethers with one hand, and then his eyes went wide. "We can't be in Elsewhere."

"And why is that?"

"Now I feel shame."

"That's all up here." Kazimir pointed to his head. "It is the affairs of the body that have no bearing here. The need to shog or piss. To eat or drink. Even the air you breath is your mind working out of reflex. There is no air here, only the void."

"What about you and your…" Whitney swallowed. "Hunger."

"Gone."

"I was wondering how you've been resisting this handsome, bare neck."

"Just because the need is gone doesn't mean I wouldn't take pleasure in draining you, thief. You're just lucky Elsewhere seems to have a purpose for you."

"If I can't feel, why did I feel you kick me?"

"Oh, the pain of violence remains very, very real."

Whitney felt his heart racing but figured that was a trick of his mind as well. He tried to let the repetitive motion of rowing soothe him. It wasn't working, but it kept him occupied if not distracted.

"You've been here before?" he asked.

"Every time I close my eyes," Kazimir responded.

"A bit dramatic, don't you think?"

"I am not being dramatic," he said. "It is why we do not sleep. We upyr are already dead. When we allow ourselves to drift, we find ourselves in this very place. It is how I know our guide. It is how I know the beast."

"So, we're in your dream?"

"No. Dead men don't dream."

Kazimir lay back and closed his eyes regardless. Whitney tried to get him to keep talking a few times, but if the upyr couldn't sleep, he was an excellent actor. With his arms folded over his chest, Whitney wished he'd place them lower.

An indeterminable amount of time passed as he rowed, no end in sight. There was no sun or moons to track the day or night. The sky remained dark red, same as the water only still. There were no gulls or spouting whales, just the gentle song of the spirits. Whitney's eyelids grew heavy. His head fell off to the side a few times as he struggled to stay awake. He leaned on the oar and finally gave in.

"You can't sleep in a dream," he told himself. "Sora's going to wake me up with a bucket of water back on the sea." He blinked a few times, minutes passing each time as he dozed off. Then, suddenly, they reopened, and he noticed a few bumps sticking out from the endless seascape through a layer of fog.

"Hey," Whitney said.

No answer.

He extended his leg and kicked Kazimir in the foot without looking over at his disgustingly pale, naked body. The upyr didn't argue or respond, just sat up.

"What's that?" Whitney asked. "Is that land?"

Kazimir peeked over. "Looks like mountains."

"Yes! They are, aren't they! Oh, gods, get me off this boat, and I'll worship all of you for the rest of my life." Whitney started rowing harder, the resistance of the spirits growing stronger.

He kept at it. His arms burned with soreness even though he'd hoped Kazimir had been wrong and he wouldn't feel pain here. Nobody gets hurt in dreams after all.

"Uh, why are those mountains moving?" Whitney asked.

The more he rowed, the more land appeared on either side of the mountains, extending to the horizon in either direction. The land drew closer, gaining shape through the fog, but the hills never seemed to grow no matter how close they got. Then, they vanished beneath the sea. Whitney's brow furrowed. A break in the land, the mouth of a narrow river, appeared. Whitney felt the current pulling on the oar and stopped rowing, but it was like no river entry he'd ever seen. The water drained in front of them as it towed the boat forward.

"Those were no mountains," Kazimir said, eyes snapping all the way open. "He's returned." He hopped to his feet just as a massive tentacle, missing its tip, shot up into the air and slammed down in front of their boat. Whitney soared back as the water swelled, but Kazimir caught him and tossed him down. He pried the oar out of Whitney's grasp which had tightened out of reflex.

Kazimir stabbed it out over the bow and struck the beast in an eye, eliciting a roar that would have stopped Whitney's heart if adrenaline didn't have it thumping against its rib cage.

"I thought you said it didn't want to hurt me!" Whitney said.

"The ferryman is gone. Now you're just in the way." A tentacle lashed at him, and he sprawled out to duck under it. Whitney stayed on the floor of the boat and dared not rise. He considered kicking the upyr overboard to save his own skin—it was the least the upyr deserved for all he'd done—but Whitney's muscles had seized.

A tentacle burst through the bottom of the boat, rising like a disgusting column of lumpy skin and suction cups. They soared into the air, Kazimir nearly flipping over the side of the boat and doing Whitney's work for him. The vessel tilted forward, and they both slid toward the bow.

Whitney found himself staring down into the face of a creature larger than a dozen zhulong. Its many tentacular appendages waved around beneath and above the surface like so many snakes preparing to strike. Its two large eyes stared back at him, wider than any wagon wheel in Yarrington, and both of them as dark and soulless as Kazimir's, like they were related somehow.

It let out a primal scream—something Whitney would have never considered possible from any sea creature. With its giant maw open, rows upon rows of razor sharp teeth could be seen, hunks of flesh lodged between them, and they were being lowered into it.

"I'm dreaming," Whitney told himself. "I'm dreaming, I'm dreaming."

"It is not time yet, beast!" Kazimir shouted. He snapped the oar in half with his foot. The wianu shook the boat, and Kazimir flipped over the side, falling straight toward its mouth. He grabbed onto a tentacle before being carved to pieces. Swinging, broken end of the oar in hand, he stabbed it into one of the beast's eyes.

The wianu cried out, the sound so primordial it snapped Whitney back to attention. Its tentacles thrashed, and the boat went with them, snapping in half at the stern. Whitney held onto the front half as it flew through the air over the beast, then slammed into the mouth of the river.

Kazimir leaped from tentacle to tentacle as it tried to grab him. He didn't move lightning fast as he had back in Winde Port, but Whitney had never seen such precision.

The beast's head exploded from the surface behind him, blood black as pitch leaking from its eye. Its teeth gnashed, and it caught Kazimir on the back with one last desperate swipe of a tentacle, knocking him into the river ahead of the half-a-boat Whitney clung to.

Whitney stuck a leg out as the boat went by, now caught in the river's current. Kazimir grabbed hold of it, and Whitney reeled him in.

The wianu crawled up onto the land, a mess of tentacles allowing it to stand. Its screeches filled the air, but it didn't follow. Whitney didn't know if it was because the river grew too narrow, or Kazimir's blow had hurt it too badly, but he wouldn't complain.

"What the hell did you do to piss that thing off!" Whitney yelled.

"Only what I had to," Kazimir said through a series of coughs.

The swift current whipped them around a bend in the river which got thinner and thinner. They hit a rock, and the front of the boat broke open before it started spinning. Now Whitney and Kazimir held onto what was essentially a piece of debris.

The rapids whipped them until Whitney could feel his fingers beginning to give way. He cursed himself for rowing so hard toward mountains that turned out to be a giant octopus monster. Brackish water filled his mouth, beat against his eyes.

Then he let go.

He tumbled through the water, blind, terrified. His shoulder hit a rock, lucky it wasn't his head, and he flipped around. He screamed, though only bubbles came out. He found himself so dizzy he wasn't sure which way was up. Then something squeezed the back of his neck and heaved him out of the water. Whitney looked from side to side, in shock. Gone was the raging river carrying them in from the sea. Gone were the echoes of the crying wianu. He wasn't sure how he'd been drowning, because now they were within a gentle stream. Kazimir stood in the chest-high water, holding Whitney up, allowing him to cough up water. The remnants of the boat floated on ahead.

Kazimir gazed back, eyes still bright with adrenaline. Then he drew a long, tired breath. "We're safe from it here, I think."

"You mean you're safe." Whitney shook himself free and fell back into the water again. His head dipped, but his feet found purchase in the soft river-bed.

"Do not think the beast innocent. It hungers for souls and would not hesitate to devour yours."

"Maybe I should have left you back there so we could test that."

Kazimir didn't reply, but he didn't have to. Now that things had calmed Whitney couldn't help but wonder more about what he was thinking saving the upyr who'd only just threatened to kill him back with Sora. He imagined Kazimir wondered the same.

He cursed his talent for acting first and thinking later.

"So where is here?" Whitney asked once he waded through the water enough for it to be at his waist, where he finally felt like he could breathe. Whether the air around him was real or imagined, he was desperate for it.

"The boat's destination is different for all who arrive in this realm."

"Are your answers to everything so vague?"

"It is the nature of this place."

Whitney stifled a groan. Hills rose and fell, there was a forest downriver, and smokestacks billowing from beyond the river's crest. He put a hand through his hair, grimacing from his sore shoulder. "Shog in a barrel," he said as he took another look from side to side.

"What is it now?" Kazimir questioned.

"Shog. In. A. Barrel."

"What is wrong?" Kazimir asked more directly.

Before Whitney could answer, a young boy came jogging down a path toward them through the brush.

"Greetings travelers!" he exclaimed. "Welcome to Troborough!"

IV

THE KNIGHT

Torsten's dirty, bloodstained hands wrapped the rusty bars of his own personal cell in the deepest dungeon beneath the Glass Castle. From there, he imagined how many wrongdoers and miscreants had stood in that very spot—how many of them he'd put there. Cultists, murderers, and thieves, like Whitney.

Now, he was stuck on the same side as all of them. Damned to hear the eternal grousing of those in the dark, dank cells around him who proclaimed their innocence as if they'd forgotten how to say anything else.

If Elsewhere was as legends described—a place where one was cursed to endure their greatest fear over and over for the rest of eternity—Torsten couldn't imagine worse. His only solace was knowing he wouldn't be one of the prisoners left to decay, forgotten. Redstar wouldn't have that. One morning, Torsten would be dragged outside and hanged before his people as a traitor.

And that was what broke his heart the most, even though he knew it was wrong. He knew his only concern should be the Glass Kingdom, left in the hands of those with unclear motives, but if Redstar had proven anything, it was how weak Torsten truly was.

His fingers slipped from the cold metal, and he fell back against the stone floor. Cobwebs in the corner were his only company, gathered around a stick-shaped object which he dared not get closer to observe. Some cells had port-holes, but not his. His had chain-links hanging from the ceiling and more on the floor. Attached to one was a solid, iron mask with only a few holes poked in for air.

Redstar was a cruel and spiteful bastard, putting Torsten in the very cell he himself had occupied after Torsten brought him back from the Webbed Woods. The very cell he'd been chained in, accused of cursing the then-Prince and purporting himself as Uriah Davies, before suddenly, nobody seemed to care anymore.

Torsten fought the urge to pound his fists into the stone. Instead, he used them to prop himself up onto his knees. He regarded the moldy ceiling and closed his eyes.

"Iam," he said.

"Ain't no gods down here!" an old coot in the adjacent cell cackled.

Torsten ignored him, sliding further into the cell and lowered his voice to a whisper. "Iam, I cannot say if You have abandoned me, though I would not question it if You have. I have failed You, mind and body. I have sinned beyond forgiveness in the murder of a brother of the Shield, Sir Havel Tralen. And I have failed to bring to justice a rebel responsible for so much death."

He paused to gather his breath. For so long, when he spoke with Iam, he could feel his God around him, as if wrapped in His loving embrace. Now, Torsten felt hollow.

"Forget me if You must," he said. "Let me rot down here, but do not forget about them. A devil wearing human flesh walks amongst Your most devout, plying them with a silver tongue. Perhaps we have allowed Your light to wane in this past years, but You mustn't abandon them. They need You now more than ever."

"You think your god can hear you all the way down here?" Redstar said, his voice like needles stabbing Torsten's brain. He leaned against the bars of the cell, the light of a torch illuminating him so that the mark covering half his face was like pooling blood.

Torsten didn't answer.

Redstar picked something from his teeth, probably leftovers from some great feast had in honor of the 'Hero of Winde Port.'

"The realm of the buried belongs to a different deity," he said. "Perhaps you appeal to her?"

"Did you come here to gloat, Redstar?"

"Gloat? Why ever would I do that?"

"Because you've stolen everything you've ever wanted."

"Oh, Torsten. You have me all wrong. It pains me so to see you like this. Pains me to have been forced to do what I did for the good of the kingdom."

"Then walk upstairs and tell the King of your lies. Tell him exactly how you cursed him, and not all the fiction of you helping him see the truth. But how you wanted revenge for being shunned by your sister and left behind in the tundra by Liam. Tell him how you stole the face of Sir Uriah Davies."

Redstar sighed. "I can do all of that, and you'll still be the only one of us whose hands claimed the life of a fellow King's Shieldsman."

"Just leave me to exile!" Torsten barked, his fist pounding the wall. His knuckles split open against the immovable stone.

"Oh, but I have come to like you so much. After everything that's happened between us, it's almost as if… as if I created this version of you. As if I'm writing your story."

"You're no god, Redstar."

"Now that we agree on, but I do know one thing. This, in here, is not where or how your story ends. The Buried Goddess promises so much more."

"Do you truly believe all the lies you spout? You foretold her glorious return back in the Webbed Woods, but where is she?"

"Sitting on the throne you so cherish, in the ears of your king."

Torsten scoffed. "Face it, Redstar. She remains buried as she ever was. I looked into Pi's eyes; I saw no all-powerful goddess in them. I saw his father."

Redstar allowed a grimace to show just for a second before he regained his infamous, shog-eating grin. "Nesilia's time is coming. She lies just beyond the veil, waiting to step back into the world she helped create at Iam's side."

"But she isn't here." Torsten leaned forward, realizing that he finally had the upper hand in one of their spats. "You didn't expect that, did you? All this scheming is just you biding time."

"Preparing her domain for her true arrival."

"Just admit it. You're as lost as the rest of us."

"Do you remember the hymn I recited in the Woods? 'Eye always wary and never known fear—'"

"Not this drivel again." Torsten rolled his eyes.

"'Abruptly disrupted by a single shed tear,'" Redstar continued. "'Beneath soil and stone, the Lady awaits. The heart of her lover shall ne'er abate.'"

"Enough. I remember the damn song."

"Then perhaps you can help me." Redstar sat and folded his legs. "I've studied those ancient etchings of the God Feud endlessly alongside the hymn inscribed around its border. It was supposed to bring her back from Elsewhere, you see. The blood of Bliss spilled by a servant of both Iam and Nesilia. We killed the Spider Queen together. You buried her blood with Pi's orepul beneath Mount Lister. Yet all that rose was the boy and her whispers. My Lady's true essence remains trapped in the prison made by Iam."

Torsten's throat went dry. *The orepul?* He'd been so busy with the kingdom; he never examined the night Pi was reborn in detail. He'd believed it was Iam's hand, or Redstar's curse finally wearing off. But now he knew why the boy king was so unpredictable and disconnected. If it wasn't a miracle of Iam that brought him back, it was unnatural, dark magic that should never have been trifled with.

He's a liar, Torsten reminded himself. Every word from his mouth is poison.

"You didn't put all that together yet?" Redstar remarked, clearly noticing the shock written all over Torsten face. "Yes, my thick-headed friend. Pi lives again thanks to blood magic."

"He died from it too," Torsten snapped.

"That was never my intention, but I can't say it's been bad for me." He raised his arms, gesturing to the fact that he was free.

"Yet your goddess remains buried."

"Not for long." He scooted closer like he was listening to a lecture from Holy Wren. "There's something in all the signs that I'm missing or ignoring. Something forgotten."

Then she will arise, in glorious day
Through will and through fire, her enemies slain
Forgotten, abandoned, but no longer bound
From Elsewhere and exile, she'll receive her crown

"She will arise," Redstar said. "But when? How? Something is missing."

"Well, I hope you search forever."

"If that is what it takes. But I hear her, even now, telling me the answers I seek are somehow connected to you."

"I'll die before I help you."

"Oh, please. A few days down here, you'll be looking forward to my visits. Don't worry, dear Torsten. Together we'll find out what was missing, and by the time this year's Dawning comes, our Lord and Lady will be reunited in this realm again."

"Leave him be, brother."

Torsten was ready to drive his fists even harder into the stone from frustration when he heard Oleander's familiar voice, somehow both soothing and authoritative at the same time.

"Sister!" Redstar exclaimed. He pulled himself to his feet. "What a delightful surprise. Come to visit your favorite knight?"

"What I've come for is none of your business," she replied.

"Of course. The former Wearer and I were merely discussing his responsibilities in this transition of power. It will be so difficult deciding on a new Wearer who can finally live up to the reputation of Sir Uriah Davies. I'd take on the mantle myself but, Arch Warlock, dradinengor, Prime Minister; my responsibilities are endless these days."

"I'm sure you'll find a way. Now leave us."

Redstar turned to Torsten. The way the flame caught his brown eyes and marked face made him appear like a demon. "I look forward to seeing your story unfold, Torsten Unger."

"I suggest you hang me now then," Torsten said, seething. "Because the only way this ends is with my sword in your spine."

"I'd best be sure not to wear armor then to make things easier for you."

Redstar bowed with a grin and a flourish, then left. He bumped into Oleander on his way out, offering a halfhearted apology. A moment later, the Queen Mother appeared at the bars. She wore a pleased expression, her nose turned up at Torsten as if he were any other prisoner. But he could see the pain behind her bright, blue eyes. The dungeons weren't a fitting place for a woman of her majesty. Dust caked across the bottom of the same exquisite dress she'd worn in the Throne Room.

He rushed across the cell, wrapped his bloodied hands around the bars again and stuck his face through as far as he could.

"Oleander, I—"

"You were supposed to kill him," she cut him off.

"I was supposed to do many things, but we... I... underestimated Muskigo."

"I spent every second you were gone enduring my son's chastising until he finally began to speak to me somewhat like his mother again. I saw my precious boy in him. And now Redstar arrives to continue whispering in his ear and warping his mind. Already Pi ignores me."

"Then you kill Redstar!"

Her hand struck with the quickness of a desert snake, slapping Torsten across the face. Her long, manicured nails scratched his cheek. When he looked back up, he could see the pangs of regret painting her features before she forced her lips into a straight line.

He took her hand. "My Queen," Torsten said.

She pulled away. "You are not Wearer anymore. Dare touch me again, and you'll lose your hand on top of your dignity."

Torsten drew a deep breath. "I failed him, Oleander. For that, I am sorrier than you could possibly imagine."

"Do you know what it's like, seeing Redstar walk these halls with that damn grin on his face, barking commands? He was a rotten boy, and I was happy to leave him behind in the north when my Liam came. I never thought he could get worse."

"Then stand up to him. Help Pi see what a snake he really is."

"You think I haven't tried? Magic, parlor tricks, and heroics… I can't compete with that. All I can offer is my love and whatever happened to him when he passed on for those short days; I don't think he can feel love again."

"So, you allowed Redstar to throw me in here and take control of the King's Shield? Why, because you're scared Pi would be upset with you?"

"Because I don't want to lose him again!" she screamed. The way her voice echoed in the dungeon sent a shiver up Torsten's spine. A few other prisoners hollered lewd remarks, and they were lucky she was so focused on him otherwise they might've found their necks in a noose.

It was then that Torsten noticed the handmaiden lurking in Oleander's shadow and he remembered Tessa, the handmaiden she had so ruthlessly executed in a fit of rage. He'd spent so long trusting that Oleander and her soft spot for him was the key to fixing everything, but had somehow ignored how things got so bad in the first place. He forgot who ran things after Liam grew too sick to talk, or when Pi was unconscious and dead.

It all made him feel incredibly foolish ever thinking Oleander might've supported him back in the Throne Room. He knew everything she did was only for her son. And he knew what lengths she was willing to go to for him.

"The kingdom of Iam is in peril, Your Grace," Torsten said, unwilling to back down. "I know how much you care for Pi, but we've both been played for fools. If we don't try something drastic, we—"

"Fools?" The laugh that followed dripped with sarcasm. She was back to her old tricks. "How dare you. You had one simple task Torsten, and you didn't just fail to kill him, you let him become the greatest hero the kingdom has known since my husband."

"You think I don't know that? For Iam's sake, I'm in a dungeon!" He squeezed the bars so tight his hands lost their color. "I know all you want to do is earn Pi's affection, but someone has to stand up to him. Someone has to show him the light of Iam."

"Of all people, you should see," she bristled. "Iam has abandoned us. We're all we have."

Torsten lost his grip and staggered backward. To hear her say that… She had been born in the same land as Redstar but spent most of her life in Yarrington at Liam's side. She became as much a woman of the Glass as anyone. It wasn't acting. From the moment a younger Wren bathed her in Iam's light and cleansed her soul, Iam became a part of her.

"You can't believe that," Torsten stammered.

"You're blind not to. He teaches us not to kill, but do you know what I felt when I had all those people hanged?" Torsten's heart nearly stopped. In the months since that happened, never once had Oleander brought up what she'd done. "Nothing. Iam didn't stop me. He didn't punish me. All I wanted was to embrace my child again, and now that's possible."

"Then protect him from the monster upstairs, at least."

"Redstar now claims it was him and his goddess who brought Pi back."

"Redstar claims a lot of things."

"I don't care how it happened, only that it did. I will earn my son's love in the manner of my choosing, but you were meant to kill Redstar so that he never blamed me for stealing an uncle he admires for whatever gods-forsaken reason."

"Then let me out of here, and I'll do it. Even if it means I suffer an eternity in Elsewhere, I'll do it for this kingdom. For you."

"So you can find a way to make him more powerful?"

"What then? What would you ask of me?"

"Nothing. It's too late now, Torsten. If Redstar isn't lying and all his nonsense about the Buried Goddess is true... I won't let my rotten brother cause any more harm to my child if I insult her by having her voice on this plane killed."

"Oleander, please listen to me. These past months I have seen miracles with my own eyes, and they did not belong to him. There is no her."

"There is in the land I come from. And if I simply appeased my brother when he visited muttering his madness about fallen gods a year ago, none of this would have ever happened."

"So, you'd turn your back on Iam? After all His light has blessed you with?"

"I turn my back on all but my son." As if to demonstrate her words, she whipped around and snapped her fingers for her handmaiden. The young girl hurried forward and placed a bowl of steaming, fresh stew on the floor. She went to slide it under the bars, but Oleander clicked her tongue in disapproval, and she left it outside the cell. It was within reach, but the message was clear enough.

"That is for all you have done in service to my family," she said, her back still turned. "Enjoy it. It's the last thing you'll ever get from me."

She started walking away. Torsten mustered the courage to press his face back against the cold metal.

"Answer me this, my Queen," he said. She stopped. "Why did you come to my room that night if you don't trust me? In your heart, you must know that all I want is what's best for this kingdom."

Finally, she turned back and approached the bars. There was rage in her eyes, but also a playfulness that reminded Torsten all too much of her brother. He'd never seen a resemblance between them until that moment.

"I did trust you, more than anyone in this damned castle," she said. "But like I said then, my husband got to have all the fun in the world with every whore in every corner of Pantego, from here to Panping. Why shouldn't I get to?"

Torsten sunk back, wondering how he could have been such a fool. Blinded by the touch of her lips. He'd lived so long, hoping that he was a better man than the vagabonds in taverns groping at barmaids, but now he knew he had all the same weaknesses. Perhaps he'd had them all along.

"Oleander," he said softly, "can you do one last thing for me at least?"

She didn't answer, but she didn't leave. She simply kept glowering. He knew her well enough to know that meant she was listening.

"Send for Wren to visit me," Torsten said. "If I am to die in the cell, I'd like to talk to Iam one last time, and it's clear He's listening to me no longer."

"Goodbye, Torsten."

"Please, Your Grace."

She left without a response, her handmaiden scurrying after her like a trained wolf. Torsten knew well enough that a non-answer from her wasn't a no. She could be incredibly impish when she was agitated, much like her brother.

Now she and Redstar were the only two speaking into Pi's ear, and Nesilia if Redstar was to be believed. The only two influencing the fate of the kingdom Liam had brought to such heights. Torsten wondered if maybe deep inside, Oleander wanted to see the kingdom crumble. For the man she claimed to love so deeply, she often cursed with equal vim.

Liam wasn't perfect.

It was a hard truth to admit, but it was true nonetheless. He'd had his vices, a short temper with his wife who took so long to produce a male heir or a lust for any woman who flashed a smile and a bit of flesh. In the end, that was likely what got him sick. Yet, Iam had chosen him to spread the word of his chosen kingdom. For all the death and suffering he brought to Pantego in that crusade—death which inspired men like Muskigo to rebel—he also brought a decade of peace not known in all of history.

As Torsten leaned back and stared into the surrounding darkness, he vowed not to sulk and let everything he loved fade. If Liam was flawed, Torsten was a monster, but so long as he drew breath, he would come up with a way to unseat Redstar. Whatever it took.

The Glass Kingdom had nobody else left…

V

THE DESERTER

Rand Langley woke the same way he had nearly every time he'd allowed himself to drift asleep over the last few months. Drenched in sweat. It didn't matter that it was the heart of winter in the dead of night and so cold that frost hadn't abandoned the tiny window of his tiny apartment since before he could remember. He'd become exhausted from fighting sleep, hoping to ward off the terrors.

Exhaustion won.

"It's okay, Rand," his sister Sigrid whispered. She rolled over in her bed. Their narrow mattresses rested side by side against the wall, a dusting of snow at their feet, blowing in from an ever-growing crack in their window.

Rand continued to breathe heavy, squeezing his eyes shut to drive out the noise that had plagued him for so long. The threads of rope stretching as it swung, creaking, over and over. It was like the sounds of docked ships rocking in the waves, only in his head, the rope wasn't moored to a quay.

"Just breathe, brother." Sigrid crawled to his bed and stroked his sweat-wet hair.

She hummed the same tune their mother used to when they were kids in Dockside. A Ship to Nowhere, about the poor dreamers sitting on the edge of the docks, wondering where the great vessels came from and where they were heading. Rand and Sigrid used to sit by the water, and he'd sing to her, but now he didn't know the words. It was before the King's Shield. Before...

"I need a drink," Rand said. He threw off his ratty sheets and edged his way passed Sigrid's bed.

"Rand, it's the middle of the night," she said. "What ye be needing is sleep." She spoke with a Dockside affection; one Rand managed to break as he rose through the King's Shield and spent more time amongst nobles.

He ignored her while pawing around the room in the darkness, only a bit of moonlight coming through the clouds lighting his world. Their last candle was a melted clump of wax in the center of their only table, which Rand banged his knee into and cursed. Then he found an empty bottle of wine and cursed louder, throwing it down in disgust.

"Rand, please," his sister said, taking his hand. "We can't afford anymore."

He shook her off. "You're a barmaiden," he replied. "Take some."

He rifled through their cupboard and found a jug of ale. Not even bothering with a mug, he lifted it to his lips. Only a few, stale drops remained. "Gods-damned, empty yigging…"

Rand's voice trailed off as he slammed the clay jug on the table just as Sigrid went to stop him. Shards flew out in every direction, and a chunk of table snapped off.

"Dammit, Rand!" she squealed.

Rand stood, fuming. The taste of ale was just enough to make the terrors of his mind worse. *Creak, creak, creak,* the taut rope swung like his own mind was taunting him. He raised his hands to his temples and screamed. It was the only way to stop the thoughts.

A neighbor banged on the thin wall to quiet him, dust billowing through the thin ray of moonlight.

Rand fell to his knees, panting. The creaking rope was now accompanied by the sound of thick blood trickling to the floor. More waking nightmares. He could see the bulging eyes of the handmaiden Tessa as if she were right in front of him, tongue swollen, purple, and hanging limply from her lips. Only there has been no blood dripping from those he hanged.

Rand opened his eyes and saw his sister, seated on her bed. The tear on her cheek glistened with Celeste's light, but she fought back any more as she clutched her hand. A piece of the jar had left a deep gash on her palm.

"Sigrid, I'm so..." he stammered. He crawled over and took her arm. Blood streamed down her forearm onto the floor, seeping through the cracks in the faded wooden planks. She pulled away, unable to look at him. He tore a strip off his bedsheets and gently wrapped her hand. She was the injured one, yet his fingers shook as his body yearned for another drink.

"Yer getting worse, Rand," she said softly. "Yer going to kill yerself drinking so much. I... I don't know if I can keep helping ye."

"I know. It's just," he paused, looking up at her. "It's the only thing that helps me stop seeing her face. All the others, they're blank. The same. But hers, I can still see the tears streaming from her eyes as the white went red and her neck tensed. She was the most beautiful girl I'd ever known and I—"

Sigrid finally gave in and clutched his face. Rand could smell the iron in the blood on her hand, but he didn't care. "It wasn't yer fault," she said. "The Queen made ye."

"I could have run."

She put on a smirk. Rand knew it was all a façade to try and cheer him up. "And never see me again?"

"I just wished I'd told her how I felt. That from the moment I entered the castle, she made even the Queen seem hideous. That I'd offer anything to see her smile in the hall as I passed. One last time."

"And I'd offer anything to see ye smiling again, li'l brother."

Rand swallowed the lump forming in his throat. "Then help me."

"I'm scared I can't." She stood and crossed the room. She picked up a single, bronze autla from a bowl. It scraped as she slid it over the rough wood. "This be the last of the pay for yer prior cycle in the Shield. Everything I earn downstairs goes to keeping this dump. It's all we've got, Rand."

"We'll find a way."

"We keep saying that, but we don't. I can't be the only fighter. I know ye can't return to yer post, especially after ignoring the call to Winde Port, but there's got to be something ye can do. Someone in this city is always looking for muscle."

"I don't want to hurt anyone ever again."

"Then haul cargo down by the docks. More Longboats from the Drav Cra're arriving every day now they're allies. Do something, Rand. I… I feel like I'm falling apart supporting us both these past months. I can't even imagine what ye've been through, but I can't be doing this alone no more."

"You're right. You should be off getting married to some great man. Having children on a farm outside of Westvale. You deserve the world."

"Listen to ye, speaking all proper-like. I don't care about deserving; I just want to survive winter." She returned and kneeled in front of Rand, staring straight into his eyes. "Please, find a way to forgive yerself. We can go to church and kneel in the light of Iam if ye want. He can show ye that none of this is yer fault."

Rand didn't respond. For months, his sister had been begging him to attend service, but how could he bring himself to stand before Iam after what he'd done?

"Fine," Sigrid said. "I guess we'll both freeze in this awful place together." She stood and grabbed a cloak from a hook on the wall.

"Where are you going?"

"On a walk. If ye won't go and seek out Iam, then I will."

"Sigrid, wa—"

The door slammed before he could get the words out. Her footsteps echoed down the hall, then nothing. All he was left with was the soft whistle of wind coming through their window.

For those few seconds alone, he stared at his sister's blood and considered never taking to the drink again. Then a gust of snow powder blasted his cheek and stirred his thoughts. Salty, fishy air mixed with the faint smell of blood. He wondered how those hanging bodies faired against the elements when winter took, if the cold frosted their eyes like glass.

Rand looked up at the rotting, wood ceiling which warped down to one corner. "You really have abandoned us, haven't you?"

He pulled himself to his feet and peered out the window. Sigrid walked through the alley out to Port Street, drawing her cloak tight for warmth.

The clarity in which he could see her, even through the dirty glass, meant dawn was approaching. He didn't have much time.

He rushed to the door and grabbed the bronzer—blood money—then headed out without bothering to lock the door behind him. There was freedom in knowing they had nothing worth stealing. The dark hall on the second floor of the Maiden's Mugs Tavern had a few more rundown apartments, but Rand was interested in the tavern itself.

His eyes closed as he descended the stairs. The floor of the tavern wasn't much better, but he'd manage. Relief was so close. Not a soul was around, and the bar was cleaned up nice. Gideon Trapp ran a clean establishment, which was a lot to say for Dockside. He didn't, however, take good care of his lodgers.

The storage room was locked, but the tapped barrels of ale stacked along the wall were merely plugged. Rand unsealed one, grabbed a mug, and let it pour. *Stealing...* It went against everything a member of the King's Shieldsman should stand for.

He didn't care. *Trapp shouldn't make it so easy.*

He let the mug fill halfway, then raised it to his lips and guzzled it down. The Dockside stuff had a sour tinge—nothing like Old Yarrington mead—but he was so used to it now, it went down like water. And every ounce down his throat was like one turn of a gear loosening the vice squeezing his head. He hated himself for breaking his vow so quickly, but after Tessa's horrid, decaying face began to blur in his mind, the guilt vanished. He wiped his lips, then went to fill the mug again. He was just about topped off when a hand slapped the bar counter behind him.

"Ye gonna pay for that?" a man asked.

Rand turned slowly, mug in hand, and saw Gideon Trapp standing behind him. The man had a gut the size of one of the kegs and shaggy mutton chops running down the sides of his head to draw attention away from his balding pate. His teeth were a rotten shade of yellow, like any man born in Dockside who never left.

"Are you going to fix our window before my sister freezes to death?" Rand asked, taking a step closer, looking down on the man. Months of wallowing had eaten away much of the muscle he'd earned in King's Shield training, but he still towered over most Docksiders.

"I told you, I can't do nothing till we thaw out a bit."

"By then you'll be scraping our bodies off the cold floor."

"Better than the streets. Now, I'll ask again, are ye gonna pay for that?"

The portly man didn't back down, just puffed out his soft chest then grabbed Rand's wrist. Rand's forearm shot forward and barred Trapp's throat, slamming him against the stack of barrels. He pushed harder and harder until spit bubbled in the corner of the Trapp's mouth as he struggled to speak. It was only when Rand heard that familiar gurgling of a clenched airway that he realized what he was doing and backed off.

Trapp fell to the floor, gasping and pawing at his throat. The sight made Rand envision another of his victims besides Tessa's. With full clarity, the bearded visage of the Royal Physician, Deturo, flailing as the noose tightened and the color fled his cheeks passed before his eyes. He blinked a dozen times, trying to force the vision away.

Rand reached into his pocket, removed the last bronzer he had left to his name, and slapped it down on the counter. In the same motion, he grabbed the mug and headed upstairs.

"Yer lucky yer sister has such great… mugs… or ye'd both be out in the cold!" Trapp rasped.

Rand stopped and regarded the man. In a district so poor, only the dishonest were so obese. Rand could have killed the fat slob in a second if it wouldn't have left his sister without a proper way to make a living. There were worse taverns, which would ask more of her than to show skin.

"Speak about her like that again, and I'll drown you in your ale," Rand said.

"I don't care what you used to be; you won't get the jump on me again. Now get out of here. One more screw-up, and I'll tell yer sister she's through! Don't care how pretty she be. Ye can take it up with Valin, or go crawling back to your friends at the Glass Castle, deserter."

It was no secret to anyone in Dockside who Rand was, or what he'd done. There weren't many from the place who rose so high. The only reason the crown didn't barge through his door to drag him away and punish him as a deserter was because Docksiders kept their mouths shut.

"Just leave her out of this," he growled.

Rand's hands quaked as he turned to leave. He used both hands to grip the mug, ale sloshing over the rim. It wasn't rage, though he was desperate to unleash some on the man. Just the thought of being so near the sweet release had his entire body aching.

He waited until he was back in his room. Downing a second full mug of Dockside ale was enough to make him feel light as a feather. It tasted like swill, but that just meant it kicked like an angry zhulong. Plus, he'd been drunk so long, it was like his body forgot how to act any other way.

"I'll show ye a screw-up," he hiccuped to himself, his accent breaking through training. He made it two steps across his room before he tripped over the chair leg and came crashing down on the floor face-first. His lip split open, and splinters drove into his hand as he failed to break the fall.

Rand couldn't bring himself to get back up, laid flat across the floor, and that was when he noticed the glimmer of the armor tucked under his bed, the metal forged with glaruium from the heart of Mount Lister.

Despite the dust and snow powder covering the room, somehow the King's Shield armor remained clean, so polished he could see his reflection in the chestplate. There wasn't even the faintest dent or scratch, for even though he'd claimed the lives of dozens whilst wearing it in the name of the Queen, it had never seen battle.

He barely recognized the man who stared back in its reflection. Bleeding, eyes puffy and red, cheeks gaunt from malnourishment. He reached out to crawl toward it, and his fingers brushed through his sister's still-wet blood on the floor. Now, Gideon Trapp would be riding her even harder thanks to Rand causing more issues downstairs. Drunkenly stumbling through the tavern, knocking over tables every other day was bad enough, but striking the owner?

"Some knight," he whispered as he dragged the armor out and lay it across his hay bed. He could remember proudly standing in it, still donning the helm of the Wearer of White before Torsten returned to reclaim it. He could remember being in the castle bailey, ordering his men to string up the innocent at the command of the mad Queen Regent. He could recall Tessa's face, heartbroken, knowing the feelings he'd held inside for so long and feeling them just the same.

And even then, Rand had said nothing. Even then, he was a loyal knight serving his monarch. All he had to do was speak out, and maybe Oleander's wrath would have turned to him instead of her handmaiden. It could have been him hung from the walls like meat in a butcher shop, putting an end to his miserable life.

It was then he knew what needed to doing. For the first time in a long time, Rand's mind was clear.

"I'm so sorry, Sigrid," he whispered as he tore his sheet out from under the armor, then took his sister's. He tied the ends together while muttering, "Ye'll be better off, ye will."

He stood on the bed, tying one side securely around a ceiling beam, and with the other, he tied a tight noose around his neck.

Staring down at his armor, he began reciting the words of the King's Shield. "We are the Armor of Yer Holy Kingdom. Our lives are given freely under the sight of Yer Vigilant Eye so Yer children may thrive in this world Ye have blessed us with." He sniveled, closed his eyes and drew a deep breath.

"I shielded nobody but meself," he sputtered through tears before mustering the courage to continue.

"We are the right hand of Iam. The sword of His justice, and the Shield that guards the light of this world." He hung his head. A tear rolled down his cheek and splattered on his armor. He wasn't sure how long he stood there, a minute or an hour. To take one's own life was a sin by the teachings of Iam, but he was bound for Elsewhere anyway. Eternal torment in the bowels of the underworld was all he deserved.

There was a knock at the door. The sound startled him, and his feet slid hard to the side, knocking the mangy bed out from under him. His feet dropped, stopping a good half-meter from the floor. His neck wrenched upward, the cloth tightening around his throat so fast the corners of his vision went blotchy.

Sigrid! he thought, imagining his sister finding him like this. He grasped at the cloth and flailed his legs to try and pull the bed back. His toe caught its edge, but the wood frame cracked, and the bed tipped. His body swung the other way, his vision growing blurrier as he struggled.

At a certain point, he gave in and allowed his eyes to close. There was no fighting anymore. He could almost see the other side and the end to his torment. All he could hear was the creaking of the cloth pulling on wood.

Suddenly, something wrapped his legs and lifted him. Air rushed down his throat, filling his lungs with new life. He gasped awake from the precipice of unconsciousness. He rolled his eyes to look down with his peripherals and saw two arms around them. Then, taking another breath, they became more manifest, covered in the loose sleeves of a white robe. Just as suddenly, they vanished, and Rand's weight once again pulled him toward doom.

Just before he could wonder what cruel trick this was, the bed reappeared beneath his feet. He tapped with his bare feet until he found footing. The relief was immediate, unlike anything he'd ever experienced. Even laying down after a hard day at training under Sir Unger or Sir Jolly couldn't compare.

He felt a body against his and fingers against his neck. The handmade noose lifted over his ears, and without the support of it, his wobbly legs gave out. He collapsed onto a man's chest.

Chest stinging from exertion, throat burning, he steadied his breathing, every one like a tendril of ice as the cold air went down.

"It's okay, my child," the man said, laying Rand down on the bed, his voice still indistinct. "Breathe."

The world came slowly into focus, and with it, the man hovering above him. Rand thought he'd died and gone to Elsewhere when he saw him, that this was some demon's trick. For cradling him and rubbing his back as if to beckon the air in, was the unmistakable face of Wren the Holy, High Priest of the Church of Iam.

VI

THE MYSTIC

As a lover of music, Sora could say with certainty what she was listening to was no such thing. Three of her new pirate companions picked and plucked at strange, homemade-looking instruments of a variety Sora had never seen before and hoped she'd never hear again.

To see such hardened and grizzled men drinking and being merry, laughing and joking; it was unsettling.

She'd only been on Gold Grin's pirate ship for a few hours, but already she wanted to go back to her little captain's quarters and sleep. If she weren't afraid of offending Gold Grin, she'd have already retired into the small quarters they'd provided for her far below the deck. It being separate from the rest of the crews' bunks by only a curtain didn't have her any more eager.

Aquira was already there although she'd protested at letting Sora wander off unprotected. Sora knew it wouldn't help anyone to have a wyvern flittering about, least of all, Aquira. The pirates were all spooked by her, something about ancient Panpingese curses. In Sora's experience, Aquira had been anything but a curse. The little, winged reptile had saved her life more than once.

She let her head fall into her arms folded on the table in front of her.

She tried to imagine the music being better than it was; tried to imagine it was Fabian "Feel Good" Saravia, her favorite bard who'd frequently come through Troborough.

It was no use. It was trash. Brigands without an ear for music gallivanting around because there was nothing else to do on the high seas—besides stare at her now. She noticed one of their gazes fixed upon her while the grubby man tapped his foot along to the sorry excuse for a tune.

She turned sidewise and self-consciously raised the neckline of her dress. Then she allowed her mind to drift toward Yaolin City and her plans once she arrived. The problem was, Whitney was supposed to be her guide. She knew nothing of the city—even being Panpingese. Their customs were as foreign to her as she was to these pirates.

It reminded her of her first day of church in Troborough. Father Hullquist stood at the altar beneath the glittering Eye of Iam and read from ancient scripture. The villagers sang hymns with him, then one by one were invited up the aisle to bask in the pinhole shaft of light piercing the center of the Eye.

Those first days, fresh off the caravan of war refugees, she felt so out of place. Wetzel had barely spoken to her above an incomprehensible grumble and had her towing supplies all over town. It wasn't until a tawny-haired boy slapped her on the rump as she trembled before the priest and said, "You're up," that she was able to breathe properly. From that day, she and Whitney had been inseparable.

Until he left…

"Left," Sora spat to herself. At first, the pirates were a distraction, but now that she'd settled in, her mind returned to those dark places which had her confined to her quarters on the corsair for so long.

This wasn't like the time he'd abandoned her in Troborough and set off to find adventure she could barely dream of. She'd been responsible this time. Wherever he was, Sora had sent him there.

"Girly," came Tum Tum's voice, pulling Sora from her ruminating. "Yer gonna hafta move on someday. Why not start?"

Tum Tum was a nice enough man, even for a dwarf. Sora hadn't known many dwarves. Even those who'd plowed through Troborough on the occasional caravan usually kept to the Twilight Manor, filling Hamm's coffers with coin and their gullets with ale. But if there was anything to be learned from how she'd been treated in places like Bridleton and Winde Port, it was people are people no matter what race.

Tum Tum sat beside her and threw his feet up onto the table. He was clean. Really clean. The pirates treated them well, allowing them to bathe in heated salt water which was great for their wounds. Tum Tum's now-untangled hair and beard were combed and braided. She didn't know what the standard of beauty was for dwarves, but she'd imagined he was on the handsome end of the scale.

They were in what she assumed to be the pirate ship's galley. It was a massive galleon, so many times larger than their little corsair ship it was impossible for her to guess just how many rooms there were. All she knew was it was comforting to know that someone besides her and Tum Tum—someone who was skilled in naval fairing—was piloting the ship.

The galley, like the rest of the ship, wasn't ornate, but it was homey. It was clear the pirates took care of their vessel. Trinkets and paintings lined the walls, all appearing to come from different places—loot displayed like trophies to their greatest conquest, not unlike Liam's Throne Room

She'd have never thought such dangerous men would be so meticulous about their ship decor or the quality of their food, but they showed great care even to the smallest details. Looking down at the chopped mutton before her, drenched in thick, rich gravy, topped with kernels of corn, she wished she had an appetite.

"Haven't touched yer food," Tum Tum said.

"Where did they get sheep?" Sora asked.

Tum Tum shrugged and snatched a piece from her plate. He made a deep, satisfied moaning sound as he bit into it.

Sora once again regarded the musicians—if they could be called that. Big, toothless grins plastered their faces. One with a patch over an eye drummed on the top of a clay mug with the tips of two dirks.

"Whitney would have made some cheesy joke," she said to Tum Tum without looking at him, "about how they were a merry band of pirates. Then he'd have thought himself a genius for the play on words."

Tum Tum laughed. Sora smiled.

"Aye," he said. "Whitney could tell tales with the best of em. Never could tell where his jokes ended and his adventures began though." He took a deep breath, then lifted his pint. "To Whitney. It's a quieter life without him."

"Yeah," Sora said, not having a mug of her own to lift. "To Whitney…"

As tears welled in the corner of her eyes, she realized she hadn't cried since they left their ship. It felt like a personal record after what happened.

"What if I killed him, Tum Tum?" she asked. In the days since, she'd never been able to ask that question out loud. She couldn't bear the thought.

"Ye did what ye had to," Tum Tum said. "If ye hadn't, that gods-damned vampire'd have done it and we'd all been dead. Ye saved our lives, lass. Ye should be celebrated. I know Whitney wouldn't have had it any other way. Ye should have seen his face when I assumed the two of ye were married back in Winde Port. Cheeks red as an apple." He chuckled. "Matter of fact, make believe this party be for ye, for savin our skins and riddin the world of that monster. Ye deserve it."

"I deserve nothing!" Sora snapped. "You know what I did? I burned down a whole city, and I killed my best friend or worse."

"Now stop it!" Tum Tum stood, shoulders barely clearing the height of the table. "Ye did no such thing. That place was overrun by them gray men, and ye saved us all. In yer own way, ye even saved Whitney from a much worse fate."

The music stopped as their host, Gold Grin, appeared within the threshold of the galley. Even across the way, she could see his teeth glistening in the light of the candles.

"Carry on, boys!" he exclaimed.

The men cheered, and the music struck up again, a little more lively and a lot less in tune. The feet clomping on the floor sounded like they were keeping the beat to at least a dozen different songs.

Sora watched as Gold Grin picked up a silver goblet and made his way toward the table where she and Tum Tum sat with a skip to his step.

Sora raised her head and furiously wiped her eyes. She didn't know why, but she didn't want the man to see her in such a state. Probably something Whitney had told her. Showing weakness to pirates was the quickest way to wind up one of their wenches.

"That's more like it," Tum Tum said, his back to the pirate, not knowing the reason for her sudden change in demeanor.

"Guests!" Gold Grin addressed them. "Hoping yer comfortable?"

"Damn," Tum Tum said. "Comfortable that is. We be damn comfortable. Anything beats sailing toward nowhere."

Gold Grin looked to Sora, and she managed a nod.

"Good to hear," Gold Grin said. He pulled up a chair and sat with its back facing the wrong direction. He crossed his arms and leaned in before continuing. "Now tell me, what makes ye want to go to Yaolin… really?"

He examined Sora from head to toe. Usually, it made her shudder when men looked her over like she was meat at a butcher, but there wasn't a hint of malice in Gold Grin's eyes. For the terror of the seas he claimed to be, he seemed quite the gentleman.

"As I said, my husband died, and I want to inform his family in person," Sora said. "Whitney was an old friend, and helped us get this ship and start sailing before leaving us for the gulls."

"Codswallop," Gold Grin said. "Try again."

Sora blinked. "That's the truth."

"Aye, so let me get this straight. I save ye from certain doom, we welcome ye onto our ship, into our home, and ye lie to my face?"

Sora glanced at Tum Tum. The dwarf shrugged. "Can't say I ain't curious meself."

Sora swallowed the lump in her throat. She wasn't sure why she cared so much about guarding her true purpose. Sure, Gold Grin might not take kindly to being lied to and change his mind about taking them to Yaolin, but that wasn't the real reason. He seemed decent enough despite his title. But the last person she'd opened up to vanished, and the thought of doing it again made her stomach churn.

"Honestly, I need to know more about where I come from," she said, battling back the sick feeling. "Who I am, why I can do what I do, how to control it better." She pictured her outstretched hand back on the corsair ship and the blinding light; Whitney and Kazimir there one second, then gone another. Then she recalled the Webbed Woods when she released a blast of energy that subdued a powerful warlock, or in Winde Port when Muskigo was on the cusp of victory before her fire spread as if fueled by her rage. She even remembered Redstar's face when she healed Torsten's wounds in the forest.

It was nothing any normal blood mage without decades of experimenting like Redstar had should be capable of, she knew that now. Nothing her teacher Wetzel even knew enough to teach her.

"That's more like it!" Gold Grin slapped the table hard, and so deep in thought, Sora jumped. "Ye got yerself a special gift there, lassy. I'd been trying to learn some magic myself in my travels, but some of us just ain't got the gift."

"It's not as great as it seems," Sora said.

"Trust me, girl. I've seen more horrors at the hands of men playing with magic than any other, but I've seen some good too."

Gold Grin gently took Sora's hand. She tried to pull away out of instinct, but Grisham politely asked, "May I?" and she gave in. He slowly unwound the cloth bandage around her palm and studied the many scars.

"Blood magic, aye?" he asked.

"Yes," Sora replied softly.

"I've seen the Drav Cra use it. Very powerful, very unpredictable in weak hands. Never seen a Panpingese lass doing it, but I suppose there aren't many mystics left after the war."

Sora leaned forward. "But there are some left?"

"Ah, so it's a mystic ye want to meet?" he asked, grinning. "Rumors say they're out there. They ain't on the seas though, and impossible to find. Trust me; I've looked. It's said the ancient mystics found a way to live forever. Hogwash probably, but I'll be damned if me and my mates don't keep an ear open for the secrets. Sail the seas for all of time!"

"Live forever, ye say?" Tum Tum asked.

"What about making someone disappear?" Sora asked.

Gold Grin scratched his chin. "Not sure. What, were ye wishing ye'd make that scallywag Whitney vanish? Cus then I'd understand!"

Sora choked on her next breath. Gold Grin's brow furrowed like he knew he was on to something.

"Well, I don't know nothing about disappearing," he said, "but I heard some say the mystics learned a way to travel to Elsewhere itself. That they hid there after the war. Seeing as how nobody talks about them now, probably got stuck there, where nothing living should be."

Sora turned to Tum Tum. "You don't think Whitney—"

"I just be a dwarf good at pourin ale," Tum Tum said. "All this mumbo-jumbo talk makes me head spin."

"Look, if Whitney wronged ye, ye wouldn't be alone in wanting revenge, lass," Gold Grin said.

"He didn't wrong me," Sora said.

"Ah, so he broke your heart."

"No," she protested, but her expression must have betrayed her words because Gold Grin's smile gave credence to his name.

"The boy always did fancy himself a ladies' man. Stealing a woman like ye from her husband though, I'm impressed."

"He didn't steal me—"

Gold grin waved his hand to quiet her. "I ain't here to judge, lass. Whether yer husband truly be dead or yer going back to him after a dalliance with that lying thief, I can promise ye I've done far worse."

"I'm not sure about that." She closed her eyes and could see the flames devouring Winde Port, feeding off her anger.

"Bah," Gold Grin spat. "That rat bastard is fickle as the wind, so I say move on."

"Now, now, he wun't too bad," Tum Tum butted in. He'd had a few ales by then, and the words flowed right out of him. Sora stayed quiet and tried her best to listen, but something Gold Grin said had her distracted.

Mystics hiding in Elsewhere.

"I met him in the Dragon's Tail when I was just a mere miner," Tum Tum explained even though nobody asked. "He convinced me to follow me dream and travel south. 'Open a pub,' he said after we spent a week deep underground searching for the mythical Brike Stone."

"Did ye find it?" Gold grin interrupted.

"We found a stone all right, but it wasn't magical, much as he claimed it was. I think he just wanted to get to the fresh air. 'Why do anything we don't want to?' he always used to say and lived it too. Minute we got out, he gave me some staff he took so I could buy a lot on Winder's Wharf, much good it's doing for me now."

"You had it easy," Grisham said. "Old Whitney joined up with my crew a few years back. We were riding on my first; hand built it myself. The *Sea Hawk* was a fine vessel, but Whitney spotted a Glass Kingdom galleon alone on the Torrential. Convinced me to try and take her and start an armada. Ye know how convincing he can be."

"Like a silver-tongued devil," Tum Tum snickered.

"So, we did it, and we took it. And next thing I know, Whitney's sailing off the other way in the *Sea Hawk* with a few deserters."

Tum Tum smacked his head with his palm. "And ye didn't kill him?"

"We set off on him full tilt when I realized: somehow he'd shoved all our plundered riches into barrels and set them into the water for us to grab. All I was short was a small, mangy ship and a few unloyal crewmen. Now I've got the *Reba* and the best crew in Pantego!" His men took a momentary break from their raucousness to cheer in approval.

"Never's there been a man so equally able to frustrate and show ye everything ye really want," Tum Tum said.

"Yeah..." Sora whispered.

"So where in Elsewhere did he disappear off to then?" Grisham asked. "Always a thrill to hear about one of his great escapes, even if it came at your expense lass." He nodded Sora's way, but she stayed quiet.

"He pulled off the greatest trick of all," Tum Tum said. "There we were on that ship, beset by a vile killer. An upyr, believe ye me. He had Whitney by the neck and Sora here was going to use some of that magic to save em. A flash, then bam, they're both gone. Never seen a thing like it in me life."

Gold Grin shot Sora a knowing look. A man like him had likely seen so much of the mysterious in their world; she wasn't sure why she was surprised he'd pieced some of what happened together, at least as much as she had herself. She did her best to mask her grief, but that apparently wasn't good enough.

"I see," Gold Grin said. "Boy always was so quick with his fingers it was like magic."

"Just like magic," Sora said. Just as she went to lean on her palm, a thought popped into her head. Her eyes lit up.

Where in Elsewhere is he... For the first time in many days, a weight lifted off her heart. If the mystics could access Elsewhere, not just feel it working through them, but genuinely obtain that plane as Gold Grin said, could that be where she sent Whitney and Kazimir? It wouldn't be the first time she'd pulled off a magic feat seemingly only a powerful mystic should've been capable of. And if that's where he was, maybe they could help her get there. It made more sense than anything else.

Either he was alive and trapped there, or dead, and damned to spend eternity there. He sure as Iam wasn't destined for the Gate of Light, if it even existed. The only other option was that Kazimir had powers the books on upyrs never spoke of and somehow teleported them somewhere else.

"Look, lass," Grisham said. "If ye want to meet a mystic and figure out whatever in the gods' name happened, I can't help ye, but Yaolin is the best place to start looking."

"So, you don't care that I lied about why I wanted to go?" Sora said.

"Care?" he chuckled. "Like I said, whether it be dead husbands, fake husbands, or mysteries of magic; they don't matter to me. Ye be a friend of Whitney Fierstown, and that be enough. Plus, I've already got this!" He pulled out the half of the Glass Crown and placed it on the table. "If Whitney weren't lying, this'll be worth a fortune, broken or not. Where better to sell it then Yaolin?"

"Even *if* he's lyin again, it's got enough gems," Tum Tum said, ogling it.

"Eyes to yerself, dwarf." Gold Grin laughed and hid the crown again.

"You didn't meet the Shieldsman who caught him," Sora said. "If you had, you'd know this is one time he's being truthful."

"Shieldsman and the Glass Crown? Now, this I've got to hear." He banged his empty tankard to get one of his men's attention. "Fortist, fill me up. I've got a tale to hear."

So, Sora told him. With the glimmer of hope instilled by the information about mystics she'd learned from him, talking about Whitney didn't completely fill her with dread.

She explained all about how he'd stolen the crown from a royal masquerade celebrating the late king's last birthday, though she could only tell it how Whitney had and he tended to exaggerate. She found it strangely healing to be speaking of him, especially considering her company. Never in her life did she imagine she'd feel welcomed by a pirate with gold-clad teeth.

She finished the story of the crown, and they shared long laughs, which felt good compared to weeping in solitude. By the end, Sora was eating and drinking, and felt her spirits begin to rise a bit. Her toe even tapped along to the off-time beat and dreadful singing.

They shared more stories of adventures, not just featuring Whitney.

Gold Grin of battles on the high seas she could barely fathom, or of how his ship got its odd name, the *Reba*. He'd been lured, nearly to his doom, by the song of a mermaid by that name. When he'd shown the fortitude and strength to deny her seductions unlike any man before, she called off the many storms and waves meant to bring death to the crew and invited him to her waters.

"She was the only woman I ever loved," he said. "And she didn't even have the parts I'd once thought necessary for loving!"

Tum Tum told of crazy nights in his tavern which only he found hilarious. Sora tried to match them, but every story she told went back to Whitney. Because without him, she'd never done anything more than hide out in Wetzel's shack and learn how to make a fire in her hand.

So, she spoke of Whitneys rescue from the Yarrington dungeons by Torsten's hands, and about his rescue by her hands in the Webbed Woods, and then about how Muskigo and the Shesaitju attack rescued him just as he was about to be hung by Bartholomew Darkings. She began to see a pattern.

"Right good fellow he was," Tum Tum said, rubbing tears of laughter from his eyes at the vision of Whitney fleeing with a noose flapping in the wind at his back.

"Aye, despite him being a no good jollywanker!" Gold Grin exclaimed. They laughed again, drunker now.

Sora just smiled and closed her eyes. Whitney had a knack for being rescued, and if there was a chance, even in the slightest, that he and Kazimir were banished to Elsewhere in her blind rage—she was going to find a way to bring him back.

VII

THE THIEF

"Shog in a barrel," Whitney said for what must have been the tenth time in as many days.

"I don't know what that means, Mister, but I'm sure if we've got it, we'll be happy to share it," the boy replied. His clothes were dirty but well-kept. His hair, tawny brown and messy, his face red and blotchy like he'd just spent the afternoon rolling around by the river.

"We haven't had anyone new come through here in as long as I can remember," he went on. "Lots of folks are gonna be happy to see you both."

Whitney looked at Kazimir and suspected very few people had been happy to see him in centuries.

"Uh, yeah," Whitney started. "So, this is Troborough, you say?"

"You've never heard of it?" the boy asked. "I guess that makes sense. It's pretty small compared to Yarrington. I hope I get to go there one day." He stared off toward the barely visible mountain in the distance, peak sliced clean across. "Father says we'll go for a Dawning when I'm older."

It was then Whitney realized the deep purple sky had lightened. Little, white, puffy clouds now painted themselves against an amber sky, the color of Sora's eyes. Whitney wasn't sure when that happened. Green grass swayed along rolling hills, and the smell of horse shog in the distance met his nostrils.

"Gonna be here long?" the boy asked.

Whitney regarded Kazimir, who remained silent as a corpse. When the upyr didn't respond, he said, "Just passing through, I think."

"Travelers, huh?" The boy's eyes lit up. "Are you hungry then?" he asked.

Whitney glanced down at his stomach. After running through Winde Port without a bite to eat or a wink of sleep, then rowing across Elsewhere, he felt like he should have been starving, but Kazimir was right, his stomach neither grumbled nor cramped as it should have. The thought of food, however, had him salivating.

"Starved," he said. He both meant it and didn't, which made no sense, just like the rest of this strange place.

"Great!" the boy said. "Let me show you the farm! We've got plenty of food, and I bet Pa will let you stay in the barn. We don't get many noble visitors here."

"Noble," Whitney repeated to nobody in particular, instinctually puffing out his chest.

"It's gonna be dark soon if you want to get going. Don't wanna make Pa mad."

Again, Whitney looked to Kazimir in disbelief that he was in a position where he had to rely on the murderer. Kazimir nodded him along.

"If this is where the Ferryman wanted you, you'd be wise to follow. But remember this, thief, there's no, 'just passing through,' in Elsewhere."

"What if it isn't where he wanted me?" Whitney asked.

"Pray to whatever god you believe in it is."

Whitney found himself standing firmly in place. Everything with the upyr was grim, but that didn't stop his mind from churning with possibilities, all of them awful. The stories fathers told about Elsewhere, and how demons would pluck out your organs while you watched; all the mystical hogwash he'd ever heard was starting to feel all too real.

"C'mon, we better hurry." The boy took Whitney's hand and pulled him along in the direction of the town. The act made Whitney look down, and then he remembered what he looked like.

"Hey kid," Whitney said. "Think we could stop by the tailor and pick up some clothes first?"

The boy stopped.

"Clothes?" he asked, looking Whitney up and down like he was insane. "Those are nicer than anything you can buy here."

Whitney peered down again and noticed he was now wearing clothes —dark pants, white silk tunic, and a cloak worthy of a Darkings. Kazimir the same. They looked like proper noblemen.

"How did?" Whitney said, incredulous.

"I bought mine from the tailor, Gilly." The boy snapped his cloth collar. "Well..." He leaned in close. "I didn't buy them." He continued on his way.

Whitney touched his clothes, pulling at fabric, fingering his cloak until Kazimir nudged him in the side. He grunted for them to keep following.

As they traveled, Whitney's jaw increasingly dropped. He was dumbfounded. Troborough looked just as he'd remembered it growing up.

What mess did you get me into this time, Sora?

In the distance, he could see the Julset twins' place. The corners of his mouth peaked at the thought of afternoons spent snogging in their backyard, wondering but not caring which one it was, Becca or Kayla. Then, next door was old Charles Whelfork's place and Farmer Branson's farm. It all looked like it had when he was a kid, not like the last time he'd visited, and certainly not like it had after the Shesaitju attacked and burned it to dust and ash.

Then he saw something that made the air catch in his throat and the contents of his stomach swirl. He may not have been able to feel hunger, but he felt the sickness gurgle within at the sight of Wetzel's little shack down back at the riverside. It was the place Sora had grown up and apparently learned magic, unbeknownst to him. Wetzel was the town healer and herbalist; the place you went when prayer at the church wouldn't cut it.

Whitney started veering off the path toward it.

"Hey, Mister." The boy pulled him away. "You don't want to go there."

Whitney didn't listen. He released the boy's hand and continued on his path.

"I said, Mister! You don't want to go there."

Every muscle in Whitney's body froze a few meters away from the shack. He tried to push forward to Wetzel's door but felt compelled back to the road until he was, once again, striding alongside the boy. He wasn't even sure he could remember how he got back there.

"What are you doing, thief?" Kazimir asked.

"I don't know," he said. "I wanted to go see the shack but... I... I couldn't."

"You don't carve your own path here."

"I always do."

Kazimir ground his teeth. "The Sanguine Lords must truly be angry to strand me here with such a fool."

"The farm is just over there, beyond the town center," the boy said, pointing.

He started running again, waving Whitney and Kazimir along.

They passed the Twilight Manor and a small oak whose leaves were turning that wasn't so small the last time he'd seen it. Whitney's was so distracted by the tree that he nearly plowed over the boy when he stopped in the middle of the courtyard.

"That's the Twilight Manor," he said. "Dad says it's the porthole to Elsewhere and exile, and only rotten sinners go there."

"Sounds like something my old man would have said too," Whitney said to Kazimir. The upyr walked at a brisk pace behind them, refusing to run. He wore the jaded glare one does when being dragged to church on the turning of the moons. Like it was all too routine.

Whitney stole a glance to the sky. It returned to blood red, only now one of the moons peeked out from soft clouds. Whitney never paid much attention to the moons if he wasn't forced to during Dawnings, but now, Celeste the bright moon was nowhere to be found. Loutis hung alone in the sky, haggard and skull-like, no light shining from it and barely able to be seen.

He didn't even have a chance to ask about the moons before his gaze turned down and he noticed that the old Troborough Church of Iam stood in ruins across the plaza. The bit of stone around the altar remained standing along with half a statue of Iam's Eye, but the rest of the place was burned down, charred. Whitney couldn't remember a time when the church was in such disrepair except after the Shesaitju's razing. A blind priest sat, legs folded, before the ravaged altar. Only he too was different, with dark skin like a man from Glinthaven and not the old, white-haired priest Whitney remembered growing up.

"What happened to the church?" Whitney asked.

The boy slowed. "Not sure," he said. "Burned down before I was born and the Crown hasn't sent anyone to fix it."

"Then where do you all… you know… pray?" Whitney recalled how many hours of his life he must have spent in sermons within that unimpressive building. He'd never cared for all the pomp and circumstance, but it was undoubtedly a big part of his childhood.

The boy stopped to observe him quizzically, tilting his head, but never answered the question. After a brief moment of silence passed between them, he said, "C'mon, my house is this way," and continued down one of the roads.

"Even the creators of this place cannot abide prayer to the one who damned them here," Kazimir said, catching up to him. "This is where you grew up, isn't it?"

"How can you tell?"

"I hated where I grew up too."

Kazimir passed by as well, leaving Whitney staring at the devastated church. He swallowed the lump forming in his throat, and followed, unable to take his eyes off the out-of-place priest. A cloth wrapped his blinded eyes, but he seemed to be looking straight at Whitney, through him.

Whitney turned away quickly and jogged to catch up to the boy. Something about the imposter was familiar, and it sent a very inhuman chill up Whitney's spine.

Loutis still hung alone in the sky when their young guide led Whitney and Kazimir to a wooden fence surrounding farmland.

"Welcome to my home!" the boy announced. "I hope Ma made candied plums. Farmer Branson grows the best plums."

Whitney's legs stopped working. His mouth fell so wide he thought it might've soon touched the ground and filled with dirt.

"This is…" He couldn't get the words out.

"You are dull as a wizard's blade," Kazimir said.

"You knew?"

"I told you this isn't my first foray through this realm."

"You, mighty assassin of the Dom Nohzi, have been to this town? My house? I—I mean, my parent's house?"

"Elsewhere is different for every traveler, but nearly all the problems of men seem to stem from their homes, no matter how it looks, or who occupies it."

Whitney's home was exactly as he had remembered it—or how he'd chosen to forget it. He never even went to take a look when he'd returned to the Twilight Manor what seemed like ages ago and was challenged to steal the Glass Crown.

It was a simple farmhouse, wattle and daub with a broad, thatched roof. Over the years, Whitney's father had begun reinforcing the frame with long pieces of timber, and it looked like he was in the midst of repairing the roof. It might have been one of the nicer houses in Troborough, but that wasn't saying much.

The boy ducked under the fence and waved to them. "Come along."

"You—you live here?" Whitney asked.

The boy turned and grinned. Whitney felt the air flee his lungs.

"My name is Whitney," the boy said without prompting. "Whitney Fierstown. I know, it's a girl's name. Ha, ha, very funny." The boy stood staring, waiting eagerly for Whitney and Kazimir to respond to a joke Whitney knew too well. He'd spent his entire childhood getting ahead of the game before other children teased him first.

"My name is Kazimir," Kazimir said. Whitney had no idea he could sound so polite. The boy offered a broader smile and nod of approval. Whitney couldn't believe a child—himself—could look upon the pale upyr with his snow-white hair and dark, soulless eyes and not be gripped by terror.

The boy then turned to Whitney.

"I'm Whi—" Whitney began before Kazimir interrupted.

"Willis."

"Yeah, Willis Blisslayer." Whitney took a step, then had to grab hold of a fencepost to keep himself upright.

"Want to meet my parents?" Young Whitney asked. "I'm sure they'll love company."

"Doubtful…" Whitney said under his breath.

"Huh?" the boy said.

"Would love to," he said, forcing a smile. He didn't. In fact, he wanted to turn tail and run the other direction as fast as he could, but just as he had been led away from Wetzel's shack, he was compelled toward his childhood home. His legs moved, seemingly disconnected from his thoughts.

They walked down the dirt path Whitney had walked a million times before. He hadn't been there since the day he left at sixteen, but it all felt familiar—eerie even. A candle burned in what Whitney knew was the kitchen window. Several of them, in fact. He could remember how comforting that sight was every time he'd return after playing by the river with Sora or getting into trouble alone. His mother would be in there with a white smock covering her plump figure, probably pulling some kind of fruit pie from the oven, so it had time to cool before dinner was through.

He could smell the roast duck wafting through the window. Then, he heard something that reminded him of why he'd left in the first place.

"Iam's light, Lauryn, that's gotta be a whole week's worth of butter you used!" His father shouted, somewhere inside. "No wonder you keep growing."

Again, Whitney stopped and swallowed hard. "Maybe we should find someplace else for the night? I always preferred the Twilight Manor." He fought the urge to keep walking and finally spun around to leave, but the next time he blinked he found himself facing his childhood home again.

"Nonsense!" Young Whitney shouted. "Didn't you hear that? Pie!" He licked his lips before running toward the house. When neither Whitney nor Kazimir moved to follow, the boy called back, "Lazy as you are ugly?" He laughed.

Kazimir grinned, and not the wicked sneer that made grown men shiver that Whitney was used to, but a mortal one, like he was delighted. "This will be fun," Kazimir remarked.

"How do you figure that?" Whitney asked.

"You're about to be as annoyed by you as the rest of us are."

Whitney rolled his eyes and continued ahead, but then a thought crossed his mind that he wished would go away. "If this is Elsewhere... and you're... how do you know you didn't?"

"Because I'm here, in your Elsewhere." Kazimir shoved by him; only Whitney didn't go flying onto his rump. All that supernatural strength the upyr had displayed in Winde Port, he was now no stronger than all the countless drunks who'd nudged by Whitney over the years.

Up ahead, Young Whitney threw the front door open and cried out, "I'm home, and I've brought guests!"

"I hope it's not that little knife-ear orphan!" his father shouted.

"Hush," said the voice of a woman. Her finger was still over her lips as she rushed into the mudroom. She was large for a woman, and her messy apron couldn't cover it. But her red cheeks and warm smile were sweet as spring after winter. She'd left work at a bakery in Yarrington to live with her husband and never looked back. Just like Whitney hadn't when he left the farm behind, not even when he'd heard that a plague passed through Troborough's water supply and claimed his parents' lives.

"Hi, sweetheart," she said. "Did you have fun?"

"Did you get into more trouble this time?" his father questioned.

"No!" Young Whitney shouted defiantly.

Big Whitney knew precisely what that tone meant. He had gotten into trouble, and by the look on his face and the redness of his cheeks, it was pretty serious.

The boy's father—Whitney's father—stood in the doorway leading into the sitting room, two hundred pounds of muscle and a beard down to his heart. He looked the way he'd always looked, like he'd just worked the whole day. That's all Rocco ever did, after all. From the moment the sun rose to well after it set, taking only the yearly Dawning off to relax. For all his work, they still lived in this shog house, in a shog town, just west of nothing but more shog.

Kazimir elbowed Whitney, and he realized he'd been making a face like he smelled the shog.

"Who're these vagabonds?" Rocco asked.

"They're not vagabonds, Pa," Young Whitney said, then turned to Big Whitney and said, "Are you?" He smirked before Big Whitney could answer. "This is Willis and Kazimir," he said. "I told them they could stay for dinner and then sleep in the barn."

Rocco took a few lumbering steps toward the two. He got so close to their faces, Whitney could feel the whiskers tickling his skin.

"We look like an inn?" he asked.

"Nope, you're right," Whitney said. "We'll head right down the road to the Twilight. It'll only cost a few autlas."

"Nonsense," his mother said. "Rocco, you said it yourself, this is too much food for the three of us. Why don't we let them stay? By now, the Twilight will be full of ruffians. Nobody these two fine gentlemen would want to deal with."

Whitney thought his mother was about to receive a wallop, but instead, Rocco nodded and with a snort said, "Fine, Lauryn. They can work off their share on the farm first thing in the morning before they head off. Big harvest tomorrow."

"Yippee!" shouted Young Whitney.

"Yippee, farm work," Whitney whispered sarcastically to himself. He'd dedicated his entire life to escaping the tedium of farm work, and now, somehow, he was at risk of it again. He decided he'd play along with Elsewhere's games, enjoy his mother's cooking—which was one of very few good parts about Troborough—then slip out in the night to find a way out of… whatever this was.

"Better than spending autlas on room and board," Rocco said.

Lauryn invited them to a too-small table in a cluttered kitchen where she had the feast laid out. Roast duck with fingerling potatoes and cabbage. It looked delicious.

Whitney stared at his mother, just as he'd remembered her. When she and his father passed from illness, he'd probably been across the world on some adventure. He wouldn't have come back even if he'd known. He preferred never to see his dad again and wanted to remember his mother with some fondness. Truth was, he resented the woman for sitting by while his father did whatever he wanted, treated them both however he pleased, and slandered Sora and any other foreigner relentlessly. He was a nobody yet she let him act like he ruled Yarrington.

"Where you from, sirs?" Rocco said, shoveling a large, juicy bite of duck into his mouth.

Kazimir shot Whitney a look that said, "Think this through." He was glad for it too. He might have blurted Troborough out of reflex, and then who knows what mess would follow.

"Yarrington," he said instead.

"Figured as much," Rocco replied, mouth still full. "You don't look like the type who've done a day's work in a long time." Lauryn kicked him under the table, but he ignored her and grinned. "We'll fix that tomorrow, huh?"

Whitney held his tongue. "Yes. I suppose we will."

"Pa, if they're helping you, does that mean I don't have to?" Young Whitney asked. His mouth was full of food as he talked as well, though when he did it, it wasn't nearly as repulsive.

"What, so you can go play around with the knife-ear and the old codger who'dun took her in?" Rocco questioned.

"Not at the table Rocco," Lauryn muttered under her breath.

"The war with her kind got your aunt and uncle killed, boy!" Young Whitney's gaze snapped toward Rocco upon being scolded. For a moment, staring at the sad expression of his miniature doppelgänger, Whitney forgot which body he was in.

"If King Liam didn't decree that we take in refugees," Rocco went on, "she'd be on the streets wit—"

"You sure look awfully familiar, Willis," Lauryn said, cutting her husband off. "Have you been here before?"

After a pregnant pause, Whitney said, "No."

"Hm, guess you just have one of those faces. And where are you from?" Lauryn asked, turning to Kazimir. "I haven't seen hair that white on a man your age in all my life."

"The far north," Kazimir said.

"You don't look like a Drav Cra heathen," Rocco remarked.

"Brekliodad."

"Oh, how fun!" Lauryn said. "I've never met anyone from there. What brings you so far south?"

"Yeah, Kazimir old pal, what does bring you so far?" Whitney said.

"Work," he answered.

"Then you've come to the right place," Rocco said. "It's about time someone your age learned the meaning of hard work. Too many soft hands around these parts."

Whitney wished his old man could experience Kazimir's "work" first-hand. If he'd known what the upyr was, he'd be calling for the King's Shield. Only they'd never bother coming to such a worthless town in the first place.

"Pfft," Whitney said before he could stop himself.

"Excuse me?" Rocco's glare could have shot icepicks.

"Sorry, had a stray hair on my lip."

Young Whitney sniggered into his napkin.

"I see," Rocco said, placing another bite of duck in his mouth, eyes fixated on Big Whitney.

"My dear, you haven't touched your meal," Lauryn said to Kazimir after a brief silence.

"I'm not hungry." Kazimir regarded the food, his lip twitching with disgust. He pushed the plate away.

"I see." Lauryn frowned. Her head tilted to the side, and she stared at him so intensely it looked like she was going to cry. Whitney didn't remember her ever acting that way. "You should eat. I can make you something else." Her head tilted the other way. "I can make you something else. I can make you something else." She stood to go to the kitchen.

"This is fine." Whitney grabbed a piece of duck and held it up to Kazimir's face. "More than fine, right old friend? Nice, bloody duck meat for you."

Kazimir snagged it. Just the smell had him looking like he was going to gag. He closed his eyes, tilted his head back, and dropped it into his mouth like he was eating a worm, then he swallowed in a single gulp.

Whitney would have taken pleasure in how miserable Kazimir, the man who tried to kill him and drink Sora, appeared if his mother's strange behavior wasn't so unsettling. As soon as Kazimir had his bite, her head straightened, her smile returned, and she continued eating like nothing had happened. Neither Young Whitney nor Rocco even seemed to notice her repeating herself like Gold Grin Grisham's parrot before Whitney accidentally set it free.

"Is it pie time?" Young Whitney asked after another long moment of silence.

"Not until you're done," Rocco said. "And even then, you'd better slow down before you end up a tub of lard like your mother." He laughed a mirthless laugh and his mother chuckled awkwardly.

Big Whitney closed his eyes and clenched his jaw. He felt a hand rest upon his thigh under the table and squeeze. When he opened his eyes, he saw Kazimir giving him another warning look.

His mother said nothing and Young Whitney stuffed his mouth with all his food. Then he opened his mouth and said, "Ah" for his father to see.

"Oh, yes," Lauryn said. "Blueberry and lemongrass with flakes of ginger." She looked at Young Whitney. "Some Panpingese merchants came through today with buckets of fresh ginger. Did Sora go see them?"

Big Whitney rolled his eyes. *Typical.* His parents figured every place on earth was as small and insignificant as Troborough. As if every Panpingese person in the world knew each other, even the ones who hadn't been since birth.

"Oh, yes," Young Whitney said. "I believe that was Sora's mother you bought that ginger from. Oh, wait. No. She's dead. Maybe Uncle killed her?"

A fist landed hard on the wooden table, sending silverware and goblets soaring, their liquid contents covering the table and dripping onto the floor. The same fist reached out and grabbed Young Whitney's ear.

"You want to get funny with your mother, I'll make your ears look like that little wench's," Rocco said. "That what you want?"

He pulled so hard Big Whitney thought he might succeed in his threat. Without conscious thought, he grasped at his own ear.

A ruckus outside suddenly drew everyone's attention. The sound of the front gate opening and footsteps dragging on gravel. Whitney—Big Whitney—sat up tall and craned his neck to see out the window. Through the bare branches crisscrossing over the opening, he saw the shadows of a band of men crossing the yard.

His head spun on Young Whitney so fast he heard his neck crack.

This is that night?

"Oh, you foolish boy," Whitney said under his breath.

"What's that noise out there, dear?" Lauryn asked Rocco as if Whitney weren't already looking. "It's a little late for visits, no?"

"I don't know, but I'll see to it." Rocco got up and made his way to the front door.

"Go to your room," Big Whitney whispered to Young Whitney, quiet and intense. "Trust me."

A moment later, just as Rocco reached for the handle, the door kicked inward, splintering at the frame and slamming hard into his forehead. The blow sent him reeling backward so hard his head rebounded against the wall. Lauryn yipped.

"What is this?" Kazimir stood and asked Whitney.

"What do you think?" Whitney said. "The kid is me."

Young Whitney was midway up the stairs when the first of the men entered the room. Big Whitney's jaw dropped. He remembered the night fairly well, though he'd blocked much of his past from his conscious memory. He'd stolen jewels from the wrong travelers and was caught. Only this wasn't the thug he'd recalled breaking into their home. This was Bartholomew Darkings.

VIII

THE DESERTER

Rand blinked at the sight of the blind man whose responsibility it was to carry the voice of Iam on Pantego. It must have been a heavy burden to bear, especially when so much about Iam's caring nature now felt like a lie to Rand. Strangely still, the old man's presence brought him a sense of peace during a time that peace had been so elusive. All the pain wracking Rand's body seemed to wash away beneath Wren's gaze until Rand tried to speak.

"Father..." he rasped, his throat like the streaming magma from Kal Driscus in the far east.

Wren shushed him. "No need to speak." His wrinkled arms were frail, but somehow, he was able to prop Rand up against the wall to rest. Then Wren looked to the ceiling, traced his eyes with his fingers, and muttered something under his breath.

"I..." Rand coughed. He could barely formulate words. "Why?"

"Iam guided me here to save you from eternal damnation, Sir Langley. I'm glad I listened."

"I'm no knight."

Wren the Holy smiled, his face creasing all over, chasms digging deep into his flesh. If Rand ever pictured what Iam might look like, it was the man standing before him; a fatherly presence, with a long, white beard that spoke of many years on Pantego. The only difference was that he always imagined Iam with old eyes teeming with untold wisdom, and Wren had only gaping holes where his used to be.

"No matter what you are, life is precious," Wren said. "To take it, in anger or grief—there is no higher sin."

"Not even taking the lives of so many innocents?" Rand barely managed the question, but once he did, he saw his error.

Wren's face contorted into sadness. No, not sadness. Pain.

"Those were not your fault, my son. I know how difficult living with such things can be. How impossible it can be." He pressed the palm of his hand against the side of Rand's face. Rand could hear the coarseness of Wren's skin against his beard. "Knight or beggar, all must endure. I know it may not seem it, but the light of Iam is with you, child."

The man's touch sent Rand's skin to goosebumps. Either that, or it was a cold gust of air and snow slipping in through the crack in his window. "Trust me, Father. Nobody is with me."

"Yet, here I am."

Rand sat up. The burning in his throat had diminished slightly. It was still incredibly sore, but the act of speaking no longer felt like a trick of magic. "How?"

"Let us just say that an old friend needs your help."

Rand laughed, then coughed again. "Look at me. Who could I possibly help?"

Wren rose to pace the room, bones creaking. Somehow, even sightless and in tight confines, he didn't bump anything. He stopped by Rand's set of Shieldsman armor, leaning against the wall. Apparently, when Rand sent his bed flying his armor went with it.

"You took a vow to shield this kingdom and the faithful," Wren said. "I know what you did, Rand. I was there. And I saw what your Queen ordered you to do. You thought you were serving your kingdom."

"I was a coward."

"Then so too am I," Wren said, his vacant eye-sockets aiming toward Rand. For a moment, Rand swore the man could see him. "There were men of the cloth hung in her wrath as well. Priests I hand-picked to serve in the castle's chapel. I looked the other way because, for all the Queen's wrongdoing, Iam saw fit to raise her child from the grave, I don't care what the heathens say. He showed me that the Nothhelm family's time is not yet through."

"Maybe it should be." Rand wished he could take the words back the moment they escaped his lips. He expected the Holy Father to be shocked, but the old man nodded and wore a relieved smile as if happy to see he wasn't alone in that thought.

"Perhaps." His face turned toward the floor. "Rand, did you know that it was I who crowned our greatest king atop Mount Lister?"

Rand shook his head.

"I placed the Glass Crown upon his head, and it was one of my proudest moments as High Priest. I knew without question the man he was and who he'd become."

"He was perfection in Iam's sight."

Wren laughed this time. "He was a whoremonger with a lust for blood-shed when it suited him."

Rand nearly toppled over.

"But Iam, in His grace, found the greatness of the man to outweigh his flaws. For we are all imperfect. It is what makes us human, and it takes a long life to find the inward light of Iam in it's purest form."

Wren returned to Rand's side and lay a gentle hand upon his shoulder. "That day, crowning Liam, I felt something strong course through my veins. Hope. It is a feeling I have not felt in a long while, yet today I feel it once more. There is hope yet for the Glass Kingdom. It all starts with you."

"With all due respect, Your Holiness. I think you've come to the wrong place."

"Perhaps Sir Unger meant a different Rand Langley, former Wearer of White, who lived in a 'shoghole of a flat above a shoghole of a tavern' when he sent me here to beseech you."

Wren smiled, and Rand sat up further. The only thing more shocking than the priest's language was the name that spilled off his lips.

"Sir Unger sent you?" Rand asked.

"Directly, yes."

"I guess he tired of begging me to return himself."

"He wished he could come, but that is no longer possible. You're not the only disgraced Wearer in Yarrington any longer."

"What did she do to him?"

"She is the least of our concerns. Yarrington has been invaded. Quietly, peacefully, the enemies of Iam flood these walls from the cold, bitter North. The worst among them, Redstar, whispers in the ear of our king."

"The Queen's brother? I thought him dead."

"Dead?"

"Last I saw, Torsten returned from the Webbed Woods with him as prisoner, set to be hanged for his crimes."

"Is Dockside so forgotten by the castle you haven't heard? The Drav Cra are here, and it was by invitation of the King himself."

"Not Dockside." Rand stood and crossed the room toward a row of empty jugs of ale. He sat at the table. The urge for a drink hit him like a crashing wave now that the pain had subsided. He realized his hands were shaking. Luckily, there was nothing left to drink.

"I see," Wren said, disappointed.

"All I know is the young Prince—"

"King," Wren corrected.

"Yes, my apologies. The young King Pi came back to life, and we're at war with the Black Sands." Rand stared at the old man. That fatherly warmth was gone, replaced now with fear. "I know. Not exactly the hero Torsten painted."

"Then perhaps it is not a hero we need. Torsten said you are the only Shieldsman he can trust."

"Now I know this is a dream. I'm still hanging on that rope, aren't I? Ready to die."

"You are here, and now. The Queen's treasonous brother has stripped Torsten of his rank, claimed the ear of the King as his newly instated prime minister, and stolen victory in the battle of Winde Port. His heathens fill the capital, their warlocks spreading their lies to the faithful. If we do not act fast, there will be nothing left to save."

Rand swallowed the lump in his throat. He'd noticed an unusual number of fur-clad, Drav Cra traders passing through the Maiden's Mugs, but little else. Every day since the moment he handed Torsten back the white helm and left the castle behind was a blur. Just the ropes creaking over and over and over...

"Rand, it's time you put your armor back on," Wren said.

Rand squeezed his eyelids tight, then tried to focus on the High Priest. "I don't know what you possibly think I could do."

"'Cut the head off the true snake,' as Torsten so mildly put it. Traitors and deceivers abound, but there is only one who can be traced to all of it—one whose actions led the Queen down that horrid path you suffered."

"I didn't suffer!" Rand snapped. "They all suffered. Priests, doctors, council members... Tessa!" He couldn't believe himself, yelling at the High Priest of Iam.

"And we can never change that," Wren interjected calmly. "We can, however, ensure that Iam's light shines brightly on the future. Redstar would cover this world in darkness in the name of his Buried Goddess. He must..." Wren paused. His lips parted, but the word he was searching for didn't come. And that was likely because it was a word no man of peace like him had likely ever uttered before in such context.

"Die," Rand finished for him. "Is that what this is all about?"

"It is a sin even to think, but like your friend Torsten, I would rather suffer eternity in Elsewhere than watch Pantego succumb to madness."

"So, you come to an expert on killing?" The words stung as they came out and in the back of his mind, he could hear Tessa and the others begging for mercy.

"I come to a sworn knight of the King's Shield. A man who vowed to safeguard this realm, and who hasn't been manipulated by an imposter like the rest. Perhaps there are other Shieldsmen to be trusted, but the only one I trust is locked in a cell, and he told me to find you."

Rand shook his head. "I don't... I'm done killing."

"That is why it must be you. Our king is young and impressionable. If we wait any longer, our great cathedral will be a ruin for warlocks to dance and spill blood on. Who knows what they will do when the light goes out upon the Dawning next week. If I could do this for the kingdom of Iam, I would. But I am too old and too frail."

"And I'm a drunk."

"No one is perfect. Not me, not the great Liam. All his countless mistakes litter Elsewhere—bastards all—but we are the best he could do. We are small, jealous humans, yet he put faith in us as his creation. It's time we do something for him and protect his chosen realm from the fallen."

Rand drew a deep breath; then a chuckle slipped through his lips. Before today, he couldn't remember the last time he'd laughed at anything, no matter how slight. "The sermons in Dockside are nowhere near as poetic as yours, Your Holiness."

"That is something I will have to remedy."

"Rand, are you—" The door swung open, and Sigrid froze in the entry. The loaves of bread under her arm fell. "Your Holiness." She fell to her knees and circled her eyes with her fingers.

"Stand, dear," Wren said. "You are Rand's…"

"Sister," she finished for him. "Why are you... I mean..." Her words trailed off as her gaze stopped on the noose of tied blankets still hanging from the ceiling. Then on the upturned furniture and armor.

"We're doing Iam's work, my child." Wren stood, groaning softly as his old legs stretched out. "Now, I do think it's time to return to the cathedral. There are a few honest folks left in this city if you look hard enough, and the Dawning approaches. Must be prepared." He shuffled past Sigrid to grab his cane from against the wall. Sigrid hurried over to help him to the door.

"Your Holiness, what do you expect me to do?" Rand asked.

The High Priest stopped at the door, then glanced back, again wearing his warmest smile like it was second nature. Perhaps it was. After all, he was the father to all the faithful in Yarrington. Had Rand's own father lived long enough, his might have grown equally reassuring.

"To receive that armor is a rare thing, an honor," Wren said. "There are few in this city who have it, even fewer living beyond the castle walls. If you remain loyal to Torsten, the one you seek now sits, an imposter in the chambers you and he once occupied." Wren traced his eyes in prayer, then hobbled out of the room.

Sigrid watched the door close all the way, then turned, brow furrowed. "Am I losing my mind?" she asked.

Rand didn't respond. All he could think to do was rush across the room and wrap his arms around her.

A heavy gust of sea wind tore in through the window. The already loose knot of the tied sheets Rand had used to try and kill himself came undone, the cloth fluttering harmlessly to the floor. He squeezed Sigrid tight and kissed the top of her head.

They were all each other had since their parents died when they were still young. He stepped back and took in the sight of her. He'd almost stolen even that from her—made the shogpile she called a life even worse. He caught a whiff of her tangled hair, the familiar scent of salt and spilled ale heavy in it.

A second later and Wren might have been too late to save him. As he pulled Sigrid closer, he couldn't help but wonder if perhaps he was wrong. If Iam hadn't yet turned His eye away from him.

IX

THE MYSTIC

ora awoke to the sound of gulls. She sat up, stretched, and yawned. Aquira flopped over and snorted, ash spraying like powder from her nostrils. The warmth of her scales felt nice in contrast to the cool air beneath the deck of the *Reba*.

It took a minute or three for Sora to realize what the sound of gulls meant.

"Land!" she shouted. She sprang up from her bed and bounded toward the door, grabbing her dress on her way out. She pulled it down over her body even as she climbed the stairs. The hatch opened. Bright light poured in and blinded her. The sounds of hurried commotion assaulted her ears, and with her vision temporarily impaired, it was all overwhelming.

Gold Grin's men barked commands, ropes thrummed, and sails battled with the wind for dominance, their flapping loud as Muskigo's army marching down the streets of Winde Port. Somewhere in the distance, bells rang out.

Her eyesight returning, Sora could see the visual representation of all the sounds. Excitement stole over her, something she thought she'd never feel again, but there it was. After weeks spent on the sea, anything other than the vast bluish-gray landscape of ocean and sky was a thrill to see.

To add to all the racket, she heard the clattering of little claws against wood and looked down to see Aquira standing next to her, blearily blinking her four sets of eyelids.

Sora scooped her up and held her tight against her chest.

"We're here, girl," she said, taking a few steps out onto the deck. She turned and looked up at the helm where Gold Grin stood. It was then that she realized the ship's black sails with a bleeding skull had been switched out for unmarked white ones.

"Aye, lassie!" he shouted. "Come on up and see your homeland for the first time!"

By now, Sora had come to like the pirate. She hadn't seen much of the world, and in her limited experience adventuring with Whitney, most men were cruel brutes. Torsten thought her a monster, Bartholomew Darkings a pest, Kazimir a meal, and Whitney…

She'd been nervous to step upon the *Reba* at first, but even though Gold Grin was some dastardly pirate feared across the seas, he treated her as she would think any decent man would a woman. He reminded her of Muskigo, and that scared her, but she smiled back up at him and climbed the short flight of stairs leading to the stern-side deck.

Grisham held the wheel steady and peered off into the distance.

"Yaolin City," he said, a sense of awe in his voice. "No more beautiful nor magical place in all Pantego, except maybe Glinthaven."

Sora couldn't muster a response. She followed Grisham's gaze and saw the capital city of her people. As far as she could see, tiers upon tiers of buildings with sweeping, red-tile roofs plastered a cliff face. It seemed nearly impossible. When she squinted, she could see dark little dots scurrying like ants along the rocky terrain. Wooden staircases connected the tiers, and more little dots covered those, with waterfalls cascading amongst all of it.

"It's huge," she said.

"No place like it," Grisham repeated. He reached out to scratch Aquira beneath her chin as she flapped hard to fly along with the ship. Even Aquira had come to like the man over the weeks they'd been on the *Reba*. "No place at all."

Sora's features darkened.

"What's wrong, lass?" Grisham asked, noticing.

"How am I ever going to find what I'm looking for in a place so big? It was hard enough for Wetzel to teach me to light a candle and I'd lived in his home."

Sora had shared enough details of her life with the self-proclaimed pirate king for him to know about Wetzel and how he taught her. Grisham had been particularly interested in the many tomes explaining how to perform magic spells until he'd found out they'd been burned along with the rest of Troborough.

"Aye, difficult indeed," he said. "But I'm sure someone of your particular talents'll have no trouble."

"You're too kind," Sora said. She lifted her arm for Aquira to land, but it was more to hide her reddening cheeks. "Come on Aquira, let's go find Tum Tum. You'll excuse us?"

Gold Grin nodded. "I don't own ye, lass."

Sora hurried down a small flight of stairs to the galley where she found Tum Tum, as always, by the food.

"Aye, girly!" he exclaimed. "Pull up a crate." His beard had grown unruly during the journey. Sora couldn't believe how fast dwarf hair grew.

"But Yaolin is so close," she said. "We need to get ready."

"Sometimes I forget ye've never been on the sea, so worldly ye seem. It'll take another half-day to close that distance over water. No point goin hungry, I always say."

"Half a day?" Sora asked.

The first mate himself, a pirate named Fortist, dragged a crate toward the pot for Sora. Aquira growled. She still hadn't forgiven the man for how he handled her on the day Grisham's men boarded their old ship.

"Thank you, Fortist," Sora said, then tapped Aquira on the snout. "I'm sorry about her."

"I deserve it, miss." Fortist bowed and backed away. "Cap'n always says that a pirate who can make friends always has an army."

"Yer cap'n is as wise as his teeth be… well… gold!" Tum Tum burst out laughing, and a few others joined him. It was clear now that his belly wasn't just full of food, but that once again they'd dug into the ale despite it being just past sunrise.

Sora rolled her eyes. *They can't be perfect. They are pirates after all.*

After a hearty meal, Sora retired to her quarters to pack what meager belongings she had. The pirate crew had been kind enough to supply Sora out of their massive cache of loot with the things men had no need of. She tried not to notice the gold or jewels in the crates as well and dared not ask where they were taken from—for her own sake and peace of mind.

Her first day on board, she'd been given several changes of clothing, all in the style common to wayfaring Pantegans. She finished lacing up her leather bodice, adjusted the waistline of her pants, then put on a pair of leather gloves she'd specifically asked Gold Grin's men for. They ran high up her forearms, covering the blood magic scars. She clicked her tongue, inviting Aquira to crawl up her sleeve to perch on her shoulder.

"I wish I were a little more prepared," she whispered to Aquira. "I was really counting on Whit, you know? He knows the place. I'm not sure how I'm going to find the Bokeos to let them know about Tayvada let alone hidden mystics. Iam's light, Aquira, I'm even assuming the man still has living family and that they didn't live and die in Winde Port along with so many others."

Sora had taken to talking to the wyvern, speaking her thoughts instead of keeping them bottled up inside. It was how she passed the quiet moments without dwelling on Whitney and how she could undo what had been done.

There were times when Sora thought her little reptilian companion understood every word—like when she'd used her fire breath to rescue Sora from the hands of Kazimir in the old, battered church steeple. In the present, if Aquira understood a word, she hid it well. She scratched her head with her rear claws then rolled over on the bed, belly facing the ceiling, and stretched.

"Yeah, girl, your kind aren't used to being cooped up on boats either, are they?" Sora said.

"Lass?" Gold Grin's voice boomed from above.

"Coming!" Sora emerged to find Gold Grin waiting at the top of the hatch.

He extended his hand. "Gonna need them papers of yers."

"My papers, already?" she said, hand moving instinctively to cover the pocket of her leather pants. "For what?"

He laughed. "Ye think the govn'r of Panping tells his men to just let pirates into his capital city?"

Sora didn't argue further. She produced the papers Whitney had taken from Tayvada Bokeo's corpse back in Winde Port. Grisham snatched them, inspected them, then handed them back, grinned, and said, "On second thought, best ye handle this. I be fairly famous for the grin."

Sora reluctantly returned a smile. Making believe she was a helpless traveler on the road in need of help from a passing caravan, or Father Gorenheimer's altar server was entirely different from trying to fool the city guard in a land unfamiliar to her.

She took the papers back and glanced toward the city. They were close now, close enough that the people were no longer dots lining the cliff faces but she could even make out faces. And ears. Sure, the steel armor of Glass soldiers patrolling glimmered here and there, but thousands upon thousands of people worked, walked, and generally lived life with ears just like hers. She felt something she didn't even know she wanted because she didn't know it existed.

Belonging.

"Where are the docks?" she asked.

"Follow me," Gold Grin said, already on his way back to the helm.

He gave the wheel the slightest turn, and the course shifted toward a giant, dark hole in the face of the cliff, piercing the city and with a water-fall pouring over it. As they approached, Sora grew concerned that the tall mast wouldn't clear the opening. The closer they got, the bigger the hole appeared to be until she realized the sheer immensity of it. The *Reba* could have fit twice stacked within the cavern.

"Hold on, lads!" Grisham shouted. "Bout to get mighty wet in here!"

The ship passed beneath the pounding waterfall. The force of it knocked Aquira from Sora's shoulder, and as she sprawled to grab the wyvern, she saw that Grisham already had. He lifted Sora by the back of her shirt. One foot into Yaolin and her new clothes were already drenched.

"That's how we swab the deck round these parts." He removed his hat and flicked it to get the water off.

Light bloomed on the far end of the cavern. Every sound of the ship echoed. Waves slapped against the side of the hull, causing the wood to creak, and then bounced back to collide with the hard stone. After a moment, Sora fell into the gentle tempo of it all. It was like nature's song, peaceful, serene.

She closed her eyes and let the rhythmic sounds wash over her until a hot, white light painted her vision through her eyelids. She opened them and was immediately forced to squint.

They emerged into a great lake. The city and all its colorful, tiled roofs stretched all around it, rising up three rocky hills like the fingers of giants grasping for the clouds. Between them, walls rose high to keep out invaders, with the sea and cliffs guarding the side they'd arrived from. Hundreds of large ships were docked along the coasts, and hundreds more little fishing boats with square, ruffled sails floated within the vast waters.

"A beaut, ain't she?" Tum Tum said, sidling up to her.

He was right in every sense of the word. The sheer mass of the place made Sora wonder how Liam managed to conquer it. As she took it all in, she only saw the one entrance by sea through the waterfall, walls, and hills everywhere else.

How did he ever bring a fleet and an army through? Wetzel didn't have any books that told that story. It was a testament to the man's prowess as a military leader.

Then she thought of all the people who'd lived peaceably here before the Glass brought their heavy fist down.

"I've never…" She couldn't find the words.

"No one has until they has," Gold Grin said.

"What's that?" Sora asked, pointing at a tall tower on a small island in the middle of the lake. A series of stacked, terraced layers comprised it, made from smooth red stone carved with bands of bas-reliefs depicting men and women in robes. At each landing, tapering up to a top which vanished into the clouds, bare plants and twisting vines grew, void of all color. It was the dead of winter, but the air in Panping remained temperate, so Sora wasn't sure why they didn't grow.

More trees surrounded the base, budding from the centers of still pools of water. A bronze gate sat on four sides of the round tower, each with a large gem set in the center. One red, one blue, one yellow, and one green. Before each gate stood a row of clay statues depicting armored soldiers holding spears.

"That be the old mystic tower," Gold Grin answered.

"Was before Liam took over," Tum Tum added.

"They were a strange folk, them mystics who ruled this place. I heard tale they stored their books and secrets in that tower, but it's been sealed ever since Liam left this place."

"They say water used to fall down each layer from the top, and that plants of the wildest colors ye could imagine grew up the sides."

"Aye, it's true. I saw it once as a boy. O'course, I was peeking through the tiny slit of a prison cell, so maybe I was dreaming." Gold Grin laughed.

Sora didn't have time to think about a response before Gold Grin started throwing orders around to his crew, directing the ship toward the city's least crowded of many docks. His crew scurried around the deck and up the masts like spiders, reeling in sails, swinging booms. If the city weren't so spectacular, Sora would have been enthralled with the performance. It was better than anything the troupes passing through Troborough ever put on in the town square.

Before she knew it, they pulled up alongside the dock and secured the ship between a Glass warship and a small fishing boat. She'd expected a few bumps after how rocky the escape from Winde Port proved to be, but Grisham's crew were artists on the water.

With the ship successfully moored, Grisham "Gold Grin" Gale, one of the strangest and most powerful men Sora had ever known, placed his arms around Sora and said, "Anyone official be seeing me here without an understanding, and we might find trouble, even with this old girl wearing the white of Parlay. Get us clear to stay, and find us a way to debark without trouble, aye lass? The boys want to see what kind of trouble they can get into here and it ain't often we get hold of some legal trading papers."

"I'll stay here and wait until we're clear," Tum Tum said. " A dwarf will only complicate things down there. But you'll find me at The Ruby House at sundown. I never been here, but Whitney always said it's the best place on Xiahou Boulevard."

"The Ruby House. Xiahou Boulevard. Peaceful passage." Sora nodded then looked up at Grisham. "I can't thank you enough for this. You have no idea what it's been like since me and Whitney started adventuring together."

"Aye, trust me, I know how things be with him." He squeezed her a bit, then took her by the shoulders and looked straight into her eyes.

"Always a pleasure to have a proper lass on board. Ye tell the world that old Gold Grin ain't just a monster of the seas."

Sora chuckled. "I will."

His lip twisted. "On second thought, tell them we ravaged yer bones and made ye wish for death. Fear be a great motivator!" He laughed heartily, then opened her hand and placed a bag stuffed with gold autlas in it. It was more than she and Whitney had earned in Winde Port, and he gave it over like one would an apple.

"Give this to the guards, and they won't look twice at this ship," he said. "Now go on. There was a bargain struck between us, and I believe my end be upheld."

He gave her a gentle shove toward the lowered gangway. She stepped lightly, unsure. But as she neared the docks, she felt invigorated. Somewhere in this vast city were the answers to all her questions: who she was, why she could do the things she sometimes did, and where Whitney was.

Aquira nuzzled against her neck and closed her eyes. Sora took comfort in the wyvern's soft purrs. She stowed the coin purse, then drew in a deep breath and noted how different the air smelled compared to anywhere she'd been before. No salt from water, and no shog from men up to no good. It was fresh, crisp, and a bit like the first budding flowers of spring.

Her foot crunched onto gravel as she made landfall.

"Jinszi," said a Panpingese man waiting on the dock almost immediately. He gave Aquira little more than a cursory glance. Apparently, wyvern's weren't such a curiosity in the east.

"I… uh. I don't speak Panpingese," she said.

The man rolled his eyes, apparently a gesture that transcended culture, and said, "Papers."

"Oh, yes. Right here." Sora handed the man the trading documents.

He looked at the papers, then at her, then Aquira, then back at the papers again. He waved back to a pavilion, where Sora now noticed the host of Glass soldiers sitting around playing gems. One of them groaned, then stood to approach.

The Panpingese dockworker held up the papers for him to see. He shielded his eyes from the sun as he gave them a look-over, then snatched them out of the man's hands to scrutinize.

"You don't look like a Tayvada," he muttered.

"No," Sora said simply, then forced herself to look as sad as she could manage. "My husband. He's dead, and I've come to deliver news to his family and return with the last of his goods." She pointed to the galleon behind her.

The man followed her finger, then his bleary eyes finally opened wide enough to show concern, but it was not for her loss. His hand fell to the grip of his sword. "You do know whose ship that is, don't you?"

"I do." One look was all it took him. Perhaps she underestimated how infamous and feared Grisham truly was. Though other than switching out their black sails on approach, he didn't try to hide anything. Now that Sora wasn't on the ship or in a storm, she could see the distinctive shape of a golden mermaid statue perched on the *Reba*'s prow. There couldn't be another like it in all Pantego.

"Come on, Higgin, your turn!" shouted one of the Glass guards beneath the covering.

The guard named Higgin glanced back at them, and his expression caused them all to stir from their game. Two rose and started toward him.

"They helped me escape the fighting in Winde Port," Sora said. "I assure you, they're flying white because all they wish for is a few days on land and to trade away their wares."

"Trade *their* wares?" Higgin replied. "You do realize what pirates do, don't you, Miss Bokeo?"

The reference to her as Miss Bokeo nearly shook her, but she found her resolve and mustered the same air of nobility she's used back in Winde Port on the rebel Muskigo. All of Whitney's lessons on lying and thieving were paying off.

"I'm not a fool," she said, "but these men helped me and the Winde Trader's Guild." She acted wounded, vulnerable, even getting her eyes to water. Then she pulled out the purse and stuck it in the man's gut. "I owe them."

The guard glanced down. All his worries seemed to melt away. He raised a hand for his men to stop approaching. "Go help them," he ordered the Panpingese dockhand, pointing to another ship down the docks.

"Fine." The guard stowed the purse. "They cover that damn prow, they can stay, but you didn't deal with me." He handed the papers back. "You have one day free of charge, as is customary due to your husband—late husband's position in the guild. After that, they'll be charged the regular rate of... two hundred autlas per day. Understood?"

"Two hun—" Sora caught herself. It wasn't her money, and with the loot Grisham's boys would be selling off, that was probably pocket change. "Thank you." She forced a snivel. "I'll never forget how you've helped me."

"No, thank you, miss. And please, forget." He turned, then glared at Aquira. "And get your pet in a damn cage if you don't want to be stopped again. All those things manage is trouble."

He returned to his game of gems with his mates, and with a lot more to bet now.

"Don't listen to him," Sora said, scratching Aquira's chin. "You're no trouble."

Sora turned back to the *Reba* and waved for one of the crew to get Grisham. She couldn't believe how happy the site of him peering down over the side made her. She explained to him the terms of them staying, and the great pirate tossed her a smaller pouch of autlas of her own to help her in this strange new city.

"Good luck lass!" he shouted down as his crew hooted in celebration at being welcomed to Yaolin. "And when you see that whelp Whitney again, tell him he owes me a ship!" He burst out laughing, and his men joined in. Sora wouldn't miss the stench of their breath or how raucous they could be, but she'd never forget him.

Thanking him one last time, she headed back toward the city. She had no idea where to start, but the Winde Trader's Guild papers, a sack of autlas, and a sad story were a good place to start. It was much more than she and Whitney had when they got to Winde Port seeking passage.

She spotted the dockworker who'd greeted her and hurried to him.

"Sir?" she said as he tied a knot around a cleat to hold another ship in place. He didn't answer. It wasn't until she addressed him again that he regarded her, but didn't stop working. "Do you know where I can find the Trader's Guild?"

"That a joke?" he asked.

"I'm sorry?"

He pointed toward a giant edifice just behind them. "Big building, round dome, bronze ship statue."

"Thank you so much." Sora reached into her pocket to find an autla for him, then reconsidered. "One more thing?"

The man released a loud sigh and pursed his lips.

"Can you tell me the way to The Ruby House?" she asked.

His eyes went wide, and his face turned bright red. "Madam…" He laughed awkwardly. "I don't—why would you… such an establishment is no place for…"

Sora blushed. "Never mind. I'm sorry I asked. Thank you for your help." She handed him a coin, and he bowed three times before scuttling away.

Sora swore to herself she'd give Tum Tum a good smack for embarrassing her when the time came. Reaching up with her right hand, she scratched Aquira on the top of the head and whispered, "You ready, girl?"

The wyvern purred and readjusted herself as Sora set off down the quay. A short staircase led up to the city streets. When she reached the top, she stopped and turned back toward the lake. The view was breathtaking. She'd seen Trader's Bay near Winde Port, but that was little more than swamp and sharp rocks in comparison. This looked like the place Iam would choose for his throne.

Clear across the water she could see small pagoda style houses surrounded by bamboo forests. Personal-sized vessels lined the bay near the homes like ferryboats intended to give the illusion of being a part of the vast city. The water itself was so still, it was almost crystalline, even around the coast of the mystic's tower. Here and there, bulbous formations of rock topped with moss jutted out.

When she turned around, she was staring at the Winde Trader's Guild. The entrance was shaped like a giant ship made of bronze. She looked down and frowned, realizing how underdressed she was likely to be. There was no time to worry about that.

The interior changed her opinion. The guild hall in Winde Port had all the trappings of a noble mansion, but this one was far more reserved. Unadorned walls, with those leading deeper inside made of what seemed like paper and grids of wood. The only decoration were tapestries along the walls portraying cities from around Pantego in a symbolic nature. She recognized Yarrington by the Glass Castle and Mount Lister; Winde Port by the pier filled with ships that no longer existed.

A short and stout Panpingese gentleman awaited her in the lobby. He sat on a cushion directly on the floor behind a low desk and wore a style of clothing she was not at all familiar with. It was a bit like layered robes, but more tightly fitted, and the shoulders were broad with tassels nearly tickling the ground. He barely glanced up from a pile of papers upon which he scrawled in black ink with a thin brush.

"Shi shi," he said.

"Shi shi," Sora responded. It was all she knew in Panpingese. She'd learned how to greet travelers who made their way through Troborough long ago.

The man said something else in Panpingese and Sora raised her hands and smiled. "I'm sorry, that's all I know of your beautiful language."

"I see," the man said in perfect common, seeming disappointed. "What brings you to the guild?"

"I am looking for the Bokeo family."

The man's eyes narrowed. "What business have you with the Bokeos?"

She considered sticking with the story of her and Tayvada's ill-fated marriage, but anyone who knew the man would know that was a lie. "I know—knew their son, Tayvada," she went with instead.

"Yes, sad news."

"Oh, you've heard?" Sora asked a little too eagerly. She caught herself and toned it down. "He was a good man."

"Yes, we've all heard. The family has been in mourning since word arrived of his unfortunate murder in Winde Port. A shame what happened there. It's miraculous any of our people made it out alive, and with the rebels holing up in Nahanab, things will only be getting worse down south."

Sora nodded her agreement, the horrors of what happened in Winde Port flashing through her mind.

"Will that be all?" the man asked.

"Do you know where I can find them?" Sora asked. "I was there wh… when he… passed on. I'd like to offer my condolences."

"I'm not sure that is wise."

Aquira perked up and shuffled on Sora's shoulder, then released a shrill sound that caused the man to jump.

"I'm sorry about her," Sora said. "Aquira, stop that."

"Aquira?" the man asked, for the first time peering up enough from his work to see her. "Is that…. That's Tayvada's wyvern?"

"It is. As I said, I was there when he passed."

"Aquira didn't like anyone but Tayvada. If that is her—"

"Like I said, it is her."

"In that case, Lord Bokeo would be most interested to hear your tale, and I'm sure they'd all like to have Aquira back."

Aquira backed down but still growled softly.

"Back?" Sora asked, a wave of sadness passing over her. She'd gotten used to having the wyvern's needlelike claws digging into her shoulder, and it had been nice having someone to talk to now that Whitney was gone, even if Aquira never answered with more than a growl.

"I'd suspect so. A wyvern of that rare stock is worth its weight in gold. Is this your first time in Yaolin?"

"Unfortunately."

Again, his disappointment showed. "Okay. Just follow this road with the statues. That's Xiahou boulevard. Take a left when you reach the end and look for Bones and Tomes—Lord Bokeo owns a small bookstore, and the family lives in the home adjacent to it. If he isn't there, please, do not disturb them at home—they deserve time to grieve the loss of their son."

Sora nodded, and Aquira screeched.

"Thank you, Mr…"

"Kyoto," he finished for her.

"Thank you, Mr. Kyoto," Sora said, and turned to walk away.

"Oh, and Miss?'

Sora looked back.

"Take care of Aquira until you speak with them," he said. "You have no idea how valuable she is."

X

THE THIEF

"Is that—" Whitney didn't dare speak the name of the man who'd entered his parent's house out loud. Bartholomew Darkings was unmistakable. His fat belly was clad in a colorful silken shirt, unbuttoned halfway and more expensive than anything in the Fierstown household. His gold chains jingled, bouncing against his hairy chest.

"Elsewhere has a way of doing that," Kazimir said, also apparently recognizing the man who'd hired him to kill Whitney. "It's time to hide. This isn't our battle."

"Shouldn't we do something? You can kill all of them in the blink of an eye."

"In Elsewhere, always take the path of least resistance."

Kazimir opened the coat closet, and he and Whitney hid before the men could see them. They watched through a crack as Rocco yelled from the ground, blood dripping from his forehead.

"This is an outrage!"

"Where's that little rat?" Darkings spat, his mustaches bobbing atop his upper lip.

"How dare you!" Rocco scrambled to his feet.

Five more men shoved their way into the house and pushed him aside.

"Tear the place apart until you find it," Darkings ordered. Two men clambered upstairs and the sound of things breaking traveled down the flight.

"Rocco," Lauryn cried. "What's going on?"

"Sirs, you must leave this instant!" Rocco demanded.

Darkings ignored him and sauntered into the kitchen.

"Oh, roast duck," he said, eyes unfolding over the dinner table. "How quaint. And is that blueberry?"

"Blueberry and lemongrass… w-with a t-touch of ginger," Whitney's mother stammered, though there was no mistaking the hint of pride in her tone even as her voice quivered.

"Get out of my home!" Rocco shouted.

"Boys, shut him up." Darkings snapped his fingers before pulling out his father's chair and picking up a fork and knife. He stabbed a piece of duck and shoved it into his mouth, then moaned in ecstasy.

The remaining three thugs accosted Rocco, two grabbing his arms and a third punching him in the gut.

"Please, don't!" Lauryn cried, starting to stand.

Darkings pointed his knife at her and said, "Sit."

She returned to her seat and smoothed her apron.

Whitney took a step, but Kazimir held him back.

"Did this happen?" he asked.

Whitney nodded. It did. His younger self even managed to squirm upstairs and hide during the brunt of the action. He drew on the deepest chasms of his memory to try and piece the rest together.

"Then don't make things worse," Kazimir said.

"I can't just watch this."

"They aren't really your parents. Just wait."

Rocco's lips pursed in anger just before he took a balled fist to the face. He clattered to the floor, taking a table and flower vase with him.

Darkings took another bite of the duck then looked at Lauryn. "You made this? Quite good, quite good."

"W-what are you d-doing in my home?" she asked.

"Is there anyone else here?"

Lauryn looked to Rocco, and his father shook his bloody head. "No," she said.

"It turns out there's a young boy who lives here, your son perhaps?"

Darkings waited, but Lauryn said nothing. "Well, he stole from the wrong man today. We're just here to recover what was lost and teach the boy a lesson."

"Boss!" one of the thugs called down. His footsteps grew louder as he clomped down the stairs. He held Young Whitney by the scruff of the neck. "This him?"

Darkings stood, wiped the corners of his lips with a napkin, and threw it down over the plate. He made his way to the bottom of the stairs.

"Get off me!" Young Whitney shouted, kicking his feet frantically. "It wasn't me."

Darkings grabbed him by the jaw and forced him to look into his eyes. "You stole from me. Me! Do you know who I am, boy?"

"By the look of it," Young Whitney said, teeth clenched, "the King's jester."

Darkings slapped the boy hard with a ring-covered hand. Big Whitney seethed.

"No!" Lauryn yelled, finally getting up the courage to leave the kitchen table.

Darkings pointed a finger at her and said, "Stop, before you join your husband and make things worse for your boy."

"Please, just leave them alone," Rocco grated. "You got what you came for now get out of my house. He's just a boy."

Big Whitney's gaze turned to Rocco, bloody-nosed and eyes that would surely be black and blue in the morning. He remembered all this happening, though not the parts where his father tried to protect him.

Just then, another thug came barreling downstairs waving King Liam's Glass Crown in his hand. "Got it, Mr. Darkings."

"I don't know how it got in there!" Young Whitney shouted. I swear it wasn't me. "What the yig-and-shog?" Big Whitney whispered. His younger self had only stolen jewelry that day, not the Glass Crown.

"You don't get away with anything in Elsewhere, thief," Kazimir said.
"Wonderful."

Darkings removed a dagger with a red jewel buried into the hilt from his belt and raised it to Young Whitney's nose.

Lauryn whimpered.

"Get out, now," Rocco warned. "I had two guests here, sent them after the bailiff the moment we saw you coming."

"You heard him, boys, it's about that time to head off." He lowered his dagger, and his man dropped Young Whitney, who ran to his mother. Then they began ransacking the cupboards and all their unfinished dinner. That's what the real thugs did before punching Rocco one last time and burning the barn down on their way out.

Whitney finally recollected how he'd been punished for months after. He had to help his father rebuild the barn, harvest the fall crops, help the Father Hullquist—who wasn't the father in this version of Troborough— prepare for post-Dawning festivities and wasn't allowed outside their fence. Work had him too exhausted even to sneak out. It was the longest he'd gone without being able to spend time with Sora until he left Troborough for good.

"Your boy's got talent," Darkings said. "But he's got to learn that there are consequences to getting caught." Darkings plucked a candle off a window-sill and headed for the back door. He grabbed Young Whitney again on his way, tearing him from Lauryn's arms. The boy kicked and thrashed, but was too small and weak.

"Let him go!" Rocco started to rise, but one of the thugs kicked him hard, ensuring he stays put.

This was the moment. That first time Whitney got caught nipping more than a bronzer. The thug hadn't hurt him, only tossed him in the dirt and made him watch as the barn burned. Besides being punished, his father never let it go, and his mother never looked at him the same. Smiling when he returned for supper grew more and more difficult for her, until it stopped altogether.

Before Kazimir could stop him, Big Whitney threw the door to the closet open.

"Stop!" he shouted. "I did it!"

"I don't know who you are," Darkings said, stopping by the door. "but we saw the boy do it."

"You think that little punk-kid is capable of devising a plan like that? I did it. Paid him to help because I figured even a boy could rob fools like you."

Darkings looked back at Young Whitney. "Is that true boy?"

Young Whitney looked at his ma and pa, then nodded. "Yes, sir," he said, just as Whitney imagined his younger self would, eager never to take the blame. "He told me I was doing the right thing."

"That's right, it was me," Big Whitney said. "Whit… I mean Willis Blisslayer, bester of brigands, the filcher fantastic himself. So, let him go."

The thugs dropped Young Whitney to the floor and moved toward Big Whitney, seizing him and dragging him to Darkings. Whitney had hoped, by that point, Kazimir would've burst out and made quick work of them, but the upyr remained hidden.

So much for saving him from that sea beast…

"Do you know who I am?" Darkings asked.

"Pretty sure the boy just told us all," Whitney said. "Court jester?"

"Everyone here is a comedian. What an entertaining little town. What's this little shoghole called?" Darkings turned back to his thugs.

"Troborough, boss."

"Well, why don't you teach this Troborough trash a lesson? It's a shame; we'd have let the kid go. He's just a kid, after all. But if you did it…" He frowned at Whitney. "Well, that's a different story."

One of the thugs approached Whitney wielding a heavy club.

"You don't have to do this, Barty," Whitney pleaded. "You got the Crown back, right? No harm done."

"What did you call me?" He seemed confused, then looked at his thug. "Make it hurt, would you?"

The club-wielding thug reared back. At the same time, two things happened: Rocco rose and propelled himself at the man, and Whitney heard the sound of a door opening behind him. The club came down hard. Whitney winced, clenching his eyes shut.

A white blur passed him on his right, and Kazimir unleashed a flurry of attacks on the men, though in Elsewhere he was too slow to stop everything and the club found purchase with a loud crack, and a groan. Only, the groan wasn't Whitney's.

Whitney cracked open one eye to see Rocco, his father, on the ground, face scrunched up in pain and holding his knee. The thugs who'd been holding Whitney faced Kazimir's wrath and were face-down on the floor, dead.

"Get him!" Darkings shouted.

Kazimir used his momentum to spear another thug, driving him to the floor. The upyr rolled to his feet.

Whitney, now free, elbowed Darkings in the nose and blood flowed freely.

The remaining thugs dropped into what passed as fighting stances, although they were little more than brutes using their size and raw strength instead of any real skill.

Kazimir reached back, and in one fluid motion, grabbed two knives from the table and threw one. It lodged itself in one of the thug's throats. He then wrapped his arm around Bartholomew Darkings, who was holding his probably-broken nose, and pulled him in, the other knife at his throat.

"Tell your men to get out of here and never return unless every one of you wants to look like that." Kazimir wrenched Darkings' neck, pointing his eyes down at the gurgling thug.

"You will not get away with this," Darkings said.

Kazimir flicked his wrist, and the tip of the blade caught Bartholomew Darkings' ear.

"Okay, okay!" he blubbered. "Let's go boys."

Kazimir waited until the surviving thugs were out of the house before walking Darkings to the front door and shoving him down the front steps.

"Do not return," Kazimir said.

Whitney sidled up to him in the doorway and threw the Crown. "Don't forget this!" It hit Darkings in the back of the head, and the fat man stumbled before turning to snatch it up.

Whitney turned to see Young Whitney staring, stunned and speechless. Lauryn knelt by Rocco's side, cradling his head. Whitney gave his younger counterpart a sidelong glance and the boy wiped his nose with his sleeve.

"Rocco," Lauryn whispered.

His father groaned and sucked in air through his teeth.

"Are you okay?" she asked.

"Where's the vagabond?" he asked.

"Right here, Whitney said.

"Thank you for what you did, taking the fall for my boy," he groaned.

Whitney could tell the man was in incredible pain. "It was stupid, but thank you."

"He was aiming for me," Whitney said, unable to believe what he was seeing. This was not how the night he remembered had unfolded.

"You were trying to keep my boy safe, and for that, you have my eternal gratitude."

Whitney never heard his father say a single kind thing about him growing up. He glanced over at Young Whitney, who hid his face. Big Whitney grabbed Rocco's wrist and tried to lift him, but the man squealed and crumpled back to the floor.

"Are you okay?" Whitney asked. He couldn't believe he was asking that question of his father.

"I can't feel my legs, he said. He gritted his teeth and squeezed his eyes shut.

"Oh, Rocco," his mother said, crying. After a moment hugging Rocco, she pulled back and yelled, "Whitney! Go get Father Drimmond and Wetzel, now!"

Big Whitney nearly started running, then remembered who she was talking to.

"C'mon," Kazimir said, grabbing Whitney. "Let them handle their own affairs. Let's get rid of this body."

Whitney got stuck carrying the thug by the heavy end. Weight didn't seem to be any different in Elsewhere, the thug may as well have weighed a ton. Whitney had to stop a few times to catch his breath on what Kazimir had assured him wasn't air before they reached the creek at the back of his family's property.

"Right here," Whitney said, groaning. He and Kazimir tossed the body of the dead thug into the brush by the creek. He remembered burying stolen treasures nearby as a kid and even saw the glint of something shiny under a pile of rocks.

He gave the body an extra hard kick into the current so it wouldn't ever come back on the Fierstowns. Someone might find it down a ways in some other worthless town, bloated and unrecognizable—if there even were other towns in Elsewhere.

Whitney exhaled and fell against a tree stump. He couldn't die from hunger in Elsewhere, but he was exhausted all the same. Kazimir too seemed winded without his supernatural, upyr abilities.

"You were *supposed* to jump out with me," Whitney said.

"I warned you to take the path of least resistance," Kazimir replied.

"What's the point of having an upyr companion if I can't beat up some thugs who have it coming?"

"Do you still not realize where you are, you ignorant, son of a—"

"Hard to insult her now that you've met her, isn't it?"

Kazimir exhaled through his teeth. "You said this is all your memory, didn't you?"

"Sort of, only I didn't rob Darkings, and it wasn't the Glass Crown." Whitney stuck out his chest. "It took a more refined thief to pull those off."

Kazimir appeared to hold back another insult. "Was your father hurt then?"

"No, just a few bruises from being punched. They burned down the barn and made me watch as punishment, and I—well, younger me—got stuck helping rebuild it for months."

"All these years and you still haven't learned there are consequences."

"What, I was just supposed to watch it happen again? What is the point of the place if I'm just supposed to relive every yigging memory?"

"That is precisely the point, thief." Kazimir stood and brushed his pants. "This isn't your game. It's theirs." He looked around, and Whitney followed his gaze but saw nothing but trees. "Give an opening, and you'll lose your mind faster. So, stop acting like an impetuous child and let's hope your father is all right. There's no telling what *they'll* do if he's not."

They set off back toward the house. Whitney took a second or three to let the words sink in. He knew Elsewhere tortured fallen souls, at least that's what the Church of Iam preached. Good, honest people went to live out eternity in paradise through the Gate of Light, but what happened to those who were magically exiled to Elsewhere by their best friend along-side an upyr?

He hurried and caught up to Kazimir. "You should have taken down that fellow with a club before he ever started his swing," Whitney said. "I've seen you move ten times faster."

Kazimir bit his lip. Whitney noticed it wasn't only anger twisting his features, but frustration. "I didn't this time."

A few clever quips popped into Whitney's head. He settled on silence. Maybe the upyr had even fewer of his abilities than Whitney thought, as slow now as an average man. Even if that were true, Whitney was smart enough to know he still couldn't take him in a one on one fight without a chance to cheat.

As they approached the farmhouse, the town father—who was now of Glintish decent for whatever reason—caned his way out of the house toward the exit gate at the edge of the Fierstown property. Whitney held it open for him.

"Thank you, my son," he said. "Praise the Fallen."

Whitney froze in the gateway, and it wasn't because of the priest's refusal to praise Iam, but because of the man's face. The cloth wrapped around his eyes made it difficult to tell, but it was clearly not Father Hullquist. Not only in skin color, but the man looked exactly like Torsten Unger.

"Torsten?" Whitney said, but the man ignored him as if he'd said nothing at all.

Whitney blinked hard. Still Torsten. It was just like how Darkings had appeared as another figure from his childhood.

It's just Elsewhere messing with you, Whitney told himself. *Just play along, like the blood-sucking upyr said. You always wanted to try your hand in an acting troupe.*

Wetzel suddenly plowed by Whitney. The old codger wore his usual rags, hollowed out shells and dried fruits dangling from his neck, each holding odd potions and powders. He was the strangest man Whitney had ever met, and Sora, as a child, used to say the same. She said they rarely spoke, meanwhile he'd secretly been training her in blood magic.

Seeing him made Whitney wonder if she had any other secrets, such as having exiled someone else to Elsewhere with her power before. Then he worried that she might be with him—he wasn't ready to see her.

Luckily, only Lauryn and Young Whitney followed behind, the latter looking anxious and cowering behind her. Whitney couldn't tell if his nervousness was for his father, or for the repercussions of what he'd done. He had no experience in worrying over Rocco after all.

"How is he?" Whitney asked.

Kazimir stood off to the side, watching, but not speaking.

Wetzel stopped and scrutinized Big Whitney. "Who is this?" he asked, leaning in uncomfortably close. His skin stunk of muck from trolling the riverbank, searching for herbs. He pulled something from one of his many pockets, a feather, and waved it in the shape of an eight front of Whitney's face. His eyes widened, he opened his mouth, then closed it again.

"Wetzel, this is Willis," Lauryn said. Her eyes were puffy and red.

Wetzel craned his neck to look into Whitney's ear, then grumbled, "Your color is wrong."

"What?" Whitney asked.

"Your color. It is wrong."

"Uh, thanks?" Whitney said.

Wetzel grumbled again, then continued back into town, all the strange containers hanging all over his rags clattering.

"You'll have to excuse him," Lauryn said. "He means the best, and he is the only healer we have."

"What did he say?" Whitney asked.

"Father Drimmond prayed for him. Blessed him. He's asleep now." Her voice shook. "Wetzel said… he said…"

"It's okay, take your time."

"He's... he's...." Lauryn's face fell into her hands as she tried to mask her sobbing.

"His back is broken," Young Whitney said for her. "They said he's never gonna walk again without a miracle from the fallen gods."

"I thought I told you to stay inside!" Lauryn snapped.

"I—I didn't mean for this." Tears welled in the corner of his eyes, then his head sunk and he sulked back toward the house. Big Whitney found it strange seeing himself so somber. He hated being sad; in fact, he couldn't remember the last time he let that feeling overtake him. He rolled with life, improvised—and now he wondered if it was that nature Elsewhere planned to prey on.

"I'm sure he never imagined this could happen," Whitney said.

"He's always getting into trouble," Lauryn said, voice clogged from crying. "It was bound to catch up to him eventually."

Whitney frowned. Burned barn or crippled father, the result was the same. His mother's love would wane every time she looked at him.

"I don't know what we're gonna do," Lauryn sobbed. "The farm. The house. Who's going to finish the roof? Tend the land? We can barely afford help right now, and the King's taxes keep going up with the wars in the South. Oh, gods…"

Whitney thought about the sacrifice Rocco made, then the things Kazimir had said to him. He didn't like the upyr, but he'd had experience with Elsewhere. It was Whitney's fault the man—this version of him at least—was crippled. Had he just stayed in that stupid closet, everything would have been fine.

"Don't you worry about a thing," Whitney said. He turned to Kazimir and said, "We'll help."

"You will?" Lauryn's eyes lit up. "We don't have much to pay, but…"

Whitney shook his head. "Forget about that. We have nowhere else in this whole world to be. We've been looking to settle down."

"Oh, bless you, kind sirs." She threw her arms around Whitney. He nearly hugged her in return before remembering that as far as she knew they'd just met. He didn't realize, however, how much he'd missed the warmth of her hugs.

"I won't let you do it for free," she said, barely able to contain her excitement. "How's ten bronzers a day sound, and you can sleep in the barn, and have supper for as long as you're here? "

"That's fine, right Kazimir?" Whitney nudged the upyr and earned a glare that made his heart feel like it'd jumped into his throat.

"Bless you ten times over!" She went to hug Kazimir, but the man's demeanor was enough to scare off a starving Westvale whore. She settled for a bow.

"You have no idea how much this means to us," she said. "And it'll do good for Whitney to have such fine gentleman as you. Especially with his father…" She paused, and her enthusiasm faded. "Well, anyway… I'll talk to Rocco about the details. For now, there's more than enough room in the barn, and I'll set down blankets. Sorry we don't have more."

"We've slept on worse." Whitney grinned, and she did the same though hers brimmed with sadness.

"Path of least resistance, right?" Whitney said, pleased with himself as she waddled away back to the house. "What can be more simple and boring than farming? It's why I left to find some excitement."

Kazimir grimaced, said nothing, and headed off toward the barn. Whitney all but patted himself on the back. If Elsewhere wanted to try and throw him, he was up for the challenge. He could play the good guy in their game until he found a way out of this gods-forsaken place.

X I

THE DESERTER

"What will ye do?" Sigrid asked.

She and Rand sat side by side in the mouth of an alley at the end of the docks, a blanket wrapped around their shoulders. They were at their favorite spot in Autlas' Inlet, named after the first King of Glass. Once home to the wealthy and influential of the city, the area was destroyed by a storm off the Torrential Sea the likes of which none had seen since. Those who survived moved to higher ground, taking up residence in the district just beyond the castle walls in what is known as Old Yarrington. Now surrounded by the slums of Dockside, the homage to the Father of Glass was one small step away from insulting.

In the warmer months, Gunter, a merchant old as the docks themselves, worked a stand behind them. He peddled the best mussels this side of the gorge and likely beyond. Rand wouldn't know. He'd never traveled so far. He used to toss them one every day when they were children. Now Gunter wanted coin like everyone else.

He'd been Wearer of White, but he'd never been anywhere. Given the highest honor the Kingdom offered someone without a noble name, yet he'd only seen their little corner.

He sneezed. On top of it all, he felt as if he was coming down with sickness.

A stiff breeze blew in from the ocean, carrying flurries of snow with it. Tall waves from the Torrential Sea broke against jetties at the mouth of the inlet, tossing ships in the ice-cold water within. Most belonged to the Glass Kingdom, but there was an unusual number of longboats moored along the curved docks. Glassmen from Crowfall and further north would see those square, patterned sails and pointed prows bearing the imagery of the Buried Goddess carved into the wood and fear for their lives. They were the ships of Drav Cra raiders and having never been farther north than Westvale, Rand had never seen them before.

Presently, one sailed in from the darkness of the sea before them. A fur-clad warrior at the bow barked orders to more than a dozen rowers. Their shields hung along the sides of the hull, painted in all manner of heathen imagery.

It had always been custom for Liam's training Shieldsmen to be sent north to protect towns against Drav Cra raiders, but as peace painted the land and the Glass grew stronger, there'd been fewer raiding parties to defend against. When Uriah Davies wore the helm, he'd been known to still send his men into the cold to test their mettle—but Torsten had been too preoccupied with a dying king to focus much on his men.

Rand didn't blame the man—after all, look at what he himself had accomplished during his tenure as Wearer serving under the foreign Queen Oleander. Nothing but murder. She was one of the northerners in another life after all.

After Liam's illness became visible and he was kept within the castle to maintain appearances, and Sir Uriah disappeared, Rand started to hear tales of the Drav Cra returning to their old ways. The heathens had once again begun looting, raping, and pillaging as much as they could manage before vanishing to return to their tundra in ships just like the one before him. Rand knew it was true because half the uprooted refugees wound up in Dockside after their homes were torched.

If Wren could be believed, these Drav Cra killers were now taking up residence in the very castle Rand swore to protect.

"Rand," Sigrid said, tearing Rand from his reverie.

"Sorry." Rand shook out his head. "It's just those ships; I'm not used to seeing them here."

"Yer just noticing, are ye?"

"Apparently."

"Been getting worse for a month now, brother. They come into the Maiden's Mugs, trying to trade trinkets for ale or just slamming down an axe. We're all too scared to ask for autlas."

Rand shivered as the wind picked up.

"Here," Sigrid said. She went to share more of the blanket with him, but he pushed it back.

"I'm fine," he said, sneezing again.

His hands would tremble regardless, his body desperate for a drink. His head throbbed as well. It'd been so long since he allowed himself to feel anything, he almost welcomed the pain to accompany his sore throat.

"Ye ain't fine," she said. "If Wren didn't show when he did ye'd have—"

"But he did," Rand interrupted before she could remind him.

"Was a miracle, it was."

"It was an old man come calling at a lucky hour." He didn't even know why he was being so stubborn. He too had wondered whether Iam's hand had intervened.

"Is that all ye'd call it?"

"No," he said, then pulled a bit of the blanket over him and scooted closer to his sister. "A reminder, maybe. That the vow to take the Shield is one made for life, and I turned my back on it. I should have been killed the moment that happened, but Sir Unger never lost faith, even though I had."

"Ye aren't considering going back for true, are ye?"

Rand hung his head. He couldn't help but picture Torsten chained up in a dungeon like an animal. "I don't know."

"After the things ye did? All they made ye do? I spent months keeping Sir Unger away from ye, brother. Look at what they done to ye." She clasped one of his hands in both of hers. "I know it was Wren the Holy they sent this time, but they don't deserve ye."

Although Rand knew the love with which they were offered, the words stung him harder than a slap in the face. "Torsten Unger was the most honorable man I ever met in that gods-forsaken castle. Perhaps he is the most honorable man I've ever known."

"Where was he when the Queen Mother started hanging everyone in her way?"

"Doing whatever it took to serve the kingdom the right way."

She squeezed his hands tighter. "Iam gave ye a second chance. Don't throw it away acting as their murdering thug. Let's leave all of it behind. Leave this place, go somewhere south where it's warmer."

"With all my heart, I wish I could."

"So, yer going back?"

"It's my duty; I'm just… I'm not sure I can do what they need me to."

"Of course, ye can't. Ye ain't a killer, Rand, I don't care who they're needing to die. Ye never have been. Ye joined them to protect people, just like ye've always looked out for me."

"Not recently." He turned and looked straight into her eyes. She looked so much like their mother. "I'm so sorry for everything I've put you through."

A tear rolled down her cheek as she stared back. She released his hands so she could wipe it away, then turned to snivel.

"For the first time in months, I don't feel like yer a stranger. I don't want them to destroy the good man ye are again."

"I can never bring back those who died so senselessly, but if I have a chance to help bring them justice? The chance to stop the person behind all of this?"

"Rand, I won't stop ye, but—"

The blanket snapped from off their shoulders. Rand whipped around to see a group of three Drav Cra men. Their skin was white as the snow falling around them. Thick, braided beards dropped from their chins, getting lost in the gray pelt of their furs.

The biggest of them scrutinized the ratty blanket. "No wonder why so many of you Glassmen freeze in the deep winter." He laughed. The others joined him.

"Such a pretty thing under there though," another said, gawking at Sigrid. He was gaunt with a sharp, hawkish nose permanently broken in two places.

"Give it back," Sigrid demanded.

"And such fire too."

"I think you fellows are lost." Rand stood and positioned himself in front of his sister. His heart began to race, reminding him how sore his ribs were from nearly hanging to death.

"Damn right we are," the big one said. "We just sailed in at Drad Skaardi's request expecting to see the grand city of Yarrington, and all I see is yig and shog."

"Except you, little lady," the hawkish one said. "I hear southern ladies'll do anything."

"If you're looking for women, I suggest you head down the other end of Dockside," Rand said. "Valin Tehr runs a brothel called the Vineyard where you could get whatever you can imagine."

"Oh, but I never had much of an imagination," he said, taking a step closer. "I want her. She looks so… ripe."

The man grabbed Sigrid's arm. Rand shoved him away.

"Don't touch her!" he snapped. A few locals strolled by, glancing over, but otherwise minding their own business. That was how things were in Dockside. Nobody got involved in another's business unless they were left with no other choice. As for guards, they were rarely seen. It was why Rand joined the King's Shield in the first place. To try and make the forgotten corner of Yarrington he grew up in a better place.

The big one drew a hatchet and raised it to Rand's throat. The sharp edge scraped across the short hairs on his neck.

"Or what?" the man asked. "Look at you, shaking like a true southern flower."

Rand caught a glimpse of his hands, still involuntarily shaking. "I'm warning you," he said.

"Haven't you heard, Glassman? We share this city now. It's only right for you to share her with my friend here. It's… what do they call it? The law."

The hawkish one grabbed Sigrid and yanked her forward, wrapping his arms around her. She squirmed and tried to push him away, calling for Rand to help, but his whole body seized. All he could see was Tessa and the others, necks forced into nooses on the command of the Crown.

Sigrid elbowed the man in the groin and broke free. He grabbed the back of her shirt as she tried to escape. It tore in half before she slipped on the icy dock and hit the wood hard. The savage grabbed her leg and dragged her back screaming.

"Rand!"

The leader chortled. "That this puny little man's name? More like runt."

The screams of all the voices of those who'd suffered filled Rand's mind, mixing until, through the chaos, he heard his sister scream his name. His vision focused. His eyelids peeled open. Suddenly, he was back with Sigrid, the freezing air biting at his nose. His years of training for the King's Shield kicked in, and he didn't think—he just acted.

He punched upward, catching the big one in the elbow. It didn't break the bone but extended his tendons so he couldn't get any strength behind his swipe at Rand's neck. The blade sliced off a few hairs from Rand's unshaved chin as he twisted out of the way. The big man lost his balance, and a kick to the jaw finished the job. He tumbled off the docks and into freezing water.

Rand heard the unmistakable hum of steel through the air. He ducked beneath the swinging hatchet of one of the others, then barreled into him shoulder first. They hit the floor and rolled over. Rand held the man's weapon-arm back with both hands and earned blow after blow to the ribs. Rand head-butted the Drav Cra heathen just above the ridge of his nose. They both came away dazed, but Rand had existed in a fog for months now. He recovered quicker and pried the hatchet out of the man's loosened grip.

He drew it across the man's throat, shoved him aside, and faced the belligerent savage who'd first grabbed his sister. The man had a knife to Sigrid's throat. Tears filled her eyes, already starting to freeze upon her cheeks as she cried Rand's name.

"You're gonna regret that, Glassman," the savage said.

Rand squeezed the grip of the hatchet so tight the wood creaked. *Creak, creak, creak.*

"Let her go!" he roared, focusing his anger.

"Or what?" The savage slid the blade closer to her jugular, drawing a bit of blood. "I swear, I'll gut the pretty whore like a fish and make you watch as I take her—"

Without so much as a warning, Rand threw the hatchet as hard as he could. The blade sunk into man's forehead, the front of his skull crunching. He collapsed, and Sigrid twisted her body with him so that his knife only drew a shallow scrape along her neck. She gasped for air as she crawled out from under his arm.

Rand ran to help Sigrid to her feet. Only once she was upright did he take a moment to breathe. One of their assailants gurgled, blood pouring out of his split throat. The big one splashed around in the water, his movements slowing as the cold set it. He was dead already but didn't know it, and the one who started it all was still, eyes stuck wide open in shock. A flake of snow fell upon one, landing like a speck of dust on glass.

Rand scanned his surroundings. A homeless woman cowered in an alley, burying the face of her child against her bosom to shield him from the horrors. A dockhand gripped his broom, unable to move. A few more down the way helped the incoming Drav Cra longboat into a slip.

"Rand… they… they were going to…" Sigrid was shivering uncontrollably, both from terror and from all the snow filling her torn and tattered dress. Rand could feel the goosebumps all along her exposed skin.

"I know," he said. "They can't hurt you now."

"Are you sure they're…"

"They're dead."

He yanked the hatchet free of the man's cranium with a satisfying *thunk*, hung it from his belt, then swept up Sigrid and helped her toward the Maiden's Mugs. Not a soul approached them or the bodies. No one said a word. In the deep winter, if you died in an alley, your rotting corpse might not be found until Spring. That was the way of things in Dockside, the strip of Yarrington by the water's edge in South Corner.

Halfway home, Rand locked eyes with one of the Drav Cra standing on the prow of the arriving ship. There was a wild look in them. Rand quickly turned Sigrid down an alley and away from the man's gaze. A few beggars who'd taken up residence beneath strung up tents rattled pewter mugs for money, not realizing that Rand and Sigrid were equally poor now thanks to Rand's weakness.

They reached the Maiden's Mugs and quietly made their way for the hearth. A few drunkards looked Sigrid over on her way by, unable to help themselves with her dress so torn. All those men in for an early round before her shift had likely dreamed of seeing more of her. Her smooth, milky skin showed now even more than in her barmaid uniform. It didn't matter that her lip was split and her teeth chattered from the cold.

Rand stopped to pull the neckline of her ripped dress up as high as he could, then noticed a pair of Drav Cra seated in the corner, speaking in their heathen language and laughing over pints. He led her as far away from them as possible on his route to the hearth. A fire crackled, and he carefully set his sister down on one of the tavern's few cushioned chairs.

"There ye are, Sigrid!" Gideon Trapp called over. He approached from the side, cleaning out a mug. "Almost sundown. Ye'd better get dressed."

"Get her a blanket," Rand asked.

"What'd ye say to me, thief?"

"I said to get her a gods-damned blanket!" Rand slammed on the nearest table. Every pair of eyes in the room fell upon him, except those of the Drav Cra.

Trapp's face twisted with rage. Rand could tell he was preparing to curse in response until he got closer and noticed Sigrid'a condition.

"Who did that?" he said. Not in a way that showed concern for her, but as if a precious possession of his had been damaged.

"I'm not going to ask again, Trapp."

Finally, the portly man hopped to and went to storage, returning a moment later with frayed sackcloth probably used to cover barrels. Rand tore it from his hands and wrapped it around Sigrid's shoulders.

"There you go, Sig," he whispered. Now it was she who shook uncontrollably, and it was Rand's turn to care for her. He tucked the cloth tightly over her chest. She stared up at him, eyes agape in horror, but no other part of her moved. Seeing her in such a state of complete shock made Rand feel ill. He may have been the Shieldsman, but she'd always been the tough one—always wanting to go hunting with Rand and their father when they were younger, never shying away from elbowing a handsy customer in the gut as a barmaiden.

"Either of ye gonna tell me what happened?" Trapp questioned, his hairy arms crossed over his belly.

"What happened is you're going to keep her right here by the fire for the rest of the night," Rand said.

"No way. She can clean up, but I need her on the floor tonight. She's all I got."

Rand's fist and jaw clenched. He rose to his full height and glowered down at the man. "If I hear you have her working, I swear to Iam, you'll pay."

Gideon Trapp didn't back down. He rose up on his toes and shoved his face toward Rand's. "Who the yig do ye think you are? She don't work, yer both out on the streets."

"I am a…" His voice trailed off. He wanted to say what he was, to claim he was a knight of the King's Shield out loud, but his brain wouldn't let him. Instead, he said, "I swear to you, Trapp, one word she's working, and someone will hear about what's in the crates shipping through your basement for Valin Tehr. I may not have any friends left at the castle, but I know how to get word to them." Rand kept his voice low so nobody, especially the Drav Cra in the corner would hear.

The color fled Trapp's chubby, red cheeks.

"Drinking doesn't make me blind," Rand said. "Now fetch her some warm tea."

Trapp grumbled something under his breath as he turned. Rand made sure he headed straight for the bar. All the barkeep did was help smuggle in manaroot from the Eastern Panping Region for one of Yarrington's more vocal leaders of the underworld. That was tame for Dockside, but the root was outlawed after the Panping Wars. Panpingese Soothsayers were said to use it to help magnify their connection with Elsewhere. For everyone else, it was a powerful sensory amplifying drug popular in brothels.

What Rand didn't mention was that it was his sister who'd told him about Trapp's dealings soon after he moved in with her. Somehow, in his alcohol filled stupor, Rand held on to that bit of knowledge. All those long months she'd managed to take care of him alone after he abdicated his duty and came stumbling home to hide in forgotten Dockside, he couldn't even do the same for her without needing a bit of her help.

"Everything is going to be all right, Sig," he said as he kneeled by her side and took her hand. He could tell she wanted to thank him for dealing with Trapp, but her lips merely parted. "Just stay right here and keep warm."

"Wh—what are ye gonna—gonna do?" she replied, teeth still chattering.

"Keep you safe this time." He kissed her on the top of the head, realizing it was the same thing their mother used to do when one of them got hurt, then he headed for the stairs. He paused at the bottom, eying a full mug of ale in the grip of some grimy, off-duty dockhand. He watched the liquid foaming, sloshing against the side. His whole body tingled merely from the sight, but he shook his head out and scaled the stairs.

It was clear now what he had to do, and he couldn't do it with his head in a fog and his vision blurred. He threw open his door and strode to the opposite side of the tiny room. Then he stopped and stared down into the reflection of his armor.

It was time to wear it again. Time to serve Iam and those closest to Him.

Redstar, the wicked man who'd cursed the Queen Mother's son and driven her into a spiteful rampage, needed to die. And he wasn't going to do it for Wren or Torsten or the King's Shield. He was going to do it for his sister and Dockside who'd suffer under the Drav Cra occupation more than any other part of Yarrington and to find justice for those murdered at his own hand like Tessa.

No matter what it took.

XII

THE MYSTIC

Sora walked slowly, cautiously. Yaolin City was larger than any place she'd ever been and unfamiliar in all regards.

Statues of all shapes and sizes rose on both sides of the street, every ten paces. Upon closer examination, Sora noticed they'd all had their faces rearranged. None of them were exactly alike, but she knew without a doubt, they were intended to be the visage of King Liam the Conqueror.

Her heart sank for her people. These statues must have been idols of Panpingese emperors or gods, but now they were all desecrated—history abolished for the sake of a far-off king who was now dead.

And now, from this vantage, she was even more in awe of Liam managing to conquer such a massive city. It was twice the size of Yarrington at least, not to mention it had been ruled by mystics capable of bending the world to their wills.

It was immediately clear, however, that the Glass presence in Yaolin City remained strong. Blue and white flags hung from many buildings, totally out of place against the earthy tones and terra-cotta roofs, guards posted at every corner. It was more security than Winde Port had by a long shot, despite being twice as far from the Glass Castle. Muskigo's active rebellion probably didn't help with that.

Still, through shop windows and on the streets, Sora saw smiling faces and generally happy-looking people, both Panpingese and Glassmen. It was a jarring juxtaposition to the Panping Ghetto in Winde Port where she'd seen children begging for coin or scraps of food.

"Come off the adventure, miss?" a lady said, appearing in front of her. Dresses and fine clothing hung along the porch beside them. "A pretty girl like you could use some proper clothing. Take your measurements?"

"I… no, thank you." Sora ducked away.

"Finest dumplings at port!" shouted another. The aroma coming from his stand was intoxicating, but she didn't have time to waste on trying food just yet.

As she traveled down the statue-lined boulevard, she read all the store signs—or she tried to. Half or more were in Panpingese, others had both languages but used strange words she didn't understand. She stopped when she spotted one that said: Clairvoyant of the Mystic Arts.

"It can't be that easy," Sora said to Aquira who wasn't listening. She was huddled against Sora's neck, probably terrified by the busy streets.

Sora stepped up to the threshold, and a Panpingese woman wearing a dress covered in jangling jewelry emerged from behind a shimmering curtain. She wore a ridiculous amount of makeup that made her look like a street performer.

"Welcome to—" she stopped, her eyes widening. "I am sorry, madam. I am sorry." She dropped to her knees and kowtowed. "Here. Here."

She gathered a pouch from beneath the folds of her dress with one hand and raised it without looking up. Sora didn't take it, and the bag fell to the floor, spilling open to reveal dozens of gold autlas, enough to live comfortably for a year.

"I've not been able to pay in some time," she said. "Business has been scarce since the seas became unstable from the war to the west."

Sora knelt quickly and shoved the bag back toward the woman. "What are you talking about?" she asked. A few minutes in Yaolin and people were trying to give her more autlas than she'd ever need. No wonder Whitney loved this place.

"Lady, please forgive me," the woman said. "There's far more there than I owe. Spare me, I beg."

"Stand up," Sora said.

The woman was reluctant, but she stood.

"Who are you?" Sora asked.

"I'm no one, my Lady," she said, still purposefully avoiding eye-contact.

"I'm no lady. Why do you call me that?"

The woman laughed, but then her expression quickly grew dour. "This is a test? You are one of the..." she lowered her voice, "...Secret Council, are you not? Your aura, your power... It is—"

"Me?" Sora said. "What in Iam's name is the Secret Council? Wait." Sora leaned in close, a glimmer in her eyes. "Are you talking about the Mystic Council?"

"You charlatan! Thief!" the woman shouted, wiping her tears. "You have wasted my time and brought fear upon me without reason. Please, leave this place." In an instant, she swept back into her shop, the curtain fluttering behind her.

"Mistress!" Sora shouted. She pulled the veil back and called again, but there was no answer. The room was empty but for a circular table with a small, glass orb set upon it.

"Iam's light," Sora exhaled. "What was that?" Aquira flew off her shoulder and landed on the table, circling the orb and sniffing it. Sora approached slowly. The walls were all white and unadorned, the ceiling black as night. But there were no other trinkets on shelves like there would be in a shop of curiosities.

She reached for the orb and gently lifted it from a jade stand with prongs like dragon claws on three sides. She felt nothing. It was heavier than it looked, but nothing more than a globe. She returned it and extended an arm for Aquira.

"Come on, girl," she said. "We need to find your family."

She headed back outside onto Xiahou Boulevard, bustling with traders, guards, performers, and all manner of other things that go on in capital cities. Most people shared her features, but most men wore the same strange silk robes as Mr. Kyoto and most women, flowered dresses with flowing fabric belts tied into bows. It was then that she realized how far from home she truly was, and how little she understood about this new world, even if she had been born there.

Sora shuffled along until she saw a large sign with words written in

Panpingese. She recognized the letters but couldn't read the words. The image of two bones and a book spread open was burned into the wood, which indicated she'd found the place she was searching for.

Sora felt Aquira peep over her shoulder and the wyvern began to purr.

"You recognize this place, huh?" Sora asked.

The wyvern made a series of chirping noises.

As Sora approached, two Glass soldiers stomped toward her from the opposite direction.

"Clear the streets!" they shouted absentmindedly as they talked to one another, laughing. "Clear the streets!" People listened, flooding away from the road without protest or delay. However, those with shop stands took longer. One earned a shove, knocking over the beautiful calligraphy pieces he was selling.

"Speed it up!" the guards ordered.

Sora continued ahead, the distance between them closing and the bookstore resting in between.

"Aye! You!" one shouted. She stopped, and they filled the gap. "If you don't speak the common tongue, you are in violation of the law."

"I do!" she said.

"Then you're just insolent?"

"Me? No! What?" Sora stammered.

"We said, 'off the streets!' yet, here you are."

"I'm just trying to get home," she lied. "I'm sorry. I live right there." She pointed to the rooms above the bookstore, and the men let their eyes follow.

They regarded her suspiciously for a moment, then one said, "Get going. Now! We have a parade to set up for."

"Sorry," she said and rushed by.

She felt a yanking behind her, then heard a squeal.

"What's this?" one of the guards asked.

She turned around and saw the men prodding Aquira who was being held by the frills and throat, wings batting against the man's armor. The way he held her kept her from being able to open her mouth and spray fire or claw at the man. This wasn't the first time they'd dealt with a wyvern.

"Put her down!" Sora demanded.

"Oh, found your voice, huh, wench?" The other guards pulled their swords halfway from their sheaths.

Wench?

Sora couldn't believe what she was seeing. She thought Panping would be different, that somehow being in her own land, she wouldn't suffer the same prejudices. Apparently, she was wrong.

She felt the gentle tugging of Elsewhere from deep within, begging her to make the sacrifice necessary to burn the men to a crisp but she stifled it before it managed to take hold.

"She is my friend, and you are hurting her," Sora said calmly. "Please, put her down."

"Aye, that's a bit better. But what if we want to keep her?" He turned to the other man. "Never ate dragon before, have you?"

They laughed.

Aquira squirmed, her muffled squeals somehow even more distressing than if she were permitted to howl.

"Maybe we bring them both to the Overlord?" the guard said.

"Supposed to call him Governor Nantby in public," whispered the other. He had an incongruously small head and a pugnacious goiter on his neck.

"Whatever," said the first, running his fingers along Aquira's tail.

"She's a wyvern," Sora said, "and I think you're making her angry."

"I know what she is, *girl*. And they aren't supposed to be on the streets without a muzzle, by word of the Governor." The guard, still laughing, leaned in and scratched Aquira under the chin. "Aw, is the little pest getting angry?"

Aquira thrashed hard enough to shift the man's grip so she could snap at him, taking a chunk off the man's finger. He dropped her and swore.

"Kill that little shogger!" he commanded.

The other guard hesitated as Aquira reared back, spreading her wings wide. Her wingspan couldn't have been more than a meter, but she still cut an intimidating figure.

They gathered their nerve and began inching forward, Aquira let out a shrill cry, and a blast of flames burst forth from her maw toward the sky. Sora could tell it was restrained. Had she wanted to, Sora was sure the little wyvern could have burned them all in their armor and watched as their ashes filled the wind.

Aquira flapped her wings and rose, hovering at about head-height, then screamed again.

This time, the guards didn't stick around. "Get that thing under control or else!" one yelled as they turned and ran down the street, nearly knocking each other over with the effort. Once they were a safe distance, Sora reached out and coaxed Aquira back to her shoulder.

"Let's go before they bring more," she said. "And thank you for holding back on those creeps."

She squeaked what Sora liked to imagine as 'you're welcome,' and then they continued into the bookstore. The door jingled on her way through, which startled Sora. She looked up to see a bell tied to a string in front of the door.

Clever, she thought.

"Hello?" she said softly. When no one answered, she called a little louder.

Books were everywhere—on shelves, tables, stacked on the floor. More books than Sora had ever seen. The closest she'd ever been to such a library was in Wetzel's shack, but those sprawled around the floor could have fit on one of the hundred shelves throughout the store.

She strolled through, taking it all in, reading the spines of the books. There were stories as well as learning books. Another shelf had nothing but scrolls piled nearly to the ceiling. Most were in Panpingese, but some were in common, or... she wondered what they called her language here. *Glassenese?* Others still were in languages she'd never seen before.

She stopped at a shelf with leather-bound tomes and fingered a few of them.

"Hello?" she called again as she walked toward the rear of the room.

She rounded a corner, putting the shelves behind her, and found another section of the store. More shelves lined the walls, but these had various artifacts resting on them. There were skulls and bones, jars, both large and small, filled with liquid, strange creatures floating within.

Aquira hissed. Sora turned around and saw bottles similar to Wetzel's potion bottles at an alchemy table. Within were concoctions, none of which Sora recognized, made with powders and herbs ground up using the mortar and pestle beside them.

"Ah, I thought I heard someone," said a voice from behind her.

Sora's hand instinctually fell to her knife as she spun around, bumping a shelf and causing a jar to topple. Aquira swooped down and caught it before any real damage could occur.

The man laughed as he slid closed the translucent door leading to an adjoining room. He wore a robe similar to the doorman at the Winde Traders Guild, but this one looked expensive—judging by the patterned, gold threading.

"I'm sorry," Sora said. She glanced down, realized she still had her fingers wrapped around the grip of her knife, and quickly let go. "I called out, but no one answered."

"You've done nothing wrong, dear," the man said. "Welcome to my humble shop. Are you finding things as you desire them to be?"

His back was impossibly straight, hands folded behind his back. After the initial shock wore off, Sora noticed the resemblance.

"Lord Bokeo?" she said.

"At your service." He bowed, which she found odd for anyone called Lord to do to anyone not a king.

"I am—"

"I know who you are Sora." He took a couple of steps, smiled wide and said, "Aquira."

The wyvern flapped her wings and soared to the man. She purred and nuzzled up against his face.

"Warm as ever, aren't you?" he said. "Have you been well?"

Aquira nodded.

Sora's mouth opened slightly.

"Are you still sure about this one?" he asked Aquira who nodded again. "Excellent."

Aquira rose up again and returned to Sora.

"Did you just..." Sora started. "Did you understand him?"

Aquira squeaked and bobbed her head.

"She understands?" Sora asked Lord Bokeo.

"She does a lot more than understand," he replied. "You are an extraordinary young woman, Sora."

"What do you mean?"

"Oh, dear, there's so much to discuss." Lord Bokeo took a few steps and reached out, offering her his arm. "We've been waiting for you."

"That's impossible," Sora said, backing up. "No one knew I was coming here. No one. I came to tell you of your son's unfortunate death, but apparently, you already knew about it."

"Knew about it? I've been expecting it."

The breath fled Sora's lungs. "What?"

"The Ancients have been waiting for you for some time, my dear. I knew—Tayvada knew that someday the gods would come calling."

"His death is the work of no god!" Sora bristled, thinking about Kazimir. "It was the work of a monster."

"All things are works of the gods."

Aquira purred, and Sora jumped. She had been so distracted by the man's words she almost forgot the wyvern on her shoulder.

"Relax, my dear, and I'll show you the world," Lord Bokeo said.

It sounded like something Whitney would have said. She stood, mouth agape that a man across Pantego somehow knew her name, just as the demons in the Webbed Woods had.

"I know this is a lot to take in, Sora," Lord Bokeo said, stepping closer. "There is much you do not know, and much you will discover, but as it turns out, time is short."

"Short for what?" she said. "Do you not even care about your son's passing?"

"My son made the sacrifice expected of him. We all have our purpose, dear. That was his."

Sora grew frustrated. She'd wasted valuable time away from her quest to find out what happened to Whitney. All to give her best to Tayvada's family and tell them how beloved he was in Winde Port. Apparently for no reason.

"Tell me, what is on your arm?" Lord Bokeo asked.

"My arm?" she said, surprised by the sudden shift in conversation.

"I mean upon your skin." He inched toward her, cautiously.

Sora pulled back.

"Please, Sora, I mean you no harm," he said. "Trust an old man. If you cannot trust me, trust your friend." He pointed to Aquira.

"I'm starting to feel deceived by everyone, including her."

"You cannot tell me you never suspected she understood your words?"

Sora couldn't deny it. The wyvern was either incredibly perceptive, or she took instruction through spoken language. The answer was probably both.

Aquira whined and lowered herself to the floor.

"Do not blame her," Lord Bokeo protested. "She was merely following commands."

The wyvern nuzzled against Sora's leg. Her warmth and the roughness of her skin oddly comforting.

"Now, may I?" Lord Bokeo asked.

Sora bit her lip and conceded. "Fine."

He moved close enough to roll her sleeve back. When the marks on the top of her forearm revealed themselves, she reeled back, but he tugged a bit on her wrist, straightening her elbow. Then he started to pull down her gloves.

"Just as I imagined. What are these?" he asked, pointing to the scars.

"None of your business," she said. Ever since Wetzel allowed her to practice blood magic, she'd been self-conscious of the scars on her hands and arms. Not only because the Glass Kingdom outlawed blood magic, but because nobody else had them. It was hard enough to fit in as a Panpingese refugee in a small town raised by the town kook.

"They are precisely my business." Lord Bokeo walked toward the shelf housing jars of fine powders. He pulled one, seemingly at random, and returned to Sora. While he perused the shelf, she considered running away, but still, curiosity had her pinned to the floor.

"What is that?" she asked.

"Will you trust me? I believe I possess the answers to all of your questions."

Sora nodded.

Lord Bokeo unscrewed the jar's cover and swirled the contents. "Stay still, even if it burns a little."

Sora flinched ever so slightly as he shook the contents of the jar onto her arm, careful to coat each scar. He was right, it burned, but she'd experienced worse pain every time she sliced herself to access the powers of Elsewhere.

After the burning subsided, Lord Bokeo bent over and blew away the powder.

Sora sneezed. When she opened her eyes, every scar on her arm and hand was gone.

"What the yig and shog?" She covered her mouth. "Excuse me, I'm sorry, Lord Bokeo."

He chuckled. "It is fine."

Her eyes went wide, and she said, "Wait, you do magic?"

"It was not magic, my dear. It is what learned men call alchemy."

"I know what that is." She'd watched Wetzel brew potions and toxins enough. She'd rarely seen him perform any blood magic himself, but he preferred to think of alchemy in the same light.

"Then you know that in many ways, it works like magic," he said, echoing Wetzel's sentiments. "But Alchemy calls upon the laws of Pantego and its elements. Magic breaks those laws through Elsewhere, and always it comes with a cost." He took her other hand and revealed those scars.

"So then, you know?" Sora said.

"That you do magic? Yes, but those days are over. Soon, you'll never need to mutilate your body again."

"You don't understand," she said. "I must do magic. I have to…" She was going to tell him of her need to see Whitney returned to this world, but remembered she had only just met the man, even if he'd somehow known her by name.

"I did not say you wouldn't do magic. But this barbaric way, this blood magic. That is the way of animals who would defile this world. You are above it. If you allow, I can make preparations for your training."

"Training for what?"

"Your bond to Elsewhere is strong, Sora. The gift courses through your veins. It always has. We wish to teach it which veins to travel. Wetzel could only instruct so far."

Sora swallowed.

Lord Bokeo smiled. "Yes, I know of the old badger as well." He put his arm on her shoulder and led her to a wall with a painting the size of a man. "You've not been forgotten, Sora. The Secret Council has watched you for some time."

Sora was too stunned to fight his guidance. The painting depicted three Panpingese warriors dressed in blue robes. She wasn't sure how she knew they were warriors, they held no weapons, but even in the painting, they bore a particular strength.

Rolling his fingers along the edge of the frame, Lord Bokeo stopped toward the bottom. Sora heard an audible click. Rising, he gave the frame a hard yank. The painting swung away from the wall, revealing a stone staircase.

"Come," Lord Bokeo said. Aquira screeched and flapped forward, following him as he descended.

"You expect me to follow you down there?"

When no response came, Sora looked from side to side. All the room held were dusty old books, and there was hardly anything fearful about a librarian. She hoped. Regardless, Tayvada's strange father clearly had a more intimate knowledge of Elsewhere, and that was precisely what she needed.

She took a deep breath, then hurried to catch up. She did, however, have the good sense to keep her hand on her weapon as she did. She was about halfway down the dark stairwell when she heard a creak as the painting closed behind her. All the light disappeared except for a faint, bluish glow emanating from the bottom of the staircase.

"Almost there," Lord Bokeo said.

"What is this place?" she asked.

"It is the Dixia Shanyow, or roughly translated, The Underground."

"Dixia Shanyow," Sora repeated softly.

"Many years ago, even before King Liam the Conqueror arrived and sowed discourse amongst our people, the Mystic Council became keenly aware of a time to come where they would not be welcome with arms wide open as they had been for so many centuries."

They reached the landing which opened into a chamber of engraved stone. Great statues of beasts Sora didn't recognize lined the walls on both sides. Water spewed from their mouths into pools, the ceaselessly rippling water, mesmerizing. In the middle, a platform bridged one side to the other.

"Those are wianu," he said, yanking her from her reverie. "The great sea beasts. Legend says they retreated when the Drav Cra expanded their tent stakes into lower Pantego. They have not been seen since the establishment of Westvale, their first city."

"They are…"

"Beautiful," Lord Bokeo finished for her.

"I was going to say terrifying, but I suppose beauty can be scary."

"Yes," he said, giving her a sidelong glare, "I believe that to be true as well."

"You were saying something about the Secret Council?"

"Ah, yes," he said, slowly proceeding across the bridge. He raised his voice over the gurgling of the fountains. "The Mystic Council decided it would be best to find quiet solace for a time, to bide time and wait for the age of Glass to fall."

"That could take centuries."

"For the remaining Ancients of the Mystic Order, centuries would be like days. They do not fear time and death the way the rest of us do. They can afford to wait."

"You mean to say they are immortal?"

"Not exactly," he said as they reached the other side. "They can be killed, but there are none outside of Elsewhere who we believe possess the power to do it. They went to great pains to survive after the culling of King Liam, sacrificing much of their power in this mortal realm to endure. All to ensure your future."

Sora assumed he meant the future of all Panpingese, but still, the words caught in the back of her mind somewhere as if they were intended only for her.

Massive, stone doors stood in their path, intricate markings covering both sides. Sora recognized some of the letters as the Panpingese alphabet, although she couldn't say what any of the words meant. Other lines and circles created patterns and shapes, but if they represented anything, she couldn't tell.

"How are you involved in all of this?" she asked.

"There will be much time to answer questions, although I believe you'll find all your questions will be answered in short time," he said. "To sate your curiosity regarding me, I am but a gatekeeper. My family was not blessed with the gift, my son especially, but our loyalty to the Council has never waned."

That explained why Kazimir didn't take to Tayvada's blood like a drug after he drained him. Before Sora could inquire further, Lord Bokeo raised his hand to the door and fit his finger within one of the engraved circles. Tracing it around, then to another, and then a straight line down to another series of loops. A deep growl sounded and shook the very stone upon which they stood. Dust billowed, and the door cracked open.

"Speak only when spoken to, Sora," he said. "This is very important."

Sora nodded. She wasn't sure what else to do.

Inside, she expected to see a giant, soaring cavern, but instead, it was a reasonably sized, circular room—twenty or thirty paces across. She followed Lord Bokeo to a raised dais the same shape as the room itself. The chamber was cold. Unnaturally cold. The chill pierced through Sora's layers as if she were naked and even then, her skin did nothing to keep it away from her bones.

She shivered.

Lord Bokeo stepped up onto the dais and beckoned Sora to follow. He climbed. She climbed. When he sat in the center with legs crossed over one another, Sora watched.

Placing his hands together, palms flat, Lord Bokeo inhaled, and in one breath said, "*Lu hwan, oolanxio!*"

Suddenly, as if reality itself changed, Sora saw seven thrones materialize around her in a circle. She looked to Lord Bokeo, who held a finger against pursed lips.

Turning back to the thrones, Sora now saw figures seated upon them. The one straight ahead of her wore a robe of blue, and the others wore yellow flecked with darker shades of yellow. All seven raised their hands and grabbed hold of their hoods, drawing them up, casting deep shadows over their faces.

"Sora, the one with no place to call home." A voice spoke, but Sora wasn't sure from which of the figures it had come.

Sora remembered what Lord Bokeo said about staying quiet and looked to him. He gestured for her to respond, though she wasn't sure how to.

"It is... I," she stammered and immediately felt ridiculous. It's what Whitney would've said, never the one to feel out of place no matter how bizarre the situation. She regarded Lord Bokeo again, and he nodded in approval.

"Aran Bokeo, we thank you for your service," the voice spoke again. "You may leave."

"Wait," Sora said, then cringed.

Lord Bokeo flinched but still rose and walked toward the door. He shot Sora a look that seemed to convey his condolences for the wrath she was about to suffer. Aquira shifted nervously as well, reminding Sora she was there.

The blue robed figure stood and stepped down from the throne. "Bokeo, wait." The voice sounded feminine as it hovered in the air.

Sora heard the shuffling of Bokeo's boots as he stopped.

"Our guest wishes for you to stay," the figure said. "Is that right?"

"I… uh…. Yes, my Lady," Sora said, hoping she addressed her correctly. She wasn't sure why she cared if Lord Bokeo, a relative stranger, remained, but even a face familiar for but minutes was preferable to these robed figures who reminded her of Redstar's followers in the Webbed Woods.

"Then please, stay."

"Yes, Ancient One," Lord Bokeo responded, bowing. Sora took note of the title.

"Do you know why you are here, Sora?" the woman asked.

"No, Ancient One," Sora replied.

"Aquira tells us you are special."

"May I ask you something about that?" Sora asked.

The Ancient urged her to continue with an elegant wave of her hand.

"I do not understand how Aquira told you anything when she's been with me since nearly the day we met," Sora said.

"Aquira is not average, just as you are not average." The woman turned her shrouded face toward Aran Bokeo as if waiting for approval, and they exchanged a nod. "Many years ago, when the gods spoke of Tayvada's sacrifice, we sent Aquira to wait for you."

"For me? I'm sorry, I still do not understand. I… I grew up in a small village far from all of this. An orphan of war, that's all."

"The Well of Wisdom showed us that in Tayvada's passing, you would finally be ready to return to us. To fulfill your destiny."

"My what?" Sora fought back the sick feeling within her belly. To think, Tayvada might have died because of her, just as Whitney possibly had. She couldn't believe it. "Tayvada didn't pass, he was murdered by an upyr who was hunting another… my friend."

"The cause of his death matters not. Only that his lifeblood was spilt. Aquira knew the moment she met you at the guild that you were the one for which we have waited so long. When she told Tayvada, he accepted his fate, as you must."

Sora looked to Aquira. The wyvern blinked her two sets of eyelids, then bobbed her head, frills wriggling.

"She speaks now?" Sora asked.

"Not with words. In time, you will learn to communicate with her, and she will be your aid as we embark upon this great journey. It is time to fulfill your destiny."

"And if I refuse?"

Behind her, Aran Bokeo winced. She was uncomfortably aware of the eyes of the other six hooded figures on her even though their faces were shrouded.

"You will not," the Ancient One said. "Allow me to show you the glory that awaits you in the new Mystic Order. This may be jarring at first…"

"Wait—" Sora said, but it was too late.

The Ancient One stalked toward her, and no sooner had Sora reached for her knife then the mysterious woman waved a hand in front of her eyes. Sora felt a sensation she'd become all too familiar with. Elsewhere tugged, just as it had when the guards held Aquira, as it had when she knew Kazimir was around, as it had so many times before. Only, usually the haunting sensation came from within, but this time it seemed to envelop her.

Heat washed over her body and sweat poured down her brow. Her head swam like it had when Whitney bought her a second drink at The Lofty Mare back in Yarrington.

Without thinking, she took a step and felt faint, then the familiar sting of Aquira's claws digging into her shoulder vanished. She spun, searching for her wyvern companion who was nowhere to be found. The quick movement almost made her fall over. Something about the room was wrong now. The lines didn't match up. The place where the wall would normally meet the floor now connected with another wall. Come to think of it, she wasn't even sure the floor was the floor anymore.

The thrones were gone, and so were the figures seated upon them.

"Lord Bokeo?" Sora called, but he was gone too.

Another shift, and Sora found herself falling to the side. She tumbled from the dais and expected to feel pain as her shoulder collided with the floor, but she felt nothing.

She hadn't even realized she was clenching her eyes shut. When she opened them, she was floating.

"Sora," spoke a matronly voice from somewhere. At first, Sora thought it was the Ancient One, but the voice was different. It sounded far off and distant, like someone talking under water.

Sora tried to turn, but with her feet no longer touching the ground, even the smallest movement came at an incredible cost. She finally managed to rotate and face the doorway leading into the room with the bridge and water. Breathing was difficult. Everything around her, she noticed, was the wrong color. No, not color, just shade. Everything was darker, redder.

Something raced toward her, wings flapping. A bird maybe. No. The wings were too big, flapping hard, fast. She recoiled as it got nearer, but it went right through her.

Then fire came. Hot fire. Bright, blinding. She shielded her face from the sudden onslaught of heat.

When it passed, she heard another sound. Her name. The voice was familiar and screaming. Over and over she heard the voice calling her name. There was panic within the word, desperation even. She knew immediately, the voice belonged to Whitney.

"Whitney!" Sora shouted and heard her name come back in reply. She fought against everything to find him, wading through darkness just to get a glimpse. She peeled away another layer of darkness and could just make out his face in the distance, but as she went to call out again, another presence stepped before him. Pale of face, eyes like daggers; a nightmare. Kazimir.

The mere sight of him caused her to jump, and then she fell. She screamed Whitney's name and could hear him shouting hers, the sound growing more and more faint as she plummeted. Then she stopped, and his presence was gone.

"Whitney?" she said. A series of torches surrounded her and suddenly ignited. Sensation returned to the flats of her feet, dirt between her toes. Everything was still wrong, red, purple, different—plus, now, she was no longer inside Dixia Shanyow. Those words came easily to her, like she'd known them all her life.

"*Dixia Shanyow,*" she said aloud, and then, "*Tsu shensughu ywen zhun tahuet feng yaris tsu weyong ywen hou.*"

She not only spoke the words in Panpingese, but she understood them. Earlier that day, she could do little more than say hello in the foreign tongue, now she was speaking sentences.

"*The spirit of the gods is found in the one with the will of fire,*" the Ancient One's voice echoed, translating what she'd said back into common.

A sudden rumble tore her from her reverie, and the ground began to shake. Her feet stayed rooted, even as winds blew fiercely, whipping dirt and sand. Slowly, like a worm wriggling from beneath the soil, a rock poked through the surface of the ground. It continued to rise, eternally, yet in an instant. Time meant nothing to Sora as she watched.

When it stopped, she stood staring at something she'd only seen from a great distance. Mount Lister, in all her glory, cast a long shadow over her. She recalled the only other time she'd seen it close up, when she stole off from Wetzel's shack in search of Whitney and wasn't there to protect him from raiders. She'd only made it to the hills in the western fields before she became overwhelmed by the size of Yarrington.

Even then, she'd never seen it like this.

It was then she realized she'd only thought the mountain stopped rising. It continued into the clouds, ever growing.

The earth shook once more, but this time Sora found it difficult to stand. Small stones pelted her feet and ankles, and she backed away from the spot where dirt and grass collapsed into the earth. A pale hand broke through the surface, grabbing hold of anything it could. Its muscles flexed, and an elbow appeared, then a shoulder.

She expected rent flesh and yellowing bone like that of a dead man, but the hand was smooth as a newborn babe.

A second arm broke through, and with it, a face.

Before she could register the terror in her heart, she stood face to face with the most beautiful woman she'd ever seen. Her long, black hair, flowed like a flock of ravens behind her, catching the wind. Her eyes were entirely white; her irises only a shade off-color. She wore the most beautiful dress Sora had ever seen—a burial gown fit for a queen.

Her pale skin wriggled all over, and Sora feared maggots covered her until she realized what caused the movement. Small, budding roots and they sprouted leaves.

This strange, buried woman should have been a vile thing of the grave. Instead, she was perfect. Her arm extended. A long finger traced the outline of Sora's face.

"Yes," the woman said. "Yes."

Sora tried to step back but couldn't.

"Do you know me?" the woman asked.

Sora took a deep breath and said, "I know of you." She wasn't sure how, but she knew exactly who she was looking at. Nesilia, the Buried Goddess. She who Redstar and his wicked warlocks worshipped above all else. Nesilia was magnificent, stunning. A power pulsed from her like all the waters of the oceans coalescing into one massive tidal wave.

Nesilia's brow furrowed, drawing attention to the fact that they were little more than lines of moss across her forehead. "Then tell me what you know of me," she said. The words came as a gentle request, not a command.

"Awful things, yet now I fear they are mostly lies and myths, my Lady," Sora said. She hadn't even meant to call her that, but in the goddess' presence, she struggled to find any other title.

Nesilia smiled, then gestured for her to continue.

"I've heard from the men who worship Iam that you were… are the false goddess. Evil and without a heart—but I met evil. Bliss was pure evil. You… you're something else."

Nesilia still smiled but said nothing.

"I've heard from your followers in the North that you and Iam were lovers, that he saved you by cursing Bliss—the One Who Remained—but I think both tales are too different for either to be trusted in their entirety and both people too flawed." As the answers flowed through her lips, Sora wasn't even sure if she was in control of what she was saying, like her deepest, unconscious thoughts were slipping out.

"Smart girl." As Nesilia spoke, vines spread from her feet and ankles, slinking ever closer to Sora who didn't dare move. "But what do you believe?"

"Truly?"

"Truly."

"In my heart, I chose to believe the story of love. That Iam created Elsewhere for the gods and goddesses who rebelled, but you, he loved. After cursing Bliss, he let you stay buried beneath his throne so he'd never be far from you."

Something new washed over the goddess' face like a shifting shadow.

"I'm sorry, my Lady, if I offended," Sora said.

"He wanted to punish that witch… that vile and heinous creature," Nesilia said, her voice growing louder. "She thought herself so beautiful, so perfect. So, he stole her looks. Cursed her to become the creature you met. He thought it would be the ultimate punishment. Send all the rebels to Elsewhere except the one who struck out against me, his love, his Queen!"

As she said the last word, the ground shook, and sharp, jagged rocks rose up around them like the talons of a carrion bird.

"He cursed her, but he blessed her as well! She may have become a beast, but he let her retain that which gods love most: the fear of our creation. All of the world feared her—even those who didn't know she existed. Each time they saw an eight-legged pest scurry across their floors, their fear fueled her."

"But for me..." Nesilia pressed a hand against her heart. "He said he loved me! Said he wanted me close. He could have saved me, built me a throne upon His Mountain. Instead, the very earth healed me."

Nesilia stroked the vines which now covered her arms.

"Even the lesser gods were free to rule Elsewhere," she went on, "but I was the one who was cursed! What's worse than being a dreadful beast?"

When she hesitated, Sora wasn't sure if she expected a response. Sora stuttered until Nesilia's chin fell to her chest, and a black tear, like sap, ran down her cheek.

"Being forgotten," Nesilia said softly.

"My Lady… I…" Sora stopped. All her life, she'd heard the Church of Iam preach against Nesilia and her role in starting the God Feud, even more so than the other fallen gods. Then, she heard Redstar speak of her glory and giving her life out of love. At the time she thought little of it, but now, as Sora looked upon the Buried Goddess, she could only feel pity.

"I am so sorry," Sora finished.

"For what?" Nesilia questioned. "It was not you who abandoned me."

"I—no… it was not."

"Why have you come to this plane?" Nesilia asked, jolted from her sadness in an instant.

"I was sent by an ancient mystic, I think. She said I would see the glory that awaits me."

"So, look upon me, girl. Feast upon my glory and do not forget it!"

The world began to swirl again. The mountain rumbled as Nesilia's scream rang out, then it broke into countless pieces, scattering and showering down around Sora. She cried out even though none of the stones touched her.

Suddenly, Nesilia's face was all she could see, filled with fury. Yet there was something else there. That sorrow and loneliness remained within her colorless eyes even as her features twisted with rage. In that moment, Sora wanted nothing more than to be close to the goddess, to embrace her and soothe her pain.

And with that, Sora's entire world collapsed around her.

XIII

THE THIEF

Following a hearty breakfast made by Lauryn, accompanied by the kind of awkward silence one would expect at the table after a thieving son gets his father crippled, Whitney and Kazimir set out to harvest.

It had been a long time since Whitney gripped a sickle, but it didn't take long to find his rhythm. It also didn't take long before he remembered all the reasons he'd left the farm to begin with. Between the fragments of vegetation pelting his skin, the hot sun, and the bugs buzzing around, he was itchy and irritable.

Young Whitney was outside as well, supposed to be helping, but instead kicking around rocks by the barn with his head down. Whitney didn't bother him. He couldn't believe his younger self would feel such guilt, but then again, the real version of himself had never got his father's back broken. Barns are easier to mend than bones.

"You know what I hate?" Whitney asked.

Kazimir ignored him, as he'd been doing all morning. He simply worked, quiet and drone-like, hacking away. After all this time together, Whitney still couldn't get a read on the man. The ruthless, rule-bending killer, happy to fall in line and listen to all the ingrates in this phantom Troborough. It was hard to fear him now.

"The color brown," Whitney answered himself. "I miss anything that isn't brown. Look around you. Brown fields, brown houses, brown roofs. Even the horses and goats are brown. Shog, even their shog is brown. That's why I left this place—well, that and a million other reasons."

"Yet, here we are, harvesting barley in Elsewhere," Kazimir said.

"You know what I realized?" Whitney threw his sickle to the ground. The tedium of work gnawed at him like a swarm of angry locusts.

"What?" Kazimir didn't even bother looking up from his work.

"We wouldn't be here at all if not for you."

"Is that so?"

"Let's see," Whitney started as he approached the upyr. "First, you appear like a creep from the shadows of some murdered guy's bedroom. Then, you kidnap my… friend. Then, you try to kill us both."

"And I'd have succeeded if your mystic *friend* had the slightest clue how to wield her magic," Kazimir growled. He stabbed his sickle down and looked to the sky. "Trapped here, thanks to an accident."

"Oh, poor you," Whitney shoved him.

"You're going to regret that."

"You aren't as tough without your spiky teeth, dung breath." He wasn't sure what came over him. Kazimir was right; he was the one who'd committed to helping run the farm. Kazimir just played along for reasons Whitney still couldn't understand. But Whitney pushed him again, harder this time.

As Kazimir stumbled back, a sound drew Whitney's focus to the creek. Young Whitney was behind the barn out of view of his house, throwing stones at fence posts with a young, Panpingese girl with long, jet-black hair. Whitney hadn't even noticed that the boy had somehow slipped away.

"Sora…"

It was the only word Whitney got out before he felt Kazimir's balled fist connect with the side of his head, and then the cold earth came up to meet him.

Whitney came to, sprung to his feet, and dropped into a fighting stance, but Kazimir was nowhere around. It was no longer morning. The sky was dark again, and to Whitney's chagrin, a deep purplish maroon, as unnatural as could be. Whitney realized he must have been knocked out cold. His ears rang, and he saw starry blotches before his eyes.

A high-pitched laugh came from behind him, and he spun. It echoed, and he turned again. Soon, the sound surrounded him, feeling vaguely familiar. Suddenly, a horned head popped up from beneath the barley field. Its golden yellow eyes gleamed as it cackled. It was dark, so Whitney couldn't make out its features as it climbed free of the ground, but he immediately recognized the satyr.

When he, Torsten, and Sora were in the Webbed Woods, they'd encountered the beasts and only survived through the interference of Redstar disguised as Uriah and his dire wolf, Gryff.

Gryff wasn't around to help this time.

Another satyr arose, snickering. Then another. And another still. They soon surrounded Whitney and were closing in. One spoke, its voice sounding feminine, but distant and difficult to understand.

As they grew ever closer, their features began to form, and Whitney blanched.

"Sora?" he whispered.

Each of them looked the same, and each of them looked like her. They were arm's length away, and he felt the heat of their breath. One opened its maw, and its Sora-like features began melting away and their faces morphed into thousands of little bugs. Some flitted around, snapping their tiny mouths at him. Instead of the expected buzzing sound, their collective wings mimicked Sora's voice, and it sounded pained.

Whitney felt something crawling on his leg and looked down. Spiders covered his feet and ankles. He tried to shake them off, but he couldn't move. His heart pounded, his clothing, soaked with sweat. He wanted to throw up but couldn't.

The flying insects swarmed, swirling around him. His vision was now completely obscured, shrouded in total darkness. From within the darkness, a giant spider emerged. As his eyes followed from the ground up, the legs and thorax faded into the body of a woman. She was completely naked.

Bliss, the spider queen and the One Who Remained.

He tried again to run, tried to do anything. He opened his mouth to scream, and it was immediately filled with hundreds of bugs. He felt them teeming on his tongue.

Bliss spoke, and his gaze met hers, but once again, instead of the face of Bliss Whitney had encountered in the Webbed Woods, Sora's stared back at him.

She charged him, and when he fell backward, his world went black again.

Someone screamed Sora's name, hysterical.

After a few shouts, Whitney realized it was him. His eyes protested but finally shot open, and he was staring into the glaring sun, surrounded by blue skies. He heard himself, his younger self, talking to him, but couldn't make out the words. Then he heard another voice. When he shifted his eyes, all he saw was a giant white blotch. He blinked, trying to focus.

"Why is he screaming my name?" the voice asked.

"I don't know. Say, Mr. Willis, why are you calling my friend's name?" Young Whitney asked. "How do you know her? Are you okay? Where's your friend?"

Big Whitney sat up. Finally, he could see clearly, and he was face to face with Sora, exactly how he'd remembered her looking as a kid. From her hair and her scrawny frame to her stunningly amber eyes.

"Why are you calling me?" Sora asked.

"I was dreaming," Big Whitney said.

"Ick." She looked repulsed. "About me?"

"I—I don't. No, I have a friend named Sora, too."

"You do?" Sora asked. There was something in her voice Young Whitney wouldn't have noticed, but Big Whitney did. Hope.

Whitney cleared his throat and stood. He stared at the little girl, the spitting image of Sora—because it was her. It was every bit her as the woman he'd left on a ship in the middle of Trader's Bay. Every bit her as the one who'd saved him from Redstar... twice.

"Mister? You know another Sora?" Young Whitney asked.

"Yes," Whitney said, clearing his throat again, and tussling her hair. "She's beautiful, just like you."

Little Sora blushed.

Young Whitney scowled. "Gross," he said.

"Be nice, Whitney," Sora said. "Didn't he take credit for that dumb stunt you pulled yesterday?"

"Yeah," Big Whitney said. "I've been waiting for a thank you."

"A lot of good it did..." he grumbled. "Come on." He grabbed Sora by the arm. "Let's go."

"It's almost supper time, won't your mother—"

"I need a break from their sad faces, and besides, that guy's too old for you."

"Stop it!" Sora punched Young Whitney in the arm before they ran off toward the creek, though not before he shot Big Whitney another dirty look. The sight of them together made Whitney's eyes well up.

"She used to punch me like that," Whitney whispered as they skipped away.

Whitney wiped sweat from his brow, still shaken up from the vision. Then he swatted a bug on his neck. He stuck his tongue out as he wiped its guts off on his pants.

He decided that his younger self was right; a break was in order. He made his way to the house, drawn by the scent of a fresh cherry pie. The back door was always open, and he let himself in.

"Mrs. Fierstown?" he called. It was weird calling her that, and he'd, more than a few times, almost called her 'ma' already.

"Where's your friend?" Rocco asked. The day after his injury, Whitney and Kazimir carried a bed down from upstairs and set it up in a downstairs room with a window that looked out over the farm. He'd barked all morning for Young Whitney to get to work before passing out in his bed, subdued by herbs brought over by Wetzel.

"Not sure. Probably off skulking in shadows," Whitney said.

"What's that supposed to mean?"

"I don't know," Whitney snapped.

The words hadn't any sooner left his lips than he'd regretted them. Memories of being badgered by his father returned, and he couldn't help himself. He braced, waiting for his father's wrath.

"Fine." Was all Rocco said, which pissed Whitney off more. If he'd lashed out like that when he was a child, he'd have a painful date with a belt.

"Fine?" he questioned. "That's it? Fine? If I'd have said that to you twenty years ago, you'd have threatened to tear my ass from my hind or some crazy thing that made no sense. Fine?"

"Twenty years ago? What is wrong with you, boy? The sun… the heat's getting to you. You'd better rest." Then he muttered under his breath, "Nobles."

"Are you yigging kidding me? Rest? Since when is anyone allowed to rest around this gods-damned farm?"

Whitney was now directly in front of Rocco and shouting in his face, spittle speckling his lips. The fact that the man was laying down and couldn't even get up completely escaped him.

"Enough."

Kazimir appeared out of what might as well have been thin air and stood between Whitney and Rocco.

Rocco's fists were clenched along with his jaw. "I thank you for this kindness, but get your friend some water and shade or you'll both be without a bed tonight, that understood?"

"Maybe we'll just—" Kazimir gripped Whitney by the arm and shoved him outside before he could finish.

"Yes, sir," Kazimir said. "It's just the sun, I'm sure."

Rocco gave Whitney one last glance, then closed his eyes, moaning. "I knew they couldn't be trusted with this," he grumbled.

Kazimir gave Whitney another push on his way out the door.

"Get off me," Whitney bristled.

"If you insist on acting like a child, I will treat you like one," Kazimir said.

"If you haven't noticed," Whitney said, voice still raised, "the child version of me is down there by the river. He'd leave now if he knew what's good for him. Take Sora with him."

"A roof. Fresh food any time. I would have killed to grow up in a place like this. I did kill."

Whitney stared for a moment, then huffed. "You don't get it. The bastard is impossible."

"Excuse me?"

"My father," he spat the word from his mouth like it was a bit of maggot-filled meat.

"You get him crippled, now complain about an attitude you instigated?"

"This isn't really…" Whitney drew a long breath. "He and I just shouldn't be in the same place for long."

"Well, this was your idea. 'Simple and easy,' you said."

"You don't understand," Whitney whispered, shaking his head.

"What, a Glassman who hates his father? You're as predictable as the day I caught you."

"Do you have any idea how predictable everything about you is? Just cos you're a bloodsucking demon doesn't mean you have to look like… like this." He flattened his palm and lifted and lowered it, gesturing like he was showing off a cow at market. "You're the spitting image of my childhood nightmares."

"A nap in the dirt wasn't enough? I should kill you where your stand."

"It wouldn't count," Whitney retorted.

"What?"

"That's right. This ***fool*** is starting to figure things out. You can't toss me away and leave me here, can you?" Whitney scoffed. "Your Sang-whatever Lords won't count it as dead and clear your blood pact. That's why you're following me around like a hen. Hoping we come out of this crazy place side-by-side."

"My desire was the orphan mystic. And neither you nor this foul place will keep me from her."

"Well, there she is!" Whitney smirked, gesturing back toward the river. "I may be many things, but I know how to sniff out a liar. I've learned from the best." He nodded in the direction of his younger doppelgänger. "You're scared to fail. No, wait… you think the sandwind Lor—"

"Sanguine ," Kazimir growled.

"Whatever. You think they're keeping you here as punishment because you went too far and still couldn't get the job done. Killing Tayvada, bloodletting Sora. They know you've been naughty."

Kazimir's features twisted with rage. Whitney placed his hands behind his back so a part of him could twitch with fear while the rest of him stood strong. He'd taken his gamble, and now he had to stick with it. He laughed.

"Ruthless Kazimir is superstitious!"

Kazimir's whole body tensed and Whitney prepared for another blow to the head. Instead, the upyr stalked away. "When I do get out of here and find your friend, thief, know that I'm going to drain her in the most painful ways imaginable."

"*If* you find her. Far as I can tell, we aren't leaving this place, and the Sora here doesn't know mystics from cow dung."

Kazimir didn't stop walking.

"Hey! Where the yig are you going?"

"I'm done arguing with a child," Kazimir answered without turning around or stopping. "I'm going to rest for the first time in longer than I can remember. You can handle this problem yourself."

"What is wrong with you?" Whitney asked, following him into the dark barn. "You're a gods-damned upyr, and you're acting like a trained house cat."

"When you've been here as many times as I have, you learn a thing or two. No one is saving you. Nothing you do will make anything better. Play by their rules, and you might get along easy. I'm not a cat, and I'm sure as this is Elsewhere not an upyr anymore. Not here, at least."

"Well, you might give up, but I won't. I'm going to get out of here. I've escaped the Glass Castle more times than I can count—and that was just in the past few months."

"One day and you nearly got yourself kicked out of here. Tell me, what do you think you'll be doing in Elsewhere if you can't handle farming. Hanging from the Eye of Iam to be picked out by ravens for all eternity. I see no other possibility for you. This isn't the Glass Castle. You're playing in the territory of angry gods now." Kazimir laid down on the hay and closed his eyes.

"Yeah well, these gods haven't met me. I killed a goddess, and I'll kill every one of them if I have to. I'm done playing. I won't waste any more of my life here." Whitney picked up a sickle, slammed the barn doors open, then started off toward the edge of the property.

"You're wasting your time," Kazimir said, having abandoned his hay to follow.

Whitney ignored him. He thought he could handle playing the helpful stranger, but it was clear that was a bad idea. He had them—bad ideas—from time to time, albeit very rarely. He crossed back through Troborough. As usual, nothing was going on. Whitney heard some of the townsfolk discussing the latest gossip, and almost all of them seemed to be talking about what happened to Rocco and the strange travelers kind enough to help him like that was the biggest thing that had happened in all of their lifetimes.

"I'll give you a game," Whitney grumbled. "Damn, lazy upyr tricking me into sitting around doing nothing." He swung the sickle in anger, and the townsfolk gathered outside the Twilight Manor stared at him.

"Just a mysterious traveler passing through!" he shouted.

Their heads turned with him. It made his skin crawl. Even the priest version of Torsten watched him though he had no eyes.

Whitney held his breath and picked up his pace.

"Ferryman!" he shouted as he walked down to where they'd been dropped off in the river. Wetzel's shack sat far to the left of him, roof covered in moss and a broken water-wheel off to the side. The old codger fumbled with something out back, cursing to himself.

"Ferryman!" Whitney yelled again. He sloshed into the water and looked from side to side, as if the boat would appear, completely repaired.

"Yigging exile," he cursed. He looked back toward town and saw that a few of the townsfolk had gathered atop the hill, still watching him, whispering to one another. He snapped the sickle shaft over his knee and stormed up passed them, pants soaking wet.

He found the town stables to be empty, wondering why he'd ever thought there'd be a convenience like horses in Elsewhere. So, he marched down the main, western road on his own, doing his best to ignore all the prying eyes of anyone he passed.

"Not going to wait around in this dump," he grumbled. "I'll go where things happen."

He stopped at the edge of town, rolling hills before him. Eventually, the dirt road would intersect with the grand, stone-paved Glass Road which led straight to Yarrington. He turned back. Dozens of townsfolk were now congregated, Wetzel among them, and out-of-place Torsten, even Lauryn, staring at him like she had no idea who he was.

"Have a good eternity," he said, performing an exaggerated bow, then set off down the road. Just as a smile crossed his face, he slammed into something he couldn't see, and collapsed to the ground, his tailbone landing on a rock. Pain shot all the way up his spine and further. His nose hurt… his whole face hurt.

"What the…" He popped back up and crept forward with his hand flat. It pressed against an invisible boundary. He whipped back around, brow furrowed, and all the townsfolk began to break away.

"Drunken fool," one said.

"Poor, lost soul," said another.

Whitney patted the unseen surface separating him from the Glass Road, taunting him. He sensed a shadow creeping up on him.

"Wonderful," he said. "We're stuck here, aren't we?"

He turned, and Kazimir stood in the road. They'd spent the entire day bickering, but now Whitney saw an unfamiliar expression on the upyr's face. It seemed like pity.

"You're starting to get it," Kazimir said.

"There has to be a way out."

"Not for you." Kazimir walked by him and stretched his hand through the invisible wall. The world rippled around his fingers like water as it passed through.

"What the!" Whitney nudged him aside and slapped his palms against the same part, only for them to be blocked. "No, there has to be a way out."

"There isn't."

"You're a yigging liar!" Whitney kept going, skirted along the barrier and running his hand along it as if it were a wall. "There's a way out; there's always a way out." He kept going, running now, until he found himself back around on the other side of Wetzel's shack, shin-deep in the river.

"What kind of place is this!" Whitney shouted. He kicked at the water, then fell to his knees.

"I've been trying to tell you," Kazimir said. "I have all of Elsewhere I could be, but I'm staying here because this is your Elsewhere, and just as you are unable to leave, the wianu are forbidden to enter."

"So, you're scared?"

"The beast exists beyond life and death. Only it can destroy me, and I have too much left to do before I die."

"If it can kill you, doesn't that mean it can do the opposite. You know, send you back?"

"I do not know. We do not face them here by choice, where they're at their most powerful."

"But you can leave? You can go find one of the fallen gods or whatever and tell them we don't belong here."

"And they would care not. For you do belong here, and I belong nowhere."

"I don't. You were there, on that ship. We didn't die."

"But you're here, and only the dead inhabit this place. Mistake or not, your soul is in exile. Never to return."

"You said it yourself. You've been here before many times. Not just when you closed your eyes."

"It is the nature of becoming upyr. To become of both realms as the wianu is. Untethered. The newest of us always pass through this place, and encounter all its challenges as their minds come to grips with what they are. Knowing I was going to wake from this nightmare as the Sanguine Lords saw fit, I never cared."

Whitney looked up at him, tears in his eyes. "So now you've come to gloat?"

"No. Seeing a man grasp for purpose when there is none, even if it is you, brings me no pleasure. You're dead Whitney Fierstown. There is no going back. The Sanguine Lords punish me, but not because you failed to die, but because I wasn't the one who killed you."

Whitney's throat went dry. "So, you expect me to just… stay here?"

"It is all you can do. I hoped you would see on your own, but the people I've sent here aren't expecting miracles. They're dead, and they know it."

"Well, I'm not. There's a way out of everything, and if this really is all Sora's fault, she's up there figuring out how to reverse it."

Kazimir exhaled, then laid a hand on Whitney's shoulder. Whitney winced out of reflex.

"I've seen many strange things, but for men, Elsewhere is permanent," Kazimir said. "There is nothing your friend can do. Fight the truth if you must, but do yourself a favor and make things easier on yourself. Be the man you think it's impossible for you to be, because there is no worse torture, and that is all this foul place feeds on. One day, the Sanguine Lords will pardon my failure. I will wake up on the other side, and I won't be here to keep you from turning this nightmare into true exile. Until then, don't ruin my rest."

The upyr walked away, leaving Whitney to stare down into the water at his reflection. Dead him still looked like the him he knew, at least until the broken shaft of the sickle floated into his knee and disturbed the water. He grabbed it and considered ramming the pointy end through his own chest. His hands shook but eventually dropped it.

If Elsewhere was like this, he couldn't imagine where he'd wind up should he die a second time. He looked up and saw Wetzel hurrying Young Sora indoors. Apparently, she had returned from the Fierstown's, probably kicked out once Whitney's parents saw her. She looked at him before the door slammed behind her. Straight at him.

Ever since he'd gotten to Elsewhere, he'd had this eerie feeling like people were looking through him, but not her.

"He's wrong," Whitney told himself. He stood, clenching the shaft so hard his knuckles turned white. "Maybe I am dead, but I don't belong here."

An invisible wall may have trapped him in Troborough, but he'd been trapped in worse places. He'd find a way out, and if he couldn't, he still had Sora out there in Pantego, seeking out true magic from the mystics. She'd sent him here, the girl who'd grown up in that shack, and he had to hope she wouldn't stop until she found a way to undo it.

Even if it took years, he'd wait. He'd keep his mind. If Elsewhere wanted him to live out the nightmare of being a worthless farmer in a worthless town, he'd be the best damn farmer there ever was.

XIV

THE DESERTER

Rand's armor felt heavy as he made his way to the heart of Yarrington. Every suit of Shieldsman armor was reinforced with glaruium mined from within Mount Lister, the sturdiest and rarest ore Pantego offered. They were passed down from generations, refitted for each man by the castle's eldest blacksmith, Hovom Nitebrittle, who'd trained beneath dwarven artisans to become the only Glassman possessed of the skills to work the metal.

Now, Rand's had a loose fit. He hadn't realized how much muscle he'd lost since he fled his post. The vast, open fields he'd spent days and nights training and exercising in had been replaced by a room the size of a horse's pen and enough alcohol to drown the horse.

The training of a Shieldsman, however, was eternal. He'd learned that lesson well at the docks. He may have never wanted to kill again, but defending Sigrid was different. As Wren said, he would agonize in the bowels of Elsewhere if it meant creating a better world in which for her to live. He was already destined for that rotten place anyway. Until the Drav Cra were driven from the city, a Docksider like her would never be safe.

Yarrington Square was different from Rand's memory. Usually, when a harsh winter came, the merchants kept to the southern portions of the kingdom. But with the Drav Cra in town—they were an entirely new customer base. Maybe they didn't have autlas, but they were out in droves buying things that were of no use to nomads living in the far north. Formal clothing, pottery, furniture; items they'd never seen before, but they seemed eager to get a taste of Yarrington.

They traded their weapons and furs for all the southern trinkets and fineries, hauling it all back to leather tents just beyond the city walls, where their women, children, and elders lived while their army helped secure the kingdom.

There are so many. Have they all abandoned Drav Cra? Rand wondered.

It all seemed so incredibly innocent until Rand looked a little closer. For all the Drav Cra marveling at useless items, they were also sharing their clothing with Yarrington. Furs from bear and wolves—oversized coats, boots and gloves—all crafted by masters of keeping warm through the coldest winters, and in that way, they were winning over the locals. Even in the square, painted warlocks by the walls invited Glassmen into their circles for prayer, drawing bloody symbols on and around a slain goat, and surrounding it with candles and burning incense.

Idols to the Buried Goddess were worshiped without fear of reprisal.

"Yarrington is being invaded. Quietly, peacefully, the enemies of Iam flood these walls from the Drav Cra." Wren's words echoed in Rand's mind.

He could see why even young King Pi might see the beauty in this blending of cultures. But it all seemed incredibly calculated.

The Drav Cra never stayed put for long. They were raiders and nomads, playing the part of wholesome guests until they decided to be raiders and nomads again. They were used to striking at small villages around Crowfall and even as far east as Hornsheim, yet here they were, welcomed into the walls of Yarrington. Perhaps the number of warriors present was few with others out fighting rebellion, but he'd already seen firsthand how little they thought of southern men and women. All the realm believed that the rebels were south in the Black Sands, but they were forgetting to look right underneath their noses.

"Repent!" shouted an old man on a podium where the Square met the Royal Avenue. He wore tattered, brown robes and had his head shaved with the eye of Iam painted large and sloppily across his forehead, indicating him a monk of a more fanatic sect of the Church of Iam known as the Order of the Holy Eye. They rejected the Kings of Glass as chosen and heeded only the direct word of their God.

"Brothers and sisters, you must repent!" he continued. "You welcome these heathens and destroyers with open arms. Those who would deny our holy Lord His glory!"

A crowd of Glassmen started to gather around him. Guards took notice and inched closer. As Rand instinctually did the same, he remembered that, as far as the world could see, he was one of them—higher ranking, in fact, than any of them.

"The boy seated upon the throne does not speak for us!" the man continued. Spittle flew from his mouth as he spoke with such vim it looked like he might burst a blood vessel. "Only Iam can. How many of these monsters slaughtered our kin in the North? They are children of the great deceiver. She who tricked the heathen gods in the feud over Pantego. She who lies buried beneath that very mountain!" He stuck a finger out toward the flattened summit of Mount Lister presiding over the city.

"Bah! You'd all be roasting on Shesaitju spits if not for us," said a Drav Cra warrior who'd remained behind with his people as he passed.

"Even now, they mock us!" the monk said. A few grumbles of agreement broke out. "These corrupt men. These depraved men. Heathens!" The monk turned his wrinkled finger in the direction of the warrior who'd spoken. In that moment, the surface of peace melted away as a dozen angry eyes fell upon the warrior.

"We must not stand idly by while they ravage the realm of Iam. Brothers, we must take up the sword and drench His holy realm with their heathen blood. We must bury them with their goddess, or they will do the same to us!"

More cheers rang out, this time with more vigor. The crowd, stirred like a nest of angry hornets, turned upon the nearest Drav Cra warrior. The guards battled against the masses to reach the rabble-rousing monk.

"How many of your kin have died in their raids!" the monk shouted.

"My brother died in Crowfall thanks to them," a man in the crowd called out.

"How many of your children have been sacrificed to the wicked cults who worship the false goddess with them? They are the very spawn of

Elsewhere! It is time we tear the imposter, Redstar, from his seat in the castle and burn him in the fires. We will ensure he'll never see the Gate of Light nor his blasphemous Skorravik."

"Aye, why don't you savages go back to your tundra!" another voice cried out to the Drav Cra warrior who'd spoken up.

The warrior didn't leave. In true Drav Cra fashion, he turned to face his accusers and drew his battle-axe. "Which one of you wants to die first, then?"

Rand took a few steps closer. In the faces of the incensed crowd, he could see the truth of the situation. The tension boiling over would eventually lead to Yarrington's ruin. If the entire Drav Cra horde was near the city, even a small squabble like this could ignite the flames of open war. Perhaps that was what Redstar wanted. He'd already done enough horrible things to weasel his way into power, and Rand likely didn't know the half of it.

"That's what I thought," the warrior spat. "A bunch of southern flowers."

"Heathen scum!"

A man burst through the crowd and charged the Drav Cra warrior. The swing of his battle-axe sent the Glassman back onto his rump. But the Glassman wasn't alone. All it took was one to show bravery, and now a good portion of the crowd stalked toward the warrior.

"Kill the savage!" a local screamed, waving his hand to coax the mob forward, but his body froze mid-stride. His eyes darted side to side, the only part of him able to move.

"Nesilia is the one true!" Three men, garbed in crimson robes, wearing emotionless white masks appeared behind the warrior. Each had one hand raised, fresh blood trickling from their palms, and gripping a knife in the other. They weren't Drav Cra warlocks, but members of the Cult of the Buried Goddess. They were a group Rand had dealt with even in his short time as a Shieldsman. Usually relegated to abandoned basements or caverns beyond the city, now, they found themselves emboldened by unexpected allies.

"Donning masks doesn't make you one of us!" The warrior whipped around and slashed even at his saviors. They retreated just as more guards arrived to hold back the swelling mob.

The Glassman attacker let out a breath as he collapsed to the dirt only to be trampled by his own people with sights on both the cultists and warrior.

"See how they turn us all against each other!" the monk yelled. "Tricksters and demons in human form!"

The chaos allowed Rand to shove his way through the edges of the crowd and seize the monk. There was truth to what the man was saying, but men like him had a knack for starting fires.

"You want to get everybody killed?" Rand questioned as he dragged the monk west along Royal Avenue toward the Glass Castle. The glass spire presided proudly over the city, shining even with the sun veiled by snow and clouds.

"I speak only the truth," he answered.

"Well, you can enlighten everyone in the dungeons."

"Don't you see?" he cried, manic. "You have been deceived!"

"Would you shut it? I'm on your side."

With his armor on, no one questioned Rand as he entered the Old Yarrington. He kept his head down so he wouldn't be recognized, but he had no idea where his post should be. He wasn't even sure he was supposed to be in Yarrington and not out in the field subduing the rebel Black Sandsmen. At least with a rabble-rousing fanatic from the Order of the Holy Eye in tow, he'd be subject to fewer inquiries unless he ran into the Shieldsmen's Taskmaster, Lars Kesselman.

They reached the bend in the road where it ran parallel to the castle's outer walls. The sight of them stopped Rand in his tracks. The walls were bare now, the wind howling along their flat faces, but he could still picture the bodies, ropes tied around their necks, creaking together as if part of a symphony.

Rand squeezed his eyes shut. "Focus," he whispered to himself, hands trembling and head aching.

"You are troubled, brother," the monk said. "We of the Holy Eye can help you."

"Quiet," he grumbled. He opened his eyes, and the bodies were gone.

Soon I'll be free of them, he told himself. Soon all will be made right.

They reached the gates, where a few Glass soldiers stood guard. He expected them to question him, but instead, they parted for him to pass.

Redstar may have set up camp in the castle, but Rand's order still held sway among the commoners.

"Sir, allow me?" one of the guards said, motioning to the monk.

"Excuse me?" Rand said, surprised.

"Is he a prisoner? I'll take him to the dungeons."

Rand swore under his breath. He'd hoped to use the monk as a means to traverse the castle with a ready excuse. "I've got him," he said.

"Sir, I insist. You shouldn't have to sully your armor in that pit. Please, let me do my job?"

It was a sincere request from a good soldier. Rand sensed a future Shieldsman in that armor. "What's your name?" he asked.

"Garihad, sir. Garihad Yulniz."

"Yulniz, eh?" Rand said.

"Yes, sir. I believe you must know my father."

"I've heard of him." Phillip Yulniz was a revered and retired member of the Shield and had served as Taskmaster under King Liam and Uriah Davies years back.

Rand sighed and handed the monk over. "He's a rabble-rouser from down in the Square," he said. "Do what you do, soldier."

The soldier pounded on his chestplate in salute, pride on his face, then grabbed the monk and headed around the back of the castle. Rand considered giving the monk a message for Torsten before he was gone but decided against it. After Redstar was removed from the equation, Torsten would be free. Plus, according to Wren, Torsten occupied the lowest, most secure sanctum of the castle dungeons. It was nowhere a mere fanatical preacher would be held.

Rand slowly crossed the bailey. A legion of young Shieldsmen trained on one side. Sir Nikserof Pasic sat overlooking them, chatting with Hovom, the castle blacksmith, and another Shieldsman Rand recognized as Sir Austun Mulliner. Nikserof behaved like a commander, but Rand had only known of two King's Shieldsmen able to act in such a way in Yarrington. There were captains in every city throughout the kingdom, but here, Torsten was the commander, and if he wasn't around, Sir Wardric Jolly had always been his second, just as he was for Torsten's predecessor.

Neither was present now.

Sir Nikserof wasn't green at least. Rand remembered a few lessons he'd received from him in swordsmanship. He was an expert at that subject, but still, he was no Torsten Unger.

Rand drew a deep breath when he realized he was standing still again. Being back at the castle brought all the horrid memories to the forefront of his mind. He turned his head away from the Shieldsman and continued toward the castle gates. Even with his now-shaggy hair and beard, he might be recognized. His days as Wearer, although few, were memorable.

He turned, facing the other end of the bailey where a group of Drav Cra warriors practiced throwing their axes at dummies. Their chief strode through their ranks, barking at them in their harsh language. He had a beard that looked like it'd never been cut, with a bald portion along the right side of his jaw where a series of deep scars lay. The white paint covering the right half his face only seemed to accentuate them, like he was proud of how near he'd come to death.

It was as strange a sight as Rand had ever seen. Painted, fur-clad Drav Cra warriors before the backdrop of the Glass Castle. And while tension remained between the commoners in the Square, these groups of soldiers paid no attention to each other, whether good or bad. Whatever had happened in Winde Port left them fused by battle.

Savages, literally at the gates, trusted enough that nobody was keeping so much as a wary eye on them. So much had changed it made Rand's head throb. He tried to gather himself, leaning against the statue of King Fentomir flanking the Great Hall entry.

He looked up and saw the visage of the Fentomir, then let his eye wander down the line until it rested on King Liam's statue. After a moment, his gaze drifted to the slab of rock that would eventually be carved into the likeness of King Pi. Rand couldn't help but wonder what kind of legacy the young boy would leave.

In his mind, the image shifted into the birthmarked face of the chieftain Redstar. He shuddered at the thought of the Glass Kingdom falling into Drav Cra hands.

He was pulled from his reverie when, out of the corner of his eye, he noticed the outer wall's gate crank where he and his soldiers had forced Tessa to her death. He could remember that look on her face like he was there. Betrayal, sorrow; a mixture of all the awful things a person could feel.

"I shouldn't have come here," he whispered.

He knew he was drawing attention to himself, muttering under his breath and shaking his head like a madman, but he couldn't help it. Her shrieks hammered around in his skull. Calling out his name, just like how Sigrid had when the savages got their hands on her.

Am I really any better?

"You," someone addressed him.

He turned and saw the source of all his pain. Oleander Nothhelm, wife of Liam the Conqueror and the mother of the Miracle King, approached him. Her dress was long and lovely, the same deep blue color of her lips and nails. The last Rand saw her, she was frazzled and broken, yet now she was the picture of royalty. Even after everything she'd done.

"Are you dull?" she asked, snapping her fingers in front of his face. "Shieldsman, I'm talking to you."

"Y-y-your Grace," Rand managed to squeeze through lips, paralyzed by an onslaught of emotion. His hand fell to the pommel of his longsword before he could think about it.

She leaned down and stared into his eyes. She was going to recognize him, blow the whole thing. She was going to recognize him, and he'd have no choice but to kill her, no matter how much he fought the desire.

"Will you just stare at me?" she asked. "I swear, ever since Torsten went away, the quality of your order is..." She grabbed Rand's jaw. "Would you look at your Queen." She emphasized each word like she was scolding a child.

The front of Rand's head pulsed with pain as he forced his blank stare to meet Oleander's. He didn't want to look at her. He never wanted to look at her again. His fingers slowly wrapped the handle of his sword. All he had to do was draw it, and the source of all his pain would be wiped from the face of Pantego.

"That's better," she said, then released him. "Since the kingdom is left without a Wearer, I need you to go fetch my impetuous brother."

Rand swallowed. She was literally inviting him to the room of his target. All so easy. All he had to do was hold steady, and he could fix everything. "What..." His voice cracked, and he cleared his throat. He felt like he was holding his breath deep underwater. "What shall I tell him?"

"Tell him his king needs him. And Shieldsman, your duty is to do what

I ask and nothing more." She groaned and stormed away, her heels clacking along the courtyard's marble perimeter. "These Shieldsmen are going to be the death of me," she muttered before disappearing into the castle.

Looking down, Rand released a mouthful of air and realized his sword was halfway out of its sheath.

Shieldsman.

Everything she'd put him through, and she had no idea who he even was. He could see it written all over her face like she was talking to any inferior whose name she'd never bothered to learn. She'd rarely gotten his name correct even when he stood guard as Wearer directly outside her chambers.

"By Iam I need a drink." He shook out his hands, then headed across the courtyard toward the West Tower, keeping his head low. If she didn't recognize him, he doubted anyone else would, but he still had to be safe.

Three guards walked by chatting. "I hear Sir Unger let the rebel afhem escape down at Winde Port," one said. "Probably helped Yuri Darkings free the Caleef too."

"No, Sir Nikserof was there," said another. "Said he fought like a madman to get them out alive, then just snapped and lost it, blood-crazed."

"I heard he drove his blade straight through Xander's heart back in Winde Port, he did," said the third.

"Yeah? I heard worse, that it was he who slew Sir Wardric Jolly outside Winde Port, not that Darkings traitor."

A wave of sadness passed over Rand. He'd served under the old Shieldsman Wardric who'd been around in the order forever and refused to wear the White after Uriah Davies died. There was no finer Shieldsman, and now, while Rand drank himself to oblivion, Wardric had been killed at the hands of traitors. Rand understood very few rumors in his drunken spell, but the news of Yuri Darkings, the former Master of Coin, conspiring to free Caleef Rakun of the Shesaitju from King Pi's grasp was information he retained.

"Don't be ridiculous," the first guard said.

"Fine... was a Black Sand's wench at the Vineyard who told me, I'll admit."

The other two laughed.

"All that time sharing the mad Queen's bed, I'd lose it too—" his comrade nudged him as they noticed Rand passing. They nodded in acknowledgment.

Sharing her bed? Freeing Rebels? Killing Sir Wardric? Rand couldn't believe how busy Redstar had been sullying Torsten's good name. One would think the vile heathen would honor a debt of gratitude to Torsten for allowing him to return alive from the Webbed Woods. Now, instead of answering for his crimes against the Prince, Redstar now served directly under young Pi as prime minister, a position which had gone unoccupied for many kings passed.

Rand glanced back one last time at the slab of stone that would be King Pi's statue. He circled his eyes and ducked into the East Tower. As he turned back, he collided with something and heard a clattering on the floor. A younger gentleman stumbled, and Rand reached out to keep him from falling too.

"My apologies," Rand said.

"Yes, yes, yes," said the young man.

Rand recognized him, thought him an assistant to the Master of Rolls before realizing he had a young page following behind him. Then he remembered that he'd been there when the former holder of the title, Frederick Holgrass, was hanged at the request of the Queen—that he'd fulfilled her request.

Focus, Rand, he told himself as his hands balled into fists.

Liars, monsters, and strangers abounded in the castle where he once happily served. It could all be traced back to Redstar. From Uriah Davies vanishing, to the cursed Prince nearly dying and driving Oleander to do unspeakable things.

He had to trust Wren the Holy. He had to trust Torsten.

He rushed by the new Master of Rolls without bothering to help with the mess. It earned him a glare, but there was no time to dawdle. If he were discovered, everything would be for naught. He'd be hanged for abandoning his post, or worse, thrown into a dungeon to live forever with what he'd done.

He scaled the stairs of the West Tower two at a time. Wren said Redstar was in the Wearer's chambers—Torsten's chambers—and Rand knew well where they were. Another noble or council member Rand didn't recognize passed by as if Oleander had driven away every familiar face in the castle.

He reached the long hall at the second highest level of the castle, where councilmen and other dignitaries kept their quarters. The Wearer of White's room was first down the line as if he were meant to protect all the rest. The shield of the kingdom's noblest nobles.

A Drav Cra warlock stood outside, wearing a ratty cloak and discolored furs. A necklace of bones and totems fell to her narrow waist. Her expressionless face aimed forward, with eyes staring off into nothingness as if her soul was already in Elsewhere. She may have been pretty once, before she let her hair go wild and covered her face with paint like a demon, white beneath her nose and solid black above.

Rand grew up like any other proper Glassmen, attending services at the changing of the moons in the name of Iam, receiving His light at the weekly congregation his end of Dockside, honoring the Dawning. Other than being forced to shirk the lazy accent of his upbringing, he'd never been good at learning; otherwise, he might have gone on to study the holy scripture. But he was always good at fighting, at defending his sister even though she rarely needed it. The King's Shield—sworn protectors of the Iam's chosen kingdom—seemed the only possible choice.

To see a faithful servant of the Buried Goddess guarding the very chambers reserved for Rand's leader... suddenly it put everything into perspective. He knew what he had to do. He knew why he had to do it. But only now was he entirely sure he was going to.

The corridor was empty except for the warlock.

"I must speak with Redstar, by request of the Queen Mother," Rand said.

The woman didn't bother to face him. "Arch Warlock, Drad Redstar is busy and must not be disturbed. Tell her she can wait."

"She said it's in regards to King Pi. It seemed urgent."

"There is only one being who requires urgency."

"Please..." Rand begged, letting his shoulders sag. "Do you know what the Queen Mother will do to me if I return to her alone?"

"His convention with the goddess will conclude in due time. You are free to wait, but hers is the only scorn you should fear, knight."

"Okay, I'll, uh... I'll wait right here."

He went to step by the warlock, keeping his defeated tone and posture. The warlock's eyes stayed unfocused. Rand took two steps, then whipped around and swung. His glaruium-hard gauntlet crashed into the warlock's jaw, and she went down in an instant. He'd never been one to hit a woman, but chivalry died for her when she chose to be a warlock.

Rand waited for her to spring up, but she remained still.

"So much for your goddess' powers," he whispered. He approached the door cautiously. It was unlocked. The knob turned with a barely audible click, and he slowly pushed it in. First, he saw the familiar relics of Shieldsmen past lining the walls. Then, sitting with his legs folded in the center of the room, was Redstar.

He was completely naked, palms raised to the ceiling, and covered in thick blood. His infamous birthmark stretched down the side of his neck and over his shoulder. Rand never realized it was so extensive. Every inch of his back was scarred—sword marks, frost burn, and even animal bites. All the windows were covered in sackcloth, the wavering light of dozens of candles surrounding, illuminating him.

Redstar muttered under his breath in a strange language, his fingers twitching. Arrayed on the floor before him was a series of stone shards fitted together like a puzzle to create a mural of imagery reminiscent of the stained glass designs of the God Feud found in Yarrington Cathedral. He recognized Mount Lister in the center and the Eye of Iam above it, but much of the rest was unclear including strange, florid inscriptions which wrapped its border in a foreign language.

Rand slowly unsheathed his longsword and approached him. He drew steady breaths, kept his footsteps light, and forced his mind clear. It took all his King's Shield training to do the latter, but he managed. At the same time, he battled his training—battled his instincts of knowing that stabbing an unarmed, unarmored man in the back wasn't the way of a Shieldsman. But he was a Shieldsman only in appearance, and even then, barely. He'd failed a long time ago. At least this failure might right all his wrongs. He knew such an act would likely keep him from entering the Gate of Light and earn him a place in Elsewhere, but he didn't care. As he prepared to strike, he hoped that maybe, perhaps, he was performing the work of Iam.

Remember me well, Sig, he thought to himself.

One last step and he thrust his sword toward the base of Redstar's skull. The tip stopped just short as if a shield had blocked it, but there was only air.

Rand glanced up from the blade and saw one of Redstar's bloody hands closed into a fist, blood squeezing out from the creases.

"I wondered how long it would take you to get out, Torsten," Redstar said, flippantly.

He stood and strolled to his bed. The muscles in Rand's arms tensed as he struggled, but his arm was frozen along with the rest of him.

He tried to speak, but even his mouth was forced shut by the magic.

"Ah, not Torsten. You two share the same aura." He chuckled as he put on his robe. He released his fist and said, "Speak."

"What devilry is this!" Rand questioned.

Redstar turned. He had a grin smeared across his face. "The same aura, indeed. He sent you, didn't he?"

Rand said nothing; he merely grimaced as he continued his futile attempts to move.

"Your eyes betray you, knight," Redstar said. He picked up a dagger from atop the stone mural. The handle was carved from bone and the blade curved. The same foreign language found on the mural was etched into the hilt. The edge was still wet with the blood from his sliced hands.

"And your heart betrays you, heathen," Rand snapped. "You will not make it out of this room alive."

"Another insufferable zealot? I swear, I thought only your former master was cut from so rigid a cloth."

Sweat glistened on Redstar's forehead, and streaks, commingled with blood, drew lines on his crimson birthmark. Redstar kept his voice firm, but Rand could see the dark rings hanging beneath his eyes like bloated coin purses. Whatever dark ceremony he had just been involved in clearly had him drained.

"Wait," Redstar said. "I recognize you." He squinted as he scrutinized Rand's face, then began to cackle. "You're the Wearer who replaced Torsten, aren't you? The coward who tucked tailed and ran from my lovely sister? Just like everyone else."

"Release me from whatever this is, and I'll show you cowardice," Rand growled.

Redstar leaned in close. His grin vanished and his features darkened.

"You? A deserter and a drunk? I can smell the ale in your sweat. It reeks of weakness. Are you the best Torsten could find to come for me? I suppose after his little performance at Winde Port, the Shield is even less loyal to him than I expected. I thought perhaps that Pasic fellow, Nikserof, but you? I'm insulted."

"You—"

"Don't speak!" Redstar raised his other hand and pressed his fingers together. Rand's lips sealed again, and this time he couldn't even groan. Redstar then glanced back at the stone mural and the circle of candles around it. "Is this another test, my goddess? I have done everything you ask. Why do you not return to your realm in full?"

Rand remained frozen but noticed that Redstar had to take a breath before the last sentence. He was straining, winded. All the signs were showing of a man in a sparring duel ready to be overtaken, down to the way he held his slumped shoulders.

So Rand pushed with all his might to move his sword. It stung with unimaginable ferocity, but he didn't back down. He wanted to scream at the top of his voice, but his lips were sealed. He pictured Sigrid with a knife to her throat from one of Redstar's savage followers. He pictured Tessa's rotting corpse swinging in the wind at the command of the sister Redstar drove to madness. And then, he remembered himself, vision going black as the sheet tightened around his throat. Ready to give up until Iam's highest servant arrived to give him one final task, to give him purpose.

His lips suddenly parted, and he released a scream that shook the heavens. His sword hand twitched, and while he wasn't in complete control, he was able to swipe upward. The blade, forged by Hovom, the castle smith, cleaved Redstar's hand from his wrist. The Arch Warlock stumbled backward, gawking down at the stump on the end of his arm as blood gushed.

"The madness ends today!" Rand declared. Suddenly, he was free of the dark magic. He charged forward and swung at Redstar, who ducked and spun around. Redstar's gaze fell to his dagger, still gripped by the cloven hand.

Rand came at him again. The tip of his blade sliced Redstar's robe as he evaded another blow. He was quick as the dire wolves of his homeland, but Rand didn't stop. He measured his attacks, desperate to finish him.

"Enough!" Redstar finally roared.

Rand's blade stopped inches from the warlock's heart, then flew from his grip as he soared backward. He slammed into the stone wall so hard it cracked, arms and legs spread. Redstar remained on the other end of the room, panting like a wild beast. Two streams of blood trickled down from his nostrils, and his pupils filled the entire iris of his eyes.

He used his stump of a wrist to hold up his other arm and thrust them both forward. Rand felt as if the magic intensified by a hundred times as it crushed him against the wall.

"You think you have weakened me?" he growled. "The more of my blood that falls to the earth, the stronger my connection to her power!" His fingertips remained inward, and Rand's glaruium armor started to tighten around his body, constricting his throat, bending his ribs. Rand could do nothing but gurgle.

"Do you feel that?" Redstar said. "You fools have spent centuries mining the stone imbued with Nesilia's power after Bliss struck her down and Iam was too weak to save her. Coating yourselves in a shell of her protection. None of you were bright enough to even question why the stuff was so strong." He clenched his fingers more, and the armor squeezed so tight Rand couldn't breathe. "Others are difficult to control but you, Shieldsman, it's like you're wearing strings."

Darkness nipped at Rand's vision. He felt like he was back in his shoddy room above The Maiden's Mugs, swinging from the rafters with a noose around his neck. *Failing Sigrid. Failing himself. Failing everybody.*

"You thought that you could destroy me, her Hand?" Redstar said. "You pathetic, little fool. I will wear your bones."

"You will not lay a finger on another of Iam's children," someone said from the doorway.

The pressure exerted by Redstar's magic let up. Rand was still pressed against the wall, but as his armor expanded back to its proper form, he found himself able to breathe again. He and Redstar both looked to the entrance, and Rand was greeted by a familiar sight to eyes blurred by strangulation. Wren the Holy shuffled in with his cane. His scarred face where his eyes had once been scrunched up, leaving crow's feet as if he were in pain.

"I suggest you leave, old man," Redstar said. "We wouldn't want you breaking anything."

"Wren… go," Rand rasped.

"I will leave when you let the boy go." He walked in further and positioned himself between Rand and Redstar. "Not before."

"You would protect a murderer willing to stab an unarmed man in the back?" Redstar asked. "Though I suppose that was the way of your God's champion, Liam. Win, no matter how many orphans are left behind."

"Enough posturing!" Wren said, projecting his voice with a timbre no man his age should bear. "Your pettiness and lust for revenge are going to bring this kingdom to ruin."

"Then I will sleep in its ashes." Redstar raised his hand high again, and Rand was compressed from every direction.

"This man came at my request. If you must have blood, take mine, but you will let him go."

"No, Your Holiness," Rand grated. "You still have a part to play."

"Release him!" Wren slammed his cane down in front of him with both hands. The floor cracked like he had the strength of a giant and the crystalline Eye of Iam carved upon the handle began to glow. The blinding light folded in front of them as if it were a shield. Redstar's hold completely vanished, and Rand collapsed to the floor, gasping for air.

"Yours isn't the only deity with tricks up her sleeve," Wren said. Redstar's bloody limbs remained outstretched, the air between them rippling from magical energy. Wren's shield blocked it all and seemed even to push Redstar back. The sheets whipped off the bed and the many relics around the room clattered to the stone floor, several shattering. The rest of the warlock's face went red to match his birthmark as he drew on Elsewhere to break through.

Even once air filled his lungs, Rand remained frozen on the floor, shocked. People often spoke of Wren and other priests performing feats of healing that could be described as no less than magic, but he'd never seen any of them do anything like this. Wren turned back to face him. Heavy beads of sweat ran down the High Priest's forehead, and Rand wondered if the man could somehow see even without his eyes.

"You must run, Rand Langley of Yarrington," Wren said.

Rand stared at the spot where the man's eyes should have been.

"I won't leave you." Rand reached down, grasping his fallen longsword, and went to charge, but Wren stuck one of his arms out to impede him. The cane shook in his other hand, the preternatural light beginning to flicker.

"I cannot retain him much longer." Now he sounded every bit as old and brittle as he appeared. "He's stronger now than either of us ever imagined."

"He'll kill you."

"He'll kill us all," Wren said. "Torsten put his faith in you and so did Iam. Prove it was not misplaced."

"I… I don't know what to do," Rand said, voice quavering.

Wren's lips creased into a smile. "I never have. Now go. Perhaps Torsten was wrong in thinking this great act could be completed alone."

Rand's gaze darted between them. Redstar slowly battled the energy expelled from Wren's light shield and approached the cane. He wore the expression of a wolf crouched above its prey, ravenous and ready to pounce—barely even human.

"You've gone too far now, holy man!" Redstar shouted, crowing like a madman. "My Lady and I will break you!"

Darkness now filled even the whites of the Arch Warlock's eyes. Wren's legs and arms quaked.

"I won't fail you," Rand said. "I'll find another way." He bolted for the door. He stepped over the unconscious body of the female warlock, then heard shouting. He glanced the other way and saw a host of Glass soldiers bearing down on him. That was when he realized he was leaving the private chambers of the royal uncle with a bloodstained sword and armor, standing over a body.

They were coming from further down the corridor, so he took off toward the stairs that would lead back to the bailey. As he skidded around the corner, a Shieldsman was ascending. The knight went for his sword, but Rand leaped over him, slamming into the wall at the next landing. A blade hummed toward his head, but he ducked under it before continuing down the stairs.

Horns sounded throughout the castle, vibrating in the stone. Some were familiar, belonging to the Shieldsmen. Others had a wild sound to them, and he recalled the terror of Drav Cra longboats lining the docks in South Corner.

Rand knocked a candelabra down behind him to slow the Shieldsman at his back, then hurried for the Great Hall. He slowed his pace when he reached it, remembering what he was wearing. He sheathed his sword where the blood was most apparent and kept his head down as chaos broke out all around him.

He had no idea what to do. Wren placed his faith in him again, even after his latest failure, and he'd gotten himself surrounded. He considered making a run for the dungeons to free Torsten, but he'd never make it down now that the castle was swarming—the whole city likely too. An assassination attempt on a member of the royal family, no matter how awful he was, couldn't go unanswered.

Dockside was the only place in Yarrington he knew he could hide out and regroup. The poor folk there never talked, proven by how he'd remained there even after deserting the shield. Torsten had found him, but he imagined that more a result of the man's prowess than anyone ratting.

Rand veered toward the front gates and picked up his pace. Shieldsmen and Drav Cra flowed in from the bailey in a steady stream, none seeming to notice them. Rand was nearly through the gates when the Shieldsman from the stairs hollered, "Seize him!"

Rand glanced back and dozens of eyes fell upon him. He didn't wait around. He sprinted through the great doors into the bailey. Horses were tied up along the wall, and he sliced the rope on one before mounting it. A soldier was already at the castle gates, cranking them closed.

Rand spurred the horse onward, kicking at its side, driving it to pound its hooves into the dirt. Once the gate sealed, he'd be doomed. Barking sounded as dire wolves raced out from the bailey's stables and gave chase. Rand's horse squeezed through the closing gates just in time, barreling through a few guards. The wolves scratched at the wood and howled. Arrows clacked against the snow-covered street behind him from archers on the wall.

He yanked on the reins and sent the horse toward the busy marketplace. A quick glance over his shoulder revealed a few glass soldiers on horseback. He kicked his horse's haunches again, but they were going downhill, and the streets were slick with frost. The horse's front hooves slid apart, and it dipped, launching Rand forward.

He slammed into the street, and he skidded into a mob, knocking the legs out of many before rolling to his feet. Things had heated up since he left the Square, and guards were busy keeping the tensions between the populace at bay. The din of cursing citizens drowned out the horns from the castle.

Rand took one quick look up at the men chasing him, then shoved his way through the mob. By the time he was through, he'd lost them and was safely into the back alleys leading down to South Corner and Dockside.

Wren the Holy had called upon Iam to give Rand a second chance at making things right in Yarrington. The next time he'd be ready, he just had to figure out his next move. One thing was clear after witnessing Redstar's power firsthand—he couldn't do it alone.

XV

THE MYSTIC

The moment the darkness around Sora faded, she found herself standing within the circular chamber where Lord Bokeo brought her to meet the Ancient One and who Sora surmised were what remained of the mystics Liam conquered. She slapped her hands against something soft and supple out of reflex. Lord Bokeo took the hits like he deserved them.

"It is fine, my dear," he said, grabbing her arms to stop her. "Tell me, what did you see?"

Sora spun a quick circle, desperate to find Nesilia. At that very moment, she needed more than anything to see her again.

"Nesilia!" she cried out, but no answer came.

Lord Bokeo pulled her close, eyes wide like saucers. "You saw the Goddess of Earth? Where?"

"I was there," Sora said, eyes still darting around the room as if she'd suddenly appear again. "I was in Elsewhere."

"Elsewhere…. You were in Elsewhere?" he said, urgency saturating his words. "What did you see?"

"I told you." She pulled herself free. "I must go back. I have to go back. Send me back!"

"Sora, please. Stop," he said. "The Ancient One, Aihara Na, would not have sent you to Elsewhere."

"There's no mistaking that feeling, Lord Bokeo. I was there. I heard my friend who is stuck there. I saw Nesilia. It was all so real. I... I know what communing with Elsewhere feels like and I was there."

The emptiness she'd been feeling in Whitney's absence was now magnified by her being with him, even fleetingly in the ethereal realm, and the hole left in the wake of Nesilia. Her presence was intoxicating. Sora had never wanted to be closer to anyone ever, and that brought a sense of guilt. Whitney was trapped in a nightmare with the monster Kazimir, and she let herself be distracted from that awful fact in the presence of Nesilia.

Sora surveyed the room and the now-empty thrones. "Where are... they?"

"You were unconscious for some time. They gave me the honor of waiting for your return."

"Aquira," Sora said, suddenly and turned quickly, looking for any signs of the wyvern.

Lord Bokeo squeezed her shoulder and tried to get her to focus on him. "Breathe, Sora. Do not worry. Aquira is well known to the Council. They are... catching up."

Sora shook him off. "Would you just tell me what's going on? Why did she send me there? Why?"

"The Ancient One sent you nowhere. She merely shows you the truest parts of your soul."

Whitney, Sora thought.

"She gives you insight into what was and what is to come," he continued. "If you saw the goddess... please, try to have peace. I know this is all very confusing and hard to grasp, but the Ancients—they've been expecting you for many years, well before Aquira told them your time had come."

"But I came here. I chose to be here. I..." Sora finally drew a few deep breaths to calm herself. Enough to look the man in the eyes. "How did they know? I don't understand anything she told me."

"It has been heard on the wind and in the waters. The call of nature beckons forth the heart of the gods."

More riddles. If this is what was left of the once mighty Mystic Order

Sora had read about, able to move earth and summon storms, they now reminded her more of Redstar. Always talking in circles. But what Lord Bokeo said reminded Sora of something that happened in her vision of Elsewhere.

"While I was in Elsewhere—"

"You were not there," Lord Bokeo interrupted. "You must trust me on this."

"Wherever it was then. I heard something—or rather, I said something. It doesn't make sense to me but, maybe you could?"

"Tell me," Lord Bokeo said.

"Tsu shensughu ywen zhun tahuet feng yaris tsu weyong ywen hou."

"How do you—"

"When I was in Else—there, it was like… I don't know how to explain it, but I can understand your language. *Yi zhu naji mei tong.* I guess... I can speak it now too."

A smile spread wide across Lord Bokeo's face. "They were right."

"Who was right?" Sora asked.

"The spirit of the gods," Lord Bokeo, whispered to himself as he took her by the arm and pulled her down the stone steps, "is found in the one with the will of fire."

"I know how it translates but what does it mean?"

In response, he took her by the arm and said, "Come. It means time is shorter than I'd thought."

Lord Bokeo led her back out to the bookstore. It was still light outside, but the sun was well along its descent. Sora pulled back on him at the door to stop them. He'd been in such a rush it caused him to stumble and knock over a few worn books.

"Lord Bokeo, I'm not going a step further until you give me some answers!" she demanded.

He promptly released her and tended to the fallen books. She thought she could hear him whispering to them under his breath. When he finished, he glanced up.

"Please, indulge me just a moment longer," he said. "I promise the answers will become clear to you. We aren't going far."

She bit her lip, looked back at the dark staircase they'd emerged from, then conceded. *I've come this far already…*

Lord Bokeo led her outside and rushed through the streets, forcing her to keep up. They dodged Glass soldiers along the way who were finishing clearing Xiahou Boulevard.

"What is all this?" Sora asked, referring to the barricades stanchioning off the road, fearing it truly was Winde Port all over again.

"Tonight begins a weeklong celebration called, *Gyuan Jie*—"

"Festival of Ghosts," Sora translated without a second thought.

"Yes, indeed. It is an ancient celebration of our people—those who have passed on to be with the gods."

"And the Glassmen allow this?" she asked, thinking about the defaced statues which now all resembled King Liam.

"King Liam didn't, but when he left Panping in the hands of Lord Phillipi Nantby, the Governor welcomed it. They enjoy it as much as we, and it leads into the Dawning, providing extra time for leisure. With as much drinking and carousing as goes on—they care not what reason we give them for partaking."

As they continued, Sora saw a building that stood out, wrapped by a porch on all four sides. Upon its gates sat two stone monkeys. Their hands were broken off at the wrists and patched in between them, as if an afterthought, was an Eye of Iam.

"What is that place?" Sora asked.

"In the days of the Council, it was a temple to Heragi, God of Misfortune. Now, it is like all of our temples, a Church of Iam."

"That is awful," Sora said.

"It makes them comfortable, which keeps everyone happy."

"It still seems wrong."

"The people have taken to the Glassmen's faith in the name of peace, but we know the other gods are stirring. These are sacred sites of communing with gods. Just because the effigies and the names change, does not mean the power does. It is something the Glassmen could never understand."

They walked the rest of the way in silence, climbing marble flights of stairs until they came to a stop at a long, public balcony overlooking the lake where Gold Grin's ship docked.

"Beautiful, isn't it?" Lord Bokeo said.

From so high, the lake looked like a mirror, the setting sun casting a pinkish hue over it. The shadow of the abandoned tower of the defeated Mystic Council stretched long toward an outcrop of rock at the edge of the lake. Sora followed the shadow to the shore where it fell upon another tall structure. She followed the coast, noting several such spires. That was when Sora realized that the mystic tower also served as a massive sundial.

"Breathtaking," she marveled.

"Sora," Lord Bokeo said, turning to her, "what do you know of the gods?"

"Which gods?"

"Our people once worshiped the Many and the Few—*Pinyun tsu chahn ji duo.* Or simply *Pinyun.* Now they embrace Iam. Iam is not our enemy, but his followers have created him to be such."

"I know little of your gods, only of Iam and a bit about Nesilia. I—my friends and I, ended the life of another whom we were told was a goddess. But I am not so sure. I didn't think gods could die."

"Bliss—the One Who Remained."

"Yes!" Sora said, then her eyes narrowed. "How did you know?"

"Your fame precedes you in many ways. The destruction of the deformed goddess brought confirmation to the now-Secret Council of your preparedness. It was no accident you found Aquira soon after."

"That is what the Ancient said, but I still don't understand."

"May I tell you a story of the gods?" Lord Bokeo asked.

"Will it explain everything?"

He smiled. "Perhaps everything. Perhaps nothing." He motioned to a stone bench facing the lake, and they took a seat.

"Many centuries ago, before the molding of man, before even the forging of the dwarves by Meungor the Sharp Axe, the gods made tabernacle upon this earth," he began. "Pantego was vast, far vaster than any world in which they'd dwelt before.

"Upon this very spot, rising above these cliffs stood a majestic mountain, and the gods all called it home. It was rare to find any of them upon it, they were far too busy playing and shaping the world, but it was home nonetheless.

"One spring morning, when the dew was just so, and the flowers bloomed, bringing with them the fragrance of the eternal planes, the gods were spread widely throughout the land. Our legend tells of the Emperor

God—the most powerful of all gods—call him Iam if you'd like, but our people did not. He decided the mountain should reflect the beauty of its inhabitants. So, with his great hand, he scooped up the rock, grass, and all that was within, and carried it far across the western horizon, searching for the place of greatest beauty. When he found a vast ocean and green, fertile land, he left it. Weary from his travels, he rested before making the trek back to the others to share with them the news of his findings."

"Mount Lister…" Sora whispered.

Lord Bokeo nodded "When the gods and goddesses returned," he continued, "and saw their beloved home was gone, they wept until they were dry and their tears filled the chasm left by the mountain. They created something new and possibly more beautiful even than the mountain. This very lake. But the gods would not be content; they missed their mountain. They cried out to one another, demanding justice be served to their Emperor God. One rose up, higher than the rest. The Goddess of Death and Darkness. You knew her as Bliss."

"She, more than any, would not stand the barb at the hand of the Emperor, for she still did not know that what he did was for all their benefits. So, she called together the thousands—gods and lesser gods. Even those who'd long since abandoned the mountain in hopes of forging their own peoples and lands—Meungor the Sharp Axe, god of dwarves, Bilnor god of the giants, Vilnor, his brother, god of the frost giants, and many more.

"When they found the Emperor God, he slept peacefully upon his new home. Only he wasn't alone. For it was only with the help of the Goddess of Earth that he moved the mountain, and she saw his wisdom. Bliss led the charge, even though the Goddess was her sister, carrying with her the full weight of the scorned gods. But none could match the Emperor's strength, and none would hear his words."

"Before long, the gods had forgotten why they battled or who they were angry against. They turned on one another, fury driving them to destroy each other. The violence of gods tore a rift in the fabric of reality, creating Elsewhere and damning them all within. Now they all, the *Pinyun*, crave to once again return to this land. But we cannot allow it. This is why I know the wise Aihara Na would not have opened up a gateway to Elsewhere. It is too dangerous."

It was quiet for some time after he finished and they stared upon the lake. The shadow of the tower stretched so far now in the fading daylight it scraped along the western coast of the city.

"The tower," Sora said, breaking the silence. "What is it really?"

"It was once a place full of life and magic. The Red Tower—the home of the Mystic Order for millennia. Liam, when he outlawed magic, first made the Mystic Council seal it—with magic of all things! Could you imagine? As if that could stop those few mystics who remain. Within lies the knowledge of every mystic ever to walk Pantego, where the Well of Wisdom still bubbles."

"Then we should go," Sora said.

Aran Bokeo laughed. "Your eagerness may be the end of you, Sora. Tonight is an important night for our people. I would encourage you to clear your mind of all this until the time has come for your training."

"Why not start now?"

Lord Bokeo's legend of the gods sounded just like all the others she'd heard, a story, nothing more. The mystics might have feared opening Elsewhere because of them, but that meant they knew how. Which meant she could learn.

"The time will come quickly, and it will not be easy," Lord Bokeo said. "Do not rush it, for it will not be pleasant. Tonight will be a night you will not soon forget, as will the nights thereafter. There is much to appreciate about the Festival of Ghosts. Just try to take it all in. Do you have any autlas?"

"Plenty," she said.

"Good, good, good. Then I recommend you head to the Emperor's Quilt and ask for a room overlooking the lake. The views tonight will be spectacular. If they are booked, tell them I sent you."

"And they'll believe me, just like that?" She wasn't sure if the Panpingese were just an overly trusting people, but in the Glass, people required proof.

Lord Bokeo chuckled. "I own the place."

"Of course you do…"

"Now, I suggest you try to enjoy the night. Forget about all this and see your homeland for the jewel it truly is." Lord Bokeo stood and brushed off his robe.

"Wait. You said my questions would be answered. You've only given me more."

"Sometimes, the quickest route to enlightenment is the longest path around the desert." He bowed, then left her.

Sora watched as he descended the marble stairs and disappeared. She considered following him, but couldn't take any more riddles. Then she considered seeking out Tum Tum, but the thought of finding him in a brothel brought a sour taste to her lips.

Instead, she decided to heed Lord Bokeo's suggestion. She was exhausted, mentally and physically, and a plush bed at an inn owned by a wealthy member the Winde Traders Guild—and evidently the Secret Council—sounded about right.

Finding the Emperor's Quilt was no trouble at all, especially now that she could understand Panpingese. She could even read it now. She rented a room using Lord Bokeo's name and plopped down on a luxurious bed. The cool lake air blew in through an open balcony. At least, it felt cold to her. She'd gotten used to sharing a bed with Aquira out on the sea, who was like an oven when she slumbered.

Sleep was impossible to come by anyway. Sora's mind replayed the meeting with the mystics, and then Nesilia, the sound of Whitney's voice calling to her. Her mind swam in the many mysteries.

She'd heard Whitney there in Elsewhere, just like Gold Grin said. She was sure of it. All she needed to do was enter again, find him, and figure a way to bring him out. If she'd put him there alongside Kazimir in the first place, certainly she could remove him. And if anyone could teach her how, it was the strange, hidden mystics she'd just encountered.

But it wasn't only that. For so long she'd sought to belong. The mystics were her people, both in race and in their ability to answer why she had this strange power that seemed to extend beyond any normal blood mages. She'd set off with Whitney to find them, and now, she had.

A chance to understand.

So, as she lay, staring at the wooden ceiling, she decided she would see it through. Whatever it was the mystics wanted. It was the only way. She would learn about her power, bring Whitney back alive before it was too late, and leave Kazimir behind where he could never harm another innocent soul like Tayvada Bokeo again.

Having a clear path calmed her enough to finally start to doze off, until a loud bang caused her to shoot upright. Shouting followed, coming from downstairs in the streets.

She swung her feet off the bed, but two more deafening blasts had her covering her head and ears. Terrified.

XVI

THE DESERTER

Watchtower bells echoed from every direction. Guards flocked down streets, sending Rand through back alleys. By the time he passed through South Corner and into Dockside, their footsteps were distant, lost to the chimes of moored ships and the rasp of beggars.

Nobody would question him here, and the guards were so scarce it'd take some time for the search to reach the grimy place. Rand threw his back against the nearest wall and finally took a moment to breathe. He couldn't get air down fast enough. His chest felt like it was going to implode, and the armor still felt tight from Redstar's dark magic even though it was normal again.

He considered tearing it off, then noticed the dirt-covered boy kneeling next to him, a tin outstretched and rattling.

"Spare a bronzer, Sir Shieldsman?" he asked, then coughed.

Rand regarded the child, skin and bones, a product of Dockside. *Saving the realm is enough.* He could worry about saving Dockside later, plus, the child likely had more autlas to his name than Rand did.

Rand started off at a brisk walk without a backward glance. Keeping his shoulders straight, he bore the proper poise of a true Shieldsman. He took steady, slow breaths through his teeth, so he wouldn't appear anxious. The cold air made his teeth sting, but the pain made it easier to focus. Docksiders didn't talk to guards, but during the winter months, when there was little to do but survive and gossip, rumors spread like wildfire. A Shieldsman decked out in armor having a panic attack wouldn't remain a mystery for long.

It was dusk by the time he reached the Maiden's Mugs. Before anything, he had to grab Sigrid and get her out. Trapp knew his name, and so did Redstar. It wouldn't be long before word reached these parts and while Docksiders didn't talk, money did. The reward for turning him in would be too much for a sleazy tavern owner like Gideon Trapp to deny.

Grab Sigrid, find shelter, free Torsten. That was the best plan he could come up with. It was clear he couldn't take down Redstar alone, but with him maimed, the two of them might be able to. Torsten's renown as a warrior was unparalleled. Wren had provided Rand a chance to strike again and he…

Wren, Rand thought solemnly. All his church-going life, he'd received Iam's light, but he'd never seen such a display of power in His name. He could only imagine what Redstar would do to the High Priest once he broke through the shield of light the old man had summoned. Rand vowed not to let the distraction go to waste.

He stopped outside the doors of the Maiden's Mugs, drew a few deep breaths. The regulars would be arriving soon, finished with their shifts down at the docks. One had already arrived.

"Shieldsman blessin our li'l corner today?" a drunkard arriving at the same time said. Rand recognized him from other nights imbibing.

"Impossible to get a proper pint in the castle," Rand replied. Stay calm. Act superior. Don't draw attention.

"Impossible to find a proper lass too, eh?" he chuckled. "There be a bar wench here who's pretty as spring. A li'l flower blossom for winter."

Rand knew who he was referring to, but let it slide. "I'm not here for chitchat, just a drink."

The man shrugged. "Suit yerself."

He pushed the door open and stepped inside. Rand followed close behind and bumped into his back when he suddenly stopped. Rand was about to curse him as any Shieldsman would a drunkard, then realized what caused it.

The tavern was abandoned, tables overturned, ale spilled all over the floors. All of Trapp's storage barrels, broken apart, the bar cleaved in two. There were no bodies, but a few splatters of blood were counted on the floor, mixing with ale.

Rand heard a whimper and pushed the drunkard aside to rush toward the sound. Gideon Trapp slumped against the wall behind the bar, ale trickling onto the top of his head from a broken tap. One of his legs bent like a galler's, the wrong way at the knee. His nose was broken and bleeding profusely.

"Trapp, what happened?" Rand questioned, kneeling at his side.

The man's bleary eyes blinked open. His gaze went from Rand's face to his armor, then widened. "So… it is true?" he wheezed.

Rand took him by the shoulders and shook. "Trapp!"

"The savage… he… every guard in Dockside went running toward bells; then he stormed the place."

"Where's my sis—" Footsteps creaked upstairs. Trapp raised one trembling arm and pointed to the ceiling.

Rand shoved him aside and ran for the stairs, unsheathing his sword as he went. A thud followed heavy footsteps and low voices speaking in Drav Crava. Besides his, there were a few apartments upstairs—every door was open revealing ransacked rooms. Beds were flipped, cabinets raided, and in the first room, a man lay sprawled out, groaning on the floor. His face was a flat, bloody mess.

"Where's the one who did this, girl?" a deep voice questioned.

It was coming from the direction of Sigrid's room. Rand couldn't hear the response, but it was muffled and frantic.

"You dragged me here for a girl?" another Drav Cra man answered. "Nesilia's grave… don't you know you can pay for them here?"

"Quiet. I'll never hold an axe again thanks to this little wench."

"Is it just your axe your worried about holding?" The second man cackled.

Rand stopped just outside his door and peered in. A Drav Cra warrior he didn't recognize sat on the table—his table—biting on a piece of the stale bread Sigrid had only recently brought home. A wooden shortbow was slung over one shoulder and a full quiver over the other. A hatchet-axe still dangled from his hip. Apparently, ransacking the place was too easy for him to bother using it.

Behind him, the savage Rand had pushed into the bay had Sigrid pinned against the cabinetry by the throat with his left forearm. His weapon hand hung slack at his side, empty, the skin of his half-clenched fingers discolored from frostbite.

"Now, you whore," he said, "I'm not going to ask again. Where is your man?"

One eating, one crippled. Rand was out of practice, but he liked his odds. He was just about to speak up and answer the devil when Sigrid grabbed a kitchen knife and stabbed her assailant in the shoulder just below the neck. He dropped her and staggered, but didn't go down, the stab missing anything vital.

Sigrid scrambled to the far corner of the room with nowhere to go.

"Bitch!" he barked, tearing the knife out. He stalked toward her, blood staining his furs red. His compatriot burst out laughing, at least until Rand stormed in and cleaved his head from his shoulders in a single, mighty swipe.

"Step away from her," he ordered, his sword directing the remaining savage with a twist of the wrist.

The Drav Cra warrior turned, a steady stream of blood now pouring down his shoulder and chest. As soon as his eyes laid upon Rand, the corner of lips, still purple from the swim in ice-cold water, curled into a smile.

"And here I thought I'd have to go looking for you," he said. He playfully flipped the knife and dropped into a fighting stance, but the man's feet were set wrong, telling Rand it wasn't his dominant hand.

"I'm right here," Rand said. "Sig, get behind me."

She went to move, but the warrior slowly rotated so that he'd be directly between her and Rand. "She's going to watch you die, soldier-boy. No water to push me in this time."

"They're all right about you people. Infesting this city like a sickness with your vile ways."

"I've seen very well what Glassman are capable of. You were probably a pup when the coward Liam invaded my clan to take his Queen. Oleander isn't the only one of us who got forced to bed that night."

"The Queen came of her own free will because she saw what it was like to live in the light."

"'The light,'" he chortled. "All I see outside are clouds."

"You'll see black soon."

Rand charged him and swung. After striking air twice, it was clear to him that he'd gotten lucky down on the docks accidentally knocking this one into the water so fast. The man was nimble as a hare. Rand went high, and the Drav Cra spun around low, slicing Rand where his armor bent at the knee.

"Rand!" Sigrid yelped. She was at his back now, both of them with nowhere to go.

"Stay back," he told her.

The Drav Cra warrior rolled his shoulders and cracked his neck. "Been a long time since I had a fair fight, but I only need one hand to kill you."

Rand charged him again and brought his sword crashing down. The man evaded, rolling to the side. Grabbing Rand by the neck, he flung him into the cabinets headfirst. Rand's ears and forehead were stung by splinters.

"Now where were we, girl?" the man asked, turning to Sigrid who now fully cowered in the corner.

Rand pulled himself free and leaped back into the fight. The warrior dodged without looking, then whipped his frostbitten forearm around and smashed Rand in the face. Rand stumbled back, but not before thrusting his weapon. The man purposefully caught the end of the blade with the palm of his crippled hand. Skin sliced as the metal sunk through, but if he could feel it at all, it didn't show. Once the sword pierced through the other side, he wrenched it out of Rand's grip.

The warrior placed his foot against the wall to spring toward Rand. It went through the thin wall like a sheet of parchment. Rand tried to take advantage, but before he knew what hit him, the warrior lashed out. The now bloody, frozen wrist forced Rand's head down and kept it there as the savage's knee rose to meet Rand's jaw.

Rand flew back, the table cracking in half beneath the full weight of his body and armor. He saw stars but felt the savage on top of him. Blood still poured from the man's neck, now drenching Rand.

"Because of you, I'll never be a dradinengor!" His good fist slammed into Rand's face. "I'm going to drag you into the water. And you'll freeze as I show your girl what a true man is like." He flipped the knife over again and held the blade to Rand's eye.

"Get off him!" Sigrid screamed as she came at him.

His frozen hand snapped up, smacked her across the face, sending her to her knees.

"Don't touch her!" Rand shouted. He went to push the savage off, but the knife returned to his eye, blade glinting so close he could see how red they were in the reflection. He hadn't had a good night's sleep in days, and now after all he'd been through since he decided to string himself up by the neck, he was going to die by the hands of a coward picking on a woman half his size.

Rand, in a last-ditch effort, forced his hand up and dug his gauntleted finger into the man's neck wound. The savage screamed, but easily swatted Rand's hand away.

"Stop fighting, flower picker," the Drav Cra warrior said. "You'll be with the Goddess underground soon. You just—"

Blood sprayed across Rand's face, and the full weight of the warrior fell onto his chest. Rand dragged himself backward, wiped his eyes, and saw the arrow sticking through the savage's neck.

Sigrid stood holding the savage's shortbow, the string still thrumming. Her cheek was split open. His gaze went there first, then to her usually calm eyes. He'd never seen such rage in them.

"Monster!" she yelled. She tore another arrow from the quiver, took two long strides, then straddled over the savage. He still clutched at his neck as he gurgled on a mouthful of blood. She screamed again and brought the arrow down into his chest. Once, twice, again and again, until his eyelids froze open and his limbs wilted, his chest looking like a pincushion.

Tears streamed down her cheeks as she screamed and threw the bow aside, then kicked the fallen assailant repeatedly in the face. Rand regretted how long it took for him to get up and comfort her, but eventually, he caught her arms and pulled her into a tight embrace.

"It's okay now, Sig," he whispered. "I'm back now."

She squeezed him, then shoved away and punched him in the chest. "I heard the bells, I thought…"

"I failed, but I got out. I had to get back here to you, but it seems you didn't need me. How in Iam's name did you learn to shoot like that?"

She sniveled, then released a low chuckle. "Ye weren't the only one paying attention when father took us hunting."

"Father's still saving us from beyond the grave."

"It was a lucky shot," she confessed.

"I'm starting not to believe in luck. Come on." His knees were still shaky, and his legs burned with soreness now that the adrenaline stopped pumping. After months of sitting around drinking, he'd been through more real fights in the last day than his entire service in the King's Shield.

It was clear someone wanted him alive.

"Where are we going?" Sigrid asked.

"Anywhere but here. Redstar's turned the whole Shield against Torsten as he performs some dark ritual in the Wearer's own chambers. We have to stop him, but it's clear I can't do it alone."

He took a step away, but Sigrid's hand fell upon his cheek, and she turned him back. "It's not your fight anymore."

Rand nuzzled her hand, then removed it. "It is. I don't know why, but it's like this is what I was born for. If I don't, Redstar will make this city a playground for his heathen horde, and more good women will be..."

"I understand," she replied solemnly. "But if ye can't do it alone, who can help?"

"Redstar has Wren the Holy in his grips now too, and the King's trust. So, I'm going to free Torsten so the King's Shield may do what it's meant to and shield this kingdom. He defeated Redstar once before, and he made a mistake putting his faith in me alone. But right now, we need to get out of here before the guards arrive."

Sigrid nodded, hurried to the table beside her bed, and grabbed a few items including a necklace. Rand recognized it. The thing belonged to their mother; a bit of bone from a Panpingese sea creature whose name Rand couldn't remember carved into the shape of a water droplet on a rusty, metal band. Then, she hefted the shortbow and slung it over her shoulder. "Just in case," she said, shrugging.

"Smart," Rand replied. He retrieved his sword and a loaf of bread. He had no keepsake from their parents to take with him. No belongings but for the Shieldsman armor on his back. The very armor he'd earned in the name of his parents to try and make Dockside—their home—a little brighter.

"Okay, let's go," Rand said. He took Sigrid's arm and caught her staring at the body of the man she'd killed. The first one was always the toughest, even if it was a monster. "He deserved it," Rand assured her.

"I know." She swallowed hard. "Iam forgive me anyway."

"He will. Now we just have to make sure He has a kingdom left to watch over."

Rand towed her along back down the hall. Groans sounded from within the other rooms as the victims of the Drav Cra recovered from the raid. Downstairs, Gideon Trapp lethargically swept up broken bottles, his wounds slowing him down. The drunkard Rand had arrived with sat at the bar with a pint in hand, utterly oblivious to the chaos. A few others had trickled in as well.

Rand understood well. Most people from Dockside needed to drown out the thoughts of their shoggy lives, and no mess would keep them from their favorite watering hole.

"There ye are," Trapp snapped. He tossed aside his broom and met them at the base of the stairs. "This were yer fault, weren't it? First, ye get my best server hurt, now this?"

"We're leaving, Trapp," Rand said. He went to shove by, but Trapp stood his ground.

"Oh no, ye don't. Ye'll both be working to pay off all of this, ye hear me?"

"She's done here. We both are."

"I don't care what ye think ye know," Trapp said, "ye ain't getting out of this. Valin will hear about this."

"He cares so much he didn't even have a guard looking over the place. Sigrid is done. Step aside."

Gideon Trapp turned to her and softened his tone. "Siggy, don't listen to this drunken brute. There ain't no better work than this in Dockside for a lady like you. Haven't I been good to ye?"

Sigrid shoved a ball of fabric into his gut.

"What's this?" Trapp said. He held it up. It was the skippy outfit he made her wear while serving.

"He ain't a drunken brute," she said. "He's my brother, and yer a right piece of shog ."

Rand flashed Trapp a grin, and then he and Sigrid pushed by.

"Don't ye dare walk away!" Trapp shouted. "I own ye, ye filthy whore's daughter. When Valin finds out what ye cost him—"

"And what did they cost me, Trapp old chum?"

The front door swung open and in strode the last person in Dockside Rand ever wanted to see. Out of instinct, he stopped to place one arm in front of Sigrid while the other hand fell to the grip of his longsword. Dockside had no mayor or constable, only a guard captain who kept as close to Yarrington proper as he could. Even the Master of Ships stayed at the castle and rarely visited.

Valin Tehr was the power. He had been for all of Rand's life. If you stepped into a shop or tavern, it was likely he received taxes from the owners on top of what they paid the Crown. His right leg, scrawny and deformed from birth, made the man walk with a permanent limp and use a cane plated in gold. Even his face, with its oversized chin and wide-set eyes, was nothing to look at, but his mind more than made up for it.

Valin had been a thorn in the side of the King's Shield for many years, though some felt him a necessary scourge. With fear and gold, he kept Dockside in line and its people working hard enough that the Crown turned a blind eye to his more nefarious dealings.

"Mr. Tehr, sir... I...I," Trapp stammered like he was talking to a king. With the way the gangster dressed, however, he may as well have been. And while the man had no King's Shield, a dozen or so thugs entered alongside him.

"Who did you insult this time to bring such destruction?" Valin asked.

"It wasn't me, sir. This, this, drunkard angered the Drav Cra. They came bursting in before we opened, right through the lock."

"Drav Cra and a Shieldsman? I pay you good money to stay inconspicuous."

"Sir, if you don't mind, me and my sister were leaving," Rand said. He took a step, the thugs shadowed his movement, grinning like wild men.

"Not so fast." Valin dragged his misshapen leg forward to get a closer look at Rand. "I know you, don't I, kid?"

"Please, Mr. Tehr," Sigrid said. "We really need to be gone."

"I say who is 'gone' anywhere here!" Valin barked, emphasizing Sigrid's Dockside accent. He spoke with the refinement of a true noble.

Rand pulled his sister back, his fingers wrapping the hilt of his sword now. "In the name of the King's Shield, move aside."

"Yes, no one has more respect for the Shield than I, isn't that right boys?" His crew laughed. One went behind the bar, filled a mug and passed it to another who'd shoved aside the drunk and stole his seat. "Thing is, you're Rand Langley. Wearer for a day, disgraced for a lifetime. And the word is you tried to murder the King's uncle in his own chambers earlier today."

Rand's throat went dry. His palms started to sweat. Inch by inch, he slid his sword out of its sheath.

Valin clicked his tongue in disapproval. "I know everyone in Dockside, kid. You can hide from the Crown. You can hide from Iam. But you can't hide from me." He began to pace, every thud of his cane unnerving Rand further. "I've been keeping an eye on you. Not every day a Docksider earns the Shield," he went on, "but every time I reached out so you might use your post to help this place we call home, you ignored my call."

"I have no quarrel with you, Valin," Rand said. "My father worked at your dock when he was alive, and you paid him well, kept food on our table. I meant no offense in rejecting your advances; I merely wanted to focus on my training."

"Who am I to scorn good old-fashioned hard work? Still, it hurts me that you went off and forgot this place. You had so much potential."

"I never forgot I… Look, I know what you bring in through this place. Let us go, and the secret goes with us.

Valin edged closer, and Rand's heart raced. The man could hardly walk, and he didn't bother carrying a weapon when his thugs could handle things for him, but growing up in Dockside, there wasn't a soul who didn't know that crossing Valin Tehr meant taking a nice swim out into the Torrential Sea.

"Are you threatening me, Rand Langley?" he asked. "You gonna get your Queen to hang me over the walls like the others?"

Rand pictured Tessa and the others swinging in the wind but squeezed his eyes to drive out the image. People in Dockside didn't pay attention to

Glass Castle affairs. It was what made it such a good place for him to shirk his duties. Clearly, Valin knew enough for the whole district.

"No threat… I just… we need to leave," Rand said.

"Going to take another swipe at Redstar? Castle halls not bloody enough for you?"

Rand didn't say a word. Instead, he drew his sword a little further, wary of the thugs surrounding him. Sigrid clutched his arm.

"Why didn't you cut out his black heart the first time, you fool!" Valin laughed and banged him in the pauldron with his cane. His men joined in, and after a short while, Rand forced a nervous chuckle as well.

"If you let us go, I will," Rand said.

Valin eyed one of his men. Unlike the others, this one was older, more refined. His shirt was neatly tucked, and his graying hair combed. All Rand could focus on, however, was his glass eye painted entirely white. He had the sharp nose and noble brow of a man from Brekliodad, as well as a curled, white mustache no westerner could possibly grow.

"Confident, chap, isn't he, Codar?" Valin asked the man.

"Indeed, sir," Codar answered, Breklian accent thick as syrup.

"Too bad. You've got the whole guard in a mad scramble looking for you, kid. Like you're more important than the missing Caleef." Tehr smiled. "You don't have the Caleef, do you?" He leaned in, pretending to look behind Rand. "You aren't getting close enough to that filthy warlock to smell him now, let alone kill him."

"I don't have a choice," Rand said. "Iam needs me."

"The boy is needed by Iam Himself?" More chuckles from the thugs sounded, now nearer.

"They would do well to watch their manners," Sigrid bristled. "Wren the Holy himself asked this of him."

"Ha! The Holy Father asked a sinner to sin?" Valin looked toward the ceiling, closed his eyes, and traced one of them with his finger. "Guess its better to use a sinner than a saint, if there are any left. What is this city coming to?" He looked to Codar as if expecting an answer.

"It is impossible to tell," Codar said.

"Barbarians surrounding us, sharing our mead and nobody in the castle can do a damn thing. Hell, I don't even know a soul in that place anymore, and I used to have the whole council on retainer. You hung a few who owed me a favor."

"Redstar started it all," Rand said. "Now he'll see us fall to ruin."

"And you're going to stop him? You, the hangman who let the mad Queen run wild? If you ask me, it's about time we got a whole new family up in that keep, but I'm happy here in my little fiefdom so long as whoever's on the throne keeps out of it."

"As long as Redstar has the King's ear, the Dockside you know will become a hunting ground for barbarians. I can help stop it."

"Not alone you can't." Valin smirked, then turned to his men. "Get this place cleaned up and grab my shipment. A Shieldsman needs our help rooting out the savages, and I live to serve the Crown."

XVII

THE KNIGHT

Torsten tossed a tiny rock against the wall and let it roll back to him. Then again, and again. It was the best way he'd found of staying sane in the dungeon. Even then, he wasn't sure it was working.

Sitting, waiting for news from Wren the Holy about Rand Langley's mission made it even worse. He'd staked the fate on the kingdom first on Oleander showing a shred of mercy and sending for Wren. When she did, he'd put even more trust in a deserter of the King's Shield to take down an Arch Warlock.

He was running out of faith.

"Yer gonna to need something bigger than that to break out," the old kook in the adjacent cell said. When he wasn't snoring, he couldn't go more than five minutes without having something to say.

"I'm not trying to break out," Torsten replied.

"Ye'll be the first then."

Torsten remained silent, rolling the stone over in his fingers.

"I gave up too." The old man coughed loudly. "Been so many years down here, I dun't know what I'd do outside no how. I be a charm of good luck though. Ye go, try and break out. I bet ye do it."

Torsten clenched his jaw and held his tongue. He had no interest in making friends, but there was nothing else to do. And in the stifling dark-ness, the silence was an easy place to lose oneself.

"Please, by Iam, tell me how an old man trapped down here could possibly be a good luck charm?" Torsten said.

"Each bastard what gets shut in near me, gets out. Not long ago, upstairs, some handsome devil tricked me into tryin and got out himself instead." He hacked out a laugh and a cough simultaneously. "Called himself the greatest thief in Pantego. Stole my freedom, he did."

Torsten allowed his head to sink back against the wall. He couldn't help but smirk. There was no question in his mind who the man was refer-ring to.

"Then, they shoved me down here and some Drav Cra warlock, all metal, and masks, get's put right where you are," the old man continued. "Ye think I talk too much; guy wouldn't shut it for a second even after they muzzled him."

Torsten sat up. He crawled over to the bars and stuck his head through as far as it would go. "Redstar?" he said.

"Yeah that… that sounds familiar."

"He escaped?"

The old coot peeked through as well, made visible by the flickering torch outside his cell. His face was so loose with age it looked like it was melting off his skull. Only a handful of rotting teeth remained in his mouth, and when he grinned Torsten caught a whiff of the foulest smell imaginable, and he'd endured the sewers of Winde Port.

"Ye shoulda seen it," he said, ignoring the question. "The gods damned new King hisself came down here every night and talked to him. Sat right outside the cell yer in now. I swear on me bastard son, there ain't never even been a Royal Councilman willing to stay down here, and I been locked up since Liam could walk. I'm innocent of course, but ain't no one with them decision-making ears be willin to listen."

"You didn't answer my question. Did Redstar escape?"

"I wouldn't say that."

Torsten slammed on the bars. "Old man! I need to know."

"Iam's light, ye really are a nutter ain't ye? The King let him out hisself. I know it was him because of the crown, ye see, and the stature. I

888

didn't even know Liam had a son." He cackled. "But I'm guessin he didn't when I was locked in."

Torsten backed away and hung his head. "Did you hear anything they had to say, or were you too busy yammering?"

"If I did, I wun't tell you." Torsten heard the man's knees drag across the floor as he slinked back into the corner.

"I don't have time for this. What did they say?"

"Ye have all the time in Pantego, ye biff. Gods… even the warlock'd be better company than ye—least he sang some songs."

Torsten squeezed his fist and slowly drew air through his teeth. "Please, tell me."

"Now that's better!" The man guffawed. "It wasn't too much really. Just some apologizin for doing what had to be done to open eyes, talk about Iam and the Buried Goddess. All borin stuff. The warlock was much more entertainin when he was mutterin to hisself alone. But, of course, he got invited right out by the King hisself. See? Charm of good luck."

"If only it were thanks to you. That man is a foul, no good—"

"Monster," someone addressed him from the opposite direction. Soft footsteps approached from around the corner, then a familiar face outside his cell was painted orange by the dim torchlight, the birthmark covering half of it as dark as red wine.

"Redstar," Torsten growled.

"That's the man!" the old coot said excitedly. "Walked right on outta here like he—"

"Quiet." Redstar raised his left hand and squeezed his fingers, a bloody bandage wound around his palm. The old man went silent in an instant. "I told you I would be visiting, old friend," he addressed Torsten. "How are you faring down here?"

"I preferred when it was quiet," Torsten said.

"Must you always be such a grouser? Come, Torsten, I'd like to show you something."

"If you open that door, I will kill you."

"And them?" Redstar snapped his fingers, and two King's Shieldsmen approached, their heavy boots shaking dust from the walls. The first was Sir Nikserof Pasic, the most veteran of his order remaining within the Glass Castle. His arm wound had healed. The other, Sir Austun Mulliner, whom Torsten had wounded so deeply outside Winde Port. "Will you murder them too, just like last time?"

Torsten hurried to the bars and looked Nikserof in the eye. The Shieldsman refused to look back. "Nikserof, you must not listen to a word he says," Torsten pled. "Can't you see how he's deceived you all?"

"They are under strict orders to keep me safe, by the King himself," Redstar said. "After a man of your order—former order—tried to kill me in my quarters, they're lucky they aren't all hanged. But that man wasn't really one of them, was he, Torsten?"

Torsten's heart sank. He hadn't yet heard from anyone, but that meant Wren the Holy was able to reach out to Sir Rand Langley to redeem himself through the death of Redstar. Clearly, he'd failed.

"What did you do to him?" Torsten questioned.

"Far less than I should have. He escaped like the spineless rat he is."

"Turning to a Deserter?" Sir Mulliner said. "By Iam, what happened to you in Winde Port?"

Sir Nikserof didn't say a word.

"I thought you were better than turning to deserters and ale-soaked cowards to do your dirty work," Redstar said. "You have abandoned honor in your mad quest to prove me something I'm not. Your men see it too."

Torsten again tried to get Nikserof to acknowledge him, but now understood why he wouldn't. Taking the vows of the King's Shield meant serving for life, and Rand Langley had abandoned the castle after Torsten returned, leaving nobody to answer for why so many had died. By their code, he should have been hanged.

Torsten realized then that he could have attempted asking Nikserof to do what was necessary and take down Redstar. They had fought together in Winde Port, bled together. Instead, Torsten went to a deserter for help— failed—and again played right into Redstar's hands.

Torsten shifted his gaze to Mulliner, who stared back, eyes full of frustration and judgment. Torsten closed his eyes and let his chin fall to his chest.

Sir Nikserof removed a ring of keys from his belt and began unlocking the cell door.

"Nikserof, whatever this is, there's still time," Torsten said without looking up. "I know I don't deserve to wear the White, but he will destroy you. Hang me if you must, but set him beside me."

"Sir Pasic," was Nikserof's only reply as the keys fumbled within the lock. *He's nervous. Perhaps he might still welcome the opportunity to tear the warlock down.*

"Some of the King's Shield know how to obey the command of their king," Redstar said. "It shouldn't be so difficult as it's in the name, but you seem intent on undermining him at every turn."

The lock clicked, and the door swung open. Nikserof and Mulliner entered and seized Torsten's arms to cuff them. Austun then gave him a hard tug.

"Would you listen to me!" Torsten implored. "He doesn't serve the King; he only serves himself!"

"Relax, Torsten," Redstar groaned. "This isn't your execution. I simply want to show you something."

"Nothing you show me will change a thing."

"We shall see." Redstar grinned. "Come."

The Shieldsmen dragged Torsten along. Behind their group, he noticed Freydis following, soundless and reserved, yet Torsten knew madness stirred just below her surface. Nikserof still refused to look at him, and Torsten wondered if he were being controlled by black magic at their hands. The old coot in the adjacent cell sat against the wall, pawing at his mouth, seemingly unable to open it.

Torsten paused to look in, and Redstar took notice.

"Ah, my apologies," the Arch Warlock said. "The Lady has been so kind to me with her power of late, sometimes I forget." He spread his fingers, and the old man gasped for air. He remained cowering in the corner, quiet for once.

They led Torsten to the castle's entry hall. He'd made himself busy the entire way trying to talk sense into Nikserof, and not getting an answer. He even tried talking to Mulliner, although he knew it would do no good.

When they reached the vast space, drowned in the colorful light of all the stained glass in the clerestory, he was silenced. Glass soldiers, Shieldsmen and Drav Cra warriors patrolled and guarded the castle's every corner. The Northern savages were no longer merely at the gates, but inside them making themselves comfortable.

Torsten stole a glance into the Throne Room. Pi stood in the center of the room, engaged in a heated conversation with Oleander. Or, rather, it was heated on one end. Oleander towered over the boy. She was tall by any standards, but next to her son, she appeared a giant. Her cheeks were flushed, and her hands whipped around dramatically as she spoke, but Pi remained the same stoic boy he'd been since emerging from the Royal Crypt.

Oleander threw her arms up in frustration. Pi shook his head solemnly, then turned and headed toward his throne. Oleander made a move toward the Great Hall and locked gazes with Torsten through the open doors. He expected a glower, but she seemed relieved to see him.

"Torsten, I must have a word with you immediate—"

The doors slammed shut in her face without anyone pushing them. Torsten heard Freydis snicker and looked back. She had a bloody hand raised. Oleander pounded from the other side, her muffled shouting indiscernible.

Torsten's pulse raced. He was about to have a chance to beseech the King again.

"Take him to my quarters," Redstar said, smiling. "He won't want to miss this."

Torsten veered toward the doors and was about to call out to Oleander when his escorts jerked him back.

"Please, I must speak with her and the King," Torsten protested. "I must speak with them!" He thrashed with the full weight of his towering body. The Shieldsmen had to anchor their feet to keep him in place.

"Sir Unger, this isn't the time," Nikserof whispered into his ear.

Hearing his title whispered caused Torsten to stop fighting, and he was promptly towed to the stairs of the West Tower. It meant that at least a smidgeon of respect still remained. That didn't change how foolish he felt. All his life in the Shield, he'd hauled hundreds of criminals to the dungeons. He always wondered where they found the gumption to fight the inevitable. Nearly all of them struggled as if they had a chance against soldiers or Shieldsmen with their hands cuffed.

Now Torsten understood. They fought it because in their hearts they believed they were innocent. Not every criminal was as self-aware as Whitney had been. Torsten couldn't help but doubt himself—to wonder if maybe he was wrong. If somehow, he'd imagined Redstar's many slights. After all, the only others there that night, a year ago, when Redstar cursed Pi and fled, were Uriah, who died shortly after, and Queen Oleander. When it came to Pi, the Queen never saw things clearly.

No, Torsten told himself, shaking the thoughts out of his head as Nikserof and Mulliner dragged him onto the stairs. The wolves were circling no longer. They now made their home within the camp, and their pack leader would devour everything in his path.

"Nikserof, Mulliner, you have to see the madness in this," Torsten said as they ascended the stairs. "Drav Cra in our very halls." He nodded back toward Freydis who followed them at a safe distance.

"Now isn't the time for this," Nikserof said. Mulliner remained silent.

"Soon there will be no time."

They pulled him to a halt at the landing of the second highest floor of the castle, just around the corner from Torsten's old chambers. Nikserof leaned in to whisper in his ear. "Many of our men defend against the Black Sands. We're outnumbered."

"And we don't need a traitor's help," Mulliner snapped.

He shoved Torsten into the passageway. Torsten staggered forward but couldn't mask his smirk as he found his balance. Mulliner may have been unreachable, but Sir Nikserof wasn't lost to lies.

I'm not alone.

They stopped outside of Torsten's former Wearer's chambers. Two Drav Cra warlocks stood outside, rags and trinkets draped all over them. Both turned simultaneously toward them as if they were connected.

They extended their arms and silently beckoned Torsten into the room. Freydis rattled off to them in Drav Crava. One left, and she took his place guarding the door.

"You may enter," she said.

The Shieldsmen released Torsten, and he took a few cautious steps toward the doorway. These were his chambers, but he couldn't help but feel that something was different. He stopped.

"Are we still the Shield that guards this kingdom?" he asked Nikserof.

"Always." The knight replied.

"We are," Mulliner said at the same time, indicating that Torsten wasn't one of them. Then they set off back toward the stairwell.

Spirits lifted by one of their answers, Torsten entered the chambers that had served him and so many Wearers of White before him. He barely recognized it anymore. All the arms of former Wearers which once festooned the walls like relics were askew or fallen. An entire wall was cracked as if a boulder had slammed into its center. Droplets of blood covered the floor, the largest splatter on a mural, its stone canvas pieced together like a puzzle.

That uplifted feeling vanished almost as soon as it'd arrived. Torsten could never forget that painting Redstar once showed him which depicted the God Feud in a way that painted Nesilia, the Buried Goddess, as Iam's ally and lover. The notion itself was ridiculous, contradicting the Holy Scripture and every glass shard of artwork decorating churches of Iam—both ancient and new. In true history, Nesilia and the One Who Remained, whom Redstar called Bliss, were the two instigators of the feud that nearly reduced Pantego to rubble. Hundreds of gods and goddesses died or fled, never to be heard from again. The One Who Remained defeated Nesilia after they turned on each other.

Iam watched in horror as all his kin ravaged the land that, together, they created. With all others weakened, he created Elsewhere and banished what remained of the gods there for all eternity. All the horrid creations of unspeakable power they conceived to help in their feud joined them. Iam was left with both the feeblest and fairest of their creations; dwarves and men, beings of flesh, blood, and bone. He shed his light upon them from the heavens above, hoping for a day when all the fighting initiated by his fallen ilk might end.

It was the sad story of Pantego's birth, once intended to be the crowning achievement of the gods. But even they fell prey to jealousy and contempt. Only Iam stayed true, and Torsten had long ago dedicated his life to that truth by following King Liam. His conquest to bring all Pantego under a single banner was everything Iam loathed, but Liam understood the cost. To do whatever it took, even sacrifice the sanctity his very soul to create a peaceful world of tomorrow. A world where man would stop squabbling over false idols and dedicate themselves to the light of the One True.

Now, Redstar sought to undo all of Liam's painstaking work.

Torsten squeezed his fists tight. There were ancient weapons all around him. If he could find a way to break the chains on his wrists, he could get out and finish what Rand couldn't. He wasn't sure why he trusted the broken-down deserter to take down an Arch Warlock alone.

The axe of Sir Quenton Carlsbad lay on the floor, its shaft cracked in half a century ago in a war with the dwarven kingdom of Elnor. If Torsten could get the right angle, he might be able to snap the chain. He'd have to deal with the two warlocks outside, who may be listening to his very thoughts for all he knew. All he'd have to—

"Fair Yarrington!" someone announced. Torsten was immediately drawn to the window which looked down over the castle's entry gate. Redstar stood atop it with Pi on one side and Wren the Holy on the other. In the bailey, at their backs, were all the members of the now-worthless Royal Council. Arrayed behind them, King's Shieldsmen and Drav Cra warlocks and warriors, Nikserof at the head of the former, and Drad Mak, the latter.

A crowd had formed down on Royal Avenue, staring up at their lords. It was common-folk, mostly; the only people stirred by affairs of the kingdom. The nobles down the way were happy to stay in their Old Yarrington estates, letting the world pass them by so long as their coffers remained full.

"I stand before you, humbled by the acceptance of my people, and the trust of your king," Redstar continued. It was only then that Torsten realized it was he who'd been speaking. He'd never heard the Arch Warlock project his voice so loudly. "It has not been easy coming to this strange, vast city. I've been working hard to learn how things work so that I might earn the title given me by your King as Prime Minister, his right hand."

"Ain't no Drav Cra ever be one of us!" a member of the crowd shouted, encouraged by a smattering of cheers.

"You don't belong here!" cried another.

"I have heard all the rumors and lies about how I came to be your Prime Minister!" Redstar said, ignoring them. "But today I stand before you, begging you to put aside our differences. Do you not remember we all hail from Drav Cra long ago? Oh, what the years have done to our minds, our memory fails us. Has this alliance not brought us back to simpler times? Times when we were one? Has it not proven the brilliance of your late King in taking my lovely sister, Oleander, as his wife?"

Torsten scanned the platform. Oleander wasn't present. As Queen Mother, she should've been standing by the side of her son, but Redstar stood there in her stead.

"Lovely as gold-plated shog!" someone else in the crowd hollered, drawing laughs.

"Where is the murderous shrew?" asked another.

Pi glared in their direction. Without anyone needing to ask, two hulking Drav Cra warriors delved into the crowd, grabbed the men who'd spoken out, and hauled them, screaming, back through the bailey.

"There are still those who ignore fact," Redstar continued. "Since the moment King Pi was brave enough to call on his family for help we have claimed resounding victory at Winde Port, as only Liam could have done. All of Pantego now fears our great army again, but there are still some among us who deny this success." Redstar lifted his arm and drew back his sleeve. The crowd gasped, Torsten did as well. There was only a stump where his hand used to be.

"A member of your King's Shield accosted me as I slept. A man, still loyal to the former Wearer Torsten Unger, whose mind was so ravaged by battle he took the life of one of his own. I have been left scarred but not disheartened. For as my life seemed to be coming to an end, a sign—a light from the heavens shown. Wren the Holy arrived at my room at the exact moment of betrayal and disarmed my would-be assassin." Redstar extended his remaining hand and placed it on Wren's shoulder, and smiled warmly. "The voice of Iam saved my life."

Murmurs broke out. Wren limped forward, leaning on his cane, his hands shaking so much Torsten could see it even where he stood. Wren moved like a decrepit old man, and even nodding in agreement with Redstar seemed a struggle. Torsten had seen him only days earlier when he sent him to find Rand, and he appeared healthy. He'd been an old man since Torsten first met him, but never had he been feeble.

"Some of you are loathed even to speak the name of the Buried Goddess!" Redstar announced, stepping forward, arm around Wren's hunched back. "Some of you believe she is wicked. The bringer of the God Feud. Deceiver. Just as we, for so long, thought Iam our enemy. But it is all of us who have been deceived. History, twisted over eons by liars and cheats who have forgotten the love shared by our holy Father and Mother."

"Blasphemer!" someone in the crowd called out.

"Hang him!"

"Crucify him!"

"Silence!" Pi bellowed. His voice, like that of a giant, filled the air, sending a chill up Torsten's spine. In an instant, the crowd grew so quiet he could hear the clattering of glaruium armor far down below. "You speak ill of my uncle and your Prime Minister. The next who does shall speak no more."

With that, the silence lasted. There was no question that the common-folk of Yarrington remembered the sight of Oleander's slaughter, dozens swinging from the walls by their necks. Torsten wasn't sure if Pi would do the same. He'd seen such a glimmer of hope in the boy outside of Redstar's influence—but that was the problem. There they stood, side by side.

"Thank you, Your Grace." Redstar bowed to him, then turned back to the crowd. "For too long we have fought in mind and body! We have imagined our gods to be enemies until we believed it ourselves, down to our very cores. But I have seen the truth. I have seen it written in texts older than the Glass Kingdom itself, and I have seen it here." Redstar faced Pi. "Our Miracle King, brought back from the earth."

He returned to Wren's side, knelt, and took the holy man's hand. "And only yesterday, this great vessel of wisdom was sent to my chambers at the exact moment I was to die," Redstar said. "The voice of Iam on Pantego sent to save me, the voice of Nesilia—as if it were fated. That after all these long centuries of fighting, we might come together once more, as was always intended."

"Lord Redstar s-s-speaks the truth," Wren said, stammering.

Torsten grabbed hold of the window-sill and squeezed. Something was very wrong with the High Priest. He'd only just been a part of planning the assassination of Redstar, yet now was supporting him and speaking with a stutter he'd never had before. As if this were his first time speaking in front of a crowd rather than the ten-thousandth.

"I see now how foolish we've been," Wren continued. "T-t-torn apart by unknown grudges when it is so clear. The light of the sun cast upon

Pantego is worthless without the earth to bear its warmth. We must come together."

"And we shall." Redstar stood and approached the edge of the wall. "The Goddess below and the God above shall be together once more. In the name of our King, Pi Nothhelm, the Miracle Prince, first of his name and son of Liam the Conqueror, we beseech you, therefore, brethren, today, shed your hate and see what we can become. Nesilia, the Buried Goddess stands with you. Iam, the Vigilant Eye stands with you. Your King stands with you!"

Redstar pointed back at Pi, and the crowd erupted. Torsten hadn't seen anything like it in many, many years. All those loyal servants of Iam, roaring in approval. They probably had no idea what they were even celebrating, but it was clear now that Redstar's silver tongue made even Whitney's seem like mere bronze.

Pi stepped forward. "Together, we will finish what my father started," he pronounced. "I know now that this is why the gods brought me back." He wasn't enthusiastic, and nowhere near as florid as Redstar's speech, but his voice carried. More cheers rained upon him, and when he opened his arms, the soldiers in the bailey marched out. Drav Cra, Glass soldiers, and Shieldsmen marched out side by side through the parting crowd.

"Rebellion still rages in the Southern sands," Pi said. "I hereby name Sir Nikserof Pasic of the King's Shield and Drad Mak the Mountainous of the Drav Cra, Co-Wearers of White. They shall lead our armies under a single banner in bringing Afhem Muskigo to justice."

That was when Torsten noticed. The White Helm he'd worn now resided on Nikserof's head. His cape and a single pauldron were fitted snugly over the Drav Cra chief's patchwork of fur armor. Nikserof had only just been with Torsten and wore no such thing, which meant all this had just happened down in the bailey. The most experienced Shieldsman, and likely the only one with the pull to stand up to this new shifting of power, was being sent far away to war where he could do naught but serve his kingdom through blood.

No other Shieldsman deserved the honor more, but Torsten knew it wasn't intended to be one.

"Let Iam's light s-shhine upon our brave soldiers as they bring peace to this world," Wren the Holy exclaimed, lifting his cane, so the eye of Iam atop it caught sunlight and refracted a rainbow of colors.

"And let Nesilia bring them swiftly across the earth, from here and back again." Redstar grasped the cane right above Wren and raised it higher. King Pi stood before them, still calmly taking in the revelry of his subjects.

Redstar glanced back over his shoulder, looking directly up at the window where Torsten stood. Then he grinned. Torsten's blood boiled. All the most experienced King's Shieldsmen he might be able to trust in—many of which had fought at his side in Winde Port—were being sent away to finish the war. And all that'd be left behind would be green Shieldsmen and men like Mulliner whose loyalties could be more easily swayed by the promises of survival or glory.

There's no time for patience.

Torsten whipped around, remembering his intent to free himself, take Redstar down, and end his influence over the impressionable young King. Freydis stood directly in front of him. He went to swing at her, but her hand dripped with blood, and her magic held him back.

Before he knew it, more Drav Cra warriors flooded into the room, and he was hauled back to his cell, deep below the castle, damned to do nothing while Iam's kingdom was usurped from within.

XVIII

THE MYSTIC

Sora lifted her hands off her ears and peered through her eyelashes at the window. A series of softer pops followed the booms. A sickly green glow emanated through the window, then morphed to blue.

She drew her knife and crept toward the opening, keeping the blade against her palm just in case. A few more blasts on the way made her wince, but when she got close enough to peer over the sill, she saw their source. It left him breathless.

High above the Red Tower and all across Lake Yaolin, flames burst in the night sky like fiery paint on a dark canvas. Only they were all types of colors, not just the orange of fire—blue, purple, green. She also realized that the shouting which proceeded every blast wasn't frantic, but instead, celebratory. A grouping of people stood downstairs on the patio over-looking the lake.

"What in the name of Iam?" she whispered just before another splash of color painted the sky red. Finally, she didn't flinch at the sound. She was just glad nobody had been around to see her hiding from something that didn't seem to be hurting anyone.

She found herself in the lobby of the Emperor's Quilt, approaching the crowd of people appreciating the light show. She'd planned on staying in her room all night, waiting to hear from Lord Bokeo again, getting much-needed rest, but her heart raced too fast now.

She tapped someone on the shoulder, but they ignored her. She nudged another. The man leaned back but didn't remove his eyes from the spectacle.

"What is that?" she asked, nearly forced to shout over the noise.

"What's what?" replied the man.

Sora leaned in and pointed over the man's shoulder. She'd never seen anything that could compare. Perhaps the mystics were in hiding, but magic was surely not absent from this place.

"You serious?" he asked. "They're fireworks. This your first Festival of Ghosts?"

"No, of course not," she lied. "I…" She was trying to think of something to say when she realized the man was no longer listening anyway. Then, as suddenly as the fireworks started, they stopped, and everyone cheered, hooting and hollering, clapping their hands. As one, they turned and walked straight by Sora as if she didn't exist.

"Time for the fun!" said one woman as she passed.

"Let the trouble commence," said another.

Sora turned and watched them leave, wondering what manner of "fun" and "trouble" they were talking about.

A pit formed in her stomach. Both of those words reminded her of Whitney in the worst way. There was nothing he loved more than fun and trouble, and here she was, running off toward it alone. She was so out of her element, lost in a world she was unfamiliar with, and confused about everything, down to the question of who she was.

She shook her head. "How often are you in Yaolin City?" she asked herself, since Aquira wasn't around to listen. "You can sleep another night."

So, she decided to treat herself to a night out in this strange new city. With the autlas from Gold Grin and Aran Bokeo, she could do whatever she wanted short of buying a mansion and still be fine for a very long time. She'd see what this Festival of Ghosts was about, sample the local cuisine—now that it was quieter she couldn't help but hear her stomach grumble—clear her mind, and maybe even learn something about her people. She deserved it after the mess this week had become, and tomorrow, she'd storm back to Lord Bokeo's shop and demand they get started.

The Emperor's Quilt was off the beaten path, perched on a cliff on the east side of Yaolin. Although the din of celebration seemed to fill every corner of the city, it wasn't until she reached Xiahou Boulevard that she saw the sheer magnitude of the event.

People were everywhere, parading down the streets dressed to the hilt in costumes. She saw lich lords and wraiths, skeletons and walking dead. There was even a group of four, all wearing the same zhulong costume, dancing about, knocking into people and causing a ruckus.

She pushed through the crowd, and no one seemed to mind. The shop stands she'd seen the guards remove earlier had returned, now gathered into squares adjacent to Xiahou Boulevard. The scent drew her to the one selling something called dumplings, and her stomach did the rest. Next thing she knew she'd purchased one, devoured it, and then brought another back to the street. In the West, they'd never wrap meat in dough in such a manner, but they were missing out. And the spices... Sora's taste buds had never been so grateful.

On the way out, another salesman offered for her to buy a carafe of liquid. She didn't have time to ask what it was before he pushed it on her. It was both sweet and a bit tangy, going down with a bite. She couldn't say she enjoyed it, though she couldn't help but wash down every bite with a sip.

Filling her stomach improved her mood. All the street performers doing their tricks were far more enticing, juggling balls of fire or swallowing swords. A line of revelers passed her, each wearing a part of a dragon costume and moving in a serpentine, so they appeared like one of the great, ancient beasts. They wrapped a tight circle around her, the reptilian face swaying right in front of her, then spun away to circle someone else.

A blast of fire at her back sent Sora spinning again.

"Experience the breath of dragons!" shouted the old, bearded man responsible for it. Before him stood a table with many jars and glass bottles. "Feel the heat of their flames and the roar of their bellies!"

Sora scrutinized the setup.

"Come to see magic?" he asked her in a loud, booming voice.

Sora stared at him as he absentmindedly poured two liquids into one vial.

"Come on, girl," he whispered, "just play along."

"Sure… show me." Sora moved in closer and nodded at him. He cleared his throat, and Sora noticed a few more people sidle up next to her while she pretended to be interested. With that, the man feverishly began mixing various potions and herbs. She couldn't help but be reminded of old Wetzel as steam rose from one of the vials.

"Long ago, a strapping, young man, with only the leather on his back and his father's old, rusty sword, set out on a trek into the cold, unforgiving Dragon's Tail Mountains," the man said, emphasizing every word with his hands as any good performer would.

He grabbed hold of the vial, tipped his hand, and poured out the contents. It was a slow, agonizing drip, flowing like tree sap. When it touched the man's hand, it turned into a fine powder. He threw it, and it hit the crowd, cold as ice.

They all laughed and brushed the snowy substance off their cloaks.

"The snow beat down upon him," the man continued, "but he pressed forward, sure there was treasure within the many caverns." He reached beneath the table and brought out a thin, brown leather mat which he laid upon the surface, flattening it with his palm.

"One such cavern called to him." He covered his mouth with his hand, and a voice came from behind Sora.

"Hello!" it said, almost seeming to echo. She spun, as did the others. There was no doubt it was the performer's voice, but how he'd managed to send it behind them, Sora had no idea. She turned back to the man and clapped. The others joined in.

Maybe he isn't just a trickster.

"As he entered, his footsteps echoed within the high ceiling." The performer carefully set small piles of gray rock at varying intervals on the mat. With a finger, he tapped the edge of the mat and the stones popped in series, sounding like footfalls against the leather.

Sora found herself enchanted by the man's story.

"Darkness surrounded the young man," he continued. "A darkness fell unlike any he'd ever experienced, as if it blanketed his very soul, and a cold chill came over him, colder than any snowstorm could produce."

Sora could have been imagining it, but goosebumps rose up all over her body.

The old man reached into a pouch on his belt and produced an orange powder. He held it above a basin filled with liquid.

"That was when he heard it," he said, dropping the handful of powder. Sora jumped, and the now-large gathering cried out in surprise when the roar of a great beast sounded from the bowl. "The dragon was awake. It was true, there was a vast treasure trove within that mountain, but there was, too, a guardian."

"He drew his sword, slowly approaching. One step, and then another." He tapped the mat again and the rocks leaped. "He could hear, in the darkness, a shifting, a rattle like metal on metal. He knew it was the beast's scales rubbing against one another. A mighty thwack, a dragon tail, rising and failing, over and over like a drum or the beating of a heart."

Sora was so caught up in the moment, she'd hardly even noticed the sound. Thump, thump. Thump, thump.

"He readied his sword, lifting it high above his head," the performer went on. His knees buckled, shaking like leaves on a windy day. Then, without warning, the reptilian nightmare unleashed a breath of fire that tore through the cavern, singeing even the man's eyebrows."

The performer quickly swigged a small vile, lifted his other hand to his mouth, tilted his head back, and blew a flame from his mouth that reached the rooftops.

The unified cry of fear and delight rose so loudly around Sora, she clenched her teeth together. The heat was intense, causing little beads of sweat to form on her forehead.

When the flame subsided, the crowd erupted in applause, Sora included. The old man bowed, then rose and waved his hands, encouraging his audience to be quiet.

"The young man was so frightened. You could imagine, could you not?" the performer said. The onlookers laughed and nodded. "He abruptly lowered his sword and turned to run. The rusty blade fell against his neck and carved a deep wound."

"Did he die?" shouted a man in the back.

The performer laughed. "What do you think?"

"The dragon ate him whole!" called a girl, so young Sora wondered why she wasn't in bed.

"Surely, it didn't. How then would the man know the tale!" said the child's mother.

"Right you are," said the performer. Then he reached up and grabbed the neckline of his tunic and dragged it down, revealing a long scar stretching from earlobe to collarbone. "I ran like Elsewhere had just unleashed her demon hordes."

A collective gasp sounded, then murmurs bounced around from person to person, many whispers and expressions of awe.

"I thank you, fair people of Yaolin and elsewhere, for listening to my story. If you enjoyed it, please help an old man who never did find the dragon's treasure." The performer shook a tin cup, a few coins scraping around on the bottom.

Men and women rushed forward to fill it with autlas, and the old man smiled, nodding his appreciation. Sora happily added a few bronzers. When the man gave a disapproving glare, she reached into her bag and added a silver piece, thanked him in Panpingese for his show, and turned to walk away.

"You know they're watching you," he said.

Sora turned back. "What?"

The man wasn't looking. He fiddled with his props, preparing them for the next show. She rushed to his side and took his arm. "What did you say?"

"Huh?" he said. "I said nothing."

"You said they were watching me. Who's watching me? The mystics? Are you one of them?"

"Look, girl, all this here is just a trick of alchemy. Anyone who knew a lick about real magic died in the war or is smart enough to hide from the Glassmen. Now please, leave me alone so I can prepare. Time is money!"

Sora released the man's robe, and he brushed the wrinkles away before returning to his bottles. She glanced around, looking for where the voice might have originated, but the performer's onlookers had dispersed, leaving only the costumed revelers marching down the street.

She hurried along, once again caught up in the parade. By the time she'd slowed down, she was nearly at a central square, which was more of a circle. It appeared to be the spot where all the statues, presumably of the Pinyun, which now looked vaguely like an army of Liam the Conqueror, came together into what felt like an arena. A series of repurposed, domed temples, now all dedicated to Iam, encircled the fireside.

"Sora!" she thought she heard a voice call out from somewhere within the parade. However, through all the costumed bodies, all wearing masks, some colorful, some terrifying, she couldn't find its source.

They're watching you. Those words echoed in Sora's head.

She whirled, and more costumed people surrounded her. It grew dizzying. She picked up her pace through the mob, fingering the grip of her knife as she moved. Her name filled the air again; then a hand grabbed her shoulder, the grip firm but gentle.

"Aye, lass!"

Sora turned, tearing her knife free and raised it toward the neck of whoever was following. Only there was no neck. Her knife hovered over a clump of messy, red hair, and she looked down to see Tum Tum with his hands in the air.

Tum Tum laughed nervously as he slowly brushed her knife-hand aside. "If ye're ever bein snuck up on by a dwarf, ye might want to aim lower," he said, able to make a joke out of anything.

"Oh, Tum Tum !" Sora laughed and threw her arms around him. When she backed away, she saw Gold Grin behind him, wearing a long robe and... the Glass Crown upon his head. Fortist and Hestor stood at his side, one dressed like a noble and the other a jester.

"Are you mad?" Sora asked.

"What? This?" he laughed, fingering the crown. "Might be the only night I get to show it off. No one would be crazy enough to believe it was the real thing."

He bowed his head and took her hand. "Dearest Sora of Troborough. It is a pleasure to see you again."

He pressed his lips against the top of her hand. It was only then she realized that for the first time in longer than she could remember, she wasn't wearing gloves in public. Thanks to Lord Bokeo there were no scars of her unlawful practice of blood magic to hide.

"And you," she said as he gently released her hand. The act of a pirate who seemed more gentleman than monster caused her to blush, which in turn made her punch Tum Tum in the arm to draw attention from her cheeks. Unlike Whitney, Tum Tum was solid as a rock.

"Oi!" Tum Tum yelped. "What that be for!"

"For making me inquire about The Ruby House," she said. "And my subsequent red cheeks."

All four men, Gold Grin, Tum Tum, Fortist and Hestor laughed, hands to their bellies, nearly doubling over for the effort. Judging by their red cheeks and the distant look in their eyes, they'd all had a few drinks already.

"I'm supposin you din't want a room there then?" Tum Tum said.

Sora reared back again, and Tum Tum flinched, but she was sure it was just for show. "No, thank you. I've got a room at the Emperor's Quilt."

"Oh, ye tired of the *Reba*'s modest rooms, did ye?" Gold Grin said, then hiccupped. "Wanted a taste of luxury?"

"I hear there be a stand nearby that sells rice wine that'll knock you out," Tum Tum added.

"It's nothing compared to the Winder's Dwarf," Sora said, but immediately regretted it. She'd wanted to compliment Tum Tum on his wonderful pub back in Winde Port, but considering she'd been the one responsible for burning it, and the rest of Winde Port to soot and ash, she lowered her head and said, "Sorry."

"Nonsense! Nothin to be sorry for. Had that bundle of sticks not gotten torched I ain't never've been able to experience *Gu—Guin—Gway—*"

"*Gyuan Jie,*" Sora helped, then shrugged when his brow furrowed. "I've picked up a few words already."

"Bah!" the dwarf cried. "The Festival of Ghosts. Law be to speak common anyway, ain't it? Say, where's yer dragon?"

"Wyvern," she corrected, "and it's a long story."

"We ain't got time for long stories, dwarf," said Gold Grin. "Not if ye don't want us to leave ye where ye stand."

"Guess that's me cue," Tum Tum sighed.

"What? I'm not invited?" Sora asked.

"Trust me, lass, ye don't want a part of it. Old Gold Grin wants to help me open a right western pub here in his namesake. First, we have to convince an old codger to sell his place."

"Right on the lake." Gold Grin tossed his arm around her, and she realized why he was acting so strangely. He was so drunk, he could hardly stand. Extending one arm as if gesturing to something grand, he said, "There be no more perfect place for Gold Grin's Grotto. Can you picture it?"

Sora chuckled. "Stunning."

Tum Tum shrugged. "Pirates," he muttered to her. "Can't say no to me only investors though!"

"Come, Tum Tum!" Gold Grin slurred, stumbling a few paces after he released Sora. His arm no sooner left her than went around one of his men, though they were in no better state. "Leave this fair lady to her business. We have a shop to pillage—" His lagging gaze met Sora's, and he blinked. "Purchase. That's the word."

"I'll see ye around, aye?" Tum Tum said to Sora. "Ye know where to find me."

"If you think I'm going to come calling for you at the Ruby House like some desperate damsel..."

Tum Tum chortled. "I'll be findin you then. And the moment I've got me own place up and running, first drink's on me."

"I look forward to it."

Gold Grin shot her an awkward, crooked smile, then he, Tum Tum, and the rest staggered off. They were quite the sight, hulking man the pirate king was, shoulder to shoulder with the small, stout dwarf. Sora couldn't help but chuckle.

They were barely out of view when Sora heard a screech and saw a familiar shape zip by her face. At least, she thought she did. She wondered if she'd accidentally tried some of that strong rice wine Tum Tum referred to and that's why she was hearing and seeing things.

"Excuse me," she said, running. And, "Pardon," then finally, "Move!"

She didn't even care that she'd knocked several people to the ground, all of them berating her verbally as she put them behind her.

The line of people in their dragon costume passed in front of her, and she slid beneath their shuffling feet. She heard another cry, looked up, and saw Aquira. The wyvern flapped her wings and soared overhead, swooping in and out of a grouping of revelers with flags on posts, waving them to and fro.

"Aquira!" Sora shouted. She followed her wyvern friend up a flight of stone steps. If Aquira had heard her, she was ignoring her, which was very unusual.

Something is wrong.

When Sora reached the top of the stairs, Aquira was nowhere in sight. She searched, frantic, but there was no sign of her, nothing to clue her into where Aquira had gone until…

A frightened screech rang out. Sora dug her heels in and pushed off toward the sound. She slid around a corner and gasped. She was before an open, circular temple with a domed roof held upright by marble columns, Eyes of Iam dangling from gold chains between them.

The seven mystics from earlier stood around a young boy lying horizontally on a stone slab in the center. He was tied down, struggling to wriggle free as he cried. The mystics' faces remained shrouded by the loose-hanging hoods of their robes. The Ancient One, Aihara Na, wielded a crude weapon, little more than a sharp rock, and had it raised above her head. Aquira hovered, watching but not interfering.

Aihara Na spoke words in Panpingese, words that Sora wouldn't have understood the day before, but now they met her ears with clarity. She wished she didn't understand.

"Blood of babe, bone of child, bring forth the power of Elsewhere's fire." Aihara rotated the weapon so that the razor-sharp edge was facing the boy's chest. Sora's mind instantly drew on rumors she'd heard from passersby and even Torsten in the Webbed Woods, about how the old mystics used to experiment on their people in the name of magic. She'd thought them to be exaggerated stories like everything else, but she'd thought the same about Nesilia.

Sora didn't think, she just reacted.

"Aquira, move!" she said as she sliced her arm with her knife. Blood flowed, and Sora barely noticed the pain. She entered the temple and raised her hand, knowing that she needed to be careful not to harm the boy she was trying to save.

Aihara Na and the other mystics turned to face her, Aihara lowering her shiv. All their expressions remained hard as stone, unfazed by her arrival. It was then that Sora realized how gravely outnumbered she was. But it didn't matter.

All manner of thoughts passed through her mind in the moments it took to call upon Elsewhere, turning her hand into a deadly, fiery war-machine. Fear gripped her at the thought of turning another city into cindery ash, but she had to do something to save the child.

"Lower your hand, girl," Aihara Na spoke, her voice like thunder. "The boy's life is the sacrifice to commune with the other side. With Elsewhere. It must be done, lest we fade to ashes."

Elsewhere. Sora froze, flame wreathed around her hand. Of all the places for Aquira to lead her, it was to this clandestine ceremony where the Secret Council sought to connect with Elsewhere.

"Aquira led you here with reason," Aihara Na said as if reading her mind. "Breaching the other side is the key to unlimited power. To eternal life and resurrection! It can be yours as well. For that is why you sought us out, is it not?"

Sora found herself unable to reply. The other mystics returned to the ceremony, surrounding the struggling child, chanting in Panpingese and other languages. Every language. They blended, one beginning where the other took off, overlapping. Their voices hummed, and the air crackled as air swirled around the temple. In fact, now she realized that around that structure, all she could see was darkness as if Yaolin City had disappeared.

"Come, Sora," Aihara beckoned. Before she knew it, Sora had lowered her hand and approached the boy. "Fulfill your destiny and join us. Rip open the fabric of this world as the gods did so long ago, and become as powerful as a goddess yourself!"

Sora felt Aihara Na place the stone in her hands but didn't see her. All she could focus on was that boy, thrashing, begging to survive. Fire closed in over the weapon as Sora gripped it. From within her, she could feel her power bubbling to the surface, her very soul drawing upon the world between worlds, on Elsewhere. Only now it was different, the sensation stronger. It was like a dam she didn't know existed broke open, and her power flooded through her.

She raised the stone over the boy. The blackness around them took shape, and again she could see Whitney in a realm of shadow and obscurity. He called out to her, so near yet impossibly far. All she had to do was complete the ritual, and she could tear him free from the torment she'd exiled him to.

Only, he wasn't alone.

She also heard Nesilia, whispering her name, her voice both matronly and seductive. She could see her pale, colorless eyes reflected in those of the boy. "I know you," she whispered. "I've always known you."

"Sora!" Whitney called out.

Sora's hand's shook as she gripped the weapon. Her fire was intense now, the stone itself glowed. She struggled to focus as more power than should have been possible through her bleeding hand crackled on her fingertips. And then, in the faintest whisper, she heard the boy's cries again.

"Please don't hurt me…" he whimpered. "I'll do anything..."

"No!" Sora screamed. She brought the stone around and stopped it a finger's length away from Aihara Na's throat. The darkness surrounding her whisked away, and the city and the temple grew visible again along with the other yellow-clad mystics.

"I'll die before I hurt an innocent child," she said.

Aihara Na stalked forward, unperturbed by the sharp object at her throat. Her hands were folded in front of her chest as if praying to Iam. Sora backed away but kept the blade raised.

"Don't touch him!" Her anger fueled the flame along the stone, and its tendrils now lashed out at Aihara Na. The mystic's skin should have been boiling, but it didn't appear to harm her at all.

"Brave," Aihara Na said. "It appears the Will of Fire is true." She waved her hand toward the boy, and all his bindings came undone. "Go child. And remember that we are not lost." The child didn't wait for her to finish speaking before he scurried away.

"What are—"

Aihara whipped suddenly around and placed her finger against Sora's forehead. She whispered something in Panpingese, too quiet for Sora to understand, and Sora's fire extinguished in an instant. Her vision blurred.

Before her world went black, she realized that she'd rejected the chance to open Elsewhere and save Whitney in exchange for a child she didn't know. She wondered if she'd missed out on her only opportunity, but she didn't regret it. No matter what happened in the Webbed Woods or Winde Port, no matter what she really was, she knew one thing—she wasn't a killer like Kazimir or Muskigo.

XIX

THE DESERTER

"Are ye sure this is smart?" Sigrid whispered into Rand's ear as they followed Valin Tehr and his cronies through the winding Dockside streets. Night had fallen upon Yarrington. While clouds obscured Celeste's normally bright glow, snow blanketed the streets, making it more like home for the Drav Cra.

"We need to disappear, and nobody does it better," Rand said.

"But still, Father always said he was a man never to get in bed with."

"The King's Shield deals with pretend-lords like him all the time. I know enough about his operation to keep us safe."

"Keep up, Shieldsman!" Valin hollered back. "I shouldn't be able to outpace you on this leg."

Sigrid took Rand's arm. "I trust ye; ye know that. And I missed ye."

"I've been with you this whole time," Rand said.

Sigrid leveled a glare at him. The kind that said, 'No you haven't,' and he couldn't deny it. Perhaps in body, but his mind had been absent for far too long. He put on an abashed smile. All things considered, she seemed to be handling her first kill well.

"I'm with ye now," he said, his Dockside speech returning, if only for a moment. No matter how badly his head ached or his body sweat as it longed for a sip of ale, he vowed silently, staring upon her face, never to touch the stuff again. He'd broken the vows he'd made to the King's Shield, but one made in her name, he'd keep.

"I hope so."

"You don't have to worry about me anymore. What about you? I know what it's like to take a life. Better than most. I—"

"I'm fine brother. It was him or watching ye die, and I'd do the same every time."

"You're stronger than I am."

"Yer finally noticing?"

They exchanged a smile and a nod, then caught up to Valin who crutched along the docks. A line of Drav Cra longboats swayed in the water. A group of them sat outside a tavern, drinking with no signs of stopping. They remained outside as if the worst winter Rand had known in his life were summer. They even had some of their animal-skin tents set up in the yard.

"Look at them, Rand Langley," Valin said. "They flood the district, autlas like trinkets to them, our women like toys. They pay for nothing and intimidate inns for ale and lodging. Some have scared my people from their homes and taken them for their own."

"They have no respect for us," Rand agreed.

"They have no need for that kind of respect. I don't fault them for how they treat this city. In the North, survival is all that matters. But they're bad for business." He stopped and pointed to the tavern's owner. The man poured them another round, shaking, braving the cold instead of making them come inside. "I control that tavern. I decide what everything costs. Jipper there is a good fellow, always pays on time. But when my people are more frightened of the foreigners than me... that's when I have a problem."

"Then why don't ye drive them off?" Sigrid said. "Yer owing them protection, just like yer owing it to Trapp. Ain't that how it works?"

Valin scowled. "It isn't so simple, girl. After they returned victorious from Winde Port, more came. There are now more than twice as many of them here than men on my payroll. The depravities Old Yarrington shirks as being for us poorer souls, the Drav Cra adore. I can't protect it all now."

"Only your drugs, huh?" Rand glanced back at the crate one of Valin's men grabbed from the basement of Maiden's Mugs before leaving. People all over the city used manaroot, the powerful sensory amplifier Valin smuggled into the city from the far east—the perks of owning the dockworkers. Rand had even found some in the castle kitchens once. The chef swore he was trying a new dish.

"Careful, Rand. You may wear that armor, but you're an outlaw, now, in the company of outlaws."

"Trust me, I know."

Valin started walking again, and everyone kept to his leisurely pace. "In the end, the Drav Cra are bad for us all," he said. "But make no mistake. If they came down here with gold instead of furs and relics, I'd have handed you over to Redstar already."

"Some champion of Dockside," Sigrid murmured under her breath. Rand nudged her.

"Did you know that some of the servants your brother executed for the Queen were from here?" Valin said. "Rose to the highest place a man or woman from Dockside incapable of fighting could rise, only to be cut down at his hands."

"She didn't leave him a choice."

"My dear, there is always a choice. I merely have the means to see mine through."

Sigrid grunted but kept quiet. Rand focused on keeping the memories of those executions at bay. He hadn't known any of his victims were from Dockside, but why would he? Neither he nor the Queen gave them a fair trial. All he could do was wonder if her beautiful, sweet, handmaiden Tessa had grown up right down the street from him, or if they'd played on the docks together as children, angered old Gunter together.

"Spare a coin, Lord Tehr?" a beggar asked. He kowtowed on the street, hands upturned, an Eye of Iam etched in the snow before him. A group of others doing the same had gathered on a lane down to Fortune's Landing, the small, well-off part of Dockside, if any part of it could be called well-off.

Rand knew the place well and knew that The Vineyard—the brothel Valin made his headquarters—would be just down the way. There was no sign on the door saying that was where to find him, but everyone in Dockside knew it.

Rand and Sigrid fell back a bit while Valin reached into a coin purse and removed a handful of silver autlas. He placed them in the beggar's hand, and before the man could run, grabbed him by the wrist.

"Share this, or it is the last that shall come," he said.

"Yes, me lord," the beggar said. "Praise Iam."

"There is no Iam here."

Valin continued walking by as the filthy beggar handed out alms for him. He'd made the man an employee without him even realizing, and all the others stroked Valin's arms and praised him as he passed, like he was Wren the Holy himself.

"Valin, we discussed this," Codar, his Breklian advisor said, speaking for the first time since the Maiden's Mugs. "The more you hand out to these people… they'll keep coming back like stray cats."

"Oh, Codar, have a bit of fun," Valin said. A dirt-coated woman took his hand and shook it in gratitude.

"So long as the Drav Cra are here, we can't afford to give—"

"Codar, do you know why you have stayed here all this time, instead of returning to Brekliodad to handle the coffers of one of your fancy oligarchs?"

"Because you pay better than anybody else."

"Exactly. And if, or when, all these poor souls are forced to rise and take iron to the Drav Cra, they'll do it for me. Loyalty, old friend. That's all that matters in this life."

"Valin Tehr!" a husky voice barked. "Just the man I've been looking for."

Rand saw the sheen of armor first, then grabbed Sigrid and ducked into the shadow of the nearest overhang. Captain Henry of the Dockside guard stood outside of the Vineyard with a few other Glass soldiers.

He was an unimpressive man, as one would expect for the soldier tasked with keeping Dockside safe. Rand didn't know him well, but having been a city guard before The King's Shield took him in, Rand had spent a year serving beneath Henry.

"Captain Henry," Valin said, leaning on his good leg so he could bow with a flourish. "To what do I owe this great pleasure?" He strutted right up to him, seemingly without concern that being carried behind him was a crate of outlawed manaroot as well as the most wanted man in Yarrington.

"What do we do?" Sigrid whispered into Rand's ear.

"Just wait," he answered. He kept his head low, hoping the darkness and the falling snow would be enough to conceal him.

"Crazy happenings down by the castle," Captain Henry said.

"Are there?" Valin replied. "I haven't heard of anything."

Captain Henry's fat lips went straight. "What's in the crate, Valin?"

"A cake from my favorite baker. It's Codar's birthday, you see."

Henry and his men circled him, stopping by the thug carrying the crate. Valin and Codar watched calmly.

"I love birthdays," Captain Henry said. He slapped the top of the crate. "You wouldn't mind if I crack it open, try a piece?"

"I would prefer you didn't," Valin said.

Captain Henry started to lift the lid, but the brute holding it glowered down at him and he backed off. Rand also noticed Codar's hand wrapped around the blade of a dirk sheathed behind his back.

"I'm full anyway," Captain Henry grumbled. He went to turn, and his gaze froze upon Rand. "Got Shieldsman working for you now, do you?"

"One can't be too careful in these days," Valin said.

"Ain't that the truth. Thing is, the Crown has us all keeping on the lookout for a traitor to the Order. One of them took a shot at our new Prime Minister, the hero of Winde Port and the King's own uncle."

"Why, that is awful."

"You wouldn't happen to know anything about that, would you?" Captain Henry started toward Rand, but Valin was unexpectedly quick on his cane and got in front of him.

"Nothing at all. But we'll keep a weather eye out for the traitor, in the name of the King. To kill the royal uncle, no matter what he did in the past... why, that I cannot abide."

Rand thought he saw something pass quickly between their hands. The captain looked Valin over once more, then grinned.

"Long reign the Miracle King," Captain Henry said.

"Now," Valin guided him back the other way, "why don't you go make sure your armory is secure before the savages take everything? Leave our busy streets to me."

"Aye boys, I think we will." He waved his hand in a circle for them to move along, then grabbed Valin by the collar. "You're up to something, Tehr," he whispered. "Whatever it is, I want in."

"I assure you," Valin said, removing the man's hand with two fingers, "I only mean to celebrate the life of my dear friend Codar amongst good company."

"I want in," Captain Henry whispered again before catching up to his men. He offered Rand a salute on his way by, a few of his men chuckling, then seized one of the beggars and shoved him along. "Clear the streets, ye filth. No begging beyond the church grounds. All of you!"

Rand rarely thought about it, but now he remembered why he was so eager to get out of the Dockside guard. Most of them were less honorable than Valin's thugs, and they did a hell of a lot less for Dockside. Rand also knew he should've been concerned that the guard captain recognized him, but he wasn't. So long as Valin kept the man's mouth full and his pocket's stuffed, serving the Crown came second.

"I detest that man," Codar said, releasing his weapon.

"Now, now, old friend, don't bite the hand that appeases us," Valin said.

Codar didn't respond.

Rand hadn't known many people from the mountainous lands of northeast Pantego, with their hair as white as the land and accents just as harsh, but all those whom he'd ever met were equally short with words.

"Come along, Shieldsman," Valin beckoned. "There are others who would take justice into their own hands, even if Redstar is a bloody savage."

Rand retook Sigrid's hand, and they followed Valin. Only two structures in Dockside were more prominent than The Vineyard—both were churches, both were on either side of Fortune's Landing, and both were in far worse shape. The chapel of sins, which made Valin Tehr the wealthiest man in Yarrington outside of castle halls, sat like a jewel within a field of gray stone. A balcony lined the second floor, oak railings sculpted to appear like grapevines and big-bosomed women. On warmer days, the terrace would be packed with wenches and rich, old men.

Rand never imagined he'd be bringing his sister anywhere near the place. He'd never been there himself. One step inside reminded him why he'd never had any desire.

A wall of hot, humid air accosted him. He was grateful for the warmth, but not the stench—sweat, ale, sex, and Iam knows what else. It was enough to send the aches of withdrawal soaring to the front of his mind and make him want to vomit. He found himself squeezing Sigrid's hand with a sweaty one of his own.

Whores strutted around in every direction, wearing naught but beads and frills. They chatted with men of all types and classes, feigning laughs and interest. A group of off-duty guards sat in the corner. A man dressed as a noble lounged in a booth by the bar, three women all over him.

It was like they'd left Pantego itself.

A single hearth gave the big space a hellish, red glow. The outside balcony was mirrored inside with the same oak railings. Rand followed a Panpingese man with his eyes as a whore led him behind one of the many curtains. Back on ground level, a musician troupe kept the racket of the upstairs dealings quiet, playing eerie tunes on stringed instruments Rand hadn't seen before. They appeared Shesaitju in origin but weren't loud enough to completely mask the loud moans and grinding bodies echoing all around like a percussion line.

Valin held out an arm. A bulky man crashed through the second-floor railing and hit the floor in front of them. Rand jumped back, Sigrid yelped. Men Rand recognized as more of Valin's thugs rushed down the stairs and grabbed the fat man. A young, Glintish girl burst out of a room upstairs, covering her breasts as she shouted in her language. She had a cut on both her chin and brow. Rand caught himself staring at the girl from Glinthaven and hoped Sigrid didn't notice. Their strange beauty had always enraptured him, skin the color of dark chocolate like Torsten's. The music paused, only momentarily, as Valin's men grabbed hold of the fat man and heaved him through the open doors and onto the Dockside streets. Not a moment later, everything returned to business as usual.

"And that is why I'm glad I never had a daughter," Valin remarked, brushing dust from his sleeve. "Clean this shog up. Now! It's bad for business."

"Rand, I have a bad feeling about this," Sigrid whispered.

"It's fine," Rand replied. He drew her close, then noticed a booth with at least a dozen Drav Cra warriors crowded around. A naked woman danced in the middle of them, and they all gawked, motionless.

"Manaroot," Valin said as if reading Rand's mind. "It makes the simplest things appear like magic, and it keeps the savages from tearing this place and my girls to pieces."

"A costly solution," Codar added.

"And a temporary one."

Valin snapped his fingers to two large men guarding a door behind the bar. They stepped aside to reveal a dark stairway. The sounds of merriment and stringed instruments were replaced by pounding. Rand saw light filtering through a curtain at the end of a long passage. The people beyond went silent, then half gasped and half broke out into raucous cheering.

One of Valin's men opened the door to their right and beckoned them in before Rand could see what was beyond the curtain.

"Weapons," the thug said, offering a hand. Rand glanced at Sigrid, who was busy looking to him for what to do.

"I assure you, it's merely a formality," Valin said. "I can't tell you how many people want me dead. It gets exhausting."

"I could say the same for myself," Rand replied. "How do I know you won't tie me up and hand me over to Redstar?"

"Do you think that sword of yours is all that's stopping me? Stop being a fool like all the other sanctimonious Shieldsmen. You aren't one any longer."

Rand regarded his sister again. He could tell she didn't like where they were, but it was too late now. He nodded her along, then unbuckled his sheath and handed it over. Sigrid did the same with the Drav Cra shortbow and bone-tipped arrows she'd taken from the Maiden's Mugs.

The guard stepped aside. Everyone else but Codar stayed in the hall. Rand guessed they were now in Valin's personal office, judging by the fine mahogany desk stacked with writs and pay logs. Men like Valin didn't stay rich without keeping track of everything.

Months back, the Shield would have killed to be in this room, with access to enough shady dealings to wipe Valin Tehr and his gang from the face of Pantego for good. Valin didn't care to blend in or lay low like the other gangs of Dockside or South Corner. He was happy to flaunt his debauchery and wealth, and Rand was starting to wonder if the Shield ever even wanted to take him down.

A raid on The Vineyard wouldn't cost many lives, and few within its walls were innocent. But a number of gangs vying for Valin's underground kingdom, eager to make a name for themselves, sounded far worse than organized chaos beneath a self-proclaimed king. And if Rand previously had doubts Valin viewed himself that way, now he was sure.

Valin's self-portrait donned the wall behind his desk, an image of him leaning on his cane. It wasn't exactly the same as the portraits of Glass Kingdom monarchs lining the Glass Castle halls, clutching a scepter topped with the Eye of Iam, but the parallels were clear enough. All around the room, more stunning works of art and foreign trinkets covered walls and filled shelves. There was a fishing spear with a shaft of Shesaitju blackwood and a stone point—it had to be centuries old. Across from it was a dwarven helm centuries older, patterns etched into the bronze with such precision craftsmanship, only gods seemed capable of crafting it.

The room contained enough wealth for Valin to build a castle for himself, which had Rand questioning why he chose to remain in his under-world kingdom of shog-stained streets.

"Codar, please fetch our guests here some of that Breklian brandy I love so much," Valin requested, taking a seat behind his desk. He lifted his malformed leg onto the mahogany, groaned, and rubbed the knee.

"I shouldn't," Rand said, a hint of desperation in his tone. Valin must have noticed it because his brow raised.

"Ah yes, a man battling his vices," Valin said, waving Codar to stop. "You'll find few who understand better than I."

"Or how to get rich off them," Sigrid remarked. Again, Rand nudged her to stay quiet. She'd always been the more rebellious of the two. The one to want to explore the streets after their parents put them down for bed. All her pent-up anger dealing with Trapp, just to have a place to live, clearly bubbling to the surface. The guilt of having to kill a man likely wasn't helping either, even if she thought she was 'fine.'

"See what we get for offering our hospitality?" Valin said to Codar. The Breklian merely shook his head in disapproval. He remained by the door, hands crossed behind his back, eyes on everything. "One can only profit off what he knows best, dear."

"Those girls upstairs—"

"Those girls live better than half the louts in Dockside. And you saw what happens when a visitor doesn't treat them like they're my own flesh and blood."

"Then why don't ye take one of their places on a bed."

"Siggy, stop," Rand snapped.

"I heard about more than just manaroot working for Trapp," she continued, ignoring Rand.

"All lovely things, I'm sure?" Valin said calmly.

"Now there's a word for it."

Valin laughed and clapped his hands. "Your sister has fire, Rand Langley. Eyes closed, and I'd question which one of you was the knight. A woman like her could—"

Now it was Rand's turn to step forward and grit his teeth. "Don't you dare."

Valin shrugged. "Your loss. Men come here because they think they want a chance to control something for once in their gods-forsaken lives. They stay so they can lose control of everything in the arms of a goddess."

Rand lost his train of thought. Sigrid's cheeks turned the same color as her ginger hair. Valin swung his leg down, then came limping around his desk toward Sigrid.

"Yes, I see it now," he said. "Gideon Trapp was a fool to keep you all to himself in that dump." He circled her and drew back her messy hair to accentuate her features. She shrugged him away. "Just a little polish, you could rival the Queen of Glass herself."

"Yer disgusting," Sigrid spat.

"Please, Mr. Tehr." Rand stepped closer and took Valin by the arm. Out of the corner of his eyes, he noticed Codar's forearm tense out of reflex, ready to draw his dirk. Rand released Valin quickly and backed away. "You brought me here to discuss removing Redstar. We can't waste any more time."

"By Iam, you're right." Valin turned back toward his desk. "These young ones do hate conversation, Codar."

"A shame," Codar remarked.

"Always wanting to get right to the destination when the riches are in the journey." He plopped back down into his chair, and again, stretched out his leg. "So, tell me, Rand Langley. Why should we work together rather than fetch the hefty price your head is worth? Enough to buy your fair sister a farm of her own."

"Because together we can free the kingdom from Redstar's grip."

"And why would you want that? He's not hanging anyone like his sister. All he's done is root out a traitor in the Royal Council, and drive a rebel army away from Winde Port."

"But… you said you wanted to get rid of him." If Rand wasn't nervous already, he was now.

"I said I wanted to get rid of the Drav Cra. Tell me, have you considered what happens when you murder their Arch Warlock in cold blood? When their people go rampaging through the streets out for revenge?"

"I…"

"See, Codar? Even the deserter is like any other knight. Short-sighted. Charging ahead like a starved boar."

"If you don't want to help, why did you invite me here?" Rand questioned.

"I simply want you to understand what you're asking. Removing the Drav Cra now, while much of their army is off fighting the Crown's war, is the sensible decision. I can live with the carnage; chaos is profitable. Can you?"

Rand turned to Sigrid. She bit her lip, deep in thought, her eyes dull with sorrow. Rand knew why. They'd always been able to tell what the other was thinking.

More death on my hands.

He took Sigrid's hand and nodded. Her head sunk.

"The longer we give them to drive their roots into our streets, the more fighting there will be," Rand decided. "My Wearer, and the very mouth of Iam asked this of me. If I hide again, what am I?"

Valin chuckled. "A smart man. But, assuming you're insane, what is your plan to eliminate the imposter?"

Rand drew a deep breath. "We free Sir Torsten Unger from the dungeons. I know what cell he's in. Wren the Holy believes he still has enough support to get the King's Shield back on his side."

"Torsten Unger?" Valin's brow furrowed.

"Yes, he is the rightful Wearer of White, Commander of the King's armies, and one of the greatest warriors alive. I've faced Redstar alone and failed. Torsten is strong, experienced in fighting him, and together we can—"

Valin erupted in laughter until tears rolled down his cheeks. Even Codar let a slight snigger slip through his lips.

"What's so funny?" Sigrid questioned.

"Torsten yigging Unger? That is what you're offering? The location of another disgraced Wearer?" Again, Valin stood and limped right up to Sigrid. "Do you fools think I don't have people that can tell me where Torsten is?"

"They don't know the castle," Rand said.

"They sweep up the damn shog!" He slammed his cane on the ground. "All the kingdom knows that Torsten is a traitor who murdered one of their own. Who do you think would help him? Sir Nikserof Pasic was sent off to war. Who else is there from Uriah's old guard? Wren the Holy just stood beside Redstar and the King and declared Iam and Nesilia kin."

"What? No," Rand said, incredulous. "That's impossible. Wren came to me. He sent me on this quest."

"An imagined visit. Brought about by the drowning of your sorrows, I'd wager."

"He was there! And he saved my life from Redstar when he unleashed his dark magic by summoning a shield of light. It was as if Iam worked through him just to keep me alive."

Valin scoffed. "Are you so desperate for a purpose to believe that?"

"Iam chose me!" Rand screamed. He didn't care who he was talking to, but the harshness in his tone caused Codar to reach for his dirk again.

"Don't hurt him!" Sigrid shouted, but Valin slammed his cane again, and she froze.

"He chose me!" Rand's knees went wobbly, and he had to crouch to keep from passing out. Shouting made his head hurt so bad, it felt like someone was dragging a knife around the rim of his skull. "I have to fix what I started..." he said weakly. "I executed all those people for her. Drove away anyone who could stand up to Redstar."

"Get up, you sniveling fool." Valin placed his cane under Rand's jaw and lifted.

"Rand." Sigrid wrapped her arms around him and helped him to his feet.

"It seems power isn't for everyone," Valin said to Codar as he clacked back to his desk.

"Please, Mr. Tehr, you have to listen to me," Rand said. "I don't know why, but I know now that only Torsten can kill Redstar. Whatever they started in the Webbed Woods, it has to be him. I tried to do it myself, but Wren the Holy is right."

"Codar, come here." The Breklian lifted his dirk away and moved to Valin's side where they held a private conversation. The former remained staid as ever while they talked. Valin, however, couldn't help but glance over and grin.

"He's not lying," Sigrid said to them. "I was there, too. I saw Wren come to my brother after he tried to..." She regarded Rand mournfully. "All that matters is that he was there."

Valin seemed to take what she said to heart. Eventually, Codar stepped aside and calmly folded his hands behind his back.

"Okay, Shieldsman," Valin said. "We're going to help you break Torsten out. I miss my feuds with the stubborn, former Wearer. No matter how hard I tried, he remained… incorruptible. You have to respect that sort of blind obedience."

"Thank you, sir, I—"

Valin raised a hand to silence him. "Who am I to strike down a man chosen by Iam Himself? But this isn't charity anymore. If I do this, you're going to help me with something. A task worthy of a warrior of the King's Shield."

Rand swallowed. "What do you need?"

Valin leaned forward, steepled his fingers, and smiled. "Isn't that always the question?"

XX

THE MYSTIC

It wasn't exactly that Sora woke up; she hadn't been sleeping. She'd experienced the whole journey after whatever Aihara Na did to her, eyes wide-open. The problem was that although she saw everything, she couldn't process anything. It was as if she was under the influence of one of Wetzel's potions for some life-threatening malady, one that would require the patient to be relieved from the very feeling of existence.

That was how she felt, like she was relieved from feeling anything at all. She'd felt cobbled roads, and seen water. She remembered climbing stairs and seeing people—but all those things might have been true of any place in the city.

She was hopelessly confused.

A finger pressed against her forehead, same as before, and she snapped to. Her fists waved around as if trying to punch out an army by herself.

Sora's vision became clear again. She stood alone in a room with Aihara Na. Unlike most of Yaolin City with its wood and sweeping tile roofs, this room was hard, cold, red stone. The ceiling extended high above, braziers of fire hanging at varying intervals.

"There you are," Aihara Na said. "Everything is all right." For the first time, the woman had her hood drawn back, and Sora could see the details of her face. High, proud, cheekbones and a long chin creased with wrinkles at the point. She wasn't ancient like Wetzel, despite the title Lord Bokeo gave her, but it was evident she'd seen much of the world. Her expression spoke of decades of disappointment, exhaustion.

"What are you doing to me?" Sora was instantly reminded of the time, not too long ago in Winde Port, that Kazimir had her chained up in the steeple of a church. But this time, she realized, she wasn't chained up. Aihara Na wasn't even looking at her. Sora was completely free and uninhibited, yet still found incapacitated. It was like her mind had to relearn how to operate her body.

Aihara Na moved toward Sora, and Sora would have shrunk back if she could've. "We've already told you what we will do. We are going to train you in the mystic arts."

"Train me? I want nothing to do with you or your wicked rituals. You're no better than the Drav Cra, sacrificing life to get what you want."

Aihara merely smirked in response.

Just then, Aquira crawled out from behind a column.

"Aquira," Sora said. Her foot finally budged, and she stomped forward hard without meaning to. Now it was Aquira's turn to shrink back. Her eyes blinked fast, and Sora recognized a look of sadness when she saw one.

"How could you lead me to that?" Sora asked. "I… I"

"Stop," Aihara Na said. "Do not blame her. She may understand your words, but she is still a beast and knew not what was done. She only followed the command of those she knew cared for her."

Sora slowly crept forward and knelt before the wyvern. "You have no love for her if you'd treat her that way." She stretched out her arm for Aquira to climb up, but Aquira remained skittish.

"If it helps," Aihara Na said, "there was no real danger."

Sora turned, slowly. "Excuse me?"

"It was a test. You passed."

"A test?" Her brow furrowed, and as she went to stand, Aquira finally hopped onto her arm. One of her claws scraped Sora's arm, making her yelp. The wyvern flapped away again, fearful.

"What if I didn't try to stop you?" Sora asked. "You mean to tell me you wouldn't have killed that boy?"

"He was inconsequential, just an orphan."

"*Just an orphan?*" Sora took several steps toward her, cheeks hot with rage. "I was just an orphan."

Aihara's laugh was as hard and rigid as her face.

"That isn't funny," Sora said.

"Girl, you have no idea what you are," Aihara Na said. "Who you are. Of what you are capable. But we do, and we want to teach you."

"If that means sacrificing more people, I'm not interested." It took all her effort to force that ultimatum out, knowing it meant there would be no second chance for saving Whitney, but she had to believe he'd feel the same way. She hoped. There was a big heart hiding somewhere behind that selfish shell.

"As I said, it was a test. We are not savages. I apologize if our current way of living has made us numb to your value of life. You can remain upset that a nobody might have died, but we were confident in your resolve. You proved us correct. You saved his life."

"Correct about what?"

"That you would not sit back and watch as we opened a porthole to Elsewhere. That was the true test. In that, you passed."

"So, what? You were going to open up a gateway to Elsewhere by killing that boy?"

"Of course not. That was not a real spell. Could you imagine? It was just a silly limerick meant to test your fortitude."

"But the things I saw there…" Sora hung her head, and Aquira must have noticed her heartache because she returned to Sora's shoulder and nestled against her face.

"Only visions. We can, all of us, peer into Elsewhere, but the one thing that must never be done is creating a portal. You didn't even know that, and your intuition persevered."

"I only cared about saving that boy," she grumbled.

"It matters not. You have seen what evil it is to open a bridge to the source of our power."

"But it can be done?" she asked impulsively. It was hard to hold back. Opening Elsewhere was the truest reason she'd been so eager to meet with mystics.

"Can what be done?" Aihara Na responded slowly.

"A gateway, a portal to Elsewhere."

"Yes."

"And you can do it?"

"We guard that ability with our very lives. It is why the Order was founded in the first place. To keep those with the gift from undoing our world with power they scant understand."

"But I thought you all hid from the Glass Kingdom there, in Elsewhere. Isn't that how you survived?"

"So those legends reached even your ears. Lies told to appease a murderous foreign king. To make him stop his search for us. Once there were thousands of our kind, but we seven of the council who remain do so because we draw on every ounce of our power to stay hidden."

Aihara approached Sora, extended her hand, and gestured toward it.

Sora hesitated, though, she wasn't sure why. For so long she'd longed to meet the mystics, but seeing them test her with the feigned sacrifice of a child was difficult to pass over. What if all the awful rumors about them weren't just lies spread by their conquerors.

"Go on, take it," Aihara Na said.

Sora finally gave in, but her hand went right through Aihara Na's as if the woman were little more than air. Her eyes darted between her hand and Aihara's, words stuck on the tip of her tongue.

"To draw on Elsewhere's power so fully nearly destroyed us," Aihara Na said. "But it was necessary for the Order to survive. We remain, not in Elsewhere, but in-between. Tethered here barely of body, but eternal."

Now Sora understood what Aran Bokeo meant about them being close to immortal. "Couldn't you just have hidden in Elsewhere and returned?"

"No!" Aihara Na bellowed, making the very walls shake. Sora winced. Aihara drew a long breath to calm herself, and Sora wondered if she even needed to breathe in her form, or if it was a habit, leftovers from when she was human.

"Elsewhere is the realm of more than fallen gods," Aihara Na said. "It is the well of our magic in this corporeal realm, and in that power, there is more than fire. To open Elsewhere, we invite demons, lesser gods, and dead men who refuse to believe their time here is through. If those with our gift traveled there and returned, it would not be as themselves."

"What would happen?"

"What is this about, Sora?"

"Curiosity," she lied. "It's just that… when you gave me that vision back in that chamber with Lord Bokeo, I think I saw—"

"What you saw was only what lies within, nothing more. And a connection to Elsewhere lies within all mystics. It is the gift with which we are born. What makes us special. And it is that connection we seek to sharpen into a razor's edge here on Pantego."

"But it felt like I was there. I saw—"

"You were not there." Aihara Na interrupted again, staring straight into Sora's eyes. "Listen to me Sora, and listen closely. I have trained many mystics in the centuries I've lived. Some, promising, living within these very walls. But far more perish, and there is no fate ghastlier than when a rebellious or clumsy soul finds itself possessed by a being of Elsewhere. That which goes there must stay. Too many born with the gift have come to us seeking training, driven by the desire to bring back those who have passed on from Pantego. We mystics are capable of many great feats."

Aihara Na flicked her hands and murmured in that same manner of mixed languages she had in the temple. Her words flowed as gracefully as her body, which whipped around in a dance of martial arts. A powerful gust of air zipped by Sora and swirled around the mystic, then turned into a globe of water over her hand. She swept it in a wide arc, and the water turned to ice. Then, slamming her fist into the floor, a circle of cracks spread wide. One zigzagged beneath Sora's feet, but as the mystic rose again, the cracks reversed and vanished.

"We can manipulate the elements that bind this world, mend wounds, extend our lives beyond comprehension," Aihara Na said. If Sora wasn't paying attention, she wouldn't have noticed the mystic was panting. "We can even see beyond this realm, but we do not travel there, and we do not bring the fallen back. We mustn't. I know the temptation might be strong. What is dead must remain dead. We have all lost, or will lose loved ones, but it is far too dangerous. Do you understand?"

Sora managed a nod. She couldn't tell Aihara that she'd just revealed that the mystics were capable of the very thing she'd come to Yaolin City to learn. If it would bring Whitney back, she didn't care if it was dangerous, as long as nobody had to die to do it.

"Where are we, Ancient One?" Sora asked Aihara Na, deciding it was time to stop resisting and play along.

"You do not know?" Aihara Na replied. If she was pleased with Sora's use of her formal title, her seemingly always staid façade didn't show it.

"How could I? You did that… thing… and then I was here."

"Yes," the mystic said, now standing with her back to Sora. "I do apologize for that. I had to be sure you'd come, and I wasn't sure what kinds of lies you've heard of this place. Liam spread so many after he destroyed the Council."

Aihara Na placed the palm of her hand against the wall, and the stones shifted, overlapping one another, some moving out and creating a platform on the exterior of the building, others folding inward. When it had finished, Sora was looking out over Lake Yaolin, enclosed on all sides by the city.

She approached the new opening, breathless. They were twenty stories above the water. Perhaps more.

"Welcome to the Red Tower," Aihara Na said.

By now, Aquira was comfortably perched on Sora's shoulder, purring softly. Sora stroked her beneath the chin. She couldn't help it.

"I thought Liam made you seal this place up?" Sora asked.

"He was a fool to believe we would use our own magic to keep us from the place where all magic is born. He also thinks us all dead. He grossly underestimated the lengths we'd go to protect the knowledge of proper magic on this plane."

Aihara Na turned to walk away from the window, and her body passed through Sora. Sora clutched at her heart, such cold stealing over her she thought she might pass out. The feeling left her nearly as soon as it had come.

"Come, Sora," Aihara Na said. "Let me show you around. This will be your home until training is complete."

"How long will that be?"

"As long as it takes. Not a moment less or more."

Sora thought to retort, but the truth was, she had nowhere better to be. Troborough was gone, as was everyone she ever loved or loved her. In his own demented way, Wetzel loved her, and he was now ash. Her feelings for Whitney confused her, but vexing others was Whitney's goal in life. She longed to be so frustrated by him that she had to punch him in the arm, yet at the same time, wanted to wrap her arms around him and squeeze. This was her only chance to have that feeling back.

Aihara Na led her down a spiraling flight of stairs, and then another. As they descended further, Sora couldn't believe she'd climbed all these steps while under the influence of Aihara Na's magic. She didn't remember any of it.

When they reached a landing, she had lost count of how many flights they'd gone. She breathed heavily, but Aihara Na wasn't affected in the slightest. The perks of having an ethereal body.

"This way." Aihara rolled her fingers, and a light bloomed in the center, revealing a hallway with rooms along the outside. They made their way to the other side of the tower, passing dozens of empty rooms until Aihara Na stopped at one, completely nondescript.

"It is not The Emperor's Quilt, but it should do," she said.

"It is lovely," Sora said as the door opened, and she meant it. The room had a window, and even though it was little more than an arrowslit carved into the stone, it was a vast improvement over Wetzel's basement where she'd grown up or even her bed on Gold Grin's ship. There was a bed as well, instead of a pile of hay, and it looked comfortable enough.

"What's through that door?" Sora asked.

"A space for you to take a bath and clear your mind. The Glassman see no value in a clean soul, but you're in Panping now. We can finish the tour after supper if you'd prefer. It has been a trying day."

Aquira flapped her wings and soared toward the large, plush bed. She turned a few circles, then curled up and closed her eyes.

"No," Sora said, not wanting to waste any more time. Whitney had been trapped in Elsewhere with Kazimir for long enough. She didn't deserve rest yet. "Let's continue."

"As you wish."

Aihara continued to lead her down the stairs.

"How will I know how to get back to my chambers?" Sora asked.

"It will not be difficult."

Sora realized she would need to get used to terse responses from everyone in this strange place. Living such a secluded life had clearly left them cold. Sora could understand that. Being cooped up with Wetzel every day gave her a tendency to be short with him as well.

"You will do most of your training here," Aihara said, stopping at a floor a long way down containing a single, rectangular room that was far too large to fit within the tower. The walls, ceiling, floor; everything was white.

"How can—"

"We don't rebuild the world," Aihara responded before Sora could finish. "We are now beneath the waters." She gestured to the walls, emphasizing the size of the room. "Madam Neelangam Jayasin will handle much of your teaching."

Sora hadn't even noticed the yellow-robed woman seated in the middle of the room, one of the seven remaining mystics. Seeing her there brought a sense of wonder at the immensity of the place. It was bigger than any room she'd ever been in, except maybe the Throne Room in the Glass Castle.

The woman rose and joined them by the entrance to the room. She bowed, and said, "Greetings Sora. You may call me Madam Jaya."

"Madam Jaya," Sora said and returned the bow.

"It is a pleasure."

"The pleasure is mine, I'm sure."

"When will she be starting?" Madam Jaya asked Aihara Na.

"First thing in the morning," Aihara Na replied. "Time is always of the essence. Are things prepared?"

"As they'll ever be."

"Excellent," Aihara said with a bow. "We will see you at supper."

Their next stop was just a few floors down, but at the end of the stairwell, the bottommost level. A large pair of stone doors stood before them, the image of a lush tree carved onto them and glowing blue.

"Beyond those doors is something few have ever seen," Aihara Na said. "Power beyond fathoming. Are you ready?"

Sora nodded.

Aihara Na had been locked up for a long time, but Sora was sure nothing could be worse than facing Queen Bliss or Afhem Muskigo's army. The mystic waved her hand, muttered under her breath, and the doors opened.

Bright blue light poured out, forcing Sora to raise her hand to shield her eyes.

"Come," Aihara said, walking forward.

"What is it?" Sora said, wonder filling her every fiber. A pool of blue liquid bubbled within, steam rising from it. Inside the fluid, floating on the surface, were hundreds of flower petals.

"This is the Well of Wisdom." She led Sora to its edge. "This place is the beginning and end of all of our journeys."

"What does it do?"

"Everything and nothing. Everything for the one who truly desires its gifts, but nothing for him who thinks it a weapon."

Another cryptic response.

"I see that answer doesn't satisfy you?" Aihara Na said.

"How could it?"

"As you'll see, there are no books in this tower. We have no library of records like kings keep locked away. The Well of Wisdom contains the collective memories of our Order since the first Mystic Council and visions of those who've looked beyond. It is here we learned you would return to us after the passing of poor Tayvada Bokeo, that you would be one blessed enough by the Gift to help us rebuild our fractured Order. The one with the Will of Fire."

"You wish to use me?"

"Is a blade demeaned by it being used to draw blood? To be used for that which you were created is a gift from the gods. Tayvada accepted his fate long before you knew of your power."

"You knew so long, but didn't save him?"

"For all our power, we cannot control fate. He is an example of what can happen when one accepts who they are. He lived life to the fullest, knowing the end was imminent, and helped so many of our people abroad, as you have seen."

Sora's lip twisted. *He died a hero to them*, she thought, but couldn't manage to say out loud.

"When you are done with your training—and only when you are done —you will enter and see what the gods would like you to see," Aihara Na said.

The liquid looked as if it would burn Sora alive, bubbling as it was. She couldn't imagine going into the pool and found herself glad it would be a matter for another day.

"Are you hungry?" Aihara Na asked, abruptly. "I apologize, it has been a long while, and I sometimes forget what hunger is like."

Sora nodded.

Aihara Na guided her back up to one of the ground levels where many Panpingese men and women gathered in brown and gray hooded robes. Sora couldn't help but remember Redstar's cultist haven in that dwarven ruin south of Oxgate.

"Who are all these people? Trainees as well?" Sora asked.

"Servants."

The word didn't sit well in Sora's belly, like foul food curdling in the acids. "Slaves," she muttered, thinking about Winde Port and the Ghetto, about Darkings and his 'servants.'

"*Willing* servants," Aihara corrected.

"I hope so."

"Many wish to see the return of the mystics as a governing power within the Panping Region; those who are not so blessed with the Gift as you will take decades to see it manifest within them. They have chosen to hide in this place with us and serve our wills, never to leave unless commanded to. Lord Bokeo is among them, and his late son." Aihara stepped toward Sora. "I know you do not yet trust us."

"You were going to kill a boy just to test me," Sora retorted before she could help herself. "Now you force people to stay locked in here?" The thought of Tayvada dying for their vision had her frustrated. A handful of servants within earshot spun, now staring at the two.

Aihara's hand lashed out, slapping hard against Sora's face. Sora pawed at her cheek, not sure how the mystic had suddenly become corporeal again.

"You may not yet understand our ways and methods, but you will not question them here," Aihara Na said sternly, anger contorting her features. She glared around the room, and the servants turned away. "We are, you are, this place is so much bigger than some poor street urchin roaming around Yaolin City. You have looked upon the Well of Wisdom, seen beyond our veil. You are an apprentice of the Mystic Order now, and while you are here training, you will keep your opinions to yourself. Is that understood?"

Sora expected to feel Elsewhere rising inside of her, but she felt nothing. She just narrowed her eyes, staring into Aihara's.

"Yes," she said.

"Yes, Ancient One," Aihara prompted. "I am your master now."

"Yes, Ancient One," Sora said through gritted teeth.

"Understand that I have known lifetimes worth of opinions. I have seen things you could not possibly imagine. When I am passed, and you sit upon the council, then, and only then, will your opinions on this world matter. And when that time comes, I am certain you will see the world as we do."

"And how is that?"

Aihara Na continued staring for a brief moment in silence, then turned and walked away. Only then did Sora realize the mystic's steps made no sound. "Enjoy a meal," she said. "You begin training in the morning."

XXI

THE DESERTER

Valin opened the door back into The Vineyard's downstairs hallway, inviting Rand to follow. He barred the opening with his cane when Sigrid tried to do the same.

"Where we're going is no place for a lady such as yourself," Valin said.

"Ye don't know nothing about me," she bristled.

He sighed. "A young girl from Dockside with parents who loved her. She didn't like that her brother got all the attention, taught to fight and drink like a man of Dockside should, so she tagged along and learned some herself. Her parents died young, as they often do here, and she and her brother were left alone for years. He looked out for her when lechers like Trapp would have sold her skin until he left her for greener pastures. So, she learned to look out for herself, and then when he came crawling back and needed her, she started to learn how strong she truly was..."

"Enough," Sigrid said, refusing to look at him.

"I've seen every story Dockside has to offer one hundred times over, girl. Neither of you is special. Understand that. My only care is to make sure those stories don't end before they're meant to."

"Ain't ye such a hero?"

"This isn't a place for heroes. But even a lawless land needs someone to keep the order. We're animals deep down, and without them we'd rip each other to shreds the first chance we got."

"Says only those who turn their back on Iam," Rand said.

"And how has that faith worked out for the King's Shield, good knight?"

Rand bit his lip. He regretted thinking Valin was a worthwhile ally with a sincere heart for Dockside. Perhaps his grim vision of the world was the necessary evil Dockside needed to survive, or maybe it was men like him keeping the district from bathing in the light of Iam like the rest of the capital. For now, he was a tool only to help reach Torsten.

"We've wasted enough time," Rand said. "You said we could make a deal, so let's make one."

Valin laughed. "There he is! Not a meek little deserter hiding from the wicked Queen anymore, are you? Still, I must insist that your sister stay behind for now."

Rand was about to protest when Sigrid took his hand. "It's fine, Rand," she said. "I need a break from this bastard anyway."

"Excellent," Valin said. "You'll be well guarded here." He turned to one of his thugs. "Fetch her a drink and some hog's head broth. Best in Dockside."

Sigrid grunted a response, then returned to Valin's office.

"Codar, bring the bounty and meet us," Valin ordered. His Breklian aid bowed, then hurried off. Turning, Valin led Rand down the hall toward the curtain, flanked by a few cronies—most of whom were missing teeth. Rand tried not to stare, despite the fact they didn't return the favor. He imagined how ridiculous he must've looked, donned head to toe in Shieldsman armor in a place where Iam's Eye wouldn't dare glimpse.

"Your sister will be fine," Codar said. "Bloodsport has a way of... riling men. It's no place for women."

"Bloodsport?"

Valin grinned in response. It was then that Rand noticed the discolored stone of the walls as they went deeper into the passage. Red in places, bleached in others from trying to wipe the red away. And with every step, cheering grew louder. Dust poured down from the ceiling now as feet slammed in thunderous unison.

Valin pushed the curtain aside with his cane, and Rand saw the source of the tumult. An arena was sunken into the earth, surrounded by rows of wooden stands. Every inch was filled with patrons, screaming and spilling their drinks—hundreds of them. Rand had never seen an arena like it in all his life. Supposedly, there was a great coliseum built onto an island off the coast of Latiapur in which the Shesaitju warlords proved their mettle, but he'd never traveled so far. Yet this was right in his hometown.

On the sands of the arena, a man lay against some rocks, his weapon lying out of reach. A shaggy-bearded giant screamed to the crowd, the single eye in the center of his flat forehead open wide. Rand had seen giants before, mostly on construction crews in Old Yarrington. They were tall as most homes after all, with biceps the size of barrels.

The giant squeezed his massive fist, then drove it down into the combatant's arm with the force of a battering ram. The bone snapped like a twig, and the man rolled off the rocks, howling in agony. Rand had to turn from the carnage, but the drunken crowd went crazy. Autlas were passed around in bets, Valin's cronies collecting around the top of the arena. Rand couldn't imagine anyone would bet against the giant.

Two men entered the arena from a metal portcullis to drag the loser out.

"If the Shield knew about this..." Rand said as he followed Valin around the concourse.

"Do you imagine the former Master of Coin didn't take his cut?" Valin said.

"The traitor, Darkings, you mean?"

"From the mouth of a traitor? I assure you, Mister Langley, not a soul enters that arena who doesn't know the cost. And nobody gets killed… mostly."

A narrow stairwell led up to a private promontory looking out over the arena. Valin collapsed onto a plush couch that was severely out of place around so much stone. He winced in pain as he stretched his leg out beside a platter of luxuriant fruits from all over, places where it didn't winter.

From their vantage point, they could see everything within the arena, but nobody could see them unless they craned their necks. Rand moved to the edge and looked over. An announcer called out the giant's next opponent, and more bets flew around the crowd. A warrior entered the arena, hoisting a battle-axe into the air and roaring. His pale skin, painted face, and many piercings made it easy to tell he was Drav Cra, but as tremendous and musclebound as the Northman was, the giant was as tall as two of him.

"I thought you said the Drav Cra cost you money?" Rand said, realizing just how much coin was being tossed around.

"People pay to watch the savages die for now," Valin replied. "It won't last long. My champion, Uhlvark, never loses anyway."

"How is it fair to pit that against a man?"

"It isn't. But a desperate man will try anything, and get a few drinks into a Drav Cra, they'll claim they can slay anything. Unless you have an issue with thinning their herd?"

"I—"

Valin waved his hand in dismissal. "Spare me the sermon, please. The people want what they want. I am here only to appease them."

"And what? You want me to fight down there, is that what this is? A Shieldsman in your arena?"

He scratched his chin. "You know, I hadn't thought of that."

"I won't spill blood for you."

"You will do whatever I ask if you want to see Unger freed."

The crowd roared. The next fight started, and the Drav Cra warrior circled Uhlvark, axe in hand. The giant spun in place, grunting indecipherable words. Their ilk were considered simpletons, and his battle-stance proved it. He had none. Without his size, the Drav Cra warrior, trained from birth for battle, would have cut him to pieces. Still, the warrior was playing it smart, keeping his distance and slashing at the giant's hand's every time he tried to grasp him.

"So, what do you want?" Rand asked.

Just then Rand heard chains rattling behind him. He turned to see Codar returning, and he wasn't alone. He had a bald man in tow, wearing naught but a loincloth, with chains around his wrists and ankles. His gray skin screamed Shesaitju.

"Valin, how long are you planning to delay this?" asked another man who entered behind the Black Sandsman, going silent when he noticed Rand. He had a thin mustache and large belly that his delicate, satin tunic couldn't hide. He looked like a noble and held himself like one too. Rand was sure he'd seen him before, though couldn't place where.

Codar sent the Shesaitju man to his knees, earning a few curses in Saitjuese.

"Who is this?" Rand questioned.

"The most important man in Yarrington," Valin said. "Until Redstar took over, that is."

"We had a deal, Valin," the nobleman said. "You dare hand us over to the Shield?"

"Relax, young Darkings. This is no mere Shieldsman. He's the deserter who sent your father fleeing for his life."

"The Mad Queen's Hangman?"

"The very same."

The nobleman grinned, teeth yellow and rotten despite how wealthy he appeared. That was when Rand put things together. He had seen that smile before, only on a grayer head belonging to the man's father. This was Bartholomew Darkings, son of the former Master of Coin, Yuri Darkings, who had fled the capital during Oleander's rage, then returned only to betray the Crown and conspire to aid the Shesaitju rebellion.

That means… "Is that?"

"Caleef Sidar Rakun, the embodiment of God of Sand and Sea, and the root of the war in the South," Valin pronounced. "There's that Shieldsman intuition I've become accustomed to. The mind works better minus the drink, doesn't it, Sir Langley?"

"How did you find him?"

"I didn't. A peculiar mercenary company led by a dwarf happened upon him on the road. Wouldn't you know it, that one of them knew I'd pay better than the Crown. I thought about selling him back to young King Pi, and then Yuri Darkings offered so much more."

"And the rest comes when you get him back to Latiapur, Valin," Bartholomew Darkings said. "Remember that."

Valin rolled his eyes. "Like you'd ever let me forget."

"This man started a war," Rand said, a harsh edge to his tone.

"Your King started it," Caleef Rakun snapped. "I came in peace, offered my help in what ways I could. He locked me in a room and expected my afhems to sit on their thumbs?"

"Quiet." Codar yanked on his chains so hard the Caleef fell forward onto his face.

"It does not matter to me who caused it," Valin said. "The Caleef is mine now, and he will be sent to the party which has shown they desire him more. War has already started." Valin grabbed a bellot from a platter set before his couch and took a bite. Juice from the yellow melon grown only in southern Panping ran down his chin. He offered the fruit to Rand, then continued with a mouthful.

"Tell me, Rand, what good is having him here as prisoner inspiring more to Muskigo's ranks?" Valin said. "More fighting so that more fine people of Dockside can be conscripted to march off to their deaths."

"That is the King's decision," Rand said, stewing.

Valin threw his hands up in frustration. "You Shieldsman astound me. You want help removing Redstar, yet you would judge me for this?"

"It's not the same. Redstar is—"

"The King's uncle and Prime Minister of all the Glass," Valin finished. "Ridiculous as that may be. And you would be remiss to know that Torsten Unger, the very accused traitor you wish to save, advised against imprisoning the Caleef in the first place."

Rand looked to the gray-skinned Caleef, stripped and disgraced. He was usually painted entirely black from head to toe, and now only a few smudges remained behind his ears. His sad eyes told the truth in what Valin had said, leaving Rand without a response.

"So, Rand Langley, this is what I need from you." Valin stood and limped around Rand's back. He tossed the bellot pit into the sands below where the Drav Cra was still taunting the big giant. "In two days time, the Dawning will be upon us, and the King's Shield in the Glass Castle will be lax. We have always respected the Dawning as a solemn day of reflection, but foreigners are amongst us. We can't play by the rules either."

"The Dawning," Rand mouthed to himself. He hadn't even realized it was coming up. For Iam's followers, there was no day more sacred. It was at the heart of winter, the tenth day of Freefrost, when Pantego's two moons passed across the sun at dusk, forcing an early, fleeting night. Celeste, matching its path across the sky, kept the world in twilight until it fell behind the horizon for the night. A time without Iam's light, when his flock was forced to look within for it.

Rand was surprised Valin Tehr, and his underworld would respect such a day. He also knew, from experience, that he was right, the guard would be light. Most people didn't work on the Dawning. They spent the day in sermons and amongst family, then the night in prayer and fasting, waiting awake to see the first dawn of the new year. Even children endured the long, quiet night. Most of the Shieldsmen and castle guard would be given the day off, with a skeleton crew left behind of the greenest among them—those who hadn't yet earned respite.

All gates and entries to the Glass Castle would be sealed off as the Royal Council observed the holy day. Then, the King and Wren the Holy —If Wren was even still alive—would walk outside the next morning, side by side, and declare the new year.

"Even if there are few Glassmen, the castle will be swarming with heathens," Rand said. Even if the worst Glassmen, like Valin, recognized the Dawning as a day of peace, Redstar wouldn't.

"More of their herd to thin then," Valin said. "I cannot promise Unger's freedom without spilling a bit of blood, but at least on that day, it will be savage blood alone."

"The castle will be sealed off."

"Dwarves don't celebrate the Dawning. The hairy bastards always live in darkness." He laughed, drawing a smirk from Codar and Bartholomew. "You and my men will enter the dungeons through the damaged Royal Crypt. The ceiling is nearly rebuilt, but there remains one opening."

"They'll keep heavy guard there to keep the pilgrims and crazies out," Rand said. "Especially during the Dawning, people will crowd Mount Lister for sermons."

"This is the man you claim will help us?" Bartholomew said. "He questions everything."

"You are in no position to be picky, Bartholomew," Valin replied. He turned back to Rand. "Yuri Darkings knows the dwarven foreman performing repairs, and he'll let us through."

Rand regarded the revolting son of the traitorous Master of Coin. "I don't feel comfortable leaving this in the hands of a Darkings. They're traitors. What would stop them from having us gutted the moment we get in?"

"You would be wise to look at the company you keep, knight," Bartholomew snapped.

"Even I have my limits." Rand took a hard step toward him.

"Enough!" Valin barked. He distracted half the crowd downstairs from the fight, and the warriors as well. The Drav Cra man glimpsed up toward Valin's private viewing chamber, and at that moment the giant got his hands around his waist. The savage hacked at Uhlvark's enormous forearm, but the giant raised him above his head and pulled with both hands. The crunch as the Drav Cra warrior was torn in two made Rand's stomach turn over. The crowd went into a frenzy.

Uhlvark tilted his head back, letting the savage's blood pour into his mouth. The giant spit the blood in a spray above his head, and the mist carried into the crowd. It only made them cheer louder.

"He put up a good fight," Valin remarked, as if he'd been somehow keeping an eye on the battle the entire time, then he returned his attention to Rand. "Yuri Darkings speaks only one language." Valin squeezed the bridge of his nose. "The dwarf will be paid amply to get us through."

"No small price, indeed," Bartholomew said. "Greedy buggers, as if our coins aren't made of the very rock they sleep on."

Rand breathed in through his teeth. Knowing the people he was plotting with was more sickening than watching a man torn in two, but he had to trust in the path Iam placed him on. "So, we get into the crypt, then what?"

"The rest is up to you. You'll sneak or fight your way through the catacombs to the castle's lowest dungeon. Codar and a few of my most trusted men will accompany you in case it comes to fighting."

"No killing Glassmen," Rand said.

"We will try our best. I may not look it, Rand, but I am a pious man. You think I want my hands stained with the blood of our people on the Dawning?"

"You're right," Rand said, finally picking up a bellot and taking a bite. "You don't look it."

Valin grinned. "And that's it. We will free Unger, and then you'll have your chance to repay me."

"How?"

"The distraction Torsten causes along with the Dawning will be the perfect cover for the Caleef to be escorted out of the city that very night. You will lead a company of men along with Bartholomew, and deliver him back to his people as promised."

Rand was mid-bite, and the bellot nearly slipped through his fingers. "You want me to guard a rebel king?"

"Look at him," Valin pointed to the Caleef. The man had a soft body and his old, gray eyes brimmed with fear. His were a race of renowned warriors, but it was clear the same could not be said for their ruler. "Who better to guard the god-king of the Shesaitju than a Shieldsman of the Glass? In your armor, no one will question you at the gates on the Dawning. And bandits or worse will be less apt to attack."

"And what of Redstar?" Rand questioned. "Even if I agree to that. I can't promise that Torsten and I will be able to handle him by the end of the night."

"Who said anything about Redstar? We arrange to free Torsten Unger so that he may handle the imposter. That is what you agreed to in exchange for my help."

"So, what? I open Torsten's cage and then leave him in a castle full of enemies to fend for himself?"

"In simpler terms," Valin agreed.

"So that I can help you commit high treason alongside a family that has already done so? I heard men say that Yuri Darkings killed Sir Wardric Jolly. He was a good man who helped train me. Loyal to the Crown and I am."

"Is that the name of the Shieldsman who tried to stop us?" Bartholomew said. "Squealed like a pig when I sliced his gut open."

"You son of a—" Rand charged at him, but didn't get far before Codar's dirk was at his throat. Rand had the satisfaction of seeing the cowardly nobleman flinch, however.

"Codar, if this worm makes another move, cut out his throat." Valin's cane clicked behind him as he made his way around. Gone was the calculating, visage he usually wore. Replaced instead by the controlled rage that was the reason he was the most feared man in Dockside.

"Now is not the time to be brazen, boy," Valin said. "I could just as easily tear that armor off your body and give it to one of my men. It doesn't belong to you anymore anyway. But in open battle, a Shieldsman is worth his weight in glaruium, and I'm feeling generous toward a fellow Docksider who rose so high and fell so spectacularly."

"You said..." Rand cleared his throat. "You said you wanted Redstar and his people gone. Leaving Torsten alone in a castle where he has no allies left is murder."

"I consider it a calculated risk. I won't have my people seen assassinating a member of the royal family. Necessary or not, that kind of attention is bad for business."

"Then let me help him. Together we can see an end to this silent invasion, and then I'll do whatever you need. Even if it means helping this worthless sack of shog." He pointed to Bartholomew, who seemed amused at the title.

"And risk my opportunity to move during the Dawning while the castle is distracted?" Valin said. "Or losing you?"

"I'll give you my yigging armor!"

"Do not think for one second that this is a negotiation, Mister Langley."

"Isn't everything you do?" Rand replied. His head turned, and the point of Codar's blade pushed gently into his jaw.

Valin wasn't entertained. "Bartholomew, make sure his highness doesn't scamper away." Everyone glanced over to find Caleef Rakun crawling to the exit, hoping nobody would notice him. Bartholomew stomped down on his ankle. The Caleef cried out, then whimpered.

"Bring him." Valin waved them forward to look down upon the arena. Codar didn't leave Rand much choice but to follow.

A cleaning crew was busy dragging away the two halves of the Drav Cra warrior's body. Nobody cared to swab up the blood or entrails. The crowd trickled out, seeing as how the foreign warrior perishing was likely the main event. The giant, Uhlvark, sat on some rocks, chomping on a cow's thigh as if it had once belonged to a chicken.

"I think it is time you understand exactly where you are," Valin said. "You've spent too much time away in grand castles, you forget who owns this district. You think I don't know the threats you made to poor Gideon Trapp about exposing my shipments there?"

Codar shoved Rand against the rail, then pressed the point of his dagger against the weak point at the base of his skull. Valin leaned over next to him.

"My friends!" Valin called down to the dwindling crowd. "Why do you leave? I have a special performance for you. I give you a traitor's sister, and the only one who can save her would rather keep his pride!"

There was motion down by the lower entrance to the arena. Rand extended his neck to get a better view and saw Sigrid shoved out by a group of thugs. Her clothes were shredded beyond recognition. Whistles sounded all around the arena as the crowd returned to their seats. Ale showered down from flagons and drenched her wild hair.

"Rand?" she cried out as she spun, voice cracking. "Rand!"

"What is this?" Rand asked. "What in the name of Iam are you doing!" The angrier he got, the harder Codar pressed the blade into the back of his neck. Too fast a move and he'd be dead before he got a finger on Valin.

"Teaching you some respect." Valin flicked his hand. One of his men in the stands tossed Sigrid her Drav Cra bow and quiver.

The giant finished his meal at the same time and noticed her. The single eye in his pear-shaped face went wide. "Prettyyy giirl," he said, enough drool to fill a tub dripping from his lips. The ground shook as he stood, then more as he lumbered toward her. The quake sent Sigrid staggering, but she grabbed the bow and arrows and found her footing.

"Please, let me out of here!" she screamed. "Rand!"

"Let her go, Valin!" Rand felt a kick and dropped to his knees. Codar's blade slipped around in front, pointing at his trachea. One of his arms was wrenched behind his back and Codar's boot pressed against the back of his legs. The Breklian was extremely well-trained.

Valin leaned in and whispered into Rand's ear. "I need you to listen and listen close, boy or your strong, pretty sister will be split in half by that oaf in ways you don't want to imagine."

"Please, Valin, be reasonable. She's a good Docksider. Please."

The giant grasped at Sigrid, but she rolled out of the way, tearing a bit more of her dress. The crowd yapped in delight.

"Reasonable?" Valin grabbed Rand's jaw and pulled it so near Rand could smell the wine on his breath." I trade in favors and gold. You come here, with nothing to offer me but your sword and your identity. And you dare try to push away my generosity?"

"Whatever you want, I'll do, just let her go. I'm begging you."

The giant charged again, and Sigrid struggled to thread her bow. Rand now knew how well she could do it, but nerves had her hands shaking like

Rand's had his first day of training under Sir Torsten and Sir Wardic. She got a shot off, and it slashed the Giant's shoulder on the way to stabbing into the stands, right next to a drunkard's head.

The giant grabbed her. She stabbed an arrow into his wrist, and he flung her aside. The fall wasn't far, but the magnificent creature didn't know his own strength. Her side hit the sand, and she rolled all the way across, slamming hard into the wall. The giant's eye narrowed with rage, and he roared.

"Valin!" Rand screamed.

The giant took two clumsy steps, then Valin raised a hand. "Stop, friend Uhlvark," he said, barely needing to raise his voice. "Please, return to your room."

The giant did as commanded and looked up toward them. "Yes, Papa…" he said. Then he grabbed the stripped cow bone and ran off through the lower gates. The crowd moaned in disapproval as if watching the ravaging of an innocent woman was worthwhile entertainment.

"That is but a taste of what will happen if you betray me, Rand Langley," Valin said. Codar released him and stepped in front of his leader, leaving Rand hanging onto the railing to keep from collapsing. He could barely feel his legs. Some of Valin's men ran out and grabbed Sigrid. She got a swing in at one with an arrow, slicing his calf, but he slapped her. Her gaze found Rand's as they dragged her away, and all he could do was wish he'd listened to her and they'd run.

"You're worse than any of them," Rand whispered once she was gone.

"You're going to hurt my feelings." Valin clacked toward the other end of the room. Bartholomew wore a smirk, but the Caleef looked horrified. A foreign rebel, the most human of them all.

"Now, you are going to help Codar free Unger so that he may cause all manner of chaos for the city guard in his mad quest for vengeance," Valin said. "Then, you will meet Bartholomew and the Caleef at the South Corner gates, and help transport him south to his people. If you are discovered, the Crown will blame you, the deserter who tried to kill the Prime Minister and you will not say otherwise. If you do this, your sister will come to no more harm, and you will find a fruitful place in my employ."

"I'll never work with—"

Valin clicked his tongue and wagged his finger to silence him. "If you fail in any of this, your sister will taste all the rotten men of Yarrington until they've had their fill. Only then will I allow her to die."

Valin turned to leave, and before Rand could shout at him, Codar smashed him in the side of the head. He hit the floor like a sack of dirt, his vision blurry and blackness closing in.

"You went off to serve in the King's Shield, and you forgot where you're from," Valin said. "Now, boy, I hope that you remember."

Rand looked down into a full mug of ale. He didn't drink from it, only stared until the foam dissipated, and he could see his pale reflection in the amber liquid.

"You may as well have one," someone behind him said. "Codar says his people drink their full before every battle. It takes away their fear. Dulls their pain."

Rand glanced back and saw Valin limping toward him across The Vineyard, wearing a warm smile. His brothel was mostly empty now that it was the morning of the Dawning. A few stragglers remained, unable to spend even a day avoiding sin.

"I want to feel everything," Rand said, squeezing the mug so tight his fingernails made marks in his palm. He'd been kept in a small room below The Vineyard for two days, forbidden from seeing his sister or talking to anyone.

Now Rand knew he'd led them straight into the house of a snake. Their father always told them to stay away from Valin because before you knew it, you'd be working for him. It was a slow end, like the venom of a Shesaitju sand snake, breaking you down piece by piece until your body seized.

Valin had his fangs in Rand now, and there was no wriggling free. He just had to focus on the task at hand. Torsten was a mighty warrior, and there was no man in Pantego closer to Iam. If anyone could end Redstar's insurrection, it was him.

The legs of a stool screeched. Valin lifted himself onto the velour seat, wincing. Codar stood a short distance behind, just out of sight and easy to forget about, ever vigilant.

"I hope there are no hard feelings between us," Codar said.

"You threatened my sister's life."

"I threaten lives daily. Don't take it personally."

Rand squeezed the mug harder until he could feel the area under his thumb ready to crack. "Don't you have more fights to put on?"

"Even I take a little break this holiest of days."

Finally, Rand decided to look at Valin and noticed the luminescent paint under his eyes. All the children of Iam wore it on the day of the Dawning, spread onto their faces by priests during morning service. It shimmered with Iam's light and also allowed people to observe the eclipse of the sun without winding up as blind as the priests themselves.

"You don't deserve to wear that," Rand bristled.

"Is it my fault you were too stubborn to see the right path in front of you? You'll thank me in the end. A man like you could do far more for this district at my side than in the King's Shield, and get rich doing it."

"Gold isn't everything."

"Now that's where you're wrong," Valin said, slapping the bar. "The only reason places like Dockside exist is so the pampered ingrates on the other side of the fence can feel better about what they have. We're a frame of reference, kid. A novelty."

"And men like you will keep us there forever."

Valin chuckled. "Ah, the eternal battle. Pragmatist versus dreamer. I've met countless men like you who thought the same, yet I'm still here, and men like you end up dead or in a gutter more often than not."

"Is there a purpose to this conversation?"

"I have every right to check up on my investment before he leaves. But really, I came to invite you to see your sister one last time before you go."

Rand turned so fast he knocked over the mug, ale quickly spreading across the bar. "If you hurt her anymore."

"She's fine, I assure you. I have no desire to harm her or to see you fail —on the contrary, I root for all my people to rise as far as they can."

"We aren't your people."

"Such the perfect little Shieldsman." Valin slid off the stool and made his way to the stairs. "Come, I'll take you to her."

Rand followed him up to the second floor overlooking the lobby of The

Vineyard. Curtains leading into semi-private rooms lined the walls, usually all full, this morning they were mostly open. They did pass one with deep moans emanating from within. A thug stood guard out front. Rand's heart fell to his feet, thinking Sigrid was inside, but Valin continued past.

He turned down a hallway running along the empty, outdoor balcony. It was a quiet day, snowflakes fluttering about from a patchy, blue sky. A perfect day for the dawning. Too many clouds and the eclipse would have been barely visible.

They turned again and reached a door guarded by two thugs. All that was beyond it was silence.

"Let him in," Valin ordered.

"The screaming wench finally got a client?" one of them joked.

Rand had his forearm against the man's throat in a heartbeat, pinning him against the wall. "If you touch her, I'll rip out your tongue."

"Relax, Rand," Valin said. "I said she would not be harmed unless you betray me, and my word is my bond."

Rand backed off, then noticed Codar in his peripherals. The mustached Breklian stood directly behind Valin, his weapon-hand, whether full or empty, was concealed behind his back.

The thug coughed and rubbed his neck. "Someone ought to teach this knight some manners," he rasped.

"A lesson I am certain you wouldn't survive," Valin said. "Now, let him in."

The other guard rattled through some keys and gave the door a push. It creaked open, and Rand saw his sister curled up on a bed, a metal cuff around her ankle that kept her chained to the bedpost. A ratty dress was draped over her body, but at the very least, this one wasn't ripped and adequately covered her.

His whole world melted away, and all that remained was her. Rand ran in and wrapped his arms around her. He could feel her shaking like she probably had been since a giant tried to have his way with her. She had a few scrapes on her forehead from falling in the arena, and her hands were cut up far worse.

"Are you okay?" he asked. "Did they lay another hand on you?"

"Not since the arena," she replied, voice shaking.

He squeezed her again, then held her at arm's length. "I'm so sorry for letting us come here. I should have never trusted him."

"No, ye shouldn't have." She forced a smile. It stung Rand's heart to see how difficult it seemed for her to do.

"And I was always so good at listening to Father, too."

"He'd be so disappointed."

Rand laughed, then his features darkened. He would've been. The day he died in a riot at the docks, crushed by fallen debris, was the day Rand promised to help fix Dockside. He'd failed in spectacular fashion. He couldn't even protect his own sister.

"I'm going to get you out of here," Rand said.

"I'll be fine," she said. "Ye've got to finish what ye started."

"You're not fine. Valin is a monster, and if I don't do what he says he'll… I won't let him hurt you anymore."

"I'm tougher than I look."

"I don't know... you look pretty tough." This time he got her to actually smile. It was a sight he'd missed more than anything. All his wallowing, he'd forgotten how much he enjoyed being around her. Sigrid was his best and only friend.

"What's he makin ye do?" she asked.

Rand bit his lip and looked to the floor.

"That bad?" She took his hand and pulled it to her face. Her skin was cold, like the empty room. Everything was freezing these days. "Don't tell me, just promise me something."

"Anything."

"Don't let this city fall to the Drav Cra for me. I can handle whatever Valin throws at me; I been practicing with Trapp for years. But I can't handle ye being crushed again."

Rand held his head high. "By the morning, after the Dawning, Redstar will no longer be poisoning the ears of the King. He and his people will return to their frozen tundra where they belong."

Or Torsten will die trying. He didn't add that last part, but it was the truth. A part of him felt like he might betray Valin, help Torsten, and rush back to kill Valin and save Sigrid before the king of the underworld knew what hit him. But now that he saw her, frightened and alone in a room meant for Valin's whores, he knew exactly what he had to do.

There was a hard knock on the door. "All right, enough," one of Valin's thugs grated.

"I'll be back for you before you know it," Rand said. He took Sigrid in his embrace again, wishing he didn't have to leave.

"Just come back the same man ye are now," she whispered into his ear. "I missed him, and I don't want to lose him again."

"You won't." Rand kissed the top of her head. "Ever again."

Two sets of hands grabbed him and pulled him from her. He didn't fight it. Not with her life in the balance. Instead, he held her gaze until the door slammed shut. Just before it closed, he could see the stark terror in her eyes. Worse even than when those Drav Cra monsters had her by the neck.

"We have our opening," Codar said. "Time to go."

Rand allowed a final wave of sadness to wash over him, then turned. Valin was gone, leaving only Codar and three thugs behind. Their grand raiding party to break Torsten out of his cell.

"No farewell from your boss?" Rand questioned.

"None required."

He set off down the hall, and Rand followed. They headed downstairs to the exit where another one of Valin's cronies handed Rand's sword to Codar.

"Try anything, and it will find its sheath in you," Codar warned, then presented the weapon.

"I wouldn't dream of it," Rand said as he took it.

"Walk straight, head down. Remember, you are the most wanted man in Yarrington, but the people are distracted, the guard is light, and few would know you at first glance." Codar snapped his fingers, and a man dressed in rags stood from the bar and shuffled over. His eyes were burned out—as were any priest's, but he banged into every table on the way over. Most went through enough training at the convents to move fluidly despite lack of sight, learning how to rely on faith and senses. He held a bowl filled with luminescent paint made from the poppies that grew on the banks of Mount Lister, and it sloshed over the rim as he swayed.

"He will help," Codar said.

"Always happy to serve." The blind man bowed, hiccuped, and almost spilled the bowl. Codar had to keep him upright.

"Get a hold of yourself, Father," he hissed.

The blind man wriggled himself free, then took Rand's face and went to paint it. Rand pulled away.

"Only priests are meant to do this," Rand protested.

"I am one!" he slurred. "Father Morningweg of Fessix... or I was before those filthy savages razed it a few years back."

"Many combatants won't enter the arena before unburdening their souls," Codar explained.

"And I'm a gr... great listener."

The Father grasped Rand's head, then nearly toppled over. Rand wound up holding the man upright while he spread the paint around his eyes. It was sloppy, dripping down Rand's cheeks and over his nose in a way that masked much of his features. By the time he finished, Rand figured he looked more like one of the Drav Cra heathens than a Glassman on the Dawning.

"Priase Iam, my son," he said when he'd finished. His breath reeked as Rand imagined his own had for so long. "May His light always be with you. Praise be the Vigilant Eye." Father Morningweg circled his vacant eye sockets in the gesture of prayer. "Good'nuf for you?"

"We're all going to Elsewhere," Rand said.

"Not where I'm from," Codar said. The drunken priest then painted his face, along with the three of Valin's thugs accompanying them. Rand didn't bother learning their names.

"All right..." the priest said. "Good.. uh... luck boys. May Iam watch your feet or whatever." He took a step, stumbled into Rand's chest, then put on a nervous smile as he patted his arm and went to pass.

"No, you don't." Codar grabbed the priest and shoved him out the door. "Valin is paying you well enough. You'll escort us to the mountain."

One of the thugs nudged Rand in the side. "Ain't nobody gonna question a priest's party on the Dawning. Valin's a genius."

"That's a word for it," Rand mumbled.

Rand watched as the cold air greeted the priest's face. His cheeks went green, and he leaned over on the patio to vomit. The sight sent a shiver up Rand's spine. Sorrow had sent him on a similar path of sin. If a priest, willing to burn his own eyes out in the name of Iam, could fall to vices so severely, he couldn't have imagined what would have happened to him had Wren not shown up...

I would have been a corpse swinging from the ceiling, he reminded himself. Just like Tessa and the rest.

"Keep your eyes up," Codar said, forcefully tilting Rand's head back toward the door. "No distractions. You are a Shieldsman from the moment we step out that door."

"You told me to keep my head down," Rand said. "Make up your mind."

Codar wasn't amused.

"Do you think this is my first mission?" Rand questioned.

"It is your first with me." Codar folded his hands behind his back and headed outside, giving the priest another shove to get him moving. The thugs sneered at Rand as they all followed.

The air was warmer than it had been in many weeks. It still snowed lightly, but Iam's mercy was upon the city for the Dawning. The street was empty. No line of beggars waiting for handouts from the richest man they knew of. Everyone was off to church, nary a guard in sight.

Valin was right about something. It was the perfect day for Rand to walk the streets without drawing suspicion.

"Today's your lucky day, my son," Father Morningweg said, wiping his mouth with his sleeve.

"Why is that?" Rand asked.

"Not everyone gets to die on the Dawning."

XXII

THE KNIGHT

The steel doors of Torsten's cell flung open, slamming hard against themselves. He jumped up, not even realizing he'd fallen asleep. So deep underground, it was impossible to know night from day. His sleeping came in spurts whenever exhaustion finally took him. After seeing Redstar's plans further unfold, he was trying his best to stay awake. He had to keep his eyes open, searching for a chance to escape and put an end to the Arch Warlock.

Torsten heard a commotion as Sir Austun Mulliner stormed in, grabbed Torsten by his dirty tunic, and chained his wrists while another unlocked his ankles.

"Come on," Mulliner said as they hauled him out of the cell.

"What is this?" Torsten questioned. Out of his peripherals, he saw two warlocks leering from the darkness. "Another of Redstar's tricks?"

Nobody answered. Mulliner simply dragged him along while the warlocks followed in their shadows. With Nikserof gone, Torsten had seemingly lost his greatest potential ally in the castle. His only potential ally—just like Redstar wanted. Nearly all the distinguished members of the Royal Council were strangers after Oleander chased so many away or hung them, and while he knew the Queen Mother better than anyone else alive, she was unpredictable. She'd fetched Wren for him as was his last request, and there was that moment outside the throne room when she seemed eager to ask him something, but when last they spoke she remained furious with him for not killing Redstar and refused to support his position with Pi. Her fury rarely waned.

Mulliner took him out of the dungeons, through the courtyard, and then down dark castle halls until they were at the entrance to the royal stable. The ground was splotches of white and brown. They dragged him through the snow, not caring to avoid puddles or piles of shog, throwing him down in front of a stable gate.

"Thank you, Sir Mulliner," Oleander said. She turned from brushing the mane of her beloved horse, a trim, Panpingese Whitehair gifted to her by Liam after the last war in the East. The beast came from perfect stock.

"You can leave us."

"Your Grace, he is a—"

"A criminal?" she interrupted the Shieldsman. "A killer? I've been called the same thing. Now leave us, or you'll find out why."

"Right away, Your Grace." He didn't seem pleased, but Oleander either didn't notice his insolent tone or ignored it. "We'll be right over there with them. Prime Minister's orders." Mulliner pointed to the warlocks, standing on the opposite side of the grounds in their ratty cloaks, watching their every move.

Oleander exhaled and clenched her jaw. "What joy."

Mulliner released Torsten.

"Do you know why I prefer horses to men?" Oleander asked.

"What is it, Oleander?" Torsten said. He'd always been proper around her, even diffident, but now that his arms were chained and he wore rags he couldn't find a reason to be. All he could think about was her silence back in the Throne Room when he needed her help more than ever.

She ignored him and continued stroking her horse's mane. "They cannot speak, or lie, or cheat. I hated this horse when Liam brought her home to me. I knew what it meant when Liam gave me an extravagant gift. Now, I have nobody else in this gods-forsaken castle."

"Oleander, what do you want?" Torsten took a hard step toward her and heard the rasp of Mulliner's blade sliding from its sheath. Torsten acknowledged the threat and gave her space. Oleander didn't let it stand.

She turned all the way from her horse to take Torsten's hand and drew herself closer.

"Must the Queen Mother have a reason to call upon a knight?" she asked.

"I'm a prisoner now, no thanks to you."

"Oh, Torsten, don't be so dramatic."

"Dramatic? I stood by you, after everything you did. Not just hanging those men. For a year you ruled this kingdom in Liam's sickness, and you ran our coffers dry with parties you barely wanted to attend, let our streets and trading agreements wither, our armies rust."

"Sounds like you weren't a very good advisor."

"Advisor? That's never been my job. I was simply the only one on the Royal Council who wasn't terrified of being near you. Even Yuri Darkings chose to keep his distance and now… he'd rather betray the kingdom he's served loyally for decades."

As it had in the dungeons, the back of her hand lashed out. Torsten winced, but she stopped just short of his face. He couldn't say he didn't deserve it, but he'd had far too much time to think in his cell—about every little thing that had happened since the day Liam's sickness had become known.

Oleander lowered her hand. "And I asked you to do one thing as Wearer," she growled, keeping her voice low so as not to be overheard by their watchers. "More than ending the rebellion or proving the might of your arms, I demanded he not return home."

"I guess we're both inspired failures."

He could tell she was about to continue scolding him when she heard what he said. Torsten noticed a grin pull at the corner of her lips.

"I suppose we are," she said. She sauntered to the other side of her horse and continued brushing. "Why were you never so honest with me before?"

Torsten rolled his shoulders. "Chains have a way of bringing it out."

"I like it."

"I'm glad someone does."

A long moment of silence passed between them. All he could hear was the sound of her brush against coarse fur.

"Thank you for sending Wren," he said.

"I'm sorry, Torsten," she said softly at the same time.

His brow furrowed. Those were words he wasn't sure he'd ever heard her speak, let alone sound genuine saying them.

"My Queen?"

"After Liam grew ill, I had no idea what to do," she continued. "I knew what everyone called me. How they looked at me—the Council like I was an imposter, you and the other soldiers like they were all keeping secrets about my husband. I was just so…"

"Angry?" Torsten finished for her. "It isn't too late to make amends."

"Just because your prison has a name doesn't mean you're the only person in one. They watch me everywhere I go. I had to ask my brother's permission just to speak with you outside of that foul-smelling dungeon, like I'm a child."

"And why did you invite me here?"

Her brush got caught on a knot in the horse's mane. The horse snorted, and frustration twisted Oleander's features, but she kept her composure as she calmly smoothed it out. "Would it sound unqueenly to say I just wanted to talk?"

"Not at all."

She inhaled deeply. "I was getting through to Pi while you were off to war. I know it. And the moment Redstar returned, it all vanished. He's not even cruel anymore, Torsten. He just ignores me so he can spend every waking moment with the beloved uncle who destroyed his childhood. They're out joining the hunt for the Caleef right now as a 'lesson.'"

"I should have left him to rot on the cold dirt of the Webbed Woods. Maybe we would have lost Winde Port without the Drav Cra at our side, but we wouldn't have lost the throne."

"Every night, as my head hits the pillow, I find myself wishing Liam were here. Even after his mind started to go, or as he screamed at me for not bearing him a son. I wonder what he'd think of his heir now?"

"A child who's been through what King Pi has needs a father. Redstar saw that and took advantage of it. We were always a step behind."

"It should have been you."

Torsten choked on his next breath. "Your Grace?"

"To help bring him up strong like his father. Guide him. You're the closest man to Liam I've ever known, the good parts at least."

"I'm barely a shred of him." He stared up at her and saw her nose twitch like it always did when she was annoyed. He hadn't ever realized he knew that about her, but he'd spent a lot of time watching over her; listening to her rants about every 'worthless wretch' living in the castle.

"Thank you, my Queen," he said softly. At the same time, he reached around the horse with his chained hands and took hers. "We've had our differences, but I know you did the best you could. To live in the shadow of so great a leader for so long; none of us were prepared to take the reins, even knowing his days were numbered. It is all our failings."

"No, it is him." She released Torsten's hands and glared at the warlocks. "My vile brother."

"I wish that were true. I've had a lot of time to think down there, and I'm certain about a few things now. Redstar cannot stay, but we gave him the power he now possesses. We let the people feel scared and neglected in the absence of their King. Pi's rebirth comforted them for a short while, and then he kidnapped the Caleef. They grew fearful of the cold, of rebellion, of—"

"Of me." Oleander turned her gaze to the floor. "No need to be coy, Torsten."

Torsten reached out further and lifted her chin. Mulliner cleared his throat, and Torsten ignored him. "I threw blame around for a long time. Now we're both killers. Redstar isn't a plague destroying us; he's a symptom of what was already here."

"Then enough of us wallowing. End him like you were supposed to. I'd kill him myself at this point if I ever had a moment alone. Anything is better than this."

Torsten rattled his chains. "As would I. But it's been left in the hands of Iam now."

"You're blind as a priest, aren't you?" She patted her horse on the back. "She's the fastest steed in all the West." She leaned close and whispered. "Take her. Find a blacksmith to break your chains, and do what the assassin you sent failed to. I'm sure that oaf in the castle, Hovor, Hovom? No matter, I'm sure he would do it. I hear him muttering incessantly about having to repair weapons for the savages who raided his home when he was a child."

Torsten repositioned himself in front of Oleander so their watchers couldn't read her lips. "You can't be serious? Who knows what he'll do to you."

"He's robbed me of the love of my only son. There is no worse he can do."

Torsten swallowed and looked down at his bindings. He remembered when Redstar enraged him enough to kill one of his own men, him posing as Sir Uriah Davies in the Webbed Woods, ready to murder Torsten and his companions. "Trust me, my Queen. There are no limits for him."

"Am I not still your Queen?"

"Always, Your Grace."

"Then you will steal this horse and escape. Find your assassin. Band together. Do it whatever it takes to get back here and take our city back before his lies spread too deep."

Torsten glanced down and saw that Oleander had unlatched the gate —the only thing between a mounted horse and freedom. The impressive beast took one step forward, and soon he'd have no choice but to mount her before she trotted out onto the grounds alone. He looked back to Oleander. Happy was never a word he'd used to describe her, but she seemed content in her decision to openly defy her brother. He then glanced back at Mulliner and the warlocks. They watched, but the stables were too darkened for them to be able to see what was happening.

"No more fear of false gods?" Torsten asked.

"Let them smite me," Oleander sneered.

"Then this time I will not fail you."

"I hope not. I don't know how many more times I can bring myself to forgive you, my dear, sweet Torsten."

The horse took another step, and Torsten grabbed a handful of her mane.

"At least once more." Torsten smiled.

The wall into the castle gardens was low enough for a Panpingese Whitehair to jump. After that, using a few secret doorways groundskeepers used so they could keep out of sight, he could traverse the outer fortifications toward one of the main gates and escape through the guard exits. If he was fast enough, all he'd have to do was barrel past a few sleepy guards. Nobody would even need to die. There were blacksmiths in South Corner or Dockside who would break his chains without question. Then he could return and do what Rand couldn't.

He didn't blame the kid. He had no idea what he was up against, but Torsten knew all Redstar's tricks. And he knew the castle better than anyone. He'd grown up in it. He could find Redstar when he was at his most vulnerable, fulfill the will of his Queen, and let Iam decide where his actions would send him.

"I will help your son, my King, see the light again, and you will know his love once more," Torsten told her. He pulled on the mane to yank himself up onto the horse and then raced by Oleander, the wind brushing back her exquisite dress.

Mulliner and the others had grown lax and scrambled after him. Torsten kicked the horse and set his sights on the garden wall. He went to spur it a second time when suddenly, the horse stopped in her tracks and flung him off.

He skidded through the snow so hard his head rebounded against the stable wall. The horse whinnied and reared back, and as he gathered his bearings, he noticed the vines growing from the frozen dirt now wrapped around her back hooves so tight she was rendered immobile.

Oleander sprinted down from the stables. "What is this?" she shouted.

"Redstar hoped you could be trusted," Freydis said, emerging from behind the stables. Her sliced hand dripped blood into the fresh snow, turning it pink. "He hoped there was a bit of the tundra left in you. I let him have faith for his sake, but I knew you'd betray him. That you would choose lust over blood."

Oleander pointed to her horse with a long finger. "Let her go, you filthy daughter of a—"

"Silence." Freydis ran a bloody finger across her lips and Oleander's sealed shut.

"You will release your Queen!" Torsten hopped to his feet and charged at her, but Freydis slid a knife out and swung it toward Oleander's stomach. It didn't cut her, but she kept it close enough to make an incision in her stomach should Torsten come nearer.

He froze.

"Careful, Redstar may have a soft spot for her, but accidents happen when criminals try to break out of their holes." Freydis clicked her tongue to the guards, and they hurried over like trained pups. Mulliner and the other Shieldsman seized Torsten while the two warlocks drew their daggers and watched.

"Let her go," Torsten said, seething. "I stole the horse. She had nothing to do with it."

"I heard everything." Freydis placed her mouth right against Oleander's ear. "All your *scheming*."

"Freydis, I'm warning you. Release her."

"The ex-Wearer is right," Mulliner said, reluctant. "The Queen Mother must answer to the Prime Minister and the King for her actions. We will bring him back to his cell, and she should be returned to her quarters until they return from the hunt."

"But what punishment befits such betrayal of blood?" Freydis asked, circling Oleander. The Queen grunted, but her lips remained magically sealed. "I have no tundra to abandon her in with nothing but a broken clan like she did to us so long ago."

"Sir Mulliner, she is the Queen Mother," Torsten said, desperate to appeal to the Shieldsman's better nature despite how he might feel about him. "You have to see reason. This is wrong." Torsten felt the grip on his chains loosen. A little more and he might be able to pull free and do something before any of the warlocks could assail him with blood magic.

"That's it," Freydis said. "I'll leave her alone. More alone than she's ever been." She strolled toward the Queen's beloved horse and raised her dagger to its neck. Oleander's muffled screams resounded as she fell to her knees, unable to even beg.

"That horse is the property of the royal Nothhelms!" Torsten shouted. "You will not touch it!" Mulliner's grip on him loosened a little more. That's it, a little more doubt. Torsten was about to break free and charge when the castle doors swung open and Redstar strolled out.

"Now, now, Freydis," he said. "We mustn't blame the beast for the faults of her master." He approached the horse with Pi in front of him, hands on the boy's shoulders like a proud father teaching a lesson.

"Such a fine specimen," Redstar went on. "Panpingese? A gift from your late husband, no doubt. He kept you locked up here tighter than these noble beasts. I wonder what the whore he was apologizing for looked like."

"Shut your cursed mouth," Torsten said.

Redstar ignored him. "Perhaps I will ride her in celebration after we defeat Muskigo. What do you think, my King?"

"My father's gift would get far more use than standing around here," Pi said. He glanced at his frantic mother, not a hint of worry in his eyes. His lips, straight as an arrow.

"My thoughts exactly."

"Drad Redstar, it was as I warned," Freydis said, reeling her dagger back to her side. "Your sister tried to free the traitor. She is not one of us."

"She hasn't been for a long time, but still, she is the Queen Mother," Redstar scolded. "While I am ever thankful for your loyalty, you will take her to her quarters. I will deal with her betrayal shortly."

Freydis regarded Oleander, bit her lip, then said, "Of course, Arch Warlock." She grabbed Oleander's arm and shoved her along, still keeping the Queen Mother from speaking. Torsten locked eyes with Oleander as they left, holding her gaze until she was out of sight. The vines around the horse's hooves, withered, and the Whitehair ran back to her pen.

Redstar leaned down, close to Pi's ear. "My King, perhaps it is time for you to rest as well? It was a trying day, hunting for the lost Caleef. Alas, the search continues."

"Yes, Uncle," Pi replied. "I should rest if I want to stay awake through the Dawning."

"Ah yes, how could I forget? Soon, when the moons cast out the light, all will be illuminated." He rustled Pi's hair, and the boy strode off with perfect posture. He didn't even acknowledge Torsten's existence as he turned to leave.

"I'm disappointed in you, Torsten," Redstar said. "Using my sister to get to me?"

"I'll do far worse when I get out of these chains." Torsten lurched forward, and the knights reeled him back. "You'll handle her? What exactly does that mean? Please, tell these fair knights who believe you to be a hero."

"They serve their King, just as I do." Redstar bowed in their direction. "And he has already made his decision on you. Take him away. And you two." He gestured to the two warlocks. "Do not leave his sight and allow no visitors but me. Especially not the Queen Mother."

The two knights started pulling Torsten along, but he noticed something before the metal chafed his wrists again. Hesitation. Maybe it was little more than hope beyond reason that with Nikserof gone, there was still someone in the Shield he could get through to, but he swore he felt it.

"Rand already took a piece of you," Torsten snarled. "I look forward to taking the rest."

Redstar stopped them. He raised his arm so his sleeve fell back and fully revealed the stump he had for a right hand. "He took nothing, Torsten. I did tell you that you would help me discover the secret, and so you did. The power I felt when the deserter you sent for me took this… the connection to her. You showed me why we failed to bring her all back in fullness."

"You failed because she's gone. Defeated as you will soon be."

"I failed because I wasn't willing to sacrifice everything. Now I understand." Redstar waved for the men to continue dragging Torsten away. "Enjoy the Dawning from below the Earth, Torsten," he said as they passed. "It's the last time My Lady will ever have to. Soon she will wake, and the world will know the truth."

XXIII

THE MYSTIC

The next morning came and with it, a fresh blaze within Sora. She rose, leaving Aquira asleep on the bed in her room inside the Red Tower. She stared through the arrowslit window at Yaolin City and the lake surrounding them. Dark, gray clouds loomed high above, casting shadows. Although, compared to Winde Port, life seemed to be pretty good here for her people, she tried to imagine what it would have been like when the mystics ruled, before King Liam brought his army and drove them into hiding.

Then, she recalled—as if she could forget—that poor boy Madam Aihara was ready to slaughter for the sake of a lesson. She thought of the repurposed temples now serving Iam, which the locals happily attended. She remembered how that clairvoyant kowtowed at the sight of Sora, thinking her a member of the mystic's Secret Council.

It wasn't only men like Liam and Torsten who feared their power. Whitney had tons of lessons, but none of them involved willfully murdering anyone to make a point. Maybe the mystics needed governing, needed to be chased away.

No, that can't be.

Mad as they might seem, their rule had to be better than living under the control of a far-off king, forced to worship a God that was not their own and serve a Crown they barely knew. She simply didn't understand the mystics yet, and Wetzel had taught her never to discount anything without first studying it.

A knock on the door startled her. Aquira nearly flew into the ceiling before growling toward the disturbance. Sora quickly threw on a Panpingese dress she'd heard called a kimono.

"Come in."

The heavy door swung and in walked a young Panpingese man. His brown robes looked worn and old, although he couldn't have been long past adolescence.

Aquira swooped down to a dresser near the door and continued growling. The man didn't seem frightened in the slightest.

"Aquira, it's fine," Sora scolded as she hurried over to grab the wyvern and place her on her shoulder. "Sorry about her. She's protective, even though she's a liar." Sora shot Aquira a smirk, and the wyvern features darkened. Smoke billowed from her nostrils as she huffed.

"I'm sorry, Miss," the man said. He carried a tray. "The madams wished me to bring you this breakfast. They didn't want you hungry for your first full day of training."

"Thank you…"

"Kai, Miss."

"Thank you, Kai. Would you please put it down there?" She pointed to a table by the bed.

After placing the tray down, he turned, bowed, and went to take his leave.

"Kai?" Sora said, stopping him at the door.

"Yes, Miss?"

"First, my name is Sora. You may call me that."

"Yes, Miss Sora—"

"Just Sora."

He blushed and nodded.

"Could I ask you a question, Kai?" she asked.

"Oh, uh—Sora, you are permitted to ask anything you'd like of me," he said.

"How do they treat you?"

"They?"

"The mystics. Aihara Na and the rest."

"I live to serve," he answered. "That is why we are here. To assist the Secret Council with all of our beings."

She noticed his eyes wander toward the red, stone floor.

"That is not an answer to what I asked," Sora said.

"Miss Sora, please, I have much to do this morning and time is dwindling."

His face betrayed something his words did not; that the mystics were listening and he couldn't speak freely. Or at least that's what she thought his face said. Considering they could seemingly appear at a whim in their spirit-like state, Sora wasn't sure how she'd slept so soundly the night before.

"Thank you for the breakfast, Kai." Sora bowed, and Kai returned the gesture before hurriedly exiting the room.

Left in silence, Sora sat down and pulled the lid off a delicious looking fried turnip cake and orange dumplings. She ate it all, washing it down with a large cup of rice milk.

She looked around the spartan room. A storage chest sat in the corner, a desk by the window, and the bed in the middle. In the far corner, she saw something she couldn't believe she'd forgotten. She slid open the semi-transparent paper door and was greeted by a bright room, though she couldn't find the source of the light. Steam rose from a tub in the center but there was no room to fan a flame beneath it—a self-heating bath.

Sora nearly tripped over herself in her haste to remove the clothing she'd only just put on. She hadn't had a hot bath since she'd been a guest of that brute Muskigo in Winde Port, and that had only been her first time experiencing one. She shuddered at the thought of the afhem.

Evil like Kazimir's, she could understand—his thirst made him wicked and forced him to see other human life as little more than cattle. Muskigo's evil she could not. He had been kind and hospitable to her, as well as his handmaid Shiva, yet only moments before had led a massacre of innocent people in Winde Porte. And not long before that, had razed Troborough and so many other villages.

Sora had experienced more in the past couple of months than nearly her whole life combined, and so much of it was evil. Sure, she'd survived a war she didn't remember, traveled across Pantego in a refugee wagon, lived within a crazy old man's house who happened to have an interest in the occult, and gotten into her fair share of mischief with Whitney, but that was nothing.

If she closed her eyes, she could find herself back in the Webbed Woods, listening to Whitney poke egg sacs of monstrous spiders that he didn't know were egg sacs. She'd seen creatures she didn't know existed. She'd be lying if she said she hadn't woken up in a puddle of sweat after a nightmare over the demonic satyrs or Redstar's dire wolves.

But right now, all she wanted to think about was hot water.

Sora drove the memories from her head and tried to enjoy a moment for once. She climbed the stone steps of the bath and tested the waters with her toe. It was hot, but not scalding—the perfect temperature. Soon, she was waist deep. She hadn't even realized how her bones ached until they found relief. She dipped below the surface, allowing the hot water to soak her hair and face. Eyes closed, she blew bubbles, slowly releasing the lung of air, then came up for air, pushing her hair back.

"Better than a pirate's cabin, isn't it?" she said to Aquira who flapped into the room and perched on the rim.

The wyvern screeched in response.

"Yeah. Maybe we won't burn this one down."

Sora stretched her arms out, extending one toward the creature. Seeing smooth and not scarred skin on her limbs surprised her once again. She'd grown so used to water making the fresh cuts on her hands sting. Aquira nuzzled her warm nose into Sora's palm, the steam pouring from her nostrils making the hot water seem cold.

"Friends again?" Sora asked.

Aquira chirped. Sora smiled ear to ear. They had been apart for less than a day, but she missed her tiny friend. All the deception wasn't her fault. Even had she'd been told Tayvada was going to die in the process of sending Sora to them like they somehow foresaw, Sora wasn't sure she truly understood what death meant. The permanence of it that even the mystics apparently couldn't undo. Or rather, refused to.

"Sora, report to training room posthaste," someone said suddenly. The voice echoed like it had been shouted in the Pikeback Mountains—not that Sora would've known what that sounded like, not really. She searched the room, but it was empty.

Then Sora recognized that the voice belonged to Madam Jaya, her new teacher, as Aihara Na had called her. She reluctantly exited the bath. She didn't see a towel, so she pricked her thumb on Aquira's tail to summon warmth from within. Once dry, she slid on her kimono again and slipped into her heavy boots.

She considered bringing her knife, then decided against it. If she needed weapons, she was sure Madam Jaya would provide them, plus she wanted to seem open to their instruction rather than nervous. It was her first day as a mystic acolyte, after all, and she had no idea what training even entailed.

"Aquira, are you coming?"

Aquira, who had already made herself comfortable on Sora's bed, cracked one eye open and released a mouthful of air as she yawned. Then she turned her head and trilled her tongue.

Sora took it as a 'no' and left the room.

She reached the level of the tower below the lake without incident. Staring at the door to the training facility, she took a deep breath, then knocked. When no answer came, she decided to push her way inside. When she'd come with Madam Aihara, she hadn't had the time to take in the room. It was massive; she knew that. She didn't, however, notice how high the ceiling was.

There were no windows or secondary doors, just the exit behind her and the white walls before her. Sora took a few steps toward the center of the room. An overwhelming sense of its magnitude washed over her. She felt vulnerable.

"Hello?" she said, listening to only her echo as a reply. "Madam Jaya?"

The sound of metal scraping metal bounced off the walls. Sora spun but still saw nothing. Footsteps pounded behind her, but again there was nothing.

"Who's there?" she asked, her voice shaking.

Sora felt a dull thud against her lower back, followed by pins and needles up her spine, and then a hard crack as her face hit the floor. Stunned, she barely managed to roll over before a familiar face bore down on her.

Muskigo's gray skin and tattoos were unmistakable.

Sora scrabbled backward, kicking with her feet at his impossibly hard abdomen. She rolled over and drew up to her knees. Her heart sank as she reached for her knife. *Why would I leave it behind after everything?* The better question would have been how Muskigo entered the Red Tower, but she was too distracted to give it much thought.

Not daring to take her eyes off him for more than a split second, she used her peripherals to search the room, hoping to see a weapons rack she'd missed, something that might help her fend off the afhem. There was nothing. Just a stark, empty room with supernaturally tall ceilings, and no exit beyond the one she'd come in. And now, Muskigo stood squarely between her and it.

"What do you want?" she huffed.

His scimitar glistened, reflecting the light of a burning brazier. Elsewhere begged her to draw on its power, sacrificing her blood, but there was nothing to be done without a blade. Muskigo charged her, rearing his weapon back and preparing to slice down. She sidestepped so the sharp edge of the blade would gash her arm. If he drew blood, then she would rain fire down upon him, delivering him swiftly into the arms of the fallen gods.

He rotated the scimitar just in time to slap her hard with the flat of the blade. It would be sure to leave a bruise, but it drew no blood.

He lashed out again, but Sora rolled out of the way.

"Stop this!" she panted as he pursued again. "The mystics will be here any moment, and you'll be killed. Stop now, and they might spare you."

He only smiled and pressed again, that debonair grin that hid the monster he truly was. Sora punched him, but Muskigo palmed her fist and forced her to the ground. He dropped the scimitar, and it clattered against the stone. Straddling her, his gray hands wrapped tightly around her wrists, he leaned in, breathing into her ear. She squirmed, but couldn't move, couldn't break free.

"Without blood, you are useless." She heard the words, but they weren't in Muskigo's smooth, accented voice.

"Madam Jaya?"

"See me now for who I really am," she said.

Before Sora's eyes, Muskigo's visage changed, color coming into his skin, tattoos disappearing. The muscles disappeared, giving way to a pair of unclothed breasts. Suddenly, the weight of the mystic's body vanished as well, and she rolled over, her limbs passing through Sora to quickly find her footing. Sora remained, back on the ground.

"Wha… Why?"

"Tell me, child," Madam Jaya started. "What did you see?" She rolled her hand, and her yellow robe materialized out of thin air. As she dressed, Sora climbed to her feet.

"I saw Afhem Muskigo of the Black Sands. How did you…"

"Curious. Very curious."

"I'm sorry, what's curious?" Sora asked.

"The spell I used was designed to show you the image of that which you most fear. Most people see themselves or their parents. Who is this Muskigo, and why do you believe you hold such fear in your heart for him?"

The question gave Sora pause. If asked who she most feared, she'd have thought Kazimir would have been the obvious answer. The upyr had terrified her, nearly killed her, held her captive, and tortured her—mentally if not physically. But as she heard this, she realized the truth.

"He destroyed my home. Killed the man who raised me, everything I loved." Even Whitney was gone because of Muskigo, though she didn't say that part out loud. If not for Muskigo's rebellion, they'd have passed right through Winde Port. They wouldn't have needed a ship, leading Bartholomew Darkings to find them and sic the Dom Nohzi upyr on Whitney in vengeance. Which meant Tayvada wouldn't have been killed to serve as prey for them…

He wouldn't have been killed.

Her eyes went wide. She'd never even thought of that, how even Tayvada's death could be traced back to Muskigo. Kazimir was a wolf on a hunt, but Muskigo's very existence had sent her life hurtling toward this place like it was fated for them to meet.

"For all our power, we cannot control fate." Sora couldn't help but recall those words from Aihara Na.

"Interesting," Madam Jaya said. "Did he harm you?"

"No," Sora said. "Even after I attacked him, he never did."

"But others have?"

"Many." She grimaced. "Too many to count."

"Family and friends, they mean the most to you, do they not?" Madam Jaya circled Sora. Sora's gaze followed until it could not, then she turned her head, her body.

"I never had a family," Sora said.

"Oh, but you did. Blood is not everything—as you have learned today. You were completely at my mercy. It is a wonder you've survived as long as you have." She raised her hand to stop Sora's retort before it started. "Do not misunderstand, child, you've done well—but it is time you stop relying upon spilled blood like a common bloodfiend."

"I survived no thanks to this place." Sora couldn't help herself. "I always thought Panping was going to be some gods-forsaken, desolate place where people murdered each other for food. The way I was abandoned and shipped off to the Glass, you'd have thought there wasn't a street to spare. But everyone here seems to be living peaceably. Why did I have to grow up in a place only to watch it burn."

"You were left in good and necessary hands to keep you safe until you were ready. I know it is difficult to see, but there is no teacher like the open world. You've been training for this all your life, Sora of Troborough."

"What do you know of Troborough?" Sora questioned. "Do you know of its ashes? Of the lives lost? Most of the people there may never have cared much for me, they barely even noticed me, but not one of them deserved what they got."

"I know many things, and you would be wise to remember that. Do not forget your role, even in your anger." Madam Jaya stopped in front of Sora. "I know that Wetzel never made it past meager blooding. He died tragically before he could try, but without being a true mystic he never would have been able to."

"If he wasn't a mystic, then what was he?"

"A servant of our Order, looking after one strong with the Gift. Like Kai, or the Bokeos."

"Why do you call them that?"

"What?"

"Servants. If they're so willing to be here, the word seems…"

"Harsh?" Madam Jaya finished. "You will find that some words do not translate well from Panpingese to common. The definition may remain the same, but here, to be a servant is not considered an insult. Perhaps, acolyte is a more apt term, but there is no greater calling than to choose to serve that which is greater than you." She began to pace the room.

"You will come to find that there is no logic to those that are chosen by fate to wield the Gift," she continued. "Some never even realize the font of power growing within them. Some escape our gaze and the Well of Wisdom; even the most attuned clairvoyants. Only the gods decide, but that does not mean the lowliest member of our Order is of no importance. We are not all seeing, and the nature of this world is relentless even to those given the ability to change the rules. Without cleanliness, we could be taken by disease beyond healing. Without farms, we would starve."

"So, everyone in Panping exists to take care of the few people within this tower?"

"Existed. And I may not be as strict as Master Aihara Na, but consider your tone." She turned quickly and glowered at Sora, her robe snapping up behind her. "You explain the nature of our very world. Did the vassals of King Liam not serve him and his kingdom? Did the warlords of Latiapur not serve their Caleef? Yet they cannot summon rain in the driest summer, nor will crops to grow in stubborn dirt."

Sora lowered her head. "No, they can't."

"Precisely. Ours is a world of give and take. The masses provide for their lords so that they may be kept fed, safe. The lord provides for the masses, so he is not massacred out of desperation and hunger. It is the same with magic. Wetzel spoke to you about sacrifice, and so you scarred your body. We will teach you how to channel your blood from within in order to bring the magic of Elsewhere to bear."

"Is that what you do? Sacrifice blood from within?"

"In a way. It takes many years to learn the channeling in a way that will not leave you clinging to life even with the most tenuous of spells, that is why we have this." She produced a necklace from the folds of her robe. A periapt hung from it, a golden disc surrounded by six small, stones, each etched with a unique, symbolic marking. They seemed like characters in a written language, but Sora had no idea which.

"What is it?" Sora asked.

"Turn."

Sora hesitated.

"If you are going to be here, you must learn trust. Go on."

Sora conceded and turned her back to Madam Jaya. She felt the unnaturally cold metal against her skin and heard it clasp behind her. It hung heavy around her neck, yet it was oddly comforting.

"This is a bar guai," Madam Jaya said. "It will help you in casting without mutilation until such a time that you learn to channel from within. We must bind it to your blood. Please be still, this will only sting for a moment."

Sora was used to pain, but she did not expect what came next. Madam Jaya pressed her finger to the front of the flat disc and said a phrase in a language that wasn't precisely Panpingese. It sounded older, rougher.

A sudden, stabbing pain—no, not one, but several sharp stabs broke the flesh beneath the disc. It felt like she was being branded. She looked down and saw the round disc boring into her skin. Blood poured down her front, soaking her clothes.

She tried to cry out, but no sound would come. Then, as quickly as it started, it stopped. The pain stopped. The sharpness stopped. The chain fell from the periapt, but that didn't matter, the disc and the connected stones were now firmly embedded in her skin.

"It is not like true channeling, and it is far more limited, but you are powerful Sora—more than you know," Madam Jaya said. "Your blood is unique and strong in its bond to Elsewhere. Perhaps that is why, in the vision Aihara Na gave, you saw that realm in detail. The bar guai will allow you to use that power, harness it."

Sora touched the disc. She wiggled it, but it wouldn't budge.

"The bar guai will not come free except by my word when you are ready for channeling," Madam Jaya said. "You will come to appreciate it and what it can do for you."

"You did not…" Sora gasped. "I did not…"

"What? Ask your permission? I am your teacher now, Sora of Troborough. I need not your permission, and you need not worry about anything other than proving to me that you are ready to be more than a simple blood mage. Someday, when the Order is rebuilt, you will be a mystic, and you will understand the weight that comes with the title."

Her words, although harsh, did not come across that way. There was a softness to her tone, a gentleness that put Sora at ease.

"Why me?" Sora asked.

"Why not?" Madam Jaya replied.

Sora rolled her eyes, a bit of Whitney's influence coming through.

"Do not speak with your eyes, child," Madam Jaya scolded. "If you've something to say, use words."

"Fine. I didn't ask for any of this. I was practically kidnapped and brought here, and although I enjoyed two lavish meals and a hot bath, I've also been attacked by a man I hoped never to see again. I think it's time someone explains something, anything."

"After you learn to use your bar guai, you will have all the answers you will ever need."

"I'm not asking for all the answers, only—"

"Sora, the process you are about to go through has taken all the mystics, including me, decades. We have all gone through our period with the bar guai. In the time of the Mystic Order, some apprentices never grew beyond its crutch. Some were consumed by the power it unlocks. If patience was our first lesson, you are failing."

Hearing the word 'lesson' reminded Sora why she was doing this in the first place. She considered all Whitney must be going through, all the suffering. She had to do whatever it took.

"I am sorry, Madam Jaya," she said. "Please, teach me. Teach me everything."

XXIV

THE DESERTER

Rand and the others kept to backroads on their way up from Dockside, avoiding churches, where people were gathered in great numbers, waiting to receive their blessings for the new year. Even the Drav Cra set up camps to watch a phenomenon probably as strange to them as summer. A day without labor, Rand imagined them saying. In the harsh lands they came from, that would probably spell certain death.

Father Morningweg had sobered up a bit in the frigid air, at least enough that his swerving could be chalked up to a blind man walking without a cane. Codar kept him moving briskly, however, and he only stopped once more to clear out the contents of his stomach.

They were headed northwest of Yarrington, for the base of Mount Lister where the royal crypt's ceiling had broken open months back on the day of Pi's rebirth. The magnificent stone spires gleamed in the low winter sun, and the glass Eye of Iam atop it painted a rainbow across a vast crowd. The faces of those who'd already been blessed with the luminescent paint of God reflected the vibrant colors.

It was a magical sight; one Rand looked forward to every year… until now. For standing before the tall open doors of the cathedral wasn't just

High Priest Wren the Holy and his circle of bishops, but Redstar and his warlocks too. Their faces were painted white on the bottom, their mouths and chins, and black across their brows as usual as if mocking Iam's own followers. The petrifying, female warlock beside Redstar was the one Rand had knocked out in the castle. If only he'd known how important she was, to stand directly at the Arch Warlock's side, he wished he'd killed her instead.

The sight gave Rand pause. Not long ago, he'd watched Wren stand against Redstar with a shield of light, proud and mighty. Now he looked like nothing more than an old, tired man, leaning on his cane more than ever before. His wrinkles were deeper, his cheeks saggier, and his hair somehow whiter, wispier. Gone was the man who appeared as Yarrington's all-loving father, replaced instead by the visage of a vagrant.

"Long has this kingdom stood alone in the light of Iam!" Redstar announced. "And on this day, year by year, you stand in the absence of it, looking within. No longer." He took Wren's cane and raised it. "Today, as the light falls away, know that Nesilia is with you. Her love is eternal, always within us and the earth, buried but not dead. After all these long centuries, you may be open to it again."

"Buried, not dead," the warlocks alongside him chanted. Buried Goddess cultists and Drav Cra civilians in the crowd repeated the words as well. Rand only then noticed how many of the former there seemed to be with their chilling, expressionless white masks.

"The light of Iam never leaves you, for you cannot have light without shadow," Wren said, voice weathered and raspy. Rand had heard him give sermons before, and he usually spoke with enough verve to inspire a stone to the faith. Now, he could barely be heard. "Praise be the Vigilant Eye." He circled his burned eye-sockets, hands trembling as he did. The Glassmen in the crowd mimicked him.

The female warlock handed Redstar a horn. He scooped out a glob of black paint and ran it over Wren's sightless eyes in the very same manner as his warlocks wore it.

"There is no more time for spectating," Codar said, taking Rand by the arm and tugging him along until the Cathedral Square was out of view.

"How can they stand there and watch that... atrocity?" Rand said.

"Their king accepts Redstar. Their High Priest now does as well."

"Sheep will always follow the shepherd," Father Morningweg said, burping. "Even to the slaughter. That bastard was there when they ravaged my home. Now he's up there, and I'm down here."

Rand yanked his arm free. "Whatever he did to the High Priest, getting him to speak like that, he can't get away with it."

"That is not for us to decide," Codar replied, still hurrying them along.

"You can help us end it. Valin won't even have to know. You have to realize that there won't be a Glass Kingdom anymore if they win."

"I do not serve the Glass Kingdom."

"Then there won't be anything left for you to exploit!" Rand shouted, stopping.

Codar stopped and glared daggers at him. "Keep trying to persuade me to betray Mister Tehr, and you will do so without a tongue."

"Gentleman," the Father slurred. He slipped his way between them, then beckoned them along. "This way. I was promised revenge on Redstar too."

They continued skirting around Old Yarrington, along bridleways toward the northern gates of the city which stood a short distance directly behind the cathedral. The road led straight to the trails up Mount Lister. A group of guards passed by, offering Father Morningweg a circle of prayer. They didn't even give Rand a passing glance.

"See, just follow my lead." The priest started walking, then stopped to dry heave and nearly toppled over.

"Is there no depth Valin Tehr won't sink to?" Rand asked. "That man needs help."

"That man lost everything," Codar said. "His home, his flock. All to Redstar and his horde of savages. Mister Tehr gives purpose to those who would otherwise hang… like you."

"How did you wind up working for the bastard then? A resourceful man like you, I'm sure you could make a fine living back home."

"Have you ever been to Brekliodad?"

Rand shook his head. He'd never been to Winde Port, let alone beyond the Dragon's Tail to the Pikeback Mountains of Brekliodad and their colorful palaces.

"Then do not assume what I could do back home," Codar said.

"Did he take your sister hostage too then?"

"He gave me purpose when I could no longer return home. And now my purpose is to help you get what you want." He touched his temple with his forefinger. "You would be wise not to forget that, and maybe, one day, if you return from your duty in the South, you will see that there is as much work to be done in the shadows as there is in the light."

"Praise be! Light shines brightest in the shadows." Father Morningweg cheered, pumping his fist in the air.

He rounded a corner and fell in with a line of citizens headed out to the base of Mount Lister. Every year, people camped around it, for there was no more splendid a place to watch the Dawning than the site where Iam brought an end to the God Feud. The most faithful would climb to the flattened peak of Mount Lister itself for the event. After sermons throughout the city, Wren the Holy and the King would ride up to join them. Rand had never been, as he was still in training at the last one.

So much had happened in just a year.

The slope started off shallow and smooth, stairs weaving back and forth until the angle sharpened at the center and they had to wrap the mountain. Areas around the entries to the glaruium mines were known to be unstable, and the rock toward the top was so thick the path grew thin enough to be traversed only in a single file.

Anyone seeking to reach the flat peak by foot before the eclipse had to start the climb in the morning, and there were already Shieldsmen and warlocks doing so as the sun crept over the horizon. Rand didn't spot any civilians making the climb this year, however.

Once within the flow of the river of the faithful, Rand and his odd party were rendered nearly invisible. Only the fur-covered Drav Cra and masked cultists sprinkled throughout the throng drew any real attention. The base of the mountain had become a Drav Cra trading camp, the savages hoping to take advantage of the pilgrims, hawking their thick furs. On the trail, priests stood at intervals, praying out loud.

"They're using us," Rand said, then he remembered to whom he spoke.

"Everyone is using someone," Codar said. He nudged Rand in the arm, then pointed through a mob of sojourners to an area at the base of the

Mountain that was blocked off by a low, spiked wooden wall and a line of Glass soldiers. "Crypt is through there."

"It'll take us an hour to shove through," Rand complained.

Codar turned Father Morningweg toward the crypt entry. "Act convincing for once," he said.

"I'll have you know, there wasn't a soul in Fessix who missed my sermons," the Father replied.

"Then pretend they aren't all food for worms somewhere up north."

The priest's cheeks went from a pale green to white. His gaze grew distant, and it was a look Rand recognized. He wore the same one every time he pictured Tessa and the others hanging from the walls of the Glass Castle. He then realized that it'd been some time since he last thought of that. Now, when he closed his eyes, all he saw was what horror might befall Sigrid should he fail.

"Come on, Father," Rand said. He took him by the arm and helped him walk. "Just because you don't have a church any longer, doesn't mean you aren't a priest. Every man and woman of Fessix looks down upon you now from the Gate of Light. You mustn't disappoint them."

The crowd parted easily, and after a short while, the Father's gait was brimming with renewed confidence. "Bless you, my son," he would say as the people shifted. "Iam watch over us," he said to another. "May His light shine eternally upon you."

By the end of the walk, he no longer swayed. Reminding him of what he used to be seemed to sober him up, and it got them through the dense crowd faster than Rand could have wished for.

"Tell Valin I'll take double," Father Morningweg said when they stopped a short distance from the crypt's guards.

"You'll take what was agreed upon," Codar said.

"Yeah? Why don't I mosey over to those guards and tell them what you're planning then?"

Codar's hand shot forward, fast as a crossbow bolt, to clutch the father by his robes. Murmuring broke out around them just as quickly. Rand didn't need to hear the words. A Breklian grabbing a priest in obvious anger on the day of the Dawning... it was bound not to go well.

"Valin wouldn't hurt a priest now, would he?" the Father said.

Codar's bushy, white mustache wriggled as he grit his teeth, and he released him. "You god-worshippers are all the same. He reached into a pouch and drew a few gold autlas. "For your trouble, Father," he said as he pulled the man close and slipped them into his hand.

Father Morningweg bowed and circled his eyes. "Bless you, child of Brekliodad," he said. "May the light of Iam guide you on your journey in sending that bastard Redstar straight to exile." He flashed a grin, then strutted off.

All the pride Rand felt at helping the priest regain a fragment of his poise instantly melted away. Men who took the vow of sightlessness swore off all wealth and finery, and evidently, Morningweg had been changed too much by the horrors of war. Or perhaps, he had always been corrupt, and Valin Tehr was there to feed that darkness, to prey on his weakness to accomplish his goals like he had with Rand.

"Did you hope his kind was above greed?" Codar asked.

"I hoped many things weren't as they are," Rand replied.

"The old gods have abandoned us. Soon, you people will see as mine have, that all we are is flesh and desire."

"How much is Valin paying you to try and coax me toward loyal service to him?"

Codar didn't bother responding. "Come. Tell the guards you are here to see Foreman Orebreaker. That we are more masons to help finish the job." He gestured to Valin's three thugs accompanying them.

"And if they recognize me?"

"The Rand they knew wasn't a drunk with a beard patchy as a goat with mange." Codar again poked Rand's jaw to lift it. "Head up. Avoid their gaze like you're above them. Breklian emissaries are not renowned for being on the winning side of deals because they are special, but because everyone thinks they are."

Codar continued along with Valin's men. They strolled right up to the guards at the fence as if they were invited in until two spears closed before them.

"Sorry," one of the guards said. "All revelry is to be kept east of the break."

"We are here to help with repairs," Codar replied.

"On the Dawning?"

"I'm not a Glassman and they're masons from east of Crowfall. Wouldn't know Iam from Meungor."

The guards exchanged a confused look. "Sorry, we have orders."

Rand took that as his cue to step in or risk failing. They'd given him a loose sense of the plan, but Codar didn't speak much when Valin was around.

"Now you've got new ones," he said, stepping forward. He did his best to sound commanding, drawing on his memories of Torsten and Wardric.

"Sir," they both saluted.

"The Crown doesn't want construction to stop on account of the holiday, and there aren't enough dwarves alone," Rand said.

"I ...uh... we heard nothing about it," one of them stammered.

"And that's why you're out here. Now let us through to the foreman."

"Yes, sir... right away, sir."

Their spears parted, and Rand walked through first. Codar and the others followed. He knew the way many Shieldsmen spoke to their underlings even if it had never been how he treated other men of the Glass. He'd been a meager guard before, been spoken to the same.

"Well done, *knight*," Codar said, the title oozing with mockery.

"Keep walking."

Inside, a barricade retained massive hunks of fallen rock on the mountain-side of the trail. On the day of Pi's rebirth, it was said Mount Lister split open as if bearing him from her womb. The metaphor was apter than Rand expected. A gash ran down a portion of the mountainside all the way to the base, ending directly above the buried Royal Crypt.

They climbed over and through a pile of boulders, then arrived at the construction site. A handful of dwarves stood in a clearing surrounded by piles of rough, jagged stone, the size of which made the dwarves seem even smaller. A few of their construction machinations sat beside the gap in the earth leading down to the Royal Crypt—huge contraptions able to lift stone into place with a system of pulleys and levers. A few more Glass guards stood around the area, making sure no curious pilgrims tried to sneak in and disturb things. One of them wore glaruium armor, a Shieldsman Rand didn't recognize.

"For such small folks, everything they build is huge," Rand remarked.

"Whatever it takes to prove they're better than us," Codar replied.

"Aye, who let you pass!" the Shieldsman called, rushing over. The two Glass soldiers took their time following.

"They're here to help with construction," Rand said. He purposefully turned his body and head to face Codar, and never turned all the way back.

"Today?"

"No delays."

A lift rose to the surface out of the maw, a burly dwarf perched atop, chest thick as an iron keg and beard full as an oak in summer. He noticed Codar and the features on his grime-covered face lit up.

"There ye be, lazy bugger!" he exclaimed. "Been waitin for you."

"Why didn't you mention anything?" the Shieldsman asked.

"Last I heard, I report to the Leuvero Messier, Master of Masons, who reports to the Prime Minister," the foreman said.

"You report to the Crown, of which I am an extension."

"So is he." The dwarf stuck one of his stubby, calloused fingers toward Rand. "Found him this morning and sent him to fetch this crew by the gates. Barely a soul working today, festivities tomorrow; you lazy flower pickers hate work." He and his crew burst out in laughter.

The Shieldsman wasn't entertained. "We don't fall behind on our work."

"A mountain filled with metal makin iron seem like parchment split open and collapsed on a crypt. Ye try stickin to a deadline."

The Shieldsman groaned. "Fine, get them working. But anything goes wrong, and it'll be your head on the Prime Minister's spike."

Even the Shieldsmen are recognizing Redstar's new position, Rand noted.

Codar approached the dwarf, and they exchanged some quiet words as the dwarf invited Valin's men onto the lift. Nothing passed between hands like with the priest, but that arrangement was likely already taken care of.

Rand took a step toward them, but the other Shieldsman did the same and got in between them. "What are you doing, *knight*?" he questioned.

Rand stopped. He kept his gaze fixed on Codar, refusing to look the Shieldsman in the eye. "Taskmaster Lars asked if I could fill in at the dungeon today," Rand replied. Lying wasn't his forte, and with all the turnover he wasn't sure that the old scribe in charge of organizing the day-to-day affairs of the King's Shield barracks was still in place. The name didn't appear to surprise the Shieldsman.

"There may not be a new wearer yet," Rand added, "but we still have to work, right?"

"No new Wearer?" the Shieldsman's brow furrowed. "They named Sir Nikserof co-wearer just the other day."

Rand's throat went dry. Codar had mentioned that in their prep over the last few days and it completely escaped his mind. "Sir Nikserof? Really? I just transferred down from Crowfall, and nobody bothered to tell me?"

The man gave him another look over, then sighed. "Not surprising. It's been a mess since Sir Unger lost his mind."

"Were you there?"

"Aye. He was like a mad bull, never seen anything like it. Would have killed me if I were in the way but I was lucky to be behind the giant."

"By Iam..."

"These are strange times sure. Rebellion, warlocks on the streets, a Wearer sharing the white with a barbarian..." Rand nodded along with the man until his train of thought seemed to end. "Anyway, what were you saying?"

"I was hoping to pass through the crypt. Just got stationed back here so I've got dungeon duty on the Dawning of all days."

"Well, that's an active work zone," the Shieldsman replied, pointing. "Only masons allowed while they finish the dome. You'll have to head back to the castle the long way."

Rand gestured back to the northern gate. "Back though that crowd? It'll take me all day."

"You should've thought of that before taking on an escort that any guard in Yarrington could have handled."

"C'mon Sir..." Rand made the mistake of locking eyes with the man momentarily as he lingered on the word, waiting for a name.

"Childress," the Shieldsman said.

"Sir Childress. I didn't even know about the new Wearer, let alone how best to get around the city these days."

"And you didn't think that the Royal Crypt might still be dangerous?"

"To be honest, I figured it was done by now."

The man grimaced. "Then you haven't worked with dwarves. Only thing that gets those short runts to move is gold, and the war in the South has the coffers low."

Rand thought back to the man's earlier conversation with the dwarven foreman and remembered the constant butting heads between the Glass and the dwarven kingdoms. He wasn't used to his mind being so sharp as it was of late. He could get used to it.

"You're telling me," Rand said, acting exhausted. "It's amazing any of us in Crowfall has a bronzer to spend with how many of the little-men live near there."

Sir Childress' stance appeared to relax. "Fine, I'll let you through just this once, but don't tell anyone."

"Thank you, Sir." Rand saluted and took a step, but the Shieldsman wasn't done talking.

"How is the old snow city?" he asked. "I grew up there myself."

"Did you, now?" It wasn't hard to feign the excitement in his tone. Of all the cities in the kingdom he could've picked, of course, he chose the one where the Shieldsman grew up.

"Aye." He snickered. "You probably came up a few years earlier than me, green as you are, but I'm Crow through and through. Trained under the Sir Barvadi. He still up there?"

"Still a pain. Barely made it a day in training without him screaming at me."

"You sure it was him? Sir Barvadi lost his tongue to Drav Cra raiders."

Rand cursed himself inwardly. Another slip up. All he needed to do was get out of this conversation. "Of course, figure of speech. His glare was worse than words."

Sir Childress took a step forward and looked Rand straight in the eyes. "What did you say your name was?"

"I didn't." Rand forced a smile to mask how hard he swallowed next as if all moisture left his mouth. "I really ought to be going. Thanks for letting me through. Always a pleasure to meet a fellow Crow." Rand banged his chest-plate in salute again, then moved for the lift. Childress grabbed his arm.

"Wait, I know you, don't I?" he asked, leaning in close.

"Maybe we trained together one day up there?"

"No, that's not it, I... wait. You're..." He didn't get a chance to finish his sentence. A knife stabbed through the back of his neck, the point dripping red through his throat. As he fell, Rand saw Codar, arm outstretched, hand open like he'd thrown it.

The two soldiers in the clearing reached for their weapons, but Valin's men bolted into action. Rand wasn't sure where they drew knives from, but two of them gutted a soldier so fast he collapsed at Rand's feet before he could step back. The other was able to get his sword from its sheath in time and cut open the third thug's belly. Valin's man crumpled, pawing to hold his innards in before toppling over.

In the confusion, Rand nearly betrayed his feelings, thrilled to see the brute get cut down.

"Traitors!" the soldier barked. He charged at Rand, but Codar slipped between them. He was both incredibly quick and elegant, like a dancer in a southern troupe. He deflected two blows, used the guard's weight against him to affect his balance, then spun low and kicked out the soldier's feet. In the same motion, Codar brought the tip of his blade around and shoved it through the soldier's eye.

The Breklian wiped his blade off on the end of his tunic as he stood.

Rand was stunned by the carnage. Foreman Oarbreaker and the other dwarven masons were similarly dumbfounded. The Shieldsman still gurgled, somehow having risen to his hands and knees. One of Valin's men kicked him over and released a chuckle.

Rand shot forward, seized Codar, and threw him to the ground. "We said no killing Glassmen!" he roared. He heard metal scraping, then felt something sharp at his belly, but it didn't stop him.

"*I* didn't," Codar replied.

"Your boss did."

"But I didn't," he repeated. "That man recognized you. We do not have time for this."

"Time for this? You murdered a Shieldsman. He never even reached for his sword, he might have just thought I was someone else."

"Well, next time you try to deceive a well-trained man, don't slip twice. Now release me before it's too late."

Rand's fists squeezed tight, then he shoved Codar down for good measure and stood. The Breklian kicked back up to his feet and pointed at

Foreman Oarbreaker. "Get these bodies down into the crypt. I don't care where you bury them."

The dwarf remained frozen, staring at Sir Childress' now twitching body.

"Now, dwarf!"

Foreman Oarbreaker shook out his head. "Aye lads, ye heard him. It'll be our heads too if these're found."

The dwarves grabbed the bodies of the soldiers and Valin's fallen thug and dragged them onto the lift, grumbling to each other the whole way. Codar hopped up some rocks to take a look beyond the construction site.

"Nobody saw," he said. "You're lucky, Glassman."

"Lucky that you killed these men?" Rand said.

"*We*. Like it or not you're one of us now, and it was them or us."

"I…" Rand lost his train of thought. He wasn't sure why he was shocked that foul men like these would do something so horrid beyond the gaze of their equally monstrous boss. "You could have knocked them out."

"Incapacitation is a risk. Death leaves no room for regret."

Codar backed onto the lift alongside his men, the dwarves, and the bodies. Rand had no choice but to join them. He was in too deep now. All he could hope was that saving Torsten would be enough.

One of the dwarves climbed onto the pulley, and the lift began its descent. Now that the initial shock was out of the way, the little men seemed peculiarly calm amidst all the death.

"Valin's gonna be payin a lot more for this," Foreman Oarbreaker griped.

"I'm sure he'll be happy to renegotiate," Codar replied.

"Renego... I'll be visitin him on our way out. Soon as yer through, this is the last time ye'll see us in Yarrington."

"What about finishing the Royal Crypt?" Rand wasn't sure why that was a concern at a time like this, but he'd only been down once before during training. Sir Torsten and Sir Wardric liked to show new recruits the incredible breadth of history they protected.

As they descended into the massive, domed space, it was impossible for its majesty not to overshadow Rand's anger at Codar. Caskets made of glass wrapped the walls, allowing the preserved bodies of former kings to be viewed. Every inch of stone was carved with imagery from both the history of the Glass Kingdom and Iam himself. Flawless work that only the greatest artisans in history were capable of. The very floor was a mosaic telling the story of how Iam ended the God Feud, took man under his wing, led them all those centuries ago from the wintery wasteland of Drav Cra, and inspired the first King of the Glass, Autlas Nothhelm, to found Yarrington at the foot of Mount Lister.

The damage from the quake which ruptured the Mountain above was nearly all repaired. Some scaffolding still lined the walls, as some of the low, arched openings within which the caskets were slotted had collapsed. A portion of the domed ceiling was ruptured, and an area of the vast hall encasing the space had its columns knocked out, supported temporarily by wood. The scepters of old Kings sat in alcoves along it, and some were now damaged and could likely never be replicated. Hallways shot out between them toward lesser crypts for the families of the kings, some of those blocked off by rubble.

"Good enough job for me," the dwarf said. "You humans want to keep burying people underground, maybe you should learn how to build down here."

"Quiet," Codar demanded. "Are there any guards in the crypt?"

"The softies preferred the fresh air until they got too cold." He glanced down at the Shieldsman's corpse and stuck his tongue out in disgust. "They'll be awful cold now."

"What about Drav Cra? Have you seen them in the castle tunnels?"

"This a quiz? I come, I work stone, and I go home. If ye wanted me spyin on the castle, ye should have made an offer, Breklian."

"Dwarves," Codar grumbled. The lift clanked to a stop in a cloud of dust, and he stepped off. "Hide them in one of the family crypts."

"Which one?"

"I don't care." Codar removed his entire purse of autlas and flung it at the dwarves feet. "Just don't let them be found, and consider that final payment."

Foreman Oarbreaker kneeled and pulled back his beard so he could peak into the bag, then snatched it up. "Aye, boys. Ye heard him. Got one more thing to bury before we head off." He and his crew slung the bodies over their shoulders, two per man, like they were carrying logs, then headed off toward one of the lesser crypts.

"Those are sacred places," Rand said. "This is wrong."

"You wanted to get inside; this is the cost."

"Are you truly that cold? They didn't have to die. They at least deserve to be put to rest properly."

"Brek is cold. Those men, you're welcome to dig them out and do so after we're done."

Codar brushed by him, heading for one of the catacombs branching off from the Royal Crypt. A locked gate stood in the opening, each iron bar as thick as Rand's forearm, impossible to bash open. Codar grabbed a burning torch from the stone wall and raised it to the lock.

"You," he said to one of Valin's thugs. "Get to work."

The man cracked his knuckles, then knelt before the gate with a pin and started picking the lock. Rand wasn't sure where to look as he did it. He had to avoid facing the Royal Crypt where it felt like the eyes of every fallen king were watching, judging him. He couldn't face the surrounding colonnade through which he could hear the dwarves fumbling with bodies. He couldn't even stare at the wall or floors, or he'd see stories of Iam.

So, he closed his eyes. He felt ridiculous doing it, like a child who'd broken a rule down by the docks, but his entire life had become so absurd. The only thing he was sure of was that he wasn't doing the work of Iam any longer. That was up to Torsten. From being the Queen's hangman to this… his hands were covered in too much innocent blood.

The lock clicked, and the gate creaked inward. The thug rubbed his hands together. "Easy as a Vineyard wench." The remark instantly drew Rand's glower, and the man smirked. "Most of em anyways."

Rand pushed him aside and moved into the entrance. "Let's just get this over with," he said. "I think I know the way to the lower dungeons from here."

"Lead on," Codar said.

"Do you have another pouch of gold?" Rand asked. "What do we do if we have to buy someone else's silence?"

"A favor owed from Valin Tehr is worth far more than gold," he replied, without even needing to give it a second's thought, like he didn't sense the venom in Rand's tone.

"Then I hope we don't run into anyone else."

"Now you are learning." Codar slid his dirk back out of the sheath on the small of his back. Valin's two remaining men drew daggers as well and held them backward, concealed by their wrists and forearms.

Rand moved ahead. "I'll go first. My armor will make any guards hesitate. No more killing."

Codar grabbed Rand and pulled him out of the hall. Rand was about to protest when the Breklian held a finger to his lips. He gestured back down the tunnel. Two men passed by the nearest fork, a torch revealing their pale skin, furs, and leather armor. One spoke in Drav Crava, and the other laughed.

"And what about them, knight?" Codar asked.

Rand didn't dignify him with a response. Instead, they waited for the savages to pass, but they both knew the answer. They were here to help stop the spread of the Drav Cra into Yarrington, and if one of them got in the way, Rand wouldn't falter.

"Let's go." Rand took the torch and headed into the catacombs. The light would give away their position, but any guard in the tunnels was required to keep a torch with them. He didn't draw his sword either, so as not to look threatening at first glance, but he held his hand on the pommel as they moved. The Dawning had cleared the passage out until they were all the way to the end of the catacombs. Down the passage, where stairs led up to the castle courtyard, stood two Glass soldiers.

Rand positioned the torch directly in front of his chest so the shadow he cast would make Codar and the others invisible. He walked straight, shoulders proud, and the guards didn't seem to care about his presence at all. He did appear to be a Shieldsman after all, and he was too far for them to distinguish his face. He stopped at an entrance to a more cramped tunnel that led to the lower dungeons and allowed Codar and the others to slip behind him unseen.

"Well done," Codar said.

"Just keep walking," Rand replied. "The Dawning has helped, but the dungeons won't be empty."

A warren of tunnels crisscrossed beneath the castle. Some said it was an old dwarven city before the first king, Autlas Nothhelm, had his capital built above it centuries ago. Rand followed the light, avoiding the corridors where he could see the shimmer of torchlight on the moist stone walls. He may have appeared a Shieldsman, but he didn't want to encounter anyone else unless there was no choice.

The longer route avoiding patrols took them through storage halls—food, supplies, everything the castle might need to withstand a siege for months if it ever came to that. They had to slow on their way through as two Drav Cra warriors were passed out on a mat after looting some of it and eating their fill.

A staircase led to the lower dungeons where all the most rotten criminals the Crown got their hands on rotted for the rest of their lives. That was where Torsten would be, like some sort of mad killer. He, a man who had so loyally served the Crown for so long and faced untold evil just to bring back a doll Queen Oleander thought would save her son. Considering that the very next day King Pi rose from his casket alive and well, Rand couldn't deny that she might have been right and that Torsten's actions, insane as they might've been, had saved the Nothhelm line.

Rand now knew all the rumors about what Torsten did at the battle of Winde Port; killing a Shieldsman in rage, failing to capture the rebel Afhem Muskigo on purpose. Rand knew it was all hogwash. Sir Torsten Unger had trained Rand to serve the King's Shield far better than he ever had, and there was nobody who cared more for the realm.

"Is this the lower dungeons?" Codar asked as they reached the bottom of the stairs. So far below the ground, the air was dank and stale. The narrow hall extended two ways, barred cells lining it on either side. There were barely enough torches set on the walls to see anything. It was quiet, save for the soft echo of madness and the occasional scream.

"I'm surprised you've never been here," Rand replied.

"Perks of serving Valin Tehr. Now, where would they keep you, Torsten Unger?"

"There." Two Drav Cra warlocks stood outside one of the cells and a Glass soldier at a desk in a nearby nook. He was the unfortunate soul forced to endure the smell of shog and the din of insanity in the lower dungeons while the city above celebrated the Dawning. That meant he'd be the one with the keys.

"Your move, knight," Codar said.

Rand drew a deep breath. Warlocks were dangerous, as he'd learned in Redstar's chambers, but Rand had them outnumbered, four to three. Any other day of the year that number might have been tripled, but Valin Tehr was brilliant as he was wicked.

"We take out the warlocks, then convince the guard to open the cell," Rand said.

"And if he doesn't?"

"We take the keys and leave him in Torsten's cell. He doesn't die."

"Then don't let him see my face," Codar said, shoving Rand. "Go. This has taken too long already, and we have a schedule to keep."

Rand stumbled forward, the clatter of his armor drawing the attention of the warlocks. He had no choice but to proceed. They turned to face him simultaneously, two men with their faces painted black and white. Their heads were shaved, the black continuing all the way over their skulls. Ragged furs hung over their bodies, stitched together from various animals, and bone trinkets rattled around on their necks. Luckily, they weren't the ones who'd been outside Redstar's room.

The guard scrambled to his feet and saluted as Rand passed. The warlocks slowly repositioned themselves, now facing Rand, side by side.

"What is it you require, Shieldsman?" they asked. Hearing them speak in synchronization gave Rand momentary pause.

"I have to speak with Sir Unger," Rand said.

"Only Drad Redstar can order that."

Rand lifted his chin. "I was sent by the King himself."

"And we serve the Arch Warlock."

"You are in King Pi's castle, in our castle," Rand said sternly. "You will obey a direct order, or you will feel the might of the Glass Kingdom."

"We are that might. The former wearer is not to be—"

A knife zipped by Rand's ear. The warlock it was aimed at somehow predicted the attack and was able to slide out of the way, the blade stabbing into his shoulder. Rand swung at the other warlock with his torch without thinking twice and bashed him across the face.

Reeling from the knife, the first warlock raised a hand, and suddenly, the flame on the end of the torch jumped onto Rand's arm. His armor was infused with glaruium yet it caught fire like a thistle in a drought. One of Valin's men squeezed around him in the narrow passage and leaped onto the warlock Rand had struck, plunging the dagger into his chest over and over. The warlock murmured in Drav Crava as it happened, calmly, as if he felt no pain. When Valin's man glanced back up, all the deadly wounds he'd inflicted in the warlock showed on his chest as well, identical. He toppled over, dead in an instant.

The Glass guard grabbed his bludgeon and swung at Rand, but Codar parried the attack. "No!" Rand shouted as Codar swiftly ducked around the man and got his knife to his throat. Codar stopped centimeters away from shredding the man's throat.

The injured, remaining warlock stepped forward, chanting in Drav Crava. His eyes were wild, gray but glowing like hot coals, and the fire he'd summoned wrapped like a serpent up Rand's limb. He could feel his skin boiling beneath his armor, the pain so intense he could barely move. Valin's other thug stood to the side, the one who'd picked the lock, too petrified by the dark magic to move. The fire leaped from Rand's arm onto the thug like a living thing, and without armor, the man's clothing caught quickly. He shrieked, falling to the ground and rolling.

Rand fought through the pain. The heat was on his neck now, the skin beginning to blister, but he drew his sword and charged. The warlock backed up and sliced his own wrist with a knife so deep blood instantly gushed out. The body of the other warlock flew off the ground, knocking Rand from his feet and crushing Valin's lockpicker's head against the wall.

Rand groped for his sword, but the fire only grew brighter, hotter. He caught a glimpse of Codar and the guard out of the corner of his eye.

"There is no choice," Codar said. He was about to slit the man's throat so he could join the fight when all of a sudden the fire dwindled. Rand found his sword and got to his feet, only to see the warlock with his back against the bars of Torsten's cell. A chain was wrapped around his throat, scraping the white paint off until the man's throat crunched.

"You'll never get away with this," the glass guard rasped as Codar choked him. Rather than answering, the Breklian bashed him in the back of the head with the guard's cudgel and knocked him out.

"Rand, is that you?" a gruff, haggard voice asked. It didn't sound anything like the booming voice Rand remembered, but it couldn't be anyone else in the cell but the man who'd left Rand as Wearer while he saved the kingdom, only for Rand to ruin everything.

Rand wasn't sure why he hesitated, but it took all the strength in his limbs to drag his body in front of the cell. It was Torsten inside, still tall and strong as an ox with skin like pitch. He had a chain in one hand which hung from the ceiling, the end around the Warlock's throat keeping him from collapsing in a heap of tangled limbs. His ankles were chained like common livestock for slaughter.

"Sir Unger," Rand struck his chest and bowed his head. "I received your message."

XXV

THE MYSTIC

Wetzel was a strict teacher. Sora could remember the feeling of his cane against her knuckles every time she messed up or didn't listen, but he often wound up more upset with himself for not being able to teach her correctly. Then he'd storm off alone, rambling like a madman that he couldn't do it.

Madam Jaya was calmer, which she made up for in both unpredictability and ambiguity.

For days, Madam Jaya forced Sora to meditate, to clear her mind—as if she could focus on anything other than Whitney and his torment in Elsewhere.

Finally, after days of solitude, Madam Jaya finally returned. Just when Sora thought she'd gain some reprieve, the mystic told her she couldn't leave the training area until she'd summoned flame without the drawing of blood. She left with no further explanation of the bar guai and sealed the door behind her.

Sora stared down at the disc embedded in her skin, puzzled. "I guess this is teaching me." She drew a long, beleaguered breath. "Okay. Summon fire. You've done it a thousand times."

She closed her eyes and reached inward how she always used to. Ever since the first time Wetzel's teachings had unlocked her powers, the presence of Elsewhere had always called out in return. But they could only ever communicate if she drew blood.

Presently, Sora heard only the echo of her thoughts. Eyes closed, she pictured fire, roaring, its arms reaching out to devour everything in its path. Then, she thrust her arm forward. Nothing happened.

She shook out her limb, took another breath and tried again. And again. And once more, until she wasn't only thinking about fire, she was consumed by it. She imagined herself back in Winde Port, tongues of flame licking all around her. She could feel the terror. She heard a laugh and spun around only to see Kazimir chuckling as he slid a bloody blade across his tongue. She tripped over her own feet as she scrambled backward and away from the upyr.

"My dear, you've fallen," said another. "Allow me." A gray hand extended to her, and she looked up to see Muskigo smiling down at her.

"Get away from me!" she yelled, jumping to her feet. When her heels hit the ground, she found herself in the training room again.

"What did… Madam Jaya?" Nobody answered.

Sora struggled to catch her breath, and once she did, she felt a sharp pain in the center of her chest. Painful memories often helped her fuel her power after she cut herself, and the bar guai seemed to enhance that sensation, to send her deeper into her fears and emotions until she was lost in them.

"It's this yigging thing," she said as she dug her fingers beneath the disc and tried to pry it out of her chest, but she couldn't find purchase.

"As I said, you are not yet capable of removing it," Madam Jaya said.

Sora spun. The door remained closed, but the mystic was suddenly standing before her again.

"You said I had all day," Sora said.

"You did. It is now night."

"What? How? I… I… I guess I lost track of time."

The woman's thin lips creased into a pathetic excuse for a grin. "Nobody casts through the bar guai on their first attempt. I told you that patience would be your first lesson."

Sora sighed. "Another test."

"All life is a test. I tell you this, so you do not blame yourself for not being able to do in a day without instruction what has taken others years, no matter who they were.”

“It’s just… I can feel the power of Elsewhere within me still, but it’s like it’s ignoring me. Telling me I must bleed.”

Madam Jaya sat and folded her legs. She invited Sora to sit beside her, and now that Sora knew how long she’d been struggling to find her power, she was eager for the break.

“We spoke of sacrifice, and without it, Elsewhere remains blocked off for all of us.”

“Then why can’t I use my knife?” Sora snapped, her frustration peeking through. “Sorry, Madam, it’s been a long day.”

“I understand. It is rare for one of our apprentices to be so accomplished in blood magic before reaching us. Their comprehension of Elsewhere’s power and what it means to sacrifice often winds up tainted. It can take time to retrain your mind.”

“Time…” Sora sighed. “Madam Jaya, can I tell you something?”

The mystic nodded.

“I believe I have already opened Elsewhere, but there was no sacrifice.”

Madam Jaya turned her head but betrayed no emotion. “Tell me.”

“When I was in Winde Port, I was attacked, hunted by a monster. He’d finally cornered me and, without knowing, I sent him to Elsewhere.” Still unsure of what they might think about it, she decided to leave Whitney out of it altogether.

“How do you know that is where he went?”

“I…” Sora swallowed. “I saw him in the chamber beneath Lord Bokeo’s bookstore when the Ancient One gave me that vision.”

“Does this monster have a name?”

“He is an upyr,” Sora admitted. “His name is Kazimir.”

“Ah,” Madam Jaya breathed out in relief.

“Why are you smiling?” Sora asked.

“The upyr are very different from us. Their powers come from an otherworldly attachment to Elsewhere, and at a high price. For an upyr to even close his or her eyes is to see Elsewhere. Each time they blink, there it is, waiting for them. It was not your power alone that cast him into that abyss. It was his already strong connection to the place that allowed it.”

Sora felt something she couldn't immediately pinpoint. It might have been relief—relief that perhaps she hadn't been wholly responsible for Whitney's fate.

"Rest assured," Madam Jaya continued, "you alone will never open Elsewhere without sacrifice. In this case, the upyr already made the sacrifice long ago. For you, it remains blocked off and this," she motioned to the disc buried in Sora's chest. "The bar guai acts as a conduit for what we call a makros."

"A makros?

"It is when the power of a casting is stored within an object, making it able to be called upon at will without sacrifice. I know that amulet seems like nothing, but there is no object in this realm of greater value. For centuries, mystics have poured bits of their power into those stones, bound by runic magic, carved in the language of the gods."

"So, the sacrifice has already been made?"

Madam Jaya nodded, taking no effort to hide her self-satisfaction at triggering the realization. "Exactly. You failed because you called on the wrong place. Self-channeling through Elsewhere takes decades to master, so for now, you must channel through the stone as all new apprentices learn to do. Walk before you run, or so they say. Where once you could cast fire through thought, now you must call upon the rune by name."

Sora stared down at the six strange symbols glowing on her chest. "I don't know their names."

"You know one. The most gifted mystics are born with an affinity for a certain element. You've always been drawn to one."

"Fire." She didn't even have to think twice.

"Yes. The giver and the destroyer. It is the power that blossomed within you naturally, and that which burned your home to the ground. It saved you from certain death in the Webbed Woods, yet made you fear your own abilities in Winde Port. In you, the fire is two sides of the same coin, and its name lies on its ridge."

Sora was too overwhelmed to wonder how Madam Jaya knew about what happened in those places. She'd come to assume that her new caretakers knew everything about her past.

"I don't..." she stammered.

"Look within," Madam Jaya said. "The runes speak, but the language of the gods is unique in us all, as we were all made unique. I can show you the way, but only you can find the word. Imagine it like a flower, blossoming in spring—you are the flower. Within you holds the power of life, the seed that will grow into a great field."

Sora looked to her teacher, but the woman remained stone-faced. So, she closed her eyes again, and this time didn't allow herself to go to dark places. She searched inside herself, into her memories, until she felt that sharp pain in her chest again.

"Aquira!" She blurted the word out before realizing what could happen. Energy roiled beneath the surface. Her eyes snapped open, and air flooded her lungs. One of the bar guai's runes glowed blue like the door to the Well of Wisdom.

"Of course," Madam Jaya said. "Yours was a destined meeting. The fulcrum on which your future rests. Now, try again."

Sora stood, feeling like she'd just woken from an extended rest. She raised her hand and looked inward. She could always feel the presence of Elsewhere staring back if she searched deep enough, haunting her, tempting her to push beyond her limitations and sacrifice a piece of herself, but now she only heard the thumping of her heart.

She whispered the name of her wyvern friend, and a spark ignited at her fingertips. Then she spoke it louder, and flame wrapped her hand as it always had after blooding.

"Marvelous!" Madam Jaya applauded, showing enthusiasm for the first time.

Sora exhaled, and the flame extinguished. Usually, summoning fire left her weakened, as if her power were a muscle to be exerted. Thanks to the bar guai, she felt perfectly fine.

"Do not get used to how little it drains you," Madam Jaya said. "The makros imbued in the stones is limited. With practice, you will grow more efficient, but draw on them too much, and you will find magic as impossible to wield as a commoner."

"So then how do I learn to channel as you do?"

"By not getting ahead of yourself." Madam Jaya stood and guided Sora's hand to her side.

"I don't mean to be difficult. It's just, I don't understand how learning to use a crutch will help."

"It is a good question. A crutch, by any definition, is meant to help one who is weak become strong. Channeling requires extreme knowledge of oneself. Through blood sacrifice, Elsewhere responds, begs even, for you to unleash its power here on Pantego. It is why we admonish blood magic. For those without your natural gift, it can be impossible to control the rage it fosters. Elsewhere can consume the host or turn them into vengeful husks bent on consuming all before them."

"Like an upyr," Sora remarked.

"In a way, yes. An upyr with no sense of what they once were. The bar guai allows you to see only your own reflection, and thus it is purer. More controllable. When you learn to channel, it is from within yourself you must draw. You will come to find that Elsewhere isn't a parasite you answer to, but a tool to be wielded."

"But I thought you said that using our abilities in Pantego meant a sacrifice is needed. Spilling blood, I understand. Other mystics, they gave their power to store in this stone. But if you can channel it through your own body, what is the sacrifice?"

"That, Sora of Troborough, is an answer for another time."

"Please, I'd like to know." And she meant it. She knew Whitney needed her as soon as possible, but these answers were why they'd set out from Yarrington in the first place. For her to discover her true identity. It was difficult to look away now.

Madam Jaya stared longingly in Sora's direction, through her. "With every spell, we give a piece of ourselves."

"What do you mean?"

"Not a piece made of flesh or bone, but a shred of who we are. Our personality, our memory, but not our sanity as with blooding. It is why the first of us created the Well of Wisdom. So that we may remind ourselves of who we are if we stray too far. Abuse your power, and who you are will cease to be in both mind and body. A spectre." Madam Jaya reached out to touch Sora's cheek, and her hand passed through.

The grief twisting her features was unmistakable. Since she found them, Sora had looked upon the mystics only with fear, awe, and disdain. Now, she pitied the woman before her who had been reduced to air.

"Is that why Aihara is so coarse?" she said, grinning impishly.

Madam Jaya looked shocked, then allowed a smile to show as well. *So, they do have a sense of humor.*

"I suppose," Madam Jaya said. "*The Ancient One*," she stressed the mystic's title, "has been around for a long, long time. She clings to this realm for the good of our Order. Do you know why she speaks for us when there are seven of us who remain on our Council?"

Sora shook her head.

"For a mystic, there is no greater achievement than age. The focus and honing of the power it takes to exist here in Pantego for three hundred and six years is beyond comprehension."

"Three hundred and six?" Sora asked, jaw dropping.

"Before Liam the Conqueror was even a thought. When there was an Order of our people to lead, the eight eldest sat atop the Tower ruling over us. We are the Council now, only because we remain, waiting for our eight to restart our great order."

"How old are you?"

"Alas, I am only one hundred and fifty-two."

"Only..." Sora muttered.

"I see your spirits are higher now, Apprentice Sora, and I am glad of it. For next, you will find the god-word for another spell. Tell me, since your Gift first manifested, have you found a proclivity for another type of magic?"

"I've healed people, but it's always been much more difficult and drained me far more. There was a time with... well... I healed a rancher after a dire wolf attacked him and it nearly killed me."

"There is no art nobler than healing, but it draws on two of the fundamental elements in your bar guai. Power over flame, as you know, and over water. If fire is the life giver and the destroyer, water is the life-essence that flows within all of us and the land upon which we live. It is within your blood, within your flesh, as it is within the earth."

"Okay... I think I can do that."

"Many have thought." She snapped her fingers, and the door to the room opened. In walked two of what they called servants, carrying a table. Sora felt her stomach turn over. On the table lay Kai, stripped completely bare, with a gash cut across his chest.

"What did you do!" Sora ran directly through Madam Jaya to the men.

She inspected Kai's wound. He was breathing well and had the muscle tone to ensure that the cut wasn't too deep, but it still looked incredibly painful.

"What did they do to you?" she questioned as she pushed the other servants away.

Kai took her hand and squeezed. His palm dripped with sweat, as did his brow. "I'm helping with your training," he rasped.

"Relax, Sora," Madam Jaya said.

"Relax?" Sora glared at her, Elsewhere in her eyes.

"The wound is not fatal, and in this place, it cannot get infected. It is only the pain he feels, and we must learn to conquer pain. Kai understands this."

"It is all right, Miss Sora," he said. "I trust you."

"This is wrong," Sora said.

"As I said, all members of the Order have their part to play. Not only us. Kai bleeds so that others who are at your mercy do not have to."

"You could bleed yourself."

Madam Jaya raised her hand and stared at it, longingly. "We no longer can. Now, eat." A bowl of lumpy soup suddenly appeared in her ethereal hand. She shoved it toward Sora's gut. "Maintain your strength and stay focused. I will return in the morning to see if you have healed his wound.

At that, Madam Jaya soundlessly exited the room, the two healthy servants at her side. "Wait, but I don't—" Sora chased after her, stopping when she noticed Aihara Na standing in the entry, appraising her. Her hard glare sent a chill up Sora's spine. Then, the door sealed shut.

Sora turned back to Kai. He seemed calm enough despite being treated like a test subject... *as* a test subject.

"You'll be fine, Miss Sora," Kai said. "Find the power within, and you'll be okay."

"I'm not worried about me," she said, softly. She returned to his side. "Is this what they do to you? Treat you like meat?"

"The Secret Council is in no need of training. I do this for you, and only you."

Sora swallowed. She extended her hands over his bloody chest and wriggled her fingers in preparation. "Then I won't let you down."

XXVI

THE KNIGHT

Torsten couldn't believe his eyes. He'd sent Wren to Rand's home to try and find an ally who hadn't yet been manipulated by Redstar, but it'd been so long he'd nearly given up. Especially after seeing Wren, broken and subservient, agreeing to Redstar's every word before the people of Yarrington.

"Rand Langley," Torsten said. He released the chain he'd used to strangle one of Redstar's warlocks, letting the body crumple. Stepping toward the bars, he said, "From Iam's Eye to mine, it's really you."

Rand raised his head to regard him. The young man looked even worse than the last time Torsten had seen him, weeks after he surrendered the white helm and fled the castle. His face was gaunt, almost skeletal, and a patchy beard sheltered a bony jaw. The luminescent paint around his eyes masked just how tired and dark they were.

"No warlock tricks, Sir," Rand said. "I came just as you asked."

"I was worried Wren never made it to you."

"He did. I... I tried to take down Redstar myself, but if not for the High Priest, I'd be dead. Whatever Redstar did to him, he's—"

"I know. I saw. He's another puppet to the deceiver's will now, just like our poor king."

"The reunion is over," said another who accompanied Rand. "Time to go, Rand Langley." The man stepped forward and tried a few keys in the cell's lock before its gate swung open. He was a Breklian, judging by his white hair and mustache, and the feathered muffin cap topping his head. Torsten swore he knew him from somewhere. It wasn't often Breklians came so far south outside of trading vessels.

"He's not free yet." Rand snatched the keys from the man's hand, then hurried into the cell. He kneeled before Torsten to unlock the cuffs chaining his ankles to the wall.

"What did he do to the High Priest?" Torsten asked. A cuff fell off his leg, and the stale air against his irritated skin stung. He welcomed the pain.

"I don't know, but he has to be stopped," Rand replied. "I maimed him, but it only seemed to make him more powerful."

"So that was you who took his hand?"

Rand released the second cuff, then stood and nodded. "Spilling blood only seemed to make him stronger."

"It is the font of wickedness his kind draws on. You've done well, Sir Langley. It won't be forgotten. Now, it's time we end this nightmare once and for all. Redstar said that on the Dawning, light and darkness would be one. Whatever he's planning, it must be stopped."

"He mentioned something similar to me."

"You Glassman would see all the wonder wiped from this world, wouldn't you?" the mustached Breklian interrupted. "Unfortunately, the young deserter has made a deal, and I take those seriously. You are on your own from here, Sir Knight."

"Rand, what is he talking about?" Torsten asked. "I can't do this alone. But together, two Wearers stripped of their honor—thanks to Redstar's treachery—we can win back the King's Shield." Torsten lay a hand on Rand's armored shoulder. "I may not know the faces of those who remain, but I know their hearts."

"The Crown is not everything to all of you. Move, Rand."

Rand glanced back at the Breklian, then Torsten, and then his gaze fell to the floor.

"I won't ask again," the Breklian warned, stepping into the entry of the cell. The burning torch, lying on the ground, cast light on his face.

"Wait, I do recognize you," Torsten said. "You're Valin Tehr's man, aren't you? Codar, is it?"

The Breklian bowed. "He sends his regards and says that he misses your squabbles. You were too good for us after you put on the White Helm."

"The whole world is too good for you lot." Torsten turned back to Rand who seemed heartbroken. "What do they have on you? I swear, help me now, and when the kingdom we once knew is restored, they won't be able to touch you."

"We don't need to touch him," Codar said. He scraped his dagger up one of the cell's bars, the screech causing nearby inmates to cry out in anger. "Let's go."

"Rand… what did you do?"

"Whatever it took to get you out." Rand bowed his head to Torsten. "You didn't give up on me, sir, when all the world's light seemed to go out. You don't need me. This kingdom never has. Now fix what I helped start."

Rand hurried past Codar as if he didn't want a chance to second guess his decision. The Breklian's mustache lifted with a grin. "Good luck, knight. We look forward to what happens next." The man sunk back into the shadow, and when Torsten rushed to the open gate, he saw their shadows fading down the dark tunnel.

"Rand!" he called out.

The young man stopped and glanced back.

"You had nothing to do with this," Torsten continued. "Whatever it is you think you did wrong, you are forgiven. Thanks to your strength we have hope again."

"If only you knew what I have done," Rand said softly. Then he and Codar headed upstairs and out of the lower dungeons. Again, Torsten was alone with the ravings of madmen asking why they too weren't freed.

Torsten knew well of Valin Tehr and his exploitation of Dockside. He'd grown up in the South Corner, just beyond the docks, where Valin's influence over the many cobblers and tailors dotting the clothing district were continually butting heads with his thugs. His years in the King's Shield consisted of many days cleaning up Valin Tehr's messes. However, the wretch always seemed to avoid a cell. Eventually, Torsten moved on to kingdom-wide concerns, but Tehr's gang remained a nagging pain in the King's Shield's side.

He couldn't imagine what Rand had offered in exchange for their help, but as Torsten crossed over into the anteroom, he whispered a silent prayer for him. Then he looked to the moss-covered ceiling.

"Not all of us have lost our faith, Iam." He fell to one knee. "Give me the strength on this, the holiest of days, to see Your will done. To cast Your enemies from this sacred land once and for all, and return light upon Your chosen kingdom."

He traced his eyes, noticing that for the first time in his life, he hadn't received the blessing of a priest on the day of the Dawning. And he wouldn't. For today, he planned to do the work of his kingdom, even if it meant he'd never reach the Gate of Light.

Whatever it took.

He and Redstar had danced for too long, and he wasn't sure why he'd expected it to end with him anything but alone. He grabbed the unconscious guard's cudgel, then headed for the exit. The other prisoners begged him to free them as well, but if he was guilty of killing one of his own Order, he couldn't imagine what they'd done.

He climbed the stairs and headed down the dank tunnels toward the castle. The Dawning would mean fewer guards to deal with, at least any Glassmen standing in his way who believed him a traitor. Any Drav Cra would face the unadulterated wrath of Iam.

Two Glass soldiers stood guard at the stairs leading into the castle courtyard. Torsten headed straight for them.

"Halt!" one shouted. "Who are you?"

Torsten didn't stop, didn't respond, just continued onward until the torchlight was enough to reveal his features. The sentry's eyes went wide.

"Sir Unger? You're not supposed to be—"

"Step aside," Torsten ordered.

Their hands fell to the grips of their swords. "We have strict orders."

Torsten closed his eyes. "Forgive me," he whispered.

"For?"

Torsten swung the cudgel and swept one of them off his feet. The other got his sword free and slashed, but Torsten grabbed his forearm first and bashed it into the wall, knocking the weapon loose. He drove his head hard into the bridge of the man's nose. As he turned, he brought his foot down on the other's face, knocking him out cold as well. They'd be fine save for some bumps and bruises.

He quickly dragged their unconscious bodies into a near-empty storage nook, used some rope from sacks of potatoes to tie them down, and covered their mouths with a shred of torn cloth. Checking their armor for anything useful, he found that only the chainmail hauberk of one of them fit his tremendous build, and even then, it was a tight fit. Ever since his days as a squire, he'd needed the castle blacksmith Hovom Nitebrittle to craft his armor specially to fit him even when such meager work was beneath him.

It wasn't the full uniform of a castle guard, but it would have to do. At the very least, the hauberk had the Eye of Iam painted in blue on the chest. One also wore a kettle helmet that Torsten could barely squeeze around his skull, but it would be enough to disguise his face at first glance.

As he stood, a flash in his peripherals distracted him. He rolled quickly. An axe struck the stone floor right behind him and sent sparks flying. A Drav Cra brute reeled back and swung again. Torsten grabbed one of the guard's longswords and raised it in time to deflect the blow. It still sent him staggering back into a row of storage barrels. The weapon was worthless compared to his claymore which now rested at the bottom of a canal in Winde Port.

"And they said staying in the castle today wouldn't be fun!" The mass of muscle came at Torsten again before he could get up, but he was all power. Torsten ducked out of the way of two more swipes until the man's axe crashed into a barrel and sunk through the wood. Grain leaked out as Torsten rolled forward and slashed up. Blood poured into the meal as the swipe severed the man's arm off at the elbow. Before the man could scream, Torsten covered his mouth and propelled him to his knees.

"Where is Redstar?" Torsten growled. He waited for the man to stop squirming before removing his hand, but received only a wad of spit on his chest. Before the man could curse him, Torsten cleaved his head from his shoulders.

"Your time in my castle is over," he said.

Torsten wiped the blade on the savage's furs, then headed upstairs into snow-covered grounds of the western courtyard. A now-bare cherry tree presided over the frozen dragon fountain.

Torsten could remember being in that very courtyard, holding Oleander on the night Pi threw himself from the tower just behind him.

He sighed and took a step out into the frigid air. He wasn't sure where Redstar would be. It was the day of the Dawning, and Redstar had intimated he would be spending it with Pi, but surrounded by the castle building and the sky brushed with clouds, he couldn't tell how late it was or if they'd have begun the trek up to the summit of Mount Lister yet. His former Wearer's quarters where Redstar made home seemed a good place to look first.

"Quickly, a prisoner has escaped!" Torsten shouted, noting two Glass soldiers patrolling the arcade bordering the grounds.

The guards sprung to action, running toward him without a second glance. Torsten stole one's sword as they raced by and slammed the door shut behind them. He jammed the weapon through the handles to lock them in. They shouted, banging gauntleted fists against the wood, but it was a long way to any other exit.

Not caring to hear their cries, Torsten headed toward the castle chapel adjacent the courtyard, facing northwest toward Mount Lister as all churches in the kingdom did. He peered in first. Although he couldn't see the whole room, the crystalline altar was empty as he expected. Anyone important would be traveling to the summit of the mountain for the Dawning.

Torsten swept in and made it a few steps down the aisle when he heard a cough. He looked left, hands squeezing the grip of his stolen sword when he saw Hovom, the castle blacksmith, seated on the far end of a pew all alone.

"Wren said you'd pass through here," Hovom said. "I guess the old man was right." Hovom stood. He had the longest beard of any man Torsten had ever known, nearly down to his waist. Burn marks from a smithing accident covered half his body, but there was no finer blacksmith in all Pantego, dwarves considered. It was said the secret to smelting glaruium to use in weapons and armor had been passed down in his family since the first kings. He was an odd, quiet man, who rarely left the heat of his irons for anything, even the call of food or drink—only for prayer.

Torsten set his feet and tensed. "Hovom, just let me pass, and you won't be bothered."

Hovom approached, sword held out in front of him. Torsten prepared to fend him off when the blacksmith flipped the claymore around and presented Torsten with the hilt, bowing his head.

"Relax, my friend," he said. "I have no quarrel with you."

Torsten let his shoulders loosen, but not his grip on his sword. After everything, he couldn't afford to trust anyone. There was no saying who had Redstar's claws in them. "I'm afraid I'm not 'friend' to many these days," Torsten said.

"Not all have lost faith in you or Iam." He ran his hand tenderly along the blade while he remained bowed. "Wren came to me days ago before the deserter attempted to kill Redstar. He spoke in riddles, but I think I understood."

"What are you talking about."

"He'd expected you'd be needing this." He shuffled forward, urging Torsten to take the massive claymore. That was when Torsten finally let himself observe the hilt and his eyes went wide. His stolen longsword fell from his grasp. The claymore's cross-guard extended from a sculpture of the Eye of Iam, a grip of beautiful leather threaded with gold, and a pommel, silver and sculpted in the shape of a dragon's head. The sword had belonged to King Liam, buried with him in the Royal Crypt.

"That's..."

"*Salvation*. The sword of King Liam. The blade broke when the earth-quake ravaged the Royal Crypt. Wren gave me very specific instructions to reforge it. He made me vow in the name of Iam to tell nobody of it, not even the King, until you found me here on the Dawning."

Torsten reached out and let his fingers run across the handle. Then he pulled back. "I cannot accept this," he said. "The sword of Liam the Conqueror can find no home within the hands of a sinner."

"The sword's name says otherwise. Wren said you would need it."

"Wren is broken, you must have seen it from your quarters."

"Whatever his Holiness has become, the Wren we knew said you would pass through here at this exact moment." Hovom closed his eyes and inhaled. "What other proof do you need. I've always said, the sword chooses the man, not the other way around."

Hovom released the weapon, causing Torsten to catch it out of reflex. The heft and length were about the same as his old claymore, though this one was heavier. He turned it over and flicked the blade. "No glaruium?"

"Wren insisted I reforge the blade without it."

"It is perfect, nonetheless." Torsten's heart sank. "Still, I cannot accept this." He extended it for Hovom to take, but the blacksmith folded his arms behind his back.

"Then you must leave it on the floor. Its time with its maker has come to an end." He walked by Torsten, stopped, and picked up the rusty longsword he'd stolen. He spun it, and even through his thick beard, Torsten could see his heartbreak. "When all this is over, tell the King our men need new weapons. My children grow old."

"Wait," Torsten called. "Do you know where Redstar is?"

Hovom didn't look back. He pointed up, then continued on his way toward the chapel's front doors. Torsten stood, dumbfounded, staring down at the sword which once filled the hand of the greatest King Pantego had ever known. When he looked up again, Hovom was gone.

Torsten exhaled. *Who am I to question the will of Iam? Perhaps he hasn't lost faith in me yet.*

"With this sword, I will reclaim your holy kingdom, Your Grace," he spoke aloud to the sword. "Then it will find you at the Gate of Light once more."

Without another word, Torsten crossed the chapel to a side door that had direct access to the western tower, so the King could visit the chapel without being bothered. Hovom indicated that Redstar was above, so Torsten felt confident in checking his own quarters first. The door was locked, but no entry was built to withstand Torsten's frame. He rammed into it with his shoulder once, then the second time tore it from its hinges.

Drav Crava protests met his ears immediately. A white-faced warlock was descending the stairs and upon seeing Torsten's drawn weapon, immediately sliced his thigh. A stream of ice struck Torsten in the shoulder and thrust him into the wall. Even though it was ice, it stung like fire and was a spell he'd never faced from a warlock before.

Torsten fell back behind the turn of the spiral stairs, but the warlock shot ice across the landing between them, making it slick so Torsten wouldn't be able to pass.

"Stop!" A Shieldsman charged in from the other direction and aimed a spear at Torsten's chest. Not just any Shieldsman, but Sir Austun Mulliner.

He wore the luminescent paint of the Dawning, apparently having attended service before his duty. "Torsten," he spat.

Torsten kept his new sword raised toward the warlock. "Sir Mulliner, you have to listen to me."

"How many times are you going to try this?"

"Then just walk away. You don't need to be a party to this."

Mulliner didn't flinch. His grip on his weapon tightened. "Trespassers in the Glass Castle on the Dawning receive no quarter. Maybe this time, Sir Havel will finally get justice."

"He is a criminal," the warlock said. "Kill him, Glassman."

"Do you really believe that abomination speaks for the Crown?" Torsten asked. "I don't care what you saw in Winde Port, Redstar is no hero. He is a deceiver."

Mulliner's armor was so shiny and unsullied that Torsten saw in its reflection that the warlock had slit his hand. Ice shot forth from his palm, and Torsten grasped Mulliner's spear and turned them both, so the stream of magic hit the wood shaft. It froze solid in an instant. Torsten cracked off the spear end and threw it at the warlock, the point piercing his heart.

By the time the warlock hit the ground, he was already dead, with no ability to draw power from the mass exodus of blood. Torsten promptly used the railing and his sword to propel himself over the landing still slick from mystical ice. He turned back. Austun stood at the edge, and in his heavy Shieldsman armor, it would be difficult for him to get over with ease.

"You won't stop, will you?" Mulliner said, grimacing. "Until the King hangs our entire Order for your treason."

"Sound the bells of alarm," Torsten said, pointing his claymore toward Mulliner. "Don't find yourself on the end of a noose on my behalf if I fail." The knight remained still. "Trust me or not, I'm here for Redstar and Redstar alone. The King is in no danger."

Mulliner didn't answer, but he slowly backed away to find another way around. That meant Torsten wouldn't have long before the castle gates were sealed and the intruder alarms rang out. He took the stairs three at a time, all the way to the second highest floor below the King's chambers.

He slowed at the landing and sidled up against the wall. A single warlock guarded the door to the Wearer's chambers. Another stood a few meters off, staring in the opposite direction. Two of Redstar's apostles sharing a floor meant to house members of the Royal Council and nary a Glass soldier in sight. What a disgrace. Torsten recognized neither from his previous encounters with Redstar, and no Freydis.

Torsten rested *Salvation* against the wall, knowing that if he cut but didn't kill either of these men, their magic would be unleashed. He quickly lashed out and wrapped his massive sword-arm around the nearest warlock's neck. With the other, he wrenched the warlock's hands so the man wouldn't be able to cut himself. He was growing more proficient at handling the blood mages.

"Move," Torsten growled. The warlock cursed back in Drav Crava, then called to his comrade. The other warlock pulled out a dagger, dragged it along his palm, and turned to face them. Fire bloomed around his hand, but he didn't throw it yet.

"Drop him!" he hissed.

"First, we need to talk!" Torsten answered. He glanced left, sensing motion. One of the chambers had its door open, and inside was the young Master of Rolls. He looked terrified, and as Torsten passed with the warlock in his grasp, the young Master of Rolls slowly shut his door.

The castle bells sounded and drew both warlock's attention, distracting them just long enough for Torsten to throw the warlock he held against the wall headfirst and charge the other. A stream of flame shot over his shoulder, so hot his bald head immediately started to sweat. His shoulder slammed into the warlock and drove him to the ground. White-hot hands grasped his bicep, melting through his hauberk and keeping him from furthering his attack. The warlock muttered under his breath in Drav Crava, the whites of his eyes bright against the black paint surrounding them. Torsten fought the pain, grasped the skinny man by the throat and crushed his windpipe until his arms fell limp.

He jumped to his feet and retrieved *Salvation* from near the stairs. Then he positioned himself in front of the room he'd called home for over a year. He built up momentum and kicked through the door.

The splinters peppering his face were a bracing reminder of how much had changed. As was the sight that greeted him. Redstar's pieced-together mural remained on the floor, and strung up on the wall was the Queen Mother, Oleander. She was stripped completely bare.

"Torsten," she said. "By Iam, I never thought I'd be so glad to see you."

Torsten averted his gaze out of reflex as he approached.

"Grow up, knight," she said. "Have you never seen a woman before?"

He swallowed the lump in his throat and turned back. There wasn't a scratch on her, but Redstar had many ways to inflict pain. Her lithe limbs were spread wide by the ropes stringing her up, leaving little to the imagination. Someone had sloppily painted her face in the manner of warlocks, the black and white dripping down onto her bosom.

"Who did this to you?" Torsten asked. He had to raise his voice since the window was open and the castle bells continued to chime.

"Who do you think?"

"You're his," Torsten caught his breath, "sister."

"Apparently, I'm a 'foreign whore, and it's time I look like one.' Now get me down so I can rip that traitorous bastard's throat out myself!"

Torsten didn't answer. He could barely summon words. Seeing his Queen in such condition broke his heart. She'd never been good at ruling, and after the night she attempted to seduce Torsten, her figure had filled his dreams. But not like this. It was no way for the widow of Liam Nothhelm to be treated, no matter what the cause.

He started untying one of her ankles, then heard gurgling. A vine had crept in through the open window and wrapped around her throat. Her foot got free, and she pointed it to the doorway. The warlock Torsten had thrown against the wall lay in the threshold, stretching his bloody hand through the opening.

"Only Iam gives life," Torsten said. He lifted his sword, strode over to the man, and plunged it down into his back, straight through the heart. His magical vine loosened, allowing Oleander to cough, then crackled away into dust.

He was about to return to Oleander when Sir Mulliner and a host of Glass Soldiers appeared behind him, weapons drawn.

"Drop your weapon and surrender," Mulliner demanded. "I won't ask again."

Torsten backed slowly into the room, and as the soldiers followed him, they realized who was on the wall. "W—what have you done?" Mulliner stuttered.

"Stand down, all of you," Oleander rasped. "How far do you think your true Wearer has fallen that he would do this to me?"

"He killed one of our own!" Mulliner and the others kept their eyes fixed on Torsten, refusing to regard their Queen in such a manner. Mulliner edged forward until the tip of his sword was a hair's breadth from Torsten's throat.

Torsten lowered *Salvation*. "It's true Austun," he said. "I did. I didn't mean to, but it happened, and Iam will judge me for that. But I had nothing to do with this."

He pointed back to Redstar's mural telling a false version of the God Feud that painted Nesilia a hero. "Look upon that heathen's blasphemy, he and his horde of devils. He did this to your Queen, his own sister."

"Do you plan on letting me hang here all day?" Oleander spat.

Torsten took a step toward her, but Mulliner positioned himself between them. He gestured to two of the soldiers and sent them to untie Oleander.

"I have made many mistakes," Torsten said to Mulliner. "I should have been closer with you, with all of our Order. Then perhaps you all would see Redstar for what he truly is and not the savior he claims to be."

"Watch your hand, knave!" Oleander yelped and kicked one of the soldiers in the face.

Torsten smirked. He knew it wasn't the time, but he couldn't help himself. He was so used to being on the receiving end of her barbs, it was nice to hear someone else facing them.

"You dare laugh at a time like this?" Mulliner said.

"All my mistakes, but my loyalty to the Crown has never been in question. I would die for any Nothhelm, and that means now too. So, you have two options, Sir Mulliner. Try to kill me and fail, or watch me and the Queen walk away."

"Must everything you do be so dramatic?" Queen Oleander said as a soldier helped her down. She shook him away without even a 'thank you,' and strode across the room to the bed, taking no care to cover herself. The entire room went silent. She picked a dark blue dress off the bed and began dressing. That was when Torsten noticed one of her handmaidens lying over the side of the bed with her throat slit.

One of the soldiers went to help her with her dress, but she slapped his hand. "Don't dare touch me," she snapped. She got it on without tying the back, then yanked the blankets out from under the body of her handmaiden. The poor girl's corpse rolled off and thudded against the floor.

"You will stand down, and Torsten and I will walk out of here together as he said," Oleander said, using the blankets to wipe the paint off her face. "There are no options."

Mulliner didn't lower his weapon, but his hand started to shake. "We were ordered by the King to follow only the Prime Minister. Not you."

"And after I rip out my brother's tongue, where would you like me to hang you for treason? I hear the sun is warm on the south side of the wall."

"Your Grace, I..."

"Unless your next words are an apology, I suggest you keep your mouth shut! Now, Torsten, dear, come and help me tie my dress."

"Yes, Your Grace." Torsten backed away slowly from Mulliner's blade until he was behind Oleander, then tied the back of her dress as he'd seen Tessa and her other unfortunate handmaidens do so many times before. Hers was an uneven history filled with sorrow and actions Iam would never approve of, but Torsten had never been more grateful for her hard hand and the fear she instilled in men.

Mulliner drew a deep breath. "Come, men, there's nothing here for us."

"But—" one of them began before being cut off.

"I said let's move. You, silence the bells." He turned to leave, but stopped in the doorway and glanced back at Torsten. All his resentment dripped away and gave way to sadness. "You killed my friend, and I can't ever forgive that."

"You don't have to," Torsten said.

"But any man who'd be willing to do that to his sister doesn't deserve the King's ear. I hope I'm wrong about you. Otherwise, I'll see you in Elsewhere."

"You're a good knight," Torsten said. "You all are. Uriah Davies made sure of that. I never deserved to wear the White, but now I go to make sure that Sir Nikserof can do so with honor. He's worthier than I ever was."

At that, Mulliner left Torsten and the Queen behind, standing before the bed on which she'd once tried to seduce him. He'd been nervous then, but not anymore.

"My Queen, where is your brother?" Torsten asked.

"I thought you'd never be rid of them." She straightened her dress and strode away from him. "He's already on his way to the summit with my son for the Dawning, along with that useless ingrate Wren who now has decided he'd rather hold hands with Redstar. Said he planned to show him the true reason why the sun goes out today."

"More tricks, Your Grace."

"It doesn't matter. When I see Redstar again, I'm going to kill him as my husband should have decades ago."

"No." Torsten took her hand, turning her toward him, and stared into her fierce, blue eyes. "No more blood on your hands. As the light of Iam fades upon the Dawning, Redstar's games end with it. By my sword."

XXVII

THE MYSTIC

Despite her best efforts, Sora let Kai down.

Hours passed as she looked within, searching her mind for the answer to healing him, but all she found was fire. She forced herself to remain calm for his sake. After those hours, after he'd finally fallen asleep, Sora collapsed to the stone floor.

Not being able to summon fire was frustrating, but watching the blood trickling off the table, beginning to pool next to her on the floor made her feel like more of a failure than ever before.

Early on, she'd torn a piece of her kimono and laid it over the wound so she could keep pressure on it. Her hands were covered in blood now and shaking. She whispered, conversing with herself in search of solutions. A few times she looked too far inward and wound up encircled by her fears, thanks again to the bar guai. Kai's face became Whitney's, begging her to help him, asking why she didn't care enough about him.

"Sora," someone said. "Sora."

"I've always cared!" she screamed. Her head shot up. She glanced side to side in a daze, not even realizing that at some point, she'd fallen asleep with her head against the leg of the table. Madam Jaya now stood beside her. Sora sprang to her feet.

"I see you haven't found your answer," Madam Jaya said.

"Please, you have to help him," Sora pled. She turned and went to grab Madam Jaya's arm, but her hands slipped through. Her knees hit the ground again. "He's lost a lot of blood."

"What a disappointment," another, deeper voice spoke. Aihara Na strode into the room, arms folded behind her back. "I thought you'd find the bar guai simple to master."

Madam Jaya bowed to her. "She is a quick study, Ancient One, but she has not had much time."

"Time enough for one so gifted as she."

"I'll work harder, Ancient One. I promise," Sora said, still on her knees. Her legs felt like sand. She'd been standing a long time, and even with her short break, it hadn't done much to return the feeling to her lower extremities. "Just please, heal him."

"It is not for lack of trying that you fail," Aihara Na said. "It is a lack of focus. You wanted to be here with us, but you are not here with us, not really. You are distracted. Your thoughts are... *elsewhere*."

The way she said the word made Sora wonder if she knew the deeper desires of her heart. That she wasn't just here to find a place she belonged and an answer to her powers but to free Whitney. To do the one thing their Order forbade.

"Please, just help him, then deal with me," Sora said.

"Ancient One, she found the word of fire in mere minutes after I explained how the bar guai works," Madam Jaya said, stepping between them. "If she is distracted, it is because I revealed too much, filled her mind with thoughts she didn't need."

"We will discuss your tactics later," Aihara Na said.

"It has been so many long years since I had a pupil and I... my mind has not been the same since... this." She motioned to her incorporeal body.

Aihara Na stopped and placed her hand upon Jaya's cheek. Her hand didn't pass through. "You have forgotten more than most will ever know. I do not blame you for this."

"You are too forgiving, Master." Madam Jaya backed away, bowing low. Aihara Na stepped forward. Sora had never realized how tall she was.

"Tell me, Sora of Troborough," Aihara Na said. "In all your years practicing blood magic, have you ever managed to heal yourself of even the slightest injury?"

"Never," Sora said, her voice shaky. "Wetzel told me never to try, that it was too dangerous."

"It is indeed. It is the key to possession for a blood mage. To draw on the power of Elsewhere to use it on oneself. It is an ability few but the most powerful can accomplish without drawing too deeply and leaving themselves vulnerable to Elsewhere's darker side."

"Then I won't ever try! Just help him." Sora lifted her head, her eyes bleary from lack of sleep and budding tears. She saw Kai's hand hanging from the table, slack.

"With the bar guai, self-healing is difficult, but not impossible. The power and focus required will drain the makros faster than any other spell. To do so as a mystic, without sacrificing too much of oneself, is an ability few have accomplished, a power few have been found able to wield. It is that singular focus on oneself, in applied power and mind, that over-whelms even masters of channeling. Back when I was more than a shade in this world, even I could mend little more than a scratch on my own being."

"Why are you telling me this.?"

"Because if you are as gifted as the Well of Wisdom promises you are, then healing should be your greatest strength. Training a mystic apprentice to gain a full understanding of their abilities is a slow, tedious process. Each of our connections to Elsewhere is unique. We are all born with natural affinities for different spells and elements. It can take years to uncover." Aihara Na grabbed Sora by the arm, now physical, and hauled her to her feet. "But sometimes, the best means of instruction is a push."

Sora's eyes darted nervously between Madams Aihara and Jaya. Upon those words, even Jaya's features darkened with fear.

"Ancient One, she is not re—"

Aihara Na took Sora's arm. Then, from the folds of her robes, Aihara Na produced Sora's own knife and slashed her wrist vertically. Sora had cut herself countless times, but never so deep, and never upward. That was one of Wetzel's first warnings.

Blood drooled onto the stone floor in puddles and Sora fell to all fours. She was too shocked to feel pain, but it had been mere seconds, and she'd never seen so much of her own blood. She could hear Elsewhere begging her to its waiting bosom; for her to give in, let the power overtake her.

It came in the form of Nesilia whispering her name now. But with the bar guai buried in her chest, she found she couldn't access the power through her blood as she once had. Every time her mind surrendered to Elsewhere, her chest stung and threw her back into focus.

"Fight the urge, Sora," Aihara Na said. "Don't allow your baser instincts to grab hold. Do not call upon your sacrifice, use the bar guai. Call upon the gods who built this world. Who built you. Call upon the mystics of old who sacrificed themselves so you may rise."

"I… I can't…" Sora whimpered.

"Yes, you can," Madam Jaya said. "It is your destiny."

"I can't!" Sora was on the ground now, eyes clenched shut. The shock waned, and the pain began to take hold. Her arm felt like burning flames. "I can't!"

"Do not be weak," Aihara Na said. "Do not be fractured. Focus on who you are. Too much longer and you will die. Unlike the servant, your wound is fatal."

Sora could feel her heart beating faster, and as it pumped, more blood gushed from the wound. She drew a few long, steady breaths and remembered how she'd learned to use fire.

Calm, she told herself. *You must stay calm. Calm for Whitney.*

She ignored the urging of Elsewhere that was so present yet impossible to access. The wound burned. She thought she felt bubbles roiling around it. Whether it was blistering skin or her blood boiling from Elsewhere's fires, she didn't know, but she kept digging.

The inferno in her mind dwindled, and through it, water began to cascade, gurgling as it gushed over rocks and around bends. She saw the small homes of Troborough—the Julset twins, the Whelforks, Wetzel's shack. And she realized she stood in the narrow river running behind it. Her old caretaker was in the river with her, washing her messy hair. Only, she couldn't have been more than three or four.

She remembered that day, so long ago, like a memory grasping at the threads of her mind. Her refugee caravan had finally let her off into the arms of an old man. She was so grimy from the long trip, Wetzel dragged her right out to the river, and as he scrubbed her, a young boy strolled by, tossing a rock into the air again and again. He stopped when he saw her.

"What's wrong with your ears?" he'd asked, gawking. Then Wetzel shooed him, both hands flailing in the air like the town kook he was.

"Shellnak," Sora said the name of Troborough's puny river. She felt a rush of power again, starting in her chest. Her eyes opened, and another of the runes in the bar guai started to glow. "Aquira-Shellnak." She chanted again, the rune of fire illuminating as well.

The whole of her body tingled then grew numb as she focused on the wound. The pain became unbearable, causing her to scream. It radiated to her chest, then pulsed, and as she fought to stay conscious, she felt the blood rushing to her gashed limb.

She squinted at it through the sweat coating her brow. Her arm and hand trembled, but the deep gash began to close. It went from a blanket of blood to sinew, to her skin threading back together as if made from strands of yarn on a loom. She embraced the pain until the flesh sealed, then released a mouthful of air. All that remained on her arm was quickly drying blood.

"I did it?" she whispered. A laugh snuck through her lips without her intending to do so. "I did it."

"Well done, Sora," Madam Jaya said, smiling.

"As I said, sometimes all it takes is a push," Aihara Na said. She extended a hand to help Sora to her feet, but Sora didn't take it.

Unlike summoning fire through the bar guai, healing herself left her so weak she felt like she'd just run from Troborough to Yarrington and back again. But she didn't care. She scrambled to her feet, ran through Madam Aihara, and to Kai's side.

She placed her hands over his wound and began incanting, focusing her mind on that key memory of water, on the feeling it brought her. Kai's injury started sealing just as hers had. It was nearly halfway closed when her legs wobbled, and she grasped the table to stay upright. The pain in her own chest grew so intense she stopped trying to breathe. Only after Kai's wound closed did she stagger back, dizzy.

She tried to say something to her masters, but her words came out in a garbled mess of languages. She caught the table for balance, then her hand slipped, slick with hers and Kai's blood. Kai sprung awake and tried to catch her, but was too late. She hit the ground hard, skull slamming against the floor.

XXVIII

THE THIEF

After Kazimir revealed to Whitney why he was really sticking around, Whitney returned to the Fierstown farm as promised. Never in his life had he thought mundane work would be exactly what he needed to keep him from doing something stupid. But focusing on the bugs biting him, or the sweat, or how tedious it was, it helped him ignore the misery of his situation. Helped the days go by while he waited for night to come so he could seek a way through his personal Elsewhere's barrier without prying eyes.

The spring harvest came and went, but there was never downtime as a farmhand. Pigs and cows needed constant attention, and the moment he finished fixing the roof of his childhood home, something else broke that required the hands of someone who could stand since Rocco couldn't.

Days turned to weeks. Whitney tried his best to keep quiet and disturb nothing. All he had to do was bite his lip around his father to avoid his basic instinct to battle with him. Perhaps it was his injuries, but the man was far more docile then Whitney remembered.

Weeks turned to months. Lauryn kept Whitney well-fed. Rocco ensured that payment was timely, and they even gave Whitney a raise when the fall harvest hit. Even though he couldn't leave Troborough, the people there still took autlas. The cost of a drink at the Twilight Manor was torturous—a week's pay alone, far more than in real Troborough—but it helped remind Whitney this wasn't the real Troborough.

In his off-hours, Whitney and Rocco constructed a wheeling chair to keep Rocco from complaining so much. Occasionally, Whitney would roll him down, and Rocco's condition earned a few free rounds, which made hearing his stories about what Troborough was like a decade ago tolerable.

Whitney even heard a few he'd never had before or had never paid attention to, like when conscript officers for the Panping War passed through. Rocco wanted to go off on an adventure like never before and serve his kingdom, but Whitney was born only days before, so Rocco stayed for him.

Whitney couldn't imagine his unworldly father ever wanting to set foot in a place that wasn't Troborough, but this version of him seemed to long for adventure. It was like losing his legs showed him everything he'd missed out on.

Sometimes Kazimir was around, quietly watching from the corner. He'd taken up residence in an apartment above the Twilight Manor. Mostly, Kazimir kept to himself, locked in his room, doing gods know what. From time to time the upyr helped on the farm, and since he had less need for autlas, because he didn't eat or drink, Whitney got the bonus. Maybe he hadn't needed food to survive, but Whitney had found eating to be a tough addiction to break and a soothing one. Though he did discover that he couldn't get drunk, not even a smidge.

Winter came and went.

It was a brutal one, and it battered the farm, which meant more repairs. The cold was worse than any Whitney had known before, and Rocco couldn't handle it. He passed away from his injuries around the time when the Dawning should have occurred but didn't, and they buried him in the cemetery behind the broken-down church.

Whitney couldn't say how he felt about watching Fake Torsten lay his father down, but even stranger was the fact that Whitney attended. He'd known this shattered version of his father for a few months, even shared a few laughs, and it seemed right considering he was part of the reason his back wound up broken. Lauryn wept, holding Young Whitney in her arms as he did the same. Although his father's condition and subsequent death was Young Whitney's fault, Lauryn's buried resentment toward the boy waned now that he'd became the only family she had.

Whitney was sure as shog his real mother never would have done that. In real life, a burned down barn made her regard him like a monster. Here, she hugged Young Whitney every time he came home, whispered to him that it wasn't his fault every time Rocco was brought up. She even allowed Sora over for supper almost nightly, treating her like a daughter.

Whitney took his useless food to the barn those nights. He knew being around Sora wouldn't be wise. It was easiest that way. Every time this Troborough got too strange for him, he just held his tongue and went to sleep. Sometimes Kazimir was there, and even if they didn't talk, it was comforting having someone around who knew he didn't belong. It helped him remember what he was waiting for.

Months turned to years, and Whitney never stopped hoping for Sora to find a way to reverse what had happened. He'd learned more about farming than he ever wanted to, and construction too. Things grew too somber around the Fierstown home with Rocco gone, having to hear his mother cry from time to time. Young Whitney stopped sticking around to help around the house during the day, barely showed up for dinner, and when he did, it sounded like Sora had forced him. When he misbehaved, Lauryn forced herself not to be mad, Big Whitney could see it in her eyes. And he got into trouble often, more so than even Whitney could remember doing as a child. Everyone else had, but Whitney's doppelgänger didn't seem to change in the slightest. Even Big Whitney now boasted a pathetic, patchy beard so nobody would notice how alike he and Lauryn's son were. Not that anybody in Elsewhere seemed to notice that sort of thing.

And it was one unspectacular night after Young Whitney promised to have supper with his mom and failed to show up, sending her to tears, that Whitney found himself at the Twilight Manor. He offered to stick around for supper, but she'd asked to be left alone.

"What's the difference between a Westvale whore and a dwarf?" Whitney asked, clothes still stained from a day's work at the Fierstown farm. "One's short, fat, and has a beard. The other lives in the tunnels of the Dragon's Tail."

Hamm, the owner of the place, and all the other men burst into laughter. Whitney joined them, and it was only when the laughter died down that his heart sunk as it sometimes did over the last six years in Elsewhere. It wasn't that Whitney hated being in this Troborough as much as he hated how comfortable he was becoming in this Troborough. His life had been many things, but never before had it been… well… plain. Boring. Like he was any average serf in the Glass Kingdom

A bard by the name of Fabian "Feel Good" Saravia plucked his lute, singing a song about a grimuar. Whitney had never seen the hawk-face beasts in the Pikeback Mountains near Glinthaven. In fact, if he'd not been seated at a tavern in Elsewhere, he'd likely still think them myth, but now, nothing was unbelievable to him.

"My Lord," the barmaiden Alless said, placing another flagon of ale down in front of Whitney.

Whitney's face lit up. Who'd have thought it would take going back in time to the one place he hated more any anywhere else to finally be called 'my Lord?' Sure, his letters patent were gone, and no one but Torsten and Sora remembered him ever becoming Whitney Blisslayer, but that didn't stop him from enjoying the attention.

"Thanks, Alless. Looking good tonight," he said with a wink. Her cheeks turned pink. She dressed modestly, and her strawberry blonde hair was worn long and braided into two pigtails. He'd forgotten how pretty she was back in the day.

"Sure, you don't wanna sit for a spell?" Whitney said.

She looked over her shoulder. "Hamm wouldn't take kindly to that. Lots of folks in here tonight, and all of them looking to be served."

"Chair's always open…" Just as he said it, a lumbering oaf from the north side of town plopped down in it. "Till it's not," Whitney laughed.

She giggled. "I'll have a break soon. I'll find you." She curtsied, then walked away to keep working.

She's old enough to be your mother, Whitney reminded himself. *Oh, and she isn't real.*

There were more than a few times Whitney had considered abandoning his nightly searches, leaving his bed unused, and staying in hers. He'd have to close his eyes and tell himself 'path of least resistance.' Laying with an apparition was the definition of resistance.

"Eyes to yourself, Willis," Hamm said.

"Have you considered some male help then?" Whitney remarked. "An old man. I'm talking saggy and gray."

"I'll think on it." Hamm chuckled. He served someone else while cleaning a mug and continuing the conversation. He was a damn good barkeep in his prime. If Troborough could boast anything, it was that. Best Whitney had ever known save for Tum Tum…

The spell of longing hit Whitney harder this time.

"What's wrong, friend?" Hamm asked. "You look like you've seen a ghost."

"Nothing, I… I'm just tired," he said.

"Old lady Fierstown working you to the bone, is she?"

"That's a word for it."

"It isn't easy work making an honest living, I'll tell you that." Hamm placed his hand on Whitney's shoulder, and Whitney didn't have a chance to respond before the man laughed at the joke building inside his own head. "But that's what taverns are for!"

"Here, here!" a few men down the bar slammed their tankards. The bard took it as recognition for the finishing of a song and began to play louder.

"Truer words never were spoken," Whitney said.

"I'll tell ya, I would have run after Rocco passed, but it's a damn good thing you're doing there," Hamm went on. "Can't tell you how many times I caught that Young Whitney trying to steal from my stores. I don't know how you deal with that little menace."

Whitney wondered if that was how Hamm had viewed him back in the day before saying, "Mostly, I don't see him. Especially after Rocco died. He's got that dirty look plastered on his face every time we run into each other, then he rushes by." All of that was true. Whitney had no love for Troborough, but he never remembered being so angry growing up.

"Well, a boy needs a man around he can respect if he doesn't want to grow up rotten," Hamm said. "And a woman like Lauryn needs a ma…"

Whitney choked on his next sip of ale. "Wait, you don't think…"

"Hey, I ain't one to judge. Rocco's been dead for five years now, and a man from noble stock like you is still around."

Whitney had to cover his mouth to keep from vomiting. "It's nothing like that you horny codger. She just makes a mean pie."

"Damn right she does! Well if you aren't... you wouldn't mind if I asked her to..."

"Please don't finish," Whitney blurted. "But yeah, fine. I'm not her father, why would I care?" The strangeness of this words didn't hit him until after he'd said them. Still, the way Hamm's eyes lit up when he heard Lauryn was available made Whitney feel a bit better. Still disgusted, but this version of his mother deserved some bit of happiness.

Whitney scanned the room. After continually trying to sneak into the Twilight Manor as a young boy, it never stopped being strange to him, drinking side-by-side with the men he'd had thought so old all those years ago. He liked it.

As a child, he never got to hear from all the townsman who'd fought in Liam's wars, who'd had great adventures and then settled down. They weren't all like Rocco who was born on his farm and never left until the day he died. And traders passed through town, even here. Men from Brekliodad and Glinthaven, everywhere. As a child, they'd ignored him, so he'd pick their pockets for trinkets. Now, they'd share grand tales of Pantego, then ride off the next morning along a road Whitney still couldn't travel.

For once, he'd mostly sit back and listen. He couldn't tell any of his stories because they were all in the future—and on a completely different plane. If Lauryn found out he wasn't really a nobleman looking for a simpler life, but a world-renowned thief, he might lose his cushy gig while waiting for Sora.

An odd something in the dark corner of the dining hall tore him from his thoughts. Crouching at the side of the bar, out of the sight of Hamm and the others, was a young Panpingese girl—only the truth was, she wasn't so young anymore. Over the course of time Whitney had been stuck in Troborough, she'd blossomed into quite the young lady, and Whitney couldn't imagine how foolish he'd been to leave her behind. Growing up every day with her, he'd probably never realized how stunning she was until that fateful day they were reunited.

Presently, he had little relationship with her. From time to time he'd stroll by Wetzel's shack to remind himself of the hope he had for her older version, but talking with her was too complicated, and Elsewhere never let him get close enough to peek inside regardless.

The Sora he knew had always told him of the nights she'd snuck into the Manor to hear the bards play, but he'd assumed she'd been telling tall tales in an attempt to one-up him. They did that sort of thing. Yet there she was, crouching, hidden from all view, a big smile plastered on her face. Upon noticing Whitney eyeballing her, she winced, then retreated into the shadows, but not before placing a finger over her lips in hopes of convincing him not to rat her out.

All these years and she was the one who'd accomplished something he'd never been able to. He couldn't help wonder how she'd gotten in unseen, or why she'd never showed his younger self the way.

He stood, his chair scraping the wood floor. He took a few steps before remembering his ale. Even though it did nothing to make him dizzy and forgetful in this place, it always served to buoy his heart.

"Heading off?" Hamm asked.

"Got to take a piss," he said.

He headed out back to take care of his business, but more so with the intention of looking around the building for where Sora might have gotten in. It was brisk, the late autumn air biting at his cheeks, which meant every window was locked.

"How in Iam's name does she do it?" he asked himself

Hamm guarded the place like a damn golem. He made sure that if anyone was sleeping upstairs, or sleeping with someone sleeping upstairs, they were paying him autlas. He knew every face that entered the hall and expected them all to be drinking or eating if they were taking up space.

"You lost?" The sound of Alless' voice simultaneously startled and excited Whitney.

He turned, and with his back against the wall, said, "No, just getting some fresh air."

She drew herself so close to him their hips were touching. "Fresh air is overrated. It's finally breaktime if you…"

She didn't finish the sentence, but let her fingers finish the implication, crawling up his chest. She leaned in to kiss him, but he ducked under her so that now she was against the wall.

"What's the matter?" she said, smirking, not backing down. "All talk? You do find me… attractive, don't you? Unless it's always someone behind me you're staring at,"

"More than you could possibly…" His voice cracked. He cleared his throat and said, "imagine."

She sauntered toward him again. "Then what's the problem, farmboy?"

Other than how much he hated being called farmboy, that was a great question. It was one he asked himself nightly, and one he figured he'd be asking himself for years to come. The gorgeous barmaid in his hometown that all the young men, including Whitney, only dreamed about growing up. He always told himself that it was because she wasn't the real Alless, but after so long, she was as real as any of the others.

"It's just—"

"You ain't a boy lover, are you?" she interrupted.

"Gods no! I just… I had a lot to drink, and I wouldn't want to take advantage of you."

She smiled. "I didn't have anything to drink. You sure it's me who'd be taken advantage of?"

"You're right," Whitney said, now smiling as well. "What kind of lady are you?"

"A bored one." She wrapped both arms around his neck and pulled herself in close. He could feel the warmth of her breath, real as anything else. "Always the same men asking me out around here since I was a girl. And the traders just want to move on. Why does the man I desire constantly refuse me?"

Whitney slipped her grasp before his heart beat any faster, making sure not to spill his drink, and started off toward the town center. "I'm just waiting for the right time."

She bit her lip in frustration. "Well, I won't be waiting around here forever!"

I will, he thought, then cursed himself for letting it pop into his head. He didn't want to hurt the girl's feelings, real or not, but she just wasn't… Sora. Just as he thought of her, her younger version crept across the darkness ahead, back to Wetzel's shack after her time skulking around the Twilight Manor.

Whitney stopped. "It's been six years, Whitney," he said to himself. "Even if she hasn't forgotten you, she's probably married by now, has kids."

He turned back to the Twilight Manor. Alless remained leaning against the wall, looking as disappointed as every night when Whitney dodged her and promised a future romantic gesture that never came.

"Why do you continue to deny yourself?" Kazimir asked.

Whitney looked toward the origin of the voice and saw the upyr, sitting on the edge of the well in the center of the square, gazing up toward the sky. The sound of the bard's playing echoed soothingly on the air. The ruins of Iam's chapel loomed behind him where Father Fake-Torsten sat, legs folded before a non-existent altar.

"Stupidity probably," Whitney said.

Kazimir cracked a smirk, and Whitney sat beside him. He took a sip of his ale before offering it to Kazimir. In all their time in Troborough, Whitney had never seen Kazimir eat or drink anything save for the bite of duck he'd been force-fed on the night of their arrival. Whitney had also never seen someone so content to simply sit and enjoy the air.

"So, you'll continue your nightly search instead?" Kazimir asked, ignoring the ale.

"It's the best way to keep out of trouble. Good for both of us, no?

"It is. And I'll continue to tell you that you won't be sneaking out of here."

"Kazimir, my friend." He patted him on the back. "If I had a gold autla for every time I've been told that, I'd be rich."

If anyone would have told Whitney six years ago that he'd be sitting in Troborough with the upyr who'd tried to kill him and Sora in Winde Port —or that'd he'd be calling him 'friend'—Whitney would have laughed. Of course, Winde Port seemed a lifetime ago.

They went quiet for a short while as Fabian, the bard, finished up a song.

"You know how many times I've escaped from the Yarrington dungeons?" Whitney said, finally. "There was this one time, some dirty, old man named Reese—"

"I've heard it," Kazimir replied. "Save your breath."

"Yeah, well, that was easy. Another time, these giants in the Pikebacks held me—"

Kazimir shot him a sidelong glare that he knew meant he'd heard it.

Whitney pursed his lips. He'd been a drifter for so long that he'd never been around someone enough for them to have heard all his stories.

Whitney took a sip of his ale. "When did you decide to be happy here?" he asked.

"I'm not happy here," Kazimir replied. "But I am here still, and I must accept my fate, as you must."

"Hey, I accept it," Whitney said.

"Your map says otherwise."

"Well, I need something to do besides farm, and you convinced me to play the good guy."

"Is company not enough?" He nodded toward Alless, who'd already headed back inside from her break, shoulders sagging in disappointment. Whitney didn't have a good answer. Six years ago, he probably would have snapped and started a fight with the upyr, but he'd gotten better at not irritating the extremely easy to irritate and only other person in Troborough who knew his plight.

"Six years," Whitney sighed. "Did you imagine you'd be here this long?"

Kazimir looked back to the sky. "Six years for a man who has lived hundreds is like the blink of an eye. The Sanguine Lords will punish me for my failings as they see fit."

"How old are you, anyway?"

"Old enough to have tasted the blood of the first mystics in their fallen Order."

Whitney chuckled. "One day you'll give a real number."

"You misunderstand. I can't. Calendars changed, kingdoms fell—eventually, I stopped keeping count. You will too after enough time here."

Whitney opened his mouth to respond, stopped, then exhaled through his teeth. "It already feels like forever."

"Until it isn't. I've been in this realm many times as you know, and this visit has by far been the most pleasant. For that, you have my thanks. Most times, I spend relative years dodging the wianu. It's been nice being away from the chaos. To stand out in the sun, false as it may be. It's been nice not having to… feed."

It was the first time Kazimir had spoken about that particular affliction since they'd arrived, but Whitney had taken notice. The more time passed, the calmer Kazimir seemed. Whitney still felt things like the need to eat and drink—not hunger or thirst, but the compulsion. Not Kazimir. Whitney wondered what it would be like for all basic instinct to disappear enough to turn a monster willing to murder and drain a man like Tayvada into a stargazer.

"Well, I'm glad my exile is your vacation," Whitney said.

Seeing pangs of regret ripple across Kazimir's face never got normal. "That's not what I meant. Dakel un Ghastrin lives out there, stuck between worlds as all the wianu are, lusting for me as I lusted for your friend, Sora."

"There's more than one?" Whitney asked.

"Many more."

"Then how do you know your squid monster is the same every time?"

"Oh, he's the same," Kazimir assured Whitney. "He knows me, and I, him. Each upyr has one. Just one who will hunt us until the day one of us is destroyed. He knows as well as I do that in this life, its either him or me."

"But you're already dead."

"Not dead. Not alive."

Whitney waved his hands in the air and said, "Wooooooo," like he'd seen a ghost, then reached for his ale.

"Make jokes if you will." Kazimir's face betrayed his grave tone. Whitney had always said he was like a fine wine, and the more time together, the more the upyr seemed to appreciate his jokes.

"Okay, fine," Whitney said. "So are you finally going to tell me why this thing gives a hot shog about you? Why are you so special?"

"I'm not special," Kazimir said. "But my power belongs to him. At least that's what he would say if the vile thing could speak. I devoured a piece of him."

Whitney's cheeks went white. "I hate squid."

"It was that or die," Kazimir said, resignedly. "I was young, in love. I refused to leave Pantego until I was ready. Now I can't even remember her face."

"Listen to you, Kazzy in love." Whitney nudged him playfully and earned a glower. The upyr hadn't changed too much, and he hated when Whitney used that nickname.

"Tread carefully."

"Fine, fine. But do you really expect me to feel bad?"

"I expect nothing."

"Well, at least you've got hundreds of years out of it, powers I can't dream of. I'm stuck here forever, according to you, and I'll never see the woman I… I grew up with." Whitney nearly allowed frustration get the better of him, but he took a moment to gather himself. "The truth is, I'm happy you're stuck here. I hope you never get out of Elsewhere to fulfill your dream of drinking Sora's blood."

"Then I will make you a deal." Kazimir stood. He still wore a knife, even though he didn't need it. Whitney winced when Kazimir drew the blade, then the upyr dragged it across his palm and extended the blade to Whitney. "When I return to Pantego with the blessing of my Lords, I will not hunt your friend. And I will indulge in her blood only if she offers it freely."

"No offering," Whitney said. "No blood."

"Don't push me, thief. Should my hunger return, I doubt I could resist. But the blood pact is a sacred oath, more binding than gold or silver. Failing one is the reason I am here, and I do not intend to return soon."

Whitney took the knife, sticking his tongue out as he wiped the blade. "What happens after?"

"You trust me, as Darkings did."

"*You.* An upyr. You're growing on me, but I'm not sure I'm there yet. Here is one thing, but back home?"

"You gave me six years of sunlight and peaceful dreams when you could have turned this place into madness incarnate. You pulled me out of the water when you could have left me for Dakel."

"Six years!" Whitney threw his arms into the air. "Six years I've been waiting for a thank you. Man, was that worth it. Sora, you can let me out now!" he shouted to the sky.

Kazimir wasn't amused. "It is my only offer, thief."

"Ah, screw it." Whitney drew the faintest line of red in the center of his hand. "I've always wondered what it felt like for her anyway." He clasped Kazimir's hand and felt nothing. He wasn't sure why he was expecting some rush of energy.

"That's it?" Whitney asked. "No sacred words or prayers? Torsten had a million."

"The blood says all."

"Well, speaking of wastes of time. I'm going to go see to my map before I do something stupid and ruin your good time." He downed his ale and tossed it into the well, listening as it clanged off the walls then splashed. "Perhaps tonight's the night I get out."

Kazimir nodded to him, then returned to staring up at the night sky. "Perhaps indeed."

"Fare thee well, fair upyr," Whitney hollered. "I hope I never see you again!" He bowed, spun on his heels, and headed down the road. Pillars of smoke rose from all the chimneys in the peaceful little town.

"Goodnight, Father Torsten!" Whitney called out as he passed by the ruined church. The out-of-place priest didn't even acknowledge him.

He said hello to a few more townsfolk on his way home. They were people whose names he'd never even bothered to learn growing up, but now he knew every soul in Troborough. He knew how long they'd been there. Hell, he knew what most of them had in their homes as he'd been invited into plenty. Nothing worth stealing, that was for sure.

He paused by the gate into the Fierstown farm. Lauryn was out front, hanging up some clothes to dry. He wasn't sure why Rocco was always so rude about her weight. Sure, she wasn't a beauty like the Queen of Glass, but she would make this Hamm a lucky man if he ever grew the courage to ask her out.

She acknowledged him, and he her, then he continued on. Around the back of their land stood the small cottage he'd built for himself shortly after Rocco died, when things got too somber for his taste. Lauryn crying, Young Whitney making things worse—Whitney couldn't concentrate on his nighttime activities without quiet.

The cottage was shoddy, slightly crooked, with gaps between every plank. The roof was perfectly set—he'd had plenty of practice—but that was about it. Still, as he opened the creaky door, there was no denying it was one of his favorite possessions he'd ever had, honest or stolen.

The table wilted to one side. He owned only a single chair, and while most of the home was hand-built, he'd admittedly bought it from Lauryn.

After the stress of helping construct Rocco's wheeling chair, he was done with chairs. The whole place was one room, though, he never had guests.

"All right, where should we check tonight?" he asked himself as if anyone was listening. He lit a candle, then looked at his pantry which was mysteriously unlocked. He nudged open the doors with his foot. He never kept any food inside, only his map which wasn't there.

"What the…" He placed the candle down and scoured the tiny compartment, looking under shelves. "No…no…no…" He even lifted the loose floorboard he hadn't bothered fixing. "No, don't do this!"

His map was gone.

XXIX

THE MYSTIC

Fading into sleep and waking in a new place was becoming a feeling all too common to Sora. She lay upon something soft and could feel Aquira breathing softly on her lap, her warm body making Sora sweat. Sora guessed she was in her quarters. Her eyelids protested movement, so she stared at their insides, a soft pink glow shining through and no shadows of movement. She was alone.

She'd dreamed of Whitney, of the voice she'd heard in Elsewhere twice now, and was more convinced than ever that he was alive and lost in that realm. She remembered the desperation in his voice, calling out to her. He would have to hold tight until she figured out how to access Elsewhere without sacrificing some poor orphan child.

Stirring slightly, she stopped as she heard two others outside her door speaking in hushed tones. She couldn't see them, but she'd begun to notice a chilling sensation whenever the spectral mystics were around. And despite Aquira's warmth, her feet were cold.

Sora focused on listening to them even though her head was foggy. "She's not ready," the voice said, unmistakably Madam Aihara Na.

"She summoned fire in a day without blood," Madam Jaya replied. "Healed a fatal wound in herself. Nobody has done that so quickly since—"

"I'm aware. She also couldn't help herself from healing Kai while weakened, when he was in no danger of dying. She could have killed herself, just like..."

"But she didn't. You always say that time is short, that the age of the Glass is coming to an end. We can't rebuild our Order in this state, you know that. We are too weak to instruct through example; our bodies too close to leaving this plane for good."

"Patience, dear Jaya. You preach it to her, and forget it yourself."

"You are wise as always Master, but excuse me for saying this: I think your fading essence has made you blind to see the risks if we are not honest with her. She's headstrong, impetuous. She's already seen and done too much, more than ever we thought she would when she was sent to hiding."

"She asks too many questions, just like someone else I knew."

"And if we hold back, we risk driving her away. Not in my lifetime has there been one so strong in her bond with Elsewhere. She should understand why she is here, who she is—should have the same knowledge as the rest of us."

"You know the risks of showing her the truth. In her past lies clarity, but also the knowledge to open Elsewhere, in which she's displayed far too much curiosity. She's still too considerate. Too stuck on the foolish idea that she can save everyone, and I can see it in her heart, that extends to those who are lost."

"But Ancient One—"

"Enough," Aihara Na said sternly. "We cannot risk a breaching of our realm. Not when there are those so desperate to break free. You heard who Sora saw within, and she is not strong enough to withstand it."

"Then perhaps just something. Not the full truth, but at least who her mother was."

"I will meditate on it, Jaya. For now, continue training her with the bar guai once she is rested. Only when she masters the basic elemental magic held within the runes will I consider showing her the true breadth of her ability."

"Yes, Ancient one."

There were no retreating footsteps, but Sora took the silence to mean that they were gone. It took all her willpower to stay quiet when they mentioned her mother. All of a sudden, everything that had come to pass since she and Whitney left Yarrington felt worth it. She'd wanted to travel to Yaolin City to figure out who she was, and apparently, the real answers were far below her in the Well of Wisdom. And not just that, but the secrets to opening Elsewhere.

All she had to do was stay quiet and train with her new masters until they thought she was ready—masters who'd lived for centuries and grown indifferent to human emotion. It could be years; years of Whitney lost in Elsewhere with Kazimir until he went insane or the upyr killed him, if that was even possible there. The Whitney she knew couldn't very well avoid either for too long.

"Aquira," Sora whispered. "Aquira, wake up."

The wyvern's yellow eyes peeled open from beneath her two sets of eyelids, and she hopped across Sora's chest to lick her face.

"I'm fine, girl," Sora said. She sat up. Moving her head made her woozy. She reached up and didn't feel a bandage, but it was clear she'd hit her head hard. Either her masters couldn't mend the pain within her rattled skull, or they chose to leave it as a reminder of how impulsive Sora had been.

And if they were going to hold back from her, it was time she proved them correct. It was what Whitney would do. If she was going to save him, it was time to do more than just think like him. She needed to start acting like him.

"Aquira, how would you feel about going on another adventure?" Sora asked.

The wyvern screeched.

"Yeah, I know, me too." She tossed the covers and slid her feet off the side of her bed. She had to take a moment to settle her head, then stood. She looked down, pleased that the intrusive mystics hadn't undressed her at the very least. She gathered her belt, and this time hooked her knife to it. Just in case.

Aquira swooped in front of her, landing on the dresser, then released a throaty clicking noise.

"Don't worry, girl. I'm not going to fight them," Sora said. "You heard them; they think I'm special, which means even if they catch me, they won't hurt me... I hope."

Aquira's head and tail drooped.

"I may fit in here, finally, but I have to take the risk. It's the least he deserves." She straightened her kimono and made sure her knife was secure. Her fingertips brushed the bar guai. Madam Jaya had been relatively kind to her and she hated to disappoint anyone. But she'd stood idly and watched after Aihara Na cut Sora's arm open and left her to bleed out, while Aihara Na pretended to sacrifice an orphan simply to make a point.

"Maybe I was meant to be more than some orphan blood mage," Sora said to Aquira. "But if it means becoming like her, maybe I don't want to."

She extended her arm for Aquira, then noticed the bumpy scar running up her wrist from where Aihara cut her. Evidently, she hadn't healed herself enough to get rid of it. Before Aquira hopped up to her shoulder, she decided she'd keep this scar and never feel self-conscious. This one wasn't like the others.

She stopped at the door and glanced up at her friend on her shoulder. "I'm glad you're still with me, Aquira," she said. "Tayvada would have been proud, no matter what they claim he wanted." She nestled her cheek against Aquira, and then they strode out into the hall.

Through the windows along the spiral stairs, she could see the colorful smoke settling over the lake from the all the fireworks during the week-long Festival of Ghosts. She had figured them magic, but now in the daylight, she realized that they came from boats sitting on the lake, shot out of strange tubes.

Not magic at all.

Above it all, she could see the pale silhouettes of Pantego's moons in the blue sky, inching closer toward covering the sun and reminding Sora of what this night meant in the Glass Kingdom. The Dawning. She'd forgotten that the Gyuan Jie ended at the same time. Forgotten entirely that the Dawning was coming, she'd so lost track of time.

"Ah, Miss Sora."

She whipped around, looking as guilty as one could possibly look even though she only descended stairs. A mystic she hadn't met—or rather whose face she hadn't yet seen from under drawn hoods—stood before her, his face dignified and eyes distant. He appeared far older than Madam Jaya, his cheeks pockmarked from age, and his hair a wispy tuft of gray on top of a pointed skull.

"My apologies for startling you," he said, bowing.

"That's all right, Master…"

"Huyshi," he said. "I am glad to see you are feeling better."

"I am, thank you." She lowered her foot to the next step, and he walked beside her. She kept a brisk pace that didn't appear to tire him in the slightest.

"Training is never easy, but I would not presume to know what you're going through. It is unique for you as it was for us all."

"Did they stab you?"

"I can't heal. Never could. Even with the bar guai," he pointed to her chest. "I went to drastic measures to try and learn, but it's not for all of us to play with matters of life and death."

He wiggled his sleeve, and out of the corner of her eye, Sora noticed his left arm ended at a stump above his bicep. She slowed. She'd been in such a rush she wasn't sure how she'd missed it.

"They did that to you?" she asked, incredulous.

"Gods no. I cut this limb to pieces trying to find the power, it got infected, and I had to go to a human physician in Yarrington—of all places—to have it properly amputated. Now, I keep it as a reminder that we are not invincible."

"Sometimes it doesn't feel like that."

"I understand that better than most." He stopped at a landing, and Sora found herself stopping with him. He didn't have a kind face, but he did his best to force an unnatural smile. "I didn't find this place and start training until I was sixty years old. It has been a century since, and I remain one of the weakest ever to sit upon the Council. But we are all that remains. Stay the course, Sora. Learn all you can."

He extended his only hand and lay it over Sora's bar guai. She found his presence so comforting that she didn't fight it, and Aquira didn't even growl. He closed his eyes and inhaled. "The gods' Gift is strong in you. I know it is difficult, but you will rule this place. You will help usher in a new age of mystics, and we old, soulless leeches will fade into the mist."

"You truly believe that?" Sora asked.

"The Well of Wisdom shows what has been and what might come to pass. The future is in constant motion, but we have seen great things for you. Great things."

"What if I don't want greatness?"

"Those who reach such heights rarely do." He opened his eyes. "For now, keep growing, learning. Madam Jaya awaits you in the training room. She taught me everything I know about the mystic arts. I resisted too hard because I looked twice her age, but you're in good hands. She has two of them at least." He smiled, then turned and strolled down the hallway onto whatever level of the tower they were on.

His words gave her pause. All her life, she'd felt like she never belonged, yet here, everyone seemed to have been waiting a lifetime for her to arrive. *Can I really just throw that all away?*

"I have to," she said, more to herself than Aquira. "For Whitney."

She continued down the stairs until she reached the common area. The servants were inside preparing supper. She noticed Kai among them, carrying a sack of flour to the back room, in perfect health.

She pressed on before he turned and noticed her watching. She passed by the training room. Madam Jaya sat legs folded in the center, meditating, looking as if she were floating within an all-white sea.

There were no guards to keep her from the glowing door of the Well of Wisdom at the bottom of the stairwell. She peeked around the corner and didn't spot any of the mystics either. They trusted her, or they trusted that their gate could not be breached.

"Okay Aquira, here we go," she said.

The wyvern screeched.

Sora stepped before the great stone doors, large enough to allow a giant passage if one of their kind could even become a mystic. "Aquira, watch the stairs and screech if you spy anyone," Sora said.

The wyvern chirped, then pushed off her shoulder and landed on the railing. She stared intently upward, never letting her sight waver.

Sora tried waving her hand at the door as she'd seen Aihara Na do. As expected, it failed. So, she pressed her palms against the cold stone, hoping to feel something. Nothing.

She looked within as Madam Jaya had taught her, found nothing still. She lay her ear against the surface and heard nothing.

She sighed. "There has to be a way." She started to pace in front of it, thinking about every word the mystics had spoken to her from the moment she met Aihara Na. She knew there had to be a hint somewhere. "Think, Sora. Think."

She ran through the events of the last few days in her mind over and over. Lord Bokeo was the gatekeeper, but that didn't seem to mean this gate, only introduction to the Secret Council itself. Still, she kept going back to him. Tayvada, Aquira, all the things that had been placed in her path to lead her here.

"*Tsu shensughu ywen zhun tahuet feng yaris tsu weyong ywen hou,*" she said aloud, her eyes going wide. Those were the first words she'd spoken in Panpingese during the vision Aihara Na gave her. "'The spirit of the gods is found in the one with the will of fire.'"

"Aquira," she spoke with vigor, finding that raging inferno within. At the same time, Aquira returned to her shoulder and stared into her eyes. It broke her concentration, and she was about to tell the wyvern to return to the stairs when she recognized the coincidence.

"Together?" she said. Aquira bobbed her frilly head. "Okay." She spoke the wyvern's name again, louder this time, and the rune in her chest began to glow. The flame danced up her arms, and she extended both palms to focus it into the center of the doors as a stream like liquid, molten lava. She could feel the sweltering heat against her face. Aquira growled, then blew fire into the same spot.

In her mind, she brought herself back to all those memories of fire, both of pain and triumph. She saw herself defeating Redstar, razing Winde Port to the ground, and in the midst of that, saving Torsten from Muski-go's wrath. She saw Troborough on fire, with her too late to save it or Wetzel. And she recalled how it led her back to Whitney.

She didn't just think about those moments, she traveled there. She could literally taste the ash on her tongue; feel it brushing against her shins, great gusts of wind blowing hot against her. And as she did, her chest stung, the pain excruciating. The rune in her bar guai she'd come to understand as fire, grew so bright, that between it and the dual streams of flame, she couldn't see anything when she opened her eyes.

Her legs quaked, but she didn't back down. The bar guai pricked deeper, like it was trying to find its way to her heart. The pain had her screaming, and there was no way the mystics and their servants wouldn't hear her.

The rune on the bar guai suddenly burst into pieces, and the blast sent her to her knees. She kept her arms outstretched, and the fire kept flowing. She wasn't sure how as it seemed that the fire rune was fractured. Once more she felt that familiar pull of Elsewhere. That haunting whisper.

If she was channeling from within, she wasn't sure. But she wouldn't risk it. She accepted the temptation of Elsewhere, keeping one hand raised to continue the blaze and with the other, she drew her knife. Slicing horizontally over her sole scar a few times, she found it no longer hurt her. It was almost pleasurable.

The fire burned brighter and hotter, turning blue now. Aquira's claws dug into her shoulder as her wyvern friend released more fire. Sora sliced her other arm to further fuel the blaze.

Sora could hear Nesilia whispering her name. And not only her, countless voices of Elsewhere mixed and blended, Whitney's among them. When she heard it, she roared, the act making her throat hurt.

Sora released one final blast.

Then there was silence.

Sora was on her hands and knees panting, blood dripping from her arms, surrounded by smoke. She was so exhausted her head felt like stone, but she fought to lift it. A hole had been burned through the thick door, crackling blue at the edges.

"We did it," she rasped, turning to Aquira. The wyvern blinked blearily, took one step, then tumbled off Sora's shoulder into her waiting hands. She was panting, smoke slipping through her flared nostrils.

"It's okay, girl," she whispered. "I've got you." She cradled her against her chest and crawled through the hole. Her muscles were so exhausted she couldn't stand even if she wanted to. Her chest still burned hot, and she noticed a stream of blood running between her breasts from the ruptured rune.

She ignored all the aches and kept crawling. The bubbling pool of blue liquid awaited her, steam rising to meet the stone ceiling. Apart from the preternatural coloring, it was so unassuming, like a natural spring, yet according to her masters contained all the knowledge she could ever want. Sora set Aquira down on the pool's edge.

"Sora, no!"

She glanced back and saw Madam Jaya at the base of the tower stairs.

She raised her hand as if to perform a spell, and Sora didn't wait to find out. She pulled herself into the pool headfirst and plunged. She expected to meet the bottom, but the water seemed to descend as deep as an ocean to the heart of the world.

She rolled over, waving with her arms to find the surface. The water was warm but not hot, refreshing. Her fresh wounds didn't sting, but red coalesced with the pristine, blue liquid into beautiful shapes.

She reached the top and gasped for air, and as she did, a rush of thoughts and feelings poured over her like an enormous wave in the Torrential Sea. Colors, shapes, sounds, light, everything all at once.

The shapes and colors began materializing into silhouettes and then full images. Trees, hills, mountains, the vast expanse of Pantego splayed out before her. She could see the harsh, cold lands of Brotlebir and Drav Cra. North even of there, she noted the land of Brekliodad from where the upyr Kazimir hailed. The Dragon's Tail Mountains intersected with the Pikeback like a great **T** upon the land.

Her vision shifted down past Glinthaven and south to the Jarein Gorge and the Walled Lake. She saw Yarrington and Troborough, Winde Port and Bridleton. It was all there, lain before her as if she were looking down upon a living map. As her view drifted across to the Panping Region, she saw a massive army gathered at the western walls of Yaolin City as well as a fleet amassed off the southern shores. The flotilla consisted of ships belonging to both the Glass Kingdom and the Black Sands as if they were allies.

In an instant, she stood amidst the men at the wall, soldiers of the Glass Kingdom. The sounds of them preparing for battle met her ears. Steel sharpening on whetstones, fires crackling while men sang songs of war.

Sora walked, feeling the grass beneath her feet. She'd had an experience like this before when she met Nesilia, but in that vision, she knew where she was—it was Elsewhere, no question. Now, she wasn't sure.

Did she see the past? Were these men huddled just beyond the walls of Yaolin prepared to take it by force?

Then she wondered if she saw the future, the Fourth Panping War, and the army preparing. She thought to look for Torsten, knowing that if she indeed saw the future, he would be there leading his men.

That was when the answer to her question came with certainty. From the slit in a grand tent strode a man no one alive would mistake. King Liam the Conqueror, with his sober expression and eyes a hue of hazel much like amber. His hair was black, the color of youth, long before sickness overtook him enough for Whitney to pluck the Glass Crown from his head. She couldn't help but notice how handsome he was, striking in his bright white and blue armor.

"Men!" he said. "Glory in the name of Holy Iam awaits! Today we prepare to finish that which my father and his father's father could not. But with the furthering of His kingdom in mind, we possess something neither of them had."

The men outside the tent grunted in agreement. They too wore white, and Sora noticed the one standing next to Liam, helmet tucked under his arm. A sinking feeling like she'd swallowed a rock hit her. Relief only came when her mind relaxed and made the distinction between Redstar posing as Uriah and this man, Uriah Davies, the Wearer of White himself.

It was uncanny. Redstar had impersonated Uriah so thoroughly, and if not for this version appearing younger, it would have been impossible to tell the difference.

Liam placed his hand on Uriah's shoulder.

"We attempted this peaceably, did we not?" he asked Uriah who nodded. "I hold no distaste for these fine people, but my mandate is clear. If the salvation of the people requires the blood of their masters, then blood shall run this day!"

Each of the men, who Sora assumed were Liam's highest generals in the King's Shield, roared.

Once they'd settled, he spoke softly. "We occupy and demand the seat of their council. If they attack first, we lay waste to their lands. Spare the women and children unless otherwise necessary. The mystics are tricksters in true form, and they will not hesitate to throw anything they can summon at us. But we are not Drav Cra savages."

His men nodded and grunted in agreement.

"Get some rest," Liam said. "Uriah, see to it that all preparations are complete. Tomorrow, we march."

Liam turned toward his tent, then stopped halfway. He stared up at the wall of the city in the distance where two women stood, their long robes flapping in the wind. They stared back. Sora couldn't make out who they were, but from their outfits, they appeared to be mystics. One wore the red of the Ancient One, the other yellow.

As Sora took a step to get a closer look, the world frayed to blackness all around her. Footsteps crashed like a thundering herd of zhulong. She panicked. Soldiers formed up, and she expected to be trampled, only they passed right through her, just as she had the mystics so many times before.

She spun. Balls of fire painted the sky orange, filling it with smoke. Bolts of lightning slashed the dirt, and massive vines broke through the earth to restrain Glass soldiers, knocking over even the Panpingese in the effort.

"Forward!" a man shouted. "Iam stands with us!"

"Torsten!" Sora exclaimed. She ran to him, but he didn't notice her. He thrust his sword into the air and raised his shield, painted with the Eye of Iam. He wasn't wearing Shieldsman armor, nor did he wear the white helm, since Uriah was still alive, but he did have on glaruium bracers. He must have been a Shieldsman in training during the siege of Yaolin City.

Soldiers rallied to him nonetheless and charged. A natural leader.

They were through the gates, engaging what remained of the Panping army after years of warfare. Another ball of fire came down, this one slamming into Torsten's shield and knocking him back, but Sir Uriah Davies was there to catch him and continue the charge.

The Glass army was massive, and Sora could see the fear in the Panpingese even as their mystic leaders flung spells of destruction at their enemies. There were Shieldsmen, dwarven and Shesaitju mercenaries, and others, Glintish men and women, skin like Torsten's, and even those from Brekliodad. Everything it took for Liam the Conqueror to vanquish these people of, what he considered, false gods.

Sora ducked out of reflex as Torsten swung at an enemy right over her head. That was when she noticed priests of Iam walking with them into the fray, somehow summoning shields of light to dispel mystic spells as they strolled forward, blind and clutching Eyes of Iam.

"Retreat!" the Panpingese yelled in their language. Their men looked overwhelmed with terror. They turned to flee down the streets of Yaolin when walking toward them came a mystic. They halted at the sight of her. Sora searched through them and felt her heart leap into her throat. It was

Aihara Na, flanked on either side by Madam Jaya and Huyshi, but she wasn't wearing red. Another legion of Panpingese soldiers stood behind her. Unlike Liam, Aihara Na didn't look a day younger. The only difference was that her stare wasn't so distant and hollow.

"Stand your ground cowards, or feel our wrath instead," Aihara Na said. She didn't shout, but her words carried on the air with authority. The men stopped, frightened as if trapped between two enemies, invaders and their beloved masters.

Aihara Na and the other mystics joined hands and began a chant. Sora saw the Red Tower standing tall over the rooftops behind them. The ground shook, then a tremendous wave rushed down the street. The water split around the mystics and the army behind them but washed through their own people on route to pushing the Glass army back.

Torsten reached out, and Sora tried to grab his hand before the water carried him away in its strong current. She wasn't moved by it. When the water settled, men of both armies littered the streets, disoriented.

"Kill the Glassmen," Aihara Na ordered to the legion behind her. "Kill them all."

The Panpingese soldiers stared at their people stuck between them and the Glass army, gagging on water, some with their bodies crushed against buildings. They didn't charge.

"Why are we fighting for them?" one at the front said.

"King Liam said any who stood against the mystics would receive mercy," spoke another.

"You think he will show you mercy?" Aihara Na spat. "The liar will slaughter every single one of you. The streets will run red with your blood."

"They already do!"

"Insolent fool!" Aihara Na swung her hand, and the man flew across the street. His back snapped against a column. "This is our city. Defend it, or die!"

One of the Panpingese soldiers glared at her, then tossed his curved blade aside. A few more did the same, until Aihara Na and the other mystics weren't facing the recovering Glass army, but their own people.

"You fools!" she roared. A storm brewed overhead, lower than any storm cloud should naturally be. "Can you not see who the true enemy is?"

"They see, as I do," a deep, basso voice shouted from the gates. King Liam strode in, carrying a sword at his side.

"You!" Aihara Na bellowed. She marched forward, magically pushing all her remaining soldiers out of the way.

"Your people no longer wish to be tools for your profane tests," Liam said. Sir Uriah had recovered from the flood and tried to stop him, but King Liam gestured for him to step aside and unlike Aihara's men, he did so without a fuss. "They no longer wish to suffer as you strive to conquer death."

"And how many of them have died in your quest to rule this world?"

"I gave them the choice to bend the knee," he said solemnly, "to see Iam as their one true savior. It is your kind that denies them peace."

"There can be no peace with the likes of you!" She raised her arms, and a bolt of lightning shot out of the clouds above toward Liam.

"My Lord, no!" Torsten scrambled to his feet and leaped in front of it, but the coruscating stream of light froze right in front of his chest. Torsten hit the ground, clutching his necklace, staring as the bolt vacillated, making the air crackle with energy.

"Enough," spoke a soft voice that, like Aihara Na's, carried. Another Mystic walked out onto the street, more beautiful than any mortal woman Sora had ever seen. She wore the red of the Ancient One, and she stepped in front of Aihara.

"Long have I stood by while we fought back, but for what?" she said.

"Ancient One Sumati, I—" Aihara started, but was cut off by the newcomer.

"No, it is time you listen. I am the eldest on the council, and I will not see any more death. Today, we show them that Iam is with us as well. Perhaps they see no others, but perhaps we see too many."

The woman spun to face King Liam and the Glass soldiers. Sora swore there was something familiar about her, but she wasn't sure what. She was the Ancient One of the time, which meant that she had to be hundreds of years old, but she didn't look a day older than Sora.

Ancient One Sumati fell to her knees and bowed her head. "Let this fighting come to an end, King Liam. Do what you will with us." She gestured back to the Panpingese soldiers. "But spare them."

Liam didn't answer. He merely stared across the smoldering battlefield and into the ageless eyes of the elder mystic. After a few seconds, a smile touched the corner of his lips. What happened next, Sora couldn't see. Again, the world frayed at the edges, and before she knew it, she stood in a dark, candlelit room. An arrowslit window revealed that they were high up in the Red Tower.

Ancient One Sumati lay on a bed wearing nothing but a nightgown, no longer the mystic warrior on the battlefield. Sora considered shielding her eyes, believing she was about to see something meant to be private. She heard screaming, but not pleasurable ones. The woman's swollen belly rose and fell in sharp intervals.

Two others were in the room in addition to the laboring, soon-to-be-mother. Liam Nothhelm sat at the bedside, holding the Ancient One's hand. A handmaiden kneeled by her feet preparing to deliver the child.

Something wasn't right. Sora had seen births in Troborough before, but the mystic seemed to be in even more pain. Sweat drenched every part of her, and the sheets beneath her legs were soaked with blood.

"What's taking so long?" Liam demanded.

"I… she doesn't seem to be able to push. Your Grace," the handmaiden replied.

"Is it blocked?" Sumati grated.

"It doesn't seem…"

"I'm afraid the child will never see the light of this world," Aihara Na said, entering. "Its heart is too weak for this realm. It will not survive the stress and should be dead already."

"What are you talking about, witch?" Liam asked.

"She hasn't told you? Your child should have been stillborn, but Ancient One Sumati has drawn on all her power to keep her breathing."

Liam squeezed the Ancient One's hand. "What is she talking about?" The woman struggled to speak, and Liam yelled. "Answer me!" Then softer, "Please?"

"Never has a mystic been so skilled in the art of healing, but this is beyond her," Aihara Na said. "Elsewhere desires the soul it was meant to have, and it will not be denied. Even our power has its limits."

"Aihara," Ancient One Sumati wheezed. "I can't… I can't hold on much longer. You must save the child."

"You are asking me to do something against all that we believe," Aihara said.

"Please…" Ancient One Sumati said.

"What is this?" Liam hovered over the Ancient One's face. "Why didn't you tell me?"

She stroked his cheek, her hand trembling. "I couldn't bear to see you unhappy."

Liam took her hand in both of his. He now shook as well. "This is impossible. Iam spoke to me. He told me that this union was destined."

"Perhaps your savage Queen cursed it," Aihara Na said. "Her people are known for that."

"Do not speak of her!" Liam snapped.

"Aihara, please… save our child," Ancient One Sumati moaned, sweat pouring off her forehead, matting her long black hair. "I know we've had our differences, but you must save her."

"And risk splitting the veil?" Aihara Na said. "You know what it requires."

"I can hold Elsewhere at bay. Why else live so long as I have?" She chuckled weakly, then coughed.

"No, Madam. Perhaps you could have, but it is too dangerous now. If you were not in so fragile a state, you would see that."

"You can save her?" Liam asked, standing.

"Only one of them. The mother, or the child. But it is too—"

"I am your new King," Liam stated.

"And as our new King, you've made it very clear that our magic is outlawed. An act of this magnitude has consequences."

"I know what your people are capable of. You will use any power at your disposal to save them both, is that clear? Queen Oleander has yet to bear me a child. I will not lose my first."

Ancient One Sumati grabbed Liam's hand, groaning in pain from the simple act. Blood had thoroughly saturated the bed by now. "It's okay, Liam," she said. "I've lived a good, long life, rose to the top of the Mystic Order, saw this awful thing called war end peaceably," she paused and stroked his hand, "by finding the peace in you." She rubbed her stomach. "Our child deserves the same chance."

Liam bit his lip. His eyes welled, but he did not weep. A man like him couldn't afford to show weakness, even in a time like this. He leaned over and placed a gentle kiss upon her cheek, then he turned to Aihara Na, his glower hard as glaruium.

"I am your King. I do not ask," he said. "Do what must be done to save the child."

"Ancient One, please," Aihara Na pled. Sora didn't think the woman capable of looking so terrified.

"I can control it." Ancient One Sumati howled in pain and clutched her stomach. "Blessed be the union between our two peoples. Do not fight it."

Liam drew his sword and raised it to Aihara's neck. It was then, as she heard the rasp of another sword drawn from a sheath that Sora noticed Sir Uriah Davies quietly standing guard by the door.

"Listen to her, or I swear to Iam I will burn this tower to the ground," Liam growled. "Prove that it is not just wickedness that springs from this place, and save our innocent child."

Aihara Na swallowed hard. "King Liam," she spoke softly. "Are you asking me to call upon the gods and use their Gift?"

"Do it, Aihara," Liam said. "I won't ask again."

"Do you not care to know the conse—"

"I said, do it!"

Madam Aihara approached Ancient One Sumati. "Move, girl," Aihara ordered the handmaiden.

"But, she—"

"Move!"

Aihara Na flicked her wrist, and the handmaiden slid across the floor and was pinned against the wall by an unseen force. She then placed a hand upon Ancient One Sumati's bulging belly and began to speak low, steady words, multiple languages blending and overlapping. They grew in volume, blanketing the room and making Sora's insides chatter, and then she raised her other hand toward Liam.

"What are you doing?" he questioned.

"Your will." She touched Liam's chest while still leaving her other hand on the mother's stomach as if forming a conduit between them. Ancient One Sumati screamed in agony.

"You're hurting her !" Liam said.

"Then you may want to close your eyes." Aihara Na began to chant louder, and Ancient One Sumati screamed louder. Her body began to stagger, just as Sora's vision did as she shifted within the revelations of the Well of Wisdom. Liam dropped his sword and fell to a knee. He too groaned in torment.

"Unhand the King!" Sir Uriah Davies stormed forward but was thrown back by the aura that pulsed from Aihara Na. Ancient One Sumati's screams grew even louder.

"I can feel the tear," Aihara yelled over the sound of the entire room shaking. "Madam, we must stop."

"No!" Madam Sumati yelled. "I can hold it." Her neck arched, and a stream of dark red smoke forced its way through her eyes. Sora could hear whispers in a strange, demonic language echoing around her. She could feel the chill of evil even though she wasn't there. "My life I give freely in her name! You will hold no sway over me bastards of Elsewhere."

"What is this place?" a familiar voice muttered. Sora spun in a circle. It undoubtedly belonged to Nesilia, and Sora soon realized that the words were being spoken through Ancient One Sumati's lips. "How long have I been asleep?"

"You will not pass to this realm!" Ancient One Sumati yelled.

"Master, I can't… hold…" Aihara Na could hardly keep her arms up anymore. Liam shouted in pain, now as loud as all the others.

"They have forgotten me?" Nesilia spoke again. "I am buried, not dead, yet they have forgotten me!" A spectral arm extended from Ancient One Sumati's chest which now glowed blue like the Well of Wisdom, like the smoke from Sora's healing. It lashed across the ceiling, rending a large crack.

"Be gone!"

A flash of light—just like the light which Sora had summoned in the Webbed Woods or on the Breklian ship—flung Aihara Na and King Liam against the wall. Even though Sora wasn't physically present, it did the same to her. When she gathered her bearings and ran back to the bed, Ancient One Sumati was gone. Only her clothing and blood remained, and lying in a pool of it in the center of the bed was a crying infant.

Aihara Na panted uncontrollably, unable to stand. Liam scrambled across the room and to the bed. He grasped at the sheets from his knees.

"My dearest Sora, don't do this. Come back to me. Please, Iam, hear my prayers."

Sora's eyes went wide. Liam's shoulders shook as he allowed himself to cry. He rubbed the bloody sheets against his face. "May Iam see you suited to walk through the Gate of Light," he sniveled. He raised his quaking hands to circle his eyes in prayer, then squeezed them shut. Sora could see his lips moving as he murmured a prayer to himself. She was too shocked by the name he'd used to hear the words.

As he cried, Aihara Na finally mustered the strength to walk over and lay a hand upon his shoulder.

"You did this!" he roared as he spun on her.

"At your word, I did only what I could to save the child," she replied, not shrinking back at all in the face of the legend. "You, my King, demanded I keep this child alive. Ancient One Sora Sumati, my master, is dead because of you. Your daughter is alive through my hand because she willed it, but her heart is yours."

"My daughter." His gaze snapped back to bed as if he'd forgotten about the infant. He reached out, still shaking, and lifted the crying girl. She sounded healthy, her voice strong. "My daughter." He held her close and kissed her forehead. "She sounds healthy."

"She is, thanks to Sora Sumati. Elsewhere demanded a soul and so the bridge was opened. She risked everything for that child."

"Our child."

"But my master was not alone in sacrifice. The child was not meant for this world, and more sacrifice was needed in defying the fate of the gods. Sora was too weak from preserving your daughter's life for so long in the womb, so the child is alive only by your lifeblood, sharing your heart. As she grows, you will pass from this life. Only in her death can you be free of this bond."

"This cannot be," Liam said, breathless.

"It is. You will gray long before your time. Your mind will become fitful and be filled with unrest, and eventually, you will find yourself present only in body. That is the price you agreed to, my King. A soul for Elsewhere, and a heart for a bastard daughter."

Without even a sound or warning, the world frayed again, and Sora stood on an unfamiliar street in Yaolin City. It was night, No, not night. Celeste and Loutis covered the sun. The Dawning.

Once again, King Liam stood next to her, surrounded by men wearing the white of the King's Shield.

"Leave us!" the King shouted. His men clomped away, leaving Liam standing beside Aihara Na who now wore a hooded red robe. With Master Sumati's death, it appeared she had taken on the role of eldest in the Mystic Order.

"I only trust you because I trusted her, you know that right?" Liam said.

Aihara Na nodded.

"Do not make me regret it," Liam warned.

"Your trust is well-placed, my King," she said. "If you claim the child publicly, it will only draw questions. She cannot rule in your world as a woman anyway. This is best."

"No one will know?"

"None."

"Send wagons filled with Panpingese war refugees all over the realm. Make it seem like she is any other. Place her with someone you trust to keep her safe, in a place no one cares about at all. Never tell me where she is and I will never ask."

Liam looked down at his daughter, swaddled in a cloth in his arms. She had his amber-hued eyes. He stroked her fine, black wisps of hair. "Daughter or son, you are my first, and I do this to protect you," he whispered. "I fear what I might do as my mind slips should I know where you are, so I mustn't." He held her out so he could look upon her in her entirety.

"So much like your mother," he smiled. "We will never see each other again, but know this; when you are grown, and I pass from this world, I give my heart willingly, as your mother gave hers. Iam saw fit to give you this second chance, born on the Dawning as if you, my Sora, are my light from within. You will find greatness. It is in your blood."

He kissed her on the forehead, and then another gut-wrenching pull made the world fold inward and brought Sora before the Red Tower. Now it was true night.

"Do it now!" King Liam shouted.

Sora turned back to the tower to see all the mystics, hundreds of them, on their knees on the small island beneath the tall, red structure. Each of them was held in place at the tip of a King's Shieldsman's sword. Uriah Davies had his against Aihara Na's neck.

"My King, please do not do this," Aihara Na begged from her knees, her hands cuffed.

"Call it what you will, but your magic is no different from the Drav Cra," Liam said. "I shall let no other share my fate."

"Your Grace, this is what you wanted."

"And I thank you for it. Know that because of your master, I do not do this out hate, but out of love."

"You call this love?" Aihara Na shouted. "We have sealed the tower for good. Cut off our connection to the Well. What else could we possibly do to keep you happy?"

Uriah kneed the small of her back, and she fell to her face. He barked at her to stay quiet. Liam kneeled to whisper in her ear. "Nothing. But so long as any of you know of my daughter, she is not safe. Not from me, not from you."

Liam rose to face his men. "We have tried peace, but Iam has made it clear to me, we cannot possibly coexist with these heathens. Their time presiding over Panping has come to an end. We will not share our rule."

He drew a deep breath, closed his eyes, then looked to his Wearer of White. "Uriah, do it."

It was all he needed to say.

Before most of the mystics could react, they had glaruium blades shoved through their throats. Most of them folded to the ground, dead and covered in the very blood that gave them power. But Madam Aihara and a few others—Madam Jaya among them, resisted. Aihara Na's chains turned to ice and shattered. She stabbed one of the shards into Uriah's leg and fled onto the lake. The water solidified beneath her every step. A few others killed Shieldsmen to escape, including Madam Jaya.

"Find them and kill them!" Liam demanded. "The Mystic Order is over." His men raced to their boats and set off after the dozen or so escaped mystics. Others fired arrows across the lake. One raced toward Madam Jaya.

Sora yelled out to warn Madam Jaya when the ground suddenly

vanished, and Sora felt herself falling. Letters and symbols from every language in Pantego blew past her. She landed with a splash, the familiar scent of boiling flowers in the air. Then she emerged from the Well of Wisdom, gasping for air.

In the present, Aihara Na, Madam Jaya, Master Huyshi, and the four other surviving mystics stood at the edge of the waters looking down at her, faces wracked by concern. "Sora, are you all right?"

She wanted to respond, but couldn't find the words. The truth was almost too much to bear.

XXX

THE KNIGHT

The Queen Mother's white mare was as feisty as she was, but she was as advertised—faster than any horse Torsten had ever ridden. He sat up front on her saddle, snapping the reins as he shouted for the crowd outside Yarrington to part in the name of the Queen Mother.

Faces smeared with luminescent paint were everywhere. The cold didn't matter. All the pious souls of Yarrington and beyond gathered in knots to witness this yearly ritual when they were tested in the darkness. Priests gave sermons on every hillside and promontory. Only they weren't alone. Warlock rituals and sacrifices were scattered amongst them attended by masked cultists while Drav Cra civilians sold furs.

It was a sight Torsten never thought he'd witness, and one he'd make sure he never did again. Allying with the barbarians and heathens of the North was one thing, but inviting them and exiled cultists to participate in this holiest of day, one in which they even didn't believe was another. It was like he'd gone to the dungeons and stepped out into an Elsewhere itself—his own personal exile.

"Would you go faster?" Oleander said. "The Dawning approaches, and whatever my brother plans to show my son, I don't trust him." She sat at Torsten's back, arms wrapped around his waist. It had taken a long time, but Torsten finally felt all those hours catering to her every need was worth it. She was the only ally he had left who saw Redstar for the monster he was.

"I'm trying," Torsten replied. He pulled on the reins to dart around a mob, then nearly toppled over a line of dwarves who'd scurried in front of them. The mare reared back, and Oleander tightened her hold. Torsten and the leader of the dwarven group met gazes momentarily. It was Oathbreaker, Oarbringer—Tosten couldn't remember his name—but he knew it was the construction foreman working to repair the Royal Crypt. The little men darted beneath the horse's belly, and Torsten grabbed Oleander's wrist tight.

"The next fool that gets in our way," Oleander snapped, "plow them over!"

Torsten didn't listen, but he weaved his way to the bottom of the trail leading up the mountain. A warlock and a handful of Drav Cra warriors camped in the path. Two dire wolves lay perched on an outcrop of rock beside them, chewing the meat off the bones of some poor animal. Torsten brought the horse to a halt in front of them.

"Sorry, nobody gets by," the biggest of the warriors said, standing and hefting an axe with both hands. "Orders from the Arch Warlock."

"Do you know who I am?" Oleander questioned.

"Fresh meat?"

"You insolent—"

"Let me handle this." Torsten stopped her from hopping off the horse and doing something stupid. "You speak with the Queen Mother. She wishes to spend the first Dawning after his miracle rebirth with her son."

The warrior sneered. "We're especially not supposed to let her pass."

"I suggest you reconsider. She isn't known for leniency."

"You think we're afraid of the 'Flower of the Drav Cra?' You should try meeting a real Northern woman."

"Stop wasting breath!" Oleander kicked the sides of her horse, and it darted forward. Torsten caught his balance on the reins with one hand and drew his claymore from his back sheath with the other. It slit the warlock's neck as it slipped free, and as the heathen toppled over, fire sprayed from his hand in an explosive blast, blowing back the Drav Cra warriors.

"Get them!" one roared.

The pounding paws and barking that followed were all too familiar sounds. After his trek to the Webbed Woods with Whitney, he hoped never to be caught fleeing dire wolves again, but he'd hoped for much that hadn't come to pass. He spurred Oleander's horse around the first sharp turn on switchbacks.

"You're worse than Fierstown!" Torsten shouted back at Oleander. "Next time warn me."

"It's your sacred duty to know every want and need of your Queen," she replied.

"I'm no longer a Shieldsman."

"You're as much one as I am a Queen."

A snarl made the hair's on Torsten's neck stand on end. Oleander squeezed him harder, and he glanced back to see the two dire wolves bounding after them. Their maws snapped, saliva flinging, and their yellow eyes pierced the white of the snow-coated slope.

They had a lead on the beasts, but the ground was slick, and every time the horse took a turn, the wolves claws allowed them to dig in and take it sharper. Heavy flakes of snow pelted Torsten's face as they ascended higher, and through a break in the clouds, he saw that both moons were now visible, edging ever closer to eclipse the sun.

"Grotesque beast!" Oleander yelped.

Torsten glanced back as they took another corner and saw one of the wolves literally chomping at her heels. Its head was the size of Oleander's torso, and one bite would rip her foot clean off.

"We'll never make it up with them after us!" Torsten yelled.

"I hadn't realized!" She squealed as the wolf snapped at the bottom of her dress and tore off a shred. Torsten grabbed her so the force of the bite wouldn't yank her from the saddle. Then he stretched her hands around him and slotted the reins into her palms.

"I'll handle them," Torsten said. "When I let go, don't stop."

"What? I am your Queen, and I order you to—"

As the horse dug in to make the next turn, Torsten pushed off the side. He flew through the air, slamming into the dire wolf trailing behind which hadn't yet made the turn. He plunged his claymore into its chest, squeezing the handle with all his might. They skidded to a stop at the edge of the rocky path, a hands-length from plummeting together to their doom.

The wolf howled, and its head lilted off to the side, but Torsten's gambit paid off. Wolves were pack animals, and as he stood and slid his blade out of the beast, he saw that the other wolf had stopped in its pursuit of Oleander to face him. Torsten set his feet and tightened his grip. They were a long way up the mountain now, where the slope began to sharpen and grow rocky. The wolf glared down at him from the incline, claws digging into the snow, eyes like ice.

Torsten looked over his shoulder. At his back was certain death, and at his front, a wolf the size of a bovine, with fangs as long as his forearm.

"Come beast!" he bellowed. "I will not be stopped by you."

The horrifying creature prepared to pounce, but just as its hind legs left the ground Oleander's Whitehair's back hooves kicked it in the side. True to its name, the mare was as white as the snow and close to invisible on the trail. The wolf scrambled to find a grip with razor-sharp claws, but the snow was too slick, and it tumbled over the ledge. Bouncing its way down, its whimpers echoed, no doubt drawing the attention of many a pilgrim. Torsten didn't waste time seeing how far it went.

"Must I handle everything?" Oleander called down.

"I told you not to stop!"

"And you promised to kill my brother. Now hurry up, it's freezing."

Torsten stowed *Salvation* on his back and jogged up to the horse. Oleander didn't slide back to make room for him to take the reins. "She listens better to me," she said. "Keep me warm, knight."

After she likely saved his life, there wasn't much Torsten could say. He pulled himself up behind her, and they took off through the snow and freezing wind.

Up they went until the silence of the mountain grew more unnerving than the snarling wolves. The higher they climbed, the straighter the path became, no longer slicing back and forth but instead was carved around the entire circumference of the mountain. They passed the top entry to the glaruium mine and Torsten could see the glow of the rare element through the cracks. In its natural form, it glimmered in the darkness like stars compressed into stone.

Clouds rolled in, shrouding Pantego in shadow. The sun wasn't yet covered, but the cold was brutal. Every breath was like a chain of icicles down Torsten's throat. He could feel Oleander shivering and wrapped her tighter. The cold was unquestionably getting to her as she'd stopped speaking, and he was used to her sharp tongue no matter the situation. They circled once more around the mountain, and then her horse released a heart-wrenching cry before collapsing to the snow.

Torsten threw his leg over the side of the mare and yanked Oleander off before being crushed beneath the weight of it. He wiped the snow from his face. Off to the side, the horse labored to breathe. He was sure the beast hadn't been in so high an altitude or such cold in all its life. There was good reason people climbed to the summit of Mount Lister earlier in the day or rode mules or stocky Quarter Horses intended for hauling.

"Sora!" Oleander cried out. She scrambled out of Torsten's grip and lay her hand upon the horse's head.

Torsten had seen the Queen be many things, but sympathetic wasn't one of them. As she looked up at him, he swore a tear rolled down her cheek. It froze so quickly it could have easily been a snowflake. "We can't leave her," she shivered.

"We must." Torsten lay his hand on Oleander's shoulder. "Her place is in the Gate of Light now. We're close."

"Then you must end her suffering."

Torsten moved Oleander aside and knelt before the horse.

"Sora," Oleander whispered again.

"Sora," Torsten repeated, the familiarity of the name finally striking him. "I didn't realize that was your horse's name."

"You don't know everything about me, knight."

"It's just a curious name."

"Liam had already named her before she was gifted to me. He said she was as rare as I was. I never asked him the true story of where he got her. I never wanted to know."

"Like I've told you. No matter what was said or done, he loved you, Oleander."

"How could he not?" She stood and turned away. "Now hurry up and get on with it."

"Your Grace?"

"I will not have her suffer. Do what you knights do."

Torsten rubbed the horse's snout and drew *Salvation*. Of all the things Oleander was, he'd never pegged her for one who'd be unable to watch this mercy. But those Drav Cra warriors were right. She was far from one of them anymore. At that moment, she had more compassion in one of her blonde, nearly silver hairs, than all of them combined.

"Be in the light now," he whispered as he drove the sword straight into Sora's heart. "Suffer no more." He thought he could hear Oleander whimpering, but he showed her the respect of keeping his sympathy to himself. He stood, wrapped his arm around her, and continued up the path.

"Why didn't you carve the fur from those infernal wolves?" she asked.

Torsten smiled, glad to see she hadn't lost all her venom. "My failures abound, Your Grace."He kept her moving the rest of the climb. Oleander's body resisted, but there was no time to rest. To stop under these conditions would mean death. The day had started warmer and brighter, but all that changed. Never in all his life could he remember such a harsh Dawning atop Mount Lister. He couldn't help feeling it was an omen.

The icy wind, for him, was preferable to rotting in the dungeon, breathing in stale air that reeked of shog. His training had prepared him for this. Every Shieldsman was sworn in on the flat top of Mount Lister. He had knelt before Uriah Davies to take the vows as had so many countless others, forced to make the climb alone, with naught but his own two feet.

This was so similar. From a boy, counted out and growing up in squalor, to be raised by Liam Nothhelm to stand as one of his elite soldiers. Now he was an exiled Shieldsman, making the same climb thanks to Liam's widow. It was as if he'd grown close with her, against all odds, just for this moment; for a chance to save the kingdom when so much hung in the balance.

He peered to the right, over Oleander's head, through the fog and snow. She hunched over, breathing into her dress to stay warm, every step a struggle. The edges of the moons were passing across the sun now like a door closing, casting eerie darkness across the kingdom that grew deeper and deeper each second. Eyelids for Iam's world.

Torsten stopped.

"What is it?" Oleander asked softly.

"We're here." Now that it grew darker, he could see the glow of torchlight a short distance above. Indistinguishable voices carried on the wind as he propped Oleander up within a nook that protected against the wind. "Let me go first."

"And miss out on a chance to help end my detestable brother?" she bristled.

"I don't know what's waiting up there, but I do know what he did to you in my chambers. He's been trying some mad ritual to bring his goddess back all this time, and he'll stop at nothing. If I fail, you may be the only one left who can get close enough to him."

Oleander pursed her lips in anger, then her features softened. "Is it wrong that a part of me wants you to fail so that I can have the satisfaction?"

"I would expect nothing less. Stay here." He turned to leave, but she grabbed him.

"Torsten."

"Yes, My Queen."

"Don't let anything happen to my son. Do you hear me? He's all I have left, and after Redstar is gone, I know he'll be fine."

"On my life, the King will come to no harm."

She leaned up to whisper into his ear. "I always knew I could trust you, my dear, loyal Torsten." She pressed her ice-cold lips against his cheek. "I'm so sorry I didn't stand by you after you returned."

"I wouldn't have either." He held her at arm's length, and for the first time in his life, stared into her eyes without a sense of trepidation bubbling up from within. "Liam built this great country for us and for your boy. Today we take it back." He released her and slowly backed away. He'd had his doubts about her for a long time, but here she stood, braving deathly cold for the sake of the Glass. He knew it was likely a prayer, but he couldn't help feeling that after all the madness was over, she might become the Queen Liam always knew she could be, and not the one her people had come to hate and fear.

He believed in her, always had. And as he turned away and their gazes broke, he could tell she believed in him too. That was enough. He drew *Salvation* and pushed his aching limbs to finish the climb.

XXXI

THE DESERTER

Rand stopped at the corner where Poplar and Newton Streets intersected in South Corner. He followed the spread of a shadow across the dirt, up the wall of an old plaster building, to the moons passing over the sun. A silver glow reflected off the castle's glass spire and cast the city in an unnatural twilight.

The silence was unsettling. Most of Yarrington either sat before the base of Mount Lister, or they had returned home to be with their families to fast before the great feast that would occur when the sun rose the next morning. For a man of the Glass army, there was no more peaceful day, though Rand was usually with his sister by this time every year.

Rand closed his eyes and drew a deep, steadying breath. Remembering where he was and what he was doing, he let out the breath, and his heart plummeted. Torsten was free, and Rand and Codar had made it out of the Royal Crypt without a hitch. But he would never forget the bodies stuffed into graves by greedy dwarves, never to be found again. He'd recited a prayer for Childress and his family, and the others on his way up the construction lift, but he doubted Iam was listening. Not to him. He'd done all he could to rescue Torsten, to finish what he'd started, and now he found himself hoping Iam had turned His Eye away.

"Come, Rand," Codar said. "There is no time to waste."

"I'm just wondering how I got here," Rand said.

"Survival."

Rand opened his eyes and looked upon the callous, mustached man from Brekliodad. Not even his childhood nightmares could've provided such an unexpected situation.

"I don't give a rat's shog about that," Rand said.

"Not yours," Codar replied.

"Buried not dead!" a crazed, masked cultist of Nesilia screamed suddenly as he emerged from seemingly nowhere and raced by. "Buried not dead. Buried not dead!"

Rand spun to watch him, whispering, "What in Iam's name?"

The cultist danced around, continuing his chant, red robe sloshing through the snow, kicking up powder as he twirled and skipped.

A Glass soldier, wearing the mark of the city guard stepped to block the cultist's path. "Off the streets, devil," he ordered. "Just because we have to trust the Drav Cra means nothing for the likes of you."

The cultist stopped, tilting his head, but didn't respond.

"Did you hear me?" the guard questioned. He grabbed the cultist by the collar. "I said, get off the yigging streets. Show so resp—"

The cultist extended his arm, and a knife fell through his sleeve into his waiting hand. It all happened so fast the guard couldn't have done anything. The cultist jammed the knife between the laces of the man's armor. It sank deep into the man's side. "Buried, not dead," the cultist continued as if nothing happened, skipping, dancing, and cackling like a madman.

The guard folded over and clutched the wound. "Seize him!" he shouted to Rand, apparently noticing his armor.

Rand took a step toward the cultist—he couldn't help himself—but Codar tugged him back onto their course toward the gate and their freedom.

"There is nothing you can do," he said. "We must leave, now."

"I'm helping you, aren't I?" Rand bristled. "Valin said nothing about refusing to help othe—" Another cultist appeared from around a corner and drove a second knife into the back of the guard's neck.

"Iam's Light," Rand gasped. He ignored Codar and started off toward the man when, from the opposite direction, two more cultists emerged from an alley and kicked through a door into a shanty-home. The shrill cries of terror of those within gave Rand goosebumps.

Rand didn't think twice. He drew his sword, shoved by Codar, and stormed into the cottage. A cultist had a woman by the hair and dragged her across the floor directly in front of him. Her husband sat on a chair, head drooped back with his throat slit. Children huddled in the corner on the other side of the home, a second cultist bearing down on them.

"Unhand her!" Rand yelled.

The cultist turned his head. His hood was up, and his expressionless porcelain mask with a bloody tear beneath one eye and dark holes for seeing, shimmered with the hearth fire.

"Sacrifice for the Lady," the man hissed, then after a shrill laugh, he raised his knife. Rand darted forward, slicing off the man's arm before he could complete his attack. Rand's own sword found a home, plunging into the cultist's chest.

"My babies!" the woman shrieked.

Rand turned and saw that the other cultist had now cornered the children and was brandishing his dagger. Rand threw a chair out of the way and sprinted, but the cultist turned the dagger on himself and slit his own throat. Blood poured out onto the crying children, and the gargling corpse of the cultist thudded at Rand's feet.

The sight gave Rand pause, but he remembered his training. He recovered quickly and grabbed the children. "Hide in the pantry," he said. "All of you. Hide in there now and don't come out!" He gave a gentle push to get the crying children past their dead father into the arms of their mother.

"Thank you, Shieldsman," she whimpered, but she wasn't looking at Rand. She showered her children with kisses. "Thank you."

"Don't thank me," Rand said. "Just keep them safe."

Bedlam outside drew Rand back to the door where he found Codar already standing on the stack of boards they called a porch.

"You can't help them all, Rand," Codar said. He calmly wiped his dagger on his sleeve, staining it red. Another dead cultist lay a few meters away.

Rand looked past him. With the sun growing dimmer, cultists ran rampant throughout the district. Emboldened by the Drav Cra presence, or invited by Redstar himself, they sowed chaos in South Corner with so few on duty to protect its citizens. South Corner, Dockside, and the rest of Yarrington's poor district were mostly wood and thatch. Thick billows of black smoke hovered over the homes and shops, and a soft, flickering, orange glow painted the abnormally dark sky. The constant snowfall kept the blaze from spreading as it had in Winde Port. The cultists raced around, dozens of them, using the smoke for cover and causing mayhem—flipping parked trading carts, raiding shops for supplies only to dump them all over the streets.

It took Rand a few moments to find his voice. "How could this happen?" he asked.

"How could it not?" Codar said. "You people let a child rule because of his blood and expect peace?"

"This has nothing to do with the King. This is Redstar. I... I told you we needed to stop him first!"

"Is it? Redstar was imprisoned when your King decided to condemn the Caleef. Because of him, the rebels took Winde Port, only to be driven out by Redstar and hand him all the leverage he needed."

Rand didn't have an answer.

"In freeing the Caleef, Mister Tehr will undo the mistake made by lesser men and children," Codar said. "In Brek, it doesn't matter what family you're born into, only what's in here." He pointed to his head.

"There have been many mistakes."

Codar scoffed. "You Shieldsmen... you only ever see what's right in front of you!" He whipped around and flung his dirk right by Rand's head, so close it scraped his pauldron. Rand fell back against the wall of a building and was about to curse the Breklian, when the body of another cultist toppled over, bumping into him. The dirk sticking out from between his eyes caused his mask to crack in half upon impact, revealing the face of an adolescent boy.

"You asked why I'm here. I came to the Glass, sent by my father, to learn from the great Liam the Conqueror. Arrived to find him drooling on himself like a baby." Codar tore the blade out of the boy's skull, his tone agitated.

"Instead, I found Valin, a cripple born from shog," he went on. "And he's more a man than any of your kings or you worthless knights. Now let's go, and no more stopping to play hero. That's not your life anymore. He'll help you be better if you'd open your damn eyes."

Codar hauled Rand to his feet then set off around the building without another word. Rand took one more look at the pandemonium before following. The Breklian was right about one thing—Rand couldn't do anything about this. There was nobody to warn with so much of the city guard off duty, especially in South Corner. Eventually, someone would see the flames and rouse the city guards, but not before the devastation was exhaustive. And if Rand died fighting an unpredictable foe willing to kill themselves to sow terror, his sister would die with him.

He and Codar kept to the alleyways to avoid the brunt of the chaos. They stopped at an opening to a major avenue running along the city wall. "The southern gate is across the way," he said.

"Then let's get this over with." Rand went to move, but Codar grabbed his wrist.

"No, this is where I leave you," Codar said. "Your company awaits in a caravan by the gate. You'll have no trouble getting through, even with the rioting."

"I thought saving the Caleef was heroic since Valin wanted it? Now you run?"

"My face is known to the guards, and so I cannot come. Remember, Valin's role in this affair is one of ignorance. You know what happens to Sigrid should you do anything to change that, or should you fail."

Rand bit back his initial response. He was eager to escape the watchful eye of the heartless Breklian, so willing to wield Rand's sister's name like a weapon. "Tell your boss not to worry. I won't fail," Rand said. "But I have to ask. All this insanity—was it Redstar who inspired it, or was it our mutual friend?"

Rand turned to face Codar, but the Breklian was gone. When he looked back, a cultist stood before the alley staring at him from behind his mask. Rand's hand fell to the grip of his sword.

"Walk away," he warned.

The cultist didn't respond. Instead, he ran a rusty blade across his palm and attempted to use blood magic like a true warlock. The spell backfired, and he wound up setting himself ablaze. "One for the Lady, one for the

Lord!" He screamed as he ran by Rand, flailing his arms. The snow would have easily extinguished him, but he merely let himself burn.

Poor, lost souls...

Rand cringed and averted his gaze. He stepped out of the alley and focused on the summit of Mount Lister where, above it, the two moons had nearly come into alignment in front of the sun. The Dawning had arrived.

"End this madness, Sir Unger," Rand whispered, then set off for the southern gate at a brisk pace. He didn't have to search far to find the men he was looking for. A trading caravan sat before the closed portcullis. A dwarf stood on the back of the cart with a long red beard and eyes which looked two ways at the same time. He had an axe in hand, swinging madly at a group of looters bent upon taking advantage of the riots. Two heavily-armored human mercenaries stood on the street on either side of him, swords at the ready.

"Back ye fiends!" the dwarf shouted. "Ye ain't touchin a blood-soaked thing."

One of the humans swiped at a looter, but they didn't get close enough to attack.

"Do ye plan on helpin?" the dwarf shouted up to the guard tower above the arched gate. Two soldiers were on duty, aiming down over the ramparts with bows but not firing. Only the most inexperienced were put to work on the Dawning, and Rand could see the sweat glistening on their foreheads.

It was time to act like a Shieldsman again. Straightening his shoulders, Rand approached the caravan with his weapon drawn.

"Step back from those traders!" he barked at the looters. "In the name of the King."

The men offered him little regard. "A hand of Iam, come to set us straight," one of them sneered.

"Can't you see?" said another, gesturing toward the covered sun, then the chaos overrunning the district. "There is no light to judge us now. Iam is gone."

A boom shook the earth as if in response to the man's words, like the quake which had preceded the splitting of the Royal Crypt and Pi's rebirth. Then there was a flash atop Mount Lister, blinding at first, then it appeared more like a vortex. Light and shadow, swirling, distorting all the air around it so even the eclipse wasn't visible.

All the city likely trembled in fear from the sight of the anomaly, but not Rand. He knew what it was: Redstar's dark magic corrupting the world because Torsten had made it out of the Glass Castle to face him down.

I should be at his side, he thought, anger mounting within him. But he'd put himself in this position. He directed that rage toward the looters and took a hard step toward them. They fled like the cowards they were.

"Ye better run!" the dwarf shouted. He hopped down from the back of the cart and approached Rand. "What in the name of Meungor's axe was that up there?"

"A chance to end this lunacy," Rand replied.

"Looks more like the opposite to me. Either way, I be glad we're gettin out of here. You must be the one Valin sent." The dwarf stowed a battle-axe a few sizes too large for him behind his back.

"He did."

"About time." He bowed. "Grint Strongiron at your service, Sir Knight."

Rand thought about correcting him, but he wasn't even sure if he should use his real name.

"That's Zane and Dorblo," Grint continued before Rand could respond. "Fine warriors, but barely got one brain between the two of em."

"Watch it, Grint," Zane said as the two mercenaries moved to the front of the cart where the horse waited. They looked so similar they could've been brothers, perhaps even twins.

Grint set his hands on his broad hips and stared back into the city. Rand joined him. Screams still echoed as the cultists' reign of terror endured. Far down the street, through a brush of smoke, Rand saw a guard chasing one who held what looked like a swaddled infant. Others flung torches through the stained glass windows of a South Corner chapel. Citizens flocked to the streets, sprinting in every direction, faces painted for a Dawning they would never forget.

It was the kind of unholy anarchy Shieldsmen trained for but never imagined they'd see.

"Bastards wouldn't open the gate, even when we were attacked," the dwarf said. "Care to prod them along before we wind up as sacrifices?"

All the screams blended, and in them, Rand could hear those of Tessa and the others he'd hung. All sounding so similar, desperate not to die when all hope seemed lost. Rand felt that familiar aching for a drink swell up in him. Anything to take the edge off; to help him abdicate his sworn duties to the Glass without guilt overwhelming him.

"Move yer arse, Shieldsman." Grint nudged him in the side. "Ain't no good, me dying here and not bein able to spend what Valin's payin."

Rand shook out his head and realized that he wasn't as helpless as he thought. Maybe he couldn't fight the rioters, but he could offer the people of South Corner and Dockside a way out. They were trapped within the walls like chickens in a coup filled with wolves.

"You!" he shouted up to one of the gate guards. "Open up and let these people out!"

"We ain't supposed to!" he replied, voice shaking. "City's on lock-down at night ever since the Caleef got out."

"In the name of the King and the King's Shield, open that gate and let these people out or there will be nobody left to fill this city!"

The guard ducked out of sight, and Rand swore inwardly. He couldn't blame them for not being prepared to handle such a dire situation—he didn't fare much better in his. He was about to climb the gate himself when the portcullis finally stirred, then started to rattle open.

"Well done." Grint slapped Rand on the back and climbed up onto the front of the caravan to take the reins. Either Zane or Dorblo—Rand didn't know one from another—offered to help him up, but he denied the man with a flurry of dwarven curses. "Ye comin?" he shouted back.

"One second." Rand turned back to the city and walked to the center of the snowy road. A cultist tried to scurry past, but Rand grabbed him by the robe and slammed him to the ground. "Flee the city!" he yelled. "Let them take your homes, but never your light! Run!"

All it took was one person to find sense in the pandemonium for Rand's orders to start spreading. "Run for the gate!" a woman cried out. "The gates are open!" shouted another. Then the handful of guards trying to impede rampaging cultists relayed the order.

It wasn't much, but it was the best Rand could do.

He jogged back and kept pace with the caravan as it rolled through the archway. People trickled through around them, out into the frozen farmland where they'd be safe as long as they kept away from the Drav Cra camps outside Yarrington's main entry. If Rand knew anything, it was that structures could be repaired, but horror lived in men forever, scratching away at their sanity, and all these cultists were after was madness. The more people who escaped that, the better off they'd be, homeless or not.

A young woman tripped on a rock on her way by, her baby tumbling from her arms. Rand knelt to pick up the crying infant.

"Rand Langley, the great deserter," someone said. "What is it Valin Tehr's got his hands into this time?"

Rand handed the baby over and helped the women up, then glared at the source of the voice. Captain Henry of the Dockside guard stood before the caravan with a group of Glass soldiers who looked like they might as well belong to Valin's gang as well. Grimy, hawkish, aching for a fight when they should be in the city helping the innocent.

"Dunno what yer talkin about," Grint said. "We be nothin but traders tryin to survive. Ye seen what's going on back th—"

"Shut your filthy mouth, dwarf!" Henry snapped.

The brother mercenaries stood out front of the horse, and their hands fell to the hilts of their swords. "Only we speak to him like that," one said.

"Would you really assault a captain of the Glass army?" Henry asked.

Rand hurried between them before things escalated and faced the guard captain he had served under so many moons ago. "Move aside, or you'll find out."

Henry grinned, half his teeth black and rotten. "You hear that boys? The Queen's hangman has decided to move up from hanging priests and handmaidens." The others laughed with him.

Rand didn't ask politely a second time. He unsheathed his sword and pointed it at the crooked captain. He knew it probably wasn't the smartest move, but the craziness at his back had his adrenaline pumping. "Do not test me. Not today."

Henry didn't back down. "How about you show me what's inside that there cart first?"

"Furs," Grint said.

"Don't have enough of that around here?" Henry nodded toward the distant glow of Drav Cra campfires by the city's main gates.

"That's why we be leavin with them."

"You think you're smarter than me, half-pint?" Henry spat, stomping forward.

The mercenary brothers drew their weapons as well.

"Now," Henry said, "I ain't gonna ask again. Let me take a gander inside the caravan, and I'll see what we can do about letting you pass. No traders allowed to leave the city without inspection these days, haven't you heard?"

"You know we can't let you," Rand said. "So why don't you go back into the city and help the people you're sworn to?"

"Says the man who took a more sacred oath. Shouldn't you be helping them? No, instead you're here, deserting your people again. I saw those bodies you helped sling over the wall for our whore Queen. One of them was my baby cousin. A rotten scoundrel he was, but blood is blood."

"Step aside, or I'll show you blood," Rand said through clenched teeth.

"You going to make us carve through you? This ought to be good. By Iam, what could Valin possibly have in there? The Glass-yigging-Crown?"

"Like he said, just furs," one of the mercenaries repeated.

"Then what's there to hide? I can keep a secret. I saw Valin take the deserter here in right after he tried to murder the Prime Minister and didn't tell a soul. Just open it up and give us a stake, and we can all move on with our lives."

"One more word and the only person who'll get hurt is you," Rand said.

"I'd like to see you try." Henry stepped closer, not even bothering to reveal his weapon. "You aren't a killer, boy. You weren't when you were a guard, and you aren't now. You're a coward, hanging old men and women for made-up crimes."

He took another step, and Rand flinched without meaning to. The captain's words brought those memories he constantly fought so hard to keep down surging back in full force. The rope creaking, bodies swinging in the wind, Tessa...

"You won't touch a Glass soldier," Henry said. "You don't have the balls. So, move, you cowardly son of a whore, before someone gives you what you deserv—"

"Enough!" Rand screamed. He slashed the man's right leg and sent him to a knee, then kicked him onto his back. The other guards armed themselves and circled him, but Rand held his blade to Henry's neck. His hand quaked, the tip of his swords inches away from taking another Glassman's life. It took every ounce of his willpower not to let rage consume him and drive him to deal the killing blow.

Henry laughed through the pain. "See boys?" He stifled a grimace. "He doesn't have it in him to kill me. I'm not weak enough prey."

"You're plenty weak," Rand said, seething. He steadied his sword and glared up at the circling guards. "I may be done killing Glassman, but my employer isn't. You will go back and help the people of this city, or he'll hear about this." Rand turned his attention back to Henry. "I'm sure his giant would love a word with you."

For the first time, Henry's expression darkened. Rand tried not to show how much it stung him inside to speak those words—to finally claim out loud that no matter what the reason was, he worked for Valin Tehr now.

"Now get up." Rand grabbed Henry by the collar and dragged him out of the way of the caravan.

"Shouldn't we kill them?" Dorblo asked quietly. "You know, just in case."

"These men won't say a word," Rand said. "I know cowards when I see them, I've been one. Now, Captain, go and serve your people the right way while I tend to mine."

Henry's brow furrowed, and Rand realized what his words might sound like, that he'd betrayed the Glass Kingdom and now served a new monarch when really all he meant was Sigrid. Through everything, she was the only constant—the only person he had left. And if acting like a heartless mercenary under Valin's thumb was what it took to win her freedom, he'd become like Codar if he had to.

"Go!" he roared.

Henry's men scampered away. Two stopped to help Henry to his feet. "Valin may have your back now," the captain snarled, limping along. "But if I ever see you again, it'll be the end of you, deserter. I'll hang you off the shogging barrack's tower! You hear me!"

"Well done, knight," Grint said. The two mercenaries agreed.

Rand sheathed his sword while gazing back toward Yarrington. He hadn't noticed, but the strange anomaly atop Mount Lister had subsided, and now only Celeste blocked the sun on its descent behind the mountain. That meant that either Torsten or Redstar had finally claimed the other.

The reddish glow of fire hung over the city itself, pillars of smoke rising here and there. Most of the rioting seemed to keep toward South Corner and Dockside, where the guard presence was due to be lighter, especially with Henry and his men away. More frightened families poured through the southern gate, making Grint's caravan seem like it was just a part of the exodus.

Then Rand turned toward the road. He'd been on it before, but only this time did his heart race. Someone within the carriage pulled the tarp back and startled him. "They're gone, why are we still sitting around?" Bartholomew Darkings asked. He wore the familiar scowl of a nobleman who thought himself superior to everyone around him, like so many who occupied the Glass Castle. In the back of the carriage, the Caleef sat, dressed in rags like an ordinary Shesaitju peasant. A muzzle covered his mouth, and his arms and legs were bound.

"Ye heard the man." Grint snapped on the reins.

As the rickety, wooden wheels turned, the sound of ropes creaking once again crept into Rand's head along with the desire for a drink. This time, he quickly silenced them. Instead, he pictured his sister's crooked smile, the way she snapped back at handsy drunkards, and more than anything, the way she never gave up on him. Failure to his Order, now a traitor to the Crown—but he refused to desert her.

"For you, Sig," Rand whispered to himself, "and only you," then he set off away from the only home he'd ever known, with a foreign king in tow.

XXXII

THE THIEF

Whitney swept through his cottage, tearing through the cupboards, checking under his hay-filled mattress looking for the map he'd been drawing for years now. He was about to flip the bed over in frustration when he noticed that the back window wasn't closed, rattling from a slight breeze.

He hurried over to it and checked the lock. Busted. He peered outside and saw that the grass leading up to it was disturbed, the barely visible path leading into the forest.

"Still sloppy, you little devil." He left the candle behind and went back outside. He didn't need light to find his old hiding place. "I knew I saw him—er, me—snooping around," he grumbled.

The path of trampled brush led through the forest to the creek, the same spot he and Kazimir had disposed of that thug's body what felt like a lifetime ago. It was the point exactly halfway between Whitney and Sora's homes where they met up nearly every day; where he had hidden so many of his prizes—as if there was anything to call a prize in Troborough.

Whitney saw the candlelight and slowed to a creep. If there was anything he knew he could do, it was sneak up on himself. He sneaked up behind a thick tree trunk and peered over at Young Whitney. Only he wasn't alone. He and Sora kneeled in the dirt side by side, pouring over Big Whitney's map.

"All right, you thieving whelp, give that here!" Whitney jumped out and shouted.

His younger self nearly leaped out of his shoes. Sora flinched, then reached down for the whittling knife strapped to her belt. Only, she had no intention to wield it against Big Whitney. Her hand was exposed, and the candlelight revealed a few pale scars. She hid it behind her back when she noticed hin looking.

So, Wetzel started training her even before I left? Whitney wondered how he'd missed that when they were together so often. Were kids really that oblivious?

"I knew you were a freak, Willis." The name dripped with venom off Young Whitney's lips, as if he somehow didn't realize they looked exactly the same. In fact, Big Whitney had shown no signs of aging in six years, and soon they'd be twins.

Young Whitney tossed the unfurled map onto the ground. It was a hand-drawn plan of Troborough with an amorphous barrier drawn around it. Arrows lined the entire thing with notes scrawled around the edges. Houses had **X**'s over them, the Twilight Manor, Gilly's tailor shop—all places he'd searched ceiling to cellar for a break in Elsewhere's barrier.

He'd grown up thinking Troborough was small, but when every inch had to be covered, it seemed endless. Still, after years there was nary a blank spot on the drawing. His next plan was to start climbing trees and searching higher up on the invisible barrier. Then there was that curious mental block anytime Whitney tried to go near Wetzel's shack as if Elsewhere was determined to keep him away.

"What in the name of the fallen gods is this?" Young Whitney hissed.

Whitney surrendered his position of power without thinking. He fell to his knees and gathered the map. It was only a matter of time before his troublesome younger self ran out of people to rob and turned to him.

"I've always known it was off, you showing up out of the blue one day and never leaving," Young Whitney went on. "What the yig do you want with us?"

"Relax, Whitney," Sora said. "I'm sure there's a perfectly good explanation."

Ever the optimist, Big Whitney thought.

There wasn't one. Even the truth seemed foolish after every conversation with Kazimir reinforced how pointless this project was. Luckily, Whitney had been preparing for just this moment.

"I was a cartographer before I came here," he said. "I do it to pass the time."

"Liar." Young Whitney ripped the map out from under him and held it up, earning a scolding from Sora for being cruel. He ignored her. "Look, right here. It says barrier. There isn't anything natural about that. You're with the Crown, aren't you? They're going to turn this place into a fortress before the Black Sands invade, aren't they?"

"I swear, I just make maps." He extended his hand for it. Young Whitney pulled it back, crumpling the edge.

"C'mon, Whit," Sora implored. "Look at his face. He's being honest."

"That's just because you're bad at reading people," Young Whitney said. "You thought my father was kind."

Big Whitney considered smacking his younger self before realizing he wasn't just doing it for Sora's sake, but for his father's—a man he'd spent a lifetime hating before watching the life drain slowly from his crippled body.

"Just give it back, and I won't tell your mother," Big Whitney said.

"You think I care what you tell her?" Young Whitney retorted.

Now Big Whitney was pushing his tongue against the back of his teeth to keep from shouting at the boy. The truth was, what happened to Rocco had only made Young Whitney more of a brat, unpleasant to be around even in the minimal time Big Whitney spent with him. He wasn't just a scamp, as Big Whitney admittedly was and had been, but he was an angry one. And Lauryn let him get away with pretty much anything… if he even showed his face around the farm, he never helped tend.

"If your father were around—" Big Whitney said.

"He isn't," Young Whitney snapped. "I thought you were protecting me when I was little, but I'm not so stupid now. You were up to something, taking credit like that, getting dad beaten. Now, this?" He raised the map in one hand and picked up his candle with the other. "You're going to tell me the truth, or I'm going to burn it."

"Whitney, you're being ridiculous," Sora said. "All he's done is help."

"And know your name somehow when he first arrived. Maybe you forgot that, but I haven't. If you never showed up that day, maybe they would have just taken it out on me. You weaseled yourself into our home, got rid of my father. Now you live next door. By the gods... have you been trying to get close with my mother, you sick freak?"

"Why does everyone keep thinking that?" Big Whitney said, and immediately wished he hadn't.

Young Whitney's face contorted with rage. It was then that Big Whitney realized this must have been bubbling up in his doppelgänger for years. That mistake his first day in Elsewhere, when he still thought Kazimir's words of caution were foolishness. He'd barely spoken a sentence to Young Whitney in years, hardly seen him, but seeing the map brought it all erupting to the surface.

"Look, I'm telling you the truth," Big Whitney said. "The map is worthless; it's just a hobby. There's no fortress, no plans, and I for sure have no feelings for your mother besides gratitude. I'm practically wedded to Alless from the Manor for Iam's sake!"

Iam's name drew a curious look from Sora. Most of the time, when he wasn't careful with his language in Elsewhere, people stared or repeated themselves on a loop. Not her. She simply looked confused.

"Then you won't mind if I do this?" Young Whitney said. He raised the candle to the corner of the parchment, and the flame took to it. "Too bad. This gods-forsaken place would be better off as a fortress."

"No!" Big Whitney yelped.

"Whitney what are you doing!" Sora shouted. She shoved by him, knocking him onto a pile of sticks. Without thinking, she sliced her palm on the whittling knife, then held it over the burning map. The fire leaped off it and into her palm where it dissipated. A few seconds later, the map lay on the ground, only the corner burned away.

Young Whitney stared at her, then the map, aghast. Big Whitney did the same. It'd been so long since he'd seen her blood magic it caught him off guard.

It took a moment for Sora to grasp what she'd done. "Whitney, I..." she said.

"You can..." Young Whitney said at the same time.

"I can explain."

"Is anyone honest around here?" Young Whitney glowered at Big Whitney one more time, then stormed off into the forest.

"Whitney, wait!" Sora called after him and followed.

Big Whitney kneeled by the map he'd spent so many tireless hours crafting. Ashes from it brushed against his cheek, carried on the wind.

"What game is this now?" he said. He swore he'd locked his pantry same as any other day. And he'd made the lock, which meant it was far beyond his younger self's skills to pick and it hadn't been broken. A quarter of his hard work, ruined. Months of labor, as if Elsewhere were telling him to stop seeking passage.

He clutched it against his chest. "I'm trying my best," he whispered. "Isn't that enough?" Nothing and nobody answered—not even Kazimir appeared behind him as the wraithlike upyr often did when he lost his way —only silence. All he could be sure of was that his insistence on searching for holes in the barrier had caused Young Whitney to witness Sora's blood magic, something he'd never done until years after leaving Troborough.

What it meant, he wasn't sure. All he could do was brace himself and hope that the history he knew hadn't strayed too far this time.

"Whitney!" Sora shouted again as Young Whitney disappeared into the brush.

Whitney sighed, folded the map and tucked it into his pocket, sighed again, then stood. He lightly jogged after them, knowing he needed to give them a chance to work things out. If he'd seen Sora use blood magic at their age, after all that time knowing he'd been lied to, he would not have been okay.

He shoved his way past sharp branches, swatting them as they poked and scratched at his face and arms, but he continued.

"This part of your game?" Whitney whispered at the sky. "Fallen god bastards. Where's Iam when you need him?"

The terrain dove into a steep slope down a hillside coated in years worth of rotting leaves. Whitney slid a bit, but it was on purpose. Sure-footed as a goat, he used stumps and roots to slow his descent.

"Whitney!" Sora shouted up ahead. The boy's head twitched slightly, almost turning around, but instead, he hopped a few rocks to the other side of the stream. Sora followed.

Little bastard is fast. It was a poor choice of words, what with Rocco's passing.

He wasn't real!

But he was, and that meant Young Whitney was every bit as real as Big Whitney was. This was his world now as much as he resisted it. As he got closer, Sora caught up to Young Whitney. Big Whitney crouched behind some bushes within earshot to give them a bit of privacy—but only a bit.

"Were you planning on telling me you were a gods damned witch?" Young Whitney asked.

"Witch?" Sora looked hurt. "I'm not a witch. I can do a little blood magic, that's all."

"Right, and old Mrs. Dodson only drinks a little."

"That's not fair, Whitney." Sora pointed her finger. "I would have told you, but I knew you'd act exactly like this."

"Well, aren't you some kind of a genius? You knew that if your best and only friend in the world found out you'd been lying to him for, how long? A year? Two? Ten? You just somehow knew he'd react in a completely normal and rational way. Bravo." Whitney clapped his hands slowly.

"You're a real piece of shog, you know that?" Sora punched Whitney in the arm, and this time it wasn't playful. "It's not like I chose this, you know."

"Oh, someone forced you to cut yourself and throw fireballs?"

"That's not what I meant. You have parents—"

"Had."

Sora growled. "You're insufferable. You know what I meant! My parents died so long ago I don't even know what they looked like. Do you know I don't even know their names? Wetzel is all I've ever had, and he's taught me a few ways to protect myself. Take care of myself."

"It's a good thing he did. If he's *all you ever had,* then I guess I'm not needed anymore. Good luck with your life, Sora."

Sora grabbed hold of his tunic, but he yanked it away then turned around and said, "It's too late. You're the only reason I stuck around in this gods-forsaken town, and even you can't be honest with me."

"Oh, c'mon Whitney, you know that's not what I meant."

"It's all a yigging joke."

"What?"

"Life. My mom won't scream at me no matter what I do or how much she wants to. Her *employee's* a fraud. Everyone remembers my dad as this kind, loyal man, and now you. Nobody's honest, nobody cares. Why should I?"

"Whitney…"

"No, I can't take it anymore." And with that, Whitney took off, scaling the cliffside.

"Whitney, wait!" Sora shrieked, tears welling in the corners of her eyes.

"It's too late, knife-ear. Goodbye."

Hearing that term seemed to stop Sora in her tracks. "Fine, go you selfish child!" Sora screamed. "You think your father was cruel, you're so much worse you're a… a" She threw her hands up in frustration then ran directly toward Big Whitney. She was so distracted she didn't even see him, but he could see the shimmer of tears on her cheeks.

That little shog-faced prick.

As soon as Sora passed, Whitney made his way for the small cliff. His fingertips found a jutting rock, and he started the climb. Fire stirred inside of him. He imagined this was how Sora felt anytime she called upon Elsewhere. It was like molten lava burning a hole in his chest, begging to escape by any means necessary.

The wall was smooth, but he found plenty of hand and footholds. It would have challenged most, but it was easier than scaling the Whispering Wizards tower, and he'd done that carrying the Splintering Staff in his teeth on the way back down. Close to the top, he felt something pelt his shoulder. Figuring it was just a stone bouncing down from above, disturbed by Young Whitney or an animal, he kept going. Then he felt another and another. The fourth one hit him squarely on the head.

"Hey!" he shouted, looking up to see Young Whitney throwing rocks down at him. "Cut it out!"

"Then leave me alone, freak," Young Whitney yelled back. All his talk of leaving yet he hadn't made it far. "This is none of your business."

"You, have, no…" Whitney huffed, throwing his leg up and rolling onto the clearing, "…idea, how wrong, you are."

"This isn't about you," Young Whitney said. "You can go back to your little house on my farm and finish out your days doing gods-know-what with my mom. I'm done. This place is shog, and I'm through living in it."

He turned to walk away again, and Big Whitney grabbed his shoulder.

"Geez, kid, just stop for a second," he said, still panting. "You're acting like a lunatic."

Young Whitney stopped but didn't turn around. His shoulders heaved like he was holding back rage.

"You don't want to do this," Big Whitney said. "Trust me."

"Why's that?" he barked, whipping back around. There was something about his eyes, something violent and unrestrained.

Big Whitney raised his hands, palms out. "Just calm down, and you'll see reason."

"Reason? I see reason better than ever before. This place is worthless. The people are worthless liars. There's something more out there, and I'm going to find it. Something real."

"I get that," Whitney said. "More than you could ever understand, I get it. But here's the thing… it's going to seem like a good idea for a while. A long while, really. Truthfully, up until right now."

"What are you talking about?"

"Leaving here. The world is amazing. I've seen more than I could fit in a million books. Dwarves, dragons, big, strange octopus-looking things called wianu, giants, giant women."

"What is your point?"

"My point is that nothing in this world is more important than what you have right here, right now."

"Which is what? A mom who's been broken since dad died? I have exactly one friend here, and she's been lying to me for ages. Why shouldn't I leave?"

"You love her," Big Whitney said.

"You'd better yigging take that back."

"Why can't you just admit it?"

Young Whitney, who Big Whitney had to admit wasn't very young anymore, drew his fist back to punch. Whitney had always been fast—that was what being a thief was all about—but farming for so long made him strong as well. His hand snapped up and his fingers closed around Young Whitney's balled fist.

"Stop it," Big Whitney said, but the boy kicked at him instead. Big Whitney scooped under his leg, still holding his fist and lowered him to the ground. Young Whitney thrashed.

"I don't want to hurt you."

"Well, I want to hurt you, home wrecker," Young Whitney said.

"You're out of your mind," Big Whitney said through his teeth as he struggled to hold the boy down. "Mother—your mother is not my type. She's… old."

"She's like your age, shog-breath."

Whitney flipped the boy over onto his stomach and wrenched his arm behind his back, pulling it up with a sharp jab.

Young Whitney screamed.

"If I let you go, will you stop attacking me?" Big Whitney asked.

He didn't respond, but Whitney took it as a 'yes.' Before releasing him, Big Whitney slapped the boy hard in the side of the head. "Don't you ever call her knife-ear again, do you understand me?"

Young Whitney clenched his jaw.

Big Whitney hit him again. "Yes?"

"Yes," Young Whitney said reluctantly.

"Yes, sir?"

"Suck shog."

Big Whitney laughed and let the boy go. He rolled away the moment he was free, then sprung to his feet, defensive.

"You gonna leave me alone now?" Young Whitney asked.

"Not a chance," Big Whitney said.

"What are you really doing here, *Willis*?"

"Clearly, the gods sent me here to make sure you don't make the same mistakes I did and run from here, you worthless piece of shog."

"Gods, huh?" Young Whitney scoffed. "I heard you talking about Iam. No one talks about Iam here. Not even Father Drimmond. So, you show up talking about that evil bastard, you've got a map of our town with **X**'s marked all over it, you kill my dad—"

"I didn't kill your father."

"Whatever," he continued. "He wouldn't have died if you hadn't interfered."

"He wouldn't have died if you didn't steal that crown!"

"Crown? What yigging crown?" Young Whitney asked. "It was a necklace. I knew it, man, you're crazy."

That gave Whitney a reason to pause. Was he crazy? Was he imagining this? At the start of this adventure into death, he'd believed he was dreaming. Was he right and had never woken up?

"You some kind of Shieldsman?" Young Whitney asked.

Whitney laughed harder than he remembered doing since before Sora exiled him. The thought of wearing that ridiculous costume like Torsten. He wiped a tear from his eye and said, "You've got no idea how funny that is."

"Well, your story makes no sense. So either start talking about why you really want me here or I'm walking."

Big Whitney considered telling him everything but worried what might happen if he did.

"Okay, fine." Young Whitney turned to walk away again.

"I'm you!" Big Whitney blurted, forcing the boy to turn back.

Young Whitney's head tilted. All the anger fled his eyes, instead replaced by a blank stare that Whitney found far more chilling. "What does that mean?" his younger self said. "What does that mean?" It wasn't the first time Whitney heard someone in Elsewhere respond on a loop and it rarely, if ever, meant anything good was about to happen. "What does that mean?"

"Not really, I mean," Big Whitney clarified. "I've made the same dumb mistakes you have. I told you I had a friend named Sora. She was more than a friend, way more, and I left her just like you're planning to leave yours."

Young Whitney's head straightened and his eyes refocused. "We aren't like that."

"I've seen how she looks at you." It was true, and Whitney couldn't believe he'd never seen it when he was younger. "Shog, kid, I've seen the way you look at her."

"Like I said, crazy."

"If you don't have feelings for her at all, then go back there and tell her goodbye. For real. Tell her you're going off on some grand adventure to see the world, that you'd rather run away from your problems than face them. Tell her this is for the best. Do it. I dare you."

Young Whitney blew out a breath. "You're a dick." He shook his head and started back on his path to wherever the wind was going to take him.

"You can't. Because it'll hurt too much."

Big Whitney watched for a few seconds. The Elsewhere barrier was just beyond a large tree, and Young Whitney was about to pass through it.

"Coward," he said.

"Liar," Young Whitney replied.

And with that, Young Whitney crossed through the barrier. Whitney watched as light coruscated across the now rippling surface of the transparent wall which he now saw stretched over the whole town like a dome.

As the barrier undulated, Whitney caught a glimpse of something beyond it, darkness unlike any he'd seen before in his life, and then as quickly as it started, it ended, leaving only eerie silence.

He thought about Sora, both Soras. He'd just had to witness one of them experience the same heartache his own must have when he'd been the petulant, selfish child who couldn't even gather enough guts to say a proper goodbye. Sadness—no, not sadness… that word wasn't nearly strong enough. Sorrow filled every pound of him. Six years. It took six years in this shogpile to figure out a lesson as simple as how horrible a human being he had been.

A sudden shift made Whitney's heart leap and his stomach flip. No longer was he surrounded by thick trees and the sound of a bubbling brook, but instead, he found himself on the bank of the Shellnak River. He looked over each of his shoulders in turn, searching for something, anything to tell him what had just happened.

After a moment, he realized he was standing in the same place he and Kazimir had arrived so many years ago, but the remnants of the Ferryman's boat were no longer there.

Did I do it? Did I escape Elsewhere?

Hope flooded over him, enveloping him like a warm blanket. He turned and saw Mount Lister practically sparkling in the distance. Puffy, white clouds frolicked along against a sky painted bright blue. Then, something happened. The blue sky darkened, turning a harsh shade of reddish-purple. The clouds disappeared. Loutis stained the sky alone, pale and pathetic as ever.

"No, no, no," Whitney said, the rush of hope drowned by despair. "No, no, no, no, no, no, no, no, no, no, no, no."

He heard footsteps shuffling behind him. Thinking it to be Kazimir, appearing as usual in the worst moments, he spun. Instead, he saw a small, familiar boy with tawny brown hair, wind-swept and dirty.

"No, no, no, no, no."

"Welcome to Troborough!" the boy exclaimed, his features bright, life not yet turning him into a hateful prick.

"No way," Whitney said. He rushed forward, placed the palm of his hand on Even-Younger-Whitney's head, and shoved him to the side "Out of my way shog-for-brains."

"Excuse me?" the boy said, his voice already far in the distance.

Whitney knew exactly what he needed to do. His map, which he could still feel in his pocket, was covered in marks and Xs, but there was one place he was saving for last. The one place Elsewhere seemed to refuse him access.

Wetzel's shack stood at the base of a tiny hill. Whitney crossed a field of yellow daffodils, small bugs stirring with each step.

"Hey, mister!" Young Whitney shouted. "You don't want to go there!"

"Yeah, I really do, kid," Whitney called back over his shoulder.

"You don't want to go there! You don't want to go there! You don't want to go there!" The boy's word echoed over and over again, and it just kept going as Whitney got closer to the hut.

Again, his body froze outside the shack, every muscle unable to press forward. He fought, but nothing happened. He remembered Kazimir's warning, "You don't carve your own path here."

But Kazimir was wrong. Kazimir had damned himself to this place, Whitney hadn't. Besides, where was the upyr now?

Whitney did the only thing he could think of. He didn't have faith in gods or goddesses; he'd never needed them before. All he knew was all those many years ago he'd made a mistake, and his mistake hurt the only person who'd ever truly mattered to him.

"Sora!" Whitney shouted. "Sora!"

He summoned whatever strength he had in his body, and farming had made him sturdy as an ox. Still, it took every ounce of his energy to lift his left leg. But it moved. Ever so slightly, it moved.

That gave him hope again. He reached deep inside of himself, pushing away all thoughts of Iam or any other god. He thought only of reaching Sora again. His right foot lifted and he placed it down, one step closer.

"Ha!" Whitney shouted loud enough for Yarrington to hear—if there was a Yarrington in Elsewhere. "Suck shog, gods!"

Behind him, he could still hear the boy saying, "You don't want to go there!" on repeat. But Whitney did.

He focused and moved his other foot. He did it, again and again, until he stood right at the threshold of Wetzel's shack. He considered knocking but didn't care. It wasn't even real Wetzel. He'd seen that the barrier of this realm extended all the way across the sky. If there were any connection between Elsewhere and Pantego, it would be in that shack where Sora had grown up. It was the only place he hadn't looked.

He reached down, turned the knob, and the door opened.

Inside, there was nothing at all.

No tables, no chairs, no stacks of strange tomes, no bed, no potions. Nothing at all.

Whitney's chin hit his chest.

"Whitney?" came a voice from behind him.

As he turned, he saw the spectral form of a Panpingese woman, more beautiful and radiant than anything he'd ever seen before. Her long, dark hair fell just past her shoulders, her eyes practically glowed, amber like the sun.

"Sora?" he said. "Sora!"

Whitney tried to move again, but he was stuck. He pushed but still couldn't budge.

"Sora!" he screamed again.

"You could have told me the truth," Sora said, her voice distant, floating on air.

"What? What do you mean? Sora, I knew you didn't forget about me! Oh, gods." He squeezed his eyelids shut, worried he was seeing things. When he opened them again, she remained in front of him. "Sora, I know you didn't mean to do this, but only you can get me out!"

"Did he know?" Sora said.

Whitney looked over his shoulder at Wetzel's shack, not understanding. "Did who know?"

"At least he never lied."

"You're right, I'm sorry. I've lied to about so much. But I want you to know the truth. How I fee—"

"In time?" she interrupted.

"No," Whitney said, "Now. Just get me out, and I'll tell you everything. I'm so sorry." He ran to her and went to embrace her, but his arms passed right through.

"Forgiveness?"

Whitney spun back to her. Her face grew angry and then suddenly, her form disappeared and in its place was just a charred patch of grass. Whitney was suddenly free to move again and fell to his knees, clawing at the ground, tears flowing more freely than he'd ever remembered.

"Why!" he sobbed, staring down. "Sora, come back to me. Sora!" He looked up to the bloodstained sky. "What kind of sick game is this!" he screamed.

He heard the shuffling of feet, expected to see Kazimir, and then Younger Whitney appeared before him. All this bedlam he'd been causing was bound to bring Kazimir around and beg him to stay calm so he can remain on his vacation, but it was clear to Whitney now. That conversation they'd had, and that deal—the upyr only made it because his time in Elsewhere was over. He was gone... free.

The thought of Kazimir getting to leave despite all the awful things he'd done made Whitney even angrier. Sure, they'd moved on from being enemies, he was the only thing he had here, his only connection to the real world. Big Whitney gritted his teeth and began to rise, his head lifting first. He was done playing Elsewhere's games.

"You bring her bac—"

Whitney's words were cut short as he saw the boy, no longer the boy. His face looked as if it were melting like wax under a hot flame. Beneath the pink flesh that had been, there was dark, blood red, scaly hide. Blood poured down his face from two holes in his forehead where horns were growing. He showed his teeth, sharp, long, needle thin.

Whitney fell back on his hands and crab crawled backward until his head slammed against the door of Wetzel's shack.

"Whitney, you stupid man," his deformed doppelgänger said, voice now so deep Whitney could feel it in his bones.

"What... what are you?" he asked as if he didn't already know. Churches of Iam and cults depicted enough demon spirits of Elsewhere for him to take a guess at what one might look like.

"That does not matter anymore. You've been so concerned about what the barrier was keeping in," the demon said, approaching him, "that you've failed to wonder what it might be keeping out. Heragi, God of Misfortune had his fun with you in this realm of mischief, but the will of fire has broken the barrier, and I've had my eyes on you since you fled Troborough. A heartless thief like you deserves torture far worse than this."

Wetzel's shack suddenly exploded from within throwing Whitney into the river. Wood splintered like arrows, some piercing his flesh. A deafening sound so horrific it belonged in nightmares filled the sky, making all other sounds nonexistent. Whitney couldn't even hear himself breath. He rose to his feet, knees shaking.

Demons, hundreds of them, all unique but equally terrifying, poured out of the rupture beneath the shack. They gathered behind the demon that was Young Whitney. One had more eyes than Whitney could count, blinking all at once. A sharp, hooked beak protruded from another's face. And yet another appeared like a goat with ears and tusks like a mammoth.

A blinding light flashed somewhere beyond the town square. Whitney chanced looking away from the horde to see something bright white and in the shape of an Eye of Iam. Dozens of figures moved around within the light, but Whitney couldn't make any of them out.

He tried to speak, but nothing came out. He looked back to the demons.

The one who was Young Whitney smiled, each needle-like tooth digging into its own flesh and producing pinpricks of blood. "Run."

XXXIII

THE MYSTIC

In so many ways, Wetzel hadn't done his job to prepare Sora for the world at large. Sure, she knew there were beasts and evil—but never could she have imagined the kind of evil she'd faced with Whitney and Torsten these last few months. Sora had never been in trouble with the law before Whitney. She hadn't even been in deep trouble with Wetzel other than the time she'd set one of his bookshelves ablaze while practicing blood magic.

Presently, she stood outside a dark room that resembled the one Lord Aran Bokeo had taken her to beneath his bookstore. The mystics had their servants carry her from the Well of Wisdom to the highest floor of the tower, where it tapered to fit only a single, circular room. She was too exhausted to protest, both in mind and body. Summoning enough fire to rupture her bar guai, seeing into the past—it was a struggle just to stay upright, let alone fight.

The servants placed Sora on her feet just within the threshold and dared not go further. She caught Kai's eye as he turned to leave. The gravity of his expression was enough for her to know she was in trouble. He nodded to her as if offering good luck, but said nothing as he and the others left.

Two huge doors slammed shut behind her and startled Sora forward. A bridge led her to a circular dais in the center surrounded by rushing water. Floating, blue torches lit alongside it as she went. When she reached the platform, the bridge disappeared.

Statues of those same creatures Lord Bokeo had called wianu jutted out from the red walls, spitting water from a slit of a mouth. Their two giant eyes, all fashioned from gems more precious than Sora had ever seen, although unmoving, sparkled with the pride of life. She hadn't noticed in the other chamber, likely because the waters didn't rage like this, but tendril-like appendages thrust up from the surface, creating white foam breaks.

Aihara Na, leader of the Secret Council of Mystics, and the most frightening woman Sora had ever met—Queen Bliss included—sat on her throne. Seven others dotted the perimeter of the dais, each with its own yellow-robed mystic seated atop except one. They no longer shrouded their faces with hoods. She recognized Madam Jaya and Master Huyshi, and the others whose names she didn't know. They all looked different, yet had a sameness—an ageless quality, even though some looked no younger or older than Sora and yet others, gray and withered.

Maybe it was their eyes, holding all the wisdom of every mystic come and gone, both calming and terrifying at the same time.

Scary as the Council might've been, Sora refused to cow before them. They'd held back far too much and lied about far more. Even now, she could feel defiance growing once again. She wished she had Aquira with her, wished she could command her little wyvern friend to shoot forth and burn them all to a crisp, but she hadn't seen Aquira since fainting of exhaustion outside the Well of Wisdom.

Aihara Na steepled her fingers, elbows pressed firmly into the fabric of her armrests. Those ageless eyes looked over her overlong fingertips, calculating.

Sora took a deep breath to steady herself for the verbal onslaught she knew was coming.

"Sora of Troborough," Aihara began, "you are brought here before—"

"Why don't you call me by my real name?" she interrupted. She couldn't help herself. Seeing the mystics again now that she'd had time to collect her thoughts caused the words to cascade off her tongue like a waterfall pounding against the rocks with unbridled fury. She was too weary to be coy. "Is it Nothhelm? Sumati?"

"Silence!" Madam Aihara Na bellowed as she stood from her throne and took two steps forward. Each footfall which was previously silent, now sounded like a thunderclap, resonating through Sora's very soul. "You stand here, guilty of willful rebellion against the Secret Council—"

"Rebellion? I don't remember swearing allegiance to anyone."

"If you open your mouth out of turn one more time, I will seal it shut permanently, is that understood? No, don't respond. Just stay silent." Madam Aihara returned to her throne, and this time Sora listened. The Mystic fell into her grand seat and waited a few long, calculating seconds before speaking again. "Your open *rebellion*, disregard for rules, and disrespect of our most sacred ritual place you before us for judgment. How do you plead?"

"Plead?" Sora asked. "I plead taken advantage of. Used by the mystics and lied to for reasons I do not understand."

"You were never lied to," Madam Jaya spoke up. "You simply weren't ready to know."

"It's all the same." Sora almost felt sorry for snapping at the mystic who'd she'd spent so much time training with, but she didn't let it stop her. "I spent my entire life wondering who I was, who my parents were. I... how long were you going to wait to tell me? Until I was over a century old?"

"Half a year ago, who were you?" Aihara continued. "No one. You were little more than some heathen blood mage holed up beneath some backwoods town's crazy healer's shack."

"You know nothing of Wetzel or Troborough."

"Final warning," Aihara said, drawing her fingers across her lips like a zipper.

"The Well of Wisdom is not some trinket to trifle with, yet you treated it as such," Aihara said. "You have opened your mind to the deepest depths, a veritable chasm of knowledge, and you've tainted the waters with your uneducated thoughts and frivolous human attachments like that to this… Whitney Blisslayer who fills your mind."

Sora felt the air flee her lungs. Now, words didn't come to her. She still hadn't told any of them about Whitney.

Madam Aihara paused, her lips tightening to a thin line, yet the corners pulled just barely. "You act surprised?"

"It's just… I…"

"Did you not think Madam Jaya would tell her superior of your dealings with the upyr?"

"I didn't think anything," Sora said, "but I made no mention of anyone but him." She looked to Madam Jaya, her instructor, whose expression betrayed her disappointment.

"Our vision pierces time and flesh," Madam Jaya said. "We've known all along what tethers you, what keeps you from dedicating yourself to this order. You must understand, Sora. Whitney is dead. Forever gone. Nothing you can do will bring him back."

"You're wrong," Sora said, despite the previous two warnings.

"Insolent girl." Aihara raised her hand, swiping it hard in one direction. Even from so great a distance, several meters away, Sora felt the slap against her face. Her cheeks grew hot as burning embers.

"Death is the nature of Elsewhere," Aihara said. "It is the other side which every living being in this world fights to stay away from until the fight leaves them. It is why only death can bridge the realms."

Sora pushed off the cold stone and returned to her feet. "I don't believe you."

"You dare question the Ancient One?" a mystic she hadn't met snapped.

"No, no. Ghing, let her speak. Perhaps she, in her short time on this world uncovered some great truth we've missed all these *centuries*."

"You said sacrifice was necessary to open Elsewhere, but I've done it without loss," Sora said.

"I've already told you, that was the upyr's doing, not your own, child," Madam Jaya said.

"I didn't tell you the whole truth."

"Tell me then, Sora, what do you think happened?" Madam Jaya said. She didn't even look disappointed anymore. Sora saw pity on the woman's face.

Sora recounted the story aboard Kazimir's ship, how she'd sent both Whitney and Kazimir to Elsewhere before the upyr could kill him.

"You do not call that a sacrifice?" Aihara said. "Come, now, Sora.

You've been grasping to willow branches in the middle of the Boiling Waters."

"At least I'm being honest!" Sora yelled. "I didn't kill anyone. Both Kazimir and Whitney still live within that place, I just… I know it."

"It was because of the upyr, Sora," Madam Jaya said.

"You saw them?" Madam Aihara said, ignoring Jaya.

Sora nodded.

"Then they have passed into that gods-forsaken realm," Aihara Na said. "They are gone, Sora, and it is high time you come to terms with it." She steepled her fingers again. "And even if they do live, what makes you so certain the gods would let them return if even they themselves cannot?"

A response died on the tip of Sora's tongue. She hadn't thought much about how to remove them once she'd opened the portal to Elsewhere. Call it blind faith, but she was sure things would come together once the deed was done.

"Many of us have sacrificed deeply for you, Sora Sumati," Aihara Na said. "Even your friend Aquira clings to life in your room after you forced her to nearly drain her body of flame. Without Madam Jaya's healing, she surely would have died."

Sora looked at Madam Jaya. Her teacher hung her head.

"I know what you saw in the Well," Aihara Na said. "How can you not understand how dangerous it is to resist Elsewhere now that you know?"

The news about Aquira caught her off guard, but Sora closed her eyes and tried to focus. She couldn't back down now. "It's different. I was still here, not in Elsewhere."

"Our entire Order crumbled because you were born when Elsewhere should have claimed you!" Aihara's voice made the room quake. "Your mother gave her life in your stead. She opened herself to Elsewhere and in doing so roused a fallen Goddess, inspiring the one called Redstar to cause so much death in the West. Even Liam, the man responsible for our ruin, died for you. An Order of hundreds, and now only seven. We've gone to great stakes to hide you away because my master—your mother—begged us to protect you. You think Wetzel was a stranger to us?"

She'd figured out by now that they knew him, but she had no idea how. "He was a mystic?" Sora asked, hopeful.

"Gods, no." Aihara looked aghast. "He was a student who outgrew the tower. He was headstrong, broke rules, and tried to take a shortcut with blood magic. We exiled him. Then, after your birth signaled our destruction, we needed someone we could trust. Someone right under Liam's nose where he would never think to look if he decided to end his curse by killing you, and where we wouldn't be tempted to bring you here before you were ready."

"Clearly, we didn't wait long enough," the mystic named Ghing chimed in.

"Or too long," said Huyshi.

"We knew Wetzel would do anything to earn our trust again," Aihara went on. "You see, rule breakers can still receive redemption from the Council."

"He died without knowing he did," Sora said, a harsh edge creeping into her tone. She took a moment to calm herself lest she earn more punishment.

"He continued to pursue blood magic against our wishes, and so, tainted you." Aihara stood.

"Did he know?" Sora asked abruptly.

"About who you are? Of course not." Hearing Aihara scoff in dismissal only served to fuel Sora's frustration. "All he knew was to look after a gifted child and impart what little knowledge he could."

"At least he never lied." She found relief in knowing he was ignorant. She was as close to the old codger as he would let anyone get to him, but he still raised her, opened up her mind. She couldn't bear the thought of being lied to by him as well.

"Sora, you miss the lesson. Wetzel betrayed us as you did, but forgiveness remains for those who atone. Even for you, who stole Madam Sumati, my master, from this world, stole even her name. But life itself was not your choice, and for that, you will not be punished any differently than any other apprentice who once walked these halls."

Sora shook her head. "I saw what happened. You did this. You allowed me to live. You killed Madam Sum—my mother—" Just saying it made her feel strange all over. "You cursed King Liam."

Aihara raised her hand and squeezed her fist. Sora's legs flew out from under her, and she slammed into the ground. Madam Jaya had to look away. The pain made Sora feel the familiar surge of Elsewhere, but along with it, her seared chest. The place where the bar guai rested throbbed. The ruptured fire amulet had left a dark, charred patch of skin between her breasts.

"You will not speak of the atrocities you saw within the Well of Wisdom again," Aihara said. She took several booming steps toward Sora. "You didn't see with eyes of understanding. Your refusal to wait until ready made sure of that. I did not kill your mother. I loved her like any student should their master. She gave her soul up to Elsewhere, siphoning her life away in sacrifice until even this pathetic, spectral form was beyond her."

Aihara extended a hand to grasp Sora's, but it passed right through. She turned her back and drew a long, beleaguered breath.

"Helping my master preserve your life when I knew it was against everything we believe in is my greatest regret," Aihara said, "but it is also why I refuse to give up on you. It is clear to me now that much of the fault in your disobedience lies with us. We should not have rushed you, especially after leaving you with a disobedient former student like Wetzel."

"You could have told me the truth," Sora said. She knew she should fight the anger swelling in her, but she was too tired. Nobody answered her remark. The mystics all remained still and silent except Huyshi who nodded meekly like he agreed with her.

"I tried to teach you the importance of patience," Madam Jaya said after a short while. "I should have tried harder Sora, and that is my failure as well."

"Should you choose the road to forgiveness, vowing to obey even the smallest command of this Council, to let go of this… mortal, Whitney, and forsake your endeavors to bring him back, we will allow you to remain within these walls as a servant. You will watch, observe and learn what it means to be a member of this Order. In time, when we think you are ready, you will be permitted to resume your training in the mystic arts."

"In time?" Sora said, incredulous.

"Yes. We hoped Wetzel would have you more prepared for the mystic studies, but we were wrong. He led you astray, but at the very least, he kept you alive and in a time when our allies were few, that was enough. When you are many years older and wiser, should your wisdom allow you to make better choices, we will revisit this council."

"It is a great honor, Sora," Huyshi said. "You are young, younger than most we ever took on in the golden days of the Order. Age will refine you. The fault of rushing you lies with us."

"He's right, Sora," Madam Jaya added. "Under your mother, any who violated the Well of Wisdom would have been exiled, or worse."

Aihara stopped pacing and stared straight into Sora's eyes. "Do you accept forgiveness, Sora Sumati?"

Sora's brow furrowed. She stared back at Ancient One Aihara Na, a thousand different responses bouncing around her head. Her entire life, she sought a place she could fit in. She hoped more than anything it could be this tower, once filled with people touched with the same Gift as her. Now, she felt more alone and out of place than ever before.

She couldn't help but imagine what Whitney would have said to people like this, who would have tied him down and kept him from the world—from adventure.

"Forgiveness?" she said, voice dripping with indignation. "I don't know why you think I need to receive forgiveness. You people have access to truth and you horde it away for yourselves. When I got to Yaolin, I wondered why my people seemed so content to live under their conquerors, but I see it now. You think that what I saw in the Well was corrupted, but I think you're wrong. I saw you, forcing our people to fight a war they no longer wanted to, and I saw my mother protecting them."

Aihara bit her lip. "Careful what you say next, girl."

"You've all been here so long and used so much power you've forgotten what it's like to be human. You think that makes you better, but you're wrong, and I think my mother saw it. I think that's why she did what she did that night, knowing how Liam would react. She found love after centuries and saw the need to rebuild the Order because all of you had become so… heartless."

"How dare you speak of her like that!" Aihara roared. She raised her hand and Sora flew back, sliding across the stone and nearly into the rushing waters. Aihara held her there, intense pressure building on all her limbs.

"Aihara, stop!" Madam Jaya shouted.

"No. It is time she learned respect!" Aihara pushed her hand forward, and Sora felt like she was being crushed. She hung over the ledge, further and further. She felt the water beat against her hair. She couldn't breathe or speak—it was the same feeling as when Redstar threatened to kill her, Whitney, and Torsten in the Webbed Woods. His may have been blood magic, but now Sora knew that all magic came from sacrifice, inside or out.

"She just found out who she is," Madam Jaya said. "Of course she's not thinking clearly."

"She just needs time," Huyshi said.

"We have no time," spoke another whom Sora hadn't heard before. "I've seen enough. She is no savior."

"I concur," said Ghing.

Aihara stalked forward, muttering in a mixture of languages. Elsewhere beckoned Sora as she struggled for air as it had before she stopped Redstar or banished Kazimir, burning in her chest.

No, not Elsewhere.

Sora couldn't move her head, but she turned her eyes downward and saw the bar guai. Each of the remaining five stones glowed as the disc spun, lifting from her chest.

She couldn't scream, but the pain was like nothing she'd ever experienced. Elsewhere called to her, the power begging her to return the call, but with the bar guai there, she couldn't answer. Her body felt like it was tearing in two.

"You *will* remain here without magic," Aihara said. "And you will learn the respect and patience required of a mystic. *My* Sora did not sacrifice her life so you could insult her people! Our visions said you would rebuild this broken Order, so you will serve until you're old and gray and every shred of beauty has left your cheeks if that's what it takes for you to learn. Another fifty years is like a blink of an eye to us."

The bar guai exploded from Sora's body and flew into Aihara's hand. Sora collapsed and gasped for air. She clutched her chest, feeling all the blood, hot and sticky. For a fleeting moment, dread gripped her until she realized something—she could answer Elsewhere's whispers again. She could feel that familiar pull again.

Sora heard Whitney's voice, frantic and desperate. Nesilia's sultry, seductive tones begged her to join her in the red mist. They were distant, but growing louder as more blood leaked from her wound.

Sora got onto all fours. "No," she rasped. "You've let me live a lie my whole life. I wanted answers, I got them."

"You got only what your eyes witnessed, but you fail to see the bigger picture," Aihara said. "You want your mother to have been as rebellious as you are, but it simply isn't true."

"I didn't mean about her."

Sora reached for her knife, but as her fingers closed around the grip, the water churned, the waves reached out and washed the knife into the pool.

Sora turned to see Aihara Na's hand outstretched to the moat. Then she rushed forward and pressed her palm to Sora's chest. The wound inflicted by removing the bar guai began to heal.

"You have no power here," Aihara said. "Now, you will start doing as told. It will take many months to repair the door to the Well of Wisdom. I suggest we start your service there."

Sora's hands balled into fists. "I didn't only use blood magic to open that door," she said, seething. "Or the bar guai." She thought back to her mother on that bed, channeling her power to offer her own life to Elsewhere. Opening that realm so Sora could live when she wasn't intended to.

Aihara removed her hand, revealing Sora's wholly healed chest. Sora closed her eyes and looked inward, focusing on the blood running through her veins, on her heartbeat. Fire crackled at her fingertips, swirling around her hands even though she didn't bleed. They were little more than embers, but they were there.

"What is this?" Aihara Na questioned. "What is she doing, Jaya? She cannot channel."

"'Blood of babe,'" Sora quoted Aihara's own false sacrifice back to her. "'Bone of child...'"

"Stop it. That's not real."

"Bring forth the power of Elsewhere's fire.'"

Sora could barely hear their responses, but the shock on Aihara's face was enough to know she'd figured it out. Their ritual may have been nothing, but in every good lie held specks of truth. Whitney had taught her that, and his insane view of the world often proved correct.

The secret to opening Elsewhere, and all that came with it which the mystics feared so much was the sacrifice of a life. Her own. And she didn't need a knife to sacrifice what was required to open Elsewhere and reach Whitney. She didn't need anything but herself. She knew that now. And even if she never found a way to bring him back, at least she'd be with someone who accepted her.

Every word in the room became distant and removed, obscured by the vague whispers of Elsewhere. Sora wasn't sure how she did it back at the Well, but she had channeled from within like a true mystic. Like her mother, an Ancient One who seemed without equal.

She kept digging within for the answer. Nothing and no one existed except for her own soul, and she offered it willingly, just as her mother had. She couldn't say what channeling her power felt like, but she knew she was doing it. Embers churned around her hands now in a heavy current floating around her eyes. It felt like the energy when she released a stream of fire from her fingertips only it was focused within, rushing through her veins toward her chest.

Aihara used her power to become corporeal and grabbed Sora's face. "Sora, you know not what powers you're flirting with! Control yourself!"

"Let me go!" she roared. Light exploded from her just as it had in the Webbed Woods. Then the room seemed to fade away into a thick reddish haze, the cries of the mystics replaced by foreign shrieks.

Splayed out before her were the kingdoms of the world. She could see it all like in her visions, yet with no detail. A deep, purple sky loomed over everything, and the ground was rent, molten liquid pouring from the fissure. Sora spun when she recognized the feeling of solid ground. She saw sharp, yellow teeth just before they sank into her flesh, only they didn't sink in. They passed through her. Hundreds of the creatures did the same, a cold, empty feeling washing over her as they did. Some had skulls capped by a series of horns, but each one was different. There were faces with large beaks filled with razor-sharp teeth. Others had a dozen eyes, at least, covering a flat area beneath the facial crests.

Sinewy muscle flexed as they beat the dirt, running on all fours. Their blood red skin glistened, and pockets of pus oozed from what looked like open sores.

"Shog! Shog! Shog!" She heard him before she saw him, but knew without any question—it was Whitney.

His dirty blonde hair bobbed beyond the mass of creatures, red, horned, and scaly beasts, ugly as could be.

"Well done, my child." Sora turned when she heard her. She'd heard that voice before, sensual, intoxicating, euphoric even. "I can feel it. My power, returning from its buried prison after so long."

"Nesilia?" Sora asked. "Where are you?"

The Buried Goddess stood in the distance, towering over a dark figure. Sora could hear indistinct shouting—words spoken with conviction. She closed the gap, and as she did, saw Torsten wrestling with someone clothed in red. At first, she thought it to be one of the mystics. Before she could better assess the scene, she saw Whitney again, running toward her.

No demons followed him this time. She hiked up her kimono and forsook all as she ran toward him.

"Whitney!" she called out.

"Sora!" came a cry from somewhere behind her. She looked over her shoulder at Aihara Na's vacillating form but didn't stop. The old mystic cradled something in her arms and shouted at it. "Stop the sacrifice! There's still a chance to stop!"

Sora continued ignoring her. She saw Torsten, face covered in blood and surrounded by snow, but that didn't matter. She saw a young nobleman wearing a crown, floating in the air, but he didn't matter either. All that mattered was Whitney, and suddenly they were wrapped in each other's arms. Chaos surrounded them, as it always had, but as she looked at him, she felt more at peace than ever before.

"Whit." She was laughing and crying at the same time. "Whitney. I never thought I'd see you again... I... I'm so sorry, I..."

"Shut up," Whitney said as he squeezed her. "You're ruining the moment." His arms were stronger than she remembered. He even had a patchy beard that itched her neck.

Sora laughed again and allowed herself to get lost in his embrace. And it was while she was there, looking over his shoulder, that she noticed where they were. The quaint, wooden homes were unmistakable.

She pulled away, struggling to catch her breath. "Are we in—"

"Troborough," Whitney finished for her. "Welcome home."

She stumbled over what to say next, then settled on her grabbing his face and kissing him deeply, just as she wished she'd done back on that ship in Winde Port before she and her powers ruined everything.

Whitney's eyes went wide, shocked. It wasn't the reaction she expected. She was about to pull back and punch him in his arm when he grabbed her tighter and dragged her to the ground. An axe whizzed by as they hit the dirt. A thunk sounded as it buried into the chest of a King's Shieldsman behind them.

"A Shieldsman?" Whitney said, breathless. Sora wasn't sure if it was due to the kiss or dodging certain death. "How in the world?"

Sora recalled who she'd seen when she entered Elsewhere. "Torsten is here too!" She pointed at the tear in the world she'd passed. She now saw that it was within what appeared like a ruined Church of Iam. The air around it coruscated with energy, but she could see a haze of snow against a backdrop of a black circle surrounded by a ring of fire.

"There, by the church!" They saw him and then he was gone, hidden behind a wall of demons.

"Oh," Whitney said. "That's not really Torsten. Elsewhere is awful."

"No, right there!" she shouted, but a heap of demons obstructed their view.

"Shog in a barrel," Whitney said. "We've gotta get out of here." Whitney started pulling Sora away from the demons and the portal. "Keeps getting better."

Sora looked behind her, the mass of Elsewhere's hounds was already moving away from them, but before them stood two snarling demons. Sora glanced down, then realized her knife remained in the water of the Mystic Council's throne room. She could still hear Aihara Na whispering to her, chanting with the others like they were miles away. She couldn't go back for the weapon now.

"Hold on," Whitney said. He kneeled and pried the sword out of the fallen Shieldsman's gauntleted hands, then pointed it at the beasts.

"Let me." Sora extended her hand for him to cut it, but instead, he sneered.

"Come at me, demon!" he roared. She wasn't sure what he'd been doing for the last weeks, but he didn't seem afraid in the slightest. Almost eager to fight rather than sneak around it.

In response, one of the beasts bounded toward him, but Whitney rolled aside, then came up waving the weapon before him.

"Goooood dog," he said. "Good dog."

The creature snapped at him while the other paced back and forth behind it. The demon rushed at Whitney again. Once more, he attempted to roll out of the way, but this time, the beast was ready for it and thrust its claws out.

They raked Whitney's thigh, drawing three long, bloody lines. The demon snapped out its arm once more, and as Whitney dodged the swipe, he dove toward the monster. His sword found purchase, digging into the demon's flesh. Whitney pulled hard, dragging the blade across the demon's chest. Blood poured from the chasm as the creature collapsed on top of him.

Whitney let out a groan, and his hand slammed hard against the dirt. His sword was pinned under the massive corpse, making an attack impossible as the second demon pounced. Whitney rolled and used the corpse as a shield. He was flat on his back, unable to tear his arm and weapon free. It snapped its jaws wildly at him as he struggled to hold it back with the other hand.

Sòra rushed in. It wasn't a smart move. With her bar guai shattered and no weapon with which to draw blood, she resorted to punching the creature. Its hide was thick as a zhulong.

"Get off him, vile creature!" Sora shouted as she punched it again and again. The demon momentarily stopped gnashing at Whitney, turned, and regarded Sora with deep-set eyes so red they appeared to bleed. Its right arm snapped out, throwing Sora far and hard. She hit the ground with a grunt but didn't let it stop her.

She rolled and stood, preparing to continue the barrage. As she started, she noticed something red out of the corner of her eye. Her arm was bleeding. The demon must have scratched her with one of its claws.

Focusing, she tried to call forth the fires of Elsewhere, but that familiar feeling wasn't there. Perhaps it was because she was now in Elsewhere, she wasn't sure.

The demon set its focus back on Whitney, snarling gutturally in some demonic tongue. Spit showered Whitney as he scrambled to defend himself.

"A little help?" he shouted.

"I can't!" she shouted.

"Do something!" he cried. "Anything!"

Sora tried again to call upon Elsewhere to bring forth flames. When there was still no response, she dug down deep to channel like a mystic as she just had when opening Elsewhere. No crackling power raced toward her heart from within, nothing.

"Aquira!" she cried, thrusting her hand out before her. Nothing happened. She shook out her hand, rolled her neck, and took a deep breath, watching as the demon's bite grew ever closer to Whitney's exposed face. He tried relentlessly to stab it, but the angle was all wrong.

"Aquira!" She tried the word that signaled her bar guai, desperate.

Whitney thrashed around.

"It's not working! I... I can't call fire!"

The beast's razor-sharp teeth punctured Whitney's shoulder, and he squealed. Sora conceded to charging it again, hoping to knock it free so she might be able to reach the sword.

"Kaaazaaamiiiiir."

The name of the upyr who'd tried to devour her filled the air, a deep and cavernous bellow. The creature stopped gnawing and looked up, past her. She wasn't sure what terror looked like on the face of such a monster, but she was sure it was there. It unmounted Whitney and scurried away.

"You better run!" Whitney screamed, flipping over and grabbed his sword. Then he too saw whatever was behind Sora and the color fled his cheeks. She almost didn't want to look but did anyway.

Barrelling toward them was a blob of tentacles, rising tall as the Cathedral of Yarrington itself. It whipped a group of demons out of the way, swatting them through the air like flies. More massive tentacles unfurled, revealing a maw filled with thousands of teeth, above which sat two giant eyes, one scarred and calloused. The mere sight of them made Sora's spine tingle.

"What in Iam's name is that?" Sora asked.

"A friend of Kazimir's," Whitney replied. He tried lifting the sword with his good arm, but the wound in his shoulder made him grimace.

"Is he still here?"

"It's complicated."

"What do we do?"

The monster roared, making the very air tremble. One of its tentacles slapped down into the Shellnak, so tremendous it nearly drained the river. A deep furrow cut through the ground, fleeing demons tumbling into it.

"Run!"

Whitney took Sora's hand, and they took off into the town. A tentacle slammed through farmer Branson's house, crushing the roof. They ducked under the flying debris and veered right toward the town center.

"He's not here!" Whitney shouted back at it.

Another tentacle crushed the Twilight Manor and sent them back the other way toward Mrs. Dodson's place. Two more landed with a quake and blocked off the road.

They found themselves cornered into the ruins of the old Troborough Church of Iam. They backed up against what was left of the stone wall behind the altar, nowhere to go. Torsten stood in the center of the aisle, stretching his hand toward a floating child who was within the center of a strange rift in the air that seemed to be following him. His face wracked with pain, he didn't seem to notice them.

"Torsten, watch out!" Whitney shouted just as a tentacle came slithering over the broken walls. Then more.

Sora thought she saw the face of a familiar woman in the rift before the tentacles covered Torsten and it stopped before the altar. The hideous beast drew itself over the roofless church, casting them both in shadow. Sora and Whitney went to grasp each other's hands at the same time.

"I can't believe after all our years here together, Kazimir's going to get me... whatever happens when you die here," Whitney said.

"Years?" Sora asked.

The ground trembled as the beast drew closer, leaning down so she could look into its bulbous eyes. She could smell its rank breath like a graveyard with all the graves turned over.

"Six, in case you lost count. Some nights I worried you'd forgotten me, but that kiss... I'm glad I held out." Whitney laughed nervously. His grip on her hand tightened. He talked when scared. He must have been terrified.

The great, tentacled beast tried to attack, but an invisible field kept it at bay, making its limbs stretch over them as if the bars of a cage.

"What the—"

"I'm here now," she said, ignoring the thing that wanted them dead, not bothering to tell him it'd only been weeks on Pantego. She sandwiched his hands with hers. "I'm so sorry Whitney. I... I'll never leave your side again."

"I'm the one who left you. Besides..." Whitney nodded toward the monster looming over them. "Not really anywhere else for us to run this time."

Sora turned from the monster and their impending doom and stared at him. He looked no older. Messier, yes, but he was still the young, dashing rogue she remembered. It was in his eyes that she saw it, however. That weariness she'd never seen there before. It pained her to think she was responsible for him being stuck for what, to him, felt like years in Elsewhere. All because the mystics decided not to tell her what she was until the time was right.

"I love you, Whitney," Sora blurted out. "I have since the beginning."

"Who wouldn't." She punched him in the arm, he grinned. Despite all the chaos around them. "I love you, too." He looked to the sky as if seeing something beyond the horrifying monstrosity.

"See, you little whelp? It isn't that hard to admit."

He pulled her close, and she, him. The razor-sharp teeth of the beast above glinted, ready to devour them if not for the barrier. Even still, Sora decided there was no place she'd rather be than here, with Whitney. Everything that had happened, him leaving her, her exiling him—everything. None of it mattered now that they were together at the end.

"For Liam!" Torsten's voice rang out. Then a burst of energy in the aisle sent the beast reeling back, stumbling through the front of the ruined Church. Stone crumbled as its diabolical screams had Sora's eardrums ready to burst.

"You have stopped nothing... nothing... nothing..." the sensuous voice of a woman echoed.

Robed figures circled them as well, mystics and warlocks—denizens of Elsewhere's magic—their chanting like a hymn on the air.

Sora searched from side to side as more of the church crumbled away, the ground too until she and Whitney stood upon blackness.

Torsten appeared again in the center of it all, faint like an apparition, holding onto the boy he'd been reaching for. The rift in the air hung over him again, faded now just like him. Mist rose from the chest of the boy, forming the most beautiful woman Sora had ever seen.

"Uh, Sora... what in Elsewhere is going on?" Whitney walked toward Torsten and waved his hand through him, unable to make contact.

"I... I don't know," she replied.

"Are those mystics?" Whitney turned to her, and a smirk crossed his face. Sora couldn't fathom how much she'd missed that smug look until she saw it. "I knew you'd find them. Whitney and Sora... even Elsewhere can't stop uhh—"

His last word trailed off as the blackness gave way beneath him. The rift that followed Torsten engulfed Whitney now, both the ground and the air, sizzling with energy.

"Whitney!" Sora ran to him and grabbed his hand. She tried to pull him up, but something in the darkness resisted her. Torsten's silhouette was now below them, spectral as Aihara Na and the mystics.

"Sora, what is..." Whitney got his free hand up to try and pull himself free, but an invisible forced yanked him back.

Sora didn't let go. The energy exuding off the strange rift surrounding him grew, so instead, she could feel it tickling her skin. Still, she held on. Then a hand, pale as winter's snow, wrapped around her arm.

"Sora, I've been waiting for you," Nesilia whispered. Her voice was the same as always, sensual but warm.

Sora's stomach turned over. She recalled how she'd felt the last time she'd been in Nesilia's presence and felt every bit the same. She wanted nothing more than to be with her, unendingly, forever. She fought it with all her being, but one of her fingers released Whitney.

"Uh... Sora!" he yelled.

"Why have you kept me waiting all these years?" Nesilia said. "Tell me, are you ready for your destiny?"

"Who the yig are you?" Whitney asked. Sora barely heard him, so enthralled she was by the goddess.

"We are the same, Sora, you and I," Nesilia continued. "Connected since the day of your birth so many Dawnings ago. Can't you feel it?"

The mention of that traumatic night with Sora's mother and Liam snapped her mind back to the moment. She closed her hand tighter around Whitney's and continued pulling.

"No!" Sora said. "I'm through being used."

"We were both forgotten by those who once loved us," Nesilia said. "Tell me it's not true. Abandoned by your own father to live underground. Underground, like me."

"I've dealt with these Elsewhere tricks, Sora," Whitney said. "Ignore her. Let's run while we have the chance!"

Nesilia's hand slid down Sora's arm until it reached Whitney's fingers. She unlatched one, and he yelped in fright.

"No, stop!" Sora shouted.

She unhooked another, and Sora couldn't stop her.

"Don't hurt him!" Sora yelled. "Please, don't hurt him. I'll do anything. Just don't hurt him."

"It's time to let go of what makes you normal, Sora." A smile played at the corners of Nesilia's mouth. She leaned down by Whitney's ear and whispered something Sora couldn't hear. His eyes went wide with horror, then she tore his hand free of Sora's, and Whitney plummeted through the darkness toward Torsten's apparition.

The energy of the rift coruscated with bright lines of distortion. Sora heard his screams grow distant, then stop altogether. The air settled, blackness returning to the ground around Sora, and as she patted it, searching for a way through. Both Whitney and Torsten were nowhere to be found.

"Whitney!" Sora cried out. "What did you do with him!"

"It wasn't yet his time," Nesilia said, softly. "You know that. It was you who put him here because you lost control, but Sora, my love," Nesilia said. "My sweet. Together there is nothing we can't do."

"Come back to us, Sora." Sora heard the distant, familiar voice of Aihara Na again. Then, chanting in a multitude of languages echoed from her, and Madam Jaya, and all the others. She saw them surrounding her again, no warlocks present this time.

"Don't surrender yourself over nothing," Aihara Na went on. "Your future is bright as your fire."

"They would keep you from your destiny!" Nesilia's voice boomed. "Just as the Shieldsman bars me from returning in my own true form. He would keep me buried and forgotten. They would keep you trapped in a tower." Her finger stroked Sora's chin. "But together we can make them all bow."

Another blinding, searing light shone, causing Sora to see nothing but white. A rush of energy made her heart feel like it was going to explode. Then came a tugging sensation. It dragged her backward toward the circling mystics. She clawed at the blackness to try and reach the spot where Whitney vanished.

"No!" Sora screamed. "Not again! Bring me back to him. Whitney!"

More magical chanting enveloped her. Sora tried to grasp onto the ground and tried to crawl forward, but there was nothing but smooth, black. Elsewhere began to tear around her, offering glimpses of the Red Tower throne room and mystics surrounding her.

"Don't be afraid," Nesilia whispered. Sora lost grip with one hand and her legs whipped up into the air. Nesilia kneeled before her, her face a thing of beauty, her eyes completely white and glowing.

"There is nothing for you here any longer," she said. She lay her hand upon Sora's. "It's time to let go."

Sora lost her grip, and everything zoomed past her. Both worlds, all through history, from the days of Liam to her terrible present. She gasped for air, real air, the chamber atop the Red Tower now surrounding her in perfect clarity. Aihara Na was on her knees before her, weak.

"By the gods, she's still alive," the Ancient One of the Secret Mystic Order wheezed.

Sora's head turned from side to side. All the mystics surrounded her, palms outstretched in her direction, save for Huyshi who had only one. Madam Jaya breathed a sigh of relief.

Sora opened her mouth to speak, but no words came out. Then, out of the corner of her eye, she noticed Wetzel's old knife glinting beneath the calm waters around the platform. A smile spread over her face, going all the way to her eyes.

XXXIV

THE KNIGHT

Torsten lifted one heavy leg after the other up the stairs carved into the mountainside which led up to the summit flattened ages ago in the God Feud. Statues of kings lined the holy walk, each of them leaning on a sword with two hands, eyes closed. At the top, stood an archway fashioned in the shape of the Eye of Iam, made from pure glaruium that would sparkle like glass in the sunlight.

Only now, the sunlight had faded, and an eerie twilight had fallen upon the realm as Pantego's two moons drew closer to one another and threatened to cover the sun completely. Only dim torchlight showed Torsten the way.

No guards stood in his path. His legs were stiff. His lungs burned. He had to close his eyes and focus on every icy breath, so he didn't inhale too vigorously. He'd already drawn *Salvation* to use as a walking stick, the sound of it scraping across rock drowned out by whistling wind and the distant voices.

Then, after what felt like an eternity, his foot possessed the summit. He opened his eyes. The driving snow dwindled around the clearing as if Iam wanted Torsten to see what waited there—the parting clouds, and the Dawning in all its glory.

Shieldsmen and Drav Cra warriors lined the edge of the plateau, alter-nating and staring inward. A vast Eye of Iam was etched into the icy surface as always, only this time it wasn't alone. Within the pupil, a triangle, the symbol of Nesilia—her mountainous tomb—large enough for a man to fit inside, was painted in blood. At least two dozen Drav Cra warlocks encircled it, holding hands, faces aimed toward the eclipse. Freydis strolled around them, lighting small basins of fire with her blood magic.

Within that circle stood King Pi wearing his new Glass Crown, Wren the Holy, leaning on his cane with quaking arms, and Redstar, clutching Pi's old orepul, still stained beyond recognition by Bliss' blood. Blood also coated each of their hands as if they'd been the ones to desecrate the summit of Mount Lister with the symbol of Nesilia. Torsten remembered the night before he set off to the Webbed Woods to find Redstar, when he caught Pi, mad and rambling, scribbling bloody symbols upon the walls of his bedroom.

"Redstar!" Torsten bellowed. All eyes snapped toward him. "Enough of this madness."

"Torsten, my friend!" Redstar replied. "I was wondering when you would arrive."

"Do not act unsurprised!" Torsten shoved his sword into the ground.

"Surprised? I knew you wouldn't want to miss this."

"You will unhand the King. Now!"

"The King is here of his own volition."

"We both know that's not true."

"Remove this traitor," Pi ordered. "He is a prisoner now, nothing more." All the Shieldsmen and Drav Cra warriors drew their weapons.

Redstar lay his hand on the boy's shoulder, making sure the orepul—that seemingly innocuous doll that had been with Pi when he rose from the apparent-dead, which had been there when they slew the monster Bliss—was visible.

"That's all right, Your Grace," Redstar said. "I think he should see. All those who doubt the strength of our unified faith should see."

Pi raised his hand, and the guards took a step back, lowering their weapons. He still commanded respect as King, but it was like Torsten had always feared: Redstar led through him.

Torsten slowly edged forward. "Pi, you must listen to me," he said.

"He's using you for… for whatever this madness is. He thinks he can bring his goddess back, but she is gone."

"She helped bring me back," Pi said. "After you allowed me to die!"

"You know in your heart that isn't true! He filled your mind with visions and lies. Now he plays the part of loving uncle. I've seen what he did to your mother just for disobeying him. You cannot trust him."

"My mother refuses to see reason," Pi spat. "She got what she deserved."

Torsten pleaded silently with Iam that Oleander not be within hearing. "Your mother loves you! More than anything."

"My sister is a murdering shrew," Redstar said. "She would see this kingdom and all its inhabitants crumble of her own foolish pride. But we, we seek to raise it beyond even the heights of Liam."

"You dare speak his name!" Torsten lifted his *Salvation*, the sword wielded by King Liam himself in so many battles, and pointed it at the Arch Warlock. He heard the unified rasp of blades drawn around the circle. He was now surrounded and he hadn't even realized it.

"This profane ritual is nothing but cultish madness," Torsten addressed the Shieldsmen. "You have to see that."

"You are wrong, Torsten," Redstar said. He turned with his hand on Pi's shoulder to face the eclipse. The two moons were nearly kissing now, and soon they would cover the sun in its entirety. "This is the way of the future. Bound in love, our God and Goddess shall be reunited. For He is the light above, and She is below, buried, not dead."

He raised the doll. "Blood of the enemy. Of the Lord and the Lady. Perhaps you weren't as pious as I thought, but this man is, and he stands with us now." He smiled and touched Wren's wrinkled face. The old priest remained hunched over, looking frail as death.

"That is not the Wren I know," Torsten said.

"That is because you refuse to see how your kingdom is changing. Evolving."

"Wren, I know you are in there. Put a stop to this. Tell these Shieldsmen the truth."

Wren raised one hand off his cane. It trembled, more bone and sinew than skin. He reached toward Redstar's neck. For a moment, Torsten thought he saw something in the Arch Warlock's eyes. Fear? But it was gone before Torsten could identify it. Freydis sidled up behind the old man, and his hand fell back to the cane.

"We have lived blindly in our faith for too long. I now see the folly," Wren said. "It is you who are blind, Torsten Unger. The Dawning shall set us free." His head remained sagging. But something else was wrong. Though it was his voice that came out of his mouth, his lips weren't moving. Instead, the warlock Freydis spoke through him, controlled him. Blood stained her face and lips. The sight made Torsten want to vomit, and the moment Wren finished speaking, his entire body fell weak. He fell onto his cane with all his weight just to stay upright.

"Light above," Redstar started, "earth below. Soon all Pantego will know our truth. It is time now for the union of the Dawning."

"I'm ready, uncle," Pi said. "I'm ready to open my eyes."

"Resist him, my King!" Torsten thundered. "Step out from that circle, and I will never let him harm you again. Your mother waits for you, ready to beg forgiveness for all that she's done in your name."

Redstar sighed. "Perhaps our King is right. How many times are you going to go through this, Torsten? My Lady said that no matter what I did you'd be here, but I tire of this. Men, in the name of Pi Nothhelm, the Miracle King, son of Liam Nothhelm, first of his name, and heir to be Dradinengor of the Ruuhar Clan, seize the criminal. Take him alive."

Soldiers closed in, Drav Cra and Shieldsmen alike. Torsten spun to face those who once swore allegiance to him. "I have failed you, men," he said. "I look upon your faces, and I don't recognize them. I should. I should know each and every one of you... as Sir Uriah Davies did. I will pay for that negligence for the rest of my days, but I know your armor. I know what you stand for."

Redstar spoke in Drav Crava, and all at once, the circle of warlocks around him sliced their forearms. They clasped hands, blood flowing down between each of their wrists. In a monotonous roar, they chanted in their language. Redstar did the same, standing between Pi and Wren who remained silent. Pi's orepul lifted into the air. Pi flinched, betraying a bit of the child still beneath the cold exterior, but Redstar took his hand.

"Look inside yourselves and find the light!" Torsten implored. He brandished *Salvation* now, ready to do whatever necessary.

"There is no light today," hissed a woman, voice like a serpent. With soldiers on either side, Freydis appeared in front of him. Her knees bent in a battle-stance, tossing a dagger playfully between her hands while she licked her bloody lips.

Torsten closed his eyes. "Iam, guide my hand," he whispered, then he charged. An axe swung at his legs, but without his armor, he was nimble, and leaped over it. Then, falling into a roll, he dodged another swipe and brought *Salvation* crashing toward Freydis' head. She parried left, sliced her palm, and flung a ball of fire at Torsten, but he was ready for it. It flew by his ear and slammed into the chest of a Drav Cra warrior, sending the savage flying back into a few more. Torsten rebuffed the attack of a Shieldsman, then grabbed him and shoved him into even more of the attackers. Torsten winced as an axe grazed his torso and cut his shirt, but he spun, slashing one of the heathens across the chest. A hand grabbed his arm, stopping him mid-backswing. Torsten wasted no time, caught it in turn, and flipped the man over his massive shoulders.

Torsten froze as *Salvation* drove downward to stab into the assailant. A Shieldsman stared up at him, not afraid, ready to die for what he thought was their cause in serving the King of the Glass Kingdom—Torsten's kingdom. That moment of hesitation allowed Freydis to slide behind Torsten and flay the backs of both his thighs.

He howled as he fell to his knees. An axe knocked *Salvation* from his grasp, and more hands wrenched his arms between them. He thrashed, but it was no use, like he was back in Winde Port again.

"Release me!" he roared. "Can't you see what he's doing? He'll destroy your King. He'll destroy us all!"

Behind Freydis, tiny droplets of blood trickled out of the floating orepul and began to swirl around it, a web of red lines. Pi's arms were now outstretched, and he too levitated. A spectral presence stretched out from his chest, taking shape like an illuminated wisp of fog.

"Drad Redstar elevates him," Freydis said. She knelt before Torsten and ran her bloody dagger across his cheek. The whites of her eyes shone within the crusting black paint on her brow, freezing off in flakes. "Soon you will see."

Torsten threw his weight at her, but warlocks promptly hauled him back. Though the Drav Cra restrained him without a second thought, the eyes of the Shieldsman present darted nervously between him and the ritual. It was one thing to hear promises of an alliance between gods, but its must have been quite another to see their wicked magic raising their King from the ground; tapping the very light of his soul.

"Look around you men," Torsten whispered. "Is this where you thought you'd find yourselves when you took the oath? Party to the Buried Goddess' blood rituals? If you no longer trust me, I understand. I let hate for anything foreign to us cloud my mind and turn me to rage instead of seeing what was right before me. You, loyal Glassmen. Children of Iam, I should have looked to you and not into the darkness. So, let me pass on, but trust your hearts. Perhaps not all Drav Cra are evil, but that man is."

Chanting in the circle grew louder, Drav Crava filled the air like a brewing storm, and now Pi didn't just float before his orepul, but the air around and between them crackled with energy. Streaks of it distorted the view, and Torsten could see momentary glimpses of somewhere else through them; a small village shrouded in red.

"Drad Redstar says to let you watch," Freydis whispered in Torsten's ear. "But he says nothing about speaking." She grabbed his jaw as he tried to appeal to his men again and held her dagger to his lips.

"Unhand him, witch!"

Torsten peered out of the corner of his eye to see Oleander standing at the top of the stairs, surrounded by the Eye-of-Iam-shaped gate. Sir Austun Mulliner stood at her side, a bow in his hands. A thrum sent an arrow toward the female warlock and sliced her cheek, knocking her back, then continued forward. Torsten turned with her, thinking he knew where it was going to strike until it stabbed into Pi's floating orepul, finally landing on the opposite edge of the summit.

The distortion in the air around Pi suddenly stopped, and the strange wisp of light swirling around him began to diminish. The boy looked from side to side, and for the first time since his reawakening—even for the year before that—he didn't seem emotionless. He was frightened. He continued searching until his gaze fell upon Oleander.

"Mama?" he whimpered.

"Redstar left the wife of Liam Nothhelm to bleed," Austun shouted. "No matter what she has done, no matter who Torsten has killed—we must still protect our own." He drew his sword, and a host of Glass soldiers behind him did the same. "Iam smite me if I am wrong, but this is not the King's Shield to which I swore an oath. Brothers, it is time to take it back!"

He charged, and the men followed him. Drav Cra warriors broke away from Torsten to meet them head-on. The Shieldsmen committed to Redstar were confused. Torsten found himself thrilled that Mulliner saw beyond his hatred enough to do what was right— precisely what Torsten had failed to do.

In the confusion, Torsten broke free of his Shieldsman captor, kicking a downed-Freydis in the face in the process, then ran for the orepul.

"Continue the summoning!" Redstar ordered. "And you." He stopped in front of Wren and laid his stump of a hand over his shoulder. "No more half-measures this time. One for the Lord. A true sacrifice." He drew a dagger and placed it in Wren's hand, then burst through the circle, racing toward the orepul as well.

"The blood of the enemy shall bring rise to her!" Redstar shouted.

"I should have destroyed it when I had the chance!" Torsten cried out. He barreled into him. They tumbled across the snowy surface, stopping just out of reach of the doll. Redstar had no weapon, and in hand to hand combat, Torsten was far more proficient. He pinned the Arch Warlock down and drove fist after fist into his nose. Redstar pawed at Torsten's face with his one hand, clubbing him with his other. The more blood Torsten drew from Redstar's mouth, the more he felt it—fire building within Redstar's palm. The Arch Warlock spread his long fingers, and the heat made Torsten's skin bubble.

"When will you learn to kill me?" Redstar hissed. He squeezed until the pain was too much for Torsten to bear. Torsten fell off him, the imprint of Redstar's hand branded onto his face.

"Perhaps it is time you live like those you bow to," Redstar said. "Like all the Glassmen. Blind."

He stretched his hand across Torsten's eyes. Torsten lashed out, punching Redstar in the ribs, feeling the bone crack beneath his fists, but Redstar held him down. The heat augmented, burning Torsten's eyelids first and then his eyeballs.

"Get off of him!" Oleander shouted. Torsten's eyes were covered, but he heard the soft crunch of a blade stabbing through flesh. Redstar screamed and slid to the side, tumbling off Torsten. Torsten's eyes were so damaged by the magical fire, he could see nothing but shapes, but that was enough. A knife stuck out of the center of Redstar's back, placed there by the Queen Mother.

"Whore Queen!" Redstar snarled. Red-hot fire leaped from his fingertips into Oleander's chest and sent her flying. Then Redstar stood and limped to the orepul. Torsten pawed at the blur of his legs and slowed him, but without sight, Redstar was easily able to kick him away.

Gathering the orepul, Redstar started back toward the blood circle, only to find it compromised. With Sir Mulliner's reinforcements, the Drav Cra warriors were outnumbered. A handful stood with their backs to the circle of warlocks, Freydis at their center. They faced at least a dozen knights and the same amount of Glass soldiers. It seemed that even if they wouldn't fight for their disgraced ex-Wearer, they chose to fight beside their own.

"You fools!" Redstar rasped. "You cannot stop this." He reached behind his back and wrenched out the knife his sister wedged there. With it, he sliced his own wrist, deep, like he didn't care about bleeding out. "Like I told the last of you who thought to rebel, your armor is of the mountain. And what is below the peak, belongs to my Lady."

He lifted his hand and squeezed.

"What the—" one of the Shieldsmen gasped.

"Iam's light!" cried another.

More and more of them shouted in pain as Redstar's arms moved slowly to the side. "Your armor is mine!" Redstar yelled.

Shieldsmen threw themselves into one another without regard. One grabbed a Glass soldier and hurled him over the ridge of the summit, his screams rending the very air.

"Freydis," Redstar shouted, "kill them all!"

She clasped her bloody hands then pulled them apart. The ground split beneath the Glassmen, wide enough for ten abreast to lose their footing. The remaining Drav Cra warriors attacked.

Redstar made his way back into the circle where the warlocks chanted. He raised the orepul, and Pi went from a terrified boy, back to impassive. His body arched and the spirit continued lifting from his chest.

During it all, Torsten dragged himself toward Oleander's body. His vision was still impaired, but it didn't take much to recognize the massive burns coating half of her like a boar left over a hot spit.

"My Queen," Torsten whispered, pawing for her hand in the snow. Finding it, he squeezed.

"T… Torsten," she stuttered. "My sweet, loyal, Torsten."

"Come. I must get you to safety."

He tried to lift her, but she slapped him away. The blow was weak, not like all the countless times she'd done it before, but he got the message. "You made a vow to protect my boy. I… I…" She swallowed back her pain. He could see the red staining her teeth. "I order you to uphold it."

"My Qu… Oleander."

"Redstar thinks he must take his own life. Kill the bastard… for me." Torsten hesitated a moment more, and she pushed him. "Go!"

Staggering forward, still seeing the world only in shapes and contrast of light, Torsten roared, "Redstar!"

The ritual illuminated the entire summit now, and Torsten realized why. The moons and the sun were in complete alignment; the Dawning was upon them. Just a ring of light surrounded them as Iam looked away and allowed his people to find the light within themselves.

Torsten wouldn't ignore the call. He trudged forward, nearly sightless, body battered. Through the circle of warlocks, Redstar eyed him.

"Biding her time, her pain like a flood. Alone in the darkness, she longs for the blood. In the name of the Lady, in the name of the Lord, Shall settle it all with power and sword," Redstar chanted. He lifted his knife, and Wren mimicked his every move with the dagger in his quaking hand. Torsten realized that the poor old man whispered the words along with him as well.

"Then she will arise, in glorious day," Redstar continued. "Through will and through fire, her enemies slain. Forgotten, abandoned, but no longer bound. From Elsewhere and exile, she'll receive her crown." Side by side, Redstar and Wren plunged their blades into their own chests.

Torsten stopped and clutched his own. It stung him deep within to see, even through bleary eyes, the holy leader of his church forced to take his own life—a blasphemy, an abomination unto their God. As they dropped to their knees, the spirit poured out of Pi, taking the shape of a woman whose whispers Torsten heard on the air. It was almost imperceptible, but it was there.

The blood from the orepul fed into it and the very air around them fractured, again revealing a hellish world between worlds. Torsten knew without question what it was. As the fabric of reality had been split in the God Feud when Iam made Elsewhere, now it was being reopened.

"Torsten!" Austun yelled.

Torsten looked right and saw the vague and blurred shape of the Shieldsman on his knees. Freydis had summoned vines from the ice to lash him down. She controlled them with one hand while with the other she stabbed a Glass soldier in the chest repeatedly. Austun tossed something to Torsten. He heard it clatter on the ground and found grip on it. He'd only had King Liam's sword for a short time, but already, *Salvation* felt at home within his tight grasp.

The space between the circle of warlocks was narrow. Torsten's vision was getting worse, so he closed his eyes and listened only to the laughing of the madmen King Autlas had abandoned in the North so long ago. He drew *Salvation* overhead, reared back with both hands, and released. In all the chaos, he focused on the thrum as it sliced through the air, pommel over blade, again and again.

It found its place buried within Redstar's chest. Torsten barreled through the warlocks to finish the job, and as he passed their circle toward the rift in the air, he found himself in what seemed to be a new realm. He could see perfectly now, but the world itself had grown red and blurry, darkness tattering the edges. The sounds of battle and the chants of heathens were drowned out by an otherworldly whirr. All that remained was a surface of life upon which Torsten, Wren, Redstar, and Pi remained.

He spun. Around him, he could see countless places—towns, villages, kingdoms, and plains, but all without focus. He blinked and tried to breathe, then saw something he least expected. Unholy monsters, demons the likes of which Torsten had never seen, chased a man and woman through a village. It all happened so fast, and the vision was unclear, simultaneously all around him and nowhere at all. He spun again and saw a circle of robed figures who looked like the mystics Torsten had fought so long ago by Liam's side. They had their hands outstretched toward a curled-up body.

Between them all, Pi remained affixed in midair, enveloped by what was now the ghastly figure of a beautiful woman.

"Well done, my child," she whispered, voice sensuous, intoxicating. "I can feel it. My power, returning from its buried prison after so long."

The last thing Torsten expected was for Nesilia to look as favorably in reality as Redstar's mural depicted. But behind that beauty were callous, colorless eyes set on devouring the world.

A force pulled at Torsten's ankles as he struggled to move. It seemed to be affecting Redstar as well. His dagger lay before him, and he crawled for it, *Salvation* skewering his chest. Torsten was able to reach it first and kick it aside.

"You can't stop it," Redstar gurgled. "In killing Bliss, we opened this world to her spirit, but with our sacrifice, the goddess herself may return."

"I can," Torsten replied. In this strange realm, even his own voice echoed, as if a hundred of himself he were whispering from all around. "Today, you die by my hand!" Unseen forces tried to hold him back, but Torsten fought with all his might to grab *Salvation's* hilt and shove it deeper into Redstar, all the way down to the crossguard.

Redstar cried out in pain, Nesilia's spirit with him. The world flashed, and for a moment, the circle of warlocks and the fighting Shieldsmen were revealed. Then, Torsten was back in what he assumed was Elsewhere. He looked up and saw Pi still in the air.

"I will not fail you," he whispered, although the boy couldn't hear him. He took a step toward Pi when the two people fleeing demons raced by him. For a moment Torsten thought he recognized them, though he couldn't believe his eyes in this other world, then tendrils of darkness closed in around them, coating their faces in shadow as they stopped to kiss. A circle of chanting warlocks halted the darkness, forming a magical shield that glowed red hot. Their screams rang out as the tendrils tore into them, worlds literally colliding.

Torsten ignored it all and extended his hand toward the young King. He could feel Nesilia's power, or perhaps Elsewhere itself pushing him back. The bones of his fingers felt like they were going to snap as they passed through the Buried Goddess' spectral form. His arm pushed forward, and he felt the pain in his forearm, then his elbow.

"Your world is open, and I shall walk it again," Nesilia said. "All those who have forgotten me will be punished!"

"We are the right hand of Iam," Torsten groaned through clenched teeth, desperate to distract himself from both Nesilia's words and the unbearable pain afflicting him. "We are the sword of His justice, and the Shield that guards the light of this world." Her fingers wrapped Pi's skinny arm. "For Liam!" he shouted and yanked backward.

He and Pi fell and slammed into the snow, his arms wrapped around the boy. Above him, the portal stayed open, sizzling in the sky like fat over a flame. Torsten covered Pi's ears and searched his surroundings, his vision impaired again now that he was beyond Elsewhere. Another blurry body soared across the rift. It slammed through a group of warlocks before rolling to a stop.

"You have stopped nothing," Nesilia's voice lingered on the air. "Deny my body this world, but the will of fire is mine…" And with that, she went silent, and the summit along with it. Torsten rolled over and saw with his blurred vision that the moons were now parting, revealing the light of the sun again.

Glass soldiers now surrounded the six remaining warlocks who hadn't been slaughtered by demons, Sir Mulliner at their lead. They looked from side to side, confused, weak. The ritual had melted the paint on the heathens faces, revealing only pale, scared appearances.

A red-stained hand suddenly grasped at Pi. Torsten wrenched it back and pulled the man it belonged to close.

"It's over, Redstar!" he cried over the sound of Elsewhere's veil.

"It can't be…" Redstar choked on blood. "It was her time..."

"It is yours alone."

Torsten wished his eyes worked properly so he could see every ounce of anguish in Redstar's eyes before he rolled over and his last breaths rattled through his lips. His arm fell limp into the bloody snow.

"Drad Redstar!" Freydis abandoned her defense and ran to Redstar's side. She cradled him as blood dripped from his mouth. "Help me with him, you fools!" she hissed at the other warlocks.

"They killed him," one said nervously.

"How could this happen?" asked another.

"Now your time comes to an end, witch." Austun lifted his blade and went at Freydis, but Torsten raised a hand.

"No," he rasped. "Enough have died today."

The warlocks looked to each other, then ran for the stairs. The soldiers let them go. They were all so weakened by the ritual they were no longer any harm to anyone if they even made it down the mountain.

"Cowards!" Freydis shrieked. She pulled Redstar close and whispered to him in Drav Crava. Her lips fell upon his, blood and all. A few guards ignored Torsten's orders and attempted to seize her. She slashed one in the leg, howled like a wild dire wolf, and went to slit her own throat. She was bashed in the back of the head before she could and crumpled atop her master.

"Sir Unger?" a small voice spoke beneath him. Torsten released Pi so he could look upon his face, but his vision was worse than ever as the magical burns Redstar left him with settled. All Torsten could tell was that Pi no longer sounded twice his age.

"You're all right, Your Gra—"

"Mother!" Pi interrupted him.

He squirmed free and ran to his mother, too far for Torsten to see clearly. He could hear the boy crying, shedding love upon Oleander as if the past year had been a nightmare and he'd only then woken. Sir Uriah Davies always spoke of how kind the son of Liam Nothhelm and Oleander Ruuhar was. Now, after all this time, Torsten saw the truth in that.

For a moment, Torsten's heart grew heavy, then he saw that Oleander's chest still rose and fell. He exhaled and rolled onto his back to face the brightening sun, as Loutis moved off and Celeste half-covered her path toward the horizon. His hand brushed against a seemingly harmless little doll a devoted mother had made for her son on the day of his birth. He raised it toward the light.

"You held onto that thing all this time?" The voice that spoke those words sounded familiar but was so overwhelmed by exhaustion it was hard to tell.

Torsten rolled his head to face whoever it was. He could see only splotches and shapes, but that was all he needed to recognize the face. Whitney Blisslayer, formerly the bane of his existence, lay in the trampled snow where the warlocks had been.

Torsten let his head fall back and hoped he was dreaming. When he looked back, his vision was even worse, and Whitney remained.

"I thought I was dreaming too," Whitney said. "But it's really you, isn't it? You're really here."

"Against all odds." Torsten drew a long, deep breath of the cold air.

"That means I'm here…" Whitney patted his own chest. "And she's…"

"Sir, who is this?" Sir Mulliner placed his sword against Whitney's neck. The thief crawled backward until the body of a fallen warlock blocked his way.

"I'm a friend to the Crown," Whitney said, raising his hands. "Lord Blisslayer, the master thief who helped your Wearer steal that doll."

"He isn't Wearer any longer," Mulliner said.

"Seems to be a theme with him."

"Forget the thief," Torsten said. "Get the King and his mother to safety and see to her wounds."

Mulliner hesitated for a second, then sheathed his sword. "You heard him," he said to the soldiers. "Help them and lock up any heathens who still breathe."

"Oh, and Sir Mulliner," Torsten tossed the doll at the Shieldsman's feet. "Burn this."

"After all we went through to get it?" Whitney asked.

"He's right. For Iam's sake, drown the ashes in the Torrential Sea." He let his head fall back into the snow. The loving arms of exhaustion wrapped their proverbial arms around him, and he gave in. Whitney said something, but he didn't hear him.

For the first time in a long time, concern over the future of the kingdom didn't make rest impossible to come by. Neither the impetuous thief nor the cold—nothing could keep him from it.

XXXV

THE THIEF

"Torsten, wake up," Whitney said. "Torsten!"

The big Shieldsman shot upright in his bed. They were in the physician's hall in the Glass Castle, where Torsten had remained resting for the better part of a day. Whitney wasn't exactly sure what had happened to cause so much upheaval since they parted in Winde Port—something about Redstar taking over and Torsten being imprisoned.

Masked Cultists of Nesilia had rioted throughout the city during the Dawning, burning down half of South Corner. Eventually, the city guard put them down, and when the Shieldsmen returned from the mountain, they began rounding up the Drav Cra and sending them out to their tents. Things were safer within the castle, that was for sure.

All Whitney knew was none of it could have been stranger than what he'd gone through. Just breathing the Pantego air again was a thing of beauty, even if the room smelled like stale blood and piss.

"Who is that?" Torsten grumbled. He rolled his head to face Whitney, but a bloody bandage covered his eyes.

"Your very best friend," Whitney replied.

"Whitney? You're still here?"

"You were in rough shape up there. I couldn't just leave you."

"And they let you in here?" Torsten asked, incredulous.

"Wouldn't you know it. One of the Shieldsmen remembered you ennobling me. I always knew that would come in handy."

"What happened… I… the King and Queen."

He tried to slide his legs off the bed, grimaced. Whitney placed a hand on his shoulder to stop him. Whatever had happened, he was fairly beat up beyond being unable to see.

"They say the Queen will live at the cost of her beauty," Whitney said. "Though if you heard her screaming echoing down the hall, you wouldn't think it. And the King is well, talking again."

"I need to speak with them."

"Hold your zhulong, old friend. If I let you up too soon, they'll never let me back here."

"That's fine because you aren't supposed to be here." Torsten tried to adjust his position, winced in pain some more, then laid back. "How did you get up there anyway?"

"You wouldn't believe me if I told you."

"After what I saw on the mountain, there's nothing I wouldn't believe."

"Honestly? Elsewhere."

"What?"

"I was there for years, trapped by Sora thanks to a spell gone wrong."

Torsten turned over. "C'mon, thief. I said I'd believe anything, but must you always push your stories too far?"

"Hey, I'm serious! There was an upyr, and Barty Darkings, and Troborough wasn't burned down, and… you have no idea how good it feels to be out of that place." He considered telling Torsten that he too was there, as a blind priest, but it seemed like it would only sound like an insult considering his current state. He'd learned a thing or two in Elsewhere about watching his tongue around people that could beat him to death like Kazimir.

"Sounds like a bad dream."

"I hoped so too until I was spat out onto Mount Lister after Sora freed me. Any chance you've seen her?"

Torsten tugged on the bandage over his eyes. "I don't see much of anything now, thief. Besides, as you know, I've been here."

Whitney's head hung. "I just meant… Maybe you'd heard something about a Panpingese woman around here from guards passing through. I don't know." Whitney didn't add that was the real reason he was sticking around. Hoping Sora had been thrown out of the rift between worlds in another direction and was close, and that she wasn't still stuck in Elsewhere with that goddess.

Goddess? You know who that was Whitney.

Torsten turned back. "I haven't heard a thing about anyone except cultists and Drav Cra refusing to be kicked out to their camp. Last I saw Sora was barely a month ago."

"What? Really? How was she?" Whitney asked.

"You tell me. You were there, floating away from Winde Port on a stolen ship after helping me walk right into an ambush thanks to those Darkings traitors."

"A month?" Whitney recoiled. "It's only been a month here?"

He felt sick. He knew it hadn't been six years in Pantego while he was gone. He wasn't stupid. The Prince—or King—didn't appear much older after all and neither did Sora. Six years imagining her face, he would have noticed any extra wrinkles. He'd figured at least one year had passed and he'd arrived at the next Dawning. He couldn't stomach asking any guards on the way down from Mount Lister, but now he knew.

"Whatever really happened to bring you to that mountaintop did a number on you, didn't it, kid?" Torsten said. "Did Redstar put a spell on you to go after the orepul or something?"

"Something like that... I... look." Whitney slid across the bed to get closer to Torsten's head. "If Sora isn't here, then I think she's in Panping, and she's in trouble. I saw mystics around her, and..." He swallowed the lump forming in his throat. "Nesilia."

"You had a bad dream, Whitney. There are no mystics anymore, and Redstar's attempt at reviving the Buried Goddess failed. He's gone." Whitney could tell the knight didn't even believe his own words.

"Torsten, it wasn't a dream. I was in Elsewhere for six years. You can't make that up."

"Then maybe you'll do a bit of good in your life, so next time you'll reach the Gate of Light."

"You really don't believe me?"

"I'm sorry Redstar's evil got to you, Whitney. I truly am. But it's over now. The madness is finished, and it's time to rebuild this broken kingdom from the inside out. The people have lost trust in the Crown and in Iam. Rebellion still rages in the Black Sands. The King is… I don't know why I'm telling you all this."

"Because we're best friends, like I said."

Torsten groaned. Whitney smiled.

"You're still a stubborn old mule; you know that?" Whitney said.

"And you're still a rotten thief," Torsten replied.

"So, I guess that means you aren't going to help me find Sora? Because I faintly remember there was a bargain struck in Winde Port that if I helped you, you'd help me save her. Considering she saved herself, you still owe me."

Torsten tapped his forehead. "Wouldn't be much help looking for anything now, would I?"

"I suppose not."

A period of silence passed between them. Torsten's expression grew dourer than ever from another reminder of his injury.

"I never had a chance to thank you, Whitney," Torsten said, finally.

"Go on," Whitney said.

"You kept your word in Winde Port when no one else did. Your distraction of Muskigo was exceptional."

"Exceptional, eh?"

"Don't let it go to your head."

"Too late," Whitney joked.

Whitney thought he heard a soft chuckle slip through the Shieldman's lips.

"That's two thank yous in as many days from men I never thought I'd get them from," Whitney said. "All those years in Elsewhere have really improved my influence."

"You're really going to stick with that story?" Torsten said.

"I always tell the truth."

"You're impossible."

"I missed this." Whitney slapped Torsten on the shoulder, forgetting his many injuries. The Shieldsman winced but didn't make a sound. Then Whitney hopped to his feet.

"Well, since you're all right, I guess it's time I head off," he said. "Better get out of this city before something else crazy happens to me."

"Whitney." Torsten grabbed his wrist. "That was you and Sora I saw together when I entered that hellish breach in the world, wasn't it?"

"So, you do believe me!"

"I don't know what I believe anymore, but it seems every time I have all reason to give up hope, your friend Sora is there to make sure I don't."

"She's the best there is."

Torsten nodded. "Whatever happened, I hope you find her again. I mean it. Even you deserve some sort of happiness in this broken world of ours."

"Torsten Unger, you continue to surprise me."

He scoffed. "Before you go, would you mind getting this thing off me?" He fought through the pain to swing his legs around and sit upright.

"Why?" Whitney said. "You look like one of your priests; it's fitting."

"Whitney."

"I don't want to get into trouble."

"Just do it. I need to know."

Whitney sighed. He sat beside Torsten and began unwinding the bandage covering his eyes. The sight underneath was grizzly. His brown skin was ragged and bubbled across his brow, and his eyelids were nearly burned shut, the lashes seared away. What little of his eyes Whitney could see were gray and calloused.

Torsten turned his head from side to side after the bandage fell free. He looked up, down, then straight toward Whitney. Whitney didn't need the Shieldsman's words for him to know he could see nothing. He'd played the part of blind priest before.

"Anything?" Whitney said anyway.

Torsten shook his head, but he didn't seem saddened by the revelation. "Not even blurs now."

"I'm sorry Torsten."

"Don't be. Thank Iam for letting my vision linger long enough to stop Redstar before he dug this kingdom any deeper into exile." He reached up slowly, one of his arms shaking from the pain. Whitney helped it the rest of the way so that the Shieldsman could circle his worthless eyes in prayer to Iam. He didn't say it, but he nodded to Whitney in thanks for helping him.

"If you don't mind, I'd like to be alone with Him right now," Torsten said.

"Always at his side, just like in Elsewhere," Whitney said.

"I won't even pretend to understand what you're talking about."

"I never do." Whitney stood and took a few long strides toward the exit. He stopped and fell into an exaggerated bow. "Fare thee well, fair knight. Good luck with rebuilding your kingdom. I'm off to find my lady. See you soon—er, until we meet again."

"I have little doubt we will. Goodbye, thief."

At that, Whitney spun on his heel and made his way out the door. He nearly bumped a masked physician on the way out, mumbling his apologies as he sidestepped.

As soon as he was alone his smile faded and his features darkened. He even had to stop for a moment to lean on the wall and breathe. It wasn't just seeing the mighty Shieldsman so vulnerable that affected him. It was everything.

It'd been six years for him since they'd last talked, and he had to act as if no time at all had passed. It was a lie. Maybe Whitney looked the same, but when they traversed the Webbed Woods together, it felt like he was still only a kid. A kid with a crush he refused to recognize that had become so much more.

He drew himself to a window and stared off across the snowy plains. Sora was somewhere out there, and she was in trouble. He wasn't sure how he knew it, but he did. He could never forget that look on her face in Elsewhere right before they were split apart once again. The sheer terror.

Maybe it was the mystics' fault or the Buried Goddess. Perhaps both or something unimaginably worse. It didn't matter. Sora had sought out a people thought to be extinct just to save him, now he was going to do the same for her. Wherever it took him.

XXXVI

THE MYSTIC

Sora heard screams. They weren't the cries of demon spawn in Elsewhere, they were human, and they were horrified. She tried desperately to open her eyes, but she couldn't. The bright light, still searing, still blinding, forced her eyes shut although she fought. It was as if her eyes were controlled by someone, something else. The smell of iron filled her nostrils, a scent she'd become far too familiar with over the course of her lifetime. It was part of her, and she, it.

Blood.

Lots of blood.

"Please, don't." She heard the voice but couldn't see its owner. Even so, she didn't need her eyes to know it was Aihara Na. The voice came from below Sora like she was standing and the other was kneeling. "Together we can start afresh."

"Yes," said a voice, familiar and loud. It belonged to Nesilia. Sora had encountered her enough times to know. And it was loud like it came from within Sora's head.

A sudden flash in Sora's vision revealed the walls of the Red Tower. How had she gotten back there? Was it another vision? Another flash showed the color red, deep like blood. This time her eyes stayed open and her insides roiled around, gurgling, threatening to make her heave.

Dead mystics littered the floor, Madam Jaya, Huyshi and the others, their blood spattered all over the walls. Red on red. She had no idea they could even bleed, but it was like their spectral forms had been undone. Their blood formed crimson streams, coalescing into one current and pouring into the rushing waters of the chamber of the Secret Council. It frothed beneath the spray of the wianu statues, and Sora could've sworn she saw one of them move.

Her stomach lurched, and she threw up. As she looked down, she saw the bile pooling in front of Aihara Na. The woman was on her knees and didn't flinch as the vomit sprinkled her robes.

That was when Sora realized the blood soaking her shredded kimono and covering her own hands. Wetzel's knife was gripped in one of them.

"Please, Sora, don't do this," Ancient One Aihara Na sniveled, groveling. "I was wrong about you, your power. We can still save Panping and the Order. Together."

"What—what happened?" Sora asked.

Madam Aihara looked scared and confused.

Sora searched the room. Madam Jaya wasn't merely bleeding, she had a gash across her throat left there by a blade. Sora regarded her hands again. She staggered back, the knife slipping through her fingers, landing in the pool of red with a loud clatter.

"You know the truth," came a voice from within, sultry and hypnotic. "No more lies."

"Nesilia?" Sora asked.

From the depths of the waters, vines began to grow, climbing the impossibly high walls and ceiling. Leaves, branches, and thorns congregated together, thick like the Webbed Woods. They weren't just sprouting from the waters. Sora saw them coming from her own hands.

Panic drove Sora to her knees.

"Please, spare me?" Aihara said. The vines wrapped the mystic's calves and throat, slowly squeezing the life from her. Her form was corporeal now as well. "The others they could not see, but I know now this is the form of our saving. Your forgiveness, no? I offer you mine."

She gagged as the vines tightened. Her cheeks went pale. Tears welled in her eyes. A fearless, centuries-old being she no longer seemed, but instead, an old human woman who'd realized she didn't want to die yet.

Sora didn't think she could pity the cruel woman, but she did, and the vines stopped tightening. Seeing her fear made her mind drift to Whitney and the way he looked at her before they were split apart.

"Stop fighting." Sora heard the words echoing all around her. Her thoughts were promptly yanked back to her present. The smell of blood gave way to the scent of dirt. "You no longer have to struggle, my love. I will take care of everything." Sora shook like a tall tree amidst a great storm. "Give in!"

Sora's head snapped back, eyes rolling upward. She felt her back straighten, arch, then her feet touched down. It was as if Sora watched herself from within. Not in control. She screamed and begged for answers, but her cries only seemed to fill the formless void she now inhabited, whispers in the dark, like when she used to call upon Elsewhere and heard it responding but couldn't understand, only now, her mind rumbled with Nesilia's words.

The door to the chamber suddenly creaked, and Sora's body whipped around. Aquira stood in the entry, her big, bright eyes blinking. Sora's hand rose, beyond her control, and the jagged vines extended toward the little creature.

Sora screamed Aquira's name into the darkness. She poured every ounce of her soul into the word, and the little wyvern's eyes went wide. She screeched, then soared, dodging a snapping vine. She blew fire at another as she twisted back around.

Sora's body turned to watch Aquira spin sideways and zip through one of the tower's narrow, arrowslit windows. She simultaneously felt anger and relief, not sure which emotion belonged to her any longer.

Cloth brushed stone.

"Where are you going, mystic?" said the voice of Nesilia. This time, it came from Sora's own lips. Aihara Na had been crawling away thanks to Aquira's distraction, but the vines rose to wrap her limbs and throat again.

Aihara Na struggled to speak the vines grew so tight. "I'll pledge myself to you," she gagged. "With your power, we could once again rule Panping."

The vines loosened, and Aihara Na collapsed onto her hands and knees, coughing like a mere mortal.

"Why settle for Panping?" Nesilia said. "With this body, together, we can rule it all."

EPILOGUE

Sigrid sat silently in a booth on the ground floor of the Vineyard. Valin had let her out of her room, though she wasn't sure why. Screams sounded outside in Dockside, like a war had broken out, some so shrill and filled with terror they made Sigrid wince.

None of it fazed Valin. He sat across from her with his bad leg stretched out on the seat, massaging his knee. With his other hand, he used a fork to enjoy a steak, drenched in gravy, the pieces already cut for him. Two thugs remained so she couldn't do anything but watch him indulge. The rest of the rotten place was empty. Even the few wenches and their regulars who didn't care to honor the Dawning had filed out.

"What do you want?" Sigrid asked meekly. A scream, louder than all the others, made her heart feel like it was going to burst through her chest. What sounded like glass shattering followed it. "What's going on?"

"Progress, my dear," Valin said, chewing on a chunk of meat.

"I don't understand. Can't you help them?"

A flash of orange streaked across a window, accompanied by cheering.

"Save your prayers for your brother," Valin said.

Sigrid slid along the booth toward Valin, but one of the thugs flaunted his cudgel to keep her still.

"Is he out there still?" she asked.

"Not if he cares a lick about you." Sigrid hung her head, and Valin finally glanced over at her. "Relax. I have a good feeling about him. It took some work, but I think I finally got through to him."

The doors swung open, and Codar strode inside. Blood spatter covered half his face, a few spots staining his usually neat, white mustache. Valin sat up at the sight of him. Codar took a moment to gather his breath as if refusing to speak until he collected himself. "They passed through the gates," he said. "I feared Rand might try and come back for her, but it seems he finally sees reason."

"Excellent!" Valin clapped his hands. He stood and waved up to the balcony. Sigrid hadn't noticed before, but one of his thugs had a crossbow perched on the railing aimed at her. The man lowered it and backed away.

A chill ran up Sigrid's spine. Before she could speak, Valin laid his hand on her shoulder. "Just a precaution, my dear," he said, a warmth to his tone that somehow made her feel worse. "I had every faith in him—"

A torch broke through the window of the Vineyard and landed on one of the tables. The dry wood instantly caught fire.

Codar whipped around just before a masked cultist of Nesilia plowed into him. He fended off a fury of stabs and gutted the assailant. Another leaped through the broken window and ran toward the booth where Sigrid sat. He screamed mad, indecipherable words until a crossbow bolt struck him in the chest and knocked him over.

"Yigging savages!" Valin yelled. He slammed his fist on the table, flipping his meal and sending his fork clattering to the ground. "Get this cleaned up. And call for Uhlvark and place him outside on guard. That ought to scare the crazies off."

The two thugs hurried to put out the flames. Valin grabbed his crutch and went to stand, then noticed Sigrid.

"Get her locked up safe upstairs," Valin said. "We wouldn't want anything happening to her."

The thug with the crossbow rushed down the stairs to the booth. "Let's go beautiful," he said. He gave Sigrid's arm a gentle tug despite only just having been prepared to do to her what he'd done to the cultist. Sigrid's gaze darted between Valin as he crutched away and Codar, busy trying to roll the corpse off him.

"I said, let's go, wench!" This time he pulled hard on her arm.

Sigrid instantly recalled the feeling of helplessness when the Drav Cra men tried to rape her. She ripped free and reached under the booth. The thug grabbed her foot and dragged her. She pawed at the floor as she slid until her fingers found the handle of Valin's fork.

The thug yanked her so hard she crashed onto the floor, and when he went to lift her, she stabbed the fork into his eye. His scream made those echoing outside the doors seem tame. Valin stopped by the exit to his office and looked back. Sigrid made eye contact with him, then bolted for the front door.

The crimelord of Dockside didn't seem concerned. "Codar, retrieve her," he groaned, rolling his eyes.

The Breklian pushed the body atop him aside and rolled over. He slashed at Sigrid's legs on her way by, cutting her calf. She fell through the doorway and tumbled down the stairs, but she didn't let it stop her. She hopped back to her feet and limped, glancing back to see Codar leisurely walking after her.

"Get away from me!" she shouted. A crash drew her vision back in front of her. A cart of supplies toppled over, and fish slid from barrels across the snow. Her gaze then rose to see the Dockside church she'd spent many a sermon in over the years entirely consumed by fire. Terrified citizens ran this way and that, some being chased by cultists in their billowing red robes and white masks.

Sigrid slipped and nearly lost her footing. She glanced back to see Codar gaining on her, and when she turned back around, she bumped into a cultist.

"Buried, not dead," the man behind the mask hissed before scurrying away.

Sigrid went to take another step, then her legs went weak, and she fell to a knee. When she looked down, she saw the tip of the cultist's dagger jutting out of her stomach, buried all the way down to the hilt. She'd been so frantic she didn't even feel him stab her.

She grabbed the handle, blood covering her hands.

Codar grabbed her shoulders and gently laid her back upon the street.

"You had to run," he sighed. He inspected the wound, and his expression told Sigrid all she needed to know.

She was going to die.

Sigrid struggled for words, but none came. She didn't feel pain, only a cold sensation spreading within her, a coldness that made the harsh winter air seem warm.

"Rand…" she managed to eke out through quivering lips.

"At least you will die knowing he loved you," Codar said. "You westerners care terribly for being loved." He yanked, removing the blade and stared down into Sigrid's eyes. "Don't worry, girl, it will all be over soon."

He held the blade to her throat, but as he did, his gaze lifted away from her. His face twisted with terror.

"Kazimir?" he said softly.

"Why would you sully such potential with death?" a man said. His voice was nearly as cold as the ground beneath Sigrid. "I can feel the rage within her—power like you never had."

Whoever it was, his presence rendered Codar speechless. Sigrid couldn't speak either, only watch and listen as the numbness spread within her. The newcomer circled them, and the dagger fell from Codar's grasp as he staggered back.

"Grandfather, H… how are you here?" Codar stammered.

"I asked myself that when my eyes finally opened after so many years in Elsewhere and this chaos surrounded me. Now I see. I denied the Sanguine Lords a blood pact owed, and so it is time I offer them a new vessel."

The stranger had silken, white hair just like Codar. But when he knelt before Sigrid, she saw that his face was smooth as a young man despite Codar calling him his grandfather. He kneeled and dragged his finger through Sigrid's blood, then brought it to his lips. His eyes closed, lids flickering like he was in ecstasy.

"How I missed this," he said. Then he stared straight into Sigrid's eyes. His were dark, soulless—the stuff of nightmares, yet she couldn't look away.

"No more a woman than a girl and already your life draws to an abrupt end," he whispered to her. He ran the back of his now bloody hand across her cheek. "Don't be afraid. I'm not here to kill you. Quite the opposite, really."

Sigrid listened but didn't speak—couldn't speak. The stranger leaned down, drawing himself to her ear. She felt no warmth on his breath. She felt nothing.

"Do you not wish to live?" he said. "Do you not wish for more?"

THIS CONCLUDES REDSTAR RISING
(Books 1-3 of the Buried Goddess Saga)
Redstar's rise to power may have been thwarted, but the story isn't over. Continue on with Book 4 in the Buried Goddess Saga, *Way of Gods*, as our heroes are thrust into new and unexpected situations. Nesilia's plans to claim vengeance on the world which forgot her may be delayed, but her time is coming.

- Kazimir and Sigrid… that's quite the team. Rand is gonna be yigging pissed.
- Wow. Did Sora just kill… everyone?
- Whitney is free of Elsewhere, but is he really?
- Torsten gave all to bring down Redstar. What else has he to live for? What else has he to gain?
- War is ravaging the Black Sands. Will a new leader rise up?

**Find out what happens next! Grab *Way of Gods* now!
Or pick up *The Saga So Far*.**

JOIN THE KING'S SHIELD

Sign up to the *free* and exclusive King's Shield Newsletter at www.jaimecastle.com to receive early looks and new novels, peeks at conceptual art that breathes life into Pantego as well as exclusive access to short stories called "Legends of Pantego." Learn more about the characters and the world you love.

Did you know we have a Facebook group too? All the same perks as the email readers group plus instant interaction with Rhett and Jaime! Search for: The Official King's Shield Fan Club.

THANK YOU!

FROM THE PUBLISHER

Check out the rest of our catalogue or sign up to receive updates regarding all new releases at www.aethonbooks.com.

If you liked this book, check out the rest of our catalogue at www.aethonbooks.com. To sign up to receive a FREE collection from some of our best authors as well as updates regarding all new releases, visit www.subscribepage.com/AethonReadersGroup.